Remembrance of
Things Past

VOLUME TWO

Remembrance of Things Past

MARCEL PROUST

VOLUME TWO
Cities of the Plain, The Captive,
The Sweet Cheat Gone,
Time Regained

Translated by
C. K. SCOTT MONCRIEFF
& STEPHEN HUDSON

WORDSWORTH CLASSICS
OF WORLD LITERATURE

For my husband
ANTHONY JOHN RANSON
with love from your wife, the publisher.
Eternally grateful for your unconditional love.

Readers who are interested in other titles from
Wordsworth Editions are invited to visit our website at
www.wordsworth-editions.com

For our latest list and a full mail-order service, contact
Bibliophile Books, 5 Datapoint, South Crescent, London E16 4TL
TEL: +44 (0)20 7474 2474 FAX: +44 (0)20 7474 8589
ORDERS: orders@bibliophilebooks.com
WEBSITE: www.bibliophilebooks.com

This edition published 2006 by Wordsworth Editions Limited
8B East Street, Ware, Hertfordshire SG12 9HJ

ISBN 978 1 84022 147 3

© Wordsworth Editions Limited 2006
Introduction © Ingrid Wassenaar 2006

Wordsworth® is a registered trade mark of
Wordsworth Editions Limited

Wordsworth Editions
is the company founded in 1987 by
MICHAEL TRAYLER

Typeset in Great Britain by Antony Gray
Printed and bound by Clays Ltd, St Ives plc

Contents

CITIES OF THE PLAIN

THE CAPTIVE

THE SWEET CHEAT GONE

TIME REGAINED

Cities of the Plain

Translated by
C. K. SCOTT MONCRIEFF

To
RICHARD & MYRTLE KURT
and Their Creator

PISA, 1927

C.K.S.M.

PART I

Introducing the men-women, descendants of those of the inhabitants of Sodom who were spared by the fire from heaven.

La femme aura Gomorrhe et l'homme aura Sodome.
ALFRED DE VIGNY

T HE READER will remember that, long before going that day (on the evening of which the Princesse de Guermantes was to give her party) to pay the Duke and Duchess the visit which I have just described, I had kept watch for their return and had made, in the course of my vigil, a discovery which, albeit concerning M. de Charlus in particular, was in itself so important that I have until now, until the moment when I could give it the prominence and treat it with the fullness that it demanded, postponed giving any account of it. I had, as I have said, left the marvellous point of vantage, so snugly contrived for me at the top of the house, commanding the broken and irregular slopes leading up to the Hôtel de Bréquigny, and gaily decorated in the Italian manner by the rose-pink campanile of the Marquis de Frécourt's stables. I had felt it to be more convenient, when I thought that the Duke and Duchess were on the point of returning, to post myself on the staircase. I regretted somewhat the abandonment of my watchtower. But at that time of day, namely the hour immediately following luncheon, I had less cause for regret, for I should not then have seen, as in the morning, the footmen of the Bréquigny-Tresmes household, converted by distance into minute figures in a picture, make their leisurely ascent of the abrupt precipice, feather-brush in hand, behind the large, transparent flakes of mica which stood out so charmingly upon its ruddy bastions. Failing the geologist's field of contemplation, I had at least that of the botanist, and was peering through the shutters of the staircase window at the Duchess's little tree and at the precious plant, exposed in the courtyard with that insistence with which mothers 'bring out' their marriageable offspring, and asking myself whether the unlikely insect would come, by a providential hazard, to visit the offered and neglected pistil. My curiosity emboldening me by degrees, I went down to the ground-floor window, which also stood open with its shutters ajar. I could hear distinctly, as he got ready to go out, Jupien who could not detect me behind my blind, where I stood perfectly still until the moment when I drew quickly aside in order not to be seen by M. de Charlus, who, on his way to call upon Mme de Villeparisis, was slowly crossing the courtyard, a pursy figure, aged by the strong light, his hair visibly grey. Nothing short of an indisposition of Mme de Villeparisis (consequent on the illness of the Marquis de Fierbois, with whom he personally was at daggers drawn) could have made M. de Charlus pay a call, perhaps for the first time in his life, at that hour of the day. For with that eccentricity of the Guermantes, who, instead of conforming to the ways of society, used to modify them to suit their own personal habits (habits not, they thought, social, and deserving in consequence the abasement before them of that thing of no value, Society – thus it was that Mme de Marsantes had no regular 'day', but was at home to her friends every morning between ten o'clock and noon), the Baron, reserving those hours for reading, hunting for old curiosities and so forth, paid calls only between four and six in the afternoon. At six o'clock he went to the Jockey Club, or took a stroll in the Bois. A moment later, I again recoiled, in order not to be seen by Jupien. It was nearly time for him to start for the office, from which he would return only for dinner, and not even then always during the last week, his niece and her apprentices having gone to the country to finish a dress there for a customer. Then, realising that no one could see me, I decided not to let myself be disturbed again, for fear of missing, should the miracle be fated to occur, the arrival, almost beyond the possibility of hope (across so many obstacles of distance, of adverse risks, of dangers), of the insect sent from so far as ambassador to the virgin who had so long been waiting for him to appear. I knew that this expectancy was no more passive than in the male flower, whose stamens had spontaneously curved so that the insect might more easily receive their offering; similarly the female flower that stood here, if the insect came, would coquettishly arch her styles; and, to be more effectively penetrated by him, would imperceptibly advance, like a hypocritical but ardent damsel, to meet him halfway. The laws of the vegetable kingdom are themselves governed by other laws, increasingly exalted. If the visit of an insect, that is to say, the transportation of the seed of one flower is generally necessary for the fertilisation of another, that is because autofecundation, the fertilisation of a flower by itself, would lead, like a succession of intermarriages in the same family, to degeneracy and sterility, whereas the crossing effected by the insects gives to the subsequent generations of the same species a vigour unknown to their forebears. This invigoration may, however, prove excessive, the species develop out of all proportion; then, as an antitoxin protects us against disease, as the thyroid gland regulates our adiposity, as defeat comes to punish pride, fatigue indulgence, and as sleep in turn depends upon fatigue, so an exceptional act of autofecundation comes at a given point to apply its turn of the screw, its pull on the curb, brings back within normal limits the flower that has exaggerated its transgression of them. My reflections had followed a tendency which I shall describe in due course, and I had already drawn from the visible stratagems of flowers a conclusion that bore upon a whole unconscious element of literary work, when I saw M. de Charlus coming away from the Marquise. Perhaps he had learned from his elderly relative herself, or merely from a servant, the great improvement, or rather her complete recovery from what had been nothing more than a slight indisposition. At this moment, when he did not suspect that anyone was watching him, his eyelids lowered as a screen against the sun, M. de Charlus had relaxed that tension in his face, deadened that artificial vitality, which the animation of his talk and the force of his will kept in evidence there as a rule. Pale as marble, his nose stood out firmly, his fine features no longer received from an expression deliberately assumed a different meaning which altered the beauty of their modelling; nothing more now than a Guermantes, he seemed already carved in stone, he Palamède the Fifteenth, in their chapel at Combray. These general features of a whole family took on, however, in the face of M. de Charlus a fineness more spiritualised, above all more gentle. I regretted for his sake that he should habitually adulterate with so many acts of violence, offensive oddities, tale-bearings, with such harshness, susceptibility and arrogance, that he should conceal beneath a false brutality the amenity, the kindness which, at the moment of his emerging from Mme de Villeparisis', I could see displayed so innocently upon his face. Blinking his eyes in the sunlight, he seemed almost to be smiling, I found in his face seen thus in repose and, so to speak, in its natural state something so affectionate, so disarmed, that I could not help thinking how angry M. de Charlus would have been could he have known that he was being watched; for what was suggested to me by the sight of this man who was so insistent, who prided himself so upon his virility, to whom all other men seemed odiously effeminate, what he made me suddenly think of, so far had he momentarily assumed her features, expression, smile, was a woman.

I was about to change my position again, so that he should not catch sight of me; I had neither the time nor the need to do so. What did I see? Face to face, in that courtyard where certainly they had never met before (M. de Charlus coming to the Hôtel de Guermantes only in the afternoon, during the time when Jupien was at his office), the Baron, having suddenly opened wide his half-shut eyes, was studying with unusual attention the ex-tailor poised on the threshold of his shop, while the latter, fastened suddenly to the ground before M. de Charlus, taking root in it like a plant, was contemplating with a look of amazement the plump form of the middle-aged Baron. But, more astounding still, M. de Charlus's attitude having changed, Jupien's, as though in obedience to the laws of an occult art, at once brought itself into harmony with it. The Baron, who was now seeking to conceal the impression that had been made on him, and yet, in spite of his affectation of indifference, seemed unable to move away without regret, went, came, looked vaguely into the distance in the way which, he felt, most enhanced the beauty of his eyes, assumed a complacent, careless, fatuous air. Meanwhile Jupien, shedding at once the humble, honest expression which I had always associated with him, had – in perfect symmetry with the Baron – thrown up his head, given a becoming tilt to his body, placed his hand with a grotesque impertinence on his hip, stuck out his behind, posed himself with the coquetry that the orchid might have adopted on the providential arrival of the bee. I had not supposed that he could appear so repellent. But I was equally unaware that he was capable of improvising his part in this sort of dumb charade, which (albeit he found himself for the first time in the presence of M. de Charlus) seemed to have been long and carefully rehearsed; one does not arrive spontaneously at that pitch of perfection except when one meets in a foreign country a compatriot with whom an understanding then grows up of itself, both parties speaking the same language, even though they have never seen one another before.

This scene was not, however, positively comic, it was stamped with a strangeness, or if you like a naturalness, the beauty of which steadily increased. M. de Charlus might indeed assume a detached air, indifferently let his eyelids droop; every now and then he raised them, and at such moments turned on Jupien an attentive gaze. But (doubtless because he felt that such a scene could not be prolonged indefinitely in this place, whether for reasons which we shall learn later on, or possibly from that feeling of the brevity of all things which makes us determine that every blow must strike home, and renders so moving the spectacle of every kind of love), each time that M. de Charlus looked at Jupien, he took care that his glance should be accompanied by a spoken word, which made it infinitely unlike the glances we usually direct at a person whom we do or do not know; he stared at Jupien with the peculiar fixity of the person who is about to say to us: 'Excuse my taking the liberty, but you have a long white thread hanging down your back,' or else: 'Surely I can't be mistaken, you come from Zurich

too; I'm certain I must have seen you there often in the curiosity shop.'
Thus, every other minute, the same question seemed to be being intensely
put to Jupien in the stare of M. de Charlus, like those questioning phrases of
Beethoven indefinitely repeated at regular intervals, and intended – with an
exaggerated lavishness of preparation – to introduce a new theme, a change
of tone, a 're-entry'. On the other hand, the beauty of the reciprocal glances
of M. de Charlus and Jupien arose precisely from the fact that they did not,
for the moment at least, seem to be intended to lead to anything further.
This beauty, it was the first time that I had seen the Baron and Jupien
display it. In the eyes of both of them, it was the sky not of Zurich but of
some Oriental city, the name of which I had not yet divined, that I saw
reflected. Whatever the point might be that held M. de Charlus and the ex-
tailor thus arrested, their pact seemed concluded and these superfluous
glances to be but ritual preliminaries, like the parties that people give before
a marriage which has been definitely 'arranged'. Nearer still to nature – and
the multiplicity of these analogies is itself all the more natural in that the
same man, if we examine him for a few minutes, appears in turn as a man, a
man-bird or man-insect, and so forth – one would have called them a pair of
birds, the male and the female, the male seeking to make advances, the
female – Jupien – no longer giving any sign of response to these overtures,
but regarding her new friend without surprise, with an inattentive fixity of
gaze, which she doubtless felt to be more disturbing and the only effective
method, once the male had taken the first steps, and had fallen back upon
preening his feathers. At length Jupien's indifference seemed to suffice him
no longer; from this certainty of having conquered, to making himself be
pursued and desired was but the next stage, and Jupien, deciding to go off to
his work, passed through the carriage gate. It was only, however, after
turning his head two or three times that he escaped into the street towards
which the Baron, trembling lest he should lose the trail (boldly humming a
tune, not forgetting to fling a 'Good-day' to the porter, who, half-tipsy
himself and engaged in treating a few friends in his back kitchen, did not
even hear him), hurried briskly to overtake him. At the same instant, just as
M. de Charlus disappeared through the gate humming like a great bumble-
bee, another, a real bee this time, came into the courtyard. For all I knew
this might be the one so long awaited by the orchid, which was coming to
bring it that rare pollen without which it must die a virgin. But I was
distracted from following the gyrations of the insect for, a few minutes later,
engaging my attention afresh, Jupien (perhaps to pick up a parcel which he
did take away with him eventually and so, presumably, in the emotion
aroused by the apparition of M. de Charlus, had forgotten, perhaps simply

for a more natural reason) returned, followed by the Baron. The latter, deciding to cut short the preliminaries, asked the tailor for a light, but at once observed: 'I ask you for a light, but I find that I have left my cigars at home.' The laws of hospitality prevailed over those of coquetry. 'Come inside, you shall have everything you require,' said the tailor, on whose features disdain now gave place to joy. The door of the shop closed behind them and I could hear no more. I had lost sight of the bee. I did not know whether he was the insect that the orchid needed, but I had no longer any doubt, in the case of an extremely rare insect and a captive flower, of the miraculous possibility of their conjunction when M. de Charlus (this is simply a comparison of providential hazards, whatever they may be, without the slightest scientific claim to establish a relation between certain laws and what is sometimes, most ineptly, termed homosexuality), who for years past had never come to the house except at hours when Jupien was not there, by the mere accident of Mme de Villeparisis' illness had encountered the tailor, and with him the good fortune reserved for men of the type of the Baron by one of those fellow-creatures who may indeed be, as we shall see, infinitely younger than Jupien and better looking, the man predestined to exist in order that they may have their share of sensual pleasure on this earth; the man who cares only for elderly gentlemen.

All that I have just said, however, I was not to understand until several minutes had elapsed; so much is reality encumbered by those properties of invisibility until a chance occurrence has divested it of them. Anyhow, for the moment I was greatly annoyed at not being able to hear any more of the conversation between the ex-tailor and the Baron. I then bethought myself of the vacant shop, separated from Jupien's only by a partition that was extremely slender. I had, in order to get to it, merely to go up to our flat, pass through the kitchen, go down by the service stair to the cellars, make my way through them across the breadth of the courtyard above, and on coming to the right place underground, where the joiner had, a few months ago, still been storing his timber and where Jupien intended to keep his coal, climb the flight of steps which led to the interior of the shop. Thus the whole of my journey would be made under cover, I should not be seen by anyone. This was the most prudent method. It was not the one that I adopted, but, keeping close to the walls, I made a circuit in the open air of the courtyard, trying not to let myself be seen. If I was not, I owe it more, I am sure, to chance than to my own sagacity. And for the fact that I took so imprudent a course, when the way through the cellar was so safe, I can see three possible reasons, assuming that I had any reason at all. First of all, my impatience. Secondly, perhaps, a dim memory of the scene at Montjouvain, when I stood concealed outside Mlle Vinteuil's window. Certainly, the affairs of this sort of which I have been a spectator have always been presented in a setting of the most imprudent and least probable character, as if such revelations were to be the reward of an action full of risk, though in part clandestine. Lastly, I hardly dare, so childish does it appear, to confess the third reason, which was, I am quite sure, unconsciously decisive. Since, in order to follow – and see controverted – the military principles enunciated by Saint-Loup, I had followed in close detail the course of the Boer war, I had been led on from that to read again old accounts of explorations, narratives of travel. These stories had excited me, and I applied them to the events of my daily life to stimulate my courage. When attacks of illness had compelled me to remain for several days and nights on end not only without sleep but without lying down, without tasting food or drink, at the moment when my pain and exhaustion became so intense that I felt that I should never escape from them, I would think of some traveller cast on the beach, poisoned by noxious herbs, shivering with fever in clothes drenched by the salt water, who nevertheless in a day or two felt stronger, rose and went blindly upon his way, in search of possible inhabitants who might, when he came to them, prove cannibals. His example acted on me as a tonic, restored my hope, and I felt ashamed of my momentary discouragement. Thinking of the Boers who, with British armies facing them, were not afraid to expose themselves at the moment when they had to cross, in order to reach a covered position, a tract of open country: 'It would be a fine thing,' I thought to myself, 'if I were to show less courage when the theatre of operations is simply the human heart, and when the only steel that I, who engaged in more than one duel without fear at the time of the Dreyfus case, have to fear is that of the eyes of the neighbours who have other things to do besides looking into the courtyard,'

But when I was inside the shop, taking care not to let any plank in the floor make the slightest creak, as I found that the least sound in Jupien's shop could be heard from the other, I thought to myself how rash Jupien and M. de Charlus had been, and how wonderfully fortune had favoured them.

I did not dare move. The Guermantes groom, taking advantage no doubt of his master's absence, had, as it happened, transferred to the shop in which I now stood a ladder which hitherto had been kept in the coach-house, and if I had climbed this I could have opened the ventilator above and heard as well as if I had been in Jupien's shop itself. But I was afraid of making a noise. Besides, it was unnecessary. I had not even cause to regret my not having arrived in the shop until several minutes had elapsed. For from what I heard at first in Jupien's shop, which was only a series of inarticulate sounds, I imagine that few words had been exchanged. It is true that these sounds were so violent that, if one set had not always been taken up an octave higher by a parallel plaint, I might have thought that one person was strangling another within a few feet of me, and that subsequently the murderer and his resuscitated victim were taking a bath to wash away the traces of the crime. I concluded from this later on that there is another thing as vociferous as pain, namely pleasure, especially when there is added to it – failing the fear of an eventual parturition, which could not be present in this case, despite the hardly convincing example in the *Golden Legend* – an immediate afterthought of cleanliness. Finally, after about half an hour (during which time I had climbed on tiptoe up my ladder so as to peep through the ventilator which I did not open), a conversation began. Jupien refused with insistence the money that M. de Charlus was pressing upon him.

'Why do you have your chin shaved like that,' he inquired of the Baron in a cajoling tone. 'It's so becoming, a nice beard.' 'Ugh! It's disgusting,' the Baron replied. Meanwhile he still lingered upon the threshold and plied Jupien with questions about the neighbourhood. 'You don't know anything about the man who sells chestnuts at the corner, not the one on the left, he's a horror, but the other way, a great, dark fellow? And the chemist opposite, he has a charming cyclist who delivers his parcels.' These questions must have ruffled Jupien, for, drawing himself up with the scorn of a great courtesan who has been forsaken, he replied: 'I can see you are completely heartless.' Uttered in a pained, frigid, affected tone, this reproach must have made its sting felt by M. de Charlus, who, to counteract the bad impression made by his curiosity, addressed to Jupien, in too low a tone for me to be able to make out his words, a request the granting of which would doubtless necessitate their prolonging their sojourn in the shop, and which moved the tailor sufficiently to make him forget his annoyance, for he studied the Baron's face, plump and flushed beneath his grey hair, with the supremely blissful air of a person whose self-esteem has just been profoundly flattered, and, deciding to grant M. de Charlus the favour that he had just asked of him, after various remarks lacking in refinement such as: 'Aren't you naughty!' said to the Baron with a smiling, emotional, superior and grateful air: 'All right, you big baby, come along!'

'If I hark back to the question of the tram conductor,' M. de Charlus went on imperturbably, 'it is because, apart from anything else, he might offer me some entertainment on my homeward journey. For it falls to my lot, now and then, like the Caliph who used to roam the streets of Bagdad in the guise of a common merchant, to condescend to follow some curious little person whose profile may have taken my fancy.' I made at this point the same observation that I had made on Bergotte. If he should ever have to plead before a bench, he would employ not the sentences calculated to convince his judges, but such Bergottesque sentences as his peculiar literary temperament suggested to him and made him find pleasure in using. Similarly M. de Charlus, in conversing with the tailor, made use of the same language that he would have used to fashionable people of his own set, even exaggerating its eccentricities, whether because the shyness which he was striving to overcome drove him to an excess of pride or, by preventing him from mastering himself (for we are always less at our ease in the company of someone who is not of our station), forced him to unveil, to lay bare his true nature, which was, in fact, arrogant and a trifle mad, as Mme de Guermantes had remarked. 'So as not to lose the trail,' he went on, 'I spring like a little usher, like a young and good-looking doctor, into the same car as the little person herself, of whom we speak in the feminine gender only so as to conform with the rules of grammar (as we say, in speaking of a Prince, 'Is His Highness enjoying her usual health'). If she changes her car, I take, with possibly the germs of the plague, that incredible thing called a 'transfer', a number, and one which, albeit it is presented to *me*, is not always number one! I change 'carriages' in this way as many as three or four times, I end up sometimes at eleven o'clock at night at the Orléans station and have to come home. Still, if it were only the Orléans station! Once, I must tell you, not having managed to get into conversation sooner, I went all the way to Orléans itself, in one of those frightful compartments where one has, to rest one's eyes upon, between triangles of what is known as 'string-work', photographs of the principal architectural features of the line. There was only one vacant seat; I had in front of me, as an historic edifice, a 'view' of the Cathedral of Orléans, quite the ugliest in France, and as tiring a thing to have to stare at in that way against my will as if somebody had forced me to focus its towers in the lens of one of those optical penholders which give one ophthalmia. I got out of the train at Les Aubrais together with my young person, for whom alas his family (when I had imagined him to possess every defect except that of having a family) were waiting on the platform! My sole consolation, as I waited for a train to take me back to Paris, was the house of Diane de Poitiers. She may indeed have charmed one of my royal ancestors, I should have preferred a more living beauty. That is why, as an antidote to the boredom of returning home by myself, I should rather like to make friends with a sleeping-car attendant or the conductor of an omnibus. Now, don't be shocked,' the Baron wound up, 'it is all a question of class. With what you call 'young gentlemen', for instance, I feel no desire actually to have them, but I am never satisfied until I have touched them, I don't mean physically, but touched a responsive chord. As soon as, instead of leaving my letters unanswered, a young man starts writing to me incessantly, when he is morally at my disposal, I grow calm again, or at least I should grow calm were I not immediately caught by the attraction of another. Rather curious, ain't it? – Speaking of 'young gentlemen', those that come to the house here, do you know any of them?' 'No, baby. Oh, yes, I do, a dark one, very tall, with an eye-glass, who keeps smiling and turning round.' 'I don't know who you mean.' Jupien filled in the portrait, but M. de Charlus could not succeed in identifying its subject, not knowing that the ex-tailor was one of those persons, more common than is generally supposed, who never remember the colour of the hair of people they do not know well. But to me, who was aware of this infirmity in Jupien and substituted 'fair' for 'dark', the portrait appeared to be an exact description of the Duc de Châtellerault. 'To return to young men not of the lower orders,' the Baron went on, 'at the present moment my head has been turned by a strange little fellow, an intelligent little cit who shows with regard to myself a prodigious want of civility. He has absolutely no idea of the prodigious personage that I am, and of the microscopic animalcule that he is in comparison. After all, what does it matter, the little ass may bray his head off before my august bishop's mantle.' 'Bishop!' cried Jupien, who had understood nothing of M. de Charlus's concluding remarks, but was completely taken aback by the word bishop. 'But that sort of thing doesn't go with religion,' he said. 'I have three Popes in my family,' replied M. de Charlus, 'and enjoy the right to mantle in gules by virtue of a cardinalatial title, the niece of the Cardinal, my great-uncle, having conveyed to my grandfather the title of Duke which was substituted for it. I see, though, that metaphor leaves you deaf and French history cold. Besides,' he added, less perhaps by way of conclusion than as a warning, 'this attraction that I feel towards the young people who avoid me, from fear of course, for only their natural respect stops their mouths from crying out to me that they love me, requires in them an outstanding social position. And again, their feint of indifference may produce, in spite of that, the directly opposite effect. Fatuously prolonged, it sickens me. To take an example from a class with which you are more familiar, when they were doing up my Hôtel, so as not to create jealousies among all the duchesses who were vying with one another for the honour of being able to say that they had given me a lodging, I went for a few days to an 'hotel', as they call inns nowadays. One of the bedroom valets I knew, I pointed out to him an interesting little page who used to open and shut the front door, and who remained refractory to my proposals. Finally, losing my temper, in order to prove to him that my intentions were pure, I made him an offer of a ridiculously high sum simply to come upstairs and talk to me for five minutes in my room. I waited for him in vain. I then took such a dislike to him that I used to go out by the service door so as not to see his villainous little mug at the other. I learned afterwards that he had never had any of my notes, which had been intercepted, the first by the bedroom valet, who was jealous, the next by the day porter, who was virtuous, the third by the night porter, who was in love with the little page, and used to couch with him at the hour when Dian rose. But my disgust persisted none the less, and were they to bring me the page, simply like a dish of venison on a silver platter, I should thrust him away with a retching stomach. But there's the unfortunate part of it, we have spoken of serious matters, and now all is over between us, there can be no more question of what I hoped to secure. But you could render me great services, act as my agent; why no, the mere thought of such a thing restores my vigour, and I can see that all is by no means over.'

From the beginning of this scene a revolution, in my unsealed eyes, had occurred in M. de Charlus, as complete, as immediate as if he had been touched by a magician's wand. Until then, because I had not understood, I had not seen. The vice (we use the word for convenience only), the vice of each of us accompanies him through life after the manner of the familiar genius who was invisible to men so long as they were unaware of his presence. Our goodness, our meanness, our name, our social relations do not disclose themselves to the eye, we carry them hidden within us. Even Ulysses did not at once recognise Athena. But the gods are immediately perceptible to one another, as quickly like to like, and so too had M. de Charlus been to Jupien. Until that moment I had been, in the presence of M. de Charlus, in the position of an absent-minded man who, standing before a pregnant woman whose distended outline he has failed to remark, persists, while she smilingly reiterates: 'Yes, I am a little tired just now,' in asking her indiscreetly: 'Why, what is the matter with you?' But let someone say to him: 'She is expecting a child,' suddenly he catches sight of her abdomen and ceases to see anything else. It is the explanation that opens our eyes; the dispelling of an error gives us an additional sense.

Those of my readers who do not care to refer, for examples of this law, to the Messieurs de Charlus of their acquaintance, whom for long years they had never suspected, until the day when, upon the smooth surface of the individual just like everyone else, there suddenly appeared, traced in an ink hitherto invisible, the characters that compose the word dear to the ancient Greeks, have only, in order to convince themselves that the world which surrounds them appears to them at first naked, bare of a thousand ornaments which it offers to the eyes of others better informed, to remind themselves how many times in the course of their lives they have found themselves on the point of making a blunder. Nothing upon the blank, undocumented face of this man or that could have led them to suppose that he was precisely the brother, or the intended husband, or the lover of a woman of whom they were just going to remark: 'What a cow!' But then, fortunately, a word whispered to them by someone standing near arrests the fatal expression on their lips. At once there appear, like a *Mené, Tekel, Upharsin*, the words: 'He is engaged to,' or, 'he is the brother of,' or 'he is the lover of the woman whom we ought not to describe, in his hearing, as a cow.' And this one new conception will bring about an entire regrouping, thrusting some back, others forward, of the fractional conceptions, henceforward a complete whole, which we possessed of the rest of the family. In M. de Charlus another creature might indeed have coupled itself with him which made him as different from other men as the horse makes the centaur, this creature might indeed have incorporated itself in the Baron, I had never caught a glimpse of it. Now the abstraction had become materialised, the creature at last discerned had lost its power of remaining invisible, and the transformation of M. de Charlus into a new person was so complete that not only the contrasts of his face, of his voice, but, in retrospect, the very ups and downs of his relations with myself, everything that hitherto had seemed to my mind incoherent, became intelligible, brought itself into evidence, just as a sentence which presents no meaning so long as it remains broken up in letters scattered at random upon a table, expresses, if these letters be rearranged in the proper order, a thought which one can never afterwards forget.

I now understood, moreover, how, earlier in the day, when I had seen him coming away from Mme de Villeparisis', I had managed to arrive at the conclusion that M. de Charlus looked like a woman: he was one! He belonged to that race of beings, less paradoxical than they appear, whose ideal is manly simply because their temperament is feminine and who in their life resemble in appearance only the rest of men; there where each of us carries, inscribed in those eyes through which he beholds everything in the universe, a human outline engraved on the surface of the pupil, for them it is that not of a nymph but of a youth. Race upon which a curse weighs and which must live amid falsehood and perjury, because it knows the world to regard as a punishable and a scandalous, as an inadmissible thing, its desire, that which constitutes for every human creature the greatest happiness in life; which must deny its God, since even Christians, when at the bar of justice they appear and are arraigned, must before Christ and in His Name defend themselves, as from a calumny, from the charge of what to them is life itself; sons without a mother, to whom they are obliged to lie all her life long and even in the hour when they close her dying eyes; friends without friendships, despite all those which their charm, frequently recognised, inspires and their hearts, often generous, would gladly feel; but can we describe as friendship those relations which flourish only by virtue of a lie and from which the first outburst of confidence and sincerity in which they might be tempted to indulge would make them be expelled with disgust, unless they are dealing with an impartial, that is to say a sympathetic mind, which however in that case, misled with regard to them by a conventional psychology, will suppose to spring from the vice confessed the very affection that is most alien to it, just as certain judges assume and are more inclined to pardon murder in inverts and treason in Jews for reasons derived from original sin and racial predestination. And lastly – according at least to the first theory which I sketched in outline at the time and which we shall see subjected to some modification in the sequel, a theory by which this would have angered them above all things, had not the paradox been hidden from their eyes by the very illusion that made them see and live – lovers from whom is always precluded the possibility of that love the hope of which gives them the strength to endure so many risks and so much loneliness, since they fall in love with precisely that type of man who has nothing feminine about him, who is not an invert and consequently cannot love them in return; with the result that their desire would be for ever insatiable did not their money procure for them real men, and their imagination end by making them take for real men the inverts to whom they had prostituted themselves. Their honour precarious, their liberty provisional, lasting only until the discovery of their crime; their position unstable, like that of the poet who one day was feasted at every table, applauded in every theatre in London, and on the next was driven from every lodging, unable to find a pillow upon which to lay his head, turning the mill like Samson and saying like him: 'The two sexes shall die, each in a place apart!'; excluded even, save on the days of general disaster when the majority rally round the victim as the Jews rallied round Dreyfus, from the sympathy – at times from the society – of their fellows, in whom they inspire only disgust at seeing themselves as they are, portrayed in a mirror which, ceasing to flatter them, accentuates every blemish that they have refused to observe in themselves, and makes them understand that what they have been calling their love (a thing to which, playing upon the word, they have by association annexed all that poetry, painting, music, chivalry, asceticism have contrived to add to love) springs not from an ideal of beauty which they have chosen but from an incurable malady; like the Jews again (save some who will associate only

with others of their race and have always on their lips ritual words and
consecrated pleasantries), shunning one another, seeking out those who are
most directly their opposite, who do not desire their company, pardoning
their rebuffs, moved to ecstasy by their condescension; but also brought into
the company of their own kind by the ostracism that strikes them, the
opprobrium under which they have fallen, having finally been invested,
by a persecution similar to that of Israel, with the physical and moral
characteristics of a race, sometimes beautiful, often hideous, finding (in
spite of all the mockery with which he who, more closely blended with,
better assimilated to the opposing race, is relatively, in appearance, the least
inverted, heaps upon him who has remained more so) a relief in frequenting
the society of their kind, and even some corroboration of their own life, so
much so that, while steadfastly denying that they are a race (the name of
which is the vilest of insults), those who succeed in concealing the fact that
they belong to it they readily unmask, with a view less to injuring them,
though they have no scruple about that, than to excusing themselves; and,
going in search (as a doctor seeks cases of appendicitis) of cases of inversion
in history, taking pleasure in recalling that Socrates was one of themselves,
as the Israelites claim that Jesus was one of them, without reflecting that
there were no abnormals when homosexuality was the norm, no anti-
Christians before Christ, that the disgrace alone makes the crime because it
has allowed to survive only those who remained obdurate to every warning,
to every example, to every punishment, by virtue of an innate disposition so
peculiar that it is more repugnant to other men (even though it may be
accompanied by exalted moral qualities) than certain other vices which
exclude those qualities, such as theft, cruelty, breach of faith, vices better
understood and so more readily excused by the generality of men; forming a
freemasonry far more extensive, more powerful and less suspected than that
of the Lodges, for it rests upon an identity of tastes, needs, habits, dangers,
apprenticeship, knowledge, traffic, glossary, and one in which the members
themselves, who intend not to know one another, recognise one another
immediately by natural or conventional, involuntary or deliberate signs
which indicate one of his congeners to the beggar in the street, in the great
nobleman whose carriage door he is shutting, to the father in the suitor for
his daughter's hand, to him who has sought healing, absolution, defence, in
the doctor, the priest, the barrister to whom he has had recourse; all of them
obliged to protect their own secret but having their part in a secret shared
with the others, which the rest of humanity does not suspect and which
means that to them the most wildly improbable tales of adventure seem
true, for in this romantic, anachronistic life the ambassador is a bosom

friend of the felon, the prince, with a certain independence of action with which his aristocratic breeding has furnished him, and which the trembling little cit would lack, on leaving the duchess's party goes off to confer in private with the hooligan; a reprobate part of the human whole, but an important part, suspected where it does not exist, flaunting itself, insolent and unpunished, where its existence is never guessed; numbering its adherents everywhere, among the people, in the army, in the church, in the prison, on the throne; living, in short, at least to a great extent, in a playful and perilous intimacy with the men of the other race, provoking them, playing with them by speaking of its vice as of something alien to it; a game that is rendered easy by the blindness or duplicity of the others, a game that may be kept up for years until the day of the scandal, on which these lion-tamers are devoured; until then, obliged to make a secret of their lives, to turn away their eyes from the things on which they would naturally fasten them, to fasten them upon those from which they would naturally turn away, to change the gender of many of the words in their vocabulary, a social constraint, slight in comparison with the inward constraint which their vice, or what is improperly so called, imposes upon them with regard not so much now to others as to themselves, and in such a way that to themselves it does not appear a vice. But certain among them, more practical, busier men who have not the time to go and drive their own bargains, or to dispense with the simplification of life and that saving of time which may result from cooperation, have formed two societies of which the second is composed exclusively of persons similar to themselves.

This is noticeable in those who are poor and have come up from the country, without friends, with nothing but their ambition to be some day a celebrated doctor or barrister, with a mind still barren of opinions, a person unadorned with manners, which they intend, as soon as possible, to decorate, just as they would buy furniture for their little attic in the Latin quarter, copying whatever they had observed in those who had already 'arrived' in the useful and serious profession in which they also intend to establish themselves and to become famous; in these their special taste, unconsciously inherited like a weakness for drawing, for music, a weakness of vision, is perhaps the only living and despotic originality – which on certain evenings compels them to miss some meeting, advantageous to their career, with people whose ways, in other respect, of speaking, thinking, dressing, parting their hair, they have adopted. In their quarter, where otherwise they mix only with their brother students, their teachers or some fellow-provincial who has succeeded and can help them on, they have speedily discovered other young men whom the same peculiar taste attracts to them, as in a small town one sees an intimacy grow up between the assistant master and the lawyer, who are both interested in chamber music or mediaeval ivories; applying to the object of their distraction the same utilitarian instinct, the same professional spirit which guides them in their career, they meet these young men at gatherings to which no profane outsider is admitted any more than to those that bring together collectors of old snuff-boxes, Japanese prints or rare flowers, and at which, what with the pleasure of gaining information, the practical value of making exchanges and the fear of competition, there prevail simultaneously, as in a saleroom of postage stamps, the close cooperation of the specialists and the fierce rivalries of the collectors. No one moreover in the café where they have their table knows what the gathering is, whether it is that of an angling club, of an editorial staff, or of the 'Sons of the Indre', so correct is their attire, so cold and reserved their manner, so modestly do they refrain from anything more than the most covert glances at the young men of fashion, the young 'lions' who, a few feet away, are making a great clamour about their mistresses, and among whom those who are admiring them without venturing to raise their eyes will learn only twenty years later, when they themselves are on the eve of admission to the Academy, and the others are middle-aged gentlemen in club windows, that the most seductive among them, now a stout and grizzled Charlus, was in reality akin to themselves, but differently, in another world, beneath other external symbols, with foreign labels, the strangeness of which led them into error. But these groups are at varying stages of advancement; and, just as the 'Union of the Left' differs from the 'Socialist Federation' or some Mendelssohnian musical club from the Schola Cantorum, on certain evenings, at another table, there are extremists who allow a bracelet to slip down from beneath a cuff, sometimes a necklace to gleam in the gap of a collar, who by their persistent stares, their cooings, their laughter, their mutual caresses, oblige a band of students to depart in hot haste, and are served with a civility beneath which indignation boils by a waiter who, as on the evenings when he has to serve Dreyfusards, would find pleasure in summoning the police did he not find profit in pocketing their gratuities.

It is with these professional organisations that the mind contrasts the taste of the solitaries, and in one respect without straining the points of difference, since it is doing no more than copy the solitaries themselves who imagine that nothing differs more widely from organised vice than what appears to them to be a misunderstood love, but with some strain nevertheless, for these different classes correspond, no less than to diverse physiological types, to successive stages in a pathological or merely social evolution. And it is, in fact, very rarely that, one day or another, it is not in some such organisation that the solitaries come to merge themselves, sometimes from simple weariness, or for convenience (just as the people who have been most strongly opposed to such innovations end by having the telephone installed, inviting the Iénas to their parties, or dealing with Potin). They meet there, for that matter, with none too friendly a reception as a rule, for, in their relatively pure lives, their want of experience, the saturation in dreams to which they have been reduced, have branded more strongly upon them those special marks of effeminacy which the professionals have sought to efface. And it must be admitted that, among certain of these newcomers, the woman is not only inwardly united to the man but hideously visible, agitated as one sees them by a hysterical spasm, by a shrill laugh which convulses their knees and hands, looking no more like the common run of men than those monkeys with melancholy, shadowed eyes and prehensile feet who dress up in dinner-jackets and black bow ties; so that these new recruits are judged by others, less chaste for all that themselves, to be compromising associates, and their admission is hedged with difficulties; they are accepted, nevertheless, and they benefit then by those facilities by which commerce, great undertakings have transformed the lives of individuals, and have brought within their reach commodities hitherto too costly to acquire and indeed hard to find, which now submerge them beneath the plethora of what by themselves they had never succeeded in discovering amid the densest crowds. But, even with these innumerable outlets, the burden of social constraint is still too heavy for some, recruited principally among those who have not made a practice of self-control, and who still take to be rarer than it actually is their way of love. Let us leave out of consideration for the moment those who, the exceptional character of their inclinations making them regard themselves as superior to the other sex, look down upon women, make homosexuality the privilege of great genius and of glorious epochs of history, and, when they seek to communicate their taste to others, approach not so much those who seem to them to be predisposed towards it (as the morphino-maniac does with his morphia) as those who seem to them to be worthy of it, from apostolic zeal, just as others preach Zionism, conscientious objection to military service, Saint-Simonism, vegetarianism or anarchy. Here is one who, should we intrude upon him in the morning, still in bed, will present to our gaze an admirable female head, so general is its expression and typical of the sex as a whole; his very hair affirms this, so feminine is its ripple; unbrushed, it falls so naturally in long curls over the cheek that one marvels how the young woman, the girl, the Galatea barely awakened to life, in the unconscious mass of this male body in which she is imprisoned, has contrived so ingeniously by herself, without instruction from anyone, to make use of the narrowest apertures in her prison wall to find what was necessary to her existence. No doubt the young man who sports this delicious head does not say: 'I am a woman.' Even if – for any of the countless possible reasons – he lives with a woman, he can deny to her that he is himself one, can swear to her that he has never had intercourse with men. But let her look at him as we have just revealed him, lying back in bed, in pyjamas, his arms bare, his throat and neck bare also beneath the darkness of his hair. The pyjama jacket becomes a woman's shift, the head that of a pretty Spanish girl. The mistress is astounded by these confidences offered to her gaze, truer than any spoken confidence could be, or indeed any action, which his actions, indeed, if they have not already done so, cannot fail later on to confirm, for every creature follows the line of his own pleasure, and if this creature is not too vicious he will seek it in a sex complementary to his own. And for the invert vice begins, not when he forms relations (for there are all sorts of reasons that may enjoin these), but when he takes his pleasure with women. The young man whom we have been attempting to portray was so evidently a woman that the women who looked upon him with longing were doomed (failing a special taste on their part) to the same disappointment as those who in Shakespeare's comedies are taken in by a girl in disguise who passes as a youth. The deception is mutual, the invert is himself aware of it, he guesses the disillusionment which, once the mask is removed, the woman will experience, and feels to what an extent this mistake as to sex is a source of poetical imaginings. Besides, even from his exacting mistress, in vain does he keep back the admission (if she, that is to say, be not herself a denizen of Gomorrah): 'I am a woman!' when all the time with what stratagems, what agility, what obstinacy as of a climbing plant the unconscious but visible woman in him seeks the masculine organ. We have only to look at that head of curling hair on the white pillow to understand that if, in the evening, this young man slips through his guardians' fingers, in spite of anything that they, or he himself can do to restrain him, it will not be to go in pursuit of women. His mistress may chastise him, may lock him up; next day, the man-woman will have found some way of attaching himself to a man, as the convolvulus throws out its tendrils wherever it finds a convenient post or rake. Why, when we admire in the face of this person a delicacy that touches our hearts, a gracefulness, a spontaneous affability such as men do not possess, should we be dismayed to learn that this young man runs after boxers? They are different aspects of an identical reality. And indeed, what repels us is the most touching thing of all, more touching than any refinement of delicacy, for it represents an admirable though unconscious effort on the part of nature: the recognition of his sex by itself, in spite of the sexual deception, becomes apparent, the unconfessed attempt to escape from itself towards what an initial error on the part of society has segregated from it. Some, those no doubt who have been most timid in childhood, are scarcely concerned with the material kind of the pleasure they receive, provided that they can associate it with a masculine face. Whereas others, whose sensuality is doubtless more violent, imperiously restrict their material pleasure within certain definite limitations. These live perhaps less exclusively beneath the sway of Saturn's outrider, since for them women are not entirely barred, as for the former sort, in whose eyes women would have no existence apart from conversation, flirtation, loves not of the heart but of the head. But the second sort seek out those women who love other women; who can procure for them a young man, enhance the pleasure which they feel on finding themselves in his company; better still, they can, in the same fashion, enjoy with such women the same pleasure as with a man. Whence it arises that jealousy is kindled in those who love the first sort only by the pleasure which they may be enjoying with a man, which alone seems to their lovers a betrayal, since these do not participate in the love of women, have practised it only as a habit, and, so as to reserve for themselves the possibility of eventual marriage, representing to themselves so little the pleasure that it is capable of giving that they cannot be distressed by the thought that he whom they love is enjoying that pleasure; whereas the other sort often inspire jealousy by their love-affairs with women. For, in the relations which they have with her, they play, for the woman who loves her own sex, the part of another woman, and she offers them at the same time more or less what they find in other men, so that the jealous friend suffers from the feeling that he whom he loves is riveted to her who is to him almost a man, and at the same time feels his beloved almost escape him because, to these women, he is something which the lover himself cannot conceive, a sort of woman. We need not pause here to consider those young fools who by a sort of arrested development, to tease their friends or to shock their families, proceed with a kind of frenzy to choose clothes that resemble women's dress, to redden their lips and blacken their eyelashes; we may leave them out of account, for they are those whom we shall find later on, when they have suffered the all too cruel penalty of their affectation, spending what remains of their lifetime in vain attempts to repair by a sternly protestant demeanour the wrong that they did to themselves when they were carried away by the same demon that urges young women of the Faubourg Saint-Germain to live in a scandalous fashion, to set every convention at defiance, to scoff at the entreaties of their relatives, until the day when they set themselves with perseverance but without success to re-ascend the slope down which it had seemed to them that it would be so amusing to glide, down which they had found it so amusing, or rather had not been able to stop themselves from gliding. Finally, let us leave to a later volume the men who have sealed a pact with Gomorrah. We shall deal with them when M. de Charlus comes to know them. Let us leave out for the present all those, of one sort or another, who will appear each in his turn, and, to conclude this first sketch of the subject, let us say a word only of those whom we began to mention just now, the solitary class. Supposing their vice to be more exceptional than it is, they have retired into solitude from the day on which they discovered it, after having carried it within themselves for a long time without knowing it, for a longer time only than certain other men. For no one can tell at first that he is an invert or a poet or a snob or a scoundrel. The boy who has been reading erotic poetry or looking at indecent pictures, if he then presses his body against a schoolfellow's, imagines himself only to be communing with him in an identical desire for a woman. How should he suppose that he is not like everybody else when he recognises the substance of what he feels on reading Mme de Lafayette, Racine, Baudelaire, Walter Scott, at a time when he is still too little capable of observing himself to take into account what he has added from his own store to the picture, and that if the sentiment be the same the object differs, that what he desires is Rob Roy, and not Diana Vernon? With many, by a defensive prudence on the part of the instinct that precedes the clearer vision of the intellect, the mirror and walls of their bedroom vanish beneath a cloud of coloured prints of actresses; they compose poetry such as:

> I love but Chloe in the world,
>   For Chloe is divine;
> Her golden hair is sweetly curled,
>   For her my heart doth pine.

   Must we on that account attribute to the opening phase of such lives a taste which we shall never find in them later on, like those flaxen ringlets on the heads of children which are destined to change to the darkest brown? Who can tell whether the photographs of women are not a first sign of hypocrisy, a first sign also of horror at other inverts? But the solitary kind are precisely those to whom hypocrisy is painful. Possibly even the example of the Jews, of a different type of colony, is not strong enough to account for the frail hold that their upbringing has upon them, or for the artfulness with which they find their way back (perhaps not to anything so sheerly terrible as the suicide to which maniacs, whatever precautions one may take with them, return, and, pulled out of the river into which they have flung themselves, take poison, procure revolvers, and so forth; but) to a life of which the men of the other race not only do not understand, cannot imagine, abominate the essential pleasures but would be filled with horror by the thought of its frequent danger and everlasting shame. Perhaps, to form a picture of these, we ought to think, if not of the wild animals that never become domesticated, of the lion-cubs said to be tame but lions still at heart, then at least of the negroes whom the comfortable existence of the white man renders desperately unhappy and who prefer the risks of a life of savagery and its incomprehensible joys. When the day has dawned on which they have discovered themselves to be incapable at once of lying to others and of lying to themselves, they go away to live in the country, shunning the society of their own kind (whom they believe to be few in number) from horror of the monstrosity or fear of the temptation, and that of the rest of humanity from shame. Never having arrived at true maturity, plunged in a constant melancholy, now and again, some Sunday evening when there is no moon, they go for a solitary walk as far as a crossroads where, although not a word has been said, there has come to meet them one of their boyhood's friends who is living in a house in the neighbourhood. And they begin again the pastimes of long ago, on the grass, in the night, neither uttering a word. During the week, they meet in their respective houses, talk of no matter what, without any allusion to what has occurred between them, exactly as though they had done nothing and were not to do anything again, save, in their relations, a trace of coldness, of irony, of irritability and rancour, at times of hatred. Then the neighbour sets out on a strenuous expedition on horseback, and, on a mule, climbs mountain peaks, sleeps in the snow; his friend, who identifies his own vice with a weakness of temperament, the cabined and timid life, realises that vice can no longer exist in his friend now emancipated, so many thousands of feet above sea-level. And, sure enough, the other takes a wife. And yet the abandoned one is not cured (in spite of the cases in which, as we shall see, inversion is curable). He insists upon going down himself every morning to the kitchen to receive the milk from the hands of the dairyman's boy, and on the evenings when desire is too strong for him will go out of his way to set a drunkard on the right road or to 'adjust the dress' of a blind man. No doubt the life of certain inverts appears at times to change, their vice (as it is called) is no longer apparent in their habits; but nothing is ever lost; a missing jewel turns up again; when the quantity of a sick man's urine decreases, it is because he is perspiring more freely, but the excretion must invariably occur. One day this homosexual hears of the death of a young cousin, and from his inconsolable grief we learned that it was to this love, chaste possibly and aimed rather at retaining esteem than at obtaining possession, that his desires have passed by a sort of virement, as, in a budget, without any alteration in the total, certain expenditure is carried under another head. As is the case with invalids in whom a sudden attack of urticaria makes their chronic ailments temporarily disappear, this pure love for a young relative seems, in the invert, to have momentarily replaced, by metastasis, habits that will, one day or another, return to fill the place of the vicarious, cured malady.

Meanwhile the married neighbour of our recluse has returned; before the beauty of the young bride and the demonstrative affection of her husband, on the day when their friend is obliged to invite them to dinner, he feels ashamed of the past. Already in an interesting condition, she must return home early, leaving her husband behind; he, when the time has come for him to go home also, asks his host to accompany him for part of the way; at first, no suspicion enters his mind, but at the crossroads he finds himself thrown down on the grass, with not a word said, by the mountaineer who is shortly to become a father. And their meetings begin again, and continue until the day when there comes to live not far off a cousin of the young woman, with whom her husband is now constantly to be seen. And he, if the twice-abandoned friend calls in the evening and endeavours to approach him, is furious, and repulses him with indignation that the other has not had the tact to foresee the disgust which he must henceforward inspire. Once, however, there appears a stranger, sent to him by his faithless friend; but being busy at the time, the abandoned one cannot see him, and only afterwards learns with what object his visitor came.

Then the solitary languishes alone. He has no other diversion than to go to the neighbouring watering-place to ask for some information or other from a certain railwayman there. But the latter has obtained promotion, has been transferred to the other end of the country; the solitary will no longer be able to go and ask him the times of the trains or the price of a first class ticket, and, before retiring to dream, Griselda-like, in his tower, loiters upon the beach, a strange Andromeda whom no Argonaut will come to free, a sterile Medusa that must perish upon the sand, or else he stands idly, until his train starts, upon the platform, casting over the crowd of passengers a gaze that will seem indifferent, contemptuous or distracted to those of another race, but, like the luminous glow with which certain insects bedeck themselves in order to attract others of their species, or like the nectar which certain flowers offer to attract the insects that will fertilise them, would not deceive the almost undiscoverable sharer of a pleasure too singular, too hard to place, which is offered him, the colleague with whom our specialist could converse in the half-forgotten tongue; in which last, at the most, some seedy loafer upon the platform will put up a show of interest, but for pecuniary gain alone, like those people who, at the Collège de France, in the room in which the Professor of Sanskrit lectures without an audience, attend his course but only because the room itself is heated. Medusa! Orchid! When I followed my instinct only, the medusa used to revolt me at Balbec; but if I had the eyes to regard it, like Michelet, from the standpoint of natural history, and aesthetic, I saw an exquisite wheel of azure flame. Are they not, with the transparent velvet of their petals, as it were the mauve orchids of the sea? Like so many creatures of the animal and vegetable kingdoms, like the plant which would produce vanilla but, because in its structure the male organ is divided by a partition from the female, remains sterile unless the humming-birds or certain tiny bees convey the pollen from one to the other, or man fertilises them by artificial means, M. de Charlus (and here the word fertilise must be understood in a moral sense, since in the physical sense the union of male with male is and must be sterile, but it is no small matter that a person may encounter the sole pleasure which he is capable of enjoying, and that every 'creature here below' can impart to some other 'his music, or his fragrance or his flame'), M. de Charlus was one of those men who may be called exceptional, because however many they may be, the satisfaction, so easy in others, of their sexual requirements depends upon the coincidence of too many conditions, and of conditions too difficult to ensure. For men like M. de Charlus (leaving out of account the compromises which will appear in the course of this story and which the reader may already have foreseen, enforced by the need of pleasure which resigns itself to partial acceptations), mutual love, apart from the difficulties, so great as to be almost insurmountable, which it meets in the ordinary man, adds to these others so exceptional that what is always extremely rare for everyone becomes in their case well nigh impossible, and, if there should befall them an encounter which is really fortunate, or which nature makes appear so to them, their good fortune, far more than that of the normal lover, has about it something extraordinary, selective, profoundly necessary. The feud of the Capulets and Montagues was as nothing compared with the obstacles of every sort which must have been surmounted, the special eliminations which nature has had to submit to the hazards, already far from common, which result in love, before a retired tailor, who was intending to set off soberly for his office, can stand quivering in ecstasy before a stoutish man of fifty; this Romeo and this Juliet may believe with good reason that their love

is not the caprice of a moment but a true predestination, prepared by the
harmonies of their temperaments, and not only by their own personal
temperaments but by those of their ancestors, by their most distant strains
of heredity, so much so that the fellow creature who is conjoined with them
has belonged to them from before their birth, has attracted them by a force
comparable to that which governs the worlds on which we passed our
former lives. M. de Charlus had distracted me from looking to see whether
the bee was bringing to the orchid the pollen it had so long been waiting to
receive, and had no chance of receiving save by an accident so unlikely that
one might call it a sort of miracle. But this was a miracle also that I had just
witnessed, almost of the same order and no less marvellous. As soon as I had
considered their meeting from this point of view, everything about it
seemed to me instinct with beauty. The most extraordinary devices that
nature has invented to compel insects to ensure the fertilisation of flowers
which without their intervention could not be fertilised because the male
flower is too far away from the female – or when, if it is the wind that must
provide for the transportation of the pollen, she makes that pollen so much
more simply detachable from the male, so much more easily arrested in its
flight by the female flower, by eliminating the secretion of nectar which is
no longer of any use since there is no insect to be attracted, and, that the
flower may be kept free for the pollen which it needs, which can fructify
only in itself, makes it secrete a liquid which renders it immune to all other
pollens – seemed to me no more marvellous than the existence of the sub-
variety of inverts destined to guarantee the pleasures of love to the invert
who is growing old: men who are attracted not by all other men, but – by a
phenomenon of correspondence and harmony similar to those that precede
the fertilisation of heterostyle trimorphous flowers like the *lythrum salicoria* –
only by men considerably older than themselves. Of this sub-variety
Jupien had just furnished me with an example less striking however than
certain others, which every collector of a human herbary, every moral
botanist can observe in spite of their rarity, and which will present to the eye
a delicate youth who is waiting for the advances of a robust and paunchy
quinquagenarian, remaining as indifferent to those of other young men as
the hermaphrodite flowers of the short-styled *primula veris* so long as they
are fertilised only by other *primulae veris* of short style also, whereas they
welcome with joy the pollen of the *primula veris* with the long styles. As for
M. de Charlus's part in the transaction, I noticed afterwards that there were
for him various kinds of conjunction, some of which, by their multiplicity,
their almost invisible speed and above all the absence of contact between the
two actors, recalled still more forcibly those flowers that in a garden are

fertilised by the pollen of a neighbouring flower which they may never touch. There were in fact certain persons whom it was sufficient for him to make come to his house, hold for an hour or two under the domination of his talk, for his desire, quickened by some earlier encounter, to be assuaged. By a simple use of words the conjunction was effected, as simply as it can be among the infusoria. Sometimes, as had doubtless been the case with me on the evening on which I had been summoned by him after the Guermantes dinner-party, the relief was effected by a violent ejaculation which the Baron made in his visitor's face, just as certain flowers, furnished with a hidden spring, sprinkle from within the unconsciously collaborating and disconcerted insect. M. de Charlus, from vanquished turning victor, feeling himself purged of his uneasiness and calmed, would send away the visitor who had at once ceased to appear to him desirable. Finally, inasmuch as inversion itself springs from the fact that the invert is too closely akin to woman to be capable of having any effective relations with her, it comes under a higher law which ordains that so many hermaphrodite flowers shall remain unfertile, that is to say the law of the sterility of autofecundation. It is true that inverts, in their search for a male person, will often be found to put up with other inverts as effeminate as themselves. But it is enough that they do not belong to the female sex, of which they have in them an embryo which they can put to no useful purpose, such as we find in so many hermaphrodite flowers, and even in certain hermaphrodite animals, such as the snail, which cannot be fertilised by themselves, but can by other hermaphrodites. In this respect the race of inverts, who eagerly connect themselves with Oriental antiquity or the Golden Age in Greece, might be traced back farther still, to those experimental epochs in which there existed neither plants nor monosexual animals, to that initial hermaphroditism of which certain rudiments of male organs in the anatomy of the woman and of female organs in that of the man seem still to preserve the trace. I found the pantomime, incomprehensible to me at first, of Jupien and M. de Charlus as curious as those seductive gestures addressed, Darwin tells us, to insects not only by the flowers called composite which erect the florets of their capitals so as to be seen from a greater distance, such as a certain heterostyle which turns back its stamens and bends them to open the way for the insect, or offers him an ablution, or, to take an immediate instance, the nectar-fragrance and vivid hue of the corollae that were at that moment attracting insects to our courtyard. From this day onwards M. de Charlus was to alter the time of his visits to Mme de Villeparisis, not that he could not see Jupien elsewhere and with greater convenience, but because to him just as much as to me the afternoon sunshine and the blossoming plant were, no doubt, linked together in memory. Apart from this, he did not confine himself to recommending the Jupiens to Mme de Villeparisis, to the Duchesse de Guermantes, to a whole brilliant list of patrons, who were all the more assiduous in their attentions to the young seamstress when they saw that the few ladies who had held out, or had merely delayed their submission, were subjected to the direst reprisals by the Baron, whether in order that they might serve as an example, or because they had aroused his wrath and had stood out against his attempted domination; he made Jupien's position more and more lucrative, until he definitely engaged him as his secretary and established him in the state in which we shall see him later on. 'Ah, now! There is a happy man, if you like, that Jupien,' said Françoise, who had a tendency to minimise or exaggerate people's generosity according as it was bestowed on herself or on others. Not that, in this instance, she had any need to exaggerate, nor for that matter did she feel any jealousy, being genuinely fond of Jupien. 'Oh, he's such a good man, the Baron,' she went on, 'such a well-behaved, religious, proper sort of man. If I had a daughter to marry and was one of the rich myself, I would give her to the Baron with my eyes shut.' 'But, Françoise,' my mother observed gently, 'she'd be well supplied with husbands, that daughter of yours. Don't forget you've already promised her to Jupien.' 'Ah! Lordy, now,' replied Françoise, 'there's another of them that would make a woman happy. It doesn't matter whether you're rich or poor, it makes no difference to your nature. The Baron and Jupien, they're just the same sort of person.'

However, I greatly exaggerated at the time, on the strength of this first revelation, the elective character of so carefully selected a combination. Admittedly, every man of the kind of M. de Charlus is an extraordinary creature since, if he does not make concessions to the possibilities of life, he seeks out essentially the love of a man of the other race, that is to say a man who is a lover of women (and incapable consequently of loving him); in contradiction of what I had imagined in the courtyard, where I had seen Jupien turning towards M. de Charlus like the orchid making overtures to the bee, these exceptional creatures whom we commiserate are a vast crowd, as we shall see in the course of this work, for a reason which will be disclosed only at the end of it, and commiserate themselves for being too many rather than too few. For the two angels who were posted at the gates of Sodom to learn whether its inhabitants (according to Genesis) had indeed done all the things the report of which had ascended to the Eternal Throne must have been, and of this one can only be glad, exceedingly ill chosen by the Lord, Who ought not to have entrusted the task to any but a Sodomite. Such an one the excuses: 'Father of six children – I keep two mistresses,' and so forth could never have persuaded benevolently to lower his flaming sword and to mitigate the punishment; he would have answered: 'Yes, and your wife lives in a torment of jealousy. But even when these women have not been chosen by you from Gomorrah, you spend your nights with a watcher of flocks upon Hebron.' And he would at once have made him retrace his steps to the city which the rain of fire and brimstone was to destroy. On the contrary, they allowed to escape all the shamefaced Sodomites, even if these, on catching sight of a boy, turned their heads, like Lot's wife, though without being on that account changed like her into pillars of salt. With the result that they engendered a numerous posterity with whom this gesture has continued to be habitual, like that of the dissolute women who, while apparently studying a row of shoes displayed in a shop window, turn their heads to keep track of a passing student. These descendants of the Sodomites, so numerous that we may apply to them that other verse of Genesis: 'If a man can number the dust of the earth, then shall thy seed also be numbered,' have established themselves throughout the entire world; they have had access to every profession and pass so easily into the most exclusive clubs that, whenever a Sodomite fails to secure election, the blackballs are, for the most part, cast by other Sodomites, who are anxious to penalise sodomy, having inherited the falsehood that enabled their ancestors to escape from the accursed city. It is possible that they may return there one day. Certainly they form in every land an Oriental colony, cultured, musical, malicious, which has certain charming qualities and intolerable defects. We shall study them with greater thoroughness in the course of the following pages; but I have thought it as well to utter here a provisional warning against the lamentable error of proposing (just as people have encouraged a Zionist movement) to create a Sodomist movement and to rebuild Sodom. For, no sooner had they arrived there than the Sodomites would leave the town so as not to have the appearance of belonging to it, would take wives, keep mistresses in other cities where they would find, incidentally, every diversion that appealed to them. They would repair to Sodom only on days of supreme necessity, when their own town was empty, at those seasons when hunger drives the wolf from the woods; in other words, everything would go on very much as it does today in London, Berlin, Rome, Petrograd or Paris.

Anyhow, on the day in question, before paying my call on the Duchess, I did not look so far ahead, and I was distressed to find that I had, by my engrossment in the Jupien-Charlus conjunction, missed perhaps an opportunity of witnessing the fertilisation of the blossom by the bee.

PART II

Chapter One

M. de Charlus in Society – A physician – Typical physiognomy of Mme
de Vaugoubert – Mme d'Arpajon, the Hubert Robert fountain and the
merriment of the Grand Duke Vladimir – Mmes d'Amoncourt, de
Citri, de Saint-Euverte, etc. – Curious conversation between Swann and
the Prince de Guermantes – Albertine on the telephone – My social life
in the interval before my second and final visit to Balbec –
Arrival at Balbec: The heart's intermissions.

As I was in no haste to arrive at this party at the Guermantes', to which I
was not certain that I had been invited, I remained sauntering out of doors;
but the summer day seemed to be in no greater haste than myself to stir.
Albeit it was after nine o'clock, it was still the light of day that on the Place
de la Concorde was giving the Luxor obelisk the appearance of being made
of pink nougat. Then it diluted the tint and changed the surface to a
metallic substance, so that the obelisk not only became more precious but
seemed to have grown more slender and almost flexible. You imagined that
you might have twisted it in your fingers, had perhaps already slightly
distorted its outline. The moon was now in the sky like a section of orange
delicately peeled although slightly bruised. But presently she was to be
fashioned of the most enduring gold. Sheltering alone behind her, a poor
little star was to serve as sole companion to the lonely moon, while she,
keeping her friend protected, but bolder and striding ahead, would brandish
like an irresistible weapon, like an Oriental symbol, her broad and
marvellous crescent of gold.

Outside the mansion of the Princesse de Guermantes, I met the Duc de
Châtellerault; I no longer remembered that half an hour earlier I had still
been persecuted by the fear – which, for that matter, was speedily to grip me
again – that I might be entering the house uninvited. We grow uneasy, and
it is sometimes long after the hour of danger, which a subsequent distraction
has made us forget, that we remember our uneasiness. I greeted the young
Duke and made my way into the house. But here I must first of all record a

trifling incident, which will enable us to understand something that was presently to occur.

There was one person who, on that evening as on the previous evenings, had been thinking a great deal about the Duc de Châtellerault, without however suspecting who he was: this was the usher (styled at that time the *aboyeur*) of Mme de Guermantes. M. de Châtellerault, so far from being one of the Princess's intimate friends, albeit he was one of her cousins, had been invited to her house for the first time. His parents, who had not been on speaking terms with her for the last ten years, had been reconciled to her within the last fortnight, and, obliged to be out of Paris that evening, had requested their son to fill their place. Now, a few days earlier, the Princess's usher had met in the Champs-Elysées a young man whom he had found charming but whose identity he had been unable to establish. Not that the young man had not shown himself as obliging as he had been generous. All the favours that the usher had supposed that he would have to bestow upon so young a gentleman, he had on the contrary received. But M. de Châtellerault was as reticent as he was rash; he was all the more determined not to disclose his incognito since he did not know with what sort of person he was dealing; his fear would have been far greater, although quite unfounded, if he had known. He had confined himself to posing as an Englishman, and to all the passionate questions with which he was plied by the usher, desirous to meet again a person to whom he was indebted for so much pleasure and so ample a gratuity, the Duke had merely replied, from one end of the Avenue Gabriel to the other: 'I do not speak French.'

Albeit, in spite of everything – remembering his cousin Gilbert's maternal ancestry – the Duc de Guermantes pretended to find a touch of Courvoisier in the drawing-room of the Princesse de Guermantes-Bavière, the general estimate of that lady's initiative spirit and intellectual superiority was based upon an innovation that was to be found nowhere else in her set. After dinner, however important the party that was to follow, the chairs, at the Princesse de Guermantes's, were arranged in such a way as to form little groups, in which people might have to turn their backs upon one another. The Princess then displayed her social sense by going to sit down, as though by preference, in one of these. Not that she was afraid to pick out and attract to herself a member of another group. If, for instance, she had remarked to M. Détaille, who naturally agreed with her, on the beauty of Mme de Villemur's neck, of which that lady's position in another group made her present a back view, the Princess did not hesitate to raise her voice: 'Madame de Villemur, M. Détaille, with his wonderful painter's eye, has just been admiring your neck.' Mme de Villemur interpreted this as a direct invitation to join in the conversation; with the agility of a practised horsewoman, she made her chair rotate slowly through three quadrants of a circle, and, without in the least disturbing her neighbours, came to rest almost facing the Princess. 'You don't know M. Détaille?' exclaimed their hostess, for whom her guest's nimble and modest tergiversation was not sufficient. 'I do not know him, but I know his work,' replied Mme de Villemur, with a respectful, engaging air, and a promptitude which many of the onlookers envied her, addressing the while to the celebrated painter whom this invocation had not been sufficient to introduce to her in a formal manner, an imperceptible bow. 'Come, Monsieur Détaille,' said the Princess, 'let me introduce you to Mme de Villemur.' That lady thereupon showed as great ingenuity in making room for the creator of the *Dream* as she had shown a moment earlier in wheeling round to face him. And the Princess drew forward a chair for herself; she had indeed invoked Mme de Villemur only to have an excuse for quitting the first group, in which she had spent the statutory ten minutes, and bestowing a similar allowance of her time upon the second. In three quarters of an hour, all the groups had received a visit from her, which seemed to have been determined in each instance by impulse and predilection, but had the paramount object of making it apparent how naturally 'a great lady knows how to entertain.' But now the guests for the party were beginning to arrive, and the lady of the house was seated not far from the door – erect and proud in her semi-regal majesty, her eyes ablaze with their own incandescence – between two unattractive Royalties and the Spanish Ambassadress.

I stood waiting behind a number of guests who had arrived before me. Facing me was the Princess, whose beauty is probably not the only thing, where there were so many beauties, that reminds me of this party. But the face of my hostess was so perfect; stamped like so beautiful a medal, that it has retained a commemorative force in my mind. The Princess was in the habit of saying to her guests when she met them a day or two before one of her parties: 'You will come, won't you?' as though she felt a great desire to talk to them. But as, on the contrary, she had nothing to talk to them about, when they entered her presence she contented herself, without rising, with breaking off for an instant her vapid conversation with the two Royalties and the Ambassadress and thanking them with: 'How good of you to have come,' not that she thought that the guest had shown his goodness by coming, but to enhance her own; then, at once dropping him back into the stream, she would add: 'You will find M. de Guermantes by the garden door,' so that the guest proceeded on his way and ceased to bother her. To some indeed she said nothing, contenting herself with showing them her admirable onyx eyes, as though they had come merely to visit an exhibition of precious stones.

The person immediately in front of me was the Duc de Châtellerault.

Having to respond to all the smiles, all the greetings waved to him from inside the drawing-room, he had not noticed the usher. But from the first moment the usher had recognised him. The identity of this stranger, which he had so ardently desired to learn, in another minute he would know. When he asked his 'Englishman' of the other evening what name he was to announce, the usher was not merely stirred, he considered that he was being indiscreet, indelicate. He felt that he was about to reveal to the whole world (which would, however, suspect nothing) a secret which it was criminal of him to force like this and to proclaim in public. Upon hearing the guest's reply: 'Le duc de Châtellerault', he felt such a burst of pride that he remained for a moment speechless. The Duke looked at him, recognised him, saw himself ruined, while the servant, who had recovered his composure and was sufficiently versed in heraldry to complete for himself an appellation that was too modest, shouted with a professional vehemence softened by an emotional tenderness: 'Son Altesse Monseigneur le duc de Châtellerault!' But it was now my turn to be announced. Absorbed in contemplation of my hostess, who had not yet seen me, I had not thought of the function – terrible to me, although not in the same sense as to M. de Châtellerault – of this usher garbed in black like a headsman, surrounded by a group of lackeys in the most cheerful livery, lusty fellows ready to seize hold of an intruder and cast him out of doors. The usher asked me my name, I told him it as mechanically as the condemned man allows himself to be strapped to the block. At once he lifted his head majestically and, before I could beg him to announce me in a lowered tone so as to spare my own feelings if I were not invited and those of the Princesse de Guermantes if I were, shouted the disturbing syllables with a force capable of bringing down the roof.

The famous Huxley (whose grandson occupies an unassailable position in the English literary world of today) relates that one of his patients dared not continue to go into society because often, on the actual chair that was pointed out to her with a courteous gesture, she saw an old gentleman already seated. She could be quite certain that either the gesture of invitation or the old gentleman's presence was a hallucination, for her hostess would not have offered her a chair that was already occupied. And when Huxley, to cure her, forced her to reappear in society, she felt a moment of painful hesitation when she asked herself whether the friendly sign that was being made to her was the real thing, or, in obedience to a non-existent vision, she was about to sit down in public upon the knees of a gentleman in flesh and blood. Her brief uncertainty was agonising. Less so perhaps than mine. From the moment at which I had taken in the sound of my name, like the rumble that warns us of a possible cataclysm, I was bound to plead my own good faith in either event, and as though I were not tormented by any doubt, to advance towards the Princess with a resolute air.

She caught sight of me when I was still a few feet away and (to leave me in no doubt that I was the victim of a conspiracy), instead of remaining seated, as she had done for her other guests, rose and came towards me. A moment later, I was able to heave the sigh of relief of Huxley's patient when, having made up her mind to sit down on the chair, she found it vacant and realised that it was the old gentleman that was a hallucination. The Princess had just held out her hand to me with a smile. She remained standing for some moments with the kind of charm enshrined in the verse of Malherbe which ends: 'To do them honour all the angels rise.'

She apologised because the Duchess had not yet come, as though I must be bored there without her. In order to give me this greeting, she wheeled round me, holding me by the hand, in a graceful revolution by the whirl of which I felt myself carried off my feet. I almost expected that she would next offer me, like the leader of a cotillon, an ivory-headed cane or a watch-bracelet. She did not, however, give me anything of the sort, and as though, instead of dancing the boston, she had been listening to a sacred quartet by Beethoven the sublime strains of which she was afraid of interrupting, she cut short the conversation there and then, or rather did not begin it, and, still radiant at having seen me come in, merely informed me where the Prince was to be found.

I moved away from her and did not venture to approach her again, feeling that she had absolutely nothing to say to me and that, in her vast kindness, this woman marvellously tall and handsome, noble as were so many great ladies who stepped so proudly upon the scaffold, could only, short of offering me a draught of honeydew, repeat what she had already said to me twice: 'You will find the Prince in the garden.' Now, to go in search of the Prince was to feel my doubts revive in a fresh form.

In any case I should have to find somebody to introduce me. One could hear, above all the din of conversation, the interminable chatter of M. de Charlus, talking to H. E. the Duke of Sidonia, whose acquaintance he had just made. Members of the same profession find one another out, and so it is with a common vice. M. de Charlus and M. de Sidonia had each of them immediately detected the other's vice, which was in both cases that of soliloquising in society, to the extent of not being able to stand any interruption. Having decided at once that, in the words of a famous sonnet, there was 'no help', they had made up their minds not to be silent but each to go on talking without any regard to what the other might say. This had resulted in the confused babble produced in Molière's comedies by a number of people saying different things simultaneously. The Baron, with his deafening voice, was moreover certain of keeping the upper hand, of drowning the feeble voice of M. de Sidonia; without however discouraging him, for, whenever M. de Charlus paused for a moment to breathe, the interval was filled by the murmurs of the Grandee of Spain who had imperturbably continued his discourse. I could easily have asked M. de Charlus to introduce me to the Prince de Guermantes, but I feared (and with good reason) that he might be cross with me. I had treated him in the most ungrateful fashion by letting his offer pass unheeded for the second time and by never giving him a sign of my existence since the evening when he had so affectionately escorted me home. And yet I could not plead the excuse of having anticipated the scene which I had just witnessed, that very afternoon, enacted by himself and Jupien. I suspected nothing of the sort. It is true that shortly before this, when my parents reproached me with my laziness and with not having taken the trouble to write a line to M. de Charlus, I had violently reproached them with wishing me to accept a degrading proposal. But anger alone, and the desire to hit upon the expression that would be most offensive to them had dictated this mendacious retort. In reality, I had imagined nothing sensual, nothing sentimental even, underlying the Baron's offers. I had said this to my parents with entire irresponsibility. But sometimes the future is latent in us without our knowledge, and our words which we suppose to be false forecast an imminent reality.

M. de Charlus would doubtless have forgiven me my want of gratitude. But what made him furious was that my presence this evening at the Princesse de Guermantes's, as for some time past at her cousin's, seemed to be a defiance of his solemn declaration: 'There is no admission to those houses save through me.' A grave fault, a crime that was perhaps inexpiable, I had not followed the conventional path. M. de Charlus knew well that the thunderbolts which he hurled at those who did not comply with his orders, or to whom he had taken a dislike, were beginning to be regarded by many people, however furiously he might brandish them, as mere pasteboard, and had no longer the force to banish anybody from anywhere. But he believed perhaps that his diminished power, still considerable, remained intact in the eyes of novices like myself. And so I did not consider it well advised to ask a favour of him at a party at which the mere fact of my presence seemed an ironical denial of his pretensions.

I was buttonholed at that moment by a man of a distinctly common type, Professor E—. He had been surprised to see me at the Guermantes'. I was no less surprised to see him there, for nobody had ever seen before or was ever to see again a person of his sort at one of the Princess's parties. He had just succeeded in curing the Prince, after the last rites had been administered, of a septic pneumonia, and the special gratitude that Mme de Guermantes felt towards him was the reason for her thus departing from custom and inviting him to her house. As he knew absolutely nobody in the rooms, and could not wander about there indefinitely by himself, like a minister of death, having recognised me, he had discovered, for the first time in his life, that he had an infinite number of things to say to me, which enabled him to assume an air of composure, and this was one of the reasons for his advancing upon me. There was also another. He attached great importance to his never being mistaken in his diagnoses. Now his correspondence was so numerous that he could not always bear in mind, when he had seen a patient once only, whether the disease had really followed the course that he had traced for it. The reader may perhaps remember that, immediately after my grandmother's stroke, I had taken her to see him, on the afternoon when he was having all his decorations stitched to his coat. After so long an interval, he no longer remembered the formal announcement which had been sent to him at the time. 'Your grandmother is dead, isn't she?' he said to me in a voice in which a semi-certainty calmed a slight apprehension. 'Ah! Indeed! Well, from the moment I saw her my prognosis was extremely grave, I remember it quite well.'

It was thus that Professor E— learned or recalled the death of my grandmother, and (I must say this to his credit, which is that of the medical profession as a whole), without displaying, without perhaps feeling, any satisfaction. The mistakes made by doctors are innumerable. They err habitually on the side of optimism as to treatment, of pessimism as to the outcome. 'Wine? In moderation, it can do you no harm, it is always a tonic ... Sexual enjoyment? After all it is a natural function. I allow you to use, but not to abuse it, you understand. Excess in anything is wrong.' At once, what a temptation to the patient to renounce those two life-givers, water and chastity. If, on the other hand, he has any trouble with his heart, albumen, and so forth, it never lasts for long. Disorders that are grave but purely functional are at once ascribed to an imaginary cancer. It is useless to continue visits which are powerless to eradicate an incurable malady. Let the patient, left to his own devices, thereupon subject himself to an implacable regime, and in time recover, or merely survive, and the doctor, to whom he touches his hat in the Avenue de l'Opéra, when he supposed him to have long been lying in Père Lachaise, will interpret the gesture as an act of insolent defiance. An innocent stroll, taken beneath his nose and venerable beard, would arouse no greater wrath in the Assize Judge who, two years earlier, had sentenced the rascal, now passing him with apparent impunity, to death. Doctors (we do not here include them all, of course, and make a mental reservation of certain admirable exceptions), are in general more displeased, more irritated by the quashing of their sentence than pleased by its execution. This explains why Professor E—, despite the intellectual satisfaction that he doubtless felt at finding that he had not been mistaken, was able to speak to me only with regret of the blow that had fallen upon us. He was in no hurry to cut short the conversation, which kept him in countenance and gave him a reason for remaining. He spoke to me of the great heat through which we were passing, but, albeit he was a well-read man and capable of expressing himself in good French, said to me: 'You are none the worse for this hyperthermia?' The fact is that medicine has made some slight advance in knowledge since Molière's days, but none in its vocabulary. My companion went on: 'The great thing is to avoid the sudations that are caused by weather like this, especially in superheated rooms. You can remedy them, when you go home and feel thirsty, by the application of heat.' (by which he apparently meant hot drinks)

Owing to the circumstances of my grandmother's death, the subject interested me, and I had recently read in a book by a great specialist that perspiration was injurious to the kidneys, by making moisture pass through the skin when its proper outlet was elsewhere. I thought with regret of those dog-days at the time of my grandmother's death, and was inclined to blame them for it. I did not mention this to Dr E—, but of his own accord he said to me: 'The advantage of this very hot weather in which perspiration is abundant is that the kidney is correspondingly relieved.' Medicine is not an exact science.

Keeping me engaged in talk, Professor E— asked only not to be forced to leave me. But I had just seen, making a series of sweeping bows to right and left of the Princesse de Guermantes, stepping back a pace first, the Marquis de Vaugoubert. M. de Norpois had recently introduced me to him and I hoped that I might find in him a person capable of introducing me to our host. The proportions of this work do not permit me to explain here in consequence of what incidents in his youth M. de Vaugoubert was one of the few men (possibly the only man) in society who happened to be in what is called at Sodom the 'confidence' of M. de Charlus. But, if our Minister to the Court of King Theodosius had certain defects in common with the Baron, they were only a very pale reflection. It was merely in an infinitely softened, sentimental and simple form that he displayed those alternations of affection and hatred through which the desire to attract, and then the fear – equally imaginary – of being, if not scorned, at any rate unmasked, made the Baron pass. Made ridiculous by a chastity, a 'platonicism' (to which as a man of keen ambition he had, from the moment of passing his examination, sacrificed all pleasure), above all by his intellectual nullity, these alternations M. de Vaugoubert did, nevertheless, display. But whereas in M. de Charlus the immoderate praises were proclaimed with a positive burst of eloquence, and seasoned with the subtlest, the most mordant banter which marked a man for ever, by M. de Vaugoubert, on the other hand, the affection was expressed with the banality of a man of the lowest intelligence, and of a public official, the grievances (worked up generally into a complete indictment, as with the Baron) by a malevolence which, though relentless, was at the same time spiritless, and was all the more startling inasmuch as it was invariably a direct contradiction of what the Minister had said six months earlier and might soon perhaps be saying again: a regularity of change which gave an almost astronomic poetry to the various phases of M. de Vaugoubert's life, albeit apart from this nobody was ever less suggestive of a star.

The greeting that he gave me had nothing in common with that which I should have received from M. de Charlus. To this greeting M. de Vaugoubert, apart from the thousand mannerisms which he supposed to be indicative of good breeding and diplomacy, imparted a cavalier, brisk, smiling air, which should make him seem on the one hand to be rejoicing at being alive – at a time when he was inwardly chewing the mortification of a career with no prospect of advancement and with the threat of enforced retirement – and on the other hand young, virile and charming, when he could see and no longer ventured to go and examine in the glass the lines gathering upon a face which he would have wished to keep full of seduction. Not that he would have hoped for effective conquests, the mere thought of which filled him with terror on account of what people would say, scandals, blackmail. Having passed from an almost infantile corruption to an absolute continence dating from the day on which his thoughts had turned to the Quai d'Orsay and he had begun to plan a great career for himself, he had the air of a caged animal, casting in every direction glances expressive of fear, appetite and stupidity. This last was so dense that he did not reflect that the street-arabs of his adolescence were boys no longer, and when a news vendor bawled in his face: '*La Presse!*' even more than with longing he shuddered with terror, imagining himself recognised and denounced.

But in default of the pleasures sacrificed to the ingratitude of the Quai d'Orsay, M. de Vaugoubert – and it was for this that he was anxious still to attract – was liable to sudden stirrings of the heart. Heaven knows with how many letters he would overwhelm the Ministry (what personal ruses he would employ, the drafts that he made upon the credit of Mme de Vaugoubert, who, on account of her corpulence, her exalted birth, her masculine air, and above all the mediocrity of her husband, was reputed to be endowed with eminent capacities and to be herself for all practical purposes the Minister), to introduce without any valid reason a young man destitute of all merit into the staff of the Legation. It is true that a few months, a few years later, the insignificant attaché had only to appear, without the least trace of any hostile intention, to have shown signs of coldness towards his chief for the latter, supposing himself scorned or betrayed, to devote the same hysterical ardour to punishing him with which he had showered favours upon him in the past. He would move heaven and earth to have him recalled and the Director of Political Affairs would receive a letter daily: 'Why don't you hurry up and rid me of that lascar. Give him a dressing down in his own interest. What he needs is a slice of humble pie.' The post of attaché at the court of King Theodosius was on this account far from enjoyable. But in all other respects, thanks to his perfect common sense as a man of the world, M. de Vaugoubert was one of the best representatives of the French Government abroad. When a man who was reckoned a superior person, a Jacobin, with an expert knowledge of all subjects, replaced him later on, it was not long before war broke out between France and the country over which that monarch reigned.

M. de Vaugoubert, like M. de Charlus, did not care to be the first to give a greeting. Each of them preferred to 'respond', being constantly afraid of the gossip which the person to whom otherwise they might have offered their hand might have heard about them since their last meeting. In my case, M. de Vaugoubert had no need to ask himself this question, I had as a matter of fact gone up of my own accord to greet him, if only because of the difference in our ages. He replied with an air of wonder and delight, his eyes continuing to stray as though there had been a patch of clover on either side of me upon which he was forbidden to graze. I felt that it would be more becoming to ask him to introduce me to Mme de Vaugoubert, before effecting that introduction to the Prince which I decided not to mention to him until afterwards. The idea of making me acquainted with his wife seemed to fill him with joy, for his own sake as well as for hers, and he led me at a solemn pace towards the Marquise. Arriving in front of her, and indicating me with his hand and eyes, with every conceivable mark of consideration, he nevertheless remained silent and withdrew after a few

moments, in a sidelong fashion, leaving me alone with his wife. She had at
once given me her hand, but without knowing to whom this token of
friendship was addressed, for I realised that M. de Vaugoubert had forgotten
my name, perhaps even had failed to recognise me, and being unwilling,
from politeness, to confess his ignorance had made the introduction consist
in a mere dumb show. And so I was no further advanced; how was I to get
myself introduced to my host by a woman who did not know my name?
Worse still, I found myself obliged to remain for some moments talking to
Mme de Vaugoubert. And this annoyed me for two reasons. I had no wish to
remain all night at this party, for I had arranged with Albertine (I had given
her a box for *Phèdre*) that she was to pay me a visit shortly before midnight.
Certainly I was not in the least in love with her; I was yielding, in making her
come this evening, to a wholly sensual desire, albeit we were at that torrid
period of the year when sensuality, evaporating, visits more readily the
organ of taste, seeks above all things coolness. More than for the kiss of a
girl, it thirsts for orangeade, for a cold bath, or even to gaze at that peeled
and juicy moon which was quenching the thirst of heaven. I counted
however upon ridding myself, in Albertine's company – which, moreover,
reminded me of the coolness of the sea – of the regret that I should not fail
to feel for many charming faces (for it was a party quite as much for girls as
for married women that the Princess was giving. On the other hand, the
face of the imposing Mme de Vaugoubert, Bourbonian and morose, was in
no way attractive).

People said at the Ministry, without any suggestion of malice, that in
their household it was the husband who wore the petticoats and the wife
the trousers. Now there was more truth in this saying than was supposed.
Mme de Vaugoubert was really a man. Whether she had always been one,
or had grown to be as I saw her, matters little, for in either case we have to
deal with one of the most touching miracles of nature which, in the latter
alternative especially, makes the human kingdom resemble the kingdom of
flowers. On the former hypothesis – if the future Mme de Vaugoubert had
always been so clumsily manlike – nature, by a fiendish and beneficent ruse,
bestows on the girl the deceiving aspect of a man. And the youth who has
no love for women and is seeking to be cured greets with joy this subterfuge
of discovering a bride who figures in his eyes as a market porter. In the
alternative case, if the woman has not originally these masculine characteristics, she adopts them by degrees, to please her husband, and even
unconsciously, by that sort of mimicry which makes certain flowers assume
the appearance of the insects which they seek to attract. Her regret that she
is not loved, that she is not a man, virilises her. Indeed, quite apart from the

case that we are now considering, who has not remarked how often the most normal couples end by resembling each other, at times even by an exchange of qualities? A former German Chancellor, Prince von Bùlow, married an Italian. In the course of time, on the Pincio, it was remarked how much the Teutonic husband had absorbed of Italian delicacy, and the Italian Princess of German coarseness. To turn aside to a point without the province of the laws which we are now tracing, everyone knows an eminent French diplomat, whose origin was at first suggested only by his name, one of the most illustrious in the East. As he matured, as he grew old, there was revealed in him the Oriental whom no one had ever suspected, and now when we see him we regret the absence of the fez that would complete the picture.

To revert to habits completely unknown to the ambassador whose profile, coarsened by heredity, we have just recalled, Mme de Vaugoubert realised the acquired or predestined type, the immortal example of which is the Princess Palatine, never out of a riding habit, who, having borrowed from her husband more than his virility, championing the defects of the men who do not care for women, reports in her familiar correspondence the mutual relations of all the great noblemen of the court of Louis XIV. One of the reasons which enhance still farther the masculine air of women like Mme de Vaugoubert is that the neglect which they receive from their husbands, the shame that they feel at such neglect, destroy in them by degrees everything that is womanly. They end by acquiring both the good and the bad qualities which their husbands lack. The more frivolous, effeminate, indiscreet their husbands are, the more they grow into the effigy, devoid of charm, of the virtues which their husbands ought to practise.

Traces of abasement, boredom, indignation, marred the regular features of Mme de Vaugoubert. Alas, I felt that she was regarding me with interest and curiosity as one of those young men who appealed to M. de Vaugoubert, and one of whom she herself would so much have liked to be, now that her husband, growing old, showed a preference for youth. She was gazing at me with the close attention shown by provincial ladies who from an illustrated catalogue copy the tailor-made dress so becoming to the charming person in the picture (actually, the same person on every page, but deceptively multiplied into different creatures, thanks to the differences of pose and the variety of attire). The instinctive attraction which urged Mme de Vaugoubert towards me was so strong that she went the length of seizing my arm, so that I might take her to get a glass of orangeade. But I released myself, alleging that I must presently be going, and had not yet been introduced to our host.

This distance between me and the garden door where he stood talking to a group of people was not very great. But it alarmed me more than if, in order to cross it, I should have to expose myself to a continuous hail of fire.

A number of women from whom I felt that I might be able to secure an introduction were in the garden, where, while feigning an ecstatic admiration, they were at a loss for an occupation. Parties of this sort are as a rule premature. They have little reality until the following day, when they occupy the attention of the people who were not invited. A real author, devoid of the foolish self-esteem of so many literary people, if, when he reads an article by a critic who has always expressed the greatest admiration for his works, he sees the names of various inferior writers mentioned, but not his own, has no time to stop and consider what might be to him a matter for astonishment: his books are calling him. But a society woman has nothing to do and, on seeing in the *Figaro*: 'Last night the Prince and Princesse de Guermantes gave a large party,' etc., exclaims: 'What! Only three days ago I talked to Marie-Gilbert for an hour, and she never said a word about it!' and racks her brains to discover how she can have offended the Guermantes. It must be said that, so far as the Princess's parties were concerned, the astonishment was sometimes as great among those who were invited as among those who were not. For they would burst forth at the moment when one least expected them, and summoned in people whose existence Mme de Guermantes had forgotten for years. And almost all the people in society are so insignificant that others of their sort adopt, in judging them, only the measure of their social success, cherish them if they are invited, if they are omitted detest them. As to the latter, if it was the fact that the Princess often, even when they were her friends, did not invite them, that was often due to her fear of annoying 'Palamède', who had excommunicated them. And so I might be certain that she had not spoken of me to M. de Charlus, for otherwise I should not have found myself there. He meanwhile was posted between the house and the garden, by the side of the German Ambassador, leaning upon the balustrade of the great staircase which led from the garden to the house, so that the other guests, in spite of the three or four feminine admirers who were grouped round the Baron and almost concealed him, were obliged to greet him as they passed. He responded by naming each of them in turn. And one heard an incessant: 'Good-evening, Monsieur du Hazay, good-evening, Madame de la Tour du Pin-Verclause, good-evening, Madame de la Tour du Pin-Gouvernet, good-evening, Philibert, good-evening, my dear Ambassadress,' and so on. This created a continuous barking sound, interspersed with benevolent suggestions or inquiries (to the answers to which he paid no attention), which M. de Charlus addressed to them in a tone softened, artificial to show his indifference, and benign: 'Take care the child doesn't catch cold, it is always rather damp in the gardens. Good-evening, Madame de Brantes. Good-evening, Madame de Mecklembourg. Have you brought your daughter? Is she wearing that delicious pink frock? Good-evening, Saint-Geran.' Certainly there was an element of pride in this attitude, for M. de Charlus was aware that he was a Guermantes, and that he occupied a supreme place at this party. But there was more in it than pride, and the very word *fête* suggested, to the man with aesthetic gifts, the luxurious, curious sense that it might bear if this party were being given not by people in contemporary society but in a painting by Carpaccio or Veronese. It is indeed highly probable that the German Prince that M. de Charlus was must rather have been picturing to himself the reception that occurs in *Tannhäuser*, and himself as the Margrave, standing at the entrance to the Warburg with a kind word of condescension for each of his guests, while their procession into the castle or the park is greeted by the long phrase, a hundred times renewed, of the famous March.

I must, however, make up my mind. I could distinguish beneath the trees various women with whom I was more or less closely acquainted, but they seemed transformed because they were at the Princess's and not at her cousin's, and because I saw them seated not in front of Dresden china plates but beneath the boughs of a chestnut. The refinement of their setting mattered nothing. Had it been infinitely less refined than at Oriane's, I should have felt the same uneasiness. When the electric light in our drawing-room fails, and we are obliged to replace it with oil lamps, everything seems altered. I was recalled from my uncertainty by Mme de Souvré. 'Good-evening,' she said as she approached me. 'Have you seen the Duchesse de Guermantes lately?' She excelled in giving to speeches of this sort an intonation which proved that she was not uttering them from sheer silliness, like people who, not knowing what to talk about, come up to you a thousand times over to mention some bond of common acquaintance, often extremely slight. She had on the contrary a fine conducting wire in her glance which signified: 'Don't suppose for a moment that I haven't recognised you. You are the young man I met at the Duchesse de Guermantes. I remember quite well.' Unfortunately, this protection, extended over me by this phrase, stupid in appearance but delicate in intention, was extremely fragile, and vanished as soon as I tried to make use of it. Madame de Souvré had the art, if called upon to convey a request to some influential person, of appearing at the same time, in the petitioner's eyes, to be recommending him, and in those of the influential person not to be recommending the petitioner, so that her ambiguous gesture opened a credit balance of gratitude to her with the latter without placing her in any way in debt to the former. Encouraged by this lady's civilities to ask her to introduce me to M. de Guermantes, I found that she took advantage of a moment when our host was not looking in our direction, laid a motherly hand on my shoulder, and, smiling at the averted face of the Prince who was unable to see her, thrust me towards him with a gesture of feigned protection, but deliberately ineffective, which left me stranded almost at my starting point. Such is the cowardice of people in society.

That of a lady who came to greet me, addressing me by my name, was greater still. I tried to recall her own name as I talked to her; I remembered quite well having met her at dinner, I could remember things that she had said. But my attention, concentrated upon the inward region in which these memories of her lingered, was unable to discover her name there. It was there, nevertheless. My thoughts began playing a sort of game with it to grasp its outlines, its initial letter, and so finally to bring the whole name to light. It was labour in vain, I could more or less estimate its mass, its weight, but as for its forms, confronting them with the shadowy captive lurking in the inward night, I said to myself: 'It is not that.' Certainly my mind would have been capable of creating the most difficult names. Unfortunately, it had not to create but to reproduce. All action by the mind is easy, if it is not subjected to the test of reality. Here, I was forced to own myself beaten. Finally, in a flash, the name came back to me as a whole: 'Madame d'Arpajon'. I am wrong in saying that it came, for it did not, I think, appear to me by a spontaneous propulsion. I do not think either that the many slight memories which associated me with the lady, and to which I did not cease to appeal for help (by such exhortations as: 'Come now, it is the lady who is a friend of Mme de Souvré, who feels for Victor Hugo so artless an admiration, mingled with so much alarm and horror') – I do not believe that all these memories, hovering between me and her name, served in any way to bring it to light. In that great game of hide and seek which is played in our memory when we seek to recapture a name, there is not any series of gradual approximations. We see nothing, then suddenly the name appears in its exact form and very different from what we thought we could make out. It is not the name that has come to us. No, I believe rather that, as we go on living, we pass our time in keeping away from the zone in which a name is distinct, and it was by an exercise of my will and attention which increased the acuteness of my inward vision that all of a sudden I had pierced the semi-darkness and seen daylight. In any case, if there are transitions between oblivion and memory, then these transitions are unconscious. For the intermediate names through which we pass, before finding the real name, are themselves false, and bring us nowhere nearer to it. They are not even, properly speaking, names at all, but often mere consonants which are not to be found in the recaptured name. And yet, this operation of the mind passing from a blank to reality is so mysterious, that it is possible after all that these false consonants are really handles, awkwardly held out to enable us to seize hold of the correct name. 'All this,' the reader will remark, 'tells us nothing as to the lady's failure to oblige; but since you have made so long a digression, allow me, gentle author, to waste another moment of your time in telling you that it is a pity that, young as you were (or as your hero was, if he be not yourself), you had already so feeble a memory that you could not recall the name of a lady whom you knew quite well.' It is indeed a pity, gentle reader. And sadder than you think when one feels the time approaching when names and words will vanish from the clear zone of consciousness, and when one must for ever cease to name to oneself the people whom one has known most intimately. It is indeed a pity that one should require this effort, when one is still young, to recapture names which one knows quite well. But if this infirmity occurred only in the case of names barely known, quite naturally forgotten, names which one would not take the trouble to remember, the infirmity would not be without its advantages. 'And what are they, may I ask?' Well, Sir, that the malady alone makes us remark and apprehend, and allows us to dissect the mechanism of which otherwise we should know nothing. A man who, night after night, falls like a lump of lead upon his bed, and ceases to live until the moment when he wakes and rises, will such a man ever dream of making, I do not say great discoveries, but even minute observations upon sleep? He barely knows that he does sleep. A little insomnia is not without its value in making us appreciate sleep, in throwing a ray of light upon that darkness. A memory without fault is not a very powerful incentive to studying the phenomena of memory. 'In a word, did Mme d'Arpajon introduce you to the Prince?' No, but be quiet and let me go on with my story.

Mme d'Arpajon was even more cowardly than Mme de Souvré, but there was more excuse for her cowardice. She knew that she had always had very little influence in society. This influence, such as it was, had been reduced still farther by her connection with the Duc de Guermantes; his desertion of her dealt it the final blow. The resentment which she felt at my request that she should introduce me to the Prince produced a silence which, she was artless enough to suppose, conveyed the impression that she had not heard what I said. She was not even aware that she was knitting her brows with anger. Perhaps, on the other hand, she was aware of it, did not bother about the inconsistency, and made use of it for the lesson which she was thus able to teach me without undue rudeness; I mean a silent lesson, but none the less eloquent for that.

Apart from this, Mme d'Arpajon was extremely annoyed; many eyes were raised in the direction of a renaissance balcony at the corner of which, instead of one of those monumental statues which were so often used as ornaments at that period, there leaned, no less sculptural than they, the magnificent Marquise de Surgis-le-Duc, who had recently succeeded Mme d'Arpajon in the heart of Basin de Guermantes. Beneath the flimsy white tulle which protected her from the cool night air, one saw the supple form of a winged victory. I had no recourse left save to M. de Charlus, who had withdrawn to a room downstairs which opened on the garden. I had plenty of time (as he was pretending to be absorbed in a fictitious game of whist which enabled him to appear not to notice people) to admire the deliberate, artistic simplicity of his evening coat which, by the merest trifles which only a tailor's eye could have picked out, had the air of a 'Harmony in Black and White' by Whistler; black, white and red, rather, for M. de Charlus was wearing, hanging from a broad ribbon pinned to the lapel of his coat, the Cross, in white, black and red enamel, of a Knight of the religious Order of Malta. At that moment the Baron's game was interrupted by Mme de Gallardon, leading her nephew, the Vicomte de Courvoisier, a young man with an attractive face and an impertinent air. 'Cousin,' said Mme de Gallardon, 'allow me to introduce my nephew Adalbert. Adalbert, you remember the famous Palamède of whom you have heard so much.' 'Good-evening, Madame de Gallardon,' M. de Charlus replied. And he added, without so much as a glance at the young man: 'Good-evening, Sir,' with a truculent air and in a tone so violently discourteous that everyone in the room was stupefied. Perhaps M. de Charlus, knowing that Mme de Gallardon had her doubts as to his morals and guessing that she had not been able to resist, for once in a way, the temptation to allude to them, was determined to nip in the bud any scandal that she might have embroidered upon a friendly reception of her nephew, making at the same time a resounding profession of indifference with regard to young men in general; perhaps he had not considered that the said Adalbert had responded to his aunt's speech with a sufficiently respectful air; perhaps, desirous of making headway in time to come with so attractive a cousin, he chose to give himself the advantage of a preliminary assault, like those sovereigns who, before engaging upon diplomatic action, strengthen it by an act of war.

It was not so difficult as I supposed to secure M. de Charlus's consent to my request that he should introduce me to the Prince de Guermantes. For one thing, in the course of the last twenty years, this Don Quixote had tilted against so many windmills (often relatives who, he imagined, had behaved badly to him), he had so frequently banned people as being 'impossible to have in the house' from being invited by various male or female Guermantes, that these were beginning to be afraid of quarrelling with all the people they knew and liked, of condemning themselves to a lifelong deprivation of the society of certain newcomers whom they were curious to meet, by espousing the thunderous but unexplained rancours of a brother-in-law or cousin who expected them to abandon for his sake, wife, brother, children. More intelligent than the other Guermantes, M. de Charlus realised that people were ceasing to pay any attention, save once in a while, to his veto, and, looking to the future, fearing lest one day it might be with his society that they would dispense, he had begun to make allowances, to reduce, as the saying is, his terms. Furthermore, if he had the faculty of ascribing for months, for years on end, an identical life to a detested person – to such an one he would not have tolerated their sending an invitation, and would have fought, rather, like a trooper, against a queen, the status of the person who stood in his way ceasing to count for anything in his eyes; on the other hand, his explosions of wrath were too frequent not to be somewhat fragmentary. 'The imbecile, the rascal! We shall have to put him in his place, sweep him into the gutter, where unfortunately he will not be innocuous to the health of the town,' he would scream, even when he was alone in his own room, while reading a letter that he considered irreverent, or upon recalling some remark that had been repeated to him. But a fresh outburst against a second imbecile cancelled the first, and the former victim had only to show due deference for the crisis that he had occasioned to be forgotten, it not having lasted long enough to establish a foundation of hatred upon which to build. And so, I might perhaps – despite his ill-humour towards me – have been successful when I asked him to introduce me to the Prince, had I not been so ill-inspired as to add, from a scruple of conscience, and so that he might not suppose me guilty of the indelicacy of entering the house at a venture, counting upon him to enable me to remain there: 'You are aware that I know them quite well, the Princess has been very kind to me.' 'Very well, if you know them, why do you need me to introduce you?' he replied in a sharp tone, and, turning his back, resumed his make-believe game with the Nuncio, the German Ambassador and another personage whom I did not know by sight.

Then, from the depths of those gardens where in days past the Duc d'Aiguillon used to breed rare animals, there came to my ears, through the great, open doors, the sound of a sniffing nose that was savouring all those refinements and determined to miss none of them. The sound approached,

I moved at a venture in its direction, with the result that the words *good-evening* were murmured in my ear by M. de Bréauté, not like the rusty metallic-sound of a knife being sharpened on a grindstone, even less like the cry of the wild boar, devastator of tilled fields, but like the voice of a possible saviour.

Less influential than Mme de Souvré, but less deeply ingrained than she with the incapacity to oblige, far more at his ease with the Prince than was Mme d'Arpajon, entertaining some illusion perhaps as to my position in the Guermantes set, or perhaps knowing more about it than myself, I had nevertheless for the first few moments some difficulty in arresting his attention, for, with fluttering, distended nostrils, he was turning in every direction, inquisitively protruding his monocle, as though he found himself face to face with five hundred matchless works of art. But, having heard my request, he received it with satisfaction, led me towards the Prince and presented me to him with a relishing, ceremonious, vulgar air, as though he had been handing him, with a word of commendation, a plate of cakes. Just as the greeting of the Duc de Guermantes was, when he chose, friendly, instinct with good fellowship, cordial and familiar, so I found that of the Prince stiff, solemn, haughty. He barely smiled at me, addressed me gravely as 'Sir'. I had often heard the Duke make fun of his cousin's stiffness. But from the first words that he addressed to me, which by their cold and serious tone formed the most entire contrast with the language of Basin, I realised at once that the fundamentally disdainful man was the Duke, who spoke to you at your first meeting with him as 'man to man', and that, of the two cousins, the one who was really simple was the Prince. I found in his reserve a stronger feeling, I do not say of equality, for that would have been inconceivable to him, but at least of the consideration which one may show for an inferior, such as may be found in all strongly hierarchical societies; in the Law Courts, for instance, in a Faculty, where a public prosecutor or dean, conscious of their high charge, conceal perhaps more genuine simplicity, and, when you come to know them better, more kindness, true simplicity, cordiality, beneath their traditional aloofness than the more modern brethren beneath their jocular affectation of comradeship. 'Do you intend to follow the career of Monsieur, your father?' he said to me with a distant but interested air. I answered his question briefly, realising that he had asked it only out of politeness, and moved away to allow him to greet the fresh arrivals.

I caught sight of Swann, and meant to speak to him, but at that moment I saw that the Prince de Guermantes, instead of waiting where he was to receive the greeting of Odette's husband, had immediately, with the force of a suction pump, carried him off to the farther end of the garden, in order, as some said, 'to show him the door'.

So entirely absorbed in the company that I did not learn until two days later, from the newspapers, that a Czech orchestra had been playing throughout the evening, and that Bengal lights had been burning in constant succession, I recovered some power of attention with the idea of going to look at the celebrated fountain of Hubert Robert.

In a clearing surrounded by fine trees several of which were as old as itself, set in a place apart, one could see it in the distance, slender, immobile, stiffened, allowing the breeze to stir only the lighter fall of its pale and quivering plume. The eighteenth century had refined the elegance of its lines, but, by fixing the style of the jet, seemed to have arrested its life; at this distance one had the impression of a work of art rather than the sensation of water. The moist cloud itself that was perpetually gathering at its crest preserved the character of the period like those that in the sky assemble round the palaces of Versailles. But from a closer view one realised that, while it respected, like the stones of an ancient palace, the design traced for it beforehand, it was a constantly changing stream of water that, springing upwards and seeking to obey the architect's traditional orders, performed them to the letter only by seeming to infringe them, its thousand separate bursts succeeding only at a distance in giving the impression of a single flow. This was in reality as often interrupted as the scattering of the fall, whereas from a distance it had appeared to me unyielding, solid, unbroken in its continuity. From a little nearer, one saw that this continuity, apparently complete, was assured, at every point in the ascent of the jet, wherever it must otherwise have been broken, by the entering into line, by the lateral incorporation of a parallel jet which mounted higher than the first and was itself, at an altitude greater but already a strain upon its endurance, relieved by a third. Seen close at hand, drops without strength fell back from the column of water crossing on their way their climbing sisters and, at times, torn, caught in an eddy of the night air, disturbed by this ceaseless flow, floated awhile before being drowned in the basin. They teased with their hesitations, with their passage in the opposite direction, and blurred with their soft vapour the vertical tension of that stem, bearing aloft an oblong cloud composed of a thousand tiny drops, but apparently painted in an unchanging, golden brown which rose, unbreakable, constant, urgent, swift, to mingle with the clouds in the sky. Unfortunately, a gust of wind was enough to scatter it obliquely on the ground; at times indeed a single jet, disobeying its orders, swerved and, had they not kept a respectful distance, would have drenched to their skins the incautious crowd of gazers.

One of these little accidents, which could scarcely occur save when the breeze freshened for a moment, was distinctly unpleasant. Somebody had told Mme d'Arpajon that the Duc de Guermantes, who as a matter of fact had not yet arrived, was with Mme de Surgis in one of the galleries of pink marble to which one ascended by the double colonnade, hollowed out of the wall, which rose from the brink of the fountain. Now, just as Mme d'Arpajon was making for one of these staircases, a strong gust of warm air made the jet of water swerve and inundated the fair lady so completely that, the water streaming down from her open bosom inside her dress, she was soaked as if she had been plunged into a bath. Whereupon, a few feet away, a rhythmical roar resounded, loud enough to be heard by a whole army, and at the same time protracted in periods as though it were being addressed not to the army as a whole but to each unit in turn; it was the Grand Duke Vladimir, who was laughing wholeheartedly upon seeing the immersion of Mme d'Arpajon, one of the funniest sights, as he was never tired of repeating afterwards, that he had ever seen in his life. Some charitable persons having suggested to the Muscovite that a word of sympathy from himself was perhaps deserved and would give pleasure to the lady who, notwithstanding her tale of forty winters fully told, wiping herself with her scarf, without appealing to anyone for help, was stepping clear in spite of the water that was maliciously spilling over the edge of the basin, the Grand Duke, who had a kind heart, felt that he must say a word in season, and, before the last military tattoo of his laughter had altogether subsided, one heard a fresh roar, more vociferous even than the last. 'Bravo, old girl!' he cried, clapping his hands as though at the theatre. Mme d'Arpajon was not at all pleased that her dexterity should be commended at the expense of her youth. And when someone remarked to her, in a voice drowned by the roar of the water, over which nevertheless rose the princely thunder: 'I think His Imperial Highness said something to you.' 'No! It was to Mme de Souvré,' was her reply.

I passed through the gardens and returned by the stair, upon which the absence of the Prince, who had vanished with Swann, enlarged the crowd of guests round M. de Charlus, just as, when Louis XIV was not at Versailles, there was a more numerous attendance upon Monsieur, his brother. I was stopped on my way by the Baron, while behind me two ladies and a young man came up to greet him.

'It is nice to see you here,' he said to me, as he held out his hand. 'Good-evening, Madame de la Trémoïlle, good-evening, my dear Herminie.' But doubtless the memory of what he had said to me as to his own supreme position in the Hôtel Guermantes made him wish to appear to be feeling, with regard to a matter which annoyed him but which he had been unable to prevent, a satisfaction which his high-and-mighty impertinence and his hysterical excitement immediately invested in a cloak of exaggerated irony. 'It is nice,' he repeated, 'but it is, really, very odd.' And he broke into peals of laughter which appeared to be indicative at once of his joy and of the inadequacy of human speech to express it. Certain persons, meanwhile, who knew both how difficult he was of access and how prone to insolent retorts, had been drawn towards us by curiosity, and, with an almost indecent haste, took to their heels. 'Come, now, don't be cross,' he said to me, patting me gently on the shoulder, 'you know that I am your friend. Good-evening, Antioche, good-evening, Louis-René. Have you been to look at the fountain?' he asked me in a tone that was affirmative rather than questioning. 'It is quite pretty, ain't it? It is marvellous. It might be made better still, naturally, if certain things were removed, and then there would be nothing like it in France. But even as it stands, it is quite one of the best things. Bréauté will tell you that it was a mistake to put lamps round it, to try and make people forget that it was he who was responsible for that absurd idea. But after all he has only managed to spoil it a very little. It is far more difficult to deface a great work of art than to create one. Not that we had not a vague suspicion all the time that Bréauté was not quite a match for Hubert Robert.'

I drifted back into the stream of guests who were entering the house. 'Have you seen my delicious cousin Oriane lately?' I was asked by the Princess who had now deserted her post by the door and with whom I was making my way back to the rooms. 'She's sure to be here tonight, I saw her this afternoon,' my hostess added. 'She promised me to come. I believe too that you will be dining with us both to meet the Queen of Italy, at the Embassy, on Thursday. There are to be all the Royalties imaginable, it will be most alarming.' They could not in any way alarm the Princesse de Guermantes, whose rooms swarmed with them, and who would say: 'My little Coburgs' as she might have said 'my little dogs'. And so Mme de Guermantes said: 'It will be most alarming', out of sheer silliness, which, among people in society, overrides even their vanity. With regard to her own pedigree, she knew less than a passman in history. As for the people of her circle, she liked to show that she knew the nicknames with which they had been labelled. Having asked me whether I was dining, the week after, with the Marquise de la Pommelière, who was often called 'la Pomme', the Princess, having elicited a reply in the negative, remained silent for some moments. Then, without any other motive than a deliberate display of instinctive erudition, banality, and conformity to the prevailing spirit, she added: 'She's not a bad sort, the Pomme!'

While the Princess was talking to me, it so happened that the Duc and Duchesse de Guermantes made their entrance. But I could not go at once to greet them, for I was waylaid by the Turkish Ambassadress, who, pointing to our hostess whom I had just left, exclaimed as she seized me by the arm: 'Ah! What a delicious woman the Princess is! What a superior being! I feel sure that, if I were a man,' she went on, with a trace of Oriental servility and sensuality, 'I would give my life for that heavenly creature.' I replied that I did indeed find her charming, but that I knew her cousin, the Duchess, better. 'But there is no comparison,' said the Ambassadress. 'Oriane is a charming society woman who gets her wit from Mémé and Babal, whereas Marie-Gilbert is *somebody*.'

I never much like to be told like this, without a chance to reply, what I ought to think about people whom I know. And there was no reason why the Turkish Ambassadress should be in any way better qualified than myself to judge of the worth of the Duchesse de Guermantes.

On the other hand (and this explained also my annoyance with the Ambassadress), the defects of a mere acquaintance, and even of a friend, are to us real poisons, against which we are fortunately 'mithridated'.

But, without applying any standard of scientific comparison and talking of anaphylaxis, let us say that, at the heart of our friendly or purely social relations, there lurks a hostility momentarily cured but recurring by fits and starts. As a rule, we suffer little from these poisons, so long as people are 'natural'. By saying 'Babal' and 'Mémé' to indicate people with whom she was not acquainted, the Turkish Ambassadress suspended the effects of the 'mithridatism' which, as a rule, made me find her tolerable. She annoyed me, which was all the more unfair, inasmuch as she did not speak like this to make me think that she was an intimate friend of 'Mémé', but owing to a too rapid education which made her name these noble lords according to what she believed to be the custom of the country. She had crowded her course into a few months, and had not picked up the rules. But, on thinking it over, I found another reason for my disinclination to remain in the Ambassadress' company. It was not so very long since, at Oriane's, this same diplomatic personage had said to me, with a purposeful and serious air, that she found the Princesse de Guermantes frankly antipathetic. I felt that I need not stop to consider this change of front: the invitation to the party this evening had brought it about. The Ambassadress was perfectly sincere when she told me that the Princesse de Guermantes was a sublime creature. She had always thought so. But, having never before been invited to the Princess's house, she had felt herself bound to give this non-invitation the appearance of a deliberate abstention on principle. Now that she had been asked, and would

presumably continue to be asked in the future, she could give free expression
to her feelings. There is no need, in accounting for three out of four of the
opinions that we hold about other people, to go so far as crossed love
or exclusion from public office. Our judgment remains uncertain: the
withholding or bestowal of an invitation determines it. Anyhow, the Turkish
Ambassadress, as the Baronne de Guermantes remarked while making a
tour of inspection through the rooms with me, 'was all right'. She was,
above all, extremely useful. The real stars of society are tired of appearing
there. He who is curious to gaze at them must often migrate to another
hemisphere, where they are more or less alone. But women like the Ottoman
Ambassadress, of quite recent admission to society, are never weary of
shining there, and, so to speak, everywhere at once. They are of value at
entertainments of the sort known as *soirée* or *rout*, to which they would let
themselves be dragged from their deathbeds rather than miss one. They are
the supers upon whom a hostess can always count, determined never to miss
a party. And so, the foolish young men, unaware that they are false stars,
take them for the queens of fashion, whereas it would require a formal
lecture to explain to them by virtue of what reasons Mme Standish, who, her
existence unknown to them, lives remote from the world, painting cushions,
is at least as great a lady as the Duchesse de Doudeauville.

In the ordinary course of life, the eyes of the Duchesse de Guermantes
were absent and slightly melancholy, she made them sparkle with a flame of
wit only when she had to say how-d'ye-do to a friend; precisely as though
the said friend had been some witty remark, some charming touch, some
titbit for delicate palates, the savour of which has set on the face of the
connoisseur an expression of refined joy. But upon big evenings, as she had
too many greetings to bestow, she decided that it would be tiring to have to
switch off the light after each. Just as an ardent reader, when he goes to the
theatre to see a new piece by one of the masters of the stage, testifies to his
certainty that he is not going to spend a dull evening by having, while he
hands his hat and coat to the attendant, his lip adjusted in readiness for a
sapient smile, his eye kindled for a sardonic approval; similarly it was at the
moment of her arrival that the Duchess lighted up for the whole evening.
And while she was handing over her evening cloak, of a magnificent Tiepolo
red, exposing a huge collar of rubies round her neck, having cast over her
gown that final rapid, minute and exhaustive dressmaker's glance which is
also that of a woman of the world, Oriane made sure that her eyes, just as
much as her other jewels, were sparkling. In vain might sundry 'kind friends'
such as M. de Janville fling themselves upon the Duke to keep him from
entering: 'But don't you know that poor Mama is at his last gasp? He had

had the Sacraments.' 'I know, I know,' answered M. de Guermantes, thrusting the tiresome fellow aside in order to enter the room. 'The viaticum has acted splendidly,' he added, with a smile of pleasure at the thought of the ball which he was determined not to miss after the Prince's party. 'We did not want people to know that we had come back,' the Duchess said to me. She never suspected that the Princess had already disproved this statement by telling me that she had seen her cousin for a moment, who had promised to come. The Duke, after a protracted stare with which he proceeded to crush his wife for the space of five minutes, observed: 'I told Oriane about your misgivings.' Now that she saw that they were unfounded, and that she herself need take no action in the attempt to dispel them, she pronounced them absurd, and continued to chaff me about them. 'The idea of supposing that you were not invited! Besides, wasn't I there? Do you suppose that I should be unable to get you an invitation to my cousin's house?' I must admit that frequently, after this, she did things for me that were far more difficult; nevertheless, I took care not to interpret her words in the sense that I had been too modest. I was beginning to learn the exact value of the language, spoken or mute, of aristocratic affability, an affability that is happy to shed balm upon the sense of inferiority in those persons towards whom it is directed, though not to the point of dispelling that sense, for in that case it would no longer have any reason to exist. 'But you are our equal, if not our superior,' the Guermantes seemed, in all their actions, to be saying; and they said it in the most courteous fashion imaginable, to be loved, admired, but not to be believed; that one should discern the fictitious character of this affability was what they called being well-bred; to suppose it to be genuine, a sign of ill-breeding. I was to receive, as it happened, shortly after this, a lesson which gave me a full and perfect understanding of the extent and limitations of certain forms of aristocratic affability. It was at an afternoon party given by the Duchesse de Montmorency to meet the Queen of England; there was a sort of royal procession to the buffet, at the head of which walked Her Majesty on the arm of the Duc de Guermantes. I happened to arrive at that moment. With his disengaged hand the Duke conveyed to me, from a distance of nearly fifty yards, a thousand signs of friendly invitation, which appeared to mean that I need not be afraid to approach, that I should not be devoured alive instead of the sandwiches. But I, who was becoming word-perfect in the language of the court, instead of going even one step nearer, keeping my fifty yards' interval, made a deep how, but without smiling, the sort of bow that I should have made to someone whom I scarcely knew, then proceeded in the opposite direction. Had I written a masterpiece, the Guermantes would have given me less credit for it than I earned by that bow. Not only did it not pass unperceived by the Duke, albeit he had that day to acknowledge the greetings of more than five hundred people, it caught the eye of the Duchess, who, happening to meet my mother, told her of it, and, so far from suggesting that I had done wrong, that I ought to have gone up to him, said that her husband had been lost in admiration of my bow, that it would have been impossible for anyone to put more into it. They never ceased to find in that bow every possible merit, without however mentioning that which had seemed the most priceless of all, to wit that it had been discreet, nor did they cease either to pay me compliments which I understood to be even less a reward for the past than a hint for the future, after the fashion of the hint delicately conveyed to his pupils by the headmaster of a school: 'Do not forget, my boys, that these prizes are intended not so much for you as for your parents, so that they may send you back next term.' So it was that Mme de Marsantes, when someone from a different world entered her circle, would praise in his hearing the discreet people whom 'you find at home when you go to see them, and who at other times let you forget their existence,' as one warns by an indirect allusion a servant who has an unpleasant smell, that the practice of taking a bath is beneficial to the health.

While, before she had even left the entrance hall, I was talking to Mme de Guermantes, I could hear a voice of a sort which, for the future, I was to be able to classify without the possibility of error. It was, in this particular instance, the voice of M. de Vaugoubert talking to M. de Charlus. A skilled physician need not even make his patient unbutton his shirt, nor listen to his breathing, the sound of his voice is enough. How often, in time to come, was my ear to be caught in a drawing-room by the intonation or laughter of some man, who, for all that, was copying exactly the language of his profession or the manners of his class, affecting a stern aloofness or a coarse familiarity, but whose artificial voice was enough to indicate: 'He is a Charlus' to my trained ear, like the note of a tuning fork. At that moment the entire staff of one of the Embassies went past, pausing to greet M. de Charlus. For all that my discovery of the sort of malady in question dated only from that afternoon (when I had surprised M. de Charlus with Jupien) I should have had no need, before giving a diagnosis, to put questions, to auscultate. But M. de Vaugoubert, when talking to M. de Charlus, appeared uncertain. And yet he must have known what was in the air after the doubts of his adolescence. The invert believes himself to be the only one of his kind in the universe; it is only in later years that he imagines – another exaggeration – that the unique exception is the normal man. But, ambitious and timorous, M. de Vaugoubert had not for many years past surrendered himself to what would to him have meant pleasure. The career of diplomacy had had the same effect upon his life as a monastic profession. Combined with his assiduous frequentation of the School of Political Sciences, it had vowed him from his twentieth year to the chastity of a professing Christian. And so, as each of our senses loses its strength and vivacity, becomes atrophied when it is no longer exercised, M. de Vaugoubert, just as the civilised man is no longer capable of the feats of strength, of the acuteness of hearing of the cave-dweller, had lost that special perspicacy which was rarely at fault in M. de Charlus; and at official banquets, whether in Paris or abroad, the Minister Plenipotentiary was no longer capable of identifying those who, beneath the disguise of their uniform, were at heart his congeners. Certain names mentioned by M. de Charlus, indignant if he himself was cited for his peculiarities, but always delighted to give away those of other people, caused M. de Vaugoubert an exquisite surprise. Not that, after all these years, he dreamed of profiting by any windfall. But these rapid revelations, similar to those which in Racine's tragedies inform Athalie and Abner that Joas is of the House of David, that Esther, enthroned in the purple, comes of a Yiddish stock, changing the aspect of the X— Legation, or of one or another department of the Ministry of Foreign Affairs, rendered those palaces as mysterious, in retrospect, as the Temple of Jerusalem or the Throne-room at Susa. At the sight of the youthful staff of this Embassy advancing in a body to shake hands with M. de Charlus, M. de Vaugoubert assumed the astonished air of Elise exclaiming, in *Esther*: 'Great heavens! What a swarm of innocent beauties issuing from all sides presents itself to my gaze! How charming a modesty is depicted on their faces!' Then, athirst for more definite information, he cast at M. de Charlus a smiling glance fatuously interrogative and concupiscent. 'Why, of course they are,' said M. de Charlus with the knowing air of a learned man speaking to an ignoramus. From that instant M. de Vaugoubert (greatly to the annoyance of M. de Charlus) could not tear his eyes from these young secretaries whom the X— Ambassador to France, an old stager, had not chosen blindfold. M. de Vaugoubert remained silent, I could only watch his eyes. But, being accustomed from my childhood to apply, even to what is voiceless, the language of the classics, I made M. de Vaugoubert's eyes repeat the lines in which Esther explains to Elise that Mardochée, in his zeal for his religion, has made it a rule that only those maidens who profess it shall be employed about the Queen's person. 'And now his love for our nation has peopled this palace with daughters of Sion, young and tender flowers wafted by fate, transplanted like myself beneath a foreign sky. In a place set apart from profane eyes, he' (the worthy Ambassador) 'devotes his skill and labour to shaping them.'

At length M. de Vaugoubert spoke, otherwise than with his eyes. 'Who knows,' he said sadly, 'that in the country where I live the same thing does not exist also?' 'It is probable,' replied M. de Charlus, 'starting with King Theodosius, not that I know anything definite about him.' 'Oh, dear, no! Nothing of that sort!' 'Then he has no right to look it so completely. Besides, he has all the little tricks. He had that 'my dear' manner, which I detest more than anything in the world. I should never dare to be seen walking in the street with him. Anyhow, you must know what he is, they all call him the White Wolf.' 'You are entirely mistaken about him. He is quite charming, all the same. The day on which the agreement with France was signed, the King kissed me. I have never been so moved.' 'That was the moment to tell him what you wanted.' 'Oh, good heavens! What an idea! If he were even to suspect such a thing! But I have no fear in that direction.' A conversation which I could hear, for I was standing close by, and which made me repeat to myself: 'The King unto this day knows not who I am, and this secret keeps my tongue still enchained.'

This dialogue, half mute, half spoken, had lasted but a few moments, and I had barely entered the first of the drawing-rooms with the Duchesse de Guermantes when a little dark lady, extremely pretty, stopped her.

'I've been looking for you everywhere. D'Annunzio saw you from a box in the theatre, he has written the Princesse de T— a letter in which he says that he never saw anything so lovely. He would give his life for ten minutes' conversation with you. In any case, even if you can't or won't, the letter is in my possession. You must fix a day to come and see me. There are some secrets which I cannot tell you here. I see you don't remember me,' she added, turning to myself; 'I met you at the Princesse de Parme's' (where I had never been). 'The Emperor of Russia is anxious for your father to be sent to Petersburg. If you could come in on Monday, Isvolski himself will be there, he will talk to you about it. I have a present for you, my dear,' she went on, returning to the Duchess, 'which I should not dream of giving to anyone but you. The manuscripts of three of Ibsen's plays, which he sent to me by his old attendant. I shall keep one and give you the other two.'

The Duc de Guermantes was not over pleased by these offers. Uncertain whether Ibsen and D'Annunzio were dead or alive, he could see in his mind's eye a tribe of authors, playwrights, coming to call upon his wife and putting her in their works. People in society are too apt to think of a book as a sort of cube one side of which has been removed, so that the author can at once 'put in' the people he meets. This is obviously disloyal, and authors are a pretty low class. Certainly, it would not be a bad thing to meet them once in a way, for thanks to them, when one reads a book or an article, one can 'read between the lines', 'unmask' the characters. After all, though, the wisest thing is to stick to dead authors. M. de Guermantes considered 'quite all right' only the gentleman who did the funeral notices in the *Gaulois*. He, at any rate, confined himself to including M. de Guermantes among the people 'conspicuous by their presence' at funerals at which the Duke had given his name. When he preferred that his name should not appear, instead of giving it, he sent a letter of condolence to the relatives of the deceased, assuring them of his deep and heartfelt sympathy. If, then, the family sent to the paper 'among the letters received, we may mention one from the Duc de Guermantes' etc., this was the fault not of the ink-slinger but of the son, brother, father of the deceased whom the Duke thereupon described as upstarts, and with whom he decided for the future to have no further dealings (what he called, not being very well up in the meaning of such expressions, 'having a crow to pick'). In any event, the names of Ibsen and D'Annunzio, and his uncertainty as to their survival, brought a frown to the brows of the Duke, who was not far enough away from us to escape hearing the various blandishments of Mme Timoléon d'Amoncourt. This was a charming woman, her wit, like her beauty, so entrancing that either of them by itself would have made her shine. But, born outside the world in which she now lived, having aspired at first merely to a literary salon, the friend successively – and nothing more than a friend, for her morals were above reproach – and exclusively of every great writer, who gave her all his manuscripts, wrote books for her, chance having once introduced her into the Faubourg Saint-Germain, these literary privileges were of service to her there. She had now an established position, and no longer needed to dispense other graces than those that were shed by her presence. But, accustomed in times past to act as go-between, to render services, she persevered in them even when they were no longer necessary. She had always a state secret to reveal to you, a potentate whom you must meet, a water colour by a master to present to you. There was indeed in all these superfluous attractions a trace of falsehood, but they made her life a comedy that scintillated with complications, and it was no exaggeration to say that she appointed prefects and generals.

As she strolled by my side, the Duchesse de Guermantes allowed the azure light of her eyes to float in front of her, but vaguely, so as to avoid the people with whom she did not wish to enter into relations, whose presence she discerned at times, like a menacing reef in the distance. We advanced between a double hedge of guests, who, conscious that they would never come to know 'Oriane', were anxious at least to point her out, as a curiosity, to their wives: 'Quick, Ursule, come and look at Madame de Guermantes talking to that young man.' And one felt that in another moment they would be clambering upon the chairs, for a better view, as at the Military Review on the 14th of July, or the Grand Prix. Not that the Duchesse de Guermantes had a more aristocratic salon than her cousin. The former's was frequented by people whom the latter would never have been willing to invite, principally on account of her husband. She would never have been at home to Mme Alphonse de Rothschild, who, an intimate friend of Mme de la Trémoïlle and of Mme de Sagan, as was Oriane herself, was constantly to be seen in the house of the last-named. It was the same with Baron Hirsch, whom the Prince of Wales had brought to see her, but not to the Princess, who would not have approved of him, and also with certain outstandingly notorious Bonapartists or even Republicans, whom the Duchess found interesting but whom the Prince, a convinced Royalist, would not have allowed inside his house. His anti-semitism also being founded on principle did not yield before any social distinction, however strongly accredited, and if he was at home to Swann, whose friend he had been since their boyhood, being, however, the only one of the Guermantes who addressed him as Swann and not as Charles, this was because, knowing that Swann's grandmother, a Protestant married to a Jew, had been the Duc de Berri's mistress, he endeavoured, from time to time, to believe in the legend which made out Swann's father to be a natural son of that Prince. By this hypothesis, which incidentally was false, Swann, the son of a Catholic father, himself the son of a Bourbon by a Catholic mother, was a Christian to his fingertips.

'What, you don't know these glories?' said the Duchess, referring to the rooms through which we were moving. But, having given its due meed of praise to her cousin's 'palace', she hastened to add that she a thousand times preferred her own 'humble den'. 'This is an admirable house to visit. But I should die of misery if I had to stay behind and sleep in rooms that have witnessed so many historic events. It would give me the feeling of having been left after closing-time, forgotten, in the Château of Blois, or Fontainebleau, or even the Louvre, with no antidote to my depression except to tell myself that I was in the room in which Monaldeschi was murdered. As a sedative, that is not good enough. Why, here comes Mme de Saint-Euverte. We've just been dining with her. As she is giving her great annual beanfeast tomorrow, I supposed she would be going straight to bed. But she can never miss a party. If this one had been in the country, she would have jumped on a lorry rather than not go to it.'

As a matter of fact, Mme de Saint-Euverte had come this evening, less for the pleasure of not missing another person's party than in order to ensure the success of her own, recruit the latest additions to her list, and, so to speak, hold an eleventh hour review of the troops who were on the morrow to perform such brilliant evolutions at her garden party. For, in the long course of years, the guests at the Saint-Euverte parties had almost entirely changed. The female celebrities of the Guermantes world, formerly so sparsely scattered, had – loaded with attentions by their hostess – begun gradually to bring their friends. At the same time, by an enterprise equally progressive, but in the opposite direction, Mme de Saint-Euverte had, year by year, reduced the number of persons unknown to the world of fashion. You had ceased to see first one of them, then another. For some time the 'batch' system was in operation, which enabled her, thanks to parties over which a veil of silence was drawn, to summon the ineligibles separately to entertain one another, which dispensed her from having to invite them with the nice people. What cause had they for complaint? Were they not given (*panem et circenses*) light refreshments and a select musical programme? And so, in a kind of symmetry with the two exiled duchesses whom, in years past, when the Saint-Euverte salon was only starting, one used to see holding up, like a pair of Caryatides, its unstable crest, in these later years one could distinguish, mingling with the fashionable throng, only two heterogeneous persons, old Mme de Cambremer and the architect's wife with a fine voice who was always having to be asked to sing. But, no longer knowing anybody at Mme de Saint-Euverte's, bewailing their lost comrades, feeling that they were in the way, they stood about with a frozen-to-death air, like two swallows that have not migrated in time. And so, the following year, they were not invited; Mme de Franquetot made an attempt on behalf of her cousin, who was so fond of music. But as she could obtain for her no more explicit reply than the words: 'Why, people can always come in and listen to music, if they like; there is nothing criminal about that!' Mme de Cambremer did not find the invitation sufficiently pressing, and abstained.

Such a transformation having been effected by Mme de Saint-Euverte, from a leper hospice to a gathering of great ladies (the latest form, apparently in the height of fashion, that it had assumed), it might seem odd that the person who on the following day was to give the most brilliant party of the season should need to appear overnight to address a last word of command to her troops. But the fact was that the pre-eminence of Mme de Saint-Euverte's drawing-room existed only for those whose social life consists entirely in reading the accounts of afternoon and evening parties in the *Gaulois* or *Figaro*, without ever having been present at one. To these worldlings who see the world only as reflected in the newspapers, the enumeration of the British, Austrian etc. Ambassadresses, of the Duchesses d'Uzès, de la Trémoïlle, etc., etc., was sufficient to make them instinctively imagine the Saint-Euverte drawing-room to be the first in Paris, whereas it was among the last. Not that the reports were mendacious. The majority of the persons mentioned had indeed been present. But each of them had come in response to entreaties, civilities, services, and with the sense of doing infinite honour to Mme de Saint-Euverte. Such drawing-rooms, shunned rather than sought after, to which people are so to speak roped in, deceive no one but the fair readers of the 'Society' column. They pass over a really fashionable party, the sort at which the hostess, who could have had all the duchesses in existence, they being athirst to be 'numbered among the elect', invites only two or three and does not send any list of her guests to the papers. And so these hostesses, ignorant or contemptuous of the power that publicity has acquired today, are considered fashionable by the Queen of Spain but are overlooked by the crowd, because the former knows and the latter does not know who they are.

Mme de Saint-Euverte was not one of these women, and, with an eye to the main chance, had come to gather up for the morrow everyone who had been invited. M. de Charlus was not among these, he had always refused to go to her house. But he had quarrelled with so many people that Mme de Saint-Euverte might put this down to his peculiar nature.

Assuredly, if it had been only Oriane, Mme de Saint-Euverte need not have put herself to the trouble, for the invitation had been given by word of mouth, and, what was more, accepted with that charming, deceiving grace in the exercise of which those Academicians are unsurpassed from whose door the candidate emerges with a melting heart, never doubting that he can count upon their support. But there were others as well. The Prince d'Agrigente, would he come? And Mme de Durfort? And so, with an eye to business, Mme de Saint-Euverte had thought it expedient to appear on the scene in person. Insinuating with some, imperative with others, to all alike she hinted in veiled words at inconceivable attractions which could never be seen anywhere again, and promised each that he should find at her party the person he most wished, or the personage he most wanted to meet. And this sort of function with which she was invested on one day in the year – like certain public offices in the ancient world – of the person who is to give on the morrow the biggest garden-party of the season conferred upon her a momentary authority. Her lists were made up and closed, so that while she wandered slowly through the Princess's rooms to drop into one ear after another: 'You won't forget about me tomorrow,' she had the ephemeral glory of turning away her eyes, while continuing to smile, if she caught sight of some horrid creature who was to be avoided or some country squire for whom the bond of a schoolboy friendship had secured admission to

Gilbert's, and whose presence at her garden-party would be no gain. She preferred not to speak to him, so as to be able to say later on: 'I issued my invitations verbally, and unfortunately I didn't see you anywhere.' And so she, a mere Saint-Euverte, set to work with her gimlet eyes to pick and choose among the guests at the Princess's party. And she imagined herself, in so doing, to be every inch a Duchesse de Guermantes.

It must be admitted that the latter lady had not, either, whatever one might suppose, the unrestricted use of her greetings and smiles. To some extent, no doubt, when she withheld them, it was deliberately. 'But the woman bores me to tears,' she would say, 'am I expected to talk to her about her party for the next hour?'

A duchess of swarthy complexion went past, whom her ugliness and stupidity, and certain irregularities of behaviour, had exiled not from society as a whole but from certain small and fashionable circles. 'Ah!' murmured Mme de Guermantes, with the sharp, unerring glance of the connoisseur who is shown a false jewel, 'so they have that sort here?' By the mere sight of this semi-tarnished lady, whose face was burdened with a surfeit of moles from which black hairs sprouted, Mme de Guermantes gauged the mediocre importance of this party. They had been brought up together, but she had severed all relations with the lady; and responded to her greeting only with the curtest little nod. 'I cannot understand,' she said to me, 'how Marie-Gilbert can invite us with all that scum. You might say there was a deputation of paupers from every parish. Mélanie Pourtalès arranged things far better. She could have the Holy Synod and the Oratoire Chapel in her house if she liked, but at least she didn't invite us on the same day.' But, in many cases, it was from timidity, fear of a scene with her husband, who did not like her to entertain artists and suchlike (Marie-Gilbert took a kindly interest in dozens of them, you had to take care not to be accosted by some illustrious German diva), from some misgivings, too, with regard to Nationalist feeling, which, inasmuch as she was endowed, like M. de Charlus, with the wit of the Guermantes, she despised from the social point of view (people were now, for the greater glory of the General Staff, sending a plebeian general in to dinner before certain dukes), but to which, nevertheless, as she knew that she was considered unsound in her views, she made liberal concessions, even dreading the prospect of having to offer her hand to Swann in these anti-semitic surroundings. With regard to this, her mind was soon set at rest, for she learned that the Prince had refused to have Swann in the house, and had had 'a sort of an altercation' with him. There was no risk of her having to converse in public with 'poor Charles', whom she preferred to cherish in private.

'And who in the world is that?' Mme de Guermantes exclaimed, upon seeing a little lady with a slightly lost air, in a black gown so simple that you would have taken her for a pauper, greet her, as did also the lady's husband, with a sweeping bow. She did not recognise the lady and, in her insolent way, drew herself up as though offended and stared at her without responding. 'Who is that person, Basin?' she asked with an air of astonishment, while M. de Guermantes, to atone for Oriane's impoliteness, was bowing to the lady and shaking hands with her husband. 'Why, it is Mme de Chaussepierre, you were most impolite.' 'I have never heard of anybody called Chausse-pierre.' 'Old mother Chanlivault's nephew.' 'I haven't the faintest idea what you're talking about. Who is the woman, and why does she bow to me?' 'But you know her perfectly, she's Mme de Charleval's daughter, Henriette Montmorency.' 'Oh, but I knew her mother quite well, she was charming, extremely intelligent. What made her go and marry all these people I never heard of? You say that she calls herself Mme de Chaussepierre?' she said, isolating each syllable of the name with a questioning air, and as though she were afraid of making a mistake. 'It is not so ridiculous as you appear to think, to call oneself Chaussepierre! Old Chaussepierre was the brother of the aforesaid Chanlivault, of Mme de Sennecour and of the Vicomtesse de Merlerault. They're a good family.' 'Oh, do stop,' cried the Duchess, who, like a lion-tamer, never cared to appear to be allowing herself to be intimidated by the devouring glare of the animal. 'Basin, you are the joy of my life. I can't imagine where you picked up those names, but I congratulate you on them. If I did not know Chaussepierre, I have at least read Balzac, you are not the only one, and I have even read Labiche. I can appreciate Chanlivault, I do not object to Charleval, but I must confess that Merlerault is a masterpiece. However, let us admit that Chaussepierre is not bad either. You must have gone about collecting them, it's not possible. You mean to write a book,' she turned to myself, 'you ought to make a note of Charleval and Merlerault. You will find nothing better.' 'He will find himself in the dock, and will go to prison; you are giving him very bad advice, Oriane.' 'I hope, for his own sake, that he has younger people than me at his disposal if he wishes to ask for bad advice; especially if he means to follow it. But if he means to do nothing worse than write a book!' At some distance from us, a wonderful, proud young woman stood out delicately from the throng in a white dress, all diamonds and tulle. Madame de Guermantes watched her talking to a whole group of people fascinated by her grace. 'Your sister is the belle of the ball, as usual; she is charming tonight,' she said, as she took a chair, to the Prince de Chimay who went past. Colonel de Froberville (the General of that name was his uncle) came and sat down beside us, as did M.

de Bréauté, while M. de Vaugoubert, after hovering about us (by an excess of politeness which he maintained even when playing tennis when, by dint of asking leave of the eminent personages present before hitting the ball, he invariably lost the game for his partner) returned to M. de Charlus (until that moment almost concealed by the huge skirt of the Comtesse Molé, whom he professed to admire above all other women), and, as it happened, at the moment when several members of the latest diplomatic mission to Paris were greeting the Baron. At the sight of a young secretary with a particularly intelligent air, M. de Vaugoubert fastened on M. de Charlus a smile upon which there bloomed visibly one question only. M. de Charlus would, no doubt, readily have compromised someone else, but to feel himself compromised by this smile formed on another person's lips, which, moreover, could have but one meaning, exasperated him. 'I know absolutely nothing about the matter, I beg you to keep your curiosity to yourself. It leaves me more than cold. Besides, in this instance, you are making a mistake of the first order. I believe this young man to be absolutely the opposite.' Here M. de Charlus, irritated at being thus given away by a fool, was not speaking the truth. The secretary would, had the Baron been correct, have formed an exception to the rule of his Embassy. It was, as a matter of fact, composed of widely different personalities, many of them extremely second-rate, so that, if one sought to discover what could have been the motive of the selection that had brought them together, the only one possible seemed to be inversion. By setting at the head of this little diplomatic Sodom an Ambassador who on the contrary ran after women with the comic exaggeration of an old buffer in a revue, who made his battalion of male impersonators toe the line, the authorities seemed to have been obeying the law of contrasts. In spite of what he had beneath his nose, he did not believe in inversion. He gave an immediate proof of this by marrying his sister to a Chargé d'Affaires whom he believed, quite mistakenly, to be a womaniser. After this he became rather a nuisance and was soon replaced by a fresh Excellency who ensured the homogeneity of the party. Other Embassies sought to rival this one, but could never dispute the prize (as in the matriculation examinations, where a certain school always heads the list), and more than ten years had to pass before, heterogeneous attachés having been introduced into this too perfect whole, another might at last wrest the grim trophy from it and march at the head.

Reassured as to her fear of having to talk to Swann, Mme de Guermantes felt now merely curious as to the subject of the conversation he had had with their host. 'Do you know what it was about?' the Duke asked M. de Bréauté. 'I did hear,' the other replied, 'that it was about a little play which the writer

Bergotte produced at their house. It was a delightful show, as it happens. But it seems the actor made up as Gilbert, whom, as it happens, Master Bergotte had intended to take off.' 'Oh, I should have loved to see Gilbert taken off,' said the Duchess, with a dreamy smile. 'It was about this little performance,' M. de Bréauté went on, thrusting forward his rodent jaw, 'that Gilbert demanded an explanation from Swann, who merely replied what everyone thought very witty: "Why, not at all, it wasn't the least bit like you, you are far funnier!" It appears, though,' M. de Bréauté continued, 'that the little play was quite delightful. Mme Molé was there, she was immensely amused.' 'What, does Mme Molé go there?' said the Duchess in astonishment. 'Ah! That must be Mémé's doing. That is what always happens, in the end, to that sort of house. One fine day everybody begins to flock to it, and I, who have deliberately remained aloof, upon principle, find myself left to mope alone in my corner.' Already, since M. de Bréauté's speech, the Duchesse de Guermantes (with regard if not to Swann's house, at least to the hypothesis of encountering him at any moment) had, as we see, adopted a fresh point of view. 'The explanation that you have given us,' said Colonel de Froberville to M. de Bréauté, 'is entirely unfounded. I have good reason to know. The Prince purely and simply gave Swann a dressing down and would have him to know, as our forebears used to say, that he was not to show his face in the house again, seeing the opinions he flaunts. And, to my mind, my uncle Gilbert was right a thousand times over, not only in giving Swann a piece of his mind, he ought to have finished six months ago with an out-and-out Dreyfusard.'

Poor M. de Vaugoubert, changed now from a too cautious tennis-player to a mere inert tennis ball which is tossed to and fro without compunction, found himself projected towards the Duchesse de Guermantes to whom he made obeisance. He was none too well received, Oriane living in the belief that all the diplomats – or politicians – of her world were nincompoops.

M. de Froberville had greatly benefited by the social privileges that had of late been accorded to military men. Unfortunately, if the wife of his bosom was a quite authentic relative of the Guermantes, she was also an extremely poor one, and, as he himself had lost his fortune, they went scarcely anywhere, and were the sort of people who were apt to be overlooked except on great occasions, when they had the good fortune to bury or marry a relative. Then, they did really enter into communion with the world of fashion, like those nominal Catholics who approach the holy table but once in the year. Their material situation would indeed have been deplorable had not Mme de Saint-Euverte, faithful to her affection for the late General de Froberville, done everything to help the household, providing frocks and entertainments for the two girls. But the Colonel, though generally considered a good fellow, had not the spirit of gratitude. He was envious of the splendours of a benefactress who extolled them herself without pause or measure. The annual garden party was for him, his wife and children a marvellous pleasure which they would not have missed for all the gold in the world, but a pleasure poisoned by the thought of the joys of satisfied pride that Mme de Saint-Euverte derived from it. The accounts of this garden party in the newspapers, which, after giving detailed reports, would add with Machiavellian guile: 'We shall refer again to this brilliant gathering', the complementary details of the women's costume, appearing for several days in succession, all this was so obnoxious to the Frobervilles, that they, cut off from most pleasures and knowing that they could count upon the pleasure of this one afternoon, were moved every year to hope that bad weather would spoil the success of the party, to consult the barometer and to anticipate with ecstasy the threatenings of a storm that might ruin everything.

'I shall not discuss politics with you, Froberville,' said M. de Guermantes, 'but, so far as Swann is concerned, I can tell you frankly that his conduct towards ourselves has been beyond words. Introduced into society, in the past, by ourselves, by the Duc de Chartres, they tell me now that he is openly a Dreyfusard. I should never have believed it of him, an epicure, a man of practical judgment, a collector, who goes in for old books, a member of the Jockey, a man who enjoys the respect of all that know him, who knows all the good addresses, and used to send us the best port wine you could wish to drink, a dilettante, the father of a family. Oh! I have been greatly deceived. I do not complain for myself, it is understood that I am only an old fool, whose opinion counts for nothing, mere rag tag and bobtail, but if only for Oriane's sake, he ought to have openly disavowed the Jews and the partisans of the man Dreyfus.

'Yes, after the friendship my wife has always shown him,' went on the Duke, who evidently considered that to denounce Dreyfus as guilty of high treason, whatever opinion one might hold in one's own conscience as to his guilt, constituted a sort of thank-offering for the manner in which one had been received in the Faubourg Saint-Germain, 'he ought to have disassociated himself. For, you can ask Oriane, she had a real friendship for him.' The Duchess, thinking that an ingenuous, calm tone would give a more dramatic and sincere value to her words, said in a schoolgirl voice, as though she were simply letting the truth fall from her lips, merely giving a slightly melancholy expression to her eyes: 'It is quite true, I have no reason to conceal the fact that I did feel a sincere affection for Charles!'

'There, you see, I don't have to make her say it. And after that, he carries his ingratitude to the point of being a Dreyfusard!'

'Talking of Dreyfusards,' I said, 'it appears, Prince Von is one.' 'Ah, I am glad you reminded me of him,' exclaimed M. de Guermantes, 'I was forgetting that he had asked me to dine with him on Monday. But whether he is a Dreyfusard or not is entirely immaterial, since he is a foreigner. I don't give two straws for his opinion. With a Frenchman, it is another matter. It is true that Swann is a Jew. But, until today – forgive me, Froberville – I have always been foolish enough to believe that a Jew can be a Frenchman, that is to say, an honourable Jew, a man of the world. Now, Swann was that in every sense of the word. Ah, well! He forces me to admit that I have been mistaken, since he has taken the side of this Dreyfus (who, guilty or not, never moved in his world, he cannot ever have met him) against a society that had adopted him, had treated him as one of ourselves. It goes without saying, we were all of us prepared to vouch for Swann, I would have answered for his patriotism as for my own. Ah! He is rewarding us very badly: I must confess that I should never have expected such a thing from him. I thought better of him. He was a man of intelligence (in his own line, of course). I know that he had already made that insane, disgraceful marriage. By which token, shall I tell you someone who was really hurt by Swann's marriage: my wife. Oriane often has what I might call an affectation of insensibility. But at heart she feels things with extraordinary keenness.' Mme de Guermantes, delighted by this analysis of her character, listened to it with a modest air but did not utter a word, from a scrupulous reluctance to acquiesce in it, but principally from fear of cutting it short. M. de Guermantes might have gone on talking for an hour on this subject, she would have sat as still, or even stiller than if she had been listening to music. 'Very well! I remember, when she heard of Swann's marriage, she felt hurt; she considered that it was wrong in a person to whom we had given so much friendship. She was very fond of Swann; she was deeply grieved. Am I not right, Oriane?' Mme de Guermantes felt that she ought to reply to so direct a challenge, upon a point of fact, which would allow her, unobtrusively, to confirm the tribute which, she felt, had come to an end. In a shy and simple tone, and with an air all the more studied in that it sought to show genuine 'feeling', she said with a meek reserve, 'It is true, Basin is quite right.' 'Still, that was not quite the same. After all, love is love, although, in my opinion, it ought to confine itself within certain limits. I might excuse a young fellow, a mere boy, for letting himself be caught by an infatuation. But Swann, a man of intelligence, of proved refinement, a good judge of pictures, an intimate friend of the Duc de Chartres, of Gilbert himself!' The tone in which M. de Guermantes said this was, for that matter, quite inoffensive, without a trace of the vulgarity which he too often showed. He spoke with a slightly indignant melancholy, but everything about him was steeped in that gentle gravity which constitutes the broad and unctuous charm of certain portraits by Rembrandt, that of the Burgomaster Six, for example. One felt that the question of the immorality of Swann's conduct with regard to 'the Case' never even presented itself to the Duke, so confident was he of the answer; it caused him the grief of a father who sees one of his sons, for whose education he has made the utmost sacrifices, deliberately ruin the magnificent position he has created for him and dishonour, by pranks which the principles or prejudices of his family cannot allow, a respected name. It is true that M. de Guermantes had not displayed so profound and pained an astonishment when he learned that Saint-Loup was a Dreyfusard. But, for one thing, he regarded his nephew as a young man gone astray, as to whom nothing, until he began to mend his ways, could be surprising, whereas Swann was what M. de Guermantes called 'a man of weight, a man occupying a position in the front rank'. Moreover and above all, a considerable interval of time had elapsed during which, if, from the historical point of view, events had, to some extent, seemed to justify the Dreyfusard argument, the anti-Dreyfusard opposition had doubled its violence, and, from being purely political, had become social. It was now a question of militarism, of patriotism, and the waves of anger that had been stirred up in society had had time to gather the force which they never have at the beginning of a storm. 'Don't you see,' M. de Guermantes went on, 'even from the point of view of his beloved Jews, since he is absolutely determined to stand by them, Swann has made a blunder of an incalculable magnitude. He has shown that they are to some extent forced to give their support to anyone of their own race, even if they do not know him personally. It is a public danger. We have evidently been too easy-going, and the mistake Swann is making will create all the more stir since he was respected, not to say received, and was almost the only Jew that anyone knew. People will say: *Ab uno disce omnes.*' (His satisfaction at having hit, at the right moment, in his memory, upon so apt a quotation, alone brightened with a proud smile the melancholy of the great nobleman conscious of betrayal.)

I was longing to know what exactly had happened between the Prince and Swann, and to catch the latter, if he had not already gone home. 'I don't mind telling you,' the Duchess answered me when I spoke to her of this desire, 'that I for my part am not overanxious to see him, because it appears, by what I was told just now at Mme de Saint-Euverte's, that he would like me before he dies to make the acquaintance of his wife and daughter. Good heavens, it distresses me terribly that he should be ill, but, I must say, I hope it is not so serious as all that. And besides, it is not really a reason at all, because if it were it would be so childishly simple. A writer with no talent would have only to say: "Vote for me at the Academy because my wife is dying and I wish to give her this last happiness." There would be no more entertaining if one was obliged to make friends with all the dying people. My coachman might come to me with: "My daughter is seriously ill, get me an invitation to the Princesse de Parme's." I adore Charles, and I should hate having to refuse him, and so that is why I prefer to avoid the risk of his asking me. I hope with all my heart that he is not dying, as he says, but really, if it has to happen, it would not be the moment for me to make the acquaintance of those two creatures who have deprived me of the most amusing of my friends for the last fifteen years, with the additional disadvantage that I should not even be able to make use of their society to see him, since he would be dead!'

Meanwhile M. de Bréauté had not ceased to ruminate the contradiction of his story by Colonel de Froberville. 'I do not question the accuracy of your version, my dear fellow,' he said, 'but I had mine from a good source. It was the Prince de la Tour d'Auvergne who told me.'

'I am surprised that an educated man like yourself should still say "Prince de la Tour d'Auvergne",' the Duc de Guermantes broke in, 'you know that he is nothing of the kind. There is only one member of that family left. Oriane's uncle, the Duc de Bouillon.'

'The brother of Mme de Villeparisis?' I asked, remembering that she had been Mlle de Bouillon. 'Precisely. Oriane, Mme de Lambresac is bowing to you.' And indeed, one saw at certain moments form and fade like a shooting star a faint smile directed by the Duchesse de Lambresac at somebody whom she had recognised. But this smile, instead of taking definite shape in an active affirmation, in a language mute but clear, was drowned almost immediately in a sort of ideal ecstasy which expressed nothing, while her head drooped in a gesture of blissful benediction, recalling the inclination towards the crowd of communicants of the head of a somewhat senile prelate. There was not the least trace of senility about Mme de Lambresac. But I was acquainted already with this special type of old-fashioned distinction. At Combray and in Paris, all my grandmother's friends were in the habit of greeting one another at a social gathering with as seraphic an air as if they had caught sight of someone of their acquaintance in church, at the moment of the Elevation or during a funeral, and were casting him a gentle 'Good-morning' which ended in prayer. At this point a remark made by M.

de Guermantes was to complete the likeness that I was tracing. 'But you have seen the Duc de Bouillon,' he said to me. 'He was just going out of my library this afternoon as you came in, a short person with white hair.' It was the person whom I had taken for a man of business from Combray, and yet, now that I came to think it over, I could see the resemblance to Mme de Villeparisis. The similarity between the evanescent greetings of the Duchesse de Lambresac and those of my grandmother's friends had first aroused my interest, by showing me how in all narrow and exclusive societies, be they those of the minor gentry or of the great nobility, the old manners persist, allowing us to recapture, like an archaeologist, what might have been the standard of upbringing, and the side of life which it reflects, in the days of the Vicomte d'Arlincourt and Loïsa Puget. Better still now, the perfect conformity in appearance between a man of business from Combray of his generation and the Duc de Bouillon reminded me of what had already struck me so forcibly when I had seen Saint-Loup's maternal grandfather, the Duc de La Rochefoucauld, in a daguerreotype in which he was exactly similar, in dress, air and manner, to my great-uncle, that social, and even individual differences are merged when seen from a distance in the uniformity of an epoch. The truth is that the similarity of dress, and also the reflection, from a person's face, of the spirit of his age occupy so much more space than his caste, which bulks largely only in his own self-esteem and the imagination of other people, that in order to discover that a great nobleman of the time of Louis Philippe differs less from a citizen of the time of Louis Philippe than from a great nobleman of the time of Louis XV, it is not necessary to visit the galleries of the Louvre.

At that moment, a Bavarian musician with long hair, whom the Princesse de Guermantes had taken under her wing, bowed to Oriane. She responded with an inclination of her head, but the Duke, furious at seeing his wife bow to a person whom he did not know, who had a curious style, and, so far as M. de Guermantes understood, an extremely bad reputation, turned upon his wife with a terrible inquisitorial air, as much as to say: 'Who in the world is that Ostrogoth?' Poor Mme de Guermantes's position was already distinctly complicated, and if the musician had felt a little pity for this martyred wife, he would have made off as quickly as possible. But, whether from a desire not to remain under the humiliation that had just been inflicted on him in public, before the eyes of the Duke's oldest and most intimate friends, whose presence there had perhaps been responsible to some extent for his silent bow, and to show that it was on the best of grounds and not without knowing her already that he had greeted the Duchesse de Guermantes, or else in obedience to the obscure but irresistible impulse to commit a blunder

which drove him – at a moment when he ought to have trusted to the spirit –
to apply the whole letter of the law, the musician came closer to Mme de
Guermantes and said to her: 'Madame la Duchesse, I should like to request
the honour of being presented to the Duke.' Mme de Guermantes was
indeed in a quandary. But after all, she might well be a forsaken wife, she was
still Duchesse de Guermantes and could not let herself appear to have
forfeited the right to introduce to her husband the people whom she knew.
'Basin,' she said, 'allow me to present to you M. d'Herweck.'

'I need not ask whether you are going to Madame de Saint-Euverte's
tomorrow,' Colonel de Froberville said to Mme de Guermantes, to dispel
the painful impression produced by M. d'Herweck's ill-timed request. 'The
whole of Paris will be there.' Meanwhile, turning with a single movement
and as though he were carved out of a solid block towards the indiscreet
musician, the Duc de Guermantes, fronting his suppliant, monumental,
mute, wroth, like Jupiter Tonans, remained motionless like this for some
seconds, his eyes ablaze with anger and astonishment, his waving locks
seeming to issue from a crater. Then, as though carried away by an impulse
which alone enabled him to perform the act of politeness that was demanded
of him, and after appearing by his attitude of defiance to be calling the entire
company to witness that he did not know the Bavarian musician, clasping
his white-gloved hands behind his back, he jerked his body forward
and bestowed upon the musician a bow so profound, instinct with such
stupefaction and rage, so abrupt, so violent, that the trembling artist recoiled,
stooping as he went, so as not to receive a formidable butt in the stomach.
'Well, the fact is, I shall not be in Paris,' the Duchess answered Colonel de
Froberville. 'I may as well tell you (though I ought to be ashamed to confess
such a thing) that I have lived all these years without seeing the windows at
Montfort-l'Amaury. It is shocking, but there it is. And so, to make amends
for my shameful ignorance, I decided that I would go and see them
tomorrow.' M. de Bréauté smiled a subtle smile. He quite understood that,
if the Duchess had been able to live all these years without seeing the
windows at Montfort-l'Amaury, this artistic excursion did not all of a
sudden take on the urgent character of an expedition 'hotfoot' and might
without danger, after having been put off for more than twenty-five years,
be retarded for twenty-four hours. The plan that the Duchess had formed
was simply the Guermantes way of issuing the decree that the Saint-Euverte
establishment was definitely not a 'really nice' house, but a house to which
you were invited that you might be utilised afterwards in the account in the
Gaulois, a house that would set the seal of supreme smartness upon those, or
at any rate upon her (should there be but one) who did not go to it. The

delicate amusement of M. de Bréauté, enhanced by that poetical pleasure which people in society felt when they saw Mme de Guermantes do things which their own inferior position did not allow them to imitate, but the mere sight of which brought to their lips the smile of the peasant thirled to the soil when he sees freer and more fortunate men pass by above his head, this delicate pleasure could in no way be compared with the concealed but frantic ecstasy that was at once felt by M. de Froberville.

The efforts that this gentleman was making so that people should not hear his laughter had made him turn as red as a turkey-cock, in spite of which it was only with a running interruption of hiccoughs of joy that he exclaimed in a pitying tone: 'Oh! Poor Aunt Saint-Euverte, she will take to her bed! No! The unhappy woman is not to have her Duchess, what a blow, why, it is enough to kill her!' he went on, convulsed with laughter. And in his exhilaration he could not help stamping his feet and rubbing his hands. Smiling out of one eye and with the corner of her lips at M. de Froberville, whose amiable intention she appreciated, but found the deadly boredom of his society quite intolerable, Mme de Guermantes decided finally to leave him.

'Listen, I shall be obliged to bid you good-night,' she said to him as she rose with an air of melancholy resignation, and as though it had been a bitter grief to her. Beneath the magic spell of her blue eyes her gently musical voice made one think of the poetical lament of a fairy. 'Basin wants me to go and talk to Marie for a little.' In reality, she was tired of listening to Froberville, who did not cease to envy her her going to Montfort-l'Amaury, when she knew quite well that he had never heard of the windows before in his life, nor for that matter would he for anything in the world have missed going to the Saint-Euverte party. 'Goodbye, I've barely said a word to you, it is always like that at parties, we never see the people, we never say the things we should like to say, but it is the same everywhere in this life. Let us hope that when we are dead things will be better arranged. At any rate, we shall not always be having to put on low dresses. And yet, one never knows. We may perhaps have to display our bones and worms on great occasions. Why not? Look, there goes old Rampillon, do you see any great difference between her and a skeleton in an open dress? It is true that she has every right to look like that, for she must be at least a hundred. She was already one of those sacred monsters before whom I refused to bow the knee when I made my first appearance in society. I thought she had been dead for years; which for that matter would be the only possible explanation of the spectacle she presents. It is impressive and liturgical; quite *Camposanto*!' The Duchess had moved away from Froberville; he came after her: 'Just one word in your ear.' Slightly annoyed: 'Well, what is it now?' she said to him stiffly. And he, having been afraid lest, at the last moment, she might change her mind about Montfort-l'Amaury: 'I did not like to mention it for Mme de Saint-Euverte's sake, so as not to get her into trouble, but since you don't intend to be there, I may tell you that I am glad for your sake, for she has measles in the house!' 'Oh, good gracious!' said Oriane, who had a horror of illnesses. 'But that wouldn't matter to me, I've had them already. You can't get them twice.' 'So the doctors say; I know people who've had them four times. Anyhow, you are warned.' As for himself, these fictitious measles would have needed to attack him in reality and to chain him to his bed before he would have resigned himself to missing the Saint-Euverte party to which he had looked forward for so many months. He would have the pleasure of seeing so many smart people there! The still greater pleasure of remarking that certain things had gone wrong, and the supreme pleasures of being able for long afterwards to boast that he had mingled with the former and, while exaggerating or inventing them, of deploring the latter.

I took advantage of the Duchess's moving to rise also in order to make my way to the smoking-room and find out the truth about Swann. 'Do not believe a word of what Babal told us,' she said to me. 'Little Molé would never poke her nose into a place like that. They tell us that to draw us. Nobody ever goes to them and they are never asked anywhere either. He admits it himself: "We spend the evenings alone by our own fireside." As he always says we, not like royalty, but to include his wife, I do not press him. But I know all about it,' the Duchess added. We passed two young men whose great and dissimilar beauty took its origin from one and the same woman. They were the two sons of Mme de Surgis, the latest mistress of the Duc de Guermantes. Both were resplendent with their mother's perfections, but each in his own way. To one had passed, rippling through a virile body, the royal presence of Mme de Surgis and the same pallor, ardent, flushed and sacred, flooded the marble cheeks of mother and son; but his brother had received the Grecian brow, the perfect nose, the statuesque throat, the eyes of infinite depth; composed thus of separate gifts, which the goddess had shared between them, their twofold beauty offered one the abstract pleasure of thinking that the cause of that beauty was something outside themselves; one would have said that the principal attributes of their mother were incarnate in two different bodies; that one of the young men was his mother's stature and her complexion, the other her gaze, like those divine beings who were no more than the strength and beauty of Jupiter or Minerva. Full of respect for M. de Guermantes, of whom they said: 'He is a great friend of our parents', the elder nevertheless thought that it would be wiser not to come up and greet the Duchess, of whose hostility towards his mother he was aware, though without perhaps understanding the reason for it, and at the sight of us he slightly averted his head. The younger, who copied his brother in everything, because, being stupid and short-sighted to boot, he did not venture to own a personal opinion, inclined his head at the same angle, and the pair slipped past us towards the card-room, one behind the other, like a pair of allegorical figures.

Just as I reached this room, I was stopped by the Marquise de Citri, still beautiful but almost foaming at the mouth. Of decently noble birth, she had sought and made a brilliant match in marrying M. de Citri, whose great-grandmother had been an Aumale-Lorraine. But no sooner had she tasted this satisfaction than her natural cantankerousness gave her a horror of people in society which did not cut her off absolutely from social life. Not only, at a party, did she deride everyone present, her derision of them was so violent that mere laughter was not sufficiently bitter, and changed into a guttural hiss. 'Ah!' she said to me, pointing to the Duchesse de Guermantes who had now left my side and was already some way off, 'what defeats me is that she can lead this sort of existence.' Was this the speech of a righteously indignant Saint, astonished that the Gentiles did not come of their own accord to perceive the Truth, or that of an anarchist athirst for carnage? In any case there could be no possible justification for this apostrophe. In the first place, the 'existence led' by Mme de Guermantes differed hardly perceptibly (except in indignation) from that led by Mme de Citri. Mme de Citri was stupefied when she saw the Duchess capable of that mortal sacrifice: attendance at one of Marie-Gilbert's parties. It must be said in this particular instance that Mme de Citri was genuinely fond of the Princess, who was indeed the kindest of women, and knew that, by attending her party, she was giving her great pleasure. And so she had put off, in order to come to the party, a dancer whom she regarded as a genius, and who was to have initiated her into the mysteries of Russian choreography. Another reason which to some extent stultified the concentrated rage which Mme de Citri felt on seeing Oriane greet one or other of the guests was that Mme de Guermantes, albeit at a far less advanced stage, showed the symptoms of the malady that was devouring Mme de Citri. We have seen, moreover, that she had carried the germs of it from her birth. In fact, being more intelligent than Mme de Citri, Mme de Guermantes would have had better right than she to this nihilism (which was more than merely social), but it is true that certain good qualities help us rather to endure the defects of our neighbour than they make us suffer from them; and a man of great talent will normally pay less attention to other people's folly than would a fool. We have already described at sufficient length the nature of the Duchess's wit to convince the reader that, if it had nothing in common with great intellect, it was at least wit, a wit adroit in making use (like a translator) of different grammatical forms. Now nothing of this sort seemed to entitle Mme de Citri to look down upon qualities so closely akin to her own. She found everyone idiotic, but in her conversation, in her letters, showed herself distinctly inferior to the people whom she treated with such disdain. She had moreover such a thirst for destruction that, when she had almost given up society, the pleasures that she then sought were subjected, each in turn, to her terrible disintegrating force. After she had given up parties for musical evenings, she used to say: 'You like listening to that sort of thing, to music? Good gracious, it all depends on what it is. It can be simply deadly! Oh! Beethoven! What a bore!' With Wagner, then with Franck, Debussy, she did not even take the trouble to say the word *barbe*, but merely passed her hand over her face with a tonsorial gesture.

Presently, everything became boring. 'Beautiful things are such a bore. Oh! Pictures! They're enough to drive one mad. How right you are, it is such a bore having to write letters!' Finally it was life itself that she declared to be *rasante*, leaving her hearers to wonder where she applied the term.

I do not know whether it was the effect of what the Duchesse de Guermantes, on the evening when I first dined at her house, had said of this interior, but the card- or smoking-room, with its pictorial floor, its tripods, its figures of gods and animals that gazed at you, the sphinxes stretched out along the arms of the chairs, and most of all the huge table, of marble or enamelled mosaic, covered with symbolical signs more or less imitated from Etruscan and Egyptian art, gave me the impression of a magician's cell. And, on a chair drawn up to the glittering, augural table, M. de Charlus, in person, never touching a card, unconscious of what was going on round about him, incapable of observing that I had entered the room, seemed precisely a magician applying all the force of his will and reason to drawing a horoscope. Not only that, but, like the eyes of a Pythian on her tripod, his eyes were starting from his head, and that nothing might distract him from labours which required the cessation of the most simple movements, he had (like a calculator who will do nothing else until he has solved his problem) laid down beside him the cigar which he had previously been holding between his lips, but had no longer the necessary detachment of mind to think of smoking. Seeing the two crouching deities borne upon the arms of the chair that stood facing him, one might have thought that the Baron was endeavouring to solve the enigma of the Sphinx, had it not been that, rather, of a young and living Oedipus, seated in that very armchair, where he had come to join in the game. Now, the figure to which M. de Charlus was applying with such concentration all his mental powers, and which was not, to tell the truth, one of the sort that are commonly studied *more geometrico*, was that of the proposition set him by the lineaments of the young Comte de Surgis; it appeared, so profound was M. de Charlus's absorption in front of it, to be some rebus, some riddle, some algebraical problem, of which he must try to penetrate the mystery or to work out the formula. In front of him the sibylline signs and the figures inscribed upon that Table of the Law seemed the gramarye which would enable the old sorcerer to tell in what direction the young man's destiny was shaping. Suddenly he became aware that I was watching him, raised his head as though he were waking from a dream, smiled at me and blushed. At that moment Mme de Surgis's other son came up behind the one who was playing, to look at his cards. When M. de Charlus had learned from me that they were brothers, his features could not conceal the admiration that he felt for a family which could create masterpieces so splendid and so diverse. And what added to the Baron's enthusiasm was the discovery that the two sons of Mme de Surgis-le-Duc were sons not only of the same mother but of the same father. The children of Jupiter are dissimilar, but that is because he married first Metis, whose destiny was to bring into the world wise children, then Themis, and after her Eurynome, and Mnemosyne, and Leto, and only as a last resort Juno. But to a single father Mme de Surgis had borne these two sons who had each received beauty from her, but a different beauty.

I had at length the pleasure of seeing Swann come into this room, which was very big, so big that he did not at first catch sight of me. A pleasure mingled with sorrow, with a sorrow which the other guests did not, perhaps, feel, their feeling consisting rather in that sort of fascination which is exercised by the strange and unexpected forms of an approaching death, a death that a man already has, in the popular saying, written on his face. And it was with a stupefaction that was almost offensive, into which entered indiscreet curiosity, cruelty, a scrutiny at once quiet and anxious (a blend of *suave mari magno* and *memento quia pulvis*, Robert would have said), that all eyes were fastened upon that face the cheeks of which had been so eaten away by disease, like a waning moon, that, except at a certain angle, the angle doubtless at which Swann looked at himself, they stopped short like a flimsy piece of scenery to which only an optical illusion can add the appearance of solidity. Whether because of the absence of those cheeks, no longer there to modify it, or because arteriosclerosis, which also is a form of intoxication, had reddened it, as would drunkenness, or deformed it, as would morphine, Swann's punchinello nose, absorbed for long years in an attractive face, seemed now enormous, tumid, crimson, the nose of an old Hebrew rather than of a dilettante Valois. Perhaps too in him, in these last days, the race was making appear more pronounced the physical type that characterises it, at the same time as the sentiment of a moral solidarity with the rest of the Jews, a solidarity which Swann seemed to have forgotten throughout his life, and which, one after another, his mortal illness, the Dreyfus case and the anti-semitic propaganda had revived. There are certain Israelites, superior people for all that and refined men of the world, in whom there remain in reserve and in the wings, ready to enter at a given moment in their lives, as in a play, a bounder and a prophet. Swann had arrived at the age of the prophet. Certainly, with his face from which, by the action of his disease, whole segments had vanished, as when a block of ice melts and slabs of it fall off bodily, he had greatly altered. But I could not help being struck by the discovery how far more he had altered in relation to myself. This man, excellent, cultivated, whom I was far from annoyed at meeting, I could not bring myself to understand how I had been able to invest him long ago in a mystery so great that his appearance in the Champs-Elysées used to make my heart beat so violently that I was too bashful to approach his silk-lined cape, that at the door of the flat in which such a being dwelt I could not ring the bell without being overcome by boundless emotion and dismay; all this had vanished not only from his home, but from his person, and the idea of talking to him might or might not be agreeable to me, but had no effect whatever upon my nervous system.

And besides, how he had altered since that very afternoon, when I had met him – after all, only a few hours earlier – in the Duc de Guermantes's study. Had he really had a scene with the Prince, and had it left him crushed? The supposition was not necessary. The slightest efforts that are demanded of a person who is very ill quickly become for him an excessive strain. He has only to be exposed, when already tired, to the heat of a crowded drawing-room, for his countenance to decompose and turn blue, as happens in a few hours with an overripe pear or milk that is ready to turn. Besides, Swann's hair was worn thin in patches, and, as Mme de Guermantes remarked, needed attention from the furrier, looked as if it had been camphored, and camphored badly. I was just crossing the room to speak to Swann when unfortunately a hand fell upon my shoulder.

'Hallo, old boy, I am in Paris for forty-eight hours. I called at your house, they told me you were here, so that it is to you that my aunt is indebted for the honour of my company at her party.' It was Saint-Loup. I told him how greatly I admired the house. 'Yes, it makes quite a historic edifice. Personally, I think it appalling. We mustn't go near my uncle Palamède, or we shall be caught. Now that Mme Molé has gone (for it is she that is ruling the roost just now), he is quite at a loose end. It seems it was as good as a play, he never let her out of his sight for a moment, and only left her when he had put her safely into her carriage. I bear my uncle no ill will, only I do think it odd that my family council, which has always been so hard on me, should be composed of the very ones who have led giddy lives themselves, beginning with the giddiest of the lot, my uncle Charlus, who is my official guardian, has had more women than Don Juan, and is still carrying on in spite of his age. There was a talk at one time of having me made a ward of court. I bet, when all those gay old dogs met to consider the question, and had me up to preach to me and tell me that I was breaking my mother's heart, they dared not look one another in the face for fear of laughing. Just think of the fellows who formed the council, you would think they had deliberately chosen the biggest womanisers.' Leaving out of account M. de Charlus, with regard to whom my friend's astonishment no longer seemed to me to be justified, but for different reasons, and reasons which, moreover, were afterwards to undergo modification in my mind, Robert was quite wrong in finding it extraordinary that lessons in worldly wisdom should be given to a young man by people who had done foolish things, or were still doing them.

Even if we take into account only atavism, family likenesses, it is inevitable that the uncle who delivers the lecture should have more or less the same faults as the nephew whom he has been deputed to scold. Nor is the uncle in the least hypocritical in so doing, taken in as he is by the faculty that people have of believing, in every fresh experience, that 'this is quite different', a faculty which allows them to adopt artistic, political and other errors without perceiving that they are the same errors which they exposed, ten years ago, in another school of painters, whom they condemned, another political affair which, they considered, merited a loathing that they no longer feel, and espouse those errors without recognising them in a fresh disguise. Besides, even if the faults of the uncle are different from those of the nephew, heredity may none the less be responsible, for the effect does not always resemble the cause, as a copy resembles its original, and even if the uncle's faults are worse, he may easily believe them to be less serious.

When M. de Charlus made indignant remonstrances to Robert, who moreover was unaware of his uncle's true inclinations, at that time, and indeed if it had still been the time when the Baron used to scarify his own inclinations, he might perfectly well have been sincere in considering, from the point of view of a man of the world, that Robert was infinitely more to blame than himself. Had not Robert, at the very moment when his uncle had been deputed to make him listen to reason, come within an inch of getting himself ostracised by society, had he not very nearly been blackballed at the Jockey, had he not made himself a public laughing stock by the vast sums that he threw away upon a woman of the lowest order, by his friendships with people – authors, actors, Jews – not one of whom moved in society, by his opinions, which were indistinguishable from those held by traitors, by the grief he was causing to all his relatives? In what respect could it be compared, this scandalous existence, with that of M. de Charlus who had managed, so far, not only to retain but to enhance still further his position as a Guermantes, being in society an absolutely privileged person, sought after, adulated in the most exclusive circles, and a man who, married to a Bourbon Princess, a woman of eminence, had been able to ensure her happiness, had shown a devotion to her memory more fervent, more scrupulous than is customary in society, and had thus been as good a husband as a son!

'But are you sure that M. de Charlus has had all those mistresses?' I asked, not, of course, with any diabolical intent of revealing to Robert the secret that I had surprised, but irritated, nevertheless, at hearing him maintain an erroneous theory with so much certainty and assurance. He merely shrugged his shoulders in response to what he took for ingenuousness on my part. 'Not that I blame him in the least, I consider that he is perfectly right.' And he began to sketch in outline a theory of conduct that would have horrified him at Balbec (where he was not content with denouncing seducers, death seeming to him then the only punishment adequate to their crime). Then, however, he had still been in love and jealous. He went so far as to sing me the praises of houses of assignation. 'They're the only places where you can find a shoe to fit you, sheath your weapon, as we say in the regiment.' He no longer felt for places of that sort the disgust that had inflamed him at Balbec when I made an allusion to them, and, hearing what he now said, I told him that Bloch had introduced me to one, but Robert replied that the one which Bloch frequented must be 'extremely mixed, the poor man's paradise! – It all depends, though: where is it?' I remained vague, for I had just remembered that it was the same house at which one used to have for a louis that Rachel whom Robert had so passionately loved. 'Anyhow, I can take you to some far better ones, full of stunning women.' Hearing me express the desire that he would take me as soon as possible to the ones he knew, which must indeed be far superior to the house to which Bloch had taken me, he expressed a sincere regret that he could not, on this occasion, as he would have to leave Paris next day. 'It will have to be my next leave,' he said. 'You'll see, there are young girls there, even,' he added with an air of mystery. 'There is a little Mademoiselle de . . . I think it's d'Orgeville, I can let you have the exact name, who is the daughter of quite tiptop people; her mother was by way of being a La Croix-l'Evêque, and they're a really decent family, in fact they're more or less related, if I'm not mistaken, to my aunt Oriane. Anyhow, you have only to see the child, you can tell at once that she comes of decent people.' (I could detect, hovering for a moment over Robert's voice, the shadow of the genius of the Guermantes, which passed like a cloud, but at a great height and without stopping.) 'It seems to me to promise marvellous developments. The parents are always ill and can't look after her. Gad, the child must have some amusement, and I count upon you to provide it!' 'Oh! When are you coming back?' 'I don't know, if you don't absolutely insist upon Duchesses,' (Duchess being in aristocracy the only title that denotes a particularly brilliant rank, as the lower orders talk of 'Princesses') 'in a different class of goods, there is Mme Putbus's maid.'

At this moment, Mme de Surgis entered the room in search of her sons. As soon as he saw her M. de Charlus went up to her with a friendliness by which the Marquise was all the more agreeably surprised, in that an icy frigidity was what she had expected from the Baron, who had always posed as Oriane's protector and alone of the family – the rest being too often inclined to forgive the Duke his irregularities by the glamour of his position and their own jealousy of the Duchess – kept his brother's mistresses pitilessly at a distance. And so Mme de Surgis had fully understood the motives of the attitude that she dreaded to find in the Baron, but never for a moment suspected those of the wholly different welcome that she did receive from him. He spoke to her with admiration of the portrait that Jacquet had painted of her years before. This admiration waxed indeed to an enthusiasm which, if it was partly deliberate, with the object of preventing the Marquise from going away, of 'hooking' her, as Robert used to say of enemy armies when you seek to keep their effective strength engaged at one point, might also be sincere. For, if everyone was delighted to admire in her sons the regal bearing and eyes of Mme de Surgis, the Baron could taste an inverse but no less keen pleasure in finding those charms combined in the mother, as in a portrait which does not by itself excite desire, but feeds with the aesthetic admiration that it does excite the desires that it revives. These came now to give, in retrospect, a voluptuous charm to Jacquet's portrait itself, and at that moment the Baron would gladly have purchased it to study upon its surface the physiognomic pedigree of the two young Surgis.

'You see, I wasn't exaggerating,' Robert said in my ear. 'Just look at the way my uncle is running after Mme de Surgis. Though I must say, that does surprise me. If Oriane knew, she would be furious. Really, there are enough women in the world without his having to go and sprawl over that one,' he went on; like everybody who is not in love, he imagined that one chose the person whom one loved after endless deliberations and on the strength of various qualities and advantages. Besides, while completely mistaken about his uncle, whom he supposed to be devoted to women, Robert, in his rancour, spoke too lightly of M. de Charlus. We are not always somebody's nephew with impunity. It is often through him that a hereditary habit is transmitted to us sooner or later. We might indeed arrange a whole gallery of portraits, named like the German comedy: *Uncle and Nephew*, in which we should see the uncle watching jealously, albeit unconsciously, for his nephew to end by becoming like himself.

I go so far as to say that this gallery would be incomplete were we not to include in it the uncles who are not really related by blood, being the uncles only of their nephews' wives. The Messieurs de Charlus are indeed so convinced that they themselves are the only good husbands, what is more the only husbands of whom their wives are not jealous, that generally, out of affection for their niece, they make her marry another Charlus. Which tangles the skein of family likenesses. And, to affection for the niece, is added at times affection for her betrothed as well. Such marriages are not uncommon, and are often what are called happy.

'What were we talking about? Oh yes, that big, fair girl, Mme Putbus's maid. She goes with women too, but I don't suppose you mind that, I can tell you frankly, I have never seen such a gorgeous creature.' 'I imagine her rather Giorgione?' 'Wildly Giorgione! Oh, if I only had a little time in Paris, what wonderful things there are to be done! And then, one goes on to the next. For love is all rot, mind you, I've finished with all that.' I soon discovered, to my surprise, that he had equally finished with literature, whereas it was merely with regard to literary men that he had struck me as being disillusioned at our last meeting. ('They're practically all a pack of scoundrels,' he had said to me, a saying that might be explained by his justified resentment towards certain of Rachel's friends. They had indeed persuaded her that she would never have any talent if she allowed 'Robert, scion of an alien race' to acquire an influence over her, and with her used to make fun of him, to his face, at the dinners to which he entertained them.) But in reality Robert's love of Letters was in no sense profound, did not spring from his true nature, was only a by-product of his love of Rachel, and he had got rid of it, at the same time as of his horror of voluptuaries and his religious respect for the virtue of women.

'There is something very strange about those two young men. Look at that curious passion for gambling, Marquise,' said M. de Charlus, drawing Mme de Surgis's attention to her own sons, as though he were completely unaware of their identity. 'They must be a pair of Orientals, they have certain characteristic features, they are perhaps Turks,' he went on, so as both to give further support to his feint of innocence and to exhibit a vague antipathy, which, when in due course it gave place to affability, would prove that the latter was addressed to the young men solely in their capacity as sons of Mme de Surgis, having begun only when the Baron discovered who they were. Perhaps too M. de Charlus, whose insolence was a natural gift which he delighted in exercising, took advantage of the few moments in which he was supposed not to know the name of these two young men to have a little fun at Mme de Surgis's expense, and to indulge in his habitual sarcasm, as Scapin takes advantage of his master's disguise to give him a sound drubbing.

'They are my sons,' said Mme de Surgis, with a blush which would not have coloured her cheeks had she been more discerning, without necessarily being more virtuous. She would then have understood that the air of absolute indifference or of sarcasm which M. de Charlus displayed towards a young man was no more sincere than the wholly superficial admiration which he showed for a woman, did not express his true nature. The woman to whom he could go on indefinitely paying the prettiest compliments might well be jealous of the look which, while talking to her, he shot at a man whom he would pretend afterwards not to have noticed. For that look was not of the sort which M. de Charlus kept for women; a special look, springing from the depths, which even at a party could not help straying innocently in the direction of the young men, like the look in a tailor's eye which betrays his profession by immediately fastening upon your attire.

'Oh, how very strange!' replied M. de Charlus, not without insolence, as though his mind had to make a long journey to arrive at a reality so different from what he had pretended to suppose. 'But I don't know them!' he added, fearing lest he might have gone a little too far in the expression of his antipathy, and have thus paralysed the Marquise's intention to let him make their acquaintance. 'Would you allow me to introduce them to you?' Mme de Surgis enquired timidly. 'Why, good gracious, just as you please, I shall be delighted, I am perhaps not very entertaining company for such young people,' M. de Charlus intoned with the air of hesitation and coldness of a person who is letting himself be forced into an act of politeness.

'Arnulphe, Victurnien, come here at once,' said Mme de Surgis. Victurnien rose with decision. Arnulphe, though he could not see where his brother was going, followed him meekly.

'It's the sons' turn, now,' muttered Saint-Loup. 'It's enough to make one die with laughing. He tries to curry favour with everyone, down to the dog in the yard. It is all the funnier, as my uncle detests pretty boys. And just look how seriously he is listening to them. If it had been I who tried to introduce them to him, he would have given me what for. Listen, I shall have to go and say how d'ye do to Oriane. I have so little time in Paris that I want to try and see all the people here that I ought to leave cards on.'

'What a well-bred air they have, what charming manners,' M. de Charlus was saying. 'You think so?' Mme de Surgis replied, highly delighted.

Swann having caught sight of me came over to Saint-Loup and myself. His Jewish gaiety was less refined than his witticisms as a man of the world. 'Good-evening,' he said to us. 'Heavens! All three of us together, people will think it is a meeting of the Syndicate. In another minute they'll be looking for the safe!' He had not observed that M. de Beaucerfeuil was just behind his back and could hear what he said. The General could not help wincing. We heard the voice of M. de Charlus close beside us: 'What, you are called Victurnien, after the *Cabinet des Antiques*,' the Baron was saying, to prolong his conversation with the two young men. 'By Balzac, yes,' replied the elder Surgis, who had never read a line of that novelist's work, but to whom his tutor had remarked, a few days earlier, upon the similarity of his Christian name and d'Esgrignon's. Mme de Surgis was delighted to see her son shine, and at M. de Charlus's ecstasy before such a display of learning.

'It appears that Loubet is entirely on our side, I have it from an absolutely trustworthy source,' Swann informed Saint-Loup, but this time in a lower tone so as not to be overheard by the General. Swann had begun to find his wife's Republican connections more interesting now that the Dreyfus case had become his chief preoccupation. 'I tell you this because I know that your heart is with us.'

'Not quite to that extent; you are entirely mistaken,' was Robert's answer. 'It's a bad business, and I'm sorry I ever had a finger in it. It was no affair of mine. If it were to begin over again, I should keep well clear of it. I am a soldier, and my first duty is to support the Army. If you will stay with M. Swann for a moment, I shall be back presently, I must go and talk to my aunt.' But I saw that it was with Mlle d'Ambresac that he went to talk, and was distressed by the thought that he had lied to me about the possibility of their engagement. My mind was set at rest when I learned that he had been introduced to her half an hour earlier by Mme de Marsantes, who was anxious for the marriage, the Ambresacs being extremely rich.

'At last,' said M. de Charlus to Mme de Surgis, 'I find a young man with some education, who has read, who knows what is meant by Balzac. And it gives me all the more pleasure to meet him where that sort of thing has become most rare, in the house of one of my peers, one of ourselves,' he added, laying stress upon the words. It was all very well for the Guermantes to profess to regard all men as equal; on the great occasions when they found themselves among people who were 'born', especially if they were not quite so well born as themselves, whom they were anxious and able to flatter, they did not hesitate to trot out old family memories. 'At one time,' the Baron went on, 'the word aristocrat meant the best people, in intellect, in heart. Now, here is the first person I find among ourselves who has ever heard of Victurnien d'Esgrignon. I am wrong in saying the first. There are also a Polignac and a Montesquieu,' added M. de Charlus, who knew that this twofold association must inevitably thrill the Marquise. 'However, your sons have every reason to be learned, their maternal grandfather had a famous collection of eighteenth century stuff. I will show you mine if you will do me the pleasure of coming to luncheon with me one day,' he said to the young Victurnien. 'I can show you an interesting edition of the *Cabinet des Antiques* with corrections in Balzac's own hand. I shall be charmed to bring the two Victurniens face to face.'

I could not bring myself to leave Swann. He had arrived at that stage of exhaustion in which a sick man's body becomes a mere retort in which we study chemical reactions. His face was mottled with tiny spots of Prussian blue, which seemed not to belong to the world of living things, and emitted the sort of odour which, at school, after the 'experiments', makes it so unpleasant to have to remain in a 'science' classroom. I asked him whether he had not had a long conversation with the Prince de Guermantes and if he would tell me what it had been about. 'Yes,' he said, 'but go for a moment first with M. de Charlus and Mme de Surgis, I shall wait for you here.'

Indeed, M. de Charlus, having suggested to Mme de Surgis that they should leave this room which was too hot, and go and sit for a little in another, had invited not the two sons to accompany their mother, but myself. In this way he made himself appear, after he had successfully hooked them, to have lost all interest in the two young men. He was moreover paying me an inexpensive compliment, Mme de Surgis being in distinctly bad odour.

Unfortunately, no sooner had we sat down in an alcove from which there was no way of escape than Mme de Saint-Euverte, a butt for the Baron's jibes, came past. She, perhaps to mask or else openly to show her contempt for the ill will which she inspired in M. de Charlus, and above all to show that she was on intimate terms with a woman who was talking so familiarly to him, gave a disdainfully friendly greeting to the famous beauty, who acknowledged it, peeping out of the corner of her eye at M. de Charlus with a mocking smile. But the alcove was so narrow that Mme de Saint-Euverte, when she tried to continue, behind our backs, her canvass of her guests for the morrow, found herself a prisoner, and had some difficulty in escaping, a precious moment which M. de Charlus, anxious that his insolent wit should shine before the mother of the two young men, took good care not to let slip. A silly question which I had put to him, without malice aforethought, gave him the opportunity for a hymn of triumph of which the poor Saint-Euverte, almost immobilised behind us, could not have lost a word. 'Would you believe it, this impertinent young man,' he said, indicating me to Mme de Surgis, 'asked me just now, without any sign of that modesty which makes us keep such expeditions private, if I was going to Mme de Saint-Euverte's, which is to say, I suppose, if I was suffering from the colic. I should endeavour, in any case, to relieve myself in some more comfortable place than the house of a person who, if my memory serves me, was celebrating her centenary when I first began to go about town, though not, of course, to her house. And yet who could be more interesting to listen to? What a host of historic memories, seen and lived through in the days of the First Empire and the Restoration, and secret history too, which could certainly have nothing of the "saint" about it, but must be decidedly "verdant" if we are to judge by the amount of kick still left in the old trot's shanks. What would prevent me from questioning her about those passionate times is the acuteness of my olfactory organ. The proximity of the lady is enough. I say to myself all at once: oh, good lord, someone has broken the lid of my cesspool, when it is simply the Marquise opening her mouth to emit some invitation. And you can understand that if I had the misfortune to go to her house, the cesspool would be magnified into a formidable sewage-cart. She bears a mystic name, though, which has always made me think with jubilation, although she has long since passed the date of her jubilee, of that stupid line of poetry called deliquescent: "Ah, green, how green my soul was on that day . . ." But I require a cleaner sort of verdure. They tell me that the indefatigable old streetwalker gives "garden-parties", I should describe them as "invitations to explore the sewers". Are you going to wallow there?' he asked Mme de Surgis, who this time was annoyed. Wishing to pretend for the Baron's benefit that she was not going, and knowing that she would give days of her life rather than miss the Saint-Euverte party, she got out of it by taking a middle course, that is to say uncertainty. This uncertainty took so clumsily amateurish, so sordidly material a form, that M. de Charlus, with no fear of offending Mme de Surgis, whom nevertheless he was anxious to please, began to laugh to show her that 'it cut no ice with him'.

'I always admire people who make plans,' she said; 'I often change mine at the last moment. There is a question of a summer frock which may alter everything. I shall act upon the inspiration of the moment.'

For my part, I was furious at the abominable little speech that M. de Charlus had just made. I would have liked to shower blessings upon the giver of garden-parties. Unfortunately, in the social as in the political world, the victims are such cowards that one cannot for long remain indignant with their tormentors. Mme de Saint-Euverte, who had succeeded in escaping from the alcove to which we were barring the entry, brushed against the Baron inadvertently as she passed him, and, by a reflex action of snobbishness which wiped out all her anger, perhaps even in the hope of securing an opening, at which this could not be the first attempt, exclaimed: 'Oh! I beg your pardon, Monsieur de Charlus, I hope I did not hurt you,' as though she were kneeling before her lord and master. The latter did not deign to reply save by a broad ironical smile, and conceded only a 'Good-evening', which, uttered as though he were only now made aware of the Marquise's presence after she had greeted him, was an insult the more. Lastly, with a supreme want of spirit which pained me for her sake, Mme de Saint-Euverte came up to me and, drawing me aside, said in my ear: 'Tell me, what have I done to offend M. de Charlus? They say that he doesn't consider me smart enough for him,' she said, laughing from ear to ear. I remained serious. For one thing, I thought it stupid of her to appear to believe or to wish other people to believe that nobody, really, was as smart as herself. For another thing, people who laugh so heartily at what they themselves have said, when it is not funny, dispense us accordingly, by taking upon themselves the responsibility for the mirth, from joining in it.

'Other people assure me that he is cross because I do not invite him. But he does not give me much encouragement. He seems to avoid me.' (This expression struck me as inadequate.) 'Try to find out, and come and tell me tomorrow. And if he feels remorseful and wishes to come too, bring him. I shall forgive and forget. Indeed, I shall be quite glad to see him, because it will annoy Mme de Surgis. I give you a free hand. You have the most perfect judgment in these matters and I do not wish to appear to be begging my guests to come. In any case, I count upon you absolutely.'

It occurred to me that Swann must be getting tired of waiting for me. I did not wish, moreover, to be too late in returning home, because of Albertine, and, taking leave of Mme de Surgis and M. de Charlus, I went in search of my sick man in the card-room. I asked him whether what he had said to the Prince in their conversation in the garden was really what M. de Bréauté (whom I did not name) had reported to us, about a little play by Bergotte. He burst out laughing: 'There is not a word of truth in it, not one, it is entirely made up and would have been an utterly stupid thing to say. Really, it is unheard of, this spontaneous generation of falsehood. I do not ask who it was that told you, but it would be really interesting, in a field as limited as this, to work back from one person to another and find out how the story arose. Anyhow, what concern can it be of other people, what the Prince said to me? People are very inquisitive. I have never been inquisitive, except when I was in love, and when I was jealous. And a lot I ever learned! Are you jealous?' I told Swann that I had never experienced jealousy, that I did not even know what it was. 'Indeed! I congratulate you. A little jealousy is not at all a bad thing, from two points of view. For one thing, because it enables people who are not inquisitive to take an interest in the lives of others, or of one other at any rate. And besides, it makes one feel the pleasure of possession, of getting into a carriage with a woman, of not allowing her to go about by herself. But that occurs only in the very first stages of the disease, or when the cure is almost complete. In the interval, it is the most agonising torment. However, even the two pleasures I have mentioned, I must own to you that I have tasted very little of them: the first, by the fault of my own nature, which is incapable of sustained reflection; the second, by force of circumstances, by the fault of the woman, I should say the women, of whom I have been jealous. But that makes no difference. Even when one is no longer interested in things, it is still something to have been interested in them; because it was always for reasons which other people did not grasp. The memory of those sentiments is, we feel, to be found only in ourselves; we must go back into ourselves to study it. You mustn't laugh at this idealistic jargon, what I mean to say is that I have been very fond of life and very fond of art. Very well! Now that I am a little too weary to live with other people, those old sentiments, so personal and individual, that I felt in the past, seem to me – it is the mania of all collectors – very precious. I open my heart to myself like a sort of showcase, and examine one by one ever so many love affairs of which the rest of the world can have known nothing. And of this collection, to which I am now even more attached than to my others, I say to myself, rather as Mazarin said of his library, but still without any keen regret, that it will be very tiresome to have to leave it all. But, to come back to my conversation with the Prince, I shall repeat it to one person only, and that person is going to be yourself.' My attention was distracted by the conversation that M. de Charlus, who had returned to the card-room, was prolonging indefinitely close beside us. 'And are you a reader too? What do you do?' he asked Comte Arnulphe, who had never heard even the name of Balzac. But his short-sightedness, as he saw everything very small, gave him the appearance of seeing to great distances, so that, rare poetry in a sculptural Greek god, there seemed to be engraved upon his pupils remote, mysterious stars.

'Suppose we took a turn in the garden, Sir,' I said to Swann, while Comte Arnulphe, in a lisping voice which seemed to indicate that mentally at least his development was incomplete, replied to M. de Charlus with an artlessly obliging precision: 'I, oh, golf chiefly, tennis, football, running, polo I'm really keen on.' So Minerva, being subdivided, ceased in certain cities to be the goddess of wisdom, and incarnated part of herself in a purely sporting, horse-loving deity, Athene Hippia. And he went to Saint Moritz also to ski, for Pallas Trilogeneia frequents the high peaks and outruns swift horsemen. 'Ah!' replied M. de Charlus with the transcendent smile of the intellectual who does not even take the trouble to conceal his derision, but, on the other hand, feels himself so superior to other people and so far despises the intelligence of those who are the least stupid, that he barely differentiates between them and the most stupid, the moment they can be attractive to him in some other way. While talking to Arnulphe, M. de Charlus felt that by the mere act of addressing him he was conferring upon him a superiority which everyone else must recognise and envy. 'No,' Swann replied, 'I am too tired to walk about, let us sit down somewhere in a corner, I cannot remain on my feet any longer.' This was true, and yet the act of beginning to talk had already given him back a certain vivacity. This was because, in the most genuine exhaustion, there is, especially in neurotic people, an element that depends upon attracting their attention and is kept going only by an act of memory. We at once feel tired as soon as we are afraid of feeling tired, and, to throw off our fatigue, it suffices us to forget about it. To be sure, Swann was far from being one of those indefatigable invalids who, entering a room worn out and ready to drop, revive in conversation like a flower in water and are able for hours on end to draw from their own words a reserve of strength which they do not, alas, communicate to their hearers, who appear more and more exhausted the more the talker comes back to life. But Swann belonged to that stout Jewish race, in whose vital energy, its resistance to death, its individual members seem to share. Stricken severally by their own diseases, as it is stricken itself by persecution, they continue indefinitely to struggle against terrible suffering which may be prolonged beyond every apparently possible limit, when already one sees nothing more than a prophet's beard surmounted by a huge nose which dilates to inhale its last breath, before the hour strikes for the ritual prayers and the punctual procession begins of distant relatives advancing with mechanical movements, as upon an Assyrian frieze.

We went to sit down, but, before moving away from the group formed by M. de Charlus with the two young Surgis and their mother, Swann could not resist fastening upon the lady's bosom the slow expansive concupiscent gaze of a connoisseur. He put up his monocle, for a better view, and, while he talked to me, kept glancing in the direction of the lady. 'This is, word for word,' he said to me when we were seated, 'my conversation with the Prince, and if you remember what I said to you just now, you will see why I choose you as my confidant. There is another reason as well, which you shall one day learn. – "My dear Swann," the Prince de Guermantes said to me, "you must forgive me if I have appeared to be avoiding you for some time past." (I had never even noticed it, having been ill and avoiding society myself.) "In the first place, I had heard it said that, as I fully expected, in the unhappy affair which is splitting the country in two your views were diametrically opposed to mine. Now, it would have been extremely painful to me to have to hear you express them. So sensitive were my nerves that when the Princess, two years ago, heard her brother-in-law, the Grand Duke of Hesse, say that Dreyfus was innocent, she was not content with promptly denying the assertion but refrained from repeating it to me in order not to upset me. About the same time, the Crown Prince of Sweden came to Paris and, having probably heard someone say that the Empress Eugénie was a Dreyfusist, confused her with the Princess (a strange confusion, you will admit, between a woman of the rank of my wife and a Spaniard, a great deal less well born than people make out, and married to a mere Bonaparte), and said to her: Princess, I am doubly glad to meet you, for I know that you hold the same view as myself of the Dreyfus case, which does not surprise me since Your Highness is Bavarian. Which drew down upon the Prince the answer: Sir, I am nothing now but a French Princess, and I share the views of all my fellow-countrymen. Now, my dear Swann, about eighteen months ago, a conversation I had with General de Beaucerfeuil made me suspect that not an error, but grave illegalities had been committed in the procedure of the trial." '

We were interrupted (Swann did not wish people to overhear his story) by the voice of M. de Charlus who (without, as it happened, paying us the slightest attention) came past escorting Mme de Surgis, and stopped in the hope of detaining her for a moment longer, whether on account of her sons or from that reluctance common to all the Guermantes to bring anything to an end, which kept them plunged in a sort of anxious inertia. Swann informed me, in this connection, a little later, of something that stripped the name Surgis-le-Duc, for me, of all the poetry that I had found in it. The Marquise de Surgis-le-Duc boasted a far higher social position, far finer connections by marriage than her cousin the Comte de Surgis, who had no money and lived on his estate in the country. But the words that ended her title 'le Duc' had not at all the origin which I ascribed to them, and which had made me associate it in my imagination with Bourg-l'Abbé, Bois-le-Roi, etc. All that had happened was that a Comte de Surgis had married, during the Restoration, the daughter of an immensely rich industrial magnate, M. Leduc, or Le Duc, himself the son of a chemical manufacturer, the richest man of his day, and a Peer of France. King Charles X had created for the son born of this marriage the Marquisate of Surgis-le-Duc, a Marquisate of Surgis existing already in the family. The addition of the plebeian surname had not prevented this branch from allying itself, on the strength of its enormous fortune, with the first families of the realm. And the present Marquise de Surgis-le-Duc, herself of exalted birth, might have moved in the very highest circles. A demon of perversity had driven her, scorning the position ready made for her, to flee from the conjugal roof, to live a life of open scandal. Whereupon the world which she had scorned at twenty, when it was at her feet, had cruelly failed her at thirty, when, after ten years, everybody, except a few faithful friends, had ceased to bow to her, and she set to work to reconquer laboriously, inch by inch, what she had possessed as a birthright. (An outward and return journey which are not uncommon.)

As for the great nobles, her kinsmen, whom she had disowned in the past, and who in their turn had now disowned her, she found an excuse for the joy that she would feel in gathering them again to her bosom in the memories of childhood that they would be able to recall. And in so saying, to cloak her snobbishness, she was perhaps less untruthful than she supposed. 'Basin is all my girlhood!' she said on the day on which he came back to her. And as a matter of fact there was a grain of truth in the statement. But she had miscalculated when she chose him for her lover. For all the women friends of the Duchesse de Guermantes were to rally round her, and so Mme de Surgis must descend for the second time that slope up which she had so laboriously toiled. 'Well!' M. de Charlus was saying to her, in his attempt to prolong the conversation. 'You will lay my tribute at the feet of the beautiful portrait. How is it? What has become of it?' 'Why,' replied Mme de Surgis, 'you know I haven't got it now; my husband wasn't pleased with it.' 'Not pleased! With one of the greatest works of art of our time, equal to Nattier's *Duchesse de Châteauroux*, and, moreover, perpetuating no less majestic and heart-shattering a goddess. Oh! That little blue collar! I swear, Vermeer himself never painted a fabric more consummately, but we must not say it too loud or Swann will fall upon us to avenge his favourite painter, the Master of Delft.' The Marquise, turning round, addressed a smile and held out her hand to Swann, who had risen to greet her. But almost without concealment, whether in his declining days he had lost all wish for concealment, by indifference to opinion, or the physical power, by the excitement of his desire and the weakening of the control that helps us to conceal it, as soon as Swann, on taking the Marquise's hand, saw her bosom at close range and from above, he plunged an attentive, serious, absorbed, almost anxious gaze into the cavity of her bodice, and his nostrils, drugged by the lady's perfume, quivered like the wings of a butterfly about to alight upon a half-hidden flower. He checked himself abruptly on the edge of the precipice, and Mme de Surgis herself, albeit annoyed, stifled a deep sigh, so contagious can desire prove at times. 'The painter was cross,' she said to M. de Charlus, 'and took it back. I have heard that it is now at Diane de Saint-Euverte's.' 'I decline to believe,' said the Baron, 'that a great picture can have such bad taste.'

'He is talking to her about her portrait. I could talk to her about that portrait just as well as Charlus,' said Swann, affecting a drawling, slangy tone as he followed the retreating couple with his gaze. 'And I should certainly enjoy talking about it more than Charlus,' he added. I asked him whether the things that were said about M. de Charlus were true, in doing which I was lying twice over, for, if I had no proof that anybody ever had said anything, I had on the other hand been perfectly aware for some hours past that what I was hinting at was true. Swann shrugged his shoulders, as though I had suggested something quite absurd. 'It's quite true that he's a charming friend. But, need I add, his friendship is purely platonic. He is more sentimental than other men, that is all; on the other hand, as he never goes very far with women, that has given a sort of plausibility to the idiotic rumours to which you refer. Charlus is perhaps greatly attached to his men friends, but you may be quite certain that the attachment is only in his head and in his heart. At last, we may perhaps be left in peace for a moment. Well, the Prince de Guermantes went on to say: "I don't mind telling you that this idea of a possible illegality in the procedure of the trial was extremely painful to me, because I have always, as you know, worshipped the army; I discussed the matter again with the General, and, alas, there could be no two ways of looking at it. I don't mind telling you frankly that, all this time, the idea that an innocent man might be undergoing the most degrading punishment had never even entered my mind. But, starting from this idea of illegality, I began to study what I had always declined to read, and then the possibility not, this time, of illegal procedure but of the prisoner's innocence began to haunt me. I did not feel that I could talk about it to the Princess. Heaven knows that she has become just as French as myself. You may say what you like, from the day of our marriage, I took such pride in showing her our country in all its beauty, and what to me is the most splendid thing in it, our

Army, that it would have been too painful to me to tell her of my suspicions, which involved, it is true, a few officers only. But I come of a family of soldiers, I did not like to think that officers could be mistaken. I discussed the case again with Beaucerfeuil, he admitted that there had been culpable intrigues, that the *bordereau* was possibly not in Dreyfus's writing, but that an overwhelming proof of his guilt did exist. This was the Henry document. And, a few days later, we learned that it was a forgery. After that, without letting the Princess see me, I began to read the *Siècle* and the *Aurore* every day; soon I had no doubt left, it kept me awake all night. I confided my distress to our friend, the abbé Poiré, who, I was astonished to find, held the same conviction, and I got him to say masses for the intention of Dreyfus, his unfortunate wife and their children. Meanwhile, one morning as I was going to the Princess's room, I saw her maid trying to hide something from me that she had in her hand. I asked her, chaffingly, what it was, she blushed and refused to tell me. I had the fullest confidence in my wife, but this incident disturbed me considerably (and the Princess too, no doubt, who must have heard of it from her woman), for my dear Marie barely uttered a word to me that day at luncheon. I asked the abbé Poiré whether he could say my mass for Dreyfus on the following morning . . . " And so much for that!' exclaimed Swann, breaking off his narrative. I looked up, and saw the Duc de Guermantes bearing down upon us. 'Forgive me for interrupting you, boys. My lad,' he went on, addressing myself, 'I am instructed to give you a message from Oriane. Marie and Gilbert have asked her to stay and have supper at their table with only five or six other people: the Princess of Hesse, Mme de Ligné, Mme de Tarente, Mme de Chevreuse, the Duchesse d'Arenberg. Unfortunately, we can't wait, we are going on to a little ball of sorts.' I was listening, but whenever we have something definite to do at a given moment, we depute a certain person who is accustomed to that sort of duty to keep an eye on the clock and warn us in time. This in-dwelling servant reminded me, as I had asked him to remind me a few hours before, that Albertine, who at the moment was far from my thoughts, was to come and see me immediately after the theatre. And so I declined the invitation to supper. This does not mean that I was not enjoying myself at the Princesse de Guermantes's. The truth is that men can have several sorts of pleasure. The true pleasure is that for which they abandon the other. But the latter, if it is apparent, or rather if it alone is apparent, may put people off the scent of the other, reassure or mislead the jealous, create a false impression. And yet, all that is needed to make us sacrifice it to the other is a little happiness or a little suffering. Sometimes a third order of pleasures, more serious but more essential, does not yet exist for us, in whom its potential existence is indicated only by its arousing regrets, discouragement. And yet it is to these pleasures that we shall devote ourselves in time to come. To give an example of quite secondary importance, a soldier in time of peace will sacrifice a social existence to love, but, once war is declared (and without there being any need to introduce the idea of a patriotic duty), will sacrifice love to the passion, stronger than love, for fighting. It was all very well Swann's saying that he enjoyed telling me his story, I could feel that his conversation with me, because of the lateness of the hour, and because he himself was too ill, was one of those fatigues at which those who know that they are killing themselves by sitting up late, by overexerting themselves, feel when they return home an angry regret, similar to that felt at the wild extravagance of which they have again been guilty by the spendthrifts who will not, for all that, be able to restrain themselves tomorrow from throwing money out of the windows. After we have passed a certain degree of enfeeblement, whether it be caused by age or by ill health, all pleasure taken at the expense of sleep, in departure from our habits, every breach of the rules becomes a nuisance. The talker continues to talk, out of politeness, from excitement, but he knows that the hour at which he might still have been able to go to sleep has already passed, and he knows also the reproaches that he will heap upon himself during the insomnia and fatigue that must ensue. Already, moreover, even the momentary pleasure has come to an end, body and brain are too far drained of their strength to welcome with any readiness what seems to the other person entertaining. They are like a house on the morning before a journey or removal, where visitors become a perfect plague, to be received sitting upon locked trunks, with our eyes on the clock. 'At last we are alone,' he said; 'I quite forget where I was. Oh yes, I had just told you, hadn't I, that the Prince asked the abbé Poiré if he could say his mass next day for Dreyfus. "No, the abbé informed me" (I say *me* to you,' Swann explained to me, 'because it is the Prince who is speaking, you understand?), "for I have another mass that I have been asked to say for him tomorrow as well. – What, I said to him, is there another Catholic as well as myself who is convinced of his innocence? – It appears so. – But this other supporter's conviction must be of more recent growth than mine. – Maybe, but this other was making me say masses when you still believed Dreyfus guilty. – Ah, I can see that it is not anyone in our world. – On the contrary! – Indeed! There are Dreyfusists among us, are there? You intrigue me; I should like to unbosom myself to this rare bird, if I know him. – You do know him. – His name? – The Princesse de Guermantes. While I was afraid of shocking the Nationalist opinions, the French faith of my dear wife, she had been afraid of alarming my religious opinions, my patriotic sentiments.

But privately she had been thinking as I did, though for longer than I had.
And what her maid had been hiding as she went into her room, what she
went out to buy for her every morning, was the *Aurore*. My dear Swann,
from that moment I thought of the pleasure that I should give you when I
told you how closely akin my views upon this matter were to yours; forgive
me for not having done so sooner. If you bear in mind that I had never said
a word to the Princess, it will not surprise you to be told that thinking the
same as yourself must at that time have kept me farther apart from you than
thinking differently. For it was an extremely painful topic for me to
approach. The more I believe that an error, that crimes even have been
committed, the more my heart bleeds for the Army. It had never occurred
to me that opinions like mine could possibly cause you similar pain, until I
was told the other day that you were emphatically protesting against the
insults to the Army and against the Dreyfusists for consenting to ally
themselves with those who insulted it. That settled it, I admit that it has
been most painful for me to confess to you what I think of certain officers,
few in number fortunately, but it is a relief to me not to have to keep at arms'
length from you any longer, and especially that you should quite understand
that if I was able to entertain other sentiments, it was because I had not a
shadow of doubt as to the soundness of the verdict. As soon as my doubts
began, I could wish for only one thing, that the mistake should be rectified."
I must tell you that this speech of the Prince de Guermantes moved me
profoundly. If you knew him as I do, if you could realise the distance he has
had to traverse in order to reach his present position, you would admire him
as he deserves. Not that his opinion surprises me, his is such a straightforward nature!' Swann was forgetting that in the afternoon he had on the
contrary told me that people's opinions as to the Dreyfus case were dictated
by atavism. At the most he had made an exception in favour of intelligence,
because in Saint-Loup it had managed to overcome atavism and had made a
Dreyfusard of him. Now he had just seen that this victory had been of short
duration and that Saint-Loup had passed into the opposite camp. And so it
was to straightforwardness now that he assigned the part which had
previously devolved upon intelligence. In reality we always discover afterwards that our adversaries had a reason for being on the side they espoused,
which has nothing to do with any element of right that there may be on that
side, and that those who think as we do do so because their intelligence, if
their moral nature is too base to be invoked, or their straightforwardness, if
their penetration is feeble, has compelled them.

    Swann now found equally intelligent anybody who was of his opinion, his
old friend the Prince de Guermantes and my schoolfellow Bloch, whom

previously he had avoided and whom he now invited to luncheon. Swann
interested Bloch greatly by telling him that the Prince de Guermantes was a
Dreyfusard. 'We must ask him to sign our appeal for Picquart; a name like
his would have a tremendous effect.' But Swann, blending with his ardent
conviction as an Israelite the diplomatic moderation of a man of the world,
whose habits he had too thoroughly acquired to be able to shed them at this
late hour, refused to allow Bloch to send the Prince a circular to sign, even
on his own initiative. 'He cannot do such a thing, we must not expect the
impossible,' Swann repeated. 'There you have a charming man who has
travelled thousands of miles to come over to our side. He can be very useful
to us. If he were to sign your list, he would simply be compromising himself
with his own people, would be made to suffer on our account, might even
repent of his confidences and not confide in us again.' Nor was this all,
Swann refused his own signature. He felt that his name was too Hebraic not
to create a bad effect. Besides, even if he approved of all the attempts to
secure a fresh trial, he did not wish to be mixed up in any way in the anti-
militarist campaign. He wore, a thing he had never done previously, the
decoration he had won as a young militiaman, in '70, and added a codicil to
his will asking that, contrary to his previous dispositions, he might be buried
with the military honours due to his rank as Chevalier of the Legion of
Honour. A request which assembled round the church of Combray a whole
squadron of those troopers over whose fate Françoise used to weep in days
gone by, when she envisaged the prospect of a war. In short, Swann refused
to sign Bloch's circular, with the result that, if he passed in the eyes of many
people as a fanatical Dreyfusard, my friend found him lukewarm, infected
with Nationalism, and a militarist. Swann left me without shaking hands so
as not to be forced into a general leave-taking in this room which swarmed
with his friends, but said to me: 'You ought to come and see your friend
Gilberte. She has really grown up now and altered, you would not know her.
She would be so pleased!' I was no longer in love with Gilberte. She was for
me like a dead person for whom one has long mourned, then forgetfulness
has come, and if she were to be resuscitated, she could no longer find any
place in a life which has ceased to be fashioned for her. I had no desire now
to see her, not even that desire to show her that I did not wish to see her
which, every day, when I was in love with her, I vowed to myself that I would
flaunt before her, when I should be in love with her no longer.

And so, seeking now only to give myself, in Gilberte's eyes, the air of
having longed with all my heart to meet her again and of having been
prevented by circumstances of the kind called 'beyond our control' albeit
they only occur, with any certainty at least, when we have done nothing to

prevent them, so far from accepting Swann's invitation with reserve, I would not let him go until he had promised to explain in detail to his daughter the mischances that had prevented and would continue to prevent me from going to see her. 'Anyhow, I am going to write to her as soon as I go home,' I added. 'But be sure you tell her it will be a threatening letter, for in a month or two I shall be quite free, and then let her tremble, for I shall be coming to your house as regularly as in the old days.'

Before parting from Swann, I said a word to him about his health. 'No, it is not as bad as all that,' he told me. 'Still, as I was saying, I am quite worn out, and I accept with resignation whatever may be in store for me. Only, I must say that it would be most annoying to die before the end of the Dreyfus case. Those scoundrels have more than one card up their sleeves. I have no doubt of their being defeated in the end, but still they are very powerful, they have supporters everywhere. Just as everything is going on splendidly, it all collapses. I should like to live long enough to see Dreyfus rehabilitated and Picquart a colonel.'

When Swann had left, I returned to the great drawing-room in which was to be found that Princesse de Guermantes with whom I did not then know that I was one day to be so intimate. Her passion for M. de Charlus did not reveal itself to me at first. I noticed only that the Baron, after a certain date, and without having taken one of those sudden dislikes, which were not surprising in him, to the Princesse de Guermantes, while continuing to feel for her just as strong an affection, a stronger affection perhaps than ever, appeared worried and annoyed whenever anyone mentioned her name to him. He never included it now in his list of the people whom he wished to meet at dinner.

It is true that before this time I had heard an extremely malicious man about town say that the Princess had completely changed, that she was in love with M. de Charlus, but this slander had appeared to me absurd and had made me angry. I had indeed remarked with astonishment that, when I was telling her something that concerned myself, if M. de Charlus's name cropped up in the middle, the Princess immediately screwed up her attention to the narrower focus of a sick man who, hearing us talk about ourselves, and listening, in consequence, in a careless and distracted fashion, suddenly realises that a name we have mentioned is that of the disease from which he is suffering, which at once interests and delights him. So, if I said to her: 'Why, M. de Charlus told me . . . ' the Princess at once gathered up the slackened reins of her attention. And having on one occasion said in her hearing that M. de Charlus had at that moment a warm regard for a certain person, I was astonished to see appear in the Princess's eyes that momentary change of colour, like the line of a fissure in the pupil, which is due to a thought which our words have unconsciously aroused in the mind of the person to whom we are talking, a secret thought that will not find expression in words, but will rise from the depths which we have stirred to the surface – altered for an instant – of his gaze. But if my remark had moved the Princess, I did not then suspect in what fashion.

Anyhow, shortly after this, she began to talk to me about M. de Charlus, and almost without ambiguity. If she made any allusion to the rumours which a few people here and there were spreading about the Baron, it was merely as though to absurd and scandalous inventions. But, on the other hand, she said: 'I feel that any woman who fell in love with a man of such priceless worth as Palamède ought to have sufficient breadth of mind, enough devotion, to accept him and understand him as a whole, for what he is, to respect his freedom, humour his fancies, seek only to smooth out his difficulties and console him in his griefs.' Now, by such a speech, vague as it was, the Princesse de Guermantes revealed the weakness of the character she was seeking to extol, just as M. de Charlus himself did at times. Have I not heard him, over and again, say to people who until then had been uncertain whether or not he was being slandered: 'I, who have climbed many hills and crossed many valleys in my life, who have known all manner of people, burglars as well as kings, and indeed, I must confess, with a slight preference for the burglars, who have pursued beauty in all its forms,' and so forth; and by these words which he thought adroit, and in contradicting rumours the currency of which no one suspected (or to introduce, from inclination, moderation, love of accuracy, an element of truth which he was alone in regarding as insignificant), he removed the last doubts of some of his hearers, inspired others, who had not yet begun to doubt him, with their first. For the most dangerous of all forms of concealment is that of the crime itself in the mind of the guilty party. His permanent consciousness of it prevents him from imagining how generally it is unknown, how readily a complete lie would be accepted, and on the other hand from realising at what degree of truth other people will detect, in words which he believes to be innocent, a confession. Not that he would not be entirely wrong in seeking to hush it up, for there is no vice that does not find ready support in the best society, and one has seen a country house turned upside down in order that two sisters might sleep in adjoining rooms as soon as their hostess learned that theirs was a more than sisterly affection. But what revealed to me all of a sudden the Princess's love was a trifling incident upon which I shall not dwell here, for it forms part of quite another story, in which M. de Charlus allowed a Queen to die rather than miss an appointment with the hairdresser who was to singe his hair for the benefit of an omnibus conductor who filled him with alarm. However, to be done with the Princess's love, let us say what the trifle was that opened my eyes. I was, on the day in question, alone with her in her carriage. As we were passing a post office she stopped the coachman. She had come out without a footman. She half drew a letter from her muff and was preparing to step down from the carriage to put it into the box. I tried to stop her, she made a show of resistance, and we both realised that our instinctive movements had been, hers compromising, in appearing to be guarding a secret, mine indiscreet, in attempting to pass that guard. She was the first to recover. Suddenly turning very red, she gave me the letter. I no longer dared not to take it, but, as I slipped it into the box, I could not help seeing that it was addressed to M. de Charlus.

To return to this first evening at the Princesse de Guermantes's, I went to bid her good-night, for her cousins, who had promised to take me home, were in a hurry to be gone. M. de Guermantes wished, however, to say goodbye to his brother, Mme de Surgis having found time to mention to the Duke as she left that M. de Charlus had been charming to her and to her sons. This great courtesy on his brother's part, the first moreover that he had ever shown in that line, touched Basin deeply and aroused in him old family sentiments which were never asleep for long. At the moment when we were saying goodbye to the Princess he was attempting, without actually thanking M. de Charlus, to give expression to his fondness for him, whether because he really found a difficulty in controlling it or in order that the Baron might remember that actions of the sort that he had performed this evening did not escape the eyes of a brother, just as, with the object of creating a chain of pleasant associations in the future, we give sugar to a dog that has done its trick. 'Well, little brother!' said the Duke, stopping M. de Charlus and taking him lovingly by the arm, 'so this is how one walks past one's elders and betters without so much as a word. I never see you now, Mémé, and you can't think how I miss you. I was turning over some old letters just now and came upon some from poor Mamma, which are all so full of love for you.' 'Thank you, Basin,' replied M. de Charlus in a broken voice, for he could never speak without emotion of their mother. 'You must make up your mind to let me fix up bachelor quarters for you at Guermantes,' the Duke went on. 'It is nice to see the two brothers so affectionate towards each other,' the Princess said to Oriane. 'Yes, indeed! I don't suppose you could find many brothers like that. I shall invite you to meet him,' she promised me. 'You've not quarrelled with him? . . . But what can they be talking about?' she added in an anxious tone, for she could catch only an occasional word of what they were saying. She had always felt a certain jealousy of the pleasure that M. de Guermantes found in talking to his brother of a past from which he was inclined to keep his wife shut out. She felt that, when they were happy at being together like this, and she, unable to restrain her impatient curiosity, came and joined them, her coming did not add to their pleasure. But this evening, this habitual jealousy was reinforced by another. For if Mme de Surgis had told M. de Guermantes how kind his brother had been to her so that the Duke might thank his brother, at the same time certain devoted female friends of the Guermantes couple had felt it their duty to warn the Duchess that her husband's mistress had been seen in close conversation with his brother. And this information was torture to Mme de Guermantes. 'Think of the fun we used to have at Guermantes long ago,' the Duke went on. 'If you came down sometimes in summer we could take up our old life again. Do you remember old Father Courveau: "Why is Pascal vexing? Because he is vec . . . vec . . . " ' '*Said*!' put in M. de Charlus as though he were still answering his tutor's question. 'And why is Pascal vexed; because he is vec . . . because he is vec . . . *Sing*! Very good, you will pass, you are certain to be mentioned, and Madame la Duchesse will give you a Chinese dictionary.' 'How it all comes back to me, young Mémé, and the old china vase Hervey brought you from Saint-Denis, I can see it now. You used to threaten us that you would go and spend your life in China, you were so fond of the country; even then you used to love wandering about all night. Ah! You were a peculiar type, for I can honestly say that never in anything did you have the same tastes as other people . . . ' But no sooner had he uttered these words than the Duke flamed up, as the saying is, for he was aware of his brother's reputation, if not of his actual habits. As he never made any allusion to them before his brother, he was all the more annoyed at having said something which might be taken to refer to them, and more still at having shown his annoyance. After a moment's silence: 'Who knows,' he said, to cancel the effect of his previous speech, 'you were perhaps in love with a Chinese girl, before loving so many white ones and finding favour with them, if I am to judge by a certain lady to whom you have given great pleasure this evening by talking to her. She was delighted with you.' The Duke had vowed that he would not mention Mme de Surgis, but, in the confusion that the blunder he had just made had wrought in his ideas, he had fallen upon the first that occurred to him, which happened to be precisely the one that ought not to have appeared in the conversation, although it had started it. But M. de Charlus had observed his brother's blush. And, like guilty persons who do not wish to appear embarrassed that you should talk in their presence of the crime which they are supposed not to have committed, and feel that they ought to prolong a dangerous conversation: 'I am charmed to hear it,' he replied, 'but I should like to go back to what you were saying before, which struck me as being profoundly true. You were saying that I never had the same ideas as other people, how right you are, you said that I had peculiar tastes.' 'No,' protested M. de Guermantes who, as a matter of fact, had not used those words, and may not have believed that their meaning was applicable to his brother. Besides, what right had he to bully him about eccentricities which in any case were vague enough or secret enough to have in no way impaired the Baron's tremendous position in society? What was more, feeling that the resources of his brother's position were about to be placed at the service of his mistresses, the Duke told himself that this was well worth a little tolerance in exchange; had he at that moment known of some 'peculiar' intimacy of his brother, M. de Guermantes would, in the hope of the support that the other was going to give him, have passed it over, shutting his eyes to it, and if need be lending a hand. 'Come along, Basin; good-night, Palamède,' said the Duchess, who, devoured by rage and curiosity, could endure no more, 'if you have made up your minds to spend the night here, we might just as well have stayed to supper. You have been keeping Marie and me standing for the last half-hour.' The Duke parted from his brother after a significant pressure of his hand, and the three of us began to descend the immense staircase of the Princess's house.

On either side of us, on the topmost steps, were scattered couples who were waiting for their carriages to come to the door. Erect, isolated, flanked by her husband and myself, the Duchess kept to the left of the staircase, already wrapped in her Tiepolo cloak, her throat clasped in its band of rubies, devoured by the eyes of women and men alike, who sought to divine the secret of her beauty and distinction. Waiting for her carriage upon the same step of the stair as Mme de Guermantes, but at the opposite side of it, Mme de Gallardon, who had long abandoned all hope of ever receiving a visit from her cousin, turned her back so as not to appear to have seen her, and, what was more important, so as not to furnish a proof of the fact that the other did not greet her. Mme de Gallardon was in an extremely bad temper because some gentlemen in her company had taken it upon themselves to speak to her of Oriane: 'I have not the slightest desire to see her,' she had replied to them, 'I did see her, as a matter of fact, just now, she is beginning to show her age; it seems she can't get over it. Basin says so himself. And, good lord, I can understand that, for, as she has no brains, is as mischievous as a weevil, and has shocking manners, she must know very well that, once her looks go, she will have nothing left to fall back upon.'

I had put on my greatcoat, for which M. de Guermantes, who dreaded chills, reproached me, as we went down together, because of the heated atmosphere indoors. And the generation of noblemen which more or less passed through the hands of Mgr Dupanloup speaks such bad French (except the Castellane brothers) that the Duke expressed what was in his mind thus: 'It is better not to put on your coat before going out of doors, at least *as a general rule.*' I can see all that departing crowd now, I can see, if I be not mistaken in placing him upon that staircase, a portrait detached from its frame, the Prince de Sagan, whose last appearance in society this must have been, baring his head to offer his homage to the Duchess, with so sweeping a revolution of his tall hat in his white-gloved hand (harmonising with the gardenia in his buttonhole), that one felt surprised that it was not a plumed felt hat of the old regime, several ancestral faces from which were exactly reproduced in the face of this great gentleman. He stopped for but a short time in front of her, but even his momentary attitudes were sufficient to compose a complete *tableau vivant*, and, as it were, an historical scene. Moreover, as he has since then died, and as I never had more than a glimpse of him in his lifetime, he has so far become for me a character in history, social history at least, that I am quite astonished when I think that a woman and a man whom I know are his sister and nephew.

While we were going downstairs, there came up, with an air of weariness that became her, a woman who appeared to be about forty, but was really older. This was the Princesse d'Orvillers, a natural daughter, it was said, of the Duke of Parma, whose pleasant voice rang with a vaguely Austrian accent. She advanced, tall, stooping, in a gown of white flowered silk, her exquisite, throbbing, cankered bosom heaving beneath a harness of diamonds and sapphires. Tossing her head like a royal palfrey embarrassed by its halter of pearls, of an incalculable value but an inconvenient weight, she let fall here and there a gentle, charming gaze, of an azure which, as time began to fade it, became more caressing than ever, and greeted most of the departing guests with a friendly nod. 'You choose a nice time to arrive, Paulette!' said the Duchess. 'Yes, I am so sorry! But really it was a physical impossibility,' replied the Princesse d'Orvillers, who had acquired this sort of expression from the Duchesse de Guermantes, but added to it her own natural sweetness and the air of sincerity conveyed by the force of a remotely Teutonic accent in so tender a voice. She appeared to be alluding to complications of life too elaborate to be related, and not merely to evening parties, although she had just come on from a succession of these. But it was not they that obliged her to come so late. As the Prince de Guermantes had for many years forbidden his wife to receive Mme d'Orvillers, that lady, when the ban was withdrawn, contented herself with replying to the other's invitations, so as not to appear to be thirsting after them, by simply leaving cards. After two or three years of this method, she came in person, but very late, as though after the theatre. In this way she gave herself the appearance of attaching no importance to the party, nor to being seen at it, but simply of having come to pay the Prince and Princess a visit, for their own sakes, because she liked them, at an hour when, the great majority of their guests having already gone, she would 'have them more to herself'.

'Oriane has really sunk very low,' muttered Mme de Gallardon. 'I cannot understand Basin's allowing her to speak to Mme d'Orvillers. I am sure M. de Gallardon would never have allowed me.' For my part, I had recognised in Mme d'Orvillers the woman who, outside the Hôtel Guermantes, used to cast languishing glances at me, turn round, stop and gaze into shop windows. Mme de Guermantes introduced me, Mme d'Orvillers was charming, neither too friendly nor annoyed. She gazed at me as at everyone else out of her gentle eyes . . . But I was never again, when I met her, to receive from her one of those overtures with which she had seemed to be offering herself. There is a special kind of glance, apparently of recognition, which a young man never receives from certain women – nor from certain men – after the day on which they have made his acquaintance and have learned that he is the friend of people with whom they too are intimate.

We were told that the carriage was at the door. Mme de Guermantes gathered up her red skirt as though to go downstairs and get into the carriage, but, seized perhaps by remorse, or by the desire to give pleasure, and above all to profit by the brevity which the material obstacle to prolonging it imposed upon so boring an action, looked at Mme de Gallardon; then, as though she had only just caught sight of her, acting upon a sudden inspiration, before going down tripped across the whole width of the step and, upon reaching her delighted cousin, held out her hand. 'Such a long time,' said the Duchess who then, so as not to have to develop all the regrets and legitimate excuses that this formula might be supposed to contain, turned with a look of alarm towards the Duke, who as a matter of fact, having gone down with me to the carriage, was storming with rage when he saw that his wife had gone over to Mme de Gallardon and was holding up the stream of carriages behind. 'Oriane is still very good looking, after all!' said Mme de Gallardon. 'People amuse me when they say that we have quarrelled; we may (for reasons which we have no need to tell other people) go for years without seeing one another, we have too many memories in common ever to be separated, and in her heart she must know that she cares far more for me than for all sorts of people whom she sees every day and who are not of her rank.' Mme de Gallardon was in fact like those scorned lovers who try desperately to make people believe that they are better loved than those whom their fair one cherishes. And (by the praises which, without heeding their contradiction of what she had been saying a moment earlier, she now lavished in speaking of the Duchesse de Guermantes) she proved indirectly that the other was thoroughly conversant with the maxims that ought to guide in her career a great lady of fashion who, at the selfsame moment when her most marvellous gown is exciting an admiration not unmixed with envy, must be able to cross the whole width of a staircase to disarm it. 'Do at least take care not to wet your shoes' (a brief but heavy shower of rain had fallen), said the Duke, who was still furious at having been kept waiting.

On our homeward drive, in the confined space of the coupé, the red shoes were of necessity very close to mine, and Mme de Guermantes, fearing that she might actually have touched me, said to the Duke: 'This young man will have to say to me, like the person in the caricature: "Madame, tell me at once that you love me, but don't tread on my feet like that." ' My thoughts, however, were far from Mme de Guermantes. Ever since Saint-Loup had spoken to me of a young girl of good family who frequented a house of ill-fame, and of the Baroness Putbus's maid, it was in these two persons that were coalesced and embodied the desires inspired in me day by day by countless beauties of two classes, on the one hand the plebeian and magnificent, the majestic lady's maids of great houses, swollen with pride and saying 'we' when they spoke of Duchesses, on the other hand those girls of whom it was enough for me sometimes, without even having seen them go past in carriages or on foot, to have read the names in the account of a ball for me to fall in love with them and, having conscientiously searched the yearbook for the country houses in which they spent the summer (as often as not letting myself be led astray by a similarity of names), to dream alternately of going to live amid the plains of the West, the sandhills of the North, the pine-forests of the South. But in vain might I fuse together all the most exquisite fleshly matter to compose, after the ideal outline traced for me by Saint-Loup, the young girl of easy virtue and Mme Putbus's maid, my two possessible beauties still lacked what I should never know until I had seen them: individual character. I was to wear myself out in seeking to form a mental picture, during the months in which I would have preferred a lady's maid, of the maid of Mme Putbus. But what peace of mind after having been perpetually troubled by my restless desires, for so many fugitive creatures whose very names I often did not know, who were in any case so hard to find again, harder still to become acquainted with, impossible perhaps to captivate, to have subtracted from all that scattered, fugitive, anonymous beauty, two choice specimens duly labelled, whom I was at least certain of being able to procure when I chose. I kept putting off the hour for devoting myself to this twofold pleasure, as I put off that for beginning to work, but the certainty of having it whenever I chose dispensed me almost from the necessity of taking it, like those soporific tablets which one has only to have within reach of one's hand not to need them and to fall asleep. In the whole universe I desired only two women, of whose faces I could not, it is true, form any picture, but whose names Saint-Loup had told me and had guaranteed their consent. So that, if he had, by what he had said this evening, set my imagination a heavy task, he had at the same time procured an appreciable relaxation, a prolonged rest for my will.

'Well!' said the Duchess to me, 'apart from your balls, can't I be of any use to you? Have you found a house where you would like me to introduce you?' I replied that I was afraid the only one that tempted me was hardly fashionable enough for her. 'Whose is that?' she asked in a hoarse and menacing voice, scarcely opening her lips. 'Baroness Putbus.' This time she pretended to be really angry. 'No, not that! I believe you're trying to make a fool of me. I don't even know how I come to have heard the creature's name. But she is the dregs of society. It's just as though you were to ask me for an introduction to my milliner. And worse than that, for my milliner is charming. You are a little bit cracked, my poor boy. In any case, I beg that you will be polite to the people to whom I have introduced you, leave cards on them, and go and see them, and not talk to them about Baroness Putbus of whom they have never heard.' I asked whether Mme d'Orvillers was not inclined to be flighty. 'Oh, not in the least, you are thinking of someone else, why, she's rather a prude, if anything. Ain't she, Basin?' 'Yes, in any case I don't think there has ever been anything to be said about her,' said the Duke.

'You won't come with us to the ball?' he asked me. 'I can lend you a Venetian cloak and I know someone who will be damned glad to see you there – Oriane for one, that I needn't say – but the Princesse de Parme. She's never tired of singing your praises, and swears by you alone. It's fortunate for you – since she is a trifle mature – that she is the model of virtue. Otherwise she would certainly have chosen you as a sigisbee, as it was called in my young days, a sort of *cavalière servente*.'

I was interested not in the ball but in my appointment with Albertine. And so I refused. The carriage had stopped, the footman was shouting for the gate to be opened, the horses pawing the ground until it was flung apart and the carriage passed into the courtyard. 'Till we meet again,' said the Duke. 'I have sometimes regretted living so close to Marie,' the Duchess said to me, 'because I may be very fond of her, but I am not quite so fond of her company. But have never regretted it so much as tonight, since it has allowed me so little of yours.' 'Come, Oriane, no speechmaking.' The Duchess would have liked me to come inside for a minute. She laughed heartily, as did the Duke, when I said that I could not because I was expecting a girl to call at any moment. 'You choose a funny time to receive visitors,' she said to me.

'Come along, my child, there is no time to waste,' said M. de Guermantes to his wife. 'It is a quarter to twelve, and time we were dressed . . .' He came in collision, outside his front door which they were grimly guarding, with the two ladies of the walking-sticks, who had not been afraid to descend at dead of night from their mountain-top to prevent a scandal. 'Basin, we felt we must warn you, in case you were seen at that ball: poor Amanien has just passed away, an hour ago.' The Duke felt a momentary alarm. He saw the delights of the famous ball snatched from him as soon as these accursed mountaineers had informed him of the death of M. d'Osmond. But he quickly recovered himself and flung at his cousins a retort into which he introduced, with his determination not to forego a pleasure, his incapacity to assimilate exactly the niceties of the French language: 'He is dead! No, no, they exaggerate, they exaggerate!' And without giving a further thought to his two relatives who, armed with their alpenstocks, were preparing to make their nocturnal ascent, he fired off a string of questions at his valet: 'Are you sure my helmet has come?' 'Yes, Monsieur le Duc.' 'You're sure there's a hole in it I can breathe through? I don't want to be suffocated, damn it!' 'Yes, Monsieur le Duc.' 'Oh, thunder of heaven, this is an unlucky evening. Oriane, I forgot to ask Babal whether the shoes with pointed toes were for you!' 'But, my dear, the dresser from the Opéra-Comique is here, he will tell us. I don't see how they could go with your spurs.' 'Let us go and find the dresser,' said the Duke. 'Goodbye, my boy, I should ask you to come in while we are trying on, it would amuse you. But we should only waste time talking, it is nearly midnight and we must not be late in getting there or we shall spoil the set.'

I too was in a hurry to get away from M. and Mme de Guermantes as quickly as possible. *Phèdre* finished at about half past eleven. Albertine must have arrived by now. I went straight to Françoise: 'Is Mlle Albertine in the house?' 'No one has called.'

Good God, that meant that no one would call! I was in torment, Albertine's visit seeming to me now all the more desirable, the less certain it had become.

Françoise was cross too, but for quite a different reason. She had just installed her daughter at the table for a succulent repast. But, on hearing me come in, and seeing that there was not time to whip away the dishes and put out needles and thread as though it were a work party and not a supper party: 'She has just been taking a spoonful of soup,' Françoise explained to me, 'I forced her to gnaw a bit of bone,' to reduce thus to nothing her daughter's supper, as though the crime lay in its abundance. Even at luncheon or dinner, if I committed the error of entering the kitchen, Françoise would pretend that they had finished, and would even excuse herself with 'I just felt I could eat a *scrap*,' or 'a *mouthful*'. But I was speedily reassured on seeing the multitude of the plates that covered the table, which Françoise, surprised by my sudden entry, like a thief in the night which she was not, had not had time to conjure out of sight. Then she added: 'Go along to your bed now, you have done enough work today' (for she wished to make it appear that her daughter not only cost us nothing, lived by privations, but was actually working herself to death in our service). 'You are only crowding up the kitchen, and disturbing Master, who is expecting a visitor. Go on, upstairs,' she repeated, as though she were obliged to use her authority to send her daughter to bed, who, the moment supper was out of the question, remained in the kitchen only for appearance's sake, and if I had stayed five minutes longer would have withdrawn of her own accord. And turning to me, in that charming popular and yet, somehow, personal French which was her spoken language: 'Master doesn't see that her face is just cut in two with want of sleep.' I remained, delighted at not having to talk to Françoise's daughter.

I have said that she came from a small village which was quite close to her mother's, and yet different from it in the nature of the soil, its cultivation, in dialect; above all in certain characteristics of the inhabitants. Thus the 'butcheress' and Françoise's niece did not get on at all well together, but had this point in common, that, when they went out on an errand, they would linger for hours at 'the sister's' or 'the cousin's', being themselves incapable of finishing a conversation, in the course of which the purpose with which they had set out faded so completely from their minds that, if we said to them on their return: 'Well! Will M. le Marquis de Norpois be at home at a quarter past six?' they did not even beat their brows and say: 'Oh, I forgot all about it,' but 'Oh! I didn't understand that Master wanted to know that, I thought I had just to go and bid him good-day.' If they 'lost their heads' in this manner about a thing that had been said to them an hour earlier, it was on the other hand impossible to get out of their heads what they had once heard said, by 'the' sister or cousin. Thus, if the butcheress had heard it said that the English made war upon us in '70 at the same time as the Prussians, and I had explained to her until I was tired that this was not the case, every three weeks the butcheress would repeat to me in the course of conversation: 'It's all because of that war the English made on us in '70, with the Prussians.' 'But I've told you a hundred times that you are wrong.' – She would then answer, implying that her conviction was in no way shaken: 'In any case, that's no reason for wishing them any harm. Plenty of water has run under the bridges since '70,' and so forth. On another occasion, advocating a war with England which I opposed, she said: 'To be sure, it's always better not to go to war; but when you must, it's best to do it at once. As the sister was explaining just now, ever since that war the English made on us in '70, the commercial treaties have ruined us. After we've beaten them, we won't allow one Englishman into France, unless he pays three hundred francs to come in, as we have to pay now to land in England.'

Such was, in addition to great honesty and, when they were speaking, an obstinate refusal to allow any interruption, going back twenty times over to the point at which they had been interrupted, which ended by giving to their talk the unshakable solidity of a Bach fugue, the character of the inhabitants of this tiny village which did not boast five hundred, set among its chestnuts, its willows, and its fields of potatoes and beetroot.

Françoise's daughter, on the other hand, spoke (regarding herself as an up-to-date woman who had got out of the old ruts) Parisian slang and was well versed in all the jokes of the day. Françoise having told her that I had come from the house of a Princess: 'Oh, indeed! The Princess of Brazil, I suppose, where the nuts come from.' Seeing that I was expecting a visitor, she pretended to suppose that my name was Charles. I replied innocently that it was not, which enabled her to get in: 'Oh, I thought it was! And I was just saying to myself, *Charles attend* (charlatan).' This was not in the best of taste. But I was less unmoved when, to console me for Albertine's delay, she said to me: 'I expect you'll go on waiting till doomsday. She's never coming. Oh! Those modern flappers!'

And so her speech differed from her mother's; but, what is more curious, her mother's speech was not the same as that of her grandmother, a native of Bailleau-le-Pin, which was so close to Françoise's village. And yet the dialects differed slightly, like the scenery. Françoise's mother's village, scrambling down a steep bank into a ravine, was overgrown with willows. And, miles away from either of them, there was, on the contrary, a small district of France where the people spoke almost precisely the same dialect as at Méséglise. I made this discovery only to feel its drawbacks. In fact, I once came upon Françoise eagerly conversing with a neighbour's housemaid, who came from this village and spoke its dialect. They could more or less understand one another, I did not understand a word, they knew this but did not however cease (excused, they felt, by the joy of being fellow-countrywomen although born so far apart) to converse in this strange tongue in front of me, like people who do not wish to be understood. These picturesque studies in linguistic geography and comradeship below stairs were continued weekly in the kitchen, without my deriving any pleasure from them.

Since, whenever the outer gate opened, the doorkeeper pressed an electric button which lighted the stairs, and since all the occupants of the building had already come in, I left the kitchen immediately and went to sit down in the hall, keeping watch, at a point where the curtains did not quite meet over the glass panel of the outer door, leaving visible a vertical strip of semi-darkness on the stair. If, all of a sudden, this strip turned to a golden yellow, that would mean that Albertine had just entered the building and would be with me in a minute; nobody else could be coming at that time of night. And I sat there, unable to take my eyes from the strip which persisted in remaining dark; I bent my whole body forward to make certain of noticing any change; but, gaze as I might, the vertical black band, despite my impassioned longing, did not give me the intoxicating delight that I should have felt had I seen it changed by a sudden and significant magic to a luminous bar of gold. This was a great to do to make about that Albertine to whom I had not given three minutes' thought during the Guermantes party! But, reviving my feelings when in the past I had been kept waiting by other girls, Gilberte especially, when she delayed her coming, the prospect of having to forego a simple bodily pleasure caused me an intense mental suffering.

I was obliged to retire to my room. Françoise followed me. She felt that, as I had come away from my party, there was no point in my keeping the rose that I had in my buttonhole, and approached to take it from me. Her action, by reminding me that Albertine was perhaps not coming, and by obliging me also to confess that I wished to look smart for her benefit, caused an irritation that was increased by the fact that, in tugging myself free, I crushed the flower and Françoise said to me: 'It would have been better to let me take it than to go and spoil it like that.' But anything that she might say exasperated me. When we are kept waiting, we suffer so keenly from the absence of the person for whom we are longing that we cannot endure the presence of anyone else.

When Françoise had left my room, it occurred to me that, if it only meant that now I wanted to look my best before Albertine, it was a pity that I had so many times let her see me unshaved, with several days' growth of beard, on the evenings when I let her come in to renew our caresses. I felt that she took no interest in me and was giving me the cold shoulder. To make my room look a little brighter, in case Albertine should still come, and because it was one of the prettiest things that I possessed, I set out, for the first time for years, on the table by my bed, the turquoise-studded cover which Gilberte had had made for me to hold Bergotte's pamphlet, and which, for so long a time, I had insisted on keeping by me while I slept, with the agate marble. Besides, as much perhaps as Albertine herself, who still did not come, her presence at that moment in an 'alibi' which she had evidently found more attractive, and of which I knew nothing, gave me a painful feeling which, in spite of what I had said, barely an hour before, to Swann, as to my incapacity for being jealous, might, if I had seen my friend at less protracted intervals, have changed into an anxious need to know where, with whom, she was spending her time. I dared not send round to Albertine's house, it was too late, but in the hope that, having supper perhaps with some other girls, in a café, she might take it into her head to telephone to me, I turned the switch and, restoring the connection to my own room, cut it off between the post office and the porter's lodge to which it was generally switched at that hour. A receiver in the little passage on which Françoise's room opened would have been simpler, less inconvenient, but useless. The advance of civilisation enables each of us to display unsuspected merits or fresh defects which make him dearer or more insupportable to his friends. Thus Dr. Bell's invention had enabled Françoise to acquire an additional defect, which was that of refusing, however important, however urgent the occasion might be, to make use of the telephone. She would manage to disappear whenever anybody was going to teach her how to use it, as people disappear when it is time for them to be vaccinated. And so the telephone was installed in my bedroom, and, that it might not disturb my parents, a rattle had been substituted for the bell. I did not move, for fear of not hearing it sound. So motionless did I remain that, for the first time for months, I noticed the tick of the clock. Françoise came in to make the room tidy. She began talking to me, but I hated her conversation, beneath the uniformly trivial continuity of which my feelings were changing from one minute to another, passing from fear to anxiety; from anxiety to complete disappointment. Belying the words of vague satisfaction which I thought myself obliged to address to her, I could feel that my face was so wretched that I pretended to be suffering from rheumatism, to account for the discrepancy between my feigned indifference and my woebegone expression; besides, I was afraid that her talk, which, for that matter, Françoise carried on in an undertone (not on account of Albertine, for she considered that all possibility of her coming was long past), might prevent me from hearing the saving call which now would not sound. At length Françoise went off to bed; I dismissed her with an abrupt civility, so that the noise she made in leaving the room should not drown that of the telephone. And I settled down again to listen, to suffer; when we are kept waiting, from the ear which takes in sounds to the mind which dissects and analyses them, and from the mind to the heart, to which it transmits its results, the double journey is so rapid that we cannot even detect its course, and imagine that we have been listening directly with our heart.

I was tortured by the incessant recurrence of my longing, ever more anxious and never to be gratified, for the sound of a call; arrived at the culminating point of a tortuous ascent through the coils of my lonely anguish, from the heart of the populous, nocturnal Paris that had suddenly come close to me, there beside my bookcase, I heard all at once, mechanical and sublime, like, in *Tristan*, the fluttering veil or the shepherd's pipe, the purr of the telephone. I sprang to the instrument, it was Albertine. 'I'm not disturbing you, ringing you up at this hour?' 'Not at all . . . ' I said, restraining my joy, for her remark about the lateness of the hour was doubtless meant as an apology for coming, in a moment, so late, and did not mean that she was not coming. 'Are you coming round?' I asked in a tone of indifference. 'Why . . . no, unless you absolutely must see me.'

Part of me which the other part sought to join was in Albertine. It was essential that she come, but I did not tell her so at first; now that we were in communication, I said to myself that I could always oblige her at the last moment either to come to me or to let me hasten to her. 'Yes, I am near home,' she said, 'and miles away from you; I hadn't read your note properly. I have just found it again and was afraid you might be waiting up for me.' I felt sure that she was lying, and it was now, in my fury, from a desire not so much to see her as to upset her plans that I determined to make her come. But I felt it better to refuse at first what in a few moments I should try to obtain from her. But where was she? With the sound of her voice were blended other sounds: the braying of a bicyclist's horn, a woman's voice singing, a brass band in the distance rang out as distinctly as the beloved voice, as though to show me that it was indeed Albertine in her actual surroundings who was beside me at that moment, like a clod of earth with which we have carried away all the grass that was growing from it. The same sounds that I heard were striking her ear also, and were distracting her attention: details of truth, extraneous to the subject under discussion, valueless in themselves, all the more necessary to our perception of the miracle for what it was; elements sober and charming, descriptive of some street in Paris, elements heart-rending also and cruel of some unknown festivity which, after she came away from *Phèdre*, had prevented Albertine from coming to me. 'I must warn you first of all that I don't in the least want you to come, because, at this time of night, it will be a frightful nuisance . . .' I said to her, 'I'm dropping with sleep. Besides, oh, well, there are endless complications. I am bound to say that there was no possibility of your misunderstanding my letter. You answered that it was all right. Very well, if you hadn't understood, what did you mean by that?' 'I said it was all right, only I couldn't quite remember what we had arranged. But I see you're cross with me, I'm sorry. I wish now I'd never gone to *Phèdre*. If I'd known there was going to be all this fuss about it . . .' she went on, as people invariably do when, being in the wrong over one thing, they pretend to suppose that they are being blamed for another. 'I am not in the least annoyed about *Phèdre*, seeing it was I that asked you to go to it.' 'Then you are angry with me; it's a nuisance it's so late now, otherwise I should have come to you, but I shall call tomorrow or the day after and make it up.' 'Oh, please, Albertine, I beg of you not to, after making me waste an entire evening, the least you can do is to leave me in peace for the next few days. I shan't be free for a fortnight or three weeks. Listen, if it worries you to think that we seem to be parting in anger, and perhaps you are right, after all, then I greatly prefer, all things considered, since I have been waiting for you all this time and you have not gone home yet, that you should come at once. I shall take a cup of coffee to keep myself awake.' 'Couldn't you possibly put it off till tomorrow? Because the trouble is . . . ' As I listened to these words of deprecation, uttered as though she did not intend to come, I felt that, with the longing to see again the velvet-blooming face which in the past, at Balbec, used to point all my days to the moment when, by the mauve September sea, I should be walking by the side of that roseate flower, a very different element was painfully endeavouring to combine. This terrible need of a person, at Combray I had learned to know it in the case of my mother, and to the pitch of wanting to die if she sent word to me by Françoise that she could not come upstairs. This effort on the part of the old sentiment, to combine and form but a single element with the other, more recent, which had for its voluptuous object only the coloured surface, the rosy complexion of a flower of the beach, this effort results often only in creating (in the chemical sense) a new body, which can last for but a few moments. This evening, at any rate, and for long afterwards, the two elements remained apart. But already, from the last words that had reached me over the telephone, I was beginning to understand that Albertine's life was situated (not in a material sense, of course) at so great a distance from mine that I should always have to make a strenuous exploration before I could lay my hand on her, and, what was more, organised like a system of earthworks, and, for greater security, after the fashion which, at a later period, we learned to call camouflaged. Albertine, in fact, belonged, although at a slightly higher social level, to that class of persons to whom their doorkeeper promises your messenger that she will deliver your letter when she comes in (until the day when you realise that it is precisely she, the person whom you met out of doors, and to whom you have allowed yourself to write, who is the doorkeeper. So that she does indeed live (but in the lodge, only) at the address she has given you, which for that matter is that of a private brothel, in which the doorkeeper acts as pander), or who gives as her address a house where she is known to accomplices who will not betray her secret to you, from which your letters will be forwarded to her, but in which she does not live, keeps at the most a few articles of toilet. Lives entrenched behind five or six lines of defence, so that when you try to see the woman, or to find out about her, you invariably arrive too far to the right, or to the left, or too early, or too late, and may remain for months on end, for years even, knowing nothing. About Albertine, I felt that I should never find out anything, that, out of that tangled mass of details of fact and falsehood, I should never unravel the truth: and that it would always be so, unless I were to shut her up in prison (but prisoners escape) until the end. This evening, this conviction gave me only a vague uneasiness, in which however I could detect a shuddering anticipation of long periods of suffering to come.

'No,' I replied, 'I told you a moment ago that I should not be free for the next three weeks – no more tomorrow than any other day.' 'Very well, in that case . . . I shall come this very instant . . . it's a nuisance, because I am at a friend's house, and she . . . ' I saw that she had not believed that I would accept her offer to come, which therefore was not sincere, and I decided to force her hand. 'What do you suppose I care about your friend, either come or don't, it's for you to decide, it wasn't I that asked you to come, it was you who suggested it to me.' 'Don't be angry with me, I am going to jump into a cab now and shall be with you in ten minutes.' And so from that Paris out of whose murky depths there had already emanated as far as my room, delimiting the sphere of action of an absent person, a voice which was now about to emerge and appear, after this preliminary announcement, it was that Albertine whom I had known long ago beneath the sky of Balbec, when the waiters of the Grand Hotel, as they laid the tables, were blinded by the glow of the setting sun, when, the glass having been removed from all the windows, every faintest murmur of the evening passed freely from the beach where the last strolling couples still lingered, into the vast dining-room in which the first diners had not yet taken their places, and, across the mirror placed behind the cashier's desk, there passed the red reflection of the hull, and lingered long after it the grey reflection of the smoke of the last steamer for Rivebelle. I no longer asked myself what could have made Albertine late, and, when Françoise came into my room to inform me: 'Mademoiselle Albertine is here', if I answered without even turning my head, that was only to conceal my emotion: 'What in the world makes Mademoiselle Albertine come at this time of night!' But then, raising my eyes to look at Françoise, as though curious to hear her answer which must corroborate the apparent sincerity of my question, I perceived, with admiration and wrath, that, capable of rivalling Berma herself in the art of endowing with speech inanimate garments and the lines of her face, Françoise had taught their part to her bodice, her hair – the whitest threads of which had been brought to the surface, were displayed there like a birth-certificate – her neck bowed by weariness and obedience. They commiserated her for having been dragged from her sleep and from her warm bed, in the middle of the night, at her age, obliged to bundle into her clothes in haste, at the risk of catching pneumonia. And so, afraid that I might have seemed to be apologising for Albertine's late arrival: 'Anyhow, I'm very glad she has come, it's just what I wanted,' and I gave free vent to my profound joy. It did not long remain unclouded, when I had heard Françoise's reply. Without uttering a word of complaint, seeming indeed to be doing her best to stifle an irrepressible cough, and simply folding her shawl over her bosom as though she were feeling cold, she began by telling me everything that she had said to Albertine, whom she had not forgotten to ask after her aunt's health. 'I was just saying, Monsieur must have been afraid that Mademoiselle was not coming, because this is no time to pay visits, it's nearly morning. But she must have been in some place where she was enjoying herself, because she never even said as much as that she was sorry she had kept Monsieur waiting, she answered me with a devil-may-care look, "Better late than never!" ' And Françoise added, in words that pierced my heart: 'When she spoke like that she gave herself away. She would have liked to hide what she was thinking, perhaps, but . . . '

I had no cause for astonishment. I said, a few pages back, that Françoise rarely paid attention, when she was sent with a message, if not to what she herself had said, which she would willingly relate in detail, at any rate to the answer that we were awaiting. But if, making an exception, she repeated to us the things that our friends had said, however short they might be, she generally arranged, appealing if need be to the expression, the tone that, she assured us, had accompanied them, to make them in some way or other wounding. At a pinch, she would bow her head beneath an insult (probably quite imaginary) which she had received from a tradesman to whom we had sent her, provided that, being addressed to her as our representative, who was speaking in our name, the insult might indirectly injure us. The only thing would have been to tell her that she had misunderstood the man, that she was suffering from persecution mania and that the shopkeepers were not at all in league against her. However, their sentiments affected me little. It was a very different matter, what Albertine's sentiments were. And, as she repeated the ironical words: 'Better late than never!' Françoise at once made me see the friends in whose company Albertine had finished the evening, preferring their company, therefore, to mine. 'She's a comical sight, she has a little flat hat on, with those big eyes of hers, it does make her look funny, especially with her cloak which she did ought to have sent to the amender's, for it's all in holes. She amuses me,' added, as though laughing at Albertine, Françoise who rarely shared my impressions, but felt a need to communicate her own. I refused even to appear to understand that this laugh was indicative of scorn, but, to give tit for tat, replied, although I had never seen the little hat to which she referred: 'What you call a "little flat hat" is a simply charming . . . ' 'That is to say, it's just nothing at all,' said Françoise, giving expression, frankly this time, to her genuine contempt. Then (in a mild and leisurely tone so that my mendacious answer might appear to be the expression not of my anger but of the truth), wasting no time, however, so as not to keep Albertine waiting, I heaped upon Françoise these cruel words: 'You are excellent,' I said to her in a honeyed voice, 'you are kind, you have a thousand merits, but you have never learned a single thing since the day when you first came to Paris, either about ladies' clothes or about how to pronounce words without making silly blunders.' And this reproach was particularly stupid, for those French words which we are so proud of pronouncing accurately are themselves only blunders made by the Gallic lips which mispronounced Latin or Saxon, our language being merely a defective pronunciation of several others.

The genius of language in a living state, the future and past of French, that is what ought to have interested me in Françoise's mistakes. Her 'amender' for 'mender' was not so curious as those animals that survive from remote ages, such as the whale or the giraffe, and show us the states through which animal life has passed. 'And,' I went on, 'since you haven't managed to learn in all these years, you never will. But don't let that distress you, it doesn't prevent you from being a very good soul, and making spiced beef with jelly to perfection, and lots of other things as well. The hat that you think so simple is copied from a hat belonging to the Princesse de Guermantes which cost five hundred francs. However, I mean to give Mlle Albertine an even finer one very soon.' I knew that what would annoy Françoise more than anything was the thought of my spending money upon people whom she disliked. She answered me in a few words which were made almost unintelligible by a sudden attack of breathlessness. When I discovered afterwards that she had a weak heart, how remorseful I felt that I had never denied myself the fierce and sterile pleasure of making these retorts to her speeches. Françoise detested Albertine, moreover, because, being poor, Albertine could not enhance what Françoise regarded as my superior position. She smiled benevolently whenever I was invited by Mme de Villeparisis. On the other hand, she was indignant that Albertine did not practice reciprocity. It came to my being obliged to invent fictitious presents which she was supposed to have given me, in the existence of which Françoise never for an instant believed. This want of reciprocity shocked her most of all in the matter of food. That Albertine should accept dinners from Mamma, when we were not invited to Mme Bontemps's (who for that matter spent half her time out of Paris, her husband accepting 'posts' as in the old days when he had had enough of the Ministry), seemed to her an indelicacy on the part of my friend which she rebuked indirectly by repeating a saying current at Combray:

'Let's eat my bread.'
'Ay, that's the stuff.'
'Let's eat thy bread.'
'I've had enough.'

I pretended that I was obliged to write a letter. 'To whom were you writing?' Albertine asked me as she entered the room. 'To a pretty little friend of mine, Gilberte Swann. Don't you know her?' 'No.' I decided not to question Albertine as to how she had spent the evening, I felt that I should only find fault with her and that we should not have any time left, seeing how late it was already, to be reconciled sufficiently to pass to kisses and caresses. And so it was with these that I chose to begin from the first moment. Besides, if I was a little calmer, I was not feeling happy. The loss of all orientation, of all sense of direction that we feel when we are kept waiting, still continues, after the coming of the person awaited, and, taking the place, inside us, of the calm spirit in which we were picturing her coming as so great a pleasure, prevents us from deriving any from it. Albertine was in the room: my unstrung nerves, continuing to flutter, were still expecting her. 'I want a nice kiss, Albertine.' 'As many as you like,' she said to me in her kindest manner. I had never seen her looking so pretty. 'Another?' 'Why, you know it's a great, great pleasure to me.' 'And a thousand times greater to me,' she replied. 'Oh! What a pretty book-cover you have there!' 'Take it, I give it to you as a keepsake.' 'You are too kind . . .' People would be cured for ever of romanticism if they could make up their minds, in thinking of the girl they love, to try to be the man they will be when they are no longer in love with her. Gilberte's book-cover, her agate marble, must have derived their importance in the past from some purely inward distinction, since now they were to me a book-cover, a marble like any others.

I asked Albertine if she would like something to drink. 'I seem to see oranges over there and water,' she said. 'That will be perfect.' I was thus able to taste with her kisses that refreshing coolness which had seemed to me to be better than they, at the Princesse de Guermantes's. And the orange squeezed into the water seemed to yield to me, as I drank, the secret life of its ripening growth, its beneficent action upon certain states of that human body which belongs to so different a kingdom, its powerlessness to make that body live, but on the other hand the process of irrigation by which it was able to benefit it, a hundred mysteries concealed by the fruit from my senses, but not from my intellect.

When Albertine had gone, I remembered that I had promised Swann that I would write to Gilberte, and courtesy, I felt, demanded that I should do so at once. It was without emotion and as though drawing a line at the foot of a boring school essay, that I traced upon the envelope the name *Gilberte Swann*, with which at one time I used to cover my exercise-books to give myself the illusion that I was corresponding with her. For if, in the past, it had been I who wrote that name, now the task had been deputed by Habit to one of the many secretaries whom she employs. He could write down Gilberte's name with all the more calm, in that, placed with me only recently by Habit, having but recently entered my service, he had never known Gilberte, and knew only, without attaching any reality to the words, because he had heard me speak of her, that she was a girl with whom I had once been in love.

I could not accuse her of hardness. The person that I now was in relation to her was the clearest possible proof of what she herself had been: the book-cover, the agate marble had simply become for me in relation to Albertine what they had been for Gilberte, what they would have been to anybody who had not suffused them with the glow of an internal flame. But now I felt a fresh disturbance which in its turn destroyed the very real power of things and words. And when Albertine said to me, in a further outburst of gratitude:

'I do love turquoises!' I answered her: 'Do not let them die,' entrusting to them as to some precious jewel the future of our friendship which however was no more capable of inspiring a sentiment in Albertine than it had been of preserving the sentiment that had bound me in the past to Gilberte.

There appeared about this time a phenomenon which deserves mention only because it recurs in every important period of history. At the same moment when I was writing to Gilberte, M. de Guermantes, just home from his ball, still wearing his helmet, was thinking that next day he would be compelled to go into formal mourning, and decided to proceed a week earlier to the cure that he had been ordered to take. When he returned from it three weeks later (to anticipate for a moment, since I am still finishing my letter to Gilberte), those friends of the Duke who had seen him, so indifferent at the start, turn into a raving anti-Dreyfusard, were left speechless with amazement when they heard him (as though the action of the cure had not been confined to his bladder) answer: 'Oh, well, there'll be a fresh trial and he'll be acquitted; you can't sentence a fellow without any evidence against him. Did you ever see anyone so gaga as Forcheville? An officer, leading the French people to the shambles, heading straight for war. Strange times we live in.' The fact was that, in the interval, the Duke had met, at the spa, three charming ladies (an Italian princess and her two sisters-in-law). After hearing them make a few remarks about the books they were reading, a play that was being given at the Casino, the Duke had at once understood that he was dealing with women of superior intellect, by whom, as he expressed it, he would be knocked out in the first round. He was all the more delighted to be asked to play bridge by the Princess. But, the moment he entered her sitting room, as he began, in the fervour of his double-dyed anti-Dreyfusism: 'Well, we don't hear very much more of the famous Dreyfus and his appeal,' his stupefaction had been great when he heard the Princess and her sisters-in-law say: 'It's becoming more certain every day. They can't keep a man in prison who has done nothing.' 'Eh? Eh?' the Duke had gasped at first, as at the discovery of a fantastic nickname employed in this household to turn to ridicule a person whom he had always regarded as intelligent. But, after a few days, as, from cowardice and the spirit of imitation, we shout 'Hallo, Jojotte' without knowing why at a great artist whom we hear so addressed by the rest of the household, the Duke, still greatly embarrassed by the novelty of this attitude, began nevertheless to say: 'After all, if there is no evidence against him.' The three charming ladies decided that he was not progressing rapidly enough and began to bully him: 'But really, nobody with a grain of intelligence can ever have believed for a moment that there was anything.' Whenever any revelation came out that was 'damning' to Dreyfus, and the

Duke, supposing that now he was going to convert the three charming ladies, came to inform them of it, they burst out laughing and had no difficulty in proving to him, with great dialectic subtlety, that his argument was worthless and quite absurd. The Duke had returned to Paris a frantic Dreyfusard. And certainly we do not suggest that the three charming ladies were not, in this instance, messengers of truth. But it is to be observed that, every ten years or so, when we have left a man filled with a genuine conviction, it so happens that an intelligent couple, or simply a charming lady, come in touch with him and after a few months he is won over to the opposite camp. And in this respect there are plenty of countries that behave like the sincere man, plenty of countries which we have left full of hatred for another race, and which, six months later, have changed their attitude and broken off all their alliances.

I ceased for some time to see Albertine, but continued, failing Mme de Guermantes who no longer spoke to my imagination, to visit other fairies and their dwellings, as inseparable from themselves as is from the mollusc that fashioned it and takes shelter within it, the pearly or enamelled valve or crenellated turret of its shell. I should not have been able to classify these ladies, the difficulty being that the problem was so vague in its terms and impossible not merely to solve but to set. Before coming to the lady, one had first to approach the faery mansion. Now as one of them was always at home after luncheon in the summer months, before I reached her house I was obliged to close the hood of my cab, so scorching were the sun's rays, the memory of which was, without my realising it, to enter into my general impression. I supposed that I was merely being driven to the Cours-la-Reine; in reality, before arriving at the gathering which a man of wider experience would perhaps have despised, I received, as though on a journey through Italy, a delicious, dazzled sensation from which the house was never afterwards to be separated in my memory. What was more, in view of the heat of the season and the hour, the lady had hermetically closed the shutters of the vast rectangular saloons on the ground floor in which she entertained her friends. I had difficulty at first in recognising my hostess and her guests, even the Duchesse de Guermantes, who in her hoarse voice bade me come and sit down next to her, in a Beauvais armchair illustrating the Rape of Europa. Then I began to make out on the walls the huge eighteenth century tapestries representing vessels whose masts were hollyhocks in blossom, beneath which I sat as though in the palace not of the Seine but of Neptune, by the brink of the river Oceanus, where the Duchesse de Guermantes became a sort of goddess of the waters. I should never stop if I began to describe all the different types of drawing-room. This example is sufficient to show that I introduced into my social judgments poetical impressions which I never included among the items when I came to add up the sum, so that, when I was calculating the importance of a drawing-room, my total was never correct.

Certainly, these were by no means the only sources of error, but I have no time left now, before my departure for Balbec (where to my sorrow I am going to make a second stay which will also be my last), to start upon a series of pictures of society which will find their place in due course. I need here say only that to this first erroneous reason (my relatively frivolous existence which made people suppose that I was fond of society) for my letter to Gilberte, and for that reconciliation with the Swann family to which it seemed to point, Odette might very well, and with equal inaccuracy, have added a second. I have suggested hitherto the different aspects that the social world assumes in the eyes of a single person only by supposing that, if a woman who, the other day, knew nobody now goes everywhere, and another who occupied a commanding position is ostracised, one is inclined to regard these changes merely as those purely personal ups and downs of fortune which from time to time bring about in a given section of society, in consequence of speculations on the stock exchange, a crashing downfall or enrichment beyond the dreams of avarice. But there is more in it than that. To a certain extent social manifestations (vastly less important than artistic movements, political crises, the evolution that sweeps the public taste in the direction of the theatre of ideas, then of impressionist painting, then of music that is German and complicated, then of music that is Russian and simple, or of ideas of social service, justice, religious reaction, patriotic outbursts) are nevertheless an echo of them, remote, broken, uncertain, disturbed, changing. So that even drawing-rooms cannot be portrayed in a static immobility which has been conventionally employed up to this point for the study of characters, though these too must be carried along in an almost historical flow. The thirst for novelty that leads men of the world who are more or less sincere in their eagerness for information as to intellectual evolution to frequent the circles in which they can trace its development makes them prefer as a rule some hostess as yet undiscovered, who represents still in their first freshness the hopes of a superior culture so faded and tarnished in the women who for long years have wielded the social sceptre and who, having no secrets from these men, no longer appeal to their imagination. And every age finds itself personified thus in fresh women, in a fresh group of women, who, closely adhering to whatever may at that moment be the latest object of interest, seem, in their attire, to be at that moment making their first public appearance, like an unknown species, born of the last deluge, irresistible beauties of each new Consulate, each new Directory. But very often the new hostess is simply like certain statesmen who may be in office for the first time but have for the last forty years been knocking at every door without seeing any open, women who were not known in society but who nevertheless had been receiving, for years past, and failing anything better, a few 'chosen friends' from its ranks. To be sure, this is not always the case, and when, with the prodigious flowering of the Russian Ballet, revealing one after another Bakst, Nijinski, Benoist, the genius of Stravinski, Princess Yourbeletiev, the youthful sponsor of all these new great men, appeared bearing on her head an immense, quivering egret, unknown to the women of Paris, which they all sought to copy, one might have supposed that this marvellous creature had been imported in their innumerable baggage, and as their most priceless treasure, by the Russian dancers; but when presently, by her side, in her stage box, we see, at every performance of the 'Russians', seated like a true fairy godmother, unknown until that moment to the aristocracy, Mme Verdurin, we shall be able to tell the society people who naturally supposed that Mme Verdurin had recently entered the country with Diaghilev's troupe, that this lady had already existed in different periods, and had passed through various avatars of which this is remarkable only in being the first that is bringing to pass at last, assured henceforth, and at an increasingly rapid pace, the success so long awaited by the Mistress. In Mme Swann's case, it is true, the novelty she represented had not the same collective character. Her drawing-room was crystallised round a man, a dying man, who had almost in an instant passed, at the moment when his talent was exhausted, from obscurity to a blaze of glory. The passion for Bergotte's works was unbounded. He spent the whole day, on show, at Mme Swann's, who would whisper to some influential man: 'I shall say a word to him, he will write an article for you.' He was, for that matter, quite capable of doing so and even of writing a little play for Mme Swann. A stage nearer to death, he was not quite so feeble as at the time when he used to come and enquire after my grandmother. This was because intense physical suffering had enforced a regime on him. Illness is the doctor to whom we pay most heed: to kindness, to knowledge we make promises only; pain we obey.

It is true that the Verdurins and their little clan had at this time a far more vital interest than the drawing-room, faintly nationalist, more markedly literary, and pre-eminently Bergottic, of Mme Swann. The little clan was in fact the active centre of a long political crisis which had reached its maximum of intensity: Dreyfusism. But society people were for the most part so violently opposed to the appeal that a Dreyfusian house seemed to them as inconceivable a thing as, at an earlier period, a Communard house. The Principessa di Caprarola, who had made Mme Verdurin's acquaintance over a big exhibition which she had organised, had indeed been to pay her a long call, in the hope of seducing a few interesting specimens of the little clan and incorporating them in her own drawing-room, a call in the course of which the Princess (playing the Duchesse de Guermantes in miniature) had made a stand against current ideas, declared that the people in her world were idiots, all of which, thought Mme Verdurin, showed great courage. But this courage was not, in the sequel, to go the length of venturing, under fire of the gaze of nationalist ladies, to bow to Mme Verdurin at the Balbec races. With Mme Swann, on the contrary, the anti-Dreyfusards gave her credit for being 'sound', which, in a woman married to a Jew, was doubly meritorious. Nevertheless, the people who had never been to her house imagined her as visited only by a few obscure Israelites and disciples of Bergotte. In this way we place women far more outstanding than Mme Swann on the lowest rung of the social ladder, whether on account of their origin, or because they do not care about dinner parties and receptions at which we never see them, and suppose this, erroneously, to be due to their not having been invited, or because they never speak of their social connections, but only of literature and art, or because people conceal the fact that they go to their houses, or they, to avoid impoliteness to yet other people, conceal the fact that they open their doors to these, in short for a thousand reasons which, added together, make of one or other of them in certain people's eyes, the sort of woman whom one does not know. So it was with Odette. Mme d'Epinoy, when busy collecting some subscription for the 'Patrie Française', having been obliged to go and see her, as she would have gone to her dressmaker, convinced moreover that she would find only a lot of faces that were not so much impossible as completely unknown, stood rooted to the ground when the door opened not upon the drawing-room she imagined but upon a magic hall in which, as in the transformation scene of a pantomime, she recognised in the dazzling chorus, half reclining upon divans, seated in armchairs, addressing their hostess by her Christian name, the royalties, the duchesses, whom she, the Princesse d'Epinoy, had the greatest difficulty in enticing into her own drawing-room, and to whom at that moment, beneath the benevolent eyes of Odette, the Marquis du Lau, Comte Louis de Turenne, Prince Borghese, the Duc d'Estrées, carrying orangeade and cakes, were acting as cupbearers and henchmen. The Princesse d'Epinoy, as she instinctively made people's social value inherent in themselves, was obliged to disincarnate Mme Swann and reincarnate her in a fashionable woman. Our ignorance of the real existence led by the women who do not advertise it in the newspapers draws thus over certain situations (thereby helping to differentiate one house from another) a veil of mystery. In Odette's case, at the start, a few men of the highest society, anxious to meet Bergotte, had gone to dine, quite quietly, at her house. She had had the tact, recently acquired, not to advertise their presence, they found when they went there, a memory perhaps of the little nucleus, whose traditions Odette had preserved in spite of the schism, a place laid for them at table, and so forth. Odette took them with Bergotte (whom these excursions, incidentally, finished off) to interesting first nights. They spoke of her to various women of their own world who were capable of taking an interest in such a novelty. These women were convinced that Odette, an intimate friend of Bergotte, had more or less collaborated in his works, and believed her to be a thousand times more intelligent than the most outstanding women of the Faubourg, for the same reason that made them pin all their political faith to certain Republicans of the right shade such as M. Doumer and M. Deschanel, whereas they saw France doomed to destruction were her destinies entrusted to the Monarchy men who were in the habit of dining with them, men like Charette or Doudeauville. This change in Odette's status was carried out, so far as she was concerned, with a discretion that made it more secure and more rapid but allowed no suspicion to filter through to the public that is prone to refer to the social columns of the *Gaulois* for evidence as to the advance or decline of a house, with the result that one day, at the dress rehearsal of a play by Bergotte, given in one of the most fashionable theatres in aid of a charity, the really dramatic moment was when people saw enter the box opposite, which was that reserved for the author, and sit down by the side of Mme Swann, Mme de Marsantes and her who, by the gradual self-effacement of the Duchesse de Guermantes (glutted with fame, and retiring to save the trouble of going on), was on the way to becoming the lion, the queen of the age, Comtesse Molé. 'We never even supposed that she had begun to climb,' people said of Odette as they saw Comtesse Molé enter her box, 'and look, she has reached the top of the ladder.' So that Mme Swann might suppose that it was from snobbishness that I was taking up again with her daughter.

Odette, notwithstanding her brilliant escort, listened with close attention to the play, as though she had come there solely to see it performed, just as in the past she used to walk across the Bois for her health, as a form of exercise. Men who in the past had shown less interest in her came to the edge of the box, disturbing the whole audience, to reach up to her hand and so approach the imposing circle that surrounded her. She, with a smile that was still more friendly than ironical, replied patiently to their questions, affecting greater calm than might have been expected, a calm which was, perhaps, sincere, this exhibition being only the belated revelation of a habitual and discreetly hidden intimacy. Behind these three ladies to whom every eye was drawn was Bergotte flanked by the Prince d'Agrigente, Comte Louis de Turenne, and the Marquis de Bréauté. And it is easy to understand that, to men who were received everywhere and could not expect any further advancement save as a reward for original research, this demonstration of their merit which they considered that they were making in letting themselves succumb to a hostess with a reputation for profound intellectuality, in whose house they expected to meet all the dramatists and novelists of the day, was more exciting, more lively than those evenings at the Princesse de Guermantes's, which, without any change of programme or fresh attraction, had been going on year after year, all more or less like the one we have described in such detail. In that exalted sphere, the sphere of the Guermantes, in which people were beginning to lose interest, the latest intellectual fashions were not incarnate in entertainments fashioned in their image, as in those sketches that Bergotte used to write for Mme Swann, or those positive committees of public safety (had society been capable of taking an interest in the Dreyfus case) at which, in Mme Verdurin's drawing-room, used to assemble Picquart, Clemenceau, Zola, Reinach and Labori.

Gilberte, too, helped to strengthen her mother's position, for an uncle of Swann had just left nearly twenty-four million francs to the girl, which meant that the Faubourg Saint-Germain was beginning to take notice of her. The reverse of the medal was that Swann (who, however, was dying) held Dreyfusard opinions, though this as a matter of fact did not injure his wife, but was actually of service to her. It did not injure her because people said: 'He is dotty, his mind has quite gone, nobody pays any attention to him, his wife is the only person who counts and she is charming.' But even Swann's Dreyfusism was useful to Odette. Left to herself, she would quite possibly have allowed herself to make advances to fashionable women which would have been her undoing. Whereas on the evenings when she dragged her husband out to dine in the Faubourg Saint-Germain, Swann, sitting sullenly in his corner, would not hesitate, if he saw Odette seeking an introduction to some Nationalist lady, to exclaim aloud: 'Really, Odette, you are mad. Why can't you keep yourself to yourself? It is idiotic of you to get yourself introduced to anti-Semites, I forbid you.' People in society whom everyone else runs after are not accustomed either to such pride or to such ill-breeding. For the first time they beheld someone who thought himself 'superior' to them. The fame of Swann's mutterings was spread abroad, and cards with turned-down corners rained upon Odette. When she came to call upon Mme d'Arpajon there was a brisk movement of friendly curiosity. 'You didn't mind my introducing her to you,' said Mme d'Arpajon. 'She is so nice. It was Marie de Marsantes that told me about her.' 'No, not at all, I hear she's so wonderfully clever, and she is charming. I had been longing to meet her; do tell me where she lives.' Mme d'Arpajon told Mme Swann that she had enjoyed herself hugely at the latter's house the other evening, and had joyfully forsaken Mme de Saint-Euverte for her. And it was true, for to prefer Mme Swann was to show that one was intelligent, like going to concerts instead of to tea-parties. But when Mme de Saint-Euverte called on Mme d'Arpajon at the same time as Odette, as Mme de Saint-Euverte was a great snob and Mme d'Arpajon, albeit she treated her without ceremony, valued her invitations, she did not introduce Odette, so that Mme de Saint-Euverte should not know who it was. The Marquise imagined that it must be some Princess who never went anywhere, since she had never seen her before, prolonged her call, replied indirectly to what Odette was saying, but Mme d'Arpajon remained adamant. And when Mme Saint-Euverte owned herself defeated and took her leave: 'I did not introduce you,' her hostess told Odette, 'because people don't much care about going to her parties and she is always inviting one; you would never hear the last of her.' 'Oh, that is all right,' said Odette with a pang of regret. But she retained the idea that people did not care about going to Mme de Saint-Euverte's, which was to a certain extent true, and concluded that she herself held a position in society vastly superior to Mme de Saint-Euverte's, albeit that lady held a very high position, and Odette, so far, had none at all.

That made no difference to her, and, albeit all Mme de Guermantes's friends were friends also of Mme d'Arpajon, whenever the latter invited Mme Swann, Odette would say with an air of compunction: 'I am going to Mme d'Arpajon's; you will think me dreadfully old-fashioned, I know, but I hate going, for Mme de Guermantes's sake' (whom, as it happened, she had never met). The distinguished men thought that the fact that Mme Swann knew hardly anyone in good society meant that she must be a superior woman, probably a great musician, and that it would be a sort of extra distinction, as for a Duke to be a Doctor of Science, to go to her house. The completely unintelligent women were attracted by Odette for a diametrically opposite reason; hearing that she attended the Colonne concerts and professed herself a Wagnerian, they concluded from this that she must be 'rather a lark', and were greatly excited by the idea of getting to know her. But, being themselves none too firmly established, they were afraid of compromising themselves in public if they appeared to be on friendly terms with Odette, and if, at a charity concert, they caught sight of Mme Swann, would turn away their heads, deeming it impossible to bow, beneath the very nose of Mme de Rochechouart, to a woman who was perfectly capable of having been to Bayreuth, which was as good as saying that she would stick at nothing. Everybody becomes different upon entering another person's house. Not to speak of the marvellous metamorphoses that were accomplished thus in the faery palaces, in Mme Swann's drawing-room, M. de Bréauté, acquiring a sudden importance from the absence of the people by whom he was normally surrounded, by his air of satisfaction at finding himself there, just as if instead of going out to a party he had slipped on his spectacles to shut himself up in his study and read the *Revue des Deux Mondes*, the mystic rite that he appeared to be performing in coming to see Odette, M. de Bréauté himself seemed another man. I would have given anything to see what alterations the Duchesse de Montmorency-Luxembourg would undergo in this new environment. But she was one of the people who could never be induced to meet Odette. Mme de Montmorency, a great deal kinder to Oriane than Oriane was to her, surprised me greatly by saying, with regard to Mme de Guermantes: 'She knows some quite clever people, everybody likes her, I believe that if she had just had a slightly more coherent mind, she would have succeeded in forming a salon. The fact is, she never bothered about it, she is quite right, she is very well off as she is, with everybody running after her.' If Mme de Guermantes had not a 'salon', what in the world could a 'salon' be? The stupefaction in which this speech plunged me was no greater than that which I caused Mme de Guermantes when I told her that I should like to be invited to Mme de Montmorency's. Oriane thought her an old idiot. 'I go there,' she said, 'because I'm forced to, she's my aunt, but you! She doesn't even know how to get nice people to come to her house.' Mme de Guermantes did not realise that nice people left me cold, that when she spoke to me of the Arpajon drawing-room I saw a yellow butterfly, and the Swann drawing-room (Mme Swann was at home in the winter months between 6 and 7) a black butterfly, its wings powdered with snow. Even this last drawing-room, which was not a 'salon' at all, she considered, albeit out of bounds for herself, permissible to me, on account of the 'clever people' to be found there. But Mme de Luxembourg! Had I already produced something that had attracted attention, she would have concluded that an element of snobbishness may be combined with talent. But I put the finishing touch to her disillusionment; I confessed to her that I did not go to Mme de Montmorency's (as she supposed) to 'take notes' and 'make a study'. Mme de Guermantes was in this respect no more in error than the social novelists who analyse mercilessly from outside the actions of a snob or supposed snob, but never place themselves in his position, at the moment when a whole social springtime is bursting into blossom in his imagination. I myself, when I sought to discover what was the great pleasure that I found in going to Mme de Montmorency's, was somewhat taken aback. She occupied, in the Faubourg Saint-Germain, an old mansion ramifying into pavilions which were separated by small gardens. In the outer hall a statuette, said to be by Falconnet, represented a spring which did, as it happened, exude a perpetual moisture. A little farther on the doorkeeper, her eyes always red, whether from grief or neurasthenia, a headache or a cold in the head, never answered your enquiry, waved her arm vaguely to indicate that the Duchess was at home, and let a drop or two trickle from her eyelids into a bowl filled with forget-me-nots. The pleasure that I felt on seeing the statuette, because it reminded me of a 'little gardener' in plaster that stood in one of the Combray gardens, was nothing to that which was given me by the great staircase, damp and resonant, full of echoes, like the stairs in certain old-fashioned bathing establishments, with the vases filled with cinerarias – blue against blue – in the entrance hall and most of all the tinkle of the bell, which was exactly that of the bell in Eulalie's room. This tinkle raised my enthusiasm to a climax, but seemed to me too humble a matter for me to be able to explain it to Mme de Montmorency, with the result that she invariably saw me in a state of rapture of which she might never guess the cause.

*   *   *

My second arrival at Balbec was very different from the other. The manager had come in person to meet me at Pont-à-Couleuvre, reiterating how greatly he valued his titled patrons, which made me afraid that he had ennobled me, until I realised that, in the obscurity of his grammatical memory, *titré* meant simply *attitré*, or accredited. In fact, the more new languages he learned the worse he spoke the others. He informed me that he had placed me at the very top of the hotel. 'I hope,' he said, 'that you will not interpolate this as a want of discourtesy, I was sorry to give you a room of which you are unworthy, but I did it in connection with the noise, because in that room you will not have anyone above your head to disturb your trapanum (tympanum). Don't be alarmed, I shall have the windows closed, so that they shan't bang. Upon that point, I am intolerable' (the last word expressing not his own thought, which was that he would always be found inexorable in that respect, but, quite possibly, the thoughts of his underlings). The rooms were, as it proved, those we had had before. They were no humbler, but I had risen in the manager's esteem. I could light a fire if I liked (for, by the doctors' orders, I had left Paris at Easter), but he was afraid there might be 'fixtures' in the ceiling. 'See that you always wait before alighting a fire until the preceding one is extenuated' (extinct). 'The important thing is to take care not to avoid setting fire to the chimney, especially as, to cheer things up a bit, I have put an old china pottage on the mantelpiece which might become insured.'

He informed me with great sorrow of the death of the leader of the Cherbourg bar. 'He was an old retainer,' he said (meaning probably 'campaigner') and gave me to understand that his end had been hastened by the quickness, otherwise the fastness, of his life. 'For some time past I noticed that after dinner he would take a doss in the reading-room' (take a doze, presumably). 'The last times, he was so changed that if you hadn't known who it was, to look at him, he was barely recognisant' (presumably, recognisable).

A happy compensation: the chief magistrate of Caen had just received his 'bags' (badge) as Commander of the Legion of Honour. 'Surely to goodness, he has capacities, but seems they gave him it principally because of his general "impotence".' There was a mention of this decoration, as it happened, in the previous day's *Echo de Paris*, of which the manager had as yet read only 'the first paradox' (meaning paragraph). The paper dealt admirably with M. Caillaux's policy. 'I consider, they're quite right,' he said. 'He is putting us too much under the thimble of Germany' (under the thumb). As the discussion of a subject of this sort with a hotel-keeper seemed to me boring, I ceased to listen. I thought of the visual images that had made me decide to return to Balbec. They were very different from those of the earlier time, the vision in quest of which I came was as dazzlingly clear as the former had been clouded; they were to prove deceitful nevertheless. The images selected by memory are as arbitrary, as narrow, as intangible as those which imagination had formed and reality has destroyed. There is no reason why, existing outside ourselves, a real place should conform to the pictures in our memory rather than to those in our dreams. And besides, a fresh reality will perhaps make us forget, detest even, the desires that led us forth upon our journey.

Those that had led me forth to Balbec sprang to some extent from my discovery that the Verdurins (whose invitations I had invariably declined, and who would certainly be delighted to see me, if I went to call upon them in the country with apologies for never having been able to call upon them in Paris), knowing that several of the faithful would be spending the holidays upon that part of the coast, and having, for that reason, taken for the whole season one of M. de Cambremer's houses (la Raspelière), had invited Mme Putbus to stay with them. The evening on which I learned this (in Paris) I lost my head completely and sent our young footman to find out whether the lady would be taking her abigail to Balbec with her. It was eleven o'clock. Her porter was a long time in opening the front door, and, for a wonder, did not send my messenger packing, did not call the police, merely gave him a dressing down, but with it the information that I desired. He said that the head lady's maid would indeed be accompanying her mistress, first of all to the waters in Germany, then to Biarritz, and at the end of the season to Mme Verdurin's. From that moment my mind had been at rest, and glad to have this iron in the fire, I had been able to dispense with those pursuits in the streets, in which I had not that letter of intro-duction to the beauties I encountered which I should have to the 'Giorgione' in the fact of my having dined that very evening, at the Verdurins', with her mistress. Besides, she might form a still better opinion of me perhaps when she learned that I knew not merely the middle class tenants of la Raspelière but its owners, and above all Saint-Loup who, prevented from commending me personally to the maid (who did not know him by name), had written an enthusiastic letter about me to the Cambremers. He believed that, quite apart from any service that they might be able to render me, Mme de Cambremer, the Legrandin daughter-in-law, would interest me by her conversation. 'She is an intelligent woman,' he had assured me. 'She won't say anything final' (*final* having taken the place of *sublime* things with Robert, who, every five or six years, would modify a few of his favourite expressions, while preserving the more important intact), 'but it is an interesting nature, she has a personality, intuition; she has the right word for everything. Every now and then she is maddening, she says stupid things on purpose, to seem smart, which is all the more ridiculous as nobody could be less smart than the Cambremers, she is not always in the picture, but, taking her all round, she is one of the people it is more or less possible to talk to.'

No sooner had Robert's letter of introduction reached them than the Cambremers, whether from a snobbishness that made them anxious to oblige Saint-Loup, even indirectly, or from gratitude for what he had done for one of their nephews at Doncières, or (what was most likely) from kindness of heart and traditions of hospitality, had written long letters insisting that I should stay with them, or, if I preferred to be more independent, offering to find me lodgings. When Saint-Loup had pointed out that I should be staying at the Grand Hotel, Balbec, they replied that at least they would expect a call from me as soon as I arrived and, if I did not appear, would come without fail to hunt me out and invite me to their garden parties.

No doubt there was no essential connection between Mme Putbus's maid and the country round Balbec; she would not be for me like the peasant girl whom, as I strayed alone along the Méséglise way, I had so often sought in vain to evoke, with all the force of my desire.

But I had long since given up trying to extract from a woman as it might be the square root of her unknown quantity, the mystery of which a mere introduction was generally enough to dispel. Anyhow at Balbec, where I had not been for so long, I should have this advantage, failing the necessary connection which did not exist between the place and this particular woman, that my sense of reality would not be destroyed by familiarity, as in Paris, where, whether in my own home or in a bedroom that I already knew, pleasure indulged in with a woman could not give me for one instant, amid everyday surroundings, the illusion that it was opening the door for me to a new life. (For if habit is a second nature, it prevents us from knowing our original nature, whose cruelties it lacks and also its enchantments.) Now this illusion I might perhaps feel in a strange place, where one's sensibility is revived by a ray of sunshine, and where my ardour would be raised to a climax by the lady's maid whom I desired: we shall see, in the course of events, not only that this woman did not come to Balbec, but that I dreaded nothing so much as the possibility of her coming, so that the principal object of my expedition was neither attained, nor indeed pursued. It was true that Mme Putbus was not to be at the Verdurins' so early in the season; but these pleasures which we have chosen beforehand may be remote, if their coming is assured, and if, in the interval of waiting, we can devote ourselves to the pastime of seeking to attract, while powerless to love. Moreover, I was not going to Balbec in the same practical frame of mind as before; there is always less egoism in pure imagination than in recollection; and I knew that I was going to find myself in one of those very places where fair strangers most abound; a beach presents them as numerously as a ballroom, and I looked forward to strolling up and down outside the hotel, on the front, with the same sort of pleasure that Mme de Guermantes would have procured me if, instead of making other hostesses invite me to brilliant dinner-parties, she had given my name more frequently for their lists of partners to those of them who gave dances. To make female acquaintances at Balbec would be as easy for me now as it had been difficult before, for I was now as well supplied with friends and resources there as I had been destitute of them on my former visit.

I was roused from my meditations by the voice of the manager, to whose political dissertations I had not been listening. Changing the subject, he told me of the chief magistrate's joy on hearing of my arrival, and that he was coming to pay me a visit in my room, that very evening. The thought of this visit so alarmed me (for I was beginning to feel tired) that I begged him to prevent it (which he promised to do, and, as a further precaution, to post members of his staff on guard, for the first night, on my landing). He did not seem over-fond of his staff. 'I am obliged to keep running after them all the time because they are lacking in inertia. If I was not there they would never stir. I shall post the lift-boy on sentry outside your door.' I asked him if the boy had yet become 'head page'. 'He is not old enough yet in the house,' was the answer. 'He has comrades more aged than he is. It would cause an outcry. We must act with granulation in everything. I quite admit that he strikes a good aptitude' (meaning attitude) 'at the door of his lift. But he is still a trifle young for such positions. With others in the place of longer standing, it would make a contrast. He is a little wanting in seriousness, which is the primitive quality' (doubtless, the primordial, the most important quality). 'He needs his leg screwed on a bit tighter' (my informant meant to say his head). 'Anyhow, he can leave it all to me. I know what I'm about. Before I won my stripes as manager of the Grand Hotel, I smelt powder under M. Paillard.' I was impressed by this simile, and thanked the manager for having come in person as far as Pont-à-Couleuvre. 'Oh, that's nothing! The loss of time has been quite infinite' (for infinitesimal). Meanwhile, we had arrived.

Complete physical collapse. On the first night, as I was suffering from cardiac exhaustion, trying to master my pain, I bent down slowly and cautiously to take off my boots. But no sooner had I touched the topmost button than my bosom swelled, filled with an unknown, a divine presence, I shook with sobs, tears streamed from my eyes. The person who came to my rescue, who saved me from barrenness of spirit, was the same who, years before, in a moment of identical distress and loneliness, in a moment when I was no longer in any way myself, had come in, and had restored me to myself, for that person was myself and more than myself (the container that is greater than the contents, which it was bringing to me). I had just perceived, in my memory, bending over my weariness, the tender, preoccupied, dejected face of my grandmother, as she had been on that first evening of our arrival, the face not of that grandmother whom I was astonished – and reproached myself – to find that I regretted so little and who was no more of her than just her name, but of my own true grandmother, of whom, for the first time since that afternoon in the Champs-Elysées on which she had had her stroke, I now recaptured, by an instinctive and complete act of recollection, the living reality. That reality has no existence for us, so long as it has not been created anew by our mind (otherwise the men who have been engaged in a Titanic conflict would all of them be great epic poets); and so, in my insane desire to fling myself into her arms, it was not until this moment, more than a year after her burial, because of that anachronism which so often prevents the calendar of facts from corresponding to that of our feelings, that I became conscious that she was dead. I had often spoken about her in the interval, and thought of her also, but behind my words and thoughts, those of an ungrateful, selfish, cruel youngster, there had never been anything that resembled my grand-mother, because, in my frivolity, my love of pleasure, my familiarity with the spectacle of her ill health, I retained only in a potential state the memory of what she had been. At whatever moment we estimate it, the total value of our spiritual nature is more or less fictitious, notwithstanding the long inventory of its treasures, for now one, now another of these is unrealisable, whether we are considering actual treasures or those of the imagination, and, in my own case, fully as much as the ancient name of Guermantes, this other, how far more important item, my real memory of my grandmother. For with the troubles of memory are closely linked the heart's intermissions. It is, no doubt, the existence of our body, which we may compare to a jar containing our spiritual nature, that leads us to suppose that all our inward wealth, our past joys, all our sorrows, are perpetually in our possession. Perhaps it is equally inexact to suppose that they escape or return. In any case, if they remain within us, it is, for most of the time, in an unknown region where they are of no service to us, and where even the most ordinary are crowded out by memories of a different kind, which preclude any simultaneous occurrence of them in our con-sciousness. But if the setting of sensations in which they are preserved be recaptured, they acquire in turn the same power of expelling everything that is incompatible with them, of installing alone in us the self that originally lived them. Now, inasmuch as the self that I had just suddenly become once again had not existed since that evening long ago when my grandmother undressed me after my arrival at Balbec, it was quite naturally, not at the end of the day that had just passed, of which that self knew nothing, but – as though there were in time different and parallel series – without loss of continuity, immediately after the first evening at Balbec long ago, that I clung to the minute in which my grandmother had leaned over me. The self that I then was, that had so long disappeared, was once again so close to me that I seemed still to hear the words that had just been spoken, albeit they were nothing more now than illusion, as a man who is half awake thinks he can still make out close at hand the sounds of his receding dream. I was nothing now but the person who sought a refuge in his grandmother's arms, sought to wipe away the traces of his suffering by giving her kisses, that person whom I should have had as great difficulty in imagining when I was one or other of those persons which, for some time past, I had successively been, as the efforts, doomed in any event to sterility, that I should now have had to make to feel the desires and joys of any of those which, for a time at least, I no longer was. I reminded myself how, an hour before the moment at which my grandmother had stooped down like that, in her dressing gown, to unfasten my boots, as I wandered along the stiflingly hot street, past the pastry-cook's, I had felt that I could never, in my need to feel her arms round me, live through the hour that I had still to spend without her. And now that this same need was reviving in me, I knew that I might wait hour after hour, that she would never again be by my side. I had only just discovered this because I had only just, on feeling her for the first time, alive, authentic, making my heart swell to breaking-point, on finding her at last, learned that I had lost her for ever. Lost for ever; I could not understand and was struggling to bear the anguish of this contradiction: on the one hand an existence, an affection, surviving in me as I had known them, that is to say created for me, a love in whose eyes everything found in me so entirely its complement, its goal, its constant lodestar, that the genius of great men, all the genius that might have existed from the beginning of the world would have been less precious to my grandmother than a single one of my defects; and on the other hand, as soon as I had lived over again that bliss, as though it were present, feeling it shot through by the certainty, throbbing like a physical anguish, of an annihilation that had effaced my image of that affection, had destroyed that existence, abolished in retrospect our interwoven destiny, made of my grandmother at the moment when I found her again as in a mirror, a mere stranger whom chance had allowed to spend a few years in my company, as it might have been in anyone's else, but to whom, before and after those years, I was, I could be nothing.

Instead of the pleasures that I had been experiencing of late, the only pleasure that it would have been possible for me to enjoy at that moment would have been, by modifying the past, to diminish the sorrows and sufferings of my grandmother's life. Now, I did not recall her only in that dressing-gown, a garment so appropriate as to have become almost their symbol to the labours, foolish no doubt but so lovable also, that she performed for me, gradually I began to remember all the opportunities that I had seized, by letting her perceive, by exaggerating if necessary my sufferings, to cause her a grief which I imagined as being obliterated immediately by my kisses, as though my affection had been as capable as my happiness of creating hers; and, what was worse, I, who could conceive no other happiness now than in finding happiness shed in my memory over the contours of that face, moulded and bowed by love, had set to work with frantic efforts, in the past, to destroy even its most modest pleasures, as on the day when Saint-Loup had taken my grandmother's photograph and I, unable to conceal from her what I thought of the ridiculous childishness of the coquetry with which she posed for him, with her wide-brimmed hat, in a flattering half light, had allowed myself to mutter a few impatient, wounding words, which, I had perceived from a contraction of her features, had carried, had pierced her; it was I whose heart they were rending now that there was no longer possible, ever again, the consolation of a thousand kisses.

But never should I be able to wipe out of my memory that contraction of her face, that anguish of her heart, or rather of my own: for as the dead exist only in us, it is ourselves that we strike without ceasing when we persist in recalling the blows that we have dealt them. To these griefs, cruel as they were. I clung with all my might and main, for I realised that they were the effect of my memory of my grandmother, the proof that this memory which I had of her was really present within me. I felt that I did not really recall her save by grief and should have liked to feel driven yet deeper into me these nails which fastened the memory of her to my consciousness. I did not seek to mitigate my suffering, to set it off, to pretend that my grandmother was only somewhere else and momentarily invisible, by addressing to her photograph (the one taken by Saint-Loup, which I had beside me) words and prayers as to a person who is separated from us but, retaining his personality, knows us and remains bound to us by an indissoluble harmony. Never did I do this, for I was determined not merely to suffer, but to respect the original form of my suffering, as it had suddenly come upon me unawares, and I wished to continue to feel it, according to its own laws, whenever those strange contradictory impressions of survival and obliteration crossed one another again in my mind. This painful and, at the moment, incomprehensible impression, I knew – not, forsooth, whether I should one day distil a grain of truth from it – but that if I ever should succeed in extracting that grain of truth, it could only be from it, from so singular, so spontaneous an impression, which had been neither traced by my intellect nor attenuated by my pusillanimity, but which death itself, the sudden revelation of death, had, like a stroke of lightning, carved upon me, along a supernatural, inhuman channel, a twofold and mysterious furrow. (As for the state of forgetfulness of my grandmother in which I had been living until that moment, I could not even think of turning to it to extract truth from it; since in itself it was nothing but a negation, a weakening of the mind incapable of recreating a real moment of life and obliged to substitute for it conventional and neutral images.) Perhaps, however, as the instinct of preservation, the ingenuity of the mind in safeguarding us from grief, had begun already to build upon still smouldering ruins, to lay the first courses of its serviceable and ill-omened structure, I relished too keenly the delight of recalling this or that opinion held by my dear one, recalling them as though she had been able to hold them still, as though she existed, as though I continued to exist for her. But as soon as I had succeeded in falling asleep, at that more truthful hour when my eyes closed to the things of the outer world, the world of sleep (on whose frontier intellect and will, momentarily paralysed, could no longer strive to rescue me from the cruelty of my real impressions) reflected, refracted the agonising synthesis of survival and annihilation, in the mysteriously lightened darkness of my organs. World of sleep in which our inner consciousness, placed in bondage to the disturbances of our organs, quickens the rhythm of heart or breath because a similar dose of terror, sorrow, remorse acts with a strength magnified an hundredfold if it is thus injected into our veins; as soon as, to traverse the arteries of the subterranean city, we have embarked upon the dark current of our own blood as upon an inward Lethe meandering sixfold, huge solemn forms appear to us, approach and glide away, leaving us in tears. I sought in vain for my grandmother's form when I had stepped ashore beneath the sombre portals; I knew, indeed, that she did still exist, but with a diminished vitality, as pale as that of memory; the darkness was increasing, and the wind; my father, who was to take me where she was, did not appear. Suddenly my breath failed me, I felt my heart turn to stone; I had just remembered that for week after week I had forgotten to write to my grandmother. What must she be thinking of me? 'Great God!' I said to myself, 'how wretched she must be in that little room which they have taken for her, no bigger than what one would take for an old servant, where she is all alone with the nurse they have put there to look after her, from which she cannot stir, for she is still slightly paralysed and has always refused to rise from her bed. She must be thinking that I have forgotten her now that she is dead; how lonely she must be feeling, how deserted! Oh, I must run to see her, I mustn't lose a minute, I mustn't wait for my father to come, even – but where is it, how can I have forgotten the address, will she know me again, I wonder? How can I have forgotten her all these months?' It is so dark, I shall not find her; the wind is keeping me back; but look! there is my father walking ahead of me; I call out to him: 'Where is grandmother? Tell me her address. Is she all right? Are you quite sure she has everything she wants?' 'Why,' says my father, 'you need not alarm yourself. Her nurse is well trained. We send her a trifle, from time to time, so that she can get your grandmother anything she may need. She asks, sometimes, how you are getting on. She was told that you were going to write a book. She seemed pleased. She wiped away a tear.' And then I fancied I could remember that, a little time after her death, my grandmother had said to me, crying, with a humble expression, like an old servant who has been given notice to leave, like a stranger, in fact: 'You will let me see something of you occasionally, won't you; don't let too many years go by without visiting me. Remember that you were my grandson, once, and that grandmothers never forget.' And seeing again that face, so submissive, so sad, so tender, which was hers, I wanted to run to her at once and say to her, as I ought to have said to her then: 'Why, grandmother, you can see me as often as you like, I have only you in the world, I shall never leave you any more.' What tears my silence must have made her shed through all those months in which I have never been to the place where she lies, what can she have been saying to herself about me? And it is in a voice choked with tears that I too shout to my father: 'Quick, quick, her address, take me to her.' But he says: 'Well . . . I don't know whether you will be able to see her. Besides, you know, she is very frail now, very frail, she is not at all herself, I am afraid you would find it rather painful. And I can't be quite certain of the number of the avenue.' 'But tell me, you who know, it is not true that the dead have ceased to exist. It can't possibly be true, in spite of what they say, because grandmother does exist still.' My father smiled a mournful smile: 'Oh, hardly at all, you know, hardly at all. I think that it would be better if you did not go. She has everything that she wants. They come and keep the place tidy for her.' 'But she is often left alone?' 'Yes, but that is better for her. It is better for her not to think, which could only be bad for her. It often hurts her, when she tries to think. Besides, you know, she is quite lifeless now. I shall leave a note of the exact address, so that you can go to her; but I don't see what good you can do there, and I don't suppose the nurse will allow you to see her.' 'You know quite well I shall always stay beside her, dear, deer, deer, Francis Jammes, fork.' But already I had retraced the dark meanderings of the stream, had ascended to the surface where the world of living people opens, so that if I still repeated: 'Francis Jammes, deer, deer', the sequence of these words no longer offered me the limpid meaning and logic which they had expressed to me so naturally an instant earlier and which I could not now recall. I could not even understand why the word 'Alas' which my father had just said to me, had immediately signified: 'Take care you don't catch cold', without any possible doubt. I had forgotten to close the shutters, and so probably the daylight had awakened me. But I could not bear to have before my eyes those waves of the sea which my grandmother could formerly contemplate for hours on end; the fresh image of their heedless beauty was at once supplemented by the thought that she did not see them; I should have liked to stop my ears against their sound, for now the luminous plenitude of the beach carved out an emptiness in my heart; everything seemed to be saying to me, like those paths and lawns of a public garden in which I had once lost her, long ago, when I was still a child: 'We have not seen her', and beneath the hemisphere of the pale vault of heaven I felt myself crushed as though beneath a huge bell of bluish glass, enclosing an horizon within which my grandmother was not. To escape from the sight of it, I turned to the wall, but alas what was now facing me was that partition which used to serve us as a morning messenger, that partition which, as responsive as a violin in rendering every fine shade of sentiment, reported so exactly to my grandmother my fear at once of waking her and, if she were already awake, of not being heard by her and so of her not coming, then immediately, like a second instrument taking up the melody, informed me that she was coming and bade me be calm. I dared not put out my hand to that wall, any more than to a piano on which my grandmother had played and which still throbbed from her touch. I knew that I might knock now, even louder, that I should hear no response, that my grandmother would never come again. And I asked nothing better of God, if a Paradise exists, than to be able, there, to knock upon that wall the three little raps which my grandmother would know among a thousand, and to which she would reply with those other raps which said: 'Don't be alarmed, little mouse, I know you are impatient, but I am just coming', and that He would let me remain with her throughout eternity which would not be too long for us.

The manager came in to ask whether I would not like to come down. He had most carefully supervised my 'placement' in the dining-room. As he had seen no sign of me, he had been afraid that I might have had another of my choking fits. He hoped that it might be only a little 'sore throats' and assured me that he had heard it said that they could be soothed with what he called 'calyptus'.

He brought me a message from Albertine. She was not supposed to be coming to Balbec that year but, having changed her plans, had been for the last three days not in Balbec itself but ten minutes away by the tram at a neighbouring watering-place. Fearing that I might be tired after the journey, she had stayed away the first evening, but sent word now to ask when I could see her. I enquired whether she had called in person, not that I wished to see her, but so that I might arrange not to see her. 'Yes,' replied the manager. 'But she would like it to be as soon as possible, unless you have not some quite necessitous reasons. You see,' he concluded, 'that everybody here desires you, definitively.' But for my part, I wished to see nobody.

And yet the day before, on my arrival, I had felt myself recaptured by the indolent charm of a seaside existence. The same taciturn lift-boy, silent this time from respect and not from scorn, and glowing with pleasure, had set the lift in motion. As I rose upon the ascending column, I had passed once again through what had formerly been for me the mystery of a strange hotel, in which when you arrive, a tourist without protection or position, each old resident returning to his room, each chambermaid passing along the eery perspective of a corridor, not to mention the young lady from America with her companion, on their way down to dinner, give you a look in which you can read nothing that you would have liked to see. This time on the contrary I had felt the entirely soothing pleasure of passing up through an hotel that I knew, where I felt myself at home, where I had performed once again that operation which we must always start afresh, longer, more difficult than the turning outside in of an eyelid, which consists in investing things with the spirit that is familiar to us instead of their own which we found alarming. Must I always, I had asked myself, little thinking of the sudden change of mood that was in store for me, be going to strange hotels where I should be dining for the first time, where Habit would not yet have killed upon each landing, outside every door, the terrible dragon that seemed to be watching over an enchanted life, where I should have to approach those strange women whom fashionable hotels, casinos, watering-places, seem to draw together and endow with a common existence.

I had found pleasure even in the thought that the boring chief magistrate was so eager to see me, I could see, on that first evening, the waves, the azure mountain ranges of the sea, its glaciers and its cataracts, its elevation and its careless majesty – merely upon smelling for the first time after so long an interval, as I washed my hands, that peculiar odour of the over-scented soaps of the Grand Hotel – which, seeming to belong at once to the present moment and to my past visit, floated between them like the real charm of a particular form of existence to which one returns only to change one's necktie. The sheets on my bed, too fine, too light, too large, impossible to tuck in, to keep in position, which billowed out from beneath the blankets in moving whorls had distressed me before. Now they merely cradled upon the awkward, swelling fullness of their sails the glorious sunrise, big with hopes, of my first morning. But that sun had not time to appear. In the dead of night, the awful, godlike presence had returned to life. I asked the manager to leave me, and to give orders that no one was to enter my room. I told him that I should remain in bed and rejected his offer to send to the chemist's for the excellent drug. He was delighted by my refusal for he was afraid that other visitors might be annoyed by the smell of the 'calyptus'. It earned me the compliment: 'You are in the movement' (he meant: 'in the right'), and the warning: 'take care you don't defile yourself at the door, I've had the lock "elucidated" with oil; if any of the servants dares to knock at your door, he'll be beaten "black and white". And they can mark my words, for I'm not a repeater' (this evidently meant that he did not say a thing twice). 'But wouldn't you care for a drop of old wine, just to set you up; I have a pig's head of it downstairs' (presumably hogshead). 'I shan't bring it to you on a silver dish like the head of Jonathan, and I warn you that it is not Château-Lafite, but it is virtuously equivocal' (virtually equivalent). 'And as it's quite light, they might fry you a little sole.' I declined everything, but was surprised to hear the name of the fish (sole) pronounced like that of the King of Israel, Saul, by a man who must have ordered so many in his life.

Despite the manager's promises, they brought me in a little later the turned down card of the Marquise de Cambremer. Having come over to see me, the old lady had sent to enquire whether I was there and when she heard that I had arrived only the day before, and was unwell, had not insisted, but (not without stopping, doubtless, at the chemist's or the haberdasher's, while the footman jumped down from the box and went in to pay a bill or to give an order) had driven back to Féterne, in her old barouche upon eight springs, drawn by a pair of horses. Not infrequently did one hear the rumble and admire the pomp of this carriage in the streets of Balbec and of various other little places along the coast, between Balbec and Féterne. Not that these halts outside shops were the object of these excursions. It was on the contrary some tea-party or garden-party at the house of some squire or functionary, socially quite unworthy of the Marquise. But she, although completely overshadowing, by her birth and wealth, the petty nobility of the district, was in her perfect goodness and simplicity of heart so afraid of disappointing anyone who had sent her an invitation that she would attend all the most insignificant social gatherings in the neighbourhood. Certainly, rather than travel such a distance to listen, in the stifling heat of a tiny drawing-room, to a singer who generally had no voice and whom in her capacity as the lady bountiful of the countryside and as a famous musician she would afterwards be compelled to congratulate with exaggerated warmth, Mme de Cambremer would have preferred to go for a drive or to remain in her marvellous gardens at Féterne, at the foot of which the drowsy waters of a little bay float in to die amid the flowers. But she knew that the probability of her coming had been announced by the host, whether he was a noble or a free burgess of Maineville-la Teinturière or of Chattoncourt-l'Orgueilleux.

And if Mme de Cambremer had driven out that afternoon without making a formal appearance at the party, any of the guests who had come from one or other of the little places that lined the coast might have seen and heard the Marquise's barouche, which would deprive her of the excuse that she had not been able to get away from Féterne. On the other hand, these hosts might have seen Mme de Cambremer, time and again, appear at concerts given in houses which, they considered, were no place for her; the slight depreciation caused thereby, in their eyes, to the position of the too obliging Marquise vanished as soon as it was they who were entertaining her, and it was with feverish anxiety that they kept asking themselves whether or not they were going to have her at their 'small party'. What an allaying of the doubts and fears of days if, after the first song had been sung by the daughter of the house or by some amateur on holiday in the neighbourhood, one of the guests announced (an infallible sign that the Marquise was coming to the party) that he had seen the famous barouche and pair drawn up outside the watchmaker's or the chemist's! Thereupon Mme de Cambremer (who indeed was to enter before long followed by her daughter-in-law, the guests who were staying with her at the moment and whom she had asked permission, granted with such joy, to bring) shone once more with undiminished lustre in the eyes of her host and hostess, to whom the hoped-for reward of her coming had perhaps been the determining if unavowed cause of the decision they had made a month earlier: to burden themselves with the trouble and expense of an afternoon party. Seeing the Marquise present at their gathering, they remembered no longer her readiness to attend those given by their less deserving neighbours, but the antiquity of her family, the splendour of her house, the rudeness of her daughter-in-law, born Legrandin, who by her arrogance emphasised the slightly insipid good-nature of the dowager. Already they could see in their mind's eye, in the social column of the *Gaulois*, the paragraph which they would draft themselves in the family circle, with all the doors shut and barred, upon 'the little corner of Brittany which is at present a whirl of gaiety, the select party from which the guests could hardly tear themselves away, promising their charming host and hostess that they would soon pay them another visit'. Day after day they watched for the newspaper to arrive, worried that they had not yet seen any notice in it of their party, and afraid lest they should have had Mme de Cambremer for their other guests alone and not for the whole reading public. At length the blessed day arrived: 'The season is exceptionally brilliant this year at Balbec. Small afternoon concerts are the fashion . . . ' Heaven be praised, Mme de Cambremer's name was spelt correctly, and included 'among others we may mention' but at the head of the list. All that remained was to appear annoyed at this journalistic indiscretion which might get them into difficulties with people whom they had not been able to invite, and to ask hypocritically in Mme de Cambremer's hearing who could have been so treacherous as to send the notice, upon which the Marquise, every inch the lady bountiful, said: 'I can understand your being annoyed, but I must say I am only too delighted that people should know I was at your party.'

On the card that was brought me, Mme de Cambremer had scribbled the message that she was giving an afternoon party 'the day after tomorrow'. To be sure, as recently as the day before yesterday, tired as I was of the social round, it would have been a real pleasure to me to taste it, transplanted amid those gardens in which there grew in the open air, thanks to the exposure of Féterne, fig trees, palms, rose bushes extending down to a sea as blue and calm often as the Mediterranean, upon which the host's little yacht sped across, before the party began, to fetch from the places on the other side of the bay the most important guests, served, with its awnings spread to shut out the sun, after the party had assembled, as an open air refreshment room, and set sail again in the evening to take back those whom it had brought. A charming luxury, but so costly that it was partly to meet the expenditure that it entailed that Mme de Cambremer had sought to increase her income in various ways, and notably by letting, for the first time, one of her properties very different from Féterne: la Raspelière. Yes, two days earlier, how welcome such a party, peopled with minor nobles all unknown to me, would have been to me as a change from the 'high life' of Paris. But now pleasures had no longer any meaning for me. And so I wrote to Mme de Cambremer to decline, just as, an hour ago, I had put off Albertine: grief had destroyed in me the possibility of desire as completely as a high fever takes away one's appetite ... My mother was to arrive on the morrow. I felt that I was less unworthy to live in her company, that I should understand her better, now that an alien and degrading existence had wholly given place to the resurging, heart-rending memories that wreathed and ennobled my soul, like her own, with their crown of thorns. I thought so: in reality there is a world of difference between real griefs, like my mother's, which literally crush out our life for years if not for ever, when we have lost the person we love – and those other griefs, transitory when all is said, as mine was to be, which pass as quickly as they have been slow in coming, which we do not realise until long after the event, because, in order to feel them, we need first to understand them; griefs such as so many people feel, from which the grief that was torturing me at this moment differed only in assuming the form of unconscious memory.

That I was one day to experience a grief as profound as that of my mother, we shall find in the course of this narrative, but it was neither then nor thus that I imagined it. Nevertheless, like a principal actor who ought to have learned his part and to have been in his place long beforehand but has arrived only at the last moment and, having read over once only what he has to say, manages to 'gag' so skilfully when his cue comes that nobody notices his unpunctuality, my new-found grief enabled me, when my mother came, to talk to her as though it had existed always. She supposed merely that the sight of these places which I had visited with my grandmother (which was not at all the case) had revived it. For the first time then, and because I felt a sorrow which was nothing compared with hers, but which opened my eyes, I realised and was appalled to think what she must be suffering. For the first time I understood that the fixed and tearless gaze (which made Françoise withhold her sympathy) that she had worn since my grandmother's death had been arrested by that incomprehensible contradiction of memory and nonexistence. Besides, since she was, although still in deep mourning, more fashionably dressed in this strange place, I was more struck by the transformation that had occurred in her. It is not enough to say that she had lost all her gaiety; melted, congealed into a sort of imploring image, she seemed to be afraid of shocking by too sudden a movement, by too loud a tone, the sorrowful presence that never parted from her. But, what struck me most of all, when I saw her cloak of crape, was – what had never occurred to me in Paris – that it was no longer my mother that I saw before me, but my grandmother. As, in royal and princely families, upon the death of the head of the house his son takes his title and, from being Duc d'Orléans, Prince de Tarente or Prince des Laumes, becomes King of France, Duc de la Trémoïlle, Duc de Guermantes, so by an accession of a different order and more remote origin, the dead man takes possession of the living who becomes his image and successor, carries on his interrupted life. Perhaps the great sorrow that follows, in a daughter such as Mamma, the death of her mother only makes the chrysalis break open a little sooner, hastens the metamorphosis and the appearance of a person whom we carry within us and who, but for this crisis which annihilates time and space, would have come more gradually to the surface. Perhaps, in our regret for her who is no more, there is a sort of auto-suggestion which ends by bringing out on our features resemblances which potentially we already bore, and above all a cessation of our most characteristically personal activity (in my mother, her common sense, the sarcastic gaiety that she inherited from her father) which we did not shrink, so long as the beloved was alive, from exercising, even at her expense, and which counterbalanced the traits that we derived exclusively from her. Once she is dead, we should hesitate to be different, we begin to admire only what she was, what we ourselves already were only blended with something else, and what in future we are to be exclusively. It is in this sense (and not in that other, so vague, so false, in which the phrase is generally used) that we may say that death is not in vain, that the dead man continues to react upon us. He reacts even more than a living man because, true reality being discoverable only by the mind, being the object of a spiritual operation, we acquire a true knowledge only of things that we are obliged to create anew by thought, things that are hidden from us in everyday life ... Lastly, in our mourning for our dead we pay an idolatrous worship to the things that they liked. Not only could not my mother bear to be parted from my grandmother's bag, become more precious than if it had been studded with sapphires and diamonds, from her muff, from all those garments which served to enhance their personal resemblance, but even from the volumes of Mme de Sévigné which my grandmother took with her everywhere, copies which my mother would not have exchanged for the original manuscript of the letters. She had often teased my grandmother who could never write to her without quoting some phrase of Mme de Sévigné or Mme de Beausergent. In each of the three letters that I received from Mamma before her arrival at Balbec, she quoted Mme de Sévigné to me, as though those three letters had been written not by her to me but by my grandmother and to her. She must at once go out upon the front to see that beach of which my grandmother had spoken to her every day in her letters. Carrying her mother's sunshade, I saw her from my window advance, a sable figure, with timid, pious steps, over the sands that beloved feet had trodden before her, and she looked as though she were going down to find a corpse which the waves would cast up at her feet. So that she should not have to dine by herself, I was to join her downstairs. The chief magistrate and the barrister's widow asked to be introduced to her. And everything that was in any way connected with my grandmother was so precious to her that she was deeply touched, remembered ever afterwards with gratitude what the chief magistrate had said to her, just as she was hurt and indignant that the barrister's wife had not a word to say in memory of the dead. In reality, the chief magistrate was no more concerned about my grandmother than the barrister's wife. The heartfelt words of the one and the other's silence, for all that my mother imagined so vast a difference between them, were but alternative ways of expressing that indifference which we feel towards the dead. But I think that my mother found most comfort in the words in which, quite involuntarily, I conveyed to her a little of my own anguish. It could not but make Mamma happy (notwithstanding all her affection for myself), like everything else that guaranteed my grandmother survival in our hearts. Daily after this my mother went down and sat upon the beach, so as to do exactly what her mother had done, and read her mother's two favourite books, the *Memoirs* of Madame de Beausergent and the *Letters* of Madame de Sévigné. She, like all the rest of us, could not bear to hear the latter lady called the 'spirituelle Marquise' any more than to hear La Fontaine called 'le Bonhomme' but when, in reading the *Letters*, she came upon the words: 'My daughter', she seemed to be listening to her mother's voice.

She had the misfortune, upon one of these pilgrimages during which she did not like to be disturbed, to meet upon the beach a lady from Combray, accompanied by her daughters. Her name was, I think, Madame Poussin. But among ourselves we always referred to her as the 'Pretty Kettle of Fish', for it was by the perpetual repetition of this phrase that she warned her daughters of the evils that they were laying up for themselves, saying for instance if one of them was rubbing her eyes: 'When you go and get ophthalmia, that will be a pretty kettle of fish.' She greeted my mother from afar with slow and melancholy bows, a sign not of condolence but of the nature of her social training. We might never have lost my grandmother, or had any reason to be anything but happy. Living in comparative retirement at Combray within the walls of her large garden, she could never find anything soft enough to her liking, and subjected to a softening process the words and even the proper names of the French language. She felt 'spoon' to be too hard a word to apply to the piece of silver which measured out her syrups, and said, in consequence, 'spune'; she would have been afraid of hurting the feelings of the sweet singer of Télémaque by calling him bluntly Fénelon – as I myself said with a clear conscience, having had as a friend the dearest and cleverest of men, good and gallant, never to be forgotten by any that knew him, Bertrand de Fénelon – and never said anything but 'Fénelon', feeling that the acute accent added a certain softness. The far from soft son-in-law of this Madame Poussin, whose name I have forgotten, having been a lawyer at Combray, ran off with the contents of the safe, and relieved my uncle among others of a considerable sum of money. But most of the people of Combray were on such friendly terms with the rest of the family that no coolness ensued and her neighbours said merely that they were sorry for Madame Poussin. She never entertained, but whenever people passed by her railings they would stop to admire the delicious shade of her trees, which was the only thing that could be made out. She gave us no trouble at Balbec, where I encountered her only once, at a moment when she was saying to a daughter who was biting her nails: 'When they begin to fester, that will be a pretty kettle of fish.'

While Mamma sat reading on the beach I remained in my room by myself. I recalled the last weeks of my grandmother's life, and everything connected with them, the outer door of the flat which had been propped open when I went out with her for the last time. In contrast to all this the rest of the world seemed scarcely real and my anguish poisoned everything in it. Finally my mother insisted upon my going out. But at every step, some forgotten view of the casino, of the street along which, as I waited until she was ready, that first evening, I had walked as far as the monument to Duguay-Trouin, prevented me, like a wind against which it is hopeless to struggle, from going farther; I lowered my eyes in order not to see. And after I had recovered my strength a little I turned back towards the hotel, the hotel in which I knew that it was henceforth impossible that, however long I might wait, I should find my grandmother, whom I had found there before, on the evening of our arrival. As it was the first time that I had gone out of doors, a number of servants whom I had not yet seen were gazing at me curiously. Upon the very threshold of the hotel a young page took off his cap to greet me and at once put it on again. I supposed that Aimé had, to borrow his own expression, 'given him the office' to treat me with respect. But I saw a moment later that, as some one else entered the hotel, he doffed it again. The fact of the matter was that this young man had no other occupation in life than to take off and put on his cap, and did it to perfection. Having realised that he was incapable of doing anything else and that in this art he excelled, he practised it as often as was possible daily, which won him a discreet but widespread regard from the visitors, coupled with great regard from the hall porter upon whom devolved the duty of engaging the boys and who, until this rare bird alighted, had never succeeded in finding one who did not receive notice within a week, greatly to the astonishment of Aimé who used to say: 'After all, in that job they've only got to be polite, which can't be so very difficult.' The manager required in addition that they should have what he called a good 'presence', meaning thereby that they should not be absent from their posts, or perhaps having heard the word 'presence' used of personal appearance. The appearance of the lawn behind the hotel had been altered by the creation of several flower-beds and by the removal not only of an exotic shrub but of the page who, at the time of my former visit, used to provide an external decoration with the supple stem of his figure crowned by the curious colouring of his hair. He had gone with a Polish countess who had taken him as her secretary, following the example of his two elder brothers and their typist sister, torn from the hotel by persons of different race and sex who had been attracted by their charm. The only one remaining was the youngest, whom nobody wanted, because he squinted. He was highly delighted when the Polish countess or the protectors of the other two brothers came on a visit to the hotel at Balbec. For, albeit he was jealous of his brothers, he was fond of them and could in this way cultivate his family affections for a few weeks in the year. Was not the Abbess of Fontevrault accustomed, deserting her nuns for the occasion, to come and partake of the hospitality which Louis XIV offered to that other Mortemart, his mistress, Madame de Montespan? The boy was still in his first year at Balbec; he did not as yet know me, but having heard his comrades of longer standing supplement the word 'Monsieur', when they addressed me, with my surname, he copied them from the first with an air of satisfaction, whether at showing his familiarity with a person whom he supposed to be well-known, or at conforming with a custom of which five minutes earlier he had never heard but which he felt it to be indispensable that he should not fail to observe. I could quite well appreciate the charm that this great 'Palace' might have for certain persons. It was arranged like a theatre, and a numerous cast filled it to the doors with animation. For all that the visitor was only a sort of spectator, he was perpetually taking part in the performance, and that not as in one of those theatres where the actors perform a play among the audience, but as though the life of the spectator were going on amid the sumptuous fittings of the stage. The lawn-tennis player might come in wearing a white flannel blazer, the porter would have put on a blue frock-coat with silver braid before handing him his letters. If this lawn-tennis player did not choose to walk upstairs, he was equally involved with the actors in having by his side, to propel the lift, its attendant no less richly attired. The corridors on each landing engulfed a flying band of nymphlike chambermaids, fair visions against the sea, at whose modest chambers the admirers of feminine beauty arrived by cunning detours. Downstairs, it was the masculine element that predominated and made this hotel, in view of the extreme and effortless youth of the servants, a sort of Judaeo-Christian tragedy given bodily form and perpetually in performance. And so I could not help repeating to myself, when I saw them, not indeed the lines of Racine that had come into my head at the Princesse de Guermantes's while M. de Vaugoubert stood watching young secretaries of embassy greet M. de Charlus, but other lines of Racine, taken this time not from *Esther* but from *Athalie*: for in the doorway of the hall, what in the seventeenth century was called the portico, 'a flourishing race' of young pages clustered, especially at teatime, like the young Israelites of Racine's choruses. But I do not believe that one of them could have given even the vague answer that Joas finds to satisfy Athalie when she enquires of the infant Prince: 'What is your office, then?' for they had none. At the most, if one had asked of any of them, like the new Queen: 'But all this race, what do they then, imprisoned in this place?' he might have said: 'I watch the solemn pomp and bear my part.' Now and then one of the young supers would approach some more important personage, then this young beauty would rejoin the chorus, and, unless it were the moment for a spell of contemplative relaxation, they would proceed with their useless, reverent, decorative, daily evolutions. For, except on their 'day off', 'reared in seclusion from the world' and never crossing the threshold, they led the same ecclesiastical existence as the Levites in *Athalie*, and as I gazed at that 'young and faithful troop' playing at the foot of the steps draped with sumptuous carpets, I felt inclined to ask myself whether I were entering the Grand Hotel at Balbec or the Temple of Solomon.

I went straight up to my room. My thoughts kept constantly turning to the last days of my grandmother's illness, to her sufferings which I lived over again, intensifying them with that element which is even harder to endure than the sufferings of other people, and is added to them by our merciless pity; when we think that we are merely reviving the pains of a beloved friend, our pity exaggerates them; but perhaps it is our pity that is in the right, more than the sufferers' own consciousness of their pains, they being blind to that tragedy of their own existence which pity sees and deplores. Certainly my pity would have taken fresh strength and far exceeded my grandmother's sufferings had I known then what I did not know until long afterwards, that my grandmother, on the eve of her death, in a moment of consciousness and after making sure that I was not in the room, had taken Mamma's hand, and, after pressing her fevered lips to it, had said: 'Farewell, my child, farewell for ever.' And this may perhaps have been the memory upon which my mother never ceased to gaze so fixedly. Then more pleasant memories returned to me. She was my grandmother and I was her grandson. Her facial expressions seemed written in a language intended for me alone; she was everything in my life, other people existed merely in relation to her, to the judgment that she would pass upon them; but no, our relations were too fleeting to have been anything but accidental. She no longer knew me, I should never see her again. We had not been created solely for one another, she was a stranger to me. This stranger was before my eyes at the moment in the photograph taken of her by Saint-Loup. Mamma, who had met Albertine, insisted upon my seeing her, because of the nice things that she had said about my grandmother and myself. I had accordingly made an appointment with her. I told the manager that she was coming, and asked him to let her wait for me in the drawing-room. He informed me that he had known her for years, her and her friends, long before they had attained 'the age of purity' but that he was annoyed with them because of certain things that they had said about the hotel. 'They can't be very "gentlemanly" if they talk like that. Unless people have been slandering them.' I had no difficulty in guessing that 'purity' here meant 'puberty'. As I waited until it should be time to go down and meet Albertine, I was keeping my eyes fixed, as upon a picture which one ceases to see by dint of staring at it, upon the photograph that Saint-Loup had taken, when all of a sudden I thought once again: 'It's grandmother, I am her grandson' as a man who has lost his memory remembers his name, as a sick man changes his personality. Françoise came in to tell me that Albertine was there, and, catching sight of the photograph: 'Poor Madame; it's the very image of her, even the beauty spot on her cheek; that day the Marquis took her picture, she was very poorly, she had been taken bad twice. "Whatever happens, Françoise", she said, "you must never let my grandson know." And she kept it to herself, she was always bright with other people. When she was by herself, though, I used to find that she seemed to be in rather monotonous spirits now and then. But that soon passed away. And then she said to me, she said: "If anything were to happen to me, he ought to have a picture of me to keep. And I have never had one done in my life." So then she sent me along with a message to the Marquis, and he was never to let you know that it was she who had asked him, but could he take her photograph. But when I came back and told her that he would, she had changed her mind again, because she was looking so poorly. "It would be even worse," she said to me, "than no picture at all." But she was a clever one, she was, and in the end she got herself up so well in that big shady hat that it didn't show at all when she was out of the sun. She was very glad to have that photograph, because at that time she didn't think she would ever leave Balbec alive. It was no use my saying to her: "Madame, it's wrong to talk like that, I don't like to hear Madame talk like that," she had got it into her head. And, lord, there were plenty days when she couldn't eat a thing. That was why she used to make Monsieur go and dine away out in the country with M. le Marquis. Then, instead of going in to dinner, she would pretend to be reading a book, and as soon as the Marquis's carriage had started, up she would go to bed. Some days she wanted to send word to Madame, to come down and see her in time. And then she was afraid of alarming her, as she had said nothing to her about it. "It will be better for her to stay with her husband, don't you see, Françoise." ' Looking me in the face, Françoise asked me all of a sudden if I was 'feeling indisposed'. I said that I was not; whereupon she: 'And you make me waste my time talking to you. Your visitor has been here all this time. I must go down and tell her. She is not the sort of person to have here.

Why, a fast one like that, she may be gone again by now. She doesn't like to be kept waiting. Oh, nowadays, Mademoiselle Albertine, she's somebody!' 'You are quite wrong, she is a very respectable person, too respectable for this place. But go and tell her that I shan't be able to see her today.'

What compassionate declamations I should have provoked from Françoise if she had seen me cry. I carefully hid myself from her. Otherwise I should have had her sympathy. But I gave her mine. We do not put ourselves sufficiently in the place of these poor maidservants who cannot bear to see us cry, as though crying were bad for us; or bad, perhaps, for them, for Françoise used to say to me when I was a child: 'Don't cry like that, I don't like to see you crying like that.' We dislike highfalutin language, asseverations, we are wrong, we close our hearts to the pathos of the countryside, to the legend which the poor servant girl, dismissed, unjustly perhaps, for theft, pale as death, grown suddenly more humble than if it were a crime merely to be accused, unfolds, invoking her father's honesty, her mother's principles, her grandam's counsels. It is true that those same servants who cannot bear our tears will have no hesitation in letting us catch pneumonia, because the maid downstairs likes draughts and it would not be polite to her to shut the windows. For it is necessary that even those who are right, like Françoise, should be wrong also, so that Justice may be made an impossible thing. Even the humble pleasures of servants provoke either the refusal or the ridicule of their masters. For it is always a mere nothing, but foolishly sentimental, unhygienic. And so, they are in a position to say: 'How is it that I ask for only this one thing in the whole year, and am not allowed it.' And yet the masters will allow them something far more difficult, which was not stupid and dangerous for the servants – or for themselves. To be sure, the humility of the wretched maid, trembling, ready to confess the crime that she has not committed, saying 'I shall leave tonight if you wish it', is a thing that nobody can resist. But we must learn also not to remain unmoved, despite the solemn, menacing fatuity of the things that she says, her maternal heritage and the dignity of the family 'kailyard', before an old cook draped in the honour of her life and of her ancestry, wielding her broom like a sceptre, donning the tragic buskin, stifling her speech with sobs, drawing herself up with majesty. That afternoon, I remembered or imagined scenes of this sort which I associated with our old servant, and from then onwards, in spite of all the harm that she might do to Albertine, I loved Françoise with an affection, intermittent it is true, but of the strongest kind, the kind that is founded upon pity.

To be sure, I suffered agonies all that day, as I sat gazing at my grandmother's photograph. It tortured me. Not so acutely, though, as the visit I received that evening from the manager. After I had spoken to him about my grandmother, and he had reiterated his condolences, I heard him say (for he enjoyed using the words that he pronounced wrongly): 'Like the day when Madame your grandmother had that sincup, I wanted to tell you about it, because of the other visitors, don't you know, it might have given the place a bad name. She ought really to have left that evening. But she begged me to say nothing about it and promised me that she wouldn't have another sincup, or the first time she had one, she would go. The floor waiter reported to me that she had had another. But, lord, you were old friends that we try to please, and so long as nobody made any complaint.' And so my grandmother had had syncopes which she had never mentioned to me. Perhaps at the very moment when I was being most beastly to her, when she was obliged, amid her pain, to see that she kept her temper, so as not to anger me, and her looks, so as not to be turned out of the hotel. 'Sincup' was a word which, so pronounced, I should never have imagined, which might perhaps, applied to other people, have struck me as ridiculous, but which in its strange sonorous novelty, like that of an original discord, long retained the faculty of arousing in me the most painful sensations.

Next day I went, at Mamma's request, to lie down for a little on the sands, or rather among the dunes, where one is hidden by their folds, and I knew that Albertine and her friends would not be able to find me. My drooping eyelids allowed but one kind of light to pass, all rosy, the light of the inner walls of the eyes. Then they shut altogether. Whereupon my grandmother appeared to me, seated in an armchair. So feeble she was, she seemed to be less alive than other people. And yet I could hear her breathe; now and again she made a sign to show that she had understood what we were saying, my father and I. But in vain might I take her in my arms, I failed utterly to kindle a spark of affection in her eyes, a flush of colour in her cheeks. Absent from herself, she appeared somehow not to love me, not to know me, perhaps not to see me. I could not interpret the secret of her indifference, of her dejection, of her silent resentment. I drew my father aside. 'You can see, all the same,' I said to him, 'there's no doubt about it, she understands everything perfectly. It is a perfect imitation of life. If we could have your cousin here, who maintains that the dead don't live. Why, she's been dead for more than a year now, and she's still alive. But why won't she give me a kiss?' 'Look her poor head is drooping again.' 'But she wants to go, now, to the Champs-Elysées.' 'It's madness!' 'You really think it can do her any harm, that she can die any further? It isn't possible that she no longer loves me. I keep on hugging her, won't she ever smile at me again?' 'What can you expect, when people are dead they are dead.'

A few days later I was able to look with pleasure at the photograph that Saint-Loup had taken of her; it did not revive the memory of what Françoise had told me, because that memory had never left me and I was growing used to it. But with regard to the idea that I had received of the state of her health – so grave, so painful – on that day, the photograph, still profiting by the ruses that my grandmother had adopted, which succeeded in taking me in even after they had been disclosed to me, showed me her so smart, so carefree, beneath the hat which partly hid her face, that I saw her looking less unhappy and in better health than I had imagined. And yet, her cheeks having unconsciously assumed an expression of their own, livid, haggard, like the expression of an animal that feels that it has been marked down for slaughter, my grandmother had an air of being under sentence of death, an air involuntarily sombre, unconsciously tragic, which passed unperceived by me but prevented Mamma from ever looking at that photograph, that photograph which seemed to her a photograph not so much of her mother as of her mother's disease, of an insult that the disease was offering to the brutally buffeted face of my grandmother.

Then one day I decided to send word to Albertine that I would see her presently. This was because, on a morning of intense and premature heat, the myriad cries of children at play, of bathers disporting themselves, of news vendors, had traced for me in lines of fire, in wheeling, interlacing flashes, the scorching beach which the little waves came up one after another to sprinkle with their coolness; then had begun the symphonic concert mingled with the splashing of the water, through which the violins hummed like a swarm of bees that had strayed out over the sea. At once I had longed to hear again Albertine's laughter, to see her friends, those girls outlined against the waves who had remained in my memory the inseparable charm, the typical flora of Balbec; and I had determined to send a line by Françoise to Albertine, making an appointment for the following week, while, gently rising, the sea as each wave uncurled completely buried in layers of crystal the melody whose phrases appeared to be separated from one another like those angel lutanists which on the roof of the Italian cathedral rise between the peaks of blue porphyry and foaming jasper. But on the day on which Albertine came, the weather had turned dull and cold again, and moreover I had no opportunity of hearing her laugh; she was in a very bad temper. 'Balbec is deadly dull this year,' she said to me. 'I don't mean to stay any longer than I can help. You know I've been here since Easter, that's more than a month. There's not a soul here. You can imagine what fun it is.' Notwithstanding the recent rain and a sky that changed every moment, after escorting Albertine as far as Epreville, for she was, to borrow her expression, 'on the run' between that little watering-place, where Mme Bontemps had her villa, and Incarville, where she had been taken 'en pension' by Rosemonde's family, I went off by myself in the direction of the highroad that Mme de Villeparisis' carriage had taken when we went for a drive with my grandmother; pools of water which the sun, now bright again, had not dried made a regular quagmire of the ground, and I thought of my grandmother who, in the old days, could not walk a yard without covering herself with mud. But on reaching the road I found a dazzling spectacle. Where I had seen with my grandmother in the month of August only the green leaves and, so to speak, the disposition of the apple trees, as far as the eye could reach they were in full bloom, marvellous in their splendour, their feet in the mire beneath their ball-dresses, taking no precaution not to spoil the most marvellous pink satin that was ever seen, which glittered in the sunlight; the distant horizon of the sea gave the trees the background of a Japanese print; if I raised my head to gaze at the sky through the blossom, which made its serene blue appear almost violent, the trees seemed to be drawing apart to reveal the immensity of their paradise. Beneath that azure a faint but cold breeze set the blushing bouquets gently trembling. Blue tits came and perched upon the branches and fluttered among the flowers, indulgent, as though it had been an amateur of exotic art and colours who had artificially created this living beauty. But it moved one to tears because, to whatever lengths the artist went in the refinement of his creation, one felt that it was natural, that these apple trees were there in the heart of the country, like peasants, upon one of the highroads of France. Then the rays of the sun gave place suddenly to those of the rain; they streaked the whole horizon, caught the line of apple trees in their grey net. But they continued to hold aloft their beauty, pink and blooming, in the wind that had turned icy beneath the drenching rain: it was a day in spring.

Chapter Two

*The mysteries of Albertine – The girls whom she sees reflected in the glass –
The other woman – The lift-boy – Madame de Cambremer – The
pleasures of M. Nissim Bernard – Outline of the strange character
of Morel – M. de Charlus dines with the Verdurins*

In my fear lest the pleasure I found in this solitary excursion might weaken my memory of my grandmother, I sought to revive this by thinking of some great mental suffering that she had undergone; in response to my appeal that suffering tried to build itself in my heart, threw up vast pillars there; but my heart was doubtless too small for it, I had not the strength to bear so great a grief, my attention was distracted at the moment when it was approaching completion, and its arches collapsed before joining as, before they have perfected their curve, the waves of the sea totter and break.

And yet, if only from my dreams when I was asleep, I might have learned that my grief for my grandmother's death was diminishing, for she appeared in them less crushed by the idea that I had formed of her non-existence. I saw her an invalid still, but on the road to recovery, I found her in better health. And if she made any allusion to what she had suffered, I stopped her mouth with my kisses and assured her that she was now permanently cured. I should have liked to call the sceptics to witness that death is indeed a malady from which one recovers. Only, I no longer found in my grandmother the rich spontaneity of old times. Her words were no more than a feeble, docile response, almost a mere echo of mine; she was nothing more than the reflection of my own thoughts.

Incapable as I still was of feeling any fresh physical desire, Albertine was beginning nevertheless to inspire in me a desire for happiness. Certain dreams of shared affection, always floating on the surface of our minds, ally themselves readily by a sort of affinity with the memory (provided that this has already become slightly vague) of a woman with whom we have taken our pleasure. This sentiment recalled to me aspects of Albertine's face, more gentle, less gay, quite different from those that would have been evoked by physical desire; and as it was also less pressing than that desire I would gladly have postponed its realisation until the following winter, without seeking to see Albertine again at Balbec, before her departure. But even in the midst of a grief that is still keen physical desire will revive. From my bed, where I was made to spend hours every day resting, I longed for Albertine to come and resume our former amusements. Do we not see, in the very room in which they have lost a child, its parents soon come together again to give the little angel a baby brother? I tried to distract my mind from this desire by going to the window to look at that day's sea. As in the former year, the seas, from one day to another, were rarely the same. Nor, however, did they at all resemble those of that first year, whether because we were now in spring with its storms, or because even if I had come down at the same time as before, the different, more changeable weather might have discouraged from visiting this coast certain seas, indolent, vaporous and fragile, which I had seen throughout long, scorching days, asleep upon the beach, their bluish bosoms, only, faintly stirring, with a soft palpitation, or, as was most probable, because my eyes, taught by Elstir to retain precisely those elements that before I had deliberately rejected, would now gaze for hours at what in the former year they had been incapable of seeing. The contrast that used then to strike me so forcibly between the country drives that I took with Mme de Villeparisis and this proximity, fluid, inaccessible, mythological, of the eternal Ocean, no longer existed for me. And there were days now when, on the contrary, the sea itself seemed almost rural. On the days, few and far between, of really fine weather, the heat had traced upon the waters, as it might be across country, a dusty white track, at the end of which the pointed mast of a fishing-boat stood up like a village steeple. A tug, of which one could see only the funnel, was smoking in the distance like a factory amid the fields, while alone against the horizon a convex patch of white, sketched there doubtless by a sail but apparently a solid plastered surface, made one think of the sunlit wall of some isolated building, a hospital or a school. And the clouds and the wind, on days when these were added to the sun, completed if not the error of judgment, at any rate the illusion of the first glance, the suggestion that it aroused in the imagination. For the alternation of sharply defined patches of colour like those produced in the country by the proximity of different crops, the rough, yellow, almost muddy irregularities of the marine surface, the banks, the slopes that hid from sight a vessel upon which a crew of nimble sailors seemed to be reaping a harvest, all this upon stormy days made the ocean a thing as varied, as solid, as broken, as populous, as civilised as the earth with its carriage roads over which I used to travel, and was soon to be travelling again. And once, unable any longer to hold out against my desire, instead of going back to bed I put on my clothes and started off to

Incarville, to find Albertine. I would ask her to come with me to Douville, where I would pay calls at Féterne upon Mme de Cambremer and at la Raspelière upon Mme Verdurin. Albertine would wait for me meanwhile upon the beach and we would return together after dark. I went to take the train on the local light railway, of which I had picked up, the time before, from Albertine and her friends all the nicknames current in the district, where it was known as the *Twister* because of its numberless windings, the *Crawler* because the train never seemed to move, the *Transatlantic* because of a horrible siren which it sounded to clear people off the line, the *Decauville* and the *Funi*, albeit there was nothing funicular about it but because it climbed the cliff, and, although not, strictly speaking, a Decauville, had a 60 centimetre gauge, the *B. A. G.* because it ran between Balbec and Grattevast *via* Angerville, the *Tram* and the *T. S. N.* because it was a branch of the Tramways of Southern Normandy. I took my seat in a compartment in which I was alone; it was a day of glorious sunshine, and stiflingly hot; I drew down the blue blind which shut off all but a single ray of sunlight. But immediately I beheld my grandmother, as she had appeared sitting in the train, on our leaving Paris for Balbec, when, in her sorrow at seeing me drink beer, she had preferred not to look, to shut her eyes and pretend to be asleep. I, who in my childhood had been unable to endure her anguish when my grandfather tasted brandy, I had inflicted this anguish upon her, not merely of seeing me accept, at the invitation of another, a drink which she regarded as bad for me, I had forced her to leave me free to swill it down to my heart's content, worse still, by my bursts of passion, my choking fits, I had forced her to help, to advise me to do so, with a supreme resignation of which I saw now in my memory the mute, despairing image, her eyes closed to shut out the sight. So vivid a memory had, like the stroke of a magic wand, restored the mood that I had been gradually outgrowing for some time past; what had I to do with Rosemonde when my lips were wholly possessed by the desperate longing to kiss a dead woman, what had I to say to the Cambremers and Verdurins when my heart was beating so violently because at every moment there was being renewed in it the pain that my grandmother had suffered? I could not remain in the compartment. As soon as the train stopped at Maineville-la-Teinturiere, abandoning all my plans, I alighted. Maineville had of late acquired considerable importance and a reputation all its own, because a director of various casinos, a caterer in pleasure, had set up, just outside it, with a luxurious display of bad taste that could vie with that of any smart hotel, an establishment to which we shall return anon, and which was, to put it briefly, the first brothel for 'exclusive' people that it had occurred to anyone to build upon the coast of France. It was the only one. True, every port has its own, but intended for sailors only, and for lovers of the picturesque whom it amuses to see, next door to the primeval parish church, the bawd, hardly less ancient, venerable and moss-grown, standing outside her ill-famed door, waiting for the return of the fishing fleet.

Hurrying past the glittering house of 'pleasure', insolently erected there despite the protests which the heads of families had addressed in vain to the mayor, I reached the cliff and followed its winding paths in the direction of Balbec. I heard, without responding to it, the appeal of the hawthorns. Neighbours, in humbler circumstances, of the blossoming apple trees, they found them very coarse, without denying the fresh complexion of the rosy-petalled daughters of those wealthy brewers of cider. They knew that, with a lesser dowry, they were more sought after, and were attractive enough by themselves in their tattered whiteness.

On my return, the hotel porter handed me a black-bordered letter in which the Marquis and the Marquise de Gonneville, the Vicomte and the Vicomtesse d'Amfreville, the Comte and the Comtesse de Berneville, the Marquis and the Marquise de Graincourt, the Comte d'Amenoncourt, the Comtesse de Maineville, the Comte and the Comtesse de Franquetot, the Comtesse de Chaverny *née* d'Aigleville, begged to announce, and from which I understood at length why it had been sent to me when I caught sight of the names of the Marquise de Cambremer *née* du Mesnil la Guichard, the Marquis and the Marquise de Cambremer, and saw that the deceased, a cousin of the Cambremers, was named Eléonore-Euphrasie-Humbertine de Cambremer, Comtesse de Criquetot. In the whole extent of this provincial family, the enumeration of which filled the closely printed lines, not a single commoner, and on the other hand not a single title that one knew, but the entire muster-roll of the nobles of the region who made their names – those of all the interesting spots in the neighbourhood – ring out their joyous endings in *ville*, in *court*, sometimes on a duller note (in *tot*). Garbed in the roof-tiles of their castle or in the roughcast of their parish church, their nodding heads barely reaching above the vault of the nave or banqueting hall, and then only to cap themselves with the Norman lantern or the dovecot of the pepperpot turret, they gave the impression of having sounded the rallying call to all the charming villages straggling or scattered over a radius of fifty leagues, and to have paraded them in massed formation, without one absentee, one intruder, on the compact, rectangular draught-board of the aristocratic letter edged with black.

My mother had gone upstairs to her room, meditating the phrase of Madame de Sévigné: 'I see nothing of the people who seek to distract me from you; the truth of the matter is that they are seeking to prevent me from thinking of you, and that annoys me.' – because the chief magistrate had told her that she ought to find some distraction. To me he whispered: 'That's the Princesse de Parme!' My fears were dispelled when I saw that the woman whom the magistrate pointed out to me bore not the slightest resemblance to Her Royal Highness. But as she had engaged a room in which to spend the night after paying a visit to Mme de Luxembourg, the report of her coming had the effect upon many people of making them take each newcomer for the Princesse de Parme – and upon me of making me go and shut myself up in my attic.

I had no wish to remain there by myself. It was barely four o'clock. I asked Françoise to go and find Albertine, so that she might spend the rest of the afternoon with me.

It would be untrue, I think, to say that there were already symptoms of that painful and perpetual mistrust which Albertine was to inspire in me, not to mention the special character, emphatically Gomorrhan, which that mistrust was to assume. Certainly, even that afternoon – but this was not the first time – I grew anxious as I was kept waiting. Françoise, once she had started, stayed away so long that I began to despair. I had not lighted the lamp. The daylight had almost gone. The wind was making the flag over the casino flap. And, fainter still in the silence of the beach over which the tide was rising, and like a voice rendering and enhancing the troubling emptiness of this restless, unnatural hour, a little barrel organ that had stopped outside the hotel was playing Viennese waltzes. At length Françoise arrived, but unaccompanied. 'I have been as quick as I could but she wouldn't come because she didn't think she was looking smart enough. If she was five minutes painting herself and powdering herself, she was an hour by the clock. You'll be having a regular scent shop in here. She's coming, she stayed behind to tidy herself at the glass. I thought I should find her here.' There was still a long time to wait before Albertine appeared. But the gaiety, the charm that she showed on this occasion dispelled my sorrow. She informed me (in contradiction of what she had said the other day) that she would be staying for the whole season and asked me whether we could not arrange, as in the former year, to meet daily. I told her that at the moment I was too melancholy and that I would rather send for her from time to time at the last moment, as I did in Paris. 'If ever you're feeling worried, or feel that you want me, do not hesitate,' she told me, 'to send for me, I shall come immediately, and if you are not afraid of its creating a scandal in the hotel, I shall stay as long as you like.' Françoise, in bringing her to me, had assumed the joyous air she wore whenever she had gone out of her way to please me and had been successful. But Albertine herself contributed nothing to her joy, and the very next day Françoise was to greet me with the profound observation: 'Monsieur ought not to see that young lady. I know quite well the sort she is, she'll land you in trouble.' As I escorted Albertine to the door I saw in the lighted dining-room the Princesse de Parme. I merely gave her a glance, taking care not to be seen. But I must say that I found a certain grandeur in the royal politeness which had made me smile at the Guermantes'. It is a fundamental rule that sovereign princes are at home wherever they are, and this rule is conventionally expressed in obsolete and useless customs such as that which requires the host to carry his hat in his hand, in his own house, to show that he is not in his own home but in the Prince's. Now the Princesse de Parme may not have formulated this idea to herself, but she was so imbued with it that all her actions, spontaneously invented to suit the circumstances, pointed to it. When she rose from table she handed a lavish tip to Aimé, as though he had been there solely for her and she were rewarding, before leaving a country house, a footman who had been detailed to wait upon her. Nor did she stop at the tip, but with a gracious smile bestowed on him a few friendly, flattering words, with a store of which her mother had provided her. Another moment, and she would have told him that, just as the hotel was perfectly managed, so Normandy was a garden of roses and that she preferred France to any other country in the world. Another coin slipped from the Princess's fingers, for the wine waiter, for whom she had sent and to whom she made a point of expressing her satisfaction like a general after an inspection. The lift-boy had come up at that moment with a message for her; he too received a little speech, a smile and a tip, all this interspersed with encouraging and humble words intended to prove to them that she was only one of themselves. As Aimé, the wine waiter, the lift-boy and the rest felt that it would be impolite not to grin from ear to ear at a person who smiled at them, she was presently surrounded by a cluster of servants with whom she chatted kindly; such ways being unfamiliar in smart hotels, the people who passed by, not knowing who she was, thought they beheld a permanent resident at Balbec, who, because of her humble origin, or for professional reasons (she was perhaps the wife of an agent for champagne) was less different from the domestics than the really smart visitors. As for me, I thought of the palace at Parma, of the counsels, partly religious, partly political, given to this Princess, who behaved towards the lower orders as though she had been obliged to conciliate them in order to reign over them one day. All the more, as if she were already reigning.

I went upstairs again to my room, but I was not alone there. I could hear someone softly playing Schumann. No doubt it happens at times that people, even those whom we love best, become saturated with the melancholy or irritation that emanates from us. There is nevertheless an inanimate object which is capable of a power of exasperation to which no human being will ever attain: to wit, a piano.

Albertine had made me take a note of the dates on which she would be going away for a few days to visit various girl friends, and had made me write down their addresses as well, in case I should want her on one of those evenings, for none of them lived very far away. This meant that when I tried to find her, going from one girl to another, she became more and more entwined in ropes of flowers. I must confess that many of her friends – I was not yet in love with her – gave me, at one watering-place or another, moments of pleasure. These obliging young comrades did not seem to me to be very many. But recently I have thought it over, their names have recurred to me. I counted that, in that one season, a dozen conferred on me their ephemeral favours. A name came back to me later, which made thirteen. I then, with almost a child's delight in cruelty, dwelt upon that number. Alas, I realised that I had forgotten the first of them all, Albertine who no longer existed and who made the fourteenth.

I had, to resume the thread of my narrative, written down the names and addresses of the girls with whom I should find her upon the days when she was not to be at Incarville, but privately had decided that I would devote those days rather to calling upon Mme Verdurin. In any case, our desire for different women varies in intensity. One evening we cannot bear to let one out of our sight who, after that, for the next month or two, will never enter our mind. Then there is the law of change, for a study of which this is not the place, under which, after an over-exertion of the flesh, the woman whose image haunts our momentary senility is one to whom we would barely give more than a kiss on the brow. As for Albertine, I saw her seldom, and only upon the very infrequent evenings when I felt that I could not live without her. If this desire seized me when she was too far from Balbec for Françoise to be able to go and fetch her, I used to send the lift-boy to Egreville, to La Sogne, to Saint-Frichoux, asking him to finish his work a little earlier than usual. He would come into my room, but would leave the door open for, albeit he was conscientious at his 'job' which was pretty hard, consisting in endless cleanings from five o'clock in the morning, he could never bring himself to make the effort to shut a door, and, if one were to remark to him that it was open, would turn back and, summoning up all his strength, give it a gentle push. With the democratic pride that marked him, a pride to which, in more liberal careers, the members of a profession that is at all numerous never attain, barristers, doctors and men of letters speaking simply of a 'brother' barrister, doctor or man of letters, he, employing, and rightly, a term that is confined to close corporations like the Academy, would say to me in speaking of a page who was in charge of the lift upon alternate days: 'I shall get my *colleague* to take my place.' This pride did not prevent him from accepting, with a view to increasing what he called his 'salary', remuneration for his errands, a fact which had made Françoise take a dislike to him: 'Yes, the first time you see him you would give him the sacrament without confession, but there are days when his tongue is as smooth as a prison door. It's your money he's after.' This was the category in which she had so often included Eulalie, and in which, alas (when I think of all the trouble that was one day to come of it), she already placed Albertine, because she saw me often asking Mamma, on behalf of my impecunious friend, for trinkets and other little presents, which Françoise held to be inexcusable because Mme Bontemps had only a general servant. A moment later the lift-boy, having removed what I should have called his livery and he called his tunic, appeared wearing a straw hat, carrying a cane, holding himself stiffly erect, for his mother had warned him never to adopt the 'working-class' or 'pageboy' style. Just as, thanks to books, all knowledge is open to a working man, who ceases to be such when he has finished his work, so, thanks to a 'boater' hat and a pair of gloves, elegance became accessible to the lift-boy who, having ceased for the evening to take the visitors upstairs, imagined himself, like a young surgeon who has taken off his overall, or Serjeant Saint-Loup out of uniform, a typical young man about town. He was not for that matter lacking in ambition, or in talent either in manipulating his machine and not bringing you to a standstill between two floors. But his vocabulary was defective. I credited him with ambition because he said in speaking of the porter, under whom he served: 'My porter', in the same tone in which a man who owned what the page would have called a 'private mansion' in Paris would have referred to his footman. As for the lift-boy's vocabulary, it is curious that anybody who heard people, fifty times a day, calling for the 'lift', should never himself call it anything but a 'left'. There were certain things about this boy that were extremely annoying: whatever I might be saying to him he would interrupt with a phrase: 'I should say so!' or 'I say!' which seemed either to imply that my remark was so obvious that anybody would have thought of it, or else to take all the credit for it to himself, as though it were he that was drawing my attention to the subject. 'I should say so!' or 'I say!' exclaimed with the utmost emphasis, issued from his lips every other minute, over matters to which he had never given a thought, a trick which irritated me so much that

I immediately began to say the opposite to show him that he knew nothing about it. But to my second assertion, albeit it was incompatible with the first, he replied none the less stoutly: 'I should say so!' 'I say!' as though these words were inevitable. I found it difficult, also, to forgive him the trick of employing certain terms proper to his calling, which would therefore have sounded perfectly correct in their literal sense, in a figurative sense only, which gave them an air of feeble witticism, for instance the verb to pedal. He never used it when he had gone anywhere on his bicycle. But if, on foot, he had hurried to arrive somewhere in time, then, to indicate that he had walked fast, he would exclaim: 'I should say I didn't half pedal!' The lift-boy was on the small side, clumsily built and by no means good looking. This did not prevent him, whenever one spoke to him of some tall, slim, handsome young man, from saying: 'Oh, yes, I know, a fellow who is just my height.' And one day when I was expecting him to bring me the answer to a message, hearing somebody come upstairs, I had in my impatience opened the door of my room and caught sight of a page as beautiful as Endymion, with incredibly perfect features, who was bringing a message to a lady whom I did not know. When the lift-boy returned, in telling him how impatiently I had waited for the answer, I mentioned to him that I had thought I heard him come upstairs but that it had turned out to be a page from the Hôtel de Normandie. 'Oh, yes, I know,' he said, 'they have only the one, a boy about my build. He's so like me in face, too, that we're always being mistaken; anybody would think he was my brother.' Lastly, he always wanted to appear to have understood you perfectly from the first second, which meant that as soon as you asked him to do anything he would say: 'Yes, yes, yes, yes, I understand all that,' with a precision and a tone of intelligence which for some time deceived me; but other people, as we get to know them, are like a metal dipped in an acid bath, and we see them gradually lose their good qualities (and their bad qualities too, at times). Before giving him my instructions, I saw that he had left the door open; I pointed this out to him, I was afraid that people might hear us; he acceded to my request and returned, having reduced the gap. 'Anything to oblige. But there's nobody on this floor except us two.' Immediately I heard one, then a second, then a third person go by. This annoyed me partly because of the risk of my being overheard, but more still because I could see that it did not in the least surprise him and was a perfectly normal occurrence. 'Yes, that'll be the maid next door going for her things. Oh, that's of no importance, it's the bottler putting away his keys. No, no, it's nothing, you can say what you want, it's my colleague just going on duty.' Then, as the reasons that all these people had for passing did not diminish my dislike of the thought that they might overhear me, at a formal order from me he went, not to shut the door, which was beyond the strength of this bicyclist who longed for a 'motor', but to push it a little closer to. 'Now we shall be quite quiet.' So quiet were we that an American lady burst in and withdrew with apologies for having mistaken the number of her room. 'You are going to bring this young lady back with you,' I told him, after first going and banging the door with all my might (which brought in another page to see whether a window had been left open). 'You remember the name: Mlle Albertine Simonet. Anyhow, it's on the envelope. You need only say to her that it's from me. She will be delighted to come,' I added, to encourage him and preserve a scrap of my own self-esteem. 'I should say so!' 'Not at all, there is not the slightest reason to suppose that she will be glad to come. It's a great nuisance getting here from Berneville.' 'I understand!' 'You will tell her to come with you.' 'Yes, yes, yes, yes, I understand perfectly,' he replied, in that sharp, precise tone which had long ceased to make a 'good impression' upon me because I knew that it was almost mechanical and covered with its apparent clearness plenty of uncertainty and stupidity. 'When will you be back?' 'Haven't any too much time,' said the lift-boy, who, carrying to extremes the grammatical rule that forbids the repetition of personal pronouns before coordinate verbs, omitted the pronoun altogether. 'Can go there all right. Leave was stopped this afternoon, because there was a dinner for twenty at luncheon. And it was my turn off duty today. So it's all right if I go out a bit this evening. Take my bike with me. Get there in no time.' And an hour later he reappeared and said: 'Monsieur's had to wait, but the young lady's come with me. She's down below.' 'Oh, thanks very much; the porter won't be cross with me?' 'Monsieur Paul? Doesn't even know where I've been. The head of the door himself can't say a word.' But once, after I had told him: 'You absolutely must bring her back with you,' he reported to me with a smile: 'You know, I couldn't find her. She's not there. Couldn't wait any longer; was afraid of getting it like my colleague who was "missed from the hotel" ' (for the lift-boy, who used the word 'rejoin' of a profession which one joined for the first time, 'I should like to rejoin the post-office,' to make up for this, or to mitigate the calamity, were his own career at stake, or to insinuate it more delicately and treacherously were the victim someone else, elided the prefix and said: 'I know he's been "missed" '). It was not with any evil intent that he smiled, but from sheer timidity. He thought that he was diminishing the magnitude of his crime by making a joke of it. In the same way, if he had said to me: 'You know, I couldn't find her,' this did not mean that he really thought that I knew it already. On the contrary, he was all too certain that I did not know it, and, what was more, was afraid to tell me. And so he said 'you know' to ward off the terror which menaced him as he uttered the words that were to bring me the knowledge. We ought never to lose our tempers with people who, when we find fault with them, begin to titter. They do so not because they are laughing at us, but because they are trembling lest we should be angry. Let us show all pity and tenderness to those who laugh. For all the world like a stroke, the lift-boy's anxiety had wrought in him not merely an apoplectic flush but an alteration in his speech which had suddenly become familiar. He wound up by telling me that Albertine was not at Egreville, that she would not be coming back there before nine o'clock, and that if betimes (which meant, by chance) she came back earlier, my message would be given her, and in any case she would be with me before one o'clock in the morning.*

It was not this evening, however, that my cruel mistrust began to take solid form. No, to make no mystery about it, although the incident did not occur until some weeks later, it arose out of a remark made by Cottard. Albertine and her friends had insisted that day upon dragging me to the casino at Incarville where, as luck would have it, I should not have joined them (having intended to go and see Mme Verdurin who had invited me again and again), had I not been held up at Incarville itself by a breakdown of the tram which it would take a considerable time to repair. As I strolled up and down waiting for the men to finish working at it, I found myself all of a sudden face to face with Doctor Cottard, who had come to Incarville to see a patient. I almost hesitated to greet him as he had not answered any of my letters. But friendship does not express itself in the same way in different people. Not having been brought up to observe the same fixed rules of behaviour as well-bred people, Cottard was full of good intentions of which one knew nothing, even denying their existence, until the day when he had an opportunity of displaying them. He apologised, had indeed received my letters, had reported my whereabouts to the Verdurins who were most anxious to see me and whom he urged me to go and see. He even proposed to take me to them there and then, for he was waiting for the little local train to take him back there for dinner. As I hesitated and he had still some time before his train (for there was bound to be still a considerable delay), I made him come with me to the little casino, one of those that had struck me as being so gloomy on the evening of my first arrival, now filled with the tumult of the girls, who, in the absence of male partners, were dancing together. Andrée came sliding along the floor towards me; I was meaning to

* Translator's note: In the French text of *Sodome et Gomorrhe*, Volume I ends at this point.

go off with Cottard in a moment to the Verdurins', when I definitely declined his offer, seized by an irresistible desire to stay with Albertine. The fact was, I had just heard her laugh. And her laugh at once suggested the rosy flesh, the fragrant portals between which it had just made its way, seeming also, as strong, sensual and revealing as the scent of geraniums, to carry with it some microscopic particles of their substance, irritant and secret.

One of the girls, a stranger to me, sat down at the piano, and Andrée invited Albertine to waltz with her. Happy in the thought that I was going to remain in this little casino with these girls, I remarked to Cottard how well they danced together. But he, taking the professional point of view of a doctor and with an ill-breeding which overlooked the fact that they were my friends, although he must have seen me shaking hands with them, replied: 'Yes, but parents are very rash to allow their daughters to form such habits. I should certainly never let mine come here. Are they nice-looking, though? I can't see their faces. There now, look,' he went on, pointing to Albertine and Andrée who were waltzing slowly, tightly clasped together, 'I have left my glasses behind and I don't see very well, but they are certainly keenly roused. It is not sufficiently known that women derive most excitement from their breasts. And theirs, as you see, are completely touching.' And indeed the contact had been unbroken between the breasts of Andrée and of Albertine. I do not know whether they heard or guessed Cottard's observation, but they gently broke the contact while continuing to waltz. At that moment Andrée said something to Albertine, who laughed, the same deep and penetrating laugh that I had heard before. But all that it wafted to me this time was a feeling of pain; Albertine appeared to be revealing by it, to be making Andrée share some exquisite, secret thrill. It rang out like the first or the last strains of a ball to which one has not been invited. I left the place with Cottard, distracted by his conversation, thinking only at odd moments of the scene I had just witnessed. This does not mean that Cottard's conversation was interesting. It had indeed, at that moment, become bitter, for we had just seen Doctor du Boulbon go past without noticing us. He had come down to spend some time on the other side of Balbec bay, where he was greatly in demand. Now, albeit Cottard was in the habit of declaring that he did no professional work during the holidays, he had hoped to build up a select practice along the coast, a hope which du Boulbon's presence there doomed to disappointment. Certainly, the Balbec doctor could not stand in Cottard's way. He was merely a thoroughly conscientious doctor who knew everything, and to whom you could not mention the slightest irritation of the skin without his immediately prescribing, in a complicated formula, the ointment, lotion or liniment that would put you right. As Marie Gineste used to say, in her charming speech, he knew how to 'charm' cuts and sores. But he was in no way eminent. He had indeed caused Cottard some slight annoyance. The latter, now that he was anxious to exchange his Chair for that of Therapeutics, had begun to specialise in toxic actions. These, a perilous innovation in medicine, give an excuse for changing the labels in the chemists' shops, where every preparation is declared to be in no way toxic, unlike its substitutes, and indeed to be disintoxicant. It is the fashionable cry; at the most there may survive below in illegible lettering, like the faint trace of an older fashion, the assurance that the preparation has been carefully disinfected. Toxic actions serve also to reassure the patient, who learns with joy that his paralysis is merely a toxic disturbance. Now, a Grand Duke who had come for a few days to Balbec and whose eye was extremely swollen had sent for Cottard who, in return for a wad of hundred-franc notes (the Professor refused to see anyone for less), had put down the inflammation to a toxic condition and prescribed a disintoxicant treatment. As the swelling did not go down, the Grand Duke fell back upon the general practitioner of Balbec, who in five minutes had removed a speck of dust. The following day, the swelling had gone. A celebrated specialist in nervous diseases was, however, a more dangerous rival. He was a rubicund, jovial person, since, for one thing, the constant society of nervous wrecks did not prevent him from enjoying excellent health, but also so as to reassure his patients by the hearty merriment of his 'Good-morning' and 'Goodbye', while quite ready to lend the strength of his muscular arms to fastening them in strait-waistcoats later on. Nevertheless, whenever you spoke to him at a party, whether of politics or of literature, he would listen to you with a kindly attention, as though he were saying: 'What is it all about?' without at once giving an opinion, as though it were a matter for consultation. But anyhow he, whatever his talent might be, was a specialist. And so the whole of Cottard's rage was heaped upon du Boulbon. But I soon bade goodbye to the Verdurins' professional friend, and returned to Balbec, after promising him that I would pay them a visit before long.

The mischief that his remarks about Albertine and Andrée had done me was extreme, but its worst effects were not immediately felt by me, as happens with those forms of poisoning which begin to act only after a certain time.

Albertine, on the night after the lift-boy had gone in search of her, did not appear, notwithstanding his assurances. Certainly, personal charm is a less frequent cause of love than a speech such as: 'No, this evening I shall not be free.' We barely notice this speech if we are with friends; we are gay all the evening, a certain image never enters our mind; during those hours it remains dipped in the necessary solution; when we return home we find the plate developed and perfectly clear. We become aware that life is no longer the life which we would have surrendered for a trifle the day before, because, even if we continue not to fear death, we no longer dare think of a parting.

From, however, not one o'clock in the morning (the limit fixed by the lift-boy), but three o'clock, I no longer felt as in former times the anguish of seeing the chance of her coming diminish. The certainty that she would not now come brought me a complete, refreshing calm; this night was simply a night like all the rest during which I did not see her, such was the idea from which I started. After which, the thought that I should see her in the morning, or some other day, outlining itself upon the blank which I submissively accepted, became pleasant. Sometimes, during these nights of waiting, our anguish is due to a drug which we have taken. The sufferer, misinterpreting his own symptoms, thinks that he is anxious about the woman who fails to appear. Love is engendered in these cases, as are certain nervous maladies, by the inaccurate explanation of a state of discomfort. An explanation which it is useless to correct, at any rate so far as love is concerned, a sentiment which (whatever its cause) is invariably in error.

Next day, when Albertine wrote to me that she had only just got back to Epreville, and so had not received my note in time, and was coming, if she might, to see me that evening, behind the words of her letter, as behind those that she had said to me once over the telephone, I thought I could detect the presence of pleasures, of people whom she had preferred to me. Once again, I was stirred from head to foot by the painful longing to know what she could have been doing, by the latent love which we always carry within us; I almost thought for a moment that it was going to attach me to Albertine, but it confined itself to a stationary throbbing, the last echo of which died away without the machine's having been set in motion.

I had failed during my first visit to Balbec – and perhaps, for that matter, Andrée had failed equally – to understand Albertine's character. I had put it down as frivolous, but had not known whether our combined supplications might not succeed in keeping her with us and making her forego a garden-party, a donkey ride, a picnic. During my second visit to Balbec, I began to suspect that this frivolity was only for show, the garden-party a mere screen, if not an invention. She showed herself in various colours in the following incident (by which I mean the incident as seen by me, from my side of the glass which was by no means transparent, and without my having any means of determining what reality there was on the other side). Albertine was making me the most passionate protestations of affection. She looked at the time because she had to go and call upon a lady who was at home, it appeared, every afternoon at five o'clock, at Infreville. Tormented by suspicion, and feeling at the same time far from well, I asked Albertine, I implored her to remain with me. It was impossible (and indeed she could wait only five minutes longer) because it would annoy the lady who was far from hospitable, highly susceptible and, said Albertine, a perfect nuisance. 'But one can easily cut a call.' 'No, my aunt has always told me that the chief thing is politeness.' 'But I have so often seen you being impolite.' 'It's not the same thing, the lady would be angry with me and would say nasty things about me to my aunt. I'm pretty well in her bad books already. She expects me to go and see her.' 'But if she's at home every day?' Here Albertine, feeling that she was caught, changed her line of argument. 'So she is at home every day. But today I've made arrangements to meet some other girls there. It will be less boring that way.' 'So then, Albertine, you prefer this lady and your friends to me, since, rather than miss paying an admittedly boring call, you prefer to leave me here alone, sick and wretched?' 'I don't care if it is boring. I'm going for their sake. I shall bring them home in my trap. Otherwise they won't have any way of getting back.' I pointed out to Albertine that there were trains from Infreville up to ten o'clock at night. 'Quite true, but don't you see, it is possible that we may be asked to stay to dinner. She is very hospitable.' 'Very well then, you won't.' 'I should only make my aunt angry.' 'Besides, you can dine with her and catch the ten o'clock train.' 'It's cutting it rather fine.' 'Then I can never go and dine in town and come back by train. But listen, Albertine. We are going to do something quite simple, I feel that the fresh air will do me good; since you can't give up your lady, I am going to come with you to Infreville. Don't be alarmed, I shan't go as far as the Tour Elisabeth' (the lady's villa), 'I shall see neither the lady nor your friends.' Albertine started as though she had received a violent blow. For a moment, she was unable to speak. She explained that the sea bathing was not doing her any good. 'If you don't want me to come with you?' 'How can you say such a thing, you know there's nothing I enjoy more than going out with you.' A sudden change of tactics had occurred. 'Since we are going for a drive together,' she said to me, 'why not go out in the other direction, we might dine together. It would be so nice. After all, that side of Balbec is much the prettier. I'm getting sick of Infreville and all those little spinach-bed places.' 'But your aunt's friend will be annoyed if you don't go and see her.' 'Very well, let her be.' 'No, it is wrong to annoy people.' 'But she won't even notice that I'm not there, she has people every day; I can go tomorrow, the next day, next week, the week after, it's exactly the same.' 'And what about your friends?' 'Oh, they've cut me often enough. It's my turn now.' 'But from the side you suggest there's no train back after nine.' 'Well, what's the matter with that? Nine will do perfectly. Besides, one need never think about getting back. We can always find a cart, a bike, if the worse comes to the worst, we have legs.' 'We can always find, Albertine, how you go on! Out Infreville way, where the villages run into one another, well and good. But the other way, it's a very different matter.' 'That way too. I promise to bring you back safe and sound.' I felt that Albertine was giving up for my sake some plan arranged beforehand of which she refused to tell me, and that there was someone else who would be as unhappy as I was. Seeing that what she had intended to do was out of the question, since I insisted upon accompanying her, she gave it up altogether. She knew that the loss was not irremediable. For, like all women who have a number of irons in the fire, she had one resource that never failed: suspicion and jealousy. Of course she did not seek to arouse them, quite the contrary. But lovers are so suspicious that they instantly scent out falsehood. With the result that Albertine, being no better than anyone else, knew by experience (without for a moment imagining that she owed her experience to jealousy) that she could always be certain of meeting people again after she had failed to keep an appointment. The stranger whom she was deserting for me would be hurt, would love her all the more for that (though Albertine did not know that this was the reason), and, so as not to prolong the agony, would return to her of his own accord, as I should have done. But I had no desire either to give pain to another, or to tire myself, or to enter upon the terrible course of investigation, of multiform, unending vigilance. 'No, Albertine, I do not wish to spoil your pleasure, go to your lady at Infreville, or rather to the person you really mean to see, it is all the same to me. The real reason why I am not coming with you is that you do not wish it, the outing you would be taking with me is not the one you meant to take, which is proved by your having contradicted yourself at least five times without noticing it.' Poor Albertine was afraid that her contradictions, which she had not noticed, had been more serious than they were. Not knowing exactly what fibs she had told me: 'It is quite on the cards that I did contradict myself. The sea air makes me lose my head altogether. I'm always calling things by the wrong names.' And (what proved to me that she would not, now, require many tender affirmations to make me believe her) I felt a stab in my heart as I listened to this admission of what I had but faintly imagined. 'Very well, that's settled, I'm off,' she said in a tragic tone, not without looking at the time to see whether she was making herself late for the other person, now that I had provided her with an excuse for not spending the evening with myself. 'It's too bad of you. I alter all my plans to spend a nice, long evening with you, and it's you that won't have it, and you accuse me of telling lies. I've never known you to be so cruel. The sea shall be my tomb. I will never see you any more.' (My heart leaped at these words, albeit I was certain that she would come again next day, as she did.) 'I shall drown myself, I shall throw myself into the water.' 'Like Sappho.' 'There you go, insulting me again. You suspect not only what I say but what I do.' 'But, my lamb, I didn't mean anything, I swear to you, you know Sappho flung herself into the sea.' 'Yes, yes, you have no faith in me.' She saw that it was twenty minutes to the hour by the clock; she was afraid of missing her appointment, and choosing the shortest form of farewell (for which as it happened she apologised by coming to see me again next day, the other person presumably not being free then), she dashed from the room, crying: 'Goodbye for ever', in a heartbroken tone. And perhaps she was heartbroken. For knowing what she was about at that moment better than I, being at the same time more strict and more indulgent towards herself than I was towards her, she may all the same have had a fear that I might refuse to see her again after the way in which she had left me. And I believe that she was attached to me, so much so that the other person was more jealous than I was.

Some days later, at Balbec, while we were in the ballroom of the casino, there entered Bloch's sister and cousin, who had both turned out quite pretty, but whom I refrained from greeting on account of my girl friends, because the younger one, the cousin, was notoriously living with the actress whose acquaintance she had made during my first visit. Andrée, at a murmured allusion to this scandal, said to me: 'Oh! About that sort of thing I'm like Albertine; there's nothing we both loathe so much as that sort of thing.' As for Albertine, on sitting down to talk to me upon the sofa, she had turned her back on the disreputable pair. I had noticed, however, that, before she changed her position, at the moment when Mlle Bloch and her cousin appeared, my friend's eyes had flashed with that sudden, close attention which now and again imparted to the face of this frivolous girl a serious, indeed a grave air, and left her pensive afterwards. But Albertine had at once turned towards myself a gaze which nevertheless remained singularly fixed and meditative. Mlle Bloch and her cousin having finally left the room after laughing and shouting in a loud and vulgar manner, I asked Albertine whether the little fair one (the one who was so intimate with the actress) was not the girl who had won the prize the day before in the procession of flowers. 'I don't know,' said Albertine, 'is one of them fair? I must confess they don't interest me particularly, I have never looked at them. Is one of them fair?' she asked her three girl friends with a detached air of enquiry. When applied to people whom Albertine passed every day on the front, this ignorance seemed to me too profound to be genuine. 'They didn't appear to be looking at us much either,' I said to Albertine, perhaps (on the assumption, which I did not however consciously form, that Albertine loved her own sex) to free her from any regret by pointing out to her that she had not attracted the attention of these girls and that, generally speaking, it is not customary even for the most vicious of women to take an interest in girls whom they do not know. 'They weren't looking at us!' was Albertine's astonished reply. 'Why, they did nothing else the whole time.' 'But you can't possibly tell,' I said to her, 'you had your back to them.' 'Very well, and what about that?' she replied, pointing out to me, set in the wall in front of us, a large mirror which I had not noticed and upon which I now realised that my friend, while talking to me, had never ceased to fix her troubled, preoccupied eyes.

Ever since the day when Cottard had accompanied me into the little casino at Incarville, albeit I did not share the opinion that he had expressed, Albertine had seemed to me different; the sight of her made me lose my temper. I myself had changed, quite as much as she had changed in my eyes. I had ceased to bear her any good will; to her face, behind her back when there was a chance of my words being repeated to her, I spoke of her in the most insulting language. There were, however, intervals of calmer feeling. One day I learned that Albertine and Andrée had both accepted an invitation to Elstir's. Feeling certain that this was in order that they might, on the return journey, amuse themselves like schoolgirls on holiday by imitating the manners of fast young women, and in so doing find an unmaidenly pleasure the thought of which wrung my heart, without announcing my intention, to embarrass them and to deprive Albertine of the pleasure on which she was reckoning, I paid an unexpected call at his studio. But I found only Andrée there. Albertine had chosen another day when her aunt was to go there with her. Then I said to myself that Cottard must have been mistaken; the favourable impression that I received from Andrée's presence there without her friend remained with me and made me feel more kindly disposed towards Albertine. But this feeling lasted no longer than the healthy moments of delicate people subject to passing maladies, who are prostrated again by the merest trifle. Albertine incited Andrée to actions which, without going very far, were perhaps not altogether innocent; pained by this suspicion, I managed in the end to repel it. No sooner was I healed of it than it revived under another form. I had just seen Andrée, with one of

those graceful gestures that came naturally to her, lay her head coaxingly on
Albertine's shoulder, kiss her on the throat, half shutting her eyes; or else
they had exchanged a glance; a remark had been made by somebody who
had seen them going down together to bathe: little trifles such as habitually
float in the surrounding atmosphere where the majority of people absorb
them all day long without injury to their health or alteration of their mood,
but which have a morbid effect and breed fresh sufferings in a nature
predisposed to receive them. Sometimes even without my having seen
Albertine again, without anyone's having spoken to me about her, there
would flash from my memory some vision of her with Gisèle in an attitude
which had seemed to me innocent at the time; it was enough now to destroy
the peace of mind that I had managed to recover, I had no longer any need
to go and breathe dangerous germs outside, I had, as Cottard would have
said, supplied my own toxin. I thought then of all that I had been told about
Swann's love for Odette, of the way in which Swann had been tricked all his
life. Indeed, when I come to think of it, the hypothesis that made me
gradually build up the whole of Albertine's character and give a painful
interpretation to every moment of a life that I could not control in its
entirety, was the memory, the rooted idea of Mme Swann's character, as it
had been described to me. These accounts helped my imagination, in after
years, to take the line of supposing that Albertine might, instead of being a
good girl, have had the same immorality, the same faculty of deception as a
reformed prostitute, and I thought of all the sufferings that would in that
case have been in store for me had I ever really been her lover.

One day, outside the Grand Hotel, where we were gathered on the front,
I had just been addressing Albertine in the harshest, most humiliating
language, and Rosemonde was saying: 'Oh, how you have changed your
mind about her; why, she used to be everything, it was she who ruled the
roost, and now she isn't even fit to be thrown to the dogs.' I was beginning,
in order to make my attitude towards Albertine still more marked, to say all
the nicest things I could think of to Andrée, who, if she was tainted with the
same vice, seemed to me to have more excuse for it since she was sickly and
neurasthenic, when we saw emerging at the steady trot of its pair of horses
into the street at right angles to the front, at the corner of which we were
standing, Mme de Cambremer's barouche. The chief magistrate who, at
that moment, was advancing towards us, sprang back upon recognising the
carriage, in order not to be seen in our company; then, when he thought
that the Marquise's eye might catch his, bowed to her with an immense
sweep of his hat. But the carriage, instead of continuing, as might have been
expected, along the Rue de la Mer, disappeared through the gate of the

hotel. It was quite ten minutes later when the lift-boy, out of breath, came to announce to me: 'It's the Marquise de Camembert, she's come here to see Monsieur. I've been up to the room, I looked in the reading-room, I couldn't find Monsieur anywhere. Luckily I thought of looking on the beach.' He had barely ended this speech when, followed by her daughter-in-law and by an extremely ceremonious gentleman, the Marquise advanced towards me, coming on probably from some afternoon tea-party in the neighbourhood, and bowed down not so much by age as by the mass of costly trinkets with which she felt it more sociable and more befitting her rank to cover herself, in order to appear as 'well dressed' as possible to the people whom she went to visit. It was in fact that 'landing' of the Cambremers at the hotel which my grandmother had so greatly dreaded long ago when she wanted us not to let Legrandin know that we might perhaps be going to Balbec. Then Mamma used to laugh at these fears inspired by an event which she considered impossible. And here it was actually happening, but by different channels and without Legrandin's having had any part in it. 'Do you mind my staying here, if I shan't be in your way?' asked Albertine (in whose eyes there lingered, brought there by the cruel things I had just been saying to her, a pair of tears which I observed without seeming to see them, but not without rejoicing inwardly at the sight), 'there is something I want to say to you.' A hat with feathers, itself surmounted by a sapphire pin, was perched haphazard upon Mme de Cambremer's wig, like a badge the display of which was necessary but sufficient, its place immaterial, its elegance conventional and its stability superfluous. Notwithstanding the heat, the good lady had put on a jet cloak, like a dalmatic, over which hung an ermine stole the wearing of which seemed to depend not upon the temperature and season, but upon the nature of the ceremony. And on Mme de Cambremer's bosom a baronial torse, fastened to a chain, dangled like a pectoral cross. The gentleman was an eminent lawyer from Paris, of noble family, who had come down to spend a few days with the Cambremers. He was one of those men whom their vast professional experience inclines to look down upon their profession, and who say, for instance: 'I know that I am a good pleader, so it no longer amuses me to plead', or: 'I'm no longer interested in operating, I know that I'm a good operator.' Men of intelligence, *artists*, they see themselves in their maturity, richly endowed by success, shining with that intellect, that artistic nature which their professional brethren recognise in them and which confer upon them a kind of taste and discernment. They form a passion for the paintings not of a great artist, but of an artist who nevertheless is highly distinguished, and spend upon the purchase of his work the large sums that their career procures for them. Le Sidaner was the artist chosen by the Cambremers' friend, who incidentally was a delightful person. He talked well about books, but not about the books of the true masters, those who have mastered themselves. The only irritating habit that this amateur displayed was his constant use of certain ready made expressions, such as 'for the most part', which gave an air of importance and incompleteness to the matter of which he was speaking. Madame de Cambremer had taken the opportunity, she told me, of a party which some friends of hers had been giving that afternoon in the Balbec direction to come and call upon me, as she had promised Robert de Saint-Loup. 'You know he's coming down to these parts quite soon for a few days: His uncle Charlus is staying near here with his sister-in-law, the Duchesse de Luxembourg, and M. de Saint-Loup means to take the opportunity of paying his aunt a visit and going to see his old regiment, where he is very popular, highly respected. We often have visits from officers who are never tired of singing his praises. How nice it would be if you and he would give us the pleasure of coming together to Féterne.' I presented Albertine and her friends. Mme de Cambremer introduced us all to her daughter-in-law. The latter, so frigid towards the petty nobility with whom her seclusion at Féterne forced her to associate, so reserved, so afraid of compromising herself, held out her hand to me with a radiant smile, safe as she felt herself and delighted at seeing a friend of Robert de Saint-Loup, whom he, possessing a sharper social intuition than he allowed to appear, had mentioned to her as being a great friend of the Guermantes. So, unlike her mother-in-law, Mme de Cambremer employed two vastly different forms of politeness. It was at the most the former kind, dry, insupportable, that she would have conceded me had I met her through her brother Legrandin. But for a friend of the Guermantes she had not smiles enough. The most convenient room in the hotel for entertaining visitors was the reading-room, that place once so terrible into which I now went a dozen times every day, emerging freely, my own master, like those mildly afflicted lunatics who have so long been inmates of an asylum that the superintendent trusts them with a latchkey. And so I offered to take Mme de Cambremer there. And as this room no longer filled me with shyness and no longer held any charm for me, since the faces of things change for us like the faces of people, it was without the slightest emotion that I made this suggestion. But she declined it, preferring to remain out of doors, and we sat down in the open air, on the terrace of the hotel. I found there and rescued a volume of Madame de Sévigné which Mamma had not had time to carry off in her precipitate flight, when she heard that visitors had called for me. No less than my grandmother, she dreaded these invasions of strangers, and, in her fear of being too late to escape if she let herself be seen, would fly from the room with a rapidity which always made my father and me laugh at her. Madame de Cambremer carried in her hand, with the handle of a sunshade, a number of embroidered bags, a holdall, a gold purse from which there dangled strings of garnets, and a lace handkerchief. I could not help thinking that it would be more convenient for her to deposit them on a chair; but I felt that it would be unbecoming and useless to ask her to lay aside the ornaments of her pastoral visitation and her social priesthood. We gazed at the calm sea upon which, here and there, a few gulls floated like white petals. Because of the 'mean level' to which social conversation reduces us and also of our desire to attract not by means of those qualities of which we are ourselves unaware but of those which, we suppose, ought to be appreciated by the people who are with us, I began instinctively to talk to Mme de Cambremer *née* Legrandin in the strain in which her brother might have talked. 'They appear,' I said, referring to the gulls, 'as motionless and as white as water-lilies.' And indeed they did appear to be offering a lifeless object to the little waves which tossed them about, so much so that the waves, by contrast, seemed in their pursuit of them to be animated by a deliberate intention, to have acquired life. The dowager Marquise could not find words enough to do justice to the superb view of the sea that we had from Balbec, or to say how she envied it, she who from la Raspelière (where for that matter she was not living that year) had only such a distant glimpse of the waves. She had two remarkable habits, due at once to her exalted passion for the arts (especially for the art of music), and to her want of teeth. Whenever she talked of aesthetic subjects her salivary glands – like those of certain animals when in rut – became so overcharged that the old lady's edentulous mouth allowed to escape from the corners of her faintly moustached lips a trickle of moisture for which that was not the proper place. Immediately she drew it in again with a deep sigh, like a person recovering his breath. Secondly, if her subject were some piece of music of surpassing beauty, in her enthusiasm she would raise her arms and utter a few decisive opinions, vigorously chewed and at a pinch issuing from her nose. Now it had never occurred to me that the vulgar beach at Balbec could indeed offer a 'seascape', and Mme de Cambremer's simple words changed my ideas in that respect. On the other hand, as I told her, I had always heard people praise the matchless view from la Raspelière, perched on the summit of the hill, where, in a great drawing-room with two fireplaces, one whole row of windows swept the gardens, and, through the branches of the trees, the sea as far as Balbec and beyond it, and the other row the valley. 'How nice of you to say so, and how well you put it: the sea through the branches. It is exquisite, one would say . . . a painted fan.' And I gathered from a deep breath intended to catch the falling spittle and dry the moustaches, that the compliment was sincere. But the Marquise *née* Legrandin remained cold, to show her contempt not for my words but for those of her mother-in-law. Besides, she not only despised the other's intellect but deplored her affability, being always afraid that people might not form a sufficiently high idea of the Cambremers. 'And how charming the name is', said I. 'One would like to know the origin of all those names.' 'That one I can tell you,' the old lady answered modestly. 'It is a family place, it came from my grandmother Arrachepel, not an illustrious family, but a decent and very old country stock.' 'What! Not illustrious!' her daughter-in-law tartly interrupted her. 'A whole window in Bayeux cathedral is filled with their arms, and the principal church at Avranches has their tombs. If these old names interest you,' she added, 'you've come a year too late. We managed to appoint to the living of Criquetot, in spite of all the difficulties about changing from one diocese to another, the parish priest of a place where I myself have some land, a long way from here, Combray, where the worthy cleric felt that he was becoming neurasthenic. Unfortunately, the sea air was no good to him at his age; his neurasthenia grew worse and he has returned to Combray. But he amused himself while he was our neighbour in going about looking up all the old charters, and he compiled quite an interesting little pamphlet on the place names of the district. It has given him a fresh interest, too, for it seems he is spending his last years in writing a great work upon Combray and its surroundings. I shall send you his pamphlet on the surroundings of Féterne. It is worthy of a Benedictine. You will find the most interesting things in it about our old Raspelière, of which my mother-in-law speaks far too modestly.' 'In any case, this year,' replied the dowager Mme de Cambremer, 'la Raspelière is no longer ours and does not belong to me. But I can see that you have a painter's instincts; I am sure you sketch, and I should so like to show you Féterne, which is far finer than la Raspelière.' For as soon as the Cambremers had let this latter residence to the Verdurins, its commanding situation had at once ceased to appear to them as it had appeared for so many years past, that is to say to offer the advantage, without parallel in the neighbourhood, of looking out over both sea and valley, and had on the other hand, suddenly and retrospectively, presented the drawback that one had always to go up or down hill to get to or from it. In short, one might have supposed that if Mme de Cambremer had let it, it was not so much to add to her income as to spare her horses. And she proclaimed herself delighted at being able at last to have the sea always so close at hand, at Féterne, she who for so many years (forgetting the two months that she spent there) had seen it only from up above and as though in a panorama. 'I am discovering it at my age,' she said, 'and how I enjoy it! It does me a world of good. I would let la Raspelière for nothing so as to be obliged to live at Féterne.'

'To return to more interesting topics', went on Legrandin's sister, who addressed the old Marquise as 'Mother', but with the passage of years had come to treat her with insolence, 'you mentioned water-lilies: I suppose you know Claude Monet's pictures of them. What a genius! They interest me particularly because near Combray, that place where I told you I had some land . . . ' But she preferred not to talk too much about Combray. 'Why! That must be the series that Elstir told us about, the greatest painter of this generation,' exclaimed Albertine, who had said nothing so far. 'Ah! I can see that this young lady loves the arts,' cried Mme de Cambremer and, drawing a long breath, recaptured a trail of spittle. 'You will allow me to put Le Sidaner before him, Mademoiselle,' said the lawyer, smiling with the air of an expert. And, as he had enjoyed, or seen people enjoy, years ago, certain 'daring' work by Elstir, he added: 'Elstir was gifted, indeed he was one of the advance guard, but for some reason or other he never kept up, he has wasted his life.' Mme de Cambremer disagreed with the lawyer, so far as Elstir was concerned, but, greatly to the annoyance of her guest, bracketed Monet with Le Sidaner. It would be untrue to say that she was a fool; she was overflowing with a kind of intelligence that meant nothing to me. As the sun was beginning to set, the seagulls were now yellow, like the water-lilies on another canvas of that series by Monet. I said that I knew it, and (continuing to copy the diction of her brother, whom I had not yet dared to name) added that it was a pity that she had not thought of coming a day earlier, for, at the same hour, there would have been a Poussin light for her to admire. Had some Norman squireen, unknown to the Guermantes, told her that she ought to have come a day earlier, Mme de Cambremer-Legrandin would doubtless have drawn herself up with an offended air. But I might have been far more familiar still, and she would have been all smiles and sweetness; I might in the warmth of that fine afternoon devour my fill of that rich honey cake which Mme de Cambremer so rarely was and which took the place of the dish of pastry that it had not occurred to me to offer my guests. But the name of Poussin, without altering the amenity of the society lady, called forth the protests of the connoisseur. On hearing that name, she produced six times in almost continuous succession that little smack of the tongue against the lips which serves to convey to a child who is misbehaving at once a reproach for having begun and a warning not to continue. 'In heaven's

name, after a painter like Monet, who is an absolute genius, don't go and
mention an old hack without a vestige of talent, like Poussin. I don't mind
telling you frankly that I find him the deadliest bore. I mean to say, you can't
really call that sort of thing painting. Monet, Degas, Manet, yes, there are
painters if you like! It is a curious thing,' she went on, fixing a scrutinous and
ecstatic gaze upon a vague point in space where she could see what was in
her mind, 'it is a curious thing, I used at one time to prefer Manet.
Nowadays, I still admire Manet, of course, but I believe I like Monet even
more. Oh! The *Cathedrals*!' She was as scrupulous as she was condescending
in informing me of the evolution of her taste. And one felt that the phases
through which that taste had evolved were not, in her eyes, any less
important than the different manners of Monet himself. Not that I had any
reason to feel flattered by her taking me into her confidence as to her
preferences, for even in the presence of the narrowest of provincial ladies
she could not remain for five minutes without feeling the need to confess
them. When a noble dame of Avranches, who would have been incapable of
distinguishing between Mozart and Wagner, said in Mme de Cambremer's
hearing: 'We saw nothing of any interest while we were in Paris, we went
once to the Opéra-Comique, they were doing *Pelléas et Mélisande*, it's
dreadful stuff', Mme de Cambremer not only boiled with rage but felt
obliged to exclaim: 'Not at all, it's a little gem', and to 'argue the point'.
It was perhaps a Combray habit which she had picked up from my
grandmother's sisters, who called it 'fighting in the good cause', and loved
the dinner-parties at which they knew all through the week that they would
have to defend their idols against the Philistines. Similarly, Mme de
Cambremer liked to 'fly into a passion' and wrangle about art, as other
people do about politics. She stood up for Debussy as she would have stood
up for a woman friend whose conduct had been criticised. She must
however have known very well that when she said: 'Not at all, it's a little
gem', she could not improvise in the other lady, whom she was putting in
her place, the whole progressive development of artistic culture on the
completion of which they would come naturally to an agreement without
any need of discussion. 'I must ask Le Sidaner what he thinks of Poussin,'
the lawyer remarked to me. 'He's a regular recluse, never opens his mouth,
but I know how to get things out of him.'

'Anyhow,' Mme de Cambremer went on, 'I have a horror of sunsets,
they're so romantic, so operatic. That is why I can't abide my mother-in-
law's house, with its tropical plants. You will see it, it's just like a public
garden at Monte-Carlo. That's why I prefer your coast, here. It is more
sombre, more sincere; there's a little lane from which one doesn't see the

sea. On rainy days, there's nothing but mud, it's a little world apart. It's just the same at Venice, I detest the Grand Canal and I don't know anything so touching as the little alleys. But it's all a question of one's surroundings.' 'But,' I remarked to her, feeling that the only way to rehabilitate Poussin in Mme de Cambremer's eyes was to inform her that he was once more in fashion, 'M. Degas assures us that he knows nothing more beautiful than the Poussins at Chantilly.' 'Indeed? I don't know the ones at Chantilly,' said Mme de Cambremer who had no wish to differ from Degas, 'but I can speak about the ones in the Louvre, which are appalling.' 'He admires them immensely too.' 'I must look at them again. My impressions of them are rather distant,' she replied after a moment's silence, and as though the favourable opinion which she was certain, before very long, to form of Poussin would depend, not upon the information that I had just communicated to her, but upon the supplementary and, this time, final examination that she intended to make of the Poussins in the Louvre in order to be in a position to change her mind. Contenting myself with what was a first step towards retraction since, if she did not yet admire the Poussins, she was adjourning the matter for further consideration, in order not to keep her on tenterhooks any longer, I told her mother-in-law how much I had heard of the wonderful flowers at Féterne. In modest terms she spoke of the little presbytery garden that she had behind the house, into which in the mornings, by simply pushing open a door, she went in her wrapper to feed her peacocks, hunt for new-laid eggs, and gather the zinnias or roses which, on the sideboard, framing the creamed eggs or fried fish in a border of flowers, reminded her of her garden paths. 'It is true, we have a great many roses,' she told me, 'our rose garden is almost too near the house, there are days when it makes my head ache. It is nicer on the terrace at la Raspelière where the breeze carries the scent of the roses, but it is not so heady.' I turned to her daughter-in-law. 'It is just like *Pelléas*,' I said to her, to gratify her taste for the modern, 'that scent of roses wafted up to the terraces. It is so strong in the score that, as I suffer from hay-fever and rose-fever, it sets me sneezing every time I listen to that scene.'

'What a marvellous thing *Pelléas* is,' cried Mme de Cambremer, 'I'm mad about it;' and, drawing closer to me with the gestures of a savage woman seeking to captivate me, using her fingers to pick out imaginary notes, she began to hum something which, I supposed, represented to her the farewells of Pelléas, and continued with a vehement persistence as though it had been important that Mme de Cambremer should at that moment remind me of that scene or rather should prove to me that she herself remembered it. 'I think it is even finer than *Parsifal*,' she added, 'because in *Parsifal* the most beautiful things are surrounded with a sort of halo of melodious phrases, which are bad simply because they are melodious.' 'I know you are a great musician, Madame,' I said to the dowager. 'I should so much like to hear you play.' Mme de Cambremer-Legrandin gazed at the sea so as not to be drawn into the conversation. Being of the opinion that what her mother-in-law liked was not music at all, she regarded the talent, a sham talent according to her, though in reality of the very highest order that the other was admitted to possess, as a technical accomplishment devoid of interest. It was true that Chopin's only surviving pupil declared, and with justice, that the Master's style of playing, his 'feeling' had been transmitted, through herself, to Mme de Cambremer alone, but to play like Chopin was far from being a recommendation in the eyes of Legrandin's sister, who despised nobody so much as the Polish composer. 'Oh! They are flying away,' exclaimed Albertine, pointing to the gulls which, casting aside for a moment their flowery incognito, were rising in a body towards the sun. 'Their giant wings from walking hinder them,' quoted Mme de Cambremer, confusing the seagull with the albatross. 'I do love them; I used to see them at Amsterdam,' said Albertine. 'They smell of the sea, they come and breathe the salt air through the paving stones even.' 'Oh! So you have been in Holland, you know the Vermeers?' Mme de Cambremer asked imperiously, in the tone in which she would have said: 'You know the Guermantes?' for snobbishness in changing its subject does not change its accent. Albertine replied in the negative, thinking that they were living people. But her mistake was not apparent. 'I should be delighted to play to you,' Mme de Cambremer said to me. 'But you know I only play things that no longer appeal to your generation. I was brought up in the worship of Chopin,' she said in a lowered tone, for she was afraid of her daughter-in-law, and knew that to the latter, who considered that Chopin was not music, playing him well or badly were meaningless terms. She admitted that her mother-in-law had technique, was a finished pianist. 'Nothing will ever make me say that she is a musician,' was Mme de Cambremer-Legrandin's conclusion. Because she considered herself 'advanced', because (in matters of art only) 'one could never move far enough to the Left,' she said, she maintained not merely that music progressed, but that it progressed along one straight line, and that Debussy was in a sense a super-Wagner, slightly more advanced again than Wagner. She did not take into account the fact that if Debussy was not as independent of Wagner as she herself was to suppose in a few years' time, because we must always make use of the weapons that we have captured to free ourselves finally from the foe whom we have for the moment overpowered, he was seeking nevertheless, after the feeling of satiety that people were beginning to derive from work that was too complete, in which everything was expressed, to satisfy an opposite demand. There were theories of course, to support this reaction for the time being, like those theories which, in politics, come to the support of the laws against religious communities, of wars in the East (unnatural teaching, the Yellow Peril, etc., etc.). People said that an age of speed required rapidity in art, precisely as they might have said that the next war could not last longer than a fortnight, or that the coming of railways would kill the little places beloved of the coaches, which the motorcar, for all that, was to restore to favour. Composers were warned not to strain the attention of their audience, as though we had not at our disposal different degrees of attention, among which it rests precisely with the artist himself to arouse the highest. For the people who yawn with boredom after ten lines of a mediocre article have journeyed year after year to Bayreuth to listen to the *Ring*. Besides, the day was to come when, for a season, Debussy would be pronounced as trivial as Massenet, and the trills of Mélisande degraded to the level of Manon's. For theories and schools, like microbes and corpuscles, devour one another and by their warfare ensure the continuity of existence. But that time was still to come.

As on the Stock Exchange, when a rise occurs, a whole group of securities benefit by it, so a certain number of despised composers were gaining by the reaction, either because they did not deserve such scorn, or simply – which enabled one to be original when one sang their praises – because they had incurred it. And people even went the length of seeking out, in an isolated past, men of independent talent upon whose reputation the present movement did not seem calculated to have any influence, but of whom one of the new masters was understood to have spoken favourably. Often it was because a master, whoever he may be, however exclusive his school, judges in the light of his own untutored instincts, does justice to talent wherever it be found, or rather not so much to talent as to some agreeable inspiration which he has enjoyed in the past, which reminds him of a precious moment in his adolescence. Or, it may be, because certain artists of an earlier generation have in some fragment of their work realised something that resembles what the master has gradually become aware that he himself meant at one time to create. Then he sees the old master as a sort of precursor; he values in him, under a wholly different form, an effort that is momentarily, partially fraternal. There are bits of Turner in the work of Poussin, we find a phrase of Flaubert in Montesquieu. Sometimes, again, this rumoured predilection of the Master was due to an error, starting heaven knows where and circulated through the school. But in that case the name mentioned profited by the auspices under which it was introduced in the nick of time, for if there is an element of free will, some genuine taste expressed in the master's choice, the schools themselves go only by theory. Thus it is that the mind, following its habitual course which advances by digression, inclining first in one direction, then in the other, had brought back into the light of day a number of works to which the need for justice, or for a renewal of standards, or the taste of Debussy, or his caprice, or some remark that he had perhaps never made had added the works of Chopin. Commended by the judges in whom one had entire confidence, profiting by the admiration that was aroused by *Pelléas*, they had acquired a fresh lustre, and even the people who had not heard them again were so anxious to admire them that they did so in spite of themselves, albeit preserving the illusion of free will. But Mme de Cambremer-Legrandin spent part of the year in the country. Even in Paris, being an invalid, she was largely confined to her own room. It is true that the drawbacks of this mode of existence were noticeable chiefly in her choice of expressions which she supposed to be fashionable and which would have been more appropriate to the written language, a distinction that she did not perceive, for she derived them more from reading than from conversation. The latter is not so necessary for an exact knowledge of current opinion as of the latest expressions. Unfortunately this revival of the *Nocturnes* had not yet been announced by the critics. The news of it had been transmitted only by word of mouth among the 'younger' people. It remained unknown to Mme de Cambremer-Legrandin. I gave myself the pleasure of informing her, but by addressing my remark to her mother-in-law, as when at billiards in order to hit a ball one aims at the cushion, that Chopin, so far from being out of date, was Debussy's favourite composer. 'Indeed, that's quaint,' said the daughter-in-law with a subtle smile as though it had been merely a deliberate paradox on the part of the composer of *Pelléas*. Nevertheless it was now quite certain that in future she would always listen to Chopin with respect and even pleasure. Moreover my words which had sounded the hour of deliverance for the dowager produced on her face an expression of gratitude to myself and above all of joy. Her eyes shone like the eyes of Latude in the play entitled *Latude, or Thirty-five Years in Captivity*, and her bosom inhaled the sea air with that dilatation which Beethoven has so well described in *Fidelio*, at the point where his prisoners at last breathe again 'this life-giving air'. As for the dowager, I thought that she was going to press her hirsute lips to my cheek. 'What, you like Chopin? He likes Chopin, he likes Chopin,' she cried with a nasal trumpet-tone of passion; she might have been saying: 'What, you know Mme de Franquetot too?'

with this difference, that my relations with Mme de Franquetot would have left her completely indifferent, whereas my knowledge of Chopin plunged her in a sort of artistic delirium. Her salivary super-secretion no longer sufficed. Not having attempted even to understand the part played by Debussy in the rediscovery of Chopin, she felt only that my judgment of him was favourable. Her musical enthusiasm overpowered her. 'Elodie! Elodie! He likes Chopin!' Her bosom rose and she beat the air with her arms. 'Ah! I knew at once that you were a musician,' she cried. 'I can quite understand an artist such as you are liking him. He's so lovely!' And her voice was as pebbly as if, to express her ardour for Chopin, she had copied Demosthenes and filled her mouth with all the shingle on the beach. Then came the turn of the tide, reaching as far as her veil which she had not time to lift out of harm's way and which was flooded; and lastly the Marquise wiped away with her embroidered handkerchief the tidemark of foam in which the memory of Chopin had steeped her moustaches.

'Good heavens,' Mme de Cambremer-Legrandin remarked to me, 'I'm afraid my mother-in-law's cutting it rather fine, she's forgotten that we've got my Uncle de Ch'nouville dining. Besides, Cancan doesn't like to be kept waiting.' The word 'Cancan' was beyond me, and I supposed that she might perhaps be referring to a dog. But as for the Chenouville relatives, the explanation was as follows. With the lapse of time the young Marquise had outgrown the pleasure that she had once found in pronouncing their name in this manner. And yet it was the prospect of enjoying that pleasure that had decided her choice of a husband. In other social circles, when one referred to the Chenouville family, the custom was (whenever, that is to say, the particle was preceded by a word ending in a vowel sound, for otherwise you were obliged to lay stress upon the *de*, the tongue refusing to utter Madame d'Ch'nonceaux) that it was the mute *e* of the particle that was sacrificed. One said: 'Monsieur d'Chenouville'. The Cambremer tradition was different, but no less imperious. It was the mute *e* of Chenouville that was suppressed. Whether the name was preceded by *mon cousin* or by *ma cousine*, it was always *de Ch'nouville* and never *de Chenouville*. (Of the father of these Chenouvilles, one said 'our Uncle' for they were not sufficiently 'smart set' at Féterne to pronounce the word 'Unk' like the Guermantes, whose deliberate jargon, suppressing consonants and naturalising foreign words, was as difficult to understand as Old French or a modern dialect.) Every newcomer into the family circle at once received, in the matter of the Chenouvilles, a lesson which Mme de Cambremer-Legrandin had not required. When, paying a call one day, she had heard a girl say: 'My Aunt d'Uzai', 'My Unk de Rouan', she had not at first recognised the illustrious

names which she was in the habit of pronouncing: Uzès, and Rolîan, she had
felt the astonishment, embarrassment and shame of a person who sees
before him on the table a recently invented implement of which he does not
know the proper use and with which he dares not begin to eat. But during
that night and the next day she had rapturously repeated: 'My Aunt Uzai',
with that suppression of the final s, a suppression that had stupefied her the
day before, but which it now seemed to her so vulgar not to know that, one
of her friends having spoken to her of a bust of the Duchesse d'Uzès, Mlle
Legrandin had answered her crossly, and in an arrogant tone: 'You might at
least pronounce her name properly: Mme d'Uzai.' From that moment she
had realised that, by virtue of the transmutation of solid bodies into more
and more subtle elements, the considerable and so honourably acquired
fortune that she had inherited from her father, the finished education that
she had received, her regular attendance at the Sorbonne, whether at Caro's
lectures or at Brunetière's, and at the Lamoureux concerts, all this was to be
rendered volatile, to find its utmost sublimation in the pleasure of being able
one day to say: 'My Aunt d'Uzai'. This did not exclude the thought that she
would continue to associate, in the earlier days, at least, of her married life,
not indeed with certain women friends whom she liked and had resigned
herself to sacrificing, but with certain others whom she did not like and to
whom she looked forward to being able to say (since that, after all, was why
she was marrying): 'I must introduce you to my Aunt d'Uzai', and, when she
saw that such an alliance was beyond her reach, 'I must introduce you to my
Aunt de Ch'nouville', and 'I shall ask you to dine to meet the Uzai.' Her
marriage to M. de Cambremer had procured for Mlle Legrandin the
opportunity to use the former of these phrases but not the latter, the circle
in which her parents-in-law moved not being that which she had supposed
and of which she continued to dream. After saying to me of Saint-Loup
(adopting for the occasion one of his expressions, for if in talking to her I
used those expressions of Legrandin, she by a reverse suggestion answered
me in Robert's dialect which she did not know to be borrowed from
Rachel), bringing her thumb and forefinger together and half-shutting her
eyes as though she were gazing at something infinitely delicate which she
had succeeded in capturing: 'He has a charming quality of mind', she began
to extol him with such warmth that one might have supposed that she was in
love with him (it had indeed been alleged that, some time back, when he was
at Doncières, Robert had been her lover), in reality simply that I might
repeat her words to him, and ended up with: 'You are a great friend of the
Duchesse de Guermantes. I am an invalid, I never go anywhere, and I know
that she sticks to a close circle of chosen friends, which I do think so wise of

her, and so I know her very slightly, but I know she is a really remarkable woman.' Aware that Mme de Carnbremer barely knew her, and anxious to reduce myself to her level, I avoided the subject and answered the Marquise that the person whom I did know well was her brother, M. Legrandin. At the sound of his name she assumed the same evasive air as myself over the name of Mme de Guermantes, but combined with it an expression of annoyance, for she supposed that I had said this with the object of humiliating not myself but her. Was she gnawed by despair at having been born a Legrandin? So at least her husband's sisters and sisters-in-law asserted, ladies of the provincial nobility who knew nobody and nothing, and were jealous of Mme de Cambremer's intelligence, her education, her fortune, the physical attractions that she had possessed before her illness. 'She can think of nothing else, that is what is killing her,' these slanderers would say whenever they spoke of Mme de Cambremer to no matter whom, but preferably to a plebeian, whether, were he conceited and stupid, to enhance, by this affirmation of the shamefulness of a plebeian origin, the value of the affability that they were showing him, or, if he were shy and clever and applied the remark to himself, to give themselves the pleasure, while receiving him hospitably, of insulting him indirectly. But if these ladies thought that they were speaking the truth about their sister-in-law, they were mistaken. She suffered not at all from having been born Legrandin, for she had forgotten the fact altogether. She was annoyed at my reminding her of it, and remained silent as though she had not understood, not thinking it necessary to enlarge upon or even to confirm my statement.

'Our cousins are not the chief reason for our cutting short our visit,' said the dowager Mme de Cambremer, who was probably more satiated than her daughter-in-law with the pleasure to be derived from saying 'Ch'nou-ville'. 'But, so as not to bother you with too many people, Monsieur,' she went on, indicating the lawyer, 'was afraid to bring his wife and son to the hotel. They are waiting for us on the beach, and they will be growing impatient.' I asked for an exact description of them and hastened in search of them. The wife had a round face like certain flowers of the ranunculus family, and a large vegetable growth at the corner of her eye. And as the generations of mankind preserve their characteristic like a family of plants, just as on the blemished face of his mother, an identical mole, which might have helped one in classifying a variety of the species, protruded below the eye of the son. The lawyer was touched by my civility to his wife and son. He showed an interest in the subject of my stay at Balbec. 'You must find yourself rather out of your element, for the people here are for the most part foreigners.' And he kept his eye on me as he spoke, for, not caring for foreigners, albeit he had many foreign clients, he wished to make sure that I was not hostile to his xenophobia, in which case he would have beaten a retreat saying: 'Of course, Mme X— may be a charming woman. It's a question of principle.' As at that time I had no definite opinion about foreigners, I showed no sign of disapproval; he felt himself to be on safe ground. He went so far as to invite me to come one day, in Paris, to see his collection of Le Sidaner, and to bring with me the Cambremers, with whom he evidently supposed me to be on intimate terms. 'I shall invite you to meet Le Sidaner,' he said to me, confident that from that moment I would live only in expectation of that happy day. 'You shall see what a delightful man he is. And his pictures will enchant you. Of course, I can't compete with the great collectors, but I do believe that I am the one that possesses the greatest number of his favourite canvases. They will interest you all the more, coming from Balbec, since they are marine subjects, for the most part, at least.' The wife and son, blessed with a vegetable nature, listened composedly. One felt that their house in Paris was a sort of temple of Le Sidaner. Temples of this sort are not without their use. When the god has doubts as to his own merits, he can easily stop the cracks in his opinion of himself with the irrefutable testimony of people who have devoted their lives to his work.

At a signal from her daughter-in-law, Mme de Cambremer prepared to depart, and said to me: 'Since you won't come and stay at Féterne, won't you at least come to luncheon, one day this week, tomorrow for instance?' And in her bounty, to make the invitation irresistible, she added: 'You will *find* the Comte de Crisenoy', whom I had never lost, for the simple reason that I did not know him. She was beginning to dazzle me with yet further temptations, but stopped short. The chief magistrate who, on returning to the hotel, had been told that she was on the premises had crept about searching for her everywhere, then waited his opportunity, and pretending to have caught sight of her by chance, came up now to greet her. I gathered that Mme de Cambremer did not mean to extend to him the invitation to luncheon that she had just addressed to me. And yet he had known her far longer than I, having for years past been one of the regular guests at the afternoon parties at Féterne whom I used so to envy during my former visit to Balbec. But old acquaintance is not the only thing that counts in society. And hostesses are more inclined to reserve their luncheons for new acquaintances who still whet their curiosity, especially when they arrive preceded by a glowing and irresistible recommendation like Saint-Loup's of me. Mme de Cambremer decided that the chief magistrate could not have heard what she was saying to me, but, to calm her guilty conscience, began addressing him in the kindest tone. In the sunlight that flooded, on the horizon, the golden coastline, invisible as a rule, of Rivebelle, we could just make out, barely distinguishable from the luminous azure, rising from the water, rosy, silvery, faint, the little bells that were sounding the angelus round about Féterne. 'That is rather *Pelléas*, too,' I suggested to Mme de Cambremer-Legrandin. 'You know the scene I mean.' 'Of course I do!' was what she said; but 'I haven't the faintest idea' was the message proclaimed by her voice and features which did not mould themselves to the shape of any recollection and by a smile that floated without support in the air. The dowager could not get over her astonishment that the sound of the bells should carry so far, and rose, reminded of the time. 'But, as a rule,' I said, 'we never see that part of the coast from Balbec, nor hear it either. The weather must have changed and enlarged the horizon in more ways than one. Unless, that is to say, the bells have come to look for you, since I see that they are making you leave; to you they are a dinner bell.' The chief magistrate, little interested in the bells, glanced furtively along the front, on which he was sorry to see so few people that evening. 'You are a true poet,' said Mme de Cambremer to me. 'One feels you are so responsive, so artistic, come, I will play you Chopin,' she went on, raising her arms with an air of ecstasy and pronouncing the words in a raucous voice like the shifting of shingle on the beach. Then came the deglutition of spittle, and the old lady instinctively wiped the stubble of her moustaches with her handkerchief. The chief magistrate did me, unconsciously, a great service by offering the Marquise his arm to escort her to her carriage, a certain blend of vulgarity, boldness and love of ostentation prompting him to actions which other people would have hesitated to risk, and which are by no means unsuccessful in society. He was, moreover, and had been for years past far more in the habit of these actions than myself. While blessing him for what he did I did not venture to copy him, and walked by the side of Mme de Cambremer-Legrandin who insisted upon seeing the book that I had in my hand. The name of Madame de Sévigné drew a grimace from her; and using a word which she had seen in certain newspapers, but which, used in speech and given a feminine form, and applied to a seventeenth century writer, had an odd effect, she asked me: 'Do you think her really masterly?' The Marquise gave her footman the address of a pastry-cook where she had to call before taking the road, rosy with the evening haze, through which loomed one beyond another the dusky walls of cliff. She asked her old coachman whether one of the horses which was apt to catch cold had been kept warm enough, whether the other's shoe were not hurting him. 'I shall write to you and make a definite engagement,' she murmured to me. 'I heard you talking about literature to my daughter-in-law, she's a darling,' she went on, not that she really thought so, but she had acquired the habit – and kept it up in her kindness of heart – of saying so, in order that her son might not appear to have married for money. 'Besides,' she added with a final enthusiastic gnashing of her teeth, 'she's so harttissttick!' With this she stepped into her carriage, nodding her head, holding the crook of her sunshade aloft like a crozier, and set off through the streets of Balbec, overloaded with the ornaments of her priesthood, like an old Bishop on a confirmation tour.

'She has asked you to luncheon,' the chief magistrate said to me sternly when the carriage had passed out of sight and I came indoors with the girls. 'We're not on the best of terms just now. She feels that I neglect her. Gad, I'm easy enough to get on with. If anybody needs me, I'm always there to say: Adsum! But they tried to force my hand. That, now,' he went on with an air of subtlety, holding up his finger as though making and arguing a distinction, 'that is a thing I do not allow. It is a threat to the liberty of my holidays. I was obliged to say: Stop! You seem to be in her good books. When you reach my age you will see that society is a very trumpery thing, and you will be sorry you attached so much importance to these trifles. Well, I am going to take a turn before dinner. Goodbye, children,' he shouted back at us, as though he were already fifty yards away.

When I had said goodbye to Rosemonde and Gisèle, they saw with astonishment that Albertine was staying behind instead of accompanying them. 'Why, Albertine, what are you doing, don't you know what time it is?' 'Go home,' she replied in a tone of authority. 'I want to talk to him,' she added, indicating myself with a submissive air. Rosemonde and Gisèle stared at me, filled with a new and strange respect. I enjoyed the feeling that, for a moment at least, in the eyes even of Rosemonde and Gisèle, I was to Albertine something more important than the time, than her friends, and might indeed share solemn secrets with her into which it was impossible for them to be admitted. 'Shan't we see you again this evening?' 'I don't know, it will depend on this person. Anyhow, tomorrow.' 'Let us go up to my room,' I said to her, when her friends had gone. We took the lift; she remained silent in the boy's presence. The habit of being obliged to resort to personal observation and deduction in order to find out the business of their masters, those strange beings who converse among themselves and do not speak to them, develops in 'employees' (as the lift-boy styled servants), a stronger power of divination than the 'employer' possesses. Our organs become atrophied or grow stronger or more subtle, accordingly as our need of them increases or diminishes. Since railways came into existence, the necessity of not missing the train has taught us to take account of minutes whereas among the ancient Romans, who not only had a more cursory science of astronomy but led less hurried lives, the notion not of minutes but even of fixed hours barely existed. And so the lift-boy had gathered and meant to inform his comrades that Albertine and I were preoccupied. But he talked to us without ceasing because he had no tact. And yet I could see upon his face, in place of the customary expression of friendliness and joy at taking me up in his lift, an air of extraordinary depression and uneasiness. As I knew nothing of the cause of this, in an attempt to distract his thoughts, and albeit I was more preoccupied than Albertine, I told him that the lady who had just left was called the Marquise de Cambremer and not de Camembert. On the landing at which we were pausing at the moment, I saw, carrying a pair of pails, a hideous chambermaid who greeted me with respect, hoping for a tip when I left. I should have liked to know if she were the one whom I had so ardently desired on the evening of my first arrival at Balbec, but I could never arrive at any certainty. The lift-boy swore to me with the sincerity of most false witnesses, but without shedding his expression of despair, that it was indeed by the name of Camembert that the Marquise had told him to announce her. And as a matter of fact it was quite natural that he should have heard her say a name which he already knew. Besides, having those very vague ideas of nobility, and of the names of which titles are composed, which are shared by many people who are not lift-boys, the name Camembert had seemed to him all the more probable inasmuch as, that cheese being universally known, it was not in the least surprising that people should have acquired a marquisate from so glorious a distinction, unless it were the marquisate that had bestowed its renown upon the cheese. Nevertheless as he saw that I refused to admit that I might be mistaken, and as he knew that masters like to see their most futile whims obeyed and their most obvious lies accepted, he promised me like a good servant that in future he would say Cambremer. It is true that none of the shopkeepers in the town, none of the peasants in the district, where the name and persons of the Cambremers were perfectly familiar, could ever have made the lift-boy's mistake. But the staff of the 'Grand Hotel of Balbec' were none of them natives. They came direct, with the furniture and stock, from Biarritz, Nice and Monte-Carlo, one division having been transferred to Deauville, another to Dinard and the third reserved for Balbec.

But the lift-boy's pained anxiety continued to grow. That he should thus forget to show his devotion to me by the customary smiles, some misfortune must have befallen him. Perhaps he had been 'missed'. I made up my mind in that case to try to secure his reinstatement, the manager having promised to ratify all my wishes with regard to his staff. 'You can always do just what you like, I rectify everything in advance.' Suddenly, as I stepped out of the lift, I guessed the meaning of the boy's distress, his panic-stricken air. Because Albertine was with me, I had not given him the five francs which I was in the habit of slipping into his hand when I went up. And the idiot, instead of understanding that I did not wish to make a display of generosity in front of a third person, had begun to tremble, supposing that it was all finished, that I would never give him anything again. He imagined that I was 'on the rocks' (as the Duc de Guermantes would have said), and the supposition inspired him with no pity for myself but with a terrible selfish disappointment. I told myself that I was less unreasonable than my mother thought when I dared not, one day, refrain from giving the extravagant but feverishly awaited sum that I had given the day before. But at the same time the meaning that I had until then, and without a shadow of doubt, ascribed to his habitual expression of joy, in which I had no hesitation in seeing a sign of devotion, seemed to me to have become less certain. Seeing the lift-boy ready, in his despair, to fling himself down from the fifth floor of the hotel, I asked myself whether, if our respective social stations were to be altered, in consequence let us say of a revolution, instead of politely working his lift for me, the boy, grown independent, would not have flung me down the well, and whether there was not, in certain of the lower orders, more duplicity than in society, where, no doubt, people reserve their offensive remarks until we are out of earshot, but where their attitude towards us would not be insulting if we were reduced to poverty.

One cannot however say that, in the Balbec hotel, the lift-boy was the most commercially minded. From this point of view the staff might be divided into two categories; on the one hand, those who drew distinctions between the visitors, and were more grateful for the modest tip of an old nobleman (who, moreover, was in a position to relieve them from 28 days of military service by saying a word for them to General de Beautreillis) than for the thoughtless liberalities of a cad who by his very profusion revealed a want of practice which only to his face did they call generosity. On the other hand, those to whom nobility, intellect, fame, position, manners were nonexistent, concealed under a cash valuation. For these there was but a single standard, the money one has, or rather the money one bestows. Possibly Aimé himself, albeit pretending, in view of the great number of hotels in which he had served, to a great knowledge of the world, belonged to this latter category. At the most he would give a social turn, showing that he knew who was who, to this sort of appreciation, as when he said of the Princesse de Luxembourg: 'There's a pile of money among that lot?' (the question mark at the end being to ascertain the facts or to check such information as he had already ascertained, before supplying a client with a chef for Paris, or promising him a table on the left, by the door, with a view of the sea, at Balbec). In spite of this, and albeit not free from sordid considerations, he would not have displayed them with the fatuous despair of the lift-boy. And yet, the latter's artlessness helped perhaps to simplify things. It is the convenience of a big hotel, of a house such as Rachel used at one time to frequent, that, without any intermediary, the face, frozen stiff until that moment, of a servant or a woman, at the sight of a hundred-franc note, still more of one of a thousand, even although it is being given to someone else, will melt in smiles and offers of service. Whereas in the dealings, in the relations between lover and mistress, there are too many things interposed between money and docility. So many things that the very people upon whose faces money finally evokes a smile are often incapable of following the internal process that links them together, believe themselves to be, and indeed are more refined. Besides, it rids polite conversation of such speeches as: 'There's only one thing left for me to do, you will find me tomorrow in the mortuary.' And so one meets in polite society few novelists, or poets, few of all those sublime creatures who speak of the things that are not to be mentioned.

As soon as we were alone and had moved along the corridor, Albertine began: 'What is it you have got against me?' Had my harsh treatment of her been painful to myself? Had it been merely an unconscious ruse on my part, with the object of bringing my mistress to that attitude of fear and supplication which would enable me to interrogate her, and perhaps to find out which of the alternative hypotheses that I had long since formed about her was correct? However that may be, when I heard her question, I suddenly felt the joy of one who attains to a long desired goal. Before answering her, I escorted her to the door of my room. Opening it, I scattered the roseate light that was flooding the room and turning the white muslin of the curtains drawn for the night to golden damask. I went across to the window; the gulls had settled again upon the waves; but this time they were pink. I drew Albertine's attention to them. 'Don't change the subject,' she said, 'be frank with me.' I lied. I declared to her that she must first listen to a confession, that of my passionate admiration, for some time past, of Andrée, and I made her this confession with a simplicity and frankness worthy of the stage, but seldom employed in real life except for a love which people do not feel. Harking back to the fiction I had employed with Gilberte before my first visit to Balbec, but adapting its terms, I went so far (in order to make her more ready to believe me when I told her now that I was not in love with her) as to let fall the admission that at one time I had been on the point of falling in love with her, but that too long an interval had elapsed, that she could be nothing more to me now than a good friend and comrade, and that even if I wished to feel once again a more ardent sentiment for her it would be quite beyond my power. As it happened, in taking my stand thus before Albertine on these protestations of coldness towards her, I was merely – because of a particular circumstance and with a particular object in view – making more perceptible, accentuating more markedly, that dual rhythm which love adopts in all those who have too little confidence in themselves to believe that a woman can ever fall in love with them, and also that they themselves can genuinely fall in love with her. They know themselves well enough to have observed that in the presence of the most divergent types of woman they felt the same hopes, the same agonies, invented the same romances, uttered the same words, to have deduced therefore that their sentiments, their actions bear no close and necessary relation to the woman they love, but pass by her, spatter her, surround her, like the waves that break round upon the rocks, and their sense of their own instability increases still further their misgivings that this woman, by whom they would so fain be loved, is not in love with them. Why should chance have brought it about, when she is simply an accident placed so as to catch the ebullience of our desire, that we should ourselves be the object of the desire that is animating her? And so, while we feel the need to pour out before her all those sentiments, so different from the merely human sentiments that our neighbour inspires in us, those so highly specialised sentiments which are a lover's, after we have taken a step forward, in avowing to her whom we love our affection for her, our hopes, overcome at once by the fear of offending her, ashamed too that the speech we have addressed to her was not composed expressly for her, that it has served us already, will serve us again for others, that if she does not love us she cannot understand us and we have spoken in that case with the want of taste, of modesty shown by the pedant who addresses an ignorant audience in subtle phrases which are not for them, this fear, this shame bring into play the counter-rhythm, the reflux, the need, even by first drawing back, hotly denying the affection we have already confessed, to resume the offensive, and to recapture her esteem, to dominate her; the double rhythm is percep-tible in the various periods of a single love affair, in all the corresponding periods of similar love affairs, in all those people whose self-analysis out-weighs their self-esteem. If it was however somewhat more vigorously accentuated than usual in this speech which I was now preparing to make to Albertine, that was simply to allow me to pass more speedily and more emphatically to the alternate rhythm which should sound my affection.

As though it must be painful to Albertine to believe what I was saying to her as to the impossibility of my loving her again, after so long an interval, I justified what I called an eccentricity of my nature by examples taken from people with whom I had, by their fault or my own, allowed the time for loving them to pass, and been unable, however keenly I might have desired it, to recapture it. I thus appeared at one and the same time to be apologising to her, as for a want of courtesy, for this inability to begin loving her again, and to be seeking to make her understand the psychological reasons for that incapacity as though they had been peculiar to myself. But by explaining myself in this fashion, by dwelling upon the case of Gilberte, in regard to whom the argument had indeed been strictly true which was becoming so far from true when applied to Albertine, all that I did was to render my assertions as plausible as I pretended to believe that they were not. Feeling that Albertine appreciated what she called my 'frank speech' and recognising in my deductions the clarity of the evidence, I apologised for the former by telling her that I knew that the truth was always unpleasant and in this instance must seem to her incomprehensible. She, on the contrary, thanked me for my sincerity and added that so far from being puzzled she understood perfectly a state of mind so frequent and so natural.

This avowal to Albertine of an imaginary sentiment for Andrée, and, towards herself, an indifference which, that it might appear altogether sincere and without exaggeration, I assured her incidentally, as though by a scruple of politeness, must not be taken too literally, enabled me at length, without any fear of Albertine's suspecting me of loving her, to speak to her with a tenderness which I had so long denied myself and which seemed to me exquisite. I almost caressed my confidant; as I spoke to her of her friend whom I loved, tears came to my eyes. But, coming at last to the point, I said to her that she knew what love meant, its susceptibilities, its sufferings, and that perhaps, as the old friend that she now was, she might feel it in her heart to put a stop to the bitter grief that she was causing me, not directly, since it was not herself that I loved, if I might venture to repeat that without offending her, but indirectly by wounding me in my love for Andrée. I broke off to admire and point out to Albertine a great bird, solitary and hastening, which far out in front of us, lashing the air with the regular beat of its wings, was passing at full speed over the beach stained here and there with reflections like little torn scraps of red paper, and crossing it from end to end without slackening its pace, without diverting its attention, without deviating from its path, like an envoy carrying far afield an urgent and vital message. 'He at least goes straight to the point!' said Albertine in a tone of reproach. 'You say that because you don't know what it is I was going to tell you. But it is so difficult that I prefer to give it up; I am certain that I should make you angry; and then all that will have happened will be this: I shall be in no way better off with the girl I really love and I shall have lost a good friend.' 'But when I swear to you that I will not be angry.' She had so sweet, so wistfully docile an air, as though her whole happiness depended on me, that I could barely restrain myself from kissing – with almost the same kind of pleasure that I should have taken in kissing my mother – this novel face which no longer presented the startled, blushing expression of a rebellious and perverse kitten with its little pink, tip-tilted nose, but seemed, in the fullness of its crushing sorrow, moulded in broad, flattened, drooping slabs of pure goodness. Making an abstraction of my love as of a chronic mania that had no connection with her, putting myself in her place, I let my heart be melted before this honest girl, accustomed to being treated in a friendly and loyal fashion, whom the good comrade that she might have supposed me had been pursuing for weeks past with persecutions which had at last arrived at their culminating point. It was because I placed myself at a standpoint that was purely human, external to both of us, at which my jealous love dissolved, that I felt for Albertine that profound pity, which would have been less profound if I had not loved her. However, in that rhythmical oscillation which leads from a declaration to a quarrel (the surest, the most certainly perilous way of forming by opposite and successive movements a knot which will not be loosed and attaches us firmly to a person by the strain of the movement of withdrawal which constitutes one of the two elements of the rhythm), of what use is it to analyse farther the refluences of human pity, which, the opposite of love, though springing perhaps unconsciously from the same cause, produces in every case the same effects? When we count up afterwards the total amount of all that we have done for a woman, we often discover that the actions prompted by the desire to show that we love her, to make her love us, to win her favours, bulk little if any greater than those due to the human need to repair the wrongs that we have done to the creature whom we love, from a mere sense of moral duty, as though we were not in love with her. 'But tell me, what on earth have I done?' Albertine asked me. There was a knock at the door; it was the lift-boy; Albertine's aunt, who was passing the hotel in a carriage, had stopped on the chance of finding her there, to take her home. Albertine sent word that she could not come, that they were to begin dinner without her, that she could not say at what time she would return. 'But won't your aunt be angry?' 'What do you suppose? She will understand all right.' And so, at this moment at least, a moment such as might never occur again – a conversation with myself was proved by this incident to be in Albertine's eyes a thing of such self-evident importance that it must be given precedence over everything, a thing to which, referring no doubt instinctively to a family code, enumerating certain crises in which, when the career of M. Bontemps was at stake, a journey had been made without a thought, my friend never doubted that her aunt would think it quite natural to see her sacrifice the dinner-hour. That remote hour which she passed without my company, among her own people, Albertine, having brought it to me, bestowed it on me; I might make what use of it I chose. I ended by making bold to tell her what had been reported to me about her way of living, and that notwithstanding the profound disgust that I felt for women tainted with that vice, I had not given it a thought until I had been told the name of her accomplice, and that she could readily understand, loving Andrée as I did, the grief that the news had caused me. It would have been more tactful perhaps to say that I had been given the names of other women as well, in whom I was not interested. But the sudden and terrible revelation that Cottard had made to me had entered my heart to lacerate it, complete in itself but without accretions. And just as, before that moment, it would never have occurred to me that Albertine was in love with Andrée, or at any rate could find pleasure in caressing her, if Cottard had not drawn my attention to their attitude as they waltzed together, so I had been incapable of passing from that idea to the idea, so different for me, that Albertine might have, with other women than Andrée, relations for which affection could not be pleaded in excuse. Albertine, before even swearing to me that it was not true, showed, like everyone upon learning that such things are being said about him, anger, concern, and, with regard to the unknown slanderer, a fierce curiosity to know who he was and a desire to be confronted with him so as to be able to confound him. But she assured me that she bore me, at least, no resentment. 'If it had been true, I should have told you. But Andrée and I both loathe that sort of thing. We have not lived all these years without seeing women with cropped hair who behave like men and do the things you mean, and nothing revolts us more.' Albertine gave me merely her word, a peremptory word unsupported by proof. But this was just what was best calculated to calm me, jealousy belonging to that family of sickly doubts which are better purged by the energy than by the probability of an affirmation. It is moreover the property of love to make us at once more distrustful and more credulous, to make us suspect, more readily than we should suspect anyone else, her whom we love, and be convinced more easily by her denials. We must be in love before we can care that all women are not virtuous, which is to say before we can be aware of the fact, and we must be in love too before we can hope, that is to say assure ourselves that some are. It is human to seek out what hurts us and then at once to seek to get rid of it. The statements that are capable of so relieving us seem quite naturally true, we are not inclined to cavil at a sedative that acts. Besides, however multiform may be the person with whom we are in love, she can in any case offer us two essential personalities accordingly as she appears to us as ours, or as turning her desires in another direction. The former of these personalities possesses the peculiar power which prevents us from believing in the reality of the other, the secret remedy to heal the sufferings that this latter has caused us. The beloved object is successively the malady and the remedy that suspends and aggravates it. No doubt, I had long since been prepared, by the strong impression made on my imagination and my faculty for emotion by the example of Swann, to believe in the truth of what I feared rather than of what I should have wished. And so the comfort brought me by Albertine's affirmations came near to being jeopardised for a moment, because I was reminded of the story of Odette. But I told myself that, if it was only right to allow for the worst, not only when, in order to understand Swann's sufferings, I had tried to put myself in his place, but now, when I myself was concerned, in seeking the truth as though it referred to someone else, still I must not, out of cruelty to myself, a soldier who chooses the post not where he can be of most use but where he is most exposed, end in the mistake of regarding one supposition as more true than the rest, simply because it was more painful. Was there not a vast gulf between Albertine, a girl of good, middle-class parentage, and Odette, a courtesan bartered by her mother in her childhood? There could be no comparison of their respective credibility. Besides, Albertine had in no respect the same interest in lying to me that Odette had had in lying to Swann. Moreover to him Odette had admitted what Albertine had just denied. I should therefore be guilty of an error in reasoning as serious – though in the opposite direction – as that which had inclined me towards a certain hypothesis because it had caused me less pain than the rest, were I not to take into account these material differences in their positions, but to reconstruct the real life of my mistress solely from what I had been told about the life of Odette. I had before me a new Albertine, of whom I had already, it was true, caught more than one glimpse towards the end of my previous visit to Balbec, frank and honest, an Albertine who had, out of affection for myself, forgiven me my suspicions and tried to dispel them. She made me sit down by her side upon my bed. I thanked her for what she had said to me, assured her that our reconciliation was complete, and that I would never be horrid to her again. I suggested to her that she ought, at the same time, to go home to dinner. She asked me whether I was not glad to have her with me. Drawing my head towards her for a caress which she had never before given me and which I owed perhaps to the healing of our rupture, she passed her tongue lightly over my lips which she attempted to force apart. At first I kept them tight shut. 'You are a great bear!' she informed me.

I ought to have left the place that evening and never set eyes on her again. I felt even then that in a love which is not reciprocated – I might as well say, in love, for there are people for whom there is no such thing as reciprocated love – we can enjoy only that simulacrum of happiness which had been given me at one of those unique moments in which a woman's good nature, or her caprice, or mere chance, bring to our desires, in perfect coincidence, the same words, the same actions as if we were really loved. The wiser course would have been to consider with curiosity, to possess with delight that little parcel of happiness failing which I should have died without ever suspecting what it could mean to hearts less difficult to please or more highly favoured; to suppose that it formed part of a vast and enduring happiness of which this fragment only was visible to me, and – lest the next day should expose this fiction – not to attempt to ask for any fresh favour after this, which had been due only to the artifice of an exceptional moment. I ought to have left Balbec, to have shut myself up in solitude, to have remained so in harmony with the last vibrations of the voice which I had contrived to render amorous for an instant, and of which I should have asked nothing more than that it might never address another word to me; for fear lest, by an additional word which now could only be different, it might shatter with a discord the sensitive silence in which, as though by the pressure of a pedal, there might long have survived in me the throbbing chord of happiness.

Soothed by my explanation with Albertine, I began once again to live in closer intimacy with my mother. She loved to talk to me gently about the days in which my grandmother had been younger. Fearing that I might reproach myself with the sorrows with which I had perhaps darkened the close of my grandmother's life, she preferred to turn back to the years when the first signs of my dawning intelligence had given my grandmother a satisfaction which until now had always been kept from me. We talked of the old days at Combray. My mother reminded me that there at least I used to read, and that at Balbec I might well do the same, if I was not going to work. I replied that, to surround myself with memories of Combray and of the charming coloured plates, I should like to read again the *Thousand and One Nights*. As, long ago at Combray, when she gave me books for my birthday, so it was in secret, as a surprise for me, that my mother now sent for both the *Thousand and One Nights* of Galland and the *Thousand Nights and a Night* of Mardrus. But, after casting her eye over the two translations, my mother would have preferred that I should stick to Galland's, albeit hesitating to influence me because of the respect that she felt for intellectual liberty, her dread of interfering with my intellectual life and the feeling that, being a woman, on the one hand she lacked, or so she thought, the necessary literary equipment, and on the other hand ought not to condemn because she herself was shocked by it the reading of a young man. Happening upon certain of the tales, she had been revolted by the immorality of the subject and the crudity of the expression. But above all, preserving, like precious relics, not only the brooch, the sunshade, the cloak, the volume of Madame de Sévigné, but also the habits of thought and speech of her mother, seeking on every occasion the opinion that she would have expressed, my mother could have no doubt of the horror with which my grandmother would have condemned Mardrus's book. She remembered that at Combray while before setting out for a walk, Méséglise way, I was reading Augustin Thierry, my grandmother, glad that I should be reading, and taking walks, was indignant nevertheless at seeing him whose name remained enshrined in the hemistich 'Then reigned Mérovée' called Merowig, refused to say 'Carolingians' for the 'Carlovingians' to which she remained loyal. And then I told her what my grandmother had thought of the Greek names which Bloch, following Leconte de Lisle, gave to the gods of Homer, going so far, in the simplest matters, as to make it a religious duty, in which he supposed literary talent to consist, to adopt a Greek system of spelling. Having occasion, for instance, to mention in a letter that the wine which they drank at his home was real nectar, he would write 'real nektar', with a k, which enabled him to titter at the mention of Lamartine. And if an *Odyssey* from which the names of Ulysses and Minerva were missing was no longer the *Odyssey* to her, what would she have said upon seeing corrupted even upon the cover the title of her *Thousand and One Nights*, upon no longer finding, exactly transcribed as she had all her life been in the habit of pronouncing them, the immortally familiar names of Scheherazade, of Dinarzade, in which, debaptised themselves (if one may use the expression of Musulman tales), the charming Caliph and the powerful Genies were barely recognisable, being renamed, he the 'Khalifat' and they the 'Gennis'. Still, my mother handed over both books to me, and I told her that I would read them on the days when I felt too tired to go out.

These days were not very frequent, however. We used to go out picnicking as before in a band, Albertine, her friends and myself, on the cliff or to the farm called Marie-Antoinette. But there were times when Albertine bestowed on me this great pleasure. She would say to me: 'Today I want to be alone with you for a little, it will be nicer if we are just by ourselves.' Then she would give out that she was busy, not that she need furnish any explanation, and so that the others, if they went all the same, without us, for an excursion and picnic, might not be able to find us, we would steal away like a pair of lovers, all by ourselves to Bagatelle or the Cross of Heulan, while the band, who would never think of looking for us there and never went there, waited indefinitely, in the hope of seeing us appear, at Marie-Antoinette. I recall the hot weather that we had then, when from the brow of each of the farm-labourers toiling in the sun a drop of sweat would fall, vertical, regular, intermittent, like the drop of water from a cistern, and alternate with the fall of the ripe fruit dropping from the tree in the adjoining 'closes'; they have remained, to this day, with that mystery of a woman's secret, the most substantial part of every love that offers itself to me. A woman who has been mentioned to me and to whom I would not give a moment's thought – I upset all my week's engagements to make her acquaintance, if it is a week of similar weather, and I am to meet her in some isolated farmhouse. It is no good my knowing that this kind of weather, this kind of assignation are not part of her, they are still the bait, which I know all too well, by which I allow myself to be tempted and which is sufficient to hook me. I know that this woman, in cold weather, in a town, I might perhaps have desired, but without the accompaniment of a romantic sentiment, without becoming amorous; my love for her is none the less keen as soon as, by force of circumstances, it has enthralled me – it is only the more melancholy, as in the course of life our sentiments for other people become, in proportion as we become more clearly aware of the ever smaller part that they play in our life and that the new love which we would like to be so permanent, cut short in the same moment as life itself, will be the last.

There were still but a few people at Balbec, hardly any girls. Sometimes I saw some girl resting upon the beach, devoid of charm, and yet apparently identified by various features as one whom I had been in despair at not being able to approach at the moment when she emerged with her friends from the riding school or gymnasium. If it was the same (and I took care not to mention the matter to Albertine), then the girl that I had thought so exciting did not exist. But I could not arrive at any certainty, for the face of any one of these girls did not fill any space upon the beach, did not offer a permanent form, contracted, dilated, transformed as it was by my own observation, the uneasiness of my desire or a sense of comfort that was self-sufficient, by the different clothes that she was wearing, the rapidity of her movements or her immobility. All the same, two or three of them seemed to me adorable. Whenever I saw one of these, I longed to take her away along the Avenue des Tamaris, or among the sandhills, better still upon the cliff. But, albeit into desire, as opposed to indifference, there enters already that audacity which is a first stage, if only unilateral, towards realisation, all the same, between my desire and the action that my request to be allowed to kiss her would have been, there was all the indefinite blank of hesitation, of timidity. Then I went into the pastrycook's bar, I drank, one after another, seven or eight glasses of port wine. At once, instead of the impassable gulf between my desire and action, the effect of the alcohol traced a line that joined them together. No longer was there any room for hesitation or fear. It seemed to me that the girl was about to fly into my arms. I went up to her, the words came spontaneously to my lips: 'I should like to go for a walk with you. You wouldn't care to go along the cliff, we shan't be disturbed behind the little wood that keeps the wind off the wooden bungalow that is empty just now?' All the difficulties of life were smoothed away, there was no longer any obstacle to the conjunction of our two bodies. No obstacle for me, at least. For they had not been volatilised for her, who had not been drinking port wine. Had she done so, had the outer world lost some of its reality in her eyes, the long cherished dream that would then have appeared to her to be suddenly realisable might perhaps have been not at all that of falling into my arms.

Not only were the girls few in number but at this season which was not yet 'the season' they stayed but a short time. There is one I remember with a reddish skin, green eyes and a pair of ruddy cheeks, whose slight symmetrical face resembled the winged seeds of certain trees. I cannot say what breeze wafted her to Balbec or what other bore her away. So sudden was her removal that for some days afterwards I was haunted by a grief which I made bold to confess to Albertine when I realised that the girl had gone for ever.

I should add that several of them were either girls whom I did not know at all or whom I had not seen for years. Often, before addressing them, I wrote to them. If their answer allowed me to believe in the possibility of love, what joy! We cannot, at the outset of our friendship with a woman, even if that friendship is destined to come to nothing, bear to part from those first letters that we have received from her. We like to have them beside us all the time, like a present of rare flowers, still quite fresh, at which we cease to gaze only to draw them closer to us and smell them. The sentence that we know by heart, it is pleasant to read again, and in those that we have committed less accurately to memory we like to verify the degree of affection in some expression. Did she write: 'Your dear letter'? A slight marring of our bliss, which must be ascribed either to our having read too quickly, or to the illegible handwriting of our correspondent; she did not say: 'Your dear letter' but 'From your letter'. But the rest is so tender. Oh, that more such flowers may come tomorrow. Then that is no longer enough, we must with the written words compare the writer's eyes, her face. We make an appointment, and – without her having altered, perhaps – whereas we expected, from the description given us or our personal memory, to meet the fairy Viviane, we encounter Puss-in-Boots. We make an appointment, nevertheless, for the following day, for it is, after all, *she*, and the person we desired is she. And these desires for a woman of whom we have been dreaming do not make beauty of form and feature essential. These desires are only the desire for a certain person; vague as perfumes, as styrax was the desire of Prothyraia, saffron the ethereal desire, aromatic scents the desire of Hera, myrrh the perfume of the Magi, manna the desire of Nike, incense the perfume of the sea. But these perfumes that are sung in the Orphic hymns are far fewer in number than the deities they worship. Myrrh is the perfume of the Magi, but also of Protogonos, Neptune, Nereus, Leto; incense is the perfume of the sea, but also of the fair Dike, of Themis, of Circe, of the Nine Muses, of Eos, of Mnemosyne, of the Day, of Dikaiosyne. As for styrax, manna and aromatic scents, it would be impossible to name all the deities that inhale them, so many are they. Amphietes has all the perfumes except incense, and Gaia rejects only beans and aromatic scents. So was it with these desires for different girls that I felt. Fewer in number than the girls themselves, they changed into disappointments and regrets closely similar one to another. I never wished for myrrh. I reserved it for Jupien and for the Prince de Guermantes, for it is the desire of Protogonos 'of twofold sex, who roars like a bull, of countless orgies, memorable, unspeakable, descending, joyous, to the sacrifices of the Orgiophants'.

But presently the season was in full swing; every day there was some fresh arrival, and for the sudden increase in the frequency of my outings, which took the place of the charmed perusal of the *Thousand and One Nights*, there was a reason devoid of pleasure which poisoned them all. The beach was now peopled with girls, and, since the idea suggested to me by Cottard had not indeed furnished me with fresh suspicions but had rendered me sensitive and weak in that quarter and careful not to let any suspicion take shape in my mind, as soon as a young woman arrived at Balbec, I began to feel ill at ease, I proposed to Albertine the most distant excursions, in order that she might not make the newcomer's acquaintance, and indeed, if possible, might not set eyes on her. I dreaded naturally even more those women whose dubious ways were remarked or their bad reputation already known; I tried to persuade my mistress that this bad reputation had no foundation, was a slander, perhaps, without admitting it to myself, from a fear, still unconscious, that she might seek to make friends with the depraved woman or regret her inability to do so, because of me, or might conclude from the number of examples that a vice so widespread was not to be condemned. In denying the guilt of each of them, my intention was nothing less than to pretend that sapphism did not exist. Albertine adopted my incredulity as to the viciousness of this one or that. 'No, I think it's just a pose, she wants to look the part.' But then, I regretted almost that I had pleaded the other's innocence, for it distressed me that Albertine, formerly so severe, could believe that this 'part' was a thing so flattering, so advantageous, that a woman innocent of such tastes could seek to 'look it'. I would have liked to be sure that no more women were coming to Balbec; I trembled when I thought that, as it was almost time for Mme Putbus to arrive at the Verdurins', her maid, whose tastes Saint-Loup had not concealed from me, might take it into her head to come down to the beach, and, if it were a day on which I was not with Albertine, might seek to corrupt her. I went the length of asking myself whether, as Cottard had made no secret of the fact that the Verdurins thought highly of me and, while not wishing to appear, as he put it, to be running after me, would give a great deal to have me come to their house, I might not, on the strength of promises to bring all the Guermantes in existence to call on them in Paris, induce Mme Verdurin, upon some pretext or other, to inform Mme Putbus that it was impossible to keep her there any longer and make her leave the place at once. Notwith-standing these thoughts, and as it was chiefly the presence of Andrée that was disturbing me, the soothing effect that Albertine's words had had upon me still to some extent persisted – I knew moreover that presently I should have less need of it, as Andrée would be leaving the place with Rosemonde and Gisèle just about the time when the crowd began to arrive and would be spending only a few weeks more with Albertine. During these weeks, moreover, Albertine seemed to have planned everything that she did, everything that she said, with a view to destroying my suspicions if any remained, or to prevent them from reviving. She contrived never to be left alone with Andrée, and insisted, when we came back from an excursion, upon my accompanying her to her door, upon my coming to fetch her when we were going anywhere. Andrée meanwhile took just as much trouble on her side, seemed to avoid meeting Albertine. And this apparent under-standing between them was not the only indication that Albertine must have informed her friend of our conversation and have asked her to be so kind as to calm my absurd suspicions.

About this time there occurred at the Grand Hotel a scandal which was not calculated to modify the intensity of my torment. Bloch's cousin had for some time past been indulging, with a retired actress, in secret relations which presently ceased to satisfy them. That they should be seen seemed to them to add perversity to their pleasure, they chose to flaunt their perilous sport before the eyes of all the world. They began with caresses, which might, after all, be set down to a friendly intimacy, in the card-room, by the baccarat-table. Then they grew more bold. And finally, one evening, in a corner that was not even dark of the big ballroom, on a sofa, they made no more attempt to conceal what they were doing than if they had been in bed. Two officers who happened to be near, with their wives, complained to the manager. It was thought for a moment that their protest would be effective. But they had this against them that, having come over for the evening from Netteholme, where they were staying, they could not be of any use to the manager. Whereas, without her knowing it even, and whatever remarks the manager may have made to her, there hovered over Mlle Bloch the protection of M. Nissim Bernard. I must explain why. M. Nissim Bernard carried to their highest pitch the family virtues. Every year he took a magnificent villa at Balbec for his nephew, and no invitation would have dissuaded him from going home to dine at his own table, which was in reality theirs. But he never took his luncheon at home. Every day at noon he was at the Grand Hotel. The fact of the matter was that he was keeping, as other men keep a chorus-girl from the opera, an embryo waiter of much the same type as the pages of whom we have spoken, and who made us think of the young Israelites in *Esther* and *Athalie*. It is true that the forty years' difference in age between M. Nissim Bernard and the young waiter ought to have preserved the latter from a contact that was scarcely pleasant. But, as Racine so wisely observes in those same choruses:

> Great God, with what uncertain tread
> A budding virtue 'mid such perils goes!
> What stumbling-blocks do lie before a soul
> That seeks Thee and would fain be innocent.

The young waiter might indeed have been brought up 'remote from the world' in the Temple-Caravanserai of Balbec, he had not followed the advice of Joad:

> In riches and in gold put not thy trust.

He had perhaps justified himself by saying: 'The wicked cover the earth.' However that might be, and albeit M. Nissim Bernard had not expected so rapid a conquest, on the very first day,

Were't in alarm, or anxious to caress,
He felt those childish arms about him thrown.

And by the second day, M. Nissim Bernard having taken the young waiter
out,

The dire assault his innocence destroyed.

From that moment the boy's life was altered. He might indeed carry bread
and salt, as his superior bade him, his whole face sang:

From flowers to flowers, from joys to keener joys
Let our desires now range.
Uncertain is our tale of fleeting years.
Haste we then to enjoy this life!
Honours and fame are the reward
Of blind and meek obedience.
For moping innocence
Who now would raise his voice!

Since that day, M. Nissim Bernard had never failed to come and occupy
his seat at the luncheon-table (as a man would occupy his in the stalls who
was keeping a dancer, a dancer in this case of a distinct and special type,
which still awaits its Degas). It was M. Nissim Bernard's delight to follow
over the floor of the restaurant and down the remote vista to where beneath
her palm the cashier sat enthroned, the evolutions of the adolescent hurrying
in service, in the service of everyone, and, less than anyone, of M. Nissim
Bernard, now that the latter was keeping him, whether because the young
chorister did not think it necessary to display the same friendliness to a
person by whom he supposed himself to be sufficiently well loved, or
because that love annoyed him or he feared lest, if discovered, it might make
him lose other opportunities. But this very coldness pleased M. Nissim
Bernard, because of all that it concealed; whether from Hebraic atavism or
from profanation of the Christian spirit, he took a singular pleasure, were it
Jewish or Catholic, in the Racinian ceremony. Had it been a real performance
of *Esther* or *Athalie*, M. Bernard would have regretted that the gulf of
centuries must prevent him from making the acquaintance of the author,
Jean Racine, so that he might obtain for his protégé a more substantial part.
But as the luncheon ceremony came from no author's pen, he contented
himself with being on good terms with the manager and Aimé, so that the
'young Israelite' might be promoted to the coveted post of under-waiter, or
even full waiter to a row of tables. The post of wine waiter had been offered

him. But M. Bernard made him decline it, for he would no longer have been able to come every day to watch him race about the green dining-room and to be waited upon by him like a stranger. Now this pleasure was so keen that every year M. Bernard returned to Balbec and took his luncheon away from home, habits in which M. Bloch saw, in the former a poetical fancy for the bright sunshine, the sunsets of this coast favoured above all others, in the latter the inveterate mania of an old bachelor.

As a matter of fact, the mistake made by M. Nissim Bernard's relatives, who never suspected the true reason for his annual return to Balbec and for what the pedantic Mme Bloch called his absentee palate, was really a more profound and secondary truth. For M. Nissim Bernard himself was unaware how much there was of love for the beach at Balbec, for the view one enjoyed from the restaurant over the sea, and of maniacal habits in the fancy that he had for keeping, like a dancing girl of another kind which still lacks a Degas, one of his servants the rest of whom were still girls. And so M. Nissim Bernard maintained, with the director of this theatre which was the hotel at Balbec, and with the stage-manager and producer Aimé – whose part in all this affair was anything but simple – excellent relations. One day they would intrigue to procure an important part, a place perhaps as head waiter. In the meantime M. Nissim Bernard's pleasure, poetical and calmly contemplative as it might be, reminded one a little of those women-loving men who always know – Swann, for example, in the past – that if they go out to a party they will meet their mistress. No sooner had M. Nissim Bernard taken his seat than he would see the object of his affections appear on the scene, bearing in his hand fruit or cigars upon a tray. And so every morning, after kissing his niece, bothering my friend Bloch about his work and feeding his horses with lumps of sugar from the palm of his outstretched hand, he would betray a feverish haste to arrive in time for luncheon at the Grand Hotel. Had the house been on fire, had his niece had a stroke, he would doubtless have started off just the same. So that he dreaded like the plague a cold that would confine him to his bed – for he was a hypochondriac – and would oblige him to ask Aimé to send his young friend across to visit him at home, between luncheon and teatime.

He loved moreover all the labyrinth of corridors, private offices, reception-rooms, cloakrooms, larders, galleries which composed the hotel at Balbec. With a strain of oriental atavism he loved a seraglio, and when he went out at night might be seen furtively exploring its passages. While, venturing down to the basement and endeavouring at the same time to escape notice and to avoid a scandal, M. Nissim Bernard, in his quest of the young Levites, put one in mind of those lines in La Juive:

O God of our Fathers, come down to us again,
Our mysteries veil from the eyes of wicked men!

I on the contrary would go up to the room of two sisters who had come to
Balbec, as her maids, with an old lady, a foreigner. They were what the
language of hotels called 'couriers', and that of Françoise, who imagined
that a courier was a person who was there to run his course, two 'coursers'.
The hotels have remained, more nobly, in the period when people sang:
'*C'est un courrier de cabinet.*'

Difficult as it was for a visitor to penetrate to the servants' quarters, I had
very soon formed a mutual bond of friendship, as strong as it was pure, with
these two young persons, Mademoiselle Marie Gineste and Madame Céleste
Albaret. Born at the foot of the high mountains in the centre of France, on
the banks of rivulets and torrents (the water passed actually under their old
home, turning a mill-wheel, and the house had often been damaged by
floods), they seemed to embody the features of that region. Marie Gineste
was more regularly rapid and abrupt, Céleste Albaret softer and more
languishing, spread out like a lake, but with terrible boiling rages in which
her fury suggested the peril of spates and gales that sweep everything before
them. They often came in the morning to see me when I was still in bed.
I have never known people so deliberately ignorant, who had learned
absolutely nothing at school, and yet whose language was somehow so
literary that, but for the almost savage naturalness of their tone, one would
have thought their speech affected. With a familiarity which I reproduce
verbatim, notwithstanding the praises (which I set down here in praise not
of myself but of the strange genius of Céleste) and the criticisms, equally
unfounded, in which her remarks seem to involve me, while I dipped
crescent rolls in my milk, Céleste would say to me: 'Oh! Little black devil
with hair of jet, O profound wickedness! I don't know what your mother
was thinking of when she made you, for you are just like a bird. Look, Marie,
wouldn't you say he was preening his feathers, and turning his head right
round, so light he looks, you would say he was just learning to fly. Ah! It's
fortunate for you that those who bred you brought you into the world to
rank and riches; what would ever have become of you, so wasteful as you are.
Look at him throwing away his crescent because it touched the bed. There
he goes, now, look, he's spilling his milk, wait till I tie a napkin round you,
for you could never do it for yourself, never in my life have I seen anyone so
helpless and so clumsy as you.' I would then hear the more regular sound of
the torrent of Marie Gineste who was furiously reprimanding her sister:
'Will you hold your tongue, now, Céleste. Are you mad, talking to Monsieur

like that?' Céleste merely smiled; and as I detested having a napkin tied round my neck: 'No, Marie, look at him, bang, he's shot straight up on end like a serpent. A proper serpent, I tell you.' These were but a few of her zoological similes, for, according to her, it was impossible to tell when I slept, I fluttered about all night like a butterfly, and in the daytime I was as swift as the squirrels. 'You know, Marie, the way we see them at home, so nimble that even with your eyes you can't follow them.' 'But, Céleste, you know he doesn't like having a napkin when he's eating.' 'It isn't that he doesn't like it, it's so that he can say nobody can make him do anything against his will. He's a grand gentleman and he wants to show that he is. They can change the sheets ten times over, if they must, but he won't give way. Yesterday's had served their time, but today they have only just been put on the bed and they'll have to be changed already. Oh, I was right when I said that he was never meant to be born among the poor. Look, his hair's standing on end, swelling with rage like a bird's feathers. Poor *ploumissou!*' Here it was not only Marie that protested, but myself, for I did not feel in the least like a grand gentleman. But Céleste would never believe in the sincerity of my modesty and cut me short. 'Oh! The storyteller! Oh! The flatterer! Oh! The false one! The cunning rogue! Oh! Molière!' (This was the only writer's name that she knew, but she applied it to me, meaning thereby a person who was capable both of writing plays and of acting them.) 'Céleste!' came the imperious cry from Marie, who, not knowing the name of Molière, was afraid that it might be some fresh insult. Céleste continued to smile: 'Then you haven't seen the photograph of him in his drawer, when he was little. He tried to make us believe that he was always dressed quite simply. And there, with his little cane, he's all furs and laces, such as no Prince ever wore. But that's nothing compared with his tremendous majesty and kindness which is even more profound.' 'So then,' scolded the torrent Marie, 'you go rummaging in his drawers now, do you?' To calm Marie's fears I asked her what she thought of M. Nissim Bernard's behaviour . . . 'Ah! Monsieur, there are things I wouldn't have believed could exist. One has to come here to learn.' And, for once outrivalling Céleste by an even more profound observation: 'Ah! You see, Monsieur, one can never tell what there may be in a person's life.' To change the subject, I spoke to her of the life led by my father, who toiled night and day. 'Ah! Monsieur, there are people who keep nothing of their life for themselves, not one minute, not one pleasure, the whole thing is a sacrifice for others, they are lives that are *given away*.' 'Look, Marie, he has only to put his hand on the counterpane and take his crescent, what distinction. He can do the most insignificant things, you would say that the whole nobility of France, from here to the Pyrenees, was stirring in each of his movements.'

Overpowered by this portrait so far from lifelike, I remained silent; Céleste interpreted my silence as a further instance of guile: 'Oh! Brow that looks so pure, and hides so many things, nice, cool cheeks like the inside of an almond, little hands of satin all velvety, nails like claws,' and so forth. 'There, Marie, look at him sipping his milk with a devoutness that makes me want to say my prayers. What a serious air! They ought really to take his portrait as he is just now. He's just like a child. Is it drinking milk, like them, that has kept you their bright colour? Oh! Youth! Oh! Lovely skin. You will never grow old. You are a lucky one, you will never need to raise your hand against anyone, for you have a pair of eyes that can make their will be done. Look at him now, he's angry. He shoots up, straight as a signpost.'

Françoise did not at all approve of what she called the two 'tricksters' coming to talk to me like this. The manager, who made his staff keep watch over everything that went on, even gave me a serious warning that it was not proper for a visitor to talk to servants. I, who found the 'tricksters' far better than any visitor in the hotel, merely laughed in his face, convinced that he would not understand my explanations. And the sisters returned. 'Look, Marie, at his delicate lines. Oh, perfect miniature, finer than the most precious you could see in a glass case, for he can move, and utters words you could listen to for days and nights.'

It was a miracle that a foreign lady could have brought them there, for, without knowing anything of history or geography, they heartily detested the English, the Germans, the Russians, the Italians, all foreign vermin, and cared, with certain exceptions, for French people alone. Their faces had so far preserved the moisture of the pliable clay of their native river beds, that, as soon as one mentioned a foreigner who was staying in the hotel, in order to repeat what he had said, Céleste and Marie imposed upon their faces his face, their mouths became his mouth, their eyes his eyes, one would have liked to preserve these admirable comic masks. Céleste indeed, while pretending merely to be repeating what the manager had said, or one of my friends, would insert in her little narrative fictitious remarks in which were maliciously portrayed all the defects of Bloch, the chief magistrate, etc., while apparently unconscious of doing so. It was, under the form of the delivery of a simple message which she had obligingly undertaken to convey, an inimitable portrait. They never read anything, not even a newspaper. One day, however, they found lying on my bed a book. It was a volume of the admirable but obscure poems of Saint-Léger Léger. Céleste read a few pages and said to me: 'But are you quite sure that these are poetry, wouldn't they just be riddles?' Obviously, to a person who had learned in her childhood a single poem: 'Down here the lilacs die', there was a gap in evolution. I fancy that their obstinate refusal to learn anything was due in part to the unhealthy climate of their early home. They had nevertheless all the gifts of a poet with more modesty than poets generally show. For if Céleste had said something noteworthy and, unable to remember it correctly, I asked her to repeat it, she would assure me that she had forgotten. They will never read any books, but neither will they ever write any.

Françoise was considerably impressed when she learned that the two brothers of these humble women had married, one the niece of the Archbishop of Tours, the other a relative of the Bishop of Rodez. To the manager, this would have conveyed nothing. Céleste would sometimes reproach her husband with his failure to understand her, and as for me, I was astonished that he could endure her. For at certain moments, raging, furious, destroying everything, she was detestable. It is said that the salt liquid which is our blood is only an internal survival of the primitive marine element. Similarly, I believe that Céleste, not only in her bursts of fury, but also in her hours of depression preserved the rhythm of her native streams. When she was exhausted, it was after their fashion; she had literally run dry. Nothing could then have revived her. Then all of a sudden the circulation was restored in her large body, splendid and light. The water flowed in the opaline transparence of her bluish skin. She smiled at the sun and became bluer still. At such moments she was truly celestial.

Bloch's family might never have suspected the reason which made their uncle never take his luncheon at home and have accepted it from the first as the mania of an elderly bachelor, due perhaps to the demands of his intimacy with some actress; everything that concerned M. Nissim Bernard was tabu to the manager of the Balbec hotel. And that was why, without even referring to the uncle, he had finally not ventured to find fault with the niece, albeit recommending her to be a little more circumspect. And so the girl and her friend who, for some days, had pictured themselves as excluded from the casino and the Grand Hotel, seeing that everything was settled, were delighted to show those fathers of families who held aloof from them that they might with impunity take the utmost liberties. No doubt they did not go so far as to repeat the public exhibition which had revolted everybody. But gradually they returned to their old ways. And one evening as I came out of the casino which was half in darkness with Albertine and Bloch whom we had met there, they came towards us, linked together, kissing each other incessantly, and, as they passed us, crowed and laughed, uttering indecent cries. Bloch lowered his eyes, so as to seem not to have recognised his cousin, and as for myself I was tortured by the thought that this occult, appalling language was addressed perhaps to Albertine.

Another incident turned my thoughts even more in the direction of Gomorrah. I had noticed upon the beach a handsome young woman, erect and pale, whose eyes, round their centre, scattered rays so geometrically luminous that one was reminded, on meeting her gaze, of some constellation. I thought how much more beautiful this girl was than Albertine, and that it would be wiser to give up the other. Only, the face of this beautiful young woman had been smoothed by the invisible plane of an utterly low life, of the constant acceptance of vulgar expedients, so much so that her eyes, more noble however than the rest of her face, could radiate nothing but appetites and desires. Well, on the following day, this young woman being seated a long way away from us in the casino, I saw that she never ceased to fasten upon Albertine the alternate, circling fires of her gaze. One would have said that she was making signals to her from a lighthouse. I dreaded my friend's seeing that she was being so closely observed, I was afraid that these incessantly rekindled glances might have the conventional meaning of an amorous assignation for the morrow. For all I knew, this assignation might not be the first. The young woman with the radiant eyes might have come another year to Balbec. It was perhaps because Albertine had already yielded to her desires, or to those of a friend, that this woman allowed herself to address to her those flashing signals. If so, they did more than demand something for the present, they found a justification in pleasant hours in the past.

This assignation, in that case, must be not the first, but the sequel to adventures shared in past years. And indeed her glance did not say: 'Will you?' As soon as the young woman had caught sight of Albertine, she had turned her head and beamed upon her glances charged with recollection, as though she were terribly afraid that my friend might not remember. Albertine, who could see her plainly, remained phlegmatically motionless, with the result that the other, with the same sort of discretion as a man who sees his old mistress with a new lover, ceased to look at her and paid no more attention to her than if she had not existed.

But, a day or two later, I received a proof of this young woman's tendencies, and also of the probability of her having known Albertine in the past. Often, in the hall of the casino, when two girls were smitten with mutual desire, a luminous phenomenon occurred, a sort of phosphorescent train passing from one to the other. Let us note in passing that it is by the aid of such materialisations, even if they be imponderable, by these astral signs that set fire to a whole section of the atmosphere, that the scattered

Gomorrah tends, in every town, in every village, to reunite its separated members, to reform the biblical city while everywhere the same efforts are being made, be it in view of but a momentary reconstruction, by the nostalgic, the hypocritical, sometimes by the courageous exiles from Sodom.

Once I saw the stranger whom Albertine had appeared not to recognise, just at the moment when Bloch's cousin was approaching her. The young woman's eyes flashed, but it was quite evident that she did not know the Israelite maiden. She beheld her for the first time, felt a desire, a shadow of doubt, by no means the same certainty as in the case of Albertine, Albertine upon whose comradeship she must so far have reckoned that, in the face of her coldness, she had felt the surprise of a foreigner familiar with Paris but not resident there, who, having returned to spend a few weeks there, on the site of the little theatre where he was in the habit of spending pleasant evenings, sees that they have now built a bank.

Bloch's cousin went and sat down at a table where she turned the pages of a magazine. Presently the young woman came and sat down, with an abstracted air, by her side. But under the table one could presently see their feet wriggling, then their legs and hands, in a confused heap. Words followed, a conversation began, and the young woman's innocent husband, who had been looking everywhere for her, was astonished to find her making plans for that very evening with a girl whom he did not know. His wife introduced Bloch's cousin to him as a friend of her childhood, by an inaudible name, for she had forgotten to ask her what her name was. But the husband's presence made their intimacy advance a stage farther, for they addressed each other as tu, having known each other at their convent, an incident at which they laughed heartily later on, as well as at the hoodwinked husband, with a gaiety which afforded them an excuse for more caresses.

As for Albertine, I cannot say that anywhere in the casino or on the beach was her behaviour with any girl unduly free. I found in it indeed an excess of coldness and indifference which seemed to be more than good breeding, to be a ruse planned to avert suspicion. When questioned by some girl, she had a quick, icy, decent way of replying in a very loud voice: 'Yes, I shall be going to the tennis court about five. I shall bathe tomorrow morning about eight,' and of at once turning away from the person to whom she had said this – all of which had a horrible appearance of being meant to put people off the scent, and either to make an assignation, or, the assignation already made in a whisper, to utter this speech, harmless enough in itself, aloud, so as not to attract attention. And when later on I saw her mount her bicycle and scorch away into the distance, I could not help thinking that she was hurrying to overtake the girl to whom she had barely spoken.

Only, when some handsome young woman stepped out of a motorcar at the end of the beach, Albertine could not help turning round. And she at once explained: 'I was looking at the new flag they've put up over the bathing place. The old one was pretty moth-eaten. But I really think this one is mouldier still.'

On one occasion Albertine was not content with cold indifference, and this made me all the more wretched. She knew that I was annoyed by the possibility of her sometimes meeting a friend of her aunt, who had a 'bad style' and came now and again to spend a few days with Mme Bontemps. Albertine had pleased me by telling me that she would not speak to her again. And when this woman came to Incarville, Albertine said: 'By the way, you know she's here. Have they told you?' as though to show me that she was not seeing her in secret. One day, when she told me this, she added: 'Yes, I ran into her on the beach, and knocked against her as I passed, on purpose, to be rude to her.' When Albertine told me this, there came back to my mind a remark made by Mme Bontemps, to which I had never given a second thought, when she had said to Mme Swann in my presence how brazen her niece Albertine was, as though that were a merit, and told her how Albertine had reminded some official's wife that her father had been employed in a kitchen. But a thing said by her whom we love does not long retain its purity; it withers, it decays. An evening or two later, I thought again of Albertine's remark, and it was no longer the ill breeding of which she was so proud – and which could only make me smile – that it seemed to me to signify, it was something else, to wit that Albertine, perhaps even without any definite object, to irritate this woman's senses, or wantonly to remind her of former proposals, accepted perhaps in the past, had swiftly brushed against her, thought that I had perhaps heard of this as it had been done in public, and had wished to forestall an unfavourable interpretation.

However, the jealousy that was caused me by the women whom Albertine perhaps loved was abruptly to cease.

We were waiting, Albertine and I, at the Balbec station of the little local railway. We had driven there in the hotel omnibus, because it was raining. Not far away from us was M. Nissim Bernard, with a black eye. He had recently forsaken the chorister from *Athalie* for the waiter at a much frequented farmhouse in the neighbourhood, known as the 'Cherry Orchard'. This rubicund youth, with his blunt features, appeared for all the world to have a tomato instead of a head. A tomato exactly similar served as head to

his twin brother. To the detached observer there is this attraction about these
perfect resemblances between pairs of twins, that nature, becoming for the
moment industrialised, seems to be offering a pattern for sale. Unfortunately
M. Nissim Bernard looked at it from another point of view, and this
resemblance was only external. Tomato II showed a frenzied zeal in furnishing
the pleasures exclusively of ladies, Tomato I did not mind condescending to
meet the wishes of certain gentlemen. Now on each occasion when, stirred,
as though by a reflex action, by the memory of pleasant hours spent with
Tomato I, M. Bernard presented himself at the Cherry Orchard, being
short-sighted (not that one need be short-sighted to mistake them), the old
Israelite, unconsciously playing Amphitryon, would accost the twin brother
with: 'Will you meet me somewhere this evening?' He at once received a
resounding smack in the face. It might even be repeated in the course of a
single meal, when he continued with the second brother the conversation he
had begun with the first. In the end this treatment so disgusted him, by
association of ideas, with tomatoes, even of the edible variety, that whenever
he heard a newcomer order that vegetable, at the next table to his own, in the
Grand Hotel, he would murmur to him: 'You must excuse me, Sir, for
addressing you, without an introduction. But I heard you order tomatoes.
They are stale today. I tell you in your own interest, for it makes no difference
to me, I never touch them myself.' The stranger would reply with effusive
thanks to this philanthropic and disinterested neighbour, call back the waiter,
pretend to have changed his mind: 'No, on second thoughts, certainly not, no
tomatoes.' Aimé, who had seen it all before, would laugh to himself, and
think: 'He's an old rascal, that Monsieur Bernard, he's gone and made
another of them change his order.' M. Bernard, as he waited for the already
overdue tram, showed no eagerness to speak to Albertine and myself, because
of his black eye. We were even less eager to speak to him. It would however
have been almost inevitable if, at that moment, a bicycle had not come
dashing towards us; the lift-boy sprang from its saddle, breathless. Madame
Verdurin had telephoned shortly after we left the hotel, to know whether I
would dine with her two days later; we shall see presently why. Then, having
given me the message in detail, the lift-boy left us, and, being one of these
democratic 'employees' who affect independence with regard to the middle
classes, and among themselves restore the principle of authority, explained: 'I
must be off, because of my chiefs.'

Albertine's girl friends had gone, and would be away for some time. I was
anxious to provide her with distractions. Even supposing that she might
have found some happiness in spending the afternoons with no company
but my own, at Balbec, I knew that such happiness is never complete, and

that Albertine, being still at the age (which some of us never outgrow) when we have not yet discovered that this imperfection resides in the person who receives the happiness and not in the person who gives it, might have been tempted to put her disappointment down to myself. I preferred that she should impute it to circumstances which, arranged by myself, would not give us an opportunity of being alone together, while at the same time preventing her from remaining in the casino and on the beach without me. And so I had asked her that day to come with me to Doncières, where I was going to meet Saint-Loup. With a similar hope of occupying her mind, I advised her to take up painting, in which she had had lessons in the past. While working she would not ask herself whether she was happy or unhappy. I would gladly have taken her also to dine now and again with the Verdurins and the Cambremers, who certainly would have been delighted to see any friend introduced by myself, but I must first make certain that Mme Putbus was not yet at la Raspelière. It was only by going there in person that I could make sure of this, and, as I knew beforehand that on the next day but one Albertine would be going on a visit with her aunt, I had seized this opportunity to send Mme Verdurin a telegram asking her whether she would be at home upon Wednesday. If Mme Putbus was there, I would manage to see her maid, ascertain whether there was any danger of her coming to Balbec, and if so find out when, so as to take Albertine out of reach on the day. The little local railway, making a loop which did not exist at the time when I had taken it with my grandmother, now extended to Doncières-la-Goupil, a big station at which important trains stopped, among them the express by which I had come down to visit Saint-Loup, from Paris, and the corresponding express by which I had returned. And, because of the bad weather, the omnibus from the Grand Hotel took Albertine and myself to the station of the little tram, Balbec-Plage.

The little train had not yet arrived, but one could see, lazy and slow, the plume of smoke that it had left in its wake, which, confined now to its own power of locomotion as an almost stationary cloud, was slowly mounting the green slope of the cliff of Criquetot. Finally the little tram, which it had preceded by taking a vertical course, arrived in its turn, at a leisurely crawl. The passengers who were waiting to board it stepped back to make way for it, but without hurrying, knowing that they were dealing with a good-natured, almost human traveller, who, guided like the bicycle of a beginner, by the obliging signals of the station-master, in the strong hands of the engine-driver, was in no danger of running over anybody, and would come to a halt at the proper place.

My telegram explained the Verdurins' telephone message and had been all the more opportune since Wednesday (the day I had fixed happened to be a Wednesday) was the day set apart for dinner-parties by Mme Verdurin, at la Raspelière, as in Paris, a fact of which I was unaware. Mme Verdurin did not give 'dinners', but she had 'Wednesdays'. These Wednesdays were works of art. While fully conscious that they had not their match anywhere, Mme Verdurin introduced shades of distinction between them. 'Last Wednesday was not as good as the one before,' she would say. 'But I believe the next will be one of the best I have ever given.' Sometimes she went so far as to admit: 'This Wednesday was not worthy of the others. But I have a big surprise for you next week.' In the closing weeks of the Paris season, before leaving for the country, the Mistress would announce the end of the Wednesdays. It gave her an opportunity to stimulate the faithful. 'There are only three more Wednesdays left, there are only two more,' she would say, in the same tone as though the world were coming to an end. 'You aren't going to miss next Wednesday, for the finale.' But this finale was a sham, for she would announce: 'Officially, there will be no more Wednesdays. Today was the last for this year. But I shall be at home all the same on Wednesday. We shall have a little Wednesday to ourselves; I dare say these little private Wednesdays will be the nicest of all.' At la Raspelière, the Wednesdays were of necessity restricted, and since, if they had discovered a friend who was passing that way, they would invite him for one or another evening, almost every day of the week became a Wednesday. 'I don't remember all the guests, but I know there's Madame la Marquise de Camembert,' the lift-boy had told me; his memory of our discussion of the name Cambremer had not succeeded in definitely supplanting that of the old world, whose syllables, familiar and full of meaning, came to the young employee's rescue when he was embarrassed by this difficult name, and were immediately preferred and re-adopted by him, not by any means from laziness or as an old and ineradicable usage, but because of the need for logic and clarity which they satisfied.

We hastened in search of an empty carriage in which I could hold Albertine in my arms throughout the journey. Having failed to find one, we got into a compartment in which there was already installed a lady with a massive face, old and ugly, with a masculine expression, very much in her Sunday best, who was reading the *Revue des Deux Mondes*. Notwithstanding her commonness, she was eclectic in her tastes, and I found amusement in asking myself to what social category she could belong; I at once concluded that she must be the manager of some large brothel, a procuress on holiday. Her face, her manner, proclaimed the fact aloud. Only, I had never yet supposed that such ladies read the *Revue des Deux Mondes*. Albertine drew my attention to her with a wink and a smile. The lady wore an air of extreme dignity; and as I, for my part, bore within me the consciousness that I was invited, two days later, to the terminal point of the little railway, by the famous Mme Verdurin, that at an intermediate station I was awaited by Robert de Saint-Loup, and that a little farther on I had it in my power to give great pleasure to Mme de Cambremer, by going to stay at Féterne, my eyes sparkled with irony as I studied this self-important lady who seemed to think that, because of her elaborate attire, the feathers in her hat, her *Revue des Deux Mondes*, she was a more considerable personage than myself. I hoped that the lady would not remain in the train much longer than M. Nissim Bernard, and that she would alight at least at Toutainville, but no. The train stopped at Evreville, she remained seated. Similarly at Mont-martin-sur-Mer, at Parville-la-Bingard, at Incarville, so that in despair, when the train had left Saint-Frichoux, which was the last station before Doncières, I began to embrace Albertine without bothering about the lady. At Doncières, Saint-Loup had come to meet me at the station, with the greatest difficulty, he told me, for, as he was staying with his aunt, my telegram had only just reached him and he could not, having been unable to make any arrangements beforehand, spare me more than an hour of his time. This hour seemed to me, alas, far too long, for as soon as we had left the train Albertine devoted her whole attention to Saint-Loup. She never talked to me, barely answered me if I addressed her, repulsed me when I approached her. With Robert, on the other hand, she laughed her provoking laugh, talked to him volubly, played with the dog he had brought with him, and, as she excited the animal, deliberately rubbed against its master. I remembered that, on the day when Albertine had allowed me to kiss her for the first time, I had had a smile of gratitude for the unknown seducer who had wrought so profound a change in her and had so far simplified my task. I thought of him now with horror. Robert must have noticed that I was not unconcerned about Albertine, for he offered no response to her provocations, which made her extremely annoyed with myself; then he spoke to me as though I had been alone, which, when she realised it, raised me again in her esteem. Robert asked me if I would not like to meet those of his friends with whom he used to make me dine every evening at Doncières, when I was staying there, who were still in the garrison. And as he himself adopted that irritating manner which he rebuked in others: 'What is the good of your having worked so hard to *charm* them if you don't want to see them again?' I declined his offer, for I did not wish to run any risk of being parted from Albertine, but also because now I was detached from them. From them, which is to say from myself. We passionately long that there may be another life in which we shall be similar to what we are here below. But we do not pause to reflect that, even without waiting for that other life, in this life, after a few years we are unfaithful to what we have been, to what we wished to remain immortally. Even without supposing that death is to alter us more completely than the changes that occur in the course of a lifetime, if in that other life we were to encounter the self that we have been, we should turn away from ourselves as from those people with whom we were once on friendly terms but whom we have not seen for years – such as Saint-Loup's friends whom I used so much to enjoy meeting again every evening at the Faisan Doré, and whose conversation would now have seemed to me merely a boring importunity. In this respect, and because I preferred not to go there in search of what had pleased me there in the past, a stroll through Doncières might have seemed to me a prefiguration of an arrival in Paradise. We dream much of Paradise, or rather of a number of successive Paradises, but each of them is, long before we die, a Paradise lost, in which we should feel ourselves lost also.

He left us at the station. 'But you may have about an hour to wait,' he told me. 'If you spend it here, you will probably see my uncle Charlus, who is going by the train to Paris, ten minutes before yours. I have said goodbye to him already, because I have to go back before his train starts. I didn't tell him about you, because I hadn't got your telegram.' To the reproaches which I heaped upon Albertine when Saint-Loup had left us, she replied that she had intended, by her coldness towards me, to destroy any idea that he might have formed if, at the moment when the train stopped, he had seen me leaning against her with my arm round her waist. He had indeed noticed this attitude (I had not caught sight of him, otherwise I should have adopted one that was more correct), and had had time to murmur in my ear: 'So that's how it is, one of those priggish little girls you told me about, who wouldn't go near Mlle de Stermaria because they thought her fast?' I had indeed mentioned to Robert, and in all sincerity, when I went down from Paris to visit him at Doncières, and when we were talking about our time at Balbec, that there was nothing to be had from Albertine, that she was the embodiment of virtue. And now that I had long since discovered for myself that this was false, I was even more anxious that Robert should believe it to be true. It would have been sufficient for me to tell Robert that I was in love with Albertine. He was one of those people who are capable of denying themselves a pleasure to spare their friend sufferings which they would feel even more keenly if they themselves were the victims. 'Yes, she is still rather childish. But you don't know anything against her?' I added anxiously. 'Nothing, except that I saw you clinging together like a pair of lovers.'

'Your attitude destroyed absolutely nothing,' I told Albertine when Saint-

Loup had left us. 'Quite true,' she said to me, 'it was stupid of me, I hurt your feelings, I'm far more unhappy about it than you are. You'll see, I shall never be like that again; forgive me,' she pleaded, holding out her hand with a sorrowful air. At that moment, from the entrance to the waiting-room in which we were sitting, I saw advance slowly, followed at a respectful distance by a porter loaded with his baggage, M. de Charlus.

In Paris, where I encountered him only in evening dress, immobile, strait-laced in a black coat, maintained in a vertical posture by his proud aloofness, his thirst for admiration, the soar of his conversation, I had never realised how far he had aged. Now, in a light travelling suit which made him appear stouter, as he swaggered through the room, balancing a pursy stomach and an almost symbolical behind, the cruel light of day broke up into paint, upon his lips, rice-powder fixed by cold cream, on the tip of his nose, black upon his dyed moustaches whose ebon tint formed a contrast to his grizzled hair, all that by artificial light had seemed the animated colouring of a man who was still young.

While I stood talking to him, though briefly, because of his train, I kept my eye on Albertine's carriage to show her that I was coming. When I turned my head towards M. de Charlus, he asked me to be so kind as to summon a soldier, a relative of his, who was standing on the other side of the platform, as though he were waiting to take our train, but in the opposite direction, away from Balbec. 'He is in his regimental band,' said M. de Charlus. 'As you are so fortunate as to be still young enough, and I unfortunately am old enough for you to save me the trouble of going across to him.' I took it upon myself to go across to the soldier he pointed out to me, and saw from the lyres embroidered on his collar that he was a bandsman. But, just as I was preparing to execute my commission, what was my surprise, and, I may say, my pleasure, on recognising Morel, the son of my uncle's valet, who recalled to me so many memories. They made me forget to convey M. de Charlus's message. 'What, you are at Doncières?' 'Yes, and they've put me in the band attached to the batteries.' But he made this answer in a dry and haughty tone. He had become an intense 'poseur', and evidently the sight of myself, reminding him of his father's profession, was not pleasing to him. Suddenly I saw M. de Charlus descending upon us. My delay had evidently taxed his patience. 'I should like to listen to a little music this evening,' he said to Morel without any preliminaries, 'I pay five hundred francs for the evening, which may perhaps be of interest to one of your friends, if you have any in the band.' Knowing as I did the insolence of M. de Charlus, I was astonished at his not even saying how d'ye do to his young friend. The Baron did not however give me time to think. Holding out his hand in the friendliest manner: 'Goodbye, my dear fellow,' he said, as a hint that I might now leave them. I had, as it happened, left my dear Albertine too long alone. 'D'you know,' I said to her as I climbed into the carriage, 'life by the seaside and travelling make me realise that the theatre of the world is stocked with fewer settings than actors, and with fewer actors than situations.' 'What makes you say that?' 'Because M. de Charlus asked me just now to fetch one of his friends, whom, this instant, on the platform of this station, I have just discovered to be one of my own.' But as I uttered these words, I began to wonder how the Baron could have bridged the social gulf to which I had not given a thought. It occurred to me first of all that it might be through Jupien, whose niece, as the reader may remember, had seemed to show a preference for the violinist. What did baffle me completely was that, when due to leave for Paris in five minutes, the Baron should have asked for a musical evening. But, visualising Jupien's niece again in my memory, I was beginning to find that 'recognitions' did indeed play an important part in life, when all of a sudden the truth flashed across my mind and I realised that I had been absurdly innocent. M. de Charlus had never in his life set eyes upon Morel, nor Morel upon M. de Charlus, who, dazzled but also terrified by a warrior, albeit he bore no weapon but a lyre, had called upon me in his emotion to bring him the person whom he never suspected that I already knew. In any case, the offer of five hundred francs must have made up to Morel for the absence of any previous relations, for I saw that they continued to talk, without reflecting that they were standing close beside our tram. As I recalled the manner in which M. de Charlus had come up to Morel and myself, I saw at once the resemblance to certain of his relatives, when they picked up a woman in the street. Only the desired object had changed its sex. After a certain age, and even if different evolutions are occurring in us, the more we become ourselves, the more our characteristic features are accentuated. For Nature, while harmoniously contributing the design of her tapestry, breaks the monotony of the composition thanks to the variety of the intercepted forms. Besides, the arrogance with which M. de Charlus had accosted the violinist is relative, and depends upon the point of view one adopts. It would have been recognised by three out of four of the men in society who nodded their heads to him, not by the prefect of police who, a few years later, was to keep him under observation.

'The Paris train is signalled, Sir,' said the porter who was carrying his luggage. 'But I am not going by the train, put it in the cloakroom, damn you!' said M. de Charlus, as he gave twenty francs to the porter, astonished by the change of plan and charmed by the tip. This generosity at once

attracted a flower-seller. 'Buy these carnations, look, this lovely rose, kind
gentlemen, it will bring you luck.' M. de Charlus, out of patience, handed
her a couple of francs, in exchange for which the woman gave him her
blessing, and her flowers as well. 'Good God, why can't she leave us alone,'
said M. de Charlus, addressing himself in an ironical and complaining tone,
as of a man distraught, to Morel, to whom he found a certain comfort in
appealing. 'We've quite enough to talk about as it is.' Perhaps the porter was
not yet out of earshot, perhaps M. de Charlus did not care to have too
numerous an audience, perhaps these incidental remarks enabled his lofty
timidity not to approach too directly the request for an assignation. The
musician, turning with a frank, imperative and decided air to the flower-
seller, raised a hand which repulsed her and indicated to her that they did
not want her flowers and that she was to get out of their way as quickly as
possible. M. de Charlus observed with ecstasy this authoritative, virile
gesture, made by the graceful hand for which it ought still to have been too
weighty, too massively brutal, with a precocious firmness and suppleness
which gave to this still beardless adolescent the air of a young David capable
of waging war against Goliath. The Baron's admiration was unconsciously
blended with the smile with which we observe in a child an expression of
gravity beyond his years. 'This is a person whom I should like to accompany
me on my travels and help me in my business. How he would simplify my
life,' M. de Charlus said to himself.

The train for Paris (which M. de Charlus did not take) started. Then we
took our seats in our own train, Albertine and I, without my knowing what
had become of M. de Charlus and Morel. 'We must never quarrel any more,
I beg your pardon again,' Albertine repeated, alluding to the Saint-Loup
incident. 'We must always be nice to each other,' she said tenderly. 'As for
your friend Saint-Loup, if you think that I am the least bit interested in him,
you are quite mistaken. All that I like about him is that he seems so very fond
of you.' 'He's a very good fellow,' I said, taking care not to supply Robert
with those imaginary excellences which I should not have failed to invent,
out of friendship for himself, had I been with anybody but Albertine. 'He's
an excellent creature, frank, devoted, loyal, a person you can rely on to do
anything.' In saying this I confined myself, held in check by my jealousy, to
telling the truth about Saint-Loup, but what I said was literally true. It
found expression in precisely the same terms that Mme de Villeparisis had
employed in speaking to me of him, when I did not yet know him, imagined
him to be so different, so proud, and said to myself: 'People think him good
because he is a great gentleman.' Just as when she had said to me: 'He would
be so pleased', I imagined, after seeing him outside the hotel, preparing to

drive away, that his aunt's speech had been a mere social banality, intended to flatter me. And I had realised afterwards that she had said what she did sincerely, thinking of the things that interested me, of my reading, and because she knew that that was what Saint-Loup liked, as it was to be my turn to say sincerely to somebody who was writing a history of his ancestor La Rochefoucauld, the author of the *Maximes*, who wished to consult Robert about him: 'He will be so pleased.' It was simply that I had learned to know him. But, when I set eyes on him for the first time, I had not supposed that an intelligence akin to my own could be enveloped in so much outward elegance of dress and attitude. By his feathers I had judged him to be a bird of another species. It was Albertine now who, perhaps a little because Saint-Loup, in his kindness to myself, had been so cold to her, said to me what I had already thought: 'Ah! He is as devoted as all that! I notice that people always find all the virtues in other people, when they belong to the Faubourg Saint-Germain.' Now that Saint-Loup belonged to the Faubourg Saint-Germain was a thing of which I had never once thought in the course of all these years in which, stripping himself of his prestige, he had displayed to me his virtues. A change in our perspective in looking at other people, more striking already in friendship than in merely social relations, but how much more striking still in love, where desire on so vast a scale increases to such proportions the slightest signs of coolness, that far less than the coolness Saint-Loup had shown me in the beginning had been enough to make me suppose at first that Albertine scorned me, imagine her friends to be creatures marvellously inhuman, and ascribe merely to the indulgence that people feel for beauty and for a certain elegance, Elstir's judgment when he said to me of the little band, with just the same sentiment as Mme de Villeparisis speaking of Saint-Loup: 'They are good girls.' But this was not the opinion that I would instinctively have formed when I heard Albertine say: 'In any case, whether he's devoted or not, I sincerely hope I shall never see him again, since he's made us quarrel. We must never quarrel again. It isn't nice.' I felt, since she had seemed to desire Saint-Loup, almost cured for the time being of the idea that she cared for women, which I had supposed to be incurable. And, faced by Albertine's mackintosh in which she seemed to have become another person, the tireless vagrant of rainy days, and which, close-fitting, malleable and grey, seemed at that moment not so much intended to protect her garments from the rain as to have been soaked by her and to be clinging to my mistress's body as though to take the imprint of her form for a sculptor, I tore apart that tunic which jealously espoused a longed-for bosom and, drawing Albertine towards me: 'But won't you, indolent traveller, dream upon my shoulder, resting your brow upon it?' I said, taking her head in my hands, and showing her the wide meadows, flooded and silent, which extended in the gathering dusk to the horizon closed by the parallel openings of valleys far and blue.

Two days later, on the famous Wednesday, in that same little train, which I had again taken, at Balbec, to go and dine at la Raspelière, I was taking care not to miss Cottard at Graincourt-Saint-Vast, where a second telephone message from Mme Verdurin had told me that I should find him. He was to join my train and would tell me where we had to get out to pick up the carriages that would be sent from la Raspelière to the station. And so, as the little train barely stopped for a moment at Graincourt, the first station after Doncières, I was standing in readiness at the open window, so afraid was I of not seeing Cottard or of his not seeing me. Vain fears! I had not realised to what an extent the little clan had moulded all its regular members after the same type, so that they, being moreover in full evening dress, as they stood waiting upon the platform, let themselves be recognised immediately by a certain air of assurance, fashion and familiarity, by a look in their eyes which seemed to sweep, like an empty space in which there was nothing to arrest their attention, the serried ranks of the common herd, watched for the arrival of some fellow-member who had taken the train at an earlier station, and sparkled in anticipation of the talk that was to come. This sign of election, with which the habit of dining together had marked the members of the little group, was not all that distinguished them; when numerous, in full strength, they were massed together, forming a more brilliant patch in the midst of the troop of passengers – what Brichot called the *pecus* – upon whose dull countenances could be read no conception of what was meant by the name Verdurin, no hope of ever dining at la Raspelière. To be sure, these common travellers would have been less interested than myself had anyone quoted in their hearing – notwithstanding the notoriety that several of them had achieved – the names of those of the faithful whom I was astonished to see continuing to dine out, when many of them had already been doing so, according to the stories that I had heard, before my birth, at a period at once so distant and so vague that I was inclined to exaggerate its remoteness. The contrast between the continuance not only of their existence, but of the fullness of their powers, and the annihilation of so many friends whom I had already seen, in one place or another, pass away, gave me the same sentiment that we feel when in the stop-press column of the newspapers we read the very announcement that we least expected, for instance that of an untimely death, which seems to us fortuitous because the causes that have led up to it have remained outside our knowledge. This is the feeling that death does not descend upon all men alike, but that a more oncoming wave of its tragic tide carries off a life placed at the same level as others which the waves that follow will long continue to spare. We shall see later on that the diversity of the forms of death that circulate invisibly is the cause of the peculiar unexpectedness presented, in the newspapers, by their obituary notices. Then I saw that, with the passage of time, not only do the real talents that may coexist with the most commonplace conversation reveal and impose themselves, but furthermore that mediocre persons arrive at those exalted positions, attached in the imagination of our child-hood to certain famous elders, when it never occurred to us that, after a certain number of years, their disciples, become masters, would be famous also, and would inspire the respect and awe that once they felt. But if the names of the faithful were unknown to the *pecus*, their aspect still singled them out in its eyes. Indeed in the train (when the coincidence of what one or another of them might have been doing during the day, assembled them all together), having to collect at a subsequent station only an isolated member, the carriage in which they were gathered, ticketed with the elbow of the sculptor Ski, flagged with Cottard's *Temps*, stood out in the distance like a special saloon, and rallied at the appointed station the tardy comrade. The only one who might, because of his semi-blindness, have missed these welcoming signals, was Brichot. But one of the party would always volunteer to keep a lookout for the blind man, and, as soon as his straw hat, his green umbrella and blue spectacles caught the eye, he would be gently but hastily guided towards the chosen compartment. So that it was inconceivable that one of the faithful, without exciting the gravest suspicions of his being 'on the loose', or even of his not having come 'by the train', should not pick up the others in the course of the journey. Sometimes the opposite process occurred: one of the faithful had been obliged to go some distance down the line during the afternoon and was obliged in consequence to make part of the journey alone before being joined by the group; but even when thus isolated, alone of his kind, he did not fail as a rule to produce a certain effect. The Future towards which he was travelling marked him out to the person on the seat opposite, who would say to himself: 'That must be somebody', would discern, round the soft hat of Cottard or of the sculptor Ski, a vague aureole and would be only half-astonished when at the next station an elegant crowd, if it were their terminal point, greeted the faithful one at the carriage door and escorted him to one of the waiting carriages, all of them reverently saluted by the factotum of Douville station, or, if it were an intermediate station, invaded the compartment. This was what was done, and with precipitation, for some of them had arrived late, just as the train which was already in the station was about to start, by the troop which

Cottard led at a run towards the carriage in the window of which he had seen me signalling. Brichot, who was among these faithful, had become more faithful than ever in the course of these years which had diminished the assiduity of others. As his sight became steadily weaker, he had been obliged, even in Paris, to reduce more and more his working hours after dark. Besides he was out of sympathy with the modern Sorbonne, where ideas of scientific exactitude, after the German model, were beginning to prevail over humanism. He now confined himself exclusively to his lectures and to his duties as an examiner; and so had a great deal more time to devote to social pursuits. That is to say, to evenings at the Verdurins', or to those parties that now and again were offered to the Verdurins by one of the faithful, tremulous with emotion. It is true that on two occasions love had almost succeeded in achieving what his work could no longer do, in detaching Brichot from the little clan. But Mme Verdurin, who kept her eyes open, and moreover, having acquired the habit in the interests of her salon, had come to take a disinterested pleasure in this sort of drama and execution, had immediately brought about a coolness between him and the dangerous person, being skilled in (as she expressed it) 'putting things in order' and 'applying the red hot iron to the wound'. This she had found all the more easy in the case of one of the dangerous persons, who was simply Brichot's laundress, and Mme Verdurin, having the right of entry into the Professor's fifth floor rooms, crimson with rage, when she deigned to climb his stairs, had only had to shut the door in the wretched woman's face. 'What!' the Mistress had said to Brichot, 'a woman like myself does you the honour of calling upon you, and you receive a creature like that?' Brichot had never forgotten the service that Mme Verdurin had rendered him by preventing his old age from foundering in the mire, and became more and more strongly attached to her, whereas, in contrast to this revival of affection and possibly because of it, the Mistress was beginning to be tired of a too docile follower, and of an obedience of which she could be certain before- hand. But Brichot derived from his intimacy with the Verdurins a distinction which set him apart from all his colleagues at the Sorbonne. They were dazzled by the accounts that he gave them of dinner-parties to which they would never be invited, by the mention made of him in the reviews, the exhibition of his portrait in the Salon, by some writer or painter of repute whose talent the occupants of the other chairs in the Faculty of Arts esteemed, but without any prospect of attracting his attention, not to mention the elegance of the mundane philosopher's attire, an elegance which they had mistaken at first for slackness until their colleague kindly explained to them that a tall hat is naturally laid on the floor, when one is paying a call, and is not the right thing for dinners in the country, however smart, where it should be replaced by a soft hat, which goes quite well with a dinner-jacket. For the first few moments after the little group had plunged into the carriage, I could not even speak to Cottard, for he was suffocated, not so much by having run in order not to miss the train as by his astonishment at having caught it so exactly. He felt more than the joy inherent in success, almost the hilarity of an excellent joke. 'Ah! That was a good one!' he said when he had recovered himself. 'A minute later! 'Pon my soul, that's what they call arriving in the nick of time!' he added, with a wink intended not so much to enquire whether the expression were apt, for he was now overflowing with assurance, but to express his satisfaction. At length he was able to introduce me to the other members of the little clan. I was annoyed to see that they were almost all in the dress which in Paris is called smoking. I had forgotten that the Verdurins were beginning a timid evolution towards fashionable ways, retarded by the Dreyfus case, accelerated by the 'new' music, an evolution which for that matter they denied, and continued to deny until it was complete, like those military objectives which a general does not announce until he has reached them, so as not to appear defeated if he fails. In addition to which, Society was quite prepared to go half way to meet them. It went so far as to regard them as people to whose house nobody in Society went but who were not in the least perturbed by the fact. The Verdurin salon was understood to be a Temple of Music. It was there, people assured you, that Vinteuil had found inspiration, encouragement. Now, even if Vinteuil's sonata remained wholly unappreciated, and almost unknown, his name, quoted as that of the greatest of modern composers, had an extraordinary effect. Moreover, certain young men of the Faubourg having decided that they ought to be more intellectual than the middle classes, there were three of them who had studied music, and among these Vinteuil's sonata enjoyed an enormous vogue. They would speak of it, on returning to their homes, to the intelligent mothers who had incited them to acquire culture. And, taking an interest in what interested their sons, at a concert these mothers would gaze with a certain respect at Mme Verdurin in her front box, following the music in the printed score. So far, this social success latent in the Verdurins was revealed by two facts only. In the first place, Mme Verdurin would say of the Principessa di Caprarola: 'Ah! She is intelligent, she is a charming woman. What I cannot endure, are the imbeciles, the people who bore me, they drive me mad.' Which would have made anybody at all perspicacious realise that the Principessa di Caprarola, a woman who moved in the highest society, had called upon Mme Verdurin. She had even mentioned her name in the course of a visit of condolence which she had paid to Mme Swann after the death of her husband, and had asked whether she knew them. 'What name did you say?' Odette had asked, with a sudden wistfulness. 'Verdurin? Oh, yes, of course,' she had continued in a plaintive tone, 'I don't know them, or rather, I know them without really knowing them, they are people I used to meet at people's houses, years ago, they are quite nice.' When the Principessa di Caprarola had gone, Odette would fain have spoken the bare truth. But the immediate falsehood was not the fruit of her calculations, but the revelation of her fears, of her desires. She denied not what it would have been adroit to deny, but what she would have liked not to have happened, even if the other person was bound to hear an hour later that it was a fact. A little later she had recovered her assurance, and would indeed anticipate questions by saying, so as not to appear to be afraid of them: 'Mme Verdurin, why, I used to know her terribly well!' with an affectation of humility, like a great lady who tells you that she has taken the tram. 'There has been a great deal of talk about the Verdurins lately,' said Mme de Souvré. Odette, with the smiling disdain of a Duchess, replied: 'Yes, I do seem to have heard a lot about them lately. Every now and then there are new people who arrive like that in society', without reflecting that she herself was among the newest. 'The Principessa di Caprarola has dined there,' Mme de Souvré went on. 'Ah!' replied Odette, accentuating her smile, 'that does not surprise me. That sort of thing always begins with the Principessa di Caprarola, and then someone else follows suit, like Comtesse Molé.' Odette, in saying this, appeared to be filled with a profound contempt for the two great ladies who made a habit of 'house warming' in recently established drawing-rooms. One felt from her tone that the implication was that she, Odette, was, like Mme de Souvré, not the sort of person to let herself in for that sort of thing.

After the admission that Mme Verdurin had made of the Principessa di Caprarola's intelligence, the second indication that the Verdurins were conscious of their future destiny was that (without, of course, their having formally requested it) they became most anxious that people should now come to dine with them in evening dress. M. Verdurin could now have been greeted without shame by his nephew, the one who was 'in the cart'.

Among those who entered my carriage at Graincourt was Saniette, who long ago had been expelled from the Verdurins' by his cousin Forcheville, but had since returned. His faults, from the social point of view, had originally been – notwithstanding his superior qualities – something like Cottard's, shyness, anxiety to please, fruitless attempts to succeed in doing so. But if the course of life, by making Cottard assume, if not at the Verdurins', where he had, because of the influence that past associations

exert over us when we find ourselves in familiar surroundings, remained
more or less the same, at least in his practice, in his hospital ward, at the
Academy of Medicine, a shell of coldness, disdain, gravity, that became
more accentuated while he rewarded his appreciative students with puns,
had made a clean cut between the old Cottard and the new, the same defects
had on the contrary become exaggerated in Saniette, the more he sought to
correct them. Conscious that he was frequently boring, that people did not
listen to him, instead of then slackening his pace as Cottard would have
done, of forcing their attention by an air of authority, not only did he try by
adopting a humorous tone to make them forgive the unduly serious turn
of his conversation, he increased his pace, cleared the ground, used
abbreviations in order to appear less long-winded, more familiar with
the matters of which he spoke, and succeeded only, by making them
unintelligible, in seeming interminable. His self-assurance was not like that
of Cottard, freezing his patients, who, when other people praised his social
graces, would reply: 'He is a different man when he receives you in his
consulting room, you with your face to the light, and he with his back to it,
and those piercing eyes.' It failed to create an effect, one felt that it was
cloaking an excessive shyness, that the merest trifle would be enough to
dispel it. Saniette, whose friends had always told him that he was wanting in
self-confidence, and who had indeed seen men whom he rightly considered
greatly inferior to himself, attain with ease to the success that was denied to
him, never began telling a story without smiling at its drollery, fearing lest a
serious air might make his hearers underestimate the value of his wares.
Sometimes, giving him credit for the comic element which he himself
appeared to find in what he was about to say, people would do him the
honour of a general silence. But the story would fall flat. A fellow-guest who
was endowed with a kind heart would sometimes convey to Saniette the
private, almost secret encouragement of a smile of approbation, making it
reach him furtively, without attracting attention, as one passes a note from
hand to hand. But nobody went so far as to assume the responsibility, to risk
the glaring publicity of an honest laugh. Long after the story was ended and
had fallen flat, Saniette, crestfallen, would remain smiling to himself, as
though relishing in it and for himself the delectation which he pretended to
find adequate and which the others had not felt. As for the sculptor Ski, so
styled on account of the difficulty they found in pronouncing his Polish
surname, and because he himself made an affectation, since he had begun to
move in a certain social sphere, of not wishing to be confused with certain
relatives, perfectly respectable but slightly boring and very numerous, he
had, at forty-four and with no pretension to good looks, a sort of boyishness,

a dreamy wistfulness which was the result of his having been, until the age of ten, the most charming prodigy imaginable, the darling of all the ladies. Mme Verdurin maintained that he was more of an artist than Elstir. Any resemblance that there may have been between them was, however, purely external. It was enough to make Elstir, who had met Ski once, feel for him the profound repulsion that is inspired in us less by the people who are our exact opposite than by those who resemble us in what is least good, in whom are displayed our worst qualities, the faults of which we have cured ourselves, who irritate by reminding us of how we may have appeared to certain other people before we became what we now are. But Mme Verdurin thought that Ski had more temperament than Elstir because there was no art in which he had not a facility of expression, and she was convinced that he would have developed that facility into talent if he had not been so lazy. This seemed to the Mistress to be actually an additional gift, being the opposite of hard work which she regarded as the lot of people devoid of genius. Ski would paint anything you asked, on cuff-links or on the panels over doors. He sang with the voice of a composer, played from memory, giving the piano the effect of an orchestra, less by his virtuosity than by his vamped basses, which suggested the inability of the fingers to indicate that at a certain point the cornet entered, which, for that matter, he would imitate with his lips. Choosing his words when he spoke so as to convey an odd impression, just as he would pause before banging out a chord to say 'Ping!' so as to let the brasses be heard, he was regarded as marvellously intelligent, but as a matter of fact his ideas could be boiled down to two or three, extremely limited. Bored with his reputation for whimsicality, he had set himself to show that he was a practical, matter-of-fact person, whence a triumphant affectation of false precision, of false common sense, aggravated by his having no memory and a fund of information that was always inaccurate. The movements of his head, neck, limbs, would have been graceful if he had been still nine years old, with golden curls, a wide lace collar and little boots of red leather. Having reached Graincourt station with Cottard and Brichot, with time to spare, he and Cottard had left Brichot in the waiting-room and had gone for a stroll. When Cottard proposed to turn back, Ski had replied: 'But there is no hurry. It isn't the local train today, it's the departmental train.' Delighted by the effect that this refinement of accuracy produced upon Cottard, he added, with reference to himself: 'Yes, because Ski loves the arts, because he models in clay, people think he's not practical. Nobody knows this line better than I do.' Nevertheless they had turned back towards the station when, all of a sudden, catching sight of the smoke of the approaching train, Cottard, with a wild shout, had exclaimed: 'We shall have to put our best foot foremost.' They did as a matter of fact arrive with not a moment to spare, the distinction between local and departmental trains having never existed save in the mind of Ski. 'But isn't the Princess on the train?' came in ringing tones from Brichot, whose huge spectacles, resplendent as the reflectors that laryngologists attach to their foreheads to throw a light into the throats of their patients, seemed to have taken their life from the Professor's eyes, and possibly because of the effort that he was making to adjust his sight to them, seemed themselves, even at the most trivial moments, to be gazing at themselves with a sustained attention and an extraordinary fixity. Brichot's malady, as it gradually deprived him of his sight, had revealed to him the beauties of that sense, just as, frequently, we have to have made up our minds to part with some object, to make a present of it for instance, before we can study it, regret it, admire it. 'No, no, the Princess went over to Maineville with some of Mme Verdurin's guests who were taking the Paris train. It is within the bounds of possibility that Mme Verdurin, who had some business at Saint-Mars, may be with her! In that case, she will be coming with us, and we shall all travel together, which will be delightful. We shall have to keep our eyes skinned at Maineville and see what we shall see! Oh, but that's nothing, you may say that we came very near to missing the bus. When I saw the train I was dumbfounded. That's what is called arriving at the psychological moment. Can't you picture us missing the train, Mme Verdurin seeing the carriages come back without us: Tableau!' added the doctor, who had not yet recovered from his emotion. 'That would be a pretty good joke, wouldn't it? Now then, Brichot, what have you to say about our little escapade?' enquired the doctor with a note of pride. 'Upon my soul,' replied Brichot, 'why, yes, if you had found the train gone, that would have been what the late Villemain used to call a wipe in the eye!' But I, distracted at first by these people who were strangers to me, was suddenly reminded of what Cottard had said to me in the ballroom of the little casino, and, just as though there were an invisible link uniting an organ to our visual memory, the vision of Albertine leaning her breasts against Andrée's caused my heart a terrible pain. This pain did not last: the idea of Albertine's having relations with women seemed no longer possible since the occasion, forty-eight hours earlier, when the advances that my mistress had made to Saint-Loup had excited in me a fresh jealousy which had made me forget the old. I was simple enough to suppose that one taste of necessity excludes another. At Harambouville, as the tram was full, a farmer in a blue blouse who had only a third class ticket got into our compartment. The doctor, feeling that the Princess must not be allowed to travel with such a person, called a porter, showed his card, describing him as medical officer to one of the big railway companies, and obliged the station-master to make the farmer get out. This incident so pained and alarmed Saniette's timid spirit that, as soon as he saw it beginning, fearing already lest, in view of the crowd of peasants on the platform, it should assume the proportions of a rising, he pretended to be suffering from a stomach ache, and, so that he might not be accused of any share in the responsibility for the doctor's violence, wandered down the corridor, pretending to be looking for what Cottard called the 'water'. Failing to find one, he stood and gazed at the scenery from the other end of the 'twister'. 'If this is your first appearance at Mme Verdurin's, Sir,' I was addressed by Brichot, anxious to show off his talents before a newcomer, 'you will find that there is no place where one feels more the "amenities of life", to quote one of the inventors of dilettantism, of pococurantism, of all sorts of words in -ism that are in fashion among our little snobbesses, I refer to M. le Prince de Talleyrand.' For, when he spoke of these great noblemen of the past, he thought it clever and 'in the period' to prefix a 'M.' to their titles, and said 'M. le Duc de La Rochefoucauld', 'M. le Cardinal de Retz', referring to these also as 'That struggle-for-lifer de Gondi', 'that Boulangist de Marcillac'. And he never failed to call Montesquieu, with a smile, when he referred to him: 'Monsieur le Président Secondat de Montesquieu'. An intelligent man of the world would have been irritated by a pedantry which reeked so of the lecture-room. But in the perfect manners of the man of the world when speaking of a Prince, there is a pedantry also, which betrays a different caste, that in which one prefixes 'the Emperor' to the name 'William' and addresses a Royal Highness in the third person. 'Ah, now that is a man,' Brichot continued, still referring to 'Monsieur le Prince de Talleyrand' – 'to whom we take off our hats. He is an ancestor.' 'It is a charming house,' Cottard told me, 'you will find a little of everything, for Mme Verdurin is not exclusive, great scholars like Brichot, the high nobility, such as the Princess Sherbatov, a great Russian lady, a friend of the Grand Duchess Eudoxie, who even sees her alone at hours when no one else is admitted.' As a matter of fact the Grand Duchess Eudoxie, not wishing Princess Sherbatov, who for years past had been cut by everyone, to come to her house when there might be other people, allowed her to come only in the early morning, when Her Imperial Highness was not at home to any of those friends to whom it would have been as unpleasant to meet the Princess as it would have been awkward for the Princess to meet them. As, for the last three years, as soon as she came away, like a manicurist, from the Grand Duchess, Mme Sherbatov would go on to Mme Verdurin, who had just awoken, and stuck to her for the rest of the day, one might say that the Princess's loyalty surpassed even that of Brichot, constant as he was at those Wednesdays, both in Paris, where he had the pleasure of fancying himself a sort of Chateaubriand at l'Abbaye-aux-Bois, and in the country, where he saw himself becoming the equivalent of what might have been in the salon of Mme de Châtelet the man whom he always named (with an erudite sarcasm and satisfaction): 'M. de Voltaire'.

Her want of friends had enabled Princess Sherbatov to show for some years past to the Verdurins a fidelity which made her more than an ordinary member of the 'faithful', the type of faithfulness, the ideal which Mme Verdurin had long thought unattainable and which now, in her later years, she at length found incarnate in this new feminine recruit. However keenly the Mistress might feel the pangs of jealousy, it was without precedent that the most assiduous of her faithful should not have 'failed' her at least once. The most stay-at-home yielded to the temptation to travel; the most continent fell from virtue; the most robust might catch influenza, the idlest be caught for his month's soldiering, the most indifferent go to close the eyes of a dying mother. And it was in vain that Mme Verdurin told them then, like the Roman Empress, that she was the sole general whom her legion must obey, like the Christ or the Kaiser that he who loved his father or mother more than her and was not prepared to leave them and follow her was not worthy of her, that instead of slacking in bed or letting themselves be made fools of by bad women they would do better to remain in her company, by her, their sole remedy and sole delight. But destiny which is sometimes pleased to brighten the closing years of a life that has passed the mortal span had made Mme Verdurin meet the Princess Sherbatov. Out of touch with her family, an exile from her native land, knowing nobody but the Baroness Putbus and the Grand Duchess Eudoxie, to whose houses, because she herself had no desire to meet the friends of the former, and the latter no desire that her friends should meet the Princess, she went only in the early morning hours when Mme Verdurin was still asleep, never once, so far as she could remember, having been confined to her room since she was twelve years old, when she had had the measles, having on the 31st of December replied to Mme Verdurin who, afraid of being left alone, had asked her whether she would not 'shake down' there for the night, in spite of its being New Year's Eve: 'Why, what is there to prevent me, any day of the year? Besides, tomorrow is a day when one stays at home, and this is my home', living in a boarding-house, and moving from it whenever the Verdurins moved, accompanying them upon their holidays, the Princess had so completely exemplified to Mme Verdurin the line of Vigny:

Thou only didst appear that which one seeks always,

that the Lady President of the little circle, anxious to make sure of one of her 'faithful' even after death, had made her promise that whichever of them survived the other should be buried by her side. Before strangers – among whom we must always reckon him to whom we lie most barefacedly because he is the person whose scorn we should most dread: ourself – Princess Sherbatov took care to represent her only three friendships – with the Grand Duchess, the Verdurins, and the Baroness Putbus – as the only ones, not which cataclysms beyond her control had allowed to emerge from the destruction of all the rest, but which a free choice had made her elect in preference to any other, and to which a certain love of solitude and simplicity had made her confine herself. 'I see *nobody* else,' she would say, insisting upon the inflexible character of what appeared to be rather a rule that one imposes upon oneself than a necessity to which one submits. She would add: 'I visit only three houses,' as a dramatist who fears that it may not run to a fourth announces that there will be only three performances of his play. Whether or not M. and Mme Verdurin believed in the truth of this fiction, they had helped the Princess to instil it into the minds of the faithful. And they in turn were persuaded both that the Princess, among the thousands of invitations that were offered her, had chosen the Verdurins alone, and that the Verdurins, courted in vain by all the higher aristocracy, had consented to make but a single exception, in favour of the Princess.

In their eyes, the Princess, too far superior to her native element not to find it boring, among all the people whose society she might have enjoyed, found the Verdurins alone entertaining, while they, in return, deaf to the overtures with which they were bombarded by the entire aristocracy, had consented to make but a single exception, in favour of a great lady of more intelligence than the rest of her kind, the Princess Sherbatov.

The Princess was very rich; she engaged for every first night a large box, to which, with the assent of Mme Verdurin, she invited the faithful and nobody else. People would point to this pale and enigmatic person who had grown old without turning white, turning red rather like certain sere and shrivelled hedgerow fruits. They admired both her influence and her humility, for, having always with her an Academician, Brichot, a famous scientist, Cottard, the leading pianist of the day, at a later date M. de Charlus, she nevertheless made a point of securing the least prominent box in the theatre, remained in the background, paid no attention to the rest of the house, lived exclusively for the little group, who, shortly before the end of the performance, would withdraw in the wake of this strange sovereign, who was not without a certain timid, fascinating, faded beauty. But if Mme Sherbatov did not look at the audience, remained in shadow, it was to try to forget that there existed a living world which she passionately desired and was unable to know: the *côterie* in a box was to her what is to certain animals their almost corpselike immobility in the presence of danger. Nevertheless the thirst for novelty and for the curious which possesses people in society made them pay even more attention perhaps to this mysterious stranger than to the celebrities in the front boxes to whom everybody paid a visit. They imagined that she must be different from the people whom they knew, that a marvellous intellect combined with a discerning bounty retained round about her that little circle of eminent men. The Princess was compelled, if you spoke to her about anyone, or introduced anyone to her, to feign an intense coldness, in order to keep up the fiction of her horror of society. Nevertheless, with the support of Cottard or Mme Verdurin, several newcomers succeeded in making her acquaintance and such was her excitement at making a fresh acquaintance that she forgot the fable of her deliberate isolation, and went to the wildest extremes to please the newcomer. If he was entirely unimportant, the rest would be astonished. 'How strange that the Princess, who refuses to know anyone, should make an exception of such an uninteresting person.' But these fertilising acquaintances were rare, and the Princess lived narrowly confined in the midst of the faithful.

Cottard said far more often: 'I shall see him on Wednesday at the Verdurins' than: 'I shall see him on Tuesday at the Academy.' He spoke, too, of the Wednesdays as of an engagement equally important and inevitable. But Cottard was one of those people, little sought after, who make it as imperious a duty to respond to an invitation as if such invitations were orders, like a military or judicial summons. It required a call from a very important patient to make him 'fail' the Verdurins on a Wednesday, the importance depending moreover rather upon the rank of the patient than upon the gravity of his complaint. For Cottard, excellent fellow as he was, would forego the delights of a Wednesday not for a workman who had had a stroke, but for a Minister's cold. Even then he would say to his wife: 'Make my apologies to Mme Verdurin. Tell her that I shall be coming later on. His Excellency might really have chosen some other day to catch cold.' One Wednesday their old cook having opened a vein in her arm, Cottard, already in his dinner-jacket to go to the Verdurins', had shrugged his shoulders when his wife had timidly enquired whether he could not bandage the cut: 'Of course I can't, Léontine,' he had groaned; 'can't you see I've got my white waistcoat on?' So as not to annoy her husband, Mme Cottard had sent post haste for his chief dresser. He, to save time, had taken a cab, with the result that, his carriage entering

the courtyard just as Cottard's was emerging to take him to the Verdurins',
five minutes had been wasted in backing to let one another pass. Mme
Cottard was worried that the dresser should see his master in evening dress.
Cottard sat cursing the delay, from remorse perhaps, and started off in a
villainous temper which it took all the Wednesday's pleasures to dispel.

If one of Cottard's patients were to ask him: 'Do you ever see the
Guermantes?' it was with the utmost sincerity that the Professor would reply:
'Perhaps not actually the Guermantes, I can't be certain. But I meet all those
people at the house of some friends of mine. You must, of course, have heard
of the Verdurins. They know everybody. Besides, they certainly are not
people who've come down in the world. They've got the goods, all right. It is
generally estimated that Mme Verdurin is worth thirty-five million. Gad,
thirty-five million, that's a pretty figure. And so she doesn't make two bites at
a cherry. You mentioned the Duchesse de Guermantes. Let me explain the
difference. Mme Verdurin is a great lady, the Duchesse de Guermantes is
probably a nobody. You see the distinction, of course. In any case, whether
the Guermantes go to Mme Verdurin's or not, she entertains all the very best
people, the d'Sherbatoffs, the d'Forchevilles, *e tutti quanti*, people of the
highest flight, all the nobility of France and Navarre, with whom you would
see me conversing as man to man. Of course, those sort of people are only too
glad to meet the princes of science,' he added, with a smile of fatuous conceit,
brought to his lips by his proud satisfaction not so much that the expression
formerly reserved for men like Potain and Charcot should now be applicable
to himself, as that he knew at last how to employ all these expressions that
were authorised by custom, and, after a long course of study, had learned
them by heart. And so, after mentioning to me Princess Sherbatov as one of
the people who went to Mme Verdurin's, Cottard added with a wink: 'That
gives you an idea of the style of the house, if you see what I mean?' He meant
that it was the very height of fashion. Now, to entertain a Russian lady who
knew nobody but the Grand Duchess Eudoxie was not fashionable at all. But
Princess Sherbatov might not have known even her, it would in no way have
diminished Cottard's estimate of the supreme elegance of the Verdurin salon
or his joy at being invited there. The splendour that seems to us to invest the
people whose houses we visit is no more intrinsic than that of kings and
queens on the stage, in dressing whom it is useless for a producer to spend
hundreds and thousands of francs in purchasing authentic costumes and real
jewels, when a great designer will procure a far more sumptuous impression
by focussing a ray of light on a doublet of coarse cloth studded with lumps of
glass and on a cloak of paper. A man may have spent his life among the great
ones of the earth, who to him have been merely boring relatives or tiresome

acquaintances, because a familiarity engendered in the cradle had stripped them of all distinction in his eyes. The same man, on the other hand, need only have been led by some chance to mix with the most obscure people, for innumerable Cottards to be permanently dazzled by the ladies of title whose drawing-rooms they imagined as the centres of aristocratic elegance, ladies who were not even what Mme de Villeparisis and her friends were (great ladies fallen from their greatness, whom the aristocracy that had been brought up with them no longer visited); no, those whose friendship has been the pride of so many men, if these men were to publish their memoirs and to give the names of those women and of the other women who came to their parties, Mme de Cambremer would be no more able than Mme de Guermantes to identify them. But what of that! A Cottard has thus his Marquise, who is to him 'the Baronne', as in Marivaux, the Baronne whose name is never mentioned, so much so that nobody supposes that she ever had a name. Cottard is all the more convinced that she embodies the aristocracy – which has never heard of the lady – in that, the more dubious titles are, the more prominently coronets are displayed upon wineglasses, silver, notepaper, luggage. Many Cottards who have supposed that they were living in the heart of the Faubourg Saint-Germain have had their imagination perhaps more enchanted by feudal dreams than the men who did really live among Princes, just as with the small shopkeeper who, on Sundays, goes sometimes to look at 'old time' buildings, it is sometimes from those buildings every stone of which is of our own time, the vaults of which have been, by the pupils of Viollet-le-Duc, painted blue and sprinkled with golden stars, that they derive the strongest sensation of the middle ages. 'The Princess will be at Maineville. She will be coming with us. But I shall not introduce you to her at once. It will be better to leave that to Mme Verdurin. Unless I find a loophole. Then you can rely on me to take the bull by the horns.' 'What were you saying?' asked Saniette, as he rejoined us, pretending to have gone out to take the air. 'I was quoting to this gentleman,' said Brichot, 'a saying, which you will remember, of the man who, to my mind, is the first of the *fins-de-siècle* (of the eighteenth century, that is), by name Charles Maurice, Abbé de Perigord. He began by promising to be an excellent journalist. But he made a bad end, by which I mean that he became a Minister! Life has these tragedies. A far from scrupulous politician to boot who, with the lofty contempt of a thoroughbred nobleman, did not hesitate to work in his time for the King of Prussia, there are no two ways about it, and died in the skin of a "Left Centre".'

At Saint-Pierre-des-Ifs we were joined by a glorious girl who, unfortunately, was not one of the little group. I could not tear my eyes from her magnolia skin, her dark eyes, her bold and admirable outlines. A moment later she wanted to open a window, for it was hot in the compartment, and not wishing to ask leave of everybody, as I alone was without a greatcoat, she said to me in a quick, cool, jocular voice: 'Do you mind a little fresh air, Sir?' I would have liked to say to her: 'Come with us to the Verdurins', or 'Give me your name and address.' I answered: 'No, fresh air doesn't bother me, Mademoiselle.' Whereupon, without stirring from her seat: 'Do your friends object to smoke?' and she lit a cigarette. At the third station she sprang from the carriage. Next day, I enquired of Albertine, who could she be. For, stupidly thinking that people could have but one sort of love, in my jealousy of Albertine's attitude towards Robert, I was reassured so far as other women were concerned. Albertine told me, I believe quite sincerely, that she did not know. 'I should so much like to see her again,' I exclaimed. 'Don't worry, one always sees people again,' replied Albertine. In this particular instance, she was wrong; I never saw again, nor did I ever identify, the pretty girl with the cigarette. We shall see, moreover, why, for a long time, I ceased to look for her. But I have not forgotten her. I find myself at times, when I think of her, seized by a wild longing. But these recurrences of desire oblige us to reflect that if we wish to rediscover these girls with the same pleasure we must also return to the year which has since been followed by ten others in the course of which her bloom has faded. We can sometimes find a person again, but we cannot abolish time. And so on until the unforeseen day, gloomy as a winter night, when we no longer seek for that girl, or for any other, when to find her would actually frighten us. For we no longer feel that we have sufficient attraction to appeal to her, or strength to love her. Not, of course, that we are, in the strict sense of the word, impotent. And as for loving, we should love her more than ever. But we feel that it is too big an undertaking for the little strength that we have left. Eternal rest has already fixed intervals which we can neither cross nor make our voice be heard across them. To set our foot on the right step is an achievement like not missing the perilous leap. To be seen in such a state by a girl we love, even if we have kept the features and all the golden locks of our youth! We can no longer undertake the strain of keeping pace with youth. All the worse if our carnal desire increases instead of failing! We procure for it a woman whom we need make no effort to attract, who will share our couch for one night only and whom we shall never see again.

'Still no news, I suppose, of the violinist,' said Cottard. The event of the day in the little clan was, in fact, the failure of Mme Verdurin's favourite violinist. Employed on military service near Doncières, he came three times a week to dine at la Raspelière, having a midnight pass. But two days ago, for the first time, the faithful had been unable to discover him on the tram. It was supposed that he had missed it. But albeit Mme Verdurin had sent to meet the next tram, and so on until the last had arrived, the carriage had returned empty. 'He's certain to have been shoved into the guardroom, there's no other explanation of his desertion. Gad! In soldiering, you know, with those fellows, it only needs a bad-tempered serjeant.' 'It will be all the more mortifying for Mme Verdurin,' said Brichot, 'if he fails again this evening, because our kind hostess has invited to dinner for the first time the neighbours from whom she has taken la Raspelière, the Marquis and Marquise de Cambremer.' 'This evening, the Marquis and Marquise de Cambremer!' exclaimed Cottard. 'But I knew absolutely nothing about it. Naturally, I knew like everybody else that they would be coming one day, but I had no idea that it was to be so soon. Sapristi!' he went on, turning to myself, 'what did I tell you? The Princess Sherbatov, the Marquis and Marquise de Cambremer.' And, after repeating these names, lulling himself with their melody: 'You see that we move in good company,' he said to me. 'However, as it's your first appearance, you'll be one of the crowd. It is going to be an exceptionally brilliant gathering.' And, turning to Brichot, he went on: 'The Mistress will be furious. It is time we appeared to lend her a hand.' Ever since Mme Verdurin had been at la Raspelière she had pretended for the benefit of the faithful to be at once feeling and regretting the necessity of inviting her landlords for one evening. By so doing she would obtain better terms next year, she explained, and was inviting them for business reasons only. But she pretended to regard with such terror, to make such a bugbear of the idea of dining with people who did not belong to the little group that she kept putting off the evil day. The prospect did for that matter alarm her slightly for the reasons which she professed, albeit exaggerating them, if at the same time it enchanted her for reasons of snobbishness which she preferred to keep to herself. She was therefore partly sincere, she believed the little clan to be something so matchless throughout the world, one of those perfect wholes which it takes centuries of time to produce, that she trembled at the thought of seeing introduced into its midst these provincials, people ignorant of the Ring and the Meistersinger, who would be unable to play their part in the concert of conversation and were capable, by coming to Mme Verdurin's, of ruining one of those famous Wednesdays, master-pieces of art incomparable and frail, like those Venetian glasses which one false note is enough to shatter. 'Besides, they are bound to be absolutely *anti*, and militarists,' M. Verdurin had said. 'Oh, as for that, I don't mind, we've heard quite enough about all that business,' had replied Mme Verdurin, who, a sincere Dreyfusard, would nevertheless have been glad to discover a social counterpoise to the preponderant Dreyfusism of her salon. For Dreyfusism was triumphant politically, but not socially. Labori, Reinach, Picquart, Zola were still, to people in society, more or less traitors, who could only keep them aloof from the little nucleus. And so, after this incursion into politics, Mme Verdurin was determined to return to the world of art. Besides were not Indy, Debussy, on the 'wrong' side in the Case? 'So far as the Case goes, we need only remember Brichot,' she said (the Don being the only one of the faithful who had sided with the General Staff, which had greatly lowered him in the esteem of Madame Verdurin). 'There is no need to be eternally discussing the Dreyfus case. No, the fact of the matter is that the Cambremers bore me.' As for the faithful, no less excited by their unconfessed desire to make the Cambremers' acquaintance than dupes of the affected reluctance which Mme Verdurin said she felt to invite them, they returned, day after day, in conversation with her, to the base arguments with which she herself supported the invitation, tried to make them irresistible. 'Make up your mind to it once and for all,' Cottard repeated, 'and you will have better terms for next year, they will pay the gardener, you will have the use of the meadow. That will be well worth a boring evening. I am thinking only of yourselves,' he added, albeit his heart had leaped on one occasion, when, in Mme Verdurin's carriage, he had met the carriage of the old Mme de Cambremer and, what was more, he had been abased in the sight of the railwaymen when, at the station, he had found himself standing beside the Marquis. For their part, the Cambremers, living far too remote from the social movement ever to suspect that certain ladies of fashion were speaking with a certain consideration of Mme Verdurin, imagined that she was a person who could know none but Bohemians, was perhaps not even legally married, and so far as people of birth were concerned would never meet any but themselves. They had resigned themselves to the thought of dining with her only to be on good terms with a tenant who, they hoped, would return again for many seasons, especially after they had, in the previous month, learned that she had recently inherited all those millions. It was in silence and without any vulgar pleasantries that they prepared themselves for the fatal day. The faithful had given up hope of its ever coming, so often had Mme Verdurin already fixed in their hearing a date that was invariably postponed. These false decisions were intended not merely to make a display of the boredom that she felt at the thought of this dinner-party, but to keep in suspense those members of the little group who were staying in the neighbourhood and were sometimes inclined to fail. Not that the Mistress guessed that the 'great day' was as delightful a prospect to them as to herself, but in order that, having persuaded them that this dinner-party was to her the most terrible of social duties, she might make an appeal to their devotion. 'You are not going to leave me all alone with those Chinese mandarins! We must assemble in full force to support the boredom. Naturally, we shan't be able to talk about any of the things in which we are interested. It will be a Wednesday spoiled, but what is one to do!'

'Indeed,' Brichot explained to me, 'I fancy that Mme Verdurin, who is highly intelligent and takes infinite pains in the elaboration of her Wednesdays, was by no means anxious to see these bumpkins of ancient lineage but scanty brains. She could not bring herself to invite the dowager Marquise, but has resigned herself to having the son and daughter-in-law.' 'Ah! We are to see the Marquise de Cambremer?' said Cottard with a smile into which he saw fit to introduce a leer of sentimentality, albeit he had no idea whether Mme de Cambremer were good-looking or not. But the title Marquise suggested to him fantastic thoughts of gallantry. 'Ah! I know her,' said Ski, who had met her once when he was out with Mme Verdurin. 'Not in the biblical sense of the word, I trust,' said the doctor, darting a sly glance through his eyeglass; this was one of his favourite pleasantries. 'She is intelligent,' Ski informed me. 'Naturally,' he went on, seeing that I said nothing, and dwelling with a smile upon each word, 'she is intelligent and at the same time she is not, she lacks education, she is frivolous, but she has an instinct for beautiful things. She may say nothing, but she will never say anything silly. And besides, her colouring is charming. She would be an amusing person to paint,' he added, half shutting his eyes, as though he saw her posing in front of him. As my opinion of her was quite the opposite of what Ski was expressing with so many fine shades, I observed merely that she was the sister of an extremely distinguished engineer, M. Legrandin. 'There, you see, you are going to be introduced to a pretty woman,' Brichot said to me, 'and one never knows what may come of that. Cleopatra was not even a great lady, she was a little woman, the unconscious, terrible little woman of our Meilhac, and just think of the consequences, not only to that idiot Antony, but to the whole of the ancient world.' 'I have already been introduced to Mme de Cambremer,' I replied. 'Ah! In that case, you will find yourself on familiar ground.' 'I shall be all the more delighted to meet her,' I answered him, 'because she has promised me a book by the former curé of Combray about the place-names of this district, and I shall be able to remind her of her promise. I am interested in that priest, and also in etymologies.' 'Don't put any faith in the ones he gives,' replied Brichot, 'there is a copy of the book at la Raspelière, which I have glanced through, but without finding anything of any value; it is a mass of error. Let me give you an example. The word Bricq is found in a number of place-names in this neighbourhood. The worthy cleric had the distinctly odd idea that it comes from Briga, a height, a fortified place. He finds it already in the Celtic tribes, Latobriges, Nemetobriges, and so forth, and traces it down to such names as Briand, Brion, and so forth. To confine ourselves to the region in which we have the pleasure of your company at this moment, Bricquebose means the wood on the height, Bricqueville the habitation on the height, Bricquebec, where we shall be stopping presently before coming to Maineville, the height by the stream. Now there is not a word of truth in all this, for the simple reason that *bricq* is the old Norse word which means simply a bridge. Just as fleur, which Mme de Cambremer's protégé takes infinite pains to connect, in one place with the Scandinavian words *floi*, *flo*, in another with the Irish word *ae* or *aer*, is, beyond any doubt, the *fjord* of the Danes, and means harbour. So too, the excellent priest thinks that the station of Saint-Mars-le-Vêtu, which adjoins la Raspelière, means Saint-Martin-le-Vieux (*vetus*). It is unquestionable that the word *vieux* has played a great part in the toponymy of this region. *Vieux* comes as a rule from *vadum*, and means a passage, as at the place called les Vieux. It is what the English call *ford* (Oxford, Hereford). But, in this particular instance, Vêtu is derived not from *vetus*, but from *vas-tatus*, a place that is devastated and bare. You have, round about here, Sottevast, the *vast* of Setold, Brillevast, the *vast* of Berold. I am all the more certain of the curé's mistake, in that Saint-Mars-le-Vêtu was formerly called Saint-Mars du Gast and even Saint-Mars-de-Terregate. Now the *v* and the *g* in these words are the same letter. We say *dévaster*, but also *gâcher*. *Jâchères* and *gatines* (from the High German *wastinna*) have the same meaning: Terregate is therefore *terra vasta*. As for Saint-Mars, formerly (save the mark) Saint-Merd, it is Saint-Medardus, which appears variously as Saint-Médard, Saint-Mard, Saint-Marc, Cinq-Mars, and even Dammas. Nor must we forget that quite close to here, places bearing the name of Mars are proof simply of a pagan origin (the god Mars) which has remained alive in this country but which the holy man refuses to see. The high places dedicated to the gods are especially frequent, such as the mount of Jupiter (Jeumont). Your curé declines to admit this, but, on the other hand, wherever Christianity has left traces, they escape his notice. He has gone so far afield as to Loctudy, a barbarian name, according to him, whereas it is simply *Locus Sancti Tudeni*, nor has he in Sammarcoles divined *Sanctus Martialis*. Your curé,' Brichot continued, seeing that I was interested, 'derives the terminations *hon*, *home*, *holm*, from the word *holl* (*hullus*), a hill, whereas it comes from the Norse *holm*, an island, with which you are familiar in Stockholm, and which is so widespread throughout this district, la Houlme, Engohomme, Tahoume, Robehomme, Néhomme, Quettehon, and so forth.' These names made me think of the day when Albertine had wished to go to Amfreville-la-Bigot (from the name of two successive lords of the manor, Brichot told me), and had then suggested that we should dine together at Robehomme. As for Maineville, we were just coming to it. 'Isn't Néhomme,' I asked, 'somewhere near Carquethuit and Clitourps?' 'Precisely; Néhomme is the *holm*, the island or peninsula of the famous Viscount Nigel, whose name has survived also in Néville. The Carquethuit and Clitourps that you mention furnish Mme de Cambremer's protégé with an occasion for further blunders. No doubt he has seen that *carque* is a church, the *Kirche* of the Germans. You will remember Querqueville, not to mention Dunkerque. For there we should do better to stop and consider the famous word *Dun*, which to the Celts meant high ground. And that you will find over the whole of France. Your abbé was hypnotised by Duneville, which recurs in the Eure-et-Loir; he would have found Châteaudun, Dun-le-Roi in the Cher, Duneau in the Sarthe, Dun in the Ariège, Dune-les-Places in the Nièvre, and many others. This word *Dun* leads him into a curious error with regard to Douville where we shall be alighting, and shall find Mme Verdurin's comfortable carriages awaiting us. Douville, in Latin *donvilla*, says he. As a matter of fact, Douville does lie at the foot of high hills. Your curé, who knows everything, feels all the same that he has made a blunder. He has, indeed, found in an old cartulary, the name *Domvilla*. Whereupon he retracts; Douville, according to him, is a fief belonging to the Abbot, *Domino Abbati*, of Mont Saint-Michel. He is delighted with the discovery, which is distinctly odd when one thinks of the scandalous life that, according to the Capitulary of Sainte-Claire sur Epte, was led at Mont Saint-Michel, though no more extraordinary than to picture the King of Denmark as suzerain of all this coast, where he encouraged the worship of Odin far more than that of Christ. On the other hand, the supposition that the n has been changed to m does not shock me, and requires less alteration than the perfectly correct Lyon, which also is derived from *Dun* (*Lugdunum*). But the fact is, the abbé is mistaken. Douville was never Donville, but Doville, *Eudonis villa*, the village of Eudes. Douville was formerly called Escalecliff, the steps up the cliff. About the year 1233, Eudes le Bouteiller, Lord of Escalecliff, set out for the Holy Land; on the eve of his departure he made over the church to the Abbey of Blanchelande. By an exchange of courtesies, the village took his name, whence we have Douville today. But I must add that toponymy, of which moreover I know little or nothing, is not an exact science; had we not this historical evidence, Douville might quite well come from Ouville, that is to say the Waters. The forms in ai (Aigues-Mortes), from *aqua*, are constantly changed to *eu* or *ou*. Now there were, quite close to Douville, certain famous springs, Carquethuit. You might suppose that the curé was only too ready to detect there a Christian origin, especially as this district seems to have been pretty hard to convert, since successive attempts were made by Saint Ursal, Saint Gofroi, Saint Barsanore, Saint Laurent of Brèvedent, who finally handed over the task to the monks of Beaubec. But as regards *thuit* the writer is mistaken, he sees in it a form of *toft*, a building, as in Cricquetot, Ectot, Yvetot, whereas it is the *thveit*, the clearing, the reclaimed land, as in Braquetuit, le Thuit, Regnetuit, and so forth. Similarly, if he recognises in Clitourps the Norman *thorp* which means village, he insists that the first syllable of the word must come from *clivus*, a slope, whereas it comes from *cliff*, a precipice. But his biggest blunders are due not so much to his ignorance as to his prejudices. However loyal a Frenchman one is, there is no need to fly in the face of the evidence and take Saint-Laurent en Bray to be the Roman priest, so famous at one time, when he is actually Saint Lawrence O'Toole, Archbishop of Dublin. But even more than his patriotic sentiments, your friend's religious bigotry leads him into strange errors. Thus you have not far from our hosts at la Raspelière two places called Montmartin, Montmartin-sur-Mer and Mont-martin-en-Graignes. In the case of Graignes, the good curé has been quite right, he has seen that Graignes, in Latin *Grania*, in Greek *Krene*, means ponds, marshes; how many instances of Cresmays, Croen, Gremeville, Lengronne, might we not adduce? But, when he comes to Montmartin, your self-styled linguist positively insists that these must be parishes dedicated to Saint Martin. He bases his opinion upon the fact that the Saint is their patron, but does not realise that he was only adopted subsequently; or rather he is blinded by his hatred of paganism; he refuses to see that we should say Mont-Saint-Martin as we say Mont Saint-Michel, if it were a question of Saint Martin, whereas the name Montmartin refers in a far more pagan fashion to temples consecrated to the god Mars, temples of which, it is true, no other vestige remains, but which the undisputed existence in the neighbourhood of vast Roman camps would render highly probable even without the name Montmartin, which removes all doubt. You see that the little pamphlet which you will find at la Raspelière is far from perfect.' I protested that at Combray the curé had often told us interesting etymologies. 'He was probably better on his own ground, the move to Normandy must have made him lose his bearings.' 'Nor did it do him any good,' I added, 'for he came here with neurasthenia and went away again with rheumatism.' 'Ah, his neurasthenia is to blame. He has lapsed from neurasthenia to philology, as my worthy master Pocquelin would have said. Tell us, Cottard, do you suppose that neurasthenia can have a disturbing effect on philology, philology a soothing effect on neurasthenia and the relief from neurasthenia lead to rheumatism?' 'Undoubtedly, rheumatism and neurasthenia are subordinate forms of neuro-arthritism. You may pass from one to the other by metastasis.' 'The eminent Professor,' said Brichot, 'expresses himself in a French as highly infused with Latin and Greek as M. Purgon himself, of Molièresque memory! My uncle, I refer to our national Sarcey . . . ' But he was prevented from finishing his sentence. The Professor had leaped from his seat with a wild shout: 'The devil!' he exclaimed on regaining his power of articulate speech, 'we have passed Maineville (d'you hear?) and Renneville too.' He had just noticed that the train was stopping at Saint-Mars-le-Vêtu, where most of the passengers alighted. 'They can't have run through without stopping. We must have failed to notice it while we were talking about the Cambremers. Listen to me, Ski, pay attention, I am going to tell you "a good one",' said Cottard, who had taken a fancy to this expression, in common use in certain medical circles. 'The Princess must be on the train, she can't have seen us, and will have got into another compartment. Come along and find her. Let's hope this won't land us in trouble!' And he led us all off in search of Princess Sherbatov. He found her in the corner of an empty compartment, reading the *Revue des Deux Mondes*. She had long ago, from fear of rebuffs, acquired the habit of keeping in her place, or remaining in her corner, in life as on the train, and of not offering her hand until the other person had greeted her. She went on reading as the faithful trooped into her carriage. I recognised her immediately; this woman who might have forfeited her position but was nevertheless of exalted birth, who in any event was the pearl of a salon such as the Verdurins', was the lady whom, on the same train, I had put down, two days earlier, as possibly the keeper of a brothel. Her social personality, which had been so vague, became clear to me as soon as I learned her name, just as when, after racking our brains over a puzzle, we at length hit upon the word which clears up all the obscurity, and which, in the case of a person, is his name. To discover two days later who the person is with whom one has travelled in the train is a far more amusing surprise than to read in the next number of a magazine the clue to the problem set in the previous number. Big restaurants, casinos, local trains, are the family portrait galleries of these social enigmas. 'Princess, we must have missed you at Maineville! May we come and sit in your compartment?' 'Why, of course,' said the Princess who, upon hearing Cottard address her, but only then, raised from her magazine a pair of eyes which, like the eyes of M. de Charlus, although gentler, saw perfectly well the people of whose presence she pretended to be unaware. Cottard, coming to the conclusion that the fact of my having been invited to meet the Cambremers was a sufficient recommendation, decided, after a momentary hesitation, to introduce me to the Princess, who bowed with great courtesy but appeared to be hearing my name for the first time. 'Cré nom!' cried the doctor, 'my wife has forgotten to make them change the buttons on my white waistcoat. Ah! Those women, they never remember anything. Don't you ever marry, my boy,' he said to me. And as this was one of the pleasantries which he considered appropriate when he had nothing else to say, he peeped out of the corner of his eye at the Princess and the rest of the faithful, who, because he was a Professor and an Academician, smiled back, admiring his good temper and freedom from pride. The Princess informed us that the young violinist had been found. He had been confined to bed the evening before by a sick headache, but was coming that evening and bringing with him a friend of his father whom he had met at Doncières. She had learned this from Mme Verdurin with whom she had taken luncheon that morning, she told us in a rapid voice, rolling her r's, with her Russian accent, softly at the back of her throat, as though they were not r's but l's. 'Ah! You had luncheon with her this morning,' Cottard said to the Princess; but turned his eyes to myself, the purport of this remark being to show me on what intimate terms the Princess was with the Mistress. 'You are indeed a faithful adherent!' 'Yes, I love the little cirlcle, so intelligent, so agleeable, neverl spiteful, quite simple, not at all snobbish, and clevel to theirl fingletips.' 'Nom d'une pipe! I must have lost my ticket, I can't find it anywhere,' cried Cottard, with an agitation that was, in the circumstances, quite unjustified. He knew that at Douville, where a couple of landaus would be awaiting us, the collector would let him pass without a ticket, and would only bare his head all the more humbly, so that the salute might furnish an explanation of his indulgence, to wit that he had of course recognised Cottard as one of the Verdurins' regular guests. 'They won't shove me in the lock-up for that,' the doctor concluded. 'You were saying, Sir,' I enquired of Brichot, 'that there used to be some famous waters near here; how do we know that?' 'The name of the next station is one of a multitude of proofs. It is called Fervaches.' 'I don't undlestand what he's talking about,' mumbled the Princess, as though she were saying to me out of politeness: 'He's rather a bore, ain't he?' 'Why, Princess, Fervaches means hot springs. Fervidae aquae. But to return to the young violinist,' Brichot went on, 'I was quite forgetting, Cottard, to tell you the great news. Had you heard that our poor friend Dechambre, who used to be Mme

Verdurin's favourite pianist, has just died? It is terribly sad.' 'He was quite young,' replied Cottard, 'but he must have had some trouble with his liver, there must have been something sadly wrong in that quarter, he had been looking very queer indeed for a long time past.' 'But he was not so young as all that,' said Brichot; 'in the days when Elstir and Swann used to come to Mme Verdurin's, Dechambre had already made himself a reputation in Paris, and, what is remarkable, without having first received the baptism of success abroad. Ah! He was no follower of the Gospel according to Saint Barnum, that fellow.' 'You are mistaken, he could not have been going to Mme Verdurin's, at that time, he was still in the nursery.' 'But, unless my old memory plays me false, I was under the impression that Dechambre used to play Vinteuil's sonata for Swann, when that clubman, who had broken with the aristocracy, had still no idea that he was one day to become the embourgeoised Prince Consort of our national Odette.' 'It is impossible, Vinteuil's sonata was played at Mme Verdurin's long after Swann ceased to come there,' said the doctor, who, like all people who work hard and think that they remember many things which they imagine to be of use to them, forget many others, a condition which enables them to go into ecstasies over the memories of people who have nothing else to do. 'You are hopelessly muddled, though your brain is as sound as ever,' said the doctor with a smile. Brichot admitted that he was mistaken. The train stopped. We were at la Sogne. The name stirred my curiosity. 'How I should like to know what all these names mean,' I said to Cottard. 'You must ask M. Brichot, he may know, perhaps.' 'Why, la Sogne is la Cicogne, *Siconia*,' replied Brichot, whom I was burning to interrogate about many other names.

Forgetting her attachment to her 'corner', Mme Sherbatov kindly offered to change places with me, so that I might talk more easily with Brichot, whom I wanted to ask about other etymologies that interested me, and assured me that she did not mind in the least whether she travelled with her face or her back to the engine, standing, or seated, or anyhow. She remained on the defensive until she had discovered a newcomer's intentions, but as soon as she had realised that these were friendly, she would do everything in her power to oblige. At length the train stopped at the station of Douville-Féterne, which being more or less equidistant from the villages of Féterne and Douville, bore for this reason their hyphenated name. 'Saperlipopette!' exclaimed Doctor Cottard, when we came to the barrier where the tickets were collected, and, pretending to have only just discovered his loss, 'I can't find my ticket, I must have lost it.' But the collector, taking off his cap, assured him that it did not matter and smiled respectfully. The Princess (giving instructions to the coachman, as though she were a sort of lady-in-waiting to Mme Verdurin, who, because of the Cambremers, had not been able to come to the station, as, for that matter, she rarely did) took me, and also Brichot, with herself in one of the carriages. The doctor, Saniette and Ski got into the other.

The driver, although quite young, was the Verdurins' first coachman, the only one who had any right to the title; he took them, in the daytime, on all their excursions, for he knew all the roads, and in the evening went down to meet the faithful and took them back to the station later on. He was accompanied by extra helpers (whom he selected if necessary). He was an excellent fellow, sober and capable, but with one of those melancholy faces on which a fixed stare indicates that the merest trifle will make the person fly into a passion, not to say nourish dark thoughts. But at the moment he was quite happy, for he had managed to secure a place for his brother, another excellent type of fellow, with the Verdurins. We began by driving through Douville. Grassy knolls ran down from the village to the sea, in wide slopes to which their saturation in moisture and salt gave a richness, a softness, a vivacity of extreme tones. The islands and indentations of Rivebelle, far nearer now than at Balbec, gave this part of the coast the appearance, novel to me, of a relief map. We passed by some little bungalows, almost all of which were let to painters; turned into a track upon which some loose cattle, as frightened as were our horses, barred our way for ten minutes, and emerged upon the cliff road. 'But, by the immortal gods,' Brichot suddenly asked, 'let us return to that poor Dechambre; do you suppose Mme Verdurin *knows*? Has anyone told *her*?' Mme Verdurin, like most people who move in society, simply because she needed the society of other people, never thought of them again for a single day, as soon as, being dead, they could no longer come to the Wednesdays, nor to the Saturdays, nor dine without dressing. And one could not say of the little clan, a type in this respect of all salons, that it was composed of more dead than living members, seeing that, as soon as one was dead, it was as though one had never existed. But, to escape the nuisance of having to speak of the deceased, in other words to postpone one of the dinners – a thing impossible to the mistress – as a token of mourning, M. Verdurin used to pretend that the death of the faithful had such an effect on his wife that, in the interest of her health, it must never be mentioned to her. Moreover, and perhaps just because the death of other people seemed to him so conclusive, so vulgar an accident, the thought of his own death filled him with horror and he shunned any consideration that might lead to it. As for Brichot, since he was the soul of honesty and completely taken in by what M. Verdurin said about his wife, he dreaded for his friend's sake the emotions that such a bereavement must cause her. 'Yes, she *knew the worst* this morning,' said the Princess, 'it was impossible to *keep it from her*.' 'Ah! Thousand thunders of Zeus!' cried Brichot. 'Ah! it must have been a terrible blow, a friend of twenty-five years' standing. There was a man who was one of us.' 'Of course, of course, what can you expect? Such incidents are bound to be painful; but Madame Verdurin is a brave woman, she is even more cerebral than emotive.' 'I don't altogether agree with the Doctor,' said the Princess, whose rapid speech, her murmured accents, certainly made her appear both sullen and rebellious. 'Mme Verdurin, beneath a cold exterior, conceals treasures of sensibility. M. Verdurin told me that he had had great difficulty in preventing her from going to Paris for the funeral; he was obliged to let her think that it was all to be held in the country.' 'The devil! She wanted to go to Paris, did she? Of course, I know that she has a heart, too much heart perhaps. Poor Dechambre! As Madame Verdurin remarked not two months ago: "Compared with him, Planté, Paderewski, Risler himself are nowhere!" Ah, he could say with better reason than that limelighter Nero, who has managed to take in even German scholarship: *Qualis artifex pereo!* But he at least, Dechambre, must have died in the fulfilment of his priesthood, in the odour of Beethovenian devotion; and gallantly, I have no doubt; he had every right, that interpreter of German music, to pass away while celebrating the *Mass in D*. But he was, when all is said, the man to greet the unseen with a cheer, for that inspired performer would produce at times from the Parisianised Champagne stock of which he came, the swagger and smartness of a guardsman.'

From the height we had now reached, the sea suggested no longer, as at Balbec, the undulations of swelling mountains, but on the contrary the view, beheld from a mountain-top or from a road winding round its flank, of a blue-green glacier or a glittering plain, situated at a lower level. The lines of the currents seemed to be fixed upon its surface, and to have traced there for ever their concentric circles; the enamelled face of the sea which changed imperceptibly in colour, assumed towards the head of the bay, where an estuary opened, the blue whiteness of milk, in which little black boats that did not move seemed entangled like flies. I felt that from nowhere could one discover a vaster prospect. But at each turn in the road a fresh expanse was added to it and when we arrived at the Douville toll-house, the spur of the cliff which until then had concealed from us half the bay, withdrew, and all of a sudden I descried upon my left a gulf as profound as that which I had already had before me, but one that changed the proportions of the other and doubled its beauty. The air at this lofty point acquired a keenness and purity that intoxicated me. I adored the Verdurins; that they should have sent a carriage for us seemed to me a touching act of kindness. I should have liked to kiss the Princess. I told her that I had never seen anything so beautiful. She professed that she too loved this spot more than any other. But I could see that to her as to the Verdurins the thing that really mattered was not to gaze at the view like tourists, but to partake of good meals there, to entertain people whom they liked, to write letters, to read books, in short to live in these surroundings, passively allowing the beauty of the scene to soak into them rather than making it the object of their attention.

After the toll-house, where the carriage had stopped for a moment at such a height above the sea that, as from a mountain-top, the sight of the blue gulf beneath almost made one dizzy, I opened the window; the sound, distinctly caught, of each wave that broke in turn had something sublime in its softness and precision. Was it not like an index of measurement which, upsetting all our ordinary impressions, shows us that vertical distances may be coordinated with horizontal, in contradiction of the idea that our mind generally forms of them; and that, though they bring the sky nearer to us in this way, they are not great; that they are indeed less great for a sound which traverses them as did the sound of those little waves, the medium through which it has to pass being purer. And in fact if one went back but a couple of yards below the toll-house, one could no longer distinguish that sound of waves, which six hundred feet of cliff had not robbed of its delicate, minute and soft precision. I said to myself that my grandmother would have listened to it with the delight that she felt in all manifestations of nature or art, in the simplicity of which one discerns grandeur. I was now at the highest pitch of exaltation, which raised everything round about me accordingly. It melted my heart that the Verdurins should have sent to meet us at the station. I said as much to the Princess, who seemed to think that I was greatly exaggerating so simple an act of courtesy. I know that she admitted subsequently to Cottard that she found me very enthusiastic; he replied that I was too emotional, required sedatives and ought to take to knitting. I pointed out to the Princess every tree, every little house smothered in its mantle of roses, I made her admire everything, I would have liked to take her in my arms and press her to my heart. She told me that she could see that I had a gift for painting, that of course I must sketch, that she was surprised that nobody had told her about it. And she confessed that the country was indeed picturesque. We drove through, where it perched upon its height, the little village of Englesqueville (*Engleberti villa*, Brichot informed us). 'But are you quite sure that there will be a party this evening, in spite of Dechambre's death, Princess?' he went on, without stopping to think that the presence at the station of the carriage in which we were sitting was in itself an answer to his question. 'Yes,' said the Princess, 'M. Verldulin insisted that it should not be put off, simply to keep his wife from *thinking*. And besides, after never failing for all these years to entertain on Wednesdays, such a change in her habits would have been bound to upset her. Her nerves are velly bad just now. M. Verdurin was particularly pleased that you were coming to dine this evening, because he knew that it would be a great distraction for Mme Verdurin,' said the Princess, forgetting her pretence of having never heard my name before. 'I think that it will be as well not to say *anything* in front of Mme Verdurin,' the Princess added. 'Ah! I am glad you warned me,' Brichot artlessly replied. 'I shall pass on your suggestion to Cottard.' The carriage stopped for a moment. It moved on again, but the sound that the wheels had been making in the village street had ceased. We had turned into the main avenue of la Raspelière where M. Verdurin stood waiting for us upon the steps. 'I did well to put on a dinner-jacket,' he said, observing with pleasure that the faithful had put on theirs, 'since I have such smart gentlemen in my party.' And as I apologised for not having changed: 'Why, that's quite all right. We're all friends here. I should be delighted to offer you one of my own dinner-jackets, but it wouldn't fit you.' The hand-clasp throbbing with emotion which, as he entered the hall of la Raspelière, and by way of condolence at the death of the pianist, Brichot gave our host elicited no response from the latter. I told him how greatly I admired the scenery. 'Ah! All the better, and you've seen nothing, we must take you round. Why not come and spend a week or two here, the air is excellent.' Brichot was afraid that his hand-clasp had not been understood. 'Ah! Poor Dechambre!' he said, but in an undertone, in case Mme Verdurin was within earshot. 'It is terrible,' replied M. Verdurin lightly. 'So young,' Brichot pursued the point. Annoyed at being detained over these futilities, M. Verdurin replied in a hasty tone and with an embittered groan, not of grief but of irritated impatience: 'Why yes, of course, but what's to be done about it, it's no use crying over spilt milk, talking about him won't bring him back to life, will it?' And, his civility returning with his joviality: 'Come along, my good Brichot, get your things off quickly. We have a *bouillabaisse* which mustn't be kept waiting. But, in heaven's name, don't start talking about Dechambre to Madame Verdurin. You know that she always hides her feelings, but she is quite morbidly sensitive. I give you my word, when she heard that Dechambre was dead, she almost cried,' said M. Verdurin in a tone of profound irony. One might have concluded, from hearing him speak, that it implied a form of insanity to regret the death of a friend of thirty years' standing, and on the other hand one gathered that the perpetual union of M. Verdurin and his wife did not preclude his constantly criticising her and her frequently irritating him. 'If you mention it to her, she will go and make herself ill again. It is deplorable, three weeks after her bronchitis. When that happens, it is I who have to be sick-nurse. You can understand that I have had more than enough of it. Grieve for Dechambre's fate in your heart as much as you like. Think of him, but do not speak about him. I was very fond of Dechambre, but you cannot blame me for being fonder still of my wife. Here's Cottard, now, you can ask him.' And indeed, he knew that a family doctor can do many little services, such as prescribing that one must not give way to grief.

The docile Cottard had said to the Mistress: 'Upset yourself like that, and tomorrow you will *give me* a temperature of 102,' as he might have said to the cook: 'Tomorrow you will give me a *riz de veau*.' Medicine, when it fails to cure the sick, busies itself with changing the sense of verbs and pronouns.

M. Verdurin was glad to find that Saniette, notwithstanding the snubs that he had had to endure two days earlier, had not deserted the little nucleus. And indeed Mme Verdurin and her husband had acquired, in their idleness, cruel instincts for which the great occasions, occurring too rarely, no longer sufficed. They had succeeded in effecting a breach between Odette and Swann, between Brichot and his mistress. They would try it again with someone else, that was understood. But the opportunity did not present itself every day. Whereas, thanks to his shuddering sensibility, his timorous and quickly aroused shyness, Saniette provided them with a whipping-block for every day in the year. And so, for fear of his failing them, they took care always to invite him with friendly and persuasive words, such as the bigger boys at school, the old soldiers in a regiment, address to a recruit whom they are anxious to beguile so that they may get him into their clutches, with the sole object of flattering him for the moment and bullying him when he can no longer escape. 'Whatever you do,' Brichot reminded Cottard, who had not heard what M. Verdurin was saying, 'mum's the word before Mme Verdurin. Have no fear, O Cottard, you are dealing with a sage, as Theocritus says. Besides, M. Verdurin is right, what is the use of lamentations,' he went on, for, being capable of assimilating forms of speech and the ideas which they suggested to him, but having no finer perception, he had admired in M. Verdurin's remarks the most courageous stoicism. 'All the same, it is a great talent that has gone from the world.' 'What, are you still talking about Dechambre,' said M. Verdurin, who had gone on ahead of us, and, seeing that we were not following him, had turned back. 'Listen,' he said to Brichot, 'nothing is gained by exaggeration. The fact of his being dead is no excuse for making him out a genius, which he was not. He played well, I admit, and what is more, he was in his proper element here; transplanted, he ceased to exist. My wife was infatuated with him and made his reputation. You know what she is. I will go farther, in the interest of his own reputation he has died at the right moment, he is done to a turn, as the *demoiselles de Caen*, grilled according to the incomparable recipe of Pampilles, are going to be, I hope (unless you keep us standing here all night with your jeremiads in this Kasbah exposed to all the winds of heaven). You don't seriously expect us all to die of hunger because Dechambre is dead, when for the last year he was obliged to practise scales before giving a concert; to recover for the moment, and for the moment only, the suppleness of his wrists. Besides, you are going to hear this evening, or at any rate to meet, for the rascal is too fond of deserting his art, after dinner, for the card-table, somebody who is a far greater artist than Dechambre, a youngster whom my wife has discovered' (as she had discovered Dechambre, and Paderewski, and everybody else): 'Morel. He has not arrived yet, the devil. He is coming with an old friend of his family whom he has picked up, and who bores him to tears, but otherwise, not to get into trouble with his father, he would have been obliged to stay down at Doncières and keep him company: the Baron de Charlus.' The faithful entered the drawing-room. M. Verdurin, who had remained behind with me while I took off my things, took my arm by way of a joke, as one's host does at a dinner-party when there is no lady for one to take in. 'Did you have a pleasant journey?' 'Yes, M. Brichot told me things which interested me greatly,' said I, thinking of the etymologies, and because I had heard that the Verdurins greatly admired Brichot. 'I am surprised to hear that he told you anything,' said M. Verdurin, 'he is such a retiring man, and talks so little about the things he knows.' This compliment did not strike me as being very apt. 'He seems charming,' I remarked. 'Exquisite, delicious, not the sort of man you meet every day, such a light, fantastic touch, my wife adores him, and so do I!' replied M. Verdurin in an exaggerated tone, as though repeating a lesson. Only then did I grasp that what he had said to me about Brichot was ironical. And I asked myself whether M. Verdurin, since those far-off days of which I had heard reports, had not shaken off the yoke of his wife's tutelage.

The sculptor was greatly astonished to learn that the Verdurins were willing to have M. de Charlus in their house. Whereas in the Faubourg Saint-Germain, where M. de Charlus was so well known, nobody ever referred to his morals (of which most people had no suspicion, others remained doubtful, crediting him rather with intense but Platonic friendships, with behaving imprudently, while the enlightened few strenuously denied, shrugging their shoulders, any insinuation upon which some malicious Gallardon might venture), those morals, the nature of which was known perhaps to a few intimate friends, were, on the other hand, being

denounced daily far from the circle in which he moved, just as, at times, the
sound of artillery fire is audible only beyond a zone of silence. Moreover, in
those professional and artistic circles where he was regarded as the typical
instance of inversion, his great position in society, his noble origin were
completely unknown, by a process analogous to that which, among the
people of Rumania, has brought it about that the name of Ronsard is known
as that of a great nobleman, while his poetical work is unknown there. Not
only that, the Rumanian estimate of Ronsard's nobility is founded upon an
error. Similarly, if in the world of painters and actors M. de Charlus had
such an evil reputation, that was due to their confusing him with a certain
Comte Leblois de Charlus who was not even related to him (or, if so, the
connection was extremely remote), and who had been arrested, possibly by
mistake, in the course of a police raid which had become historic. In short,
all the stories related of our M. de Charlus referred to the other. Many
professionals swore that they had had relations with M. de Charlus, and did
so in good faith, believing that the false M. de Charlus was the true one, the
false one possibly encouraging, partly from an affectation of nobility, partly
to conceal his vice, a confusion which to the true one (the Baron whom we
already know) was for a long time damaging, and afterwards, when he had
begun to go down the hill, became a convenience, for it enabled him
likewise to say: 'That is not myself.' And in the present instance it was not he
to whom the rumours referred. Finally, what enhanced the falsehood of the
reports of an actual fact (the Baron's tendencies), he had had an intimate and
perfectly pure friendship with an author who, in the theatrical world, had
for some reason acquired a similar reputation which he in no way deserved.
When they were seen together at a first night, people would say: 'You see,'
just as it was supposed that the Duchesse de Guermantes had immoral
relations with the Princesse de Parme; an indestructible legend, for it would
be disproved only in the presence of those two great ladies themselves, to
which the people who repeated it would presumably never come any nearer
than by staring at them through their glasses in the theatre and slandering
them to the occupant of the next stall. Given M. de Charlus's morals, the
sculptor concluded all the more readily that the Baron's social position must
be equally low, since he had no sort of information whatever as to the family
to which M. de Charlus belonged, his title or his name. Just as Cottard
imagined that everybody knew that the degree of Doctor of Medicine
implied nothing, the title of Consultant to a Hospital meant something, so
people in society are mistaken when they suppose that everybody has the
same idea of the social importance of their name as they themselves and the
other people of their set.

The Prince d'Agrigente was regarded as a swindler by a club servant to whom he owed twenty-five louis, and regained his importance only in the Faubourg Saint-Germain where he had three sisters who were Duchesses, for it is not among the humble people in whose eyes he is of small account, but among the smart people who know what is what, that the great nobleman creates an effect. M. de Charlus, for that matter, was to learn in the course of the evening that his host had the vaguest ideas about the most illustrious ducal families.

Certain that the Verdurins were making a grave mistake in allowing an individual of tarnished reputation to be admitted to so 'select' a household as theirs, the sculptor felt it his duty to take the Mistress aside. 'You are entirely mistaken, besides I never pay any attention to those tales, and even if it were true, I may be allowed to point out that it could hardly compromise me!' replied Mme Verdurin, furious, for Morel being the principal feature of the Wednesdays, the chief thing for her was not to give any offence to him. As for Cottard, he could not express an opinion, for he had asked leave to go upstairs for a moment to 'do a little job' in the *buen retiro*, and after that, in M. Verdurin's bedroom, to write an extremely urgent letter for a patient.

A great publisher from Paris who had come to call, expecting to be invited to stay to dinner, withdrew abruptly, quickly, realising that he was not smart enough for the little clan. He was a tall, stout man, very dark, with a studious and somewhat cutting air. He reminded one of an ebony paper-knife.

Mme Verdurin who, to welcome us in her immense drawing-room, in which displays of grasses, poppies, field-flowers, plucked only that morning, alternated with a similar theme painted on the walls, two centuries earlier, by an artist of exquisite taste, had risen for a moment from a game of cards which she was playing with an old friend, begged us to excuse her for just one minute while she finished her game, talking to us the while. What I told her about my impressions did not, however, seem altogether to please her. For one thing I was shocked to observe that she and her husband came indoors every day long before the hour of those sunsets which were considered so fine when seen from that cliff, and finer still from the terrace of la Raspelière, and which I would have travelled miles to see. 'Yes, it's incomparable,' said Mme Verdurin carelessly, with a glance at the huge windows which gave the room a wall of glass. 'Even though we have it always in front of us, we never grow tired of it,' and she turned her attention back to her cards. Now my very enthusiasm made me exacting. I expressed my regret that I could not see from the drawing-room the rocks of Darnetal, which, Elstir had told me, were quite lovely at that hour, when they reflected so many colours. 'Ah! You can't see them from here, you would have to go to the end of the park, to the 'view of the bay'. From the seat there, you can take in the whole panorama. But you can't go there by yourself, you will lose your way. I can take you there, if you like,' she added kindly. 'No, no, you are not satisfied with the illness you had the other day, you want to make yourself ill again. He will come back, he can see the view of the bay another time.' I did not insist, and understood that it was enough for the Verdurins to know that this sunset made its way into their drawing-room or dining-room, like a magnificent painting, like a priceless Japanese enamel, justifying the high rent that they were paying for la Raspelière, with plate and linen, but a thing to which they rarely raised their eyes; the important thing, here, for them was to live comfortably, to take drives, to feed well, to talk, to entertain agreeable friends whom they provided with amusing games of billiards, good meals, merry tea-parties. I noticed, however, later on, how intelligently they had learned to know the district, taking their guests for excursions as 'novel' as the music to which they made them listen. The part which the flowers of la Raspelière, the roads by the sea's edge, the old houses, the undiscovered churches, played in the life of M. Verdurin was so great that those people who saw him only in Paris and who, themselves, substituted for the life by the seaside and in the country the refinements of life in town could barely understand the idea that he himself formed of his own life, or the importance that his pleasures gave him in his own eyes. This importance was further enhanced by the fact that the Verdurins were convinced that la Raspelière, which they hoped to purchase, was a property without its match in the world. This superiority which their self-esteem made them attribute to la Raspelière justified in their eyes my enthusiasm which, but for that, would have annoyed them slightly, because of the disappointments which it involved (like my disappointment when long ago I had first listened to Berma) and which I frankly admitted to them.

'I hear the carriage coming back,' the Mistress suddenly murmured. Let us state briefly that Mme Verdurin, quite apart from the inevitable changes due to increasing years, no longer resembled what she had been at the time when Swann and Odette used to listen to the little phrase in her house. Even when she heard it played, she was no longer obliged to assume the air of attenuated admiration which she used to assume then, for that had become her normal expression. Under the influence of the countless neuralgias which the music of Bach, Wagner, Vinteuil, Debussy had given her, Mme Verdurin's brow had assumed enormous proportions, like limbs that are finally crippled by rheumatism. Her temples, suggestive of a pair of beautiful, pain-stricken, milk-white spheres, in which Harmony rolled endlessly, flung back upon either side her silvered tresses, and proclaimed, on the Mistress's behalf, without any need for her to say a word: 'I know what is in store for me tonight.' Her features no longer took the trouble to formulate successively aesthetic impressions of undue violence, for they had themselves become their permanent expression on a countenance ravaged and superb. This attitude of resignation to the ever impending sufferings inflicted by Beauty, and of the courage that was required to make her dress for dinner when she had barely recovered from the effects of the last sonata, had the result that Mme Verdurin, even when listening to the most heart-rending music, preserved a disdainfully impassive countenance, and actually withdrew into retirement to swallow her two spoonfuls of aspirin.

'Why, yes, here they are!' M. Verdurin cried with relief when he saw the door open to admit Morel, followed by M. de Charlus. The latter, to whom dining with the Verdurins meant not so much going into society as going into questionable surroundings, was as frightened as a schoolboy making his way for the first time into a brothel with the utmost deference towards its mistress. Moreover the persistent desire that M. de Charlus felt to appear virile and frigid was overcome (when he appeared in the open doorway) by those traditional ideas of politeness which are awakened as soon as shyness destroys an artificial attitude and makes an appeal to the resources of the subconscious. When it is a Charlus, whether he be noble or plebeian, that is stirred by such a sentiment of instinctive and atavistic politeness to strangers, it is always the spirit of a relative of the female sex, attendant like a goddess, or incarnate as a double, that undertakes to introduce him into a strange drawing-room and to mould his attitude until he comes face to face with his hostess. Thus a young painter, brought up by a godly, Protestant, female cousin, will enter a room, his head aslant and quivering, his eyes raised to the ceiling, his hands gripping an invisible muff, the remembered shape of which and its real and tutelary presence will help the frightened artist to cross without agoraphobia the yawning abyss between the hall and the inner drawing-room. Thus it was that the pious relative, whose memory is helping him today, used to enter a room years ago, and with so plaintive an air that one was asking oneself what calamity she had come to announce, when from her first words one realised, as now in the case of the painter, that she had come to pay an after-dinner call. By virtue of the same law, which requires that life, in the interests of the still unfulfilled act, shall bring into play, utilise, adulterate, in a perpetual prostitution, the most respectable, it may be the most sacred, sometimes only the most innocent legacies from the past, and albeit in this instance it engendered a different aspect, the one of Mme Cottard's nephews who distressed his family by his effeminate ways and the company he kept would always make a joyous entry as though he had a surprise in store for you or were going to inform you that he had been left a fortune, radiant with a happiness which it would have been futile to ask him to explain, it being due to his unconscious heredity and his misplaced sex. He walked upon tiptoe, was no doubt himself astonished that he was not holding a card-case, offered you his hand parting his lips as he had seen his aunt part hers, and his uneasy glance was directed at the mirror in which he seemed to wish to make certain, albeit he was bareheaded, whether his hat, as Mme Cottard had once enquired of Swann, was not askew. As for M. de Charlus, whom the society in which he had lived furnished, at this critical moment, with different examples, with other patterns of affability, and above all with the maxim that one must, in certain cases, when dealing with people of humble rank, bring into play and make use of one's rarest graces, which one normally holds in reserve, it was with a flutter, archly, and with the same sweep with which a skirt would have enlarged and impeded his waddling motion that he advanced upon Mme Verdurin with so flattered and honoured an air that one would have said that to be taken to her house was for him a supreme favour. One would have thought that it was Mme de Marsantes who was entering the room, so prominent at that moment was the woman whom a mistake on the part of Nature had enshrined in the body of M. de Charlus. It was true that the Baron had made every effort to obliterate this mistake and to assume a masculine appearance. But no sooner had he succeeded than, he having in the meantime kept the same tastes, this habit of looking at things through a woman's eyes gave him a fresh feminine appearance, due this time not to heredity but to his own way of living. And as he had gradually come to regard even social questions from the feminine point of view, and without noticing it, for it is not only by dint of lying to other people, but also by lying to oneself that one ceases to be aware that one is lying, albeit he had called upon his body to manifest (at the moment of his entering the Verdurins' drawing-room) all the courtesy of a great nobleman, that body which had fully understood what M. de Charlus had ceased to apprehend, displayed, to such an extent that the Baron would have deserved the epithet 'ladylike', all the attractions of a great lady. Not that there need be any connection between the appearance of M. de Charlus and the fact that sons, who do not always take after their fathers, even without being inverts, and though they go after women, may consummate upon their faces the profanation of their mothers. But we need not consider here a subject that deserves a chapter to itself: the Profanation of the Mother.

Albeit other reasons dictated this transformation of M. de Charlus, and purely physical ferments set his material substance 'working' and made his body pass gradually into the category of women's bodies, nevertheless the change that we record here was of spiritual origin. By dint of supposing yourself to be ill you become ill, grow thin, are too weak to rise from your bed, suffer from nervous enteritis. By dint of thinking tenderly of men you become a woman, and an imaginary spirit hampers your movements. The obsession, just as in the other instance it affects your health, may in this instance alter your sex. Morel, who accompanied him, came to shake hands with me. From that first moment, owing to a twofold change that occurred in him I formed (alas, I was not warned in time to act upon it!) a bad impression of him. I have said that Morel, having risen above his father's menial status, was generally pleased to indulge in a contemptuous familiarity. He had talked to me on the day when he brought me the photographs without once addressing me as Monsieur, treating me as an inferior. What was my surprise at Mme Verdurin's to see him bow very low before me, and before me alone, and to hear, before he had even uttered a syllable to anyone else, words of respect, most respectful – such words as I thought could not possibly flow from his pen or fall from his lips – addressed to myself. I at once suspected that he had some favour to ask of me. Taking me aside a minute later: 'Monsieur would be doing me a very great service,' he said to me, going so far this time as to address me in the third person, 'by keeping from Mme Verdurin and her guests the nature of the profession that my father practised with his uncle. It would be best to say that he was, in your family, the agent for estates so considerable as to put him almost on a level with your parents,' Morel's request annoyed me intensely because it obliged me to magnify not his father's position, in which I took not the slightest interest, but the wealth – the apparent wealth of my own, which I felt to be absurd. But he appeared so unhappy, so pressing, that I could not refuse him. 'No, before dinner,' he said in an imploring tone, 'Monsieur can easily find some excuse for taking Mme Verdurin aside.' This was what, in the end, I did, trying to enhance to the best of my ability the distinction of Morel's father, without unduly exaggerating the 'style', the 'worldly goods' of my own family. It went like a letter through the post, notwithstanding the astonishment of Mme Verdurin, who had had a nodding acquaintance with my grandfather. And as she had no tact, hated family life (that dissolvent of the little nucleus), after telling me that she remembered, long ago, seeing my great-grandfather, and after speaking of him as of somebody who was almost an idiot, who would have been incapable of understanding the little group, and who, to use her expression, 'was not one of us', she said to me: 'Families are such a bore, the only thing is to get right away from them'; and at once proceeded to tell me of a trait in my great-grandfather's character of which I was unaware, although I might have suspected it at home (I had never seen him, but they frequently spoke of him), his remarkable stinginess (in contrast to the somewhat excessive generosity of my great-uncle, the friend of the lady in pink and Morel's father's employer): 'Why, of course, if your grandparents had such a grand agent, that only shows that there are all sorts of people in a family. Your grandfather's father was so stingy that, at the end of his life, when he was almost halfwitted – between you and me, he was never anything very special, you are worth the whole lot of them – he could not bring himself to pay a penny for his ride on the omnibus. So that they were obliged to have him followed by somebody who paid his fare for him, and to let the old miser think that his friend M. de Persigny, the Cabinet Minister, had given him a permit to travel free on the omnibuses. But I am delighted to hear that *our* Morel's father held such a good position. I was under the impression that he had been a schoolmaster, but that's nothing, I must have misunderstood. In any case, it makes not the slightest difference, for I must tell you that here we appreciate only true worth, the personal contribution, what I call the participation. Provided that a person is artistic, provided in a word that he is one of the brotherhood, nothing else matters.' The way in which Morel was one of the brotherhood was – so far as I have been able to discover – that he was sufficiently fond of both women and men to satisfy either sex with the fruits of his experience of the other. But what it is essential to note here is that as soon as I had given him my word that I would speak on his behalf to Mme Verdurin, as soon, moreover, as I had actually done so, and without any possibility of subsequent retraction, Morel's 'respect' for myself vanished as though by magic, the formal language of respect melted away, and indeed for some time he avoided me, contriving to appear contemptuous of me, so that if Mme Verdurin wanted me to give him a message, to ask him to play something, he would continue to talk to one of the faithful, then move on to another, changing his seat if I approached him. The others were obliged to tell him three or four times that I had spoken to him, after which he would reply, with an air of constraint, briefly, that is to say unless we were by ourselves. When that happened, he was expansive, friendly, for there was a charming side to him. I concluded all the same from this first evening that his must be a vile nature, that he would not, at a pinch, shrink from any act of meanness, was incapable of gratitude. In which he resembled the majority of mankind. But inasmuch as I had inherited a strain of my grandmother's nature, and enjoyed the diversity of other people without expecting anything of them or resenting anything that they did, I overlooked his baseness, rejoiced in his gaiety when it was in evidence, and indeed in what I believe to have been a genuine affection on his part when, having gone the whole circuit of his false ideas of human nature, he realised (with a jerk, for he showed strange reversions to a blind and primitive savagery) that my kindness to him was disinterested, that my indulgence arose not from a want of perception but from what he called goodness; and, more important still, I was enraptured by his art which indeed was little more than an admirable virtuosity, but which made me (without his being in the intellectual sense of the word a real musician) hear again or for the first time so much good music. Moreover a manager, M. de Charlus (whom I had not suspected of such talents, albeit Mme de Guermantes, who had known him a very different person in their younger days, asserted that he had composed a sonata for her, painted a fan, and so forth), modest in regard to his true merits, but possessing talents of the first order, contrived to place this virtuosity at the service of a versatile artistic sense which increased it tenfold. Imagine a merely skilful performer in the Russian ballet, formed, educated, developed in all directions by M. Diaghilev.

I had just given Mme Verdurin the message with which Morel had charged me and was talking to M. de Charlus about Saint-Loup, when Cottard burst into the room announcing, as though the house were on fire, that the Cambremers had arrived. Mme Verdurin, not wishing to appear before strangers such as M. de Charlus (whom Cottard had not seen) and myself to attach any great importance to the arrival of the Cambremers, did not move, made no response to the announcement of these tidings, and merely said to the doctor, fanning herself gracefully, and adopting the tone of a Marquise in the Théâtre Français: 'The Baron has just been telling us . . .' This was too much for Cottard! Less abruptly than he would have done in the old days, for learning and high positions had added weight to his utterance, but with the emotion, nevertheless, which he recaptured at the Verdurins', he exclaimed: 'A Baron! What Baron? Where's the Baron?' staring around the room with an astonishment that bordered on incredulity. Mme Verdurin, with the affected indifference of a hostess when a servant has, in front of her guests, broken a valuable glass, and with the artificial, highfalutin tone of a conservatoire prize-winner acting in a play by the younger Dumas, replied, pointing with her fan to Morel's patron: 'Why, the Baron de Charlus, to whom let me introduce you, M. le Professeur Cottard.' Mme Verdurin was, for that matter, by no means sorry to have an opportunity of playing the leading lady. M. de Charlus proffered two fingers which the Professor clasped with the kindly smile of a 'Prince of Science'. But he stopped short upon seeing the Cambremers enter the room, while M. de Charlus led me into a corner to tell me something, not without feeling my muscles, which is a German habit. M. de Cambremer bore no resemblance to the old Marquise. To anyone who had only heard of him, or of letters written by him, well and forcibly expressed, his personal appearance was startling. No doubt, one would grow accustomed to it. But his nose had chosen to place itself aslant above his mouth, perhaps the only crooked line, among so many, which one would never have thought of tracing upon his face, and one that indicated a vulgar stupidity, aggravated still further by the proximity of a Norman complexion on cheeks that were like two ripe apples. It is possible that the eyes of M. de Cambremer retained behind their eyelids a trace of the sky of the Cotentin, so soft upon sunny days when the wayfarer amuses himself in watching, drawn up by the roadside, and counting in their hundreds the shadows of the poplars, but those eyelids, heavy, bleared and drooping, would have prevented the least flash of intelligence from escaping. And so, discouraged by the meagreness of that azure glance, one returned to the big crooked nose. By a transposition of the senses, M. de Cambremer looked at you with his nose. This nose of his was not ugly, it was if anything too handsome, too bold, too proud of its own importance. Arched, polished, gleaming, brand new, it was amply prepared to atone for the inadequacy of his eyes. Unfortunately, if the eyes are sometimes the organ through which our intelligence is revealed, the nose (to leave out of account the intimate solidarity and the unsuspected repercussion of one feature upon the rest), the nose is generally the organ in which stupidity is most readily displayed.

The propriety of the dark clothes which M. de Cambremer invariably wore, even in the morning, might well reassure those who were dazzled and exasperated by the insolent brightness of the seaside attire of people whom they did not know; still it was impossible to understand why the chief magistrate's wife should have declared with an air of discernment and authority, as a person who knows far more than you about the high society of Alençon, that on seeing M. de Cambremer one immediately felt oneself, even before one knew who he was, in the presence of a man of supreme distinction, of a man of perfect breeding, a change from the sort of person one saw at Balbec, a man in short in whose company one could breathe freely. He was to her, stifled by all those Balbec tourists who did not know her world, like a bottle of smelling salts. It seemed to me on the contrary that he was one of the people whom my grandmother would at once have set down as 'all wrong', and that, as she had no conception of snobbishness, she would no doubt have been stupefied that he could have succeeded in winning the hand of Mlle Legrandin, who must surely be difficult to please, having a brother who was 'so refined'. At best one might have said of M. de

Cambremer's plebeian ugliness that it was redolent of the soil and preserved a very ancient local tradition; one was reminded, on examining his faulty features, which one would have liked to correct, of those names of little Norman towns as to the etymology of which my friend the curé was mistaken because the peasants, mispronouncing the names, or having misunderstood the Latin or Norman words that underlay them, have finally fixed in a barbarism to be found already in the cartularies, as Brichot would have said, a wrong meaning and a fault of pronunciation. Life in these old towns may, for all that, be pleasant enough, and M. de Cambremer must have had his good points, for if it was in a mother's nature that the old Marquise should prefer her son to her daughter-in-law, on the other hand, she, who had other children, of whom two at least were not devoid of merit, was often heard to declare that the Marquis was, in her opinion, the best of the family. During the short time he had spent in the army, his messmates, finding Cambremer too long a name to pronounce, had given him the nickname Cancan, implying a flow of chatter, which he in no way merited. He knew how to brighten a dinner-party to which he was invited by saying when the fish (even if it were stale) or the entrée came in: 'I say, that looks a fine animal.' And his wife, who had adopted upon entering the family everything that she supposed to form part of their customs, put herself on the level of her husband's friends and perhaps sought to please him, like a mistress, and as though she had been involved in his bachelor existence, by saying in a careless tone when she was speaking of him to officers: 'You shall see Cancan presently. Cancan has gone to Balbec, but he will be back this evening.' She was furious at having compromised herself by coming to the Verdurins' and had done so only upon the entreaties of her mother-in-law and husband, in the hope of renewing the lease. But, being less well-bred than they, she made no secret of the ulterior motive and for the last fortnight had been making fun of this dinner-party to her women friends. 'You know we are going to dine with our tenants. That will be well worth an increased rent. As a matter of fact, I am rather curious to see what they have done to our poor old la Raspelière' (as though she had been born in the house, and would find there all her old family associations). 'Our old keeper told me only yesterday that you wouldn't know the place. I can't bear to think of all that must be going on there. I am sure we shall have to have the whole place disinfected before we move in again.' She arrived haughty and morose, with the air of a great lady whose castle, owing to a state of war, is occupied by the enemy, but who nevertheless feels herself at home and makes a point of showing the conquerors that they are intruding. Mme de Cambremer could not see me at first for I was in a bay at the side of the room with M. de Charlus, who was telling me that he had heard from Morel that Morel's father had been an 'agent' in my family, and that he, Charlus, credited me with sufficient intelligence and magnanimity (a term common to himself and Swann) to forego the mean and ignoble pleasure which vulgar little idiots (I was warned) would not have failed, in my place, to give themselves by revealing to our hosts details which they might regard as derogatory. 'The mere fact that I take an interest in him and extend my protection over him, gives him a pre-eminence and wipes out the past,' the Baron concluded. As I listened to him and promised the silence which I would have kept even without any hope of being considered in return intelligent and magnanimous, I was looking at Mme de Cambremer. And I had difficulty in recognising the melting, savoury morsel which I had had beside me the other afternoon at teatime, on the terrace at Balbec, in the Norman rock-cake that I now saw, hard as a rock, in which the faithful would in vain have tried to set their teeth. Irritated in anticipation by the knowledge that her husband inherited his mother's simple kindliness, which would make him assume a flattered expression whenever one of the faithful was presented to him, anxious however to perform her duty as a leader of society, when Brichot had been named to her she decided to make him and her husband acquainted, as she had seen her more fashionable friends do, but, anger or pride prevailing over the desire to show her knowledge of the world, she said, not, as she ought to have said: 'Allow me to introduce my husband,' but: 'I introduce you to my husband,' holding aloft thus the banner of the Cambremers, without avail, for her husband bowed as low before Brichot as she had expected. But all Mme de Cambremer's ill humour vanished in an instant when her eye fell on M. de Charlus, whom she knew by sight. Never had she succeeded in obtaining an introduction, even at the time of her intimacy with Swann. For as M. de Charlus always sided with the woman, with his sister-in-law against M. de Guermantes's mistresses, with Odette, at that time still unmarried, but an old flame of Swann's, against the new, he had, as a stern defender of morals and faithful protector of homes, given Odette – and kept – the promise that he would never allow himself to be presented to Mme de Cambremer. She had certainly never guessed that it was at the Verdurins' that she was at length to meet this unapproachable person. M. de Cambremer knew that this was a great joy to her, so great that he himself was moved by it and looked at his wife with an air that implied: 'You are glad now you decided to come, aren't you?' He spoke very little, knowing that he had married a superior woman. 'I, all unworthy,' he would say at every moment, and spontaneously quoted a fable of La Fontaine and one of Florian which seemed to him to apply to his ignorance, and at the same time enable him, beneath the outward form of a contemptuous flattery, to show the men of science who were not members of the Jockey that one might be a sportsman and yet have read fables. The unfortunate thing was that he knew only two of them. And so they kept cropping up. Mme de Cambremer was no fool, but she had a number of extremely irritating habits. With her the corruption of names bore absolutely no trace of aristocratic disdain. She was not the person to say, like the Duchesse de Guermantes (whom the mere fact of her birth ought to have preserved even more than Mme de Cambremer from such an absurdity), with a pretence of not remembering the unfashionable name (albeit it is now that of one of the women whom it is most difficult to approach) of Julien de Monchâteau: 'a little Madame . . . Pica della Mirandola.' No, when Mme de Cambremer said a name wrong it was out of kindness of heart, so as not to appear to know some damaging fact, and when, in her sincerity, she admitted it, she tried to conceal it by altering it. If, for instance, she was defending a woman, she would try to conceal the fact, while determined not to lie to the person who had asked her to tell the truth, that Madame So-and-so was at the moment the mistress of M. Sylvain Lévy, and would say: 'No . . . I know absolutely nothing about her, I fancy that people used to charge her with having inspired a passion in a gentleman whose name I don't know, something like Cahn, Kohn, Kuhn; anyhow, I believe the gentleman has been dead for years and that there was never anything between them.' This is an analogous, but contrary process to that adopted by liars who think that if they alter their statement of what they have been doing when they make it to a mistress or merely to another man, their listener will not immediately see that the expression (like her Cahn, Kohn, Kuhn) is interpolated, is of a different texture from the rest of the conversation, has a double meaning.

Mme Verdurin whispered in her husband's ear: 'Shall I offer my arm to the Baron de Charlus? As you will have Mme de Cambremer on your right, we might divide the honours.' 'No,' said M. Verdurin, 'since the other is higher in rank' (meaning that M. de Cambremer was a Marquis), 'M. de Charlus is, strictly speaking, his inferior.' 'Very well, I shall put him beside the Princess.' And Mme Verdurin introduced Mme Sherbatov to M. de Charlus; each of them bowed in silence, with an air of knowing all about the other and of promising a mutual secrecy. M. Verdurin introduced me to M. de Cambremer. Before he had even begun to speak in his loud and slightly stammering voice, his tall figure and high complexion displayed in their oscillation the martial hesitation of a commanding officer who tries to put you at your ease and says: 'I have heard about you, I shall see what can be done; your punishment shall be remitted; we don't thirst for blood here; it will be all right.' Then, as he shook my hand: 'I think you know my mother,' he said to me. The word 'think' seemed to him appropriate to the discretion of a first meeting, but not to imply any uncertainty, for he went on: 'I have a note for you from her.' M. de Cambremer took a childish pleasure in revisiting a place where he had lived for so long. 'I am at home again,' he said to Mme Verdurin, while his eyes marvelled at recognising the flowers painted on panels over the doors, and the marble busts on their high pedestals. He might, all the same, have felt himself at sea, for Mme Verdurin had brought with her a quantity of fine old things of her own. In this respect, Mme Verdurin, while regarded by the Cambremers as having turned everything upside down, was not revolutionary but intelligently conservative in a sense which they did not understand. They were thus wrong in accusing her of hating the old house and of degrading it by hanging plain cloth curtains instead of their rich plush, like an ignorant parish priest reproaching a diocesan architect with putting back in its place the old carved wood which the cleric had thrown on the rubbish heap, and had seen fit to replace with ornaments purchased in the Place Saint-Sulpice. Furthermore, a herb garden was beginning to take the place, in front of the mansion, of the borders that were the pride not merely of the Cambremers but of their gardener. The latter, who regarded the Cambremers as his sole masters, and groaned beneath the yoke of the Verdurins, as though the place were under occupation for the moment by an invading army, went in secret to unburden his griefs to its dispossessed mistress, grew irate at the scorn that was heaped upon his araucarias, begonias, house-leeks, double dahlias, and at anyone's daring in so grand a place to grow such common plants as camomile and maidenhair. Mme Verdurin felt this silent opposition and had made up her mind, if she took a long lease of la Raspelière or even bought the place, to make one of her conditions the dismissal of the gardener, by whom his old mistress, on the contrary, set great store. He had worked for her without payment, when times were bad, he adored her; but by that odd multiformity of opinion which we find in the lower orders, among whom the most profound moral scorn is embedded in the most passionate admiration, which in turn overlaps old and undying grudges, he used often to say of Mme de Cambremer who, in '70, in a house that she owned in the East of France, surprised by the invasion, had been obliged to endure for a month the contact of the Germans: 'What many people can't forgive Mme la Marquise is that during the war she took the side of the Prussians and even had them to stay in her house. At any other time, I could understand it; but in wartime, she ought not to have done it. It is not right.'

So that he was faithful to her unto death, venerated her for her goodness, and firmly believed that she had been guilty of treason. Mme Verdurin was annoyed that M. de Cambremer should pretend to feel so much at home at la Raspelière. 'You must notice a good many changes, all the same,' she replied. 'For one thing there were those big bronze Barbedienne devils and some horrid little plush chairs which I packed off at once to the attic, though even that is too good a place for them.' After this bitter retort to M. de Cambremer, she offered him her arm to go in to dinner. He hesitated for a moment, saying to himself: 'I can't, really, go in before M. de Charlus.' But supposing the other to be an old friend of the house, seeing that he was not set in the post of honour, he decided to take the arm that was offered him and told Mme Verdurin how proud he felt to be admitted into the symposium (so it was that he styled the little nucleus, not without a smile of satisfaction at his knowledge of the term). Cottard, who was seated next to M. de Charlus, beamed at him through his glass, to make his acquaintance and to break the ice, with a series of winks far more insistent than they would have been in the old days, and not interrupted by fits of shyness. And these engaging glances, enhanced by the smile that accompanied them, were no longer dammed by the glass but overflowed on all sides. The Baron, who readily imagined people of his own kind everywhere, had no doubt that Cottard was one, and was making eyes at him. At once he turned on the Professor the cold shoulder of the invert, as contemptuous of those whom he attracts as he is ardent in pursuit of such as attract him. No doubt, albeit each one of us speaks mendaciously of the pleasure, always refused him by destiny, of being loved, it is a general law, the application of which is by no means confined to the Charlus type, that the person whom we do not love and who does love us seems to us quite intolerable. To such a person, to a woman of whom we say not that she loves us but that she bores us, we prefer the society of any other, who has neither her charm, nor her looks, nor her brains. She will recover these, in our estimation, only when she has ceased to love us. In this light, we might see only the transposition, into odd terms, of this universal rule in the irritation aroused in an invert by a man who displeases him and runs after him. And so, whereas the ordinary man seeks to conceal what he feels, the invert is implacable in making it felt by the man who provokes it, as he would certainly not make it felt by a woman, M. de Charlus for instance by the Princesse de Guermantes, whose passion for him bored him, but flattered him. But when they see another man show a peculiar liking for them, then, whether because they fail to realise that this liking is the same as their own, or because it annoys them to be reminded that this liking, which they glorify so long as it is they themselves that feel it,

is regarded as a vice, or from a desire to rehabilitate themselves by a
sensational display in circumstances in which it costs them nothing, or from
a fear of being unmasked which they at once recover as soon as desire no
longer leads them blindfold from one imprudence to another, or from rage
at being subjected, by the equivocal attitude of another person, to the injury
which, by their own attitude, if that other person attracted them, they would
not be afraid to inflict on him, the men who do not in the least mind
following a young man for miles, never taking their eyes off him in the
theatre, even if he is with friends, and there is therefore a danger of their
compromising him with them, may be heard, if a man who does not attract
them merely looks at them, to say: 'Sir, for what do you take me?' (simply
because he takes them for what they are) 'I don't understand, no, don't
attempt to explain, you are quite mistaken,' pass if need be from words to
blows, and, to a person who knows the imprudent stranger, wax indignant:
'What, you know that loathsome creature. He stares at one so! . . . A fine
way to behave!' M. de Charlus did not go quite as far as this, but assumed the
offended, glacial air adopted, when one appears to be suspecting them, by
women who are not of easy virtue, even more by women who are. Furthermore, the invert brought face to face with an invert sees not merely an
unpleasing image of himself which, being purely inanimate, could at the
worst only injure his self-esteem, but a second self, living, acting in the same
sphere, capable therefore of injuring him in his loves. And so it is from an
instinct of self-preservation that he will speak evil of the possible rival,
whether to people who are able to do him some injury (nor does invert the
first mind being thought a liar when he thus denounces invert the second
before people who may know all about his own case), or to the young man
whom he has 'picked up', who is perhaps going to be snatched away from
him and whom it is important to persuade that the very things which it is to
his advantage to do with the speaker would be the bane of his life if he
allowed himself to do them with the other person. To M. de Charlus, who
was thinking perhaps of the – wholly imaginary – dangers in which the
presence of this Cottard whose smile he misinterpreted might involve
Morel, an invert who did not attract him was not merely a caricature of
himself, but was a deliberate rival. A tradesman, practising an uncommon
trade, who, on his arrival in the provincial town where he intends to settle
for life discovers that, in the same square, directly opposite, the same trade is
being carried on by a competitor, is no more discomfited than a Charlus
who goes down to a quiet spot to make love unobserved and, on the day of
his arrival, catches sight of the local squire or the barber, whose aspect and
manner leave no room for doubt. The tradesman often comes to regard his

competitor with hatred; this hatred degenerates at times into melancholy, and, if there be but a sufficient strain of heredity, one has seen in small towns the tradesman begin to show signs of insanity which is cured only by his deciding to sell his stock and goodwill and remove to another place. The invert's rage is even more agonising. He has realised that from the first moment the squire and the barber have desired his young companion. Even though he repeat to him a hundred times daily that the barber and the squire are scoundrels whose contact would dishonour him, he is obliged, like Harpagon, to watch over his treasure, and rises in the night to make sure that it is not being stolen. And it is this no doubt that, even more than desire, or the convenience of habits shared in common, and almost as much as that experience of oneself which is the only true experience, makes one invert detect another with a rapidity and certainty that are almost infallible. He may be mistaken for a moment, but a rapid divination brings him back to the truth. And so M. de Charlus's error was brief. His divine discernment showed him after the first minute that Cottard was not of his kind, and that he need not fear his advances either for himself, which would merely have annoyed him, or for Morel, which would have seemed to him a more serious matter. He recovered his calm, and as he was still beneath the influence of the transit of Venus Androgyne, now and again he smiled a faint smile at the Verdurins without taking the trouble to open his mouth, merely curving his lips at one corner, and for an instant kindled a coquettish light in his eyes, he so obsessed with virility, exactly as his sister-in-law the Duchesse de Guermantes might have done. 'Do you shoot much, Sir?' said M. Verdurin with a note of contempt to M. de Cambremer. 'Has Ski told you of the near shave we had today?' Cottard enquired of the mistress. 'I shoot mostly in the forest of Chantepie,' replied M. de Cambremer. 'No, I have told her nothing,' said Ski. 'Does it deserve its name?' Brichot asked M. de Cambremer, after a glance at me from the corner of his eye, for he had promised me that he would introduce the topic of derivations, begging me at the same time not to let the Cambremers know the scorn that he felt for those furnished by the Combray curé. 'I am afraid I must be very stupid, but I don't grasp your question,' said M. de Cambremer. 'I mean to say: do many pies sing in it?' replied Brichot. Cottard meanwhile could not bear Mme Verdurin's not knowing that they had nearly missed the train. 'Out with it,' Mme Cottard said to her husband encouragingly, 'tell us your odyssey.' 'Well, really, it is quite out of the ordinary,' said the doctor, and repeated his narrative from the beginning. 'When I saw that the train was in the station, I stood thunderstruck. It was all Ski's fault. You are somewhat wide of the mark in your information, my dear fellow! And there was Brichot waiting for us at the station!' 'I assumed,' said the scholar, casting around him what he could still muster of a glance and smiling with his thin lips, 'that if you had been detained at Graincourt, it would mean that you had encountered some peripatetic siren.' 'Will you hold your tongue, if my wife were to hear you!' said the Professor. 'This wife of mine, it is jealous.' 'Ah! That Brichot,' cried Ski, moved to traditional merriment by Brichot's spicy witticism, 'he is always the same'; albeit he had no reason to suppose that the university don had ever indulged in obscenity. And, to embellish this consecrated utterance with the ritual gesture, he made as though he could not resist the desire to pinch Brichot's leg. 'He never changes, the rascal,' Ski went on, and without stopping to think of the effect, at once tragic and comic, that the don's semi-blindness gave to his words: 'Always a sharp lookout for the ladies.' 'You see,' said M. de Cambremer, 'what it is to meet with a scholar. Here have I been shooting for fifteen years in the forest of Chantepie, and I've never even thought of what the name meant.' Mme de Cambremer cast a stern glance at her husband; she did not like him to humble himself thus before Brichot. She was even more annoyed when, at every 'ready-made' expression that Cancan employed, Cottard, who knew the ins and outs of them all, having himself laboriously acquired them, pointed out to the Marquis, who admitted his stupidity, that they meant nothing. 'Why "stupid as a cabbage"? Do you suppose cabbages are stupider than anything else? You say: "repeat the same thing thirty-six times". Why thirty-six? Why do you say: "sleep like a top"? Why "Thunder of Brest"? Why "play four hundred tricks"?' But at this, the defence of M. de Cambremer was taken up by Brichot who explained the origin of each of these expressions. But Mme de Cambremer was occupied principally in examining the changes that the Verdurins had introduced at la Raspelière, in order that she might be able to criticise some, and import others, or possibly the same ones, to Féterne. 'I keep wondering what that lustre is that's hanging all crooked. I can hardly recognise my old Raspelière,' she went on, with a familiarly aristocratic air, as she might have spoken of an old servant meaning not so much to indicate his age as to say that she had seen him in his cradle. And, as she was a trifle bookish in her speech: 'All the same,' she added in an undertone, 'I can't help feeling that if I were inhabiting another person's house, I should feel some compunction about altering everything like this.' 'It is a pity you didn't come with them,' said Mme Verdurin to M. de Charlus and Morel, hoping that M. de Charlus was now 'enrolled' and would submit to the rule that they must all arrive by the same train. 'You are sure that Chantepie means the singing magpie, Chochotte?' she went on, to show that, like the great hostess that she was, she could join in every conversation at the same time. 'Tell me something about this violinist,' Mme de Cambremer said to me, 'he interests me; I adore music, and it seems to me that I have heard of him before, complete my education.' She had heard that Morel had come with M. de Charlus and hoped, by getting the former to come to her house, to make friends with the latter. She added, however, so that I might not guess her reason for asking, 'M. Brichot, too, interests me.' For, even if she was highly cultivated, just as certain persons inclined to obesity eat hardly anything, and take exercise all day long without ceasing to grow visibly fatter, so Mme de Cambremer might in vain master, and especially at Féterne, a philosophy that became ever more esoteric, music that became ever more subtle, she emerged from these studies only to weave plots that would enable her to cut the middle-class friends of her girlhood and to form the connections which she had originally supposed to be part of the social life of her 'in-laws', and had then discovered to be far more exalted and remote. A philosopher who was not modern enough for her, Leibnitz, has said that the way is long from the intellect to the heart. This way Mme de Cambremer had been no more capable than her brother of traversing. Abandoning the study of John Stuart Mill only for that of Lachelier, the less she believed in the reality of the external world, the more desperately she sought to establish herself, before she died, in a good position in it. In her passion for realism in art, no object seemed to her humble enough to serve as a model to painter or writer. A fashionable picture or novel would have made her feel sick; Tolstoy's mujiks, or Millet's peasants, were the extreme social boundary beyond which she did not allow the artist to pass. But to cross the boundary that limited her own social relations, to raise herself to an intimate acquaintance with Duchesses, this was the goal of all her efforts, so ineffective had the spiritual treatment to which she subjected herself, by the study of great masterpieces, proved in overcoming the congenital and morbid snobbishness that had developed in her. This snobbishness had even succeeded in curing certain tendencies to avarice and adultery to which in her younger days she had been inclined, just as certain peculiar and permanent pathological conditions seem to render those who are subject to them immune to other maladies. I could not, all the same, refrain, as I listened to her, from giving her credit, without deriving any pleasure from them, for the refinement of her expressions. They were those that are used, at a given date, by all the people of the same intellectual breadth, so that the refined expression provides us at once, like the arc of a circle, with the means to describe and limit the entire circumference. And so the effect of these expressions is that the people who employ them bore me immediately, because I feel that I already know them, but are generally regarded as superior persons, and have often been offered me as delightful and unappreciated companions. 'You cannot fail to be aware, Madame, that many forest regions take their name from the animals that inhabit them. Next to the forest of Chantepie, you have the wood Chantereine.' 'I don't know who the queen may be, but you are not very polite to her,' said M. de Cambremer. 'One for you, Chochotte,' said Mme de Verdurin. 'And apart from that, did you have a pleasant journey?' 'We encountered only vague human beings who thronged the train. But I must answer M. de Cambremer's question; *reine*, in this instance, is not the wife of a king, but a frog. It is the name that the frog has long retained in this district, as is shown by the station, Renneville, which ought to be spelt Reineville.' 'I say, that seems a fine animal,' said M. de Cambremer to Mme Verdurin, pointing to a fish. (It was one of the compliments by means of which he considered that he paid his scot at a dinner-party, and gave an immediate return of hospitality. 'There is no need to invite them,' he would often say, in speaking of one or other couple of their friends to his wife. 'They were delighted to have us. It was they that thanked me for coming.') 'I must tell you, all the same, that I have been going every day for years to Renneville, and I have never seen any more frogs there than anywhere else. Madame de Cambremer brought the curé here from a parish where she owns a considerable property, who has very much the same turn of mind as yourself, it seems to me. He has written a book.' 'I know, I have read it with immense interest,' Brichot replied hypocritically. The satisfaction that his pride received indirectly from this answer made M. de Cambremer laugh long and loud. 'Ah! well, the author of, what shall I say, this geography, this glossary, dwells at great length upon the name of a little place of which we were formerly, if I may say so, the Lords, and which is called Pont-à-Couleuvre. Of course I am only an ignorant rustic compared with such a fountain of learning, but I have been to Pont-à-Couleuvre a thousand times if he's been there once, and devil take me if I ever saw one of his beastly serpents there, I say beastly, in spite of the tribute the worthy La Fontaine pays them.' (*The Man and the Serpent* was one of his two fables.) 'You have not seen any, and you have been quite right,' replied Brichot. 'Undoubtedly, the writer you mention knows his subject through and through, he has written a remarkable book.' 'There!' exclaimed Mme de Cambremer, 'that book, there's no other word for it, is a regular Benedictine *opus*.' 'No doubt he has consulted various polyptychs (by which we mean the lists of benefices and cures of each diocese), which may have furnished him with the names of lay patrons and ecclesiastical collators. But there are other sources. One of the most learned of my friends has delved into them. He found that the place in question was

named Pont-à-Quileuvre. This odd name encouraged him to carry his
researches farther, to a Latin text in which the bridge that your friend
supposes to be infested with serpents is styled *Pons cui aperit*: a closed bridge
that was opened only upon due payment.' 'You were speaking of frogs. I,
when I find myself among such learned folk, feel like the frog before the
areopagus,' (this being his other fable) said Cancan who often indulged,
with a hearty laugh, in this pleasantry thanks to which he imagined himself
to be making, at one and the same time, out of humility and with aptness, a
profession of ignorance and a display of learning. As for Cottard, blocked
upon one side by M. de Charlus's silence, and driven to seek an outlet
elsewhere, he turned to me with one of those questions which so impressed
his patients when it hit the mark and showed them that he could put himself
so to speak inside their bodies; if on the other hand it missed the mark, it
enabled him to check certain theories, to widen his previous point of view.
'When you come to a relatively high altitude, such as this where we now are,
do you find that the change increases your tendency to choking fits?' he
asked me with the certainty of either arousing admiration or enlarging his
own knowledge. M. de Cambremer heard the question and smiled. 'I can't
tell you how amused I am to hear that you have choking fits,' he flung at me
across the table. He did not mean that it made him happy, though as a
matter of fact it did. For this worthy man could not hear any reference to
another person's sufferings without a feeling of satisfaction and a spasm of
hilarity which speedily gave place to the instinctive pity of a kind heart. But
his words had another meaning which was indicated more precisely by the
clause that followed. 'It amuses me,' he explained, 'because my sister has
them too.' And indeed it did amuse him, as it would have amused him to
hear me mention as one of my friends a person who was constantly coming
to their house. 'How small the world is,' was the reflection which he formed
mentally and which I saw written upon his smiling face when Cottard spoke
to me of my choking fits. And these began to establish themselves, from the
evening of this dinner-party, as a sort of interest in common, after which M.
de Cambremer never failed to enquire, if only to hand on a report to his
sister. As I answered the questions with which his wife kept plying me about
Morel, my thoughts returned to a conversation I had had with my mother
that afternoon. Having, without any attempt to dissuade me from going to
the Verdurins' if there was a chance of my being amused there, suggested
that it was a house of which my grandfather would not have approved,
which would have made him exclaim: 'On guard!' my mother had gone on
to say: 'Listen, Judge Toureuil and his wife told me they had been to
luncheon with Mme Bontemps. They asked me no questions. But I

seemed to gather from what was said that your marriage to Albertine would be the joy of her aunt's life. I think the real reason is that they are all extremely fond of you. At the same time the style in which they suppose that you would be able to keep her, the sort of friends they more or less know that we have, all that is not, I fancy, left out of account, although it may be a minor consideration. I should not have mentioned it to you myself, because I attach no importance to it, but as I imagine that people will mention it to you, I prefer to get a word in first.' 'But you yourself, what do you think of her?' I asked my mother. 'Well, it's not I that am going to marry her. You might certainly do a thousand times better. But I feel that your grandmother would not have liked me to influence you. As a matter of fact, I cannot tell you what I think of Albertine; I don't think of her. I shall say to you, like Madame de Sévigné: "She has good qualities, at least I suppose so. But at this first stage I can praise her only by negatives. One thing she is not, she has not the Rennes accent. In time, I shall perhaps say, she is something else. And I shall always think well of her if she can make you happy." ' But by these very words which left it to myself to decide my own happiness, my mother had plunged me in that state of doubt in which I had been plunged long ago when, my father having allowed me to go to *Phèdre* and, what was more, to take to writing, I had suddenly felt myself burdened with too great a responsibility, the fear of distressing him, and that melancholy which we feel when we cease to obey orders which, from one day to another, keep the future hidden, and realise that we have at last begun to live in real earnest, as a grown-up person, the life, the only life that any of us has at his disposal.

Perhaps the best thing would be to wait a little longer, to begin by regarding Albertine as in the past, so as to find out whether I really loved her. I might take her, as a distraction, to see the Verdurins, and this thought reminded me that I had come there myself that evening only to learn whether Mme Putbus was staying there or was expected. In any case, she was not dining with them. 'Speaking of your friend Saint-Loup,' said Mme de Cambremer, using an expression which showed a closer sequence in her ideas than her remarks might have led one to suppose, for if she spoke to me about music she was thinking about the Guermantes; 'you know that everybody is talking about his marriage to the niece of the Princesse de Guermantes. I may tell you that, so far as I am concerned, all that society gossip leaves me cold.' I was seized by a fear that I might have spoken unfeelingly to Robert about the girl in question, a girl full of sham originality, whose mind was as mediocre as her actions were violent. Hardly ever do we hear anything that does not make us regret something that we have said. I replied to Mme de Cambremer, truthfully as it happened, that I knew nothing about it, and that anyhow I thought that the girl was still too young to be engaged. 'That is perhaps why it is not yet official, anyhow there is a lot of talk about it.' 'I ought to warn you,' Mme Verdurin observed dryly to Mme de Cambremer, having heard her talking to me about Morel and supposing, when Mme de Cambremer lowered her voice to speak of Saint-Loup's engagement, that Morel was still under discussion. 'You needn't expect any light music here. In matters of art, you know, the faithful who come to my Wednesdays, my children as I call them, are all fearfully advanced,' she added with an air of proud terror. 'I say to them sometimes: My dear people, you move too fast for your Mistress, not that she has ever been said to be afraid of anything daring. Every year it goes a little farther; I can see the day coming when they will have no more use for Wagner or Indy.' 'But it is splendid to be advanced, one can never be advanced enough,' said Mme de Cambremer, scrutinising as she spoke every corner of the dining-room, trying to identify the things that her mother-in-law had left there, those that Mme Verdurin had brought with her, and to convict the latter red-handed of want of taste. At the same time, she tried to get me to talk of the subject that interested her most, M. de Charlus. She thought it touching that he should be looking after a violinist. 'He seems intelligent.' 'Why, his mind is extremely active for a man of his age,' said I. 'Age? But he doesn't seem at all old, look, the hair is still young.' (For, during the last three or four years, the word hair had been used with the article by one of those unknown persons who launch the literary fashions, and everybody at the same radius from the centre as Mme de Cambremer would say 'the hair', not without an affected smile. At the present day, people still say 'the hair' but, from an excessive use of the article, the pronoun will be born again.) 'What interests me most about M. de Charlus,' she went on, 'is that one can feel that he has the gift. I may tell you that I attach little importance to knowledge. Things that can be learned do not interest me.' This speech was not incompatible with Mme de Cambremer's own distinction which was, in the fullest sense, imitated and acquired. But it so happened that one of the things which one had to know at that moment was that knowledge is nothing, and is not worth a straw when compared with originality. Mme de Cambremer had learned, with everything else, that one ought not to learn anything. 'That is why,' she explained to me, 'Brichot, who has an interesting side to him, for I am not one to despise a certain spicy erudition, interests me far less.' But Brichot, at that moment, was occupied with one thing only; hearing people talk about music, he trembled lest the subject should remind Mme Verdurin of the death of Dechambre. He decided to say something that would avert that harrowing memory. M. de Cambremer provided him with an opportunity with the question: 'You mean to say that wooded places always take their names from animals?' 'Not at all,' replied Brichot, proud to display his learning before so many strangers, among whom, I had told him, he would be certain to interest one at least. 'We have only to consider how often, even in the names of people, a tree is preserved, like a fern in a piece of coal. One of our Conscript Fathers is called M. de Saulces de Freycinet, which means, if I be not mistaken, a spot planted with willows and ashes, *salix et fraxinetum*; his nephew M. de Selves combines more trees still, since he is named de Selves, *de sylvis*.' Saniette was delighted to see the conversation take so animated a turn. He could, since Brichot was talking all the time, preserve a silence which would save him from being the butt of M. and Mme Verdurin's wit. And growing even more sensitive in his joy at being set free, he had been touched when he heard M. Verdurin, notwithstanding the formality of so grand a dinner-party, tell the butler to put a decanter of water in front of M. Saniette who never drank anything else. (The generals responsible for the death of most soldiers insist upon their being well fed.) Moreover, Mme Verdurin had actually smiled once at Saniette. Decidedly, they were kind people. He was not going to be tortured any more. At this moment the meal was interrupted by one of the party whom I have forgotten to mention, an eminent Norwegian philosopher who spoke French very well but very slowly, for the twofold reason that, in the first place, having learned the language only recently and not wishing to make mistakes (he did, nevertheless, make some), he referred each word to a sort of mental dictionary, and secondly, being a metaphysician, he always thought of what he intended to say while he was saying it, which, even in a Frenchman, causes slowness of utterance. He was, otherwise, a charming person, although similar in appearance to many other people, save in one respect. This man so slow in his diction (there was an interval of silence after every word) acquired a startling rapidity in escaping from the room as soon as he had said goodbye. His haste made one suppose, the first time one saw him, that he was suffering from colic or some even more urgent need.

'My dear – colleague,' he said to Brichot, after deliberating in his mind whether colleague was the correct term, 'I have a sort of – desire to know whether there are other trees in the – nomenclature of your beautiful French – Latin – Norman tongue. Madame' (he meant Madame Verdurin, although he dared not look at her) 'has told me that you know everything. Is not this precisely the moment?' 'No, it is the moment for eating,' interrupted Mme Verdurin, who saw the dinner becoming interminable. 'Very well,' the Scandinavian replied, bowing his head over his plate with a resigned and sorrowful smile. 'But I must point out to Madame that if I have permitted myself this questionnaire – pardon me, this questation – it is because I have to return tomorrow to Paris to dine at the Tour d'Argent or at the Hôtel Meurice, My French – brother – M. Boutroux is to address us there about certain seances of spiritualism – pardon me, certain spirituous evocations which he has controlled.' 'The Tour d'Argent is not nearly as good as they make out,' said Mme Verdurin sourly. 'In fact, I have had some disgusting dinners there.' 'But am I mistaken, is not the food that one consumes at Madame's table an example of the finest French cookery?' 'Well, it is not positively bad,' replied Mme Verdurin, sweetening. 'And if you come next Wednesday, it will be better.' 'But I am leaving on Monday for Algiers, and from there I am going to the Cape. And when I am at the Cape of Good Hope, I shall no longer be able to meet my illustrious colleague – pardon me, I shall no longer be able to meet my brother.' And he set to work obediently, after offering these retrospective apologies, to devour his food at a headlong pace. But Brichot was only too delighted to be able to furnish other vegetable etymologies, and replied, so greatly interesting the Norwegian that he again stopped eating, but with a sign to the servants that they might remove his plate and help him to the next course. 'One of the Forty,' said Brichot, 'is named Houssaye, or a place planted with hollies; in the name of a brilliant diplomat, d'Ormesson, you will find the elm, the *ulmus* beloved of Virgil, which has given its name to the town of Ulm; in the names of his colleagues, M. de la Boulaye, the birch (*bouleau*), M. d'Aunay, the alder (*aune*), M. de Buissière, the box (*buis*), M. Albaret, the sapwood (*aubier*)' (I made a mental note that I must tell this to Céleste), 'M. de Cholet, the cabbage (*chou*), and the apple tree (*pommier*) in the name of M. de la Pommeraye, whose lectures we used to attend, do you remember, Saniette, in the days when the worthy Porel had been sent to the farthest ends of the earth, as Proconsul in Odeonia?' 'You said that Cholet was derived from *chou*,' I remarked to Brichot. 'Am I to suppose that the name of a station I passed before reaching Doncières, Saint-Frichoux, comes from *chou* also?' 'No, Saint-Frichoux is *Sanctus Fructuosus*, as *Sanctus Ferreolus* gave rise to Saint-Fargeau, but that is not Norman in the least.' 'He knows too much, he's boring us,' the Princess muttered softly. 'There are so many other names that interest me, but I can't ask you everything at once.' And, turning to Cottard, 'Is Madame Putbus here?' I asked him. On hearing Brichot utter the name of Saniette, M. Verdurin cast at his wife and at Cottard an ironical glance which confounded their timid guest. 'No, thank heaven,' replied Mme Verdurin, who had overheard my question, 'I have managed to turn her thoughts in the direction of Venice, we are rid of her for this year.' 'I shall myself be entitled presently to two trees,' said M. de Charlus, 'for I have more or less taken a little house between Saint-Martin-du-Chêne and Saint-Pierre-des-Ifs.' 'But that is quite close to here, I hope that you will come over often with Charlie Morel. You have only to come to an arrangement with our little group about the trains, you are only a step from Doncières,' said Mme Verdurin, who hated people's not coming by the same train and not arriving at the hours when she sent carriages to meet them. She knew how stiff the climb was to la Raspelière, even if you took the zigzag path, behind Féterne, which was half-an-hour longer; she was afraid that those of her guests who kept to themselves might not find carriages to take them, or even, having in reality stayed away, might plead the excuse that they had not found a carriage at Douville-Féterne, and had not felt strong enough to make so stiff a climb on foot. To this invitation M. de Charlus responded with a silent bow. 'He's not the sort of person you can talk to any day of the week, he seems a tough customer,' the doctor whispered to Ski, for having remained quite simple, notwithstanding a surface-dressing of pride, he made no attempt to conceal the fact that Charlus had snubbed him. 'He is doubtless unaware that at all the watering-places, and even in Paris in the wards, the physicians, who naturally regard me as their 'chief', make it a point of honour to introduce me to all the noblemen present, not that they need to be asked twice. It makes my stay at the spas quite enjoyable,' he added carelessly. 'Indeed at Doncières the medical officer of the regiment, who is the doctor who attends the Colonel, invited me to luncheon to meet him, saying that I was fully entitled to dine with the General. And that General is a Monsieur *de* something. I don't know whether his title-deeds are more or less ancient than those of this Baron.' 'Don't you worry about him, his is a very humble coronet,' replied Ski in an undertone, and added some vague statement including a word of which I caught only the last syllable, -ast, being engaged in listening to what Brichot was saying to M. de Charlus. 'No, as for that, I am sorry to say, you have probably one tree only, for if Saint-Martin-du-Chêne is obviously *Sanctus Martinus juxta quercum*, on the other hand, the word *if* may be simply the root *ave*, *eve*, which means moist, as in Aveyron, Lodève, Yvette, and which you see survive in our kitchen-sinks (*éviers*). It is the word *eau* which in Breton is represented by *ster*, Stermaria, Sterlaer, Sterbouest, Ster-en-Dreuchen.' I heard no more, for whatever the pleasure I might feel on hearing again the name Stermaria, I could not help listening to Cottard, next to whom I was seated, as he murmured to Ski: 'Indeed! I was not aware of it. So he is a gentleman who has learned to look behind! He is one of the happy band, is he? He hasn't got rings of fat round his eyes, all the same. I shall have to keep my feet well under me, or he may start squeezing them. But I'm not at all surprised. I am used to seeing noblemen in the bath, in their birthday suits, they are all more or less degenerates. I don't talk to them, because after all I am in an official position and it might do me harm. But they know quite well who I am.' Saniette, whom Brichot's appeal had frightened, was beginning to breathe again, like a man who is afraid of the storm when he finds that the lightning has not been followed by any sound of thunder, when he heard M. Verdurin interrogate him, fastening upon him a stare which did not spare the wretch until he had finished speaking, so as to put him at once out of countenance and prevent him from recovering his composure. 'But you never told us that you went to those *matinées* at the Odéon, Saniette?' Trembling like a recruit before a bullying serjeant, Saniette replied, making his speech as diminutive as possible, so that it might have a better chance of escaping the blow: 'Only once, to the *Chercheuse*.' 'What's that he says?' shouted M. Verdurin, with an air of disgust and fury combined, knitting his brows as though it was all he could do to grasp something unintelligible. 'It is impossible to understand what you say, what have you got in your mouth?' enquired M. Verdurin, growing more and more furious, and alluding to Saniette's defective speech. 'Poor Saniette, I won't have him made unhappy,' said Mme Verdurin in a tone of false pity, so as to leave no one in doubt as to her husband's insolent intention. 'I was at the Ch . . . Che..' 'Che, che, try to speak distinctly,' said M. Verdurin, 'I can't understand a word you say.' Almost without exception, the faithful burst out laughing and they suggested a band of cannibals in whom the sight of a wound on a white man's skin has aroused the thirst for blood. For the instinct of imitation and absence of courage govern society and the mob alike. And we all of us laugh at a person whom we see being made fun of, which does not prevent us from venerating him ten years later in a circle where he is admired. It is in like manner that the populace banishes or acclaims its kings. 'Come, now, it is not his fault,' said Mme Verdurin. 'It is not mine either, people ought not to dine out if they can't speak properly.' 'I was at the *Chercheuse d'Esprit* by Favart.' 'What! It's the *Chercheuse d'Esprit* that you call the *Chercheuse*? Why, that's marvellous! I might have tried for a hundred years without guessing it,' cried M. Verdurin, who all the same would have decided immediately that you were not literary, were not artistic, were not 'one of us', if he had heard you quote the full title of certain works. For instance, one was expected to say the *Malade*, the *Bourgeois*; and whoso would have added *imaginaire* or *gentilhomme* would have shown that he did not understand 'shop', just as in a drawing-room a person proves that he is not in society by saying 'M. de Montesquiou-Fézensac' instead of 'M. de Montesquiou'. 'But it is not so extraordinary,' said Saniette, breathless with emotion but smiling, albeit he was in no smiling mood. Mme Verdurin could not contain herself. 'Yes, indeed!' she cried with a titter. 'You may be quite sure that nobody would ever have guessed that you meant the *Chercheuse d'Esprit*.' M. Verdurin went on in a gentler tone, addressing both Saniette and Brichot: 'It is quite a pretty piece, all the same, the *Chercheuse d'Esprit*.' Uttered in a serious tone, this simple phrase, in which one could detect no trace of malice, did Saniette as much good and aroused in him as much gratitude as a deliberate compliment. He was unable to utter a single word and preserved a happy silence. Brichot was more loquacious. 'It is true,' he replied to M. Verdurin, 'and if it could be passed off as the work of some Sarmatian or Scandinavian author, we might put forward the *Chercheuse d'Esprit* as a candidate for the vacant post of masterpiece. But, be it said without any disrespect to the shade of the gentle Favart, he had not the Ibsenian temperament.' (Immediately he blushed to the roots of his hair, remembering the Norwegian philosopher who appeared troubled because he was seeking in vain to discover what vegetable the *buis* might be that Brichot had cited a little earlier in connection with the name Bussière.) 'However, now that Porel's satrapy is filled by a functionary who is a Tolstoyist of rigorous observance, it may come to pass that we shall witness *Anna Karenina* or *Resurrection* beneath the Odeonian architrave.' 'I know the portrait of Favart to which you allude,' said M. de Charlus. 'I have seen a very fine print of it at Comtesse Molé's.' The name of Comtesse Molé made a great impression upon Mme Verdurin. 'Oh! So you go to Mme de Molé's!' she exclaimed. She supposed that people said Comtesse Molé, Madame Molé, simply as an abbreviation, as she heard people say 'the Rohans' or in contempt, as she herself said: 'Madame la Trémoïlle.' She had no doubt that Comtesse Molé, who knew the Queen of Greece and the Principessa di Caprarola, had as much right as anybody to the particle, and for once in a way had decided to bestow it upon so brilliant a personage, and one who had been extremely civil to herself. And so, to make it clear that she had spoken thus on purpose and did not grudge the Comtesse her 'de', she went on: 'But I had no idea that you knew Madame de Molé!' as though it had been doubly extraordinary, both that M. de Charlus should know the lady, and that Mme Verdurin should not know that he knew her. Now society, or at least the people to whom M. de Charlus gave that name, forms a relatively homogeneous and compact whole. And so it is comprehensible that, in the incongruous vastness of the middle classes, a barrister may say to somebody who knows one of his school friends: 'But how in the world do you come to know him?' whereas to be surprised at a Frenchman's knowing the meaning of the word *temple* or *forest* would be hardly more extraordinary than to wonder at the hazards that might have brought together M. de Charlus and the Comtesse Molé. What is more, even if such an acquaintance had not been derived quite naturally from the laws that govern society, how could there be anything strange in the fact of Mme Verdurin's not knowing of it, since she was meeting M. de Charlus for the first time, and his relations with Mme Molé were far from being the only thing that she did not know with regard to him, about whom, to tell the truth, she knew nothing. 'Who was it that played this *Chercheuse d'Esprit*, my good Saniette?' asked M. Verdurin. Albeit he felt that the storm had passed, the old antiquarian hesitated before answering. 'There you go,' said Mme Verdurin, 'you frighten him, you make fun of everything that he says, and then you expect him to answer. Come along, tell us who played the part, and you shall have some galantine to take home,' said Mme Verdurin, making a cruel allusion to the penury into which Saniette had plunged himself by trying to rescue the family of a friend. 'I can remember only that it was Mme Samary who played the Zerbine,' said Saniette. 'The Zerbine? What in the world is that,' M. Verdurin shouted, as though the house were on fire. 'It is one of the parts in the old repertory, like Captain Fracasse, as who should say the Fire-eater, the Pedant.' 'Ah, the pedant, that's yourself. The Zerbine! No, really the man's mad,' exclaimed M. Verdurin. Mme Verdurin looked at her guests and laughed as though to apologise for Saniette. 'The Zerbine, he imagines that everybody will know at once what it means. You are like M. de Longepierre, the stupidest man I know, who said to us quite calmly the other day 'the Banat'. Nobody had any idea what he meant. Finally we were informed that it was a province in Serbia.' To put an end to Saniette's torture, which hurt me more than it hurt him, I asked Brichot if he knew what the word Balbec meant. 'Balbec is probably a corruption of Dalbec,' he told me. 'One would have to consult the charters of the Kings of England, Overlords of Normandy, for Balbec was held of the Barony of Dover, for which reason it was often styled Balbec d'Outre-Mer, Balbec-en-Terre. But the Barony of Dover was itself held of the Bishopric of Bayeux, and, notwithstanding the rights that were temporarily enjoyed in the abbey by the Templars, from the time of Louis d'Harcourt, Patriarch of Jerusalem and Bishop of Bayeux, it was the Bishops of that diocese who collated to the benefice of Balbec. So it was explained to me by the incumbent of Douville, a bald person, eloquent, fantastic, and a devotee of the table, who lives by the Rule of Brillat-Savarin, and who expounded to me in slightly sibylline language a loose pedagogy, while he fed me upon some admirable fried potatoes.' While Brichot smiled to show how witty it was to combine matters so dissimilar and to employ an ironically lofty diction in treating of commonplace things, Saniette was trying to find a loophole for some clever remark which would raise him from the abyss into which he had fallen. The witty remark was what was known as a 'comparison', but had changed its form, for there is an evolution in wit as in literary styles, an epidemic that disappears has its place taken by another, and so forth . . . At one time the typical 'comparison' was the 'height of . . . ' But this was out of date, no one used it any more, there was only Cottard left to say still, on occasion, in the middle of a game of piquet: 'Do you know what is the height of absent-mindedness, it is to think that the Edict (*l'edit*) of Nantes was an English-woman.' These 'heights' had been replaced by nicknames. In reality it was still the old 'comparison', but, as the nickname was in fashion, people did not observe the survival. Unfortunately for Saniette, when these 'com-parisons' were not his own, and as a rule were unknown to the little nucleus, he produced them so timidly that, notwithstanding the laugh with which he followed them up to indicate their humorous nature, nobody saw the point. And if on the other hand the joke was his own, as he had generally hit upon it in conversation with one of the faithful, and the latter had repeated it, appropriating the authorship, the joke was in that case known, but not as being Saniette's. And so when he slipped in one of these it was recognised, but, because he was its author, he was accused of plagiarism. 'Very well, then,' Brichot continued, 'Bec, in Norman, is a stream; there is the Abbey of Bec, Mobec, the stream from the marsh (Mor or Mer meant a marsh, as in Morville, or in Bricquemar, Alvimare, Cambremer), Bricquebec the stream from the high ground coming from Briga, a fortified place, as in Bricqueville, Bricquebose, le Bric, Briand, or indeed Brice, bridge, which is the same as *bruck* in German (Innsbruck), and as the English *bridge* which ends so many place-names (Cambridge, for instance). You have moreover in Normandy many other instances of bec: Caudebec, Bolbec, le Robec, le Bec-Hellouin, Becquerel. It is the Norman form of the German *bach*, Offenbach, Anspach. Varaguebec, from the old word *varaigne*, equivalent to *warren*, preserved woods or ponds. As for Dal,' Brichot went on, 'it is a form of *thal*, a valley: Darnetal, Rosendal, and indeed, close to Louviers, Becdal. The river that has given its name to Balbec, is, by the way, charming. Seen from a *falaise* (*fels* in German, you have indeed, not far from here, standing on a height, the picturesque town of Falaise), it runs close under the spires of the church, which is actually a long way from it, and seems to be reflecting them.' 'I should think,' said I, 'that is an effect that Elstir admires greatly. I have seen several sketches of it in his studio.' 'Elstir! You know Tiche,' cried Mme Verdurin. 'But do you know that we used to be the dearest friends? Thank heaven, I never see him now. No, but ask Cottard, Brichot, he used to have his place laid at my table, he came every day. Now, there's a man of whom you can say that it has done him no good to leave our little nucleus. I shall show you presently some flowers he painted for me; you shall see the difference from the things he is doing now, which I don't care for at all, not at all! Why! I made him do me a portrait of Cottard, not to mention all the sketches he has made of me.' 'And he gave the Professor purple hair,' said Mme Cottard, forgetting that at the time her husband had not been even a Fellow of the College. 'I don't know, Sir, whether you find that my husband has purple hair.' 'That doesn't matter,' said Mme Verdurin, raising her chin with an air of contempt for Mme Cottard and of admiration for the man of whom she was speaking, 'he was a brave colourist, a fine painter. Whereas,' she added, turning again to myself, 'I don't know whether you call it painting, all those huge she-devils of composition, those vast structures he exhibits now that he has given up coming to me. For my part, I call it daubing, it's all so hackneyed, and besides, it lacks relief, personality. It's anybody's work.' 'He revives the grace of the eighteenth century, but in a modern form,' Saniette broke out, fortified and reassured by my affability. 'But I prefer Helleu.' 'He's not in the least like Helleu,' said Mme Verdurin. 'Yes, he has the fever of the eighteenth century. He's a steam Watteau,' and he began to laugh. 'Old, old as the hills, I've had that served up to me for years,' said M. Verdurin, to whom indeed Ski had once repeated the remark, but as his own invention. 'It's unfortunate that when once in a way you say something quite amusing and make it intelligible, it is not your own.' 'I'm sorry about it,' Mme Verdurin went on, 'because he was really gifted, he has wasted a charming temperament for painting. Ah! if he had stayed with us! Why, he would have become the greatest landscape painter of our day. And it is a woman that has dragged him down so low! Not that that surprises me, for he was a pleasant enough man, but common. At bottom, he was a mediocrity. I may tell you that I felt it at once. Really, he never interested me. I was very fond of him, that was all. For one thing, he was so dirty. Tell me, do you, now, really like people who never wash?' 'What is this charmingly coloured thing that we are eating?' asked Ski. 'It is called strawberry mousse,' said Mme Verdurin. 'But it is ex-qui-site. You ought to open bottles of Château-Margaux, Château-Lafite, port wine.' 'I can't tell you how he amuses me, he never drinks anything but water,' said Mme Verdurin, seeking to cloak with her delight at such a flight of fancy her alarm at the thought of so prodigal an outlay. 'But not to drink,' Ski went on, 'you shall fill all our glasses, they will bring in marvellous peaches, huge nectarines, there against the sunset; it will be as gorgeous as a fine Veronese.' 'It would cost almost as much,' M. Verdurin murmured. 'But take away those cheeses with their hideous colour,' said Ski, trying to snatch the plate from before his host, who defended his gruyère with his might and main. 'You can realise that I don't regret Elstir,' Mme Verdurin said to me, 'that one is far more gifted. Elstir is simply hard work, the man who can't make himself give up painting when he would like to. He is the good student, the slavish competitor. Ski, now, only follows his own fancy. You will see him light a cigarette in the middle of dinner.' 'After all, I can't see why you wouldn't invite his wife,' said Cottard, 'he would be with us still.' 'Will you mind what you're saying, please, I don't open my doors to street-walkers, Monsieur le Professeur,' said Mme Verdurin, who had, on the contrary, done everything in her power to make Elstir return, even with his wife. But before they were married she had tried to make them quarrel, had told Elstir that the woman he loved was stupid, dirty, immoral, a thief. For once in a way she had failed to effect a breach. It was with the Verdurin salon that Elstir had broken; and he was glad of it, as converts bless the illness or misfortune that has withdrawn them from the world and has made them learn the way of salvation. 'He really is magnificent, the Professor,' she said. 'Why not declare outright that I keep a disorderly house? Anyone would think you didn't know what Madame Elstir was like. I would sooner have the lowest street-walker at my table! Oh no, I don't stand for that sort of thing. Besides I may tell you that it would have been stupid of me to overlook the wife, when the husband no longer interests me, he is out of date, he can't even draw.' 'That is extraordinary in a man of his intelligence,' said Cottard. 'Oh, no!' replied Mme Verdurin, 'even at the time when he had talent, for he had it, the wretch, and to spare, what was tiresome about him was that he had not a spark of intelligence.' Mme Verdurin, in passing this judgment upon Elstir, had not waited for their quarrel, or until she had ceased to care for his painting. The fact was that, even at the time when he formed part of the little group, it would happen that Elstir spent the whole day in the company of some woman whom, rightly or wrongly, Mme Verdurin considered a goose, which, in her opinion, was not the conduct of an intelligent man. 'No,' she observed with an air of finality, 'I consider that his wife and he are made for one another. Heaven knows, there isn't a more boring creature on the face of the earth, and I should go mad if I had to spend a couple of hours with her. But people say that he finds her very intelligent. There's no use denying it, our Tiche was *extremely stupid*. I have seen him bowled over by people you can't conceive, worthy idiots we should never have allowed into our little clan. Well! He wrote to them, he argued with them, he, Elstir! That doesn't prevent his having charming qualities, oh, charming and deliciously absurd, naturally.' For Mme Verdurin was convinced that men who are truly remarkable are capable of all sorts of follies. A false idea in which there is nevertheless a grain of truth. Certainly, people's follies are insupportable. But a want of balance which we discover only in course of time is the consequence of the entering into a human brain of delicacies for which it is not regularly adapted. So that the oddities of charming people exasperate us, but there are few if any charming people who are not, at the same time, odd. 'Look, I shall be able to show you his flowers now,' she said to me, seeing that her husband was making signals to her to rise. And she took M. de Cambremer's arm again. M. Verdurin tried to apologise for this to M. de Charlus, as soon as he had got rid of Mme de Cambremer, and to give him his reasons, chiefly for the pleasure of discussing these social refinements with a gentleman of title, momentarily the inferior of those who assigned to him the place to which they considered him entitled. But first of all he was anxious to make it clear to M. de Charlus that intellectually he esteemed him too highly to suppose that he could pay any attention to these trivialities. 'Excuse my mentioning so small a point,' he began, 'for I can understand how little such things mean to you. Middle-class minds pay attention to them, but the others, the artists, the people who are really of our sort, don't give a rap for them. Now, from the first words we exchanged, I realised that you were one of us!' M. de Charlus, who gave a widely different meaning to this expression, drew himself erect. After the doctor's oglings, he found his host's insulting frankness suffocating. 'Don't protest, my dear Sir, you are one of us, it is plain as daylight,' replied M. Verdurin. 'Observe that I have no idea whether you practise any of the arts, but that is not necessary. It is not always sufficient. Dechambre, who has just died, played exquisitely, with the most vigorous execution, but he was not one of us, you felt at once that he was not one of us. Brichot is not one of us. Morel is, my wife is, I can feel that you are . . . ' 'What were you going to tell me?' interrupted M. de Charlus, who was beginning to feel reassured as to M. Verdurin's meaning, but preferred that he should not utter these misleading remarks quite so loud. 'Only that we put you on the left,' replied M. Verdurin. M. de Charlus, with a comprehending, genial, insolent smile, replied: 'Why! That is not of the slightest importance, *here*!' And he gave a little laugh that was all his own – a laugh that came to him probably from some Bavarian or Lorraine grandmother, who herself had inherited it, in identical form, from an ancestress, so that it had been sounding now, without change, for not a few centuries in little old-fashioned European courts, and one could relish its precious quality like that of certain old musical instruments that have now grown rare. There are times when, to paint a complete portrait of someone, we should have to add a phonetic imitation to our verbal description, and our portrait of the figure that M. de Charlus presented is liable to remain incomplete in the absence of that little laugh, so delicate, so light, just as certain compositions are never accurately rendered because our orchestras lack those 'small trumpets', with a sound so entirely their own, for which the composer wrote this or that part. 'But,' M. Verdurin explained, stung by his laugh, 'we did it on purpose. I attach no importance whatever to title of nobility,' he went on, with that contemptuous smile which I have seen so many people whom I have known, unlike my grandmother and my mother, assume when they spoke of anything that they did not possess, before others who thus, they supposed, would be prevented from using that particular advantage to crow over them. 'But, don't you see, since we happened to have M. de Cambremer here, and he is a Marquis, while you are only a Baron . . . ' 'Pardon me,' M. de Charlus replied with an arrogant air to the astonished Verdurin, 'I am also Duc de Brabant, Damoiseau de Montargis, Prince d'Oloron, de Carency, de Viareggio and des Dunes. However, it is not of the slightest importance. Please do not distress yourself,' he concluded, resuming his subtle smile which spread itself over these final words: 'I could see at a glance that you were not accustomed to society.'

Mme Verdurin came across to me to show me Elstir's flowers. If this action, to which I had grown so indifferent, of going out to dinner, had on the contrary, taking the form that made it entirely novel, of a journey along the coast, followed by an ascent in a carriage to a point six hundred feet above the sea, produced in me a sort of intoxication, this feeling had not been dispelled at la Raspelière. 'Just look at this, now,' said the Mistress, showing me some huge and splendid roses by Elstir, whose unctuous scarlet and rich white stood out, however, with almost too creamy a relief from the flower-stand upon which they were arranged. 'Do you suppose he would still have the touch to get that? Don't you call that striking? And besides, it's fine as matter, it would be amusing to handle. I can't tell you how amusing it was to watch him painting them. One could feel that he was interested in trying to get just that effect.' And the Mistress's gaze rested musingly on this present from the artist in which were combined not merely his great talent but their long friendship which survived only in these mementoes of it which he had bequeathed to her; behind the flowers which long ago he had picked for her, she seemed to see the shapely hand that had painted them, in the course of a morning, in their freshness, so that, they on the table, it leaning against the back of a chair, had been able to meet face to face at the Mistress's luncheon party, the roses still alive and their almost lifelike portrait. Almost only, for Elstir was unable to look at a flower without first transplanting it to that inner garden in which we are obliged always to remain. He had shown in this watercolour the appearance of the roses which he had seen, and which, but for him, no one would ever have known; so that one might say that they were a new variety with which this painter, like a skilful gardener, had enriched the family of the Roses. 'From the day he left the little nucleus, he was finished. It seems, my dinners made him waste his time, that I hindered the development of his *genius*,' she said in a tone of irony. 'As if the society of a woman like myself could fail to be beneficial to an artist,' she exclaimed with a burst of pride. Close beside us, M. de Cambremer, who was already seated, seeing that M. de Charlus was standing, made as though to rise and offer him his chair. This offer may have arisen, in the Marquis's mind, from nothing more than a vague wish to be polite. M. de Charlus preferred to attach to it the sense of a duty which the plain gentleman knew that he owed to a Prince, and felt that he could not establish his right to this precedence better than by declining it. And so he exclaimed: 'What are you doing? I beg of you! The idea!' The astutely vehement tone of this protest had in itself something typically 'Guermantes' which became even more evident in the imperative, superfluous and familiar gesture with which he brought both his hands down, as though to force him to remain seated, upon the shoulders of M. de Cambremer who had not risen. 'Come, come, my dear fellow,' the Baron insisted, 'this is too much. There is no reason for it! In these days we keep that for Princes of the Blood.' I made no more effect on the Cambremers than on Mme Verdurin by my enthusiasm for their house. For I remained cold to the beauties which they pointed out to me and grew excited over confused reminiscences; at times I even confessed my disappointment at not finding something correspond to what its name had made me imagine. I enraged Mme de Cambremer by telling her that I had supposed the place to be more in the country. On the other hand I broke off in an ecstasy to sniff the fragrance of a breeze that crept in through the chink of the door. 'I see you like draughts,' they said to me. My praise of the patch of green lining-cloth that had been pasted over a broken pane met with no greater success: 'How frightful!' cried the Marquise. The climax came when I said: 'My greatest joy was when I arrived. When I heard my step echoing along the gallery, I felt that I had come into some village council-office, with a map of the district on the wall.' This time, Mme de Cambremer resolutely turned her back on me. 'You don't think the arrangement too bad?' her husband asked her with the same compassionate anxiety with which he would have enquired how his wife had stood some painful ceremony. 'They have some fine things.' But, inasmuch as malice, when the hard and fast rules of sure taste do not confine it within fixed limits, finds fault with everything, in the persons or in the houses, of the people who have supplanted the critic: 'Yes, but they are not in the right places. Besides, are they really as fine as all that?' 'You noticed,' said M. de Cambremer, with a melancholy that was controlled by a note of firmness, 'there are some Jouy hangings that are worn away, some quite threadbare things in this drawing-room!' 'And that piece of stuff with its huge roses, like a peasant woman's quilt,' said Mme de Cambremer whose purely artificial culture was confined exclusively to idealist philosophy, impressionist painting and Debussy's music. And, so as not to criticise merely in the name of smartness but in that of good taste: 'And they have put up windscreens! Such bad style! What can you expect of such people, they don't know, where could they have learned? They must be retired tradespeople. It's really not bad for them.' 'I thought the chandeliers good,' said the Marquis, though it was not evident why he should make an exception of the chandeliers, just as inevitably, whenever anyone spoke of a church, whether it was the Cathedral of Chartres, or of Rheims, or of Amiens, or the church at Balbec, what he would always make a point of mentioning as admirable would be: 'the organ-loft, the pulpit and the misericords'. 'As for the garden, don't speak about it,' said Mme de Cambremer. 'It's a massacre. Those paths running all crooked.' I seized the opportunity while Mme Verdurin was pouring out coffee to go and glance over the letter which M. de Cambremer had brought me, and in which his mother invited me to dinner. With that faint trace of ink, the handwriting revealed an individuality which in the future I should be able to recognise among a thousand, without any more need to have recourse to the hypothesis of special pens, than to suppose that rare and mysteriously blended colours are necessary to enable a painter to express his original vision. Indeed a paralytic, stricken with agraphia after a seizure, and compelled to look at the script as at a drawing without being able to read it, would have gathered that Mme de Cambremer belonged to an old family in which the zealous cultivation of literature and the arts had supplied a margin to its artistocratic traditions. He would have guessed also the period in which the Marquise had learned simultaneously to write and to play Chopin's music. It was the time when well-bred people observed the rule of affability and what was called the rule of the three adjectives. Mme de Cambremer combined the two rules in one. A laudatory adjective was not enough for her, she followed it (after a little stroke of the pen) with a second, then (after another stroke), with a third. But, what was peculiar to herself was that, in defiance of the literary and social object at which she aimed, the sequence of the three epithets assumed in Mme de Cambremer's notes the aspect not of a progression but of a diminuendo. Mme de Cambremer told me in this first letter that she had seen Saint-Loup and had appreciated more than ever his 'unique – rare – real' qualities, that he was coming to them again with one of his friends (the one who was in love with her daughter-in-law), and that if I cared to come, with or without them, to dine at Féterne she would be 'delighted – happy – pleased'. Perhaps it was because her desire to be friendly outran the fertility of her imagination and the riches of her vocabulary that the lady, while determined to utter three exclamations, was incapable of making the second and third anything more than feeble echoes of the first. Add but a fourth adjective, and, of her initial friendliness, there would be nothing left. Moreover, with a certain refined simplicity which cannot have failed to produce a considerable impression upon her family and indeed in her circle of acquaintance, Mme de Cambremer had acquired the habit of substituting for the word (which might in time begin to ring false) 'sincere', the word 'true'. And to show that it was indeed by sincerity that she was impelled, she broke the conventional rule that would have placed the adjective 'true' before its noun, and planted it boldly after. Her letters ended with: *'Croyez à mon amitié vraie.' 'Croyez à ma sympathie vraie.'* Unfortunately, this had become so stereotyped a formula that the affectation of frankness was more suggestive of a polite fiction than the time-honoured formulas, of the meaning of which people have ceased to think. I was, however, hindered from reading her letter by the confused sound of conversation over which rang out the louder accents of M. de Charlus, who, still on the same topic, was saying to M. de Cambremer: 'You reminded me, when you offered me your chair, of a gentleman from whom I received a letter this morning, addressed: "To His Highness, the Baron de Charlus", and beginning "Monseigneur".' 'To be sure, your correspondent was slightly exaggerating,' replied M. de Cambremer, giving way to a discreet show of mirth. M. de Charlus had provoked this; he did not partake in it. 'Well, if it comes to that, my dear fellow,' he said, 'I may observe that, heraldically speaking, he was entirely in the right. I am not regarding it as a personal matter, you understand. I should say the same of anyone else. But one has to face the facts, history is history, we can't alter it and it is not in our power to rewrite it. I need not cite the case of the Emperor William, who at Kiel never ceased to address me as "Monseigneur". I have heard it said that he gave the same title to all the Dukes of France, which was an abuse of the privilege, but was perhaps simply a delicate attention aimed over our heads at France herself.' 'More delicate, perhaps, than sincere,' said M. de Cambremer. 'Ah! There I must differ from you. Observe that, personally, a gentleman of the lowest rank such as that Hohenzollern, a Protestant to boot, and one who has usurped the throne of my cousin the King of Hanover, can be no favourite of mine,' added M. de Charlus, with whom the annexation of Hanover seemed to rankle more than that of Alsace-Lorraine. 'But I believe the feeling that turns the Emperor in our direction to be profoundly sincere. Fools will tell you that he is a stage emperor. He is on the contrary marvellously intelligent; it is true that he knows nothing about painting, and has forced Herr Tschudi to withdraw the Elstirs from the public galleries. But Louis XIV did not appreciate the Dutch Masters, he had the same fondness for display, and yet he was, when all is said, a great Monarch. Besides, William II has armed his country from the military and naval point of view in a way that Louis XIV failed to do, and I hope that his reign will never know the reverses that darkened the closing days of him who is fatuously styled the Roi Soleil. The Republic made a great mistake, to my mind, in rejecting the overtures of the Hohenzollern, or responding to them only in driblets. He is very well aware of it himself and says, with that gift that he has for the right expression: 'What I want is a clasped hand, not a raised hat.' As a man, he is vile; he has abandoned, surrendered, denied his best friends, in circumstances in which his silence was as deplorable as theirs was grand,' continued M. de Charlus, who was irresistibly drawn by his own tendencies to the Eulenburg affair, and remembered what one of the most highly placed of the culprits had said to him: 'The Emperor must have relied upon our delicacy to have dared to allow such a trial. But he was not mistaken in trusting to our discretion. We would have gone to the scaffold with our lips sealed.' 'All that, however, has nothing to do with what I was trying to explain, which is that, in Germany, mediatised Princes like ourselves are *Durchlaucht*, and in France our rank of Highness was publicly recognised. Saint-Simon tries to make out that this was an abuse on our part, in which he is entirely mistaken. The reason that he gives, namely that Louis XIV forbade us to style him the Most Christian King and ordered us to call him simply the King, proves merely that we held our title from him, and not that we had not the rank of Prince. Otherwise, it would have to be withheld from the Duc de Lorraine and ever so many others. Besides, several of our titles come from the House of Lorraine through Thérèse d'Espinay, my great-grandmother, who was the daughter of the Damoiseau de Commercy.' Observing that Morel was listening, M. de Charlus proceeded to develop the reasons for his claim. 'I have pointed out to my brother that it is not in the third part of Gotha, but in the second, not to say the first, that the account of our family ought to be included,' he said, without stopping to think that Morel did not know what 'Gotha' was. 'But that is his affair, he is the Head of my House, and so long as he raises no objection and allows the matter to pass, I have only to shut my eyes.' 'M. Brichot interests me greatly,' I said to Mme Verdurin as she joined me, and I slipped Mme de Cambremer's letter into my pocket. 'He has a cultured mind and is an excellent man,' she replied coldly. 'Of course what he lacks is originality and taste, he has a terrible memory. They used to say of the "forebears" of the people we have here this evening, the émigrés, that they had forgotten nothing. But they had at least the excuse,' she said, borrowing one of Swann's epigrams, 'that they had learned nothing. Whereas Brichot knows everything, and hurls chunks of dictionary at our heads during dinner. I'm sure you know everything now about the names of all the towns and villages.' While Mme Verdurin was speaking, it occurred to me that I had determined to ask her something, but I could not remember what it was. I could not at this moment say what Mme Verdurin was wearing that evening. Perhaps even then I was no more able to say, for I have not an observant mind. But feeling that her dress was not unambitious I said to her something polite and even admiring. She was like almost all women, who imagine that a compliment that is paid to them is a literal statement of the truth, and is a judgment impartially, irresistibly pronounced, as though it referred to a work of art that has no connection with a person. And so it was with an earnestness which made me blush for my own hypocrisy that she replied with the proud and artless question, habitual in the circumstances: 'You like it?' 'I know you're talking about Brichot. Eh, Chantepie, Freycinet, he spared you nothing. I had my eye on you, my little Mistress!' 'I saw you, it was all I could do not to laugh.' 'You are talking about Chantepie, I am certain,' said M. Verdurin, as he came towards us. I had been alone, as I thought of my strip of green cloth and of a scent of wood, in failing to notice that, while he discussed etymologies, Brichot had been provoking derision. And inasmuch as the expressions which, for me, gave their value to things were of the sort which other people either do not feel or reject without thinking of them, as unimportant, they were entirely useless to me and had the additional drawback of making me appear stupid in the eyes of Mme Verdurin who saw that I had 'swallowed' Brichot, as before I had appeared stupid to Mme de Guermantes, because I enjoyed going to see Mme d'Arpajon. With Brichot, however, there was another reason. I was not one of the little clan. And in every clan, whether it be social, political, literary, one contracts a perverse facility in discovering in a conversation, in an official speech, in a story, in a sonnet, everything that the honest reader would never have dreamed of finding there. How many times have I found myself, after reading with a certain emotion a tale skilfully told by a learned and slightly old-fashioned Academician, on the point of saying to Bloch or

to Mme de Guermantes: 'How charming this is!' when before I had opened
my mouth they exclaimed, each in a different language: 'If you want to be
really amused, read a tale by So-and-so. Human stupidity has never sunk to
greater depths.' Bloch's scorn was aroused principally by the discovery that
certain effects of style, pleasant enough in themselves, were slightly faded;
that of Mme de Guermantes because the tale seemed to prove the direct
opposite of what the author meant, for reasons of fact which she had the
ingenuity to deduce but which would never have occurred to me. I was no
less surprised to discover the irony that underlay the Verdurins' apparent
friendliness for Brichot than to hear, some days later, at Féterne, the
Cambremers say to me, on hearing my enthusiastic praise of la Raspelière:
'It's impossible that you can be sincere, after all they've done to it.' It is true
that they admitted that the china was good. Like the shocking windscreens,
it had escaped my notice. 'Anyhow, when you go back to Balbec, you will
know what Balbec means,' said M. Verdurin ironically. It was precisely the
things Brichot had told me that interested me. As for what they called his
mind, it was exactly the same mind that had at one time been so highly
appreciated by the little clan. He talked with the same irritating fluency, but
his words no longer carried, having to overcome a hostile silence or
disagreeable echoes; what had altered was not the things that he said but the
acoustics of the room and the attitude of his audience. 'Take care,' Mme
Verdurin murmured, pointing to Brichot. The latter, whose hearing
remained keener than his vision, darted at the mistress the hastily withdrawn
gaze of a short-sighted philosopher. If his bodily eyes were less good, his
mind's eye on the contrary had begun to take a larger view of things. He saw
how little was to be expected of human affection, and resigned himself to it.
Undoubtedly the discovery pained him. It may happen that even the man
who on one evening only, in a circle where he is usually greeted with joy,
realises that the others have found him too frivolous or too pedantic or too
loud, or too forward, or whatever it may be, returns home miserable. Often
it is a difference of opinion, or of system, that has made him appear to other
people absurd or old-fashioned. Often he is perfectly well aware that those
others are inferior to himself. He could easily dissect the sophistries with
which he has been tacitly condemned, he is tempted to pay a call, to write a
letter: on second thoughts, he does nothing, awaits the invitation for the
following week. Sometimes, too, these discomfitures, instead of ending with
the evening, last for months. Arising from the instability of social judgments,
they increase that instability further. For the man who knows that Mme X
despises him, feeling that he is respected at Mme Y's, pronounces her far
superior to the other and emigrates to her house. This however is not the

proper place to describe those men, superior to the life of society but lacking the capacity to realise their own worth outside it, glad to be invited, embittered by being disparaged, discovering annually the faults of the hostess to whom they have been offering incense and the genius of her whom they have never properly appreciated, ready to return to the old love when they shall have felt the drawbacks to be found equally in the new, and when they have begun to forget those of the old. We may judge by these temporary discomfitures the grief that Brichot felt at one which he knew to be final. He was not unaware that Mme Verdurin sometimes laughed at him publicly, even at his infirmities, and knowing how little was to be expected of human affection, submitting himself to the facts, he continued nevertheless to regard the Mistress as his best friend. But, from the blush that swept over the scholar's face, Mme Verdurin saw that he had heard her, and made up her mind to be kind to him for the rest of the evening. I could not help remarking to her that she had not been very kind to Saniette. 'What! Not kind to him! Why, he adores us, you can't imagine what we are to him. My husband is sometimes a little irritated by his stupidity, and you must admit that he has every reason, but when that happens why doesn't he rise in revolt, instead of cringing like a whipped dog? It is not honest. I don't like it. That doesn't mean that I don't always try to calm my husband, because if he went too far, all that would happen would be that Saniette would stay away; and I don't want that because I may tell you that he hasn't a penny in the world, he needs his dinners. But after all, if he does mind, he can stay away, it has nothing to do with me, when a person depends on other people he should try not to be such an idiot.' 'The Duchy of Aumale was in our family for years before passing to the House of France,' M. de Charlus was explaining to M. de Cambremer, before a speechless Morel, for whom, as a matter of fact, the whole of this dissertation was, if not actually addressed to him, intended. 'We took precedence over all foreign Princes; I could give you a hundred examples. The Princesse de Croy having attempted, at the burial of Monsieur, to fall on her knees after my great-great-grandmother, that lady reminded her sharply that she had not the privilege of the hassock, made the officer on duty remove it, and reported the matter to the King, who ordered Mme de Croy to call upon Mme de Guermantes and offer her apologies. The Duc de Bourgogne having come to us with ushers with raised wands, we obtained the King's authority to have them lowered. I know it is not good form to speak of the merits of one's own family. But it is well known that our people were always to the fore in the hour of danger. Our battle-cry, after we abandoned that of the Dukes of Brabant, was *Passavant!* So that it is fair enough after all that this right to be everywhere the first, which we had established for so many centuries in war, should afterwards have been confirmed to us at Court. And, egad, it has always been admitted there. I may give you a further instance, that of the Princess of Baden. As she had so far forgotten herself as to attempt to challenge the precedence of that same Duchesse de Guermantes of whom I was speaking just now, and had attempted to go in first to the King's presence, taking advantage of a momentary hesitation which my relative may perhaps have shown (although there could be no reason for it), the King called out: 'Come in, cousin, come in; Mme de Baden knows very well what her duty is to you.' And it was as Duchesse de Guermantes that she held this rank, albeit she was of no mean family herself, since she was through her mother niece to the Queen of Poland, the Queen of Hungary, the Elector Palatine, the Prince of Savoy-Carignano and the Elector of Hanover, afterwards King of England.' '*Maecenas atavis édite regibus!*' said Brichot, addressing M. de Charlus, who acknowledged the compliment with a slight inclination of his head. 'What did you say?' Mme Verdurin asked Brichot, anxious to make amends to him for her previous speech. 'I was referring, Heaven forgive me, to a dandy who was the pick of the basket' (Mme Verdurin winced) 'about the time of Augustus' (Mme Verdurin, reassured by the remoteness in time of this basket, assumed a more serene expression), 'of a friend of Virgil and Horace who carried their sycophancy to the extent of proclaiming to his face his more than aristocratic, his royal descent, in a word I was referring to Maecenas, a bookworm who was the friend of Horace, Virgil, Augustus. I am sure that M. de Charlus knows all about Maecenas.' With a gracious, sidelong glance at Mme Verdurin, because he had heard her make an appointment with Morel for the day after next and was afraid that she might not invite him also, 'I should say,' said M. de Charlus, 'that Maecenas was more or less the Verdurin of antiquity.' Mme Verdurin could not altogether suppress a smile of satisfaction. She went over to Morel. 'He's nice, your father's friend,' she said to him. 'One can see that he's an educated man, and well bred. He will get on well in our little nucleus. What is his address in Paris?' Morel preserved a haughty silence and merely proposed a game of cards. Mme Verdurin insisted upon a little violin music first. To the general astonishment, M. de Charlus, who never referred to his own considerable gifts, accompanied, in the purest style, the closing passage (uneasy, tormented, Schumannesque, but, for all that, earlier than Franck's Sonata) of the Sonata for piano and violin by Fauré. I felt that he would furnish Morel, marvellously endowed as to tone and virtuosity, with just those qualities that he lacked, culture and style. But I thought with curiosity of this combination in a single person of a physical blemish and a spiritual gift. M. de Charlus was not very different from his brother, the Duc de Guermantes. Indeed, a moment ago (though this was rare), he had spoken as bad French as his brother. He having reproached me (doubtless in order that I might speak in glowing terms of Morel to Mme Verdurin) with never coming to see him, and I having pleaded discretion, he had replied: 'But, since it is I that asks you, there is no one but I who am in a position to take offence.' This might have been said by the Duc de Guermantes. M. de Charlus was only a Guermantes when all was said. But it had been enough that nature should upset the balance of his nervous system sufficiently to make him prefer to the woman that his brother the Duke would have chosen one of Virgil's shepherds or Plato's disciples, and at once qualities unknown to the Duc de Guermantes and often combined with this want of balance had made M. de Charlus an exquisite pianist, an amateur painter who was not devoid of taste, an eloquent talker. Who would ever have detected that the rapid, eager, charming style with which M. de Charlus played the Schumannesque passage of Fauré's Sonata had its equivalent – one dares not say its cause – in elements entirely physical, in the nervous defects of M. de Charlus? We shall explain later on what we mean by nervous defects, and why it is that a Greek of the time of Socrates, a Roman of the time of Augustus might be what we know them to have been and yet remain absolutely normal men, and not men-women such as we see around us today. Just as he had genuine artistic tendencies, which had never come to fruition, so M. de Charlus had, far more than the Duke, loved their mother, loved his own wife, and indeed, years after her death, if anyone spoke of her to him would shed tears, but superficial tears, like the perspiration of an over-stout man, whose brow will glisten with sweat at the slightest exertion. With this difference, that to the latter we say: 'How hot you are', whereas we pretend not to notice other people's tears. We, that is to say, people in society; for the humbler sort are as distressed by the sight of tears as if a sob were more serious than a haemorrhage. His sorrow after the death of his wife, thanks to the habit of falsehood, did not debar M. de Charlus from a life which was not in harmony with it. Indeed later on, he sank so low as to let it be known that, during the funeral rites, he had found an opportunity of asking the acolyte for his name and address. And it may have been true.

When the piece came to an end, I ventured to ask for some Franck, which appeared to cause Mme de Cambremer such acute pain that I did not insist. 'You can't admire that sort of thing,' she said to me. Instead she asked for Debussy's *Fêtes*, which made her exclaim: 'Ah! How sublime!' from the first note. But Morel discovered that he remembered the opening bars only,

and in a spirit of mischief, without any intention to deceive, began a
March by Meyerbeer. Unfortunately, as he left little interval and made no
announcement, everybody supposed that he was still playing Debussy, and
continued to exclaim 'Sublime!' Morel, by revealing that the composer was
that not of *Pelléas* but of *Robert le Diable* created a certain chill. Mme de
Cambremer had scarcely time to feel it, for she had just discovered a
volume of Scarlatti, and had flung herself upon it with an hysterical
impulse. 'Oh! Play this, look, this piece, it's divine,' she cried. And yet, of
this composer long despised, recently promoted to the highest honours,
what she had selected in her feverish impatience was one of those infernal
pieces which have so often kept us from sleeping, while a merciless pupil
repeats them indefinitely on the next floor. But Morel had had enough
music, and as he insisted upon cards, M. de Charlus, to be able to join in,
proposed a game of whist. 'He was telling the Master just now that he is a
Prince,' said Ski to Mme Verdurin, 'but it's not true, they're quite a humble
family of architects.' 'I want to know what it was you were saying about
Maecenas. It interests me, don't you know!' Mme Verdurin repeated to
Brichot, with an affability that carried him off his feet. And so, in order to
shine in the Mistress's eyes, and possibly in mine: 'Why, to tell you the
truth, Madame, Maecenas interests me chiefly because he is the earliest
apostle of note of that Chinese god who numbers more followers in France
today than Brahma, than Christ himself, the all-powerful God Ubedamd.'
Mme Verdurin was no longer content, upon these occasions, with burying
her head in her hands. She would descend with the suddenness of the
insects called ephemeral upon Princess Sherbatov; were the latter within
reach the Mistress would cling to her shoulder, dig her nails into it, and
hide her face against it for a few moments like a child playing at hide and
seek. Concealed by this protecting screen, she was understood to be
laughing until she cried and was as well able to think of nothing at all as
people are who while saying a prayer that is rather long take the wise
precaution of burying their faces in their hands. Mme Verdurin used to
imitate them when she listened to Beethoven quartets, so as at the same
time to let it be seen that she regarded them as a prayer and not to let it be
seen that she was asleep. 'I am quite serious, Madame,' said Brichot. 'Too
numerous, I consider, today is become the person who spends his time
gazing at his navel as though it were the hub of the universe. As a matter of
doctrine, I have no objection to offer to some Nirvana which will dissolve
us in the great Whole (which, like Munich and Oxford, is considerably
nearer to Paris than Asnières or Bois-Colombes), but it is unworthy either
of a true Frenchman, or of a true European even, when the Japanese are

possibly at the gates of our Byzantium, that socialised anti-militarists should be gravely discussing the cardinal virtues of free verse.' Mme Verdurin felt that she might dispense with the Princess's mangled shoulder, and allowed her face to become once more visible, not without pretending to wipe her eyes and gasping two or three times for breath. But Brichot was determined that I should have my share in the entertainment, and having learned, from those oral examinations which he conducted so admirably, that the best way to flatter the young is to lecture them, to make them feel themselves important, to make them regard you as a reactionary: 'I have no wish to blaspheme against the Gods of Youth,' he said, with that furtive glance at myself which a speaker turns upon a member of his audience whom he has mentioned by name. 'I have no wish to be damned as a heretic and renegade in the Mallarméan chapel in which our new friend, like all the young men of his age, must have served the esoteric mass, at least as an acolyte, and have shown himself deliquescent or Rosicrucian. But, really, we have seen more than enough of these intellectuals worshipping art with a big A, who, when they can no longer intoxicate themselves upon Zola, inject themselves with Verlaine. Become etheromaniacs out of Baudelairean devotion, they would no longer be capable of the virile effort which the country may, one day or another, demand of them, anaesthetised as they are by the great literary neurosis in the heated, enervating atmosphere, heavy with unwholesome vapours, of a symbolism of the opium-pipe.' Feeling incapable of feigning any trace of admiration for Brichot's inept and motley tirade, I turned to Ski and assured him that he was entirely mistaken as to the family to which M. de Charlus belonged; he replied that he was certain of his facts, and added that I myself had said that his real name was Gandin, Le Gandin. 'I told you,' was my answer, 'that Mme de Cambremer was the sister of an engineer, M. Legrandin. I never said a word to you about M. de Charlus. There is about as much connection between him and Mme de Cambremer as between the Great Condé and Racine.' 'Indeed! I thought there was,' said Ski lightly, with no more apology for his mistake than he had made a few hours earlier for the mistake that had nearly made his party miss the train. 'Do you intend to remain long on this coast?' Mme Verdurin asked M. de Charlus, in whom she foresaw an addition to the faithful and trembled lest he should be returning too soon to Paris. 'Good Lord, one never knows,' replied M. de Charlus in a nasal drawl. 'I should like to stay here until the end of September.' 'You are quite right,' said Mme Verdurin; 'that is the time for fine storms at sea.' 'To tell you the truth, that is not what would influence me. I have for some time past unduly neglected the Archangel Saint

Michael, my patron, and I should like to make amends to him by staying for
his feast, on the 29th of September, at the Abbey on the Mount.' 'You take
an interest in all that sort of thing?' asked Mme Verdurin, who might
perhaps have succeeded in hushing the voice of her outraged anti-clericalism,
had she not been afraid that so long an expedition might make the violinist
and the Baron 'fail' her for forty-eight hours. 'You are perhaps afflicted with
intermittent deafness,' M. de Charlus replied insolently. 'I have told you that
Saint Michael is one of my glorious patrons.' Then, smiling with a benevolent
ecstasy, his eyes gazing into the distance, his voice strengthened by an
excitement which seemed now to be not merely aesthetic but religious: 'It is
so beautiful at the offertory when Michael stands erect by the altar, in a white
robe, swinging a golden censer heaped so high with perfumes that the
fragrance of them mounts up to God.' 'We might go there in a party,'
suggested Mme Verdurin, notwithstanding her horror of the clergy. 'At that
moment, when the offertory begins,' went on M. de Charlus who, for other
reasons but in the same manner as good speakers in Parliament, never
replied to an interruption and would pretend not to have heard it, 'it would
be wonderful to see our young friend Palestrinising, indeed performing an
aria by Bach. The worthy Abbot, too, would be wild with joy, and that is the
greatest homage, at least the greatest public homage that I can pay to my
Holy Patron. What an edification for the faithful! We must mention it
presently to the young Angelico of music, a warrior like Saint Michael.'

Saniette, summoned to make a fourth, declared that he did not know how
to play whist. And Cottard, seeing that there was not much time left before
our train, embarked at once on a game of écarté with Morel. M. Verdurin
was furious, and bore down with a terrible expression upon Saniette. 'Is
there anything in the world that you can play?' he cried, furious at being
deprived of the opportunity for a game of whist, and delighted to have
found one to insult the old registrar. He, in his terror, did his best to look
clever. 'Yes, I can play the piano,' he said. Cottard and Morel were seated
face to face. 'Your deal,' said Cottard. 'Suppose we go nearer to the card-
table,' M. de Charlus, worried by the sight of Morel in Cottard's company,
suggested to M. de Cambremer. 'It is quite as interesting as those questions
of etiquette which in these days have ceased to count for very much. The
only kings that we have left, in France at least, are the kings in the pack of
cards, who seem to me to be positively swarming in the hand of our young
virtuoso,' he added a moment later, from an admiration for Morel which
extended to his way of playing cards, to flatter him also, and finally to
account for his suddenly turning to lean over the young violinist's shoulder.
'I—ee cut,' said (imitating the accent of a cardsharper) Cottard, whose

children burst out laughing, like his students and the chief dresser, whenever the master, even by the bedside of a serious case, uttered with the
emotionless face of an epileptic one of his hackneyed witticisms. 'I don't
know what to play,' said Morel, seeking advice from M. de Charlus. 'Just as
you please, you're bound to lose, whatever you play, it's all the same (*c'est
égal*).' '*Egal* . . . Ingalli?' said the doctor, with an insinuating, kindly glance at
M. de Cambremer. 'She was what we call a true diva, she was a dream, a
Carmen such as we shall never see again. She was wedded to the part. I used
to enjoy too listening to Ingalli – married.' The Marquis drew himself up
with that contemptuous vulgarity of well-bred people who do not realise
that they are insulting their host by appearing uncertain whether they ought
to associate with his guests, and adopt English manners by way of apology
for a scornful expression: 'Who is that gentleman playing cards, what does
he do for a living, what does he *sell*? I rather like to know whom I am
meeting, so as not to make friends with any Tom, Dick or Harry. But I
didn't catch his name when you did me the honour of introducing me to
him.' If M. Verdurin, availing himself of this phrase, had indeed introduced
M. de Cambremer to his fellow-guests, the other would have been greatly
annoyed. But, knowing that it was the opposite procedure that was observed,
he thought it gracious to assume a genial and modest air, without risk to
himself. The pride that M. Verdurin took in his intimacy with Cottard had
increased if anything now that the doctor had become an eminent professor.
But it no longer found expression in the artless language of earlier days.
Then, when Cottard was scarcely known to the public, if you spoke to M.
Verdurin of his wife's facial neuralgia: 'There is nothing to be done,' he
would say, with the artless self-satisfaction of people who assume that
anyone whom they know must be famous, and that everybody knows the
name of their family singing-master. 'If she had an ordinary doctor, one
might look for a second opinion, but when that doctor is called Cottard' (a
name which he pronounced as though it were Bouchard or Charcot) 'one
has simply to bow to the inevitable.' Adopting a reverse procedure, knowing
that M. de Cambremer must certainly have heard of the famous Professor
Cottard, M. Verdurin adopted a tone of simplicity. 'He's our family doctor,
a worthy soul whom we adore and who would let himself be torn in pieces
for our sakes; he is not a doctor, he is a friend, I don't suppose you have ever
heard of him or that his name would convey anything to you, in any case to
us it is the name of a very good man, of a very dear friend, Cottard.' This
name, murmured in a modest tone, took in M. de Cambremer who supposed
that his host was referring to someone else. 'Cottard? You don't mean
Professor Cottard?' At that moment one heard the voice of the said Professor

who, at an awkward point in the game, was saying as he looked at his cards: 'This is where Greek meets Greek.' 'Why, yes, to be sure, he is a professor,' said M. Verdurin. 'What! Professor Cottard! You are not making a mistake? You are quite sure it's the same man? The one who lives in the Rue du Bac?' 'Yes, his address is 43, Rue du Bac. You know him?' 'But everybody knows Professor Cottard. He's at the top of the tree! You might as well ask me if I knew Bouffe de Saint-Biaise or Courtois-Suffit. I could see when I heard him speak that he was not an ordinary person, that is why I took the liberty of asking you.' 'Come now, what shall I play, trumps?' asked Cottard. Then abruptly, with a vulgarity which would have been offensive even in heroic circumstances, as when a soldier uses a coarse expression to convey his contempt for death, but became doubly stupid in the safe pastime of a game of cards, Cottard, deciding to play a trump, assumed a sombre, suicidal air, and, borrowing the language of people who are risking their skins, played his card as though it were his life, with the exclamation: 'There it is, and be damned to it!' It was not the right card to play, but he had a consolation. In the middle of the room, in a deep armchair, Mme Cottard, yielding to the effect, which she always found irresistible, of a good dinner, had succumbed after vain efforts to the vast and gentle slumbers that were overpowering her. In vain might she sit up now and again, and smile, whether at her own absurdity or from fear of leaving unanswered some polite speech that might have been addressed to her, she sank back, in spite of herself, into the clutches of the implacable and delicious malady. More than the noise, what awakened her thus for an instant only, was the glance (which, in her wifely affection she could see even when her eyes were shut, and foresaw, for the same scene occurred every evening and haunted her dreams like the thought of the hour at which one will have to rise), the glance with which the Professor drew the attention of those present to his wife's slumbers. To begin with, he merely looked at her and smiled, for if as a doctor he disapproved of this habit of falling asleep after dinner (or at least gave this scientific reason for growing annoyed later on, but it is not certain whether it was a determining reason, so many and diverse were the views that he held about it), as an all-powerful and teasing husband, he was delighted to be able to make a fool of his wife, to rouse her only partly at first, so that she might fall asleep again and he have the pleasure of waking her afresh.

By this time, Mme Cottard was sound asleep. 'Now then, Léontine, you're snoring,' the professor called to her. 'I am listening to Mme Swann, my dear,' Mme Cottard replied faintly, and dropped back into her lethargy. 'It's perfect nonsense,' exclaimed Cottard, 'she'll be telling us presently that she wasn't asleep. She's like the patients who come to consult us and insist that they never sleep at all.' 'They imagine it, perhaps,' said M. de Cambremer with a laugh. But the doctor enjoyed contradicting no less than teasing, and would on no account allow a layman to talk medicine to him. 'People do not imagine that they never sleep,' he promulgated in a dogmatic tone. 'Ah!' replied the Marquis with a respectful bow, such as Cottard at one time would have made. 'It is easy to see,' Cottard went on, 'that you have never administered, as I have, as much as two grains of trional without succeeding in provoking somnolescence.' 'Quite so, quite so,' replied the Marquis, laughing with a superior air, 'I have never taken trional, or any of those drugs which soon cease to have any effect but ruin your stomach. When a man has been out shooting all night, like me, in the forest of Chantepie, I can assure you he doesn't need any trional to make him sleep.' 'It is only fools who say that,' replied the Professor. 'Trional frequently has a remarkable effect on the nervous tone. You mention trional, have you any idea what it is?' 'Well . . . I've heard people say that it is a drug to make one sleep.' 'You are not answering my question,' replied the Professor, who, thrice weekly, at the Faculty, sat on the board of examiners. 'I don't ask you whether it makes you sleep or not, but what it is. Can you tell me what percentage it contains of amyl and ethyl?' 'No,' replied M. de Cambremer with embarrassment. 'I prefer a good glass of old brandy or even 345 port.' 'Which are ten times as toxic,' the Professor interrupted. 'As for trional,' M. de Cambremer ventured, 'my wife goes in for all that sort of thing, you'd better talk to her about it.' 'She probably knows just as much about it as yourself. In any case, if your wife takes trional to make her sleep, you can see that mine has no need of it. Come along, Léontine, wake up, you're getting ankylosed, did you ever see me fall asleep after dinner? What will you be like when you're sixty, if you fall asleep now like an old woman? You'll go and get fat, you're arresting the circulation. She doesn't even hear what I'm saying.' 'They're bad for one's health, these little naps after dinner, ain't they, Doctor?' said M. de Cambremer, seeking to rehabilitate himself with Cottard. 'After a heavy meal one ought to take exercise.' 'Stuff and nonsense!' replied the Doctor. 'We have taken identical quantities of food from the stomach of a dog that has lain quiet and from the stomach of a dog that has been running about and it is in the former that digestion is more advanced.' 'Then it is sleep that stops digestion.' 'That depends upon whether you mean oesophagic digestion, stomachic digestion, intestinal digestion; it is useless to give you explanations which you would not understand since you have never studied medicine. Now then, Léontine, quick march, it is time we were going.' This was not true, for the doctor was going merely to continue his game, but he hoped thus to cut short in a more drastic fashion the slumbers of the deaf mute to whom he had been addressing without a word of response the most learned exhortations. Whether a determination to remain awake survived in Mme Cottard, even in the state of sleep, or because the armchair offered no support to her head, it was jerked mechanically from left to right, and up and down, in the empty air, like a lifeless object, and Mme Cottard, with her nodding poll, appeared now to be listening to music, now to be in the last throes of death. Where her husband's increasingly vehement admonitions failed of their effect, her sense of her own stupidity proved successful. 'My bath is nice and hot,' she murmured, 'but the feathers in the dictionary . . . ' she exclaimed as she sat bolt upright. 'Oh! Good lord, what a fool I am. Whatever have I been saying, I was thinking about my hat, I'm sure I said something silly, in another minute I should have been asleep, it's that wretched fire.' Everybody began to laugh, for there was no fire in the room.

'You are making fun of me,' said Mme Cottard, herself laughing, and raising her hand to her brow to wipe away, with the light touch of a hypnotist and the sureness of a woman putting her hair straight, the last traces of sleep, 'I must offer my humble apologies to dear Mme Verdurin and ask her to tell me the truth.' But her smile at once grew sorrowful, for the Professor who knew that his wife sought to please him and trembled lest she should fail, had shouted at her: 'Look at yourself in the glass, you are as red as if you had an eruption of acne, you look just like an old peasant.' 'You know, he is charming,' said Mme Verdurin, 'he has such a delightfully sarcastic side to his character. And then, he snatched my husband from the jaws of death when the whole Faculty had given him up. He spent three nights by his bedside, without ever lying down. And so Cottard to me, you know,' she went on, in a grave and almost menacing tone, raising her hand to the twin spheres, shrouded in white tresses, of her musical temples, and as though we had wished to assault the doctor, 'is sacred! He could ask me for anything in the world! As it is, I don't call him Doctor Cottard, I call him Doctor God! And even in saying that I am slandering him, for this God does everything in his power to remedy some of the disasters for which the other is responsible.' 'Play a trump,' M. de Charlus said to Morel with a delighted air. 'A trump, here goes,' said the violinist. 'You ought to have declared your king first,' said M. de Charlus, 'you're not paying attention to the game, but how well you play!' 'I have the king,' said Morel. 'He's a fine man,' replied the Professor. 'What's all that business up there with the sticks?' asked Mme Verdurin, drawing M. de Cambremer's attention to a superb escutcheon carved over the mantelpiece. 'Are they your arms?' she added with an ironical disdain. 'No, they are not ours,' replied M. de Cambremer. 'We bear, *barry of five, embattled counter-embattled or and gules, as many trefoils countercharged*. No, those are the arms of the Arrachepels, who were not of our stock, but from whom we inherited the house, and nobody of our line has ever made any changes here. The Arrachepels (formerly Pelvilains, we are told) bore *or five piles couped in base gules*. When they allied themselves with the Féterne family, their blazon changed, but remained *cantoned within twenty cross crosslets fitchee in base or, a dexter canton ermine*.' 'That's one for her!' muttered Mme de Cambremer. 'My great-grandmother was a d'Arrachepel or de Rachepel, as you please, for both forms are found in the old charters,' continued M. de Cambremer, blushing vividly, for only then did the idea for which his wife had given him credit occur to him, and he was afraid that Mme Verdurin might have applied to herself a speech which had been made without any reference to her. 'The history books say that, in the eleventh century, the first Arrachepel, Macé, named Pelvilain, showed a special aptitude, in siege warfare, in tearing up piles. Whence the name Arrachepel by which he was ennobled, and the piles which you see persisting through the centuries in their arms. These are the piles which, to render fortifications more impregnable, used to be driven, plugged, if you will pardon the expression, into the ground in front of them, and fastened together laterally. They are what you quite rightly called sticks, though they had nothing to do with the floating sticks of our good Lafontaine. For they were supposed to render a stronghold unassailable. Of course, with our modern artillery, they make one smile. But you must bear in mind that I am speaking of the eleventh century.' 'It is all rather out of date,' said Mme Verdurin, 'but the little campanile has a character.' 'You have,' said Cottard, 'the luck of . . . turlututu,' a word which he gladly repeated to avoid using Molière's. 'Do you know why the king of diamonds was turned out of the army?' 'I shouldn't mind being in his shoes,' said Morel, who was tired of military service. 'Oh! What a bad patriot,' exclaimed M. de Charlus, who could not refrain from pinching the violinist's ear. 'No, you don't know why the king of diamonds was turned out of the army,' Cottard pursued, determined to make his joke, 'it's because he has only one eye.' 'You are up against it, Doctor,' said M. de Cambremer, to show Cottard that he knew who he was. 'This young man is astonishing,' M. de Charlus interrupted innocently. 'He plays like a god.' This observation did not find favour with the doctor, who replied: 'Never too late to mend. Who laughs last, laughs longest.' 'Queen, ace,' Morel, whom fortune was favouring, announced triumphantly. The doctor bowed his head as though powerless to deny this good fortune, and admitted, spellbound: 'That's fine.' 'We are so pleased to have met M. de Charlus,' said Mme de Cambremer to Mme Verdurin. 'Had

you never met him before? He is quite nice, he is unusual, he is *of a period*'
(she would have found it difficult to say which), replied Mme Verdurin with
the satisfied smile of a connoisseur, a judge and a hostess. Mme de
Cambremer asked me if I was coming to Féterne with Saint-Loup. I could
not suppress a cry of admiration when I saw the moon hanging like an
orange lantern beneath the vault of oaks that led away from the house.
'That's nothing, presently, when the moon has risen higher and the valley is
lighted up, it will be a thousand times better.' 'Are you staying any time in
this neighbourhood, Madame?' M. de Cambremer asked Mme Cottard, a
speech that might be interpreted as a vague intention to invite and dispensed
him for the moment from making any more precise engagement. 'Oh,
certainly, Sir, I regard this annual exodus as most important for the children.
Whatever you may say, they must have fresh air. The Faculty wanted to
send me to Vichy; but it is too stuffy there, and I can look after my stomach
when those big boys of mine have grown a little bigger. Besides, the
Professor, with all the examinations he has to hold, has always got his
shoulder to the wheel, and the hot weather tires him dreadfully. I feel that a
man needs a thorough rest after he has been on the go all the year like that.
Whatever happens we shall stay another month at least.' 'Ah! In that case we
shall meet again.' 'Besides, I shall be all the more obliged to stay here as my
husband has to go on a visit to Savoy, and won't be finally settled here for
another fortnight.' 'I like the view of the valley even more than the sea view,'
Mme Verdurin went on. 'You are going to have a splendid night for your
journey.' 'We ought really to find out whether the carriages are ready, if you
are absolutely determined to go back to Balbec tonight,' M. Verdurin said
to me, 'for I see no necessity for it myself. We could drive you over
tomorrow morning. It is certain to be fine. The roads are excellent.' I said
that it was impossible. 'But in any case it is not time yet,' the Mistress
protested. 'Leave them alone, they have heaps of time. A lot of good it will
do them to arrive at the station with an hour to wait. They are far happier
here. And you, my young Mozart,' she said to Morel, not venturing to
address M. de Charlus directly, 'won't you stay the night? We have some
nice rooms facing the sea.' 'No, he can't,' M. de Charlus replied on behalf of
the absorbed card-player who had not heard. 'He has a pass until midnight
only. He must go back to bed like a good little boy, obedient, and well-
behaved,' he added in a complaisant, mannered, insistent voice, as though
he derived some sadic pleasure from the use of this chaste comparison and
also from letting his voice dwell, in passing, upon any reference to Morel,
from touching him with (failing his fingers) words that seemed to explore
his person.

From the sermon that Brichot had addressed to me, M. de Cambremer had concluded that I was a Dreyfusard. As he himself was as anti-Dreyfusard as possible, out of courtesy to a foe, he began to sing me the praises of a Jewish colonel who had always been very decent to a cousin of the Chevregny and had secured for him the promotion he deserved. 'And my cousin's opinions were the exact opposite,' said M. de Cambremer; he omitted to mention what those opinions were, but I felt that they were as antiquated and misshapen as his own face, opinions which a few families in certain small towns must long have entertained. 'Well, you know, I call that really fine!' was M. de Cambremer's conclusion. It is true that he was hardly employing the word 'fine' in the aesthetic sense in which it would have suggested to his wife and mother different works, but works, anyhow, of art. M. de Cambremer often made use of this term, when for instance he was congratulating a delicate person who had put on a little flesh. 'What, you have gained half-a-stone in two months. I say, that's fine!' Refreshments were set out on a table. Mme Verdurin invited the gentlemen to go and choose whatever drinks they preferred. M. de Charlus went and drank his glass and at once returned to a seat by the card-table from which he did not stir. Mme Verdurin asked him: 'Have you tasted my orangeade?' Upon which M. de Charlus, with a gracious smile, in a crystalline tone which he rarely sounded and with endless motions of his lips and body, replied: 'No, I preferred its neighbour, it was strawberry-juice, I think, it was delicious.' It is curious that a certain order of secret actions has the external effect of a manner of speaking or gesticulating which reveals them. If a gentleman believes or disbelieves in the Immaculate Conception, or in the innocence of Dreyfus, or in a plurality of worlds, and wishes to keep his opinion to himself, you will find nothing in his voice or in his movements that will let you read his thoughts. But on hearing M. de Charlus say in that shrill voice and with that smile and waving his arms: 'No, I preferred its neighbour, the strawberry-juice,' one could say: 'There, he likes the stronger sex,' with the same certainty as enables a judge to sentence a criminal who has not confessed, a doctor a patient suffering from general paralysis who himself is perhaps unaware of his malady but has made some mistake in pronunciation from which one can deduce that he will be dead in three years. Perhaps the people who conclude from a man's way of saying: 'No, I preferred its neighbour, the strawberry-juice', a love of the kind called unnatural, have no need of any such scientific knowledge. But that is because there is a more direct relation between the revealing sign and the secret. Without saying it in so many words to oneself, one feels that it is a gentle, smiling lady who is answering and who appears mannered because she is pretending to be a man and one is not accustomed to seeing men adopt such mannerisms. And it is perhaps more pleasant to think that for long years a certain number of angelic women have been included by mistake in the masculine sex where, in exile, ineffectually beating their wings towards men in whom they inspire a physical repulsion, they know how to arrange a drawing-room, compose 'interiors'. M. de Charlus was not in the least perturbed that Mme Verdurin should be standing, and remained installed in his armchair so as to be nearer to Morel. 'Don't you think it criminal,' said Mme Verdurin to the Baron, 'that that creature who might be enchanting us with his violin should be sitting there at a card-table? When anyone can play the violin like that!' 'He plays cards well, he does everything well, he is so intelligent,' said M. de Charlus, keeping his eye on the game, so as to be able to advise Morel. This was not his only reason, however, for not rising from his chair for Mme Verdurin. With the singular amalgam that he had made of the social conceptions at once of a great nobleman and an amateur of art, instead of being polite in the same way that a man of his world would be, he would create a sort of *tableau vivant* for himself after Saint-Simon; and at that moment was amusing himself by impersonating the Maréchal d'Uxelles, who interested him from other aspects also, and of whom it is said that he was so proud as to remain seated, with a pretence of laziness, before all the most distinguished persons at court. 'By the way, Charlus,' said Mme Verdurin, who was beginning to grow familiar, 'you don't know of any ruined old nobleman in your Faubourg who would come to me as porter?' 'Why, yes . . . why, yes,' replied M. de Charlus with a genial smile, 'but I don't advise it.' 'Why not?' 'I should be afraid for your sake, that your smart visitors would call at the lodge and go no farther.' This was the first skirmish between them. Mme Verdurin barely noticed it. There were to be others, alas, in Paris. M. de Charlus remained glued to his chair. He could not, moreover, restrain a faint smile, seeing how his favourite maxims as to aristocratic prestige and middle-class cowardice were confirmed by the so easily won submission of Mme Verdurin. The Mistress appeared not at all surprised by the Baron's posture, and if she left him it was only because she had been perturbed by seeing me taken up by M. de Cambremer. But first of all, she wished to clear up the mystery of M. de Charlus's relations with Comtesse Molé. 'You told me that you knew Mme de Molé. Does that mean, you go there?' she asked, giving to the words 'go there' the sense of being received there, of having received authority from the lady to go and call upon her. M. de Charlus replied with an inflection of disdain, an affectation of precision and in a singsong tone: 'Yes, sometimes.' This 'sometimes' inspired doubts in Mme Verdurin, who asked: 'Have you ever

met the Duc de Guermantes there?' 'Ah! That I don't remember.' 'Oh!' said
Mme Verdurin, 'you don't know the Duc de Guermantes?' 'And how
should I not know him?' replied M. de Charlus, his lips curving in a smile.
This smile was ironical; but as the Baron was afraid of letting a gold tooth be
seen, he stopped it with a reverse movement of his lips, so that the resulting
sinuosity was that of a good-natured smile. 'Why do you say: "How should
I not know him?"' 'Because he is my brother,' said M. de Charlus carelessly,
leaving Mme Verdurin plunged in stupefaction and in the uncertainty
whether her guest was making fun of her, was a natural son, or a son by
another marriage. The idea that the brother of the Duc de Guermantes
might be called Baron de Charlus never entered her head. She bore down
upon me. 'I heard M. de Cambremer invite you to dinner just now. It has
nothing to do with me, you understand. But for your own sake, I do hope
you won't go. For one thing, the place is infested with bores. Oh! If you like
dining with provincial Counts and Marquises whom nobody knows, you
will be supplied to your heart's content.' 'I think I shall be obliged to go
there once or twice. I am not altogether free, however, for I have a young
cousin whom I cannot leave by herself.' (I felt that this fictitious kinship
made it easier for me to take Albertine about) 'But as for the Cambremers,
as I have been introduced to them . . .' 'You shall do just as you please. One
thing I can tell you: it's extremely unhealthy; when you have caught
pneumonia, or a nice little chronic rheumatism, you'll be a lot better off!'
'But isn't the place itself very pretty?' 'Mmmmyess . . . If you like. For my
part, I confess frankly that I would a hundred times rather have the view
from here over this valley. To begin with, if they'd paid us I wouldn't have
taken the other house because the sea air is fatal to M. Verdurin. If your
cousin suffers at all from nerves . . . But you yourself have bad nerves, I think
you have choking fits. Very well! You shall see. Go there once, you won't
sleep for a week after it; but it's not my business.' And without thinking of
the inconsistency with what she had just been saying: 'If it would amuse you
to see the house, which is not bad, pretty is too strong a word, still it is
amusing with its old moat, and the old drawbridge, as I shall have to sacrifice
myself and dine there once, very well, come that day, I shall try to bring all
my little circle, then it will be quite nice. The day after tomorrow we are
going to Harambouville in the carriage. It's a magnificent drive, the cider is
delicious. Come with us. You, Brichot, you shall come too. And you too,
Ski. That will make a party which, as a matter of fact, my husband must have
arranged already. I don't know whom he has invited, Monsieur de Charlus,
are you one of them?' The Baron, who had not heard the whole speech, and
did not know that she was talking of an excursion to Harambouville, gave a

start. 'A strange question,' he murmured in a mocking tone by which Mme
Verdurin felt hurt. 'Anyhow,' she said to me, 'before you dine with the
Cambremers, why not bring her here, your cousin? Does she like conversation, and clever people? Is she pleasant? Yes, very well then. Bring her
with you. The Cambremers aren't the only people in the world. I can
understand their being glad to invite her, they must find it difficult to get
anyone. Here she will have plenty of fresh air, and lots of clever men. In any
case, I am counting on you not to fail me next Wednesday. I heard you were
having a tea-party at Rivebelle with your cousin, and M. de Charlus, and I
forget who else. You must arrange to bring the whole lot on here, it would
be nice if you all came in a body. It's the easiest thing in the world to get
here, the roads are charming; if you like I can send down for you. I can't
imagine what you find attractive in Rivebelle, it's infested with mosquitoes.
You are thinking perhaps of the reputation of the rock-cakes. My cook
makes them far better. I can let you have them, here, Norman rock-cakes,
the real article, and shortbread; I need say no more. Ah! If you like the filth
they give you at Rivebelle, that I won't give you, I don't poison my guests,
Sir, and even if I wished to, my cook would refuse to make such abominations
and would leave my service. Those rock-cakes you get down there, you can't
tell what they are made of. I knew a poor girl who got peritonitis from them,
which carried her off in three days. She was only seventeen. It was sad for
her poor mother,' added Mme Verdurin with a melancholy air beneath the
spheres of her temples charged with experience and suffering. 'However, go
and have tea at Rivebelle, if you enjoy being fleeced and flinging money out
of the window. But one thing I beg of you, it is a confidential mission I am
charging you with, on the stroke of six, bring all your party here, don't allow
them to go straggling away by themselves. You can bring whom you please.
I wouldn't say that to everybody. But I am sure that your friends are nice, I
can see at once that we understand one another. Apart from the little
nucleus, there are some very pleasant people coming on Wednesday. You
don't know little Madame de Longpont. She is charming, and so witty, not
in the least a snob, you will find, you'll like her immensely. And she's going
to bring a whole troop of friends too,' Mme Verdurin added to show me
that this was the right thing to do and encourage me by the other's example.
'We shall see which has most influence and brings most people, Barbe de
Longpont or you. And then I believe somebody's going to bring Bergotte,'
she added with a vague air, this meeting with a celebrity being rendered far
from likely by a paragraph which had appeared in the papers that morning,
to the effect that the great writer's health was causing grave anxiety.
'Anyhow, you will see that it will be one of my most successful Wednesdays,

I don't want to have any boring women. You mustn't judge by this evening, it has been a complete failure. Don't try to be polite, you can't have been more bored than I was, I thought myself it was deadly. It won't always be like tonight, you know! I'm not thinking of the Cambremers, who are impossible, but I have known society people who were supposed to be pleasant, well, compared with my little nucleus, they didn't exist. I heard you say that you thought Swann clever. I must say, to my mind, his cleverness was greatly exaggerated, but without speaking of the character of the man, which I have always found fundamentally antipathetic, sly, underhand, I have often had him to dinner on Wednesdays. Well, you can ask the others, even compared with Brichot, who is far from being anything wonderful, a good assistant master, whom I got into the Institute, Swann was simply nowhere. He was so dull!' And, as I expressed a contrary opinion: 'It's the truth. I don't want to say a word against him to you, since he was your friend, indeed he was very fond of you, he has spoken to me about you in the most charming way, but ask the others here if he ever said anything interesting, at our dinners. That, after all, is the supreme test. Well, I don't know why it was, but Swann, in my house, never seemed to come off, one got nothing out of him. And yet anything there ever was in him he picked up here.' I assured her that he was highly intelligent. 'No, you only think that, because you haven't known him as long as I have. One got to the end of him very soon. I was always bored to death by him.' (Which may be interpreted: 'He went to the La Trémoïlles and the Guermantes and knew that I didn't.') 'And I can put up with anything, except being bored. That, I cannot and will not stand!' Her horror of boredom was now the reason upon which Mme Verdurin relied to explain the composition of the little group. She did not yet entertain duchesses because she was incapable of enduring boredom, just as she was unable to go for a cruise, because of seasickness. I thought to myself that what Mme Verdurin said was not entirely false, and, whereas the Guermantes would have declared Brichot to be the stupidest man they had ever met, I remained uncertain whether he were not in reality superior, if not to Swann himself, at least to the other people endowed with the wit of the Guermantes who would have had the good taste to avoid and the modesty to blush at his pedantic pleasantries; I asked myself the question as though a fresh light might be thrown on the nature of the intellect by the answer that I should make, and with the earnestness of a Christian influenced by Port-Royal when he considers the problem of Grace. 'You will see,' Mme Verdurin continued, 'when one has society people together with people of real intelligence, people of our set, that's where one has to see them, the society man who is brilliant in the kingdom of the blind, is only

one-eyed here. Besides, the others don't feel at home any longer. So much
so that I'm inclined to ask myself whether, instead of attempting mixtures
that spoil everything, I shan't start special evenings confined to the bores so
as to have the full benefit of my little nucleus. However: you are coming
again with your cousin. That's settled. Good. At any rate you will both find
something to eat here. Féterne is starvation corner. Oh, by the way, if you
like rats, go there at once, you will get as many as you want. And they will
keep you there as long as you are prepared to stay. Why, you'll die of
hunger. I'm sure, when I go there, I shall have my dinner before I start. The
more the merrier, you must come here first and escort me. We shall have
high tea, and supper when we get back. Do you like apple-tarts? Yes, very
well then, our chef makes the best in the world. You see, I was quite right
when I told you that you were meant to live here. So come and stay. You
know, there is far more room in the house than people think. I don't speak
of it, so as not to let myself in for bores. You might bring your cousin to stay.
She would get a change of air from Balbec. With this air here, I maintain I
can cure incurables. I have cured them, I may tell you, and not only this
time. For I have stayed quite close to here before, a place I discovered and
got for a mere song, a very different style of house from their Raspelière. I
can show you it if we go for a drive together. But I admit that even here the
air is invigorating. Still, I don't want to say too much about it, the whole of
Paris would begin to take a fancy to my little corner. That has always been
my luck. Anyhow, give your cousin my message. We shall put you in two
nice rooms looking over the valley, you ought to see it in the morning, with
the sun shining on the mist! By the way, who is this Robert de Saint-Loup of
whom you were speaking?' she said with a troubled air, for she had heard
that I was to pay him a visit at Doncières, and was afraid that he might make
me fail her. 'Why not bring him here instead, if he's not a bore. I have heard
of him from Morel; I fancy he's one of his greatest friends,' said Mme
Verdurin with entire want of truth, for Saint-Loup and Morel were not
even aware of one another's existence. But having heard that Saint-Loup
knew M. de Charlus, she supposed that it was through the violinist, and
wished to appear to know all about them. 'He's not taking up medicine,
by any chance, or literature? You know, if you want any help about
examinations, Cottard can do anything, and I make what use of him I please.
As for the Academy later on, for I suppose he's not old enough yet, I have
several notes in my pocket. Your friend would find himself on friendly soil
here, and it might amuse him perhaps to see over the house. Life's not very
exciting at Doncières. But you shall do just what you please, then you can
arrange what you think best,' she concluded, without insisting, so as not to

appear to be trying to know people of noble birth, and because she always maintained that the system by which she governed the faithful, to wit despotism, was named liberty. 'Why, what's the matter with you,' she said, at the sight of M. Verdurin who, with gestures of impatience, was making for the wooden terrace that ran along the side of the drawing-room above the valley, like a man who is bursting with rage and must have fresh air. 'Has Saniette been annoying you again? But you know what an idiot he is, you have to resign yourself to him, don't work yourself up into such a state. I dislike this sort of thing,' she said to me, 'because it is bad for him, it sends the blood to his head. But I must say that one would need the patience of an angel at times to put up with Saniette, and one must always remember that it is a charity to have him in the house. For my part I must admit that he's so gloriously silly, I can't help enjoying him. I dare say you heard what he said after dinner: "I can't play whist, but I can the piano." Isn't it superb? It is positively colossal, and incidentally quite untrue, for he knows nothing at all about either. But my husband, beneath his rough exterior, is very sensitive, very kind-hearted, and Saniette's self-centred way of always thinking about the effect he is going to make drives him *crazy*. Come, dear, calm yourself, you know Cottard told you that it was bad for your liver. And it is I that will have to bear the brunt of it all,' said Mme Verdurin. 'Tomorrow Saniette will come back all nerves and tears. Poor man, he is very ill indeed. Still, that is no reason why he should kill other people. Besides, even at times when he is in pain, when one would like to be sorry for him, his silliness hardens one's heart. He is really too stupid. You have only to tell him quite politely that these scenes make you both ill, and he is not to come again, since that's what he's most afraid of, it will have a soothing effect on his nerves,' Mme Verdurin whispered to her husband.

One could barely make out the sea from the windows on the right. But those on the other side showed the valley, now shrouded in a snowy cloak of moonlight. Now and again one heard the voices of Morel and Cottard. 'You have a trump?' 'Yes.' 'Ah! You're in luck, you are,' said M. de Cambremer to Morel, in answer to his question, for he had seen that the doctor's hand was full of trumps. 'Here comes the lady of diamonds,' said the doctor. 'That's a trump, you know? My trick. But there isn't a Sorbonne any longer,' said the doctor to M. de Cambremer; 'there's only the University of Paris.' M. de Cambremer confessed his inability to understand why the doctor made this remark to him. 'I thought you were talking about the Sorbonne,' replied the doctor. 'I heard you say: *tu nous la sors bonne*,' he added, with a wink, to show that this was meant for a pun. 'Just wait a moment,' he said, pointing to his adversary, 'I have a Trafalgar in store for him.' And the prospect must have been excellent for the doctor, for in his joy his shoulders began to shake rapturously with laughter, which in his family, in the 'breed' of the Cottards, was an almost zoological sign of satisfaction. In the previous generation the gesture of rubbing the hands together as though one were soaping them used to accompany this movement. Cottard himself had originally employed both forms simultaneously, but one fine day, nobody ever knew by whose intervention, wifely, professorial perhaps, the rubbing of the hands had disappeared. The doctor even at dominoes, when he got his adversary on the run, and made him take the double six, which was to him the keenest of pleasures, contented himself with shaking his shoulders. And when – which was as seldom as possible – he went down to his native village for a few days, and met his first cousin, who was still at the hand-rubbing stage, he would say to Mme Cottard on his return: 'I thought poor René very common.' 'Have you the little dee–ar?' he said, turning to Morel. 'No? Then I play this old David.' 'Then you have five, you have won!' 'That's a great victory, Doctor,' said the Marquis. 'A Pyrrhic victory,' said Cottard, turning to face the Marquis and looking at him over his glasses to judge the effect of his remark. 'If there is still time,' he said to Morel, 'I give you your revenge. It is my deal. Ah! no, here come the carriages, it will have to be Friday, and I shall show you a trick you don't see every day.' M. and Mme Verdurin accompanied us to the door. The Mistress was especially coaxing with Saniette so as to make certain of his returning next time. 'But you don't look to me as if you were properly wrapped up, my boy,' said M. Verdurin, whose age allowed him to address me in this paternal tone. 'One would say the weather had changed.' These words filled me with joy, as though the profoundly hidden life, the uprising of different combinations which they implied in nature, hinted at other changes, these occurring in my own life, and created fresh possibilities in it. Merely by opening the door upon the park, before leaving, one felt that a different 'weather' had, at that moment, taken possession of the scene; cooling breezes, one of the joys of summer, were rising in the fir plantation (where long ago Mme de Cambremer had dreamed of Chopin) and almost imperceptibly, in caressing coils, capricious eddies, were beginning their gentle nocturnes. I declined the rug which, on subsequent evenings, I was to accept when Albertine was with me, more to preserve the secrecy of my pleasure than to avoid the risk of cold. A vain search was made for the Norwegian philosopher. Had he been seized by a colic? Had he been afraid of missing the train? Had an aeroplane come to fetch him? Had he been carried aloft in an Assumption? In any case he had vanished without anyone's noticing his departure, like a god. 'You are unwise,' M. de Cambremer said to me, 'it's as cold as charity.' 'Why charity?' the doctor enquired. 'Beware of choking,' the Marquis went on. 'My sister never goes out at night. However, she is in a pretty bad state at present. In any case you oughtn't to stand about bareheaded, put your tile on at once.' 'They are not frigorifie chokings,' said Cottard sententiously. 'Oh, indeed!' M. de Cambremer bowed. 'Of course, if that's your opinion . . .' 'Opinions of the press!' said the doctor, smiling round his glasses. M. de Cambremer laughed, but, feeling certain that he was in the right, insisted: 'All the same,' he said, 'whenever my sister goes out after dark, she has an attack.' 'It's no use quibbling,' replied the doctor, regardless of his want of manners. 'However, I don't practise medicine by the seaside, unless I am called in for a consultation. I am here on holiday.' He was perhaps even more on holiday than he would have liked. M. de Cambremer having said to him as they got into the carriage together: 'We are fortunate in having quite close to us (not on your side of the bay, on the opposite side, but it is quite narrow at that point) another medical celebrity, Doctor du Boulbon', Cottard, who, as a rule, from 'deontology', abstained from criticising his colleagues, could not help exclaiming, as he had exclaimed to me on the fatal day when we had visited the little casino: 'But he is not a doctor. He practises a literary medicine, it is all fantastic therapeutics, charlatanism. All the same, we are on quite good terms. I should take the boat and go over and pay him a visit, if I weren't leaving.' But, from the air which Cottard assumed in speaking of du Boulbon to M. de Cambremer, I felt that the boat which he would gladly have taken to call upon him would have greatly resembled that vessel which, in order to go and ruin the waters discovered by another literary doctor, Virgil (who took all their patients from them as well), the doctors of Salerno had chartered, but which sank with them on the voyage. 'Goodbye, my dear Saniette, don't forget to come tomorrow, you know how my husband enjoys seeing you. He enjoys your wit, your intellect; yes indeed, you know quite well, he takes sudden moods, but he can't live without seeing you. It's always the first thing he asks me: "Is Saniette coming? I do so enjoy seeing him." ' 'I never said anything of the sort,' said M. Verdurin to Saniette with a feigned frankness which seemed perfectly to reconcile what the Mistress had just said with the manner in which he treated Saniette. Then looking at his watch, doubtless so as not to prolong the leave-taking in the damp night air, he warned the coachmen not to lose any time, but to be careful when going down the hill, and assured us that we should be in plenty of time for our train. This was to set down the faithful, one at one station, another at another, ending with myself, for no one else was going as far as Balbec, and beginning with the Cambremers. They, so as not to bring their horses all the way up to la Raspelière at night, took the train with us at Douville-Féterne. The station nearest to them was indeed not this, which, being already at some distance from the village, was farther still from the mansion, but la Sogne. On arriving at the station of Douville-Féterne, M. de Cambremer made a point of giving a 'piece', as Françoise used to say, to the Verdurins' coachman (the nice, sensitive coachman, with melancholy thoughts), for M. de Cambremer was generous, and in that respect took, rather, 'after his mamma'. But, possibly because his 'papa's' strain intervened at this point, he felt a scruple, or else that there might be a mistake – either on his part, if, for instance, in the dark, he were to give a sou instead of a franc, or on the recipient's who might not perceive the importance of the present that was being given him. And so he drew attention to it: 'It is a franc I'm giving you, isn't it?' he said to the coachman, turning the coin until it gleamed in the lamplight, and so that the faithful might report his action to Mme Verdurin. 'Isn't it? Twenty sous is right, as it's only a short drive.' He and Mme de Cambremer left us at la Sogne. 'I shall tell my sister,' he repeated to me, 'that you have choking fits, I am sure she will be interested.' I understood that he meant: 'will be pleased'. As for his wife, she employed, in saying goodbye to me, two abbreviations which, even in writing, used to shock me at that time in a letter, although one has grown accustomed to them since, but which, when spoken, seem to me today even to contain in their deliberate carelessness, in their acquired familiarity, something insufferably pedantic: 'Pleased to have met you,' she said to me; 'greetings to Saint-Loup, if you see him.' In making this speech, Mme de Cambremer pronounced the name 'Saint-Loupe'. I have never discovered who had pronounced it thus in her hearing, or what had led her to suppose that it ought to be so pronounced. However it may be, for some weeks afterwards, she continued to say 'Saint-Loupe' and a man who had a great admiration for her and echoed her in every way did the same. If other people said 'Saint-Lou', they would insist, would say emphatically 'Saint-Loupe', whether to teach the others an indirect lesson or to be different from them. But, no doubt, women of greater brilliance than Mme de Cambremer told her, or gave her indirectly to understand that this was not the correct pronunciation, and that what she regarded as a sign of originality was a mistake which would make people think her little conversant with the usages of society, for shortly afterwards Mme de Cambremer was again saying 'Saint-Lou', and her admirer similarly ceased to hold out, whether because she had lectured him, or because he had noticed that she no longer sounded the final consonant, and had said to himself that if a woman of such distinction, energy and ambition had yielded, it must have been on good grounds. The worst of her admirers was her husband. Mme de Cambremer loved to tease other people in a way that was often highly impertinent. As soon as she began to attack me, or anyone else, in this fashion, M. de Cambremer would start watching her victim, laughing the while. As the Marquis had a squint – a blemish which gives an effect of wit to the mirth even of imbeciles – the effect of this laughter was to bring a segment of pupil into the otherwise complete whiteness of his eye. So a sudden rift brings a patch of blue into an otherwise clouded sky. His monocle moreover protected, like the glass over a valuable picture, this delicate operation. As for the actual intention of his laughter, it was hard to say whether it was friendly: 'Ah! You rascal! You're in an enviable position, aren't you. You have won the favour of a lady who has a pretty wit!' Or coarse: 'Well, Sir, I hope you'll learn your lesson, you've got to eat a slice of humble pie.' Or obliging: 'I'm here, you know, I take it with a laugh because it's all pure fun, but I shan't let you be ill-treated.' Or cruelly accessory: 'I don't need to add my little pinch of salt, but you can see, I'm revelling in all the insults she is showering on you. I'm wriggling like a hunchback, therefore I approve, I, the husband. And so, if you should take it into your head to answer back, you would have me to deal with, my young Sir. I should first of all give you a pair of resounding smacks, well aimed, then we should go and cross swords in the forest of Chantepie.'

Whatever the correct interpretation of the husband's merriment, the wife's whimsies soon came to an end. Whereupon M. de Cambremer ceased to laugh, the temporary pupil vanished and as one had forgotten for a minute or two to expect an entirely white eyeball, it gave this ruddy Norman an air at once anaemic and ecstatic, as though the Marquis had just undergone an operation, or were imploring heaven, through his monocle, for the palms of martyrdom.

Chapter Three

The sorrows of M. de Charlus – His sham duel – The stations on the
'Transatlantic' – Weary of Albertine I decide to break with her

I was dropping with sleep. I was taken up to my floor not by the lift-boy, but by the squinting page, who to make conversation informed me that his sister was still with the gentleman who was so rich, and that, on one occasion, when she had made up her mind to return home instead of sticking to her business, her gentleman friend had paid a visit to the mother of the squinting page and of the other more fortunate children, who had very soon made the silly creature return to her protector. 'You know, Sir, she's a fine lady, my sister is. She plays the piano, she talks Spanish. And you would never take her for the sister of the humble employee who brings you up in the lift, she denies herself nothing; Madame has a maid to herself, I shouldn't be surprised if one day she keeps her carriage. She is very pretty, if you could see her, a little too high and mighty, but, good lord, you can understand that. She's full of fun. She never leaves a hotel without doing something first in a wardrobe or a drawer, just to leave a little keepsake with the chambermaid who will have to wipe it up. Sometimes she does it in a cab, and after she's paid her fare, she'll hide behind a tree, and she doesn't half laugh when the cabby finds he's got to clean his cab after her. My father had another stroke of luck when he found my young brother that Indian Prince he used to know long ago. It's not the same style of thing, of course. But it's a superb position. The travelling by itself would be a dream. I'm the only one still on the shelf. But you never know. We're a lucky family; perhaps one day I shall be President of the Republic. But I'm keeping you talking.' (I had not uttered a single word and was beginning to fall asleep as I listened to the flow of his) 'Good-night, Sir. Oh! Thank you, Sir. If everybody had as kind a heart as you, there wouldn't be any poor people left. But, as my sister says, "there will always have to be the poor so that now I'm rich I can s—t on them". You'll pardon the expression. Good-night, Sir.'

Perhaps every night we accept the risk of facing, while we are asleep, sufferings which we regard as unreal and unimportant because they will be felt in the course of a sleep which we suppose to be unconscious. And indeed on these evenings when I came back late from la Raspelière I was very sleepy. But after the weather turned cold I could not get to sleep at once, for the fire lighted up the room as though there were a lamp burning in it. Only it was nothing more than a blazing log, and – like a lamp too, for that matter, like the day when night gathers – its too bright light was not long in fading; and I entered a state of slumber which is like a second room that we take, into which, leaving our own room, we go when we want to sleep. It has noises of its own and we are sometimes violently awakened by the sound of a bell, perfectly heard by our ears, although nobody has rung. It has its servants, its special visitors who call to take us out so that we are ready to get up when we are compelled to realise, by our almost immediate transmigration into the other room, the room of overnight, that it is empty, that nobody has called.

The race that inhabits it is, like that of our first human ancestors, androgynous. A man in it appears a moment later in the form of a woman. Things in it show a tendency to turn into men, men into friends and enemies. The time that elapses for the sleeper, during these spells of slumber, is absolutely different from the time in which the life of the waking man is passed. Sometimes its course is far more rapid, a quarter of an hour seems a day, at other times far longer, we think we have taken only a short nap, when we have slept through the day. Then, in the chariot of sleep, we descend into depths in which memory can no longer overtake it, and on the brink of which the mind has been obliged to retrace its steps. The horses of sleep, like those of the sun, move at so steady a pace, in an atmosphere in which there is no longer any resistance, that it requires some little aerolith extraneous to ourselves (hurled from the azure by some Unknown) to strike our regular sleep (which otherwise would have no reason to stop, and would continue with a similar motion world without end) and to make it swing sharply round, return towards reality, travel without pause, traverse the regions bordering on life in which presently the sleeper will hear the sounds that come from life, quite vague still, but already perceptible, albeit corrupted – and come to earth suddenly and awake. Then from those profound slumbers we awake in a dawn, not knowing who we are, being nobody, newly born, ready for anything, our brain being emptied of that past which was previously our life. And perhaps it is more pleasant still when our landing at the waking-point is abrupt and the thoughts of our sleep, hidden by a cloak of oblivion, have not time to return to us in order, before sleep ceases. Then, from the black tempest through which we seem to have passed (but we do not even say *we*), we emerge prostrate, without a thought, a we that is void of content. What hammer-blow has the person or thing that is lying there received to make it unconscious of anything, stupefied until the moment when memory, flooding back, restores to it consciousness or personality? Moreover, for both these kinds of awakening, we must avoid falling asleep, even into deep slumber, under the law of habit. For everything that habit ensnares in her nets, she watches closely, we must escape her, take our sleep at a moment when we thought we were doing anything else than sleeping, take, in a word, a sleep that does not dwell under the tutelage of foresight, in the company, albeit latent, of reflection. At least, in these awakenings which I have just described, and which I experienced as a rule when I had been dining overnight at la Raspelière, everything occurred as though by this process, and I can testify to it, I the strange human being who, while he waits for death to release him, lives behind closed shutters, knows nothing of the world, sits motionless as an owl, and like that bird begins to see things a little plainly only when darkness falls. Everything occurs as though by this process, but perhaps only a layer of wadding has prevented the sleeper from taking in the internal dialogue of memories and the incessant verbiage of sleep. For (and this may be equally manifest in the other system, vaster, more mysterious, more astral) at the moment of his entering the waking state, the sleeper hears a voice inside him saying: 'Will you come to this dinner tonight, my dear friend, it would be such fun?' and thinks: 'Yes, what fun it will be, I shall go'; then, growing wider awake, he suddenly remembers: 'My grandmother has only a few weeks to live, the Doctor assures us.' He rings, he weeps at the thought that it will not be, as in the past, his grandmother, his dying grandmother, but an indifferent waiter that will come in answer to his summons. Moreover, when sleep bore him so far away from the world inhabited by memory and thought, through an ether in which he was alone, more than alone; not having that companion in whom we perceive things, ourself, he was outside the range of time and its measures. But now the footman is in the room, and he dares not ask him the time, for he does not know whether he has slept, for how many hours he has slept (he asks himself whether it should not be how many days, returning thus with weary body and mind refreshed, his heart sick for home, as from a journey too distant not to have taken a long time). We may of course insist that there is but one time, for the futile reason that it is by looking at the clock that we have discovered to have been merely a quarter of an hour what we had supposed a day. But at the moment when we make this discovery we are a man awake, plunged in the time of waking men, we have deserted the other time. Perhaps indeed more than another time: another life. The pleasures that we enjoy in sleep, we do not include them in the list of the pleasures that we have felt in the course of our existence. To allude only to the most grossly sensual of them all, which of us, on waking, has not felt a certain irritation at having experienced in his sleep a pleasure which, if he is anxious not to tire himself, he is not, once he is awake, at liberty to repeat indefinitely during the day. It seems a positive waste. We have had pleasure, in another life, which is not ours. Sufferings and pleasures of the dream-world (which generally vanish soon enough after our waking), if we make them figure in a budget, it is not in the current account of our life.

Two times, I have said; perhaps there is only one after all, not that the time of the waking man has any validity for the sleeper, but perhaps because the other life, the life in which he sleeps, is not – in its profounder part – included in the category of time. I came to this conclusion when on the mornings after dinners at la Raspelière I used to lie so completely asleep. For this reason. I was beginning to despair, on waking, when I found that, after I had rung the bell ten times, the waiter did not appear. At the eleventh ring he came. It was only the first after all. The other ten had been mere suggestions in my sleep which still hung about me, of the peal that I had been meaning to sound. My numbed hands had never even moved. Well, on those mornings (and this is what makes me say that sleep is perhaps unconscious of the law of time) my effort to awaken consisted chiefly in an effort to make the obscure, undefined mass of the sleep in which I had just been living enter into the scale of time. It is no easy task; sleep, which does not know whether we have slept for two hours or two days, cannot provide any indication. And if we do not find one outside, not being able to re-enter time, we fall asleep again, for five minutes which seem to us three hours.

I have always said – and have proved by experiment – that the most powerful soporific is sleep itself. After having slept profoundly for two hours, having fought against so many giants, and formed so many lifelong friendships, it is far more difficult to awake than after taking several grammes of veronal. And so, reasoning from one thing to the other, I was surprised to hear from the Norwegian philosopher, who had it from M. Boutroux, 'my eminent colleague – pardon me, my brother', what M. Bergson thought of the peculiar effects upon the memory of soporific drugs. 'Naturally,' M. Bergson had said to M. Boutroux, if one was to believe the Norwegian philosopher, 'soporifics, taken from time to time in moderate doses, have no effect upon that solid memory of our everyday life which is so firmly established within us. But there are other forms of memory, loftier, but also more unstable. One of my colleagues lectures upon ancient history. He tells me that if, overnight, he has taken a tablet to make him sleep, he has great difficulty, during his lecture, in recalling the Greek quotations that he requires. The doctor who recommended these tablets assured him that they had no effect upon the memory. "That is perhaps because you do not have to quote Greek", the historian answered, not without a note of derisive pride.'

I cannot say whether this conversation between M. Bergson and M. Boutroux is accurately reported. The Norwegian philosopher, albeit so profound and so lucid, so passionately attentive, may have misunderstood. Personally, in my own experience I have found the opposite result. The moments of oblivion that come to us in the morning after we have taken certain narcotics have a resemblance that is only partial, though disturbing, to the oblivion that reigns during a night of natural and profound sleep. Now what I find myself forgetting in either case is not some line of Baudelaire, which on the other hand keeps sounding in my ear, it is not some concept of one of the philosophers above-named, it is the actual reality of the ordinary things that surround me – if I am asleep – my non-perception of which makes me an idiot; it is, if I am awakened and proceed to emerge from an artificial slumber, not the system of Porphyry or Plotinus, which I can discuss as fluently as at any other time, but the answer that I have promised to give to an invitation, the memory of which is replaced by a universal blank. The lofty thought remains in its place; what the soporific has put out of action is the power to act in little things, in everything that demands activity in order to seize – at the right moment, to grasp some memory of everyday life. In spite of all that may be said about survival after the destruction of the brain, I observe that each alteration of the brain is a partial death. We possess all our memories, but not the faculty of recalling them, said, echoing M. Bergson, the eminent Norwegian philosopher whose language I have made no attempt to imitate in order not to prolong my story unduly. But not the faculty of recalling them. But what, then, is a memory which we do not recall? Or, indeed, let us go farther. We do not recall our memories of the last thirty years; but we are wholly steeped in them; why then stop short at thirty years, why not prolong back to before our birth this anterior life? The moment that I do not know a whole section of the memories that are behind me, the moment that they are invisible to me, that I have not the faculty of calling them to me, who can assure me that in that *mass* unknown to me there are not some that extend back much farther than my human life. If I can have in me and round me so many memories which I do not remember, this oblivion (a *de facto* oblivion, at least, since I have not the faculty of seeing anything) may extend over a life which I have lived in the body of another man, even upon another planet. A common oblivion effaces all. But what, in that case, signifies that immortality of the soul the reality of which the Norwegian philosopher affirmed? The person that I shall be after death has no more reason to remember the man whom I have been since my birth than the latter to remember what I was before it.

The waiter came in. I did not mention to him that I had rung several times, for I was beginning to realise that hitherto I had only dreamed that I was ringing. I was alarmed nevertheless by the thought that this dream had had the clear precision of experience. Experience would, reciprocally, have the irreality of a dream.

Instead I asked him who it was that had been ringing so often during the night. He told me: 'Nobody,' and could prove his statement, for the bell-board would have registered any ring. And yet I could hear the repeated, almost furious peals which were still echoing in my ears and were to remain perceptible for several days. It is however seldom that sleep thus projects into our waking life memories that do not perish with it. We can count these aeroliths. If it is an idea that sleep has forged, it soon breaks up into slender, irrecoverable fragments. But, in this instance, sleep had fashioned sounds. More material and simpler, they lasted longer. I was astonished by the relative earliness of the hour, as told me by the waiter. I was none the less refreshed. It is the light sleeps that have a long duration, because, being an intermediate state between waking and sleeping, preserving a somewhat faded but permanent impression of the former, they require infinitely more time to refresh us than a profound sleep, which may be short. I felt quite comfortable for another reason. If remembering that we are tired is enough to make us feel our tiredness, saying to oneself: 'I am refreshed' is enough to create refreshment. Now I had been dreaming that M. de Charlus was a hundred and ten years old, and had just boxed the ears of his own mother, Madame Verdurin, because she had paid five thousand millions for a bunch of violets; I was therefore assured that I had slept profoundly, had dreamed the reverse of what had been in my thoughts overnight and of all the possibilities of life at the moment; this was enough to make me feel entirely refreshed.

I should greatly have astonished my mother, who could not understand M. de Charlus's assiduity in visiting the Verdurins, had I told her whom (on the very day on which Albertine's toque had been ordered, without a word about it to her, in order that it might come as a surprise) M. de Charlus had brought to dine in a private room at the Grand Hotel, Balbec. His guest was none other than the footman of a lady who was a cousin of the Cambremers. This footman was very smartly dressed, and, as he crossed the hall, with the Baron, 'did the man of fashion' as Saint-Loup would have said, in the eyes of the visitors. Indeed, the young page boys, the Levites who were swarming down the temple steps at that moment because it was the time when they came on duty, paid no attention to the two strangers, one of whom, M. de Charlus, kept his eyes lowered to show that he was paying little if any to them. He appeared to be trying to carve his way through their midst. 'Prosper, dear hope of a sacred nation,' he said, recalling a passage from Racine, and applying to it a wholly different meaning. 'Pardon?' asked the footman, who was not well up in the classics. M. de Charlus made no reply, for he took a certain pride in never answering questions and in marching straight ahead as though there were no other visitors in the hotel, or no one existed in the world except himself, Baron de Charlus. But, having continued to quote the speech of Josabeth: 'Come, come, my children', he felt a revulsion and did not, like her, add: 'Bid them approach', for these young people had not yet reached the age at which sex is completely developed, and which appealed to M. de Charlus. Moreover, if he had written to Madame de Chevregny's footman, because he had had no doubt of his docility, he had hoped to meet someone more virile. On seeing him, he found him more effeminate than he would have liked. He told him that he had been expecting someone else, for he knew by sight another of Madame de Chevregny's footmen, whom he had noticed upon the box of her carriage. This was an extremely rustic type of peasant, the very opposite of him who had come, who, on the other hand, regarding his own effeminate ways as adding to his attractiveness, and never doubting that it was this man-of-the-world air that had captivated M. de Charlus, could not even guess whom the Baron meant. 'But there is no one else in the house, except one that you can't have given the eye to, he is hideous, just like a great peasant.' And at the thought that it was perhaps this rustic whom the Baron had seen, he felt his self-esteem wounded. The Baron guessed this, and, widening his quest: 'But I have not taken a vow that I will know only Mme de Chevregny's men,' he said. 'Surely there are plenty of fellows in one house or another here or in Paris, since you are leaving soon, that you could introduce to me?' 'Oh, no!' replied the footman, 'I never go with anyone of my own class. I only speak to them on duty. But there is one very nice person I can make you know.' 'Who?' asked the Baron. 'The Prince de Guermantes.' M. de Guermantes was vexed at being offered only a man so advanced in years, one, moreover, to whom he had no need to apply to a footman for an introduction. And so he declined the offer in a dry tone and, not letting himself be discouraged by the menial's social pretensions, began to explain to him again what he wanted, the style, the type, a jockey, for instance, and so on . . . Fearing lest the solicitor, who went past at that moment, might have heard them, he thought it cunning to show that he was speaking of anything in the world rather than what his hearer might suspect, and said with emphasis and in ringing tones, but as though he were simply continuing his conversation: 'Yes, in spite of my age, I still keep up a passion for collecting, a passion for pretty things, I will do anything to secure an old bronze, an early lustre. I adore the Beautiful.' But to make the footman understand the change of subject he had so rapidly executed, M. de Charlus laid such stress upon each word, and what was more, to be heard by the solicitor, he shouted his words so loud that this charade should in itself have been enough to reveal what it concealed from ears more alert than those of the officer of the court. He suspected nothing, any more than any of the other residents in the hotel, all of whom saw a fashionable foreigner in the footman so smartly attired. On the other hand, if the gentlemen were deceived and took him for a distinguished American, no sooner did he appear before the servants than he was spotted by them, as one convict recognises another, indeed scented afar off, as certain animals scent one another. The head waiters raised their eyebrows. Aimé cast a suspicious glance. The wine waiter, shrugging his shoulders, uttered behind his hand (because he thought it polite) an offensive expression which everybody heard. And even our old Françoise, whose sight was failing and who went past at that moment at the foot of the staircase to dine with the *courriers*, raised her head, recognised a servant where the hotel guests never suspected one – as the old nurse Euryclea recognises Ulysses long before the suitors seated at the banquet – and seeing, arm in arm with him, M. de Charlus, assumed an appalled expression, as though all of a sudden slanders which she had heard repeated and had not believed had acquired a heart-rending probability in her eyes. She never spoke to me, nor to anyone else, of this incident, but it must have caused a considerable commotion in her brain, for afterwards, whenever in Paris she happened to see 'Julien', to whom until then she had been so greatly attached, she still treated him with politeness, but with a politeness that had cooled and was always tempered with a strong dose of reserve. This same incident led someone else to confide in me: this was Aimé. When I encountered M. de Charlus, he, not having expected to meet me, raised his hand and called out 'Good-evening' with the indifference – outwardly, at least – of a great nobleman who believes that everything is allowed him and thinks it better not to appear to be hiding anything. Aimé, who at that moment was watching him with a suspicious eye and saw that I greeted the companion of the person in whom he was certain that he detected a servant, asked me that same evening who he was. For, for some time past, Aimé had shown a fondness for talking, or rather, as he himself put it, doubtless in order to emphasise the character – philosophical, according to him – of these talks, 'discussing' with me. And as I often said to him that it distressed me that he should have to stand beside the table while I ate instead of being able to sit down and share my meal, he declared that he had never seen a guest show such 'sound reasoning'. He was talking at that moment to two waiters. They had bowed to me, I did not know why; their faces were unfamiliar, albeit their conversation sounded a note which seemed to me not to be novel. Aimé was scolding them both because of their matrimonial engagements, of which he disapproved. He appealed to me, I said that I could not have any opinion on the matter since I did not know them. They told me their names, reminded me that they had often waited upon me at Rivebelle. But one had let his moustache grow, the other had shaved his off and had had his head cropped; and for this reason, albeit it was the same head as before that rested upon the shoulders of each of them (and not a different head as in the faulty restorations of Notre-Dame), it had remained almost as invisible to me as those objects which escape the most minute search and are actually staring everybody in the face where nobody notices them, on the mantelpiece. As soon as I knew their names, I recognised exactly the uncertain music of their voices because I saw once more the old face which made it clear. 'They want to get married and they haven't even learned English!' Aimé said to me, without reflecting that I was little versed in the ways of hotel service, and could not be aware that a person who does not know foreign languages cannot be certain of getting a situation. I, who supposed that he would have no difficulty in finding out that the newcomer was M. de Charlus, and indeed imagined that he must remember him, having waited upon him in the dining-room when the Baron came, during my former visit to Balbec, to see Mme de Villeparisis, I told him his name. Not only did Aimé not remember the Baron de Charlus, but the name appeared to make a profound impression upon him. He told me that he would look for a letter next day in his room which I might perhaps be able to explain to him. I was all the more astonished in that M. de Charlus, when he had wished to give me one of Bergotte's books, at Balbec, the other year, had specially asked for Aimé, whom he must have recognised later on in that Paris restaurant where I had taken luncheon with Saint-Loup and his mistress and where M. de Charlus had come to spy upon us. It is true that Aimé had not been able to execute these commissions in person, being on the former occasion in bed, and on the latter engaged in waiting. I had nevertheless grave doubts as to his sincerity, when he pretended not to know M. de Charlus. For one thing, he must have appealed to the Baron. Like all the upstairs waiters of the Balbec Hotel, like several of the Prince de Guermantes's footmen, Aimé belonged to a race more ancient than that of the Prince, therefore more noble. When you asked for a sitting-room, you thought at first that you were alone. But presently, in the service-room you caught sight of a sculptural waiter, of that ruddy Etruscan kind of which Aimé was typical, slightly aged by excessive consumption of champagne and seeing the inevitable hour approach for Contrexéville water. Not all the visitors asked them merely to wait upon them. The underlings who were young, conscientious, busy, who had mistresses waiting for them outside, made off. Whereupon Aimé reproached them with not being serious. He had every right to do so. He himself was serious. He had a wife and children, and was ambitious on their behalf. And so the advances made to him by a strange lady or gentleman he never repulsed, though it meant his staying all night. For business must come before everything. He was so much of the type that attracted M. de Charlus that I suspected him of falsehood when he told me that he did not know him. I was wrong. The page had been perfectly truthful when he told the Baron that Aimé (who had given him a dressing-down for it next day) had gone to bed (or gone out), and on the other occasion was busy waiting. But imagination outreaches reality. And the page boy's embarrassment had probably aroused in M. de Charlus doubts as to the sincerity of his excuses that had wounded sentiments of which Aimé had no suspicion. We have seen moreover that Saint-Loup had prevented Aimé from going out to the carriage in which M. de Charlus, who had managed somehow or other to discover the waiter's new address, received a further disappointment. Aimé, who had not noticed him, felt an astonishment that may be imagined when, on the evening of that very day on which I had taken luncheon with Saint-Loup and his mistress, he received a letter sealed with the Guermantes arms, from which I shall quote a few passages here as an example of unilateral insanity in an intelligent man addressing an imbecile endowed with sense. 'Sir, I have been unsuccessful, notwithstanding efforts that would astonish many people who have sought in vain to be greeted and welcomed by myself, in persuading you to listen to certain explanations which you have not asked of me but which I have felt it to be incumbent upon my dignity and your own to offer you. I am going therefore to write down here what it would have been more easy to say to you in person. I shall not conceal from you that, the first time that I set eyes upon you at Balbec, I found your face frankly antipathetic.' Here followed reflections upon the resemblance – remarked only on the following day – to a deceased friend to whom M. de Charlus had been deeply attached. 'The thought then suddenly occurred to me that you might, without in any way encroaching upon the demands of your profession, come to see me and, by joining me in the card games with which his mirth used to dispel my gloom, give me the illusion that he was not dead. Whatever the nature of the more or less fatuous suppositions which you probably formed, suppositions more within the mental range of a servant (who does not even deserve the name of servant since he has declined to serve) than the comprehension of so lofty a sentiment, you probably thought that you were giving yourself importance, knowing not who I was nor what I was, by sending word to me, when I asked you to fetch me a book, that you were in bed; but it is a mistake to imagine that impolite behaviour ever adds to charm, in which you moreover are entirely lacking. I should have ended matters there had I not, by chance, the following morning, found an opportunity of speaking to you. Your resemblance to my poor friend was so accentuated, banishing even the intolerable protuberance of your too prominent chin, that I realised that it was the deceased who at that moment was lending you his own kindly expression so as to permit you to regain your hold over me and to prevent you from missing the unique opportunity that was being offered you. Indeed, although I have no wish, since there is no longer any object and it is unlikely that I shall meet you again in this life, to introduce coarse questions of material interest, I should have been only too glad to obey the prayer of my dead friend (for I believe in the Communion of Saints and in their deliberate intervention in the destiny of the living), that I should treat you as I used to treat him, who had his carriage, his servants, and to whom it was quite natural that I should consecrate the greater part of my fortune since I loved him as a father loves his son. You have decided otherwise. To my request that you should fetch me a book you sent the reply that you were obliged to go out. And this morning when I sent to ask you to come to my carriage, you then, if I may so speak without blasphemy, denied me for the third time. You will excuse my not enclosing in this envelope the lavish gratuity which I intended to give you at Balbec and to which it would be too painful to me to restrict myself in dealing with a person with whom I had thought for a moment of sharing all that I possess. At least you might spare me the trouble of making a fourth vain attempt to find you at your restaurant, to which my patience will not extend.' (Here M. de Charlus gave his address, stated the hours at which he would be at home, etc.) 'Farewell, Sir. Since I assume that, resembling so strongly the friend whom I have lost, you cannot be entirely stupid, otherwise physiognomy would be a false science, I am convinced that if, one day, you think of this incident again, it will not be without feeling some regret and some remorse. For my part, believe that I am quite sincere in saying that I retain no bitterness. I should have preferred that we should part with a less unpleasant memory than this third futile endeavour. It will soon be forgotten. We are like those vessels which you must often have seen at Balbec, which have crossed one another's course for a moment; it might have been to the advantage of each of them to stop; but one of them has decided otherwise; presently they will no longer even see one another on the horizon and their meeting is a thing out of mind; but, before this final parting, each of them salutes the other, and so at this point, Sir, wishing you all good fortune, does

THE BARON DE CHARLUS

Aimé had not even read this letter through, being able to make nothing of it and suspecting a hoax. When I had explained to him who the Baron was, he appeared to be lost in thought and to be feeling the regret that M. de Charlus had anticipated. I would not be prepared to swear that he would not at that moment have written a letter of apology to a man who gave carriages to his friends. But in the interval M. de Charlus had made Morel's acquaintance. It was true that, his relations with Morel being possibly Platonic, M. de Charlus occasionally sought to spend an evening in company such as that in which I had just met him in the hall. But he was no longer able to divert from Morel the violent sentiment which, at liberty a few years earlier, had asked nothing better than to fasten itself upon Aimé and had dictated the letter which had distressed me, for its writer's sake, when the head waiter showed me it. It was, in view of the antisocial nature of M. de Charlus's love, a more striking example of the insensible, sweeping force of these currents of passion by which the lover, like a swimmer, is very soon carried out of sight of land. No doubt the love of a normal man may also, when the lover, by the successive invention of his desires, regrets, disappointments, plans, constructs a whole romance about a woman whom he does not know, allow the two legs of the compass to gape at a quite remarkably wide angle. All the same, such an angle was singularly enlarged by the character of a passion which is not generally shared and by the difference in social position between M. de Charlus and Aimé.

Every day I went out with Albertine. She had decided to take up painting again and had chosen as the subject of her first attempts the church of Saint-Jean de la Haise which nobody ever visited and very few had even heard of, a spot difficult to describe, impossible to discover without a guide, slow of access in its isolation, more than half an hour from the Epreville station, after one had long left behind one the last houses of the village of Quette-holme. As to the name Epreville I found that the curé's book and Brichot's information were at variance. According to one, Epreville was the ancient Sprevilla; the other derived the name from Aprivilla. On our first visit we took a little train in the opposite direction from Féterne, that is to say towards Grattevast. But we were in the dog days and it had been a terrible strain simply to go out of doors immediately after luncheon. I should have preferred not to start so soon; the luminous and burning air provoked thoughts of indolence and cool retreats. It filled my mother's room and mine, according to their exposure, at varying temperatures, like rooms in a Turkish bath. Mamma's dressing-room, festooned by the sun with a dazzling, Moorish whiteness, appeared to be sunk at the bottom of a well, because of the four plastered walls on which it looked out, while far above, in the empty space, the sky, whose fleecy white waves one saw slip past, one behind another, seemed (because of the longing that one felt), whether built upon a terrace or seen reversed in a mirror hung above the window, a tank filled with blue water, reserved for bathers. Notwithstanding this scorching temperature, we had taken the one o'clock train. But Albertine had been very hot in the carriage, hotter still in the long walk across country, and I was afraid of her catching cold when she proceeded to sit still in that damp hollow where the sun's rays did not penetrate. Having, on the other hand, as long ago as our first visits to Elstir, made up my mind that she would appreciate not merely luxury but even a certain degree of comfort of which her want of money deprived her, I had made arrangements with a Balbec job-master that a carriage was to be sent every day to take us out. To escape from the heat we took the road through the forest of Chantepie. The invisibility of the innumerable birds, some of them almost sea-birds, that conversed with one another from the trees on either side of us, gave the same impression of repose that one has when one shuts one's eyes. By Albertine's side, enchained by her arms within the carriage, I listened to these Oceanides. And when by chance I caught sight of one of these musicians as he flitted from one leaf to the shelter of another, there was so little apparent connection between him and his songs that I could not believe that I beheld their cause in the little body, fluttering, humble, startled and unseeing. The carriage could not take us all the way to the church. I stopped it when we had passed through Quetteholme and bade Albertine goodbye. For she had alarmed me by saying to me of this church as of other buildings, of certain pictures: 'What a pleasure it would be to see that with you!' This pleasure was one that I did not feel myself capable of giving her. I felt it myself in front of beautiful things only if I was alone or pretended to be alone and did not speak. But since she supposed that she might, thanks to me, feel sensations of art which are not communicated thus – I thought it more prudent to say that I must leave her, would come back to fetch her at the end of the day, but that in the meantime I must go back with the carriage to pay a call on Mme Verdurin or on the Cambremers, or even spend an hour with Mamma at Balbec, but never farther afield. To begin with, that is to say. For, Albertine having once said to me petulantly: 'It's a bore that Nature has arranged things so badly and put Saint-Jean de la Haise in one direction, la Raspelière in another, so that you're imprisoned for the whole day in the part of the country you've chosen', as soon as the toque and veil had come I ordered, to my eventual undoing, a motorcar from Saint-Fargeau (*Sanctus Ferreolus*, according to the curé's book). Albertine, whom I had kept in ignorance and who had come to call for me, was surprised when she heard in front of the hotel the purr of the engine, delighted when she learned that this motor was for ourselves. I made her come upstairs for a moment to my room. She jumped for joy. 'We are going to pay a call on the Verdurins.' 'Yes, but you'd better not go dressed like that since you are going to have your motor. There, you will look better in these.' And I brought out the toque and veil which I had hidden. 'They're for me? Oh! You are an angel,' she cried, throwing her arms round my neck. Aimé who met us on the stairs, proud of Albertine's smart attire and of our means of transport, for these vehicles were still comparatively rare at Balbec, gave himself the pleasure of coming downstairs behind us. Albertine, anxious to display herself in her new garments, asked me to have the car opened, as we could shut it later on when we wished to be more private. 'Now then,' said Aimé to the driver, with whom he was not acquainted and who had not stirred, 'don't you (*tu*) hear, you're to open your roof?' For Aimé, sophisticated by hotel life, in which moreover he had won his way to exalted rank, was not as shy as the cab driver to whom Françoise was a 'lady'; notwithstanding the want of any formal introduction, plebeians whom he had never seen before he addressed as *tu*, though it was hard to say whether this was aristocratic disdain on his part or democratic fraternity. 'I am engaged,' replied the chauffeur, who did not know me by sight. 'I am ordered for Mlle Simonet. I can't take this gentleman.' Aimé burst out laughing: 'Why, you great pumpkin,' he said to the driver, whom he at once convinced, 'this is Mademoiselle Simonet, and Monsieur, who tells you to open the roof of your car, is the person who has engaged you.' And as Aimé, although personally he had no feeling for Albertine, was for my sake proud of the garments she was wearing, he whispered to the chauffeur: 'Don't get the chance of driving a Princess like that every day, do you?' On this first occasion it was not I alone that was able to go to la Raspelière as I did on other days, while Albertine painted; she decided to go there with me. She did indeed think that we might stop here and there on our way, but supposed it to be impossible to start by going to Saint-Jean de la Haise. That is to say in another direction, and to make an excursion which seemed to be reserved for a different day. She learned on the contrary from the driver that nothing could be easier than to go to Saint-Jean, which he could do in twenty minutes, and that we might stay there if we chose for hours, or go on much farther, for from Quetteholme to la Raspelière would not take more than thirty-five minutes. We realised this as soon as the vehicle, starting off, covered in one bound twenty paces of an excellent horse. Distances are only the relation of space to time and vary with that relation. We express the difficulty that we have in getting to a place in a system of miles or kilometres which becomes false as soon as that difficulty decreases. Art is modified by it also, when a village which seemed to be in a different world from some other village becomes its neighbour in a landscape whose dimensions are altered. In any case the information that there may perhaps exist a universe in which two and two make five and the straight line is not the shortest way between two points would have astonished Albertine far less than to hear the driver say that it was easy to go in a single afternoon to Saint-Jean and la Raspelière. Douville and Quetteholme, Saint-Mars le Vieux and Saint-Mars le Vêtu, Gourville and Old Balbec, Tourville and Féterne, prisoners hitherto as hermetically confined in the cells of distinct days as long ago were Méséglise and Guermantes, upon which the same eyes could not gaze in the course of one afternoon, delivered now by the giant with the seven-league boots, came and clustered about our teatime their towers and steeples, their old gardens which the encroaching wood sprang back to reveal.

Coming to the foot of the cliff road, the car took it in its stride, with a continuous sound like that of a knife being ground, while the sea falling away grew broader beneath us. The old rustic houses of Montsurvent ran towards us, clasping to their bosoms vine or rose-bush; the firs of la Raspelière, more agitated than when the evening breeze was rising, ran in every direction to escape from us and a new servant whom I had never seen before came to open the door for us on the terrace, while the gardener's son, betraying a precocious bent, devoured the machine with his gaze. As it was not a Monday we did not know whether we should find Mme Verdurin, for except upon that day, when she was at home, it was unsafe to call upon her without warning. No doubt she was 'principally' at home, but this expression, which Mme Swann employed at the time when she too was seeking to form her little clan, and to draw visitors to herself without moving towards them, an expression which she interpreted as meaning 'on principle', meant no more than 'as a general rule', that is to say with frequent exceptions. For not only did Mme Verdurin like going out, but she carried her duties as a hostess to extreme lengths, and when she had had people to luncheon, immediately after the coffee, liqueurs and cigarettes (notwithstanding the first somnolent effects of the heat and of digestion in which they would have preferred to watch through the leafy boughs of the terrace the Jersey packet passing over the enamelled sea), the programme included a series of excursions in the course of which her guests, installed by force in carriages, were conveyed, willy-nilly, to look at one or other of the views that abound in the neighbourhood of Douville. This second part of the entertainment was, as it happened (once the effort to rise and enter the carriage had been made), no less satisfactory than the other to the guests, already prepared by the succulent dishes, the vintage wines or sparkling cider to let themselves be easily intoxicated by the purity of the breeze and the magnificence of the views. Mme Verdurin used to make strangers visit these rather as though they were portions (more or less detached) of her property, which you could not help going to see the moment you came to luncheon with her and which conversely you would never have known had you not been entertained by the Mistress. This claim to arrogate to herself the exclusive right over walks and drives, as over Morel's and formerly Dechambre's playing, and to compel the landscapes to form part of the little clan, was not for that matter so absurd as it appears at first sight. Mme Verdurin deplored the want of taste which, according to her, the Cambremers showed in the furnishing of la Raspelière and the arrangement of the garden, but still more their want of initiative in the excursions that they took or made their guests take in the surrounding country. Just as, according to her, la Raspelière was only beginning to become what it should always have been now that it was the asylum of the little clan, so she insisted that the Cambremers, perpetually exploring in their barouche, along the railway line, by the shore, the one ugly road that there was in the district, had been living in the place all their lives but did not know it. There was a grain of truth in this assertion. From force of habit, lack of imagination, want of interest in a country which seemed hackneyed because it was so near, the Cambremers when they left their home went always to the same places and by the same roads. To be sure they laughed heartily at the Verdurins' offer to show them their native country. But when it came to that, they and even their coachman would have been incapable of taking us to the splendid, more or less secret places, to which M. Verdurin brought us, now forcing the barrier of a private but deserted property upon which other people would not have thought it possible to venture, now leaving the carriage to follow a path which was not wide enough for wheeled traffic, but in either case with the certain recompense of a marvellous view. Let us say in passing that the garden at la Raspelière was in a sense a compendium of all the excursions to be made in a radius of many miles. For one thing because of its commanding position, overlooking on one side the valley, on the other the sea, and also because, on one and the same side, the seaward side for instance, clearings had been made through the trees in such a way that from one point you embraced one horizon, from another another. There was at each of these points of view a bench; you went and sat down in turn upon the bench from which there was the view of Balbec, or Parville, or Douville. Even to command a single view one bench would have been placed more or less on the edge of the cliff, another farther back. From the latter you had a foreground of verdure and a horizon which seemed already the vastest imaginable, but which became infinitely larger if, continuing along a little path, you went to the next bench from which you scanned the whole amphitheatre of the sea. There you could make out exactly the sound of the waves which did not penetrate to the more secluded parts of the garden, where the sea was still visible but no longer audible. These resting-places bore at la Raspelière among the occupants of the house the name of 'views'. And indeed they assembled round the mansion the finest views of the neighbouring places, coastline or forest, seen greatly diminished by distance, as Hadrian collected in his villa reduced models of the most famous monuments of different countries. The name that followed the word 'view' was not necessarily that of a place on the coast, but often that of the opposite shore of the bay which you could make out, standing out in a certain relief notwithstanding the extent of the panorama. Just as you took a book from M. Verdurin's library to go and read for an hour at the 'view of Balbec', so if the sky was clear the liqueurs would be served at the 'view of Rivebelle', on condition however that the wind was not too strong, for, in spite of the trees planted on either side, the air up there was keen. To come back to the carriage parties that Mme Verdurin used to organise for the afternoons, the Mistress, if on her return she found the cards of some social butterfly 'on a flying visit to the coast', would pretend to be overjoyed, but was actually broken-hearted at having missed his visit and (albeit people at this date came only to 'see the house' or to make the acquaintance for a day of a woman whose artistic salon was famous, but outside the pale in Paris) would at once make M. Verdurin invite him to dine on the following Wednesday. As the tourist was often obliged to leave before that day, or was afraid to be out late, Mme Verdurin had arranged that on Mondays she was always to be found at teatime. These tea-parties were not at all large, and I had known more brilliant gatherings of the sort in Paris, at the Princesse de Guermantes's, at Mme de Gallifet's or Mme d'Arpajon's. But this was not Paris, and the charm of the setting enhanced, in my eyes, not merely the pleasantness of the party but the merits of the visitors. A meeting with some social celebrity, which in Paris would have given me no pleasure, but which at la Raspelière, whither he had come from a distance by Féterne or the forest of Chantepie, changed in character, in importance, became an agreeable incident. Sometimes it was a person whom I knew quite well and would not have gone a yard to meet at the Swanns'. But his name sounded differently upon this cliff, like the name of an actor whom one has constantly heard in a theatre, printed upon the announcement, in a different colour, of an extraordinary gala performance, where his notoriety is suddenly multiplied by the unexpectedness of the rest. As in the country people behave without ceremony, the social celebrity often took it upon him to bring the friends with whom he was staying, murmuring the excuse in Mme Verdurin's ear that he could not leave them behind as he was living in their house; to his hosts on the other hand he pretended to offer, as a sort of courtesy, the distraction, in a monotonous seaside life, of being taken to a centre of wit and intellect, of visiting a magnificent mansion and of making an excellent tea. This composed at once an assembly of several persons of semi-distinction; and if a little slice of garden with a few trees, which would seem shabby in the country, acquires an extraordinary charm in the Avenue Gabriel or let us say the Rue de Monceau, where only multi-millionaires can afford such a luxury, inversely gentlemen who are of secondary importance at a Parisian party stood out at their full value on a Monday afternoon at la Raspelière. No sooner did they sit down at the table covered with a cloth embroidered in red, beneath the painted panels, to partake of the rock cakes, Norman puff pastry, tartlets shaped like boats filled with cherries like beads of coral, 'diplomatic' cakes, than these guests were subjected, by the proximity of the great bowl of azure upon which the window opened, and which you could not help seeing when you looked at them, to a profound alteration, a transmutation which changed them into something more precious than before. What was more, even before you set eyes on them, when you came on a Monday to Mme Verdurin's, people who in Paris would scarcely turn their heads to look, so familiar was the sight of a string of smart carriages waiting outside a great house, felt their hearts throb at the sight of the two or three broken-down dog-carts drawn up in front of la Raspelière, beneath the tall firs. No doubt this was because the rustic setting was different, and social impressions thanks to this transposition regained a kind of novelty. It was also because the broken-down carriage that one hired to pay a call upon Mme Verdurin called to mind a pleasant drive and a costly bargain struck with a coachman who had demanded 'so much' for the whole day. But the slight stir of curiosity with regard to fresh arrivals, whom it was still impossible to distinguish, made everybody ask himself: 'Who can this be?' a question which it was difficult to answer, when one did not know who might have come down to spend a week with the Cambremers or elsewhere, but which people always enjoy putting to themselves in rustic, solitary lives where a meeting with a human creature whom one has not seen for a long time ceases to be the tiresome affair that it is in the life of Paris, and forms a delicious break in the empty monotony of lives that are too lonely, in which even the postman's knock becomes a pleasure. And on the day on which we arrived in a motorcar at la Raspelière, as it was not Monday, M. and Mme Verdurin must have been devoured by that craving to see people which attacks men and women and inspires a longing to throw himself out of the window in the patient who has been shut up away from his family and friends, for a cure of strict isolation. For the new and more swift-footed servant, who had already made himself familiar with these expressions, having replied that 'if Madame has not gone out she must be at the view of Douville,' and that he would go and look for her, came back immediately to tell us that she was coming to welcome us. We found her slightly dishevelled, for she came from the flower beds, farmyard and kitchen garden, where she had gone to feed her peacocks and poultry, to hunt for eggs, to gather fruit and flowers to 'make her table-centre', which would suggest her park in miniature; but on the table it conferred the distinction of making it support the burden of only such things as were useful and good to eat; for round those other presents from the garden which were the pears, the whipped eggs, rose the tall stems of bugloss, carnations, roses and coreopsis, between which one saw, as between blossoming boundary posts, move from one to another beyond the glazed windows, the ships at sea. From the astonishment which M. and Mme Verdurin, interrupted while arranging their flowers to receive the visitors that had been announced, showed upon finding that these visitors were merely Albertine and myself, it was easy to see that the new servant, full of zeal but not yet familiar with my name, had repeated it wrongly and that Mme Verdurin, hearing the names of guests whom she did not know, had nevertheless bidden him let them in, in her need of seeing somebody, no matter whom. And the new servant stood contemplating this spectacle from the door in order to learn what part we played in the household. Then he made off at a run, taking long strides, for he had entered upon his duties only the day before. When Albertine had quite finished displaying her toque and veil to the Verdurins, she gave me a warning look to remind me that we had not too much time left for what we meant to do. Mme Verdurin begged us to stay to tea, but we refused, when all of a sudden a suggestion was mooted which would have made an end of all the pleasures that I promised myself from my drive with Albertine: the Mistress, unable to face the thought of tearing herself from us, or perhaps of allowing a novel distraction to escape, decided to accompany us. Accustomed for years past to the experience that similar offers on her part were not well received, and being probably dubious whether this offer would find favour with us, she concealed beneath an excessive assurance the timidity that she felt when addressing us and, without even appearing to suppose that there could be any doubt as to our answer, asked us no question, but said to her husband, speaking of Albertine and myself, as though she were conferring a favour on us: 'I shall see them home, myself.' At the same time there hovered over her lips a smile that did not belong to them, a smile which I had already seen on the faces of certain people when they said to Bergotte with a knowledgeable air: 'I have bought your book, it's not bad', one of those collective, universal smiles which, when they feel the need of them – as we make use of railways and removal vans – individuals borrow, except a few who are extremely refined, like Swann or M. de Charlus on whose lips I have never seen that smile settle. From that moment my visit was poisoned. I pretended not to have understood. A moment later it became evident that M. Verdurin was to be one of the party. 'But it will be too far for M. Verdurin,' I objected. 'Not at all,' replied Mme Verdurin with a condescending, cheerful air, 'he says it will amuse him immensely to go with you young people over a road he has travelled so many times; if necessary, he will sit beside the engineer, that doesn't frighten him, and we shall come back quietly by the train like a good married couple. Look at him, he's quite delighted.' She seemed to be speaking of an aged and famous painter full of friendliness, who, younger than the youngest, takes a delight in scribbling figures on paper to make his grandchildren laugh. What added to my sorrow was that Albertine seemed not to share it and to find some amusement in the thought of dashing all over the countryside like this with the Verdurins. As for myself, the pleasure that I had vowed that I would take with her was so imperious that I refused to allow the Mistress to spoil it; I invented falsehoods which the irritating threats of Mme Verdurin made excusable, but which Albertine, alas, contradicted. 'But we have a call to pay,' I said. 'What call?' asked Albertine. 'You shall hear about it later, there's no getting out of it.' 'Very well, we can wait outside,' said Mme Verdurin, resigned to anything. At the last minute my anguish at seeing wrested from me a happiness for which I had so longed gave me the courage to be impolite. I refused point blank, alleging in Mme Verdurin's ear that because of some trouble which had befallen Albertine and about which she wished to consult me, it was absolutely necessary that I should be alone with her. The Mistress appeared vexed: 'All right, we shan't come,' she said to me in a voice tremulous with rage. I felt her to be so angry that, so as to appear to be giving way a little: 'But we might perhaps . . . ' I began. 'No,' she replied, more furious than ever, 'when I say no, I mean no.' I supposed that I was out of favour with her, but she called us back at the door to urge us not to 'fail' on the following Wednesday, and not to come with that contraption, which was dangerous at night, but by the train with the little group, and she made me stop the car, which was moving down hill across the park, because the footman had forgotten to put in the hood the slice of tart and the shortbread which she had had made into a parcel for us. We started off, escorted for a moment by the little houses that came running to meet us with their flowers. The face of the countryside seemed to us entirely changed, so far, in the topographical image that we form in our minds of separate places, is the notion of space from being the most important factor. We have said that the notion of time segregates them even farther. It is not the only factor either. Certain places which we see always in isolation seem to us to have no common measure with the rest, to be almost outside the world, like those people whom we have known in exceptional periods of our life, during our military service, in our childhood, and whom we associate with nothing. In my first year at Balbec there was a piece of high ground to which Mme de Villeparisis liked to take us because from it you saw only the water and the woods, and which was called Beaumont. As the road that she took to approach it, and preferred to other routes because of its old trees, went uphill all the way, her carriage was obliged to go at a crawling pace and took a very long time. When we reached the top we used to alight, stroll about for a little, get into the carriage again, return by the same road, without seeing a single village, a single country house. I knew that Beaumont was something very special, very remote, very high, I had no idea of the direction in which it was to be found, having never taken the Beaumont road to go anywhere else; besides, it took a very long time to get there in a carriage. It was obviously in the same Department (or in the same Province) as Balbec, but was situated for me on another plane, enjoyed a special privilege of extra-territoriality. But the motorcar respects no mystery, and, having passed beyond Incarville, whose houses still danced before my eyes, as we were going down the cross road that leads to Parville (*Paterni villa*), catching sight of the sea from a natural terrace over which we were passing, I asked the name of the place, and before the chauffeur had time to reply recognised Beaumont, close by which I passed thus unconsciously whenever I took the little train, for it was within two minutes of Parville. Like an officer of my regiment who might have seemed to me a creature apart, too kindly and simple to be of a great family, too remote already and

mysterious to be simply of a great family, and of whom I was afterwards to
learn that he was the brother-in-law, the cousin of people with whom I was
dining, so Beaumont, suddenly brought in contact with places from which I
supposed it to be so distinct, lost its mystery and took its place in the district,
making me think with terror that Madame Bovary and the Sanseverina
might perhaps have seemed to me to be like ordinary people, had I met
them elsewhere than in the close atmosphere of a novel. It may be thought
that my love of magic journeys by train ought to have prevented me from
sharing Albertine's wonder at the motorcar which takes even the invalid
wherever he wishes to go and destroys our conception – which I had held
hitherto – of position in space as the individual mark, the irreplaceable
essence of irremovable beauties. And no doubt this position in space was not
to the motorcar, as it had been to the railway train, when I came from Paris
to Balbec, a goal exempt from the contingencies of ordinary life, almost
ideal at the moment of departure, and, as it remains so at that of arrival, at
our arrival in that great dwelling where no one dwells and which bears only
the name of the town, the station, seeming to promise at last the accessibility
of the town, as though the station were its materialisation. No, the motorcar
did not convey us thus by magic into a town which we saw at first in the
whole that is summarised by its name, and with the illusions of a spectator in
a theatre. It made us enter that theatre by the wings which were the streets,
stopped to ask the way of an inhabitant. But, as a compensation for so
familiar a progress one has the gropings of the chauffeur uncertain of his
way and retracing his course, the 'general post' of perspective which sets a
castle dancing about with a hill, a church and the sea, while one draws nearer
to it, in spite of its vain efforts to hide beneath its primeval foliage; those ever
narrowing circles which the motorcar describes round a spellbound town
which darts off in every direction to escape it and upon which finally it drops
down, straight, into the heart of the valley where it lies palpitating on the
ground; so that this position in space, this unique point, which the motorcar
seems to have stripped of the mystery of express trains, it gives us on the
contrary the impression of discovering, of determining for ourselves as with
a compass, of helping us to feel with a more fondly exploring hand, with a
finer precision, the true geometry, the fair measure of the earth.

What unfortunately I did not know at that moment and did not learn until
more than two years later was that one of the chauffeur's patrons was M. de
Charlus, and that Morel, instructed to pay him and keeping part of the
money for himself (making the chauffeur triple and quintuple the mileage),
had become very friendly with him (while pretending not to know him
before other people) and made use of his car for long journeys. If I had

known this at the time, and that the confidence which the Verdurins were presently to feel in this chauffeur came, unknown to them, from that source, perhaps many of the sorrows of my life in Paris, in the year that followed, much of my trouble over Albertine would have been avoided, but I had not the slightest suspicion of it. In themselves M. de Charlus's excursions by motorcar with Morel were of no direct interest to me. They were moreover confined as a rule to a luncheon or dinner in some restaurant along the coast where M. de Charlus was regarded as an old and penniless servant and Morel, whose duty it was to pay the bill, as a too kind-hearted gentleman. I report the conversation at one of these meals, which may give an idea of the others. It was in a restaurant of elongated shape at Saint-Mars le Vêtu. 'Can't you get them to remove this thing?' M. de Charlus asked Morel, as though appealing to an intermediary without having to address the staff directly. 'This thing' was a vase containing three withered roses with which a well-meaning head waiter had seen fit to decorate the table. 'Yes . . . ' said Morel in embarrassment. 'You don't like roses?' 'My request ought on the contrary to prove that I do like them, since there are no roses here' (Morel appeared surprised) 'but as a matter of fact I do not care much for them. I am rather sensitive to names; and whenever a rose is at all beautiful, one learns that it is called Baronne de Rothschild or Maréchale Niel, which casts a chill. Do you like names? Have you found beautiful titles for your little concert numbers?' 'There is one that is called *Poème triste*.' 'That is horrible,' replied M. de Charlus in a shrill voice that rang out like a blow. 'But I ordered champagne?' he said to the head waiter who had supposed he was obeying the order by placing by the diners two glasses of foaming liquid. 'Yes, Sir.' 'Take away that filth, which has no connection with the worst champagne in the world. It is the emetic known as *cup*, which consists, as a rule, of three rotten strawberries swimming in a mixture of vinegar and soda-water. Yes,' he went on, turning again to Morel, 'you don't seem to know what a title is. And even in the interpretation of the things you play best, you seem not to be aware of the mediumistic side.' 'You mean to say?' asked Morel, who, not having understood one word of what the Baron had said, was afraid that he might be missing something of importance, such as an invitation to luncheon. M. de Charlus having failed to regard 'You mean to say?' as a question, Morel, having in consequence received no answer, thought it best to change the conversation and to give it a sensual turn: 'There, look at the fair girl selling the flowers you don't like; I'm certain she's got a little mistress. And the old woman dining at the table at the end, too.' 'But how do you know all that?' asked M. de Charlus, amazed at Morel's intuition. 'Oh! I can spot them in an instant. If we went out together in a crowd, you would see that I never make a mistake.' And anyone looking at Morel at that moment, with his girlish air enshrined in his masculine beauty, would have understood the obscure divination which made him no less obvious to certain women than them to him. He was anxious to supplant Jupien, vaguely desirous of adding to his regular income the profits which, he supposed, the tailor derived from the Baron. 'And with boys I am surer still, I could save you from making any mistake. We shall be having the fair soon at Balbec, we shall find lots of things there. And in Paris too, you'll see, you'll have a fine time.' But the inherited caution of a servant made him give a different turn to the sentence on which he had already embarked. So that M. de Charlus supposed that he was still referring to girls. 'Listen,' said Morel, anxious to excite in a fashion which he considered less compromising for himself (albeit it was actually more immoral) the Baron's senses, 'what I should like would be to find a girl who was quite pure, make her fall in love with me, and take her virginity.' M. de Charlus could not refrain from pinching Morel's ear affectionately, but added innocently: 'What good would that be to you? If you took her maidenhead, you would be obliged to marry her.' 'Marry her?' cried Morel, guessing that the Baron was fuddled, or else giving no thought to the man, more scrupulous in reality than he supposed, to whom he was speaking. 'Marry her? Balls! I should promise, but once the little operation was performed, I should clear out and leave her.' M. de Charlus was in the habit, when a fiction was capable of causing him a momentary sensual pleasure, of believing in its truth, while keeping himself free to withdraw his credulity altogether a minute later, when his pleasure was at an end. 'You would really do that?' he said to Morel with a laugh, squeezing him more tightly still. 'And why not?' said Morel, seeing that he was not shocking the Baron by continuing to expound to him what was indeed one of his desires. 'It is dangerous,' said M. de Charlus. 'I should have my kit packed and ready, and buzz off and leave no address.' 'And what about me?' asked M. de Charlus. 'I should take you with me, of course,' Morel made haste to add, never having thought of what would become of the Baron who was the least of his responsibilities. 'I say, there's a kid I should love to try that game on, she's a little seamstress who keeps a shop in M. le Duc's *hôtel*.' 'Jupien's girl,' the Baron exclaimed, as the wine-waiter entered the room. 'Oh! Never,' he added, whether because the presence of a third person had cooled his ardour, or because even in this sort of black mass in which he took a delight in defiling the most sacred things, he could not bring himself to allow the mention of people to whom he was bound by ties of friendship. 'Jupien is a good man, the child is charming, it would be a shame to make them unhappy.' Morel felt that he had gone too far and was silent, but his gaze continued to fix itself in imagination upon the girl for whose benefit he had once begged me to address him as 'dear great master' and from whom he had ordered a waistcoat. An industrious worker, the child had not taken any holiday, but I learned afterwards that while the violinist was in the neighbourhood of Balbec she never ceased to think of his handsome face, ennobled by the accident that having seen Morel in my company she had taken him for a 'gentleman'.

'I never heard Chopin play,' said the Baron, 'and yet I might have done so, I took lessons from Stamati, but he forbade me to go and hear the Master of the Nocturnes at my aunt Chimay's.' 'That was damned silly of him,' exclaimed Morel. 'On the contrary,' M. de Charlus retorted warmly, in a shrill voice. 'He showed his intelligence. He had realised that I had a "nature" and that I would succumb to Chopin's influence. It made no difference, because when I was quite young I gave up music, and everything else, for that matter. Besides one can more or less imagine him,' he added in a slow, nasal, drawling tone, 'there are still people who did hear him, who can give you an idea. However, Chopin was only an excuse to come back to the mediumistic aspect which you are neglecting.'

The reader will observe that, after an interpolation of common parlance, M. de Charlus had suddenly become as precious and haughty in his speech as ever. The idea of Morel's 'dropping' without compunction a girl whom he had outraged had given him a sudden and entire pleasure. From that moment his sensual appetites were satisfied for a time and the sadist (a true medium, he, if you like) who had for a few moments taken the place of M. de Charlus had fled, leaving a clear field for the real M. de Charlus, full of artistic refinement, sensibility, goodness. 'You were playing the other day the transposition for the piano of the Fifteenth Quartet, which is absurd in itself because nothing could be less pianistic. It is meant for people whose ears are hurt by the too highly strained chords of the glorious Deaf One. Whereas it is precisely that almost bitter mysticism that is divine. In any case you played it very badly and altered all the movements. You ought to play it as though you were composing it: the young Morel, afflicted with a momentary deafness and with a non-existent genius stands for an instant motionless. Then, seized by the divine frenzy, he plays, he composes the opening bars. After which, exhausted by this initial effort, he gives way, letting droop his charming forelock to please Mme Verdurin, and, what is more, gives himself time to recreate the prodigious quantity of grey matter which he has commandeered for the Pythian objectivation. Then, having regained his strength, seized by a fresh and overmastering inspiration, he flings himself upon the sublime, imperishable phrase which the virtuoso of

Berlin' (we suppose M. de Charlus to have meant by this expression Mendelssohn) 'was to imitate without ceasing. It is in this, the only really transcendent and animating fashion, that I shall make you play in Paris.' When M. de Charlus gave him advice of this sort, Morel was far more alarmed than when he saw the head waiter remove his scorned roses and 'cup', for he asked himself with anxiety what effect it would create among his 'class'. But he was unable to dwell upon these reflections, for M. de Charlus said to him imperiously: 'Ask the head waiter if he has a *Bon Chrétien*.' 'A good Christian, I don't understand.' 'Can't you see we've reached the dessert, it's a pear. You may be sure, Mme de Cambremer has them in her garden, for the Comtesse d'Escarbagnas whose double she is had them. M. Thibaudier sends her them, saying: "Here is a *Bon Chrétien* which is worth tasting".' 'No, I didn't know.' 'I can see that you know nothing. If you have never even read Molière . . . Oh, well, since you are no more capable of ordering food than of anything else, ask simply for a pear which is grown in this neighbourhood, the *Louise-Bonne d'Avranches*.' 'The?' 'Wait a minute, since you are so stupid, I shall ask him myself for others, which I prefer. Waiter, have you any *Doyennée des Cornices*? Charlie, you must read the exquisite passage about that pear by the Duchesse Emilie de Clermont-Tonnerre.' 'No, Sir, there aren't any.' 'Have you *Triomphe de Jodoigne*?' 'No, Sir.' 'Any *Virginie-Dallet*? Or *Passe-Colmar*? No? Very well, since you've nothing, we may as well go. The *Duchesse d'Angoulême* is not in season yet, come along, Charlie.' Unfortunately for M. de Charlus, his want of common sense, perhaps too the chastity of what were probably his relations with Morel, made him go out of his way at this period to shower upon the violinist strange bounties which the other was incapable of understanding, and to which his nature, impulsive in its own way, but mean and ungrateful, could respond only by a harshness or a violence that were steadily intensified and plunged M. de Charlus – formerly so proud, now quite timid – in fits of genuine despair. We shall see how, in the smallest matters, Morel, who fancied himself a M. de Charlus a thousand times more important, completely misunderstood, by taking it literally, the Baron's arrogant information with regard to the aristocracy. Let us for the moment say simply this, while Albertine waits for me at Saint-Jean de la Haise, that if there was one thing which Morel set above nobility (and this was in itself distinctly noble, especially in a person whose pleasure was to pursue little girls – on the sly – with the chauffeur), it was his artistic reputation and what the others might think of him in the violin class. No doubt it was an ugly trait in his character that because he felt M. de Charlus to be entirely devoted to him he appeared to disown him, to make fun of him, in the same way as, when I had promised not to reveal the secret of his father's position with my great-uncle, he treated me with contempt. But on the other hand his name, as that of a recognised artist, Morel, appeared to him superior to a 'name'. And when M. de Charlus, in his dreams of Platonic affection, tried to make him adopt one of his family titles, Morel stoutly refused.

When Albertine thought it better to remain at Saint-Jean de la Haise and paint, I would take the car, and it was not merely to Gourville and Féterne, but to Saint-Mars le Vêtu and as far as Criquetot that I was able to penetrate before returning to fetch her. While pretending to be occupied with anything rather than herself, and to be obliged to forsake her for other pleasures, I thought only of her. As often as not I went no farther than the great plain which overlooks Gourville, and as it resembles slightly the plain that begins above Combray, in the direction of Méséglise, even at a considerable distance from Albertine, I had the joy of thinking that if my gaze could not reach her, still, travelling farther than in my vision, that strong and gentle sea breeze which was sweeping past me must be flowing down, without anything to arrest it as far as Quetteholme, until it stirred the branches of the trees that bury Saint-Jean de la Haise in their foliage, caressing the face of my mistress, and must thus be extending a double tie between her and myself in this retreat indefinitely enlarged, but without danger, as in those games in which two children find themselves momentarily out of sight and earshot of one another, and yet, while far apart, remain together. I returned by those roads from which there is a view of the sea, and on which in the past, before it appeared among the branches, I used to shut my eyes to reflect that what I was going to see was indeed the plaintive ancestress of the earth, pursuing as in the days when no living creature yet existed its lunatic, immemorial agitation. Now, these roads were no longer simply the means of rejoining Albertine; when I recognised each of them in their uniformity, knowing how far they would run in a straight line, where they would turn, I remembered that I had followed them while I thought of Mlle de Stermaria, and also that this same eagerness to find Albertine I had felt in Paris as I walked the streets along which Mme de Guermantes might pass; they assumed for me the profound monotony, the moral significance of a sort of ruled line that my character must follow. It was natural, and yet it was not without importance; they reminded me that it was my fate to pursue only phantoms, creatures whose reality existed to a great extent in my imagination; there are people indeed – and this had been my case from my childhood – for whom all the things that have a fixed value, assessable by others, fortune, success, high positions, do not count; what they must have, is phantoms. They sacrifice all the rest, leave no stone unturned, make everything else subservient to the

capture of some phantom. But this soon fades away; then they run after
another, prepared to return later on to the first. It was not the first time that
I had gone in quest of Albertine, the girl I had seen that first year outlined
against the sea. Other women, it is true, had been interposed between the
Albertine whom I had first loved and her from whom I was scarcely separated
at this moment; other women, notably the Duchesse de Guermantes. But,
the reader will say, why give yourself so much anxiety with regard to
Gilberte, take so much trouble over Madame de Guermantes, if, when you
have become the friend of the latter, it is with the sole result of thinking no
more of her, but only of Albertine? Swann, before his own death, might have
answered the question, he who had been a lover of phantoms. Of phantoms
pursued, forgotten, sought afresh sometimes for a single meeting and in
order to establish contact with an unreal life which at once escaped, these
Balbec roads were full. When I thought that their trees, pear trees, apple
trees, tamarisks, would outlive me, I seemed to receive from them the
warning to set myself to work at last, before the hour should strike of rest
everlasting.

I left the carriage at Quetteholme, ran down the sunken path, crossed the
brook by a plank and found Albertine painting in front of the church all
spires and crockets, thorny and red, blossoming like a rose bush. The
lantern alone showed an unbroken front; and the smiling surface of the
stone was abloom with angels who continued, before the twentieth century
couple that we were, to celebrate, taper in hand, the ceremonies of the
thirteenth. It was they that Albertine was endeavouring to portray on her
prepared canvas, and, imitating Elstir, she was laying on the paint in
sweeping strokes, trying to obey the noble rhythm set, the great master had
told her, by those angels so different from any that he knew. Then she
collected her things. Leaning upon one another we walked back up the
sunken path, leaving the little church, as quiet as though it had never seen
us, to listen to the perpetual sound of the brook. Presently the car started,
taking us home by a different way. We passed Marcouville l'Orgueilleuse.
Over its church, half new, half restored, the setting sun spread its patina as
fine as that of centuries. Through it the great has-reliefs seemed to be visible
only through a floating layer, half liquid, half luminous; the Blessed Virgin,
Saint Elizabeth, Saint Joachim swam in the impalpable tide, almost on dry
land, on the water's or the sunlight's surface. Rising in a warm dust, the
many modern statues reached, on their pillars, halfway up the golden webs
of sunset. In front of the church a tall cypress seemed to be in a sort of
consecrated enclosure. We left the car for a moment to look at it and
strolled for a little. No less than of her limbs, Albertine was directly

conscious of her toque of Leghorn straw and of the silken veil (which were for her the source of no less satisfaction), and derived from them, as we strolled round the church, a different sort of impetus, revealed by a contentment which was inert but in which I found a certain charm; veil and toque which were but a recent, adventitious part of my friend, but a part that was already dear to me, as I followed its trail with my eyes, past the cypress in the evening air. She herself could not see it, but guessed that the effect was pleasing, for she smiled at me, harmonising the poise of her head with the headgear that completed it. 'I don't like it, it's restored,' she said to me, pointing to the church and remembering what Elstir had said to her about the priceless, inimitable beauty of old stone. Albertine could tell a restoration at a glance. One could not help feeling surprised at the sureness of the taste she had already acquired in architecture, as contrasted with the deplorable taste she still retained in music. I cared no more than Elstir for this church, it was with no pleasure to myself that its sunlit front had come and posed before my eyes, and I had got out of the car to examine it only out of politeness to Albertine. I found, however, that the great impressionist had contradicted himself; why exalt this fetish of its objective architectural value, and not take into account the transfiguration of the church by the sunset? 'No, certainly not,' said Albertine, 'I don't like it; I like its name *orgueilleuse*. But what I must remember to ask Brichot is why Saint-Mars is called *le Vêtu*. We shall be going there next, shan't we?' she said, gazing at me out of her black eyes over which her toque was pulled down, like her little polo cap long ago. Her veil floated behind her. I got back into the car with her, happy in the thought that we should be going next day to Saint-Mars, where, in this blazing weather when one could think only of the delights of a bath, the two ancient steeples, salmon-pink, with their lozenge-shaped tiles, gaping slightly as though for air, looked like a pair of old, sharp-snouted fish, coated in scales, moss-grown and red, which without seeming to move were rising in a blue, transparent water. On leaving Marcouville, to shorten the road, we turned aside at a crossroads where there is a farm. Sometimes Albertine made the car stop there and asked me to go alone to fetch, so that she might drink it in the car, a bottle of calvados or cider, which the people assured me was not effervescent, and which proceeded to drench us from head to foot. We sat pressed close together. The people of the farm could scarcely see Albertine in the closed car, I handed them back their bottles; we moved on again, as though to continue that private life by ourselves, that lovers' existence which they might suppose us to lead, and of which this halt for refreshment had been only an insignificant moment; a supposition that would have appeared even less far-fetched if they had seen us after Albertine had drunk her bottle of cider; she seemed then positively unable to endure the existence of an interval between herself and me which as a rule did not trouble her; beneath her linen skirt her legs were pressed against mine, she brought close against my cheeks her own cheeks which had turned pale, warm and red over the cheekbones, with something ardent and faded about them such as one sees in girls from the slums. At such moments, almost as quickly as her personality, her voice changed also, she forsook her own voice to adopt another, raucous, bold, almost dissolute. Night began to fall. What a pleasure to feel her leaning against me, with her toque and her veil, reminding me that it is always thus, seated side by side, that we meet couples who are in love. I was perhaps in love with Albertine, but as I did not venture to let her see my love, although it existed in me, it could only be like an abstract truth, of no value until one has succeeded in checking it by experiment; as it was, it seemed to me unrealisable and outside the plane of life. As for my jealousy, it urged me to leave Albertine as little as possible, although I knew that it would not be completely cured until I had parted from her for ever. I could even feel it in her presence, but would then take care that the circumstances should not be repeated which had aroused it. Once, for example, on a fine morning, we went to luncheon at Rivebelle. The great glazed doors of the dining-room and of that hall in the form of a corridor in which tea was served stood open revealing the sunlit lawns beyond, of which the huge restaurant seemed to form a part. The waiter with the flushed face and black hair that writhed like flames was flying from end to end of that vast expanse less rapidly than in the past, for he was no longer an assistant but was now in charge of a row of tables; nevertheless, owing to his natural activity, sometimes far off, in the dining-room, at other times nearer, but out of doors, serving visitors who had preferred to feed in the garden, one caught sight of him, now here, now there, like successive statues of a young god running, some in the interior, which for that matter was well lighted, of a mansion bounded by a vista of green grass, others beneath the trees, in the bright radiance of an open air life. For a moment he was close to ourselves. Albertine replied absentmindedly to what I had just said to her. She was gazing at him with rounded eyes. For a minute or two I felt that one may be close to the person whom one loves and yet not have her with one. They had the appearance of being engaged in a mysterious conversation, rendered mute by my presence, and the sequel possibly of meetings in the past of which I knew nothing, or merely of a glance that he had given her – at which I was the *terzo incomodo*, from whom the others try to hide things. Even when, forcibly recalled by his employer, he had withdrawn from us, Albertine while continuing her meal seemed to be regarding the restaurant and its gardens merely as a lighted running-track, on which there appeared here and there amid the varied scenery the swift-foot god with the black tresses. At one moment I asked myself whether she was not going to rise up and follow him, leaving me alone at my table. But in the days that followed I began to forget for ever this painful impression, for I had decided never to return to Rivebelle, I had extracted a promise from Albertine, who assured me that she had never been there before and would never return there. And I denied that the nimble-footed waiter had had eyes only for her, so that she should not believe that my company had deprived her of a pleasure. It happened now and again that I would revisit Rivebelle, but alone, and drink too much, as I had done there in the past. As I drained a final glass I gazed at a round pattern painted on the white wall, concentrated upon it the pleasure that I felt. It alone in the world had any existence for me; I pursued it, touched it and lost it by turns with my wavering glance, and felt indifferent to the future, contenting myself with my painted pattern like a butterfly circling about a poised butterfly with which it is going to end its life in an act of supreme consummation. The moment was perhaps particularly well chosen for giving up a woman whom no very recent or very keen suffering obliged me to ask for this balm for a malady which they possess who have caused it. I was calmed by these very drives, which, even if I did not think of them at the moment save as a foretaste of a morrow which itself, notwithstanding the longing with which it filled me, was not to be different from today, had the charm of having been torn from the places which Albertine had frequented hitherto and where I had not been with her, her aunt's house, those of her girl friends. The charm not of a positive joy, but only of the calming of an anxiety, and quite strong nevertheless. For at an interval of a few days, when my thoughts turned to the farm outside which we had sat drinking cider, or simply to the stroll we had taken round Saint-Mars le Vêtu, remembering that Albertine had been walking by my side in her toque, the sense of her presence added of a sudden so strong a virtue to the trivial image of the modern church that at the moment when the sunlit front came thus of its own accord to pose before me in memory, it was like a great soothing compress laid upon my heart. I dropped Albertine at Parville, but only to join her again in the evening and lie stretched out by her side, in the darkness, upon the beach. No doubt I did not see her every day, still I could say to myself: 'If she were to give an account of how she spent her time, of her life, it would still be myself that played the largest part in it;' and we spent together long hours on end which brought into my days so sweet an intoxication that even when, at Parville, she jumped from the car which I was to send to fetch her an hour later, I no more felt myself to be alone in it than if before leaving me she had strewn it with flowers. I might have dispensed with seeing her every day; I was going to be happy when I left her, and I knew that the calming effect of that happiness might be prolonged over many days. But at that moment I heard Albertine as she left me say to her aunt or to a girl friend: 'Then tomorrow at eight-thirty. We mustn't be late, the others will be ready at a quarter past.' The conversation of a woman one loves is like the soil that covers a subterranean and dangerous water; one feels at every moment beneath the words the presence, the penetrating chill of an invisible pool; one perceives here and there its treacherous percolation, but the water itself remains hidden. The moment I heard these words of Albertine, my calm was destroyed. I wanted to ask her to let me see her the following morning, so as to prevent her from going to this mysterious rendezvous at half-past eight which had been mentioned in my presence only in covert terms. She would no doubt have begun by obeying me, while regretting that she had to give up her plans; in time she would have discovered my permanent need to upset them; I should have become the person from whom one hides everything. Besides, it is probable that these gatherings from which I was excluded amounted to very little, and that it was perhaps from the fear that I might find one of the other girls there vulgar or boring that I was not invited to them. Unfortunately this life so closely involved with Albertine's had a reaction not only upon myself; to me it brought calm; to my mother it caused an anxiety, her confession of which destroyed my calm. As I entered the hotel happy in my own mind, determined to terminate, one day soon, an existence the end of which I imagined to depend upon my own volition, my mother said to me, hearing me send a message to the chauffeur to go and fetch Albertine: 'How you do waste your money.' (Françoise in her simple and expressive language said with greater force: 'That's the way the money goes.') 'Try,' Mamma went on, 'not to become like Charles de Sévigné, of whom his mother said: "His hand is a crucible in which money melts." Besides, I do really think you have gone about quite enough with Albertine. I assure you, you're overdoing it, even to her it may seem ridiculous. I was delighted to think that you found her a distraction, I am not asking you never to see her again, but simply that it may not be impossible to meet one of you without the other.' My life with Albertine, a life devoid of keen pleasures – that is to say of keen pleasures that I could feel – that life which I intended to change at any moment, choosing a calm interval, became once again suddenly and for a time necessary to me when, by these words of Mamma's, it found itself threatened. I told my mother that what she had just said would delay for perhaps two months the decision for which she asked, which otherwise I would have reached before the end of that week. Mamma began to laugh (so as not to depress me) at this instantaneous effect of her advice, and promised not to speak of the matter to me again so as not to prevent the rebirth of my good intentions. But since my grandmother's death, whenever Mamma allowed herself to laugh, the incipient laugh would be cut short and would end in an almost heartbroken expression of sorrow, whether from remorse at having been able for an instant to forget, or else from the recrudescence which this brief moment of oblivion had given to her cruel obsession. But to the thoughts aroused in her by the memory of my grandmother, which was rooted in my mother's mind, I felt that on this occasion there were added others, relative to myself, to what my mother dreaded as the sequel of my intimacy with Albertine; an intimacy to which she dared not, however, put a stop, in view of what I had just told her. But she did not appear convinced that I was not mistaken. She remembered all the years in which my grandmother and she had refrained from speaking to me of my work, and of a more wholesome rule of life which, I said, the agitation into which their exhortations threw me alone prevented me from beginning, and which, notwithstanding their obedient silence, I had failed to pursue. After dinner the car brought Albertine back; there was still a glimmer of daylight; the air was not so warm, but after a scorching day we both dreamed of strange and delicious coolness; then to our fevered eyes the narrow slip of moon appeared at first (as on the evening when I had gone to the Princesse de Guermantes's and Albertine had telephoned to me) like the slight, fine rind, then like the cool section of a fruit which an invisible knife was beginning to peel in the sky. Sometimes too, it was I that went in search of my mistress, a little later in that case; she would be waiting for me before the arcade of the market at Maineville. At first I could not make her out; I would begin to fear that she might not be coming, that she had misunderstood me. Then I saw her in her white blouse with blue spots spring into the car by my side with the light bound of a young animal rather than a girl. And it was like a dog too that she began to caress me interminably. When night had fallen and, as the manager of the hotel remarked to me, the sky was all 'studied' with stars, if we did not go for a drive in the forest with a bottle of champagne, then, without heeding the strangers who were still strolling upon the faintly lighted front, but who could not have seen anything a yard away on the dark sand, we would lie down in the shelter of the dunes; that same body in whose suppleness abode all the feminine, marine and sportive grace of the girls whom I had seen for the first time pass before a horizon of waves, I held pressed against my own, beneath the same rug, by the edge of the motionless sea divided by a tremulous path of light; and we listened to the sea without tiring and with the same pleasure, both when it held its breath, suspended for so long that one thought the reflux would never come, and when at last it gasped out at our feet the long awaited murmur. Finally I took Albertine back to Parville. When we reached her house, we were obliged to break off our kisses for fear lest someone should see us; not wishing to go to bed she returned with me to Balbec, from where I took her back for the last time to Parville; the chauffeurs of those early days of the motorcar were people who went to bed at all hours. And as a matter of fact I returned to Balbec only with the first dews of morning, alone this time, but still surrounded with the presence of my mistress, gorged with an inexhaustible provision of kisses. On my table I would find a telegram or a postcard. Albertine again! She had written them at Quetteholme when I had gone off by myself in the car, to tell me that she was thinking of me. I got into bed as I read them over. Then I caught sight, over the curtains, of the bright streak of daylight and said to myself that we must be in love with one another after all, since we had spent the night in one another's arms. When next morning I caught sight of Albertine on the front, I was so afraid of her telling me that she was not free that day, and could not accede to my request that we should go out together, that I delayed as long as possible making the request. I was all the more uneasy since she wore a cold, preoccupied air; people were passing whom she knew; doubtless she had made plans for the afternoon from which I was excluded. I looked at her, I looked at that charming body, that blushing head of Albertine, rearing in front of me the enigma of her intentions, the unknown decision which was to create the happiness or misery of my afternoon. It was a whole state of the soul, a whole future existence that had assumed before my eyes the allegorical and fatal form of a girl. And when at last I made up my mind, when with the most indifferent air that I could muster, I asked: 'Are we to go out together now, and again this evening?' and she replied: 'With the greatest pleasure,' then the sudden replacement, in the rosy face, of my long uneasiness by a delicious sense of ease made even more precious to me those outlines to which I was perpetually indebted for the comfort, the relief that we feel after a storm has broken. I repeated to myself: 'How sweet she is, what an adorable creature!' in an excitement less fertile than that caused by intoxication, scarcely more profound than that of friendship, but far superior to the excitement of social life. We cancelled our order for the car only on the days when there was a dinner-party at the Verdurins' and on those when, Albertine not being free to go out with me, I took the opportunity to inform anybody who wished to see me that I should be remaining at Balbec. I gave Saint-Loup permission to come on these days, but on these days only. For on one occasion when he had arrived unexpectedly, I had preferred to forego the pleasure of seeing Albertine rather than run the risk of his meeting her, than endanger the state of happy calm in which I had been dwelling for some time and see my jealousy revive. And I had been at my ease only after Saint-Loup had gone. And so he pledged himself, with regret, but with scrupulous observance, never to come to Balbec unless summoned there by myself. In the past, when I thought with longing of the hours that Mme de Guermantes passed in his company, how I valued the privilege of seeing him! Other people never cease to change places in relation to ourselves. In the imperceptible but eternal march of the world, we regard them as motionless in a moment of vision, too short for us to perceive the motion that is sweeping them on. But we have only to select in our memory two pictures taken of them at different moments, close enough together however for them not to have altered in themselves – perceptibly, that is to say – and the difference between the two pictures is a measure of the displacement that they have undergone in relation to us. He alarmed me dreadfully by talking to me of the Verdurins, I was afraid that he might ask me to take him there, which would have been quite enough, what with the jealousy that I should be feeling all the time, to spoil all the pleasure that I found in going there with Albertine. But fortunately Robert assured me that, on the contrary, the one thing he desired above all others was not to know them. 'No,' he said to me, 'I find that sort of clerical atmosphere maddening.' I did not at first understand the application of the adjective clerical to the Verdurins, but the end of Saint-Loup's speech threw a light on his meaning, his concessions to those fashions in words which one is often astonished to see adopted by intelligent men. 'I mean the houses,' he said, 'where people form a tribe, a religious order, a chapel. You aren't going to tell me that they're not a little sect; they're all butter and honey to the people who belong, no words bad enough for those who don't. The question is not, as for Hamlet, to be or not to be, but to belong or not to belong. You belong, my uncle Charlus belongs. I can't help it, I never have gone in for that sort of thing, it isn't my fault.'

I need hardly say that the rule which I had imposed upon Saint-Loup, never to come and see me unless I had expressly invited him, I promulgated no less strictly for all and sundry of the persons with whom I had gradually begun to associate at la Raspelière, Féterne, Montsurvent, and elsewhere; and when I saw from the hotel the smoke of the three o'clock train which in the anfractuosity of the cliffs of Parville left its stable plume which long remained hanging from the flank of the green slopes, I had no hesitation as to the identity of the visitor who was coming to tea with me and was still, like a classical deity, concealed from me by that little cloud. I am obliged to confess that this visitor, authorised by me beforehand to come, was hardly ever Saniette, and I have often reproached myself for this omission. But Saniette's own consciousness of his being a bore (far more so, naturally, when he came to pay a call than when he told a story) had the effect that, albeit he was more learned, more intelligent and a better man all round than most people, it seemed impossible to feel in his company, I do not say any pleasure, but anything save an almost intolerable irritation which spoiled one's whole afternoon. Probably if Saniette had frankly admitted this boredom which he was afraid of causing, one would not have dreaded his visits. Boredom is one of the least of the evils that we have to endure, his boringness existed perhaps only in the imagination of other people, or had been inoculated into him by them by some process of suggestion which had taken root in his charming modesty. But he was so anxious not to let it be seen that he was not sought after, that he dared not offer himself. Certainly he was right in not behaving like the people who are so glad to be able to raise their hats in a public place, that when, not having seen you for years, they catch sight of you in a box with smart people whom they do not know, they give you a furtive but resounding good-evening, seeking an excuse in the pleasure, the emotion that they felt on seeing you, on learning that you are going about again, that you are looking well, etc. Saniette, on the contrary, was lacking in courage. He might, at Mme Verdurin's or in the little tram, have told me that it would give him great pleasure to come and see me at Balbec, were he not afraid of disturbing me. Such a suggestion would not have alarmed me. On the contrary, he offered nothing, but with a tortured expression on his face and a stare as indestructible as a fired enamel, into the composition of which, however, there entered, with a passionate desire to see one – provided he did not find someone else who was more entertaining – the determination not to let this desire be manifest, said to me with a detached air: 'You don't happen to know what you will be doing in the next few days, because I shall probably be somewhere in the neighbourhood of Balbec? Not that it makes the slightest difference, I just thought I would ask you.' This air deceived nobody, and the inverse signs whereby we express our sentiments by their opposites are so clearly legible that we ask ourselves how there can still be people who say, for instance: 'I have so many invitations that I don't know where to lay my head' to conceal the fact that they have been invited nowhere. But what was more, this detached air, probably on account of the heterogeneous elements that had gone to form it, gave you, what you would never have felt in the fear of boredom or in a frank admission of the desire to see you, that is to say that sort of distaste, of repulsion, which in the category of relations of simple social courtesy corresponds to – in that of love – the disguised offer made to a lady by the lover whom she does not love to see her on the following day, he protesting the while that it does not really matter, or indeed not that offer but an attitude of false coldness. There emanated at once from Saniette's person something or other which made you answer him in the tenderest of tones: 'No, unfortunately, this week, I must explain to you . . . ' And I allowed to call upon me instead people who were a long way his inferiors but had not his gaze charged with melancholy or his mouth wrinkled with all the bitterness of all the calls which he longed, while saying nothing about them, to pay upon this person and that. Unfortunately it was very rarely that Saniette did not meet in the 'crawler' the guest who was coming to see me, if indeed the latter had not said to me at the Verdurins': 'Don't forget, I'm coming to see you on Thursday', the very day on which I had just told Saniette that I should not be at home. So that he came in the end to imagine life as filled with entertainments arranged behind his back, if not actually at his expense. On the other hand, as none of us is ever a single person, this too discreet of men was morbidly indiscreet. On the one occasion on which he happened to come and see me uninvited, a letter, I forget from whom, had been left lying on my table. After the first few minutes, I saw that he was paying only the vaguest attention to what I was saying. The letter, of whose subject he knew absolutely nothing, fascinated him and at every moment I expected his glittering eyeballs to detach themselves from their sockets and fly to the letter which, of no importance in itself, his curiosity had made magnetic. You would have called him a bird about to dash into the jaws of a serpent. Finally he could restrain himself no longer, he began by altering its position, as though he were trying to tidy my room. This not sufficing him, he took it up, turned it over, turned it back again, as though mechanically. Another form of his indiscretion was that once he had fastened himself to you he could not tear himself away. As I was feeling unwell that day, I asked him to go back by the next train, in half-an-hour's time. He did not doubt that I was feeling unwell, but replied: 'I shall stay for an hour and a quarter, and then I shall go.' Since then I have regretted that I did not tell him, whenever I had an opportunity, to come and see me. Who knows? Possibly I might have charmed away his ill fortune, other people would have invited him for whom he would immediately have deserted myself, so that my invitations would have had the twofold advantage of giving him pleasure and ridding me of his company.

On the days following those on which I had been 'at home', I naturally did not expect any visitors and the motorcar would come to fetch us, Albertine and myself. And, when we returned, Aimé, on the lowest step of the hotel, could not help looking, with passionate, curious, greedy eyes, to see what tip I was giving the chauffeur. It was no use my enclosing my coin or note in my clenched fist, Aimé's gaze tore my fingers apart. He turned his head away a moment later, for he was discreet, well bred, and indeed was himself content with relatively small wages. But the money that another person received aroused in him an irrepressible curiosity and made his mouth water. During these brief moments, he wore the attentive, feverish air of a boy reading one of Jules Verne's tales, or of a diner seated at a neighbouring table in a restaurant who, seeing the waiter carving for you a pheasant which he himself either could not afford or would not order, abandons for an instant his serious thoughts to fasten upon the bird a gaze which love and longing cause to smile.

And so, day after day, these excursions in the motorcar followed one another. But once, as I was being taken up to my room, the lift-boy said to me: 'That gentleman has been, he gave me a message for you.' The lift-boy uttered these words in an almost inaudible voice, coughing and expectorating in my face. 'I haven't half caught cold!' he went on, as though I were incapable of perceiving this for myself. 'The doctor says it's whooping-cough,' and he began once more to cough and expectorate over me. 'Don't tire yourself by trying to speak,' I said to him with an air of kindly interest, which was feigned. I was afraid of catching the whooping-cough which, with my tendency to choking fits, would have been a serious matter to me. But he made a point of honour, like a virtuoso who refuses to let himself be taken to hospital, of talking and expectorating all the time. 'No, it doesn't matter,' he said ('Perhaps not to you,' I thought, 'but to me it does'). 'Besides, I shall be returning soon to Paris.' ('Excellent, provided he doesn't give it to me first.') 'It seems,' he went on, 'that Paris is quite superb. It must be even more superb than here or Monte-Carlo, although pages, in fact visitors, and even head waiters who have been to Monte-Carlo for the season have often told me that Paris was not so superb as Monte-Carlo. They were cheated, perhaps, and yet, to be a head waiter, you've got to have your wits about you; to take all the orders, reserve tables, you need a head! I've heard it said that it's even more terrible than writing plays and books.' We had almost reached my landing when the lift-boy carried me down again to the ground floor because he found that the button was not working properly, and in a moment had put it right. I told him that I preferred to walk upstairs, by which I meant, without putting it in so many words, that I preferred not to catch whooping-cough. But with a cordial and contagious burst of coughing the boy thrust me back into the

lift. 'There's no danger now, I've fixed the button.' Seeing that he was not
ceasing to talk, preferring to learn the name of my visitor and the message
that he had left, rather than the comparative beauties of Balbec, Paris and
Monte-Carlo, I said to him (as one might say to a tenor who is wearying one
with Benjamin Godard, 'Won't you sing me some Debussy?') 'But who is
the person that called to see me?' 'It's the gentleman you went out with
yesterday. I am going to fetch his card, it's with my porter.' As, the day
before, I had dropped Robert de Saint-Loup at Doncières station before
going to meet Albertine, I supposed that the lift-boy was referring to him,
but it was the chauffeur. And by describing him in the words: 'The
gentleman you went out with,' he taught me at the same time that a working
man is just as much a gentleman as a man about town. A lesson in the use of
words only. For in point of fact I had never made any distinction between
the classes. And if I had felt, on hearing a chauffeur called a gentleman, the
same astonishment as Comte X who had only held that rank for a week and
whom, by saying: 'the Comtesse looks tired', I made turn his head round to
see who it was that I meant, it was simply because I was not familiar with that
use of the word; I had never made any difference between working men,
professional men and noblemen, and I should have been equally ready to
make any of them my friends. With a certain preference for the working
men, and after them for the noblemen, not because I liked them better, but
because I knew that one could expect greater courtesy from them towards
the working men than one finds among professional men, whether because
the great nobleman does not despise the working man as the professional
man does or else because they are naturally polite to anybody, as beautiful
women are glad to bestow a smile which they know to be so joyfully
received. I cannot however pretend that this habit that I had of putting
people of humble station on a level with people in society, even if it was
quite understood by the latter, was always entirely satisfactory to my mother.
Not that, humanly speaking, she made any difference between one person
and another, and if Françoise was ever in sorrow or in pain she was
comforted and tended by Mamma with the same devotion as her best
friend. But my mother was too much my grandmother's daughter not to
accept, in social matters, the rule of caste. People at Combray might have
kind hearts, sensitive natures, might have adopted the most perfect theories
of human equality, my mother, when a footman became emancipated,
began to say 'you' and slipped out of the habit of addressing me in the third
person, was moved by these presumptions to the same wrath that breaks out
in Saint-Simon's *Memoirs*, whenever a nobleman who is not entitled to it
seizes a pretext for assuming the style of 'Highness' in an official document,

or for not paying dukes the deference he owes to them and is gradually beginning to lay aside. There was a 'Combray spirit' so refractory that it will require centuries of good nature (my mother's was boundless), of theories of equality, to succeed in dissolving it. I cannot swear that in my mother certain particles of this spirit had not remained insoluble. She would have been as reluctant to give her hand to a footman as she would have been ready to give him ten francs (which for that matter he was far more glad to receive). To her, whether she admitted it or not, masters were masters, and servants were the people who fed in the kitchen. When she saw the driver of a motorcar dining with me in the restaurant, she was not altogether pleased, and said to me: 'It seems to me you might have a more suitable friend than a mechanic', as she might have said, had it been a question of my marriage: 'You might find somebody better than that.' This particular chauffeur (fortunately I never dreamed of inviting him to dinner) had come to tell me that the motorcar company which had sent him to Balbec for the season had ordered him to return to Paris on the following day. This excuse, especially as the chauffeur was charming and expressed himself so simply that one would always have taken anything he said for Gospel, seemed to us to be most probably true. It was only half so. There was as a matter of fact no more work for him at Balbec. And in any case, the Company being only half convinced of the veracity of the young Evangelist, bowed over the consecration cross of his steering-wheel, was anxious that he should return as soon as possible to Paris. And indeed if the young Apostle wrought a miracle in multiplying his mileage when he was calculating it for M. de Charlus, when on the other hand it was a matter of rendering his account to the Company, he divided what he had earned by six. In consequence of which the Company, coming to the conclusion either that nobody wanted a car now at Balbec, which, so late in the season, was quite probable, or that it was being robbed, decided that, upon either hypothesis, the best thing was to recall him to Paris, not that there was very much work for him there. What the chauffeur wished was to avoid, if possible, the dead season. I have said – though I was unaware of this at the time, when the knowledge of it would have saved me much annoyance – that he was on intimate terms (without their ever showing any sign of acquaintance before other people) with Morel. Starting from the day on which he was ordered back, before he realised that there was still a way out of going, we were obliged to content ourselves for our excursions with hiring a carriage, or sometimes, as an amusement for Albertine and because she was fond of riding, a pair of saddle-horses. The carriages were unsatisfactory. 'What a rattle-trap,' Albertine would say. I would often, as it happened, have preferred to be driving by myself. Without being ready to fix a date, I longed to put an end to this existence which I blamed for making me renounce not so much work as pleasure. It would happen also, however, that the habits which bound me were suddenly abolished, generally when some former self, full of the desire to live a merry life, took the place of what was my self at the moment. I felt this longing to escape especially strong one day when, having left Albertine at her aunt's, I had gone on horseback to call on the Verdurins and had taken an unfrequented path through the woods the beauty of which they had extolled to me. Clinging to the outline of the cliffs, it alternately climbed and then, hemmed in by dense woods on either side, dived into savage gorges. For a moment the barren rocks by which I was surrounded, the sea visible in their jagged intervals, swam before my eyes, like fragments of another universe: I had recognised the mountainous and marine landscape which Elstir had made the scene of those two admirable watercolours: 'Poet meeting a Muse', 'Young Man meeting a Centaur', which I had seen at the Duchesse de Guermantes's. The thought of them transported the place in which I was so far beyond the world of today that I should not have been surprised if, like the young man of the prehistoric age that Elstir painted, I had in the course of my ride come upon a mythological personage. Suddenly, my horse gave a start; he had heard a strange sound; it was all I could do to hold him and remain in the saddle, then I raised in the direction from which the sound seemed to come my eyes filled with tears and saw, not two hundred feet above my head, against the sun, between two great wings of flashing metal which were carrying him on, a creature whose barely visible face appeared to me to resemble that of a man. I was as deeply moved as a Greek upon seeing for the first time a demigod. I cried also, for I was ready to cry the moment I realised that the sound came from above my head – aeroplanes were still rare in those days – at the thought that what I was going to see for the first time was an aeroplane. Then, just as when in a newspaper one feels that one is coming to a moving passage, the mere sight of the machine was enough to make me burst into tears. Meanwhile the airman seemed to be uncertain of his course; I felt that there lay open before him – before me, had not habit made me a prisoner – all the routes in space, in life itself; he flew on, let himself glide for a few moments, over the sea, then quickly making up his mind, seeming to yield to some attraction the reverse of gravity, as though returning to his native element, with a slight movement of his golden wings, rose sheer into the sky.

To come back to the mechanic, he demanded of Morel that the Verdurins should not merely replace their brake by a motorcar (which, granted their generosity towards the faithful, was comparatively easy), but, what was less easy, replace their head coachman, the sensitive young man who was inclined to dark thoughts, by himself, the chauffeur. This change was carried out in a few days by the following device. Morel had begun by seeing that the coachman was robbed of everything that he needed for the carriage. One day it was the bit that was missing, another day the curb. At other times it was the cushion of his box-seat that had vanished, or his whip, his rug, his hammer, sponge, chamois-leather. But he always managed to borrow what he required from a neighbour; only he was late in bringing round the carriage, which put him in M. Verdurin's bad books and plunged him in a state of melancholy and dark thoughts. The chauffeur, who was in a hurry to take his place, told Morel that he would have to return to Paris. It was time to do something desperate. Morel persuaded M. Verdurin's servants that the young coachman had declared that he would set a trap for the lot of them, boasting that he could take on all six of them at once, and assured them that they could not overlook such an insult. He himself could not take any part in the quarrel, but he warned them so that they might be on their guard. It was arranged that while M. and Mme Verdurin and their guests were out walking the servants should fall upon the young man in the coach house. I may mention, although it was only the pretext for what was bound to happen, but because the people concerned interested me later on, that the Verdurins had a friend staying with them that day whom they had promised to take for a walk before his departure, which was fixed for that same evening.

What surprised me greatly when we started off for our walk was that Morel, who was coming with us, and was to play his violin under the trees, said to me: 'Listen, I have a sore arm, I don't want to say anything about it to Mme Verdurin, but you might ask her to send for one of her footmen, Howsler for instance, he can carry my things.' 'I think you ought to suggest someone else,' I replied. 'He will be wanted here for dinner.' A look of anger passed over Morel's face. 'No, I'm not going to trust my violin to any Tom, Dick or Harry.' I realised later on his reason for this selection. Howsler was the beloved brother of the young coachman, and, if he had been left at home, might have gone to his rescue. During our walk, dropping his voice so that the elder Howsler should not overhear: 'What a good fellow he is,' said Morel. 'So is his brother, for that matter. If he hadn't that fatal habit of drinking . . . ' 'Did you say drinking?' said Mme Verdurin, turning pale at the idea of having a coachman who drank. 'You've never noticed it. I always say to myself it's a miracle that he's never had an accident while he's been driving you.' 'Does he drive anyone else, then?' 'You can easily see how many spills he's had, his face today is a mass of bruises. I don't know how he's escaped being killed, he's broken his shafts.' 'I haven't seen him today,' said Mme' Verdurin, trembling at the thought of what might have happened to her, 'you appal me.' She tried to cut short the walk so as to return at once, but Morel chose an aria by Bach with endless variations to keep her away from the house. As soon as we got back she went to the stable, saw the new shaft and Howsler streaming with blood. She was on the point of telling him, without making any comment on what she had seen, that she did not require a coachman any longer, and of paying him his wages, but of his own accord, not wishing to accuse his fellow-servants, to whose animosity he attributed retrospectively the theft of all his saddlery, and seeing that further patience would only end in his being left for dead on the ground, he asked leave to go at once, which made everything quite simple. The chauffeur began his duties next day and, later on, Mme Verdurin (who had been obliged to engage another) was so well satisfied with him that she recommended him to me warmly, as a man on whom I might rely. I, knowing nothing of all this, used to engage him by the day in Paris, but I am anticipating events, I shall come to all this when I reach the story of Albertine. At the present moment we are at la Raspelière, where I have just been dining for the first time with my mistress, and M. de Charlus with Morel, the reputed son of an 'Agent' who drew a fixed salary of thirty thousand francs annually, kept his carriage, and had any number of major-domos, subordinates, gardeners, bailiffs and farmers at his beck and call. But, since I have so far anticipated, I do not wish to leave the reader under the impression that Morel was entirely wicked. He was, rather, a mass of contradictions, capable on certain days of being genuinely kind.

I was naturally greatly surprised to hear that the coachman had been dismissed, and even more surprised when I recognised his successor as the chauffeur who had been taking Albertine and myself in his car. But he poured out a complicated story, according to which he had thought that he was summoned back to Paris, where an order had come for him to go to the Verdurins, and I did not doubt his word for an instant. The coachman's dismissal was the cause of Morel's talking to me for a few minutes, to express his regret at the departure of that worthy fellow. However, even apart from the moments when I was alone, and he literally bounded towards me beaming with joy, Morel, seeing that everybody made much of me at la Raspelière and feeling that he was deliberately cutting himself off from the society of a person who could in no way imperil him, since he had made me burn my boats and had destroyed all possibility of my treating him with an air of patronage (which I had never, for that matter, dreamed of adopting), ceased to hold aloof from me. I attributed his change of attitude to the influence of M. de Charlus, which as a matter of fact did make him in certain respects less limited, more of an artist, but in others, when he interpreted literally the eloquent, insincere, and moreover transient formulas of his master, made him stupider than ever. That M. de Charlus might have said something to him was as a matter of fact the only thing that occurred to me. How was I to have guessed then what I was told afterwards (and have never been certain of its truth, Andrée's assertions as to everything that concerned Albertine, especially later on, having always seemed to me to be statements to be received with caution, for, as we have already seen, she was not genuinely fond of my mistress and was jealous of her), a thing which in any event, even if it was true, was remarkably well concealed from me by both of them: that Albertine was on the best of terms with Morel? The novel attitude which, about the time of the coachman's dismissal, Morel adopted with regard to myself, enabled me to change my opinion of him. I retained the ugly impression of his character which had been suggested by the servility which this young man had shown me when he needed my services, followed, as soon as the service had been rendered, by a scornful aloofness as though he did not even see me. I still lacked evidence of his venal relations with M. de Charlus, and also of his bestial and purposeless instincts, the non-gratification of which (when it occurred) or the complications that they involved, were the cause of his sorrows; but his character was not so uniformly vile and was full of contradictions. He resembled an old book of the middle ages, full of mistakes, of absurd traditions, of obscenities; he was extraordinarily composite. I had supposed at first that his art, in which he was really a past-master, had given him superiorities that went beyond the virtuosity of the mere performer. Once when I spoke of my wish to start work: 'Work, become famous,' he said to me. 'Who said that?' I enquired. 'Fontanes, to Chateaubriand.' He also knew certain love letters of Napoleon. Good, I thought to myself, he reads. But this phrase which he had read I know not where was doubtless the only one that he knew in the whole of ancient or modern literature, for he repeated it to me every evening. Another which he quoted even more frequently to prevent me from breathing a word about him to anybody was the following, which he considered equally literary, whereas it is barely grammatical, or at any rate makes no kind of sense, except perhaps to a mystery-loving servant: 'Beware of the wary.' As a matter of fact, if one cast back from this stupid maxim to what Fontanes had said to Chateaubriand, one explored a whole side, varied but less contradictory than one might suppose, of Morel's character. This youth who, provided there was money to be made by it, would have done anything in the world, and without remorse – perhaps not without an odd sort of vexation, amounting to nervous excitement, to which however the name remorse could not for a moment be applied – who would, had it been to his advantage, have plunged in distress, not to say mourning, whole families, this youth who set money above everything, above, not to speak of unselfish kindness, the most natural sentiments of common humanity, this same youth nevertheless set above money his certificate as first-prize winner at the Conservatoire and the risk of there being anything said to his discredit in the flute or counterpoint class. And so his most violent rages, his most sombre and unjustifiable fits of ill-temper arose from what he himself (generalising doubtless from certain particular cases in which he had met with spiteful people) called universal treachery. He flattered himself that he escaped from this fault by never speaking about anyone, by concealing his tactics, by distrusting everybody. (Alas for me, in view of what was to happen after my return to Paris, his distrust had not 'held' in the case of the Balbec chauffeur, in whom he had doubtless recognised a peer, that is to say, in contradiction of his maxim, a wary person in the good sense of the word, a wary person who remains obstinately silent before honest folk and at once comes to an understanding with a blackguard.) It seemed to him – and he was not absolutely wrong – that his distrust would enable him always to save his bacon, to slip unscathed out of the most perilous adventures, without anyone's being able not indeed to prove but even to suggest anything against him, in the institution in the Rue Bergère. He would work, become famous, would perhaps be one day, with his respectability still intact, examiner in the violin on the Board of that great and glorious Conservatoire.

But it is perhaps crediting Morel's brain with too much logic to attempt to discriminate between these contradictions. As a matter of fact his nature was just like a sheet of paper that has been folded so often in every direction that it is impossible to straighten it out. He seemed to act upon quite lofty principles, and in a magnificent hand, marred by the most elementary mistakes in spelling, spent hours writing to his brother that he had behaved badly to his sisters, that he was their elder, their natural support, etc., and to his sisters that they had shown a want of respect for himself.

Presently, as summer came to an end, when one got out of the train at Douville, the sun dimmed by the prevailing mist had ceased to be anything more in a sky that was uniformly mauve than a lump of redness. To the great peace which descends at nightfall over these tufted salt-marshes, and had tempted a number of Parisians, painters mostly, to spend their holidays at Douville, was added a moisture which made them seek shelter early in their little bungalows. In several of these the lamp was already lighted. Only a few cows remained out of doors gazing at the sea and lowing, while others, more interested in humanity, turned their attention towards our carriages. A single painter who had set up his easel where the ground rose slightly was striving to render that great calm, that hushed luminosity. Perhaps the cattle were going to serve him unconsciously and kindly as models, for their contemplative air and their solitary presence when the human beings had withdrawn, contributed in their own way to enhance the strong impression of repose that evening conveys. And, a few weeks later, the transposition was no less agreeable when, as autumn advanced, the days became really short, and we were obliged to make our journey in the dark. If I had been out anywhere in the afternoon, I had to go back to change my clothes, at the latest, by five o'clock, when at this season the round, red sun had already sunk half way down the slanting sheet of glass, which formerly I had detested, and, like a Greek fire, was inflaming the sea in the glass fronts of all my bookcases. Some wizard's gesture having revived, as I put on my dinner-jacket, the alert and frivolous self that was mine when I used to go with Saint-Loup to dine at Rivebelle and on the evening when I looked forward to taking Mme de Stermaria to dine on the island in the Bois, I began unconsciously to hum the same tune that I had hummed then; and it was only when I realised this that by the song I recognised the resurrected singer, who indeed knew no other tune. The first time that I sang it, I was beginning to be in love with Albertine, but I imagined that I would never get to know her. Later on, in Paris, it was when I had ceased to be in love with her and some days after I had enjoyed her for the first time. Now it was when I was in love with her again and on the point of going out to dinner with her, to the great regret of the manager who supposed that I would end by staying at la Raspelière altogether and deserting his hotel, and assured me that he had heard that fever was prevalent in that neighbourhood, due to the marshes of the Bec and their 'stagnous' water. I was delighted by the multiplicity in which I saw my life thus spread over three planes; and besides, when one becomes for an instant one's former self, that is to say different from what one has been for some time past, one's sensibility, being no longer dulled by habit, receives the slightest shocks of those vivid impressions which make everything that has preceded them fade into insignificance, and to which, because of their intensity, we attach ourselves with the momentary enthusiasm of a drunken man. It was already night when we got into the omnibus or carriage which was to take us to the station where we would find the little train. And in the hall the chief magistrate was saying to us: 'Ah! You are going to la Raspelière! Sapristi, she has a nerve, your Mme Verdurin, to make you travel an hour by train in the dark, simply to dine with her. And then to start off again at ten o'clock at night, with a

wind blowing like the very devil. It is easy to see that you have nothing else
to do,' he added, rubbing his hands together. No doubt he spoke thus from
annoyance at not having been invited, and also from the satisfaction that
people feel who are 'busy' – though it be with the most idiotic occupation –
at 'not having time' to do what you are doing.

Certainly it is only right that the man who draws up reports, adds up
figures, answers business letters, follows the movements of the stock
exchange, should feel when he says to you with a sneer: 'It's all very well for
you; you have nothing better to do', an agreeable sense of his own
superiority. But this would be no less contemptuous, would be even more
so (for dining out is a thing that the busy man does also) were your
recreation writing *Hamlet* or merely reading it. Wherein busy men show a
want of reflection. For the disinterested culture which seems to them a
comic pastime of idle people at the moment when they find them engaged
in it is, they ought to remember, the same that in their own profession
brings to the fore men who may not be better magistrates or administrators
than themselves but before whose rapid advancement they bow their heads,
saying: 'It appears he's a great reader, a most distinguished individual.' But
above all the chief magistrate did not take into account that what pleased
me about these dinners at la Raspelière was that, as he himself said quite
rightly, though as a criticism, they 'meant a regular journey', a journey
whose charm appeared to me all the more thrilling in that it was not an
object in itself, and no one made any attempt to find pleasure in it – that
being reserved for the party for which we were bound, and greatly modified
by all the atmosphere that surrounded it. It was already night now when I
exchanged the warmth of the hotel – the hotel that had become my home –
for the railway carriage into which I climbed with Albertine, in which a
glimmer of lamplight on the window showed, at certain halts of the panting
little train, that we had arrived at a station. So that there should be no risk of
Cottard's missing us, and not having heard the name of the station, I
opened the door, but what burst headlong into the carriage was not any of
the faithful, but the wind, the rain, the cold. In the darkness I could make
out fields, I could hear the sea, we were in the open country. Albertine,
before we were engulfed in the little nucleus, examined herself in a little
mirror, extracted from a gold bag which she carried about with her. The
fact was that on our first visit, Mme Verdurin having taken her upstairs to
her dressing-room so that she might make herself tidy before dinner, I had
felt, amid the profound calm in which I had been living for some time, a
slight stir of uneasiness and jealousy at being obliged to part from Albertine
at the foot of the stair, and had become so anxious while I was by myself in

the drawing-room, among the little clan, and asking myself what my mistress could be doing, that I had sent a telegram the next day, after finding out from M. de Charlus what the correct thing was at the moment, to order from Cartier's a bag which was the joy of Albertine's life and also of mine. It was for me a guarantee of peace of mind, and also of my mistress's solicitude. For she had evidently seen that I did not like her to be parted from me at Mme Verdurin's and arranged to make in the train all the toilet that was necessary before dinner.

Included in the number of Mme Verdurin's regular frequenters, and reckoned the most faithful of them all, had been, for some months now, M. de Charlus. Regularly, thrice weekly, the passengers who were sitting in the waiting-rooms or standing upon the platform at Doncières-Ouest used to see that stout gentleman go past with his grey hair, his black moustaches, his lips reddened with a salve less noticeable at the end of the season than in summer when the daylight made it more crude and the heat used to melt it. As he made his way towards the little train, he could not refrain (simply from force of habit, as a connoisseur, since he now had a sentiment which kept him chaste, or at least, for most of the time, faithful) from casting at the labourers, soldiers, young men in tennis flannels, a furtive glance at once inquisitorial and timorous, after which he immediately let his eyelids droop over his half-shut eyes with the unction of an ecclesiastic engaged in telling his beads, with the modesty of a bride vowed to the one love of her life or of a well-brought-up girl. The faithful were all the more convinced that he had not seen them, since he got into a different compartment from theirs (as, often enough, did Princess Sherbatov also), like a man who does not know whether people will be pleased or not to be seen with him and leaves them the option of coming and joining him if they choose. This option had not been taken, at first, by the Doctor, who had asked us to leave him by himself in his compartment. Making a virtue of his natural hesitation now that he occupied a great position in the medical world, it was with a smile, throwing back his head, looking at Ski over his glasses, that he said, either from malice or in the hope of eliciting the opinion of the 'comrades': 'You can understand that if I was by myself, a bachelor, but for my wife's sake I ask myself whether I ought to allow him to travel with us after what you have told me,' the Doctor whispered. 'What's that you're saying?' asked Mme Cottard. 'Nothing, it doesn't concern you, it's not meant for ladies to hear,' the Doctor replied with a wink, and with a majestic self-satisfaction which held the balance between the dryly malicious air he adopted before his pupils and patients and the uneasiness that used in the past to accompany his shafts of wit at the Verdurins', and went on talking in a lowered tone. Mme Cottard could make out only the words 'one of the brotherhood' and '*tapette*', and as in the Doctor's vocabulary the former expression denoted the Jewish race and the latter a wagging tongue, Mme Cottard concluded that M. de Charlus must be a garrulous Israelite. She could not understand why people should keep aloof from the Baron for that reason, felt it her duty as the senior lady of the clan to insist that he should not be left alone, and so we proceeded in a body to M. de Charlus's compartment, led by Cottard who was still perplexed. From the corner in which he was reading a volume of Balzac, M. de Charlus observed this hesitation; and yet he had not raised his eyes. But just as deaf-mutes detect, from a movement of the air imperceptible to other people, that someone is standing behind them, so he had, to warn him of other people's coldness towards him, a positive hyperaesthesia. This had, as it habitually does in every sphere, developed in M. de Charlus imaginary sufferings. Like those neuropaths who, feeling a slight lowering of the temperature, induce from this that there must be a window open on the floor above, become violently excited and start sneezing, M. de Charlus, if a person appeared preoccupied in his presence, concluded that somebody had repeated to that person a remark that he had made about him. But there was no need even for the other person to have a distracted, or a sombre, or a smiling air, he would invent them. On the other hand, cordiality completely concealed from him the slanders of which he had not heard.

Having begun by detecting Cottard's hesitation, if, greatly to the surprise of the faithful who did not suppose that their presence had yet been observed by the reader's lowered gaze, he held out his hand to them when they were at a convenient distance, he contented himself with a forward inclination of his whole person which he quickly drew back for Cottard, without taking in his own gloved hand the hand which the Doctor had held out to him. 'We felt we simply must come and keep you company, Sir, and not leave you alone like that in your little corner. It is a great pleasure to us,' Mme Cottard began in a friendly tone to the Baron. 'I am greatly honoured,' the Baron intoned, bowing coldly. 'I was so pleased to hear that you have definitely chosen this neighbourhood to set up your taber . . . ' She was going to say 'tabernacle' but it occurred to her that the word was Hebraic and discourteous to a Jew who might see an allusion in it. And so she paused for a moment to choose another of the expressions that were familiar to her, that is to say a consecrated expression: 'to set up, I should say, your *penates*.' (It is true that these deities do not appertain to the Christian religion either, but to one which has been dead for so long that it no longer claims any devotees whose feelings one need be afraid of hurting.) 'We, unfortunately, what with term beginning, and the Doctor's hospital duties, can never choose our domicile for very long in one place.' And glancing at a cardboard box: 'You see too how we poor women are less fortunate than the sterner sex; to go only such a short distance as to our friends the Verdurins, we are obliged to take a whole heap of impedimenta.' I meanwhile was examining the Baron's volume of Balzac. It was not a paper-covered copy, picked up on a bookstall, like the volume of Bergotte which he had lent me at our first meeting. It was a book from his own library, and as such bore the device: 'I belong to the Baron de Charlus', for which was substituted at times, to show the studious tastes of the Guermantes: '*In proeliis non semper*', or yet another motto: '*Non sine labore*'. But we shall see these presently replaced by others, in an attempt to please Morel. Mme Cottard, a little later, hit upon a subject which she felt to be of more personal interest to the Baron. 'I don't know whether you agree with me, Sir,' she said to him presently, 'but I hold very broad views, and, to my mind, there is a great deal of good in all religions. I am not one of the people who get hydrophobia at the sight of a . . . Protestant.' 'I was taught that mine is the true religion,' replied M. de Charlus. 'He's a fanatic,' thought Mme Cottard, 'Swann, until recently, was more tolerant; it is true that he was a converted one.' Now, so far from this being the case, the Baron was not only a Christian, as we know, but pious with a mediaeval fervour. To him as to the sculptors of the middle ages, the Christian church was, in the living sense of the word, peopled with a swarm of beings, whom he believed to be entirely real, Prophets, Apostles, Angels, holy personages of every sort, surrounding the Incarnate Word, His Mother and Her Spouse, the Eternal Father, all the Martyrs and Doctors of the Church, as they may be seen carved in high relief, thronging the porches or lining the naves of the cathedrals. Out of all these M. de Charlus had chosen as his patrons and intercessors the Archangels Michael, Gabriel and Raphael, to whom he made frequent appeals that they would convey his prayers to the Eternal Father, about Whose Throne they stand. And so Mme Cottard's mistake amused me greatly.

To leave the religious sphere, let us mention that the Doctor, who had come to Paris meagrely equipped with the counsels of a peasant mother, and had then been absorbed in the almost purely materialistic studies to which those who seek to advance in a medical career are obliged to devote themselves for a great many years, had never become cultured, had acquired increasing authority but never any experience, took the word 'honoured' in its literal meaning and was at once flattered by it because he was vain and distressed because he had a kind heart. 'That poor de Charlus,' he said to his wife that evening, 'made me feel sorry for him when he said he was honoured by travelling with us. One feels, poor devil, that he knows nobody, that he has to humble himself.'

But presently, without any need to be guided by the charitable Mme Cottard, the faithful had succeeded in overcoming the qualms which they had all more or less felt at first, on finding themselves in the company of M. de Charlus. No doubt in his presence they were incessantly reminded of Ski's revelations, and conscious of the sexual abnormality embodied in their travelling companion. But this abnormality itself had a sort of attraction for them. It gave for them to the Baron's conversation, remarkable in itself but in ways which they could scarcely appreciate, a savour which made the most interesting conversation, that of Brichot himself, appear slightly insipid in comparison. From the very outset, moreover, they had been pleased to admit that he was intelligent. 'The genius that is perhaps akin to madness,' the Doctor declaimed, and albeit the Princess, athirst for knowledge, insisted, said not another word, this axiom being all that he knew about genius and seeming to him less supported by proof than our knowledge of typhoid fever and arthritis. And as he had become proud and remained ill-bred: 'No questions, Princess, do not interrogate me, I am at the seaside for a rest. Besides, you would not understand, you know nothing about medicine.' And the Princess held her peace with apologies, deciding that Cottard was a charming man and realising that celebrities were not always approachable. In this initial period, then, they had ended by finding M. de Charlus an agreeable person notwithstanding his vice (or what is generally so named). Now it was, quite unconsciously, because of that vice that they found him more intelligent than the rest. The most simple maxims to which, adroitly provoked by the sculptor or the don, M. de Charlus gave utterance concerning love, jealousy, beauty, in view of the experience, strange, secret, refined and monstrous, upon which he founded them, assumed for the faithful that charm of unfamiliarity with which a psychology analogous to that which our own dramatic literature has always offered us bedecks itself in a Russian or Japanese play performed by native actors. One might still venture, when he was not listening, upon a malicious witticism at his expense. 'Oh!' whispered the sculptor, seeing a young railwayman with the sweeping eyelashes of a dancing girl at whom M. de Charlus could not help staring, 'if the Baron begins making eyes at the conductor, we shall never get there, the train will start going backwards. Just look at the way he's staring at him, this is not a steam-tram we're on, it's a funicular.' But when all was said, if M. de Charlus did not appear, it was almost a disappointment to be travelling only with people who were just like everybody else, and not to have by one's side this painted, paunchy, tightly-buttoned personage, reminding one of a box of exotic and dubious origin from which escapes the curious odour of fruits the mere thought of tasting which stirs the heart. From this point of view, the faithful of the masculine sex enjoyed a keener satisfaction in the short stage of the journey between Saint-Martin du Chêne, where M. de Charlus got in, and Doncières, the station at which Morel joined the party. For so long as the violinist was not there (and provided the ladies and Albertine, keeping to themselves so as not to disturb our conversation, were out of hearing), M. de Charlus made no attempt to appear to be avoiding certain subjects and did not hesitate to speak of 'what it is customary to call degenerate morals'. Albertine could not hamper him, for she was always with the ladies, like a well-bred girl who does not wish her presence to restrict the freedom of grown-up conversation. And I was quite resigned to not having her by my side, on condition however that she remained in the same carriage. For I, who no longer felt any jealousy and scarcely any love for her, never thought of what she might be doing on the days when I did not see her; on the other hand, when I was there, a mere partition which might at a pinch be concealing a betrayal was intolerable to me, and if she retired with the ladies to the next compartment, a moment later, unable to remain in my seat any longer, at the risk of offending whoever might be talking, Brichot, Cottard or Charlus, to whom I could not explain the reason for my flight, I would rise, leave them without ceremony, and, to make certain that nothing abnormal was going on, walk down the corridor. And, till we came to Doncières, M. de Charlus, without any fear of shocking his audience, would speak sometimes in the plainest terms of morals which, he declared, for his own part he did not consider either good or evil. He did this from cunning, to show his breadth of mind, convinced as he was that his own morals aroused no suspicion in the minds of the faithful. He was well aware that there did exist in the world several persons who were, to use an expression which became habitual with him later on, 'in the know' about himself. But he imagined that these persons were not more than three or four, and that none of them was at that moment upon the coast of Normandy. This illusion may appear surprising in so shrewd, so suspicious a man. Even in the case of those whom he believed to be more or less well informed, he flattered himself that their information was all quite vague, and hoped, by telling them this or that fact about anyone, to clear the person in question from all suspicion on the part of a listener who out of politeness pretended to accept his statements. Indeed, being uncertain as to what I might know or guess about him, he supposed that my opinion, which he imagined to be of far longer standing than it actually was, was quite general, and that it was sufficient for him to deny this or that detail to be believed, whereas on the contrary, if our knowledge of the whole always precedes our knowledge of details, it makes our investigation of the latter infinitely easier and having destroyed his cloak of invisibility no longer allows the pretender to conceal what he wishes to keep secret. Certainly when M. de Charlus, invited to a dinner-party by one of the faithful or of their friends, took the most complicated precautions to introduce among the names of ten people whom he mentioned that of Morel, he never imagined that for the reasons, always different, which he gave for the pleasure or convenience which he would find that evening in being invited to meet him, his hosts, while appearing to believe him implicitly, substituted a single reason, always the same, of which he supposed them to be ignorant, namely that he was in love with him. Similarly, Mme Verdurin, seeming always entirely to admit the motives, half artistic, half charitable, with which M. de Charlus accounted to her for the interest that he took in Morel, never ceased to thank the Baron with emotion for his kindness – his touching kindness, she called it – to the violinist. And how astonished M. de Charlus would have been, if, one day when Morel and he were delayed and had not come by the train, he had heard the Mistress say: 'We're all here now except the young ladies.' The Baron would have been all the more stupefied in that, going hardly anywhere save to la Raspelière, he played the part there of a family chaplain, like the abbé in a repertory company, and would sometimes (when Morel had 48 hours' leave) sleep there for two nights in succession. Mme Verdurin would then give them communicating rooms and, to put them at their ease, would say: 'If you want to have a little music, don't worry about us, the walls are as thick as a fortress, you have nobody else on your floor, and my husband sleeps like lead.' On such days M. de Charlus would relieve the Princess of the duty of going to meet strangers at the station, apologise for Mme Verdurin's absence on the grounds of a state of health which he described so vividly that the guests entered the drawing-room with solemn faces, and uttered cries of astonishment on finding the Mistress up and doing and wearing what was almost a low dress.

For M. de Charlus had for the moment become for Mme Verdurin the faithfullest of the faithful, a second Princess Sherbatov. Of his position in society she was not nearly so certain as of that of the Princess, imagining that if the latter cared to see no one outside the little nucleus it was out of contempt for other people and preference for it. As this pretence was precisely the Verdurins' own, they treating as bores everyone to whose society they were not admitted, it is incredible that the Mistress can have believed the Princess to possess a heart of steel, detesting what was fashionable. But she stuck to her guns, and was convinced that in the case of the great lady also it was in all sincerity and from a love of things intellectual that she avoided the company of bores. The latter were, as it happened, diminishing in numbers from the Verdurins' point of view. Life by the seaside robbed an introduction of the ulterior consequences which might be feared in Paris. Brilliant men who had come down to Balbec without their wives (which made everything much easier) made overtures to la Raspelière and, from being bores, became too charming. This was the case with the Prince de Guermantes, whom the absence of his Princess would not, however, have decided to go 'as a bachelor' to the Verdurins', had not the lodestone of Dreyfusism been so powerful as to carry him in one stride up the steep ascent to la Raspelière, unfortunately upon à day when the Mistress was not at home. Mme Verdurin as it happened was not certain that he and M. de Charlus moved in the same world. The Baron had indeed said that the Duc de Guermantes was his brother, but this was perhaps the untruthful boast of an adventurer. Man of the world as he had shown himself to be, so friendly, so 'faithful' to the Verdurins, the Mistress still almost hesitated to invite him to meet the Prince de Guermantes. She consulted Ski and Brichot: 'The Baron and the Prince de Guermantes, will they be all right together?' 'Good gracious, Madame, as to one of the two I think I can safely say.' 'What good is that to me?' Mme Verdurin had retorted crossly. 'I asked you whether they would mix well together.' 'Ah! Madame, that is one of the things that it is hard to tell.' Mme Verdurin had been impelled by no malice. She was certain of the Baron's morals, but when she expressed herself in these terms had not been thinking about them for a moment, but had merely wished to know whether she could invite the Prince and M. de Charlus on the same evening, without their clashing. She had no malevolent intention when she employed these ready-made expressions which are popular in artistic 'little clans'. To make the most of M. de Guermantes, she proposed to take him in the afternoon, after her luncheon-party, to a charity entertainment at which sailors from the neighbourhood would give a representation of a ship setting sail. But, not having time to attend to everything, she delegated her duties to the faithfullest of the faithful, the Baron. 'You understand, I don't want them to hang about like mussels on a rock, they must keep moving, we must see them weighing anchor, or whatever it's called. Now you are always going down to the harbour at Balbec-Plage, you can easily arrange a dress rehearsal without tiring yourself. You must know far more than I do, M. de Charlus, about getting hold of sailors. But after all, we're giving ourselves a great deal of trouble for M. de Guermantes. Perhaps he's only one of those idiots from the Jockey Club. Oh! Heavens, I'm running down the Jockey Club, and I seem to remember that you're one of them. Eh, Baron, you don't answer me, are you one of them? You don't care to come out with us? Look, here is a book that has just come, I think you'll find it interesting. It is by Roujon. The title is attractive: *Life among men*.'

For my part, I was all the more glad that M. de Charlus often took the place of Princess Sherbatov, inasmuch as I was thoroughly in her bad books, for a reason that was at once trivial and profound. One day when I was in the little train, paying every attention, as was my habit, to Princess Sherbatov, I saw Mme de Villeparisis get in. She had as a matter of fact come down to spend some weeks with the Princesse de Luxembourg, but, chained to the daily necessity of seeing Albertine, I had never replied to the repeated invitations of the Marquise and her royal hostess. I felt remorse at the sight of my grandmother's friend, and, purely from a sense of duty (without deserting Princess Sherbatov), sat talking to her for some time. I was, as it happened, entirely unaware that Mme de Villeparisis knew quite well who my companion was but did not wish to speak to her. At the next station, Mme de Villeparisis left the carriage, indeed I reproached myself with not having helped her on to the platform; I resumed my seat by the side of the Princess. But one would have thought – a cataclysm frequent among people whose position is far from stable and who are afraid that one may have heard something to their discredit, and may be looking down upon them – that the curtain had risen upon a fresh scene. Buried in her *Revue des Deux Mondes*, Madame Sherbatov barely moved her lips in reply to my questions and finally told me that I was making her head ache. I had not the faintest idea of the nature of my crime. When I bade the Princess goodbye, the customary smile did not light up her face, her chin drooped in a dry acknowledgment, she did not even offer me her hand, nor did she ever speak to me again. But she must have spoken – though what she said I cannot tell – to the Verdurins; for as soon as I asked them whether I ought not to say something polite to Princess Sherbatov, they replied in chorus: 'No! No! No! Nothing of the sort! She does not care for polite speeches!' They did not say this to effect a breach between us, but she had succeeded in making them believe that she was unmoved by civilities, that hers was a spirit unassailed by the vanities of this world. One needs to have seen the politician who was reckoned the most single-minded, the most uncompromising, the most unapproachable, so long as he was in office, one must have seen him in the hour of his disgrace, humbly soliciting, with a bright, affectionate smile, the haughty greeting of some unimportant journalist, one must have seen Cottard (whom his new patients regarded as a rod of iron) draw himself erect, one must know out of what disappointments in love, what rebuffs to snobbery were built up the apparent pride, the universally acknowledged anti-snobbery of Princess Sherbatov, in order to grasp that among the human race the rule – which admits of exceptions, naturally – is that the reputedly hard people are weak people whom nobody wants, and that the strong, caring little whether they are wanted or not, have alone that meekness which the common herd mistake for weakness.

However, I ought not to judge Princess Sherbatov severely. Her case is so common! One day, at the funeral of a Guermantes, a distinguished man who was standing next to me drew my attention to a slim person with handsome features. 'Of all the Guermantes,' my neighbour informed me, 'that is the most astonishing, the most singular. He is the Duke's brother.' I replied imprudently that he was mistaken, that the gentleman in question, who was in no way related to the Guermantes, was named Journier-Sarlovèze. The distinguished man turned his back upon me, and has never even bowed to me since.

A great musician, a member of the Institute, occupying a high official position, who was acquainted with Ski, came to Harambouville, where he had a niece staying, and appeared at one of the Verdurins' Wednesdays. M. de Charlus was especially polite to him (at Morel's request), principally in order that on his return to Paris the Academician might enable him to attend various private concerts, rehearsals and so forth, at which the violinist would be playing. The Academician, who was flattered, and was naturally a charming person, promised, and kept his promise. The Baron was deeply touched by all the consideration which this personage (who, for his own part, was exclusively and passionately a lover of women) showed him, all the facilities that he procured to enable him to see Morel in those official quarters which the profane world may not enter, all the opportunities by which the celebrated artist secured that the young virtuoso might show himself, might make himself known, by naming him in preference to others of equal talent for auditions which were likely to make a special stir. But M. de Charlus never suspected that he ought to be all the more grateful to the maestro in that the latter, doubly deserving, or, if you prefer it, guilty twice over, was completely aware of the relations between the young violinist and his noble patron. He favoured them, certainly without any sympathy for them, being unable to comprehend any other love than that for the woman who had inspired the whole of his music, but from moral indifference, a professional readiness to oblige, social affability, snobbishness. As for his doubts as to the character of those relations, they were so scanty that, at his first dinner at la Raspelière, he had enquired of Ski, speaking of M. de

Charlus and Morel, as he might have spoken of a man and his mistress:
'Have they been long together?' But, too much the man of the world to let
the parties concerned see what was in his mind, prepared, should any gossip
arise among Morel's fellow-students, to rebuke them, and to reassure Morel
by saying to him in a fatherly tone: 'One hears that sort of thing about
everybody nowadays', he did not cease to load the Baron with civilities
which the latter thought charming, but quite natural, being incapable of
suspecting the eminent maestro of so much vice or of so much virtue. For
the things that were said behind M. de Charlus's back, the expressions used
about Morel, nobody was ever base enough to repeat to him. And yet this
simple situation is enough to show that even that thing universally decried,
which would find no defender anywhere: the breath of scandal, has itself,
whether it be aimed at us and so become especially disagreeable to us, or
informs us of something about a third person of which we were unaware, a
psychological value of its own. It prevents the mind from falling asleep over
the fictitious idea that it has of what it supposes things to be when it is
actually no more than their outward appearance. It turns this appearance
inside out with the magic dexterity of an idealist philosopher and rapidly
presents to our gaze an unsuspected corner of the reverse side of the fabric.
How could M. de Charlus have imagined the remark made of him by a
certain tender relative: 'How on earth can you suppose that Mémé is in love
with me, you forget that I am a woman!' And yet she was genuinely, deeply
attached to M. de Charlus. Why then need we be surprised that in the case
of the Verdurins, whose affection and goodwill he had no title to expect, the
remarks which they made behind his back (and they did not, as we shall see,
confine themselves to remarks), were so different from what he imagined
them to be, that is to say from a mere repetition of the remarks that he
heard when he was present? The latter alone decorated with affectionate
inscriptions the little ideal tent to which M. de Charlus retired at times to
dream by himself, when he introduced his imagination for a moment into
the idea that the Verdurins held of him. Its atmosphere was so congenial, so
cordial, the repose it offered so comforting, that when M. de Charlus,
before going to sleep, had withdrawn to it for a momentary relief from his
worries, he never emerged from it without a smile. But, for each one of us, a
tent of this sort has two sides: as well as the side which we suppose to be the
only one, there is the other which is normally invisible to us, the true front,
symmetrical with the one that we know, but very different, whose decoration,
in which we should recognise nothing of what we expected to see, would
horrify us, as being composed of the hateful symbols of an unsuspected
hostility. What a shock for M. de Charlus, if he had found his way into one

of these enemy tents, by means of some piece of scandal as though by one of those service stairs where obscene drawings are scribbled outside the back doors of flats by unpaid tradesmen or dismissed servants. But, just as we do not possess that sense of direction with which certain birds are endowed, so we lack the sense of our own visibility as we lack that of distances, imagining as quite close to us the interested attention of the people who on the contrary never give us a thought, and not suspecting that we are at the same time the sole preoccupation of others. And so M. de Charlus lived in a state of deception like the fish which thinks that the water in which it is swimming extends beyond the glass wall of its aquarium which mirrors it, while it does not see close beside it in the shadow the human visitor who is amusing himself by watching its movements, or the all-powerful keeper who, at the unforeseen and fatal moment, postponed for the present in the case of the Baron (for whom the keeper, in Paris, will be Mme Verdurin), will extract it without compunction from the place in which it was happily living to cast it into another. Moreover, the races of mankind, in so far as they are not merely collections of individuals, may furnish us with examples more vast, but identical in each of their parts, of this profound, obstinate and dis-concerting blindness. Up to the present, if it was responsible for M. de Charlus's discoursing to the little clan remarks of a wasted subtlety or of an audacity which made his listeners smile at him in secret, it had not yet caused him, nor was it to cause him at Balbec any serious inconvenience. A trace of albumen, of sugar, of cardiac arrhythmia, does not prevent life from remaining normal for the man who is not even conscious of it, when only the physician sees in it a prophecy of catastrophes in store. At present the fondness – whether Platonic or not – that M. de Charlus felt for Morel merely led the Baron to say spontaneously in Morel's absence that he thought him very good-looking, supposing that this would be taken in all innocence, and thereby acting like a clever man who when summoned to make a statement before a Court of Law will not be afraid to enter into details which are apparently to his disadvantage but for that very reason are more natural and less vulgar than the conventional protestations of a stage culprit. With the same freedom, always between Saint-Martin du Chêne and Doncières-Ouest – or conversely on the return journey – M. de Charlus would readily speak of men who had, it appeared, very strange morals, and would even add: 'After all, I say strange, I don't know why, for there's nothing so very strange about that', to prove to himself how thoroughly he was at his ease with his audience. And so indeed he was, provided that it was he who retained the initiative, and that he knew his gallery to be mute and smiling, disarmed by credulity or good manners.

When M. de Charlus was not speaking of his admiration for Morel's beauty, as though it had no connection with an inclination – called a vice – he would refer to that vice, but as though he himself were in no way addicted to it. Sometimes indeed he did not hesitate to call it by its name. As after examining the fine binding of his volume of Balzac I asked him which was his favourite novel in the *Comédie Humaine*, he replied, his thoughts irresistibly attracted to the same topic: 'Either one thing or the other, a tiny miniature like the *Curé de Tours* and the *Femme abandonnée*, or one of the great frescoes like the series of *Illusions perdues*. What! You've never read *Illusions perdues*? It's wonderful. The scene where Carlos Herrera asks the name of the château he is driving past, and it turns out to be Rastignac, the home of the young man he used to love. And then the abbé falls into a reverie which Swann once called, and very aptly, the *Tristesse d'Olympio* of pederasty. And the death of Lucien! I forgot who the man of taste was who, when he was asked what event in his life had most distressed him, replied: "The death of Lucien de Rubempré in *Splendeurs et Misères*".' 'I know that Balzac is all the rage this year, as pessimism was last,' Brichot interrupted. 'But, at the risk of distressing the hearts that are smitten with the Balzacian fever, without laying any claim, damme, to being a policeman of letters, or drawing up a list of offences against the laws of grammar, I must confess that the copious improviser whose alarming lucubrations you appear to me singularly to overrate, has always struck me as being an insufficiently meticulous scribe. I have read these *Illusions perdues* of which you are telling us, Baron, flagellating myself to attain to the fervour of an initiate, and I confess in all simplicity of heart that those serial instalments of bombastic balderdash, written in double Dutch – and in triple Dutch: *Esther heureuse, Où mènent les mauvais chemins, A combien l'amour revient aux vieillards*, have always had the effect on me of the *Mystères de Rocambole*, exalted by an inexplicable preference to the precarious position of a masterpiece.' 'You say that because you know nothing of life,' said the Baron, doubly irritated, for he felt that Brichot would not understand either his aesthetic reasons or the other kind. 'I quite realise,' replied Brichot, 'that, to speak like Master François Rabelais, you mean that I am *moult sorbonagre, sorbonicole et sorboniforme*. And yet, just as much as any of the comrades, I like a book to give an impression of sincerity and real life, I am not one of those clerks . . .' 'The *quart d'heure de Rabelais*,' the Doctor broke in, with an air no longer of uncertainty but of assurance as to his own wit. ' . . . who take a vow of literature following the rule of the Abbaye-aux-Bois, yielding obedience to M. le Vicomte de Chateaubriand, Grand Master of common form, according to the strict rule of the humanists. M. le Vicomte de Chateaubriand's mistake . . .' 'With fried potatoes?' put in Dr. Cottard. 'He is the patron saint of the brotherhood,' continued Brichot, ignoring the wit of the Doctor, who, on the other hand, alarmed by the don's phrase, glanced anxiously at M. de Charlus. Brichot had seemed wanting in tact to Cottard, whose pun had brought a delicate smile to the lips of Princess Sherbatov. 'With the Professor, the mordant irony of the complete sceptic never forfeits its rights,' she said kindly, to show that the scientist's witticism had not passed unperceived by herself. 'The sage is of necessity sceptical,' replied the Doctor. 'It's not my fault. *Gnothi seauton*, said Socrates. He was quite right, excess in anything is a mistake. But I am dumbfounded when I think that those words have sufficed to keep Socrates's name alive all this time. What is there in his philosophy, very little when all is said. When one reflects that Charcot and others have done work a thousand times more remarkable, work which moreover is at least founded upon something, upon the suppression of the pupillary reflex as a syndrome of general paralysis, and that they are almost forgotten. After all, Socrates was nothing out of the common. They were people who had nothing better to do, and spent their time strolling about and splitting hairs. Like Jesus Christ: "Love one another!" It's all very pretty.' 'My dear,' Mme Cottard implored. 'Naturally my wife protests, women are all neurotic.' 'But, my dear Doctor, I am not neurotic,' murmured Mme Cottard. 'What, she is not neurotic! When her son is ill, she exhibits phenomena of insomnia. Still, I quite admit that Socrates, and all the rest of them, are necessary for a superior culture, to acquire the talent of exposition. I always quote his *gnothi seauton* to my pupils at the beginning of the course. Père Bouchard, when he heard of it, congratulated me.' 'I am not one of those who hold to form for form's sake, any more than I should treasure in poetry the rhyme millionaire,' replied Brichot. 'But all the same the *Comédie Humaine* – which is far from human – is more than the antithesis of those works in which the art exceeds the matter, as that worthy hack Ovid says. And it is permissible to choose a middle course, which leads to the presbytery of Meudon or the hermitage of Ferney, equidistant from the Valley of Wolves, in which René superbly performed the duties of a merciless pontificate, and from les Jardies, where Honoré de Balzac, browbeaten by the bailiffs, never ceased voiding upon paper to please a Polish woman, like a zealous apostle of balderdash.'

'Chateaubriand is far more alive now than you say, and Balzac is, after all, a great writer,' replied M. de Charlus, still too much impregnated with Swann's tastes not to be irritated by Brichot, 'and Balzac was acquainted with even those passions which the rest of the world ignores, or studies only to castigate them. Without referring again to the immortal *Illusions perdues;*

Sarrazine, La Fille aux yeux d'or, Une passion dans le désert, even the distinctly enigmatic *Fausse Maîtresse* can be adduced in support of my argument. When I spoke of this "unnatural" aspect of Balzac to Swann, he said to me: "You are of the same opinion as Taine." I never had the honour of knowing Monsieur Taine,' M. de Charlus continued, with that irritating habit of inserting an otiose 'Monsieur' to which people in society are addicted, as though they imagine that by styling a great writer 'Monsieur' they are doing him an honour, perhaps keeping him at his proper distance, and making it evident that they do not know him personally. 'I never knew Monsieur Taine, but I felt myself greatly honoured by being of the same opinion as he.' However, in spite of these ridiculous social affectations, M. de Charlus was extremely intelligent, and it is probable that if some remote marriage had established a connection between his family and that of Balzac, he would have felt (no less than Balzac himself, for that matter) a satisfaction which he would have been unable to help displaying as a praiseworthy sign of condescension.

Now and again, at the station after Saint-Martin du Chêne, some young men would get into the train. M. de Charlus could not refrain from looking at them, but as he cut short and concealed the attention that he was paying them, he gave it the air of hiding a secret, more personal even than his real secret; one would have said that he knew them, allowed his acquaintance to appear in spite of himself, after he had accepted the sacrifice, before turning again to us, like children who, in consequence of a quarrel among their respective parents, have been forbidden to speak to certain of their school-fellows, but who when they meet them cannot forego the temptation to raise their heads before lowering them again before their tutor's menacing cane.

At the word borrowed from the Greek with which M. de Charlus in speaking of Balzac had ended his comparison of the *Tristesse d'Olympio* with the *Splendeurs et Misères*, Ski, Brichot and Cottard had glanced at one another with a smile perhaps less ironical than stamped with that satisfaction which people at a dinner-party would show who had succeeded in making Dreyfus talk about his own case, or the Empress Eugénie about her reign. They were hoping to press him a little further upon this subject, but we were already at Doncières, where Morel joined us. In his presence, M. de Charlus kept a careful guard over his conversation and, when Ski tried to bring it back to the love of Carlos Herrera for Lucien de Rubempré, the Baron assumed the vexed, mysterious, and finally (seeing that nobody was listening to him) severe and judicial air of a father who hears people saying something indecent in front of his daughter. Ski having shown some determination to pursue the subject, M. de Charlus, his eyes starting out of his head, raised his voice and said, in a significant tone, looking at Albertine, who as a matter of fact could not hear what we were saying, being engaged in conversation with Mme Cottard and Princess Sherbatov, and with the suggestion of a double meaning of a person who wishes to teach ill-bred people a lesson: 'I think it is high time we began to talk of subjects that are likely to interest this young lady.' But I quite realised that, to him, the young lady was not Albertine but Morel; he proved, as it happened, later on, the accuracy of my interpretation by the expressions that he employed when he begged that there might be no more of such conversation in front of Morel. 'You know,' he said to me, speaking of the violinist, 'that he is not at all what you might suppose, he is a very respectable youth who has always behaved himself, he is very serious.' And one gathered from these words that M. de Charlus regarded sexual inversion as a danger as menacing to young men as prostitution is to women, and that if he employed the epithet 'respectable', of Morel it was in the sense that it has when applied to a young shop-girl. Then Brichot, to change the conversation, asked me whether I intended to remain much longer at Incarville. I had pointed out to him more than once, but in vain, that I was staying not at Incarville but at Balbec, he always repeated the mistake, for it was by the name of Incarville or Balbec-Incarville that he described this section of the coast. There are people like that, who speak of the same things as ourselves but call them by a slightly different name. A certain lady of the Faubourg Saint-Germain used invariably to ask me, when she meant to refer to the Duchesse de Guermantes, whether I had seen Zénaïde lately, or Oriane-Zénaïde, the effect of which was that at first I did not understand her. Probably there had been a time when, some relative of Mme de Guermantes being named Oriane, she herself, to avoid confusion, had been known as Oriane-Zénaïde. Perhaps, too, there had originally been a station only at Incarville, from which one went in a carriage to Balbec. 'Why, what have you been talking about?' said Albertine, astonished at the solemn, paternal tone which M. de Charlus had suddenly adopted. 'About Balzac,' the Baron hastily replied, 'and you are wearing this evening the very same clothes as the Princesse de Cadignan, not her first gown, which she wears at the dinner-party, but the second.' This coincidence was due to the fact that, in choosing Albertine's clothes, I sought inspiration in the taste that she had acquired thanks to Elstir, who greatly appreciated a sobriety which might have been called British, had it not been tempered with a gentler, more flowing grace that was purely French. As a rule the garments that he chose offered to the eye a harmonious combination of grey tones like the dress of Diane de Cadignan. M. de Charlus was almost the only person capable of appreciating Albertine's clothes at their true value; at a glance, his eye detected what constituted their rarity, justified their price; he would never have said the name of one stuff instead of another, and could always tell who had made them. Only he preferred – in women – a little more brightness and colour than Elstir would allow. And so this evening she cast a glance at me half smiling, half troubled, wrinkling her little pink cat's nose. Indeed, meeting over her skirt of grey crêpe de chine, her jacket of grey cheviot gave the impression that Albertine was dressed entirely in grey. But, making a sign to me to help her, because her puffed sleeves needed to be smoothed down or pulled up, for her to get into or out of her jacket, she took it off, and as her sleeves were of a Scottish plaid in soft colours, pink, pale blue, dull green, pigeon's breast, the effect was as though in a grey sky there had suddenly appeared a rainbow. And she asked herself whether this would find favour with M. de Charlus. 'Ah!' he exclaimed in delight, 'now we have a ray, a prism of colour. I offer you my sincerest compliments.' 'But it is this gentleman who has earned them,' Albertine replied politely, pointing to myself, for she liked to show what she had received from me. 'It is only women who do not know how to dress that are afraid of colours,' went on M. de Charlus. 'A dress may be brilliant without vulgarity and quiet without being dull. Besides, you have not the same reasons as Mme de Cadignan for wishing to appear detached from life, for that was the idea which she wished to instil into d'Arthez by her grey gown.' Albertine, who was interested in this mute language of clothes, questioned M. de Charlus about the Princesse de Cadignan. 'Oh! It is a charming tale,' said the Baron in a dreamy tone. 'I know the little garden in which Diane de Cadignan used to stroll with M. d'Espard. It belongs to one of my cousins.' 'All this talk about his cousin's garden,' Brichot murmured to Cottard, 'may, like his pedigree, be of some importance to this worthy Baron. But what interest can it have for us who are not privileged to walk in it, do not know the lady, and possess no titles of nobility?' For Brichot had no suspicion that one might be interested in a gown and in a garden as works of art, and that it was in the pages of Balzac that M. de Charlus saw, in his mind's eye, the garden paths of Mme de Cadignan. The Baron went on: 'But you know her,' he said to me, speaking of this cousin, and, by way of flattering me, addressing himself to me as to a person who, exiled amid the little clan, was to M. de Charlus, if not a citizen of his world, at any rate a visitor to it. 'Anyhow you must have seen her at Mme de Villeparisis'.' 'Is that the Marquise de Villeparisis who owns the chateau at Baucreux?' asked Brichot with a captivated air. 'Yes, do you know her?' enquired M. de Charlus dryly. 'No, not at all,' replied Brichot, 'but our colleague Norpois spends part of his holidays every year at Baucreux. I have had occasion to write to him there.' I told Morel, thinking to interest him, that M. de Norpois was a friend of my father. But not a movement of his features showed that he had heard me, so little did he think of my parents, so far short did they fall in his estimation of what my great-uncle had been, who had employed Morel's father as his valet, and, as a matter of fact, being, unlike the rest of the family, fond of not giving trouble, had left a golden memory among his servants. 'It appears that Mme de Villeparisis is a superior woman; but I have never been allowed to judge of that for myself, nor for that matter have any of my colleagues. For Norpois, who is the soul of courtesy and affability at the Institute, has never introduced any of us to the Marquise. I know of no one who has been received by her except our friend Thureau-Dangin, who had an old family connection with her, and also Gaston Boissier, whom she was anxious to meet because of an essay which interested her especially. He dined with her once and came back quite enthralled by her charm. Mme Boissier, however, was not invited.' At the sound of these names, Morel melted in a smile. 'Ah! Thureau-Dangin,' he said to me with an air of interest as great as had been his indifference when he heard me speak of the Marquis de Norpois and my father. 'Thureau-Dangin; why, he and your uncle were as thick as thieves. Whenever a lady wanted a front seat for a reception at the Academy, your uncle would say: 'I shall write to Thureau-Dangin.' And of course he got the ticket at once, for you can understand that M. Thureau-Dangin would never have dared to refuse anything to your uncle, who would have been certain to pay him out for it afterwards if he had. I can't help smiling, either, when I hear the name Boissier, for that was where your uncle ordered all the presents he used to give the ladies at the New Year. I know all about it, because I knew the person he used to send for them.' He had not only known him, the person was his father. Some of these affectionate allusions by Morel to my uncle's memory were prompted by the fact that we did not intend to remain permanently in the Hôtel de Guermantes, where we had taken an apartment only on account of my grandmother. Now and again there would be talk of a possible move. Now, to understand the advice that Charlie Morel gave me in this connection, the reader must know that my great-uncle had lived, in his day, at 40*bis* Boulevard Malesherbes. The consequence was that, in the family, as we were in the habit of frequently visiting my uncle Adolphe until the fatal day when I made a breach between my parents and him by telling them the story of the lady in pink, instead of saying 'at your uncle's' we used to say 'at 40*bis*'. If I were going to call upon some kinswoman, I would be warned to go first of all 'to 40*bis*', in order that my uncle might not be offended by my not having begun my round with him. He was the owner of the house and was, I must say, very particular as to the choice of his tenants, all of whom either were or became his personal friends. Colonel the Baron de Vatry used to look in every day and smoke a cigar with him in the hope of making him consent to pay for repairs. The carriage entrance was always kept shut. If my uncle caught sight of a cloth or a rug hanging from one of the window-sills he would dash into the room and have it removed in less time than the police would take to do so nowadays. All the same, he did let part of the house, reserving for himself only two floors and the stables. In spite of this, knowing that he was pleased when people praised the house, we used always to talk of the comfort of the 'little mansion' as though my uncle had been its sole occupant, and he allowed us to speak, without uttering the formal contradiction that might have been expected. The 'little mansion' was certainly comfortable (my uncle having installed in it all the most recent inventions). But there was nothing extraordinary about it. Only, my uncle, while saying with a false modesty 'my little hovel', was convinced, or in any case had instilled into his valet, the latter's wife, the coachman, the cook, the idea that there was no place in Paris to compare, for comfort, luxury, and general attractiveness, with the little mansion. Charles Morel had grown up in this belief. Nor had he outgrown it. And so, even on days when he was not talking to me, if in the train I mentioned to anyone else the possibility of our moving, at once he would smile at me and, with a wink of connivance, say: 'Ah! What you want is something in the style of 40*bis*! That's a place that would suit you down to the ground! Your uncle knew what he was about. I am quite sure that in the whole of Paris there's nothing to compare with 40*bis*.'

The melancholy air which M. de Charlus had assumed in speaking of the Princesse de Cadignan left me in no doubt that the tale in question had not reminded him only of the little garden of a cousin to whom he was not particularly attached. He became lost in meditation, and, as though he were talking to himself: 'The secrets of the Princesse de Cadignan!' he exclaimed, 'What a masterpiece! How profound, how heart-rending the evil reputation of Diane, who is afraid that the man she loves may hear of it. What an eternal truth, and more universal than might appear, how far it extends!' He uttered these words with a sadness in which nevertheless one felt that he found a certain charm. Certainly M. de Charlus, unaware to what extent precisely his habits were or were not known, had been trembling for some time past at the thought that when he returned to Paris and was seen there in Morel's company, the latter's family might intervene and so his future happiness be jeopardised. This eventuality had probably not appeared to him hitherto save as something profoundly disagreeable and painful. But the Baron was an artist to his finger tips. And now that he had begun to identify his own position with that described by Balzac, he took refuge, in a sense, in the tale, and for the calamity which was perhaps in store for him and did not in any case cease to alarm him, he had the consolation of finding in his own anxiety what Swann and also Saint-Loup would have called something 'quite Balzacian'. This identification of himself with the Princesse de Cadignan had been made easy for M. de Charlus by virtue of the mental transposition which was becoming habitual with him and of which he had already furnished several examples. It was enough in itself, moreover, to make the mere conversion of a woman, as the beloved object, into a young man immediately set in motion about him the whole sequence of social complications which develop round a normal love affair. When, for any reason, we introduce once and for all time a change in the calendar, or in the daily timetable, if we make the year begin a few weeks later, or if we make midnight strike a quarter of an hour earlier, as the days will still consist of twenty-four hours and the months of thirty days, everything that depends upon the measure of time will remain unaltered. Everything may have been changed without causing any disturbance, since the ratio of the figures is still the same. So it is with lives which adopt Central European time, or the Eastern calendar. It seems even that the gratification a man derives from keeping an actress played a part in these relations. When, after their first meeting, M. de Charlus had made enquiries as to Morel's actual position, he must certainly have learned that he was of humble extraction, but a girl with whom we are in love does not forfeit our esteem because she is the child of poor parents. On the other hand, the well-known musicians to whom he had addressed his enquiries, had – and not even from any personal motive, unlike the friends who, when introducing Swann to Odette, had described her to him as more difficult and more sought-after than she actually was – simply in the stereotyped manner of men in a prominent position over praising a beginner, answered the Baron: 'Ah! Great talent, has made a name for himself, of course he is still quite young, highly esteemed by the experts, will go far.' And, with the mania which leads people who are innocent of inversion to speak of masculine beauty: 'Besides, it is charming to watch him play; he looks better than anyone at a concert; he has lovely hair, holds himself so well; his head is exquisite, he reminds one of a violinist in a picture.' And so M. de Charlus, raised to a pitch of excitement moreover by Morel himself, who did not fail to let him know how many offers had been addressed to him, was flattered by the prospect of taking him home with him, of making a little nest for him to which he would often return. For during the rest of the time he wished him to enjoy his freedom, which was necessary to his career, which M. de Charlus meant him, however much money he might feel bound to give him, to continue, either because of the thoroughly 'Guermantes' idea that a man ought to do something, that he acquires merit only by his talent, and that nobility or money is simply the additional cypher that multiplies a figure, or because he was afraid lest, having nothing to do and remaining perpetually in his company, the violinist might grow bored. Moreover he did not wish to deprive himself of the pleasure which he found, at certain important concerts, in saying to himself: 'The person they are applauding at this moment is coming home with me tonight.' Fashionable people, when they are in love and whatever the nature of their love, apply their vanity to anything that may destroy the anterior advantages from which their vanity would have derived satisfaction.

Morel, feeling that I bore him no malice, being sincerely attached to M. de Charlus, and at the same time absolutely indifferent physically to both of us, ended by treating me with the same display of warm friendship as a courtesan who knows that you do not desire her and that her lover has a sincere friend in you who will not attempt to part him from her. Not only did he speak to me exactly as Rachel, Saint-Loup's mistress, had spoken to me long ago, but what was more, to judge by what M. de Charlus reported to me, he used to say to him about me in my absence the same things that Rachel had said about me to Robert. In fact M. de Charlus said to me: 'He likes you so much', as Robert had said: 'She likes you so much.' And just as the nephew on behalf of his mistress, so it was on Morel's behalf that the uncle often invited me to come and dine with them. There were, for that matter, just as many storms between them as there had been between Robert and Rachel. To be sure, after Charlie (Morel) had left us, M. de Charlus would sing his praises without ceasing, repeating – the thought of it was flattering to him – that the violinist was so good to him. But it was evident nevertheless that often Charlie, even in front of all the faithful, wore an irritated expression, instead of always appearing happy and submissive as the Baron would have wished. This irritation became so violent in course of time, owing to the weakness which led M. de Charlus to forgive Morel his want of politeness, that the violinist made no attempt to conceal, if he did not even deliberately assume it. I have seen M. de Charlus, on entering a railway carriage in which Morel was sitting with some of his soldier friends, greeted with a shrug of the musician's shoulders, accompanied by a wink in the direction of his comrades. Or else he would pretend to be asleep, as though this incursion bored him beyond words. Or he would begin to cough, and the others would laugh, derisively mimicking the affected speech of men like M. de Charlus; would draw Charlie into a corner, from which he would return, as though under compulsion, to sit by M. de

Charlus, whose heart was pierced by all these cruelties. It is inconceivable how he can have put up with them; and these ever varied forms of suffering set the problem of happiness in fresh terms for M. de Charlus, compelled him not only to demand more, but to desire something else, the previous combination being vitiated by a horrible memory. And yet, painful as these scenes came to be, it must be admitted that at first the genius of the humble son of France traced for Morel, made him assume charming forms of simplicity, of apparent frankness, even of an independent pride which seemed to be inspired by disinterestedness. This was not the case, but the advantage of this attitude was all the more on Morel's side since, whereas the person who is in love is continually forced to return to the charge, to increase his efforts, it is on the other hand easy for him who is not in love to proceed along a straight line, inflexible and graceful. It existed by virtue of the privilege of the race in the face – so open – of this Morel whose heart was so tightly shut, that face imbued with the neo-Hellenic grace which blooms in the basilicas of Champagne. Notwithstanding his affectation of pride, often when he caught sight of M. de Charlus at a moment when he was not expecting to see him, he would be embarrassed by the presence of the little clan, would blush, lower his eyes, to the delight of the Baron, who saw in this an entire romance. It was simply a sign of irritation and shame. The former sometimes found expression; for, calm and emphatically decent as Morel's attitude generally was, it was not without frequent contradictions. Sometimes, indeed, at something which the Baron said to him, Morel would come out, in the harshest tone, with an insolent retort which shocked everybody. M. de Charlus would lower his head with a sorrowful air, make no reply, and with that faculty which doting fathers possess of believing that the coldness, the rudeness of their children has passed unnoticed, would continue undeterred to sing the violinist's praises. M. de Charlus was not, indeed, always so submissive, but as a rule his attempts at rebellion proved abortive, principally because, having lived among people in society, in calculating the reactions that he might provoke he made allowance for the baser instincts, whether original or acquired. Now, instead of these, he encountered in Morel a plebeian tendency to spells of indifference. Unfortunately for M. de Charlus, he did not understand that, with Morel, everything else must give place when the Conservatoire (and the good reputation of the Conservatoire, but with this, which was to be a more serious matter, we are not at present concerned) was in question. Thus, for instance, people of the middle class will readily change their surnames out of vanity, noblemen for personal advantage. To the young violinist, on the contrary, the name Morel was inseparably linked with his first prize for the violin, and so impossible to alter. M. de Charlus would have liked Morel to take everything from himself, including a name. Going upon the facts that Morel's other name was Charles, which resembled Charlus, and that the place where they were in the habit of meeting was called les Charmes, he sought to persuade Morel that, a pleasant name, easy to pronounce, being half the battle for artistic fame, the virtuoso ought without hesitation to take the name Charmel, a discreet allusion to the scene of their intimacy. Morel shrugged his shoulders. As a conclusive argument, M. de Charlus was unfortunately inspired to add that he had a footman of that name. He succeeded only in arousing the furious indignation of the young man. 'There was a time when my ancestors were proud of the title of groom, of butler to the King.' 'There was also a time,' replied Morel haughtily, 'when my ancestors cut off your ancestors' heads.' M. de Charlus would have been greatly surprised had he been told that even if, abandoning the idea of 'Charmel', he made up his mind to adopt Morel and to confer upon him one of the titles of the Guermantes family which were at his disposal but which circumstances, as we shall see, did not permit him to offer the violinist, the other would decline, thinking of the artistic reputation attached to the name Morel, and of the things that would be said about him in 'the class'. So far above the Faubourg Saint-Germain did he place the Rue Bergère. And so M. de Charlus was obliged to content himself with having symbolical rings made for Morel, bearing the antique device: PLVS VLTRA CAR'LVS. Certainly, in the face of an adversary of a sort with which he was unfamiliar, M. de Charlus ought to have changed his tactics. But which of us is capable of that? Moreover, if M. de Charlus made blunders, Morel was not guiltless of them either. Far more than the actual circumstance which brought about the rupture between them, what was destined, provisionally, at least (but this provisional turned out to be final), to ruin him with M. de Charlus was that his nature included not only the baseness which made him lie down under harsh treatment and respond with insolence to kindness. Running parallel to this innate baseness, there was in him a complicated neurasthenia of ill breeding, which, roused to activity on every occasion when he was in the wrong or was becoming a nuisance, meant that at the very moment when he had need of all his politeness, gentleness, gaiety, to disarm the Baron, he became sombre, petulant, tried to provoke discussions on matters where he knew that the other did not agree with him, maintained his own hostile attitude with a weakness of argument and a slashing violence which enhanced that weakness. For, very soon running short of arguments, he invented fresh ones as he went along, in which he displayed the full extent of his ignorance and folly. These were barely noticeable when he was in a friendly mood and sought only to please. On the contrary, nothing else was visible in his fits of sombre humour, when, from being inoffensive, they became odious. Whereupon M. de Charlus felt that he could endure no more, that his only hope lay in a brighter morrow, while Morel, forgetting that the Baron was enabling him to live in the lap of luxury, gave an ironical smile, of condescending pity, and said: 'I have never taken anything from anybody. Which means that there is nobody to whom I owe a word of thanks.'

In the meantime, and as though he had been dealing with a man of the world, M. de Charlus continued to give vent to his rage, whether genuine or feigned, but in either case ineffective. It was not always so, however. Thus one day (which must be placed, as a matter of fact, subsequent to this initial period) when the Baron was returning with Charlie and myself from a luncheon party at the Verdurins', and expecting to spend the rest of the afternoon and the evening with the violinist at Doncières, the latter's dismissal of him, as soon as we left the train, with: 'No, I've an engagement', caused M. de Charlus so keen a disappointment, that in spite of all his attempts to meet adversity with a brave face, I saw the tears trickling down and melting the paint beneath his eyes, as he stood helpless by the carriage door. Such was his grief that, since we intended, Albertine and I, to spend the rest of the day at Doncières, I whispered to her that I would prefer that we did not leave M. de Charlus by himself, as he seemed, I could not say why, to be unhappy. The dear girl readily assented. I then asked M. de Charlus if he would not like me to accompany him for a little. He also assented, but declined to put my 'cousin' to any trouble. I found a certain charm (and one, doubtless, not to be repeated, since I had made up my mind to break with her), in saying to her quietly, as though she were my wife: 'Go back home by yourself, I shall see you this evening,' and in hearing her, as a wife might, give me permission to do as I thought fit, and authorise me, if M. de Charlus, to whom she was attached, needed my company, to place myself at his disposal. We proceeded, the Baron and I, he waddling obesely, his Jesuitical eyes downcast, and I following him, to a café where we were given beer. I felt M. de Charlus's eyes turning uneasily towards the execution of some plan. Suddenly he called for paper and ink, and began to write at an astonishing speed. While he covered sheet after sheet, his eyes glittered with furious fancies. When he had written eight pages: 'May I ask you to do me a great service?' he said to me. 'You will excuse my sealing this note. I am obliged to do so. You will take a carriage, a motorcar if you can find one, to get there as quickly as possible. You are certain to find Morel in his quarters, where he has gone to change his clothes. Poor boy, he tried to bluster a little when we parted, but you may be sure that his heart is fuller than mine. You will give him this note, and, if he asks you where you met me, you will tell him that you stopped at Doncières (which, for that matter, is the truth) to see Robert, which is not quite the truth perhaps, but that you met me with a person whom you do not know, that I seemed to be extremely angry, that you thought you heard something about sending seconds (I am, as a matter of fact, fighting a duel tomorrow). Whatever you do, don't say that I am asking for him, don't make any effort to bring him here, but if he wishes to come with you, don't prevent him from doing so. Go, my boy, it is for his good, you may be the means of averting a great tragedy. While you are away, I am going to write to my seconds. I have prevented you from spending the afternoon with your cousin. I hope that she will bear me no ill will for that, indeed I am sure of it. For hers is a noble soul, and I know that she is one of the people who are strong enough not to resist the greatness of circumstances. You must thank her on my behalf. I am personally indebted to her, and I am glad that it should be so.' I was extremely sorry for M. de Charlus; it seemed to me that Charlie might have prevented this duel, of which he was perhaps the cause, and I was revolted, if that were the case, that he should have gone off with such indifference, instead of staying to help his protector. My indignation was increased when, on reaching the house in which Morel lodged, I recognised the voice of the violinist, who, feeling the need of an outlet for his happiness, was singing boisterously: 'Some Sunday morning, when the wedding-bells rrring!' If poor M. de Charlus had heard him, he who wished me to believe, and doubtless believed himself, that Morel's heart at that moment was full! Charlie began to dance with joy when he caught sight of me. 'Hallo, old boy I (excuse me, addressing you like that; in this damned military life, one picks up bad habits) what luck, seeing you. I have nothing to do all evening. Do let's go somewhere together. We can stay here if you like, or take a boat if you prefer that, or we can have some music, it's all the same to me.' I told him that I was obliged to dine at Balbec, he seemed anxious that I should invite him to dine there also, but I refrained from doing so. 'But if you're in such a hurry, why have you come here?' 'I have brought you a note from M. de Charlus.' At that moment all his gaiety vanished; his face contracted. 'What! He can't leave me alone even here. So I'm a slave, am I? Old boy, be a sport. I'm not going to open his letter. You can tell him that you couldn't find me.' 'Wouldn't it be better to open it, I fancy it contains something serious.' 'No, certainly not, you don't know all the lies, the infernal tricks that old scoundrel's up to. It's a dodge to make me go and see him. Very well! I'm not going, I want to have an evening in peace.' 'But isn't there going to be a duel tomorrow?' I asked Morel, whom I supposed to be equally well informed. 'A duel?' he repeated with an air of stupefaction. 'I never heard a word about it. After all, it doesn't matter a damn to me, the dirty old beast can go and get plugged in the guts if he likes. But wait a minute, this is interesting, I'm going to look at his letter after all. You can tell him that you left it here for me, in case I should come in.' While Morel was speaking to me, I was looking with amazement at the beautiful books which M. de Charlus had given him, and which littered his room. The violinist having refused to accept those labelled: 'I belong to the Baron' etc., a device which he felt to be insulting to himself, as a mark of vassalage, the Baron, with the sentimental ingenuity in which his ill-starred love abounded, had substituted others, originated by his ancestors, but ordered from the binder according to the circumstances of a melancholy friendship. Sometimes they were terse and confident, as *Spes mea* or *Expectata non eludet*. Sometimes merely resigned, as *J'attendrai*. Others were gallant: *Mesmes plaisir du mestre*, or counselled chastity, such as that borrowed from the family of Simiane, sprinkled with azure towers and lilies, and given a fresh meaning: *Sustendant lilia turres*. Others, finally, were despairing, and appointed a meeting in heaven with him who had spurned the donor upon earth: *Manet ultima caelo*, and (finding the grapes which he had failed to reach too sour, pretending not to have sought what he had not secured) M. de Charlus said in one: *Non mortale quod opto*. But I had not time to examine them all.

If M. de Charlus, in dashing this letter down upon paper had seemed to be carried away by the demon that was inspiring his flying pen, as soon as Morel had broken the seal (a leopard between two roses gules, with the motto: *atavis et armis*) he began to read the letter as feverishly as M. de Charlus had written it, and over those pages covered at breakneck speed his eye ran no less rapidly than the Baron's pen. 'Good God!' he exclaimed, 'this is the last straw! But where am I to find him? Heaven only knows where he is now.' I suggested that if he made haste he might still find him perhaps at a tavern where he had ordered beer as a restorative. 'I don't know whether I shall be coming back,' he said to his landlady, and added *in petto*, 'it will depend on how the cat jumps.' A few minutes later we reached the café. I remarked M. de Charlus's expression at the moment when he caught sight of me. When he saw that I did not return unaccompanied, I could feel that his breath, his life were restored to him. Feeling that he could not get on that evening without Morel, he had pretended that somebody had told him that two officers of the regiment had spoken evil of him in connection with the violinist and that he was going to send his seconds to call upon them. Morel had foreseen the scandal, his life in the regiment made impossible, and had hastened to the spot. In doing which he had not been altogether wrong. For to make his falsehood more plausible, M. de Charlus had already written to two of his friends (one was Cottard) asking them to be his seconds. And, if the violinist had not appeared, we may be certain that, in the frantic state in which M. de Charlus then was (and to change his sorrow into rage), he would have sent them with a challenge to some officer or other with whom it would have been a relief to him to fight. During the interval, M. de Charlus, remembering that he came of a race that was of purer blood than the House of France, told himself that it was really very good of him to take so much trouble over the son of a butler whose employer he would not have condescended to know. On the other hand, if his only amusement, almost, was now in the society of disreputable persons, the profoundly ingrained habit which such persons have of not replying to a letter, of failing to keep an appointment without warning you beforehand, without apologising afterwards, aroused in him, since, often enough, his heart was involved, such a wealth of emotion and the rest of the time caused him such irritation, inconvenience and anger, that he would sometimes begin to regret the endless letters over nothing at all, the scrupulous exactitude of Ambassadors and Princes, who, even if, unfortunately, their personal charms left him cold, gave him at any rate some sort of peace of mind. Accustomed to Morel's ways, and knowing how little hold he had over him, how incapable he was of insinuating himself into a life in which friendships that were vulgar but consecrated by force of habit occupied too much space and time to leave a stray hour for the great nobleman, evicted, proud, and vainly imploring, M. de Charlus was so convinced that the musician was not coming, was so afraid of losing him for ever if he went too far, that he could barely repress a cry of joy when he saw him appear. But feeling himself the victor, he felt himself bound to dictate the terms of peace and to extract from them such advantages as he might. 'What are you doing here?' he said to him. 'And you?' he went on, gazing at myself, 'I told you, whatever you did, not to bring him back with you.' 'He didn't want to bring me,' said Morel, turning upon M. de Charlus, in the artlessness of his coquetry, a glance conventionally mournful and languorously old-fashioned, with an air, which he doubtless thought to be irresistible, of wanting to kiss the Baron and to burst into tears. 'It was I who insisted on coming in spite of him. I come, in the name of our friendship, to implore you on my bended knees not to commit this rash act.' M. de Charlus was wild with joy. The reaction was almost too much for his nerves; he managed, however, to control them. 'The friendship to which you appeal at a somewhat inopportune moment,' he replied in a dry tone, 'ought, on the contrary, to make you support me when I decide that I cannot allow the impertinences of a fool to pass unheeded. However, even if I chose to yield to the prayers of an affection which I have known better inspired, I should no longer be in a position to do so, my letters to my seconds have been sent off and I have no doubt of their consent. You have always behaved towards me like a little idiot and, instead of priding yourself, as you had every right to do, upon the predilection which I had shown for you, instead of making known to the mob of serjeants or servants among whom the law of military service compels you to live, what a source of incomparable satisfaction a friendship such as mine was to you, you have sought to make excuses for yourself, almost to make an idiotic merit of not being grateful enough. I know that in so doing,' he went on, in order not to let it appear how deeply certain scenes had humiliated him, 'you are guilty merely of having let yourself be carried away by the jealousy of others. But how is it that at your age you are childish enough (and a child ill-bred enough) not to have seen at once that your election by myself and all the advantages that must result for you from it were bound to excite jealousies, that all your comrades while they egged you on to quarrel with me were plotting to take your place? I have not thought it necessary to tell you of the letters that I have received in that connection from all the people in whom you place most confidence. I scorn the overtures of those flunkeys as I scorn their ineffective mockery. The only person for whom I care is yourself, since I am fond of you, but affection has its limits and you ought to have guessed as much.' Harsh as the word flunkey might sound in the ears of Morel, whose father had been one, but precisely because his father had been one, the explanation of all social misadventures by 'jealousy', an explanation fatuous and absurd, but of inexhaustible value, which with a certain class never fails to 'catch on' as infallibly as the old tricks of the stage with a theatrical audience or the threat of the clerical peril in a parliament, found in him an adherence hardly less solid than in Françoise, or the servants of Mme de Guermantes, for whom jealousy was the sole cause of the misfortunes that beset humanity. He had no doubt that his comrades had tried to oust him from his position and was all the more wretched at the thought of this disastrous, albeit imaginary duel. 'Oh! How dreadful!' exclaimed Charlie. 'I shall never hold up my head again. But oughtn't they to see you before they go and call upon this officer?' 'I don't know, I suppose they ought. I've sent word to one of them that I shall be here all evening and can give him his instructions.' 'I hope that before he comes I can make you listen to reason; you will, anyhow, let me stay with you,' Morel asked him tenderly. This was all that M. de Charlus wanted. He did not however yield at once. 'You would do wrong to apply in this case the

"Whoso loveth well, chasteneth well" of the proverb, for it is yourself whom I loved well, and I intend to chasten even after our parting those who have basely sought to do you an injury. Until now, their inquisitive insinuations, when they dared to ask me how a man like myself could mingle with a boy of your sort, sprung from the gutter, I have answered only in the words of the motto of my La Rochefoucauld cousins: " 'Tis my pleasure". I have indeed pointed out to you more than once that this pleasure was capable of becoming my chiefest pleasure, without there resulting from your arbitrary elevation any degradation of myself.' And in an impulse of almost insane pride he exclaimed, raising his arms in the air: '*Tantus ab uno splendor*! To condescend is not to descend,' he went on in a calmer tone, after this delirious outburst of pride and joy. 'I hope at least that my two adversaries, notwithstanding their inferior rank, are of a blood that I can shed without reproach. I have made certain discreet enquiries in that direction which have reassured me. If you retained a shred of gratitude towards me, you ought on the contrary to be proud to see that for your sake I am reviving the bellicose humour of my ancestors, saying like them in the event of a fatal issue, now that I have learned what a little rascal you are: "Death to me is life".' And M. de Charlus said this sincerely, not only because of his love for Morel, but because a martial instinct which he quaintly supposed to have come down to him from his ancestors filled him with such joy at the thought of fighting that this duel, which he had originally invented with the sole object of making Morel come to him, he could not now abandon without regret. He had never engaged in any affair of the sort without at once imagining himself the victor, and identifying himself with the illustrious Constable de Guermantes, whereas in the case of anyone else this same action of taking the field appeared to him to be of the utmost insignificance. 'I am sure it will be a fine sight,' he said to us in all sincerity, dwelling upon each word. 'To see Sarah Bernhardt in *L'Aiglon*, what is that but tripe? Mounet-Sully in *Oedipus*, tripe! At the most it assumes a certain pallid transfiguration when it is performed in the Arena of Nîmes. But what is it compared to that unimaginable spectacle, the lineal descendant of the Constable engaged in battle.' And at the mere thought of such a thing, M. de Charlus, unable to contain himself for joy, began to make passes in the air which recalled Molière, made us take the precaution of drawing our glasses closer, and fear that, when the swords crossed, the combatants, doctor and seconds would at once be wounded. 'What a tempting spectacle it would be for a painter. You who know Monsieur Elstir,' he said to me, 'you ought to bring him.' I replied that he was not in the neighbourhood. M. de Charlus suggested that he might be summoned by telegraph. 'Oh! I say it in his

interest,' he added in response to my silence. 'It is always interesting for a
master – which he is, in my opinion – to record such an instance of racial
survival. And they occur perhaps once in a century.'

But if M. de Charlus was enchanted at the thought of a duel which he had
meant at first to be entirely fictitious, Morel was thinking with terror of the
stories that might be spread abroad by the regimental band and might,
thanks to the stir that would be made by this duel, penetrate to the holy of
holies in the Rue Bergère. Seeing in his mind's eye the 'class' fully informed,
he became more and more insistent with M. de Charlus, who continued to
gesticulate before the intoxicating idea of a duel. He begged the Baron to
allow him not to leave him until the day after the next, the supposed day of
the duel, so that he might keep him within sight and try to make him listen
to the voice of reason. So tender a proposal triumphed over M. de Charlus's
final hesitations. He said that he would try to find a way out of it, that he
would postpone his final decision for two days. In this fashion, by not
making any definite arrangement at once, M. de Charlus knew that he could
keep Charlie with him for at least two days, and make use of the time to fix
future engagements with him in exchange for his abandoning the duel, an
exercise, he said, which in itself delighted him and which he would not
forego without regret. And in saying this he was quite sincere, for he had
always enjoyed taking the field when it was a question of crossing swords or
exchanging shots with an adversary. Cottard arrived at length, although
extremely late, for, delighted to act as second but even more upset by the
prospect, he had been obliged to halt at all the cafés or farms by the way,
asking the occupants to be so kind as to show him the way to 'No. 100' or 'a
certain place'. As soon as he arrived, the Baron took him into another room,
for he thought it more correct that Charlie and I should not be present at
the interview, and excelled in making the most ordinary room serve for the
time being as throne-room or council chamber. When he was alone with
Cottard he thanked him warmly, but informed him that it seemed probable
that the remark which had been repeated to him had never really been
made, and requested that, in view of this, the Doctor would be so good as let
the other second know that, barring possible complications, the incident
might be regarded as closed. Now that the prospect of danger was withdrawn, Cottard was disappointed. He was indeed tempted for a moment to
give vent to anger, but he remembered that one of his masters, who had
enjoyed the most successful medical career of his generation, having failed
to enter the Academy at his first election by two votes only, had put a brave
face on it and had gone and shaken hands with his successful rival. And so
the Doctor refrained from any expression of indignation which could have

made no difference, and, after murmuring, he the most timorous of men, that there were certain things which one could not overlook, added that it was better so, that this solution delighted him. M. de Charlus, desirous of showing his gratitude to the Doctor, just as the Duke his brother would have straightened the collar of my father's greatcoat or rather as a Duchess would put her arm round the waist of a plebeian lady, brought his chair close to the Doctor's, notwithstanding the dislike that he felt for the other. And, not only without any physical pleasure, but having first to overcome a physical repulsion, as a Guermantes, not as an invert, in taking leave of the Doctor, he clasped his hand and caressed it for a moment with the affection of a rider rubbing his horse's nose and giving it a lump of sugar. But Cottard, who had never allowed the Baron to see that he had so much as heard the vaguest rumours as to his morals, but nevertheless regarded him in his private judgment as one of the class of 'abnormals' (indeed, with his habitual inaccuracy in the choice of terms, and in the most serious tone, he said of one of M. Verdurin's footmen: 'Isn't he the Baron's mistress?'), persons of whom he had little personal experience; imagined that this stroking of his hand was the immediate prelude to an act of violence in anticipation of which, the duel being a mere pretext, he had been enticed into a trap and led by the Baron into this remote apartment where he was about to be forcibly outraged. Not daring to stir from his chair, to which fear kept him glued, he rolled his eyes in terror, as though he had fallen into the hands of a savage who, for all he could tell, fed upon human flesh. At length M. de Charlus, releasing his hand and anxious to be hospitable to the end, said: 'Won't you come and take something with us, as the saying is, what in the old days used to be called a *mazagran* or a *gloria*, drinks that are no longer to be found, as archaeological curiosities, except in the plays of Labiche and the cafés of Doncières. A *gloria* would be distinctly suitable to the place, eh, and to the occasion, what do you say?' 'I am President of the Anti-Alcohol League,' replied Cottard. 'Some country sawbones has only got to pass, and it will be said that I do not practise what I preach. *Os homini sublime dedit coelumque tueri*,' he added, not that this had any bearing on the matter, but because his stock of Latin quotations was extremely limited, albeit sufficient to astound his pupils. M. de Charlus shrugged his shoulders and led Cottard back to where we were, after exacting a promise of secrecy which was all the more important to him since the motive for the abortive duel was purely imaginary. It must on no account reach the ears of the officer whom he had arbitrarily selected as his adversary. While the four of us sat there drinking, Mme Cottard, who had been waiting for her husband outside, where M. de Charlus could see her quite well, though he had made no effort to summon her, came in and greeted the Baron, who held out his hand to her as though to a housemaid, without rising from his chair, partly in the manner of a king receiving homage, partly as a snob who does not wish a woman of humble appearance to sit down at his table, partly as an egoist who enjoys being alone with his friends, and does not wish to be bothered. So Mme Cottard remained standing while she talked to M. de Charlus and her husband. But, possibly because politeness, the knowledge of what 'ought to be done', is not the exclusive privilege of the Guermantes, and may all of a sudden illuminate and guide the most uncertain brains, or else because, himself constantly unfaithful to his wife, Cottard felt at odd moments, as a sort of compensation, the need to protect her against anyone else who failed in his duty to her, the Doctor quickly frowned, a thing I had never seen him do before, and, without consulting M. de Charlus, said in a tone of authority: 'Come, Léontine, don't stand about like that, sit down.' 'But are you sure I'm not disturbing you?' Mme Cottard enquired timidly of M. de Charlus, who, surprised by the Doctor's tone, had made no observation. Whereupon, without giving him a second chance, Cottard repeated with authority: 'I told you to sit down.'

Presently the party broke up, and then M. de Charlus said to Morel: 'I conclude from all this business, which has ended more happily than you deserved, that you are incapable of looking after yourself and that, at the expiry of your military service, I must lead you back myself to your father, like the Archangel Raphael sent by God to the young Tobias.' And the Baron began to smile with an air of grandeur, and a joy which Morel, to whom the prospect of being thus led home afforded no pleasure, did not appear to share. In the exhilaration of comparing himself to the Archangel, and Morel to the son of Tobit, M. de Charlus no longer thought of the purpose of his speech which had been to explore the ground and see whether, as he hoped, Morel would consent to come with him to Paris. Intoxicated with his love or with his self-love, the Baron did not see or pretended not to see the violinist's wry grimace, for, leaving him by himself in the café, he said to me with a proud smile: 'Did you notice how, when I compared him to the son of Tobit, he became wild with joy? That was because, being extremely intelligent, he at once understood that the Father in whose company he was henceforth to live was not his father after the flesh, who must be some horrible valet with moustaches, but his spiritual father, that is to say Myself. What a triumph for him! How proudly he reared his head! What joy he felt at having understood me. I am sure that he will now repeat day by day: "O God Who didst give the blessed Archangel Raphael as guide to thy servant Tobias, upon a long journey, grant to us,

Thy servants, that we may ever be protected by him and armed with his succour." I had no need even,' added the Baron, firmly convinced that he would one day sit before the Throne of God, 'to tell him that I was the heavenly messenger, he realised it for himself, and was struck dumb with joy!' And M. de Charlus (whom his joy, on the contrary, did not deprive of speech), regardless of the passers-by who turned to stare at him, supposing that he must be a lunatic, cried out by himself and at the top of his voice raising his hands in the air: 'Alleluia!'

This reconciliation gave but a temporary respite to M. de Charlus's torments; often, when Morel had gone out on training too far away for M. de Charlus to be able to go and visit him or to send me to talk to him, he would write the Baron desperate and affectionate letters, in which he assured him that he was going to put an end to his life because, owing to a ghastly affair, he must have twenty-five thousand francs. He did not mention what this ghastly affair was, and had he done so, it would doubtless have been an invention. As far as the money was concerned, M. de Charlus would willingly have sent him it, had he not felt that it would make Charlie independent of him and free to receive the favours of someone else. And so he refused, and his telegrams had the dry, cutting tone of his voice. When he was certain of their effect, he hoped that Morel would never forgive him, for, knowing very well that it was the contrary that would happen, he could not help dwelling upon all the drawbacks that would be revived with this inevitable tie. But, if no answer came from Morel, he lay awake all night, had not a moment's peace, so great is the number of the things of which we live in ignorance, and of the interior and profound realities that remain hidden from us. And so he would form every conceivable supposition as to the enormity which put Morel in need of twenty-five thousand francs, gave it every possible shape, labelled it with, one after another, many proper names. I believe that at such moments M. de Charlus (in spite of the fact that his snobbishness, which was now diminishing, had already been overtaken if not outstripped by his increasing curiosity as to the ways of the lower orders) must have recalled with a certain longing the lovely, many-coloured whirl of the fashionable gatherings at which the most charming men and women sought his company only for the disinterested pleasure that it afforded them, where nobody would have dreamed of 'doing him down', of inventing a 'ghastly affair', on the strength of which one is prepared to take one's life, if one does not at once receive twenty-five thousand francs. I believe that then, and perhaps because he had after all remained more 'Combray' at heart than myself, and had grafted a feudal dignity upon his Germanic pride, he must have felt that one cannot with impunity lose one's heart to a servant, that the lower orders are by no means the same thing as society, that in short he did not 'get on' with the lower orders as I have always done.

The next station upon the little railway, Maineville, reminds me of an incident in which Morel and M. de Charlus were concerned. Before I speak of it, I ought to mention that the halt of the train at Maineville (when one was escorting to Balbec a fashionable stranger, who, to avoid giving trouble, preferred not to stay at la Raspelière) was the occasion of scenes less painful than that which I am just about to describe. The stranger, having his light luggage with him in the train, generally found that the Grand Hotel was rather too far away, but, as there was nothing until one came to Balbec except small bathing places with uncomfortable villas, had, yielding to a preference for comfortable surroundings, resigned himself to the long journey when, as the train came to a standstill at Maineville, he saw the Palace staring him in the face, and never suspected that it was a house of ill fame. 'But don't let us go any farther,' he would invariably say to Mme Cottard, a woman well-known for her practical judgment and sound advice. 'There is the very thing I want. What is the use of going on to Balbec, where I certainly shan't find anything better. I can tell at a glance that it has all the modern comforts; I can quite well invite Mme Verdurin there, for I intend, in return for her hospitality, to give a few little parties in her honour. She won't have so far to come as if I stay at Balbec. This seems to me the very place for her, and for your wife, my dear Professor. There are bound to be sitting rooms, we can have the ladies there. Between you and me, I can't imagine why Mme Verdurin didn't come and settle here instead of taking la Raspelière. It is far healthier than an old house like la Raspelière, which is bound to be damp, and is not clean either, they have no hot water laid on, one can never get a wash. Now, Maineville strikes me as being far more attractive. Mme Verdurin would have played the hostess here to perfection. However, tastes differ; I intend, anyhow, to remain here. Mme Cottard, won't you come along with me; we shall have to be quick, for the train will be starting again in a minute. You can pilot me through that house, which you must know inside out, for you must often have visited it. It is the ideal setting for you.' The others would have the greatest difficulty in making the unfortunate stranger hold his tongue, and still more in preventing him from leaving the train, while he, with the obstinacy which often arises from a blunder, insisted, gathered his luggage together and refused to listen to a word until they had assured him that neither Mme Verdurin nor Mme Cottard would ever come to call upon him there. 'Anyhow, I am going to make my headquarters there. Mme Verdurin has only to write, if she wishes to see me.'

The incident that concerns Morel was of a more highly specialised order. There were others, but I confine myself at present, as the train halts and the porter calls out 'Doncières', 'Grattevast', 'Maineville', etc., to noting down the particular memory that the watering-place or garrison town recalls to me. I have already mentioned Maineville (*media villa*) and the importance that it had acquired from that luxurious establishment of women which had recently been built there, not without arousing futile protests from the mothers of families. But before I proceed to say why Maineville is associated in my memory with Morel and M. de Charlus, I must make a note of the disproportion (which I shall have occasion to examine more thoroughly later on) between the importance that Morel attached to keeping certain hours free, and the triviality of the occupations to which he pretended to devote to them, this same disproportion recurring amid the explanations of another sort which he gave to M. de Charlus. He, who played the disinterested artist for the Baron's benefit (and might do so without risk, in view of the generosity of his protector), when he wished to have the evening to himself, in order to give a lesson, etc., never failed to add to his excuse the following words, uttered with a smile of cupidity: 'Besides, there may be forty francs to be got out of it. That's always something. You will let me go, for, don't you see it's all to my advantage. Damn it all, I haven't got a regular income like you, I have my way to make in the world, it's a chance of earning a little money.' Morel, in professing his anxiety to give his lesson, was not altogether insincere. For one thing, it is false to say that money has no colour. A new way of earning them gives a fresh lustre to coins that are tarnished with use. Had he really gone out to give a lesson, it is probable that a couple of louis handed to him as he left the house by a girl pupil would have produced a different effect on him from a couple of louis coming from the hand of M. de Charlus. Besides, for a couple of louis the richest of men would travel miles, which become leagues when one is the son of a valet. But frequently M. de Charlus had his doubts as to the reality of the violin lesson, doubts which were increased by the fact that often the musician pleaded excuses of another sort, entirely disinterested from the material point of view, and at the same time absurd. In this Morel could not help presenting an image of his life, but one that deliberately, and unconsciously too, he so darkened that only certain parts of it could be made out. For a whole month he placed himself at M. de Charlus's disposal, on condition that he might keep his evenings free, for he was anxious to put in a regular attendance at a course of algebra. Come and see M. de Charlus after the class? Oh, that was impossible, the classes went on, sometimes, very late. 'Even after two o'clock in the morning?' the Baron asked. 'Sometimes.' 'But you can learn algebra just as easily from a book.' 'More easily, for I don't get very much out of the lectures.' 'Very well, then! Besides, algebra can't be of any use to you.' 'I like it. It soothes my nerves.' 'It cannot be algebra that makes him ask leave to go out at night,' M. de Charlus said to himself. 'Can he be working for the police?' In any case Morel, whatever objection might be made, reserved certain evening hours, whether for algebra or for the violin. On one occasion it was for neither, but for the Prince de Guermantes who, having come down for a few days to that part of the coast, to pay the Princesse de Luxembourg a visit, picked up the musician, without knowing who he was or being recognised by him either, and offered him fifty francs to spend the night with him in the brothel at Maineville; a twofold pleasure for Morel, in the profit received from M. de Guermantes and in the delight of being surrounded by women whose sunburned breasts would be visible to the naked eye. In some way or other M. de Charlus got wind of what had occurred and of the place appointed, but did not discover the name of the seducer. Mad with jealousy, and in the hope of finding out who he was, he telegraphed to Jupien, who arrived two days later, and when, early in the following week, Morel announced that he would again be absent, the Baron asked Jupien if he would undertake to bribe the woman who kept the establishment, and make her promise to hide the Baron and himself in some place where they could witness what occurred. 'That's all right. I'll see to it, dearie,' Jupien assured the Baron. It is hard to imagine to what extent this anxiety was agitating, and by so doing had momentarily enriched the mind of M. de Charlus. Love is responsible in this way for regular volcanic upheavals of the mind. In his, which, a few days earlier, resembled a plain so uniform that as far as the eye could reach it would have been impossible to make out an idea rising above the level surface, there had suddenly sprung into being, hard as stone, a chain of mountains, but mountains as elaborately carved as if some sculptor, instead of quarrying and carting his marble from them, had chiselled it on the spot, in which there writhed in vast titanic groups Fury, Jealousy, Curiosity, Envy, Hatred, Suffering, Pride, Terror and Love.

Meanwhile the evening on which Morel was to be absent had come. Jupien's mission had proved successful. He and the Baron were to be there about eleven o'clock, and would be put in a place of concealment. When they were still three streets away from this gorgeous house of prostitution (to which people came from all the fashionable resorts in the neighbourhood), M. de Charlus had begun to walk upon tiptoe, to disguise his voice, to beg Jupien not to speak so loud, lest Morel should hear them from inside. Whereas, on creeping stealthily into the entrance hall, M. de Charlus, who was not accustomed to places of the sort, found himself, to his terror and amazement, in a gathering more clamorous than the Stock Exchange or a sale room. It was in vain that he begged the girls who gathered round him to moderate their voices; for that matter their voices were drowned by the stream of announcements and awards made by an old 'assistant matron' in a very brown wig, her face crackled with the gravity of a Spanish attorney or priest, who kept shouting at every minute in a voice of thunder, ordering the doors to be alternately opened and shut, like a policeman regulating the flow of traffic: 'Take this gentleman to twenty-eight, the Spanish room.' 'Let no more in.' 'Open the door again, these gentlemen want Mademoiselle Noémie. She's expecting them in the Persian parlour.' M. de Charlus was as terrified as a countryman who has to cross the boulevards; while, to take a simile infinitely less sacrilegious than the subject represented on the capitals of the porch of the old church of Corleville, the voices of the young maids repeated in a lower tone, unceasingly, the assistant matron's orders, like the catechisms that we hear school children chanting beneath the echoing vault of a parish church in the country. However great his alarm, M. de Charlus who, in the street, had been trembling lest he should make himself heard, convinced in his own mind that Morel was at the window, was perhaps not so frightened after all in the din of those huge staircases on which one realised that from the rooms nothing could be seen. Coming at length to the end of his calvary, he found Mlle Noémie, who was to conceal him with Jupien, but began by shutting him up in a sumptuously furnished Persian sitting-room from which he could see nothing at all. She told him that Morel had asked for some orangeade, and that as soon as he was served the two visitors would be taken to a room with a transparent panel. In the meantime, as someone was calling for her, she promised them, like a fairy godmother, that to help them to pass the time she was going to send them a 'clever little lady'. For she herself was called away. The clever little lady wore a Persian wrapper, which she proposed to remove. M. de Charlus begged her to do nothing of the sort, and she rang for champagne which cost 40 francs a bottle. Morel, as a matter of fact, was, during this time, with the Prince de Guermantes; he had, for form's sake, pretended to go into the wrong room by mistake, had entered one in which there were two women, who had made haste to leave the two gentlemen undisturbed. M. de Charlus knew nothing of this, but was fidgeting with rage, trying to open the doors, sent for Mlle Noémie, who, hearing the clever little lady give M. de Charlus certain information about Morel which was not in accordance with what she herself had told Jupien, banished her promptly, and sent presently, as a substitute for the clever little lady, a 'dear little lady' who exhibited nothing more but told them how respectable the house was and called, like her predecessor, for champagne. The Baron, foaming with rage, sent again for Mlle Noémie, who said to them: 'Yes, it is taking rather long, the ladies are doing poses, he doesn't look as if he wanted to do anything.' Finally, yielding to the promises, the threats of the Baron, Mlle Noémie went away with an air of irritation, assuring them that they would not be kept waiting more than five minutes. The five minutes stretched out into an hour, after which Noémie came and tiptoed in front of M. de Charlus, blind with rage, and Jupien plunged in misery, to a door which stood ajar, telling them: 'You'll see splendidly from here. However, it's not very interesting just at present, he is with three ladies, he is telling them about life in his regiment.' At length the Baron was able to see through the cleft of the door and also the reflection in the mirrors beyond. But a deadly terror forced him to lean back against the wall. It was indeed Morel that he saw before him, but, as though the pagan mysteries and Enchantments still existed, it was rather the shade of Morel, Morel embalmed, not even Morel restored to life like Lazarus, an apparition of Morel, a phantom of Morel, Morel 'walking' or 'called up' in that room (in which the walls and couches everywhere repeated the emblems of sorcery), that was visible a few feet away from him, in profile. Morel had, as though he were already dead, lost all his colour; among these women, with whom one might have expected him to be making merry, he remained livid, fixed in an artificial immobility; to drink the glass of champagne that stood before him, his arm, sapped of its strength, tried in vain to reach out, and dropped back again. One had the impression of that ambiguous state implied by a religion which speaks of immorality but means by it something that does not exclude annihilation. The women were plying him with questions. 'You see,' Mlle Noémie whispered to the Baron, 'they are talking to him about his life in the regiment, it's amusing, isn't it?' – here she laughed – 'You're glad you came? He is calm, isn't he,' she added, as though she were speaking of a dying man. The women's questions came thick and fast, but Morel, inanimate, had not the strength to answer them. Even the miracle of a whispered word did not occur. M. de Charlus hesitated for barely a moment before he grasped what had really happened, namely that, whether from clumsiness on Jupien's part when he had called to make the arrangements, or from the expansive power of a secret lodged in any breast, which means that no secret is ever kept, or from the natural indiscretion of these ladies, or from their fear of the police, Morel had been told that two gentlemen had paid a large sum to be allowed to spy on him, unseen hands had spirited away the Prince de Guermantes, metamorphosed into three women, and had placed the unhappy Morel, trembling, paralysed with fear, in such a position that if M. de Charlus had but a poor view of him, he, terrorised, speechless, not daring to lift his glass for fear of letting it fall, had a perfect view of the Baron.

The story moreover had no happier ending for the Prince de Guermantes. When he had been sent away, so that M. de Charlus should not see him, furious at his disappointment, without suspecting who was responsible for it, he had implored Morel, still without letting him know who he was, to make an appointment with him for the following night in the tiny villa which he had taken and which, despite the shortness of his projected stay in it, he had, obeying the same insensate habit which we have already observed in Mme de Villeparisis, decorated with a number of family keepsakes, so that he might feel more at home. And so, next day, Morel, turning his head every moment, trembling with fear of being followed and spied upon by M. de Charlus, had finally, having failed to observe any suspicious passer-by, entered the villa. A valet showed him into the sitting-room, telling him that he would inform 'Monsieur' (his master had warned him not to utter the word 'Prince' for fear of arousing suspicions). But when Morel found himself alone, and went to the mirror to see that his forelock was not disarranged, he felt as though he were the victim of a hallucination. The photographs on the mantelpiece (which the violinist recognised, for he had seen them in M. de Charlus's room) of the Princesse de Guermantes, the Duchesse de Luxembourg, Mme de Villeparisis, left him at first petrified with fright. At the same moment he caught sight of the photograph of M. de Charlus, which was placed a little behind the rest. The Baron seemed to be concentrating upon Morel a strange, fixed glare. Mad with terror, Morel, recovering from his first stupor, never doubting that this was a trap into which M. de Charlus had led him in order to put his fidelity to the test, sprang at one bound down the steps of the villa and set off along the road as fast as his legs would carry him, and when the Prince (thinking he had kept a casual acquaintance waiting sufficiently long, and not without asking himself whether it were quite prudent and whether the person might not be dangerous) entered the room, he found nobody there. In vain did he and his valet, afraid of burglary, and armed with revolvers, search the whole house, which was not large, every corner of the garden, the basement; the companion of whose presence he had been certain had completely vanished. He met him several times in the course of the week that followed. But on each occasion it was Morel, the dangerous person, who turned tail and fled, as though the Prince were more dangerous still. Confirmed in his suspicions, Morel never outgrew them, and even in Paris the sight of the Prince de Guermantes was enough to make him take to his heels. Whereby M. de Charlus was protected from a betrayal which filled him with despair, and avenged, without ever having imagined such a thing, still less how it came about.

But already my memories of what I have been told about all this are giving place to others, for the B. A. G., resuming its slow crawl, continues to set down or take up passengers at the following stations.

At Grattevast, where his sister lived with whom he had been spending the afternoon, there would sometimes appear M. Pierre de Verjus, Comte de Crécy (who was called simply the Comte de Crécy), a gentleman without means but of the highest nobility, whom I had come to know through the Cambremers, although he was by no means intimate with them. As he was reduced to an extremely modest, almost a penurious existence, I felt that a cigar, a 'drink' were things that gave him so much pleasure that I formed the habit, on the days when I could not see Albertine, of inviting him to Balbec. A man of great refinement, endowed with a marvellous power of self-expression, snow-white hair, and a pair of charming blue eyes, he generally spoke in a faint murmur, very delicately, of the comforts of life in a country house, which he had evidently known from experience, and also of pedigrees. On my enquiring what was the badge engraved on his ring, he told me with a modest smile: 'It is a branch of verjuice.' And he added with a relish, as though sipping a vintage: 'Our arms are a branch of verjuice – symbolic, since my name is Verjus – slipped and leaved vert.' But I fancy that he would have been disappointed if at Balbec I had offered him nothing better to drink than verjuice. He liked the most expensive wines, because he had had to go without them, because of his profound knowledge of what he was going without, because he had a palate, perhaps also because he had an exorbitant thirst. And so when I invited him to dine at Balbec, he would order the meal with a refinement of skill, but ate a little too much, and drank copiously, made them warm the wines that needed warming, place those that needed cooling upon ice. Before dinner and after he would give the right date or number for a port or an old brandy, as he would have given the date of the creation of a marquisate which was not generally known but with which he was no less familiar.

As I was in Aimé's eyes a favoured customer, he was delighted that I should give these special dinners and would shout to the waiters: 'Quick, lay number 25'; he did not even say 'lay' but 'lay me', as though the table were for his own use. And, as the language of head waiters is not quite the same as of that of sub-heads, assistants, boys, and so forth, when the time came for me to ask for the bill he would say to the waiter who had served us, making a continuous, soothing gesture with the back of his hand, as though he were trying to calm a horse that was ready to take the bit in its teeth:

'Don't go too fast' (in adding up the bill), 'go gently, very gently.' Then, as the waiter was retiring with this guidance, Aimé, fearing lest his recommendations might not be carried out to the letter, would call him back: 'Here, let me make it out.' And as I told him not to bother: 'It's one of my principles that we ought never, as the saying is, to sting a customer.' As for the manager, since my guest was attired simply, always in the same clothes, which were rather threadbare (albeit nobody would so well have practised the art of dressing expensively, like one of Balzac's dandies, had he possessed the means), he confined himself, out of respect for me, to watching from a distance to see that everything was all right, and ordering, with a glance, a wedge to be placed under one leg of the table which was not steady. This was not to say that he was not qualified, though he concealed his early struggles, to lend a hand like anyone else. It required some exceptional circumstance nevertheless to induce him one day to carve the turkey-poults himself. I was out, but I heard afterwards that he carved them with a sacerdotal majesty, surrounded, at a respectful distance from the service-table, by a ring of waiters who were endeavouring thereby not so much to learn the art as to make themselves conspicuously visible, and stood gaping in open-mouthed admiration. Visible to the manager, for that matter (as he plunged a slow gaze into the flanks of his victims, and no more removed his eyes, filled with a sense of his exalted mission, from them than if he had been expected to read in them some augury), they were certainly not. The hierophant was not conscious of my absence even. When he heard of it, he was distressed: 'What, you didn't see me carving the turkey-poults myself?' I replied that having failed, so far, to see Rome, Venice, Siena, the Prado, the Dresden gallery, the Indies, Sarah in *Phèdre*, I had learned to resign myself, and that I would add his carving of turkey-poults to my list. The comparison with the dramatic art (Sarah in *Phèdre*) was the only one that he seemed to understand, for he had already been told by me that on days of gala performances the elder Coquelin had accepted a beginner's parts, even that of a character who says but a single line or nothing at all. 'It doesn't matter, I am sorry for your sake. When shall I be carving again? It will need some great event, it will need a war.' (It did, as a matter of fact, need the armistice.) From that day onwards, the calendar was changed, time was reckoned thus: 'That was the day after the day I carved the turkeys myself.' 'That's right, a week after the manager carved the turkeys himself.' And so this prosectomy furnished, like the Nativity of Christ or the Hegira, the starting point for a calendar different from the rest, but neither so extensively adopted nor so long observed.

The sadness of M. de Crécy's life was due, just as much as to his no longer keeping horses and a succulent table, to his mixing exclusively with people who were capable of supposing that Cambremers and Guermantes were one and the same thing. When he saw that I knew that Legrandin, who had now taken to calling himself Legrand de Méséglise, had no sort of right to that name, being moreover heated by the wine that he was drinking, he broke out in a transport of joy. His sister said to me with an understanding air: 'My brother is never so happy as when he has a chance of talking to you.' He felt indeed that he was alive now that he had discovered somebody who knew the unimportance of the Cambremers and the greatness of the Guermantes, somebody for whom the social universe existed. So, after the burning of all the libraries on the face of the globe and the emergence of a race entirely unlettered, an old Latin scholar would recover his confidence in life if he heard somebody quoting a line of Horace. And so, if he never left the train without saying to me: 'When is our next little gathering?', it was not so much with the hunger of a parasite as with the gluttony of a savant, and because he regarded our symposia at Balbec as an opportunity for talking about subjects which were precious to him and of which he was never able to talk to anyone else, and analogous in that way to those dinners at which assemble on certain specified dates, round the particularly succulent board of the Union Club, the Society of Bibliophiles. He was extremely modest, so far as his own family was concerned, and it was not from M. de Crécy that I learned that it was a very great family indeed, and a genuine branch transplanted to France of the English family which bears the title of Crécy. When I learned that he was a true Crécy, I told him that one of Mme de Guermantes's nieces had married an American named Charles Crécy, and said that I did not suppose there was any connection between them. 'None,' he said. 'Any more than – not, of course, that my family is so distinguished – heaps of Americans who call themselves Montgomery, Berry, Chandos or Capel have with the families of Pembroke, Buckingham or Essex, or with the Duc de Berry.' I thought more than once of telling him, as a joke, that I knew Mme Swann, who as a courtesan had been known at one time by the name Odette de Crécy; but even if the Duc d'Alencon had shown no resentment when people mentioned in front of him Émilienne d'Alencon, I did not feel that I was on sufficiently intimate terms with M. de Crécy to carry a joke so far. 'He comes of a very great family,' M. de Montsurvent said to me one day. 'His family name is Saylor.' And he went on to say that on the wall of his old castle above Incarville, which was now almost uninhabitable and which he, although born to a great fortune, was now too much impoverished to put in repair, was still to be read the old motto of the family. I thought this motto very fine, whether applied to the impatience of a predatory race niched in that eyrie from which its members must have swooped down in the past, or at the present day, to its contemplation of its own decline, awaiting the approach of death in that towering, grim retreat. It is, indeed, in this double sense that this motto plays upon the name Saylor, in the words: '*Ne sçais l'heure.*'

At Hermenonville there would get in sometimes M. de Chevregny, whose name, Brichot told us, signified like that of Mgr. de Cabrières, a place where goats assemble. He was related to the Cambremers, for which reason, and from a false idea of what was fashionable, the latter often invited him to Féterne, but only when they had no other guests to dazzle. Living all the year round at Beausoleil, M. de Chevregny had remained more provincial than they. And so when he went for a few weeks to Paris, there was not a moment to waste if he was to 'see everything' in the time; so much so that occasionally, a little dazed by the number of spectacles too rapidly digested, when he was asked if he had seen a particular play he would find that he was no longer sure. But this uncertainty was rare, for he had that detailed knowledge of Paris only to be found in people who seldom go there. He advised me which of the 'novelties' I ought to see ('It's worth your while'), regarding them however solely from the point of view of the pleasant evening that they might help to spend, and so completely ignoring the aesthetic point of view as never to suspect that they might indeed constitute a 'novelty' occasionally in the history of art. So it was that, speaking of everything in the same tone, he told us: 'We went once to the Opéra-Comique, but the show there is nothing much. It's called *Pelléas et Mélisande.* It's rubbish. Périer always acts well, but it's better to see him in something else. At the Gymnase, on the other hand, they're doing *La Châtelaine.* We went again to it twice; don't miss it, whatever you do, it's well worth seeing; besides, it's played to perfection; you have Frévalles, Marie Magnier, Baron fils'; and he went on to quote the names of actors of whom I had never heard, and without prefixing Monsieur, Madame or Mademoiselle, like the Duc de Guermantes, who used to speak in the same ceremoniously contemptuous tone of the 'songs of Mademoiselle Yvette Guilbert' and the 'experiments of Monsieur Charcot'. This was not M. de Chevregny's way, he said 'Cornaglia and Dehelly', as he might have said 'Voltaire and Montesquieu'. For in him, with regard to actors as to everything that was Parisian, the aristocrat's desire to show his scorn was overcome by the desire to appear on familiar terms of the provincial.

Immediately after the first dinner-party that I had attended at la Raspelière with what was still called at Féterne 'the young couple', albeit M. and Mme de Cambremer were no longer, by any means, in their first youth, the old Marquise had written me one of those letters which one can pick out by their handwriting from among a thousand. She said to me: 'Bring your delicious – charming – nice cousin. It will be a delight, a pleasure', always avoiding, and with such unerring dexterity, the sequence that the recipient of her letter would naturally have expected, that I finally changed my mind as to the nature of these diminuendoes, decided that they were deliberate, and found in them the same corruption of taste – transposed into the social key – that drove Sainte-Beuve to upset all the normal relations between words, to alter any expression that was at all conventional. Two methods, taught probably by different masters, came into conflict in this epistolary style, the second making Mme de Cambremer redeem the monotony of her multiple adjectives by employing them in a descending scale, by avoiding an ending upon the perfect chord. On the other hand, I was inclined to see in these inverse gradations, not an additional refinement, as when they were the handiwork of the Dowager Marquise, but an additional clumsiness whenever they were employed by the Marquis her son or by his lady cousins. For throughout the family, to quite a remote degree of kinship and in admiring imitation of aunt Zélia, the rule of the three adjectives was held in great honour, as was a certain enthusiastic way of catching your breath when you were talking. An imitation that had passed into the blood, moreover; and whenever, in the family circle, a little girl, while still in the nursery, stopped short while she was talking to swallow her saliva, her parents would say: 'She takes after aunt Zélia', would feel that as she grew up, her upper lip would soon tend to hide itself beneath a faint moustache, and would make up their minds to cultivate her inherited talent for music. It was not long before the Cambremers were on less friendly terms with Mme Verdurin than with myself, for different reasons. They felt, they must invite her to dine. The 'young' Marquise said to me contemptuously: 'I don't see why we shouldn't invite that woman, in the country one meets anybody, it needn't involve one in anything.' But being at heart considerably impressed, they never ceased to consult me as to the way in which they should carry out their desire to be polite. I thought that as they had invited Albertine and myself to dine with some friends of Saint-Loup, smart people of the neighbourhood, who owned the château of Gourville, and represented a little more than the cream of Norman society, for which Mme Verdurin, while pretending never to look at it, thirsted, I advised the Cambremers to invite the Mistress to meet them. But the lord and lady of Féterne, in their fear (so timorous were they) of offending their noble friends, or (so simple were they) that M. and Mme Verdurin might be bored by people who were not intellectual, or yet again (since they were impregnated with a spirit of routine which experience had not fertilised) of mixing different kinds of people, and making a social blunder, declared that it would not be a success, and that it would be much better to keep Mme Verdurin (whom they would invite with all her little group) for another evening. For this coming evening – the smart one, to meet Saint-Loup's friends – they invited nobody from the little nucleus but Morel, in order that M. de Charlus might indirectly be informed of the brilliant people whom they had in their house, and also that the musician might help them to entertain their guests, for he was to be asked to bring his violin. They threw in Cottard as well, because M. de Cambremer declared that he had 'a go' about him, and would be a success at the dinner-table; besides, it might turn out useful to be on friendly terms with a doctor, if they should ever have anybody ill in the house. But they invited him by himself, so as not to 'start any complications with the wife'. Mme Verdurin was furious when she heard that two members of the little group had been invited without herself to dine at Féterne 'quite quietly'. She dictated to the doctor, whose first impulse had been to accept, a stiff reply in which he said: 'We are dining that evening with Mme Verdurin', a plural which was to teach the Cambremers a lesson, and to show them that he was not detachable from Mme Cottard. As for Morel, Mme Verdurin had no need to outline a course of impolite behaviour for him, he found one of his own accord, for the following reason. If he preserved, with regard to M. de Charlus, in so far as his pleasures were concerned, an independence which distressed the Baron, we have seen that the latter's influence was making itself felt more and more in other regions, and that he had for instance enlarged the young virtuoso's knowledge of music and purified his style. But it was still, at this point in our story, at least, only an influence. At the same time there was one subject upon which anything that M. de Charlus might say was blindly accepted and put into practice by Morel. Blindly and foolishly, for not only were M. de Charlus's instructions false, but, even had they been justifiable in the case of a great gentleman, when applied literally by Morel they became grotesque. The subject as to which Morel was becoming so credulous and obeyed his master with such docility was that of social distinction. The violinist, who, before making M. de Charlus's acquaintance, had had no conception of society, had taken literally the brief and arrogant sketch of it that the Baron had outlined for him. 'There are a certain number of outstanding families,' M. de Charlus had told him, 'first and foremost the Guermantes, who claim fourteen alliances with the House of France, which is flattering to the House of France if anything, for it was to Aldonce de Guermantes and not to Louis the Fat, his consanguineous but younger brother, that the Throne of France should have passed. Under Louiv XIV, we 'draped' at the death of

Monsieur, having the same grandmother as the king; a long way below the Guermantes, one may however mention the families of La Trémoïlle, descended from the Kings of Naples and the Counts of Poitiers; of d'Uzès, scarcely old as a family, but the premier peers; of Luynes, who are of entirely recent origin, but have distinguished themselves by good marriages; of Choiseul, Harcourt, La Rochefoucauld. Add to these the family of the Noailles (notwithstanding the Comte de Toulouse), Montesquieu and Castellane, and, I think I am right in saying, those are all. As for all the little people who call themselves Marquis de Cambremerde or de Vatefairefiche, there is no difference between them and the humblest private in your regiment. It doesn't matter whether you go and p— at Comtesse S—t's or s—t at Baronne P—'s, it's exactly the same, you will have compromised yourself and have used a dirty rag instead of toilet paper. Which is not nice.' Morel had piously taken in this history lesson, which was perhaps a trifle cursory, and looked upon these matters as though he were himself a Guermantes and hoped that he might some day have an opportunity of meeting the false La Tour d'Auvergnes in order to let them see, by the contemptuous way in which he shook hands, that he did not take them very seriously. As for the Cambremers, here was his very chance to prove to them that they were no better than 'the humblest private in his regiment'. He did not answer their invitation, and on the evening of the dinner declined at the last moment by telegram, as pleased with himself as if he had behaved like a Prince of the Blood. It must be added here that it is impossible to imagine how intolerable and interfering M. de Charlus could be, in a more general fashion, and even, he who was so clever, how stupid, on all occasions when the flaws in his character came into play. We may say indeed that these flaws are like an intermittent malady of the mind. Who has not observed the fact among women, and even among men, endowed with remarkable intelligence but afflicted with nerves, when they are happy, calm, satisfied with their surroundings, we cannot help admiring their precious gifts, the words that fall from their lips are the literal truth. A touch of headache, the slightest injury to their self-esteem is enough to alter everything. The luminous intelligence, become abrupt, convulsive and narrow, reflects nothing but an irritated, suspicious, teasing self, doing everything that it can to give trouble. The Cambremers were extremely angry; and in the interval other incidents brought about a certain tension in their relations with the little clan. As we were returning, the Cottards, Charlus, Brichot, Morel and I, from a dinner at la Raspelière, one evening after the Cambremers who had been to luncheon with friends at Harambouville had accompanied us for part of our outward journey: 'You who are so fond of Balzac, and can find examples of him in the society of today,' I had remarked to M. de Charlus, 'you must feel that those Cambremers come straight out of the *Scènes de la Vie de Province*.' But M. de Charlus, for all the world as though he had been their friend, and I had offended him by my remark, at once cut me short: 'You say that because the wife is superior to the husband,' he informed me in a dry tone. 'Oh, I wasn't suggesting that she was the *Muse du département*, or Mme de Bargeton, although . . . ' M. de Charlus again interrupted me: 'Say rather, Mme de Mortsauf.' The train stopped and Brichot got out. 'Didn't you see us making signs to you? You are incorrigible.' 'What do you mean?' 'Why, have you never noticed that Brichot is madly in love with Mme de Cambremer?' I could see from the attitude of Cottard and Charlie that there was not a shadow of doubt about this in the little nucleus. I felt that it showed a trace of malice on their part. 'What, you never noticed how distressed he became when you mentioned her,' went on M. de Charlus, who liked to show that he had experience of women, and used to speak of the sentiment which they inspire with a natural air and as though this were the sentiment which he himself habitually felt. But a certain equivocally paternal tone in addressing all young men – notwithstanding his exclusive affection for Morel – gave the lie to the views of a woman-loving man which he expressed. 'Oh! These children,' he said in a shrill, mincing, singsong voice, 'one has to teach them everything, they are as innocent as a newborn babe, they can't even tell when a man is in love with a woman. I wasn't such a chicken at your age,' he added, for he liked to use the expressions of the underworld, perhaps because they appealed to him, perhaps so as not to appear, by avoiding them, to admit that he consorted with people whose current vocabulary they were. A few days later, I was obliged to yield to the force of evidence, and admit that Brichot was enamoured of the Marquise. Unfortunately he accepted several invitations to luncheon with her. Mme Verdurin decided that it was time to put a stop to these proceedings. Quite apart from the importance of such an intervention to her policy in controlling the little nucleus, explanations of this sort and the dramas to which they gave rise caused her an ever-increasing delight which idleness breeds just as much in the middle classes as in the aristocracy. It was a day of great emotion at la Raspelière when Mme Verdurin was seen to disappear for a whole hour with Brichot, whom (it was known) she proceeded to inform that Mme de Cambremer was laughing at him, that he was the joke of her drawing-room, that he would end his days in disgrace, having forfeited his position in the teaching world. She went so far as to refer in touching terms to the laundress with whom he was living in Paris, and to their little girl. She won the day, Brichot ceased to go to Féterne, but his grief was such that for two days it was thought that he would lose his sight altogether, while in any case his malady increased at a bound and held the ground it had won. In the meantime, the Cambremers, who were furious with Morel, invited M. de Charlus on one occasion, deliberately, without him. Receiving no reply from the Baron, they began to fear that they had committed a blunder, and, deciding that malice made an evil counsellor, wrote, a little late in the day, to Morel, an ineptitude which made M. de Charlus smile, as it proved to him the extent of his power. 'You shall answer for us both that I accept,' he said to Morel. When the evening of the dinner came, the party assembled in the great drawing-room of Féterne. In reality, the Cambremers were giving this dinner for those fine flowers of fashion M. and Mme Féré. But they were so much afraid of displeasing M. de Charlus, that although she had got to know the Férés through M. de Chevregny, Mme de Cambremer went into a fever when, on the afternoon before the dinner, she saw him arrive to pay a call on them at Féterne. She made every imaginable excuse for sending him back to Beausoleil as quickly as possible, not so quickly, however, that he did not pass, in the courtyard, the Férés, who were as shocked to see him dismissed like this as he himself was ashamed. But, whatever happened, the Cambremers wished to spare M. de Charlus the sight of M. de Chevregny, whom they judged to be provincial because of certain little points which are overlooked in the family circle and become important only in the presence of strangers, who are the last people in the world to notice them. But we do not like to display to them relatives who have remained at the stage which we ourselves have struggled to outgrow. As for M. and Mme Féré, they were, in the highest sense of the words, what are called 'really nice people'. In the eyes of those who so defined them, no doubt the Guermantes, the Rohans and many others were also really nice people, but their name made it unnecessary to say so. As everybody was not aware of the exalted birth of Mme Féré's mother, and the extraordinarily exclusive circle in which she and her husband moved, when you mentioned their name, you invariably added by way of explanation that they were 'the very best sort'. Did their obscure name prompt them to a sort of haughty reserve? However that may be, the fact remains that the Férés refused to know people on whom a La Trémoïlle would have called. It needed the position of queen of her particular stretch of coast, which the old Marquise de Cambremer held in the Manche, to make the Férés consent to come to one of her afternoons every year. The Cambremers had invited them to dinner and were counting largely on the effect that would be made on them by M. de Charlus. It was discreetly announced that he was to be one of the party. As it happened,

Mme Féré had never met him. Mme de Cambremer, on learning this, felt a keen satisfaction, and the smile of the chemist who is about to bring into contact for the first time two particularly important bodies hovered over her face. The door opened, and Mme de Cambremer almost fainted when she saw Morel enter the room alone. Like a private secretary charged with apologies for his Minister, like a morganatic wife who expresses the Prince's regret that he is unwell (so Mme de Clinchamp used to apologise for the Duc d'Aumale), Morel said in the airiest of tones: 'The Baron can't come. He is not feeling very well, at least I think that is why, I haven't seen him this week,' he added, these last words completing the despair of Mme de Cambremer, who had told M. and Mme Féré that Morel saw M. de Charlus at every hour of the day. The Cambremers pretended that the Baron's absence gave an additional attraction to their party, and without letting Morel hear them, said to their other guests: 'We can do very well without him, can't we, it will be all the better.' But they were furious, suspected a plot hatched by Mme Verdurin, and, tit for tat, when she invited them again to la Raspelière, M. de Cambremer, unable to resist the pleasure of seeing his house again and of mingling with the little group, came, but came alone, saying that the Marquise was so sorry, but her doctor had ordered her to stay in her room. The Cambremers hoped by this partial attendance at once to teach M. de Charlus a lesson, and to show the Verdurins that they were not obliged to treat them with more than a limited politeness, as Princesses of the Blood used in the old days to 'show out' Duchesses, but only to the middle of the second saloon. After a few weeks, they were scarcely on speaking terms. M. de Cambremer explained this to me as follows: 'I must tell you that with M. de Charlus it was rather difficult. He is an extreme Dreyfusard . . . ' 'Oh, no!' 'Yes . . . Anyhow his cousin the Prince de Guermantes is, they've come in for a lot of abuse over that. I have some relatives who are very particular about that sort of thing. I can't afford to mix with those people, I should quarrel with the whole of my family.' 'Since the Prince de Guermantes is a Dreyfusard, that will make it all the easier,' said Mme de Cambremer, 'for Saint-Loup, who is said to be going to marry his niece, is one too. Indeed, that is perhaps why he is marrying her.' 'Come now, my dear, you mustn't say that Saint-Loup, who is a great friend of ours, is a Dreyfusard. One ought not to make such allegations lightly,' said M. de Cambremer. 'You would make him highly popular in the army!' 'He was once, but he isn't any longer,' I explained to M. de Cambremer. 'As for his marrying Mlle de Guermantes-Brassac, is there any truth in that?' 'People are talking of nothing else, but you should be in a position to know.' 'But I repeat that he told me himself, he was a Dreyfusard,' said Mme de

Cambremer. 'Not that there isn't every excuse for him, the Guermantes are half German.' 'The Guermantes in the Rue de Varenne, you can say, are entirely German,' said Cancan. 'But Saint-Loup is a different matter altogether; he may have any amount of German blood, his father insisted upon maintaining his title as a great nobleman of France, he rejoined the service in 1871 and was killed in the war in the most gallant fashion. I may take rather a strong line about these matters, but it doesn't do to exaggerate either one way or the other. *In medio . . . virtus*, ah, I forget the exact words. It's a remark Doctor Cottard made. Now, there's a man who can always say the appropriate thing. You ought to have a small Larousse in the house.' To avoid having to give an opinion as to the Latin quotation, and to get away from the subject of Saint-Loup, as to whom her husband seemed to think that she was wanting in tact, Mme de Cambremer fell back upon the Mistress whose quarrel with them was even more in need of an explanation. 'We were delighted to let la Raspelière to Mme Verdurin,' said the Marquise. 'The only trouble is, she appears to imagine that with the house, and everything else that she has managed to tack on to it, the use of the meadow, the old hangings, all sorts of things which weren't in the lease at all, she should also be entitled to make friends with us. The two things are entirely distinct. Our mistake lay in our not having done everything quite simply through a lawyer or an agency. At Féterne it doesn't matter, but I can just imagine the face my aunt de Ch'nouville would make if she saw old mother Verdurin come marching in, on one of my days, with her hair streaming. As for M. de Charlus, of course, he knows some quite nice people, but he knows some very nasty people too.' I asked for details. Driven into a corner, Mme de Cambremer finally admitted: 'People say that it was he who maintained a certain Monsieur Moreau, Morille, Morue, I don't remember. Nothing to do, of course, with Morel, the violinist,' she added, blushing. 'When I realised that Mme Verdurin imagined that because she was our tenant in the Manche, she would have the right to come and call upon me in Paris, I saw that it was time to cut the cable.'

Notwithstanding this quarrel with the Mistress, the Cambremers were on quite good terms with the faithful, and would readily get into our carriage when they were travelling by the train. Just before we reached Douville, Albertine, taking out her mirror for the last time, would sometimes feel obliged to change her gloves, or to take off her hat for a moment, and, with the tortoiseshell comb which I had given her and which she wore in her hair, would smooth the plaits, pull out the puffs, and if necessary, over the undulations which descended in regular valleys to the nape of her neck, push up her chignon. Once we were in the carriages which had come to meet us, we no longer had any idea where we were; the roads were not lighted; we could tell by the louder sound of the wheels that we were passing through a village, we thought we had arrived, we found ourselves once more in the open country, we heard bells in the distance, we forgot that we were in evening dress, and had almost fallen asleep when, at the end of this wide borderland of darkness which, what with the distance we had travelled and the incidents characteristic of all railway journeys, seemed to have carried us on to a late hour of the night and almost half way back to Paris, suddenly after the crunching of the carriage wheels over a finer gravel had revealed to us that we had turned into the park, there burst forth, reintroducing us into a social existence, the dazzling lights of the drawing-room, then of the dining-room where we were suddenly taken aback by hearing eight o'clock strike, that hour which we supposed to have so long since passed, while the endless dishes and vintage wines followed one another round men in black and women with bare arms, at a dinner-party ablaze with light like any real dinner-party, surrounded only, and thereby changing its character, by the double veil, sombre and strange, that was woven for it, with a sacrifice of their first solemnity to this social purpose, by the nocturnal, rural, seaside hours of the journey there and back. The latter indeed obliged us to leave the radiant and soon forgotten splendour of the lighted drawing-room for the carriages in which I arranged to sit beside Albertine so that my mistress might not be left with other people in my absence, and often for another reason as well, which was that we could both do many things in a dark carriage, in which the jolts of the downward drive would moreover give us an excuse, should a sudden ray of light fall upon us, for clinging to one another. When M. de Cambremer was still on visiting terms with the Verdurins, he would ask me: 'You don't think that this fog will bring on your choking fits? My sister was terribly bad this morning. Ah! You have been having them too,' he said with satisfaction. 'I shall tell her that tonight. I know that, as soon as I get home, the first thing she will ask will be whether you have had any lately.' He spoke to me of my sufferings only to lead up to his sister's, and made me describe mine in detail simply that he might point out the difference between them and hers. But notwithstanding these differences, as he felt that his sister's choking fits entitled him to speak with authority, he could not believe that what 'succeeded' with hers was not indicated as a cure for mine, and it irritated him that I would not try these remedies, for if there is one thing more difficult than submitting oneself to a regime it is refraining from imposing it upon other people. 'Not that I need speak, a mere outsider, when you are here before the areopagus, at the fountainhead of wisdom. What does Professor Cottard think about them?' I saw his wife once again, as a matter of fact, because she had said that my 'cousin' had odd habits, and I wished to know what she meant by that. She denied having said it, but finally admitted that she had been speaking of a person whom she thought she had seen with my cousin. She did not know the person's name and said faintly that, if she was not mistaken, it was the wife of a banker, who was called Lina, Linette, Lisette, Lia, anyhow something like that. I felt that 'wife of a banker' was inserted merely to put me off the scent. I decided to ask Albertine whether this were true. But I preferred to speak to her with an air of knowledge rather than of curiosity. Besides Albertine would not have answered me at all, or would have answered me only with a 'no' of which the 'n' would have been too hesitating and the 'o' too emphatic. Albertine never related facts that were capable of injuring her, but always other facts which could be explained only by them, the truth being rather a current which flows from what people say to us, and which we apprehend, invisible as it may be, than the actual thing that they say. And so when I assured her that a woman whom she had known at Vichy had a bad reputation, she swore to me that this woman was not at all what I supposed, and had never attempted to make her do anything improper. But she added, another day, when I was speaking of my curiosity as to people of that sort, that the Vichy lady had a friend, whom she, Albertine, did not know, but whom the lady had '*promised* to introduce to her.' That she should have promised her this, could only mean that Albertine wished it, or that the lady had known that by offering the introduction she would be giving her pleasure. But if I had pointed this out to Albertine, I should have appeared to be depending for my information upon her, I should have put an end to it at once, I should never have learned anything more, I should have ceased to make myself feared. Besides, we were at Balbec, the Vichy lady and her friend lived at Menton; the remoteness, the impossibility of the danger made short work of my suspicions. Often when M. de Cambremer hailed me from the station I had been with Albertine making the most of the darkness, and with all the more difficulty as she had been inclined to resist, fearing that it was not dark enough. 'You know, I'm sure Cottard saw us, anyhow, if he didn't, he must have noticed how breathless we were from our voices, just when they were talking about your other kind of breathlessness,' Albertine said to me when we arrived at the Douville station where we were to take the little train home. But this homeward, like the outward journey, if, by giving me a certain poetical feeling, it awakened in me the desire to travel, to lead a new life, and so made me decide to abandon any intention of marrying Albertine, and even to break off our relations finally, also, and by the very fact of their contradictory nature, made this breach more easy. For, on the homeward journey just as much as on the other, at every station there joined us in the train or greeted us from the platform people whom we knew; the furtive pleasures of the imagination were outweighed by those other, continual pleasures of sociability which are so soothing, so soporific. Already, before the stations themselves, their names (which had suggested so many fancies to me since the day on which I first heard them, the evening on which I travelled down to Balbec with my grandmother), had grown human, had lost their strangeness since the evening when Brichot, at Albertine's request, had given us a more complete account of their etymology. I had been charmed by the 'flower' that ended certain names, such as Fiquefleur, Ronfleur, Fiers, Barfleur, Harfleur, etc., and amused by the 'beef' that comes at the end of Bricqueboeuf. But the flower vanished, and also the beef, when Brichot (and this he had told me on the first day in the train) informed us that *fleur* means a harbour (like *fiord*), and that *boeuf*, in Norman *budh*, means a hut. As he cited a number of examples, what had appeared to me a particular instance became general, Bricqueboeuf took its place by the side of Elbeuf, and indeed in a name that was at first sight as individual as the place itself, like the name Pennedepie, in which the obscurities most impossible for the mind to elucidate seemed to me to have been amalgamated from time immemorial in a word as coarse, savoury and hard as a certain Norman cheese, I was disappointed to find the Gallic *pen* which means mountain and is as recognisable in Pennemarck as in the Apennines. As at each halt of the train I felt that we should have friendly hands to shake if not visitors to receive in our carriage, I said to Albertine: 'Hurry up and ask Brichot about the names you want to know. You mentioned to me Marcouville l'Orgueilleuse.' 'Yes, I love that *orgueil*, it's a proud village,' said Albertine. 'You would find it,' Brichot replied, 'prouder still if, instead of turning it into French or even adopting a low Latinity, as we find in the Cartulary of the Bishop of Bayeux, *Marcouvilla superba*, you were to take the older form, more akin to the Norman, *Marculplinvilla superba*, the village, the domain of Merculph. In almost all these names which end in *ville*, you might see still marshalled upon this coast, the phantoms of the rude Norman invaders. At Hermenonville, you had, standing by the carriage door, only our excellent Doctor, who, obviously, has nothing of the Nordic chief about him. But, by shutting your eyes, you might have seen the illustrious Hérimund (*Herimundivilla*). Although I can never understand why people choose those roads, between Loigny and Balbec-Plage, rather than the very picturesque roads that lead from Loigny to Old Balbec, Mme Verdurin has perhaps taken you out that way in her carriage. If so, you have seen Incarville, or the village of Wiscar; and Tourville, before you come to Mme Verdurin's, is the village of Turold. And besides, there were not only the Normans. It seems that the Germans (*Alemanni*) came as far as here: Aumenancourt, *Alemanicurtis* – don't let us speak of it to that young officer I see there; he would be capable of refusing to visit his cousins there any more. There were also Saxons, as is proved by the springs of Sissonne' (the goal of one of Mme Verdurin's favourite excursions, and quite rightly), 'just as in England you have Middlesex, Wessex. And what is inexplicable, it seems that the Goths, miserable wretches as they are said to have been, came as far as this, and even the Moors, for Mortagne comes from *Mauretania*. Their trace has remained at Gourville – *Gothorumvilla*. Some vestige of the Latins subsists also, Lagny (*Latiniacum*).' 'What I should like to have is an explanation of Thorpehomme,' said M. de Charlus. 'I understand *homme*,' he added, at which the sculptor and Cottard exchanged significant glances. 'But *Thorpe*?' '*Homme* does not in the least mean what you are naturally led to suppose, Baron,' replied Brichot, glancing maliciously at Cottard and the sculptor. '*Homme* has nothing to do, in this instance, with the sex to which I am not indebted for my mother. *Homme* is *holm* which means a small island, etc . . . As for *Thorpe*, or village, we find that in a hundred words with which I have already bored our young friend. Thus in Thorpehomme there is not the name of a Norman chief, but words of the Norman language. You see how the whole of this country has been Germanised.' 'I think that is an exaggeration,' said M. de Charlus. 'Yesterday I was at Orgeville.' 'This time I give you back the man I took from you in Thorpehomme, Baron. Without wishing to be pedantic, a Charter of Robert I gives us, for Orgeville, *Otgervilla*, the domain of Otger. All these names are those of ancient lords. Octeville la Venelle is a corruption of l'Avenel. The Avenels were a family of repute in the middle ages. Bourguenolles, where Mme Verdurin took us the other day, used to be written Bourg de Môles, for that village belonged in the eleventh century to Baudoin de Môles, as also did la Chaise-Baudoin, but here we are at Doncières.' 'Heavens, look at all these subalterns trying to get in,' said M. de Charlus with feigned alarm. 'I am thinking of you, for it doesn't affect me, I am getting out here.' 'You hear, Doctor?' said Brichot. 'The Baron is afraid of officers passing over his body. And yet they have every right to appear here in their strength, for Doncières is precisely the same as Saint-Cyr, *Dominus Cyriacus*. There are plenty of names of towns in which *Sanctus* and *Sancta* are replaced by *Dominus* and *Domina*. Besides, this peaceful military town has sometimes a false air of Saint-Cyr, of Versailles, and even of Fontainebleau.'

During these homeward (as on the outward) journeys I used to tell Albertine to put on her things, for I knew very well that at Aumenancourt, Doncières, Epreville, Saint-Vast we should be receiving brief visits from friends. Nor did I at all object to these, when they took the form of (at Hermenonville – the domain of Herimund) a visit from M. de Chevregny, seizing the opportunity, when he had come down to meet other guests, of asking me to come over to luncheon next day at Beausoleil, or (at Doncières) the sudden irruption of one of Saint-Loup's charming friends sent by him (if he himself was not free) to convey to me an invitation from Captain de Borodino, from the officers' mess at the Cocq-Hardi, or the serjeants' at the Faisan Doré. If Saint-Loup often came in person, during the whole of the time that he was stationed there, I contrived, without attracting attention, to keep Albertine a prisoner under my own watch and ward, not that my vigilance was of any use. On one occasion however my watch was interrupted. When there was a long stop, Bloch, after greeting us, was making off at once to join his father, who, having just succeeded to his uncle's fortune, and having leased a country house by the name of La Commanderie, thought it befitting a country gentleman always to go about in a post-chaise, with postilions in livery. Bloch begged me to accompany him to the carriage. 'But make haste, for these quadrupeds are impatient, come, O man beloved of the gods, thou wilt give pleasure to my father.' But I could not bear to leave Albertine in the train with Saint-Loup; they might, while my back was turned, get into conversation, go into another compartment, smile at one another, touch one another; my eyes, glued to Albertine, could not detach themselves from her so long as Saint-Loup was there. Now I could see quite well that Bloch, who had asked me, as a favour, to go and say how d'ye do to his father, in the first place thought it not very polite of me to refuse when there was nothing to prevent me from doing so, the porters having told us that the train would remain for at least a quarter of an hour in the station, and almost all the passengers, without whom it would not start, having alighted; and, what was more, had not the least doubt that it was because quite decidedly – my conduct on this occasion furnished him with a definite proof of it – I was a snob. For he was well aware of the names of the people in whose company I was. In fact M. de Charlus had said to me, some time before this and without remembering or caring that the introduction had been made long ago: 'But you must introduce your friend to me, you are showing a want of respect for myself,' and had talked to Bloch, who had seemed to please him immensely, so much so that he had gratified him with an: 'I hope to meet you again.' 'Then it is irrevocable, you won't walk a hundred yards to say how d'ye do to my father, who would be so pleased,'

Bloch said to me. I was sorry to appear to be wanting in good fellowship, and even more so for the reason for which Bloch supposed that I was wanting, and to feel that he imagined that I was not the same towards my middle class friends when I was with people of 'birth'. From that day he ceased to show me the same friendly spirit and, what pained me more, had no longer the same regard for my character. But, in order to undeceive him as to the motive which made me remain in the carriage, I should have had to tell him something – to wit, that I was jealous of Albertine – which would have distressed me even more than letting him suppose that I was stupidly worldly. So it is that in theory we find that we ought always to explain ourselves frankly, to avoid misunderstandings. But very often life arranges these in such a way that, in order to dispel them, in the rare circumstances in which it might be possible to do so, we must reveal either – which was not the case here – something that would annoy our friend even more than the injustice that he imputes to us, or a secret the disclosure of which – and this was my predicament – appears to us even worse than the misunderstanding. Besides, even without my explaining to Bloch, since I could not, my reason for not going with him, if I had begged him not to be angry with me, I should only have increased his anger by showing him that I had observed it. There was nothing to be done but to bow before the decree of fate which had willed that Albertine's presence should prevent me from accompanying him, and that he should suppose that it was on the contrary the presence of people of distinction, the only effect of which, had they been a hundred times more distinguished, would have been to make me devote my attention exclusively to Bloch and reserve all my civility for him. It is sufficient that accidentally, absurdly, an incident (in this case the juxtaposition of Albertine and Saint-Loup) be interposed between two destinies whose lines have been converging towards one another, for them to deviate, stretch farther and farther apart, and never converge again. And there are friendships more precious than Bloch's for myself which have been destroyed without the involuntary author of the offence having any opportunity to explain to the offended party what would no doubt have healed the injury to his self-esteem and called back his fugitive affection.

Friendships more precious than Bloch's is not, for that matter, saying very much. He had all the faults that most annoyed me. It so happened that my affection for Albertine made them altogether intolerable. Thus in that brief moment in which I was talking to him, while keeping my eye on Robert, Bloch told me that he had been to luncheon with Mme Bontemps and that everybody had spoken about me with the warmest praise until the 'decline of Helios'. 'Good,' thought I, 'as Mme Bontemps regards Bloch as a genius, the enthusiastic support that he must have given me will do more than anything that the others can have said, it will come round to Albertine. Any day now she is bound to learn, and I am surprised that her aunt has not repeated it to her already, that I am a 'superior person'.' 'Yes,' Bloch went on, 'everybody sang your praises. I alone preserved a silence as profound as though I had absorbed, in place of the repast (poor, as it happened) that was set before us, poppies, dear to the blessed brother of Thanatos and Lethe, the divine Hypnos, who enwraps in pleasant bonds the body and the tongue. It is not that I admire you less than the band of hungry dogs with whom I had been bidden to feed. But I admire you because I understand you, and they admire you without understanding you. To tell the truth, I admire you too much to speak of you thus in public, it would have seemed to me a profanation to praise aloud what I carry in the profoundest depths of my heart. In vain might they question me about you, a sacred Pudor, daughter of Kronion, made me remain mute.' I had not the bad taste to appear annoyed, but this Pudor seemed to me akin – far more than to Kronion – to the modesty that prevents a critic who admires you from speaking of you because the secret temple in which you sit enthroned would be invaded by the mob of ignorant readers and journalists – to the modesty of the statesman who does not recommend you for a decoration because you would be lost in a crowd of people who are not your equals, to the modesty of the academician who refrains from voting for you in order to spare you the shame of being the colleague of X— who is devoid of talent, to the modesty in short, more respectable and at the same time more criminal, of the sons who implore us not to write about their dead father who abounded in merit, so that we shall not prolong his life and create a halo of glory round the poor deceased who would prefer that his name should be borne upon the lips of men to the wreaths, albeit laid there by pious hands, upon his tomb.

If Bloch, while he distressed me by his inability to understand the reason that prevented me from going to speak to his father, had exasperated me by confessing that he had depreciated me at Mme Bontemps's (I now understood why Albertine had never made any allusion to this luncheon-party and remained silent when I spoke to her of Bloch's affection for myself), the young Israelite had produced upon M. de Charlus an impression that was quite the opposite of annoyance.

Certainly Bloch now believed not only that I was unable to remain for a second out of the company of smart people, but that, jealous of the advances that they might make to him (M. de Charlus, for instance), I was trying to put a spoke in his wheel and to prevent him from making friends with them;

but for his part the Baron regretted that he had not seen more of my friend. As was his habit, he took care not to betray this feeling. He began by asking me various questions about Bloch, but in so casual a tone, with an interest that seemed so assumed, that one would have thought he did not hear the answers. With an air of detachment, an intonation that expressed not merely indifference but complete distraction, and as though simply out of politeness to myself: 'He looks intelligent, he said he wrote, has he any talent?' I told M. de Charlus that it had been very kind of him to say that he hoped to see Bloch again. The Baron made not the slightest sign of having heard my remark, and as I repeated it four times without eliciting a reply, I began to wonder whether I had not been the dupe of an acoustic mirage when I thought I heard M. de Charlus utter those words. 'He lives at Balbec?' intoned the Baron, with an air so far from questioning that it is a nuisance that the written language does not possess a sign other than the mark of interrogation with which to end these speeches which are apparently so little interrogative. It is true that such a sign would scarcely serve for M. de Charlus. 'No, they have taken a place near here, La Commanderie.' Having learned what he wished to know, M. de Charlus pretended to feel a contempt for Bloch. 'How appalling,' he exclaimed, his voice resuming all its clarion strength. 'All the places or properties called La Commanderie were built or owned by the Knights of the Order of Malta (of whom I am one), as the places called Temple or Cavalerie were by the Templars. That I should live at La Commanderie would be the most natural thing in the world. But a Jew! However, I am not surprised; it comes from a curious instinct for sacrilege, peculiar to that race. As soon as a Jew has enough money to buy a place in the country he always chooses one that is called Priory, Abbey, Minster, Chantry. I had some business once with a Jewish official, guess where he lived: at Pont-l'Evêque. When he came to grief, he had himself transferred to Brittany, to Pont-l'Abbé. When they perform in Holy Week those indecent spectacles that are called 'the Passion', half the audience are Jews, exulting in the thought that they are going to hang Christ a second time on the Cross, at least in effigy. At one of the Lamoureux concerts, I had a wealthy Jewish banker sitting next to me. They played the *Boyhood of Christ* by Berlioz, he was quite shocked. But he soon recovered his habitually blissful expression when he heard the Good Friday music. So your friend lives at the Commanderie, the wretch! What sadism! You shall show me the way to it,' he went on, resuming his air of indifference, 'so that I may go there one day and see how our former domains endure such a profanation. It is unfortunate, for he has good manners, he seems to have been well brought up. The next thing I shall hear will be that his address in

Paris is Rue du Temple!' M. de Charlus gave the impression, by these words, that he was seeking merely to find a fresh example in support of his theory; as a matter of fact he was aiming at two birds with one stone, his principal object being to find out Bloch's address. 'You are quite right,' put in Brichot, 'the Rue du Temple used to be called Rue de la Chevalerie-du-Temple. And in that connection will you allow me to make a remark, Baron?' said the don. 'What? What is it?' said M. de Charlus tartly, the proffered remark preventing him from obtaining his information. 'No, it's nothing,' replied Brichot in alarm. 'It is with regard to the etymology of Balbec, about which they were asking me. The Rue du Temple was formerly known as the Rue Barre-du-Bec, because the Abbey of Bec in Normandy had its Bar of Justice there in Paris.' M. de Charlus made no reply and looked as if he had not heard, which was one of his favourite forms of insolence. 'Where does your friend live, in Paris? As three streets out of four take their name from a church or an abbey, there seems every chance of further sacrilege there. One can't prevent Jews from living in the Boulevard de la Madeleine, Faubourg Saint-Honoré or Place Saint-Augustin. So long as they do not carry their perfidy a stage farther, and pitch their tents in the Place du Parvis-Notre-Dame, Quai de l'Archevêché, Rue Chanoinesse or Rue de l'Avemaria, we must make allowance for their difficulties.' We could not enlighten M. de Charlus, not being aware of Bloch's address at the time. But I knew that his father's office was in the Rue des Blancs-Manteaux. 'Oh! Is not that the last word in perversity?' exclaimed M. de Charlus, who appeared to find a profound satisfaction in his own cry of ironical indignation. 'Rue des Blancs-Manteaux!' he repeated, dwelling with emphasis upon each syllable and laughing as he spoke. 'What sacrilege! Imagine that these White Mantles polluted by M. Bloch were those of the mendicant brethren, styled Serfs of the Blessed Virgin, whom Saint Louis established there. And the street has always housed some religious Order. The profanation is all the more diabolical since within a stone's throw of the Rue des Blancs-Manteaux there is a street whose name escapes me, which is entirely conceded to the Jews, there are Hebrew characters over the shops, bakeries for unleavened bread, kosher butcheries, it is positively the *Judengasse* of Paris. That is where M. Bloch ought to reside. Of course,' he went on in an emphatic, arrogant tone, suited to the discussion of aesthetic matters, and giving, by an unconscious strain of heredity, the air of an old musketeer of Louis XIII to his backward-tilted face, 'I take an interest in all that sort of thing only from the point of view of art. Politics are not in my line, and I cannot condemn wholesale, because Bloch belongs to it, a nation that numbers Spinoza among its illustrious sons. And I admire Rembrandt too much not to realise the beauty that can be derived from frequenting the synagogue. But after all a ghetto is all the finer, the more homogeneous and complete it is. You may be sure, moreover, so far are business instincts and avarice mingled in that race with sadism, that the proximity of the Hebraic street of which I was telling you, the convenience of having close at hand the fleshpots of Israel will have made your friend choose the Rue des Blancs-Manteaux. How curious it all is! It was there, by the way, that there lived a strange Jew who used to boil the Host, after which I think they boiled him, which is stranger still, since it seems to suggest that the body of a Jew can be equivalent to the Body of Our Lord. Perhaps it might be possible to arrange with your friend to take us to see the church of the White Mantles. Just think that it was there that they laid the body of Louis d'Orléans after his assassination by Jean sans Peur, which unfortunately did not rid us of the Orléans. Personally, I have always been on the best of terms with my cousin the Duc de Chartres; still, after all, they are a race of usurpers who caused the assassination of Louis XVI and dethroned Charles X and Henri V. One can see where they get that from, when their ancestors include Monsieur, who was so styled doubtless because he was the most astounding old woman, and the Regent and the rest of them. What a family!' This speech, anti-Jew or pro-Hebrew – according as one regards the outward meaning of its phrases or the intentions that they concealed – had been comically interrupted for me by a remark which Morel whispered to me, to the fury of M. de Charlus. Morel, who had not failed to notice the impression that Bloch had made, murmured his thanks in my ear for having 'given him the push', adding cynically: 'He wanted to stay, it's all jealousy, he would like to take my place. Just like a yid!' 'We might have taken advantage of this halt, which still continues, to ask your friend for some explanations of his ritual. Couldn't you fetch him back?' M. de Charlus asked me, with the anxiety of uncertainty. 'No, it's impossible, he has gone away in a carriage, and besides, he is vexed with me.' 'Thank you, thank you,' Morel breathed. 'Your excuse is preposterous, one can always overtake a carriage, there is nothing to prevent your taking a motorcar,' replied M. de Charlus, in the tone of a man accustomed to see everyone yield before him. But, observing my silence: 'What is this more or less imaginary carriage?' he said to me insolently, and with a last ray of hope. 'It is an open post-chaise which must by this time have reached La Commanderie.' Before the impossible, M. de Charlus resigned himself and made a show of jocularity. 'I can understand their recoiling from the idea of a new brougham. It might have swept them clean.' At last we were warned that the train was about to start, and Saint-Loup left us. But this was the only day when by getting into our carriage he, unconsciously, caused me pain, when I thought for a moment of leaving him with Albertine in order to go with Bloch. The other times his presence did not torment me. For of her own accord Albertine, to save me from any uneasiness, would upon some pretext or other place herself in such a position that she could not even unintentionally brush against Robert, almost too far away to have to hold out her hand to him, and turning her eyes away from him would plunge, as soon as he appeared, into ostentatious and almost affected conversation with any of the other passengers, continuing this make-believe until Saint-Loup had gone. So that the visits which he paid us at Doncières, causing me no pain, no inconvenience even, were in no way discordant from the rest, all of which I found pleasing because they brought me so to speak the homage and invitation of this land. Already, as the summer drew to a close, on our journey from Balbec to Douville, when I saw in the distance the watering-place at Saint-Pierre des Ifs where, for a moment in the evening, the crest of the cliffs glittered rosy pink as the snow upon a mountain glows at sunset, it no longer recalled to my mind, I do not say the melancholy which the sight of its strange, sudden elevation had aroused in me on the first evening, when it filled me with such a longing to take the train back to Paris instead of going on to Balbec, but the spectacle that in the morning, Elstir had told me, might be enjoyed from there, at the hour before sunrise, when all the colours of the rainbow are refracted from the rocks, and when he had so often wakened the little boy who had served him, one year, as model, to paint him, nude, upon the sands. The name Saint-Pierre des Ifs announced to me merely that there would presently appear a strange, intelligent, painted man of fifty with whom I should be able to talk about Chateaubriand and Balzac. And now in the mists of evening, behind that cliff of Incarville, which had filled my mind with so many dreams in the past, what I saw, as though its old sandstone wall had become transparent, was the comfortable house of an uncle of M. de Cambremer in which I knew that I should always find a warm welcome if I did not wish to dine at la Raspelière or to return to Balbec. So that it was not merely the place-names of this district that had lost their initial mystery, but the places themselves. The names, already half-stripped of a mystery which etymology had replaced by reason, had now come down a stage farther still. On our homeward journeys, at Hermenonville, at Incarville, at Harambouville, as the train came to a standstill, we could make out shadowy forms which we did not at first identify, and which Brichot, who could see nothing at all, might perhaps have mistaken in the darkness for the phantoms of Herimund, Wiscar and Herimbald. But they came up to our carriage. It was merely M. de

Cambremer, now completely out of touch with the Verdurins, who had come to see off his own guests and, as ambassador for his wife and mother, came to ask me whether I would not let him 'carry me off' to keep me for a few days at Féterne where I should find successively a lady of great musical talent, who would sing me the whole of Gluck, and a famous chess-player, with whom I could have some splendid games, which would not interfere with the fishing expeditions and yachting trips on the bay, nor even with the Verdurin dinner-parties, for which the Marquis gave me his word of honour that he would 'lend' me, sending me there and fetching me back again, for my greater convenience and also to make sure of my returning. 'But I cannot believe that it is good for you to go so high up. I know my sister could never stand it. She would come back in a fine state! She is not at all well just now. Indeed, you have been as bad as that! Tomorrow you won't be able to stand up!' And he shook with laughter, not from malevolence but for the same reason which made him laugh whenever he saw a lame man hobbling along the street, or had to talk to a deaf person. 'And before this? What, you haven't had an attack for a fortnight. Do you know, that is simply marvellous. Really, you ought to come and stay at Féterne, you could talk about your attacks to my sister.' At Incarville it was the Marquis de Montpeyroux who, not having been able to go to Féterne, for he had been away shooting, had come 'to meet the train' in top boots, with a pheasant's feather in his hat, to shake hands with the departing guests and at the same time with myself, bidding me expect, on the day of the week that would be most convenient to me, a visit from his son, whom he thanked me for inviting, adding that he would be very glad if I would make the boy read a little; or else M. de Crécy, come out to digest his dinner, he explained, smoking his pipe, accepting a cigar or indeed more than one, and saying to me: 'Well, you haven't named a day for our next Lucullus evening? We have nothing to discuss? Allow me to remind you that we left unsettled the question of the two families of Montgomery. We really must settle it. I am relying upon you.' Others had come simply to buy newspapers. And many others came and chatted with us who, I have often suspected, were to be found upon the platform of the station nearest to their little mansion simply because they had nothing better to do than to converse for a moment with people of their acquaintance. A scene of social existence like any other, in fact, these halts on the little railway. The train itself appeared conscious of the part that had devolved upon it, had contracted a sort of human kindliness; patient, of a docile nature, it waited as long as they pleased for the stragglers, and even after it had started would stop to pick up those who signalled to it; they would then run after it panting, in which they resembled itself, but differed from it in that they were running to overtake it at full speed whereas it employed only a wise slowness. And so Hermenonville, Harambouville, Incarville no longer suggested to me even the rugged grandeurs of the Norman Conquest, not content with having entirely rid themselves of the unaccountable melancholy in which I had seen them steeped long ago in the moist evening air. Doncières! To me, even after I had come to know it and had awakened from my dream, how much had long survived in that name of pleasantly glacial streets, lighted windows, succulent flesh of birds. Doncières! Now it was nothing more than the station at which Morel joined the train, Egleville (*Aquilae villa*) that at which we generally found waiting for us Princess Sherbatov, Maineville, the station at which Albertine left the train on fine evenings, when, if she was not too tired, she felt inclined to enjoy a moment more of my company, having, if she took a footpath, little if any farther to walk than if she had alighted at Parville (*Paterni villa*). Not only did I no longer feel the anxious dread of isolation which had gripped my heart the first evening, I had no longer any need to fear its reawakening, nor to feel myself a stranger or alone in this land productive not only of chestnut trees and tamarisks, but of friendships which from beginning to end of the journey formed a long chain, interrupted like that of the blue hills, hidden here and there in the anfractuosity of the rock or behind the lime trees of the avenue, but delegating at each stage an amiable gentleman who came to interrupt my course with a cordial hand-clasp, to prevent me from feeling it too long, to offer if need be to continue the journey with me. Another would be at the next station, so that the whistle of the little tram parted us from one friend only to enable us to meet others. Between the most isolated properties and the railway which skirted them almost at the pace of a person who is walking fast, the distance was so slight that at the moment when, from the platform, outside the waiting-room, their owners hailed us, we might almost have imagined that they were doing so from their own doorstep, from their bedroom window, as though the little departmental line had been merely a street in a country town and the isolated mansion-house the town residence of a family; and even at the few stations where no 'good evening' sounded, the silence had a nourishing and calming fullness, because I knew that it was formed from the slumber of friends who had gone to bed early in the neighbouring manor, where my arrival would have been greeted with joy if I had been obliged to arouse them to ask for some hospitable office. Not to mention that a sense of familiarity so fills up our time that we have not, after a few months, a free moment in a town where on our first arrival the day offered us the absolute disposal of all its twelve hours, if one of these had by any chance fallen vacant, it would no longer have occurred to me to devote it to visiting some church for the sake of which I had come to Balbec in the past, nor even to compare a scene painted by Elstir with the sketch that I had seen of it in his studio, but rather to go and play one more game of chess at M. Féré's. It was indeed the degrading influence, as it was also the charm that this country round Balbec had had, that it should become for me in the true sense a friendly country; if its territorial distribution, its sowing, along the whole extent of the coast, with different forms of cultivation, gave of necessity to the visits which I paid to these different friends the form of a journey, they also reduced that journey to nothing more than the social amusement of a series of visits. The same place-names, so disturbing to me in the past that the mere Country House Year Book, when I turned over the chapter devoted to the Department of the Manche, caused me as keen an emotion as the railway timetable, had become so familiar to me that, in the timetable itself, I could have consulted the page headed: *Balbec to Douville via Doncières*, with the same happy tranquillity as a directory of addresses. In this too social valley, along the sides of which I felt assembled, whether visible or not, a numerous company of friends, the poetical cry of the evening was no longer that of the owl or frog, but the 'How goes it?' of M. de Criquetot or the 'Chaire!' of Brichot. Its atmosphere no longer aroused my anguish, and, charged with effluvia that were purely human, was easily breathable, indeed unduly soothing. The benefit that I did at least derive from it was that of looking at things only from a practical point of view. The idea of marrying Albertine appeared to me to be madness.

Chapter Four

I was only waiting for an opportunity for a final rupture. And, one evening, as Mamma was starting next day for Combray, where she was to attend the deathbed of one of her mother's sisters, leaving me behind so that I might get the benefit, as my grandmother would have wished, of the sea air, I had announced to her that I had irrevocably decided not to marry Albertine and would very soon stop seeing her. I was glad to have been able, by these words, to give some satisfaction to my mother on the eve of her departure. She had not concealed from me that this satisfaction was indeed extreme. I had also to come to an understanding with Albertine. As I was on my way back with her from la Raspelière, the faithful having alighted, some at Saint-Mars le Vêtu, others at Saint-Pierre des Ifs, others again at Doncières, feeling particularly happy and detached from her, I had decided, now that there were only our two selves in the carriage, to embark at length upon this subject. The truth, as a matter of fact, is that the girl of the Balbec company whom I really loved, albeit she was absent at that moment, as were the rest of her friends, but who was coming back there (I enjoyed myself with them all, because each of them had for me, as on the day when I first saw them, something of the essential quality of all the rest, as though they belonged to a race apart), was Andrée. Since she was coming back again, in a few days' time, to Balbec, it was certain that she would at once pay me a visit, and then, to be left free not to marry her if I did not wish to do so, to be able to go to Venice, but at the same time to have her, while she was at Balbec, entirely to myself, the plan that I would adopt would be that of not seeming at all eager to come to her, and as soon as she arrived, when we were talking together, I would say to her: 'What a pity it is that I didn't see you a few weeks earlier. I should have fallen in love with you; now my heart is bespoke. But that makes no difference, we shall see one another frequently, for I am unhappy about my other love, and you will help to console me.' I smiled inwardly as I thought of this conversation; by this stratagem I should be giving Andrée the impression that I was not really in love with her, and so she would not grow tired of me and I should take a joyful and pleasant advantage of her affection. But all this only made it all the more necessary that I should at length speak seriously to Albertine, so as not to behave indelicately, and, since I had decided to consecrate myself to her friend, she herself must be given clearly to understand that I was not in love with her. I must tell her so at once, as Andrée might arrive any day. But as we were getting near Parville, I felt that we should not have time that evening and that it was better to put off until the morrow what was now irrevocably settled. I confined myself, therefore, to discussing with her our dinner that evening at the Verdurins'. As she put on her cloak, the train having just left Incarville, the last station before Parville, she said to me: 'Tomorrow then, more Verdurin, you won't forget that you are coming to call for me.' I could not help answering rather sharply: 'Yes, that is if I don't "fail" them, for I am beginning to find this sort of life really stupid. In any case, if we go there, so that my time at la Raspelière may not be absolutely wasted, I must remember to ask Mme Verdurin about something that may prove of great interest to myself, provide me with a subject for study, and give me pleasure as well, for I have really had very little this year at Balbec.' 'You are not very polite to me, but I forgive you, because I can see that your nerves are bad. What is this pleasure?' 'That Mme Verdurin should let me hear some things by a musician whose work she knows very well. I know one of his things myself, but it seems there are others and I should like to know if the rest of his work is printed, if it is different from what I know.' 'What musician?' 'My dear child, when I have told you that his name is Vinteuil, will you be any the wiser?' We may have revolved every possible idea in our minds, and yet the truth has never occurred to us, and it is from without, when we are least expecting it, that it gives us its cruel stab and wounds us for all time. 'You can't think how you amuse me,' replied Albertine as she rose, for the train was slowing down. 'Not only does it mean a great deal more to me than you suppose, but even without Mme Verdurin I can get you all the information that you require. You remember my telling you about a friend older than myself, who has been a mother, a sister to me, with whom I spent the happiest years of my life at Trieste, and whom for that matter I am expecting to join in a few weeks at Cherbourg, when we shall start on our travels together (it sounds a little odd, but you know how I love the sea), very well, this friend (oh! not at all the type of woman you might suppose!) isn't this extraordinary, she is the dearest and most intimate friend of your Vinteuil's daughter, and I know Vinteuil's daughter almost as well as I know her. I always call them my two big sisters. I am not sorry to let you see that your little Albertine can be of use to you in this question of music, about

which you say, and quite rightly for that matter, that I know nothing at all.'
At the sound of these words, uttered as we were entering the station of
Parville, so far from Combray and Montjouvain, so long after the death of
Vinteuil, an image stirred in my heart, an image which I had kept in reserve
for so many years that even if I had been able to guess, when I stored it up,
long ago, that it had a noxious power, I should have supposed that in the
course of time it had entirely lost it; preserved alive in the depths of my
being – like Orestes whose death the gods had prevented in order that, on
the appointed day, he might return to his native land to punish the murderer
of Agamemnon – as a punishment, as a retribution (who can tell?) for my
having allowed my grandmother to die, perhaps; rising up suddenly from
the black night in which it seemed for ever buried, and striking, like an
Avenger, in order to inaugurate for me a novel, terrible and merited
existence, perhaps also to make dazzlingly clear to my eyes the fatal
consequences which evil actions indefinitely engender, not only for those
who have committed them, but for those who have done no more, have
thought that they were doing no more than look on at a curious and
entertaining spectacle, like myself, alas, on that afternoon long ago at
Montjouvain, concealed behind a bush where (as when I complacently
listened to an account of Swann's love affairs), I had perilously allowed to
expand within myself the fatal road, destined to cause me suffering, of
Knowledge. And at the same time, from my bitterest grief I derived a
sentiment almost of pride, almost joyful, that of a man whom the shock he
has just received has carried at a bound to a point to which no voluntary
effort could have brought him. Albertine the friend of Mlle Vinteuil and of
her friend, a practising and professional Sapphist, was, compared to what I
had imagined when I doubted her most, as are, compared to the little
acousticon of the 1889 Exhibition with which one barely hoped to be able to
transmit sound from end to end of a house, the telephones that soar over
streets, cities, fields, seas, uniting one country to another. It was a terrible
terra incognita this on which I had just landed, a fresh phase of undreamed-of
sufferings that was opening before me. And yet this deluge of reality that
engulfs us, if it is enormous compared with our timid and microscopic
suppositions, was anticipated by them. It was doubtless something akin to
what I had just learned, something akin to Albertine's friendship with Mlle
Vinteuil, something which my mind would never have been capable of
inventing, but which I obscurely apprehended when I became uneasy at the
sight of Albertine and Andrée together. It is often simply from want of the
creative spirit that we do not go to the full extent of suffering. And the most
terrible reality brings us, with our suffering, the joy of a great discovery,

because it merely gives a new and clear form to what we have long been ruminating without suspecting it. The train had stopped at Parville, and, as we were the only passengers in it, it was in a voice lowered by a sense of the futility of his task, by the force of habit which nevertheless made him perform it, and inspired in him simultaneously exactitude and indolence, and even more by a longing for sleep, that the porter shouted: 'Parville!' Albertine, who stood facing me, seeing that she had arrived at her destination stepped across the compartment in which we were and opened the door. But this movement which she was making to alight tore my heart unendurably, just as if, notwithstanding the position independent of my body which Albertine's body seemed to be occupying a yard away from it, this separation in space, which an accurate draughtsman would have been obliged to indicate between us, was only apparent, and anyone who wished to make a fresh drawing of things as they really were would now have had to place Albertine, not at a certain distance from me, but inside me. She distressed me so much by her withdrawal that, overtaking her, I caught her desperately by the arm. 'Would it be materially impossible,' I asked her, 'for you to come and spend the night at Balbec?' 'Materially, no. But I'm dropping with sleep.' 'You would be doing me an immense service . . . ' 'Very well, then, though I don't in the least understand; why didn't you tell me sooner? I'll come, though.' My mother was asleep when, after engaging a room for Albertine on a different floor, I entered my own. I sat down by the window, suppressing my sobs, so that my mother, who was separated from me only by a thin partition, might not hear me. I had not even remembered to close the shutters, for at one moment, raising my eyes, I saw facing me in the sky that same faint glow as of a dying fire which one saw in the restaurant at Rivebelle in a study that Elstir had made of a sunset effect. I remembered how thrilled I had been when I had seen from the railway on the day of my first arrival at Balbec, this same image of an evening which preceded not the night but a new day. But no day now would be new to me any more, would arouse in me the desire for an unknown happiness; it would only prolong my sufferings, until the point when I should no longer have the strength to endure them. The truth of what Cottard had said to me in the casino at Parville was now confirmed beyond a shadow of doubt. What I had long dreaded, vaguely suspected of Albertine, what my instinct deduced from her whole personality and my reason controlled by my desire had gradually made me deny, was true! Behind Albertine I no longer saw the blue mountains of the sea, but the room at Montjouvain where she was falling into the arms of Mlle Vinteuil with that laugh in which she gave utterance to the strange sound of her enjoyment. For, with a girl as pretty as Albertine, was it possible that Mlle Vinteuil, having the desires she had, had not asked her to gratify them? And the proof that Albertine had not been shocked by the request but had consented, was that they had not quarrelled, indeed their intimacy had steadily increased. And that graceful movement with which Albertine laid her chin upon Rosemonde's shoulder, gazed at her smilingly, and deposited a kiss upon her throat, that movement which had reminded me of Mlle Vinteuil, in interpreting which I had nevertheless hesitated to admit that an identical line traced by a gesture must of necessity be due to an identical inclination, for all that I knew, Albertine might simply have learned it from Mlle Vinteuil. Gradually, the lifeless sky took fire. I who until then had never awakened without a smile at the humblest things, the bowl of coffee and milk, the sound of the rain, the thunder of the wind, felt that the day which in a moment was to dawn, and all the days to come would never bring me any more the hope of an unknown happiness, but only the prolongation of my martyrdom. I clung still to life; I knew that I had nothing now that was not cruel to expect from it. I ran to the lift, regardless of the hour, to ring for the lift-boy who acted as night watchman, and asked him to go to Albertine's room, and to tell her that I had something of importance to say to her, if she could see me there. 'Mademoiselle says she would rather come to you,' was his answer. 'She will be here in a moment.' And presently, sure enough, in came Albertine in her dressing-gown. 'Albertine,' I said to her in a whisper, warning her not to raise her voice so as not to arouse my mother, from whom we were separated only by that partition whose thinness, today a nuisance, because it confined us to whispers, resembled in the past, when it so clearly expressed my grand-mother's intentions, a sort of musical transparency, 'I am ashamed to have disturbed you. Listen. To make you understand, I must tell you something which you do not know. When I came here, I left a woman whom I ought to have married, who was ready to sacrifice everything for me. She was to start on a journey this morning, and every day for the last week I have been wondering whether I should have the courage not to telegraph to her that I was coming back. I have had that courage, but it made me so wretched that I thought I would kill myself. That is why I asked you last night if you could not come and sleep at Balbec. If I had to die, I should have liked to bid you farewell.' And I gave free vent to the tears which my fiction rendered natural. 'My poor boy, if I had only known, I should have spent the night beside you,' cried Albertine, to whom the idea that I might perhaps marry this woman, and that her own chance of making a 'good marriage' was thus vanishing, never even occurred, so sincerely was she moved by a grief the cause of which I was able to conceal from her, but not its reality and strength. 'Besides,' she told me, 'last night, all the time we were coming from la Raspelière, I could see that you were nervous and unhappy, I was afraid there must be something wrong.' As a matter of fact my grief had begun only at Parville, and my nervous trouble, which was very different but which fortunately Albertine identified with it, arose from the boredom of having to spend a few more days in her company. She added: 'I shan't leave you any more, I am going to spend all my time here.' She was offering me, in fact – and she alone could offer me – the sole remedy for the poison that was burning me, a remedy akin, as it happened, to the poison, for, though one was sweet, the other bitter, both were alike derived from Albertine. At that moment, Albertine – my malady – ceasing to cause me to suffer, left me – she, Albertine the remedy – as weak as a convalescent. But I reflected that she would presently be leaving Balbec for Cherbourg, and from there going to Trieste. Her old habits would be reviving. What I wished above all things was to prevent Albertine from taking the boat, to make an attempt to carry her off to Paris. It was true that from Paris, more easily even than from Balbec, she might, if she wished, go to Trieste, but at Paris we should see; perhaps I might ask Mme de Guermantes to exert her influence indirectly upon Mlle Vinteuil's friend so that she should not remain at Trieste, to make her accept a situation elsewhere, perhaps with the Prince de —, whom I had met at Mme de Villeparisis' and, indeed, at Mme de Guermantes's. And he, even if Albertine wished to go to his house to see her friend, might, warned by Mme de Guermantes, prevent them from meeting. Of course I might have reminded myself that in Paris, if Albertine had those tastes, she would find many other people with whom to gratify them. But every impulse of jealousy is individual and bears the imprint of the creature – in this instance Mlle Vinteuil's friend – who has aroused it. It was Mlle Vinteuil's friend who remained my chief preoccupation. The mysterious passion with which I had thought in the past about Austria because it was the country from which Albertine came (her uncle had been a Counsellor of Embassy there), because its geographical peculiarities, the race that inhabited it, its historical buildings, its scenery, I could study, as in an atlas, as in an album of photographs, in Albertine's smile, her ways; this mysterious passion I still felt but, by an inversion of symbols, in the realm of horror. Yes, it was from there that Albertine came. It was there that, in every house, she could be sure of finding, if not Mlle Vinteuil's friend, others of the sort. The habits of her childhood would revive, they would be meeting in three months' time for Christmas, then for the New Year, dates which were already painful to me in themselves, owing to an instinctive memory of the misery that I had felt on those days when, long ago, they separated me, for the whole of the Christmas holidays, from Gilberte. After the long dinner-parties, after the midnight revels, when everybody was joyous, animated, Albertine would adopt the same attitudes with her friends there that I had seen her adopt with Andrée, albeit her friendship for Andrée was innocent, the same attitudes, possibly, that I had seen Mlle Vinteuil adopt, pursued by her friend, at Montjouvain. To Mlle Vinteuil, while her friend titillated her desires before subsiding upon her, I now gave the inflamed face of Albertine, of an Albertine whom I heard utter as she fled, then as she surrendered herself, her strange, deep laugh. What, in comparison with the anguish that I was now feeling, was the jealousy that I might have felt on the day when Saint-Loup had met Albertine with myself at Doncières and she had made teasing overtures to him, or that I had felt when I thought of the unknown initiator to whom I was indebted for the first kisses that she had given me in Paris, on the day when I was waiting for a letter from Mme de Stermaria? That other kind of jealousy provoked by Saint-Loup, by a young man of any sort, was nothing. I should have had at the most in that case to fear a rival over whom I should have attempted to prevail. But here the rival was not similar to myself, bore different weapons, I could not compete upon the same ground, give Albertine the same pleasures, nor indeed conceive what those pleasures might be. In many moments of our life, we would barter the whole of our future for a power that in itself is insignificant. I would at one time have foregone all the good things in life to make the acquaintance of Mme Blatin, because she was a friend of Mme Swann. Today, in order that Albertine might not go to Trieste, I would have endured every possible torment, and if that proved insufficient, would have inflicted torments upon her, would have isolated her, kept her under lock and key, would have taken from her the little money that she had so that it should be materially impossible for her to make the journey. Just as long ago, when I was anxious to go to Balbec, what urged me to start was the longing for a Persian church, for a stormy sea at daybreak, so what was now rending my heart as I thought that Albertine might perhaps be going to Trieste, was that she would be spending the night of Christmas there with Mlle Vinteuil's friend: for imagination, when it changes its nature and turns to sensibility, does not for that reason acquire control of a larger number of simultaneous images. Had anyone told me that she was not at that moment either at Cherbourg or at Trieste, that there was no possibility of her seeing Albertine, how I should have wept for joy. How my whole life and its future would have been changed! And yet I knew quite well that this localisation of my jealousy was arbitrary, that if Albertine had these desires, she could gratify them with other girls. And perhaps even these very girls, if they could have seen her elsewhere, would not have tortured my heart so acutely. It was Trieste, it was that unknown world in which I could feel that Albertine took a delight, in which were her memories, her friendships, her childish loves, that exhaled that hostile, inexplicable atmosphere, like the atmosphere that used to float up to my bedroom at Combray, from the dining-room in which I could hear talking and laughing with strangers, amid the clatter of knives and forks, Mamma who would not be coming upstairs to say good-night to me; like the atmosphere that had filled for Swann the houses to which Odette went at night in search of inconceivable joys. It was no longer as of a delicious place in which the people were pensive, the sunsets golden, the church bells melancholy, that I thought now of Trieste, but as of an accursed city which I should have liked to see go up in flames, and to eliminate from the world of real things. That city was embedded in my heart as a fixed and permanent point. The thought of letting Albertine start presently for Cherbourg and Trieste filled me with horror; as did even that of remaining at Balbec. For now that the revelation of my mistress's intimacy with Mlle Vinteuil became almost a certainty, it seemed to me that at every moment when Albertine was not with me (and there were whole days on which, because of her aunt, I was unable to see her), she was giving herself to Bloch's sister and cousin, possibly to other girls as well. The thought that that very evening she might be seeing the Bloch girls drove me mad. And so, after she had told me that for the next few days she would stay with me all the time, I replied: 'But the fact is, I want to go back to Paris. Won't you come with me? And wouldn't you like to come and stay with us for a while in Paris?' At all costs I must prevent her from being by herself, for some days at any rate, I must keep her with me, so as to be certain that she could not meet Mlle Vinteuil's friend. She would as a matter of fact be alone in the house with myself, for my mother, taking the opportunity of a tour of inspection which my father had to make, had taken it upon herself as a duty, in obedience to my grand-mother's wishes, to go down to Combray and spend a few days there with one of my grandmother's sisters. Mamma had no love for her aunt, because she had not been to my grandmother, who was so loving to her, what a sister should be. So, when they grow up, children remember with resentment the people who have been unkind to them. But Mamma, having become my grandmother, was incapable of resentment; her mother's life was to her like a pure and innocent childhood from which she would extract those memories whose sweetness or bitterness regulated her actions towards other people. Our aunt might have been able to furnish Mamma with certain priceless details, but now she would have difficulty in obtaining them, her aunt being seriously ill (they spoke of cancer), and she reproached herself for not having gone sooner, to keep my father company, found only an additional reason for doing what her mother would have done, just as she went on the anniversary of the death of my grandmother's father, who had been such a bad parent, to lay upon his grave the flowers which my grandmother had been in the habit of taking there. And so, to the side of the grave which was about to open, my mother wished to convey the kind words which my aunt had not come to offer to my grandmother. While she was at Combray, my mother would busy herself with certain things which my grandmother had always wished to be done, but only if they were done under her daughter's supervision. So that they had never yet been begun, Mamma not wishing, by leaving Paris before my father, to make him feel too keenly the burden of a grief in which he shared, but which could not afflict him as it afflicted her. 'Ah! That wouldn't be possible just at present,' Albertine assured me. 'Besides, why should you need to go back to Paris so soon, if the lady has gone?' 'Because I shall feel more at my ease in a place where I have known her than at Balbec, which she has never seen and which I have begun to loathe.' Did Albertine realise later on that this other woman had never existed, and that if that night I had really longed for death, it was because she had stupidly revealed to me that she had been on intimate terms with Mlle Vinteuil's friend? It is possible. There are moments when it appears to me probable. Anyhow, that morning, she believed in the existence of this other woman. 'But you ought to marry this lady,' she told me, 'my dear boy, it would make you happy, and I'm sure it would make her happy as well.' I replied that the thought that I might be making the other woman happy had almost made me decide; when, not long since, I had inherited a fortune which would enable me to provide my wife with ample luxury and pleasures, I had been on the point of accepting the sacrifice of her whom I loved. Intoxicated by the gratitude that I felt for Albertine's kindness, coming so soon after the atrocious suffering that she had caused me, just as one would think nothing of promising a fortune to the waiter who pours one out a sixth glass of brandy, I told her that my wife would have a motorcar, a yacht, that from that point of view, since Albertine was so fond of motoring and yachting, it was unfortunate that she was not the woman I loved, that I should have been the perfect husband for her, but that we should see, we should no doubt be able to meet on friendly terms. After all, as even when we are drunk we refrain from addressing the passers-by, for fear of blows, I was not guilty of the imprudence (if such it was) that I should have committed in Gilberte's time, of telling her that it was she, Albertine, whom I loved. 'You see, I came very near to marrying her. But I did not dare do it, after all, I should not like to make a young woman live with anyone so sickly and troublesome as myself.' 'But you must be mad, anybody would be delighted to live with you, just look how people run after you. They're always talking about you at Mme Verdurin's, and in high society too, I'm told. She can't have been at all nice to you, that lady, to make you lose confidence in yourself like that. I can see what she is, she's a wicked woman, I detest her. I'm sure, if I were in her shoes!' 'Not at all, she is very kind, far too kind. As for the Verdurins and all that, I don't care a hang. Apart from the woman I love, whom moreover I have given up, I care only for my little Albertine, she is the only person in the world who, by letting me see a great deal of her – that is, during the first few days –' I added, in order not to alarm her and to be able to ask anything of her during those days , ' – can bring me a little consolation.' I made only a vague allusion to the possibility of marriage, adding that it was quite impracticable since we should never agree. Being, in spite of myself, still pursued in my jealousy by the memory of Saint-Loup's relations with 'Rachel, when from the Lord', and of Swann's with Odette, I was too much inclined to believe that, from the moment that I was in love, I could not be loved in return, and that pecuniary interest alone could attach a woman to me. No doubt it was foolish to judge Albertine by Odette and Rachel. But it was not she, it was myself, it was the sentiments that I was capable of inspiring that my jealousy made me underestimate. And from this judgment, possibly erroneous, sprang no doubt many of the calamities that were to overwhelm us. 'Then you decline my invitation to Paris?' 'My aunt would not like me to leave just at present. Besides, even if I can come, later on, wouldn't it look rather odd, my staying with you like that? In Paris everybody will know that I'm not your cousin.' 'Very well, then. We can say that we're practically engaged. It can't make any difference, since you know that it isn't true.' Albertine's throat which emerged bodily from her nightgown, was strongly built, sunburned, of coarse grain. I kissed her as purely as if I had been kissing my mother to charm away a childish grief which as a child I did not believe that I would ever be able to eradicate from my heart. Albertine left me, in order to go and dress. Already, her devotion was beginning to falter; a moment ago she had told me that she would not leave me for a second. (And I felt sure that her resolution would not last long, since I was afraid, if we remained at Balbec, that she would that very evening, in my absence, be seeing the Bloch girls.) Now, she had just told me that she wished to call at Maineville and that she would come back and see me in the afternoon. She had not looked in there the evening before, there might be letters lying there for her, besides, her aunt might be anxious about her. I had replied: 'If that is all, we can send the lift-boy to tell your aunt that you are here and to call for your letters.' And, anxious to show herself obliging but annoyed at being tied down, she had wrinkled her brow, then, at once, very sweetly, said: 'All right' and had sent the lift-boy. Albertine had not been out of the room a moment before the boy came and tapped gently on my door. I had not realised that, while I was talking to Albertine, he had had time to go to Maineville and return. He came now to tell me that Albertine had written a note to her aunt and that she could, if I wished, come to Paris that day. It was unfortunate that she had given him this message orally, for already, despite the early hour, the manager was about, and came to me in a great state to ask me whether there was anything wrong, whether I was really leaving; whether I could not stay just a few days longer, the wind that day being rather 'tiring' (trying). I did not wish to explain to him that the one thing that mattered to me was that Albertine should have left Balbec before the hour at which the Bloch girls took the air, especially since Andrée, who alone might have protected her, was not there, and that Balbec was like one of those places in which a sick man who has difficulty in breathing is determined, should he die on the journey, not to spend another night. I should have to struggle against similar entreaties, in the hotel first of all, where the eyes of Marie Gineste and Céleste Albaret were red. (Marie, moreover, was giving vent to the swift sob of a mountain torrent. Céleste, who was gentler, urged her to keep calm; but, Marie having murmured the only poetry that she knew: 'Down here the lilacs die', Céleste could contain herself no longer, and a flood of tears spilled over her lilac-hued face; I dare say they had forgotten my existence by that evening.) After which, on the little local railway, despite all my precautions against being seen, I met M. de Cambremer who, at the sight of my boxes, turned pale, for he was counting upon me for the day after the next; he infuriated me by trying to persuade me that my choking fits were caused by the change in the weather, and that October would do them all the good in the world, and asked me whether I could not 'postpone my departure by a week', an expression the fatuity of which enraged me perhaps only because what he was suggesting to me made me feel ill. And while he talked to me in the railway carriage, at each station I was afraid of seeing, more terrible than Heribald or Guiscard, M. de Crécy imploring me to invite him, or, more dreadful still, Mme Verdurin bent upon inviting me. But this was not to happen for some hours. I had not got there yet. I had to face only the despairing entreaties of the manager. I shut the door on him, for I was afraid that, although he lowered his voice, he would end by disturbing Mamma. I remained alone in my room, that room with the too lofty ceiling in which I had been so wretched on my first arrival, in which I had thought with such longing of Mme de Stermaria, had watched for the appearance of Albertine and her friends, like migratory birds alighting upon the beach, in which I had enjoyed her with so little enjoyment after I had sent the lift-boy to fetch her, in which I had experienced my grandmother's kindness, then realised that she was dead; those shutters at the foot of which the morning light fell, I had opened the first time to look out upon the first ramparts of the sea (those shutters which Albertine made me close in case anybody should see us kissing). I became aware of my own transformations as I compared them with the identity of my surroundings. We grow accustomed to these as to people and when, all of a sudden, we recall the different meaning that they used to convey to us, then, after they had lost all meaning, the events very different from those of today which they enshrined, the diversity of actions performed beneath the same ceiling, between the same glazed bookshelves, the change in our heart and in our life that diversity implies, seem to be increased still further by the unalterable permanence of the setting, reinforced by the unity of scene.

Two or three times it occurred to me, for a moment, that the world in which this room and these bookshelves were situated and in which Albertine counted for so little, was perhaps an intellectual world, which was the sole reality, and my grief something like what we feel when we read a novel, a thing of which only a madman would make a lasting and permanent grief that prolonged itself through his life; that a tiny movement of my will would suffice, perhaps, to attain to that real world, to re-enter it, passing through my grief, as one breaks through a paper hoop, and to think no more about what Albertine had done than we think about the actions of the imaginary heroine of a novel after we have finished reading it. For that matter, the mistresses whom I have loved most passionately have never coincided with my love for them. That love was genuine, since I subordinated everything else to the need of seeing them, of keeping them to myself, and would weep aloud if, one evening, I had waited for them in vain. But it was more because they had the faculty of arousing that love, of raising it to a paroxysm, than because they were its image. When I saw them, when I heard their voices, I could find nothing in them which resembled my love and could account for it. And yet my sole joy lay in seeing them, my sole anxiety in waiting for them to come. One would have said that a virtue that had no connection with them had been attached to them artificially by nature, and that this virtue, this quasi-electric power had the effect upon me of exciting my love, that is to say of controlling all my actions and causing all my sufferings. But from this, the beauty, or the intelligence, or the kindness of these women was entirely distinct. As by an electric current that gives us a shock, I have been shaken by my love affairs, I have lived them, I have felt them: never have I succeeded in arriving at the stage of seeing or thinking them. Indeed I am inclined to believe that in these love affairs (I leave out of account the physical pleasure which is their habitual accompaniment but is not enough in itself to constitute them), beneath the form of the woman, it is to those invisible forces which are attached to her that we address ourselves as to obscure deities. It is they whose goodwill is necessary to us, with whom we seek to establish contact without finding any positive pleasure in it. With these goddesses, the woman, during our assignation with her, puts us in touch and does little more. We have, by way of oblation, promised jewels, travels, uttered formulas which mean that we adore and, at the same time, formulas which mean that we are indifferent. We have used all our power to obtain a fresh assignation, but on condition that no trouble is involved. Now would the woman herself, if she were not completed by these occult forces, make us give ourselves so much trouble, when, once she has left us, we are unable to say how she was dressed and realise that we never even looked at her?

As our vision is a deceiving sense, a human body, even when it is loved as Albertine's was, seems to us to be at a few yards', at a few inches' distance from us. And similarly with the soul that inhabits it. But something need only effect a violent change in the relative position of that soul to ourselves, to show us that she is in love with others and not with us, then by the beating of our dislocated heart we feel that it is not a yard away from us but within us that the beloved creature was. Within us, in regions more or less superficial. But the words: 'That friend is Mlle Vinteuil' had been the *Open sesame* which I should have been incapable of discovering by myself, which had made Albertine penetrate to the depths of my shattered heart. And the door that had closed behind her, I might seek for a hundred years without learning how it might be opened.

I had ceased for a moment to hear these words ringing in my ears while Albertine was with me just now. While I was kissing her, as I used to kiss my mother, at Combray, to calm my anguish, I believed almost in Albertine's innocence, or at least did not think continuously of the discovery that I had made of her vice. But now that I was alone the words began to sound afresh like those noises inside the ear which we hear as soon as the other person stops talking. Her vice now seemed to me to be beyond any doubt. The light of the approaching sunrise, by altering the appearance of the things round me, made me once again, as though it shifted my position for a moment, yet even more painfully conscious of my suffering. I had never seen the dawn of so beautiful or so painful a morning. And thinking of all the nondescript scenes that were about to be lighted up, scenes which, only yesterday, would

have filled me simply with the desire to visit them, I could not repress a sob
when, with a gesture of oblation mechanically performed which appeared to
me to symbolise the bloody sacrifice which I should have to make of all joy,
every morning, until the end of my life, a solemn renewal, celebrated as each
day dawned, of my daily grief and of the blood from my wound, the golden
egg of the sun, as though propelled by the breach of equilibrium brought
about at the moment of coagulation by a change of density, barbed with
tongues of flame as in a painting, came leaping through the curtain behind
which one had felt that it was quivering with impatience, ready to appear on
the scene and to spring aloft, the mysterious, ingrained purple of which it
flooded with waves of light. I heard the sound of my weeping. But at that
moment, to my astonishment, the door opened and, with a throbbing heart,
I seemed to see my grandmother standing before me, as in one of those
apparitions that had already visited me, but only in my sleep. Was all this
but a dream, then? Alas, I was wide awake. 'You see a likeness to your poor
grandmother,' said Mamma, for it was she, speaking gently to calm my fear,
admitting moreover the resemblance, with a fine smile of modest pride
which had always been innocent of coquetry. Her dishevelled hair, the grey
locks in which were not hidden and strayed about her troubled eyes, her
ageing cheeks, my grandmother's own dressing-gown which she was
wearing, all these had for a moment prevented me from recognising her and
had made me uncertain whether I was still asleep or my grandmother had
come back to life. For a long time past my mother had resembled my
grandmother, far more than the young and smiling Mamma that my
childhood had known. But I had ceased to think of this resemblance. So,
when we have long been sitting reading, our mind absorbed, we have not
noticed how the time was passing, and suddenly we see round about us the
sun that shone yesterday at the same hour call up the same harmonies, the
same effects of colour that precede a sunset. It was with a smile that my
mother made me aware of my mistake, for it was pleasing to her that she
should bear so strong a resemblance to her mother. 'I came,' said my
mother, 'because when I was asleep I thought I heard someone crying. It
wakened me. But how is it that you aren't in bed? And your eyes are filled
with tears. What is the matter?' I took her head in my arms: 'Mamma, listen,
I'm afraid you'll think me very changeable. But first of all, yesterday I spoke
to you not at all nicely about Albertine; what I said was unfair.' 'But what
difference can that make?' said my mother, and, catching sight of the rising
sun, she smiled sadly as she thought of her own mother, and, so that I might
not lose the benefit of a spectacle which my grandmother used to regret that
I never watched, she pointed to the window. But beyond the beach of

Balbec, the sea, the sunrise, which Mamma was pointing out to me, I saw, with movements of despair which did not escape her notice, the room at Montjouvain where Albertine, rosy and round like a great cat, with her rebellious nose, had taken the place of Mlle Vinteuil's friend and was saying amid peals of her voluptuous laughter: 'Well! If they do see us, it will be all the better. I? I wouldn't dare to spit upon that old monkey?' It was this scene that I saw, beyond the scene that was framed in the open window and was no more than a dim veil drawn over the other, superimposed upon it like a reflection. It seemed indeed almost unreal, like a painted view. Facing us, where the cliff of Parville jutted out, the little wood in which we had played 'ferret' thrust down to the sea's edge, beneath the varnish, still all golden, of the water, the picture of its foliage, as at the hour when often, at the close of day, after I had gone there to rest in the shade with Albertine, we had risen as we saw the sun sink in the sky. In the confusion of the night mists which still hung in rags of pink and blue over the water littered with the pearly fragments of the dawn, boats were going past smiling at the slanting light which gilded their sails and the point of their bowsprits as when they are homeward bound at evening: a scene imaginary, chilling and deserted, a pure evocation of the sunset which did not rest, as at evening, upon the sequence of the hours of the day which I was accustomed to see precede it, detached, interpolated, more unsubstantial even than the horrible image of Montjouvain which it did not succeed in cancelling, covering, concealing – a poetical, vain image of memory and dreams. 'But come,' my mother was saying, 'you said nothing unpleasant about her, you told me that she bored you a little, that you were glad you had given up the idea of marrying her. There is no reason for you to cry like that. Remember, your Mamma is going away today and can't bear to leave her big baby in such a state. Especially, my poor boy, as I haven't time to comfort you. Even if my things are packed, one has never any time on the morning of a journey.' 'It is not that.' And then, calculating the future, weighing well my desires, realising that such an affection on Albertine's part for Mlle Vinteuil's friend, and one of such long standing, could not have been innocent, that Albertine had been initiated, and, as every one of her instinctive actions made plain to me, had moreover been born with a predisposition towards that vice which in my uneasiness I had only too often dreaded, in which she could never have ceased to indulge (in which she was indulging perhaps at that moment, taking advantage of an instant in which I was not present), I said to my mother, knowing the pain that I was causing her, which she did not show, and which revealed itself only by that air of serious preoccupation which she wore when she was weighing the respective seriousness of making me unhappy or making me unwell, that air which she had assumed at Combray for the first time when she had resigned herself to spending the night in my room, that air which at this moment was extraordinarily like my grandmother's when she allowed me to drink brandy, I said to my mother: 'I know how what I am going to say will distress you. First of all, instead of remaining here as you wished, I want to leave by the same train as you. But that is nothing. I am not feeling well here, I would rather go home. But listen to me, don't make yourself too miserable. This is what I want to say. I was deceiving myself, I deceived you in good faith, yesterday, I have been thinking over it all night. It is absolutely necessary, and let us decide the matter at once, because I am quite clear about it now in my own mind, because I shall not change again, and I could not live without it, it is absolutely necessary that I marry Albertine.

The Captive

Translated by
C. K. SCOTT MONCRIEFF

To
LUCY LUNN

C.K.S.M.

CHAPTER ONE

Life with Albertine

AT DAYBREAK, my face still turned to the wall, and before I had seen above the big inner curtains what tone the first streaks of light assumed, I could already tell what sort of day it was. The first sounds from the street had told me, according to whether they came to my ears dulled and distorted by the moisture of the atmosphere or quivering like arrows in the resonant and empty area of a spacious, crisply frozen, pure morning; as soon as I heard the rumble of the first tramcar, I could tell whether it was sodden with rain or setting forth into the blue. And perhaps these sounds had themselves been forestalled by some swifter and more pervasive emanation which, stealing into my slumber, diffused in it a melancholy that seemed to presage snow, or gave utterance (through the lips of a little person who occasionally reappeared there) to so many hymns to the glory of the sun that, having first of all begun to smile in my sleep, having prepared my eyes, behind their shut lids, to be dazzled, I awoke finally amid deafening strains of music. It was, moreover, principally from my bedroom that I took in the life of the outer world during this period. I know that Bloch reported that, when he called to see me in the evenings, he could hear the sound of conversation; as my mother was at Combray and he never found anybody in my room, he concluded that I was talking to myself. When, much later, he learned that Albertine had been staying with me at the time, and realised that I had concealed her presence from all my friends, he declared that he saw at last the reason why, during that episode in my life, I had always refused to go out of doors. He was wrong. His mistake was, however, quite pardonable, for the truth, even if it is inevitable, is not always conceivable as a whole. People who learn some accurate detail of another person's life at once deduce consequences which are not accurate, and see in the newly discovered fact an explanation of things that have no connection with it whatsoever.

When I reflect now that my mistress had come, on our return from Balbec, to live in Paris under the same roof as myself, that she had abandoned the idea of going on a cruise, that she was installed in a bedroom within twenty paces of my own, at the end of the corridor, in my father's tapestried study, and that late every night, before leaving me, she used to slide her tongue between my lips like a portion of daily bread, a nourishing food that had the almost sacred character of all flesh upon which the sufferings that we have endured on its account have come in time to confer a sort of spiritual grace, what I at once call to mind in comparison is not the night that Captain de Borodino allowed me to spend in barracks, a favour which cured what was after all only a passing distemper, but the night on which my father sent Mamma to sleep in the little bed by the side of my own. So it is that life, if it is once again to deliver us from an anguish that has seemed inevitable, does so in conditions that are different, so diametrically opposed at times that it is almost an open sacrilege to assert the identity of the grace bestowed upon us.

When Albertine had heard from Françoise that, in the darkness of my still curtained room, I was not asleep, she had no scruple about making a noise as she took her bath, in her own dressing-room. Then, frequently, instead of waiting until later in the day, I would repair to a bathroom adjoining hers, which had a certain charm of its own. Time was, when a stage manager would spend hundreds of thousands of francs to begem with real emeralds the throne upon which a great actress would play the part of an empress. The Russian ballet has taught us that simple arrangements of light will create, if trained upon the right spot, jewels as gorgeous and more varied. This decoration, itself immaterial, is not so graceful, however, as that which, at eight o'clock in the morning, the sun substitutes for what we were accustomed to see when we did not arise before noon. The windows of our respective bathrooms, so that their occupants might not be visible from without, were not of clear glass but clouded with an artificial and old-fashioned kind of frost. All of a sudden, the sun would colour this drapery of glass, gild it, and discovering in myself an earlier young man whom habit had long concealed, would intoxicate me with memories, as though I were out in the open country gazing at a hedge of golden leaves in which even a bird was not lacking. For I could hear Albertine ceaselessly humming:

> For melancholy
> Is but folly,
> And he who heeds it is a fool.

I loved her so well that I could spare a joyous smile for her bad taste in music. This song had, as it happened, during the past summer, delighted Mme Bontemps, who presently heard people say that it was silly, with the result that, instead of asking Albertine to sing it, when she had a party, she would substitute: 'A song of farewell rises from troubled springs', which in its turn became 'an old jingle of Massenet's, the child is always dinning into our ears'.

A cloud passed, blotting out the sun; I saw extinguished and replaced by a grey monochrome the modest, screening foliage of the glass.

The partition that divided our two dressing-rooms (Albertine's, identical with my own, was a bathroom which Mamma, who had another at the other end of the flat, had never used for fear of disturbing my rest) was so slender that we could talk to each other as we washed in double privacy, carrying on a conversation that was interrupted only by the sound of the water, in that intimacy which, in hotels, is so often permitted by the smallness and proximity of the rooms, but which, in private houses in Paris, is so rare.

On other mornings, I would remain in bed, drowsing for as long as I chose, for orders had been given that no one was to enter my room until I had rung the bell, an act which, owing to the awkward position in which the electric bulb had been hung above my bed, took such a time that often, tired of feeling for it and glad to be left alone, I would lie back for some moments and almost fall asleep again. It was not that I was wholly indifferent to Albertine's presence in the house. Her separation from her girl friends had the effect of sparing my heart any fresh anguish. She kept it in a state of repose, in a semi-immobility which would help it to recover. But after all, this calm which my mistress was procuring for me was a release from suffering rather than a positive joy. Not that it did not permit me to taste many joys, from which too keen a grief had debarred me, but these joys, so far from my owing them to Albertine, in whom for that matter I could no longer see any beauty and who was beginning to bore me, with whom I was now clearly conscious that I was not in love, I tasted on the contrary when Albertine was not with me. And so, to begin the morning, I did not send for her at once, especially if it was a fine day. For some moments, knowing that he would make me happier than Albertine, I remained closeted with the little person inside me, hymning the rising sun, of whom I have already spoken. Of those elements which compose our personality, it is not the most obvious that are most essential. In myself, when ill health has succeeded in uprooting them one after another, there will still remain two or three, endowed with a hardier constitution than the rest, notably a certain philosopher who is happy only when he has discovered in two works of art, in two sensations, a common element. But the last of all, I have sometimes asked myself whether it would not be this little mannikin, very similar to another whom the optician at Combray used to set up in his shop window to forecast the weather, and who, doffing his hood when the sun shone, would put it on again if it was going to rain. This little mannikin, I know his egoism; I may be suffering from a choking fit which the mere threat of rain would calm; he pays no heed, and, at the first drops so impatiently awaited, losing his gaiety, sullenly pulls down his hood. Conversely, I dare say that in my last agony, when all my other 'selves' are dead, if a ray of sunshine steals into the room, while I am drawing my last breath, the little fellow of the barometer will feel a great relief, and will throw back his hood to sing: 'Ah! Fine weather at last!'

I rang for Françoise. I opened the *Figaro*. I scanned its columns and made sure that it did not contain an article, or so-called article, which I had sent to the editor, and which was no more than a slightly revised version of the page that had recently come to light, written long ago in Dr. Percepied's carriage, as I gazed at the spires of Martinville. Then I read Mamma's letter. She felt it to be odd, in fact shocking, that a girl should be staying in the house alone with me. On the first day, at the moment of leaving Balbec, when she saw how wretched I was, and was distressed by the prospect of leaving me by myself, my mother had perhaps been glad when she heard that Albertine was travelling with us, and saw that, side by side with our own boxes (those boxes among which I had passed a night in tears in the Balbec hotel), there had been hoisted into the 'Twister' Albertine's boxes also, narrow and black, which had seemed to me to have the appearance of coffins, and as to which I knew not whether they were bringing to my house life or death. But I had never even asked myself the question, being all overjoyed, in the radiant morning, after the fear of having to remain at Balbec, that I was taking Albertine with me. But to this proposal, if at the start my mother had not been hostile (speaking kindly to my friend like a mother whose son has been seriously wounded and who is grateful to the young mistress who is nursing him with loving care), she had acquired hostility now that it had been too completely realised, and the girl was prolonging her sojourn in our house, and moreover in the absence of my parents. I cannot, however, say that my mother ever made this hostility apparent. As in the past, when she had ceased to dare to reproach me with my nervous instability, my laziness, now she felt a hesitation – which I perhaps did not altogether perceive at the moment or refused to perceive – to run the risk, by offering any criticism of the girl to whom I had told her that I intended to make an offer of marriage, of bringing a shadow into my life, making me in time to come less devoted to my wife, of sowing perhaps for a season when she herself would no longer be there, the seeds of remorse at having grieved her by marrying Albertine. Mamma preferred to seem to be approving a choice which she felt herself powerless to make me reconsider. But people who came in contact with her at this time have since told me that in addition to her grief at having lost her mother she had an air of constant preoccupation. This mental strife, this inward debate, had the effect of overheating my mother's brow, and she was always opening the windows to let in the fresh air. But she did not succeed in coming to any decision, for fear of influencing me in the wrong direction and so spoiling what she believed to be my happiness. She could not even bring herself to forbid me to keep Albertine for the time being in our house. She did not wish to appear more strict than Mme Bontemps, who was the person principally concerned, and who saw no harm in the arrangement, which greatly surprised my mother. All the same, she regretted that she had been obliged to leave us together, by departing at that very time for Combray where she might have to remain (and did in fact remain) for months on end, during which my great-aunt required her incessant attention by day and night. Everything was made easy for her down there, thanks to the kindness, the devotion of Legrandin who, gladly undertaking any trouble that was required, kept putting off his return to Paris from week to week, not that he knew my aunt at all well, but simply, first of all, because she had been his mother's friend, and also because he knew that the invalid, condemned to die, valued his attentions and could not get on without him. Snobbishness is a serious malady of the spirit, but one that is localised and does not taint it as a whole. I, on the other hand, unlike Mamma, was extremely glad of her absence at Combray, but for which I should have been afraid (being unable to warn Albertine not to mention it) of her learning of the girl's friendship with Mlle Vinteuil. This would have been to my mother an insurmountable obstacle, not merely to a marriage as to which she had, for that matter, begged me to say nothing definite as yet to Albertine, and the thought of which was becoming more and more intolerable to myself, but even to the latter's being allowed to stay for any length of time in the house. Apart from so grave a reason, which in this case did not apply, Mamma, under the dual influence of my grandmother's liberating and edifying example, according to whom, in her admiration of George Sand, virtue consisted in nobility of heart, and of my own corruption, was now indulgent towards women whose conduct she would have condemned in the past, or even now, had they been any of her own middle-class friends in Paris or at Combray, but whose lofty natures I extolled to her and to whom she pardoned much because of their affection for myself. But when all is said, and apart from any question of propriety, I doubt whether Albertine could have put up with Mamma who had acquired from Combray, from my aunt Léonie, from all her kindred, habits of punctuality and order of which my mistress had not the remotest conception.

She would never think of shutting a door and, on the other hand, would no more hesitate to enter a room if the door stood open than would a dog or a cat. Her somewhat disturbing charm was, in fact, that of taking the place in the household not so much of a girl as of a domestic animal which comes into a room, goes out, is to be found wherever one does not expect to find it and (in her case) would – bringing me a profound sense of repose – come and lie down on my bed by my side, make a place for herself from which she never stirred, without being in my way as a person would have been. She ended, however, by conforming to my hours of sleep, and not only never attempted to enter my room but would take care not to make a sound until I had rung my bell. It was Françoise who impressed these rules of conduct upon her.

She was one of those Combray servants, conscious of their master's place in the world, and that the least that they can do is to see that he is treated with all the respect to which they consider him entitled. When a stranger on leaving after a visit gave Françoise a gratuity to be shared with the kitchen-maid, he had barely slipped his coin into her hand before Françoise, with an equal display of speed, discretion and energy, had passed the word to the kitchenmaid who came forward to thank him, not in a whisper, but openly and aloud, as Françoise had told her that she must do. The parish priest of Combray was no genius, but he also knew what was due him. Under his instruction, the daughter of some Protestant cousins of Mme Sazerat had been received into the Church, and her family had been most grateful to him: it was a question of her marriage to a young nobleman of Méséglise. The young man's relatives wrote to enquire about her in a somewhat arrogant letter, in which they expressed their dislike of her Protestant origin. The Combray priest replied in such a tone that the Méséglise nobleman, crushed and prostrate, wrote a very different letter in which he begged as the most precious favour the award of the girl's hand in marriage.

Françoise deserved no special credit for making Albertine respect my slumbers. She was imbued with tradition. From her studied silence, or the peremptory response that she made to a proposal to enter my room, or to send in some message to me, which Albertine had expressed in all innocence, the latter realised with astonishment that she was now living in an alien world, where strange customs prevailed, governed by rules of conduct which one must never dream of infringing. She had already had a foreboding of this at Balbec, but, in Paris, made no attempt to resist, and would wait patiently every morning for the sound of my bell before venturing to make any noise.

The training that Françoise gave her was of value also to our old servant herself, for it gradually stilled the lamentations which, ever since our return from Balbec, she had not ceased to utter. For, just as we were boarding the tram, she remembered that she had forgotten to say goodbye to the housekeeper of the Hotel, a whiskered dame who looked after the bedroom floors, barely knew Françoise by sight, but had been comparatively civil to her. Françoise positively insisted upon getting out of the tram, going back to the Hotel, saying goodbye properly to the housekeeper, and not leaving for Paris until the following day. Common sense, coupled with my sudden horror of Balbec, restrained me from granting her this concession, but my refusal had infected her with a feverish distemper which the change of air had not sufficed to cure and which lingered on in Paris. For, according to Françoise's code, as it is illustrated in the carvings of Saint-André-des-Champs, to wish for the death of an enemy, even to inflict it is not forbidden, but it is a horrible sin not to do what is expected of you, not to return a civility, to refrain, like a regular churl, from saying goodbye to the housekeeper before leaving a hotel. Throughout the journey, the continually recurring memory of her not having taken leave of this woman had dyed Françoise's cheeks with a scarlet flush that was quite alarming. And if she refused to taste bite or sup until we reached Paris, it was perhaps because this memory heaped a 'regular load' upon her stomach (every class of society has a pathology of its own) even more than with the intention of punishing us.

Among the reasons which led Mamma to write me a daily letter, and a letter which never failed to include some quotation from Mme de Sévigné, there was the memory of my grandmother. Mamma would write to me: 'Mme Sazerat gave us one of those little luncheons of which she possesses the secret and which, as your poor grandmother would have said, quoting Mme de Sévigné, deprive us of solitude without affording us company.' In one of my own earlier letters I was so inept as to write to Mamma: 'By those quotations, your mother would recognise you at once.' Which brought me, three days later, the reproof: 'My poor boy, if it was only to speak to me of *my mother*, your reference to Mme de Sévigné was most inappropriate. She would have answered you as she answered Mme de Grignan: "So she was nothing to you? I had supposed that you were related." '

By this time, I could hear my mistress leaving or returning to her room. I rang the bell, for it was time now for Andrée to arrive with the chauffeur, Morel's friend, lent me by the Verdurins, to take Albertine out. I had spoken to the last-named of the remote possibility of our marriage; but I had never made her any formal promise; she herself, from discretion, when I said to her: 'I can't tell, but it might perhaps be possible', had shaken her head with a melancholy sigh, as much as to say: 'Oh, no, never', in other words: 'I am too poor.' And so, while I continued to say: 'It is quite indefinite,' when speaking of future projects, at the moment I was doing everything in my power to amuse her, to make life pleasant to her, with perhaps the unconscious design of thereby making her wish to marry me. She herself laughed at my lavish generosity. 'Andrée's mother would be in a fine state if she saw me turn into a rich lady like herself, what she calls a lady who has her own "horses, carriages, pictures". What? Did I never tell you that she says that. Oh, she's a character! What surprises me is that she seems to think pictures just as important as horses and carriages.' We shall see in due course that, notwithstanding the foolish ways of speaking that she had not outgrown, Albertine had developed to an astonishing extent, which left me unmoved, the intellectual superiority of a woman friend having always interested me so little that if I have ever complimented any of my friends upon her own, it was purely out of politeness. Alone, the curious genius of Céleste might perhaps appeal to me. In spite of myself, I would continue to smile for some moments, when, for instance, having discovered that Françoise was not in my room, she accosted me with: 'Heavenly deity reclining on a bed!' 'But why, Céleste,' I would say, 'why deity?' 'Oh, if you suppose that you have anything in common with the mortals who make their pilgrimage on our vile earth, you are greatly mistaken!' 'But why "reclining" on a bed, can't you see that I'm lying in bed?' 'You never lie. Who ever saw anybody lie like that? You have just alighted there. With your white pyjamas, and the way you twist your neck, you look for all the world like a dove.'

Albertine, even in the discussion of the most trivial matters, expressed herself very differently from the little girl that she had been only a few years earlier at Balbec. She went so far as to declare, with regard to a political incident of which she disapproved: 'I consider that ominous.' And I am not sure that it was not about this time that she learned to say, when she meant that she felt a book to be written in a bad style: 'It is interesting, but really, it might have been written *by a pig.*'

The rule that she must not enter my room until I had rung amused her greatly. As she had adopted our family habit of quotation, and in following it drew upon the plays in which she had acted at her convent and for which I had expressed admiration, she always compared me to Assuérus:

> And death is the reward of whoso dares
> To venture in his presence unawares . . .
> None is exempt; nor is there any whom
> Or rank or sex can save from such a doom;

Even I myself . . .
Like all the rest, I by this law am bound;
And, to address him, I must first be found
By him, or he must call me to his side.

Physically, too, she had altered. Her blue, almond-shaped eyes, grown longer, had not kept their form; they were indeed of the same colour, but seemed to have passed into a liquid state. So much so that, when she shut them it was as though a pair of curtains had been drawn to shut out a view of the sea. It was no doubt this one of her features that I remembered most vividly each night after we had parted. For, on the contrary, every morning the ripple of her hair continued to give me the same surprise, as though it were some novelty that I had never seen before. And yet, above the smiling eyes of a girl, what could be more beautiful than that clustering coronet of black violets? The smile offers greater friendship; but the little gleaming tips of blossoming hair, more akin to the flesh, of which they seem to be a transposition into tiny waves, are more provocative of desire.

As soon as she entered my room, she sprang upon my bed and sometimes would expatiate upon my type of intellect, would vow in a transport of sincerity that she would sooner die than leave me: this was on mornings when I had shaved before sending for her. She was one of those women who can never distinguish the cause of their sensations. The pleasure that they derive from a smooth cheek they explain to themselves by the moral qualities of the man who seems to offer them a possibility of future happiness, which is capable, however, of diminishing and becoming less necessary the longer he refrains from shaving.

I enquired where she was thinking of going.

'I believe Andrée wants to take me to the Buttes-Chaumont; I have never been there.'

Of course it was impossible for me to discern among so many other words whether beneath these a falsehood lay concealed. Besides, I could trust Andrée to tell me of all the places that she visited with Albertine.

At Balbec, when I felt that I was utterly tired of Albertine, I had made up my mind to say, untruthfully, to Andrée: 'My little Andrée, if only I had met you again sooner! It is you that I would have loved. But now my heart is pledged in another quarter. All the same, we can see a great deal of each other, for my love for another is causing me great anxiety, and you will help me to find consolation.' And lo, these identical lying words had become true within the space of three weeks. Perhaps, Andrée had believed in Paris that it was indeed a lie and that I was in love with her, as she would doubtless have believed at Balbec. For the truth is so variable for each of us, that other people have difficulty in recognising themselves in it. And as I knew that she would tell me everything that she and Albertine had done, I had asked her, and she had agreed to come and call for Albertine almost every day. In this way I might without anxiety remain at home.

Also, Andrée's privileged position as one of the girls of the little band gave me confidence that she would obtain everything that I might require from Albertine. Truly, I could have said to her now in all sincerity that she would be capable of setting my mind at rest.

At the same time, my choice of Andrée (who happened to be staying in Paris, having given up her plan of returning to Balbec) as guide and companion to my mistress was prompted by what Albertine had told me of the affection that her friend had felt for me at Balbec, at a time when, on the contrary, I had supposed that I was boring her; indeed, if I had known this at the time, it is perhaps with Andrée that I would have fallen in love.

'What, you never knew,' said Albertine, 'but we were always joking about it. Do you mean to say you never noticed how she used to copy all your ways of talking and arguing? When she had just been with you, it was too obvious. She had no need to tell us whether she had seen you. As soon as she joined us, we could tell at once. We used to look at one another, and laugh. She was like a coal heaver who tries to pretend that he isn't one. He is black all over. A miller has no need to say that he is a miller, you can see the flour all over his clothes; and the mark of the sacks he has carried on his shoulder. Andrée was just the same, she would knit her eyebrows the way you do, and stretch out her long neck, and I don't know what all. When I take up a book that has been in your room, even if I'm reading it out of doors, I can tell at once that it belongs to you because it still reeks of your beastly fumigations. It's only a trifle, still it's rather a nice trifle, don't you know. Whenever anybody spoke nicely about you, seemed to think a lot of you, Andrée was in ecstasies.'

Notwithstanding all this, in case there might have been some secret plan made behind my back, I advised her to give up the Buttes-Chaumont for that day and to go instead to Saint-Cloud or somewhere else.

It was certainly not, as I was well aware, because I was the least bit in love with Albertine. Love is nothing more perhaps than the stimulation of those eddies which, in the wake of an emotion, stir the soul. Certain such eddies had indeed stirred my soul through and through when Albertine spoke to me at Balbec about Mlle Vinteuil, but these were now stilled. I was no longer in love with Albertine, for I no longer felt anything of the suffering, now healed, which I had felt in the tram at Balbec, upon learning how

Albertine had spent her girlhood, with visits perhaps to Montjouvain. All this, I had too long taken for granted, was healed. But, now and again, certain expressions used by Albertine made me suppose – why, I cannot say – that she must in the course of her life, short as it had been, have received declarations of affection, and have received them with pleasure, that is to say with sensuality. Thus, she would say, in any connection: 'Is that true? Is it really true?' Certainly, if she had said, like an Odette: 'Is it really true, that thumping lie?' I should not have been disturbed, for the absurdity of the formula would have explained itself as a stupid inanity of feminine wit. But her questioning air: 'Is that true?' gave on the one hand the strange impression of a creature incapable of judging things by herself, who appeals to you for your testimony, as though she were not endowed with the same faculties as yourself (if you said to her: 'Why, we've been out for a whole hour,' or 'It is raining,' she would ask: 'Is that true?'). Unfortunately, on the other hand, this want of facility in judging external phenomena for herself could not be the real origin of her 'Is that true? Is it really true?' It seemed rather that these words had been, from the dawn of her precocious adolescence, replies to: 'You know, I never saw anybody as pretty as you.' 'You know I am madly in love with you, I am most terribly excited.' – affirmations that were answered, with a coquettishly consenting modesty, by these repetitions of: 'Is that true? Is it really true?' which no longer served Albertine, when in my company, save to reply by a question to some such affirmation as: 'You have been asleep for more than an hour.' 'Is that true?'

Without feeling that I was the least bit in the world in love with Albertine, without including in the list of my pleasures the moments that we spent together, I was still preoccupied with the way in which she disposed of her time; had I not, indeed, fled from Balbec in order to make certain that she could no longer meet this or that person with whom I was so afraid of her misbehaving, simply as a joke (a joke at my expense, perhaps), that I had adroitly planned to sever, at one and the same time, by my departure, all her dangerous entanglements? And Albertine was so entirely passive, had so complete a faculty of forgetting things and submitting to pressure, that these relations had indeed been severed and I myself relieved of my haunting dread. But that dread is capable of assuming as many forms as the undefined evil that is its cause. So long as my jealousy was not reincarnate in fresh people, I had enjoyed after the passing of my anguish an interval of calm. But with a chronic malady, the slightest pretext serves to revive it, as also with the vice of the person who is the cause of our jealousy the slightest opportunity may serve her to practise it anew (after a lull of chastity) with different people. I had managed to separate Albertine from her accomplices, and, by so doing, to exorcise my hallucinations; even if it was possible to make her forget people, to cut short her attachments, her sensual inclination was, itself also, chronic and was perhaps only waiting for an opportunity to afford itself an outlet. Now Paris provided just as many opportunities as Balbec.

In any town whatsoever, she had no need to seek, for the evil existed not in Albertine alone, but in others to whom any opportunity for enjoyment is good. A glance from one, understood at once by the other, brings the two famished souls in contact. And it is easy for a clever woman to appear not to have seen, then five minutes later to join the person who has read her glance and is waiting for her in a side street, and, in a few words, to make an appointment. Who will ever know? And it was so simple for Albertine to tell me, in order that she might continue these practices, that she was anxious to see again some place on the outskirts of Paris that she had liked. And so it was enough that she should return later than usual, that her expedition should have taken an unaccountable time, although it was perfectly easy perhaps to account for it without introducing any sensual reason, for my malady to break out afresh, attached this time to mental pictures which were not of Balbec, and which I would set to work, as with their predecessors, to destroy, as though the destruction of an ephemeral cause could put an end to a congenital malady. I did not take into account the fact that in these acts of destruction, in which I had as an accomplice, in Albertine, her faculty of changing, her ability to forget, almost to hate the recent object of her love, I was sometimes causing a profound grief to one or other of those persons unknown with whom in turn she had taken her pleasure, and that this grief I was causing them in vain, for they would be abandoned, replaced, and, parallel to the path strewn with all the derelicts of her light-hearted infidelities, there would open for me another, pitiless path broken only by an occasional brief respite; so that my suffering could end only with Albertine's life or with my own. Even in the first days after our return to Paris, not satisfied by the information that Andrée and the chauffeur had given me as to their expeditions with my mistress, I had felt the neighbourhood of Paris to be as tormenting as that of Balbec, and had gone off for a few days in the country with Albertine. But everywhere my uncertainty as to what she might be doing was the same; the possibility that it was something wrong as abundant, vigilance even more difficult, with the result that I returned with her to Paris. In leaving Balbec, I had imagined that I was leaving Gomorrah, plucking Albertine from it; in reality, alas, Gomorrah was dispersed to all the ends of the earth. And partly out of jealousy, partly out of ignorance of such joys (a case which is rare indeed), I had arranged unawares this game of hide and seek in which Albertine was always to escape me.

I questioned her point-blank: 'Oh, by the way, Albertine, am I dreaming, or did you tell me that you knew Gilberte Swann?' 'Yes; that is to say, she used to talk to me at our classes, because she had a set of the French history notes, in fact she was very nice about it, and let me borrow them, and I gave them back the next time I saw her.' 'Is she the kind of woman that I object to?' 'Oh, not at all, quite the opposite.' But, rather than indulge in this sort of criminal investigation, I would often devote to imagining Albertine's excursion the energy that I did not employ in sharing it, and would speak to my mistress with that ardour which remains intact in our unfulfilled designs. I expressed so keen a longing to see once again some window in the Sainte-Chapelle, so keen a regret that I was not able to go there with her alone, that she said to me lovingly: 'Why, my dear boy, since you seem so keen about it, make a little effort, come with us. We can start as late as you like, whenever you're ready. And if you'd rather be alone with me, I have only to send Andrée home, she can come another time.' But these very entreaties to me to go out added to the calm which allowed me to yield to my desire to remain indoors.

It did not occur to me that the apathy that was indicated by my delegating thus to Andrée or the chauffeur the task of soothing my agitation by leaving them to keep watch over Albertine, was paralysing in me, rendering inert all those imaginative impulses of the mind, all those inspirations of the will, which enable us to guess, to forestall, what someone else is about to do; indeed the world of possibilities has always been more open to me than that of real events. This helps us to understand the human heart, but we are apt to be taken in by individuals. My jealousy was born of mental images, a form of self-torment not based upon probability. Now there may occur in the lives of men and of nations (and there was to occur, one day, in my own life) a moment when we need to have within us a superintendent of police, a clear-sighted diplomat, a master-detective, who instead of pondering over the concealed possibilities that extend to all the points of the compass, reasons accurately, says to himself: 'If Germany announces this, it means that she intends to do something else, not just "something" in the abstract but precisely this or that or the other, which she may perhaps have begun already to do.' 'If So-and-So has fled, it is not in the direction a or b or d, but to the point c, and the place to which we must direct our search for him is c.' Alas, this faculty which was not highly developed in me, I allowed to grow slack, to lose its power, to vanish, by acquiring the habit of growing calm the moment that other people were engaged in keeping watch on my behalf.

As for the reason for my reluctance to leave the house, I should not have liked to explain it to Albertine. I told her that the doctor had ordered me to stay in bed. This was not true. And if it had been true, his prescription would have been powerless to prevent me from accompanying my mistress. I asked her to excuse me from going out with herself and Andrée. I shall mention only one of my reasons, which was dictated by prudence. Whenever I went out with Albertine, if she left my side for a moment, I became anxious, began to imagine that she had spoken to, or simply cast a glance at somebody. If she was not in the best of tempers, I thought that I was causing her to miss or to postpone some appointment. Reality is never more than an allurement to an unknown element in quest of which we can never progress very far. It is better not to know, to think as little as possible, not to feed our jealousy with the slightest concrete detail. Unfortunately, even when we eliminate the outward life, incidents are created by the inward life also; though I held aloof from Albertine's expeditions, the random course of my solitary reflections furnished me at times with those tiny fragments of the truth which attract to themselves, like a magnet, an inkling of the unknown, which, from that moment, becomes painful. Even if we live in a hermetically sealed compartment, associations of ideas, memories continue to act upon us.

But these internal shocks did not occur immediately; no sooner had Albertine started on her drive than I was revivified, were it only for a few moments, by the stimulating virtues of solitude. I took my share of the pleasures of the new day; the arbitrary desire – the capricious and purely spontaneous inclination – to taste them would not have sufficed to place them within my reach, had not the peculiar state of the weather not merely reminded me of their images in the past but affirmed their reality in the present, immediately accessible to all men whom a contingent and consequently negligible circumstance did not compel to remain at home. On certain fine days the weather was so cold, one was in such full communication with the street that it seemed as though a breach had been made in the outer walls of the house, and, whenever a tramcar passed, the sound of its bell throbbed like that of a silver knife striking a wall of glass. But it was most of all in myself that I heard, with intoxication, a new sound rendered by the hidden violin. Its strings are tightened or relaxed by mere changes of temperature, of light, in the world outside. In our person, an instrument which the uniformity of habit has rendered silent, song is born of these digressions, these variations, the source of all music: the change of climate on certain days makes us pass at once from one note to another. We recapture the forgotten air the mathematical inevitability of which we might have deduced, and which for the first few moments we sing without recognising it. By themselves these modifications (which, albeit coming from without, were internal) refashioned for me the world outside. Communicating doors, long barred, opened themselves in my brain. The life of certain towns, the gaiety of certain expeditions resumed their place in my consciousness. All athrob in harmony with the vibrating string, I would have sacrificed my dull life in the past, and all my life to come, erased with the india-rubber of habit, for one of these special, unique moments.

If I had not gone out with Albertine on her long drive, my mind would stray all the farther afield, and, because I had refused to savour with my senses this particular morning, I enjoyed in imagination all the similar mornings, past or possible, or more precisely a certain type of morning of which all those of the same kind were but the intermittent apparition which I had at once recognised; for the keen air blew the book open of its own accord at the right page, and I found clearly set out before my eyes, so that I might follow it from my bed, the Gospel for the day. This ideal morning filled my mind full of a permanent reality, identical with all similar mornings, and infected me with a cheerfulness which my physical ill-health did not diminish: for, inasmuch as our sense of wellbeing is caused not so much by our sound health as by the unemployed surplus of our strength, we can attain to it, just as much as by increasing our strength, by diminishing our activity. The activity with which I was overflowing and which I kept constantly charged as I lay in bed, made me spring from side to side, with a leaping heart, like a machine which, prevented from moving in space, rotates on its own axis.

Françoise came in to light the fire, and to make it draw, threw upon it a handful of twigs, the scent of which, forgotten for a year past, traced round the fireplace a magic circle within which, perceiving myself poring over a book, now at Combray, now at Doncières, I was as joyful, while remaining in my bedroom in Paris, as if I had been on the point of starting for a walk along the Méséglise way, or of going to join Saint-Loup and his friends on the training-ground. It often happens that the pleasure which everyone takes in turning over the keepsakes that his memory has collected is keenest in those whom the tyranny of bodily ill-health and the daily hope of recovery prevent, on the one hand, from going out to seek in nature scenes that resemble those memories, and, on the other hand, leave so convinced that they will shortly be able to do so that they can remain gazing at them in a state of desire, of appetite, and not regard them merely as memories, as pictures. But, even if they were never to be anything more than memories to me, even if I, as I recalled them, saw merely pictures, immediately they

recreated in me, of me as a whole, by virtue of an identical sensation, the
boy, the youth who had first seen them. There had been not merely a
change in the weather outside, or, inside the room, the introduction of a
fresh scent, there had been in myself a difference of age, the substitution of
another person. The scent, in the frosty air, of the twigs of brushwood, was
like a fragment of the past, an invisible floe broken off from the ice of an old
winter that stole into my room, often variegated moreover with this perfume
or that light, as though with a sequence of different years, in which I found
myself plunged, overwhelmed, even before I had identified them, by the
eagerness of hopes long since abandoned. The sun's rays fell upon my bed
and passed through the transparent shell of my attenuated body, warmed
me, made me as hot as a sheet of scorching crystal. Whereupon, a famished
convalescent who has already begun to batten upon all the dishes that are
still forbidden him, I asked myself whether marriage with Albertine would
not spoil my life, as well by making me assume the burden, too heavy for my
shoulders, of consecrating myself to another person, as by forcing me to live
in absence from myself because of her continual presence and depriving me,
forever, of the delights of solitude.

    And not of these alone. Even when we ask of the day nothing but desires,
there are some – those that are excited not by things but by people – whose
character it is to be unlike any other. If, on rising from my bed, I went to the
window and drew the curtain aside for a moment, it was not merely, as a
pianist for a moment turns back the lid of his instrument, to ascertain
whether, on the balcony and in the street, the sunlight was tuned to exactly
the same pitch as in my memory, it was also to catch a glimpse of some
laundress carrying her linen-basket, a bread-seller in her blue apron, a
dairymaid in her tucker and sleeves of white linen, carrying the yoke from
which her jugs of milk are suspended, some haughty golden-haired miss
escorted by her governess, a composite image, in short, which the differences
of outline, numerically perhaps insignificant, were enough to make as
different from any other as, in a phrase of music, the difference between two
notes, an image but for the vision of which I should have impoverished my
day of the objects which it might have to offer to my desires of happiness.
But, if the surfeit of joy, brought me by the spectacle of women whom it was
impossible to imagine *a priori*, made more desirable, more deserving of
exploration, the street, the town, the world, it set me longing, for that very
reason, to recover my health, to go out of doors and, without Albertine, to
be a free man. How often, at the moment when the unknown woman who
was to haunt my dreams passed beneath the window, now on foot, now at
the full speed of her motorcar, was I made wretched that my body could not

follow my gaze which kept pace with her, and falling upon her as though shot from the embrasure of my window by an arquebus, arrest the flight of the face that held out for me the offer of a happiness which, cloistered thus, I should never know.

Of Albertine, on the other hand, I had nothing more to learn. Every day, she seemed to me less attractive. Only, the desire that she aroused in other people, when, upon hearing of it, I began to suffer afresh and was impelled to challenge their possession of her, raised her in my sight to a lofty pinnacle. Pain, she was capable of causing me; joy, never. Pain alone kept my tedious attachment alive. As soon as my pain vanished, and with it the need to soothe it, requiring all my attention, like some agonising distraction, I felt that she meant absolutely nothing to me, that I must mean absolutely nothing to her. It made me wretched that this state should persist, and, at certain moments, I longed to hear of something terrible that she had done, something that would be capable of keeping us at arm's length until I was cured, so that we might then be able to be reconciled, to refashion in a different and more flexible form the chain that bound us.

In the meantime, I was employing a thousand circumstances, a thousand pleasures to procure for her in my society the illusion of that happiness which I did not feel myself capable of giving her. I should have liked, as soon as I was cured, to set off for Venice, but how was I to manage it, if I married Albertine, I, who was so jealous of her that even in Paris whenever I decided to stir from my room it was to go out with her? Even when I stayed in the house all the afternoon, my thoughts accompanied her on her drive, traced a remote, blue horizon, created round the centre that was myself a fluctuating zone of vague uncertainty. 'How completely,' I said to myself, 'would Albertine spare me the anguish of separation if, in the course of one of these drives, seeing that I no longer say anything to her about marriage, she decided not to come back, and went off to her aunt's, without my having to bid her goodbye!' My heart, now that its scar had begun to heal, was ceasing to adhere to the heart of my mistress; I could by imagination shift her, separate her from myself without pain. No doubt, failing myself, some other man would be her husband, and in her freedom she would meet perhaps with those adventures which filled me with horror. But the day was so fine, I was so certain that she would return in the evening, that even if the idea of possible misbehaviour did enter my mind, I could, by an exercise of free will, imprison it in a part of my brain in which it had no more importance than would have had in my real life the vices of an imaginary person; bringing into play the supple hinges of my thought, I had, with an energy which I felt in my head to be at once physical and mental, as it were a muscular movement and a spiritual impulse, broken away from the state of perpetual preoccupation in which I had until then been confined, and was beginning to move in a free atmosphere, in which the idea of sacrificing everything in order to prevent Albertine from marrying someone else and to put an obstacle in the way of her fondness for women seemed as unreasonable to my own mind as to that of a person who had never known her.

However, jealousy is one of those intermittent maladies, the cause of which is capricious, imperative, always identical in the same patient, sometimes entirely different in another. There are asthmatic persons who can soothe their crises only by opening the windows, inhaling the full blast of the wind, the pure air of the mountains, others by taking refuge in the heart of the city, in a room heavy with smoke. Rare indeed is the jealous man whose jealousy does not allow certain concessions. One will consent to infidelity, provided that he is told of it, another provided that it is concealed from him, wherein they appear to be equally absurd, since if the latter is more literally deceived inasmuch as the truth is not disclosed to him, the other demands in that truth the food, the extension, the renewal of his sufferings.

What is more, these two parallel manias of jealousy extend often beyond words, whether they implore or reject confidences. We see a jealous lover who is jealous only of the women with whom his mistress has relations in his absence, but allows her to give herself to another man, if it is done with his authorisation, near at hand, and, if not actually before his eyes, under his roof. This case is not at all uncommon among elderly men who are in love with young women. Such a man feels the difficulty of winning her favour, sometimes his inability to satisfy her, and, rather than be betrayed, prefers to admit to his house, to an adjoining room, some man whom he considers incapable of giving her bad advice, but not incapable of giving her pleasure. With another man it is just the opposite; never allowing his mistress to go out by herself for a single minute in a town that he knows, he keeps her in a state of bondage, but allows her to go for a month to a place which he does not know, where he cannot form any mental picture of what she may be doing. I had with regard to Albertine both these sorts of sedative mania. I should not have been jealous if she had enjoyed her pleasures in my company, with my encouragement, pleasures over the whole of which I could have kept watch, thus avoiding any fear of falsehood; I might perhaps not have been jealous either if she had removed to a place so unfamiliar and remote that I could not imagine nor find any possibility, feel any temptation to know the manner of her life. In either alternative, my uncertainty would have been killed by a knowledge or an ignorance equally complete.

The decline of day plunging me back by an act of memory in a cool atmosphere of long ago, I breathed it with the same delight with which Orpheus inhaled the subtle air, unknown upon this earth, of the Elysian Fields.

But already the day was ending and I was overpowered by the desolation of the evening. Looking mechanically at the clock to see how many hours must elapse before Albertine's return, I saw that I had still time to dress and go downstairs to ask my landlady, Mme de Guermantes, for particulars of various becoming garments which I was anxious to procure for my mistress. Sometimes I met the Duchess in the courtyard, going out for a walk, even if the weather was bad, in a close-fitting hat and furs. I knew quite well that, to many people of intelligence, she was merely a lady like any other, the name Duchesse de Guermantes signifying nothing, now that there are no longer any sovereign Duchies or Principalities, but I had adopted a different point of view in my method of enjoying people and places. All the castles of the territories of which she was Duchess, Princess, Viscountess, this lady in furs defying the weather teemed to me to be carrying them on her person, as a figure carved over the lintel of a church door holds in his hand the cathedral that he has built or the city that he has defended. But these castles, these forests, my mind's eye alone could discern them in the left hand of the lady in furs, whom the King called cousin. My bodily eyes distinguished in it only, on days when the sky was threatening, an umbrella with which the Duchess was not afraid to arm herself. 'One can never be certain, it is wiser, I may find myself miles from home, with a cabman demanding a fare *beyond my means*.' The words 'too dear' and 'beyond my means' kept recurring all the time in the Duchess's conversation, as did also: 'I am too poor' – without its being possible to decide whether she spoke thus because she thought it amusing to say that she was poor, being so rich, or because she thought it smart, being so aristocratic, in spite of her affectation of peasant ways, not to attach to riches the importance that people give them who are merely rich and nothing else, and who look down upon the poor. Perhaps it was, rather, a habit contracted at a time in her life when, already rich, but not rich enough to satisfy her needs, considering the expense of keeping up all those properties, she felt a certain shortage of money which she did not wish to appear to be concealing. The things about which we most often jest are generally, on the contrary, the things that embarrass us, but we do not wish to appear to be embarrassed by them, and feel perhaps a secret hope of the further advantage that the person to whom we are talking, hearing us treat the matter as a joke, will conclude that it is not true.

But upon most evenings, at this hour, I could count upon finding the

Duchess at home, and I was glad of this, for it was more convenient for me to ask her in detail for the information that Albertine required. And down I went almost without thinking how extraordinary it was that I should be calling upon that mysterious Mme de Guermantes of my boyhood, simply in order to make use of her for a practical purpose, as one makes use of the telephone, a supernatural instrument before whose miracles we used to stand amazed, and which we now employ without giving it a thought, to summon our tailor or to order ices for a party.

Albertine delighted in any sort of finery. I could not deny myself the pleasure of giving her some new trifle every day. And whenever she had spoken to me with rapture of a scarf, a stole, a sunshade which, from the window or as they passed one another in the courtyard, her eyes that so quickly distinguished anything smart, had seen round the throat, over the shoulders, in the hand of Mme de Guermantes, knowing how the girl's naturally fastidious taste (refined still further by the lessons in elegance of attire which Elstir's conversation had been to her) would not be at all satisfied by any mere substitute, even of a pretty thing, such as fills its place in the eyes of the common herd, but differs from it entirely, I went in secret to make the Duchess explain to me where, how, from what model the article had been created that had taken Albertine's fancy, how I should set about to obtain one exactly similar, in what the creator's secret, the charm (what Albertine called the 'chic', the 'style') of his manner, the precise name – the beauty of the material being of importance also – and quality of the stuffs that I was to insist upon their using.

When I mentioned to Albertine, on our return from Balbec, that the Duchesse de Guermantes lived opposite to us, in the same mansion, she had assumed, on hearing the proud title and great name, that air more than indifferent, hostile, contemptuous, which is the sign of an impotent desire in proud and passionate natures. Splendid as Albertine's nature might be, the fine qualities which it contained were free to develop only amid those hindrances which are our personal tastes, or that lamentation for those of our tastes which we have been obliged to relinquish – in Albertine's case snobbishness – which is called antipathy. Albertine's antipathy to people in society occupied, for that matter, but a very small part in her nature, and appealed to me as an aspect of the revolutionary spirit – that is to say an embittered love of the nobility – engraved upon the opposite side of the French character to that which displays the aristocratic manner of Mme de Guermantes. To this aristocratic manner Albertine, in view of the impossibility of her acquiring it, would perhaps not have given a thought, but remembering that Elstir had spoken to her of the Duchess as the best-dressed woman in Paris, her republican contempt for a Duchess gave place in my mistress to a keen interest in a fashionable woman. She was always asking me to tell her about Mme de Guermantes, and was glad that I should go to the Duchess to obtain advice as to her own attire. No doubt I might have got this from Mme Swann and indeed I did once write to her with this intention. But Mme de Guermantes seemed to me to carry to an even higher pitch the art of dressing. If, on going down for a moment to call upon her, after making sure that she had not gone out and leaving word that I was to be told as soon as Albertine returned, I found the Duchess swathed in the mist of a garment of grey crêpe de chine, I accepted this aspect of her which I felt to be due to complex causes and to be quite inevitable, I let myself be overpowered by the atmosphere which it exhaled, like that of certain late afternoons cushioned in pearly grey by a vaporous fog; if, on the other hand, her indoor gown was Chinese with red and yellow flames, I gazed at it as at a glowing sunset; these garments were not a casual decoration alterable at her pleasure, but a definite and poetical reality like that of the weather, or the light peculiar to a certain hour of the day.

Of all the outdoor and indoor gowns that Mme de Guermantes wore, those which seemed most to respond to a definite intention, to be endowed with a special significance, were the garments made by Fortuny from old Venetian models. Is it their historical character, is it rather the fact that each one of them is unique that gives them so special a significance that the pose of the woman who is wearing one while she waits for you to appear or while she talks to you assumes an exceptional importance, as though the costume had been the fruit of a long deliberation and your conversation was detached from the current of everyday life like a scene in a novel? In the novels of Balzac, we see his heroines purposely put on one or another dress on the day on which they are expecting some particular visitor. The dresses of today have less character, always excepting the creations of Fortuny. There is no room for vagueness in the novelist's description, since the gown does really exist, and the merest sketch of it is as naturally preordained as a copy of a work of art. Before putting on one or another of them, the woman has had to make a choice between two garments, not more or less alike but each one profoundly individual, and answering to its name. But the dress did not prevent me from thinking of the woman.

Indeed, Mme de Guermantes seemed to me at this time more attractive than in the days when I was still in love with her. Expecting less of her (whom I no longer went to visit for her own sake), it was almost with the ease and comfort of a man in a room by himself, with his feet on the fender, that I listened to her as though I were reading a book written in the speech of long ago. My mind was sufficiently detached to enjoy in what she said that pure charm of the French language which we no longer find either in the speech or in the literature of the present day. I listened to her conversation as to a folk song deliciously and purely French, I realised that I would have allowed her to belittle Maeterlinck (whom for that matter she now admired, from a feminine weakness of intellect, influenced by those literary fashions whose rays spread slowly), as I realised that Mérimée had belittled Baudelaire, Stendhal Balzac, Paul-Louis Courier Victor Hugo, Meilhac Mallarmé. I realised that the critic had a far more restricted outlook than his victim, but also a purer vocabulary. That of Mme de Guermantes, almost as much as that of Saint-Loup's mother, was purified to an enchanting degree. It is not in the bloodless formulas of the writers of today, who say: *au fait* (for 'in reality'), *singulièrement* (for 'in particular'), étonné (for 'struck with amazement'), and the like, that we recapture the old speech and the true pronunciation of words, but in conversing with a Mme de Guermantes or a Françoise; I had learned from the latter, when I was five years old, that one did not say 'the Tarn' but 'the Tar'; not 'Béam' but 'Béar'. The effect of which was that at twenty, when I began to go into society, I had no need to be taught there that one ought not to say, like Mme Bontemps: 'Madame de Béam'.

It would be untrue to pretend that of this territorial and semi-peasant quality which survived in her the Duchess was not fully conscious, indeed she displayed a certain affectation in emphasising it. But, on her part, this was not so much the false simplicity of a great lady aping the countrywoman or the pride of a Duchess bent upon snubbing the rich ladies who express contempt for the peasants whom they do not know as the almost artistic preference of a woman who knows the charm of what belongs to her, and is not going to spoil it with a coat of modern varnish. In the same way, everybody will remember at Dives a Norman innkeeper, landlord of the Guillaume le Conquérant, who carefully refrained – which is very rare – from giving his hostelry the modern comforts of an hotel, and, albeit a millionaire, retained the speech, the blouse of a Norman peasant and allowed you to enter his kitchen and watch him prepare with his own hands, as in a farmhouse, a dinner which was nevertheless infinitely better and even more expensive than are the dinners in the most luxurious hotels.

All the local sap that survives in the old noble families is not enough, there must also be born of them a person of sufficient intelligence not to despise it, not to conceal it beneath the varnish of society. Mme de Guermantes, unfortunately clever and Parisian, who, when I first knew her, retained nothing of her native soil but its accent, had at least, when she wished to describe her life as a girl, found for her speech one of those compromises (between what would have seemed too spontaneously provincial on the one hand or artificially literary on the other), one of those compromises which form the attraction of George Sand's *La Petite Fadette* or of certain legends preserved by Chateaubriand in his *Mémoires d'Outre-Tombe*. My chief pleasure was in hearing her tell some anecdote which brought peasants into the picture with herself. The historic names, the old customs gave to these blendings of the castle with the village a distinctly attractive savour. Having remained in contact with the lands over which it once ruled, a certain class of the nobility has remained regional, with the result that the simplest remark unrolls before our eyes a political and physical map of the whole history of France.

If there was no affectation, no desire to fabricate a special language, then this manner of pronouncing words was a regular museum of French history displayed in conversation. 'My great-uncle Fitt-jam' was not at all surprising, for we know that the Fitz-James family are proud to boast that they are French nobles, and do not like to hear their name pronounced in the English fashion. One must, incidentally, admire the touching docility of the people who had previously supposed themselves obliged to pronounce certain names phonetically, and who, all of a sudden, after hearing the Duchesse de Guermantes pronounce them otherwise, adopted the pronunciation which they could never have guessed. Thus the Duchess, who had had a great-grandfather in the suite of the Comte de Chambord, liked to tease her husband for having turned Orleanist by proclaiming: 'We old Frochedorf people . . . ' The visitor, who had always imagined that he was correct in saying 'Frohsdorf', at once turned his coat, and ever afterwards might be heard saying 'Frochedorf'.

On one occasion when I asked Mme de Guermantes who a young blood was whom she had introduced to me as her nephew but whose name I had failed to catch, I was none the wiser when from the back of her throat the Duchess uttered in a very loud but quite inarticulate voice: '*C'est l'* . . . *i Eon* . . . *l* . . . *b* . . . *frère à Robert.* He makes out that he has the same shape of skull as the ancient Gauls.' Then I realised that she had said: '*C'est le petit Léon,*' and that this was the Prince de Léon, who was indeed Robert de Saint-Loup's brother-in-law. 'I know nothing about his skull,' she went on, 'but the way he dresses, and I must say he does dress quite well, is not at all in the style of those parts. Once when I was staying at Josselin, with the Rohans, we all went over to one of the pilgrimages, where there were peasants from every part of Brittany. A great hulking fellow from one of the Léon villages stood gaping open-mouthed at Robert's brother-in-law in his beige breeches! "What are you staring at me like that for?" said Léon. "I bet you don't know who I am?" The peasant admitted that he did not. "Very well," said Léon, "I'm your Prince." "Oh!" said the peasant, taking off his cap and apologising. "I thought you were an *Englische*." '

And if, taking this opportunity, I led Mme de Guermantes on to talk about the Rohans (with whom her own family had frequently intermarried), her conversation would become impregnated with a hint of the wistful charm of the Pardons, and (as that true poet Pampille would say) with 'the harsh savour of pancakes of black grain fried over a fire of rushes'.

Of the Marquis du Lau (whose tragic decline we all know, when, himself deaf, he used to be taken to call on Mme H . . . who was blind), she would recall the less tragic years when, after the day's sport, at Guermantes, he would change into slippers before taking tea with the Prince of Wales, to whom he would not admit himself inferior, and with whom, as we see, he stood upon no ceremony. She described all this so picturesquely that she seemed to invest him with the plumed musketeer bonnet of the somewhat vainglorious gentlemen of the Périgord.

But even in the mere classification of different people, her care to distinguish and indicate their native provinces was in Mme de Guermantes, when she was her natural self, a great charm which a Parisian-born woman could never have acquired, and those simple names Anjou, Poitou, the Périgord, filled her conversation with pictorial landscapes.

To revert to the pronunciation and vocabulary of Mme de Guermantes, it is in this aspect that the nobility shows itself truly conservative, with everything that the word implies at once somewhat puerile and somewhat perilous, stubborn in its resistance to evolution but interesting also to an artist. I was anxious to know the original spelling of the name Jean. I learned it when I received a letter from a nephew of Mme de Villeparisis who signs himself – as he was christened, as he figures in Gotha – Jehan de Villeparisis, with the same handsome, superfluous, heraldic h that we admire, illuminated in vermilion or ultramarine in a Book of Hours or in a window.

Unfortunately, I never had time to prolong these visits indefinitely, for I was anxious, if possible, not to return home after my mistress. But it was only in driblets that I was able to obtain from Mme de Guermantes that information as to her garments which was of use in helping me to order garments similar in style, so far as it was possible for a young girl to wear them, for Albertine. 'For instance, Madame, that evening when you dined with Mme de Saint-Euverte, and then went on to the Princesse de Guermantes, you had a dress that was all red, with red shoes, you were marvellous, you reminded me of a sort of great blood-red blossom, a blazing ruby – now, what was that dress? Is it the sort of thing that a girl can wear?'

The Duchess, imparting to her tired features the radiant expression that the Princesse des Laumes used to assume when Swann, in years past, paid her compliments, looked, with tears of merriment in her eyes, quizzingly, questioningly and delightedly at M. de Bréauté who was always there at that hour and who set beaming from behind his monocle a smile that seemed to pardon this outburst of intellectual trash for the sake of the physical excitement of youth which seemed to him to lie beneath it. The Duchess appeared to be saying: 'What is the matter with him? He must be mad.' Then turning to me with a coaxing air: 'I wasn't aware that I looked like a blazing ruby or a blood-red blossom, but I do remember, as it happens, that I had on a red dress: it was red satin, which was being worn that season. Yes, a girl can wear that sort of thing at a pinch, but you told me that your friend never went out in the evening. That is a full evening dress, not a thing that she can put on to pay calls.'

What is extraordinary is that of the evening in question, which after all was not so very remote, Mme de Guermantes should remember nothing but what she had been wearing, and should have forgotten a certain incident which nevertheless, as we shall see presently, ought to have mattered to her greatly. It seems that among men and women of action (and people in society are men and women of action on a minute, a microscopic scale, but are nevertheless men and women of action), the mind, overcharged by the need of attending to what is going to happen in an hour's time, confides only a very few things to the memory. As often as not, for instance, it was not with the object of putting his questioner in the wrong and making himself appear not to have been mistaken that M. de Norpois, when you reminded him of the prophecies he had uttered with regard to an alliance with Germany of which nothing had ever come, would say: 'You must be mistaken, I have no recollection of it whatever, it is not like me, for in that sort of conversation I am always most laconic, and I would never have predicted the success of one of those *coups d'éclat* which are often nothing more than *coups de tête* and almost always degenerate into *coups de force*. It is beyond question that in the remote future a Franco-German *rapprochement* might come into being and would be highly profitable to both countries, nor would France have the worse of the bargain, I dare say, but I have never spoken of it because the fruit is not yet ripe, and if you wish to know my opinion, in asking our late enemies to join with us in solemn wedlock, I consider that we should be setting out to meet a severe rebuff, and that the attempt could end only in disaster.' In saying this M. de Norpois was not being untruthful, he had simply forgotten. We quickly forget what we have not deeply considered, what has been dictated to us by the spirit of imitation, by the passions of our neighbours. These change, and with them our memory undergoes alteration. Even more than diplomats, politicians are unable to remember the point of view which they adopted at a certain moment, and some of their palinodes are due less to a surfeit of ambition than to a shortage of memory. As for people in society, there are very few things that they remember.

Mme de Guermantes assured me that, at the party to which she had gone in a red gown, she did not remember Mme de Chaussepierre's being present, and that I must be mistaken. And yet, heaven knows, the Chaussepierres had been present enough in the minds of both Duke and Duchess since then. For the following reason. M. de Guermantes had been the senior vice-president of the Jockey, when the president died. Certain members of the club who were not popular in society and whose sole pleasure was to blackball the men who did not invite them to their houses started a campaign against the Duc de Guermantes who, certain of being elected, and relatively indifferent to the presidency which was a small matter for a man in his social position, paid no attention. It was urged against him that the Duchess was a Dreyfusard (the Dreyfus case had long been concluded, but twenty years later people were still talking about it, and so far only two years had elapsed), and entertained the Rothschilds, that so much consideration had been shown of late to certain great international magnates like the Duc de Guermantes, who was half German. The campaign found its ground well prepared, clubs being always jealous of men who are in the public eye, and detesting great fortunes.

Chaussepierre's own fortune was no mere pittance, but nobody could take offence at it; he never spent a penny, the couple lived in a modest apartment, the wife went about dressed in black serge. A passionate music-lover, she did indeed give little afternoon parties to which many more singers were invited than to the Guermantes. But no one ever mentioned these parties, no refreshments were served, the husband did not put in an appearance even, and everything went off quite quietly in the obscurity of the Rue de la Chaise. At the Opéra, Mme de Chaussepierre passed unnoticed, always among people whose names recalled the most 'die-hard' element of the intimate circle of Charles X, but people quite obsolete, who went nowhere. On the day of the election, to the general surprise, obscurity triumphed over renown: Chaussepierre, the second vice-president, was elected president of the Jockey, and the Duc de Guermantes was left sitting – that is to say, in the senior vice-president's chair. Of course, being president of the Jockey means little or nothing to Princes of the highest rank such as the Guermantes. But not to be it when it is your turn, to see preferred to you a Chaussepierre to whose wife Oriane, two years earlier, had not merely refused to bow but had taken offence that an unknown scarecrow like that should bow to her, this the Duke did find hard to endure. He pretended to be superior to this rebuff, asserting moreover that it was his long-standing friendship with Swann that was at the root of it. Actually his anger never cooled.

One curious thing was that nobody had ever before heard the Duc de Guermantes make use of the quite commonplace expression 'out and out', but ever since the Jockey election, whenever anybody referred to the Dreyfus case, pat would come 'out and out'. 'Dreyfus case, Dreyfus case, that's soon said, and it's a misuse of the term. It is not a question of religion, it's *out and out* a political matter.' Five years might go by without your hearing him say 'out and out' again, if during that time nobody mentioned the Dreyfus case, but if, at the end of five years, the name Dreyfus cropped up, 'out and out' would at once follow automatically. The Duke could not, anyhow, bear to hear any mention of the case, 'which has been responsible,' he would say, 'for so many disasters', albeit he was really conscious of one and one only; his own failure to become president of the Jockey. And so on the afternoon in question, when I reminded Madame de Guermantes of the red gown that she had worn at her cousin's party, M. de Bréauté was none too well received when, determined to say something, by an association of ideas which remained obscure and which he did not illuminate, he began, twisting his tongue about between his pursed lips: 'Talking of the Dreyfus case – ' (why in the world of the Dreyfus case, we were talking simply of a red dress, and certainly poor Bréauté, whose only desire was to make himself agreeable, can have had no malicious intention). But the mere name of Dreyfus made the Duc de Guermantes knit his Jupiterian brows. 'I was told,' Bréauté went on, 'a jolly good thing, damned clever, 'pon my word, that was said by our friend Cartier' (we must warn the reader that this Cartier, Mme de Villefranche's brother, was in no way related to the jeweller of that name) 'not that I'm in the least surprised, for he's got plenty of brains to spare,' 'Oh!' broke in Oriane, 'he can spare me his brains. I hardly like to tell you how much your friend Cartier has always bored me, and I have never been able to understand the boundless charm that Charles de La Trémoïlle and his wife seem to find in the creature, for I meet him there every time that I go to their house.' 'My dear Dutt–yess,' replied Bréauté, who was unable to pronounce the soft c, 'I think you are very hard upon Cartier. It is true that he has perhaps made himself rather too mutt–y– at home at the La Trémoïlles', but after all he does provide Tyarles with a sort of – what shall I say? – a sort of *fidus Achates*, which has become a very rare bird indeed in these days. Anyhow, this is the story as it was told to me. Cartier appears to have said that if M. Zola had gone out of his way to stand his trial and to be convicted, it was in order to enjoy the only sensation he had never yet tried, that of being in prison.' 'And so he ran away before they could arrest him,' Oriane broke in. 'Your story doesn't hold water. Besides, even if it was plausible, I think his remark absolutely idiotic. If that's what you call being witty!' 'Good grate–ious, my dear Oriane,' replied Bréauté who, finding himself contradicted, was beginning to lose confidence, 'it's not my remark, I'm telling you it as it was told to me, take it for what's it worth. Anyhow, it earned M. Cartier a first-rate blowing up from that excellent fellow La Trémoïlle who, and quite rightly, does not like people to discuss what one might call, so to speak, current events, in his drawing-room, and was all the more annoyed because Mme Alphonse Rothschild was present. Cartier had to listen to a positive jobation from La Trémoïlle.' 'I should think so,' said the Duke, in the worst of tempers, 'the Alphonse Rothschilds, even if they have the tact never to speak of that abominable affair, are Dreyfusards at heart, like all the Jews. Indeed that is an argument *ad hominem*' (the Duke was a trifle vague in his use of the expression *ad hominem*) 'which is not sufficiently made use of to prove the dishonesty of the Jews. If a Frenchman robs or murders somebody, I do not consider myself bound, because he is a Frenchman like myself, to find him innocent. But the Jews will never admit that one of their fellow-countrymen is a traitor, although they know it perfectly well, and never think of the terrible repercussions' (the Duke was thinking, naturally, of that accursed defeat by Chaussepierre) 'which the crime of one of their people can bring even to . . . Come, Oriane, you're not going to pretend that it ain't damning to the Jews that they all support a traitor. You're not going to tell me that it ain't because they're Jews.' 'Of course not,' retorted Oriane (feeling, with a trace of irritation, a certain desire to hold her own against Jupiter Tonans and also to set 'intellect' above the Dreyfus case). 'Perhaps it is just because they are Jews and know their own race that they realise that a person can be a Jew and not necessarily a traitor and anti-French, as M. Drumont seems to maintain. Certainly, if he'd been a Christian, the Jews wouldn't have taken any interest in him, but they did so because they knew quite well that if he hadn't been a Jew people wouldn't have been so ready to think him a traitor *a priori*, as my nephew Robert would say.' 'Women never understand a thing about politics,' exclaimed the Duke, fastening his gaze upon the Duchess. 'That shocking crime is not simply a Jewish cause, but *out and out* an affair of vast national importance which may lead to the most appalling consequences for France, which ought to have driven out all the Jews, whereas I am sorry to say that the measures taken up to the present have been directed (in an ignoble fashion, which will have to be overruled) not against them but against the most eminent of their adversaries, against men of the highest rank, who have been flung into the gutter, to the ruin of our unhappy country.'

I felt that the conversation had taken a wrong turning and reverted hurriedly to the topic of clothes.

'Do you remember, Madame,' I said, 'the first time that you were friendly with me?' 'The first time that I was friendly with him,' she repeated, turning with a smile to M. de Bréauté, the tip of whose nose grew more pointed, his smile more tender out of politeness to Mme de Guermantes, while his voice, like a knife on the grindstone, emitted various vague and rusty sounds. 'You were wearing a yellow gown with big black flowers.' 'But, my dear boy, that's the same thing, those are evening dresses.' 'And your hat with the cornflowers that I liked so much! Still, those are all things of the past. I should like to order for the girl I mentioned to you a fur cloak like the one you had on yesterday morning. Would it be possible for me to see it?' 'Of course; Hannibal has to be going in a moment. You shall come to my room and my maid will show you anything you want to look at. Only, my dear boy, though I shall be delighted to lend you anything, I must warn you that if you have things from Callot's or Doucet's or Paquin's copied by some small dress-maker, the result is never the same.' 'But I never dreamed of going to a small dressmaker, I know quite well it wouldn't be the same thing, but I should be interested to hear you explain why.' 'You know quite well I can never explain anything, I am a perfect fool, I talk like a peasant. It is a question of handiwork, of style; as far as furs go, I can at least give you a line to my furrier, so that he shan't rob you. But you realise that even then it will cost you eight or nine thousand francs.' 'And that indoor gown that you were wearing the other evening, with such a curious smell, dark, fluffy, speckled, streaked with gold like a butterfly's wing?' 'Ah! That is one of Fortuny's. Your young lady can quite well wear that in the house. I have heaps of them; you shall see them presently, in fact I can give you one or two if you like. But I should like you to see one that my cousin Talleyrand has. I must write to her for the loan of it.' 'But you had such charming shoes as well, are they Fortuny's too?' 'No, I know the ones you mean, they are made of some gilded kid we came across in London, when I was shopping with Consuelo Manchester. It was amazing. I could never make out how they did it, it was just like a golden skin, simply that with a tiny diamond in front. The poor Duchess of Manchester is dead, but if it's any help to you I can write and ask Lady Warwick or the Duchess of Marlborough to try and get me some more. I wonder, now, if I haven't a piece of the stuff left. You might be able to have a pair made here. I shall look for it this evening, and let you know.'

As I endeavoured as far as possible to leave the Duchess before Albertine had returned, it often happened that I met in the courtyard as I came away from her door M. de Charlus and Morel on their way to take tea at Jupien's, a supreme favour for the Baron. I did not encounter them every day but they went there every day. Here we may perhaps remark that the regularity of a habit is generally in proportion to its absurdity. The sensational things, we do as a rule only by fits and starts. But the senseless life, in which the maniac deprives himself of all pleasure and inflicts the greatest discomforts upon himself, is the type that alters least. Every ten years, if we had the curiosity to enquire, we should find the poor wretch still asleep at the hours when he might be living his life, going out at the hours when there is nothing to do but let oneself be murdered in the streets, sipping iced drinks when he is hot, still trying desperately to cure a cold. A slight impulse of energy, for a single day, would be sufficient to change these habits for good and all. But the fact is that this sort of life is almost always the appanage of a person devoid of energy. Vices are another aspect of these monotonous existences which the exercise of will power would suffice to render less painful. These two aspects might be observed simultaneously when M. de Charlus came every day with Morel to take tea at Jupien's. A single outburst had marred this daily custom. The tailor's niece having said one day to Morel: 'That's all right then, come tomorrow and I'll stand you a tea,' the Baron had quite justifiably considered this expression very vulgar on the lips of a person whom he regarded as almost a prospective daughter-in-law, but as he enjoyed being offensive and became carried away by his own anger, instead of simply saying to Morel that he begged him to give her a lesson in polite manners, the whole of their homeward walk was a succession of violent scenes. In the most insolent, the most arrogant tone: 'So your "touch" which, I can see, is not necessarily allied to "tact", has hindered the normal development of your sense of smell, since you could allow that fetid expression "stand a tea" – at fifteen centimes, I suppose – to waft its stench of sewage to my regal nostrils? When you have come to the end of a violin solo, have you ever seen yourself in my house rewarded with a fart, instead of frenzied applause, or a silence more eloquent still, since it is due to exhaustion from the effort to restrain, not what your young woman lavishes upon you, but the sob that you have brought to my lips?'

When a public official has had similar reproaches heaped upon him by his chief, he invariably loses his post next day. Nothing, on the contrary, could have been more painful to M. de Charlus than to dismiss Morel, and, fearing indeed that he had gone a little too far, he began to sing the girl's praises in detailed terms, with an abundance of good taste mingled with impertinence. 'She is charming; as you are a musician, I suppose that she seduced you by her voice, which is very beautiful in the high notes, where she seems to await the accompaniment of your B sharp. Her lower register appeals to me less, and that must bear some relation to the triple rise of her strange and slender throat, which when it seems to have come to an end begins again; but these are trivial details, it is her outline that I admire. And as she is a dressmaker and must be handy with her scissors, you must make her give me a charming silhouette of herself cut out in paper.'

Charlie had paid but little attention to this eulogy, the charms which it extolled in his betrothed having completely escaped his notice. But he said, in reply to M. de Charlus: 'That's all right, my boy, I shall tell her off properly, and she won't talk like that again.' If Morel addressed M. de Charlus thus as his 'boy', it was not that the good-looking violinist was unaware that his own years numbered barely a third of the Baron's. Nor did he use the expression as Jupien would have done, but with that simplicity which in certain relations postulates that a suppression of the difference in age has tacitly preceded affection. A feigned affection on Morel's part. In others, a sincere affection. Thus, about this time M. de Charlus received a letter worded as follows:

My dear Palamède, when am I going to see thee again? I am longing terribly for thee and always thinking of thee.   Pierre

M. de Charlus racked his brains to discover which of his relatives it could be that took the liberty of addressing him so familiarly, and must consequently know him intimately, although he failed to recognise the handwriting. All the Princes to whom the Almanach de Gotha accords a few lines passed in procession for days on end through his mind. And then, all of a sudden, an address written on the back of the letter enlightened him: the writer was the page at a gambling club to which M. de Charlus sometimes went. This page had not felt that he was being discourteous in writing in this tone to M. de Charlus, for whom on the contrary he felt the deepest respect. But he thought that it would not be civil not to address in the second person singular a gentleman who had many times kissed one, and thereby – he imagined in his simplicity – bestowed his affection. M. de Charlus was really delighted by this familiarity. He even brought M. de Vaugoubert away from an afternoon party in order to show him the letter. And yet, heaven knows that M. de Charlus did not care to go about with M. de Vaugoubert. For the latter, his monocle in his eye, kept gazing in all directions at every passing youth. What was worse, emancipating himself when he was with M. de Charlus, he employed a form of speech which the Baron detested. He gave feminine endings to all the masculine words and, being intensely stupid, imagined this pleasantry to be extremely witty, and was continually in fits of laughter. As at the same time he attached enormous importance to his position in the diplomatic service, these deplorable outbursts of merriment in the street were perpetually interrupted by the shock caused him by the simultaneous appearance of somebody in society, or, worse still, of a civil servant. 'That little telegraph messenger,' he said, nudging the disgusted Baron with his elbow, 'I used to know her, but she's turned respectable, the wretch! Oh, that messenger from the Galeries Lafayette, what a dream! Good God, there's the head of the Commercial Department. I hope he didn't notice anything. He's quite capable of mentioning it to the Minister, who would put me on the retired list, all the more as, it appears, he's so himself.' M. de Charlus was speechless with rage. At length, to bring this infuriating walk to an end, he decided to produce the letter and give it to the Ambassador to read, but warned him to be discreet, for he liked to pretend that Charlie was jealous, in order to be able to make people think that he was enamoured. 'And,' he added with an indescribable air of benevolence, 'we ought always to try to cause as little trouble as possible.' Before we come back to Jupien's shop, the author would like to say how deeply he would regret it should any reader be offended by his portrayal of such unusual characters. On the one hand (and this is the less important aspect of the matter), it may be felt that the aristocracy is, in these pages, disproportionately accused of degeneracy in comparison with the other classes of society. Were this true, it would be in no way surprising. The oldest families end by displaying, in a red and bulbous nose, or a deformed chin, characteristic signs in which everyone admires 'blood'. But among these persistent and perpetually developing features, there are others that are not visible, to wit tendencies and tastes. It would be a more serious objection, were there any foundation for it, to say that all this is alien to us, and that we ought to extract truth from the poetry that is close at hand. Art extracted from the most familiar reality does indeed exist and its domain is perhaps the largest of any. But it is no less true that a strong interest, not to say beauty, may be found in actions inspired by a cast of mind so remote from anything that we feel, from anything that we believe, that we cannot ever succeed in understanding them, that they are displayed before our eyes like a spectacle without rhyme or reason. What could be more poetic than Xerxes, son of Darius, ordering the sea to be scourged with rods for having engulfed his fleet?

We may be certain that Morel, relying on the influence which his personal attractions give him over the girl, communicated to her, as coming from himself, the Baron's criticism, for the expression 'stand you a tea' disappeared as completely from the tailor's shop as disappears from a drawing-room some intimate friend who used to call daily, and with whom, for one reason or another, we have quarrelled, or whom we are trying to keep out of sight and meet only outside the house. M. de Charlus was satisfied by the cessation of 'stand you a tea'. He saw in it a proof of his own ascendancy over Morel and the removal of its one little blemish from the girl's perfection. In short, like everyone of his kind, while genuinely fond of Morel and of the girl who was all but engaged to him, an ardent advocate of their marriage, he thoroughly enjoyed his power to create at his pleasure more or less inoffensive little scenes, aloof from and above which he himself remained as Olympian as his brother.

Morel had told M. de Charlus that he was in love with Jupien's niece, and wished to marry her, and the Baron liked to accompany his young friend upon visits in which he played the part of father-in-law to be, indulgent and discreet. Nothing pleased him better.

My personal opinion is that 'stand you a tea' had originated with Morel himself, and that in the blindness of her love the young seamstress had adopted an expression from her beloved which clashed horribly with her own pretty way of speaking. This way of speaking, the charming manners that went with it, the patronage of M. de Charlus brought it about that many customers for whom she had worked received her as a friend, invited her to dinner, introduced her to their friends, though the girl accepted their invitations only with the Baron's permission and on the evenings that suited him. 'A young seamstress received in society?' the reader will exclaim, 'how improbable!' If you come to think of it, it was no less improbable that at one time Albertine should have come to see me at midnight, and that she should now be living in my house. And yet this might perhaps have been improbable of anyone else, but not of Albertine, a fatherless and motherless orphan, leading so uncontrolled a life that at first I had taken her, at Balbec, for the mistress of a bicyclist, a girl whose next of kin was Mme Bontemps who in the old days, at Mme Swann's, had admired nothing about her niece but her bad manners and who now shut her eyes, especially if by doing so she might be able to get rid of her by securing for her a wealthy marriage from which a little of the wealth would trickle into the aunt's pocket (in the highest society, a mother who is very well-born and quite penniless, when she has succeeded in finding a rich bride for her son, allows the young couple to support her, accepts presents of furs, a motorcar, money from a daughter-in-law whom she does not like but whom she introduces to her friends).

The day may come when dressmakers – nor should I find it at all shocking – will move in society. Jupien's niece being an exception affords us no base for calculation, for one swallow does not make a summer. In any case, if the very modest advancement of Jupien's niece did scandalise some people, Morel was not among them, for, in certain respects, his stupidity was so intense that not only did he label 'rather a fool' this girl a thousand times cleverer than himself, and foolish only perhaps in her love for himself, but he actually took to be adventuresses, dressmakers' assistants in disguise playing at being ladies, the persons of rank and position who invited her to their houses and whose invitations she accepted without a trace of vanity. Naturally these were not Guermantes, nor even people who knew the Guermantes, but rich and smart women of the middle-class, broad-minded enough to feel that it is no disgrace to invite a dressmaker to your house and at the same time servile enough to derive some satisfaction from patronising a girl whom His Highness the Baron de Charlus was in the habit – without any suggestion, of course, of impropriety – of visiting daily.

Nothing could have pleased the Baron more than the idea of this marriage, for he felt that in this way Morel would not be taken from him. It appears that Jupien's niece had been, when scarcely more than a child, 'in trouble'. And M. de Charlus, while he sang her praises to Morel, would have had no hesitation in revealing this secret to his friend, who would be furious, and thus sowing the seeds of discord. For M. de Charlus, although terribly malicious, resembled a great many good people who sing the praises of some man or woman, as a proof of their own generosity, but would avoid like poison the soothing words, so rarely uttered, that would be capable of putting an end to strife. Notwithstanding this, the Baron refrained from making any insinuation, and for two reasons. 'If I tell him,' he said to himself, 'that his lady love is not spotless, his vanity will be hurt, he will be angry with me. Besides, how am I to know that he is not in love with her? If I say nothing, this fire of straw will burn itself out before long, I shall be able to control their relations as I choose, he will love her only to the extent that I shall allow. If I tell him of his young lady's past transgression, who knows that my Charlie is not still sufficiently enamoured of her to become jealous. Then I shall by my own doing be converting a harmless and easily controlled flirtation into a serious passion, which is a difficult thing to manage.' For these reasons, M. de Charlus preserved a silence which had only the outward appearance of discretion, but was in another respect meritorious, since it is almost impossible for men of his sort to hold their tongues.

Anyhow, the girl herself was charming, and M. de Charlus, who found that she satisfied all the aesthetic interest that he was capable of feeling in women, would have liked to have hundreds of photographs of her. Not such a fool as Morel, he was delighted to hear the names of the ladies who invited her to their houses, and whom his social instinct was able to place, but he took care (as he wished to retain his power) not to mention this to Charlie who, a regular idiot in this respect, continued to believe that, apart from the 'violin class' and the Verdurins, there existed only the Guermantes, and the few almost royal houses enumerated by the Baron, all the rest being but 'dregs' or 'scum'. Charlie interpreted these expressions of M. de Charlus literally.

Among the reasons which made M. de Charlus look forward to the marriage of the young couple was this, that Jupien's niece would then be in a sense an extension of Morel's personality, and so of the Baron's power over and knowledge of him. As for 'betraying' in the conjugal sense the violinist's future wife, it would never for a moment have occurred to M. de Charlus to feel the slightest scruple about that. But to have a 'young couple' to manage, to feel himself the redoubtable and all-powerful protector of Morel's wife, who if she regarded the Baron as a god would thereby prove that Morel had inculcated this idea into her, and would thus contain in herself something of Morel, added a new variety to the form of M. de Charlus's domination and brought to light in his 'creature', Morel, a creature the more, that is to say gave the Baron something different, new, curious, to love in him. Perhaps even this domination would be stronger now than it had ever been. For whereas Morel by himself, naked so to speak, often resisted the Baron whom he felt certain of reconquering, once he was married, the thought of his home, his house, his future would alarm him more quickly, he would offer to M. de Charlus's desires a wider surface, an easier hold. All this, and even, failing anything else, on evenings when he was bored, the prospect of stirring up trouble between husband and wife (the Baron had never objected to battle-pictures) was pleasing to him. Less pleasing, however, than the thought of the state of dependence upon himself in which the young people would live. M. de Charlus's love for Morel acquired a delicious novelty when he said to himself: 'His wife too will be mine just as much as he is, they will always take care not to annoy me, they will obey my caprices, and thus she will be a sign (which hitherto I have failed to observe) of what I had almost forgotten, what is so very dear to my heart, that to all the world, to everyone who sees that I protect them, house them, to myself, Morel is mine.' This testimony in the eyes of the world and in his own pleased M. de Charlus more than anything. For the possession of what we love is an even greater joy than love itself. Very often those people who conceal this possession from the world do so only from the fear that the beloved object may be taken from them. And their happiness is diminished by this prudent reticence.

The reader may remember that Morel had once told the Baron that his great ambition was to seduce some young girl, and this girl in particular, that to succeed in his enterprise he would promise to marry her, and, the outrage accomplished, would 'cut his hook'; but this confession, what with the declarations of love for Jupien's niece which Morel had come and poured out to him, M. de Charlus had forgotten. What was more, Morel had quite possibly forgotten it himself. There was perhaps a real gap between Morel's nature – as he had cynically admitted, perhaps even artfully exaggerated it – and the moment at which it would regain control of him. As he became better acquainted with the girl, she had appealed to him, he began to like her. He knew himself so little that he doubtless imagined that he was in love with her, perhaps indeed that he would be in love with her always. To be sure his initial desire, his criminal intention remained, but glossed over by so many layers of sentiment that there is nothing to show that the violinist would not have been sincere in saying that this vicious desire was not the true motive of his action. There was, moreover, a brief period during which, without his actually admitting it to himself, this marriage appeared to him to be necessary. Morel was suffering at the time from violent cramp in the hand, and found himself obliged to contemplate the possibility of his having to give up the violin. As, in everything but his art, he was astonishingly lazy, the question who was to maintain him loomed before him, and he preferred that it should be Jupien's niece rather than M. de Charlus, this arrangement offering him greater freedom and also a wider choice of several kinds of women, ranging from the apprentices, perpetually changing, whom he would make Jupien's niece debauch for him, to the rich and beautiful ladies to whom he would prostitute her. That his future wife might refuse to lend herself to these arrangements, that she could be so perverse never entered Morel's calculations for a moment. However, they passed into the background, their place being taken by pure love, now that his cramp had ceased. His violin would suffice, together with his allowance from M. de Charlus, whose claims upon him would certainly be reduced once he, Morel, was married to the girl. Marriage was the urgent thing, because of his love, and in the interest of his freedom. He made a formal offer of marriage to Jupien, who consulted his niece. This was wholly unnecessary. The girl's passion for the violinist streamed round about her, like her hair when she let it down, like the joy in her beaming eyes. In Morel, almost everything that was agreeable or advantageous to him awakened moral emotions and words to correspond, sometimes even melting him

to tears. It was therefore sincerely – if such a word can be applied to him –
that he addressed Jupien's niece in speeches as steeped in sentimentality
(sentimental too are the speeches that so many young noblemen who look
forward to a life of complete idleness address to some charming daughter of
a middle-class millionaire) as had been steeped in unredeemed vileness the
speech he had made to M. de Charlus about the seduction and deflowering
of a virgin. Only there was another side to this virtuous enthusiasm for a
person who afforded him pleasure and the solemn engagement that he
made with her. As soon as the person ceased to afford him pleasure, or
indeed if, for example, the obligation to fulfil the promise that he had made
caused him displeasure, she at once became the object of an antipathy which
he justified in his own eyes and which, after some neurasthenic disturbance,
enabled him to prove to himself, as soon as the balance of his nervous system
was restored, that he was, even looking at the matter from a purely virtuous
point of view, released from any obligation. Thus, towards the end of his
stay at Balbec, he had managed somehow to lose all his money and, not
daring to mention the matter to M. de Charlus, looked about for someone
to whom he might appeal. He had learned from his father (who at the
same time had forbidden him ever to become a 'sponger') that in such
circumstances the correct thing is to write to the person whom you intend
to ask for a loan, 'that you have to speak to him on business', to 'ask him for
a business appointment'. This magic formula had so enchanted Morel that
he would, I believe, have been glad to lose his money, simply to have the
pleasure of asking for an appointment 'on business'. In the course of his life
he had found that the formula had not quite the virtue that he supposed. He
had discovered that certain people, to whom otherwise he would never have
written at all, did not reply within five minutes of receiving his letter asking
to speak to them 'on business'. If the afternoon went by without his
receiving an answer, it never occurred to him that, to put the best interpretation on the matter, it was quite possible that the gentleman addressed
had not yet come home, or had had other letters to write, if indeed he had
not gone away from home altogether, fallen ill, or something of that sort. If
by an extraordinary stroke of fortune Morel was given an appointment for
the following morning, he would accost his intended creditor with: 'I was
quite surprised not to get an answer, I was wondering if there was anything
wrong with you, I'm glad to see you're quite well', and so forth. Well then,
at Balbec, and without telling me that he wished to talk 'business' to him, he
had asked me to introduce him to that very Bloch to whom he had made
himself so unpleasant a week earlier in the train. Bloch had not hesitated to
lend him – or rather to secure a loan for him, from M. Nissim Bernard, of

five thousand francs. From that moment Morel had worshipped Bloch. He asked himself with tears in his eyes how he could show his indebtedness to a person who had saved his life. Finally, I undertook to ask on his behalf for a thousand francs monthly from M. de Charlus, a sum which he would at once forward to Bloch who would thus find himself repaid within quite a short time. The first month, Morel, still under the impression of Bloch's generosity, sent him the thousand francs immediately, but after this he doubtless found that a different application of the remaining four thousand francs might be more satisfactory to himself, for he began to say all sorts of unpleasant things about Bloch. The mere sight of Bloch was enough to fill his mind with dark thoughts, and Bloch himself having forgotten the exact amount that he had lent Morel, and having asked him for 3,500 francs instead of 4,000 which would have left the violinist 500 francs to the good, the latter took the line that, in view of so preposterous a fraud, not only would he not pay another centime but his creditor might think himself very fortunate if Morel did not bring an action against him for slander. As he said this his eyes blazed. He did not content himself with asserting that Bloch and M. Nissim Bernard had no cause for complaint against him, but was soon saying that they might consider themselves lucky that he made no complaint against them. Finally, M. Nissim Bernard having apparently stated that Thibaut played as well as Morel, the last-named decided that he ought to take the matter into court, such a remark being calculated to damage him in his profession, then, as there was no longer any justice in France, especially against the Jews (anti-semitism being in Morel the natural effect of a loan of 5,000 francs from an Israelite), took to never going out without a loaded revolver. A similar nervous reaction, in the wake of keen affection, was soon to occur in Morel with regard to the tailor's niece. It is true that M. de Charlus may have been unconsciously responsible, to some extent, for this change, for he was in the habit of saying, without meaning what he said for an instant, and merely to tease them, that, once they were married, he would never set eyes on them again but would leave them to fly upon their own wings. This idea was, in itself, quite insufficient to detach Morel from the girl; but, lurking in his mind, it was ready when the time came to combine with other analogous ideas, capable, once the compound was formed, of becoming a powerful disruptive agent.

It was not very often, however, that I was fated to meet M. de Charlus and Morel. Often they had already passed into Jupien's shop when I came away from the Duchess, for the pleasure that I found in her society was such that I was led to forget not merely the anxious expectation that preceded Albertine's return, but even the hour of that return.

I shall set apart from the other days on which I lingered at Mme de Guermantes's, one that was distinguished by a trivial incident the cruel significance of which entirely escaped me and did not enter my mind until long afterwards. On this particular afternoon, Mme de Guermantes had given me, knowing that I was fond of them, some branches of syringa which had been sent to her from the South. When I left the Duchess and went upstairs to our flat, Albertine had already returned, and on the staircase I ran into Andrée who seemed to be distressed by the powerful fragrance of the flowers that I was bringing home.

'What, are you back already?' I said. 'Only this moment, but Albertine had letters to write, so she sent me away.' 'You don't think she's up to any mischief?' 'Not at all, she's writing to her aunt, I think, but you know how she dislikes strong scents, she won't be particularly pleased to see those syringas.' 'How stupid of me! I shall tell Françoise to put them out on the service stair.' 'Do you imagine Albertine won't notice the scent of them on you? Next to tuberoses they've the strongest scent of any flower, I always think; anyhow, I believe Françoise has gone out shopping.' 'But in that case, as I haven't got my latchkey, how am I to get in?' 'Oh, you've only got to ring the bell. Albertine will let you in. Besides, Françoise may have come back by this time.'

I said goodbye to Andrée. I had no sooner pressed the bell than Albertine came to open the door, which required some doing, as Françoise had gone out and Albertine did not know where to turn on the light. At length she was able to let me in, but the scent of the syringas put her to flight. I took them to the kitchen, with the result that my mistress, leaving her letter unfinished (why, I did not understand), had time to go to my room, from which she called to me, and to lay herself down on my bed. Even then, at the actual moment, I saw nothing in all this that was not perfectly natural, at the most a little confused, but in any case unimportant. She had nearly been caught out with Andrée and had snatched a brief respite for herself by turning out the lights, going to my room so that I should not see the disordered state of her own bed, and pretending to be busy writing a letter. But we shall see all this later on, a situation the truth of which I never ascertained. In general, and apart from this isolated incident, everything was quite normal when I returned from my visit to the Duchess. Since Albertine never knew whether I might not wish to go out with her before dinner, I usually found in the hall her hat, cloak and umbrella, which she had left lying there in case they should be needed. As soon as, on opening the door, I caught sight of them, the atmosphere of the house became breathable once more. I felt that, instead of a rarefied air, it was happiness that filled it. I was rescued from my melancholy, the sight of these trifles gave me possession of Albertine, I ran to greet her.

On the days when I did not go down to Mme de Guermantes, to pass the time somehow, during the hour that preceded the return of my mistress, I would take up an album of Elstir's work, one of Bergotte's books, Vinteuil's sonata.

Then, just as those works of art which seem to address themselves to the eye or ear alone require that, if we are to enjoy them, our awakened intelligence shall collaborate closely with those organs, I would unconsciously evoke from myself the dreams that Albertine had inspired in me long ago, before I knew her, dreams that had been stifled by the routine of everyday life. I cast them into the composer's phrase or the painter's image as into a crucible, or used them to enrich the book that I was reading. And no doubt the book appeared all the more vivid in consequence. But Albertine herself profited just as much by being thus transported out of one of the two worlds to which we have access, and in which we can place alternately the same object, by escaping thus from the crushing weight of matter to play freely in the fluid space of mind. I found myself suddenly and for the instant capable of feeling an ardent desire for this irritating girl. She had at that moment the appearance of a work by Elstir or Bergotte, I felt a momentary enthusiasm for her, seeing her in the perspective of imagination and art.

Presently someone came to tell me that she had returned; though there was a standing order that her name was not to be mentioned if I was not alone, if for instance I had in the room with me Bloch, whom I would compel to remain with me a little longer so that there should be no risk of his meeting my mistress in the hall. For I concealed the fact that she was staying in the house, and even that I ever saw her there, so afraid was I that one of my friends might fall in love with her, and wait for her outside, or that in a momentary encounter in the passage or the hall she might make a signal and fix an appointment. Then I heard the rustle of Albertine's petticoats on her way to her own room, for out of discretion and also no doubt in that spirit in which, when we used to go to dinner at la Raspelière, she took care that I should have no cause for jealousy, she did not come to my room, knowing that I was not alone. But it was not only for this reason, as I suddenly realised. I remembered; I had known a different Albertine, then all at once she had changed into another, the Albertine of today. And for this change I could hold no one responsible but myself. The admissions that she would have made to me, easily at first, then deliberately, when we were simply friends, had ceased to flow from her as soon as she had suspected that I was in love with her, or, without perhaps naming Love, had divined the existence in me of an inquisitorial sentiment that desires to know, is pained by the knowledge, and seeks to learn yet more. Ever since that day, she had concealed everything from me. She kept away from my room if she thought that my companion was (rarely as this happened) not male but female, she whose eyes used at one time to sparkle so brightly whenever I mentioned a girl: 'You must try and get her to come here. I should like to meet her.' 'But she has what you call a bad style.' 'Of course, that makes it all the more fun.' At that moment, I might perhaps have learned all that there was to know. And indeed when in the little Casino she had withdrawn her breast from Andrée's, I believe that this was due not to my presence but to that of Cottard, who was capable, she doubtless thought, of giving her a bad reputation. And yet, even then, she had already begun to 'set', the confiding speeches no longer issued from her lips, her gestures became reserved. After this, she had stripped herself of everything that could stir my emotions. To those parts of her life of which I knew nothing she ascribed a character the inoffensiveness of which my ignorance made itself her accomplice in accentuating. And now, the transformation was completed, she went straight to her room if I was not alone, not merely from fear of disturbing me, but in order to show me that she did not care who was with me. There was one thing alone which she would never again do for me, which she would have done only in the days when it would have left me cold, which she would then have done without hesitation for that very reason, namely make me a detailed admission. I should always be obliged, like a judge, to draw indefinite conclusions from imprudences of speech that were perhaps not really inexplicable without postulating criminality. And always she would feel that I was jealous, and judging her.

As I listened to Albertine's footsteps with the consoling pleasure of thinking that she would not be going out again that evening, I thought how wonderful it was that for this girl, whom at one time I had supposed that I could never possibly succeed in knowing, the act of returning home every day was nothing else than that of entering my home. The pleasure, a blend of mystery and sensuality, which I had felt, fugitive and fragmentary, at Balbec, on the night when she had come to sleep at the hotel, was completed, stabilised, filled my dwelling, hitherto void, with a permanent store of domestic, almost conjugal bliss (radiating even into the passages) upon which all my senses, either actively, or, when I was alone, in imagination as I waited for her to return, quietly battened. When I had heard the door of Albertine's room shut behind her, if I had a friend with me, I made haste to get rid of him, not leaving him until I was quite sure that he was on the staircase, down which I might even escort him for a few steps. He warned me that I would catch cold, informing me that our house was indeed icy, a cave of the winds, and that he would not live in it if he was paid to do so. This cold weather was a source of complaint because it had just begun, and people were not yet accustomed to it, but for that very reason it released in me a joy accompanied by an unconscious memory of the first evenings of winter when, in past years, returning from the country, in order to re-establish contact with the forgotten delights of Paris, I used to go to a café-concert. And so it was with a song on my lips that, after bidding my friend goodbye, I climbed the stair again and entered the flat. Summer had flown, carrying the birds with it. But other musicians, invisible, internal, had taken their place. And the icy blast against which Bloch had inveighed, which was whistling delightfully through the ill fitting doors of our apartment was (as the fine days of summer by the woodland birds) passionately greeted with snatches, irrepressibly hummed, from Fragson, Mayol or Paulus. In the passage, Albertine was coming towards me. 'I say, while I'm taking off my things, I shall send you Andrée, she's looked in for a minute to say how d'ye do.' And still swathed in the big grey veil, falling from her chinchilla toque, which I had given her at Balbec, she turned from me and went back to her room, as though she had guessed that Andrée, whom I had charged with the duty of watching over her, would presently, by relating their day's adventures in full detail, mentioning their meeting with some person of their acquaintance, impart a certain clarity of outline to the vague regions in which that excursion had been made which had taken the whole day and which I had been incapable of imagining. Andrée's defects had become more evident; she was no longer as pleasant a companion as when I first knew her. One noticed now, on the surface, a sort of bitter uneasiness, ready to gather like a swell on the sea, merely if I happened to mention something that gave pleasure to Albertine and myself. This did not prevent Andrée from being kinder to me, liking me better – and I have had frequent proof of this – than other more sociable people. But the slightest look of happiness on a person's face, if it was not caused by herself, gave a shock to her nerves, as unpleasant as that given by a banging door. She could allow the pains in which she had no part, but not the pleasures; if she saw that I was unwell, she was distressed, was sorry for me, would have stayed to nurse me. But if I displayed a satisfaction as trifling as that of stretching myself with a blissful expression as I shut a book, saying: 'Ah! I have spent a really happy afternoon with this entertaining book,' these words, which would have given pleasure to my mother, to Albertine, to Saint-Loup, provoked in Andrée a sort of disapprobation, perhaps simply a sort of nervous irritation. My satisfactions caused her an annoyance which she was unable to conceal. These defects were supplemented by others of a more serious nature; one day when I mentioned that young man so learned in matters of racing and golf, so uneducated in all other respects, Andrée said with a sneer: 'You know that his father is a swindler, he only just missed being prosecuted. They're swaggering now more than ever, but I tell everybody about it. I should love them to bring an action for slander against me. I should be wonderful in the witness-box!' Her eyes sparkled. Well, I discovered that the father had done nothing wrong, and that Andrée knew this as well as anybody. But she had thought that the son looked down upon her, had sought for something that would embarrass him, put him to shame, had invented a long story of evidence which she imagined herself called upon to give in court, and, by dint of repeating the details to herself, was perhaps no longer aware that they were not true. And so, in her present state (and even without her fleeting, foolish hatreds), I should not have wished to see her, were it merely on account of that malicious susceptibility which clasped with a harsh and frigid girdle her warmer and better nature. But the information which she alone could give me about my mistress was of too great interest for me to be able to neglect so rare an opportunity of acquiring it. Andrée came into my room, shutting the door behind her; they had met a girl they knew, whom Albertine had never mentioned to me. 'What did they talk about?' 'I can't tell you; I took the opportunity, as Albertine wasn't alone, to go and buy some worsted.' 'Buy some worsted?' 'Yes, it was Albertine asked me to get it.' 'All the more reason not to have gone, it was perhaps a plot to get you out of the way.' 'But she asked me to go for it before we met her friend.' 'Ah!' I replied, drawing breath again. At once my suspicion revived; she might, for all I knew, have made an appointment beforehand with her friend and have provided herself with an excuse to be left alone when the time came. Besides, could I be certain that it was not my former hypothesis (according to which Andrée did not always tell me the truth) that was correct? Andrée was perhaps in the plot with Albertine. Love, I used to say to myself, at Balbec, is what we feel for a person whose actions seem rather to arouse our jealousy; we feel that if she were to tell us everything, we might perhaps easily be cured of our love for her. However skilfully jealousy is concealed by him who suffers from it, it is at once detected by her who has inspired it, and who when the time comes is no less skilful. She seeks to lead us off the trail of what might make us unhappy, and succeeds, for, to the man who is not forewarned, how should a casual utterance reveal the falsehoods that lie beneath it? We do not distinguish this utterance from the rest; spoken in terror, it is received without attention. Later on, when we are by ourselves, we shall return to this speech, it will seem to us not altogether adequate to the facts of the case. But do we remember it correctly? It seems as though there arose spontaneously in us, with regard to it and to the accuracy of our memory, an uncertainty of the sort with which, in certain nervous disorders, we can never remember whether we have bolted the door, no better after the fiftieth time than after the first, it would seem that we can repeat the action indefinitely without its ever being accompanied by a precise and liberating memory. At any rate, we can shut the door again, for the fifty-first time. Whereas the disturbing speech exists in the past in an imperfect hearing of it which it does not lie in our power to repeat. Then we concentrate our attention upon other speeches which conceal nothing and the sole remedy which we do not seek is to be ignorant of everything, so as to have no desire for further knowledge.

As soon as jealousy is discovered, it is regarded by her who is its object as a challenge which authorises deception. Moreover, in our endeavour to learn something, it is we who have taken the initiative in lying and deceit. Andrée, Aimé may promise us that they will say nothing, but will they keep their promise? Bloch could promise nothing because he knew nothing, and Albertine has only to talk to any of the three in order to learn, with the help of what Saint-Loup would have called cross-references, that we are lying to her when we pretend to be indifferent to her actions and morally incapable of having her watched. And so, replacing in this way my habitual boundless uncertainty as to what Albertine might be doing, an uncertainty too indeterminate not to remain painless, which was to jealousy what is to grief that beginning of forgetfulness in which relief is born of vagueness, the little fragment of response which Andrée had brought me at once began to raise fresh questions; the only result of my exploration of one sector of the great zone that extended round me had been to banish further from me that unknowable thing which, when we seek to form a definite idea of it, another person's life invariably is to us. I continued to question Andrée, while Albertine, from discretion and in order to leave me free (was she conscious of this?) to question the other, prolonged her toilet in her own room. 'I think that Albertine's uncle and aunt both like me,' I stupidly said to Andrée, forgetting her peculiar nature.

At once I saw her gelatinous features change. Like a syrup that has turned, her face seemed permanently clouded. Her mouth became bitter. Nothing remained in Andrée of that juvenile gaiety which, like all the little band and notwithstanding her feeble health, she had displayed in the year of my first visit to Balbec and which now (it is true that Andrée was now several years older) was so speedily eclipsed in her. But I was to make it reappear involuntarily before Andrée left me that evening to go home to dinner. 'Somebody was singing your praises to me today in the most glowing language,' I said to her. Immediately a ray of joy beamed from her eyes, she looked as though she really loved me. She avoided my gaze but smiled at the empty air with a pair of eyes that suddenly became quite round. 'Who was it?' she asked, with an artless, avid interest. I told her, and, whoever it was, she was delighted.

Then the time came for us to part, and she left me. Albertine came to my room; she had undressed, and was wearing one of the charming crêpe de chine wrappers, or one of the Japanese gowns which I had asked Mme de Guermantes to describe to me, and for some of which supplementary details had been furnished me by Mme Swann, in a letter that began: 'After your long eclipse, I felt as I read your letter about my tea-gowns that I was receiving a message from the other world.'

Albertine had on her feet a pair of black shoes studded with brilliants which Françoise indignantly called 'pattens', modelled upon the shoes which, from the drawing-room window, she had seen Mme de Guermantes wearing in the evening, just as a little later Albertine took to wearing slippers, some of gilded kid, others of chinchilla, the sight of which was pleasant to me because they were all of them signs (which other shoes would not have been) that she was living under my roof. She had also certain things which had not come to her from me, including a fine gold ring. I admired upon it the outspread wings of an eagle. 'It was my aunt gave me it,' she explained. 'She can be quite nice sometimes after all. It makes me feel terribly old, because she gave it to me on my twentieth birthday.'

Albertine took a far keener interest in all these pretty things than the Duchess, because, like every obstacle in the way of possession (in my own case the ill health which made travel so difficult and so desirable), poverty, more generous than opulence, gives to women what is better than the garments that they cannot afford to buy, the desire for those garments which is the genuine, detailed, profound knowledge of them. She, because she had never been able to afford these things, I, because in ordering them for her I was seeking to give her pleasure, we were both of us like students who already know all about the pictures which they are longing to go to Dresden or Vienna to see. Whereas rich women, amid the multitude of their hats and gowns, are like those tourists to whom the visit to a gallery, being preceded by no desire, gives merely a sensation of bewilderment, boredom and exhaustion.

A particular toque, a particular sable cloak, a particular Doucet wrapper, its sleeves lined with pink, assumed for Albertine, who had observed them, coveted them and, thanks to the exclusiveness and minute nicety that are elements of desire, had at once isolated them from everything else in a void against which the lining or the scarf stood out to perfection, and learned them by heart in every detail – and for myself who had gone to Mme de Guermantes in quest of an explanation of what constituted the peculiar merit, the superiority, the smartness of the garment and the inimitable style of the great designer – an importance, a charm which they certainly did not possess for the Duchess, surfeited before she had even acquired an appetite, and would not, indeed, have possessed for myself had I beheld them a few years earlier while accompanying some lady of fashion on one of her wearisome tours of the dressmakers' shops.

To be sure, a lady of fashion was what Albertine was gradually becoming. For, even if each of the things that I ordered for her was the prettiest of its kind, with all the refinements that had been added to it by Mme de Guermantes or Mme Swann, she was beginning to possess these things in abundance. But no matter, so long as she admired them from the first, and each of them separately.

When we have been smitten by one painter, then by another, we may end by feeling for the whole gallery an admiration that is not frigid, for it is made up of successive enthusiasms, each one exclusive in its day, which finally have joined forces and become reconciled in one whole.

She was not, for that matter, frivolous, read a great deal when she was by herself, and used to read aloud when she was with me. She had become extremely intelligent. She would say, though she was quite wrong in saying: 'I am appalled when I think that but for you I should still be quite ignorant. Don't contradict. You have opened up a world of ideas to me which I never suspected, and whatever I may have become I owe entirely to you.'

It will be remembered that she had spoken in similar terms of my influence over Andrée. Had either of them a sentimental regard for me? And, in themselves, what were Albertine and Andrée? To learn the answer, I should have to immobilise you, to cease to live in that perpetual expectation, ending always in a different presentment of you, I should have to cease to love you, in order to fix you, to cease to know your interminable and ever disconcerting arrival, oh girls, oh recurrent ray in the swirl wherein we throb with emotion upon seeing you reappear while barely recognising you, in the dizzy velocity of light. That velocity, we should perhaps remain unaware of it and everything would seem to us motionless, did not a sexual attraction set us in pursuit of you, drops of gold always different, and always passing our expectation! On each occasion a girl so little resembles what she was the time before (shattering in fragments as soon as we catch sight of her the memory that we had retained of her and the desire that we were proposing to gratify), that the stability of nature which we ascribe to her is purely fictitious and a convenience of speech. We have been told that some pretty girl is tender, loving, full of the most delicate sentiments. Our imagination accepts this assurance, and when we behold for the first time, within the woven girdle of her golden hair, the rosy disc of her face, we are almost afraid that this too virtuous sister may chill our ardour by her very virtue, that she can never be to us the lover for whom we have been longing. What secrets, at least, we confide in her from the first moment, on the strength of that nobility of heart, what plans we discuss together. But a few days later, we regret that we were so confiding, for the rose-leaf girl, at our second meeting, addresses us in the language of a lascivious Fury. As for the successive portraits which after a pulsation lasting for some days the renewal of the rosy light presents to us, it is not even certain that a momentum external to these girls has not modified their aspect, and this might well have happened with my band of girls at Balbec.

People extol to us the gentleness, the purity of a virgin. But afterwards they feel that something more seasoned would please us better, and recommend her to show more boldness. In herself was she one more than the other? Perhaps not, but capable of yielding to any number of different possibilities in the headlong current of life. With another girl, whose whole attraction lay in something implacable (which we counted upon subduing to our own will), as, for instance, with the terrible jumping girl at Balbec who grazed in her spring the bald pates of startled old gentlemen, what a disappointment when, in the fresh aspect of her, just as we were addressing her in affectionate speeches stimulated by our memory of all her cruelty to other people, we heard her, as her first move in the game, tell us that she was shy, that she could never say anything intelligent to anyone at a first introduction, so frightened was she, and that it was only after a fortnight or so that she would be able to talk to us at her ease. The steel had turned to cotton, there was nothing left for us to attempt to break, since she herself had lost all her consistency. Of her own accord, but by our fault perhaps, for the tender words which we had addressed to Severity had perhaps, even without any deliberate calculation on her part, suggested to her that she ought to be gentle.

Distressing as the change may have been to us, it was not altogether maladroit, for our gratitude for all her gentleness would exact more from us perhaps than our delight at overcoming her cruelty. I do not say that a day will not come when, even to these luminous maidens, we shall not assign sharply differentiated characters, but that will be because they have ceased to interest us, because their entry upon the scene will no longer be to our heart the apparition which it expected in a different form and which leaves it overwhelmed every time by fresh incarnations. Their immobility will spring from our indifference to them, which will hand them over to the judgment of our mind. This will not, for that matter, be expressed in any more categorical terms, for after it has decided that some defect which was prominent in one is fortunately absent from the other, it will see that this defect had as its counterpart some priceless merit. So that the false judgment of our intellect, which comes into play only when we have ceased to take any interest, will define permanent characters of girls, which will enlighten us no more than the surprising faces that used to appear every day when, in the dizzy speed of our expectation, our friends presented themselves daily, weekly, too different to allow us, as they never halted in their passage, to classify them, to award degrees of merit. As for our sentiments, we have spoken of them too often to repeat again now that as often as not love is nothing more than the association of the face of a girl (whom otherwise we should soon have found intolerable) with the heartbeats inseparable from an endless, vain expectation, and from some trick that she has played upon us. All this is true not merely of imaginative young men brought into contact with changeable girls. At the stage that our narrative has now reached, it appears, as I have since heard, that Jupien's niece had altered her opinion of Morel and M. de Charlus. My motorist, reinforcing the love that she felt for Morel, had extolled to her, as existing in the violinist, boundless refinements of delicacy in which she was all too ready to believe. And at the same time Morel never ceased to complain to her of the despotic treatment that he received from M. de Charlus, which she ascribed to malevolence, never imagining that it could be due to love. She was moreover bound to acknowledge that M. de Charlus was tyrannically present at all their meetings. In corroboration of all this, she had heard women in society speak of the Baron's terrible spite. Now, quite recently, her judgment had been completely reversed. She had discovered in Morel (without ceasing for that reason to love him) depths of malevolence and perfidy, compensated it was true by frequent kindness and genuine feeling, and in M. de Charlus an unimaginable and immense generosity blended with asperities of which she knew nothing. And so she had been unable to arrive at any more definite judgment of what, each in himself, the violinist and his protector really were, than I was able to form of Andrée, whom nevertheless I saw every day, or of Albertine who was living with me. On the evenings when the latter did not read aloud to me, she would play to me or begin a game of draughts, or a conversation, either of which I would interrupt with kisses. The simplicity of our relations made them soothing. The very emptiness of her life gave Albertine a sort of eagerness to comply with the only requests that I made of her. Behind this girl, as behind the purple light that used to filter beneath the curtains of my room at Balbec, while outside the concert blared, were shining the blue-green undulations of the sea. Was she not, after all (she in whose heart of hearts there was now regularly installed an idea of myself so familiar that, next to her aunt, I was perhaps the person whom she distinguished least from herself), the girl whom I had seen the first time at Balbec, in her flat polo-cap, with her insistent laughing eyes, a stranger still, exiguous as a silhouette projected against the waves? These effigies preserved intact in our memory, when we recapture them, we are astonished at their unlikeness to the person whom we know, and we begin to realise what a task of remodelling is performed every day by habit. In the charm that Albertine had in Paris, by my fireside, there still survived the desire that had been aroused in me by that insolent and blossoming parade along the beach, and just as Rachel retained in Saint-Loup's eyes, even after he had made her abandon it, the prestige of her life on the stage, so in this Albertine cloistered in my house, far from Balbec, from which I had hurried her away, there persisted the emotion, the social confusion, the uneasy vanity, the roving desires of life by the seaside. She was so effectively caged that on certain evenings I did not even ask her to leave her room for mine, her to whom at one time all the world gave chase, whom I had found it so hard to overtake as she sped past on her bicycle, whom the lift-boy himself was unable to capture for me, leaving me with scarcely a hope of her coming, although I sat up waiting for her all the night. Had not Albertine been – out there in front of the Hotel – like a great actress of the blazing beach, arousing jealousy when she advanced upon that natural stage, not speaking to anyone, thrusting past its regular frequenters, dominating the girls, her friends, and was not this so greatly coveted actress the same who, withdrawn by me from the stage, shut up in my house, was out of reach now of the desires of all the rest, who might hereafter seek for her in vain, sitting now in my room, now in her own, and engaged in tracing or cutting out some pattern?

No doubt, in the first days at Balbec, Albertine seemed to be on a parallel plane to that upon which I was living, but one that had drawn closer (after my visit to Elstir) and had finally become merged in it, as my relations with her, at Balbec, in Paris, then at Balbec again, grew more intimate. Besides, between the two pictures of Balbec, at my first visit and at my second, pictures composed of the same villas from which the same girls walked down to the same sea, what a difference! In Albertine's friends at the time of my second visit, whom I knew so well, whose good and bad qualities were so clearly engraved on their features, how was I to recapture those fresh, mysterious strangers who at first could not, without making my heart throb, thrust open the door of their bungalow over the grinding sand and set the tamarisks shivering as they came down the path! Their huge eyes had, in the interval, been absorbed into their faces, doubtless because they had ceased to be children, but also because those ravishing strangers, those ravishing actresses of the romantic first year, as to whom I had gone ceaselessly in quest of information, no longer held any mystery for me. They had become obedient to my caprices, a mere grove of budding girls, from among whom I was quite distinctly proud of having plucked, and carried off from them all, their fairest rose.

Between the two Balbec scenes, so different one from the other, there was the interval of several years in Paris, the long expanse of which was dotted with all the visits that Albertine had paid me. I saw her in successive years of my life occupying, with regard to myself, different positions, which made me feel the beauty of the interposed gaps, that long extent of time in which I never set eyes on her and against the diaphanous background of which the rosy person that I saw before me was modelled with mysterious shadows and in bold relief. This was due also to the superimposition not merely of the successive images which Albertine had been for me, but also of the great qualities of brain and heart, the defects of character, all alike unsuspected by me, which Albertine, in a germination, a multiplication of herself, a carnal efflorescence in sombre colours, had added to a nature that formerly could scarcely have been said to exist, but was now deep beyond plumbing. For other people, even those of whom we have so often dreamed that they have become nothing more than a picture, a figure by Benozzo Gozzoli standing out upon a background of verdure, as to whom we were prepared to believe that the only variations depended upon the point of view from which we looked at them, their distance from us, the effect of light and shade, these people, while they change in relation to ourselves, change also in themselves, and there had been an enrichment, a solidification and an increase of volume in the figure once so simply outlined against the sea. Moreover, it was not only the sea at the close of day that came to life for me in Albertine, but sometimes the drowsy murmur of the sea upon the shore on moonlit nights.

Sometimes, indeed, when I rose to fetch a book from my father's study, and had given my mistress permission to lie down while I was out of the room, she was so tired after her long outing in the morning and afternoon in the open air that, even if I had been away for a moment only, when I returned I found Albertine asleep and did not rouse her.

Stretched out at full length upon my bed, in an attitude so natural that no art could have designed it, she reminded me of a long blossoming stem that had been laid there, and so indeed she was: the faculty of dreaming which I possessed only in her absence I recovered at such moments in her presence, as though by falling asleep she had become a plant. In this way her sleep did to a certain extent make love possible. When she was present, I spoke to her, but I was too far absent from myself to be able to think. When she was asleep, I no longer needed to talk to her, I knew that she was no longer looking at me, I had no longer any need to live upon my own outer surface.

By shutting her eyes, by losing consciousness, Albertine had stripped off, one after another, the different human characters with which she had deceived me ever since the day when I had first made her acquaintance. She was animated now only by the unconscious life of vegetation, of trees, a life more different from my own, more alien, and yet one that belonged more to me. Her personality did not escape at every moment, as when we were talking, by the channels of her unacknowledged thoughts and of her gaze. She had called back into herself everything of her that lay outside, had taken refuge, enclosed, re-absorbed, in her body. In keeping her before my eyes, in my hands, I had that impression of possessing her altogether, which I never had when she was awake. Her life was submitted to me, exhaled towards me its gentle breath.

I listened to this murmuring, mysterious emanation, soft as a breeze from the sea, fairylike as that moonlight which was her sleep. So long as it lasted, I was free to think about her and at the same time to look at her, and, when her sleep grew deeper, to touch, to kiss her. What I felt then was love in the presence of something as pure, as immaterial in its feelings, as mysterious, as if I had been in the presence of those inanimate creatures which are the beauties of nature. And indeed, as soon as her sleep became at all heavy, she ceased to be merely the plant that she had been; her sleep, on the margin of which I remained musing, with a fresh delight of which I never tired, but could have gone on enjoying indefinitely, was to me an undiscovered country. Her sleep brought within my reach something as calm, as sensually delicious as those nights of full moon on the bay of Balbec, turned quiet as a lake over which the branches barely stir, where stretched out upon the sand one could listen for hours on end to the waves breaking and receding.

When I entered the room, I remained standing in the doorway, not venturing to make a sound, and hearing none but that of her breath rising to expire upon her lips at regular intervals, like the reflux of the sea, but drowsier and more gentle. And at the moment when my ear absorbed that divine sound, I felt that there was, condensed in it, the whole person, the whole life of the charming captive, outstretched there before my eyes.

Carriages went rattling past in the street, her features remained as motionless, as pure, her breath as light, reduced to the simplest expulsion of the necessary quantity of air. Then, seeing that her sleep would not be disturbed, I advanced cautiously, sat down upon the chair that stood by the bedside, then upon the bed itself.

I have spent charming evenings talking, playing games with Albertine, but never any so pleasant as when I was watching her sleep. Granted that she might have, as she chatted with me, or played cards, that spontaneity which no actress could have imitated, it was a spontaneity carried to the second degree that was offered me by her sleep. Her hair, falling all along her rosy face, was spread out beside her on the bed, and here and there a separate straight tress gave the same effect of perspective as those moonlit trees, lank and pale, which one sees standing erect and stiff in the backgrounds of Elstir's Raphaelesque pictures. If Albertine's lips were closed, her eyelids, on the other hand, seen from the point at which I was standing, seemed so loosely joined that I might almost have questioned whether she really was asleep. At the same time those drooping lids introduced into her face that perfect continuity, unbroken by any intrusion of eyes. There are people whose faces assume a quite unusual beauty and majesty the moment they cease to look out of their eyes.

I measured with my own Albertine outstretched at my feet. Now and then a slight, unaccountable tremor ran through her body, as the leaves of a tree are shaken for a few moments by a sudden breath of wind. She would touch her hair, then, not having arranged it to her liking, would raise her hand to it again with motions so consecutive, so deliberate, that I was convinced that she was about to wake. Not at all, she grew calm again in the sleep from which she had not emerged. After this she lay without moving. She had laid her hand on her bosom with a sinking of the arm so artlessly childlike that I was obliged, as I gazed at her, to suppress the smile that is provoked in us by the solemnity, the innocence and the charm of little children.

I, who was acquainted with many Albertines in one person, seemed now to see many more again, reposing by my side. Her eyebrows, arched as I had never seen them, enclosed the globes of her eyelids like a halcyon's downy nest. Races, atavisms, vices reposed upon her face. Whenever she moved her head, she created a fresh woman, often one whose existence I had never suspected. I seemed to possess not one, but innumerable girls. Her breathing, as it became gradually deeper, was now regularly stirring her bosom and, through it, her folded hands, her pearls, displaced in a different way by the same movement, like the boats, the anchor chains that are set swaying by the movement of the tide. Then, feeling that the tide of her sleep was full, that I should not ground upon reefs of consciousness covered now by the high water of profound slumber, deliberately, I crept without a sound upon the bed, lay down by her side, clasped her waist in one arm, placed my lips upon her cheek and heart, then upon every part of her body in turn laid my free hand, which also was raised, like the pearls, by Albertine's breathing; I myself was gently rocked by its regular motion: I had embarked upon the tide of Albertine's sleep. Sometimes it made me taste a pleasure that was less pure. For this I had no need to make any movement, I allowed my leg to dangle against hers, like an oar which one allows to trail in the water, imparting to it now and again a gentle oscillation like the intermittent flap given to its wing by a bird asleep in the air. I chose, in gazing at her, this aspect of her face which no one ever saw and which was so pleasing.

It is I suppose comprehensible that the letters which we receive from a person are more or less similar and combine to trace an image of the writer so different from the person whom we know as to constitute a second personality. But how much stranger is it that a woman should be conjoined, like Rosita to Doodica, with another woman whose different beauty makes us infer another character, and that in order to behold one we must look at her in profile, the other in full face. The sound of her breathing as it grew louder might give the illusion of the breathless ecstasy of pleasure and, when mine was at its climax, I could kiss her without having interrupted her sleep. I felt at such moments that I had been possessing her more completely, like an unconscious and unresisting object of dumb nature. I was not affected by the words that she muttered occasionally in her sleep, their meaning escaped me, and besides, whoever the unknown person to whom they referred, it was upon my hand, upon my cheek that her hand, as an occasional tremor recalled it to life, stiffened for an instant. I relished her sleep with a disinterested, soothing love, just as I would remain for hours listening to the unfurling of the waves.

Perhaps it is laid down that people must be capable of making us suffer intensely before, in the hours of respite, they can procure for us the same soothing calm as Nature. I had not to answer her as when we were engaged in conversation, and even if I could have remained silent, as for that matter I did when it was she that was talking, still while listening to her voice I did not penetrate so far into herself. As I continued to hear, to gather from moment to moment the murmur, soothing as a barely perceptible breeze, of her breath, it was a whole physiological existence that was spread out before me, for me; as I used to remain for hours lying on the beach, in the moonlight, so long could I have remained there gazing at her, listening to her.

Sometimes one would have said that the sea was becoming rough, that the storm was making itself felt even inside the bay, and like the bay I lay listening to the gathering roar of her breath. Sometimes, when she was too warm, she would take off, already half asleep, her kimono which she flung over my armchair. While she was asleep I would tell myself that all her correspondence was in the inner pocket of this kimono, into which she always thrust her letters. A signature, a written appointment would have sufficed to prove a lie or to dispel a suspicion. When I could see that Albertine was sound asleep, leaving the foot of the bed where I had been standing motionless in contemplation of her, I took a step forward, seized by a burning curiosity, feeling that the secret of this other life lay offering itself to me, flaccid and defenceless, in that armchair. Perhaps I took this step forward also because to stand perfectly still and watch her sleeping became tiring after a while. And so, on tiptoe, constantly turning round to make sure that Albertine was not waking, I made my way to the armchair. There I stopped short, stood for a long time gazing at the kimono, as I had stood for a long time gazing at Albertine. But (and here perhaps I was wrong) never once did I touch the kimono, put my hand in the pocket, examine the letters. In the end, realising that I would never make up my mind, I started back, on tiptoe, returned to Albertine's bedside and began again to watch her sleeping, her who would tell me nothing, whereas I could see lying across an arm of the chair that kimono which would have told me much. And just as people pay a hundred francs a day for a room at the Hotel at Balbec in order to breathe the sea air, I felt it to be quite natural that I should spend more than that upon her since I had her breath upon my cheek, between her lips which I parted with my own, through which her life flowed against my tongue.

But this pleasure of seeing her sleep, which was as precious as that of feeling her live, was cut short by another pleasure, that of seeing her wake. It was, carried to a more profound and more mysterious degree, the same pleasure that I felt in having her under my roof. It was gratifying, of course, in the afternoon, when she alighted from the carriage, that it should be to my address that she was returning. It was even more so to me that when from the underworld of sleep she climbed the last steps of the stair of dreams, it was in my room that she was reborn to consciousness and life, that she asked herself for an instant: 'Where am I?' and, seeing all the things in the room round about her, the lamp whose light scarcely made her blink her eyes, was able to assure herself that she was at home, as soon as she realised that she was waking in my home. In that first delicious moment of uncertainty, it seemed to me that once again I took a more complete possession of her since, whereas after an outing it was to her own room that she returned, it was now my room that, as soon as Albertine should have recognised it, was about to enclose, to contain her, without any sign of misgiving in the eyes of my mistress, which remained as calm as if she had never slept at all.

The uncertainty of awakening revealed by her silence was not at all revealed in her eyes. As soon as she was able to speak she said: 'My —' or 'My dearest —' followed by my Christian name, which, if we give the narrator the same name as the author of this book, would be 'My Marcel', or 'My dearest Marcel'. After this I would never allow my relatives, by calling me 'dearest', to rob of their priceless uniqueness the delicious words that Albertine uttered to me. As she uttered them, she pursed her lips in a little pout which she herself transformed into a kiss. As quickly as, earlier in the evening, she had fallen asleep, so quickly had she awoken. No more than my own progression in time, no more than the act of gazing at a girl seated opposite to me beneath the lamp, which shed upon her a different light from that of the sun when I used to behold her striding along the seashore, was this material enrichment, this autonomous progress of Albertine the determining cause of the difference between my present view of her and my original impression of her at Balbec. A longer term of years might have separated the two images without effecting so complete a change; it had come to pass, essential and sudden, when I learned that my mistress had been virtually brought up by Mlle Vinteuil's friend. If at one time I had been carried away by excitement when I thought that I saw a trace of mystery in Albertine's eyes, now I was happy only at the moments when from those eyes, from her cheeks even, as mirroring as her eyes, so gentle now but quickly turning sullen, I succeeded in expelling every trace of mystery.

The image for which I sought, upon which I reposed, against which I would have liked to lean and die, was no longer that of Albertine leading a hidden life, it was that of an Albertine as familiar to me as possible (and for this reason my love could not be lasting unless it was unhappy, for in its nature it did not satisfy my need of mystery), an Albertine who did not reflect a distant world, but desired nothing else – there were moments when this did indeed appear to be the case – than to be with me, a person like myself, an Albertine the embodiment of what belonged to me and not of the unknown. When it is in this way, from an hour of anguish caused by another person, when it is from uncertainty whether we shall be able to keep her or she will escape, that love is born, such love bears the mark of the revolution that has created it, it recalls very little of what we had previously seen when we thought of the person in question. And my first impressions at the sight of Albertine, against a background of sea, might to some small extent persist in my love of her: actually, these earlier impressions occupy but a tiny place in a love of this sort; in its strength, in its agony, in its need of comfort and its return to a calm and soothing memory with which we would prefer to abide and to learn nothing more of her whom we love, even if there be something horrible that we ought to know – would prefer still more to consult only these earlier memories – such a love is composed of very different material!

Sometimes I put out the light before she came in. It was in the darkness, barely guided by the glow of a smouldering log, that she lay down by my side. My hands, my cheeks alone identified her without my eyes beholding her, my eyes that often were afraid of finding her altered. With the result that by virtue of this unseeing love she may have felt herself bathed in a warmer affection than usual. On other evenings, I undressed, I lay down, and, with Albertine perched on the side of my bed, we resumed our game or our conversation interrupted by kisses; and, in the desire that alone makes us take an interest in the existence and character of another person, we remain so true to our own nature (even if, at the same time, we abandon successively the different people whom we have loved in turn), that on one occasion, catching sight of myself in the glass at the moment when I was kissing Albertine and calling her my little girl, the sorrowful, passionate expression on my own face, similar to the expression it had assumed long ago with Gilberte whom I no longer remembered, and would perhaps assume one day with another girl, if I was fated ever to forget Albertine, made me think that over and above any personal considerations (instinct requiring that we consider the person of the moment as the only true person) I was performing the duties of an ardent and painful devotion dedicated as an oblation to the youth and beauty of Woman. And yet with this desire, honouring youth with an *ex voto*, with my memories also of Balbec, there was blended, in the need that I felt of keeping Albertine in this way every evening by my side, something that had hitherto been unknown, at least in my amorous existence, if it was not entirely novel in my life.

It was a soothing power the like of which I had not known since the evenings at Combray long ago when my mother, stooping over my bed, brought me repose in a kiss. To be sure, I should have been greatly astonished at that time, had anyone told me that I was not wholly virtuous, and more astonished still to be told that I would ever seek to deprive some-one else of a pleasure. I must have known myself very slightly, for my pleasure in having Albertine to live with me was much less a positive pleasure than that of having withdrawn from the world, where everyone was free to enjoy her in turn, the blossoming damsel who, if she did not bring me any great joy, was at least withholding joy from others. Ambition, fame would have left me unmoved. Even more was I incapable of feeling hatred. And yet to me to love in a carnal sense was at any rate to enjoy a triumph over countless rivals. I can never repeat it often enough; it was first and foremost a sedative.

For all that I might, before Albertine returned, have doubted her loyalty, have imagined her in the room at Montjouvain, once she was in her dressing-gown and seated facing my chair, or (if, as was more frequent, I had remained in bed) at the foot of my bed, I would deposit my doubts in her, hand them over for her to relieve me of them, with the abnegation of a worshipper uttering his prayer. All the evening she might have been there, huddled in a provoking ball upon my bed, playing with me, like a great cat; her little pink nose, the tip of which she made even tinier with a coquettish glance which gave it that sharpness which we see in certain people who are inclined to be stout, might have given her a fiery and rebellious air; she might have allowed a tress of her long, dark hair to fall over a cheek of rosy wax and, half shutting her eyes, unfolding her arms, have seemed to be saying to me: 'Do with me what you please!'; when, as the time came for her to leave me, she drew nearer to say good-night, it was a meekness that had become almost a part of my family life that I kissed on either side of her firm throat which now never seemed to me brown or freckled enough, as though these solid qualities had been in keeping with some loyal generosity in Albertine.

When it was Albertine's turn to bid me good-night, kissing me on either side of my throat, her hair caressed me like a wing of softly bristling feathers. Incomparable as were those two kisses of peace, Albertine slipped into my mouth, making me the gift of her tongue, like a gift of the Holy Spirit, conveyed to me a viaticum, left me with a provision of tranquillity almost as precious as when my mother in the evening at Combray used to lay her lips upon my brow.

'Are you coming with us tomorrow, you naughty man?' she asked before leaving me. 'Where are you going?' 'That will depend on the weather and on yourself. But have you written anything today, my little darling? No? Then it was hardly worth your while, not coming with us. Tell me, by the way, when I came in, you knew my step, you guessed at once who it was?' 'Of course. Could I possibly be mistaken, couldn't I tell my little sparrow's hop among a thousand? She must let me take her shoes off, before she goes to bed, it will be such a pleasure to me. You are so nice and pink in all that white lace.'

Such was my answer; among the sensual expressions, we may recognise others that were peculiar to my grandmother and mother for, little by little, I was beginning to resemble all my relatives, my father who – in a very different fashion from myself, no doubt, for if things do repeat themselves, it is with great variations – took so keen an interest in the weather; and not my father only, I was becoming more and more like my aunt Léonie. Otherwise, Albertine could not but have been a reason for my going out of doors, so as not to leave her by herself, beyond my control. My aunt Léonie, wrapped up in her religious observances, with whom I could have sworn that I had not a single point in common, I so passionately keen on pleasure, apparently worlds apart from that maniac who had never known any pleasure in her life and lay mumbling her rosary all day long, I who suffered from my inability to embark upon a literary career whereas she had been the one person in the family who could never understand that reading was anything more than an amusing pastime, which made reading, even at the paschal season, lawful upon Sunday, when every serious occupation is forbidden, in order that the day may be hallowed by prayer alone. Now, albeit every day I found an excuse in some particular indisposition which made me so often remain in bed, a person (not Albertine, not any person that I loved, but a person with more power over me than any beloved) had migrated into me, despotic to the extent of silencing at times my jealous suspicions or at least of preventing me from going to find out whether they had any foundation, and this was my aunt Léonie. It was quite enough that I should bear an exaggerated resemblance to my father, to the extent of not being satisfied like him with consulting the barometer, but becoming an animated barometer myself; it was quite enough that I should allow myself to be ordered by my aunt Léonie to stay at home and watch the weather, from my bedroom window or even from my bed; yet here I was talking now to Albertine, at one moment as the child that I had been at Combray used to talk to my mother, at another as my grandmother used to talk to me.

When we have passed a certain age, the soul of the child that we were and the souls of the dead from whom we spring come and bestow upon us in handfuls their treasures and their calamities, asking to be allowed to cooperate in the new sentiments which we are feeling and in which, obliterating their former image, we recast them in an original creation. Thus my whole past from my earliest years, and earlier still the past of my parents and relatives, blended with my impure love for Albertine the charm of an affection at once filial and maternal. We have to give hospitality, at a certain stage in our life, to all our relatives who have journeyed so far and gathered round us.

Before Albertine obeyed and allowed me to take off her shoes, I opened her chemise. Her two little upstanding breasts were so round that they seemed not so much to be an integral part of her body as to have ripened there like fruit; and her belly (concealing the place where a man's is marred as though by an iron clamp left sticking in a statue that has been taken down from its niche) was closed, at the junction of her thighs, by two valves of a curve as hushed, as reposeful, as cloistral as that of the horizon after the sun has set. She took off her shoes, and lay down by my side.

O mighty attitudes of Man and Woman, in which there seeks to be reunited, in the innocence of the world's first age and with the humility of clay, what creation has cloven apart, in which Eve is astonished and submissive before the Man by whose side she has awoken, as he himself, alone still, before God Who has fashioned him. Albertine folded her arms behind her dark hair, her swelling hip, her leg falling with the inflection of a swan's neck that stretches upwards and then curves over towards its starting point. It was only when she was lying right on her side that one saw a certain aspect of her face (so good and handsome when one looked at it from in front) which I could not endure, hook-nosed as in some of Leonardo's caricatures, seeming to indicate the shiftiness, the greed for profit, the cunning of a spy whose presence in my house would have filled me with horror and whom that profile seemed to unmask. At once I took Albertine's face in my hands and altered its position.

'Be a good boy, promise me that if you don't come out tomorrow you will work,' said my mistress as she slipped into her chemise. 'Yes, but don't put on your dressing-gown yet.' Sometimes I ended by falling asleep by her side. The room had grown cold, more wood was wanted. I tried to find the bell above my head, but failed to do so, after fingering all the copper rods in turn save those between which it hung, and said to Albertine who had sprung from the bed so that Françoise should not find us lying side by side: 'No, come back for a moment, I can't find the bell.'

Comforting moments, gay, innocent to all appearance, and yet moments in which there accumulates in us the never suspected possibility of disaster, which makes the amorous life the most precarious of all, that in which the incalculable rain of sulphur and brimstone falls after the most radiant moments, after which, without having the courage to derive its lesson from our mishap, we set to work immediately to rebuild upon the slopes of the crater from which nothing but catastrophe can emerge. I was as careless as everyone who imagines that his happiness will endure.

It is precisely because this comfort has been necessary to bring grief to birth – and will return moreover at intervals to calm it – that men can be sincere with each other, and even with themselves, when they pride themselves upon a woman's kindness to them, although, taking things all in all, at the heart of their intimacy there lurks continually in a secret fashion, unavowed to the rest of the world, or revealed unintentionally by questions, enquiries, a painful uncertainty. But as this could not have come to birth without the preliminary comfort, as even afterwards the intermittent comfort is necessary to make suffering endurable and to prevent ruptures, their concealment of the secret hell that life can be when shared with the woman in question, carried to the pitch of an ostentatious display of an intimacy which, they pretend, is precious, expresses a genuine point of view, a universal process of cause and effect, one of the modes in which the production of grief is rendered possible.

It no longer surprised me that Albertine should be in the house, and would not be going out tomorrow save with myself or in the custody of Andrée. These habits of a life shared in common, this broad outline which defined my existence and within which nobody might penetrate but Albertine, also (in the future plan, of which I was still unaware, of my life to come, like the plan traced by an architect for monumental structures which will not be erected until long afterwards) the remoter lines, parallel to the others but vaster, that sketched in me, like a lonely hermitage, the somewhat rigid and monotonous formula of my future loves, had in reality been traced that night at Balbec when, in the little tram, after Albertine had revealed to me who it was that had brought her up, I had decided at any cost to remove her from certain influences and to prevent her from straying out of my sight for some days to come. Day after day had gone by, these habits had become mechanical, but, like those primitive rites the meaning of which historians seek to discover, I might (but would not) have said to anybody who asked me what I meant by this life of seclusion which I carried so far as not to go any more to the theatre, that its origin was the anxiety of a certain evening, and my need to prove to myself, during the days that followed, that the girl whose unfortunate childhood I had learned should not find it possible, if she wished, to expose herself to similar temptations. I no longer thought, save very rarely, of these possibilities, but they were nevertheless to remain vaguely present in my consciousness. The fact that I was destroying – or trying to destroy – them day by day was doubtless the reason why it comforted me to kiss those cheeks which were no more beautiful than many others; beneath any carnal attraction which is at all profound, there is the permanent possibility of danger.

I had promised Albertine that, if I did not go out with her, I would settle down to work, but in the morning, just as if, taking advantage of our being asleep, the house had miraculously flown, I awoke in different weather beneath another clime. We do not begin to work at the moment of landing in a strange country to the conditions of which we have to adapt ourself. But each day was for me a different country. Even my laziness itself, beneath the novel forms that it had assumed, how was I to recognise it?

Sometimes, on days when the weather was, according to everyone, past praying for, the mere act of staying in the house, situated in the midst of a steady and continuous rain, had all the gliding charm, the soothing silence, the interest of a sea voyage; at another time, on a bright day, to lie still in bed was to let the lights and shadows play around me as round a tree-trunk.

Or yet again, in the first strokes of the bell of a neighbouring convent, rare as the early morning worshippers, barely whitening the dark sky with their fluttering snowfall, melted and scattered by the warm breeze, I had discerned one of those tempestuous, disordered, delightful days, when the roofs soaked by an occasional shower and dried by a breath of wind or a ray of sunshine let fall a cooing eavesdrop, and, as they wait for the wind to resume its turn, preen in the momentary sunlight that has burnished them their pigeon's-breast of slates, one of those days filled with so many changes of weather, atmospheric incidents, storms, that the idle man does not feel that he has wasted them, because he has been taking an interest in the activity which, in default of himself, the atmosphere, acting in a sense in his stead, has displayed; days similar to those times of revolution or war which do not seem empty to the schoolboy who has played truant from his classroom, because by loitering outside the Law Courts or by reading the newspapers, he has the illusion of finding, in the events that have occurred, failing the lesson which he has not learned, an intellectual profit and an excuse for his idleness; days to which we may compare those on which there occurs in our life some exceptional crisis from which the man who has never done anything imagines that he is going to acquire, if it comes to a happy issue, laborious habits; for instance, the morning on which he sets out for a duel which is to be fought under particularly dangerous conditions; then he is suddenly made aware, at the moment when it is perhaps about to be taken from him, of the value of a life of which he might have made use to begin some important work, or merely to enjoy pleasures, and of which he has failed to make any use at all. 'If I can only not be killed,' he says to himself, 'how I shall settle down to work this very minute, and how I shall enjoy myself too.'

Life has in fact suddenly acquired, in his eyes, a higher value, because he puts into life everything that it seems to him capable of giving, instead of the little that he normally makes it give. He sees it in the light of his desire, not as his experience has taught him that he was apt to make it, that is to say so tawdry! It has, at that moment, become filled with work, travel, mountain-climbing, all the pleasant things which, he tells himself, the fatal issue of the duel may render impossible, whereas they were already impossible before there was any question of a duel, owing to the bad habits which, even had there been no duel, would have persisted. He returns home without even a scratch, but he continues to find the same obstacles to pleasures, excursions, travel, to everything of which he had feared for a moment to be for ever deprived by death; to deprive him of them life has been sufficient. As for work – exceptional circumstances having the effect of intensifying what previously existed in the man, labour in the laborious, laziness in the lazy – he takes a holiday.

I followed his example, and did as I had always done since my first resolution to become a writer, which I had made long ago, but which seemed to me to date from yesterday, because I had regarded each intervening day as non-existent. I treated this day in a similar fashion, allowing its showers of rain and bursts of sunshine to pass without doing anything, and vowing that I would begin to work on the morrow. But then I was no longer the same man beneath a cloudless sky; the golden note of the bells did not contain merely (as honey contains) light, but the sensation of light and also the sickly savour of preserved fruits (because at Combray it had often loitered like a wasp over our cleared dinner-table). On this day of dazzling sunshine, to remain until nightfall with my eyes shut was a thing permitted, customary, health-giving, pleasant, seasonable, like keeping the outside shutters closed against the heat.

It was in such weather as this that at the beginning of my second visit to Balbec I used to hear the violins of the orchestra amid the bluish flow of the rising tide. How much more fully did I possess Albertine today. There were days when the sound of a bell striking the hour bore upon the sphere of its resonance a plate so cool, so richly loaded with moisture or with light that it was like a transcription for the blind, or if you prefer a musical interpretation of the charm of rain or of the charm of the sun. So much so that, at that moment, as I lay in bed, with my eyes shut, I said to myself that everything is capable of transposition and that a universe which was merely audible might be as full of variety as the other. Travelling lazily upstream from day to day, as in a boat, and seeing appear before my eyes an endlessly changing succession of enchanted memories, which I did not select, which a moment earlier had been invisible, and which my mind presented to me one after another, without my being free to choose them, I pursued idly over that continuous expanse my stroll in the sunshine.

Those morning concerts at Balbec were not remote in time. And yet, at that comparatively recent moment, I had given but little thought to Albertine. Indeed, on the very first mornings after my arrival, I had not known that she was at Balbec. From whom then had I learned it? Oh, yes, from Aimé. It was a fine sunny day like this. He was glad to see me again. But he does not like Albertine. Not everybody can be in love with her. Yes, it was he who told me that she was at Balbec. But how did he know? Ah! he had met her, had thought that she had a bad style. At that moment, as I regarded Aimé's story from another aspect than that in which he had told me it, my thoughts, which hitherto had been sailing blissfully over these untroubled waters, exploded suddenly, as though they had struck an invisible and perilous mine, treacherously moored at this point in my memory. He had told me that he had met her, that he had thought her style bad. What had he meant by a bad style? I had understood him to mean a vulgar manner, because, to contradict him in advance, I had declared that she was most refined. But no, perhaps he had meant the style of Gomorrah. She was with another girl, perhaps their arms were round one another's waist, they were staring at other women, they were indeed displaying a 'style' which I had never seen Albertine adopt in my presence. Who was the other girl, where had Aimé met her, this odious Albertine?

I tried to recall exactly what Aimé had said to me, in order to see whether it could be made to refer to what I imagined, or he had meant nothing more than common manners. But in vain might I ask the question, the person who put it and the person who might supply the recollection were, alas, one and the same person, myself, who was momentarily duplicated but without adding anything to my stature. Question as I might, it was myself who answered, I learned nothing fresh. I no longer gave a thought to Mlle Vinteuil. Born of a novel suspicion, the fit of jealousy from which I was suffering was novel also, or rather it was only the prolongation, the extension of that suspicion, it had the same theatre, which was no longer Montjouvain, but the road upon which Aimé had met Albertine, and for its object the various friends one or other of whom might be she who had been with Albertine that day. It was perhaps a certain Elisabeth, or else perhaps those two girls whom Albertine had watched in the mirror at the Casino, while appearing not to notice them. She had doubtless been having relations with them, and also with Esther, Bloch's cousin. Such relations, had they been revealed to me by a third person, would have been enough almost to kill me, but as it was myself that was imagining them, I took care to add sufficient uncertainty to deaden the pain.

We succeed in absorbing daily, under the guise of suspicions, in enormous doses, this same idea that we are being betrayed, a quite minute quantity of which might prove fatal, if injected by the needle of a stabbing word. It is no doubt for that reason, and by a survival of the instinct of self-preservation, that the same jealous man does not hesitate to form the most terrible suspicions upon a basis of innocuous details, provided that, whenever any proof is brought to him, he may decline to accept its evidence. Anyhow, love is an incurable malady, like those diathetic states in which rheumatism affords the sufferer a brief respite only to be replaced by epileptiform headaches. Was my jealous suspicion calmed, I then felt a grudge against Albertine for not having been gentle with me, perhaps for having made fun of me to Andrée. I thought with alarm of the idea that she must have formed if Andrée had repeated all our conversations; the future loomed black and menacing. This mood of depression left me only if a fresh jealous suspicion drove me upon another quest or if, on the other hand, Albertine's display of affection made the actual state of my fortunes seem to me immaterial. Whoever this girl might be, I should have to write to Aimé, to try to see him, and then I should check his statement by talking to Albertine, hearing her confession. In the meantime, convinced that it must be Bloch's cousin, I asked Bloch himself, who had not the remotest idea of my purpose, simply to let me see her photograph, or, better still, to arrange if possible for me to meet her.

How many persons, cities, roads does not jealousy make us eager thus to know? It is a thirst for knowledge thanks to which, with regard to various isolated points, we end by acquiring every possible notion in turn except those that we require. We can never tell whether a suspicion will not arise, for, all of a sudden, we recall a sentence that was not clear, an alibi that cannot have been given us without a purpose. And yet, we have not seen the person again, but there is such a thing as a posthumous jealousy, that is born only after we have left her, a jealousy of the doorstep. Perhaps the habit that I had formed of nursing in my bosom several simultaneous desires, a desire for a young girl of good family such as I used to see pass beneath my window escorted by her governess, and especially of the girl whom Saint-Loup had mentioned to me, the one who frequented houses of ill fame, a desire for handsome lady's-maids, and especially for the maid of Mme Putbus, a desire to go to the country in early spring, to see once again hawthorns, apple trees in blossom, storms at sea, a desire for Venice, a desire to settle down to work, a desire to live like other people – perhaps the habit of storing up, without assuaging any of them, all these desires, contenting myself with the promise, made to myself, that I would not forget to satisfy them one day, perhaps this habit, so many years old already, of perpetual postponement, of what M. de Charlus used to castigate under the name of procrastination, had become so prevalent in me that it assumed control of my jealous suspicions also and, while it made me take a mental note that I would not fail, some day, to have an explanation from Albertine with regard to the girl, possibly the girls (this part of the story was confused, rubbed out, that is to say obliterated, in my memory) with whom Aimé had met her, made me also postpone this explanation. In any case, I would not mention it this evening to my mistress for fear of making her think me jealous and so offending her.

And yet when, on the following day, Bloch had sent me the photograph of his cousin Esther, I made haste to forward it to Aimé. And at the same moment I remembered that Albertine had that morning refused me a pleasure which might indeed have tired her. Was that in order to reserve it for someone else? This afternoon, perhaps? For whom?

Thus it is that jealousy is endless, for even if the beloved object, by dying for instance, can no longer provoke it by her actions, it so happens that posthumous memories, of later origin than any event, take shape suddenly in our minds as though they were events also, memories which hitherto we have never properly explored, which had seemed to us unimportant, and to which our own meditation upon them has been sufficient, without any external action, to give a new and terrible meaning. We have no need of her company, it is enough to be alone in our room, thinking, for fresh betrayals of us by our mistress to come to light, even though she be dead. And so we ought not to fear in love, as in everyday life, the future alone, but even the past which often we do not succeed in realising until the future has come and gone; and we are not speaking only of the past which we discover long afterwards, but of the past which we have long kept stored up in ourselves and learn suddenly how to interpret.

No matter, I was very glad, now that afternoon was turning to evening, that the hour was not far off when I should be able to appeal to Albertine's company for the consolation of which I stood in need. Unfortunately, the evening that followed was one of those on which this consolation was not afforded me, on which the kiss that Albertine would give me when she left me for the night, very different from her ordinary kiss, would no more soothe me than my mother's kiss had soothed me long ago, on days when she was vexed with me and I dared not send for her, but at the same time knew that I should not be able to sleep. Such evenings were now those on which Albertine had formed for the morrow some plan of which she did not wish me to know. Had she confided in me, I would have employed, to assure its successful execution, an ardour which none but Albertine could have inspired in me. But she told me nothing, nor had she any need to tell me anything; as soon as she came in, before she had even crossed the threshold of my room, as she was still wearing her hat or toque, I had already detected the unknown, restive, desperate, indomitable desire. Now, these were often the evenings when I had awaited her return with the most loving thoughts, and looked forward to throwing my arms round her neck with the warmest affection.

Alas, those misunderstandings that I had often had with my parents, whom I found cold or cross at the moment when I was running to embrace them, overflowing with love, are nothing in comparison with these that occur between lovers! The anguish then is far less superficial, far harder to endure, it has its abode in a deeper stratum of the heart. This evening, however, Albertine was obliged to mention the plan that she had in her mind; I gathered at once that she wished to go next day to pay a call on Mme Verdurin, a call to which in itself I would have had no objection. But evidently her object was to meet someone there, to prepare some future pleasure. Otherwise she would not have attached so much importance to this call. That is to say, she would not have kept on assuring me that it was of no importance. I had in the course of my life developed in the opposite direction to those races which make use of phonetic writing only after regarding the letters of the alphabet as a set of symbols; I, who for so many years had sought for the real life and thought of other people only in the direct statements with which they furnished me of their own free will, failing these had come to attach importance, on the contrary, only to the evidence that is not a rational and analytical expression of the truth; the words themselves did not enlighten me unless they could be interpreted in the same way as a sudden rush of blood to the cheeks of a person who is embarrassed, or, what is even more telling, a sudden silence.

Some subsidiary word (such as that used by M. de Cambremer when he understood that I was 'literary', and, not having spoken to me before, as he was describing a visit that he had paid to the Verdurins, turned to me with: '*Why*, Boreli was there!') bursting into flames at the unintended, sometimes perilous contact of two ideas which the speaker has not expressed, but which, by applying the appropriate methods of analysis or electrolysis I was able to extract from it, told me more than a long speech.

Albertine sometimes allowed to appear in her conversation one or other of these precious amalgams which I made haste to 'treat' so as to transform them into lucid ideas. It is by the way one of the most terrible calamities for the lover that if particular details – which only experiment, espionage, of all the possible realisations, would ever make him know – are so difficult to discover, the truth on the other hand is easy to penetrate or merely to feel by instinct.

Often I had seen her, at Balbec, fasten upon some girls who came past us

a sharp and lingering stare, like a physical contact, after which, if I knew the
girls, she would say to me: 'Suppose we asked them to join us? I should so
love to be rude to them.' And now, for some time past, doubtless since she
had succeeded in reading my character, no request to me to invite anyone,
not a word, never even a sidelong glance from her eyes, which had become
objectless and mute, and as revealing, with the vague and vacant expression
of the rest of her face, as had been their magnetic swerve before. Now it was
impossible for me to reproach her, or to ply her with questions about things
which she would have declared to be so petty, so trivial, things that I had
stored up in my mind simply for the pleasure of making mountains out of
molehills. It is hard enough to say: 'Why did you stare at that girl who went
past?' but a great deal harder to say: 'Why did you not stare at her?' And yet
I knew quite well, or at least I should have known, if I had not chosen to
believe Albertine's assertions rather than all the trivialities contained in a
glance, proved by it and by some contradiction or other in her speech, a
contradiction which often I did not perceive until long after I had left her,
which kept me on tenterhooks all the night long, which I never dared
mention to her again, but which nevertheless continued to honour my
memory from time to time with its periodical visits.

Often, in the case of these furtive or sidelong glances on the beach at
Balbec or in the streets of Paris, I might ask myself whether the person who
provoked them was not merely at the moment when she passed an object of
desire but was an old acquaintance, or else some girl who had simply been
mentioned to her, and of whom, when I heard about it, I was astonished that
anybody could have spoken to her, so utterly unlike was she to anyone that
Albertine could possibly wish to know. But the Gomorrah of today is a
dissected puzzle made up of fragments which are picked up in the places
where we least expected to find them. Thus I once saw at Rivebelle a big
dinner-party of ten women, all of whom I happened to know – at least by
name – women as unlike one another as possible, perfectly united nevertheless, so much so that I never saw a party so homogeneous, albeit so
composite.

To return to the girls whom we passed in the street, never did Albertine
gaze at an old person, man or woman, with such fixity, or on the other hand
with such reserve, and as though she saw nothing. The cuckolded husbands
who know nothing know everything all the same. But it requires more
accurate and abundant evidence to create a scene of jealousy. Besides, if
jealousy helps us to discover a certain tendency to falsehood in the woman
whom we love, it multiplies this tendency an hundredfold when the woman
has discovered that we are jealous. She lies (to an extent to which she has

never lied to us before), whether from pity, or from fear, or because she instinctively withdraws by a methodical flight from our investigations. Certainly there are love affairs in which from the start a light woman has posed as virtue incarnate in the eyes of the man who is in love with her. But how many others consist of two diametrically opposite periods? In the first, the woman speaks almost spontaneously, with slight modifications, of her zest for sensual pleasure, of the gay life which it has made her lead, things all of which she will deny later on, with the last breath in her body, to the same man – when she has felt that he is jealous of and spying upon her. He begins to think with regret of the days of those first confidences, the memory of which torments him nevertheless. If the woman continued to make them, she would furnish him almost unaided with the secret of her conduct which he has been vainly pursuing day after day. And besides, what a surrender that would mean, what trust, what friendship. If she cannot live without betraying him, at least she would be betraying him as a friend, telling him of her pleasures, associating him with them. And he thinks with regret of the sort of life which the early stages of their love seemed to promise, which the sequel has rendered impossible, making of that love a thing exquisitely painful, which will render a final parting, according to circumstances, either inevitable or impossible.

Sometimes the script from which I deciphered Albertine's falsehoods, without being ideographic needed simply to be read backwards; so this evening she had flung at me in a careless tone the message, intended to pass almost unheeded: 'It is possible that I may go tomorrow to the Verdurins', I don't in the least know whether I shall go, I don't really want to.' A childish anagram of the admission: 'I shall go tomorrow to the Verdurins', it is absolutely certain, for I attach the utmost importance to the visit.' This apparent hesitation indicated a resolute decision and was intended to diminish the importance of the visit while warning me of it. Albertine always adopted a tone of uncertainty in speaking of her irrevocable decisions. Mine was no less irrevocable. I took steps to arrange that this visit to Mme Verdurin should not take place. Jealousy is often only an uneasy need to be tyrannical, applied to matters of love. I had doubtless inherited from my father this abrupt, arbitrary desire to threaten the people whom I loved best in the hopes with which they were lulling themselves with a security that I determined to expose to them as false; when I saw that Albertine had planned without my knowledge, behind my back, an expedition which I would have done everything in the world to make easier and more pleasant for her, had she taken me into her confidence, I said carelessly, so as to make her tremble, that I intended to go out the next day myself.

I set to work to suggest to Albertine other expeditions in directions which would have made this visit to the Verdurins impossible, in words stamped with a feigned indifference beneath which I strove to conceal my excitement. But she had detected it. It encountered in her the electric shock of a contrary will which violently repulsed it; I could see the sparks flash from her eyes. Of what use, though, was it to pay attention to what her eyes were saying at that moment? How had I failed to observe long ago that Albertine's eyes belonged to the class which even in a quite ordinary person seem to be composed of a number of fragments, because of all the places which the person wishes to visit – and to conceal her desire to visit – that day. Those eyes which their falsehood keeps ever immobile and passive, but dynamic, measurable in the yards or miles to be traversed before they reach the determined, the implacably determined meeting-place, eyes that are not so much smiling at the pleasure which tempts them as they are shadowed with melancholy and discouragement because there may be a difficulty in their getting to the meeting-place. Even when you hold them in your hands, these people are fugitives. To understand the emotions which they arouse, and which other people, even better looking, do not arouse, we must take into account that they are not immobile but in motion, and add to their person a sign corresponding to what in physics is the sign that indicates velocity. If you upset their plans for the day, they confess to you the pleasure that they had hidden from you: 'I did so want to go to tea at five o'clock with So-and-So, my dearest friend.' Very well, if, six months later, you come to know the person in question, you will learn that the girl whose plans you upset, who, caught in the trap, in order that you might set her free, confessed to you that she was in the habit of taking tea like this with a dear friend, every day at the hour at which you did not see her, has never once been inside this person's house, that they have never taken tea together, and that the girl used to explain that her whole time was take up by none other than yourself. And so the person with whom she confessed that she had gone to tea, with whom she begged you to allow her to go to tea, that person, the excuse that necessity made her plead, was not the real person, there was somebody, something else! Something else, what? Someone, who?

Alas, the kaleidoscopic eyes starting off into the distance and shadowed with melancholy might enable us perhaps to measure distance, but do not indicate direction. The boundless field of possibilities extends before us, and if by any chance the reality presented itself to our gaze, it would be so far beyond the bounds of possibility that, dashing suddenly against the boundary wall, we should fall over backwards. It is not even essential that we should have proof of her movement and flight, it is enough that we should guess them. She had promised us a letter, we were calm, we were no longer in love. The letter has not come; no messenger appears with it; what can have happened? Anxiety is born afresh, and love. It is such people more than any others who inspire love in us, for our destruction. For every fresh anxiety that we feel on their account strips them in our eyes of some of their personality. We were resigned to suffering, thinking that we loved outside ourselves, and we perceive that our love is a function of our sorrow, that our love perhaps is our sorrow, and that its object is, to a very small extent only, the girl with the raven tresses. But, when all is said, it is these people more than any others who inspire love.

Generally speaking, love has not as its object a human body, except when an emotion, the fear of losing it, the uncertainty of finding it again have been infused into it. This sort of anxiety has a great affinity for bodies. It adds to them a quality which surpasses beauty even; which is one of the reasons why we see men who are indifferent to the most beautiful women fall passionately in love with others who appear to us ugly. To these people, these fugitives, their own nature, our anxiety fastens wings. And even when they are in our company the look in their eyes seems to warn us that they are about to take flight. The proof of this beauty, surpassing the beauty added by the wings, is that very often the same person is, in our eyes, alternately wingless and winged. Afraid of losing her, we forget all the others. Sure of keeping her, we compare her with those others whom at once we prefer to her. And as these emotions and these certainties may vary from week to week, a person may one week see sacrificed to her everything that gave us pleasure, in the following week be sacrificed herself, and so for weeks and months on end. All of which would be incomprehensible did we not know from the experience, which every man shares, of having at least once in a lifetime ceased to love, forgotten a woman, for how very little a person counts in herself when she is no longer – or is not yet – permeable by our emotions. And, be it understood, what we say of fugitives is equally true of those in prison, the captive women, we suppose that we are never to possess them. And so men detest procuresses, for these facilitate the flight, enhance the temptation, but if on the other hand they are in love with a cloistered woman, they willingly have recourse to a procuress to make her emerge from her prison and bring her to them. In so far as relations with women whom we abduct are less permanent than others, the reason is that the fear of not succeeding in procuring them or the dread of seeing them escape is the whole of our love for them and that once they have been carried off from their husbands, torn from their footlights, cured of the temptation to leave us, dissociated in short from our emotion whatever it may be, they are only themselves, that is to say almost nothing, and, so long desired, are soon forsaken by the very man who was so afraid of their forsaking him.

How, I have asked, did I not guess this? But had I not guessed it from the first day at Balbec? Had I not detected in Albertine one of those girls beneath whose envelope of flesh more hidden persons are stirring, than in ... I do not say a pack of cards still in its box, a cathedral or a theatre before we enter it, but the whole, vast, ever changing crowd? Not only all these persons, but the desire, the voluptuous memory, the desperate quest of all these persons. At Balbec I had not been troubled because I had never even supposed that one day I should be following a trail, even a false trail. No matter! This had given Albertine, in my eyes, the plenitude of a person filled to the brim by the superimposition of all these persons, and desires and voluptuous memories of persons. And now that she had one day let fall the words 'Mlle Vinteuil', I would have wished not to tear off her garments so as to see her body but through her body to see and read that memorandum block of her memories and her future, passionate engagements.

How suddenly do the things that are probably the most insignificant assume an extraordinary value when a person whom we love (or who has lacked only this duplicity to make us love her) conceals them from us! In itself, suffering does not of necessity inspire in us sentiments of love or hatred towards the person who causes it: a surgeon can hurt our body without arousing any personal emotion. But a woman who has continued for some time to assure us that we are everything in the world to her, without being herself everything in the world to us, a woman whom we enjoy seeing, kissing, taking upon our knee, we are astonished if we merely feel from a sudden resistance that we are not free to dispose of her life. Disappointment may then revive in us the forgotten memory of an old anguish, which we know, all the same, to have been provoked not by this woman but by others whose betrayals are milestones in our past life; if it comes to that, how have we the courage to wish to live, how can we move a finger to preserve ourselves from death, in a world in which love is provoked only by falsehood, and consists merely in our need to see our sufferings appeased by the person who has made us suffer? To restore us from the collapse which follows our discovery of her falsehood and her resistance, there is the drastic remedy of endeavouring to act against her will, with the help of people whom we feel to be more closely involved than we are in her life, upon her who is resisting us and lying to us, to play the cheat in turn, to make ourselves loathed. But the suffering caused by such a love is of the sort which must inevitably lead the sufferer to seek in a change of posture an illusory comfort.

These means of action are not wanting, alas! And the horror of the kind of love which uneasiness alone has engendered lies in the fact that we turn over and over incessantly in our cage the most trivial utterances; not to mention that rarely do the people for whom we feel this love appeal to us physically in a complex fashion, since it is not our deliberate preference, but the chance of a minute of anguish, a minute indefinitely prolonged by our weakness of character, which repeats its experiments every evening until it yields to sedatives, that chooses for us.

No doubt my love for Albertine was not the most barren of those to which, through feebleness of will, a man may descend, for it was not entirely platonic; she did give me carnal satisfaction and, besides, she was intelligent. But all this was a superfluity. What occupied my mind was not the intelligent remark that she might have made, but some chance utterance that had aroused in me a doubt as to her actions; I tried to remember whether she had said this or that, in what tone, at what moment, in response to what speech of mine, to reconstruct the whole scene of her dialogue with me, to recall at what moment she had expressed a desire to call upon the Verdurins, what words of mine had brought that look of vexation to her face. The most important matter might have been in question, without my giving myself so much trouble to establish the truth, to restore the proper atmosphere and colour. No doubt, after these anxieties have intensified to a degree which we find insupportable, we do sometimes manage to soothe them altogether for an evening. The party to which the mistress whom we love is engaged to go, the true nature of which our mind has been toiling for days to discover, we are invited to it also, our mistress has neither looks nor words for anyone but ourselves, we take her home and then we enjoy, all our anxieties dispelled, a repose as complete, as healing, as that which we enjoy at times in the profound sleep that comes after a long walk. And no doubt such repose deserves that we should pay a high price for it. But would it not have been more simple not to purchase for ourselves, deliberately, the preceding anxiety, and at a higher price still? Besides, we know all too well that however profound these momentary relaxations may be, anxiety will still be the stronger. Sometimes indeed it is revived by the words that were intended to bring us repose. But as a rule, all that we do is to change our anxiety. One of the words of the sentence that was meant to calm us sets our suspicions running upon another trail. The demands of our jealousy and the blindness of our credulity are greater than the woman whom we love could ever suppose.

When, of her own accord, she swears to us that some man is nothing more to her than a friend, she appalls us by informing us – a thing we never suspected – that he has been her friend. While she is telling us, in proof of her sincerity, how they took tea together, that very afternoon, at each word that she utters the invisible, the unsuspected takes shape before our eyes. She admits that he has asked her to be his mistress, and we suffer agonies at the thought that she can have listened to his overtures. She refused them, she says. But presently, when we recall what she told us, we shall ask ourselves whether her story is really true, for there is wanting, between the different things that she said to us, that logical and necessary connection which, more than the facts related, is a sign of the truth. Besides, there was that terrible note of scorn in her: 'I said to him no, absolutely', which is to be found in every class of society, when a woman is lying. We must nevertheless thank her for having refused, encourage her by our kindness to repeat these cruel confidences in the future. At the most, we may remark: 'But if he had already made advances to you, why did you accept his invitation to tea?' 'So that he should not be angry with me and say that I hadn't been nice to him.' And we dare not reply that by refusing she would perhaps have been nicer to us.

Albertine alarmed me further when she said that I was quite right to say, out of regard for her reputation, that I was not her lover, since 'for that matter,' she went on, 'it's perfectly true that you aren't.' I was not her lover perhaps in the full sense of the word, but then, was I to suppose that all the things that we did together she did also with all the other men whose mistress she swore to me that she had never been? The desire to know at all costs what Albertine was thinking, whom she was seeing, with whom she was in love, how strange it was that I should be sacrificing everything to this need, since I had felt the same need to know, in the case of Gilberte, names, facts, which now left me quite indifferent. I was perfectly well aware that in themselves Albertine's actions were of no greater interest. It is curious that a first love, if by the frail state in which it leaves our heart it opens the way to our subsequent loves, does not at least provide us, in view of the identity of symptoms and sufferings, with the means of curing them.

After all, is there any need to know a fact? Are we not aware beforehand, in a general fashion, of the mendacity and even the discretion of those women who have something to conceal? Is there any possibility of error? They make a virtue of their silence, when we would give anything to make them speak. And we feel certain that they have assured their accomplice: 'I never tell anything. It won't be through me that anybody will hear about it, I never tell anything.' A man may give his fortune, his life for a person, and yet know quite well that in ten years' time, more or less, he would refuse her the fortune, prefer to keep his life. For then the person would be detached from him, alone, that is to say null and void. What attaches us to people are those thousand roots, those innumerable threads which are our memories of last night, our hopes for tomorrow morning, those continuous trammels of habit from which we can never free ourselves. Just as there are misers who hoard money from generosity, so we are spendthrifts who spend from avarice, and it is not so much to a person that we sacrifice our life as to all that the person has been able to attach to herself of our hours, our days, of the things compared with which the life not yet lived, the relatively future life, seems to us more remote, more detached, less practical, less our own. What we require is to disentangle ourselves from those trammels which are so much more important than the person, but they have the effect of creating in us temporary obligations towards her, obligations which mean that we dare not leave her for fear of being misjudged by her, whereas later on we would so dare for, detached from us, she would no longer be ourself, and because in reality we create for ourselves obligations (even if, by an apparent contradiction, they should lead to suicide) towards ourself alone.

If I was not in love with Albertine (and of this I could not be sure) then there was nothing extraordinary in the place that she occupied in my life: we live only with what we do not love, with what we have brought to live with us only to kill the intolerable love, whether it be of a woman, of a place, or again of a woman embodying a place. Indeed we should be sorely afraid to begin to love again if a further separation were to occur. I had not yet reached this stage with Albertine. Her falsehoods, her admissions, left me to complete the task of elucidating the truth: her innumerable falsehoods because she was not content with merely lying, like everyone who imagines that he or she is loved, but was by nature, quite apart from this, a liar, and so inconsistent moreover that, even if she told me the truth every time, told me what, for instance, she thought of other people, she would say each time something different; her admissions, because, being so rare, so quickly cut short, they left between them, in so far as they concerned the past, huge intervals quite blank over the whole expanse of which I was obliged to retrace – and for that first of all to learn – her life.

As for the present, so far as I could interpret the sibylline utterances of Françoise, it was not only in particular details, it was as a whole that Albertine was lying to me, and 'one fine day' I would see what Françoise made a pretence of knowing, what she refused to tell me, what I dared not ask her. It was no doubt with the same jealousy that she had felt in the past with regard to Eulalie that Françoise would speak of the most improbable things, so vague that one could at the most suppose them to convey the highly improbable insinuation that the poor captive (who was a lover of women) preferred marriage with somebody who did not appear altogether to be myself. If this were so, how, notwithstanding her power of radio-telepathy, could Françoise have come to hear of it? Certainly, Albertine's statements could give me no definite enlightenment, for they were as different day by day as the colours of a spinning-top that has almost come to a standstill. However, it seemed that it was hatred, more than anything else, that impelled Françoise to speak. Not a day went by but she said to me, and I in my mother's absence endured such speeches as: 'To be sure, you yourself are kind, and I shall never forget the debt of gratitude that I owe to you' (this probably so that I might establish fresh claims upon her gratitude) 'but the house has become a plague-spot now that kindness has set up knavery in it, now that cleverness is protecting the stupidest person that ever was seen, now that refinement, good manners, wit, dignity in everything allow to lay down the law and rule the roost and put me to shame, who have been forty years in the family – vice, everything that is most vulgar and abject.'

What Françoise resented most about Albertine was having to take orders from somebody who was not one of ourselves, and also the strain of the additional housework which was affecting the health of our old servant, who would not, for all that, accept any help in the house, not being a 'good-for-nothing'. This in itself would have accounted for her nervous exhaustion, for her furious hatred. Certainly, she would have liked to see Albertine-Esther banished from the house. This was Françoise's dearest wish. And, by consoling her, its fulfilment alone would have given our old servant some repose. But to my mind there was more in it than this. So violent a hatred could have originated only in an overstrained body. And, more even than of consideration, Françoise was in need of sleep.

Albertine went to take off her things and, so as to lose no time in finding out what I wanted to know, I attempted to telephone to Andrée; I took hold of the receiver, invoked the implacable deities, but succeeded only in arousing their fury which expressed itself in the single word 'Engaged!' Andrée was indeed engaged in talking to someone else. As I waited for her to finish her conversation, I asked myself how it was – now that so many of our painters are seeking to revive the feminine portraits of the eighteenth century, in which the cleverly devised setting is a pretext for portraying expressions of expectation, spleen, interest, distraction – how it was that none of our modern Bouchers or Fragonards had yet painted, instead of 'The Letter' or 'The Harpsichord', this scene which might be entitled 'At the Telephone', in which there would come spontaneously to the lips of the listener a smile all the more genuine in that it is conscious of being unobserved. At length, Andrée was at the other end: 'You are coming to call for Albertine tomorrow?' I asked, and as I uttered Albertine's name, thought of the envy I had felt for Swann when he said to me on the day of the Princesse de Guermantes's party: 'Come and see Odette', and I had thought how, when all was said, there must be something in a Christian name which, in the eyes of the whole world including Odette herself, had on Swann's lips alone this entirely possessive sense.

Must not such an act of possession – summed up in a single word – over the whole existence of another person (I had felt whenever I was in love) be pleasant indeed! But, as a matter of fact, when we are in a position to utter it, either we no longer care, or else habit has not dulled the force of affection, but has changed its pleasure into pain. Falsehood is a very small matter, we live in the midst of it without doing anything but smile at it, we practise it without meaning to do any harm to anyone, but our jealousy is wounded by it, and sees more than the falsehood conceals (often our mistress refuses to spend the evening with us and goes to the theatre simply so that we shall not notice that she is not looking well). How blind it often remains to what the truth is concealing! But it can extract nothing, for those women who swear that they are not lying would refuse, on the scaffold, to confess their true character. I knew that I alone was in a position to say 'Albertine' in that tone to Andrée. And yet, to Albertine, to Andrée, and to myself, I felt that I was nothing. And I realised the impossibility against which love is powerless.

We imagine that love has as its object a person whom we can see lying down before our eyes, enclosed in a human body. Alas, it is the extension of that person to all the points in space and time which the person has occupied and will occupy. If we do not possess its contact with this or that place, this or that hour, we do not possess it. But we cannot touch all these points. If only they were indicated to us, we might perhaps contrive to reach out to them. But we grope for them without finding them. Hence mistrust, jealousy, persecutions. We waste precious time upon absurd clues and pass by the truth without suspecting it.

But already one of the irascible deities, whose servants speed with the agility of lightning, was annoyed, not because I was speaking, but because I was saying nothing. 'Come along, I've been holding the line for you all this time; I shall cut you off.' However, she did nothing of the sort but, as she evoked Andrée's presence, enveloped it, like the great poet that a telephone girl always is, in the atmosphere peculiar to the home, the district, the very life itself of Albertine's friend. 'Is that you?' asked Andrée, whose voice was projected towards me with an instantaneous speed by the goddess whose privilege it is to make sound more swift than light. 'Listen,' I replied; 'go wherever you like, anywhere, except to Mme Verdurin's. Whatever happens, you simply must keep Albertine away from there tomorrow.' 'Why, that's where she promised to go tomorrow.' 'Ah!'

But I was obliged to break off the conversation for a moment and to make menacing gestures, for if Françoise continued – as though it had been something as unpleasant as vaccination or as dangerous as the aeroplane – to refuse to learn to telephone, whereby she would have spared us the trouble of conversations which she might intercept without any harm, on the other hand she would at once come into the room whenever I was engaged in a conversation so private that I was particularly anxious to keep it from her ears. When she had left the room, not without lingering to take away various things that had been lying there since the previous day and might perfectly well have been left there for an hour longer, and to place in the grate a log that was quite unnecessary in view of my burning fever at the intruder's presence and my fear of finding myself 'cut off' by the operator: 'I beg your pardon,' I said to Andrée, 'I was interrupted. Is it absolutely certain that she has to go to the Verdurins' tomorrow?' 'Absolutely, but I can tell her that you don't like it.' 'No, not at all, but it is possible that I may come with you.' 'Ah!' said Andrée, in a tone of extreme annoyance and as though alarmed by my audacity, which was all the more encouraged by her opposition. 'Then I shall say good-night, and please forgive me for disturbing you for nothing.' 'Not at all,' said Andrée, and (since nowadays, the telephone having come into general use, a decorative ritual of polite speeches has grown up round it, as round the tea-tables of the past) added: 'It has been a great pleasure to hear your voice.'

I might have said the same, and with greater truth than Andrée, for I had been deeply touched by the sound of her voice, having never before noticed that it was so different from the voices of other people. Then I recalled other voices still, women's voices especially, some of them rendered slow by the precision of a question and by mental concentration, others made breathless, even silenced at moments, by the lyrical flow of what the speakers were relating; I recalled one by one the voices of all the girls whom I had known at Balbec, then Gilberte's voice, then my grandmother's, then that of Mme de Guermantes, I found them all unlike, moulded in a language peculiar to each of the speakers, each playing upon a different instrument, and I said to myself how meagre must be the concert performed in paradise by the three or four angel musicians of the old painters, when I saw mount to the Throne of God, by tens, by hundreds, by thousands, the harmonious and multisonant salutation of all the Voices. I did not leave the telephone without thanking, in a few propitiatory words, her who reigns over the swiftness of sounds for having kindly employed on behalf of my humble words a power which made them a hundred times more rapid than thunder, but my thanksgiving received no other response than that of being cut off.

When Albertine returned to my room, she was wearing a garment of black satin which had the effect of making her seem paler, of turning her into the pallid, ardent Parisian, etiolated by want of fresh air, by the atmosphere of crowds and perhaps by vicious habits, whose eyes seemed more restless because they were not brightened by any colour in her cheeks.

'Guess,' I said to her, 'to whom I've just been talking on the telephone. Andrée!' 'Andrée?' exclaimed Albertine in a harsh tone of astonishment and emotion, which so simple a piece of intelligence seemed hardly to require. 'I hope she remembered to tell you that we met Mme Verdurin the other day.' 'Mme Verdurin? I don't remember,' I replied, as though I were thinking of something else, so as to appear indifferent to this meeting and not to betray Andrée who had told me where Albertine was going on the morrow.

But how could I tell that Andrée was not herself betraying me, and would not tell Albertine tomorrow that I had asked her to prevent her at all costs from going to the Verdurins', and had not already revealed to her that I had many times made similar appeals. She had assured me that she had never repeated anything, but the value of this assertion was counterbalanced in my mind by the impression that for some time past Albertine's face had ceased to show that confidence which she had for so long reposed in me.

What is remarkable is that, a few days before this dispute with Albertine, I had already had a dispute with her, but in Andrée's presence. Now Andrée, while she gave Albertine good advice, had always appeared to be insinuating bad. 'Come, don't talk like that, hold your tongue,' she said, as though she were at the acme of happiness. Her face assumed the dry raspberry hue of those pious housekeepers who made us dismiss each of our servants in turn. While I was heaping reproaches upon Albertine which I ought never to have uttered, Andrée looked as though she were sucking a lump of barley sugar with keen enjoyment. At length she was unable to restrain an affectionate laugh. 'Come, Titine, with me. You know, I'm your dear little sister.' I was not merely exasperated by this rather sickly exhibition, I asked myself whether Andrée really felt the affection for Albertine that she pretended to feel. Seeing that Albertine, who knew Andrée far better than I did, had always shrugged her shoulders when I asked her whether she was quite certain of Andrée's affection, and had always answered that nobody in the world cared for her more, I was still convinced that Andrée's affection was sincere. Possibly, in her wealthy but provincial family, one might find an equivalent of some of the shops in the Cathedral square, where certain sweetmeats are declared to be 'the best quality'. But I do know that, for my own part, even if I had invariably come to the opposite conclusion, I had so strong an impression that Andrée was trying to rap Albertine's knuckles that my mistress at once regained my affection and my anger subsided.

Suffering, when we are in love, ceases now and then for a moment, but only to recur in a different form. We weep to see her whom we love no longer respond to us with those outbursts of sympathy, the amorous advances of former days, we suffer more keenly still when, having lost them with us, she recovers them for the benefit of others; then, from this suffering, we are distracted by a new and still more piercing grief, the suspicion that she was lying to us about how she spent the previous evening, when she doubtless played us false; this suspicion in turn is dispelled, the kindness that our mistress is showing us soothes us, but then a word that we had forgotten comes back to our mind; someone has told us that she was ardent in moments of pleasure, whereas we have always found her calm; we try to picture to ourselves what can have been these frenzies with other people, we feel how very little we are to her, we observe an air of boredom, longing, melancholy, while we are talking, we observe like a black sky the unpretentious clothes which she puts on when she is with us, keeping for other people the garments with which she used to flatter us at first. If on the contrary she is affectionate, what joy for a moment; but when we see that little tongue outstretched as though in invitation, we think of those people to whom that invitation has so often been addressed, and that perhaps even here at home, even although Albertine was not thinking of them, it has remained, by force of long habit, an automatic signal. Then the feeling that we are bored with each other returns. But suddenly this pain is reduced to nothing when we think of the unknown evil element in her life, of the places impossible to identify where she has been, where she still goes perhaps at the hours when we are not with her, if indeed she is not planning to live there altogether, those places in which she is parted from us, does not belong to us, is happier than when she is with us. Such are the revolving searchlights of jealousy.

Jealousy is moreover a demon that cannot be exorcised, but always returns to assume a fresh incarnation. Even if we could succeed in exterminating them all, in keeping for ever her whom we love, the Spirit of Evil would then adopt another form, more pathetic still, despair at having obtained fidelity only by force, despair at not being loved.

Between Albertine and myself there was often the obstacle of a silence based no doubt upon grievances which she kept to herself, because she supposed them to be irremediable. Charming as Albertine was on some evenings, she no longer showed those spontaneous impulses which I remembered at Balbec when she used to say: 'How good you are to me all the same!' and her whole heart seemed to spring towards me without the reservation of any of those grievances which she now felt and kept to herself because she supposed them no doubt to be irremediable, impossible to forget, unconfessed, but which set up nevertheless between her and myself the significant prudence of her speech or the interval of an impassable silence.

'And may one be allowed to know why you telephoned to Andrée?' 'To ask whether she had any objection to my joining you tomorrow, so that I may pay the Verdurins the call I promised them at la Raspelière.' 'Just as you like. But I warn you, there is an appalling mist this evening, and it's sure to last over tomorrow. I mention it, because I shouldn't like you to make yourself ill. Personally, you can imagine I would far rather you came with us. However,' she added with a thoughtful air: 'I'm not at all sure that I shall go to the Verdurins'. They've been so kind to me that I ought, really . . . Next to yourself, they have been nicer to me than anybody, but there are some things about them that I don't quite like. I simply must go to the Bon Marché and the Trois-Quartiers and get a white scarf to wear with this dress which is really too black.'

Allow Albertine to go by herself into a big shop crowded with people perpetually rubbing against one, furnished with so many doors that a woman can always say that when she came out she could not find the carriage which was waiting farther along the street; I was quite determined never to consent to such a thing, but the thought of it made me extremely unhappy. And yet I did not take into account that I ought long ago to have ceased to see Albertine, for she had entered, in my life, upon that lamentable period in which a person disseminated over space and time is no longer a woman, but a series of events upon which we can throw no light, a series of insoluble problems, a sea which we absurdly attempt, Xerxes-like, to scourge, in order to punish it for what it has engulfed. Once this period has begun, we are perforce vanquished. Happy are they who understand this in time not to prolong unduly a futile, exhausting struggle, hemmed in on every side by the limits of the imagination, a struggle in which jealousy plays so sorry a part that the same man who once upon a time, if the eyes of the woman who was always by his side rested for an instant upon another man, imagined an intrigue, suffered endless torments, resigns himself in time to allowing her to go out by herself, sometimes with the man whom he knows to be her lover, preferring to the unknown this torture which at least he does know! It is a question of the rhythm to be adopted, which afterwards one follows from force of habit. Neurotics who could never stay away from a dinner-party will afterwards take rest cures which never seem to them to last long enough; women who recently were still of easy virtue live for and by acts of penitence. Jealous lovers who, in order to keep a watch upon her whom they loved, cut short their own hours of sleep, deprived themselves of rest, feeling that her own personal desires, the world, so vast and so secret, time, are stronger than they, allow her to go out without them, then to travel, and finally separate from her. Jealousy thus perishes for want of nourishment and has survived so long only by clamouring incessantly for fresh food. I was still a long way from this state.

I was now at liberty to go out with Albertine as often as I chose. As there had recently sprung up all round Paris a number of aerodromes, which are to aeroplanes what harbours are to ships, and as ever since the day when, on the way to la Raspelière, that almost mythological encounter with an airman, at whose passage overhead my horse had shied, had been to me like a symbol of liberty, I often chose to end our day's excursion – with the ready approval of Albertine, a passionate lover of every form of sport – at one of these aerodromes. We went there, she and I, attracted by that incessant stir of departure and arrival which gives so much charm to a stroll along the pier, or merely upon the beach, to those who love the sea, and to loitering about an 'aviation centre' to those who love the sky. At any moment, amid the repose of the machines that lay inert and as though at anchor, we would see one, laboriously pushed by a number of mechanics, as a boat is pushed down over the sand at the bidding of a tourist who wishes to go for an hour upon the sea. Then the engine was started, the machine ran along the ground, gathered speed, until finally, all of a sudden, at right angles, it rose slowly, in the awkward, as it were paralysed ecstasy of a horizontal speed suddenly transformed into a majestic, vertical ascent. Albertine could not contain her joy, and demanded explanations of the mechanics who, now that the machine was in the air, were strolling back to the sheds. The passenger, meanwhile, was covering mile after mile; the huge skiff, upon which our eyes remained fixed, was nothing more now in the azure than a barely visible spot, which, however, would gradually recover its solidity, size, volume, when, as the time allowed for the excursion drew to an end, the moment came for landing. And we watched with envy, Albertine and I, as he sprang to earth, the passenger who had gone up like that to enjoy at large in those solitary expanses the calm and limpidity of evening. Then, whether from the aerodrome or from some museum, some church that we had been visiting, we would return home together for dinner. And yet, I did not return home calmed, as I used to be at Balbec by less frequent excursions which I rejoiced to see extend over a whole afternoon, used afterwards to contemplate standing out like clustering flowers from the rest of Albertine's life, as against an empty sky, before which we muse pleasantly, without thinking. Albertine's time did not belong to me then in such ample quantities as today. And yet, it had seemed to me then to be much more my own, because I took into account only – my love rejoicing in them as in the bestowal of a favour – the hours that she spent with me; now – my jealousy searching anxiously among them for the possibility of a betrayal – only those hours that she spent apart from me.

Well, on the morrow she was looking forward to some such hours. I must choose, either to cease from suffering, or to cease from loving. For, just as in the beginning it is formed by desire, so afterwards love is kept in existence only by painful anxiety. I felt that part of Albertine's life was escaping me. Love, in the painful anxiety as in the blissful desire, is the insistence upon a whole. It is born, it survives only if some part remains for it to conquer. We love only what we do not wholly possess. Albertine was lying when she told me that she probably would not go to the Verdurins', as I was lying when I said that I wished to go there. She was seeking merely to dissuade me from accompanying her, and I, by my abrupt announcement of this plan, which I had no intention of putting into practice, to touch what I felt to be her most sensitive spot, to track down the desire that she was concealing and to force her to admit that my company on the morrow would prevent her from gratifying it. She had virtually made this admission by ceasing at once to wish to go to see the Verdurins.

'If you don't want to go to the Verdurins',' I told her, 'there is a splendid charity show at the Trocadéro.' She listened to my urging her to attend it with a sorrowful air. I began to be harsh with her as at Balbec, at the time of my first jealousy. Her face reflected a disappointment, and I employed, to reproach my mistress, the same arguments that had been so often advanced against myself by my parents when I was little, and had appeared unintelligent and cruel to my misunderstood childhood. 'No, for all your melancholy air,' I said to Albertine, 'I cannot feel any pity for you; I should feel sorry for you if you were ill, if you were in trouble, if you had suffered some bereavement; not that you would mind that in the least, I dare say, since you pour out false sentiment over every trifle. Anyhow, I have no opinion of the feelings of people who pretend to be so fond of us and are quite incapable of doing us the slightest service, and whose minds wander so that they forget to deliver the letter we have entrusted to them, on which our whole future depends.'

These words – a great part of what we say being no more than a recitation from memory – I had heard spoken, all of them, by my mother, who was ever ready to explain to me that we ought not to confuse true feeling, what (she said) the Germans, whose language she greatly admired not-withstanding my father's horror of their nation, called *Empfindung*, and affectation or *Empfindelei*. She had gone so far, once when I was in tears, as to tell me that Nero probably suffered from his nerves and was none the better for that. Indeed, like those plants which bifurcate as they grow, side by side with the sensitive boy which was all that I had been, there was now a man of the opposite sort, full of common sense, of severity towards the morbid sensibility of others, a man resembling what my parents had been to me. No doubt, as each of us is obliged to continue in himself the life of his forebears, the balanced, cynical man who did not exist in me at the start had joined forces with the sensitive one, and it was natural that I should become in my turn what my parents had been to me.

What is more, at the moment when this new personality took shape in me, he found his language ready made in the memory of the speeches, ironical and scolding, that had been addressed to me, that I must now address to other people, and which came so naturally to my lips, whether I evoked them by mimicry and association of memories, or because the delicate and mysterious enchantments of the reproductive power had traced in me unawares, as upon the leaf of a plant, the same intonations, the same gestures, the same attitudes as had been adopted by the people from whom I sprang. For sometimes, as I was playing the wise counsellor in conversation with Albertine, I seemed to be listening to my grandmother; had it not, moreover, occurred to my mother (so many obscure unconscious currents inflected everything in me down to the tiniest movements of my fingers even, to follow the same cycles as those of my parents) to imagine that it was my father at the door, so similar was my knock to his.

On the other hand the coupling of contrary elements is the law of life, the principle of fertilisation, and, as we shall see, the cause of many disasters. As a general rule, we detest what resembles ourself, and our own faults when observed in another person infuriate us. How much the more does a man who has passed the age at which we instinctively display them, a man who, for instance, has gone through the most burning moments with an icy countenance, execrate those same faults, if it is another man, younger or simpler or stupider, that is displaying them. There are sensitive people to whom merely to see in other people's eyes the tears which they themselves have repressed is infuriating. It is because the similarity is too great that, in spite of family affection, and sometimes all the more the greater the affection is, families are divided.

Possibly in myself, and in many others, the second man that I had become was simply another aspect of the former man, excitable and sensitive in his own affairs, a sage mentor to other people. Perhaps it was so also with my parents according to whether they were regarded in relation to myself or in themselves. In the case of my grandmother and mother it was as clear as daylight that their severity towards myself was deliberate on their part and indeed cost them a serious effort, but perhaps in my father himself his coldness was but an external aspect of his sensibility. For it was perhaps the human truth of this twofold aspect: the side of private life, the side of social relations, that was expressed in a sentence which seemed to me at the time as false in its matter as it was commonplace in form, when someone remarked, speaking of my father: 'Beneath his icy chill, he conceals an extraordinary sensibility; what is really wrong with him is that he is ashamed of his own feelings.'

Did it not, after all, conceal incessant secret storms, that calm (interspersed if need be with sententious reflections, irony at the maladroit exhibitions of sensibility) which was his, but which now I too was affecting in my relations with everybody and never laid aside in certain circumstances of my relations with Albertine?

I really believe that I came near that day to making up my mind to break with her and to start for Venice. What bound me afresh in my chains had to do with Normandy, not that she showed any inclination to go to that region where I had been jealous of her (for it was my good fortune that her plans never impinged upon the painful spots in my memory), but because when I had said to her: 'It is just as though I were to speak to you of your aunt's friend who lived at Infreville,' she replied angrily, delighted – like everyone in a discussion, who is anxious to muster as many arguments as possible on his side – to show me that I was in the wrong and herself in the right: 'But my aunt never knew anybody at Infreville, and I have never been near the place.'

She had forgotten the lie that she had told me one afternoon about the susceptible lady with whom she simply must take tea, even if by going to visit this lady she were to forfeit my friendship and shorten her own life. I did not remind her of her lie. But it appalled me. And once again I postponed our rupture to another day. A person has no need of sincerity, nor even of skill in lying, in order to be loved. I here give the name of love to a mutual torment. I saw nothing reprehensible this evening in speaking to her as my grandmother – that mirror of perfection – used to speak to me, nor, when I told her that I would escort her to the Verdurins', in having adopted my father's abrupt manner, who would never inform us of any decision except in the manner calculated to cause us the maximum of agitation, out of all proportion to the decision itself. So that it was easy for him to call us absurd for appearing so distressed by so small a matter, our distress corresponding in reality to the emotion that he had aroused in us. Since – like the inflexible wisdom of my grandmother – these arbitrary moods of my father had been passed on to myself to complete the sensitive nature to which they had so long remained alien, and, throughout my whole childhood, had caused so much suffering, that sensitive nature informed them very exactly as to the points at which they must take careful aim: there is no better informer than a reformed thief, or a subject of the nation we are fighting. In certain untruthful families, a brother who has come to call upon his brother without any apparent reason and asks him, quite casually, on the doorstep, as he is going away, for some information to which he does not even appear to listen, indicates thereby to his brother that this information was the main object of his visit, for the brother is quite familiar with that air of detachment, those words uttered as though in parentheses and at the last moment, having frequently had recourse to them himself. Well, there are also pathological families, kindred sensibilities, fraternal temperaments, initiated into that mute language which enables people in the family circle to make themselves understood without speaking. And who can be more nerve-racking than a neurotic? Besides, my conduct, in these cases, may have had a more general, a more profound cause. I mean that in those brief but inevitable moments, when we detest someone whom we love – moments which last sometimes for a whole lifetime in the case of people whom we do not love – we do not wish to appear good, so as not to be pitied, but at once as wicked and as happy as possible so that our happiness may be truly hateful and may ulcerate the soul of the occasional or permanent enemy. To how many people have I not untruthfully slandered myself, simply in order that my 'successes' might seem to them immoral and make them all the more angry! The proper thing to do would be to take the opposite course, to show without arrogance that we have generous feelings, instead of taking such pains to hide them. And it would be easy if we were able never to hate, to love all the time. For then we should be so glad to say only the things that can make other people happy, melt their hearts, make them love us.

To be sure, I felt some remorse at being so irritating to Albertine, and said to myself: 'If I did not love her, she would be more grateful to me, for I should not be nasty to her; but no, it would be the same in the end, for I should also be less nice.' And I might, in order to justify myself, have told her that I loved her. But the confession of that love, apart from the fact that it could not have told Albertine anything new, would perhaps have made her colder to myself than the harshness and deceit for which love was the sole excuse. To be harsh and deceitful to the person whom we love is so natural! If the interest that we show in other people does not prevent us from being kind to them and complying with their wishes, then our interest is not sincere. A stranger leaves us indifferent, and indifference does not prompt us to unkind actions.

The evening passed. Before Albertine went to bed, there was no time to lose if we wished to make peace, to renew our embraces. Neither of us had yet taken the initiative. Feeling that, anyhow, she was angry with me already, I took advantage of her anger to mention Esther Levy. 'Bloch tells me' (this was untrue) 'that you are a great friend of his cousin Esther.' 'I shouldn't know her if I saw her,' said Albertine with a vague air. 'I have seen her photograph,' I continued angrily. I did not look at Albertine as I said this, so that I did not see her expression, which would have been her sole reply, for she said nothing.

It was no longer the peace of my mother's kiss at Combray that I felt when I was with Albertine on these evenings, but, on the contrary, the anguish of those on which my mother scarcely bade me good-night, or even did not come up at all to my room, whether because she was vexed with me or was kept downstairs by guests. This anguish – not merely its transposition in terms of love – no, this anguish itself which had at one time been specialised in love, which had been allocated to love alone when the division, the distribution of the passions took effect, seemed now to be extending again to them all, become indivisible again as in my childhood, as though all my sentiments which trembled at the thought of my not being able to keep Albertine by my bedside, at once as a mistress, a sister, a daughter; as a mother too, of whose regular good-night kiss I was beginning again to feel the childish need, had begun to coalesce, to unify in the premature evening of my life which seemed fated to be as short as a day in winter. But if I felt the anguish of my childhood, the change of person that made me feel it, the difference of the sentiment that it inspired in me, the very transformation in my character, made it impossible for me to demand the soothing of that anguish from Albertine as in the old days from my mother.

I could no longer say: 'I am unhappy.' I confined myself, with death at my heart, to speaking of unimportant things which afforded me no progress towards a happy solution. I waded knee-deep in painful platitudes. And with that intellectual egoism which, if only some insignificant fact has a bearing upon our love, makes us pay great respect to the person who has discovered it, as fortuitously perhaps as the fortune-teller who has foretold some trivial event which has afterwards come to pass, I came near to regarding Françoise as more inspired than Bergotte and Elstir because she had said to me at Balbec: 'That girl will only land you in trouble.'

Every minute brought me nearer to Albertine's good-night, which at length she said. But this evening her kiss, from which she herself was absent, and which did not encounter myself, left me so anxious that, with a throbbing heart, I watched her make her way to the door, thinking: 'If I am to find a pretext for calling her back, keeping her here, making peace with her, I must make haste; only a few steps and she will be out of the room, only two, now one, she is turning the handle; she is opening the door, it is too late, she has shut it behind her!' Perhaps it was not too late, all the same. As in the old days at Combray when my mother had left me without soothing me with her kiss, I wanted to dart in pursuit of Albertine, I felt that there would be no peace for me until I had seen her again, that this next meeting was to be something immense which no such meeting had ever yet been, and that – if I did not succeed by my own efforts in ridding myself of this melancholy – I might perhaps acquire the shameful habit of going to beg from Albertine. I sprang out of bed when she was already in her room, I paced up and down the corridor, hoping that she would come out of her room and call me; I stood without breathing outside her door for fear of failing to hear some faint summons, I returned for a moment to my own room to see whether my mistress had not by some lucky chance forgotten her handkerchief, her bag, something which I might have appeared to be afraid of her wanting during the night, and which would have given me an excuse for going to her room. No, there was nothing. I returned to my station outside her door, but the crack beneath it no longer showed any light. Albertine had put out the light, she was in bed, I remained there motionless, hoping for some lucky accident but none occurred; and long afterwards, frozen, I returned to bestow myself between my own sheets and cried all night long.

But there were certain evenings also when I had recourse to a ruse which won me Albertine's kiss. Knowing how quickly sleep came to her as soon as she lay down (she knew it also, for, instinctively, before lying down, she would take off her slippers, which I had given her, and her ring which she placed by the bedside, as she did in her own room when she went to bed), knowing how heavy her sleep was, how affectionate her awakening, I would plead the excuse of going to look for something and make her lie down upon my bed. When I returned to the room she was asleep and I saw before me the other woman that she became whenever one saw her full face. But she very soon changed her identity, for I lay down by her side and recaptured her profile. I could place my hand in her hand, on her shoulder, on her cheek. Albertine continued to sleep.

I might take her head, turn it round, press it to my lips, encircle my neck in

her arms, she continued to sleep like a watch that does not stop, like an
animal that goes on living whatever position you assign to it, like a climbing
plant, a convulvulus which continues to thrust out its tendrils whatever
support you give it. Only her breathing was altered by every touch of my
fingers, as though she had been an instrument on which I was playing and
from which I extracted modulations by drawing from first one, then another
of its strings different notes. My jealousy grew calm, for I felt that Albertine
had become a creature that breathes, that is nothing else besides, as was
indicated by that regular breathing in which is expressed that pure physiological function which, wholly fluid, has not the solidity either of speech or
of silence; and, in its ignorance of all evil, her breath, drawn (it seemed)
rather from a hollowed reed than from a human being, was truly paradisal,
was the pure song of the angels to me who, at these moments, felt Albertine
to be withdrawn from everything, not only materially but morally. And yet
in that breathing, I said to myself of a sudden that perhaps many names of
people borne on the stream of memory must be playing. Sometimes indeed
to that music the human voice was added. Albertine uttered a few words.
How I longed to catch their meaning! It happened that the name of a person
of whom we had been speaking and who had aroused my jealousy came to
her lips, but without making me unhappy, for the memory that it brought
with it seemed to be only that of the conversations that she had had with me
upon the subject. This evening, however, when with her eyes still shut she
was half awake, she said, addressing myself: 'Andrée.' I concealed my
emotion. 'You are dreaming, I am not Andrée,' I said to her, smiling. She
smiled also. 'Of course not, I wanted to ask you what Andrée was saying to
you.' 'I should have supposed that you were used to lying like this by her
side.' 'Oh no, never,' she said. Only, before making this reply, she had
hidden her face for a moment in her hands. So her silences were merely
screens, her surface affection merely kept beneath the surface a thousand
memories which would have rent my heart, her life was full of those
incidents the derisive account, the comic history of which form our daily
gossip at the expense of other people, people who do not matter, but which,
so long as a person remains lost in the dark forest of our heart, seem to us so
precious a revelation of her life that, for the privilege of exploring that
subterranean world, we would gladly sacrifice our own. Then her sleep
appeared to me a marvellous and magic world in which at certain moments
there rises from the depths of the barely translucent element the confession
of a secret which we shall not understand. But as a rule, when Albertine was
asleep, she seemed to have recovered her innocence. In the attitude which I
had imposed upon her, but which in her sleep she had speedily made her

own, she looked as though she were trusting herself to me! Her face had lost any expression of cunning or vulgarity, and between herself and me, towards whom she was raising her arm, upon whom her hand was resting, there seemed to be an absolute surrender, an indissoluble attachment. Her sleep moreover did not separate her from me and allowed her to retain her consciousness of our affection; its effect was rather to abolish everything else; I embraced her, told her that I was going to take a turn outside, she half-opened her eyes, said to me with an air of astonishment – indeed the hour was late: 'But where are you off to, my darling – ' calling me by my Christian name, and at once fell asleep again. Her sleep was only a sort of obliteration of the rest of her life, a continuous silence over which from time to time would pass in their flight words of intimate affection. By putting these words together, you would have arrived at the unalloyed conversation, the secret intimacy of a pure love. This calm slumber delighted me, as a mother is delighted, reckoning it among his virtues, by the sound sleep of her child. And her sleep was indeed that of a child. Her waking also, and so natural, so loving, before she even knew where she was, that I sometimes asked myself with terror whether she had been in the habit, before coming to live with me, of not sleeping by herself but of finding, when she opened her eyes, someone lying by her side. But her childish charm was more striking. Like a mother again, I marvelled that she should always awake in so good a humour. After a few moments she recovered consciousness, uttered charming words, unconnected with one another, mere bird-pipings. By a sort of 'general post' her throat, which as a rule passed unnoticed, now almost startlingly beautiful, had acquired the immense importance which her eyes, by being closed in sleep, had forfeited, her eyes, my regular informants to which I could no longer address myself after the lids had closed over them. Just as the closed lids impart an innocent, grave beauty to the face by suppressing all that the eyes express only too plainly, there was in the words, not devoid of meaning, but interrupted by moments of silence, which Albertine uttered as she awoke, a pure beauty that is not at every moment polluted, as is conversation, by habits of speech, commonplaces, traces of blemish. Anyhow, when I had decided to wake Albertine, I had been able to do so without fear, I knew that her awakening would bear no relation to the evening that we had passed together, but would emerge from her sleep as morning emerges from night. As soon as she had begun to open her eyes with a smile, she had offered me her lips, and before she had even uttered a word, I had tasted their fresh savour, as soothing as that of a garden still silent before the break of day.

On the morrow of that evening when Albertine had told me that she would perhaps be going, then that she would not be going to see the Verdurins, I awoke early, and, while I was still half asleep, my joy informed me that there was, interpolated in the winter, a day of spring. Outside, popular themes skilfully transposed for various instruments, from the horn of the mender of porcelain, or the trumpet of the chair weaver, to the flute of the goat driver who seemed, on a fine morning, to be a Sicilian goatherd, were lightly orchestrating the matutinal air, with an 'Overture for a Public Holiday'. Our hearing, that delicious sense, brings us the company of the street, every line of which it traces for us, sketches all the figures that pass along it, showing us their colours. The iron shutters of the baker's shop, of the dairy, which had been lowered last night over every possibility of feminine bliss, were rising now like the canvas of a ship which is setting sail and about to proceed, crossing the transparent sea, over a vision of young female assistants. This sound of the iron curtain being raised would perhaps have been my sole pleasure in a different part of the town. In this quarter a hundred other sounds contributed to my joy, of which I would not have lost a single one by remaining too long asleep. It is the magic charm of the old aristocratic quarters that they are at the same time plebeian. Just as, sometimes, cathedrals used to have them within a stone's throw of their porches (which have even preserved the name, like the porch of Rouen styled the Booksellers', because these latter used to expose their merchandise in the open air against its walls), so various minor trades, but peripatetic, used to pass in front of the noble Hôtel de Guermantes, and made one think at times of the ecclesiastical France of long ago. For the appeal which they launched at the little houses on either side had, with rare exceptions, nothing of a song. It differed from song as much as the declamation – barely coloured by imperceptible modulations – of *Boris Godounov* and *Pelléas*; but on the other hand recalled the psalmody of a priest chanting his office of which these street scenes are but the good-humoured, secular, and yet half liturgical counterpart. Never had I so delighted in them as since Albertine had come to live with me; they seemed to me a joyous signal of her awakening, and by interesting me in the life of the world outside made me all the more conscious of the soothing virtue of a beloved presence, as constant as I could wish. Several of the foodstuffs cried in the street, which personally I detested, were greatly to Albertine's liking, so much so that Françoise used to send her young footman out to buy them, slightly humiliated perhaps at finding himself mingled with the plebeian crowd. Very distinct in this peaceful quarter (where the noise was no longer a cause of lamentation to Françoise and had become a source of pleasure to myself), there came to me, each with its different modulation, recitatives declaimed by those humble folk as they would be in the music – so entirely popular – of *Boris*, where an initial intonation is barely altered by the inflection of one note which rests upon another, the music of the crowd which is more a language than a music. It was '*ah! le bigorneau, deux sous le bigorneau*', which brought people running to the cornets in which were sold those horrid little shellfish, which, if Albertine had not been there, would have disgusted me, just as the snails disgusted me which I heard cried for sale at the same hour. Here again it was of the barely lyrical declamation of Moussorgsky that the vendor reminded me, but not of it alone. For after having almost 'spoken': '*Les escargots, ils sont frais, ils sont beaux*', it was with the vague melancholy of Maeterlinck, transposed into music by Debussy, that the snail vendor, in one of those pathetic finales in which the composer of *Pelléas* shows his kinship with Rameau: 'If vanquished I must be, is it for thee to be my vanquisher?' added with a singsong melancholy: '*On les vend six sous la douzaine . . .*'

I have always found it difficult to understand why these perfectly simple words were sighed in a tone so far from appropriate, mysterious, like the secret which makes everyone look sad in the old palace to which Mélisande has not succeeded in bringing joy, and profound as one of the thoughts of the aged Arkel who seeks to utter, in the simplest words, the whole lore of wisdom and destiny. The very notes upon which rises with an increasing sweetness the voice of the old King of Allemonde or that of Goland, to say: 'We know not what is happening here, it may seem strange, maybe nought that happens is in vain', or else: 'No cause here for alarm, 'twas a poor little mysterious creature, like all the world', were those which served the snail vendor to resume, in an endless cadenza: '*On les vend six sous la douzaine . . .*' But this metaphysical lamentation had not time to expire upon the shore of the infinite, it was interrupted by a shrill trumpet. This time, it was no question of victuals, the words of the libretto were: '*Tond les chiens, coupe les chats, les queues et les oreilles.*'

It was true that the fantasy, the spirit of each vendor or vendress frequently introduced variations into the words of all these chants that I used to hear from my bed. And yet a ritual suspension interposing a silence in the middle of a word, especially when it was repeated a second time, constantly reminded me of some old church. In his little cart drawn by a she-ass which he stopped in front of each house before entering the courtyard, the old-clothes man, brandishing a whip, intoned: '*Habits, marchand d'habits, ha . . . bits*' with the same pause between the final syllables as if he had been intoning in plain chant: '*Per omnia saecula saeculo . . . rum*' or '*requiescat in pa . . . ce*' albeit he had no reason to believe in the immortality of his clothes, nor did he offer them as cerements for the supreme repose in peace. And similarly, as the motifs were beginning, even at this early hour, to become confused, a vegetable woman, pushing her little hand-cart, was using for her litany the Gregorian division:

> A la tendresse, à la verduresse,
> Artichauts tendres et beaux,
> Arti . . . chauts.

although she had probably never heard of the antiphonal, or of the seven tones that symbolise four the sciences of the *quadrivium* and three those of the *trivium*.

Drawing from a penny whistle, from a bagpipe, airs of his own southern country whose sunlight harmonised well with these fine days, a man in a blouse, wielding a bull's pizzle in his hand and wearing a basque *béret* on his head, stopped before each house in turn. It was the goatherd with two dogs driving before him his string of goats. As he came from a distance, he arrived fairly late in our quarter; and the women came running out with bowls to receive the milk that was to give strength to their little ones. But with the Pyrenean airs of this good shepherd was now blended the bell of the grinder, who cried: '*Couteaux, ciseaux, rasoirs.*' With him the saw-setter was unable to compete, for, lacking an instrument, he had to be content with calling: '*Avez-vous des scies à repasser, v'la le repasseur,*' while in a gayer mood the tinker, after enumerating the pots, pans and everything else that he repaired, intoned the refrain:

> Tam, tam, tam,
> C'est moi qui rétame
> Même le macadam,
> C'est moi qui mets des fonds partout,
> Qui bouche tous les trous, trou, trou;

and young Italians carrying big iron boxes painted red, upon which the numbers – winning and losing – were marked, and springing their rattles, gave the invitation: '*Amusez-vous, mesdames, v'là le plaisir.*'

Françoise brought in the *Figaro*. A glance was sufficient to show me that my article had not yet appeared. She told me that Albertine had asked whether she might come to my room and sent word that she had quite given up the idea of calling upon the Verdurins, and had decided to go, as I had advised her, to the 'special' matinée at the Trocadéro – what nowadays would be called, though with considerably less significance, a 'gala' matinée – after a short ride which she had promised to take with Andrée. Now that I knew that she had renounced her desire, possibly evil, to go and see Mme Verdurin, I said with a laugh: 'Tell her to come in', and told myself that she might go where she chose and that it was all the same to me. I knew that by the end of the afternoon, when dusk began to fall, I should probably be a different man, moping, attaching to every one of Albertine's movements an importance that they did not possess at this morning hour when the weather was so fine. For my indifference was accompanied by a clear notion of its cause, but was in no way modified by it. 'Françoise assured me that you were awake and that I should not be disturbing you,' said Albertine as she entered the room. And since next to making me catch cold by opening the window at the wrong moment, what Albertine most dreaded was to come into my room when I was asleep: 'I hope I have not done anything wrong,' she went on. 'I was afraid you would say to me: What insolent mortal comes here to meet his doom?' and she laughed that laugh which I always found so disturbing. I replied in the same vein of pleasantry: 'Was it for you this stern decree was made?' – and, lest she should ever venture to break it, added: 'Although I should be furious if you did wake me.' 'I know, I know, don't be frightened,' said Albertine. And, to relieve the situation, I went on, still enacting the scene from *Esther* with her, while in the street below the cries continued, drowned by our conversation: 'I find in you alone a certain grace That charms me and of which I never tire' (and to myself I thought: 'yes, she does tire me very often'). And remembering what she had said to me overnight, as I thanked her extravagantly for having given up the Verdurins, so that another time she would obey me similarly with regard to something else, I said: 'Albertine, you distrust me who love you and you place your trust in other people who do not love you' (as though it were not natural to distrust the people who love us and who alone have an interest in lying to us in order to find out things, to hinder us), and added these lying words: 'You don't really believe that I love you, which is amusing. As a matter of fact, I don't *adore* you.' She lied in her turn when she told me that she trusted nobody but myself and then became sincere when she assured me that she knew very well that I loved her. But this affirmation did not seem to imply that she did not believe me to be a liar and a spy. And she seemed to pardon me as though she had seen these defects to be the agonising consequence of a strong passion or as though she herself had felt herself to be less good. 'I beg of you, my dearest girl, no more of that *haute voltige* you were practising the other day. Just think, Albertine, if you were to meet with an accident!' Of course I did not wish her any harm. But what a pleasure it would be if, with her horses, she should take it into her head to ride off somewhere, wherever she chose, and never to return again to my house. How it would simplify everything, that she should go and live happily somewhere else, I did not even wish to know where. 'Oh! I know you wouldn't survive me for more than a day; you would commit suicide.'

So we exchanged lying speeches. But a truth more profound than that which we would utter were we sincere may sometimes be expressed and announced by another channel than that of sincerity. 'You don't mind all that noise outside,' she asked me; 'I love it. But you're such a light sleeper anyhow.' I was on the contrary an extremely heavy sleeper (as I have already said, but I am obliged to repeat it in view of what follows), especially when I did not begin to sleep until the morning. As this kind of sleep is – on an average – four times as refreshing, it seems to the awakened sleeper to have lasted four times as long, when it has really been four times as short. A splendid, sixteenfold error in multiplication which gives so much beauty to our awakening and makes life begin again on a different scale, like those great changes of rhythm which, in music, mean that in an andante a quaver has the same duration as a minim in a prestissimo, and which are unknown in our waking state. There life is almost always the same, whence the disappointments of travel. It may seem indeed that our dreams are composed of the coarsest stuff of life, but that stuff is treated, kneaded so thoroughly, with a protraction due to the fact that none of the temporal limitations of the waking state is there to prevent it from spinning itself out to heights so vast that we fail to recognise it. On the mornings after this good fortune had befallen me, after the sponge of sleep had obliterated from my brain the signs of everyday occupations that are traced upon it as upon a blackboard, I was obliged to bring my memory back to life; by the exercise of our will we can recapture what the amnesia of sleep or of a stroke has made us forget, what gradually returns to us as our eyes open or our paralysis disappears. I had lived through so many hours in a few minutes that, wishing to address Françoise, for whom I had rung, in language that corresponded to the facts of real life and was regulated by the clock, I was obliged to exert all my power of internal repression in order not to say: 'Well, Françoise, here we are at five o'clock in the evening and I haven't set eyes on you since yesterday afternoon.' And seeking to dispel my dreams, giving them the lie and lying to myself as well, I said boldly, compelling myself with all my might to silence, the direct opposite: 'Françoise, it must be at least ten!' I did not even say ten o'clock in the morning, but simply ten, so that this incredible hour might appear to be uttered in a more natural tone. And yet to say these words, instead of those that continued to run in the mind of the half-awakened sleeper that I still was, demanded the same effort of equilibrium that a man requires when he jumps out of a moving train and runs for some yards along the platform, if he is to avoid falling. He runs for a moment because the environment that he has just left was one animated by great velocity, and utterly unlike the inert soil upon which his feet find it difficult to keep their balance.

Because the dream world is not the waking world, it does not follow that the waking world is less genuine, far from it. In the world of sleep, our perceptions are so overcharged, each of them increased by a counterpart which doubles its bulk and blinds it to no purpose, that we are not able even to distinguish what is happening in the bewilderment of awakening; was it Françoise that had come to me, or I that, tired of waiting, went to her? Silence at that moment was the only way not to reveal anything, as at the moment when we are brought before a magistrate cognisant of all the charges against us, when we have not been informed of them ourselves. Was it Françoise that had come, was it I that had summoned her? Was it not, indeed, Françoise that had been asleep and I that had just awoken her; nay more, was not Françoise enclosed in my breast, for the distinction between persons and their reaction upon one another barely exists in that murky obscurity in which reality is as little translucent as in the body of a porcupine, and our all but non-existent perception may perhaps furnish an idea of the perception of certain animals. Besides, in the limpid state of unreason that precedes these heavy slumbers, if fragments of wisdom float there luminously, if the names of Taine and George Eliot are not unknown, the waking life does still retain the superiority, inasmuch as it is possible to continue it every morning, whereas it is not possible to continue the dream life every night. But are there perhaps other worlds more real than the waking world? Even it we have seen transformed by every revolution in the arts, and still more, at the same time, by the degree of proficiency and culture that distinguishes an artist from an ignorant fool.

And often an extra hour of sleep is a paralytic stroke after which we must recover the use of our limbs, learn to speak. Our will would not be adequate for this task. We have slept too long, we no longer exist. Our waking is barely felt, mechanically and without consciousness, as a water pipe might feel the turning off of a tap. A life more inanimate than that of the jellyfish follows, in which we could equally well believe that we had been drawn up from the depths of the sea or released from prison, were we but capable of thinking anything at all. But then from the highest heaven the goddess Mnemotechnia bends down and holds out to us in the formula 'the habit of ringing for our coffee' the hope of resurrection. However, the instantaneous gift of memory is not always so simple. Often we have before us, in those first minutes in which we allow ourself to slip into the waking state, a truth composed of different realities among which we imagine that we can choose, as among a pack of cards.

It is Friday morning and we have just returned from our walk, or else it is teatime by the sea. The idea of sleep and that we are lying in bed and in our nightshirt is often the last that occurs to us.

Our resurrection is not effected at once; we think that we have rung the bell, we have not done so, we utter senseless remarks. Movement alone restores our thought, and when we have actually pressed the electric button we are able to say slowly but distinctly: 'It must be at least ten o'clock, Françoise, bring me my coffee.' Oh, the miracle! Françoise could have had no suspicion of the sea of unreality in which I was still wholly immersed and through which I had had the energy to make my strange question pass. Her answer was: 'It is ten past ten.' Which made my remark appear quite reasonable, and enabled me not to let her perceive the fantastic conversations by which I had been interminably beguiled, on days when it was not a mountain of non-existence that had crushed all life out of me. By strength of will, I had reinstated myself in life. I was still enjoying the last shreds of sleep, that is to say of the only inventiveness, the only novelty that exists in storytelling, since none of our narrations in the waking state, even though they be adorned with literary graces, admit those mysterious differences from which beauty derives. It is easy to speak of the beauty created by opium. But to a man who is accustomed to sleeping only with the aid of drugs, an unexpected hour of natural sleep will reveal the vast, matutinal expanse of a country as mysterious and more refreshing. By varying the hour, the place at which we go to sleep, by wooing sleep in an artificial manner, or on the contrary by returning for once to natural sleep – the strangest kind of all to whoever is in the habit of putting himself to sleep with soporifics – we succeed in producing a thousand times as many varieties of sleep as a gardener could produce of carnations or roses. Gardeners produce flowers that are delicious dreams, and others too that are like nightmares. When I fell asleep in a certain way I used to wake up shivering, thinking that I had caught the measles, or, what was far more painful, that my grandmother (to whom I never gave a thought now) was hurt because I had laughed at her that day when, at Balbec, in the belief that she was about to die, she had wished me to have a photograph of herself. At once, albeit I was awake, I felt that I must go and explain to her that she had misunderstood me. But, already, my bodily warmth was returning. The diagnosis of measles was set aside, and my grandmother became so remote that she no longer made my heart throb. Sometimes over these different kinds of sleep there fell a sudden darkness. I was afraid to continue my walk along an entirely unlighted avenue, where I could hear prowling footsteps. Suddenly a dispute broke out between a policeman and one of those women whom one often saw driving hackney carriages, and mistook at a distance for young men. Upon her box among the shadows I could not see her, but she spoke, and in her voice I could read the perfections of her face and the youthfulness of her body. I strode towards her, in the darkness, to get into her carriage before she drove off. It was a long way. Fortunately, her dispute with the policeman continued. I overtook the carriage which was still drawn up. This part of the avenue was lighted by street lamps. The driver became visible. She was indeed a woman, but old and corpulent, with white hair tumbling beneath her hat, and a red birthmark on her face. I walked past her, thinking: Is this what happens to the youth of women? Those whom we have met in the past, if suddenly we desire to see them again, have they become old? Is the young woman whom we desire like a character on the stage, when, unable to secure the actress who created the part, the management is obliged to entrust it to a new star? But then it is no longer the same.

With this a feeling of melancholy invaded me. We have thus in our sleep a number of Pities, like the 'Pietà' of the Renaissance, but not, like them, wrought in marble, being, rather, unsubstantial. They have their purpose, however, which is to make us remember a certain outlook upon things, more tender, more human, which we are too apt to forget in the common sense, frigid, sometimes full of hostility, of the waking state. Thus I was reminded of the vow that I had made at Balbec that I would always treat Françoise with compassion. And for the whole of that morning at least I would manage to compel myself not to be irritated by Françoise's quarrels with the butler, to be gentle with Françoise to whom the others showed so little kindness. For that morning only, and I would have to try to frame a code that was a little more permanent; for, just as nations are not governed for any length of time by a policy of pure sentiment, so men are not governed by the memory of their dreams. Already this dream was beginning to fade away. In attempting to recall it in order to portray it I made it fade all the faster. My eyelids were no longer so firmly sealed over my eyes. If I tried to reconstruct my dream, they opened completely. At every moment we must choose between health and sanity on the one hand, and spiritual pleasures on the other. I have always taken the cowardly part of choosing the former. Moreover, the perilous power that I was renouncing was even more perilous than we suppose. Pities, dreams, do not fly away unaccompanied. When we alter thus the conditions in which we go to sleep, it is not our dreams alone that fade, but, for days on end, for years it may be, the faculty not merely of dreaming but of going to sleep. Sleep is divine but by no means stable; the slightest shock makes it volatile. A lover of habits, which retain it every night, being more fixed than itself, in the place set apart for it, which preserve it from all injury, but if we displace it, if it is no longer subordinated, it melts away like a vapour. It is like youth and love, never to be recaptured.

In these various forms of sleep, as likewise in music, it was the lengthening or shortening of the interval that created beauty. I enjoyed this beauty, but, on the other hand, I had lost in my sleep, however brief, a good number of the cries which render perceptible to us the peripatetic life of the tradesmen, the victuallers of Paris. And so, as a habit (without, alas, foreseeing the drama in which these late awakenings and the Draconian, Medo-Persian laws of a Racinian Assuérus were presently to involve me) I made an effort to awaken early so as to lose none of these cries.

And, more than the pleasure of knowing how fond Albertine was of them and of being out of doors myself without leaving my bed, I heard in them as it were the symbol of the atmosphere of the world outside, of the dangerous stirring life through the veins of which I did not allow her to move save under my tutelage, from which I withdrew her at the hour of my choosing to make her return home to my side. And so it was with the most perfect sincerity that I was able to say in answer to Albertine: 'On the contrary, they give me pleasure because I know that you like them.' '*A la barque, les huîtres, à la barque.*' 'Oh, oysters! I've been simply longing for some!' Fortunately Albertine, partly from inconsistency, partly from docility, quickly forgot the things for which she had been longing, and before I had time to tell her that she would find better oysters at Prunier's, she wanted in succession all the things that she heard cried by the fish hawker: '*A la crevette, à la bonne crevette, j'ai de la raie toute en vie, toute en vie.*' '*Merlans à frire, à frire.*' '*Il arrive le maquereau, maquereau frais, maquereau nouveau.*' '*Voilà le maquereau, mesdames, il est beau le maquereau.*' '*A la moule fraîche et bonne, à la moule!*' In spite of myself, the warning: '*Il arrive le maquereau*' made me shudder. But as this warning could not, I felt, apply to our chauffeur, I thought only of the fish of that name, which I detested, and my uneasiness did not last. 'Ah! Mussels,' said Albertine, 'I should so like some mussels.' 'My darling! They were all very well at Balbec, here they're not worth eating; besides, I implore you, remember what Cottard told you about mussels.' But my remark was all the more ill-chosen in that the vegetable woman who came next announced a thing that Cottard had forbidden even more strictly:

A la romaine, à la romaine!
On ne le vend pas, on la promène.

Albertine consented, however, to sacrifice her lettuces, on the condition that I would promise to buy for her in a few days' time from the woman who cried: '*J'ai de la belle asperge d'Argenteuil, j'ai de la belle asperge.*' A mysterious voice, from which one would have expected some stranger utterance, insinuated: '*Tonneaux, tonneaux!*' We were obliged to remain under the disappointment that nothing more was being offered us than barrels, for the word was almost entirely drowned by the appeal: '*Vitri, vitri–er, carreaux cassés, voilà le vitrier, vitri–er*', a Gregorian division which reminded me less, however, of the liturgy than did the appeal of the rag vendor, reproducing unconsciously one of those abrupt interruptions of sound, in the middle of a prayer, which are common enough in the ritual of the church: '*Praeceptis salutaribus moniti et divina institutione formati audemus dicere*', says the priest, ending sharply upon '*dicere*'. Without irreverence, as the populace of the middle ages used to perform plays and farces within the consecrated ground of the church, it is of that '*dicere*' that this rag vendor makes one think when, after drawling the other words, he utters the final syllable with a sharpness befitting the accentuation laid down by the great Pope of the seventh century: '*Chiffons, ferrailles à vendre*' (all this chanted slowly, as are the two syllables that follow, whereas the last concludes more briskly than '*dicere*') '*peaux d'la-pins.*' '*La Valence, la belle Valence, la fraîche orange.*' The humble leeks even: '*Voilà d'beaux poireaux*', the onions: '*Huit sous mon oignon*', sounded for me as if it were an echo of the rolling waves in which, left to herself, Albertine might have perished, and thus assumed the sweetness of a '*Suave mari magno*'. '*Voilà des carrottes à deux ronds la botte.*' 'Oh!' exclaimed Albertine, 'cabbages, carrots, oranges. All the things I want to eat. Do make Françoise go out and buy some. She shall cook us a dish of creamed carrots. Besides, it will be so nice to eat all these things together. It will be all the sounds that we hear, transformed into a good dinner . . . Oh, please, ask Françoise to give us instead a ray with black butter. It is so good!' 'My dear child, of course I will, but don't wait; if you do, you'll be asking for all the things on the vegetable-barrows.' 'Very well, I'm off, but I never want anything again for our dinners except what we've heard cried in the street. It is such fun. And to think that we shall have to wait two whole months before we hear: "*Haricots verts et tendres, haricots, v'la l'haricot vert*". How true that is: tender haricots; you know I like them as soft as soft, dripping with vinegar sauce, you wouldn't think you were eating, they melt in the mouth like drops of dew. Oh dear, it's the same with the little hearts of cream cheese,

such a long time to wait: "*Bon fromage à la cré, à la cré, bon fromage*". And the
water-grapes from Fontainebleau: "*J'ai du bon chasselas.*" ' And I thought
with dismay of all the time that I should have to spend with her before the
water-grapes were in season. 'Listen, I said that I wanted only the things
that we had heard cried, but of course I make exceptions. And so it's by no
means impossible that I may look in at Rebattet's and order an ice for the
two of us. You will tell me that it's not the season for them, but I do so want
one!' I was disturbed by this plan of going to Rebattet's, rendered more
certain and more suspicious in my eyes by the words 'it's by no means
impossible'. It was the day on which the Verdurins were at home, and, ever
since Swann had informed them that Rebattet's was the best place, it was
there that they ordered their ices and pastry. 'I have no objection to an ice,
my darling Albertine, but let me order it for you, I don't know myself
whether it will be from Poiré-Blanche's, or Rebattet's, or the Ritz, anyhow
I shall see.' 'Then you're going out?' she said with an air of distrust. She
always maintained that she would be delighted if I went out more often, but
if anything that I said could make her suppose that I would not be staying
indoors, her uneasy air made me think that the joy that she would feel in
seeing me go out every day was perhaps not altogether sincere. 'I may
perhaps go out, perhaps not, you know quite well that I never make plans
beforehand. In any case ices are not a thing that is cried, that people hawk in
the streets, why do you want one?' And then she replied in words which
showed me what a fund of intelligence and latent taste had developed in her
since Balbec, in words akin to those which, she pretended, were due entirely
to my influence, to living continually in my company, words which, however,
I should never have uttered, as though I had been in some way forbidden by
some unknown authority ever to decorate my conversation with literary
forms. Perhaps the future was not destined to be the same for Albertine as
for myself. I had almost a presentiment of this when I saw her eagerness to
employ in speech images so 'written', which seemed to me to be reserved for
another, more sacred use, of which I was still ignorant. She said to me (and
I was, in spite of everything, deeply touched, for I thought to myself:
Certainly I would not speak as she does, and yet, all the same, but for me she
would not be speaking like this, she has come profoundly under my
influence, she cannot therefore help loving me, she is my handiwork):
'What I like about these foodstuffs that are cried is that a thing which we
hear like a rhapsody changes its nature when it comes to our table and
addresses itself to my palate. As for ices (for I hope that you won't order me
one that isn't cast in one of those old-fashioned moulds which have every
architectural shape imaginable), whenever I take one, temples, churches,

obelisks, rocks, it is like an illustrated geography-book which I look at first of all and then convert its raspberry or vanilla monuments into coolness in my throat.' I thought that this was a little too well expressed, but she felt that I thought that it was well expressed, and went on, pausing for a moment when she had brought off her comparison to laugh that beautiful laugh of hers which was so painful to me because it was so voluptuous. 'Oh dear, at the Ritz I'm afraid you'll find Vendôme Columns of ice, chocolate ice or raspberry, and then you will need a lot of them so that they may look like votive pillars or pylons erected along an avenue to the glory of Coolness. They make raspberry obelisks too, which will rise up here and there in the burning desert of my thirst, and I shall make their pink granite crumble and melt deep down in my throat which they will refresh better than any oasis' (and here the deep laugh broke out, whether from satisfaction at talking so well, or in derision of herself for using such hackneyed images, or, alas, from a physical pleasure at feeling inside herself something so good, so cool, which was tantamount to a sensual satisfaction). 'Those mountains of ice at the Ritz sometimes suggest Monte Rosa, and indeed, if it is a lemon ice, I do not object to its not having a monumental shape, its being irregular, abrupt, like one of Elstir's mountains. It ought not to be too white then, but slightly yellowish, with that look of dull, dirty snow that Elstir's mountains have. The ice need not be at all big, only half an ice if you like, those lemon ices are still mountains, reduced to a tiny scale, but our imagination restores their dimensions, like those little Japanese dwarf trees which, one knows quite well, are still cedars, oaks, manchineels; so much so that if I arranged a few of them beside a little trickle of water in my room I should have a vast forest stretching down to a river, in which children would be lost. In the same way, at the foot of my yellowish lemon ice, I can see quite clearly postilions, travellers, post-chaises over which my tongue sets to work to roll down freezing avalanches that will swallow them up' (the cruel delight with which she said this excited my jealousy); 'just as,' she went on, 'I set my lips to work to destroy, pillar after pillar, those Venetian churches of a porphyry that is made with strawberries, and send what I spare of them crashing down upon the worshippers. Yes, all those monuments will pass from their stony state into my inside which throbs already with their melting coolness. But, you know, even without ices, nothing is so exciting or makes one so thirsty as the advertisements of mineral springs. At Montjouvain, at Mlle Vinteuil's, there was no good confectioner who made ices in the neighbourhood, but we used to make our own tour of France in the garden by drinking a different sparkling water every day, like Vichy water which, as soon as you pour it out, sends up from the bottom of the glass a white cloud which fades and dissolves if you don't drink it at once.' But to hear her speak of Montjouvain was too painful, I cut her short. 'I am boring you, goodbye, my dear boy.' What a change from Balbec, where I would defy Elstir himself to have been able to divine in Albertine this wealth of poetry, a poetry less strange, less personal than that of Céleste Albaret, for instance. Albertine would never have thought of the things that Céleste used to say to me, but love, even when it seems to be nearing its end, is partial. I preferred the illustrated geography-book of her ices, the somewhat facile charm of which seemed to me a reason for loving Albertine and a proof that I had an influence over her, that she was in love with me.

As soon as Albertine had gone out, I felt how tiring it was to me, this perpetual presence, insatiable of movement and life, which disturbed my sleep with its movements, made me live in a perpetual chill by that habit of leaving doors open, forced me – in order to find pretexts that would justify me in not accompanying her, without, however, appearing too unwell, and at the same time to see that she was not unaccompanied – to display every day greater ingenuity than Scheherezade. Unfortunately, if by a similar ingenuity the Persian storyteller postponed her own death, I was hastening mine. There are thus in life certain situations which are not all created, as was this, by amorous jealousy and a precarious state of health which does not permit us to share the life of a young and active person, situations in which nevertheless the problem of whether to continue a life shared with that person or to return to the separate existence of the past sets itself almost in medical terms; to which of the two sorts of repose ought we to sacrifice ourselves (by continuing the daily strain, or by returning to the agonies of separation) to that of the head or of the heart?

In any event, I was very glad that Andrée was to accompany Albertine to the Trocadéro, for certain recent and for that matter entirely trivial incidents had brought it about that while I had still, of course, the same confidence in the chauffeur's honesty, his vigilance, or at least the perspicacity of his vigilance did not seem to be quite what it had once been. It so happened that, only a short while since, I had sent Albertine alone in his charge to Versailles, and she told me that she had taken her luncheon at the Réservoirs; as the chauffeur had mentioned the restaurant Vatel, the day on which I noticed this contradiction, I found an excuse to go downstairs and speak to him (it was still the same man, whose acquaintance we had made at Balbec) while Albertine was dressing. 'You told me that you had had your luncheon at the Vatel. Mlle Albertine mentions the Réservoirs. What is the meaning of that?' The driver replied: 'Oh, I said that I had had my luncheon at the Vatel, but I cannot tell where Mademoiselle took hers. She left me as soon as we reached Versailles to take a horse cab, which she prefers when it is not a question of time.' Already I was furious at the thought that she had been alone; still, it was only during the time that she spent at her luncheon. 'You might surely,' I suggested mildly (for I did not wish to appear to be keeping Albertine actually under surveillance, which would have been humiliating to myself, and doubly so, for it would have shown that she concealed her activities from me), 'have had your luncheon, I do not say at her table, but in the same restaurant?' 'But all she told me was to meet her at six o'clock at the Place d'Armes. I had no orders to call for her after luncheon.' 'Ah!' I said, making an effort to conceal my dismay. And I returned upstairs. And so it was for more than seven hours on end that Albertine had been alone, left to her own devices. I might assure myself, it is true, that the cab had not been merely an expedient whereby to escape from the chauffeur's supervision. In town, Albertine preferred driving in a cab, saying that one had a better view, that the air was more pleasant. Nevertheless, she had spent seven hours, as to which I should never know anything. And I dared not think of the manner in which she must have employed them. I felt that the driver had been extremely clumsy, but my confidence in him was now absolute. For if he had been to the slightest extent in league with Albertine, he would never have acknowledged that he had left her unguarded from eleven o'clock in the morning to six in the afternoon. There could be but one other explanation, and it was absurd, of the chauffeur's admission. This was that some quarrel between Albertine and himself had prompted him, by making a minor disclosure to me, to show my mistress that he was not the sort of man who could be hushed, and that if, after this first gentle warning, she did not do exactly as he told her, he would take the law into his own hands. But this explanation was absurd; I should have had first of all to assume a non-existent quarrel between him and Albertine, and then to label as a con-summate blackmailer this good-looking motorist who had always shown himself so affable and obliging. Only two days later, as it happened, I saw that he was more capable than I had for a moment supposed in my frenzy of suspicion of exercising over Albertine a discreet and far-seeing vigilance. For, having managed to take him aside and talk to him of what he had told me about Versailles, I said to him in a careless, friendly tone: 'That drive to Versailles that you told me about the other day was everything that it should be, you behaved perfectly as you always do. But, if I may give you just a little hint, I have so much responsibility now that Mme Bontemps has placed her niece under my charge, I am so afraid of accidents, I reproach myself so for not going with her, that I prefer that it should be yourself, you who are so safe, so wonderfully skilful, to whom no accident can ever happen, that shall take Mlle Albertine everywhere. Then I need fear nothing.' The charming apostolic motorist smiled a subtle smile, his hand resting upon the consecration-cross of his wheel. Then he uttered these words which (banishing all the anxiety from my heart where its place was at once filled by joy) made me want to fling my arms round his neck: 'Don't be afraid,' he said to me. 'Nothing can happen to her, for, when my wheel is not guiding her, my eye follows her everywhere. At Versailles, I went quietly along and visited the town with her, as you might say. From the Réservoirs she went to the Château, from the Château to the Trianons, and I following her all the time without appearing to see her, and the astonishing thing is that she never saw me. Oh, if she had seen me, the fat would have been in the fire. It was only natural, as I had the whole day before me with nothing to do that I should visit the castle too. All the more as Mademoiselle certainly hasn't failed to notice that I've read a bit myself and take an interest in all those old curiosities' (this was true, indeed I should have been surprised if I had learned that he was a friend of Morel, so far more refined was his taste than the violinist's). 'Anyhow, she didn't see me.' 'She must have met some of her own friends, of course, for she knows a great many ladies at Versailles.' 'No, she was alone all the time.' 'Then people must have stared at her, a girl of such striking appearance, all by herself.' 'Why, of course they stared at her, but she knew nothing about it; she went all the time with her eyes glued to her guidebook, or gazing up at the pictures.' The chauffeur's story seemed to me all the more accurate in that it was indeed a 'card' with a picture of the Château, and another of the Trianons, that Albertine had sent me on the day of her visit. The care with which the obliging chauffeur had followed every step of her course touched me deeply. How was I to suppose that this correction – in the form of a generous amplification – of his account given two days earlier was due to the fact that in those two days Albertine, alarmed that the chauffeur should have spoken to me, had surrendered, and made her peace with him. This suspicion never even occurred to me. It is beyond question that this version of the driver's story, as it rid me of all fear that Albertine might have deceived me, quite naturally cooled me towards my mistress and made me take less interest in the day that she had spent at Versailles. I think, however, that the chauffeur's explanations, which, by absolving Albertine, made her even more tedious than before, would not perhaps have been sufficient to calm me so quickly. Two little pimples which for some days past my mistress had had upon her brow were perhaps even more effective in modifying the sentiments of my heart. Finally these were diverted farther still from her (so far that I was conscious of her existence only when I set eyes upon her) by the strange confidence volunteered me by

Gilberte's maid, whom I happened to meet. I learned that, when I used to
go every day to see Gilberte, she was in love with a young man of whom she
saw a great deal more than of myself. I had had an inkling of this for a
moment at the time, indeed I had questioned this very maid. But, as she
knew that I was in love with Gilberte, she had denied, sworn that never had
Mlle Swann set eyes on the young man. Now, however, knowing that my
love had long since died, that for years past I had left all her letters
unanswered – and also perhaps because she was no longer in Gilberte's
service – of her own accord she gave me a full account of the amorous
episode of which I had known nothing. This seemed to her quite natural. I
supposed, remembering her oaths at the time, that she had not been aware
of what was going on. Far from it, it was she herself who used to go, at Mme
Swann's orders, to inform the young man whenever the object of my love
was alone. The object then of my love . . . But I asked myself whether my
love of those days was as dead as I thought, for this story pained me. As I do
not believe that jealousy can revive a dead love, I supposed that my painful
impression was due, in part at least, to the injury to my self-esteem, for a
number of people whom I did not like and who at that time and even a little
later – their attitude has since altered – affected a contemptuous attitude
towards myself, knew perfectly well, while I was in love with Gilberte, that I
was her dupe. And this made me ask myself retrospectively whether in my
love for Gilberte there had not been an element of self-love, since it so
pained me now to discover that all the hours of affectionate intercourse,
which had made me so happy, were known to be nothing more than a
deliberate hoodwinking of me by my mistress, by people whom I did not
like. In any case, love or self-love, Gilberte was almost dead in me but not
entirely, and the result of this annoyance was to prevent me from worrying
myself beyond measure about Albertine, who occupied so small a place in
my heart. Nevertheless, to return to her (after so long a parenthesis) and to
her expedition to Versailles, the postcards of Versailles (is it possible, then,
to have one's heart caught in a noose like this by two simultaneous and
interwoven jealousies, each inspired by a different person?) gave me a
slightly disagreeable impression whenever, as I tidied my papers, my eye fell
upon them. And I thought that if the driver had not been such a worthy
fellow, the harmony of his second narrative with Albertine's 'cards' would
not have amounted to much, for what are the first things that people send
you from Versailles but the Château and the Trianons, unless that is to say
the card has been chosen by some person of refined taste who adores a
certain statue, or by some idiot who selects as a 'view' of Versailles the
station of the horse tramway or the goods depot. Even then I am wrong in

saying an idiot, such postcards not having always been bought by a person of that sort at random, for their interest as coming from Versailles. For two whole years men of intelligence, artists, used to find Siena, Venice, Granada a 'bore', and would say of the humblest omnibus, of every railway-carriage: 'There you have true beauty.' Then this fancy passed like the rest. Indeed, I cannot be certain that people did not revert to the 'sacrilege of destroying the noble relics of the past'. Anyhow, a first-class railway carriage ceased to be regarded as *a priori* more beautiful than St Mark's at Venice. People continued to say: 'Here you have real life, the return to the past is artificial,' but without drawing any definite conclusion. To make quite certain, without forfeiting any of my confidence in the chauffeur, in order that Albertine might not be able to send him away without his venturing to refuse for fear of her taking him for a spy, I never allowed her to go out after this without the reinforcement of Andrée, whereas for some time past I had found the chauffeur sufficient. I had even allowed her then (a thing I would never dare do now) to stay away for three whole days by herself with the chauffeur and to go almost as far as Balbec, so great was her longing to travel at high speed in an open car. Three days during which my mind had been quite at rest, although the rain of postcards that she had showered upon me did not reach me, owing to the appalling state of the Breton postal system (good in summer, but disorganised, no doubt, in winter), until a week after the return of Albertine and the chauffeur, in such health and vigour that on the very morning of their return they resumed, as though nothing had happened, their daily outings. I was delighted that Albertine should be going this afternoon to the Trocadéro, to this 'special' matinée, but still more reassured that she would have a companion there in the shape of Andrée.

Dismissing these reflections, now that Albertine had gone out, I went and took my stand for a moment at the window. There was at first a silence, amid which the whistle of the tripe vendor and the horn of the tramcar made the air ring in different octaves, like a blind piano-tuner. Thea gradually the interwoven motives became distinct, and others were combined with them. There was also a new whistle, the call of a vendor the nature of whose wares I have never discovered, a whistle that was itself exactly like the scream of the tramway, and, as it was not carried out of earshot by its own velocity, one thought of a single car, not endowed with motion, or broken down, immobilised, screaming at short intervals like a dying animal. And I felt that, should I ever have to leave this aristocratic quarter – unless it were to move to one that was entirely plebeian – the streets and boulevards of central Paris (where the fruit, fish and other trades, stabilised in huge stores, rendered superfluous the cries of the street hawkers, who for that matter would not have been able to make themselves heard) would seem to me very dreary, quite uninhabitable, stripped, drained of all these litanies of the small trades and peripatetic victuals, deprived of the orchestra that returned every morning to charm me. On the pavement a woman with no pretence to fashion (or else obedient to an ugly fashion) came past, too brightly dressed in a sack overcoat of goatskin; but no, it was not a woman, it was a chauffeur who, enveloped in his pony-skin, was proceeding on foot to his garage. Escaped from the big hotels, their winged messengers, of variegated hue, were speeding towards the termini, bent over their handlebars, to meet the arrivals by the morning trains. The throb of a violin was due at one time to the passing of a motorcar, at another to my not having put enough water in my electric kettle. In the middle of the symphony there rang out an old-fashioned 'air'; replacing the sweet seller, who generally accompanied her song with a rattle, the toy seller, to whose pipe was attached a jumping jack which he sent flying in all directions, paraded similar puppets for sale, and without heeding the ritual declamation of Gregory the Great, the reformed declamation of Palestrina or the lyrical declamation of the modern composers, entoned at the top of his voice, a belated adherent of pure melody: '*Allons les papas, allons les mamans, contentez vos petits enfants, c'est moi qui les fais, c'est moi qui les vends, et c'est moi qui boulotte l'argent. Tra la la la. Tra la la la laire, tra la la la la la la. Allons les petits!*' Some Italian boys in felt bérets made no attempt to compete with this lively aria, and it was without a word that they offered their little statuettes. Soon, however, a young fifer compelled the toy merchant to move on and to chant more inaudibly, though in brisk time: '*Allons les papas, allons les mamans.*' This young fifer, was he one of the dragoons whom I used to hear in the mornings at Doncières? No, for what followed was: '*Voilà le réparateur de faïence et de porcelaine. Je répare le verre, le marbre, le cristal, l'os, l'ivoire et objets d'antiquité. Voilà le réparateur.*' In a butcher's shop, between an aureole of sunshine on the left and a whole ox suspended from a hook on the right, an assistant, very tall and slender, with fair hair and a throat that escaped above his sky-blue collar, was displaying a lightning speed and a religious conscientiousness in putting on one side the most exquisite fillets of beef, on the other the coarsest parts of the rump, placed them upon glittering scales surmounted by a cross, from which hung down a number of beautiful chains, and – albeit he did nothing afterwards but arrange in the window a display of kidneys, steaks, ribs – was really far more suggestive of a handsome angel who, on the day of the Last Judgment, will prepare for God, according to their quality, the separation of the good and the evil and the weighing of souls. And once again the thin crawling music of the fife rose in the air, herald no longer of the destruction that

Françoise used to dread whenever a regiment of cavalry filed past, but of 'repairs' promised by an 'antiquary', simpleton or rogue, who, in either case highly eclectic, instead of specialising, applied his art to the most diverse materials. The young bread-carriers hastened to stuff into their baskets the long rolls ordered for some luncheon party, while the milk-girls attached the bottles of milk to their yokes. The sense of longing with which my eyes followed these young damsels, ought I to consider it quite justified? Would it not have been different if I had been able to detain for a few moments at close quarters one of those whom from the height of my window I saw only inside her shop or in motion? To estimate the loss that I suffered by my seclusion, that is to say the wealth that the day held in store for me, I should have had to intercept in the long unrolling of the animated frieze some girl carrying her linen or her milk, make her pass for a moment, like a silhouette from some mobile scheme of decoration, from the wings to the stage, within the proscenium of my bedroom door, and keep her there under my eye, not without eliciting some information about her which would enable me to find her again some day, like the inscribed ring which ornithologists or ichthyologists attach before setting them free to the legs or bellies of the birds or fishes whose migrations they are anxious to trace.

And so I asked Françoise, since I had a message that I wished taken, to be good enough to send up to my room, should any of them call, one or other of those girls who were always coming to take away the dirty or bring back the clean linen, or with bread, or bottles of milk, and whom she herself used often to send on errands. In doing so I was like Elstir, who, obliged to remain closeted in his studio, on certain days in spring when the knowledge that the woods were full of violets gave him a hunger to gaze at them, used to send his porter's wife out to buy him a bunch; then it was not the table upon which he had posed the little vegetable model, but the whole carpet of the underwoods where he had seen in other years, in their thousands, the serpentine stems, bowed beneath the weight of their blue beaks, that Elstir would fancy that he had before his eyes, like an imaginary zone defined in his studio by the limpid odour of the sweet, familiar flower.

Of a laundry girl, on a Sunday, there was not the slightest prospect. As for the girl who brought the bread, as ill luck would have it, she had rung the bell when Françoise was not about, had left her rolls in their basket on the landing, and had made off. The fruit girl would not call until much later. Once I had gone to order a cheese at the dairy, and, among the various young assistants, had remarked one girl, extravagantly fair, tall in stature though still little more than a child, who, among the other errand girls, seemed to be dreaming, in a distinctly haughty attitude. I had seen her in the distance only, and for so brief an instant that I could not have described her appearance, except to say that she must have grown too fast and that her head supported a fleece that gave the impression far less of capillary details than of a sculptor's conventional rendering of the separate channels of parallel drifts of snow upon a glacier. This was all that I had been able to make out, apart from a nose sharply outlined (a rare thing in a child) upon a thin face which recalled the beaks of baby vultures. Besides, this clustering of her comrades round about her had not been the only thing that prevented me from seeing her distinctly, there was also my uncertainty whether the sentiments which I might, at first sight and subsequently, inspire in her would be those of injured pride, or of irony, or of a scorn which she would express later on to her friends. These alternative suppositions which I had formed, in an instant, with regard to her, had condensed round about her the troubled atmosphere in which she disappeared, like a goddess in the cloud that is shaken by thunder. For moral uncertainty is a greater obstacle to an exact visual perception than any defect of vision would be. In this too skinny young person, who moreover attracted undue attention, the excess of what another person would perhaps have called her charms was precisely what was calculated to repel me, but had nevertheless had the effect of preventing me from perceiving even, far more from remembering anything about the other young dairymaids, whom the hooked nose of this one and her gaze – how unattractive it was! – pensive, personal, with an air of passing judgment, had plunged in perpetual night, as a white streak of lightning darkens the landscape on either side of it. And so, of my call to order a cheese, at the dairy, I had remembered (if we can say 'remember' in speaking of a face so carelessly observed that we adapt to the nullity of the face ten different noses in succession), I had remembered only this girl who had not attracted me. This is sufficient to engender love. And yet I should have forgotten the extravagantly fair girl and should never have wished to see her again, had not Françoise told me that, child as she was, she had all her wits about her and would shortly be leaving her employer, since she had been going too fast and owed money among the neighbours. It has been said that beauty is a promise of happiness. Inversely, the possibility of pleasure may be a beginning of beauty.

I began to read Mamma's letter. Beneath her quotations from Madame de Sévigné: 'If my thoughts are not entirely black at Combray, they are at least dark grey, I think of you at every moment; I long for you; your health, your affairs, your absence, what sort of cloud do you suppose they make in my sky?' I felt that my mother was vexed to find Albertine's stay in the house prolonged, and my intention of marriage, although not yet announced to my mistress, confirmed. She did not express her annoyance more directly because she was afraid that I might leave her letters lying about. Even then, veiled as her letters were, she reproached me with not informing her immediately, after each of them, that I had received it: 'You remember how Mme de Sévigné said: "When we are far apart, we no longer laugh at letters which begin with *I have received yours*." ' Without referring to what distressed her most, she said that she was annoyed by my lavish expenditure: 'Where on earth does all your money go? It is distressing enough that, like Charles de Sévigné, you do not know what you want and are 'two or three people at once', but do try at least not to be like him in spending money so that I may never have to say of you: 'he has discovered how to spend and have nothing to show, how to lose without staking and how to pay without clearing himself of debt." I had just finished Mamma's letter when Françoise returned to tell me that she had in the house that very same slightly over-bold young dairymaid of whom she had spoken to me. 'She can quite well take Monsieur's note and bring back the answer, if it's not too far. Monsieur shall see her, she's just like a Little Red Riding Hood.' Françoise withdrew to fetch the girl, and I could hear her leading the way and saying: 'Come along now, you're frightened because there's a passage, stuff and nonsense, I never thought you would be such a goose. Have I got to lead you by the hand?' And Françoise, like a good and honest servant who means to see that her master is respected as she respects him herself, had draped herself in that majesty with ennobles the matchmaker in a picture by an old master where, in comparison with her, the lover and his mistress fade into insignificance.

Elstir when he gazed at them had no need to bother about what the violets were doing. The entry of the young dairymaid at once robbed me of my contemplative calm; I could think only of how to give plausibility to the fable of the letter that she was to deliver and I began to write quickly without venturing to cast more than a furtive glance at her, so that I might not seem to have brought her into my room to be scrutinised. She was invested for me with that charm of the unknown which I should not discover in a pretty girl whom I had found in one of those houses where they come to meet one. She was neither naked nor in disguise, but a genuine dairymaid, one of those whom we imagine to be so pretty, when we have not time to approach them; she possessed something of what constitutes the eternal desire, the eternal regret of life, the twofold current of which is at length diverted, directed towards us. Twofold, for if it is a question of the unknown, of a person who must, we guess, be divine, from her stature, her proportions, her indifferent glance, her haughty calm, on the other hand we wish this woman to be thoroughly specialised in her profession, allowing us to escape from ourselves into that world which a peculiar costume makes us romantically believe different. If for that matter we seek to comprise in a formula the law of our amorous curiosities, we should have to seek it in the maximum of difference between a woman of whom we have caught sight and one whom we have approached and caressed. If the women of what used at one time to be called the closed houses, if prostitutes themselves (provided that we know them to be prostitutes) attract us so little, it is not because they are less beautiful than other women, it is because they are ready and waiting; the very object that we are seeking to attain they offer us already; it is because they are not conquests. The difference there is at a minimum. A harlot smiles at us already in the street as she will smile when she is in our room. We are sculptors. We are anxious to obtain of a woman a statue entirely different from that which she has presented to us. We have seen a girl strolling, indifferent, insolent, along the seashore, we have seen a shop-assistant, serious and active, behind her counter, who will answer us stiffly, if only so as to escape the sarcasm of her comrades, a fruit-seller who barely answers us at all. Well, we know no rest until we can discover by experiment whether the proud girl on the seashore, the shop assistant on her high horse of 'What will people say?', the preoccupied fruit-seller cannot be made, by skilful handling on our part, to relax their rectangular attitude, to throw about our neck their fruit-laden arms, to direct towards our lips, with a smile of consent, eyes hitherto frozen or absent – oh, the beauty of stern eyes – in working hours when the worker was so afraid of the gossip of her companions, eyes that avoided our beleaguering stare and, now that we have seen her alone and face to face, make their pupils yield beneath the sunlit burden of laughter when we speak of making love. Between the shopgirl, the laundress busy with her iron, the fruit-seller, the dairymaid on the one hand, and the same girl when she is about to become our mistress, the maximum of difference is attained, stretched indeed to its extreme limits, and varied by those habitual gestures of her profession which make a pair of arms, during the hours of toil, something as different as possible (regarded as an arabesque pattern) from those supple bonds that already every evening are fastened about our throat while the mouth shapes itself for a kiss. And so we pass our whole life in uneasy advances, incessantly renewed, to respectable girls whom their calling seems to separate from us. Once they are in our arms, they are no longer anything more than they originally were, the gulf that we dreamed of crossing has been bridged. But we begin afresh with other women, we devote to these enterprises all our time, all our money, all our strength, our blood boils at the too cautious driver who is perhaps going to make us miss our first assignation, we work ourself into a fever. That first meeting, we know all the same that it will mean the vanishing of an illusion. It does not so much matter that the illusion still persists; we wish to see whether we can convert it into reality, and then we think of the laundress whose coldness we remarked. Amorous curiosity is like that which is aroused in us by the names of places; perpetually disappointed, it revives and remains for ever insatiable.

Alas! As soon as she stood before me, the fair dairymaid with the ribbed tresses, stripped of all that I had imagined and of the desire that had been aroused in me, was reduced to her own proportions. The throbbing cloud of my suppositions no longer enveloped her in a shimmering haze. She acquired an almost beggarly air from having (in place of the ten, the score that I recalled in turn without being able to fix any of them in my memory) but a single nose, rounder than I had thought, which made her appear rather a fool and had in any case lost the faculty of multiplying itself. This flyaway caught on the wing, inert, crushed, incapable of adding anything to its own paltry appearance, had no longer my imagination to collaborate with it. Fallen into the inertia of reality, I sought to rebound; her cheeks, which I had not seen in the shop, appeared to me so pretty that I became alarmed, and, to put myself in countenance, said to the young dairymaid: 'Would you be so kind as to pass me the *Figaro* which is lying there, I must make sure of the address to which I am going to send you.' Thereupon, as she picked up the newspaper, she disclosed as far as her elbow the red sleeve of her jersey and handed me the conservative sheet with a neat and courteous gesture which pleased me by its intimate rapidity, its pliable contour and its scarlet hue. While I was opening the *Figaro*, in order to say something and without raising my eyes, I asked the girl: 'What do you call that red knitted thing you're wearing? It is very becoming.' She replied: 'It's my golf.' For, by a slight downward tendency common to all fashions, the garments and styles which, a few years earlier, seemed to belong to the relatively smart world of Albertine's friends, were now the portion of working girls. 'Are you quite sure it won't be giving you too much trouble,' I said, while I pretended to be searching the columns of the *Figaro*, 'if I send you rather a long way?' As soon as I myself appeared to find the service at all arduous that she would be performing by taking a message for me, she began to feel that it would be a trouble to her. 'The only thing is, I have to be going out presently on my bike. Good lord, you know, Sunday's the only day we've got.' 'But won't you catch cold, going bareheaded like that?' 'Oh, I shan't be bareheaded, I shall have my polo, and I could get on without it with all the hair I have.' I raised my eyes to the blaze of curling tresses and felt myself caught in their swirl and swept away, with a throbbing heart, amid the lightning and the blasts of a hurricane of beauty. I continued to study the newspaper, but albeit this was only to keep myself in countenance and to gain time, while I merely pretended to read, I took in nevertheless the meaning of the words that were before my eyes, and my attention was caught by the following: 'To the programme already announced for this afternoon in the great hall of the Trocadéro must be added the name of Mlle Léa who has consented to appear in *Les Fourberies de Nérine.* She will of course sustain the part of Nérine, in which she is astounding in her display of spirit and bewitching gaiety.' It was as though a hand had brutally torn from my heart the bandage beneath which its wound had begun since my return from Balbec to heal. The flood of my anguish escaped in torrents; Léa, that was the actress friend of the two girls at Balbec whom Albertine, without appearing to see them, had, one afternoon at the Casino, watched in the mirror. It was true that at Balbec Albertine, at the name of Léa, had adopted a special tone of compunction in order to say to me, almost shocked that anyone could suspect such a pattern of virtue: 'Oh no, she is not in the least that sort of woman, she is a very respectable person.' Unfortunately for me, when Albertine made a statement of this sort, it was never anything but the first stage towards other, divergent statements. Shortly after the first, came this second: 'I don't know her.' In the third phase, after Albertine had spoken to me of somebody who was 'above suspicion' and whom (in the second place) she did not know, she first of all forgot that she had said that she did not know her and then, in a speech in which she contradicted herself unawares, informed me that she did know her. This first act of oblivion completed, and the fresh, statement made, a second oblivion began, to wit that the person was above suspicion. 'Isn't So-and-So,' I would ask, 'one of those women?' 'Why, of course, everybody knows that!' Immediately the note of compunction was sounded afresh to utter a statement which was a vague echo, greatly reduced, of the first statement of all. 'I'm bound to say that she has always behaved perfectly properly with me. Of course, she knows that I would send her about her business if she tried it on. Still, that makes no difference. I am obliged to give her credit for the genuine respect she has always shown for me. It is easy to see she knew the sort of person she had to deal with.' We remember the truth because it has a name, is rooted in the past, but a makeshift lie is quickly forgotten. Albertine forgot this latest lie, her fourth, and, one day when she was anxious to gain my confidence by confiding in me, went so far as to tell me, with regard to the same person who at the outset had been so respectable and whom she did not know. 'She took quite a fancy to me at one time. She asked me, three or four times, to go home with her and to come upstairs to her room. I saw no harm in going home with her, where everybody could see us, in broad daylight, in the open air. But when we reached her front door I always made some excuse and I never went upstairs.' Shortly after this, Albertine made an allusion to the beautiful things that this lady had in her room. By proceeding from one approximation to another, I should no doubt have arrived at making her tell me the truth which was perhaps less serious than I had been led to believe, for, although perhaps easygoing with women, she preferred a male lover, and now that she had myself would not have given a thought to Léa. In any case, with regard to this person, I was still at the first stage of revelation and was not aware whether Albertine knew her. Already, in the case of many women at any rate, it would have been enough for me to collect and present to my mistress, in a synthesis, her contradictory statements, in order to convict her of her misdeeds (misdeeds which, like astronomical laws, it is a great deal easier to deduce by a process of reasoning than to observe, to surprise in the act). But then she would have preferred to say that one of her statements had been a lie, the withdrawal of which would thus bring about the collapse of my whole system of evidence, rather than admit that everything which she had told me from the start was simply a tissue of falsehood. There are similar tissues in the *Thousand and One Nights*, which we find charming. They pain us, coming from a person whom we love, and thereby enable us to penetrate a little deeper in our knowledge of human nature instead of being content to play upon the surface. Grief penetrates into us and forces us out of painful curiosity to penetrate other people. Whence emerge truths which we feel that we have no right to keep hidden, so much so that a dying atheist who has discovered them, certain of his own extinction, indifferent to fame, will nevertheless devote his last hours on earth to an attempt to make them known.

Of course, I was still at the first stage of enlightenment with regard to Léa. I was not even aware whether Albertine knew her. No matter, it all came to the same thing. I must at all costs prevent her from – at the Trocadéro – renewing this acquaintance or making the acquaintance of this stranger. I have said that I did not know whether she knew Léa; I ought, however, to have learned it at Balbec, from Albertine herself. For defective memory obliterated from my mind as well as from Albertine's a great many of the statements that she had made to me. Memory, instead of being a duplicate always present before our eyes of the various events of our life, is rather an abyss from which at odd moments a chance resemblance enables us to draw up, restored to life, dead impressions; but even then there are innumerable little details which have not fallen into that potential reservoir of memory, and which will remain for ever beyond our control. To anything that we do not know to be related to the real life of the person whom we love we pay but scant attention, we forget immediately what she has said to us about some incident or people that we do not know, and her expression while she was saying it. And so when, in due course, our jealousy is aroused by these same people, and seeks to make sure that it is not mistaken, that it is they who are responsible for the haste which our mistress shows in leaving the house, her annoyance when we have prevented her from going out by returning earlier than usual; our jealousy ransacking the past in search of a clue can find nothing; always retrospective, it is like a historian who has to write the history of a period for which he has no documents; always belated, it dashes like a mad bull to the spot where it will not find the proud and brilliant creature who is infuriating it with his darts and whom the crowd admire for his splendour and his cunning. Jealousy fights the empty air, uncertain as we are in those dreams in which we are distressed because we cannot find in his empty house a person whom we have known well in life, but who here perhaps is really another person and has merely borrowed the features of our friend, uncertain as we are even more after we awake when we seek to identify this or that detail of our dream. What was our mistress's expression when she told us this; did she not look happy, was she not actually whistling, a thing that she never does unless there is some amorous thought in her mind? In the time of our love, if our presence teased her and irritated her a little, has she not told us something that is contradicted by what she now affirms, that she knows or does not know such and such a person? We do not know, we shall never find out; we strain after the unsubstantial fragments of a dream, and all the time our life with our mistress continues, our life indifferent to what we do not know to be important to us, attentive to what is perhaps of no importance, hag-ridden by people who have no real connection with us, full of lapses of memory, gaps, vain anxieties, our life as fantastic as a dream.

I realised that the young dairymaid was still in the room. I told her that the place was certainly a long way off, that I did not need her. Whereupon she also decided that it would be too much trouble: 'There's a fine match coming off, I don't want to miss it.' I felt that she must already be devoted to sport and that in a few years' time she would be talking about 'living her own life'. I told her that I certainly did not need her any longer, and gave her five francs. Immediately, having little expected this largesse, and telling herself that if she earned five francs for doing nothing she would have a great deal more for taking my message, she began to find that her match was of no importance. 'I could easily have taken your message. I can always find

time.' But I thrust her from the room, I needed to be alone, I must at all
costs prevent Albertine from any risk of meeting Léa's girl friends at the
Trocadéro. I must try, and I must succeed; to tell the truth I did not yet see
how, and during these first moments I opened my hands, gazed at them,
cracked my knuckles, whether because the mind which cannot find what it is
seeking, in a fit of laziness allows itself to halt for an instant at a spot where
the most unimportant things are distinctly visible to it, like the blades of
grass on the embankment which we see from the carriage window trembling
in the wind, when the train halts in the open country – an immobility that is
not always more fertile than that of the captured animal which, paralysed by
fear or fascinated, gazes without moving a muscle – or that I might hold my
body in readiness – with my mind at work inside it and, in my mind, the
means of action against this or that person – as though it were no more than
a weapon from which would be fired the shot that was to separate Albertine
from Léa and her two friends. It is true that earlier in the morning, when
Françoise had come in to tell me that Albertine was going to the Trocadéro,
I had said to myself: 'Albertine is at liberty to do as she pleases' and had
supposed that until evening came, in this radiant weather, her actions would
remain without any perceptible importance to myself; but it was not only
the morning sun, as I had thought, that had made me so careless; it was
because, having obliged Albertine to abandon the plans that she might
perhaps have initiated or even completed at the Verdurins', and having
restricted her to attending a performance which I myself had chosen, so that
she could not have made any preparations, I knew that whatever she did
would of necessity be innocent. Just as, if Albertine had said a few moments
later: 'If I kill myself, it's all the same to me', it would have been because she
was certain that she would not kill herself. Surrounding myself and Albertine
there had been this morning (far more than the sunlight in the air) that
atmosphere which we do not see, but by the translucent and changing
medium of which we do see, I her actions, she the importance of her own
life, that is to say those beliefs which we do not perceive but which are no
more assimilable to a pure vacuum than is the air that surrounds us;
composing round about us a variable atmosphere, sometimes excellent,
often unbreathable, they deserve to be studied and recorded as carefully as
the temperature, the barometric pressure, the weather, for our days have
their own singularity, physical and moral. My belief, which I had failed to
remark this morning, and yet in which I had been joyously enveloped until
the moment when I had looked a second time at the *Figaro*, that Albertine
would do nothing that was not harmless, this belief had vanished. I was
living no longer in the fine sunny day, but in a day carved out of the other

by my anxiety lest Albertine might renew her acquaintance with Léa and more easily still with the two girls, should they go, as seemed to me probable, to applaud the actress at the Trocadéro where it would not be difficult for them, in one of the intervals, to come upon Albertine. I no longer thought of Mlle Vinteuil, the name of Léa had brought back to my mind, to make me jealous, the image of Albertine in the Casino watching the two girls. For I possessed in my memory only series of Albertines, separate from one another, incomplete, outlines, snapshots; and so my jealousy was restricted to an intermittent expression, at once fugitive and fixed, and to the people who had caused that expression to appear upon Albertine's face. I remembered her when, at Balbec, she received undue attention from the two girls or from women of that sort; I remembered the distress that I used to feel when I saw her face subjected to an active scrutiny, like that of a painter preparing to make a sketch, entirely covered by them, and, doubtless on account of my presence, submitting to this contact without appearing to notice it, with a passivity that was perhaps clandestinely voluptuous. And before she recovered herself and spoke to me there was an instant during which Albertine did not move, smiled into the empty air, with the same air of feigned spontaneity and concealed pleasure as if she were posing for somebody to take her photograph; or even seeking to assume before the camera a more dashing pose – that which she had adopted at Doncières when we were walking with Saint-Loup, and, laughing and passing her tongue over her lips, she pretended to be teasing a dog. Certainly at such moments she was not at all the same as when it was she that was interested in little girls who passed us. Then, on the contrary, her narrow velvety gaze fastened itself upon, glued itself to the passer-by, so adherent, so corrosive, that you felt that when she removed it must tear away the skin. But at that moment this other expression, which did at least give her a serious air, almost as though she were in pain, had seemed to me a pleasant relief after the toneless blissful expression she had worn in the presence of the two girls, and I should have preferred the sombre expression of the desire that she did perhaps feel at times to the laughing expression caused by the desire which she aroused. However she might attempt to conceal her consciousness of it, it bathed her, enveloped her, vaporous, voluptuous, made her whole face appear rosy. But everything that Albertine held at such moments suspended in herself, that radiated round her and hurt me so acutely, how could I tell whether, once my back was turned, she would continue to keep it to herself, whether to the advances of the two girls, now that I was no longer with her, she would not make some audacious response. Indeed, these memories caused me intense grief, they were like a complete admission of Albertine's failings, a general confession of her infidelity against which were powerless the various oaths that she swore to me and I wished to believe, the negative results of my incomplete researches, the assurances, made perhaps in connivance with her, of Andrée. Albertine might deny specified betrayals; by words that she let fall, more emphatic than her declarations to the contrary, by that searching gaze alone, she had made confession of what she would fain have concealed, far more than any specified incident, what she would have let herself be killed sooner than admit: her natural tendency. For there is no one who will willingly deliver up his soul. Notwithstanding the grief that these memories were causing me, could I have denied that it was the programme of the matinée at the Trocadéro that had revived my need of Albertine? She was one of those women in whom their misdeeds may at a pinch take the place of absent charms, and no less than their misdeeds the kindness that follows them and restores to us that sense of comfort which in their company, like an invalid who is never well for two days in succession, we are incessantly obliged to recapture. And then, even more than their misdeeds while we are in love with them, there are their misdeeds before we made their acquaintance, and first and foremost: their nature. What makes this sort of love painful is, in fact, that there pre-exists a sort of original sin of Woman, a sin which makes us love them, so that, when we forget it, we feel less need of them, and to begin to love afresh we must begin to suffer afresh. At this moment, the thought that she must not meet the two girls again and the question whether or not she knew Léa were what was chiefly occupying my mind, in spite of the rule that we ought not to take an interest in particular facts except in relation to their general significance, and notwithstanding the childishness, as great as that of longing to travel or to make friends with women, of shattering our curiosity against such elements of the invisible torrent of painful realities which will always remain unknown to us as have happened to crystallise in our mind. But, even if we should succeed in destroying that crystallisation, it would at once be replaced by another. Yesterday I was afraid lest Albertine should go to see Mme Verdurin. Now my only thought was of Léa. Jealousy, which wears a bandage over its eyes, is not merely powerless to discover anything in the darkness that enshrouds it, it is also one of those torments where the task must be incessantly repeated, like that of the Danaids, or of Ixion. Even if her friends were not there, what impression might she not form of Léa, beautified by her stage attire, haloed with success, what thoughts would she leave in Albertine's mind, what desires which, even if she repressed them, would in my house disgust her with a life in which she was unable to gratify them.

Besides, how could I tell that she was not acquainted with Léa, and would not pay her a visit in her dressing-room; and, even if Léa did not know her, who could assure me that, having certainly seen her at Balbec, she would not recognise her and make a signal to her from the stage that would entitle Albertine to seek admission behind the scenes? A danger seems easy to avoid after it has been conjured away. This one was not yet conjured, I was afraid that it might never be, and it seemed to me all the more terrible. And yet this love for Albertine which I felt almost vanish when I attempted to realise it, seemed in a measure to acquire a proof of its existence from the intensity of my grief at this moment. I no longer cared about anything else, I thought only of how I was to prevent her from remaining at the Trocadéro, I would have offered any sum in the world to Léa to persuade her not to go there. If then we prove our choice by the action that we perform rather than by the idea that we form, I must have been in love with Albertine. But this renewal of my suffering gave no further consistency to the image that I beheld of Albertine. She caused my calamities, like a deity that remains invisible. Making endless conjectures, I sought to shield myself from suffering without thereby realising my love. First of all, I must make certain that Léa was really going to perform at the Trocadéro. After dismissing the dairymaid, I telephoned to Bloch, whom I knew to be on friendly terms with Léa, in order to ask him. He knew nothing about it and seemed surprised that the matter could be of any importance to me. I decided that I must set to work immediately, remembered that Françoise was ready to go out and that I was not, and as I rose and dressed made her take a motor car; she was to go to the Trocadéro, engage a seat, look high and low for Albertine and give her a note from myself. In this note I told her that I was greatly upset by a letter which I had just received from that same lady on whose account she would remember that I had been so wretched one night at Balbec. I reminded her that, on the following day, she had reproached me for not having sent for her. And so I was taking the liberty, I informed her, of asking her to sacrifice her matinée and to join me at home so that we might take a little fresh air together, which might help me to recover from the shock. But as I should be a long time in getting ready, she would oblige me, seeing that she had Françoise as an escort, by calling at the Trois-Quartiers (this shop, being smaller, seemed to me less dangerous than the Bon Marché) to buy the scarf of white tulle that she required. My note was probably not superfluous. To tell the truth, I knew nothing that Albertine had done since I had come to know her, or even before. But in her conversation (she might, had I mentioned it to her, have replied that I had misunderstood her) there were certain contradictions, certain embellishments which seemed to me as decisive as catching her red-handed, but less serviceable against Albertine who, often caught out in wrongdoing like a child, had invariably, by dint of sudden, strategic changes of front, stultified my cruel onslaught and re-established her own position. Cruel, most of all, to myself. She employed, not from any refinement of style, but in order to correct her imprudences, abrupt breaches of syntax not unlike that figure which the grammarians call anacoluthon or some such name. Having allowed herself, while discussing women, to say: 'I remember, the other day, I . . . ,' she would at once catch her breath, after which 'I' became 'she': it was something that she had witnessed as an innocent spectator, not a thing that she herself had done. It was not herself that was the heroine of the anecdote. I should have liked to recall how, exactly, the sentence began, so as to conclude for myself, since she had broken off in the middle, how it would have ended. But as I had heard the end, I found it hard to remember the beginning, from which perhaps my air of interest had made her deviate, and was left still anxious to know what she was really thinking, what she really remembered. The first stages of falsehood on the part of our mistress are like the first stages of our own love, or of a religious vocation. They take shape, accumulate, pass, without our paying them any attention. When we wish to remember in what manner we began to love a woman, we are already in love with her; when we dreamed about her before falling in love, we did not say to ourself: This is the prelude to a love affair, we must pay attention! – and our dreams took us by surprise, and we barely noticed them. So also, except in cases that are comparatively rare, it is only for the convenience of my narrative that I have frequently in these pages confronted one of Albertine's false statements with her previous assertion upon the same subject. This previous assertion, as often as not, since I could not read the future and did not at the time guess what contradictory affirmation was to form a pendant to it, had slipped past unperceived, heard it is true by my ears, but without my isolating it from the continuous flow of Albertine's speech. Later on, faced with the self-evident lie, or seized by an anxious doubt, I would fain have recalled it, but in vain; my memory had not been warned in time, and had thought it unnecessary to preserve a copy.

I urged Françoise, when she had got Albertine out of the hall, to let me know by telephone, and to bring her home, whether she was willing or not. 'That would be the last straw, that she should not be willing to come and see Monsieur,' replied Françoise. 'But I don't know that she's as fond as all that of seeing me.' 'Then she must be an ungrateful wretch,' went on Françoise, in whom Albertine was renewing after all these years the same torment of envy that Eulalie used at one time to cause her in my aunt's

sickroom. Unaware that Albertine's position in my household was not of
her own seeking but had been decided by myself (a fact which, from
motives of self-esteem and to make Françoise angry, I preferred to conceal
from her), she admired and execrated the girl's dexterity, called her when
she spoke of her to the other servants a 'play-actress', a wheedler who could
twist me round her little finger. She dared not yet declare open war against
her, showed her a smiling countenance and sought to acquire merit in my
sight by the services which she performed for her in her relations with
myself, deciding that it was useless to say anything to me and that she would
gain nothing by doing so; but if the opportunity ever arose, if ever she
discovered a crack in Albertine's armour, she was fully determined to
enlarge it, and to part us for good and all. 'Ungrateful? No, Françoise, I
think it is I that am ungrateful, you don't know how good she is to me.' (It
was so soothing to give the impression that I was loved.) 'Be as quick as you
can.' 'All right, I'll get a move on.' Her daughter's influence was beginning
to contaminate Françoise's vocabulary. So it is that all languages lose their
purity by the admission of new words. For this decadence of Françoise's
speech, which I had known in its golden period, I was myself indirectly
responsible. Françoise's daughter would not have made her mother's
classic language degenerate into the vilest slang, had she been content to
converse with her in dialect. She had never given up the use of it, and when
they were both in my room at once, if they had anything private to say,
instead of shutting themselves up in the kitchen, they armed themselves,
right in the middle of my room, with a screen more impenetrable than the
most carefully shut door, by conversing in dialect. I supposed merely that
the mother and daughter were not always on the best of terms, if I was to
judge by the frequency with which they employed the only word that I could
make out: *m'esasperate* (unless it was that the object of their exasperation was
myself). Unfortunately the most unfamiliar tongue becomes intelligible in
time when we are always hearing it spoken. I was sorry that this should be
dialect, for I succeeded in picking it up, and should have been no less
successful had Françoise been in the habit of expressing herself in Persian. In
vain might Françoise, when she became aware of my progress, accelerate the
speed of her utterance, and her daughter likewise, it was no good. The
mother was greatly put out that I understood their dialect, then delighted to
hear me speak it. I am bound to admit that her delight was a mocking
delight, for albeit I came in time to pronounce the words more or less as she
herself did, she found between our two ways of pronunciation an abyss of
difference which gave her infinite joy, and she began to regret that she no
longer saw people to whom she had not given a thought for years but who,

it appeared, would have rocked with a laughter which it would have done her good to hear, if they could have heard me speaking their dialect so badly. In any case, no joy came to mitigate her sorrow that, however badly I might pronounce it, I understood it well. Keys become useless when the person whom we seek to prevent from entering can avail himself of a skeleton key or a jemmy. Dialect having become useless as a means of defence, she took to conversing with her daughter in a French which rapidly became that of the most debased epochs.

I was now ready, but Françoise had not yet telephoned; I ought perhaps to go out without waiting for a message. But how could I tell that she would find Albertine, that the latter would not have gone behind the scenes, that even if Françoise did find her, she would allow herself to be taken away? Half an hour later the telephone bell began to tinkle and my heart throbbed tumultuously with hope and fear. There came, at the bidding of an operator, a flying squadron of sounds which with an instantaneous speed brought me the words of the telephonist, not those of Françoise whom an inherited timidity and melancholy, when she was brought face to face with any object unknown to her fathers, prevented from approaching a telephone receiver, although she would readily visit a person suffering from a contagious disease. She had found Albertine in the lobby by herself, and Albertine had simply gone to warn Andrée that she was not staying any longer and then had hurried back to Françoise. 'She wasn't angry? Oh, I beg your pardon; will you please ask the person whether the young lady was angry?' 'The lady asks me to say that she wasn't at all angry, quite the contrary, in fact; anyhow, if she wasn't pleased, she didn't show it. They are starting now for the Trois-Quartiers, and will be home by two o'clock.' I gathered that two o'clock meant three, for it was past two o'clock already. But Françoise suffered from one of those peculiar, permanent, incurable defects, which we call maladies; she was never able either to read or to announce the time correctly. I have never been able to understand what went on in her head. When Françoise, after consulting her watch, if it was two o'clock, said: 'It is one' or 'it is three o'clock,' I have never been able to understand whether the phenomenon that occurred was situated in her vision or in her thought or in her speech; the one thing certain is that the phenomenon never failed to occur. Humanity is a very old institution. Heredity, cross breeding have given an irresistible force to bad habits, to vicious reflexes. One person sneezes and gasps because he is passing a rose bush, another breaks out in an eruption at the smell of wet paint, has frequent attacks of colic if he has to start on a journey, and grandchildren of thieves who are themselves millionaires and generous cannot resist the temptation to rob you of fifty francs. As for knowing in what consisted Françoise's incapacity to tell the time correctly, she herself never threw any light upon the problem. For, notwithstanding the anger that I generally displayed at her inaccurate replies, Françoise never attempted either to apologise for her mistake or to explain it. She remained silent, pretending not to hear, and thereby making me lose my temper altogether. I should have liked to hear a few words of justification, were it only that I might smite her hip and thigh; but not a word, an indifferent silence. In any case, about the timetable for today there could be no doubt; Albertine was coming home with Françoise at three o'clock, Albertine would not be meeting Léa or her friends. Whereupon the danger of her renewing relations with them, having been averted, at once began to lose its importance in my eyes and I was amazed, seeing with what ease it had been averted, that I should have supposed that I would not succeed in averting it. I felt a keen impulse of gratitude to Albertine, who, I could see, had not gone to the Trocadéro to meet Léa's friends, and showed me, by leaving the performance and coming home at a word from myself, that she belonged to me more than I had imagined. My gratitude was even greater when a bicyclist brought me a line from her bidding me be patient, and full of the charming expressions that she was in the habit of using. 'My darling, dear Marcel, I return less quickly than this cyclist, whose machine I would like to borrow in order to be with you sooner. How could you imagine that I might be angry or that I could enjoy anything better than to be with you? It will be nice to go out, just the two of us together; it would be nicer still if we never went out except together. The ideas you get into your head! What a Marcel! What a Marcel! Always and ever your Albertine.'

The frocks that I bought for her, the yacht of which I had spoken to her, the wrappers from Fortuny's, all these things having in this obedience on Albertine's part not their recompense but their complement, appeared to me now as so many privileges that I was enjoying; for the duties and expenditure of a master are part of his dominion, and define it, prove it, fully as much as his rights. And these rights which she recognised in me were precisely what gave my expenditure its true character: I had a woman of my own, who, at the first word that I sent to her unexpectedly, made my messenger telephone humbly that she was coming, that she was allowing herself to be brought home immediately. I was more of a master than I had supposed. More of a master, in other words more of a slave. I no longer felt the slightest impatience to see Albertine. The certainty that she was at this moment engaged in shopping with Françoise, or that she would return with her at an approaching moment which I would willingly have postponed, illuminated like a calm and radiant star a period of time which I would now have been far better pleased to spend alone. My love for Albertine had made me rise and get ready to go out, but it would prevent me from enjoying my outing. I reflected that on a Sunday afternoon like this little shopgirls, midinettes, prostitutes must be strolling in the Bois. And with the words *midinettes, little shopgirls* (as had often happened to me with a proper name, the name of a girl read in the account of a ball), with the image of a white bodice, a short skirt, since beneath them I placed a stranger who might perhaps come to love me, I created out of nothing desirable women, and said to myself: 'How charming they must be!' But of what use would it be to me that they were charming, seeing that I was not going out alone? Taking advantage of the fact that I still was alone, and drawing the curtains together so that the sun should not prevent me from reading the notes, I sat down at the piano, turned over the pages of Vinteuil's sonata which happened to be lying there, and began to play; seeing that Albertine's arrival was still a matter of some time but was on the other hand certain, I had at once time to spare and tranquillity of mind. Floating in the expectation, big with security, of her return escorted by Françoise and in my confidence in her docility as in the blessedness of an inward light as warming as the light of the sun, I might dispose of my thoughts, detach them for a moment from Albertine, apply them to the sonata. In the latter, indeed, I did not take pains to remark how the combinations of the voluptuous and anxious motives corresponded even more closely now to my love for Albertine, from which jealousy had been absent for so long that I had been able to confess to Swann my ignorance of that sentiment. No, taking the sonata from another point of view, regarding it in itself as the work of a great artist, I was carried back upon the tide of sound to the days at Combray – I do not mean at Montjouvain and along the Méséglise way, but to walks along the Guermantes way – when I had myself longed to become an artist. In definitely abandoning that ambition, had I forfeited something real? Could life console me for the loss of art, was there in art a more profound reality, in which our true personality finds an expression that is not afforded it by the activities of life? Every great artist seems indeed so different from all the rest, and gives us so strongly that sensation of individuality for which we seek in vain in our everyday existence. Just as I was thinking thus, I was struck by a passage in the sonata, a passage with which I was quite familiar, but sometimes our attention throws a different light upon things which we have long known, and we remark in them what we have never seen before. As I played the passage, and for all that in it Vinteuil had been trying to express a fancy which would have been wholly foreign to Wagner, I could not help murmuring '*Tristan*', with the smile of an old friend of the family discovering a trace of the grandfather in an intonation, a gesture of the grandson who never set eyes on him. And as the friend then examines a photograph which enables him to estimate the likeness, so, in front of Vinteuil's sonata, I set up on the music-rest the score of *Tristan*, a selection from which was being given that afternoon, as it happened, at the Lamoureux concert. I had not, in admiring the Bayreuth master, any of the scruples of those people whom, like Nietzsche, their sense of duty bids to shun in art as in life the beauty that tempts them, and who, tearing themselves from *Tristan* as they renounce *Parsifal*, and, in their spiritual asceticism, progressing from one mortification to another, arrive, by following the most bloody of *viae Crucis*, at exalting themselves to the pure cognition and perfect adoration of *Le Postillon de Longjumeau*. I began to perceive how much reality there is in the work of Wagner, when I saw in my mind's eye those insistent, fleeting themes which visit an act, withdraw only to return, and, sometimes distant, drowsy, almost detached, are at other moments, while remaining vague, so pressing and so near, so internal, so organic, so visceral, that one would call them the resumption not so much of a musical motive as of an attack of neuralgia.

Music, very different in this respect from Albertine's society, helped me to descend into myself, to make there a fresh discovery: that of the difference that I had sought in vain in life, in travel, a longing for which was given me, however, by this sonorous tide which sent its sunlit waves rolling to expire at my feet. A twofold difference. As the spectrum makes visible to us the composition of light, so the harmony of a Wagner, the colour of an Elstir enable us to know that essential quality of another person's sensations into which love for another person does not allow us to penetrate. Then there is diversity inside the work itself, by the sole means that it has of being effectively diverse, to wit combining diverse individualities. Where a minor composer would pretend that he was portraying a squire, or a knight, whereas he would make them both sing the same music, Wagner on the contrary allots to each denomination a different reality, and whenever a squire appears, it is an individual figure, at once complicated and simplified, that, with a joyous, feudal clash of warring sounds, inscribes itself in the vast, sonorous mass. Whence the completeness of a music that is indeed filled with so many different musics, each of which is a person. A person or the impression that is given us by a momentary aspect of nature. Even what is most independent of the sentiment that it makes us feel preserves its outward and entirely definite reality; the song of a bird, the ring of a hunter's horn, the air that a shepherd plays upon his pipe, cut out against the horizon their silhouette of sound. It is true that Wagner had still to bring these together, to make use of them, to introduce them into an orchestral whole, to make them subservient to the highest musical ideals, but always respecting their original nature, as a carpenter respects the grain, the peculiar essence of the wood that he is carving.

But notwithstanding the richness of these works in which the contemplation of nature has its place by the side of action, by the side of persons who are something more than proper names, I thought how markedly, all the same, these works participate in that quality of being – albeit marvellously – always incomplete, which is the peculiarity of all the great works of the nineteenth century, with which the greatest writers of that century have stamped their books, but, watching themselves at work as though they were at once author and critic, have derived from this self-contemplation a novel beauty, exterior and superior to the work itself, imposing upon it retrospectively a unity, a greatness which it does not possess. Without pausing to consider him who saw in his novels, after they had appeared, a *Human Comedy*, nor those who entitled heterogeneous poems or essays *The Legend of the Ages* or *The Bible of Humanity*, can we not say all the same of the last of these that he is so perfect an incarnation of the nineteenth century that the greatest beauties in Michelet are to be sought not so much in his work itself as in the attitudes that he adopts when he is considering his work, not in his *History of France* nor in his *History of the Revolution*, but in his prefaces to his books? Prefaces, that is to say pages written after the books themselves, in which he considers the books, and with which we must include here and there certain phrases beginning as a rule with a: 'Shall I say?' which is not a scholar's precaution but a musician's cadence. The other musician, he who was delighting me at this moment, Wagner, retrieving some exquisite scrap from a drawer of his writing-table to make it appear as a theme, retrospectively necessary, in a work of which he had not been thinking at the moment when he composed it, then having composed a first mythological opera, and a second, and afterwards others still, and perceiving all of a sudden that he had written a tetralogy, must have felt something of the same exhilaration as Balzac, when, casting over his works the eye at once of a stranger and of a father, finding in one the purity of Raphael, in another the simplicity of the Gospel, he suddenly decided, as he shed a retrospective illumination upon them, that they would be better brought together in a cycle in which the same characters would reappear, and added to his work, in this act of joining it together, a stroke of the brush, the last and the most sublime. A unity that was ulterior, not artificial, otherwise it would have crumbled into dust like all the other systematisations of mediocre writers who with the elaborate assistance of titles and subtitles give themselves the

appearance of having pursued a single and transcendent design. Not
fictitious, perhaps indeed all the more real for being ulterior, for being born
of a moment of enthusiasm when it is discovered to exist among fragments
which need only to be joined together. A unity that has been unaware of
itself, therefore vital and not logical, that has not banned variety, chilled
execution. It emerges (only applying itself this time to the work as a whole)
like a fragment composed separately, born of an inspiration, not required by
the artificial development of a theme, which comes in to form an integral
part of the rest. Before the great orchestral movement that precedes the
return of Yseult, it is the work itself that has attracted to it the half-forgotten
air of a shepherd's pipe. And, no doubt, just as the swelling of the orchestra
at the approach of the ship, when it takes hold of these notes on the pipe,
transforms them, infects them with its own intoxication, breaks their
rhythm, clarifies their tone, accelerates their movement, multiplies their
instrumentation, so no doubt Wagner himself was filled with joy when he
discovered in his memory a shepherd's air, incorporated it in his work, gave
it its full wealth of meaning. This joy moreover never forsakes him. In him,
however great the melancholy of the poet, it is consoled, surpassed – that is
to say destroyed, alas, too soon – by the delight of the craftsman. But then,
no less than by the similarity I had remarked just now between Vinteuil's
phrase and Wagner's, I was troubled by the thought of this Vulcan-like
craftsmanship. Could it be this that gave to great artists the illusory
appearance of a fundamental originality, incommensurable with any other,
the reflection of a more than human reality, actually the result of industrious
toil? If art be no more than that, it is not more real than life and I had less
cause for regret. I went on playing *Tristan*. Separated from Wagner by the
wall of sound, I could hear him exult, invite me to share his joy, I could hear
ring out all the louder the immortally youthful laugh and the hammer-
blows of Siegfried, in which, moreover, more marvellously struck were
those phrases, the technical skill of the craftsman serving merely to make it
easier for them to leave the earth, birds akin not to Lohengrin's swan but to
that aeroplane which I had seen at Balbec convert its energy into vertical
motion, float over the sea and lose itself in the sky. Perhaps, as the birds that
soar highest and fly most swiftly have a stronger wing, one required one of
these frankly material vehicles to explore the infinite, one of these 120
horsepower machines, marked Mystery, in which nevertheless, however
high one flies, one is prevented to some extent from enjoying the silence of
space by the overpowering roar of the engine!

    For some reason or other the course of my musings, which hitherto had
wandered among musical memories, turned now to those men who have

been the best performers of music in our day, among whom, slightly exaggerating his merit, I included Morel. At once my thoughts took a sharp turn, and it was Morel's character, certain eccentricities of his nature that I began to consider. As it happened – and this might be connected though it should not be confused with the neurasthenia to which he was a prey – Morel was in the habit of talking about his life, but always presented so shadowy a picture of it that it was difficult to make anything out. For instance, he placed himself entirely at M. de Charlus's disposal on the understanding that he must keep his evenings free, as he wished to be able after dinner to attend a course of lectures on algebra. M. de Charlus conceded this, but insisted upon seeing him after the lectures. 'Impossible, it's an old Italian painting' (this witticism means nothing when written down like this; but M. de Charlus having made Morel read *l'Éducation sentimentale*, in the penultimate chapter of which Frédéric Moreau uses this expression, it was Morel's idea of a joke never to say the word 'impossible' without following it up with 'it's an old Italian painting') 'the lectures go on very late, and I've already given a lot of trouble to the lecturer, who naturally would be annoyed if I came away in the middle.' 'But there's no need to attend lectures, algebra is not a thing like swimming, or even English, you can learn it equally well from a book,' replied M. de Charlus, who had guessed from the first that these algebra lectures were one of those images of which it was impossible to make out anything. It was perhaps some affair with a woman, or, if Morel was seeking to earn money in shady ways and had attached himself to the secret police, a nocturnal expedition with detectives, or possibly, what was even worse, an engagement as one of the young men whose services may be required in a brothel. 'A great deal easier, from a book,' Morel assured M. de Charlus, 'for it's impossible to make head or tail of the lectures.' 'Then why don't you study it in my house, where you would be far more comfortable?' M. de Charlus might have answered, but took care not to do so, knowing that at once, preserving only the same essential element that the evening hours must be set apart, the imaginary algebra course would change to a compulsory lesson in dancing or in drawing. In which M. de Charlus might have seen that he was mistaken, partially at least, for Morel did often spend his time at the Baron's in solving equations. M. de Charlus did raise the objection that algebra could be of little use to a violinist. Morel replied that it was a distraction which helped him to pass the time and to conquer his neurasthenia. No doubt M. de Charlus might have made enquiries, have tried to find out what actually were these mysterious and ineluctable lectures on algebra that were delivered only at night. But M. de Charlus was not qualified to unravel the tangled skein of Morel's occupations, being himself too much caught in the toils of social life. The visits he received or paid, the time he spent at his club, dinner-parties, evenings at the theatre prevented him from thinking about the problem, or for that matter about the violent and vindictive animosity which Morel had (it was reported) indulged and at the same time sought to conceal in the various environments, the different towns in which his life had been spent, and where people still spoke of him with a shudder, with bated breath, never venturing to say anything definite about him.

It was unfortunately one of the outbursts of this neurotic irritability that I was privileged to hear that day when, rising from the piano, I went down to the courtyard to meet Albertine, who still did not appear. As I passed by Jupien's shop, in which Morel and the girl who, I supposed, was shortly to become his wife were by themselves, Morel was screaming at the top of his voice, thereby revealing an accent that I had never heard in his speech, a rustic tone, suppressed as a rule, and very strange indeed. His words were no less strange, faulty from the point of view of the French language, but his knowledge of everything was imperfect. 'Will you get out of here, *grand pied de grue, grand pied de grue, grand pied de grue,*' he repeated to the poor girl who at first had certainly not understood what he meant, and now, trembling and indignant, stood motionless before him. 'Didn't I tell you to get out of here, *grand pied de grue, grand pied de grue*; go and fetch your uncle till I tell him what you are, you whore.' Just at that moment the voice of Jupien who was coming home talking to one of his friends was heard in the courtyard, and as I knew that Morel was an utter coward, I decided that it was unnecessary to join my forces with those of Jupien and his friend, who in another moment would have entered the shop, and I retired upstairs again to escape Morel, who, for all his having pretended to be so anxious that Jupien should be fetched (probably in order to frighten and subjugate the girl, an act of blackmail which rested probably upon no foundation), made haste to depart as soon as he heard his voice in the courtyard. The words I have set down here are nothing, they would not explain why my heart throbbed so as I went upstairs. These scenes of which we are witnesses in real life find an incalculable element of strength in what soldiers call, in speaking of a military offensive, the advantage of surprise, and however agreeably I might be soothed by the knowledge that Albertine, instead of remaining at the Trocadéro, was coming home to me, I still heard ringing in my ears the accent of those words ten times repeated: '*Grand pied de grue, grand pied de grue*', which had so appalled me.

Gradually my agitation subsided. Albertine was on her way home. I should hear her ring the bell in a moment. I felt that my life was no longer what it might have become, and that to have a woman in the house like this with whom quite naturally, when she returned home, I should have to go out, to the adornment of whose person the strength and activity of my nature were to be ever more and more diverted, made me as it were a bough that has blossomed, but is weighed down by the abundant fruit into which all its reserves of strength have passed. In contrast to the anxiety that I had been feeling only an hour earlier, the calm that I now felt at the prospect of Albertine's return was more ample than that which I had felt in the morning before she left the house. Anticipating the future, of which my mistress's docility made me practically master, more resistant, as though it were filled and stabilised by the imminent, importunate, inevitable, gentle presence, it was the calm (dispensing us from the obligation to seek our happiness in ourselves) that is born of family feeling and domestic bliss. Family and domestic: such was again, no less than the sentiment that had brought me such great peace while I was waiting for Albertine, that which I felt later on when I drove out with her. She took off her glove for a moment, whether to touch my hand, or to dazzle me by letting me see on her little finger, next to the ring that Mme Bontemps had given her, another upon which was displayed the large and liquid surface of a clear sheet of ruby. 'What! Another ring, Albertine. Your aunt is generous!' 'No, I didn't get this from my aunt,' she said with a laugh. 'It was I who bought it, now that, thanks to you, I can save up ever so much money. I don't even know whose it was before. A visitor who was short of money left it with the landlord of an hotel where I stayed at Le Mans. He didn't know what to do with it, and would have let it go for much less than it was worth. But it was still far too dear for me. Now that, thanks to you, I'm becoming a smart lady, I wrote to ask him if he still had it. And here it is.' 'That makes a great many rings, Albertine. Where will you put the one that I am going to give you? Anyhow, it is a beautiful ring, I can't quite make out what that is carved round the ruby, it looks like a man's head grinning. But my eyes aren't strong enough.' 'They might be as strong as you like, you would be no better off. I can't make it out either.' In the past it had often happened, as I read somebody's memoirs, or a novel, in which a man always goes out driving with a woman, takes tea with her, that I longed to be able to do likewise. I had thought sometimes that I was successful, as for instance when I took Saint-Loup's mistress out with me, or went to dinner with her. But in vain might I summon to my assistance the idea that I was at that moment actually impersonating the character that I had envied in the novel, that idea assured me that I ought to find pleasure in Rachel's society, and afforded me none. For, whenever we attempt to imitate something that has really existed, we forget that this something was brought about not by the desire to imitate but by an unconscious force which itself also is real; but this particular impression which I had been unable to derive from all my desire to taste a delicate pleasure in going out with Rachel, behold I was now tasting it without having made the slightest effort to procure it, but for quite different reasons, sincere, profound; to take a single instance, for the reason that my jealousy prevented me from letting Albertine go out of my sight, and, the moment that I was able to leave the house, from letting her go anywhere without me. I tasted it only now, because our knowledge is not of the external objects which we try to observe, but of involuntary sensations, because in the past a woman might be sitting in the same carriage as myself, she was not *really* by my side, so long as she was not created afresh there at every moment by a need of her such as I felt of Albertine, so long as the constant caress of my gaze did not incessantly restore to her those tints that need to be perpetually refreshed, so long as my senses, appeased it might be but still endowed with memory, did not place beneath those colours savour and substance, so long as, combined with the senses and with the imagination that exalts them, jealousy was not maintaining the woman in equilibrium by my side by a compensated attraction as powerful as the law of gravity. Our motorcar passed swiftly along the boulevards, the avenues whose lines of houses, a rosy congelation of sunshine and cold, reminded me of calling upon Mme Swann in the soft light of her chrysanthemums, before it was time to ring for the lamps.

I had barely time to make out, being divided from them by the glass of the motorcar as effectively as I should have been by that of my bedroom window, a young fruit-seller, a dairymaid, standing in the doorway of her shop, illuminated by the sunshine like a heroine whom my desire was sufficient to launch upon exquisite adventures, on the threshold of a romance which I might never know. For I could not ask Albertine to let me stop, and already the young women were no longer visible whose features my eyes had barely distinguished, barely caressed their fresh complexions in the golden vapour in which they were bathed. The emotion that I felt grip me when I caught sight of a wine-merchant's girl at her desk or a laundress chatting in the street was the emotion that we feel on recognising a goddess. Now that Olympus no longer exists, its inhabitants dwell upon the earth. And when, in composing a mythological scene, painters have engaged to pose as Venus or Ceres young women of humble birth, who follow the most sordid callings, so far from committing sacrilege, they have merely added, restored to them the quality, the various attributes which they had forfeited. 'What did you think of the Trocadéro, you little gadabout?' 'I'm jolly glad I came away from it to go out with you. As architecture, it's pretty measly, isn't

it? It's by Davioud, I fancy.' 'But how learned my little Albertine is becoming!
Of course it was Davioud who built it, but I couldn't have told you offhand.'
'While you are asleep, I read your books, you old lazybones.' 'Listen, child,
you are changing so fast and becoming so intelligent' (this was true, but even
had it not been true I was not sorry that she should have the satisfaction,
failing any other, of saying to herself that at least the time which she spent in
my house was not being entirely wasted) 'that I don't mind telling you things
that would generally be regarded as false and which are all on the way to a
truth that I am seeking. You know what is meant by impressionism?' 'Of
course!' 'Very well then, this is what I mean: you remember the church at
Marcouville l'Orgueilleuse which Elstir disliked because it was new. Isn't it
rather a denial of his own impressionism when he subtracts such buildings
from the general impression in which they are contained to bring them out
of the light in which they are dissolved and scrutinise like an archaeologist
their intrinsic merit? When he begins to paint, have not a hospital, a school,
a poster upon a hoarding the same value as a priceless cathedral which stands
by their side in a single indivisible image? Remember how the façade was
baked by the sun, how that carved frieze of saints swam upon the sea of light.
What does it matter that a building is new, if it appears to be old, or even if it
does not. All the poetry that the old quarters contain has been squeezed out
to the last drop, but if you look at some of the houses that have been built
lately for rich tradesmen, in the new districts, where the stone is all freshly
cut and still quite white, don't they seem to rend the torrid air of noon in
July, at the hour when the shopkeepers go home to luncheon in the suburbs,
with a cry as harsh as the odour of the cherries waiting for the meal to begin
in the darkened dining-room, where the prismatic glass knife-rests project a
multicoloured fire as beautiful as the windows of Chartres?' 'How wonderful
you are! If I ever do become clever, it will be entirely owing to you.' 'Why on
a fine day tear your eyes away from the Trocadéro, whose giraffe-neck
towers remind one of the Charterhouse of Pavia?' 'It reminded me also,
standing up like that on its hill, of a Mantegna that you have, I think it's of
Saint Sebastian, where in the background there's a city like an amphitheatre,
and you would swear you saw the Trocadéro.' 'There, you see! But how did
you come across my Mantegna? You are amazing!' We had now reached a
more plebeian quarter, and the installation of an ancillary Venus behind
each counter made it as it were a suburban altar at the foot of which I would
gladly have spent the rest of my life.

As one does on the eve of a premature death, I drew up a mental list of the
pleasures of which I was deprived by Albertine's setting a full stop to my
freedom. At Passy it was in the open street, so crowded were the footways,

that a group of girls, their arms encircling one another's waist, left me marvelling at their smile. I had not time to see it clearly, but it is hardly probable that I exaggerated it; in any crowd after all, in any crowd of young people, it is not unusual to come upon the effigy of a noble profile. So that these assembled masses on public holidays are to the voluptuary as precious as is to the archaeologist the congested state of a piece of ground in which digging will bring to light ancient medals. We arrived at the Bois. I reflected that, if Albertine had not come out with me, I might at this moment, in the enclosure of the Champs-Elysées, have been hearing the Wagnerian tempest set all the rigging of the orchestra ascream, draw to itself, like a light spindrift, the tune of the shepherd's pipe which I had just been playing to myself, set it flying, mould it, deform it, divide it, sweep it away in an ever-increasing whirlwind. I was determined, at any rate, that our drive should be short, and that we should return home early, for, without having mentioned it to Albertine, I had decided to go that evening to the Verdurins'. They had recently sent me an invitation which I had flung into the wastepaper basket with all the rest. But I changed my mind for this evening, for I meant to try to find out who the people were that Albertine might have been hoping to meet there in the afternoon. To tell the truth, I had reached that stage in my relations with Albertine when, if everything remains the same, if things go on normally, a woman ceases to serve us except as a starting point towards another woman. She still retains a corner in our heart, but a very small corner; we hasten out every evening in search of unknown women, especially unknown women who are known to her and can tell us about her life. Herself, after all, we have possessed, have exhausted everything that she has consented to yield to us of herself. Her life is still herself, but that part of herself which we do not know, the things as to which we have questioned her in vain and which we shall be able to gather from fresh lips.

If my life with Albertine was to prevent me from going to Venice, from travelling, at least I might in the meantime, had I been alone, have made the acquaintance of the young midinettes scattered about in the sunlight of this fine Sunday, in the sum total of whose beauty I gave a considerable place to the unknown life that animated them. The eyes that we see, are they not shot through by a gaze as to which we do not know what images, memories, expectations, disdains it carries, a gaze from which we cannot separate them? The life that the person who passes by is living, will it not impart, according to what it is, a different value to the knitting of those brows, to the dilatation of those nostrils? Albertine's presence debarred me from going to join them and perhaps also from ceasing to desire them. The man who would maintain in himself the desire to go on living, and his belief in something more delicious than the things of daily life, must go out driving; for the streets, the avenues are full of goddesses. But the goddesses do not allow us to approach them. Here and there, among the trees, at the entrance to some café, a waitress was watching like a nymph on the edge of a sacred grove, while beyond her three girls were seated by the sweeping arc of their bicycles that were stacked beside them, like three immortals leaning against the clouds or the fabulous coursers upon which they perform their mythological journeys. I remarked that, whenever Albertine looked for a moment at these girls, with a profound attention, she at once turned to gaze at myself. But I was not unduly troubled, either by the intensity of this contemplation, or by its brevity for which its intensity compensated; as for the latter, it often happened that Albertine, whether from exhaustion, or because it was an intense person's way of looking at other people, used to gaze thus in a sort of brown study at my father, it might be, or at Françoise; and as for the rapidity with which she turned to look at myself, it might be due to the fact that Albertine, knowing my suspicions, might prefer, even if they were not justified, to avoid giving them any foothold. This attention, moreover, which would have seemed to me criminal on Albertine's part (and quite as much so if it had been directed at young men), I fastened, without thinking myself reprehensible for an instant, almost deciding indeed that Albertine was reprehensible for preventing me, by her presence, from stopping the car and going to join them, upon all the midinettes. We consider it innocent to desire a thing and atrocious that the other person should desire it. And this contrast between what concerns ourselves on the one hand, and on the other the person with whom we are in love, is not confined only to desire, but extends also to falsehood. What is more usual than a lie, whether it is a question of masking the daily weakness of a constitution which we wish to be thought strong, of concealing a vice, or of going off, without offending the other person, to the thing that we prefer? It is the most necessary instrument of conversation, and the one that is most widely used. But it is this which we actually propose to banish from the life of her whom we love; we watch for it, scent it, detest it everywhere. It appalls us, it is sufficient to bring about a rupture, it seems to us to be concealing the most serious faults, except when it does so effectively conceal them that we do not suspect their existence. A strange state this in which we are so inordinately sensitive to a pathogenic agent which its universal swarming makes inoffensive to other people and so serious to the wretch who finds that he is no longer immune to it.

The life of these pretty girls (because of my long periods of seclusion, I so rarely met any) appeared to me as to everyone in whom facility of realisation has not destroyed the faculty of imagination, a thing as different from anything that I knew, as desirable as the most marvellous cities that travel holds in store for us.

The disappointment that I had felt with the women whom I had known, in the cities which I had visited, did not prevent me from letting myself be caught by the attraction of others or from believing in their reality; thus, just as seeing Venice – that Venice for which the spring weather too filled me with longing, and which marriage with Albertine would prevent me from knowing – seeing Venice in a panorama which Ski would perhaps have declared to be more beautiful in tone than the place itself, would to me have been no substitute for the journey to Venice the length of which, determined without any reference to myself, seemed to me an indispensable preliminary; similarly, however pretty she might be, the midinette whom a procuress had artificially provided for me could not possibly be a substitute for her who with her awkward figure was strolling at this moment under the trees, laughing with a friend. The girl that I might find in a house of assignation, were she even better-looking than this one, could not be the same thing, because we do not look at the eyes of a girl whom we do not know as we should look at a pair of little discs of opal or agate. We know that the little ray which colours them or the diamond dust that makes them sparkle is all that we can see of a mind, a will, a memory in which is contained the home life that we do not know, the intimate friends whom we envy. The enterprise of taking possession of all this, which is so difficult, so stubborn, is what gives its value to the gaze far more than its merely physical beauty (which may serve to explain why the same young man can awaken a whole romance in the imagination of a woman who has heard somebody say that he is the Prince of Wales, whereas she pays no more attention to him after learning that she is mistaken); to find the midinette in the house of assignation is to find her emptied of that unknown life which permeates her and which we aspire to possess with her, it is to approach a pair of eyes that have indeed become mere precious stones, a nose whose quivering is as devoid of meaning as that of a flower. No, that unknown midinette who was passing at that moment, it seemed to me as indispensable, if I wished to continue to believe in her reality, to test her resistance by adapting my behaviour to it, challenging a rebuff, returning to the charge, obtaining an assignation, waiting for her as she came away from her work, getting to know, episode by episode, all that composed the girl's life, traversing the space that, for her, enveloped the pleasure which I was seeking, and the distance which her different habits, her special mode of life, set between me and the attention, the favour which I wished to attain and capture, as making a long journey in the train if I wished to believe in the reality of Venice which I should see and which would not be merely a panoramic show in a World Exhibition. But this very parallel between desire and travel made me vow to myself that one day I would grasp a little more closely the nature of this force, invisible but as powerful as any faith, or as, in the world of physics, atmospheric pressure, which exalted to such a height cities and women so long as I did not know them, and slipped away from beneath them as soon as I had approached them, made them at once collapse and fall flat upon the dead level of the most commonplace reality.

Farther along another girl was kneeling beside her bicycle, which she was putting to rights. The repair finished, the young racer mounted her machine, but without straddling it as a man would have done. For a moment the bicycle swerved, and the young body seemed to have added to itself a sail, a huge wing; and presently we saw dart away at full speed the young creature half-human, half-winged, angel or peri, pursuing her course.

This was what a life with Albertine prevented me from enjoying. Prevented me, did I say? Should I not have thought rather: what it provided for my enjoyment. If Albertine had not been living with me, had been free, I should have imagined, and with reason, every woman to be a possible, a probable object of her desire, of her pleasure. They would have appeared to me like those dancers who, in a diabolical ballet, representing the Temptations to one person, plunge their darts in the heart of another. Midinettes, schoolgirls, actresses, how I should have hated them all! Objects of horror, I should have excepted them from the beauty of the universe. My bondage to Albertine, by permitting me not to suffer any longer on their account, restored them to the beauty of the world. Inoffensive, having lost the needle that stabs the heart with jealousy, I was able to admire them, to caress them with my eyes, another day more intimately perhaps. By secluding Albertine, I had at the same time restored to the universe all those rainbow wings which sweep past us in public gardens, ballrooms, theatres, and which became tempting once more to me because she could no longer succumb to their temptation. They composed the beauty of the world. They had at one time composed that of Albertine. It was because I had beheld her as a mysterious bird, then as a great actress of the beach, desired, perhaps won, that I had thought her wonderful. As soon as she was a captive in my house, the bird that I had seen one afternoon advancing with measured step along the front, surrounded by the congregation of the other girls like seagulls alighted from who knows whence, Albertine had lost all her colours, with all the chances that other people had of securing her for themselves. Gradually she had lost her beauty. It required excursions like this, in which I imagined her, but for my presence, accosted by some woman, or by some young man, to make me see her again amid the splendour of the beach, albeit my jealousy was on a different plane from the decline of the pleasures of my imagination. But notwithstanding these abrupt reversions in which, desired by other people, she once more became beautiful in my eyes, I might very well divide her visit to me in two periods, an earlier in which she was still, although less so every day, the glittering actress of the beach, and a later period in which, become the grey captive, reduced to her dreary self, I required those flashes in which I remembered the past to make me see her again in colour.

Sometimes, in the hours in which I felt most indifferent towards her, there came back to me the memory of a far-off moment when upon the beach, before I had made her acquaintance, a lady being near her with whom I was on bad terms and with whom I was almost certain now that she had had relations, she burst out laughing, staring me in the face in an insolent fashion. All round her hissed the blue and polished sea. In the sunshine of the beach, Albertine, in the midst of her friends, was the most beautiful of them all. She was a splendid girl, who in her familiar setting of boundless waters, had – precious in the eyes of the lady who admired her – inflicted upon me this unpardonable insult. It was unpardonable, for the lady would perhaps return to Balbec, would notice perhaps, on the luminous and echoing beach, that Albertine was absent. But she would not know that the girl was living with me, was wholly mine. The vast expanse of blue water, her forgetfulness of the fondness that she had felt for this particular girl and would divert to others, had closed over the outrage that Albertine had done me, enshrining it in a glittering and unbreakable casket. Then hatred of that woman gnawed my heart; of Albertine also, but a hatred mingled with admiration of the beautiful, courted girl, with her marvellous hair, whose laughter upon the beach had been an insult. Shame, jealousy, the memory of my earliest desires and of the brilliant setting had restored to Albertine the beauty, the intrinsic merit of other days. And thus there alternated with the somewhat oppressive boredom that I felt in her company a throbbing desire, full of splendid storms and of regrets; according to whether she was by my side in my bedroom or I set her at liberty in my memory upon the front, in her gay seaside frocks, to the sound of the musical instruments of the sea – Albertine, now extracted from that environment, possessed and of no great value, now plunged back into it, escaping from me into a past which I should never be able to know, hurting me, in her friend's presence, as much as the splash of the wave or the heat of the sun, Albertine restored to the beach or brought back again to my room, in a sort of amphibious love.

Farther on, a numerous band were playing ball. All these girls had come out to make the most of the sunshine, for these days in February, even when they are brilliant, do not last long and the splendour of their light does not postpone the hour of its decline. Before that hour drew near, we passed some time in twilight, because after we had driven as far as the Seine, where Albertine admired, and by her presence prevented me from admiring the reflections of red sails upon the wintry blue of the water, a solitary house in the distance like a single red poppy against the clear horizon, of which Saint-Cloud seemed, farther off again, to be the fragmentary, crumbling, rugged petrification, we left our motorcar and walked a long way together; indeed for some moments I gave her my arm, and it seemed to me that the ring which her arm formed round it united our two persons in a single self and linked our separate destinies together.

At our feet, our parallel shadows, where they approached and joined, traced an exquisite pattern. No doubt it already seemed to me a marvellous thing at home that Albertine should be living with me, that it should be she that came and lay down on my bed. But it was so to speak the transportation of that marvel out of doors, into the heart of nature, that by the shore of that lake in the Bois, of which I was so fond, beneath the trees, it should be her and none but her shadow, the pure and simplified shadow of her leg, of her bust, that the sun had to depict in monochrome by the side of mine upon the gravel of the path. And I found a charm that was more immaterial doubtless, but no less intimate, than in the drawing together, the fusion of our bodies, in that of our shadows. Then we returned to our car. And it chose, for our homeward journey, a succession of little winding lanes along which the wintry trees, clothed, like ruins, in ivy and brambles, seemed to be pointing the way to the dwelling of some magician. No sooner had we emerged from their dusky cover than we found, upon leaving the Bois, the daylight still so bright that I imagined that I should still have time to do everything that I wanted to do before dinner, when, only a few minutes later, at the moment when our car approached the Arc de Triomphe, it was with a sudden start of surprise and dismay that I perceived, over Paris, the moon prematurely full, like the face of a clock that has stopped and makes us think that we are late for an engagement. We had told the driver to take us home. To Albertine, this meant also coming to my home. The company of those women, however dear to us, who are obliged to leave us and return home, does not bestow that peace which I found in the company of Albertine seated in the car by my side, a company that was conveying us not to the void in which lovers have to part but to an even more stable and more sheltered union in my home, which was also hers, the material symbol of my possession of her. To be sure, in order to possess, one must first have desired. We do not possess a line, a surface, a mass unless it is occupied by our love. But

Albertine had not been for me during our drive, as Rachel had been in the past, a futile dust of flesh and clothing. The imagination of my eyes, my lips, my hands had at Balbec so solidly built, so tenderly polished her body that now in this car, to touch that body, to contain it, I had no need to press my own body against Albertine, nor even to see her; it was enough to hear her, and if she was silent to know that she was by my side; my interwoven senses enveloped her altogether and when, as we arrived at the front door, she quite naturally alighted, I stopped for a moment to tell the chauffeur to call for me later on, but my gaze enveloped her still while she passed ahead of me under the arch, and it was still the same inert, domestic calm that I felt as I saw her thus, solid, flushed, opulent and captive, returning home quite naturally with myself, as a woman who was my own property, and, protected by its walls, disappearing into our house. Unfortunately, she seemed to feel herself a prisoner there, and to share the opinion of that Mme de La Rochefoucauld who, when somebody asked her whether she was not glad to live in so beautiful a home as Liancourt, replied: 'There is no such thing as a beautiful prison'; if I was to judge by her miserable, weary expression that evening as we dined together in my room. I did not notice it at first; and it was I that was made wretched by the thought that, if it had not been for Albertine (for with her I should have suffered too acutely from jealousy in an hotel where all day long she would have been exposed to contact with a crowd of strangers), I might at that moment be dining in Venice in one of those little restaurants, barrel-vaulted like the hold of a ship, from which one looks out on the Grand Canal through arched windows framed in Moorish mouldings.

I ought to add that Albertine greatly admired in my room a big bronze by Barbedienne which with ample justification Bloch considered extremely ugly. He had perhaps less reason to be surprised at my having kept it. I had never sought, like him, to furnish for artistic effect, to compose my surroundings, I was too lazy, too indifferent to the things that I was in the habit of seeing every day. Since my taste was not involved, I had a right not to harmonise my interior. I might perhaps, even without that, have discarded the bronze. But ugly and expensive things are of great use, for they enjoy, among people who do not understand us, who have not our taste and with whom we cannot fall in love, a prestige that would not be shared by some proud object that does not reveal its beauty. Now the people who do not understand us are precisely the people with regard to whom alone it may be useful to us to employ a prestige which our intellect is enough to assure us among superior people. Albertine might indeed be beginning to show taste, she still felt a certain respect for the bronze, and this respect was reflected upon myself in a consideration which, coming from Albertine, mattered infinitely more to me than the question of keeping a bronze which was a trifle degrading, since I was in love with Albertine.

But the thought of my bondage ceased of a sudden to weigh upon me and I looked forward to prolonging it still further, because I seemed to perceive that Albertine was painfully conscious of her own. True that whenever I had asked her whether she was not bored in my house, she had always replied that she did not know where it would be possible to have a happier time. But often these words were contradicted by an air of nervous exhaustion, of longing to escape.

Certainly if she had the tastes with which I had credited her, this inhibition from ever satisfying them must have been as provoking to her as it was calming to myself, calming to such an extent that I should have decided that the hypothesis of my having accused her unjustly was the most probable, had it not been so difficult to fit into this hypothesis the extraordinary pains that Albertine was taking never to be alone, never to be disengaged, never to stop for a moment outside the front door when she came in, to insist upon being accompanied, whenever she went to the telephone, by someone who would be able to repeat to me what she had said, by Françoise or Andrée, always to leave me alone (without appearing to be doing so on purpose) with the latter, after they had been out together, so that I might obtain a detailed report of their outing. With this marvellous docility were contrasted certain quickly repressed starts of impatience, which made me ask myself whether Albertine was not planning to cast off her chain. Certain subordinate incidents seemed to corroborate my supposition. Thus, one day when I had gone out by myself, in the Passy direction, and had met Gisèle, we began to talk about one thing and another. Presently, not without pride at being able to do so, I informed her that I was constantly seeing Albertine. Gisèle asked me where she could find her, since there was something that she simply *must* tell her. 'Why, what is it?' 'Something to do with some young friends of hers.' 'What friends? I may perhaps be able to tell you, though that need not prevent you from seeing her.' 'Oh, girls she knew years ago, I don't remember their names,' Gisèle replied vaguely, and beat a retreat. She left me, supposing herself to have spoken with such prudence that the whole story must seem to me perfectly straightforward. But falsehood is so unexacting, needs so little help to make itself manifest! If it had been a question of friends of long ago, whose very names she no longer remembered, why *must* she speak about them to Albertine? This '*must*', akin to an expression dear to Mme Cottard: 'in the nick of time', could be applicable only to something particular, opportune, perhaps urgent, relating to definite persons. Besides, something about her way of opening her mouth, as though she were going to yawn, with a vague expression, as she said to me (almost drawing back her body, as though she began to reverse her engine at this point in our conversation): 'Oh, I don't know, I don't remember their names', made her face, and in harmony with it her voice, as clear a picture of falsehood as the wholly different air, tense, excited, of her previous '*must*' was of truth. I did not question Gisèle. Of what use would it have been to me? Certainly, she was not lying in the same fashion as Albertine. And certainly Albertine's lies pained me more. But they had obviously a point in common: the fact of the lie itself, which in certain cases is self-evident. Not evidence of the truth that the lie conceals. We know that each murderer in turn imagines that he has arranged everything so cleverly that he will not be caught, and so it is with liars, particularly the woman with whom we are in love. We do not know where she has been, what she has been doing. But at the very moment when she speaks, when she speaks of something else beneath which lies hidden the thing that she does not mention, the lie is immediately perceived, and our jealousy increased, since we are conscious of the lie, and cannot succeed in discovering the truth. With Albertine, the impression that she was lying was conveyed by many of the peculiarities which we have already observed in the course of this narrative, but especially by this, that, when she was lying, her story broke down either from inadequacy, omission, improbability, or on the contrary from a surfeit of petty details intended to make it seem probable. Probability, notwithstanding the idea that the liar has formed of it, is by no means the same as truth. Whenever, while listening to something that is true, we hear something that is only probable, which is perhaps more so than the truth, which is perhaps too probable, the ear that is at all sensitive feels that it is not correct, as with a line that does not scan or a word read aloud in mistake for another. Our ear feels this, and if we are in love our heart takes alarm. Why do we not reflect at the time, when we change the whole course of our life because we do not know whether a woman went along the Rue de Berri or the Rue Washington, why do we not reflect that these few hundred yards of difference, and the woman herself, will be reduced to the hundred millionth part of themselves (that is to say to dimensions far beneath our perception), if we only have the wisdom to remain for a few years without seeing the woman, and that she who has out-Gullivered Gulliver in our eyes will shrink to a Lilliputian whom no microscope – of the heart, at least, for that of the disinterested memory is more powerful and less fragile – can ever again perceive! However it may be, if there was a point in common – the lie itself – between Albertine's lies and Gisèle's, still Gisèle did not lie in the same fashion as Albertine, nor indeed in the same fashion as Andrée, but their respective lies dovetailed so neatly into one another, while presenting a great variety, that the little band had the impenetrable solidity of certain commercial houses, booksellers' for example or printing presses, where the wretched author will never succeed, notwithstanding the diversity of the persons employed in them, in discovering whether he is being swindled or not. The editor of the newspaper or review lies with an attitude of sincerity all the more solemn in that he is frequently obliged to conceal the fact that he himself does exactly the same things and indulges in the same commercial practices that he denounced in other editors or theatrical managers, in other publishers, when he chose as his battle-cry, when he raised against them the standard of Sincerity. The fact of a man's having proclaimed (as leader of a political party, or in any other capacity) that it is wicked to lie, obliges him as a rule to lie more than other people, without on that account abandoning the solemn mask, doffing the august tiara of sincerity. The 'sincere' gentleman's partner lies in a different and more ingenuous fashion. He deceives his author as he deceives his wife, with tricks from the vaudeville stage. The secretary of the firm, a blunt and honest man, lies quite simply, like an architect who promises that your house will be ready at a date when it will not have been begun. The head reader, an angelic soul, flutters from one to another of the three, and without knowing what the matter is, gives them, by a brotherly scruple and out of affectionate solidarity, the precious support of a word that is above suspicion. These four persons live in a state of perpetual dissension to which the arrival of the author puts a stop. Over and above their private quarrels, each of them remembers the paramount military duty of rallying to the support of the threatened 'corps'. Without realising it, I had long been playing the part of this author among the little band. If Gisèle had been thinking, when she used the word 'must', of someone of Albertine's friends who was proposing to go abroad with her as soon as my mistress should have found some pretext or other for leaving me, and had meant to warn Albertine that the hour had now come or would shortly strike, she, Gisèle, would have let herself be torn to pieces rather than tell me so; it was quite useless therefore to ply her with questions. Meetings such as this with Gisèle were not alone in accentuating my doubts. For instance, I admired Albertine's sketches. Albertine's sketches, the touching distractions of the captive, moved me so that I congratulated her upon them. 'No, they're dreadfully bad, but I've never had a drawing lesson in my life.' 'But one evening at Balbec you sent word to me that you had stayed at home to have a drawing lesson.' I reminded her of the day and told her that I had realised at the time that people did not have drawing lessons at that hour in the evening. Albertine blushed. 'It is true,' she said, 'I was not having drawing lessons, I told you a great many lies at first, that I admit. But I never lie to you now.' I would so much have liked to know what were the many lies that she had told me at first, but I knew beforehand that her answers would be fresh lies. And so I contented myself with kissing her. I asked her to tell me one only of those lies. She replied: 'Oh, well; for instance when I said that the sea air was bad for me.' I ceased to insist in the face of this unwillingness to reveal.

To make her chain appear lighter, the best thing was no doubt to make her believe that I was myself about to break it. In any case, I could not at that moment confide this mendacious plan to her, she had been too kind in returning from the Trocadéro that afternoon; what I could do, far from distressing her with the threat of a rupture, was at the most to keep to myself those dreams of a perpetual life together which my grateful heart kept forming. As I looked at her, I found it hard to restrain myself from pouring them out to her, and she may perhaps have noticed this. Unfortunately the expression of such dreams is not contagious. The case of an affected old woman like M. de Charlus who, by dint of never seeing in his imagination anything but a stalwart young man, thinks that he has himself become a stalwart young man, all the more so the more affected and ridiculous he becomes, this case is more general, and it is the tragedy of an impassioned lover that he does not take into account the fact that while he sees in front of him a beautiful face, his mistress is seeing his face which is not made any more beautiful, far from it, when it is distorted by the pleasure that is aroused in it by the sight of beauty. Nor indeed does love exhaust the whole of this case; we do not see our own body, which other people see, and we 'follow' our own thought, the object invisible to other people which is before our eyes. This object the artist does sometimes enable us to see in his work. Whence it arises that the admirers of his work are disappointed in its author, upon whose face that internal beauty is imperfectly reflected.

Every person whom we love, indeed to a certain extent every person is to us like Janus, presenting to us the face that we like if that person leaves us, the repellent face if we know him or her to be perpetually at our disposal. In the case of Albertine, the prospect of her continued society was painful to me in another fashion which I cannot explain in this narrative. It is terrible to have the life of another person attached to our own like a bomb which we hold in our hands, unable to get rid of it without committing a crime. But let us take as a parallel the ups and downs, the dangers, the anxieties, the fear of seeing believed in time to come false and probable things which one will not be able then to explain, feelings that one experiences if one lives in the intimate society of a madman. For instance, I pitied M. de Charlus for living with Morel (immediately the memory of the scene that afternoon made me feel the left side of my breast heavier than the other); leaving out of account the relations that may or may not have existed between them, M. de Charlus must have been unaware at the outset that Morel was mad. Morel's beauty, his stupidity, his pride must have deterred the Baron from exploring so deeply, until the days of melancholy when Morel accused M. de Charlus of responsibility for his sorrows, without being able to furnish any explanation, abused him for his want of confidence, by the aid of false but extremely subtle reasoning, threatened him with desperate resolutions, while throughout all this there persisted the most cunning regard for his own most immediate interests But all this is only a comparison. Albertine was not mad.

I learned that a death had occurred during the day which distressed me greatly, that of Bergotte. It was known that he had been ill for a long time past. Not, of course, with the illness from which he had suffered originally and which was natural. Nature hardly seems capable of giving us any but quite short illnesses. But medicine has annexed to itself the art of prolonging them. Remedies, the respite that they procure, the relapses that a temporary cessation of them provokes, compose a sham illness to which the patient grows so accustomed that he ends by making it permanent, just as children continue to give way to fits of coughing long after they have been cured of the whooping cough. Then remedies begin to have less effect, the doses are increased, they cease to do any good, but they have begun to do harm thanks to that lasting indisposition. Nature would not have offered them so long a tenure. It is a great miracle that medicine can almost equal nature in forcing a man to remain in bed, to continue on pain of death the use of some drug. From that moment the illness artificially grafted has taken root, has become a secondary but a genuine illness, with this difference only that natural illnesses are cured, but never those which medicine creates, for it knows not the secret of their cure.

For years past Bergotte had ceased to go out of doors. Anyhow, he had never cared for society, or had cared for it for a day only, to despise it as he despised everything else and in the same fashion, which was his own, namely to despise a thing not because it was beyond his reach but as soon as he had reached it. He lived so simply that nobody suspected how rich he was, and anyone who had known would still have been mistaken, for he would have thought him a miser, whereas no one was ever more generous. He was generous above all towards women – girls, one ought rather to say – who were ashamed to receive so much in return for so little. He excused himself in his own eyes because he knew that he could never produce such good work as in an atmosphere of amorous feelings. Love is too strong a word, pleasure that is at all deeply rooted in the flesh is helpful to literary work because it cancels all other pleasures, for instance the pleasures of society, those which are the same for everyone. And even if this love leads to disillusionment, it does at least stir, even by so doing, the surface of the soul which otherwise would be in danger of becoming stagnant. Desire is therefore not without its value to the writer in detaching him first of all from his fellow men and from conforming to their standards, and afterwards in restoring some degree of movement to a spiritual machine which, after a certain age, tends to become paralysed. We do not succeed in being happy but we make observation of the reasons which prevent us from being happy and which would have remained invisible to us but for these loopholes opened by disappointment. Dreams are not to be converted into reality, that we know; we would not form any, perhaps, were it not for desire, and it is useful to us to form them in order to see them fail and to be instructed by their failure. And so Bergotte said to himself: 'I am spending more than a multimillionaire would spend upon girls, but the pleasures or disappointments that they give me make me write a book which brings me money.' Economically, this argument was absurd, but no doubt he found some charm in thus transmuting gold into caresses and caresses into gold. We saw, at the time of my grandmother's death, how a weary old age loves repose. Now in society, there is nothing but conversation. It may be stupid, but it has the faculty of suppressing women who are nothing more than questions and answers. Removed from society, women become once more what is so reposeful to a weary old man, an object of contemplation. In any case, it was no longer a question of anything of this sort. I have said that Bergotte never went out of doors, and when he got out of bed for an hour in his room, he would be smothered in shawls, plaids, all the things with which a person covers himself before exposing himself to intense cold or getting into a railway train. He would apologise to the few friends whom he allowed to penetrate to his sanctuary, and, pointing to his tartan plaids, his travelling-rugs, would say merrily: 'After all, my dear fellow, life, as Anaxagoras has said, is a journey.' Thus he went on growing steadily colder, a tiny planet that offered a prophetic image of the greater, when gradually heat will withdraw from the earth, then life itself. Then the resurrection will have come to an end, for if, among future generations, the works of men are to shine, there must first of all be men. If certain kinds of animals hold out longer against the invading chill, when there are no longer any men, and if we suppose Bergotte's fame to have lasted so long, suddenly it will be extinguished for all time. It will not be the last animals that will read him, for it is scarcely probable that, like the Apostles on the

Day of Pentecost, they will be able to understand the speech of the various races of mankind without having learned it.

In the months that preceded his death, Bergotte suffered from insomnia, and what was worse, whenever he did fall asleep, from nightmares which, if he awoke, made him reluctant to go to sleep again. He had long been a lover of dreams, even of bad dreams, because thanks to them and to the contradiction they present to the reality which we have before us in our waking state, they give us, at the moment of waking if not before, the profound sensation of having slept. But Bergotte's nightmares were not like that. When he spoke of nightmares, he used in the past to mean unpleasant things that passed through his brain. Latterly, it was as though proceeding from somewhere outside himself that he would see a hand armed with a damp cloth which, passed over his face by an evil woman, kept scrubbing him awake, an intolerable itching in his thighs, the rage – because Bergotte had murmured in his sleep that he was driving badly – of a raving lunatic of a cabman who flung himself upon the writer, biting and gnawing his fingers. Finally, as soon as in his sleep it had grown sufficiently dark, nature arranged a sort of undress rehearsal of the apoplectic stroke that was to carry him off: Bergotte arrived in a carriage beneath the porch of Swann's new house, and tried to alight. A stunning giddiness glued him to his seat, the porter came forward to help him out of the carriage, he remained seated, unable to rise, to straighten his legs. He tried to pull himself up with the help of the stone pillar that was by his side, but did not find sufficient support in it to enable him to stand.

He consulted doctors who, flattered at being called in by him, saw in his virtue as an incessant worker (it was twenty years since he had written anything), in his over-strain, the cause of his ailments. They advised him not to read thrilling stories (he never read anything), to benefit more by the sunshine, which was 'indispensable to life' (he had owed a few years of comparative health only to his rigorous seclusion indoors), to take nourishment (which made him thinner, and nourished nothing but his nightmares). One of his doctors was blessed with the spirit of contradiction, and whenever Bergotte consulted him in the absence of the others, and, in order not to offend him, suggested to him as his own ideas what the others had advised, this doctor, thinking that Bergotte was seeking to have prescribed for him something that he himself liked, at once forbade it, and often for reasons invented so hurriedly to meet the case that in face of the material objections which Bergotte raised, this argumentative doctor was obliged in the same sentence to contradict himself, but, for fresh reasons, repeated the original prohibition. Bergotte returned to one of the first of these doctors, a man

who prided himself on his cleverness, especially in the presence of one of the
leading men of letters, and who, if Bergotte insinuated: 'I seem to remember,
though, that Dr. X—told me – long ago, of course – that that might congest
my kidneys and brain . . . ' would smile sardonically, raise his finger and
enounce: 'I said use, I did not say abuse. Naturally every remedy, if one takes
it in excess, becomes a two-edged sword.' There is in the human body a
certain instinct for what is beneficial to us, as there is in the heart for what is
our moral duty, an instinct which no authorisation by a Doctor of Medicine
or Divinity can replace. We know that cold baths are bad for us, we like
them, we can always find a doctor to recommend them, not to prevent them
from doing us harm. From each of these doctors Bergotte took something
which, in his own wisdom, he had forbidden himself for years past. After a
few weeks, his old troubles had reappeared, the new had become worse.
Maddened by an unintermittent pain, to which was added insomnia broken
only by brief spells of nightmare, Bergotte called in no more doctors and
tried with success, but to excess, different narcotics, hopefully reading the
prospectus that accompanied each of them, a prospectus which proclaimed
the necessity of sleep but hinted that all the preparations which induce it
(except that contained in the bottle round which the prospectus was
wrapped, which never produced any toxic effect) were toxic, and therefore
made the remedy worse than the disease. Bergotte tried them all. Some were
of a different family from those to which we are accustomed, preparations
for instance of amyl and ethyl. When we absorb a new drug, entirely
different in composition, it is always with a delicious expectancy of the
unknown. Our heart beats as at a first assignation. To what unknown forms
of sleep, of dreams, is the newcomer going to lead us? He is inside us now,
he has the control of our thoughts. In what fashion are we going to fall
asleep? And, once we are asleep, by what strange paths, up to what peaks,
into what unfathomed gulfs is he going to lead us? With what new grouping
of sensations are we to become acquainted on this journey? Will it bring us
in the end to illness? To blissful happiness? To death? Bergotte's death had
come to him overnight, when he had thus entrusted himself to one of these
friends (a friend? or an enemy, rather?) who proved too strong for him. The
circumstances of his death were as follows. An attack of uraemia, by no
means serious, had led to his being ordered to rest. But one of the critics
having written somewhere that in Vermeer's *Street in Delft* (lent by the
Gallery at The Hague for an Exhibition of Dutch painting), a picture which
he adored and imagined that he knew by heart, a little patch of yellow wall
(which he could not remember) was so well painted that it was, if one looked
at it by itself, like some priceless specimen of Chinese art, of a beauty that

was sufficient in itself, Bergotte ate a few potatoes, left the house, and went
to the exhibition. At the first few steps that he had to climb he was overcome
by giddiness. He passed in front of several pictures and was struck by the
stiffness and futility of so artificial a school, nothing of which equalled the
fresh air and sunshine of a Venetian palazzo, or of an ordinary house by the
sea. At last he came to the Vermeer which he remembered as more striking,
more different from anything else that he knew, but in which, thanks to the
critic's article, he remarked for the first time some small figures in blue, that
the ground was pink, and finally the precious substance of the tiny patch of
yellow wall. His giddiness increased; he fixed his eyes, like a child upon a
yellow butterfly which it is trying to catch, upon the precious little patch of
wall. 'That is how I ought to have written,' he said. 'My last books are too
dry, I ought to have gone over them with several coats of paint, made my
language exquisite in itself, like this little patch of yellow wall.' Meanwhile
he was not unconscious of the gravity of his condition. In a celestial balance
there appeared to him, upon one of its scales, his own life, while the other
contained the little patch of wall so beautifully painted in yellow. He felt
that he had rashly surrendered the former for the latter. 'All the same,' he
said to himself, 'I have no wish to provide the "feature" of this exhibition for
the evening papers.'

He repeated to himself: 'Little patch of yellow wall, with a sloping roof,
little patch of yellow wall.' While doing so he sank down upon a circular
divan; and then at once he ceased to think that his life was in jeopardy and,
reverting to his natural optimism, told himself: 'It is just an ordinary
indigestion from those potatoes; they weren't properly cooked; it is nothing.'
A fresh attack beat him down; he rolled from the divan to the floor, as
visitors and attendants came hurrying to his assistance. He was dead.
Permanently dead? Who shall say? Certainly our experiments in spiritualism
prove no more than the dogmas of religion that the soul survives death. All
that we can say is that everything is arranged in this life as though we
entered it carrying the burden of obligations contracted in a former life;
there is no reason inherent in the conditions of life on this earth that can
make us consider ourselves obliged to do good, to be fastidious, to be polite
even, nor make the talented artist consider himself obliged to begin over
again a score of times a piece of work the admiration aroused by which will
matter little to his body devoured by worms, like the patch of yellow wall
painted with so much knowledge and skill by an artist who must for ever
remain unknown and is barely identified under the name Vermeer. All these
obligations which have not their sanction in our present life seem to belong
to a different world, founded upon kindness, scrupulosity, self-sacrifice, a

world entirely different from this, which we leave in order to be born into this world, before perhaps returning to the other to live once again beneath the sway of those unknown laws which we have obeyed because we bore their precepts in our hearts, knowing not whose hand had traced them there – those laws to which every profound work of the intellect brings us nearer and which are invisible only – and still! – to fools. So that the idea that Bergotte was not wholly and permanently dead is by no means improbable.

They buried him, but all through the night of mourning, in the lighted windows, his books arranged three by three kept watch like angels with outspread wings and seemed, for him who was no more, the symbol of his resurrection.

I learned, I have said, that day that Bergotte was dead. And I marvelled at the carelessness of the newspapers which – each of them reproducing the same paragraph – stated that he had died the day before. For, the day before, Albertine had met him, as she informed me that very evening, and indeed she had been a little late in coming home, for she had stopped for some time talking to him. She was doubtless the last person to whom he had spoken. She knew him through myself who had long ceased to see him, but, as she had been anxious to make his acquaintance, I had, a year earlier, written to ask the old master whether I might bring her to see him. He had granted my request, a trifle hurt, I fancy, that I should be visiting him only to give pleasure to another person, which was a proof of my indifference to himself. These cases are frequent: sometimes the man or woman whom we implore to receive us not for the pleasure of conversing with them again, but on behalf of a third person, refuses so obstinately that our protégée concludes that we have boasted of an influence which we do not possess; more often the man of genius or the famous beauty consents, but, humiliated in their glory, wounded in their affection, feel for us afterwards only a diminished, sorrowful, almost contemptuous attachment. I discovered long after this that I had falsely accused the newspapers of inaccuracy, since on the day in question Albertine had not met Bergotte, but at the time I had never suspected this for a single instant, so naturally had she told me of the incident, and it was not until much later that I discovered her charming skill in lying with simplicity. The things that she said, the things that she confessed were so stamped with the character of formal evidence – what we see, what we learn from an unquestionable source – that she sowed thus in the empty spaces of her life episodes of another life the falsity of which I did not then suspect and began to perceive only at a much later date. I have used the word 'confessed', for the following reason. Sometimes a casual meeting gave me a jealous suspicion in which by her side there figured in the past, or alas in the future, another person. In order to appear certain of my facts, I mentioned the person's name, and Albertine said: 'Yes, I met her, a week ago, just outside the house. I had to be polite and answer her when she spoke to me. I walked a little way with her. But there never has been anything between us. There never will be.' Now Albertine had not even met this person, for the simple reason that the person had not been in Paris for the last ten months. But my mistress felt that a complete denial would sound hardly probable. Whence this imaginary brief encounter, related so simply that I could see the lady stop, bid her good-day, walk a little way with her. The evidence of my senses, if I had been in the street at that moment, would perhaps have informed me that the lady had not been with Albertine. But if I had knowledge of the fact, it was by one of those chains of reasoning in which the words of people in whom we have confidence insert strong links, and not by the evidence of my senses. To invoke this evidence of the senses I should have had to be in the street at that particular moment, and I had not been. We may imagine, however, that such an hypothesis is not improbable: I might have gone out, and have been passing along the street at the time at which Albertine was to tell me in the evening (not having seen me there) that she had gone a little way with the lady, and I should then have known that Albertine was lying. But is that quite certain even then? A religious obscurity would have clouded my mind, I should have begun to doubt whether I had seen her by herself, I should barely have sought to understand by what optical illusion I had failed to perceive the lady, and should not have been greatly surprised to find myself mistaken, for the stellar universe is not so difficult of comprehension as the real actions of other people, especially of the people with whom we are in love, strengthened as they are against our doubts by fables devised for their protection. For how many years on end can they not allow our apathetic love to believe that they have in some foreign country a sister, a brother, a sister-in-law who have never existed!

The evidence of the senses is also an operation of the mind in which conviction creates the evidence. We have often seen her sense of hearing convey to Françoise not the word that was uttered but what she thought to be its correct form, which was enough to prevent her from hearing the correction implied in a superior pronunciation. Our butler was cast in a similar mould. M. de Charlus was in the habit of wearing at this time – for he was constantly changing – very light trousers which were recognisable a mile off. Now our butler, who thought that the word *pissotière* (the word denoting what M. de Rambuteau had been so annoyed to hear the Duc de

Guermantes call a Rambuteau stall) was really *pistière*, never once in the whole of his life heard a single person say *pissotière*, albeit the word was frequently pronounced thus in his hearing. But error is more obstinate than faith and does not examine the grounds of its belief. Constantly the butler would say: 'I'm sure M. le Baron de Charlus must have caught a disease to stand about as long as he does in a *pistière*. That's what comes of running after the girls at his age. You can tell what he is by his trousers. This morning, Madame sent me with a message to Neuilly. As I passed the *pistière* in the Rue de Bourgogne I saw M. le Baron de Charlus go in. When I came back from Neuilly, quite an hour later, I saw his yellow trousers in the same *pistière*, in the same place, in the middle stall where he always goes so that people shan't see him.' I can think of no one more beautiful, more noble or more youthful than a certain niece of Mme de Guermantes. But I have heard the porter of a restaurant where I used sometimes to dine say as she went by: 'Just look at that old trollop, what a style! And she must be eighty, if she's a day.' As far as age went, I find it difficult to believe that he meant what he said. But the pages clustered round him, who tittered whenever she went past the hotel on her way to visit, at their house in the neighbourhood, her charming great-aunts, Mmes de Fezensac and de Bellery, saw upon the face of the young beauty the fourscore years with which, seriously or in jest, the porter had endowed the 'old trollop'. You would have made them shriek with laughter had you told them that she was more distinguished than one of the two cashiers of the hotel, who, devoured by eczema, ridiculously stout, seemed to them a fine-looking woman. Perhaps sexual desire alone would have been capable of preventing their error from taking form, if it had been brought to bear upon the passage of the alleged old trollop, and if the pages had suddenly begun to covet the young goddess. But for reasons unknown, which were most probably of a social nature, this desire had not come into play. There is moreover ample room for discussion. The universe is true for us all and dissimilar to each of us. If we were not obliged, to preserve the continuity of our story, to confine ourselves to frivolous reasons, how many more serious reasons would permit us to demonstrate the falsehood and flimsiness of the opening pages of this volume in which, from my bed, I hear the world awake, now to one sort of weather, now to another. Yes, I have been forced to whittle down the facts, and to be a liar, but it is not one universe, there are millions, almost as many as the number of human eyes and brains in existence, that awake every morning.

To return to Albertine, I have never known any woman more amply endowed than herself with the happy aptitude for a lie that is animated, coloured with the selfsame tints of life, unless it be one of her friends – one of my blossoming girls also, rose-pink as Albertine, but one whose irregular profile, concave in one place, then convex again, was exactly like certain clusters of pink flowers the name of which I have forgotten, but which have long and sinuous concavities. This girl was, from the point of view of storytelling, superior to Albertine, for she never introduced any of those painful moments, those furious innuendoes, which were frequent with my mistress. I have said, however, that she was charming when she invented a story which left no room for doubt, for one saw then in front of her the thing – albeit imaginary – which she was saying, using it as an illustration of her speech. Probability alone inspired Albertine, never the desire to make me jealous. For Albertine, without perhaps any material interest, liked people to be polite to her. And if in the course of this work I have had and shall have many occasions to show how jealousy intensifies love, it is the lover's point of view that I have adopted. But if that lover be only the least bit proud, and though he were to die of a separation, he will not respond to a supposed betrayal with a courteous speech, he will turn away, or without going will order himself to assume a mask of coldness. And so it is entirely to her own disadvantage that his mistress makes him suffer so acutely. If, on the contrary, she dispels with a tactful word, with loving caresses, the suspicions that have been torturing him for all his show of indifference, no doubt the lover does not feel that despairing increase of love to which jealousy drives him, but ceasing in an instant to suffer, happy, affectionate, relieved from strain as one is after a storm when the rain has ceased and one barely hears still splash at long intervals from the tall horse-chestnut trees the clinging drops which already the reappearing sun has dyed with colour, he does not know how to express his gratitude to her who has cured him. Albertine knew that I liked to reward her for her kindnesses, and this perhaps explained why she used to invent, to exculpate herself, confessions as natural as these stories the truth of which I never doubted, one of them being that of her meeting with Bergotte when he was already dead. Previously I had never known any of Albertine's lies save those that, at Balbec for instance, Françoise used to report to me, which I have omitted from these pages albeit they hurt me so sorely: 'As she didn't want to come, she said to me: "Couldn't you say to Monsieur that you didn't find me, that I had gone out?" ' But our 'inferiors', who love us as Françoise loved me, take pleasure in wounding us in our self-esteem.

CHAPTER TWO

The Verdurins quarrel
with M. de Charlus

After dinner, I told Albertine that, since I was out of bed, I might as well take the opportunity to go and see some of my friends, Mme de Villeparisis, Mme de Guermantes, the Cambremers, anyone in short whom I might find at home. I omitted to mention only the people whom I did intend to see, the Verdurins. I asked her if she would not come with me. She pleaded that she had no suitable clothes. 'Besides, my hair is so awful. Do you really wish me to go on doing it like this?' And by way of farewell she held out her hand to me in that abrupt fashion, the arm outstretched, the shoulders thrust back, which she used to adopt on the beach at Balbec and had since then entirely abandoned. This forgotten gesture retransformed the body which it animated into that of the Albertine who as yet scarcely knew me. It restored to Albertine, ceremonious beneath an air of rudeness, her first novelty, her strangeness, even her setting. I saw the sea behind this girl whom I had never seen shake hands with me in this fashion since I was at the seaside. 'My aunt thinks it makes me older,' she added with a sullen air. 'Oh that her aunt may be right!' thought I. 'That Albertine by looking like a child should make Mme Bontemps appear younger than she is, is all that her aunt would ask, and also that Albertine shall cost her nothing between now and the day when, by marrying me, she will repay what has been spent on her.' But that Albertine should appear less young, less pretty, should turn fewer heads in the street, that is what I, on the contrary, hoped. For the age of a duenna is less reassuring to a jealous lover than the age of the woman's face whom he loves. I regretted only that the style in which I had asked her to do her hair should appear to Albertine an additional bolt on the door of her prison. And it was henceforward this new domestic sentiment that never ceased, even when I was parted from Albertine, to form a bond attaching me to her.

I said to Albertine, who was not dressed, or so she told me, to accompany me to the Guermantes' or the Cambremers', that I could not be certain where I should go, and set off for the Verdurins'. At the moment when the thought of the concert that I was going to hear brought back to my mind the scene that afternoon: '*Grand pied de grue, grand pied de grue*' – a scene of disappointed love, of jealous love perhaps, but if so as bestial as the scene to which a woman might be subjected by, so to speak, an orang-outang that was, if one may use the expression, in love with her – at the moment when, having reached the street, I was just going to hail a cab, I heard the sound of sobs which a man who was sitting upon a kerbstone was endeavouring to stifle. I came nearer; the man, who had buried his face in his hands, appeared to be quite young, and I was surprised to see, from the gleam of white in the opening of his cloak, that he was wearing evening clothes and a white tie. As he heard my step he uncovered a face bathed in tears, but at once, having recognised me, turned away. It was Morel. He guessed that I had recognised him and, checking his tears with an effort, told me that he had stopped to rest for a moment, he was in such pain. 'I have grossly insulted, only today,' he said, 'a person for whom I had the very highest regard. It was a cowardly thing to do, for she loves me.' 'She will forget perhaps, as time goes on,' I replied, without realising that by speaking thus I made it apparent that I had overheard the scene that afternoon. But he was so much absorbed in his own grief that it never even occurred to him that I might know something about the affair. 'She may forget, perhaps,' he said. 'But I myself can never forget. I am too conscious of my degradation, I am disgusted with myself! However, what I have said I have said, and nothing can unsay it. When people make me lose my temper, I don't know what I am doing. And it is so bad for me, my nerves are all on edge', for, like all neurasthenics, he was keenly interested in his own health. If, during the afternoon, I had witnessed the amorous rage of an infuriated animal, this evening, within a few hours, centuries had elapsed and a fresh sentiment, a sentiment of shame, regret, grief, showed that a great stage had been passed in the evolution of the beast destined to be transformed into a human being. Nevertheless, I still heard ringing in my ears his '*grand pied de grue*' and dreaded an imminent return to the savage state. I had only a very vague impression, however, of what had been happening, and this was but natural, for M. de Charlus himself was totally unaware that for some days past, and especially that day, even before the shameful episode which was not a direct consequence of the violinist's condition, Morel had been suffering from a recurrence of his neurasthenia. As a matter of fact, he had, in the previous month, proceeded as rapidly as he had been able, a great deal less rapidly than he would have liked, towards the seduction of Jupien's niece with whom he was at liberty, now that they were engaged, to go out whenever he chose. But whenever he had gone a trifle far in his attempts at violation, and especially when he suggested to his betrothed that she might make friends with other girls whom she would then procure for himself, he had met with a resistance that made him furious. All at once (whether she would have proved too chaste, or on the contrary would have surrendered herself) his desire had subsided. He had decided to break with her, but feeling that the Baron, vicious as he might be, was far more moral than himself, he was afraid lest, in the event of a rupture, M. de Charlus might turn him out of the house. And so he had decided, a fortnight ago, that he would not see the girl again, would leave M. de Charlus and Jupien to clean up the mess (he employed a more realistic term) by themselves, and, before announcing the rupture, to 'b— off' to an unknown destination.

For all that his conduct towards Jupien's niece coincided exactly, in its minutest details, with the plan of conduct which he had outlined to the Baron as they were dining together at Saint-Mars le Vêtu, it is probable that his intention was entirely different, and that sentiments of a less atrocious nature, which he had not foreseen in his theory of conduct, had improved, had tinged it with sentiment in practice. The sole point in which, on the contrary, the practice was worse than the theory is this, that in theory it had not appeared to him possible that he could remain in Paris after such an act of betrayal. Now, on the contrary, actually to 'b— off' for so small a matter seemed to him quite unnecessary. It meant leaving the Baron who would probably be furious, and forfeiting his own position. He would lose all the money that the Baron was now giving him. The thought that this was inevitable made his nerves give way altogether, he cried for hours on end, and in order not to think about it any more dosed himself cautiously with morphine. Then suddenly he hit upon an idea which no doubt had gradually been taking shape in his mind and gaining strength there for some time, and this was that a rupture with the girl would not inevitably mean a complete break with M. de Charlus. To lose all the Baron's money was a serious thing in itself. Morel in his uncertainty remained for some days a prey to dark thoughts, such as came to him at the sight of Bloch. Then he decided that Jupien and his niece had been trying to set a trap for him, that they might consider themselves lucky to be rid of him so cheaply. He found in short that the girl had been in the wrong in being so clumsy, in not having managed to keep him attached to her by a sensual attraction. Not only did the sacrifice of his position with M. de Charlus seem to him absurd, he even regretted the expensive dinners he had given the girl since they became engaged, the exact cost of which he knew by heart, being a true son of the valet who used to bring his 'book' every month for my uncle's inspection. For the word book, in the singular, which means a printed volume to humanity in general, loses that meaning among Royal Princes and servants. To the latter it means their housekeeping book, to the former the register in which we inscribe our names. (At Balbec one day when the Princesse de Luxembourg told me that she had not brought a book with her, I was about to offer her *Le Pêcheur d'Islande* and *Tartarin de Tarascon*, when I realised that she had meant not that she would pass the time less agreeably, but that I should find it more difficult to pay a call upon her.)

Notwithstanding the change in Morel's point of view with regard to the consequences of his behaviour, albeit that behaviour would have seemed to him abominable two months earlier, when he was passionately in love with Jupien's niece, whereas during the last fortnight he had never ceased to assure himself that the same behaviour was natural, praiseworthy, it continued to intensify the state of nervous unrest in which, finally, he had announced the rupture that afternoon. And he was quite prepared to vent his anger, if not (save in a momentary outburst) upon the girl, for whom he still felt that lingering fear, the last trace of love, at any rate upon the Baron. He took care, however, not to say anything to him before dinner, for, valuing his own professional skill above everything, whenever he had any difficult music to play (as this evening at the Verdurins') he avoided (as far as possible, and the scene that afternoon was already more than ample) anything that might impair the flexibility of his wrists. Similarly a surgeon who is an enthusiastic motorist, does not drive when he has an operation to perform. This accounts to me for the fact that, while he was speaking to me, he kept bending his fingers gently one after another to see whether they had regained their suppleness. A slight frown seemed to indicate that there was still a trace of nervous stiffness. But, so as not to increase it, he relaxed his features, as we forbid ourself to grow irritated at not being able to sleep or to prevail upon a woman, for fear lest our rage itself may retard the moment of sleep or of satisfaction. And so, anxious to regain his serenity so that he might, as was his habit, absorb himself entirely in what he was going to play at the Verdurins', and anxious, so long as I was watching him, to let me see how unhappy he was, he decided that the simplest course was to beg me to leave him immediately. His request was superfluous, and it was a relief to me to get away from him. I had trembled lest, as we were due at the same house, within a few minutes, he might ask me to take him with me, my memory of the scene that afternoon being too vivid not to give me a certain distaste for the idea of having Morel by my side during the drive. It is quite possible that the love, and afterwards the indifference or hatred felt by Morel for Jupien's niece had been sincere. Unfortunately, it was not the first time that he had behaved thus, that he had suddenly 'dropped' a girl to whom he had sworn undying love, going so far as to produce a loaded revolver, telling her that he would blow out his brains if ever he was mean enough to desert her. He did nevertheless desert her in time, and felt instead of remorse, a sort of rancour against her. It was not the first time that he had behaved thus, it was not to be the last, with the result that the heads of many girls – girls less forgetful of him than he was of them – suffered – as Jupien's niece's head continued long afterwards to suffer, still in love with Morel although she despised him – suffered, ready to burst with the shooting of an internal pain because in each of them – like a fragment of a Greek carving – an aspect of Morel's face, hard as marble and beautiful as an antique sculpture, was embedded in her brain, with his blossoming hair, his fine eyes, his straight nose, forming a protuberance in a cranium not shaped to receive it, upon which no operation was possible. But in the fullness of time these stony fragments end by slipping into a place where they cause no undue discomfort, from which they never stir again; we are no longer conscious of their presence: I mean forgetfulness, or an indifferent memory.

Meanwhile I had gained two things in the course of the day. On the one hand, thanks to the calm that was produced in me by Albertine's docility, I found it possible, and therefore made up my mind, to break with her. There was on the other hand, the fruit of my reflections during the interval that I had spent waiting for her, at the piano, the idea that Art, to which I would try to devote my reconquered liberty, was not a thing that justified one in making a sacrifice, a thing above and beyond life, that did not share in its fatuity and futility; the appearance of real individuality obtained in works of art being due merely to the illusion created by the artist's technical skill. If my afternoon had left behind it other deposits, possibly more profound, they were not to come to my knowledge until much later. As for the two which I was able thus to weigh, they were not to be permanent; for, from this very evening my ideas about art were to rise above the depression to which they had been subjected in the afternoon, while on the other hand my calm, and consequently the freedom that would enable me to devote myself to it, was once again to be withdrawn from me.

As my cab, following the line of the embankment, was coming near the Verdurins' house, I made the driver pull up. I had just seen Brichot alighting from the tram at the foot of the Rue Bonaparte, after which he dusted his shoes with an old newspaper and put on a pair of pearl grey gloves. I went up to him on foot. For some time past, his sight having grown steadily weaker, he had been endowed – as richly as an observatory – with new spectacles of a powerful and complicated kind, which, like astronomical instruments, seemed to be screwed into his eyes; he focused their exaggerated blaze upon myself and recognised me. They – the spectacles – were in marvellous condition. But behind them I could see, minute, pallid, convulsive, expiring, a remote gaze placed under this powerful apparatus, as, in a laboratory equipped out of all proportion to the work that is done in it, you may watch the last throes of some insignificant animalcule through the latest and most perfect type of microscope. I offered him my arm to guide him on his way. 'This time it is not by great Cherbourg that we meet,' he said to me, 'but by little Dunkerque', a remark which I found extremely tiresome, as I failed to understand what he meant; and yet I dared not ask Brichot, dreading not so much his scorn as his explanations. I replied that I was longing to see the room in which Swann used to meet Odette every evening. 'What, so you know that old story, do you?' he said. 'And yet from those days to the death of Swann is what the poet rightly calls: "*Grande spatium mortalis aevi.*" '

The death of Swann had been a crushing blow to me at the time. The death of Swann! Swann, in this phrase, is something more than a noun in the possessive case. I mean by it his own particular death, the death allotted by destiny to the service of Swann. For we talk of 'death' for convenience, but there are almost as many different deaths as there are people. We are not equipped with a sense that would enable us to see, moving at every speed in every direction, these deaths, the active deaths aimed by destiny at this person or that. Often there are deaths that will not be entirely relieved of their duties until two or even three years later. They come in haste to plant a tumour in the side of a Swann, then depart to attend to their other duties, returning only when, the surgeons having performed their operation, it is necessary to plant the tumour there afresh. Then comes the moment when we read in the *Gaulois* that Swann's health has been causing anxiety but that he is now making an excellent recovery. Then, a few minutes before the breath leaves our body, death, like a sister of charity who has come to nurse, rather than to destroy us, enters to preside over our last moments, crowns with a supreme halo the cold and stiffening creature whose heart has ceased to beat. And it is this diversity among deaths, the mystery of their circuits, the colour of their fatal badge, that makes so impressive a paragraph in the newspapers such as this:

'We regret to learn that M. Charles Swann passed away yesterday at his residence in Paris, after a long and painful illness. A Parisian whose intellectual gifts were widely appreciated, a discriminating but steadfastly loyal friend, he will be universally regretted, in those literary and artistic circles where the soundness and refinement of his taste made him a willing and a welcome guest, as well as at the Jockey Club of which he was one of the oldest and most respected members. He belonged also to the Union and the Agricole. He had recently resigned his membership of the Rue Royale. His personal appearance and eminently distinguished bearing never failed to arouse public interest at all the great events of the musical and artistic seasons, especially at private views, at which he was a regular attendant until, during the last years of his life, he became almost entirely confined to the house. The funeral will take place, etc.'

From this point of view, if one is not 'somebody', the absence of a well-known title makes the process of decomposition even more rapid. No doubt it is more or less anonymously, without any personal identity, that a man still remains Duc d'Uzès. But the ducal coronet does for some time hold the elements together, as their moulds keep together those artistically designed ices which Albertine admired, whereas the names of ultra-fashionable commoners, as soon as they are dead, dissolve and lose their shape. We have seen M. de Bréauté speak of Cartier as the most intimate friend of the Duc de La Trémoïlle, as a man greatly in demand in aristocratic circles. To a later generation, Cartier has become something so formless that it would almost be adding to his importance to make him out as related to the jeweller Cartier, with whom he would have smiled to think that anybody could be so ignorant as to confuse him! Swann on the contrary was a remarkable personality, in both the intellectual and the artistic worlds; and even although he had 'produced' nothing, still he had a chance of surviving a little longer. And yet, my dear Charles —, whom I used to know when I was still so young and you were nearing your grave, it is because he whom you must have regarded as a little fool has made you the hero of one of his volumes that people are beginning to speak of you again and that your name will perhaps live. If in Tissot's picture representing the balcony of the Rue Royale club, where you figure with Galliffet, Edmond Polignac and Saint-Maurice, people are always drawing attention to yourself, it is because they know that there are some traces of you in the character of Swann.

To return to more general realities, it was of this foretold and yet unforeseen death of Swann that I had heard him speak himself to the Duchesse de Guermantes, on the evening of her cousin's party. It was the same death whose striking and specific strangeness had recurred to me one evening when, as I ran my eye over the newspaper, my attention was suddenly arrested by the announcement of it, as though traced in mysterious lines interpolated there out of place. They had sufficed to make of a living man someone who can never again respond to what you say to him, to reduce him to a mere name, a written name, that has passed in a moment from the real world to the realm of silence. It was they that even now made me anxious to make myself familiar with the house in which the Verdurins had lived, and where Swann, who at that time was not merely a row of five letters printed in a newspaper, had dined so often with Odette. I must add also (and this is what for a long time made Swann's death more painful than any other, albeit these reasons bore no relation to the individual strangeness of his death) that I had never gone to see Gilberte, as I promised him at the Princesse de Guermantes's, that he had never told me what the 'other reason' was, to which he alluded that evening, for his selecting me as the recipient of his conversation with the Prince, that a thousand questions occurred to me (as bubbles rise from the bottom of a pond) which I longed to ask him about the most different subjects: Vermeer, M. de Mouchy, Swann himself, a Boucher tapestry, Combray, questions that doubtless were not very vital since I had put off asking them from day to day, but which seemed to me of capital importance now that, his lips being sealed, no answer would ever come.

'No,' Brichot went on, 'it was not here that Swann met his future wife, or rather it was here only in the very latest period, after the disaster that partially destroyed Mme Verdurin's former home.'

Unfortunately, in my fear of displaying before the eyes of Brichot an extravagance which seemed to me out of place, since the professor had no share in its enjoyment, I had alighted too hastily from the carriage and the driver had not understood the words I had flung at him over my shoulder in order that I might be well clear of the carriage before Brichot caught sight of me. The consequence was that the driver followed us and asked me whether he was to call for me later; I answered hurriedly in the affirmative, and was regarded with a vastly increased respect by the professor who had come by omnibus.

'Ah! So you were in a carriage,' he said in solemn tones. 'Only by the purest accident. I never take one as a rule. I always travel by omnibus or on foot. However, it may perhaps entitle me to the great honour of taking you home tonight if you will oblige me by consenting to enter that rattletrap; we shall be packed rather tight. But you are always so considerate to me.' Alas, in making him this offer, I am depriving myself of nothing (I reflected) since in any case I shall be obliged to go home for Albertine's sake. Her presence in my house, at an hour when nobody could possibly call to see her, allowed me to dispose as freely of my time as I had that afternoon, when, seated at the piano, I knew that she was on her way back from the Trocadéro and that I was in no hurry to see her again. But furthermore, as also in the afternoon, I felt that I had a woman in the house and that on returning home I should not

taste the fortifying thrill of solitude. 'I accept with great good will,' replied
Brichot. 'At the period to which you allude, our friends occupied in the Rue
Montalivet a magnificent ground floor apartment with an upper landing,
and a garden behind, less sumptuous of course, and yet to my mind preferable
to the old Venetian Embassy.' Brichot informed me that this evening there
was to be at 'Quai Conti' (thus it was that the faithful spoke of the Verdurin
drawing-room since it had been transferred to that address) a great musical
'tow–row–row' got up by M. de Charlus. He went on to say that in the old
days to which I had referred, the little nucleus had been different, and its
tone not at all the same, not only because the faithful had then been younger.
He told me of elaborate jokes played by Elstir (what he called 'pure
buffooneries'), as for instance one day when the painter, having pretended to
fail at the last moment, had come disguised as an extra waiter and, as he
handed round the dishes, whispered gallant speeches in the ear of the
extremely proper Baroness Putbus, crimson with anger and alarm; then
disappearing before the end of dinner he had had a hip-bath carried into the
drawing-room, out of which, when the party left the table, he had emerged
stark naked uttering fearful oaths; and also of supper parties to which the
guests came in paper costumes, designed, cut out and coloured by Elstir,
which were masterpieces in themselves, Brichot having worn on one occasion
that of a great nobleman of the court of Charles VII, with long turned-up
points to his shoes, and another time that of Napoleon I, for which Elstir had
fashioned a Grand Cordon of the Legion of Honour out of sealing-wax. In
short Brichot, seeing again with the eyes of memory the drawing-room of
those days with its high windows, its low sofas devoured by the midday sun
which had had to be replaced, declared that he preferred it to the drawing-
room of today. Of course, I quite understood that by 'drawing-room'
Brichot meant – as the word church implies not merely the religious edifice
but the congregation of worshippers – not merely the apartment, but the
people who visited it, the special pleasures that they came to enjoy there, to
which, in his memory, those sofas had imparted their form upon which,
when you called to see Mme Verdurin in the afternoon, you waited until she
was ready, while the blossom on the horse-chestnuts outside, and on the
mantelpiece carnations in vases seemed, with a charming and kindly thought
for the visitor expressed in the smiling welcome of their rosy hues, to be
watching anxiously for the tardy appearance of the lady of the house. But if
the drawing-room seemed to him superior to what it was now, it was perhaps
because our mind is the old Proteus who cannot remain the slave of any one
shape and, even in the social world, suddenly abandons a house which has
slowly and with difficulty risen to the pitch of perfection to prefer another

which is less brilliant, just as the 'touched-up' photographs which Odette had had taken at Otto's, in which she queened it in a 'princess' gown, her hair waved by Lenthéric, did not appeal to Swann so much as a little 'cabinet picture' taken at Nice, in which, in a cloth cape, her loosely dressed hair protruding beneath a straw hat trimmed with pansies and a bow of black ribbon, instead of being twenty years younger (for women as a rule look all the older in a photograph, the earlier it is), she looked like a little servant girl twenty years older than she now was. Perhaps too he derived some pleasure from praising to me what I myself had never known, from showing me that he had tasted delights that I could never enjoy. If so, he was successful, for merely by mentioning the names of two or three people who were no longer alive and to each of whom he imparted something mysterious by his way of referring to them, to that delicious intimacy, he made me ask myself what it could have been like; I felt that everything that had been told me about the Verdurins was far too coarse; and indeed, in the case of Swann whom I had known, I reproached myself with not having paid him sufficient attention, with not having paid attention to him in a sufficiently disinterested spirit, with not having listened to him properly when he used to entertain me while we waited for his wife to come home for luncheon and he showed me his treasures, now that I knew that he was to be classed with the most brilliant talkers of the past. Just as we were coming to Mme Verdurin's doorstep, I caught sight of M. de Charlus, steering towards us the bulk of his huge body, drawing unwillingly in his wake one of those blackmailers or mendicants who nowadays, whenever he appeared, sprang up without fail even in what were to all appearance the most deserted corners, by whom this powerful monster was, evidently against his will, invariably escorted, although at a certain distance, as is the shark by its pilot, in short contrasting so markedly with the haughty stranger of my first visit to Balbec, with his stern aspect, his affectation of virility, that I seemed to be discovering, accompanied by its satellite, a planet at a wholly different period of its revolution, when one begins to see it full, or a sick man now devoured by the malady which a few years ago was but a tiny spot which was easily concealed and the gravity of which was never suspected. Although the operation that Brichot had undergone had restored a tiny portion of the sight which he had thought to be lost for ever, I do not think he had observed the ruffian following in the Baron's steps. Not that this mattered, for, ever since la Raspelière, and notwithstanding the professor's friendly regard for M. de Charlus, the sight of the latter always made him feel ill at ease. No doubt to every man the life of every other extends along shadowy paths which he does not suspect. Falsehood, however, so often treacherous, upon which all conversation is based, conceals less perfectly a feeling of hostility, or of sordid interest, or a visit which we wish to look as though we had not paid, or an escapade with the mistress of a day which we are anxious to keep from our wife, than a good reputation covers up – so as not to let their existence be guessed – evil habits. They may remain unknown to us for a lifetime; an accidental encounter upon a pier, at night, will disclose them; even then this accidental discovery is frequently misunderstood and we require a third person, who is in the secret, to supply the unimaginable clue of which everyone is unaware. But, once we know about them, they alarm us because we feel that that way madness lies, far more than by their immorality. Mme de Surgis did not possess the slightest trace of any moral feeling, and would have admitted anything of her sons that could be degraded and explained by material interest, which is comprehensible to all mankind! But she forbade them to go on visiting M. de Charlus when she learned that, by a sort of internal clockwork, he was inevitably drawn upon each of their visits, to pinch their chins and to make each of them pinch his brother's. She felt that uneasy sense of a physical mystery which makes us ask ourself whether the neighbour with whom we have been on friendly terms is not tainted with cannibalism, and to the Baron's repeated enquiry: 'When am I going to see your sons again?' she would reply, conscious of the thunderbolts that she was attracting to her defenceless head, that they were very busy working for examinations, preparing to go abroad, and so forth. Irresponsibility aggravates faults, and even crimes, whatever anyone may say. Landru (assuming that he really did kill his wives) if he did so from a financial motive, which it is possible to resist, may be pardoned, but not if his crime was due to an irresistible sadism.

Brichot's coarse pleasantries, in the early days of his friendship with the Baron, had given place, as soon as it was a question, not of uttering commonplaces, but of understanding, to an awkward feeling which concealed a certain merriment. He reassured himself by recalling pages of Plato, lines of Virgil, because, being mentally as well as physically blind, he did not understand that in those days to fall in love with a young man was like, in our day (Socrates' jokes reveal this more clearly than Plato's theories), keeping a dancing girl before one marries and settles down. M. de Charlus himself would not have understood, he who confused his mania with friendship, which does not resemble it in the least, and the athletes of Praxiteles with obliging boxers. He refused to see that for the last nineteen hundred years ('a pious courtier under a pious prince would have been an atheist under an atheist prince', as Labruyère reminds us) all conventional homosexuality – that of Plato's young friends as well as that of Virgil's shepherds – has disappeared, that what survives and increases is only the involuntary, the neurotic kind, which we conceal from other people and disguise to ourselves. And M. de Charlus would have been wrong in not denying frankly the pagan genealogy. In exchange for a little plastic beauty, how vast the moral superiority! The shepherd in Theocritus who sighs for love of a boy, later on will have no reason to be less hard of heart, less dull of wit than the other shepherd whose flute sounds for Amaryllis. For the former is not suffering from a malady, he is conforming to the customs of his time. It is the homosexuality that survives in spite of obstacles, a thing of scorn and loathing, that is the only true form, the only form that can be found conjoined in a person with an enhancement of his moral qualities. We are appalled at the apparently close relation between these and our bodily attributes, when we think of the slight dislocation of a purely physical taste, the slight blemish in one of the senses, which explain why the world of poets and musicians, so firmly barred against the Duc de Guermantes, opens its portals to M. de Charlus. That the latter should show taste in the furnishing of his home, which is that of an eclectic housewife, need not surprise us; but the narrow loophole that opens upon Beethoven and Veronese! This does not exempt the sane from a feeling of alarm when a madman who has composed a sublime poem, after explaining to them in the most logical fashion that he has been shut up by mistake, through his wife's machinations, imploring them to intercede for him with the governor of the asylum, complaining of the promiscuous company that is forced upon him, concludes as follows: 'You see that man who is waiting to speak to me on the lawn, whom I am obliged to put up with; he thinks that he is Jesus Christ. That alone will show you the sort of lunatics that I have to live among; he cannot be Christ, for I am Christ myself!' A moment earlier, you were on the point of going to assure the governor that a mistake had been made. At this final speech, even if you bear in mind the admirable poem at which this same man is working every day, you shrink from him, as Mme de Surgis's sons shrank from M. de Charlus, not that he would have done them any harm, but because of his ceaseless invitations, the ultimate purpose of which was to pinch their chins. The poet is to be pitied, who must, with no Virgil to guide him, pass through the circles of an inferno of sulphur and brimstone, to cast himself into the fire that falls from heaven, in order to rescue a few of the inhabitants of Sodom! No charm in his work; the same severity in his life as in those of the unfrocked priests who follow the strictest rule of celibacy so that no one may be able to ascribe to anything but loss of faith their discarding of the cassock.

Making a pretence of not seeing the seedy individual who was following in his wake (whenever the Baron ventured into the Boulevards or crossed the waiting-room in Saint-Lazarre station, these followers might be counted by the dozen who, in the hope of 'touching him for a dollar', never let him out of their sight), and afraid at the same time that the other might have the audacity to accost him, the Baron had devoutly lowered his darkened eyelids which, in contrast to his rice-powdered cheeks, gave him the appearance of a Grand Inquisitor painted by El Greco. But this priestly expression caused alarm, and he looked like an unfrocked priest, various compromises to which he had been driven by the need to apologise for his taste and to keep it secret having had the effect of bringing to the surface of his face precisely what the Baron sought to conceal, a debauched life indicated by moral decay. This last, indeed, whatever be its cause, is easily detected, for it is never slow in taking bodily form and proliferates upon a face, especially on the cheeks and round the eyes, as physically as the ochreous yellows accumulate there in a case of jaundice or repulsive reds in a case of skin disease. Nor was it merely in the cheeks, or rather the chaps of this painted face, in the mammiferous chest, the aggressive rump of this body allowed to deteriorate and invaded by obesity, upon which there now floated iridescent as a film of oil, the vice at one time so jealously confined by M. de Charlus in the most secret chamber of his heart. Now it overflowed in all his speech.

'So this is how you prowl the streets at night, Brichot, with a good-looking young man,' he said as he joined us, while the disappointed ruffian made off. 'A fine example. We must tell your young pupils at the Sorbonne that this is how you behave. But, I must say, the society of youth seems to be good for you, Monsieur le Professeur, you are as fresh as a rosebud. I have interrupted you, you looked as though you were enjoying yourselves like a pair of giddy girls, and had no need of an old Granny Killjoy like myself. I shan't take it to the confessional, since you are almost at your destination.' The Baron's mood was all the more blithe since he knew nothing whatever about the scene that afternoon, Jupien having decided that it was better to protect his niece against a repetition of the onslaught than to inform M. de Charlus. And so the Baron was still looking forward to the marriage, and delighting in the thought of it. One would suppose that it is a consolation to these great solitaries to give their tragic celibacy the relief of a fictitious fatherhood. 'But, upon my word, Brichot,' he went on, turning with a laugh to gaze at us, 'I feel quite awkward when I see you in such gallant company. You were like a pair of lovers. Going along arm in arm, I say, Brichot, you do go the pace!' Ought one to ascribe this speech to the senility of a particular state of mind, less capable than in the past of controlling its reflexes, which in moments of automatism lets out a secret that has been so carefully hidden for forty years? Or rather to that contempt for plebeian opinion which all the Guermantes felt in their hearts, and of which M. de Charlus's brother, the Duke, was displaying a variant form when, regardless of the fact that my mother could see him, he used to shave standing by his bedroom window in his unbuttoned nightshirt. Had M. de Charlus contracted, during the roasting journeys between Doncières and Douville, the dangerous habit of making himself at ease, and, just as he would push back his straw hat in order to cool his huge forehead, of unfastening – at first, for a few moments only – the mask that for too long had been rigorously imposed upon his true face? His conjugal attitude towards Morel might well have astonished anyone who had observed it in its full extent. But M. de Charlus had reached the stage when the monotony of the pleasures that his vice has to offer became wearying. He had sought instinctively for novel displays, and, growing tired of the strangers whom he picked up, had passed to the opposite pole, to what he used to imagine that he would always loathe, the imitation of family life, or of fatherhood. Sometimes even this did not suffice him, he required novelty, and would go and spend the night with a woman, just as a normal man may, once in his life, have wished to go to bed with a boy, from a curiosity similar though inverse, and in either case equally unhealthy. The Baron's existence as one of the 'faithful', living, for Charlie's sake, entirely among the little clan, had had, in stultifying the efforts that he had been making for years to keep up lying appearances, the same influence that a voyage of exploration or residence in the colonies has upon certain Europeans who discard the ruling principles by which they were guided at home. And yet, the internal revolution of a mind, ignorant at first of the anomaly contained in its body, then appalled at it after the discovery, and finally growing so used to it as to fail to perceive that it is not safe to confess to other people what the sinner has come in time to confess without shame to himself, had been even more effective in liberating M. de Charlus from the last vestiges of social constraint than the time that he spent at the Verdurins'. No banishment, indeed, to the South Pole, or to the summit of Mont Blanc, can separate us so entirely from our fellow creatures as a prolonged residence in the seclusion of a secret vice, that is to say of a state of mind that is different from theirs. A vice (so M. de Charlus used at one time to style it) to which the Baron now gave the genial aspect of a mere failing, extremely common, attractive on the whole and almost amusing, like laziness, absent-mindedness or greed. Conscious of the curiosity that his own striking personality aroused, M. de Charlus derived a certain pleasure from satisfying, whetting, sustaining it. Just as a Jewish journalist will come forward day after day as the champion of Catholicism, not, probably, with any hope of being taken seriously, but simply in order not to disappoint the good-natured amusement of his readers, M. de Charlus would genially denounce evil habits among the little clan, as he would have mimicked a person speaking English or imitated Mounet-Sully, without waiting to be asked, so as to pay his scot with a good grace, by displaying an amateur talent in society; so that M. de Charlus now threatened Brichot that he would report to the Sorbonne that he was in the habit of walking about with young men, exactly as the circumcised scribe keeps referring in and out of season to the 'Eldest Daughter of the Church' and the 'Sacred Heart of Jesus', that is to say without the least trace of hypocrisy, but with a distinctly histrionic effect. It was not only the change in the words themselves, so different from those that he allowed himself to use in the past, that seemed to require some explanation, there was also the change that had occurred in his intonations, his gestures, all of which now singularly resembled the type M. de Charlus used most fiercely to castigate; he would now utter unconsciously almost the same little cries (unconscious in him, and all the more deep-rooted) as are uttered consciously by the inverts who refer to one another as 'she'; as though this deliberate 'camping', against which M. de Charlus had for so long set his face, were after all merely a brilliant and faithful imitation of the manner that men of the Charlus type, whatever they may say, are compelled to adopt when they have reached a certain stage in their malady, just as sufferers from general paralysis or locomotor ataxia inevitably end by displaying certain symptoms. As a matter of fact – and this is what this purely unconscious 'camping' revealed – the difference between the stern Charlus, dressed all in black, with his stiffly brushed hair, whom I had known, and the painted young men, loaded with rings, was no more than the purely imaginary difference that exists between an excited person who talks fast, keeps moving all the time, and a neurotic who talks slowly, preserves a perpetual phlegm, but is tainted with the same neurasthenia in the eyes of the physician who knows that each of the two is devoured by the same anguish and marred by the same defects. At the same time one could tell that M. de Charlus had aged from wholly different signs, such as the extraordinary frequency in his conversation of certain expressions that had taken root in it and used now to crop up at every moment (for instance: 'the chain of circumstances') upon which the Baron's speech leaned in sentence after sentence as upon a necessary prop. 'Is Charlie here yet?' Brichot asked M. de Charlus as we came in sight of the door. 'Oh, I don't know,' said the Baron, raising his arms and half-shutting his eyes with the air of a person who does not wish anyone to accuse him of being indiscreet, all the more so as he had probably been reproached by Morel for things which he had said

and which the other, as timorous as he was vain, and as ready to deny M. de
Charlus as he was to boast of his friendship, had considered serious albeit
they were quite unimportant. 'You know, he never tells me what he's going
to do.' If the conversations of two people bound by a tie of intimacy are full
of falsehood, this occurs no less spontaneously in the conversations that a
third person holds with a lover on the subject of the person with whom the
latter is in love, whatever be the sex of that person.

'Have you seen him lately?' I asked M. de Charlus, with the object of
seeming at once not to be afraid of mentioning Morel to him and not to
believe that they were actually living together. 'He came in, as it happened,
for five minutes this morning while I was still half asleep, and sat down on
the side of my bed, as though he wanted to ravish me.' I guessed at once that
M. de Charlus had seen Charlie within the last hour, for if we ask a woman
when she last saw the man whom we know to be – and whom she may
perhaps suppose that we suspect of being – her lover, if she has just taken tea
with him, she replies: 'I saw him for an instant before luncheon.' Between
these two incidents the only difference is that one is false and the other true,
but both are equally innocent, or, if you prefer it, equally culpable. And so
we should be unable to understand why the mistress (in this case, M. de
Charlus) always chooses the false version, did we not know that such replies
are determined, unknown to the person who utters them, by a number of
factors which appear so out of proportion to the triviality of the incident
that we do not take the trouble to consider them. But to a physicist the space
occupied by the tiniest ball of pith is explained by the harmony of action, the
conflict or equilibrium, of laws of attraction or repulsion which govern far
greater worlds. Just as many different laws acting in opposite directions
dictate the more general responses with regard to the innocence, the
'platonism', or on the contrary the carnal reality of the relations that one has
with the person whom one says one saw in the morning when one has seen
him or her in the evening. Here we need merely record, without pausing to
consider them, the desire to appear natural and fearless, the instinctive
impulse to conceal a secret assignation, a blend of modesty and ostentation,
the need to confess what one finds so delightful and to show that one is
loved, a divination of what the other person knows or guesses – but does not
say – a divination which, exceeding or falling short of the other person's,
makes one now exaggerate, now underestimate it, the spontaneous longing
to play with fire and the determination to rescue something from the blaze.
At the same time, speaking generally, let us say that M. de Charlus,
notwithstanding the aggravation of his malady which perpetually urged him
to reveal, to insinuate, sometimes boldly to invent compromising details,

did intend, during this period in his life, to make it known that Charlie was not a man of the same sort as himself and that they were friends and nothing more. This did not prevent him (even though it may quite possibly have been true) from contradicting himself at times (as with regard to the hour at which they had last met), whether he forgot himself at such moments and told the truth, or invented a lie, boastingly or from a sentimental affectation or because he thought it amusing to baffle his questioner. 'You know that he is to me,' the Baron went on, 'the best of comrades, for whom I have the greatest affection, as I am certain' (was he uncertain of it, then, that he felt the need to say that he was certain?) 'he has for me, but there is nothing at all between us, nothing of that sort, you understand, nothing of that sort,' said the Baron, as naturally as though he had been speaking of a woman. 'Yes, he came in this morning to pull me out of bed. Though he knows that I hate anybody to see me in bed. You don't mind? Oh, it's horrible, it's so disturbing, one looks so perfectly hideous, of course I'm no longer five-and-twenty, they won't choose me to be Queen of the May, still one does like to feel that one is looking one's best.'

It is possible that the Baron was in earnest when he spoke of Morel as a good comrade, and that he was being even more truthful than he supposed when he said: 'I never know what he's doing; he tells me nothing about his life.'

Indeed we may mention (interrupting for a few moments our narrative, which shall be resumed immediately after the closure of this parenthesis which opens at the moment when M. de Charlus, Brichot and myself are arriving at Mme Verdurin's front door), we may mention that shortly before this evening the Baron had been plunged in grief and stupefaction by a letter which he had opened by mistake and which was addressed to Morel. This letter, which by a repercussion was to cause intense misery to myself also, was written by the actress Léa, notorious for her exclusive interest in women. And yet her letter to Morel (whom M. de Charlus had never suspected of knowing her, even) was written in the most impassioned tone. Its indelicacy prevents us from reproducing it here, but we may mention that Léa addressed him throughout in the feminine gender, with such expressions as: 'Go on, you bad woman!' or 'Of course you are so, my pretty, you know you are.' And in this letter reference was made to various other women who seemed to be no less Morel's friends than Léa's. On the other hand, Morel's sarcasm at the Baron's expense and Léa's at that of an officer who was keeping her, and of whom she said: 'He keeps writing me letters begging me to be careful! What do you say to that, my little white puss?' revealed to M. de Charlus a state of things no less unsuspected by him than

were Morel's peculiar and intimate relations with Léa. What most disturbed
the Baron was the word 'so'. Ignorant at first of its application, he had
eventually, at a time already remote in the past, learned that he himself was
'so'. And now the notion that he had acquired of this word was again put to
the challenge. When he had discovered that he was 'so', he had supposed
this to mean that his tastes, as Saint-Simon says, did not lie in the direction
of women. And here was this word 'so' applied to Morel with an extension
of meaning of which M. de Charlus was unaware, so much so that Morel
gave proof, according to this letter, of his being 'so' by having the same
taste as certain women for other women. From that moment the Baron's
jealousy had no longer any reason to confine itself to the men of Morel's
acquaintance, but began to extend to the women also. So that the people
who were 'so' were not merely those that he had supposed to be 'so', but a
whole and vast section of the inhabitants of the planet, consisting of women
as well as of men, loving not merely men but women also, and the Baron, in
the face of this novel meaning of a word that was so familiar to him, felt
himself tormented by an anxiety of the mind as well as of the heart, born
of this twofold mystery which combined an extension of the field of his
jealousy with the sudden inadequacy of a definition.

M. de Charlus had never in his life been anything but an amateur. That is
to say, incidents of this sort could never be of any use to him. He worked off
the painful impression that they might make upon him in violent scenes in
which he was a past master of eloquence, or in crafty intrigues. But to a
person endowed with the qualities of a Bergotte, for instance, they might
have been of inestimable value. This may indeed explain, to a certain extent
(since we have to grope blindfold, but choose, like the lower animals, the
herb that is good for us), why men like Bergotte have generally lived in the
company of persons who were ordinary, false and malicious. Their beauty is
sufficient for the writer's imagination, enhances his generosity, but does not
in any way alter the nature of his companion, whose life, situated thousands
of feet below the level of his own, her incredible stories, her lies carried
farther, and, what is more, in another direction than what might have been
expected, appear in occasional flashes. The lie, the perfect lie, about people
whom we know, about the relations that we have had with them, about our
motive for some action, a motive which we express in totally different terms,
the lie as to what we are, whom we love, what we feel with regard to the
person who loves us and believes that she has fashioned us in her own image
because she keeps on kissing us morning, noon and night, that lie is one of
the only things in the world that can open a window for us upon what is
novel, unknown, that can awaken in us sleeping senses to the contemplation

of universes that otherwise we should never have known. We are bound to say, in so far as M. de Charlus is concerned, that, if he was stupefied to learn with regard to Morel a certain number of things which the latter had carefully concealed from him, he was not justified in concluding from this that it was a mistake to associate too closely with the lower orders. We shall indeed see, in the concluding section of this work, M. de Charlus himself engaged in doing things which would have stupefied the members of his family and his friends far more than he could possibly have been stupefied by the revelations of Léa. (The revelation that he had found most painful had been that of a tour which Morel had made with Léa, whereas at the time he had assured M. de Charlus that he was studying music in Germany. He had found support for this falsehood in obliging friends in Germany to whom he had sent his letters, to be forwarded from there to M. de Charlus, who, as it happened, was so positive that Morel was there that he had not even looked at the postmark.) But it is time to rejoin the Baron as he advances with Brichot and myself towards the Verdurins' door.

'And what,' he went on, turning to myself, 'has become of your young Hebrew friend, whom we met at Douville? It occurred to me that, if you liked, one might perhaps invite him to the house one evening.' For M. de Charlus, who did not shrink from employing a private detective to spy upon every word and action of Morel, for all the world like a husband or a lover, had not ceased to pay attention to other young men. The vigilance which he made one of his old servants maintain, through an agency, upon Morel, was so indiscreet that his footmen thought they were being watched, and one of the housemaids could not endure the suspense, never ventured into the street, always expecting to find a policeman at her heels. 'She can do whatever she likes! It would be a waste of time and money to follow her! As if her goings on mattered to us!' the old servant ironically exclaimed, for he was so passionately devoted to his master that, albeit he in no way shared the Baron's tastes, he had come in time, with such ardour did he employ himself in their service, to speak of them as though they were his own. 'He is the very best of good fellows,' M. de Charlus would say of this old servant, for we never appreciate anyone so much as those who combine with other great virtues that of placing themselves unconditionally at the disposal of our vices. It was moreover of men alone that M. de Charlus was capable of feeling any jealousy so far as Morel was concerned. Women inspired in him no jealousy whatever. This is indeed an almost universal rule with the Charlus type. The love of the man with whom they are in love for women is something different, which occurs in another animal species (a lion does not interfere with tigers); does not distress them; if anything, reassures them.

Sometimes, it is true, in the case of those who exalt their inversion to the level of a priesthood, this love creates disgust. These men resent their friends' having succumbed to it, not as a betrayal but as a lapse from virtue. A Charlus, of a different variety from the Baron, would have been as indignant at the discovery of Morel's relations with a woman as upon reading in a newspaper that he, the interpreter of Bach and Handel, was going to play Puccini. It is, by the way, for this reason that the young men who, with an eye to their own personal advantage, condescend to the love of men like Charlus, assure them that women inspire them only with disgust, just as they would tell a doctor that they never touch alcohol, and care only for spring water. But M. de Charlus, in this respect, departed to some extent from the general rule. Since he admired everything about Morel, the latter's successes with women caused him no annoyance, gave him the same joy as his successes on the platform, or at écarté. 'But do you know, my dear fellow, he has women,' he would say, with an air of disclosure, of scandal, possibly of envy, above all of admiration. 'He is extraordinary,' he would continue. 'Everywhere, the most famous whores can look at nobody but him. They stare at him everywhere, whether it's on the underground or in the theatre. It's becoming a nuisance! I can't go out with him to a restaurant without the waiter bringing him notes from at least three women. And always pretty women too. Not that there's anything surprising in that. I was watching him yesterday, I can quite understand it, he has become so beautiful, he looks just like a Bronzino, he is really marvellous.' But M. de Charlus liked to show that he was in love with Morel, to persuade other people, possibly to persuade himself, that Morel was in love with him. He applied to the purpose of having Morel always with him (notwithstanding the harm that the young fellow might do to the Baron's social position) a sort of self-esteem. For (and this is frequent among men of good position, who are snobs, and, in their vanity, sever all their social ties in order to be seen everywhere with a mistress, a person of doubtful or a lady of tarnished reputation, whom nobody will invite, and with whom nevertheless it seems to them flattering to be associated) he had arrived at that stage at which self-esteem devotes all its energy to destroying the goals to which it has attained, whether because, under the influence of love, a man finds a prestige which he is alone in perceiving in ostentatious relations with the beloved object, or because, by the waning of social ambitions that have been gratified, and the rising of a tide of subsidiary curiosities all the more absorbing the more platonic they are, the latter have not only reached but have passed the level at which the former found it difficult to remain.

As for young men in general, M. de Charlus found that to his fondness for them Morel's existence was not an obstacle, and that indeed his brilliant reputation as a violinist or his growing fame as a composer and journalist might in certain instances prove an attraction. Did anyone introduce to the Baron a young composer of an agreeable type, it was in Morel's talents that he sought an opportunity of doing the stranger a favour. 'You must,' he would tell him, 'bring me some of your work so that Morel can play it at a concert or on tour. There is hardly any decent music written, now, for the violin. It is a godsend to find anything new. And abroad they appreciate that sort of thing enormously. Even in the provinces there are little musical societies where they love music with a fervour and intelligence that are quite admirable.' Without any greater sincerity (for all this could serve only as a bait and it was seldom that Morel condescended to fulfil these promises), Bloch having confessed that he was something of a poet (when he was 'in the mood', he had added with the sarcastic laugh with which he would accompany a platitude, when he could think of nothing original), M. de Charlus said to me: 'You must tell your young Israelite, since he writes verses, that he must really bring me some for Morel. For a composer, that is always the stumbling-block, to find something decent to set to music. One might even consider a libretto. It would not be without interest, and would acquire a certain value from the distinction of the poet, from my patronage, from a whole chain of auxiliary circumstances, among which Morel's talent would take the chief place, for he is composing a lot just now, and writing too, and very pleasantly, I must talk to you about it. As for his talent as a performer (there, as you know, he is already a past master), you shall see this evening how well the lad plays Vinteuil's music; he overwhelms me; at his age, to have such an understanding while he is still such a boy, such a kid! Oh, this evening is only to be a little rehearsal. The big affair is to come off in two or three days. But it will be much more distinguished this evening. And so we are delighted that you have come,' he went on, employing the plural pronoun doubtless because a King says: 'It is our wish'. 'The programme is so magnificent that I have advised Mme Verdurin to give two parties. One in a few days' time, at which she will have all her own friends, the other tonight at which the hostess is, to use a legal expression, 'disseized'. It is I who have issued the invitations, and I have collected a few people from another sphere, who may be useful to Charlie, and whom it will be nice for the Verdurins to meet. Don't you agree, it is all very well to have the finest music played by the greatest artists, the effect of the performance remains muffled in cotton wool, if the audience is composed of the milliner from across the way and the grocer from round the corner. You know what I think of the intellectual level of people in society, still they can play certain quite important parts, among others that which in public events devolves upon the press, and which is that of being an organ of publicity. You know what I mean; I have for instance invited my sister-in-law Oriane; it is not certain that she will come, but it is on the other hand certain that, if she does come, she will understand absolutely nothing. But one does not ask her to understand, which is beyond her capacity, but to talk, a task which is admirably suited to her, and which she never fails to perform. What is the result? Tomorrow as ever is, instead of the silence of the milliner and the grocer, an animated conversation at the Mortemarts' with Oriane telling everyone that she has heard the most marvellous music, that a certain Morel, and so forth; unspeakable rage of the people not invited, who will say: 'Palamède thought, no doubt, that we were unworthy; anyhow, who are these people who were giving the party?' a counterblast quite as useful as Oriane's praises, because Morel's name keeps cropping up all the time and is finally engraved in the memory like a lesson that one has read over a dozen times. All this forms a chain of circumstances which may be of value to the artist, to the hostess, may serve as a sort of megaphone for a performance which will thus be made audible to a remote public. Really, it is worth the trouble; you shall see what progress Charlie has made. And what is more, we have discovered a new talent in him, my dear fellow, he writes like an angel. Like an angel, I tell you.' M. de Charlus omitted to say that for some time past he had been employing Morel, like those great noblemen of the seventeenth century who scorned to sign and even to write their own slanderous attacks, to compose certain vilely calumnious little paragraphs at the expense of Comtesse Molé. Their insolence apparent even to those who merely glanced at them, how much more cruel were they to the young woman herself, who found in them, so skilfully introduced that nobody but herself saw the point, certain passages from her own correspondence, textually quoted, but interpreted in a sense which made them as deadly as the cruellest revenge. They killed the lady. But there is edited every day in Paris, Balzac would tell us, a sort of spoken newspaper, more terrible than its printed rivals. We shall see later on that this verbal press reduced to nothing the power of a Charlus who had fallen out of fashion, and exalted far above him a Morel who was not worth the millionth part of his former patron. Is this intellectual fashion really so simple, and does it sincerely believe in the nullity of a Charlus of genius, in the incontestable authority of a crass Morel? The Baron was not so innocent in his implacable vengeance. Whence, no doubt, that bitter venom on his tongue, the spreading of which seemed to dye his cheeks with jaundice when he was in a rage. 'You who knew Bergotte,' M. de Charlus went on, 'I thought at one time that you might, perhaps, by refreshing his memory with regard to the youngster's writings, collaborate in short with myself, help me to assist a twofold talent, that of a musician and a writer, which may one day acquire the prestige of that of Berlioz. As you know, the illustrious have often other things to think about, they are smothered in flattery, they take little interest except in themselves. But Bergotte, who was genuinely unpretentious and obliging, promised me that he would get into the *Gaulois*, or some such paper, those little articles, a blend of the humorist and the musician, which he really does quite charmingly now, and I am really very glad that Charlie should combine with his violin this little stroke of Ingres's pen. I know that I am prone to exaggeration, when he is concerned, like all the old fairy god-mothers of the Conservatoire. What, my dear fellow, didn't you know that? You have never observed my little weakness. I pace up and down for hours on end outside the examination hall. I'm as happy as a queen. As for Charlie's prose, Bergotte assured me that it was really very good indeed.'

M. de Charlus, who had long been acquainted with Bergotte through Swann, had indeed gone to see him a few days before his death, to ask him to find an opening for Morel in some newspaper for a sort of commentary, half-humorous, upon the music of the day. In doing so, M. de Charlus had felt some remorse, for, himself a great admirer of Bergotte, he was conscious that he never went to see him for his own sake, but in order, thanks to the respect, partly intellectual, partly social, that Bergotte felt for him, to be able to do a great service to Morel, or to some other of his friends. That he no longer made use of people in society for any other purpose did not shock M. de Charlus, but to treat Bergotte thus had appeared to him more offensive, for he felt that Bergotte had not the calculating nature of people in society, and deserved better treatment. Only, his was a busy life, and he could never find time for anything except when he was greatly interested in something, when, for instance, it affected Morel. What was more, as he was himself extremely intelligent, the conversation of an intelligent man left him comparatively cold, especially that of Bergotte who was too much the man of letters for his liking and belonged to another clan, did not share his point of view. As for Bergotte, he had observed the calculated motive of M. de Charlus's visits, but had felt no resentment, for he had been incapable, throughout his life, of any consecutive generosity, but anxious to give pleasure, broadminded, insensitive to the pleasure of administering a rebuke. As for M. de Charlus's vice, he had never partaken of it to the smallest extent, but had found in it rather an element of colour in the person affected, *fas et nefas*, for an artist, consisting not in moral examples but in memories of Plato or of Sodom. 'But you, fair youth, we never see you at Quai Conti. You don't abuse their hospitality!' I explained that I went out as a rule with my cousin. 'Do you hear that! He goes out with his cousin! What a most particularly pure young man!' said M. de Charlus to Brichot. Then, turning again to myself: 'But we are not asking you to give an account of your life, my boy. You are free to do anything that amuses you. We merely regret that we have no share in it. Besides, you show very good taste, your cousin is charming, ask Brichot, she quite turned his head at Douville. We shall regret her absence this evening. But you did just as well, perhaps, not to bring her with you. Vinteuil's music is delightful. But I have heard that we are to meet the composer's daughter and her friend, who have a terrible reputation. That sort of thing is always awkward for a girl. They are sure to be there, unless the ladies have been detained in the country, for they were to have been present without fail all afternoon at a rehearsal which Mme Verdurin was giving today, to which she had invited only the bores, her family, the people whom she could not very well have this evening. But a moment ago, before dinner, Charlie told us that the sisters Vinteuil, as we call them, for whom they were all waiting, never came.' Notwithstanding the intense pain that I had felt at the sudden association with its effect, of which alone I had been aware, of the cause, at length discovered, of Albertine's anxiety to be there that afternoon, the presence publicly announced (but of which I had been ignorant) of Mlle Vinteuil and her friend, my mind was still sufficiently detached to remark that M. de Charlus, who had told us, a few minutes earlier, that he had not seen Charlie since the morning, was now brazenly admitting that he had seen him before dinner. My pain became visible. 'Why, what is the matter with you?' said the Baron. 'You are quite green; come, let us go in, you will catch cold, you don't look at all well.' It was not any doubt as to Albertine's virtue that M. de Charlus's words had awakened in me. Many other doubts had penetrated my mind already; at each fresh doubt we feel that the measure is heaped full, that we cannot cope with it, then we manage to find room for it all the same, and once it is introduced into our vital essence it enters into competition there with so many longings to believe, so many reasons to forget, that we speedily become accustomed to it, and end by ceasing to pay it any attention. There remains only, like a partly healed pain, the menace of possible suffering, which, the counterpart of desire, a feeling of the same order, and like it become the centre of our thoughts, radiates through them to an infinite circumference a wistful melancholy, as desire radiates pleasures whose origin we fail to perceive, wherever anything may suggest the idea of the person with whom we are in love. But pain revives as soon as a fresh doubt enters our mind complete; even if we assure ourself almost immediately: 'I shall deal with this, there must be some method by which I need not suffer, it cannot be true', nevertheless there has been a first moment in which we suffered as though we believed it. If we had merely members, such as legs and arms, life would be endurable; unfortunately we carry inside us that little organ which we call the heart, which is subject to certain maladies in the course of which it is infinitely impressionable by everything that concerns the life of a certain person, so that a lie – that most harmless of things, in the midst of which we live so unconcernedly, if the lie be told by ourselves or by strangers – coming from that person, causes the little heart, which surgeons ought really to be able to excise from us, intolerable anguish. Let us not speak of the brain, for our mind may go on reasoning interminably in the course of this anguish, it does no more to mitigate it than by taking thought can we soothe an aching tooth. It is true that this person is to blame for having lied to us, for she had sworn to us that she would always tell us the truth. But we know from our own shortcomings, towards other people, how little an oath is worth. And we have deliberately believed them when they came from her, the very person to whose interest it has always been to lie to us, and whom, moreover, we did not select for her virtues. It is true that, later on, she would almost cease to have any need to lie to us – at the moment when our heart will have grown indifferent to her falsehood – because then we shall not feel any interest in her life. We know this, and, notwithstanding, we deliberately sacrifice our own lives, either by killing ourselves for her sake, or by letting ourselves be sentenced to death for having murdered her, or simply by spending, in the course of a few evenings, our whole fortune upon her, which will oblige us presently to commit suicide because we have not a penny in the world. Besides, however calm we may imagine ourselves when we are in love, we always have love in our heart in a state of unstable equilibrium. A trifle is sufficient to exalt it to the position of happiness, we radiate happiness, we smother in our affection not her whom we love, but those who have given us merit in her eyes, who have protected her from every evil temptation; we think that our mind is at ease, and a word is sufficient: 'Gilberte is not coming', 'Mademoiselle Vinteuil is expected', to make all the preconceived happiness towards which we were rising collapse, to make the sun hide his face, to open the bag of the winds and let loose the internal tempest which one day we shall be incapable of resisting. That day, the day upon which the heart has become so frail, our friends who respect us are pained that such trifles, that certain persons, can so affect us, can bring us to death's door. But what are they to do? If a poet is dying of septic pneumonia, can one imagine his friends explaining to the pneumococcus that the poet is a man of talent and that it ought to let him recover? My doubt, in so far as it referred to Mlle Vinteuil, was not entirely novel. But to a certain extent, my jealousy of the afternoon, inspired by Léa and her friends, had abolished it. Once that peril of the Trocadéro was removed, I had felt that I had recaptured for all time complete peace of mind. But what was entirely novel to me was a certain excursion as to which Andrée had told me: 'We went to this place and that, we didn't meet anyone', and during which, on the contrary, Mlle Vinteuil had evidently arranged to meet Albertine at Mme Verdurin's. At this moment I would gladly have allowed Albertine to go out by herself, to go wherever she might choose, provided that I might lock up Mlle Vinteuil and her friend somewhere and be certain that Albertine would not meet them. The fact is that jealousy is, as a rule, partial, of intermittent application, whether because it is the painful extension of an anxiety which is provoked now by one person, now by another with whom our mistress may be in love, or because of the exiguity of our thought which is able to realise only what it can represent to itself and leaves everything else in an obscurity which can cause us only a proportionately modified anguish.

Just as we were about to ring the bell we were overtaken by Saniette who informed us that Princess Sherbatov had died at six o'clock, and added that he had not at first recognised us. 'I envisaged you, however, for some time,' he told us in a breathless voice. 'Is it aught but curious that I should have hesitated?' To say 'Is it not curious' would have seemed to him wrong, and he had acquired a familiarity with obsolete forms of speech that was becoming exasperating. 'Not but what you are people whom one may acknowledge as friends.' His grey complexion seemed to be illuminated by the livid glow of a storm. His breathlessness, which had been noticeable, as recently as last summer, only when M. Verdurin 'jumped down his throat', was now continuous. 'I understand that an unknown work of Vinteuil is to be performed by excellent artists, and singularly by Morel.' 'Why singularly?' enquired the Baron who detected a criticism in the adverb. 'Our friend Saniette,' Brichot made haste to exclaim, acting as interpreter, 'is prone to speak, like the excellent scholar that he is, the language of an age in which "singularly" was equivalent to our "especially".'

As we entered the Verdurins' hall, M. de Charlus asked me whether I was engaged upon any work and as I told him that I was not, but that I was greatly interested at the moment in old dinner-services of plate and porcelain, he assured me that I could not see any finer than those that the Verdurins had; that moreover I might have seen them at la Raspelière, since, on the pretext that one's possessions are also one's friends, they were so silly as to cart everything down there with them; it would be less convenient to bring everything out for my benefit on the evening of a party; still, he would tell them to show me anything that I wished to see. I begged him not to do anything of the sort. M. de Charlus unbuttoned his greatcoat, took off his hat, and I saw that the top of his head had now turned silver in patches. But like a precious shrub which is not only coloured with autumn tints but certain leaves of which are protected by bandages of wadding or incrustations of plaster, M. de Charlus received from these few white hairs at his crest only a further variegation added to those of his face. And yet, even beneath the layers of different expressions, paint and hypocrisy which formed such a bad 'make-up', his face continued to hide from almost everyone the secret that it seemed to me to be crying aloud. I was almost put to shame by his eyes in which I was afraid of his surprising me in the act of reading it, as from an open book, by his voice which seemed to me to be repeating it in every tone, with an untiring indecency. But secrets are well kept by such people, for everyone who comes in contact with them is deaf and blind. The people who learned the truth from someone else, from the Verdurins for instance, believed it, but only for so long as they had not met M. de Charlus. His face, so far from spreading, dissipated every scandalous rumour. For we form so extravagant an idea of certain characters that we would be incapable of identifying one of them with the familiar features of a person of our acquaintance. And we find it difficult to believe in such a person's vices, just as we can never believe in the genius of a person with whom we went to the Opéra last night.

M. de Charlus was engaged in handing over his greatcoat with the instructions of a familiar guest. But the footman to whom he was handing it was a newcomer, and quite young. Now M. de Charlus had by this time begun, as people say, to 'lose his bearings' and did not always remember what might and what might not be done. The praiseworthy desire that he had felt at Balbec to show that certain topics did not alarm him, that he was not afraid to declare with regard to someone or other: 'He is a nice-looking boy', to utter, in short, the same words as might have been uttered by somebody who was not like himself, this desire he had now begun to express by saying on the contrary things which nobody could ever have said who was not like him, things upon which his mind was so constantly fixed that he forgot that they do not form part of the habitual preoccupation of people in general. And so, as he gazed at the new footman, he raised his forefinger in the air in a menacing fashion and, thinking that he was making an excellent joke: 'You are not to make eyes at me like that, do you hear?' said the Baron, and, turning to Brichot: 'He has a quaint little face, that boy, his nose is rather fun', and, completing his joke, or yielding to a desire, he lowered his forefinger horizontally, hesitated for an instant, then, unable to control himself any longer, thrust it irresistibly forwards at the footman and touched the tip of his nose, saying 'Pif!' 'That's a rum card,' the footman said to himself, and enquired of his companions whether it was a joke or what it was. 'It is just a way he has,' said the butler (who regarded the Baron as slightly 'touched', 'a bit balmy'), 'but he is one of Madame's friends for whom I have always had the greatest respect, he has a good heart.'

'Are you coming back this year to Incarville?' Brichot asked me. 'I believe that our hostess has taken la Raspelière again, for all that she has had a crow to pick with her landlords. But that is nothing, it is a cloud that passes,' he added in the optimistic tone of the newspapers that say: 'Mistakes have been made, it is true, but who does not make mistakes at times?' But I remembered the state of anguish in which I had left Balbec, and felt no desire to return there. I kept putting off to the morrow my plans for Albertine. 'Why, of course he is coming back, we need him, he is indispensable to us,' declared M. de Charlus with the authoritative and uncomprehending egoism of friendliness.

At this moment M. Verdurin appeared to welcome us. When we expressed our sympathy over Princess Sherbatov, he said: 'Yes, I believe she is rather ill.' 'No, no, she died at six o'clock,' exclaimed Saniette. 'Oh, you exaggerate everything,' was M. Verdurin's brutal retort, for, since he had not cancelled his party, he preferred the hypothesis of illness, imitating unconsciously the Duc de Guermantes. Saniette, not without fear of catching cold, for the outer door was continually being opened, stood waiting resignedly for someone to take his hat and coat. 'What are you hanging about there for, like a whipped dog?' M. Verdurin asked him. 'I am waiting until one of the persons who are charged with the cloakroom can take my coat and give me a number.' 'What is that you say?' demanded M. Verdurin with a stern expression. ' "Charged with the cloakroom?" Are you going off your head? "In charge of the cloakroom", is what we say, if we've got to teach you to speak your own language, like a man who has had a stroke.' 'Charged with a thing is the correct form,' murmured Saniette in a stifled tone; 'the abbé Le Batteux . . . ' 'You make me tired, you do,' cried M. Verdurin in a voice of thunder. 'How you do wheeze! Have you been running upstairs to an attic?' The effect of M. Verdurin's rudeness was that the servants in the cloakroom allowed other guests to take precedence of Saniette and, when he tried to hand over his things, replied: 'Wait for your turn, Sir, don't be in such a hurry.' 'There's system for you, competent fellows, that's right, my lads,' said M. Verdurin with an approving smile, in order to encourage them in their tendency to keep Saniette waiting till the end. 'Come along,' he said to us, 'the creature wants us all to catch our death hanging about in his beloved draught. Come and get warm in the drawing-room. "Charged with the cloakroom", indeed, what an idiot!' 'He is inclined to be a little precious, but he's not a bad fellow,' said Brichot. 'I never said that he was a bad fellow, I said that he was an idiot,' was M. Verdurin's harsh retort.

Meanwhile Mme Verdurin was busily engaged with Cottard and Ski. Morel had just declined (because M. de Charlus could not be present) an invitation from some friends of hers to whom she had promised the services of the violinist. The reason for Morel's refusal to perform at the party which the Verdurins' friends were giving, a reason which we shall presently see reinforced by others of a far more serious kind, might have found its justification in a habit common to the leisured classes in general but specially distinctive of the little nucleus. To be sure, if Mme Verdurin intercepted between a newcomer and one of the faithful a whispered speech which might let it be supposed that they were already acquainted, or wished to become more intimate ('On Friday, then, at So-and-So's', or 'Come to the studio any day you like; I am always there until five o'clock, I shall look forward to seeing you'), agitated, supposing the newcomer to occupy a 'position' which would make him a brilliant recruit to the little clan, the Mistress, while pretending not to have heard anything, and preserving in her fine eyes, shadowed by the habit of listening to Debussy more than they would have been by that of sniffing cocaine, the extenuated expression that they derived from musical intoxication alone, revolved nevertheless behind her splendid brow, inflated by all those quartets and the headaches that were their consequence, thoughts which were not exclusively polyphonic, and unable to contain herself any longer, unable to postpone the injection for another instant, flung herself upon the speakers, drew them apart, and said to the newcomer, pointing to the 'faithful' one: 'You wouldn't care to come and dine to meet *him*, next Saturday, shall we say, or any day you like, with some really nice people! Don't speak too loud, as I don't want to invite all this mob' (a word used to denote for five minutes the little nucleus, disdained for the moment in favour of the newcomer in whom so many hopes were placed).

But this infatuated impulse, this need to make friendly overtures, had its counterpart. Assiduous attendance at their Wednesdays aroused in the Verdurins an opposite tendency. This was the desire to quarrel, to hold aloof. It had been strengthened, had almost been wrought to a frenzy during the months spent at la Raspelière, where they were all together morning, noon and night. M. Verdurin went out of his way to prove one of his guests in the wrong, to spin webs in which he might hand over to his comrade spider some innocent fly. Failing a grievance, he would invent some absurdity. As soon as one of the faithful had been out of the house for half an hour, they would make fun of him in front of the others, would feign surprise that their guests had not noticed how his teeth were never clean, or how on the contrary he had a mania for brushing them twenty times a day. If anyone took the liberty of opening a window, this want of breeding would cause a glance of disgust to pass between host and hostess. A moment later Mme Verdurin would ask for a shawl, which gave M. Verdurin an excuse for saying in a tone of fury: 'No, I shall close the window, I wonder who had the impertinence to open it', in the hearing of the guilty wretch who blushed to the roots of his hair. You were rebuked indirectly for the quantity of wine that you had drunk. 'It won't do you any harm. Navvies thrive on it!' If two of the faithful went out together without first obtaining permission from the Mistress, their excursions led to endless comments, however innocent they might be. Those of M. de Charlus with Morel were not innocent. It was only the fact that M. de Charlus was not staying at la Raspelière (because Morel was obliged to live near his barracks) that retarded the hour of satiety, disgust, retching. That hour was, however, about to strike.

Mme Verdurin was furious and determined to 'enlighten' Morel as to the ridiculous and detestable part that M. de Charlus was making him play. 'I must add,' she went on (Mme Verdurin, when she felt that she owed anyone a debt of gratitude which would be a burden to him, and was unable to rid herself of it by killing him, would discover a serious defect in him which would honourably dispense her from showing her gratitude), 'I must add that he gives himself airs in my house which I do not at all like.' The truth was that Mme Verdurin had another more serious reason than Morel's refusal to play at her friends' party for picking a quarrel with M. de Charlus. The latter, overcome by the honour he was doing the Mistress in bringing to Quai Conti people who after all would never have come there for her sake, had, on hearing the first names that Mme Verdurin had suggested as those of people who ought to be invited, pronounced the most categorical ban upon them in a peremptory tone which blended the rancorous pride of a crotchety nobleman with the dogmatism of the expert artist in questions of entertainment who would cancel his programme and withhold his collaboration sooner than agree to concessions which, in his opinion, would endanger the success of the whole. M. de Charlus had given his approval, hedging it round with reservations, to Saintine alone, with whom, in order not to be bothered with his wife, Mme de Guermantes had passed, from a daily intimacy, to a complete severance of relations, but whom M. de Charlus, finding him intelligent, continued to see. True, it was among a middle-class set, with a cross-breeding of the minor nobility, where people are merely very rich and connected with an aristocracy whom the true aristocracy does not know, that Saintine, at one time the flower of the Guermantes set, had gone to seek his fortune and, he imagined, a social foothold. But Mme Verdurin, knowing the blue-blooded pretensions of the wife's circle, and failing to take into account the husband's position (for it is what is immediately over our head that gives us the impression of altitude and not what is almost invisible to us, so far is it lost in the clouds), felt that she ought to justify an invitation of Saintine by pointing out that he knew a great many people, 'having married Mlle —'. The ignorance which this assertion, the direct opposite of the truth, revealed in Mme Verdurin caused the Baron's painted lips to part in a smile of indulgent scorn and wide comprehension. He disdained a direct answer, but as he was always ready to express in social examples theories which showed the fertility of his mind and the arrogance of his pride, with the inherited frivolity of his occupations: 'Saintine ought to have come to me before marrying,' he said, 'there is such a thing as social as well as physiological eugenics, and I am perhaps the only specialist in existence. Saintine's case aroused no discussion, it was clear that, in making the marriage that he made, he was tying a stone to his neck, and hiding his light under a bushel. His social career was at an end. I should have explained this to him, and he would have understood me, for he is quite intelligent. On the other hand, there was a person who had everything that he required to make his position exalted, predominant, worldwide, only a terrible cable bound him to the earth. I helped him, partly by pressure, partly by force, to break his bonds and now he has won, with a triumphant joy, the freedom, the omnipotence that he owes to me; it required, perhaps, a little determination on his part, but what a reward! Thus a man can himself, when he has the sense to listen to me, become the midwife of his destiny.' It was only too clear that M. de Charlus had not been able to influence his own; action is a different thing from speech, even eloquent speech, and from thought, even the thoughts of genius. 'But, so far as I am concerned, I live the life of a philosopher who looks on with interest at the social reactions which I have foretold, but who does not assist them. And so I have continued to visit Saintine, who has always received me with the wholehearted deference which is my due. I have even dined with him in his new abode, where one is heavily bored, in the midst of the most sumptuous splendour, as one used to be amused in the old days when, living from hand to mouth, he used to assemble the best society in a wretched attic. Him, then, you may invite, I give you leave, but I rule out with my veto all the other names that you have mentioned. And you will thank me for it, for, if I am an expert in arranging marriages, I am no less an expert in arranging parties. I know the rising people who give tone to a gathering, make it go; and I know also the names that will bring it down to the ground, make it fall flat.' These exclusions were not always founded upon the Baron's personal resentments nor upon his artistic refinements, but upon his skill as an actor. When he had perfected, at the expense of somebody or something, an entirely successful epigram, he was anxious to let it be heard by the largest possible audience, but took care not to admit to the second performance the audience of the first who could have borne witness that the novelty was not novel. He would then rearrange his drawing-room, simply because he did not alter his programme, and, when he had scored a success in conversation, would, if need be, have organised a tour, and given exhibitions in the provinces. Whatever may have been the various motives for these exclusions, they did not merely annoy Mme Verdurin, who felt her authority as a hostess impaired, they also did her great damage socially, and for two reasons. The first was that M. de Charlus, even more susceptible than Jupien, used to quarrel, without anyone's ever knowing why, with the people who were most suited to be his friends. Naturally, one of the first punishments that he could inflict upon them was that of not allowing them to be invited to a party which he was giving at the Verdurins'. Now these pariahs were often people who are in the habit of ruling the roost, as the saying is, but who in M. de Charlus's eyes had ceased to rule it from the day on which he had quarrelled with them. For his imagination, in addition to finding people in the wrong in order to quarrel with them, was no less ingenious in stripping them of all importance as soon as they ceased to be his friends. If, for instance, the guilty person came of an extremely old family, whose dukedom, however, dates only from the nineteenth century, such a family as the Montesquiou, from that moment all that counted for M. de Charlus was the precedence of the dukedom, the family becoming nothing. 'They are not even Dukes,' he would exclaim. 'It is the title of the abbé de Montesquiou which passed most irregularly to a collateral, less than eighty years ago. The present Duke, if Duke he can be called, is the third. You may talk to me if you like of people like the Uzès, the La Trémoïlle, the Luynes, who are tenth or fourteenth Dukes, or my brother who is twelfth Duc de Guermantes and seventeenth Prince of Cordova. The Montesquiou are descended from an old family, what would that prove, supposing that it were proved? They have descended so far that they have reached the fourteenth storey below stairs.' Had he on the contrary quarrelled with a gentleman who possessed an ancient dukedom, who boasted the most magnificent connections, was related to ruling princes, but to whose line this distinction had come quite suddenly without any length of pedigree, a Luynes for instance, the case was altered, pedigree alone counted. 'I ask you – M. Alberti, who does not emerge from the mire until Louis XIII. What can it matter to us that favouritism at court allowed them to pick up dukedoms to which they have no right?' What was more, with M. de Charlus, the fall came immediately after the exaltation because of that tendency peculiar to the Guermantes to expect from conversation, from friendship, something that these are incapable of giving, as well as the symptomatic fear of becoming the objects of slander. And the fall was all the greater, the higher the exaltation had been. Now nobody had ever found such favour with the Baron as he had markedly shown for Comtesse Molé. By what sign of indifference did she reveal, one fine day, that she had been unworthy of it? The Comtesse always maintained that she had never been able to solve the problem. The fact remains that the mere sound of her name aroused in the Baron the most violent rage, provoked the most eloquent but the most terrible philippics. Mme Verdurin, to whom Mme Molé had been very kind, and who was founding, as we shall see, great hopes upon her and had rejoiced in anticipation at the thought that the Comtesse would meet in her house all the noblest names, as the Mistress said, 'of France and Navarre', at once proposed to invite 'Madame de Molé'. 'Oh, my God! Everyone has his own taste,' M. de Charlus had replied, 'and if you, Madame, feel a desire to converse with Mme Pipelet, Mme Gibout and Mme Joseph Prudhomme, I ask nothing better, but let it be on an evening when I am not present. I could see as soon as you opened your mouth that we do not speak the same language, since I was mentioning the names of the nobility, and you retort with the most obscure names of professional and tradespeople, dirty scandal-mongering little bounders, little women who imagine themselves patronesses of the arts because they repeat, an octave lower, the manners of my Guermantes sister-in-law, like a jay that thinks it is imitating a peacock. I must add that it would be positively indecent to admit to a party which I am pleased to give at Mme Verdurin's a person whom I have with good reason excluded from my society, a sheep devoid of birth, loyalty, intelligence, who is so idiotic as to suppose that she is capable of playing the Duchesse de Guermantes and the Princesse de Guermantes, a combination which is in itself idiotic, since the Duchesse de Guermantes and the Princesse de Guermantes are poles apart. It is as though a person should pretend to be at once Reichenberg and Sarah Bernhardt. In any case, even if it were not impossible, it would be extremely ridiculous. Even though I may, myself, smile at times at the exaggeration of one and regret the limitations of the other, that is my right. But that upstart little frog trying to blow herself out to the magnitude of two great ladies who, at all events, always reveal the incomparable distinction of blood, it is enough, as the saying is, to make a cat laugh. The Molé! That is a name which must not be uttered in my hearing, or else I must simply withdraw,' he concluded with a smile, in the tone of a doctor, who, thinking of his patient's interests in spite of that same patient's opposition, lets it be understood that he will not tolerate the collaboration of a homeopath. On the other hand, certain persons whom M. de Charlus regarded as negligible might indeed be so for him but not for Mme Verdurin. M. de Charlus, with his exalted birth, could afford to dispense with people in the height of fashion, the assemblage of whom would have made Mme Verdurin's drawing-room one of the first in Paris. She, at the same time, was beginning to feel that she had already on more than one occasion missed the coach, not to mention the enormous retardation that the social error of the Dreyfus case had inflicted upon her, not without doing her a service all the same. I forget whether I have mentioned the disapproval with which the Duchesse de Guermantes had observed certain persons of her world who, subordinating everything else to the Case, excluded fashionable women from their drawing-rooms and admitted others who were not fashionable, because they were for or against the fresh trial, and had then been criticised in her turn by those same ladies, as lukewarm, unsound in her views, and guilty of placing social distinctions above the national interests; may I appeal to the reader, as to a friend with regard to whom one completely forgets, at the end of a conversation, whether one has remembered, or had an opportunity to tell him something important? Whether I have done so or not, the attitude of the Duchesse de Guermantes can easily be imagined, and indeed if we look at it in the light of subsequent history may appear, from the social point of view, perfectly correct. M. de Cambremer regarded the Dreyfus case as a foreign machination intended to destroy the Intelligence Service, to undermine discipline, to weaken the army, to divide the French people, to pave the way for invasion. Literature being, apart from a few of La Fontaine's fables, a sealed book to the Marquis, he left it to his wife to prove that the cruelly introspective writers of the day had, by creating a spirit of irreverence, arrived by a parallel course at a similar result. 'M. Reinach and M. Hervieu are in the plot,' she would say. Nobody will accuse the Dreyfus case of having premeditated such dark designs upon society. But there it certainly has broken down the hedges. The social leaders who refuse to allow politics into society are as foreseeing as the soldiers who refuse to allow politics to permeate the army. Society is like the sexual appetite; one does not know at what forms of perversion it may not arrive, once we have allowed our choice to be dictated by aesthetic considerations. The reason that they were Nationalists gave the Faubourg Saint-Germain the habit of entertaining ladies from another class of society; the reason vanished with Nationalism, the habit remained. Mme Verdurin, by the bond of Dreyfusism, had attracted to her house certain writers of distinction who for the moment were of no advantage to her socially, because they were Dreyfusards. But political passions are like all the rest, they do not last. Fresh generations arise which are incapable of understanding them. Even the generation that felt them changes, feels political passions which, not being modelled exactly upon their predecessors, make it rehabilitate some of the excluded, the reason for exclusion having altered. Monarchists no longer cared, at the time of the Dreyfus case, whether a man had been a Republican, that is to say a Radical, that is to say Anticlerical, provided that he was an anti-Semite and a Nationalist. Should a war ever come, patriotism would assume another form and if a writer was chauvinistic nobody would stop to think whether he had or had not been a Dreyfusard. It was thus that, at each political crisis, at each artistic revival, Mme Verdurin had collected one by one, like a bird building its nest, the several items, useless for the moment, of what would one day be her Salon. The Dreyfus case had passed, Anatole France remained. Mme Verdurin's strength lay in her genuine love of art, the trouble that she used to take for her faithful, the marvellous dinners that she gave for them alone, without inviting anyone from the world of fashion. Each of the faithful was treated at her table as Bergotte had been treated at Mme Swann's. When a boon companion of this sort had turned into an illustrious man whom everybody was longing to meet, his presence at Mme Verdurin's had none of the artificial, composite effect of a dish at an official or farewell banquet, cooked by Potel or Chabot, but was merely a delicious 'ordinary' which you would have found there in the same perfection on a day when there was no party at all. At Mme Verdurin's the cast was trained to perfection, the repertory most select, all that was lacking was an audience. And now that the public taste had begun to turn from the rational and French art of a Bergotte, and to go in, above all things, for exotic forms of music, Mme Verdurin, a sort of official representative in Paris of all foreign artists, was not long in making her appearance, by the side of the exquisite Princess Yourbeletiev, an aged Fairy Godmother, grim but all-powerful, to the Russian dancers. This charming invasion, against whose seductions only the stupidest of critics protested, infected Paris, as we know, with a fever of curiosity less burning, more purely aesthetic, but quite as intense perhaps as that aroused by the Dreyfus case. There again Mme Verdurin, but with a very different result socially, was to take her place in the front row. Just as she had been seen by the side of Mme Zola, immediately under the bench, during the trial in the Assize Court, so when the new generation of humanity, in their enthusiasm for the Russian ballet, thronged to the Opéra, crowned with the latest novelty in aigrettes, they invariably saw in a stage box Mme Verdurin by the side of Princess Yourbeletief. And just as, after the emotions of the lawcourts, people used to go in the evening to Mme Verdurin's, to meet Picquart or Labori in the flesh and what was more to hear the latest news of the Case, to learn what hopes might be placed in Zurlinden, Loubet, Colonel Jouaust, the Regulations, so now, little inclined for sleep after the enthusiasm aroused by *Scheherazade* or *Prince Igor*, they repaired to Mme Verdurin's, where under the auspices of Princess Yourbeletief and their hostess an exquisite supper brought together every night the dancers themselves, who had abstained from dinner so as to be more resilient, their director, their designers, the great composers Igor Stravinski and Richard Strauss, a permanent little nucleus, around which, as round the supper-table of M. and Mme Helvétius, the greatest ladies in Paris and foreign royalties were not too proud to gather. Even those people in society who professed to be endowed with taste and drew unnecessary distinctions between the various Russian ballets, regarding the setting of the *Sylphides* as somehow 'purer' than that of *Scheherazade*, which they were almost prepared to attribute to Negro inspiration, were enchanted to meet face to face the great revivers of theatrical taste, who in an art that is perhaps a little more artificial than that of the easel had created a revolution as profound as Impressionism itself.

To revert to M. de Charlus, Mme Verdurin would not have minded so much if he had placed on his Index only Comtesse Molé and Mme Bontemps, whom she had picked out at Odette's on the strength of her love of the fine arts, and who during the Dreyfus case had come to dinner occasionally bringing her husband, whom Mme Verdurin called 'lukewarm', because he was not making any move for a fresh trial, but who, being extremely intelligent, and glad to form relations in every camp, was delighted to show his independence by dining at the same table as Labori, to whom he listened without uttering a word that might compromise himself, but managed to slip in at the right moment a tribute to the loyalty, recognised by all parties, of Jaurès. But the Baron had similarly proscribed several ladies of the aristocracy whose acquaintance Mme Verdurin, on the occasion of some musical festivity or a collection for charity, had recently formed and who, whatever M. de Charlus might think of them, would have been, far more than himself, essential to the formation of a fresh nucleus at Mme Verdurin's, this time aristocratic. Mme Verdurin had indeed been reckoning upon this party, to which M. de Charlus would be bringing her women of the same set, to mix her new friends with them, and had been relishing in anticipation the surprise that the latter would feel upon meeting at Quai Conti their own friends or relatives invited there by the Baron. She was disappointed and furious at his veto. It remained to be seen whether the evening, in these conditions, would result in profit or loss to herself. The loss would not be too serious if only M. de Charlus's guests came with so friendly a feeling for Mme Verdurin that they would become her friends in the future. In this case the mischief would be only half done, these two sections of the fashionable world, which the Baron had insisted upon keeping apart, would be united later on, he himself being excluded, of course, when the time came. And so Mme Verdurin was awaiting the Baron's guests with a certain emotion. She would not be slow in discovering the state of mind in which they came, and the degree of intimacy to which she might hope to attain. While she waited, Mme Verdurin took counsel with the faithful, but, upon seeing M. de Charlus enter the room with Brichot and myself, stopped short. Greatly to our astonishment, when Brichot told her how sorry he was to learn that her dear friend was so seriously ill, Mme Verdurin replied: 'Listen, I am obliged to confess that I am not at all sorry. It is useless to pretend to feel what one does not feel.' No doubt she spoke thus from want of energy, because she shrank from the idea of wearing a long face throughout her party, from pride, in order not to appear to be seeking excuses for not having cancelled her invitations, from self-respect also and social aptitude, because the absence of grief which she displayed was more honourable if it could be attributed to a peculiar antipathy, suddenly revealed, to the Princess, rather than to a universal insensibility, and because her hearers could not fail to be disarmed by a sincerity as to which there could be no doubt. If Mme Verdurin had not been genuinely unaffected by the death of the Princess, would she have gone on to excuse herself for giving the party, by accusing herself of a far more serious fault? Besides, one was apt to forget that Mme Verdurin would thus have admitted, while confessing her grief, that she had not had the strength of mind to forego a pleasure; whereas the indifference of the friend was something more shocking, more immoral, but less humiliating, and consequently easier to confess than the frivolity of the hostess. In matters of crime, where the culprit is in danger, it is his material interest that prompts the confession. Where the fault incurs no penalty, it is self-esteem. Whether it was that, doubtless feeling the pretext to be too hackneyed of the people who, so as not to allow a bereavement to interrupt their life of pleasure, go about saying that it seems to them useless to display the outward signs of a grief which they feel in their hearts, Mme Verdurin preferred to imitate those intelligent culprits who are revolted by the commonplaces of innocence and whose defence – a partial admission, though they do not know it – consists in saying that they would see no harm in doing what they are accused of doing, although, as it happens, they have had no occasion to do it; or that, having adopted, to explain her conduct, the theory of indifference, she found, once she had started upon the downward slope of her unnatural feeling, that it was distinctly original to have felt it, that she displayed a rare perspicacity in having managed to diagnose her own symptoms, and a certain 'nerve' in proclaiming them; anyhow, Mme Verdurin kept dwelling upon her want of grief, not without a certain proud satisfaction, as of a paradoxical psychologist and daring dramatist. 'Yes, it is very funny,' she said, 'I hardly felt it. Of course, I don't mean to say that I wouldn't rather she were still alive, she was not a bad person.' 'Yes, she was,' put in M. Verdurin. 'Ah! He doesn't approve of her because he thought that I was doing myself harm by having her here, but he is quite pig-headed about that.' 'Do me the justice to admit,' said M. Verdurin, 'that I never approved of your having her. I always told you that she had a bad reputation.' 'But I have never heard a thing against her,' protested Saniette. 'What!' exclaimed Mme Verdurin, 'everybody knew; bad isn't the word, it was scandalous, appalling. No, it has nothing to do with that. I couldn't explain, myself, what I felt; I didn't dislike her, but I took so little interest in her that, when we heard that she was seriously ill, my husband himself was quite surprised, and said: "Anyone would think that you didn't mind." Why, this evening, he offered to put off the party, and I insisted upon having it, because I should have thought it a farce to show a grief which I do not feel.' She said this because she felt that it had a curious smack of the 'independent theatre', and was at the same time singularly convenient; for an admitted insensibility or immorality simplifies life as much as does easy virtue; it converts reproachable actions, for which one no longer need seek any excuse, into a duty imposed by sincerity. And the faithful listened to Mme Verdurin's speech with the blend of admiration and misgiving which certain cruelly realistic plays, that showed a profound observation, used at one time to cause, and, while they marvelled to see their beloved Mistress display a novel aspect of her rectitude and independence, more than one of them, albeit he assured himself that after all it would not be the same thing, thought of his own death, and asked himself whether, on the day when death came to him, they would draw the blinds or give a party at Quai Conti. 'I am very glad that the party has not been put off, for my guests' sake,' said M. de Charlus, not realising that in expressing himself thus he was offending Mme Verdurin. Meanwhile I was struck, as was everybody who approached Mme Verdurin that evening, by a far from pleasant odour of rhinogomenol. The reason was as follows. We know that Mme Verdurin never expressed her artistic feelings in a moral, but always in a physical fashion, so that they might appear more inevitable and more profound. So, if one spoke to her of Vinteuil's music, her favourite, she remained unmoved, as though she expected to derive no emotion from it. But after a few minutes of a fixed, almost abstracted gaze, in a sharp, matter of fact, scarcely civil tone (as though she had said to you: 'I don't in the least mind your smoking, it's because of the carpet; it's a very fine one [not that that matters either], but it's highly inflammable, I'm dreadfully afraid of fire, and I shouldn't like to see you all roasted because someone had carelessly dropped a cigarette end on it'), she replied: 'I have no fault to find with Vinteuil; to my mind, he is the greatest composer of the age, only I can never listen to that sort of stuff without weeping all the time' (she did not apply any pathos to the word 'weeping', she would have used precisely the same tone for 'sleeping'; certain slander-mongers used indeed to insist that the latter verb would have been more applicable, though no one could ever be certain, for she listened to the music with her face buried in her hands, and certain snoring sounds might after all have been sobs). 'I don't mind weeping, not in the least; only I get the most appalling colds afterwards. It stuffs up my mucous membrane, and the day after I look like nothing on earth. I have to inhale for days on end before I can utter. However, one of Cottard's pupils, a charming person, has been treating me for it. He goes by quite an original rule: 'Prevention is better than cure.' And he greases my nose before the music begins. It is radical. I can weep like all the mothers who ever lost a child, not a trace of a cold. Sometimes a little conjunctivitis, that's all. It is absolutely efficacious. Otherwise I could never have gone on listening to Vinteuil. I was just going from one bronchitis to another.' I could not refrain from alluding to Mlle Vinteuil. 'Isn't the composer's daughter to be here,' I asked Mme Verdurin, 'with one of her friends?' 'No, I have just had a telegram,' Mme Verdurin said evasively, 'they have been obliged to remain in the country.' I felt a momentary hope that there might never have been any question of their leaving it and that Mme Verdurin had announced the presence of these representatives of the composer only in order to make a favourable impression upon the performers and their audience. 'What, didn't they come, then, to the rehearsal this afternoon?' came with a feigned curiosity from the Baron who was anxious to let it appear that he had not seen Charlie. The latter came up to greet me. I whispered a question in his ear about Mlle Vinteuil; he seemed to me to know little or nothing about her. I signalled to him not to let himself be heard and told him that we should discuss the question later on. He bowed, and assured me that he would be delighted to place himself entirely at my disposal. I observed that he was far more polite, more respectful, than he had been in the past. I spoke warmly of him – who might perhaps be able to help me to clear up my suspicions – to M. de Charlus who replied: 'He only does what is natural, there would be no point in his living among respectable people if he didn't learn good manners.' These, according to M. de Charlus, were the old manners of France, untainted by any British bluntness. Thus when Charlie, returning from a tour in the provinces or abroad, arrived in his travelling suit at the Baron's, the latter, if there were not too many people present, would kiss him without ceremony upon both cheeks, perhaps a little in order to banish by so ostentatious a display of his affection any idea of its being criminal, perhaps because he could not deny himself a pleasure, but still more, doubtless, from a literary sense, as upholding and illustrating the traditional manners of France, and, just as he would have countered the Munich or modern style of furniture by keeping in his rooms old armchairs that had come to him from a great-grandmother, countering the British phlegm with the affection of a warm-hearted father of the eighteenth century, unable to conceal his joy at beholding his son once more. Was there indeed a trace of incest in this paternal affection? It is more probable that the way in which M. de Charlus habitually appeased his vicious cravings, as to which we shall learn something in due course, was not sufficient for the need of affection, which had remained unsatisfied since the death of his wife; the fact remains that after having thought more than once of a second marriage, he was now devoured by a maniacal desire to adopt an heir. People said that he was going to adopt Morel, and there was nothing extraordinary in that. The invert who has been unable to feed his passion save on a literature written for women-loving men, who used to think of men when he read Mussel's *Nuits*, feels the need to partake, nevertheless, in all the social activities of the man who is not an invert, to keep a lover, as the old frequenter of the Opéra keeps ballet-girls, to settle down, to marry or form a permanent tie, to become a father.

M. de Charlus took Morel aside on the pretext of making him tell him what was going to be played, but above all finding a great consolation, while Charlie showed him his music, in displaying thus publicly their secret intimacy. In the meantime I myself felt a certain charm. For albeit the little clan included few girls, on the other hand girls were abundantly invited on the big evenings. There were a number present, and very pretty girls too, whom I knew. They wafted smiles of greeting to me across the room. The air was thus decorated at every moment with the charming smile of some girl. That is the manifold, occasional ornament of evening parties, as it is of days. We remember an atmosphere because girls were smiling in it.

Many people might have been greatly surprised had they overheard the furtive remarks which M. de Charlus exchanged with a number of important gentlemen at this party. These were two Dukes, a distinguished General, a great writer, a great physician, a great barrister. And the remarks in question were: 'By the way, did you notice the footman, I mean the little fellow they take on the carriage? At our cousin Guermantes', you don't know of anyone?' 'At the moment, no.' 'I say, though, outside the door, where the carriages stop, there used to be a fair little person, in breeches, who seemed to me most attractive. She called my carriage most charmingly, I would gladly have prolonged the conversation.' 'Yes, but I believe she's altogether against it, besides, she puts on airs, you like to get to business at once, you would loathe her. Anyhow, I know there's nothing doing, a friend of mine tried.' 'That is a pity, I thought the profile very fine, and the hair superb.' 'Really, as much as that? I think, if you had seen a little more of her, you would have been disillusioned. No, in the supper-room, only two months ago you would have seen a real marvel, a great fellow six foot six, a perfect skin, and loves it, too. But he's gone off to Poland.' 'Ah, that is rather a long way.' 'You never know, he may come back, perhaps. One always meets again somewhere.' There is no great social function that does not, if, in taking a section of it, we contrive to cut sufficiently deep, resemble those parties to which doctors invite their patients, who utter the most intelligent remarks, have perfect manners, and would never show that they were mad did they not whisper in our ear, pointing to some old gentleman who goes past: 'That's Joan of Arc.'

'I feel that it is our duty to enlighten him,' Mme Verdurin said to Brichot. 'Not that I have anything against Charlus, far from it. He is a pleasant fellow and as for his reputation, I don't mind saying that it is not of a sort that can do me any harm! As far as I'm concerned, in our little clan, in our table-talk, as I detest flirts, the men who talk nonsense to a woman in a corner instead of discussing interesting topics, I've never had any fear with Charlus of what happened to me with Swann, and Elstir, and lots of them. With him I was quite safe, he would come to my dinners, all the women in the world might be there, you could be certain that the general conversation would not be disturbed by flirtations and whisperings. Charlus is in a class of his own, one doesn't worry, he might be a priest. Only, he must not be allowed to take it upon himself to order about the young men who come to the house and make a nuisance of himself in our little nucleus, or he'll be worse than a man who runs after women.' And Mme Verdurin was sincere in thus proclaiming her indulgence towards Charlism. Like every ecclesiastical power she regarded human frailties as less dangerous than anything that might undermine the principle of authority, impair the orthodoxy, modify the ancient creed of her little Church. 'If he does, then I shall bare my teeth. What do you say to a gentleman who tried to prevent Charlie from coming to a rehearsal because he himself was not invited? So he's going to be taught a lesson, I hope he'll profit by it, otherwise he can simply take his hat and go. He keeps the boy under lock and key, upon my word he does.' And, using exactly the same expressions that almost anyone else might have used, for there are certain not in common currency which some particular subject, some given circumstance recalls almost inevitably to the mind of the speaker, who imagines that he is giving free expression to his thought when he is merely repeating mechanically the universal lesson, she went on: 'It's impossible to see Morel nowadays without that great lout hanging round him, like an armed escort.' M. Verdurin offered to take Charlie out of the room for a minute to explain things to him, on the pretext of asking him a question. Mme Verdurin was afraid that this might upset him, and that he would play badly in consequence. It would be better to postpone this performance until after the other. Perhaps even until a later occasion. For however Mme Verdurin might look forward to the delicious emotion that she would feel when she knew that her husband was engaged in enlightening Charlie in the next room, she was afraid, if the shot missed fire, that he would lose his temper and would fail to reappear on the sixteenth.

What ruined M. de Charlus that evening was the ill-breeding – so common in their class – of the people whom he had invited and who were now beginning to arrive. Having come there partly out of friendship for M. de Charlus and also out of curiosity to explore these novel surroundings, each Duchess made straight for the Baron as though it were he who was giving the party and said, within a yard of the Verdurins, who could hear every word: 'Show me which is mother Verdurin; do you think I really need speak to her? I do hope at least, that she won't put my name in the paper tomorrow, nobody would ever speak to me again. What! That woman with the white hair, but she looks quite presentable.' Hearing some mention of Mlle Vinteuil, who, however, was not in the room, more than one of them said: 'Ah! The sonata-man's daughter? Show me her' and, each finding a number of her friends, they formed a group by themselves, watched, sparkling with ironical curiosity, the arrival of the faithful, able at the most to point a finger at the odd way in which a person had done her hair, who, a few years later, was to make this the fashion in the very best society, and, in short, regretted that they did not find this house as different from the houses that they knew, as they had hoped to find it, feeling the disappointment of people in society who, having gone to the Boîte à Bruant in the hope that the singer would make a butt of them, find themselves greeted on their arrival with a polite bow instead of the expected:

> Ah! voyez c'te gueule, c'te binette.
> Ah! voyez c'te gueule qu'elle a.

M. de Charlus had, at Balbec, given me a perspicacious criticism of Mme de Vaugoubert who, notwithstanding her keen intellect, had brought about, after his unexpected prosperity, the irremediable disgrace of her husband. The rulers to whose Court M. de Vaugoubert was accredited, King Theodosius and Queen Eudoxia, having returned to Paris, but this time for a prolonged visit, daily festivities had been held in their honour, in the course of which the Queen, on the friendliest terms with Mme de Vaugoubert, whom she had seen for the last ten years in her own capital, and knowing neither the wife of the President of the Republic nor those of his Ministers, had neglected these ladies and kept entirely aloof with the Ambassadress. This lady, believing her own position to be unassailable – M. de Vaugoubert having been responsible for the alliance between King Theodosius and France – had derived from the preference that the Queen showed for her society a proud satisfaction but no anxiety at the peril that threatened her, which took shape a few months later in the fact, wrongly considered impossible by the too confident couple, of the brutal dismissal from the Service of M. de Vaugoubert. M. de Charlus, remarking in the 'crawler' upon the downfall of his lifelong friend, expressed his astonishment that an intelligent woman had not, in such circumstances, brought all her influence with the King and Queen to bear, so as to secure that she might not seem to possess any influence, and to make them transfer to the wives of the President and his Ministers a civility by which those ladies would have been all the more flattered, that is to say which would have made them more inclined, in their satisfaction, to be grateful to the Vaugouberts, inasmuch as they would have supposed that civility to be spontaneous, and not dictated by them. But the man who can see the mistakes of others need only be exhilarated by circumstances in order to succumb to them himself. And M. de Charlus, while his guests fought their way towards him, to come and congratulate him, thank him, as though he were the master of the house, never thought of asking them to say a few words to Mme Verdurin. Only the Queen of Naples, in whom survived the same noble blood that had flowed in the veins of her sisters the Empress Elisabeth and the Duchesse d'Alençon, made a point of talking to Mme Verdurin as though she had come for the pleasure of meeting her rather than for the music and for M. de Charlus, made endless pretty speeches to her hostess, could not cease from telling her for how long she had been wishing to make her acquaintance, expressed her admiration for the house and spoke to her of all manner of subjects as though she were paying a call. She would so much have liked to bring her niece Elisabeth, she said (the niece who shortly afterwards was to marry Prince Albert of Belgium), who would be so sorry. She stopped talking when she saw the musicians mount the platform, asking which of them was Morel. She can scarcely have been under any illusion as to the motives that led M. de Charlus to desire that the young virtuoso should be surrounded with so much glory. But the venerable wisdom of a sovereign in whose veins flowed the blood of one of the noblest races in history, one of the richest in experience, scepticism and pride, made her merely regard the inevitable defects of the people whom she loved best, such as her cousin Charlus (whose mother had been, like herself, a 'Duchess in Bavaria'), as misfortunes that rendered more precious to them the support that they might find in herself and consequently made it even more pleasant to her to provide that support. She knew that M. de Charlus would be doubly touched by her having taken the trouble to come, in the circumstances. Only, being as good as she had long ago shown herself brave, this heroic woman who, a soldier-queen, had herself fired her musket from the ramparts of Gaeta, always ready to take her place chivalrously by the weaker side, seeing Mme Verdurin alone and abandoned, and unaware (for that matter) that she ought not to leave the Queen, had sought to pretend that for her, the Queen of Naples, the centre of this party, the lodestone that had made her come was Mme Verdurin. She expressed her regret that she would not be able to remain until the end, as she had, although she never went anywhere, to go on to another party, and begged that on no account, when she had to go, should any fuss be made for her, thus discharging Mme Verdurin of the honours which the latter did not even know that she ought to render.

One must, however, do M. de Charlus the justice of saying that, if he entirely forgot Mme Verdurin and allowed her to be ignored, to a scandalous extent, by the people 'of his own world' whom he had invited, he did, on the other hand, realise that he must not allow these people to display, during the 'symphonic recital' itself, the bad manners which they were exhibiting towards the Mistress. Morel had already mounted the platform, the musicians were assembling, and one could still hear conversations, not to say laughter, speeches such as 'it appears, one has to be initiated to understand it.' Immediately M. de Charlus, drawing himself erect, as though he had entered a different body from that which I had seen, not an hour ago, crawling towards Mme Verdurin's door, assumed a prophetic expression and regarded the assembly with an earnestness which indicated that this was not the moment for laughter, whereupon one saw a rapid blush tinge the cheeks of more than one lady thus publicly rebuked, like a schoolgirl scolded by her teacher in front of the whole class. To my mind, M. de Charlus's attitude, noble as it was, was somehow slightly comic; for at one moment he pulverised his guests with a flaming glare, at another, in order to indicate to them as with a *vade mecum* the religious silence that ought to be observed, the detachment from every worldly consideration, he furnished in himself, as he raised to his fine brow his white-gloved hands, a model (to which they must conform) of gravity, already almost of ecstasy, without acknowledging the greetings of latecomers so indelicate as not to understand that it was now the time for High Art. They were all hypnotised; no one dared utter a sound, move a chair; respect for music – by virtue of Palamède's prestige – had been instantaneously inculcated in a crowd as ill-bred as it was exclusive.

When I saw appear on the little platform, not only Morel and a pianist, but performers upon other instruments as well, I supposed that the programme was to begin with works of composers other than Vinteuil. For I imagined that the only work of his in existence was his sonata for piano and violin.

Mme Verdurin sat in a place apart, the twin hemispheres of her pale, slightly roseate brow magnificently curved, her hair drawn back, partly in imitation of an eighteenth century portrait, partly from the desire for coolness of a fever-stricken patient whom modesty forbids to reveal her condition, aloof, a deity presiding over musical rites, patron saint of Wagnerism and sick-headaches, a sort of almost tragic Norn, evoked by the spell of genius in the midst of all these bores, in whose presence she would more than ordinarily scorn to express her feelings upon hearing a piece of music which she knew better than they. The concert began, I did not know what they were playing, I found myself in a strange land. Where was I to locate it? Into what composer's country had I come? I should have been glad to know, and, seeing nobody near me whom I might question, I should have liked to be a character in those *Arabian Nights* which I never tired of reading and in which, in moments of uncertainty, there arose a genie or a maiden of ravishing beauty, invisible to everyone else but not to the embarrassed hero to whom she reveals exactly what he wishes to learn. Well, at this very moment I was favoured with precisely such a magical apparition. As, in a stretch of country which we suppose to be strange to us and which as a matter of fact we have approached from a new angle, when after turning out of one road we find ourself emerging suddenly upon another every inch of which is familiar only we have not been in the habit of entering it from that end, we say to ourself immediately: 'Why, this is the lane that leads to the garden gate of my friends the X—; I shall be there in a minute', and there, indeed, is their daughter at the gate, come out to greet us as we pass; so, all of a sudden, I found myself, in the midst of this music that was novel to me, right in the heart of Vinteuil's sonata; and, more marvellous than any maiden, the little phrase, enveloped, harnessed in silver, glittering with brilliant effects of sound, as light and soft as silken scarves, came towards me, recognisable in this new guise. My joy at having found it again was enhanced by the accent, so friendlily familiar, which it adopted in addressing me, so persuasive, so simple, albeit without dimming the shimmering beauty with which it was resplendent. Its intention, however, was, this time, merely to show me the way, which was not the way of the sonata, for this was an unpublished work of Vinteuil in which he had merely amused himself, by an allusion which was explained at this point by a sentence in the programme which one ought to have been reading simultaneously, in making the little phrase reappear for a moment. No sooner was it thus recalled than it vanished, and I found myself once more in an unknown world, but I knew now, and everything that followed only confirmed my knowledge, that this world was one of those which I had never even been capable of imagining that Vinteuil could have created, for when, weary of the sonata which was to me a universe thoroughly explored, I tried to imagine others equally beautiful but different, I was merely doing what those poets do who fill their artificial paradise with meadows, flowers and streams which duplicate those existing already upon Earth. What was now before me made me feel as keen a joy as the sonata would have given me if I had not already known it, and consequently, while no less beautiful, was different. Whereas the sonata opened upon a dawn of lilied meadows, parting its slender whiteness to suspend itself over the frail and yet consistent mingling of a rustic bower of honeysuckle with white geraniums, it was upon continuous, level surfaces like those of the sea that, in the midst of a stormy morning beneath an already lurid sky, there began, in an eery silence, in an infinite void, this new masterpiece, and it was into a roseate dawn that, in order to construct itself progressively before me, this unknown universe was drawn from silence and from night. This so novel redness, so absent from the tender, rustic, pale sonata, tinged all the sky, as dawn does, with a mysterious hope. And a song already thrilled the air, a song on seven notes, but the strangest, the most different from any that I had ever imagined, from any that I could ever have been able to imagine, at once ineffable and piercing, no longer the cooing of a dove as in the sonata, but rending the air, as vivid as the scarlet tinge in which the opening bars had been bathed, something like the mystical crow of a cock, an ineffable but over-shrill appeal of the eternal morning. The cold atmosphere, soaked in rain, electric – of a quality so different, feeling wholly other pressures, in a world so remote from that, virginal and endowed only with vegetable life, of the sonata – changed at every moment, obliterating the empurpled promise of the Dawn. At noon, however, beneath a scorching though transitory sun, it seemed to fulfil itself in a dull, almost rustic bliss in which the peal of clanging, racing bells (like those which kindled the blaze of the square outside the church of Combray, which Vinteuil, who must often have heard them, had perhaps discovered at that moment in his memory like a colour which the painter's hand has conveyed to his palette) seemed to materialise the coarsest joy. To be honest, from the aesthetic point of view, this joyous motive did not appeal to me, I found it almost ugly, its rhythm dragged so laboriously along the ground that one might have succeeded in imitating almost everything that was essential to it by merely making a noise, sounds, by the tapping of drumsticks upon a table. It seemed to me that Vinteuil had been lacking, here, in inspiration, and consequently I was a little lacking also in the power of attention.

I looked at the Mistress, whose sullen immobility seemed to be protesting against the noddings – in time with the music – of the empty heads of the ladies of the Faubourg. She did not say: 'You understand that I know something about this music, and more than a little! If I had to express all that I feel, you would never hear the end of it!' She did not say this. But her upright, motionless body, her expressionless eyes, her straying locks said it for her. They spoke also of her courage, said that the musicians might go on, need not spare her nerves, that she would not flinch at the *andante*, would not cry out at the *allegro*. I looked at the musicians. The violoncellist dominated the instrument which he clutched between his knees, bowing his head to which its coarse features gave, in moments of mannerism, an involuntary expression of disgust; he leaned over it, fingered it with the same domestic patience with which he might have plucked a cabbage, while by his side the harpist (a mere girl) in a short skirt, bounded on either side by the lines of her golden quadrilateral like those which, in the magic chamber of a Sibyl, would arbitrarily denote the ether, according to the consecrated rules, seemed to be going in quest, here and there, at the point required, of an exquisite sound, just as though, a little allegorical deity, placed in front of the golden trellis of the heavenly vault, she were gathering, one by one, its stars. As for Morel, a lock, hitherto invisible and lost in the rest of his hair, had fallen loose and formed a curl upon his brow. I turned my head slightly towards the audience to discover what M. de Charlus might be feeling at the sight of this curl. But my eyes encountered only the face, or rather the hands of Mme Verdurin, for the former was entirely buried in the latter.

But very soon, the triumphant motive of the bells having been banished, dispersed by others, I succumbed once again to the music; and I began to realise that if, in the body of this septet, different elements presented themselves in turn, to combine at the close, so also Vinteuil's sonata, and, as I was to find later on, his other works as well, had been no more than timid essays, exquisite but very slight, towards the triumphant and complete masterpiece which was revealed to me at this moment. And so too, I could not help recalling how I had thought of the other worlds which Vinteuil might have created as of so many universes as hermetically sealed as each of my own love-affairs, whereas in reality I was obliged to admit that in the volume of my latest love – that is to say, my love for Albertine – my first inklings of love for her (at Balbec at the very beginning, then after the game of ferret, then on the night when she slept at the hotel, then in Paris on the foggy afternoon, then on the night of the Guermantes' party, then at Balbec again, and finally in Paris where my life was now closely linked to her own) had been nothing more than experiments; indeed, if I were to consider, not my love for Albertine, but my life as a whole, my earlier love-affairs had themselves been but slight and timid essays, experiments, which paved the way to this vaster love: my love for Albertine. And I ceased to follow the music, in order to ask myself once again whether Albertine had or had not seen Mlle Vinteuil during the last few days, as we interrogate afresh an internal pain, from which we have been distracted for a moment. For it was in myself that Albertine's possible actions were performed. Of each of the people whom we know we possess a double, but it is generally situated on the horizon of our imagination, of our memory; it remains more or less external to ourselves, and what it has done or may have done has no greater capacity to cause us pain than an object situated at a certain distance, which provides us with only the painless sensations of vision. The things that affect these people we perceive in a contemplative fashion, we are able to deplore them in appropriate language which gives other people a sense of our kindness of heart, we do not feel them; but since the wound inflicted on me at Balbec, it was in my heart, at a great depth, difficult to extract, that Albertine's double was lodged. What I saw of her hurt me, as a sick man would be hurt whose senses were so seriously deranged that the sight of a colour would be felt by him internally like a knife-thrust in his living flesh. It was fortunate that I had not already yielded to the temptation to break with Albertine; the boring thought that I should have to see her again presently, when I went home, was a trifling matter compared with the anxiety that I should have felt if the separation had been permanent at this moment when I felt a doubt about her before she had had time to become immaterial to me. At the moment when I pictured her thus to myself waiting for me at home, like a beloved wife who found the time of waiting long, and had perhaps fallen asleep for a moment in her room, I was caressed by the passage of a tender phrase, homely and domestic, of the septet. Perhaps – everything is so interwoven and superimposed in our inward life – it had been inspired in Vinteuil by his daughter's sleep – his daughter, the cause today of all my troubles – when it enveloped in its quiet, on peaceful evenings, the work of the composer, this phrase which calmed me so, by the same soft background of silence which pacifies certain of Schumann's reveries, during which, even when 'the Poet is speaking', one can tell that 'the child is asleep'. Asleep, awake, I should find her again this evening, when I chose to return home, Albertine, my little child. And yet, I said to myself, something more mysterious than Albertine's love seemed to be promised at the outset of this work, in those first cries of dawn. I endeavoured to banish the thought of my mistress, so as to think only of the composer. Indeed, he seemed to be present. One would have said that, reincarnate, the composer lived for all time in his music; one could feel the joy with which he was choosing the colour of some sound, harmonising it with the rest. For with other and more profound gifts Vinteuil combined that which few composers, and indeed few painters have possessed, of using colours not merely so lasting but so personal that, just as time has been powerless to fade them, so the disciples who imitate him who discovered them, and even the masters who surpass him do not pale their originality. The revolution that their apparition has effected does not live to see its results merge unacknowledged in the work of subsequent generations; it is liberated, it breaks out again, and alone, whenever the innovator's works are performed in all time to come. Each note underlined itself in a colour which all the rules in the world could not have taught the most learned composers to imitate, with the result that Vinteuil, albeit he had appeared at his hour and was fixed in his place in the evolution of music, would always leave that place to stand in the forefront, whenever any of his compositions was performed, which would owe its appearance of having blossomed after the works of other more recent composers to this quality, apparently paradoxical and actually deceiving, of permanent novelty. A page of symphonic music by Vinteuil, familiar already on the piano, when one heard it rendered by an orchestra, like a ray of summer sunlight which the prism of the window disintegrates before it enters a dark dining-room, revealed like an unsuspected, myriad-hued treasure all the jewels of the Arabian Nights. But how can one compare to that motionless brilliance of light what was life, perpetual and blissful motion? This Vinteuil, whom I had known so timid and sad, had been capable – when he had to select a tone, to blend another with it – of audacities, had enjoyed a good fortune, in the full sense of the word, as to which the hearing of any of his works left one in no doubt. The joy that such chords had aroused in him, the increase of strength that it had given him wherewith to discover others led the listener on also from one discovery to another, or rather it was the composer himself who guided him, deriving from the colours that he had invented a wild joy which gave him the strength to discover, to fling himself upon the others which they seemed to evoke, enraptured, quivering, as though from the shock of an electric spark, when the sublime came spontaneously to life at the clang of the brass, panting, drunken, maddened, dizzy, while he painted his great musical fresco, like Michelangelo strapped to his scaffold and dashing, from his supine position, tumultuous brush-strokes upon the ceiling of the Sistine Chapel. Vinteuil had been dead for many years; but in the sound of these instruments which he had animated, it had been given him to prolong, for an unlimited time, a part at least of his life. Of his life as a man merely? If art was indeed but a prolongation of life, was it worth while to sacrifice anything to it, was it not as unreal as life itself? If I was to listen properly to this septet, I could not pause to consider the question. No doubt the glowing septet differed singularly from the candid sonata; the timid question to which the little phrase replied, from the breathless supplication to find the fulfilment of the strange promise that had resounded, so harsh, so supernatural, so brief, setting athrob the still inert crimson of the morning sky, above the sea. And yet these so widely different phrases were composed of the same elements, for just as there was a certain universe, perceptible by us in those fragments scattered here and there, in private houses, in public galleries, which were Elstir's universe, the universe which he saw, in which he lived, so to the music of Vinteuil extended, note by note, key by key, the unknown colourings of an inestimable, unsuspected universe, made fragmentary by the gaps that occurred between the different occasions of hearing his work performed; those two so dissimilar questions which commanded the so different movements of the sonata and the septet, the former breaking into short appeals a line continuous and pure, the latter welding together into an indivisible structure a medley of scattered fragments, were nevertheless, one so calm and timid, almost detached and as though philosophic, the other so anxious, pressing, imploring, were nevertheless the same prayer, poured forth before different risings of the inward sun and merely refracted through the different mediums of other thoughts, of artistic researches carried on through the years in which he had tried to create something new. A prayer, a hope which was at heart the same, distinguishable beneath these disguises in the various works of Vinteuil, and on the other hand not to be found elsewhere than in his works. For these phrases historians of music might indeed find affinities, a pedigree in the works of other great composers, but merely for subordinate reasons, from external resemblances, from analogies which were ingeniously discovered by reasoning rather than felt by a direct impression. The impression that these phrases of Vinteuil imparted was different from any other, as though, notwithstanding the conclusions to which science seems to point, the individual did really exist. And it was precisely when he was seeking vigorously to be something new that one recognised beneath the apparent differences the profound similarities; and the deliberate resemblances that existed in the body of a work, when Vinteuil repeated once and again a single phrase, diversified it, amused himself by altering its rhythm, by making it reappear in its original form, these deliberate resemblances, the work of the intellect, inevitably superficial, never succeeded in being as striking as those resemblances, concealed, involuntary, which broke out in different colours, between the two separate masterpieces; for then Vinteuil, seeking to do something new, questioned himself, with all the force of his creative effort, reached his own essential nature at those depths, where, whatever be the question asked, it is in the same accent, that is to say its own, that it replies. Such an accent, the accent of Vinteuil, is separated from the accents of other composers by a difference far greater than that which we perceive between the voices of two people, even between the cries of two species of animal: by the difference that exists between the thoughts of those other composers and the eternal investigations of Vinteuil, the question that he put to himself in so many forms, his habitual speculation, but as free from analytical formulas of reasoning as if it were being carried out in the world of the angels, so that we can measure its depth, but without being any more able to translate it into human speech than are disincarnate spirits when, evoked by a medium, he questions them as to the mysteries of death. And even when I bore in mind the acquired originality which had struck me that afternoon, that kinship which musical critics might discover among them, it is indeed a unique accent to which rise, and return in spite of themselves those great singers that original composers are, which is a proof of the irreducibly individual existence of the soul. Though Vinteuil might try to make more solemn, more grand, or to make more sprightly and gay what he saw reflected in the mind of his audience, yet, in spite of himself, he submerged it all beneath an undercurrent which makes his song eternal and at once recognisable. This song, different from those of other singers, similar to all his own, where had Vinteuil learned, where had he heard it? Each artist seems thus to be the native of an unknown country, which he himself has forgotten, different from that from which will emerge, making for the earth, another great artist. When all is said, Vinteuil, in his latest works, seemed to have drawn nearer to that unknown country. The atmosphere was no longer the same as in the sonata, the questioning phrases became more pressing, more uneasy, the answers more mysterious; the clean-washed air of morning and evening seemed to influence even the instruments. Morel might be playing marvellously, the sounds that came from his violin seemed to me singularly piercing, almost blatant. This harshness was pleasing, and, as in certain voices, one felt in it a sort of moral virtue and intellectual superiority. But this might give offence. When his vision of the universe is modified, purified, becomes more adapted to his memory of the country of his heart, it is only natural that this should be expressed by a general alteration of sounds in the musician, as of colours in the painter. Anyhow, the more intelligent section of the public is not misled, since people declared later on that Vinteuil's last compositions were the most profound. Now no programme, no subject supplied any intellectual basis for judgment. One guessed therefore that it was a question of transposition, an increasing profundity of sound.

This lost country composers do not actually remember, but each of them remains all his life somehow attuned to it; he is wild with joy when he is singing the airs of his native land, betrays it at times in his thirst for fame, but then, in seeking fame, turns his back upon it, and it is only when he despises it that he finds it when he utters, whatever the subject with which he is dealing, that peculiar strain the monotony of which – for whatever its subject it remains identical in itself – proves the permanence of the elements that compose his soul. But is it not the fact then that from those elements, all the real residuum which we are obliged to keep to ourselves, which cannot be transmitted in talk, even by friend to friend, by master to disciple, by lover to mistress, that ineffable something which makes a difference in quality between what each of us has felt and what he is obliged to leave behind at the threshold of the phrases in which he can communicate with his fellows only by limiting himself to external points common to us all and of no interest, art, the art of a Vinteuil like that of an Elstir, makes the man himself apparent, rendering externally visible in the colours of the spectrum that intimate composition of those worlds which we call individual persons and which, without the aid of art, we should never know? A pair of wings, a different mode of breathing, which would enable us to traverse infinite space, would in no way help us, for, if we visited Mars or Venus keeping the same senses, they would clothe in the same aspect as the things of the earth everything that we should be capable of seeing. The only true voyage of discovery, the only fountain of Eternal Youth, would be not to visit strange lands but to possess other eyes, to behold the universe through the eyes of another, of a hundred others, to behold the hundred universes that each of them beholds, that each of them is; and this we can contrive with an Elstir, with a Vinteuil; with men like these we do really fly from star to star. The *andante* had just ended upon a phrase filled with a tenderness to which I had entirely abandoned myself; there followed, before the next movement, a short interval during which the performers laid down their instruments and the audience exchanged impressions. A Duke, in order to show that he knew what he was talking about, declared: 'It is a difficult thing to play well.' Other more entertaining people conversed for a moment with myself. But what were their words, which like every human and external word, left me so indifferent, compared with the heavenly phrase of music with which I had just been engaged? I was indeed like an angel who, fallen from the inebriating bliss of paradise, subsides into the most humdrum reality. And, just as certain creatures are the last surviving testimony to a form of life which nature has discarded, I asked myself if music were not the unique example of what might have been – if there had not come the invention of language, the formation of words, the analysis of ideas – the means of communication between one spirit and another. It is like a possibility which has ended in nothing; humanity has developed along other lines, those of spoken and written language. But this return to the unanalysed was so inebriating, that on emerging from that paradise, contact with people who were more or less intelligent seemed to me of an extraordinary insignificance. People – I had been able during the music to remember them, to blend them with it; or rather I had blended with the music little more than the memory of one person only, which was Albertine. And the phrase that ended the *andante* seemed to me so sublime that I said to myself that it was a pity that Albertine did not know it, and, had she known it, would not have understood what an honour it was to be blended with anything so great as this phrase which brought us together, and the pathetic voice of which she seemed to have borrowed. But, once the music was interrupted, the people who were present seemed utterly lifeless. Refreshments were handed round. M. de Charlus accosted a footman now and then with: 'How are you? Did you get

my note? Can you come?' No doubt there was in these remarks the freedom
of the great nobleman who thinks he is flattering his hearer and is himself
more one of the people than a man of the middle classes; there was also the
cunning of the criminal who imagines that anything which he volunteers is
on that account regarded as innocent. And he added, in the Guermantes
tone of Mme de Villeparisis: 'He's a good young fellow, such a good sort, I
often employ him at home.' But his adroitness turned against the Baron, for
people thought his intimate conversation and correspondence with footmen
extraordinary. The footmen themselves were not so much flattered as
embarrassed, in the presence of their comrades. Meanwhile the septet had
begun again and was moving towards its close; again and again one phrase
or another from the sonata recurred, but always changed, its rhythm and
harmony different, the same and yet something else, as things recur in life;
and they were phrases of the sort which, without our being able to
understand what affinity assigns to them as their sole and necessary home
the past life of a certain composer, are to be found only in his work, and
appear constantly in it, where they are the fairies, the dryads, the household
gods; I had at the start distinguished in the septet two or three which
reminded me of the sonata. Presently – bathed in the violet mist which rose
particularly in Vinteuil's later work, so much so that, even when he
introduced a dance measure, it remained captive in the heart of an opal – I
caught the sound of another phrase from the sonata, still hovering so
remote that I barely recognised it; hesitating, it approached, vanished as
though in alarm, then returned, joined hands with others, come, as I learned
later on, from other works, summoned yet others which became in their
turn attractive and persuasive, as soon as they were tamed, and took their
places in the ring, a ring divine but permanently invisible to the bulk of the
audience, who, having before their eyes only a thick veil through which they
saw nothing, punctuated arbitrarily with admiring exclamations a continuous
boredom which was becoming deadly. Then they withdrew, save one which
I saw reappear five times or six, without being able to distinguish its features,
but so caressing, so different – as was no doubt the little phrase in Swann's
sonata – from anything that any woman had ever made me desire, that this
phrase which offered me in so sweet a voice a happiness which would really
have been worth the struggle to obtain it, is perhaps – this invisible creature
whose language I did not know and whom I understood so well – the only
Stranger that it has ever been my good fortune to meet. Then this phrase
broke up, was transformed, like the little phrase in the sonata, and became
the mysterious appeal of the start. A phrase of a plaintive kind rose in
opposition to it, but so profound, so vague, so internal, almost so organic and

visceral that one could not tell at each of its repetitions whether they were
those of a theme or of an attack of neuralgia. Presently these two motifs were
wrestling together in a close fight in which now one disappeared entirely,
and now the listener could catch only a fragment of the other. A wrestling
match of energies only, to tell the truth; for if these creatures attacked one
another, it was rid of their physical bodies, of their appearance, of their
names, and finding in me an inward spectator, himself indifferent also to
their names and to all details, interested only in their immaterial and
dynamic combat and following with passion its sonorous changes. In the end
the joyous motif was left triumphant; it was no longer an almost anxious
appeal addressed to an empty sky, it was an ineffable joy which seemed to
come from paradise, a joy as different from that of the sonata as from a grave
and gentle angel by Bellini, playing the theorbo, would be some archangel
by Mantegna sounding a trump. I might be sure that this new tone of joy,
this appeal to a super-terrestrial joy, was a thing that I would never forget.
But should I be able, ever, to realise it? This question seemed to me all the
more important, inasmuch as this phrase was what might have seemed most
definitely to characterise – from its sharp contrast with all the rest of my life,
with the visible world – those impressions which at remote intervals
I recaptured in my life as starting-points, foundation-stones for the construction of a true life: the impression that I had felt at the sight of the
steeples of Martinville, or of a line of trees near Balbec. In any case, to
return to the particular accent of this phrase, how strange it was that the
presentiment most different from what life assigns to us on earth, the
boldest approximation to the bliss of the world beyond should have been
materialised precisely in the melancholy, respectable little old man whom
we used to meet in the Month of Mary at Combray; but, stranger still, how
did it come about that this revelation, the strangest that I had yet received,
of an unknown type of joy, should have come to me from him, since, it was
understood, when he died he left nothing behind him but his sonata, all the
rest being non-existent in indecipherable scribblings. Indecipherable they
may have been, but they had nevertheless been in the end deciphered, by
dint of patience, intelligence and respect, by the only person who had lived
sufficiently in Vinteuil's company to understand his method of working, to
interpret his orchestral indications: Mlle Vinteuil's friend. Even in the
lifetime of the great composer, she had acquired from his daughter the
reverence that the latter felt for her father. It was because of this reverence
that, in those moments in which people run counter to their natural
inclinations, the two girls had been able to find an insane pleasure in the
profanations which have already been narrated. (Her adoration of her father

was the primary condition of his daughter's sacrilege. And no doubt they ought to have foregone the delight of that sacrilege, but it did not express the whole of their natures.) And, what is more, the profanations had become rarefied until they disappeared altogether, in proportion as their morbid carnal relations, that troubled, smouldering fire, had given place to the flame of a pure and lofty friendship. Mlle Vinteuil's friend was sometimes worried by the importunate thought that she had perhaps hastened the death of Vinteuil. At any rate, by spending years in poring over the cryptic scroll left by him, in establishing the correct reading of those illegible hieroglyphs, Mlle Vinteuil's friend had the consolation of assuring the composer whose grey hairs she had sent in sorrow to the grave an immortal and compensating glory. Relations which are not consecrated by the laws establish bonds of kinship as manifold, as complex, even more solid than those which spring from marriage. Indeed, without pausing to consider relations of so special a nature, do we not find every day that adultery, when it is based upon genuine love, does not upset the family sentiment, the duties of kinship, but rather revivifies them? Adultery brings the spirit into what marriage would often have left a dead letter. A good-natured girl who merely from convention will wear mourning for her mother's second husband has not tears enough to shed for the man whom her mother has chosen out of all the world as her lover. Anyhow, Mlle Vinteuil had acted only in a spirit of sadism, which did not excuse her, but it gave me a certain consolation to think so later on. She must indeed have realised, I told myself, at the moment when she and her friend profaned her father's photograph, that what they were doing was merely morbidity, silliness, and not the true and joyous wickedness which she would have liked to feel. This idea that it was merely a pretence of wickedness spoiled her pleasure. But if this idea recurred to her mind later on, as it had spoiled her pleasure, so it must then have diminished her grief. 'It was not I,' she must have told herself, 'I was out of my mind. I myself mean still to pray for my father's soul, not to despair of his forgiveness.' Only it is possible that this idea, which had certainly presented itself to her in her pleasure, may not have presented itself in her grief. I would have liked to be able to put it into her mind. I am sure that I should have done her good and that I should have been able to re-establish between her and the memory of her father a pleasant channel of communication.

As in the illegible notebooks in which a chemist of genius, who does not know that death is at hand, jots down discoveries which will perhaps remain forever unknown, Mlle Vinteuil's friend had disentangled, from papers more illegible than strips of papyrus, dotted with a cuneiform script, the formula eternally true, forever fertile, of this unknown joy, the mystic hope of the crimson Angel of the dawn. And I to whom, albeit not so much perhaps as to Vinteuil, she had been also, she had been once more this very evening, by reviving afresh my jealousy of Albertine, she was above all in the future to be the cause of so many sufferings, it was thanks to her, in compensation, that there had been able to come to my ears the strange appeal which I should never for a moment cease to hear, as the promise and proof that there existed something other, realisable no doubt by art, than the nullity that I had found in all my pleasures and in love itself, and that if my life seemed to me so empty, at least there were still regions unexplored.

What she had enabled us, thanks to her labour, to know of Vinteuil was, to tell the truth, the whole of Vinteuil's work. Compared with this septet, certain phrases from the sonata which alone the public knew appeared so commonplace that one failed to understand how they could have aroused so much admiration. Similarly we are surprised that for years past, pieces as trivial as the *Evening Star* or *Elisabeth's Prayer* can have aroused in the concert hall fanatical worshippers who wore themselves out in applause and in crying encore at the end of what after all is poor and trite to us who know *Tristan*, the *Rheingold* and the *Meistersinger*. We are left to suppose that those featureless melodies contained already nevertheless in infinitesimal, and for that reason, perhaps, more easily assimilable quantities, something of the originality of the masterpieces which, in retrospect, are alone of importance to us, but which their very perfection may perhaps have prevented from being understood; they have been able to prepare the way for them in our hearts. Anyhow it is true that, if they gave a confused presentiment of the beauties to come, they left these in a state of complete obscurity. It was the same with Vinteuil; if at his death he had left behind him – excepting certain parts of the sonata – only what he had been able to complete, what we should have known of him would have been, in relation to his true greatness, as little as, in the case of, say, Victor Hugo, if he had died after the *Pas d'Armes du Roi Jean*, the *Fiancée du Timbalier* and *Sarah la Baigneuse*, without having written a line of the *Légende des Siècles* or the *Contemplations*: what is to us his real work would have remained purely potential, as unknown as those universes to which our perception does not attain, of which we shall never form any idea.

Anyhow, the apparent contrast, that profound union between genius (talent too and even virtue) and the sheath of vices in which, as had happened in the case of Vinteuil, it is so frequently contained, preserved, was legible, as in a popular allegory, in the mere assembly of the guests among whom I found myself once again when the music had come to an end. This assembly, albeit limited this time to Mme Verdurin's drawing-

room, resembled many others, the ingredients of which are unknown to the
general public, and which philosophical journalists, if they are at all well-
informed, call Parisian, or Panamist, or Dreyfusard, never suspecting that
they may equally well be found in Petersburg, Berlin, Madrid, and at every
epoch; if as a matter of fact the Under Secretary of State for Fine Arts, an
artist to his fingertips, well-bred and smart, several Duchesses and three
Ambassadors with their wives were present this evening at Mme Verdurin's,
the proximate, immediate cause of their presence lay in the relations that
existed between M. de Charlus and Morel, relations which made the Baron
anxious to give as wide a celebrity as possible to the artistic triumphs of his
young idol, and to obtain for him the Cross of the Legion of Honour; the
remoter cause which had made this assembly possible was that a girl living
with Mlle Vinteuil in the same way as the Baron was living with Charlie had
brought to light a whole series of works of genius which had been such a
revelation that before long a subscription was to be opened under the
patronage of the Minister of Education, with the object of erecting a statue
of Vinteuil. Moreover, these works had been assisted, no less than by Mlle
Vinteuil's relations with her friend, by the Baron's relations with Charlie, a
sort of cross-road, a short cut, thanks to which the world was enabled to
overtake these works without the preliminary circuit, if not of a want of
comprehension which would long persist, at least of a complete ignorance
which might have lasted for years. Whenever an event occurs which is
within the range of the vulgar mind of the moralising journalist, a political
event as a rule, the moralising journalists are convinced that there has been
some great change in France, that we shall never see such evenings again,
that no one will ever again admire Ibsen, Renan, Dostoevsky, D'Annunzio,
Tolstoy, Wagner, Strauss. For moralising journalists take their text from
the equivocal undercurrents of these official manifestations, in order to find
something decadent in the art which is there celebrated and which as often
as not is more austere than any other. But there is no name among those
most revered by these moralising journalists which has not quite naturally
given rise to some such strange gathering, although its strangeness may
have been less flagrant and better concealed. In the case of this gathering,
the impure elements that associated themselves with it struck me from
another aspect; to be sure, I was as well able as anyone to dissociate them,
having learned to know them separately, but anyhow it came to pass that
some of them, those which concerned Mlle Vinteuil and her friend, speaking
to me of Combray, spoke to me also of Albertine, that is to say of Balbec,
since it was because I had long ago seen Mlle Vinteuil at Montjouvain and
had learned of her friend's intimacy with Albertine, that I was presently,

when I returned home, to find, instead of solitude, Albertine awaiting me, and that the others, those which concerned Morel and M. de Charlus, speaking to me of Balbec, where I had seen, on the platform at Doncières, their intimacy begin, spoke to me of Combray and of its two 'ways', for M. de Charlus was one of those Guermantes, Counts of Combray, inhabiting Combray without having any dwelling there, between earth and heaven, like Gilbert the Bad in his window: while, after all, Morel was the son of that old valet who had enabled me to know the lady in pink, and had permitted me, years after, to identify her with Mme Swann.

M. de Charlus repeated, when, the music at an end, his guests came to say goodbye to him, the same error that he had made when they arrived. He did not ask them to shake hands with their hostess, to include her and her husband in the gratitude that was being showered on himself. There was a long queue waiting, but a queue that led to the Baron alone, a fact of which he must have been conscious, for as he said to me a little later: 'The form of the artistic celebration ended in a "few-words-in-the-vestry" touch that was quite amusing.' The guests even prolonged their expressions of gratitude with indiscriminate remarks which enabled them to remain for a moment longer in the Baron's presence, while those who had not yet congratulated him on the success of his party hung wearily in the rear. A stray husband or two may have announced his intention of going; but his wife, a snob as well as a Duchess, protested: 'No, no, even if we are kept waiting an hour, we cannot go away without thanking Palamède, who has taken so much trouble. There is nobody else left now who can give entertainments like this.' Nobody would have thought of asking to be introduced to Mme Verdurin any more than to the attendant in a theatre to which some great lady has for one evening brought the whole aristocracy. 'Were you at Eliane de Montmorency's yesterday, cousin?' asked Mme de Mortemart, seeking an excuse to prolong their conversation. 'Good gracious, no; I like Eliane, but I never can understand her invitations. I must be very stupid, I'm afraid,' he went on, parting his lips in a broad smile, while Mme de Mortemart realised that she was to be made the first recipient of 'one of Palamède's' as she had often been of 'one of Oriane's'. 'I did indeed receive a card a fortnight ago from the charming Eliane. Above the questionably authentic name of "Montmorency" was the following kind invitation: "My dear cousin, will you please remember me next Friday at half-past nine." Beneath were written two less gratifying words: "Czech Quartet". These seemed to me incomprehensible, and in any case to have no more connection with the sentence above than the words "My dear —", which you find on the back of a letter, with nothing else after them, when the writer has already begun again on the other side, and has not taken a fresh sheet, either from carelessness or in order to save paper. I am fond of Eliane: and so I felt no annoyance, I merely ignored the strange and inappropriate allusion to a Czech Quartet, and, as I am a methodical man, I placed on my chimney-piece the invitation to remember Madame de Montmorency on Friday at half-past nine. Although renowned for my obedient, punctual and meek nature, as Buffon says of the camel' – at this, laughter seemed to radiate from M. de Charlus who knew that on the contrary he was regarded as the most impossible person to live with – 'I was a few minutes late (it took me a few minutes to change my clothes), and without any undue remorse, thinking that half-past nine meant ten, at the stroke of ten in a comfortable dressing-gown, with warm slippers on my feet, I sat down in my chimney corner to remember Eliane as she had asked me and with a concentration which began to relax only at half-past ten. Tell her please that I complied strictly with her audacious request. I am sure she will be gratified.' Mme de Mortemart was helpless with laughter, in which M. de Charlus joined. 'And tomorrow,' she went on, forgetting that she had already long exceeded the time that might be allotted to her, 'are you going to our La Rochefoucauld cousins?' 'Oh, that, now, is quite impossible, they have invited me, and you too, I see, to a thing it is utterly impossible to imagine, which is called, if I am to believe their card of invitation, a 'dancing tea'. I used to be considered pretty nimble when I was young, but I doubt whether I could ever decently have drunk a cup of tea while I was dancing. No, I have never cared for eating or drinking in unnatural positions. You will remind me that my dancing days are done. But even sitting down comfortably to drink my tea – of the quality of which I am suspicious since it is called 'dancing' – I should be afraid lest other guests younger than myself, and less nimble possibly than I was at their age, might spill their cups over my clothes which would interfere with my pleasure in draining my own.' Nor indeed was M. de Charlus content with leaving Mme Verdurin out of the conversation while he spoke of all manner of subjects which he seemed to be taking pleasure in developing and varying, that cruel pleasure which he had always enjoyed of keeping indefinitely on their feet the friends who were waiting with an excruciating patience for their turn to come; he even criticised all that part of the entertainment for which Mme Verdurin was responsible. 'But, talking about cups, what in the world are those strange little bowls which remind me of the vessels in which, when I was a young man, people used to get sorbets from Poiré-Blanche. Somebody said to me just now that they were for "iced coffee". But if it comes to that, I have seen neither coffee nor ice. What curious little objects – so very ambiguous.' In saying this M. de

Charlus had placed his white-gloved hands vertically over his lips and had modestly circumscribed his indicative stare as though he were afraid of being heard, or even seen by his host and hostess. But this was a mere feint, for in a few minutes he would be offering the same criticisms to the Mistress herself, and a little later would be insolently enjoining: 'No more iced-coffee cups, remember! Give them to one of your friends whose house you wish to disfigure. But warn her not to have them in the drawing-room, or people might think that they had come into the wrong room, the things are so exactly like chamberpots.' 'But, cousin,' said the guest, lowering her own voice also, and casting a questioning glance at M. de Charlus, for she was afraid of offending not Mme Verdurin but him, 'perhaps she doesn't quite know yet . . . ' 'She shall be taught.' 'Oh!' laughed the guest, 'she couldn't have a better teacher! She is lucky! If you are in charge, one can be sure there won't be a false note.' 'There wasn't one, if it comes to that, in the music.' 'Oh! It was sublime. One of those pleasures which can never be forgotten. Talking of that marvellous violinist,' she went on, imagining in her innocence that M. de Charlus was interested in the violin 'pure and simple', 'do you happen to know one whom I heard the other day playing too wonderfully a sonata by Fauré, his name is Frank . . . ' 'Oh, he's a horror,' replied M. de Charlus, overlooking the rudeness of a contradiction which implied that his cousin was lacking in taste. 'As far as violinists are concerned, I advise you to confine yourself to mine.' This paved the way to a fresh exchange of glances, at once furtive and scrutinous, between M. de Charlus and his cousin, for, blushing and seeking by her zeal to atone for her blunder, Mme de Mortemart went on to suggest to M. de Charlus that she might give a party, to hear Morel play. Now, so far as she was concerned, this party had not the object of bringing an unknown talent into prominence, an object which she would, however, pretend to have in mind, and which was indeed that of M. de Charlus. She regarded it only as an opportunity for giving a particularly smart party and was calculating already whom she would invite and whom she would reject. This business of selection, the chief preoccupation of people who give parties (even the people whom 'society' journalists are so impudent or so foolish as to call 'the élite'), alters at once the expression – and the handwriting – of a hostess more profoundly than any hypnotic suggestion. Before she had even thought of what Morel was to play (which she regarded, and rightly, as a secondary consideration, for even if everybody this evening, from fear of M. de Charlus, had observed a polite silence during the music, it would never have occurred to anyone to listen to it), Mme de Mortemart, having decided that Mme de Valcourt was not to be one of the elect, had automatically assumed that air of conspiracy, of a secret plotting which so degrades even those women in society who can most easily afford to ignore what 'people will say'. 'Wouldn't it be possible for me to give a party, for people to hear your friend play?' murmured Mme de Mortemart, who, while addressing herself exclusively to M. de Charlus, could not refrain, as though under a fascination, from casting a glance at Mme de Valcourt (the rejected) in order to make certain that the other was too far away to hear her. 'No she cannot possibly hear what I am saying,' Mme de Mortemart concluded inwardly, reassured by her own glance which as a matter of fact had had a totally different effect upon Mme de Valcourt from that intended: 'Why,' Mme de Valcourt had said to herself when she caught this glance, 'Marie-Thérèse is planning something with Palamède which I am not to be told.' 'You mean my protégé,' M. de Charlus corrected, as merciless to his cousin's choice of words as he was to her musical endowments. Then without paying the slightest attention to her silent prayers, as she made a smiling apology: 'Why, yes . . . ' he said in a loud tone, audible throughout the room, 'although there is always a risk in that sort of exportation of a fascinating personality into surroundings that must inevitably diminish his transcendent gifts and would in any case have to be adapted to them.' Madame de Mortemart told herself that the aside, the pianissimo of her question had been a waste of trouble, after the megaphone through which the answer had issued. She was mistaken. Mme de Valcourt heard nothing, for the simple reason that she did not understand a single word. Her anxiety diminished and would rapidly have been extinguished had not Mme de Mortemart, afraid that she might have been given away and afraid of having to invite Mme de Valcourt, with whom she was on too intimate terms to be able to leave her out if the other knew about her party beforehand, raised her eyelids once again in Edith's direction, as though not to lose sight of a threatening peril, lowering them again briskly so as not to commit herself. She intended, on the morning after the party, to write her one of those letters, the complement of the revealing glance, letters which people suppose to be subtle and which are tantamount to a full and signed confession. For instance: 'Dear Edith, I am so sorry about you, I did not really expect you last night' ('How could she have expected me,' Edith would ask herself, 'since she never invited me?') 'as I know that you are not very fond of parties of that sort, which rather bore you. We should have been greatly honoured, all the same, by your company' (never did Mme de Mortemart employ the word 'honoured', except in the letters in which she attempted to cloak a lie in the semblance of truth). 'You know that you are always at home in our house, however, you were quite right, as it was a complete failure, like everything that is got up at a moment's notice.' But already the second furtive glance darted at her had enabled Edith to grasp everything that was concealed by the complicated language of M. de Charlus. This glance was indeed so violent that, after it had struck Mme de Valcourt, the obvious secrecy and mischievous intention that it embodied rebounded upon a young Peruvian whom Mme de Mortemart intended, on the contrary, to invite. But being of a suspicious nature, seeing all too plainly the mystery that was being made without realising that it was not intended to mystify him, he at once conceived a violent hatred of Mme de Mortemart and determined to play all sorts of tricks upon her, such as ordering fifty iced coffees to be sent to her house on a day when she was not giving a party, or, when she was, inserting a paragraph in the newspapers announcing that the party was postponed, and publishing false reports of her other parties, in which would figure the notorious names of all the people whom, for various reasons, a hostess does not invite or even allow to be introduced to her. Mme de Mortemart need not have bothered herself about Mme de Valcourt. M. de Charlus was about to spoil, far more effectively than the other's presence could spoil it, the projected party. 'But, my dear cousin,' she said in response to the expression 'adapting the surroundings', the meaning of which her momentary state of hyperaesthesia had enabled her to discern, 'we shall save you all the trouble. I undertake to ask Gilbert to arrange everything.' 'Not on any account, all the more as he must not be invited to it. Nothing can be arranged except by myself. The first thing is to exclude all the people who have ears and hear not.' M. de Charlus's cousin, who had been reckoning upon Morel as an attraction in order to give a party at which she could say that, unlike so many of her kinswomen, she had 'had Palamède', carried her thoughts abruptly, from this prestige of M. de Charlus, to all sorts of people with whom he would get her into trouble if he began interfering with the list of her guests. The thought that the Prince de Guermantes (on whose account, partly, she was anxious to exclude Mme de Valcourt, whom he declined to meet) was not to be invited, alarmed her. Her eyes assumed an uneasy expression. 'Is the light, which is rather too strong, hurting you?' enquired M. de Charlus with an apparent seriousness the underlying irony of which she failed to perceive. 'No, not at all, I was thinking of the difficulty, not for myself of course, but for my family, if Gilbert were to hear that I had given a party without inviting him, when he never has a cat on his housetop without . . .' 'Why of course, we must begin by eliminating the cat on the housetop, which could only miaow; I suppose that the din of talk has prevented you from realising that it was a question not of doing the civilities of a hostess but of proceeding to the rites customary at every true celebration.' Then, deciding, not that the next person had been kept waiting too long, but that it did not do to exaggerate the favours shown to one who had in mind not so much Morel as her own visiting-list, M. de Charlus, like a physician who cuts short a consultation when he considers that it has lasted long enough, gave his cousin a signal to withdraw, not by bidding her good-night but by turning to the person immediately behind her. 'Good-evening, Madame de Montesquiou, marvellous, wasn't it? I have not seen Hélène, tell her that every general abstention, even the most noble, that is to say her own, must include exceptions, if they are brilliant, as has been the case tonight. To show that one is rare is all very well, but to subordinate one's rarity, which is only negative, to what is precious is better still. In your sister's case, and I value more than anyone her systematic *absence* from places where what is in store for her is not worthy of her, here tonight, on the contrary, her presence at so memorable an exhibition as this would have been a *présidence*, and would have given your sister, already so distinguished, an additional distinction.' Then he turned to a third person, M. d'Argencourt. I was greatly astonished to see in this room, as friendly and flattering towards M. de Charlus as he was severe with him elsewhere, insisting upon Morel's being introduced to him and telling him that he hoped he would come and see him, M. d'Argencourt, that terrible scourge of men such as M. de Charlus. At the moment he was living in the thick of them. It was certainly not because he had in any sense become one of them himself. But for some time past he had practically deserted his wife for a young woman in society whom he adored. Being intelligent herself, she made him share her taste for intelligent people, and was most anxious to have M. de Charlus in her house. But above all M. d'Argencourt, extremely jealous and not unduly potent, feeling that he was failing to satisfy his captive and anxious at once to introduce her to people and to keep her amused, could do so without risk to himself only by surrounding her with innocuous men, whom he thus cast for the part of guardians of his seraglio. These men found that he had become quite pleasant and declared that he was a great deal more intelligent than they had supposed, a discovery that delighted him and his mistress.

The remainder of M. de Charlus's guests drifted away fairly rapidly. Several of them said: 'I don't want to call at the vestry' (the little room in which the Baron, with Charlie by his side, was receiving congratulations, and to which he himself had given the name), 'but I must let Palamède see me so that he shall know that I stayed to the end.' Nobody paid the slightest attention to Mme Verdurin. Some pretended not to know which was she and said good-night by mistake to Mme Cottard, appealing to me for

confirmation with a 'That *is* Mme Verdurin, ain't it?' Mme d'Arpajon
asked me, in the hearing of our hostess: 'Tell me, has there ever been a
Monsieur Verdurin?' The Duchesses, finding none of the oddities that
they expected in this place which they had hoped to find more different
from anything that they already knew, made the best of a bad job by going
into fits of laughter in front of Elstir's paintings; for all the rest of the
entertainment, which they found more in keeping than they had expected
with the style with which they were familiar, they gave the credit to M. de
Charlus, saying: 'How clever Palamède is at arranging things; if he were to
stage an opera in a stable or a bathroom, it would still be perfectly
charming.' The most noble ladies were those who showed most fervour in
congratulating M. de Charlus upon the success of a party, of the secret
motive of which some of them were by no means unaware, without,
however, being embarrassed by the knowledge, this class of society –
remembering perhaps certain epochs in history when their own family had
already arrived at an identical stage of brazenly conscious effrontery –
carrying their contempt for scruples almost as far as their respect for
etiquette. Several of them engaged Charlie on the spot for different
evenings on which he was to come and play them Vinteuil's septet, but it
never occurred to any of them to invite Mme Verdurin. This last was
already blind with fury when M. de Charlus who, his head in the clouds,
was incapable of perceiving her condition, decided that it would be only
decent to invite the Mistress to share his joy. And it was perhaps yielding to
his literary preciosity rather than to an overflow of pride that this specialist
in artistic entertainments said to Mme Verdurin: 'Well, are you satisfied? I
think you have reason to be; you see that when I set to work to give a party
there are no half-measures. I do not know whether your heraldic knowledge
enables you to gauge the precise importance of the display, the weight that
I have lifted, the volume of air that I have displaced for you. You have had
the Queen of Naples, the brother of the King of Bavaria, the three premier
peers. If Vinteuil is Mahomet, we may say that we have brought to him
some of the least movable of mountains. Bear in mind that to attend your
party the Queen of Naples has come up from Neuilly, which is a great deal
more difficult for her than evacuating the Two Sicilies,' he went on, with a
deliberate sneer, notwithstanding his admiration for the Queen. 'It is an
historic event. Just think that it is perhaps the first time she has gone
anywhere since the fall of Gaeta. It is probable that the dictionaries of dates
will record as culminating points the day of the fall of Gaeta and that of the
Verdurins' party. The fan that she laid down, the better to applaud Vinteuil,
deserves to become more famous than the fan that Mme de Metternich

broke because the audience hissed Wagner.' 'Why, she has left it here,' said Mme Verdurin, momentarily appeased by the memory of the Queen's kindness to herself, and she showed M. de Charlus the fan which was lying upon a chair. 'Oh! What a touching spectacle!' exclaimed M. de Charlus, approaching the relic with veneration. 'It is all the more touching, it is so hideous; poor little Violette is incredible!' And spasms of emotion and irony coursed through him alternately. 'Oh dear, I don't know whether you feel this sort of thing as I do. Swann would positively have died of convulsions if he had seen it. I am sure, whatever price it fetches, I shall buy the fan at the Queen's sale. For she is bound to be sold up, she hasn't a penny,' he went on, for he never ceased to intersperse the cruellest slanders with the most sincere veneration, albeit these sprang from two opposing natures, which, however, were combined in himself. They might even be brought to bear alternately upon the same incident. For M. de Charlus who in his comfortable state as a wealthy man ridiculed the poverty of the Queen was himself often to be heard extolling that poverty and, when anyone spoke of Princesse Murat, Queen of the Two Sicilies, would reply: 'I do not know to whom you are alluding. There is only one Queen of Naples, who is a sublime person and does not keep a carriage. But from her omnibus she annihilates every vehicle on the street and one could kneel down in the dust on seeing her drive past.' 'I shall bequeath it to a museum. In the meantime, it must be sent back to her, so that she need not hire a cab to come and fetch it. The wisest thing, in view of the historical interest of such an object, would be to steal the fan. But that would be awkward for her – since it is probable that she does not possess another!' he added, with a shout of laughter. 'Anyhow, you see that for my sake she came. And that is not the only miracle that I have performed. I do not believe that anyone at the present day has the power to move the people whom I have brought here. However, everyone must be given his due. Charlie and the rest of the musicians played divinely. And, my dear Mistress,' he added condescendingly, 'you yourself have played your part on this occasion. Your name will not be unrecorded. History has preserved that of the page who armed Joan of Arc when she set out for battle; indeed you have served as a connecting link, you have made possible the fusion between Vinteuil's music and its inspired interpreter, you have had the intelligence to appreciate the capital importance of the whole chain of circumstances which would enable the interpreter to benefit by the whole weight of a considerable – if I were not referring to myself, I would say providential – personage, whom you were clever enough to ask to ensure the success of the gathering, to bring before Morel's violin the ears directly attached to the tongues that have the widest hearing; no, no, it is not a small matter. There can be no small matter in so complete a realisation. Everything has its part. The Duras was marvellous. In fact, everything; that is why,' he concluded, for he loved to administer a rebuke, 'I set my face against your inviting those persons – divisors who, among the overwhelming people whom I brought you would have played the part of the decimal points in a sum, reducing the others to a merely fractional value. I have a very exact appreciation of that sort of thing. You understand, we must avoid blunders when we are giving a party which ought to be worthy of Vinteuil, of his inspired interpreter, of yourself, and, I venture to say, of me. You were prepared to invite the Molé, and everything would have been spoiled. It would have been the little contrary, neutralising drop which deprives a potion of its virtue. The electric lights would have fused, the pastry would not have come in time, the orangeade would have given everybody a stomach ache. She was the one person not to invite. At the mere sound of her name, as in a fairytale, not a note would have issued from the brass; the flute and the hautboy would have been stricken with a sudden silence. Morel himself, even if he had succeeded in playing a few bars, would not have been in tune, and instead of Vinteuil's septet you would have had a parody of it by Beckmesser, ending amid catcalls. I, who believe strongly in personal influence, could feel quite plainly in the expansion of a certain *largo*, which opened itself right out like a flower, in the supreme satisfaction of the finale, which was not merely *allegro* but incomparably *allegro*, that the absence of the Molé was inspiring the musicians and was diffusing joy among the very instruments themselves. In any case, when one is at home to Queens one does not invite one's hall-portress.' In calling her 'the Molé' (as for that matter he said quite affectionately 'the Duras') M. de Charlus was doing the lady justice. For all these women were the actresses of society and it is true also that, even regarding her from this point of view, Comtesse Molé did not justify the extraordinary reputation for intelligence that she had acquired, which made one think of those mediocre actors or novelists who, at certain periods, are hailed as men of genius, either because of the mediocrity of their competitors, among whom there is no artist capable of revealing what is meant by true talent, or because of the mediocrity of the public, which, did there exist an extraordinary individuality, would be incapable of understanding it. In Mme Molé's case it is preferable, if not absolutely fair, to stop at the former explanation. The social world being the realm of nullity, there exist between the merits of women in society only insignificant degrees, which are at best capable of rousing to madness the rancours or the imagination of M. de Charlus. And certainly, if he spoke as he had just been speaking in this language which was a precious alloy of artistic and social elements, it was because his old-womanly anger and his culture as a man of the world furnished the genuine eloquence that he possessed with none but insignificant themes. Since the world of differences does not exist on the surface of the earth, among all the countries which our perception renders uniform, all the more reason why it should not exist in the social 'world'. Does it exist anywhere else? Vinteuil's septet had seemed to tell me that it did. But where? As M. de Charlus also enjoyed repeating what one person had said of another, seeking to stir up quarrels, to divide and reign, he added: 'You have, by not inviting her, deprived Mme Molé of the opportunity of saying: "I can't think why this Mme Verdurin should invite me. I can't imagine who these people are, I don't know them." She was saying a year ago that you were boring her with your advances. She's a fool, never invite her again. After all, she's nothing so very wonderful. She can come to your house without making a fuss about it, seeing that I come here. In short,' he concluded, 'it seems to me that you have every reason to thank me, for, so far as it went, everything has been perfect. The Duchesse de Guermantes did not come, but one can't tell, it was better perhaps that she didn't. We shan't bear her any grudge, and we shall remember her all the same another time, not that one can help remembering her, her very eyes say to us "Forget me not!", for they are a pair of myosotes' (here I thought to myself how strong the Guermantes spirit – the decision to go to one house and not to another – must be, to have outweighed in the Duchess's mind her fear of Palamède). 'In the face of so complete a success, one is tempted like Bernardin de Saint-Pierre to see everywhere the hand of Providence. The Duchesse de Duras was enchanted. She even asked me to tell you so,' added M. de Charlus, dwelling upon the words as though Mme Verdurin must regard this as a sufficient honour. Sufficient and indeed barely credible, for he found it necessary, if he was to be believed, to add, completely carried away by the madness of those whom Jupiter has decided to ruin: 'She has engaged Morel to come to her house, where the same programme will be repeated, and I even think of asking her for an invitation for M. Verdurin.' This civility to the husband alone was, although no such idea even occurred to M. de Charlus, the most wounding outrage to the wife who, believing herself to possess, with regard to the violinist, by virtue of a sort of ukase which prevailed in the little clan, the right to forbid him to perform elsewhere without her express authorisation, was fully determined to forbid his appearance at Mme de Duras's party.

The Baron's volubility was in itself an irritation to Mme Verdurin who did not like people to form independent groups within their little clan. How often, even at la Raspelière, hearing M. de Charlus talking incessantly to

Charlie instead of being content with taking his part in the so harmonious chorus of the clan, she had pointed to him and exclaimed: 'What a rattle* he is! What a rattle! Oh, if it comes to rattles, he's a famous rattle!' But this time it was far worse. Inebriated with the sound of his own voice, M. de Charlus failed to realise that by cutting down the part assigned to Mme Verdurin and confining it within narrow limits, he was calling forth that feeling of hatred which was in her only a special, social form of jealousy. Mme Verdurin was genuinely fond of her regular visitors, the faithful of the little clan, but wished them to be entirely devoted to their Mistress. Willing to make some sacrifice, like those jealous lovers who will tolerate a betrayal, but only under their own roof and even before their eyes, that is to say when there is no betrayal, she would allow the men to have mistresses, lovers, on condition that the affair had no social consequence outside her own house, that the tie was formed and perpetuated in the shelter of her Wednesdays. In the old days, every furtive peal of laughter that came from Odette when she conversed with Swann had gnawed her heartstrings, and so of late had every aside exchanged by Morel and the Baron; she found one consolation alone for her griefs, which was to destroy the happiness of other people. She had not been able to endure for long that of the Baron. And here was this rash person precipitating the catastrophe by appearing to be restricting the Mistress's place in her little clan. Already she could see Morel going into society, without her, under the Baron's aegis. There was but a single remedy, to make Morel choose between the Baron and herself, and, relying upon the ascendancy that she had acquired over Morel by the display that she made of an extraordinary perspicacity, thanks to reports which she collected, to falsehoods which she invented, all of which served to corroborate what he himself was led to believe, and what would in time be made plain to him, thanks to the pitfalls which she was preparing, into which her unsuspecting victims would fall, relying upon this ascendancy, to make him choose herself in preference to the Baron. As for the society ladies who had been present and had not even asked to be introduced to her, as soon as she grasped their hesitations or indifference, she had said: 'Ah! I see what they are, the sort of old good-for-nothings that are not our style, it's the last time they shall set foot in this house.' For she would have died rather than admit that anyone had been less friendly to her than she had hoped. 'Ah! My dear General,' M. de Charlus suddenly exclaimed, abandoning Mme Verdurin, as he caught sight of General Deltour, Secretary to the President of the Republic, who

---

* Mme Verdurin uses here the word *tapette*, being probably unaware of its popular meaning. C. K. S. M.

might be of great value in securing Charlie his Cross, and who, after asking some question of Cottard, was rapidly withdrawing: 'Good-evening, my dear, delightful friend. So this is how you slip away without saying goodbye to me,' said the Baron with a genial, self-satisfied smile, for he knew quite well that people were always glad to stay behind for a moment to talk to himself. And as, in his present state of excitement, he would answer his own questions in a shrill tone: 'Well, did you enjoy it? Wasn't it really fine? The *andante*, what? It's the most touching thing that was ever written. I defy anyone to listen to the end without tears in his eyes. Charming of you to have come. Listen, I had the most perfect telegram this morning from Froberville, who tells me that as far as the Grand Chancery goes the difficulties have been smoothed away, as the saying is.' M. de Charlus's voice continued to soar at this piercing pitch, as different from his normal voice as is that of a barrister making an emphatic plea from his ordinary utterance, a phenomenon of vocal amplification by over-excitement and nervous tension analogous to that which, at her own dinner-parties, raised to so high a diapason the voice and gaze alike of Mme de Guermantes. 'I intended to send you a note tomorrow by a messenger to tell you of my enthusiasm, until I could find an opportunity of speaking to you, but you have been so surrounded! Froberville's support is not to be despised, but for my own part, I have the Minister's promise,' said the General. 'Ah! Excellent. Besides, you have seen for yourself that it is only what such talent deserves. Hoyos was delighted, I didn't manage to see the Ambassadress, was she pleased? Who would not have been, except those that have ears and hear not, which does not matter so long as they have tongues and can speak.' Taking advantage of the Baron's having withdrawn to speak to the General, Mme Verdurin made a signal to Brichot. He, not knowing what Mme Verdurin was going to say, sought to amuse her, and never suspecting the anguish that he was causing me, said to the Mistress: 'The Baron is delighted that Mlle Vinteuil and her friend did not come. They shock him terribly. He declares that their morals are appalling. You can't imagine how prudish and severe the Baron is on moral questions.' Contrary to Brichot's expectation, Mme Verdurin was not amused: 'He is obscene,' was her answer. 'Take him out of the room to smoke a cigarette with you, so that my husband can get hold of his Dulcinea without his noticing it and warn him of the abyss that is yawning at his feet.' Brichot seemed to hesitate. 'I don't mind telling you,' Mme Verdurin went on, to remove his final scruples, 'that I do not feel at all safe with a man like that in the house. I know, there are all sorts of horrible stories about him, and the police have him under supervision.' And, as she possessed a certain talent of improvisation when inspired by malice, Mme Verdurin did not stop at this: 'It seems, he has been in prison. Yes, yes, I have been told by people who knew all about it. I know, too, from a person who lives in his street, that you can't imagine the ruffians that go to his house.' And as Brichot, who often went to the Baron's, began to protest, Mme Verdurin, growing animated, exclaimed: 'But I can assure you! It is I who am telling you', an expression with which she habitually sought to give weight to an assertion flung out more or less at random. 'He will be found murdered in his bed one of these days, as those people always are. He may not go quite as far as that perhaps, because he is in the clutches of that Jupien whom he had the impudence to send to me, and who is an ex-convict, I know it, you yourself know it, yes, for certain. He has a hold on him because of some letters which are perfectly appalling, it seems. I know it from somebody who has seen them, and told me: "You would be sick on the spot if you saw them." That is how Jupien makes him toe the line and gets all the money he wants out of him. I would sooner die a thousand times over than live in a state of terror like Charlus. In any case, if Morel's family decides to bring an action against him, I have no desire to be dragged in as an accomplice. If he goes on, it will be at his own risk, but I shall have done my duty. What is one to do? It's no joke, I can tell you.' And, agreeably warmed already by the thought of her husband's impending conversation with the violinist, Mme Verdurin said to me: 'Ask Brichot whether I am not a courageous friend, and whether I am not capable of sacrificing myself to save my comrades.' (She was alluding to the circumstances in which she had, just in time, made him quarrel, first of all with his laundress, and then with Mme de Cambremer, quarrels as a result of which Brichot had become almost completely blind, and [people said] had taken to morphia.) 'An incomparable friend, far-sighted and valiant,' replied the Professor with an innocent emotion. 'Mme Verdurin prevented me from doing something extremely foolish,' Brichot told me when she had left us. 'She never hesitates to operate without anaesthetics. She is an interventionist, as our friend Cottard says. I admit, however, that the thought that the poor Baron is still unconscious of the blow that is going to fall upon him distresses me deeply. He is quite mad about that boy. If Mme Verdurin should prove successful, there is a man who is going to be very miserable. However, it is not certain that she will not fail. I am afraid that she may only succeed in creating a misunderstanding between them, which, in the end, without parting them, will only make them quarrel with her.' It was often thus with Mme Verdurin and her faithful. But it was evident that in her the need to preserve their friendship was more and more dominated by the requirement that this friendship should never be challenged by that which they might feel for one another. Homosexuality did not disgust her so long as it did not tamper with orthodoxy, but like the Church she preferred any sacrifice rather than a concession of orthodoxy. I was beginning to be afraid lest her irritation with myself might be due to her having heard that I had prevented Albertine from going to her that afternoon, and that she might presently set to work, if she had not already begun, upon the same task of separating her from me which her husband, in the case of Charlus, was now going to attempt with the musician. 'Come along, get hold of Charlus, find some excuse, there's no time to lose,' said Mme Verdurin, 'and whatever you do, don't let him come back here until I send for you. Oh! What an evening,' Mme Verdurin went on, revealing thus the true cause of her anger. 'Performing a masterpiece in front of those wooden images. I don't include the Queen of Naples, she is intelligent, she is a nice woman' (which meant: 'She has been kind to me'). 'But the others. Oh! It's enough to drive anyone mad. What can you expect, I'm no longer a girl. When I was young, people told me that one must put up with boredom, I made an effort, but now, oh no, it's too much for me, I am old enough to please myself, life is too short; bore myself, listen to idiots, smile, pretend to think them intelligent. No, I can't do it. Get along, Brichot, there's no time to lose.' 'I am going, Madame, I am going,' said Brichot, as General Deltour moved away. But first of all the Professor took me aside for a moment: 'Moral Duty,' he said, 'is less clearly imperative than our Ethics teach us. Whatever the Theosophical cafés and the Kantian beer-houses may say, we are deplorably ignorant of the nature of Good. I myself who, without wishing to boast, have lectured to my pupils, in all innocence, upon the philosophy of the said Immanuel Kant, I can see no precise ruling for the case of social casuistry with which I am now confronted in that *Critique of Practical Reason* in which the great renegade of Protestantism platonised in the German manner for a Germany prehistorically sentimental and aulic, ringing all the changes of a Pomeranian mysticism. It is still the *Symposium*, but held this time at Kônigsberg, in the local style, indigestible and reeking of sauerkraut, and without any good-looking boys. It is obvious on the one hand that I cannot refuse our excellent hostess the small service that she asks of me, in a fully orthodox conformity with traditional morals. One ought to avoid, above all things, for there are few that involve one in more foolish speeches, letting oneself be lured by words. But after all, let us not hesitate to admit that if the mothers of families were entitled to vote, the Baron would run the risk of being lamentably blackballed for the Chair of Virtue. It is unfortunately with the temperament of a rake that he pursues the vocation of a pedagogue; observe that I am not speaking evil of the Baron; that good man, who can carve a joint like nobody in the world, combines with a genius for anathema treasures of goodness. He can be most amusing as a superior sort of wag, whereas with a certain one of my colleagues, an Academician, if you please, I am bored, as Xenophon would say, at a hundred drachmae to the hour. But I am afraid that he is expending upon Morel rather more than a wholesome morality enjoins, and without knowing to what extent the young penitent shows himself docile or rebellious to the special exercises which his catechist imposes upon him by way of mortification, one need not be a learned clerk to be aware that we should be erring, as the other says, on the side of clemency with regard to this Rosicrucian who seems to have come down to us from Petronius, by way of Saint-Simon, if we granted him with our eyes shut, duly signed and sealed, permission to satanise. And yet, in keeping the man occupied while Mme Verdurin, for the sinner's good and indeed rightly tempted by such a cure of souls, proceeds – by speaking to the young fool without any concealment – to remove from him all that he loves, to deal him perhaps a fatal blow, it seems to me that I am leading him into what one might call a mantrap, and I recoil as though from a base action.' This said, he did not hesitate to commit it, but, taking him by the arm, began: 'Come, Baron, let us go and smoke a cigarette, this young man has not yet seen all the marvels of the house.' I made the excuse that I was obliged to go home. 'Just wait a moment,' said Brichot. 'You remember, you are giving me a lift, and I have not forgotten your promise.' 'Wouldn't you like me, really, to make them bring out their plate, nothing could be simpler,' said M. de Charlus. 'You promised me, remember, not a word about Morel's decoration. I mean to give him the surprise of announcing it presently when people have begun to leave, although he says that it is of no importance to an artist, but that his uncle would like him to have it.' (I blushed, for, I thought to myself, the Verdurins would know through my grandfather what Morel's uncle was) 'Then you wouldn't like me to make them bring out the best pieces,' said M. de Charlus. 'Of course, you know them already, you have seen them a dozen times at la Raspelière.' I dared not tell him that what might have interested me was not the mediocrity of even the most splendid plate in a middle-class household, but some specimen, were it only reproduced in a fine engraving, of Mme Du Barry's. I was far too gravely preoccupied – even if I had not been by this revelation as to Mlle Vinteuil's expected presence – always, in society, far too much distracted and agitated to fasten my attention upon objects that were more or less beautiful. It could have been arrested only by the appeal of some reality that addressed itself to my imagination, as might have been, this evening, a picture of that Venice of which I had thought so much during the afternoon, or some general element, common to several

forms and more genuine than they, which, of its own accord, never failed to
arouse in me an inward appreciation, normally lulled in slumber, the rising
of which to the surface of my consciousness filled me with great joy. Well, as
I emerged from the room known as the concert-room, and crossed the other
drawing-rooms with Brichot and M. de Charlus, on discovering, transposed
among others, certain pieces of furniture which I had seen at la Raspelière
and to which I had paid no attention, I perceived, between the arrangement
of the town house and that of the country house, a certain common air of
family life, a permanent identity, and I understood what Brichot meant
when he said to me with a smile: 'There, look at this room, it may perhaps
give you an idea of what things were like in Rue Montalivet, twenty-five
years ago.' From his smile, a tribute to the defunct drawing-room which he
saw with his mind's eye, I understood that what Brichot, perhaps without
realising it, preferred in the old room, more than the large windows, more
than the gay youth of his hosts and their faithful, was that unreal part (which
I myself could discern from some similarities between la Raspelière and
Quai Conti) of which, in a drawing-room as in everything else, the external,
actual part, liable to everyone's control, is but the prolongation, was that part
become purely imaginary, of a colour which no longer existed save for my
elderly guide, which he was incapable of making me see, that part which has
detached itself from the outer world, to take refuge in our soul, to which it
gives a surplus value, in which it is assimilated to its normal substance,
transforming itself – houses that have been pulled down, people long dead,
bowls of fruit at the suppers which we recall – into that translucent alabaster
of our memories, the colour of which we are incapable of displaying, since
we alone see it, which enables us to say truthfully to other people, speaking
of things past, that they cannot form any idea of them, that they do not
resemble anything that they have seen, while we are unable to think of them
ourselves without a certain emotion, remembering that it is upon the
existence of our thoughts that there depends, for a little time still, their
survival, the brilliance of the lamps that have been extinguished and the
fragrance of the arbours that will never bloom again. And possibly, for this
reason, the drawing-room in Rue Montalivet disparaged, for Brichot, the
Verdurins' present home. But on the other hand it added to this home, in the
Professor's eyes, a beauty which it could not have in those of a stranger.
Those pieces of the original furniture that had been transported here, and
sometimes arranged in the same groups, and which I myself remembered
from la Raspelière, introduced into the new drawing-room fragments of
the old which, at certain moments, recalled it so vividly as to create a
hallucination and then seemed themselves scarcely real from having evoked

in the midst of the surrounding reality fragments of a vanished world which seemed to extend round about them. A sofa that had risen up from dreamland between a pair of new and thoroughly substantial armchairs, smaller chairs upholstered in pink silk, the cloth surface of a card-table raised to the dignity of a person since, like a person, it had a past, a memory, retaining in the chill and gloom of Quai Conti the tan of its roasting by the sun through the windows of Rue Montalivet (where it could tell the time of day as accurately as Mme Verdurin herself) and through the glass doors at la Raspelière, where they had taken it and where it used to gaze out all day long over the flower-beds of the garden at the valley far below, until it was time for Cottard and the musician to sit down to their game; a posy of violets and pansies in pastel, the gift of a painter friend, now dead, the sole fragment that survived of a life that had vanished without leaving any trace, summarising a great talent and a long friendship, recalling his keen, gentle eyes, his shapely hand, plump and melancholy, while he was at work on it; the incoherent, charming disorder of the offerings of the faithful, which have followed the lady of the house on all her travels and have come in time to assume the fixity of a trait of character, of a line of destiny; a profusion of cut flowers, of chocolate-boxes which here as in the country systematised their growth in an identical mode of blossoming; the curious interpolation of those singular and superfluous objects which still appear to have been just taken from the box in which they were offered and remain for ever what they were at first, New Year's Day presents; all those things, in short, which one could not have isolated from the rest, but which for Brichot, an old frequenter of the Verdurin parties, had that patina, that velvety bloom of things to which, giving them a sort of profundity, an astral body has been added; all these things scattered before him, sounded in his ear like so many resonant keys which awakened cherished likenesses in his heart, confused reminiscences which, here in this drawing-room of the present day that was littered with them, cut out, defined, as on a fine day a shaft of sunlight cuts a section in the atmosphere, the furniture and carpets, and pursuing it from a cushion to a flower-stand, from a footstool to a lingering scent, from the lighting arrangements to the colour scheme, carved, evoked, spiritualised, called to life a form which might be called the ideal aspect, immanent in each of their successive homes, of the Verdurin drawing-room. 'We must try,' Brichot whispered in my ear, 'to get the Baron upon his favourite topic. He is astounding.' Now on the one hand I was glad of an opportunity to try to obtain from M. de Charlus information as to the coming of Mlle Vinteuil and her friend. On the other hand, I did not wish to leave Albertine too long by herself, not that she could (being uncertain of the moment of my return, not to mention that, at so late an hour, she could not have received a visitor or left the house herself without arousing comment) make any evil use of my absence, but simply so that she might not find it too long. And so I told Brichot and M. de Charlus that I must shortly leave them. 'Come with us all the same,' said the Baron, whose social excitement was beginning to flag, but feeling that need to prolong, to spin out a conversation, which I had already observed in the Duchesse de Guermantes as well as in himself, and which, while distinctive of their family, extends in a more general fashion to all those people who, offering their minds no other realisation than talk, that is to say an imperfect realisation, remain unassuaged even after hours spent in one's company, and attach themselves more and more hungrily to their exhausted companion, from whom they mistakenly expect a satiety which social pleasures are incapable of giving. 'Come, won't you,' he repeated, 'this is the pleasant moment at a party, the moment when all the guests have gone, the hour of Doña Sol; let us hope that it will end less tragically. Unfortunately you are in a hurry, in a hurry probably to go and do things which you would much better leave undone. People are always in a hurry and leave at the time when they ought to be arriving. We are here like Couture's philosophers, this is the moment in which to go over the events of the evening, to make what is called in military language a criticism of the operations. We might ask Mme Verdurin to send us in a little supper to which we should take care not to invite her, and we might request Charlie – still *Hernani* – to play for ourselves alone the sublime *adagio*. Isn't it fine, that *adagio*? But where is the young violinist, I would like to congratulate him, this is the moment for tender words and embraces. Admit, Brichot, that they played like gods, Morel especially. Did you notice the moment when that lock of hair came loose? Ah, then, my dear fellow, you saw nothing at all. There was an F sharp at which Enesco, Capet and Thibaut might have died of jealousy; I may have appeared calm enough, I can tell you that at such a sound my heart was so wrung that I could barely control my tears. The whole room sat breathless; Brichot, my dear fellow,' cried the Baron, gripping the other's arm which he shook violently, 'it was sublime. Only young Charlie preserved a stony immobility, you could not even see him breathe, he looked like one of those objects of the inanimate world of which Théodore Rousseau speaks, which make us think, but do not think themselves. And then, all of a sudden,' cried M. de Charlus with enthusiasm, making a pantomime gesture, 'then . . . the Lock! And all the time, the charming little country-dance of the *allegro vivace*. You know, that lock was the symbol of the revelation, even to the most obtuse. The Princess of Taormina, deaf until then, for there are none so deaf as those that have ears and hear not, the Princess of Taormina, confronted by the message of the miraculous lock, realised that it was music that they were playing and not poker. Oh, that was indeed a solemn moment.' 'Excuse me, Sir, for interrupting you,' I said to M. de Charlus, hoping to bring him to the subject in which I was interested, 'you told me that the composer's daughter was to be present. I should have been most interested to meet her. Are you certain that she was expected?' 'Oh, that I can't say.' M. de Charlus thus complied, perhaps unconsciously, with that universal rule by which people withhold information from a jealous lover, whether in order to show an absurd 'comradeship', as a point of honour, and even if they detest her, with the woman who has excited his jealousy, or out of malice towards her, because they guess that jealousy can only intensify love, or from that need to be disagreeable to other people which consists in revealing the truth to the rest of the world but concealing it from the jealous, ignorance increasing their torment, or so at least the tormentors suppose, who, in their desire to hurt other people are guided by what they themselves believe, wrongly perhaps, to be most painful. 'You know,' he went on, 'in this house they are a trifle prone to exaggerate, they are charming people, still they do like to catch celebrities of one sort or another. But you are not looking well, and you will catch cold in this damp room,' he said, pushing a chair towards me. 'Since you have not been well, you must take care of yourself, let me go and find you your coat. No, don't go for it yourself, you will lose your way and catch cold. How careless people are; you might be an infant in arms, you want an old nurse like me to look after you.' 'Don't trouble, Baron, let me go,' said Brichot, and left us immediately; not being precisely aware perhaps of the very warm affection that M. de Charlus felt for me and of the charming lapses into simplicity and devotion that alternated with his delirious crises of grandeur and persecution, he was afraid that M. de Charlus, whom Mme Verdurin had entrusted like a prisoner to his vigilance, might simply be seeking, under the pretext of asking for my greatcoat, to return to Morel and might thus upset the Mistress's plan.

Meanwhile Ski had sat down, uninvited, at the piano, and assuming – with a playful knitting of his brows, a remote gaze and a slight twist of his lips – what he imagined to be an artistic air, was insisting that Morel should play something by Bizet. 'What, you don't like it, that boyish music of Bizet. Why, my dear fellow,' he said, with that rolling of the letter r which was one of his peculiarities, 'it's rravishing.' Morel, who did not like Bizet, said so in exaggerated terms and (as he had the reputation in the little clan of being, though it seems incredible, a wit) Ski, pretending to take the violinist's diatribes as paradoxes, burst out laughing. His laugh was not, like M.

Verdurin's, the stifled gasp of a smoker. Ski first of all assumed a subtle air, then allowed to escape, as though against his will, a single note of laughter, like the first clang from a belfry, followed by a silence in which the subtle gaze seemed to be making a competent examination of the absurdity of what had been said, then a second peal of laughter shook the air, followed presently by a merry angelus.

I expressed to M. de Charlus my regret that M. Brichot should be taking so much trouble. 'Not at all, he is delighted, he is very fond of you, everyone is fond of you. Somebody was saying only the other day: "We never see him now, he is isolating himself!" Besides, he is such a good fellow, is Brichot,' M. de Charlus went on, never suspecting probably, in view of the affectionate, frank manner in which the Professor of Moral Philosophy conversed with him, that he had no hesitation is slandering him behind his back. 'He is a man of great merit, immensely learned, and not a bit spoiled, his learning hasn't turned him into a bookworm, like so many of them who smell of ink. He has retained a breadth of outlook, a tolerance, rare in his kind. Sometimes, when one sees how well he understands life, with what a natural grace he renders everyone his due, one asks oneself where a humble little Sorbonne professor, an ex-schoolmaster, can have picked up such breeding. I am astonished at it myself.' I was even more astonished when I saw the conversation of this Brichot, which the least refined of Mme de Guermantes's friends would have found so dull, so heavy, please the most critical of them all, M. de Charlus. But to achieve this result there had collaborated, among other influences, themselves distinct also, those by virtue of which Swann, on the one hand, had so long found favour with the little clan, when he was in love with Odette, and on the other hand, after he married, found an attraction in Mme Bontemps who, pretending to adore the Swann couple, came incessantly to call upon the wife and revelled in all the stories about the husband. Just as a writer gives the palm for intelligence, not to the most intelligent man, but to the worldling who utters a bold and tolerant comment upon the passion of a man for a woman, a comment which makes the writer's bluestocking mistress agree with him in deciding that of all the people who come to her house the least stupid is after all this old beau who shows experience in the things of love, so M. de Charlus found more intelligent than the rest of his friends Brichot, who was not merely kind to Morel, but would cull from the Greek philosophers, the Latin poets, the authors of Oriental tales, appropriate texts which decorated the Baron's propensity with a strange and charming anthology. M. de Charlus had reached the age at which a Victor Hugo chooses to surround himself, above all, with Vacqueries and

Meurices. He preferred to all others those men who tolerated his outlook upon life. 'I see a great deal of him,' he went on, in a balanced, singsong tone, allowing no movement of his lips to stir his grave, powdered mask over which were purposely lowered his prelatical eyelids. 'I attend his lectures, that atmosphere of the Latin Quarter refreshes me, there is a studious, thoughtful adolescence of young *bourgeois*, more intelligent, better read than were, in a different sphere, my own contemporaries. It is a different world, which you know probably better than I, they are young bourgeois,' he said, detaching the last word to which he prefixed a string of b's, and emphasising it from a sort of habit of elocution, corresponding itself to a taste for fine distinctions in past history, which was peculiar to him, but perhaps also from inability to resist the pleasure of giving me a flick of his insolence. This did not in any way diminish the great and affectionate pity that was inspired in me by M. de Charlus (after Mme Verdurin had revealed her plan in my hearing), it merely amused me, and indeed on any other occasion, when I should not have felt so kindly disposed towards him, would not have offended me. I derived from my grandmother such an absence of any self-importance that I might easily be found wanting in dignity. Doubtless, I was scarcely aware of this, and by dint of having seen and heard, from my schooldays onwards, my most esteemed companions take offence if anyone failed to keep an appointment, refuse to overlook any disloyal behaviour, I had come in time to exhibit in my speech and actions a second nature which was stamped with pride. I was indeed considered extremely proud, because, as I had never been timid, I had been easily led into duels, the moral prestige of which, however, I diminished by making little of them, which easily persuaded other people that they were absurd; but the true nature which we trample underfoot continues nevertheless to abide within us. Thus it is that at times, if we read the latest masterpiece of a man of genius, we are delighted to find in it all those of our own reflections which we have always despised, joys and sorrows which we have repressed, a whole world of feelings scorned by us, the value of which the book in which we discover them afresh at once teaches us. I had come in time to learn from my experience of life that it was a mistake to smile a friendly smile when somebody made a fool of me, instead of feeling annoyed. But this want of self-importance and resentment, if I had so far ceased to express it as to have become almost entirely unaware that it existed in me, was nevertheless the primitive, vital element in which I was steeped. Anger and spite came to me only in a wholly different manner, in furious crises. What was more, the sense of justice was so far lacking in me as to amount to an entire want of moral sense. I was in my heart of hearts entirely won over to the side of the weaker party, and of anyone who was in trouble. I had no opinion as to the proportion in which good and evil might be blended in the relations between Morel and M. de Charlus, but the thought of the sufferings that were being prepared for M. de Charlus was intolerable to me. I would have liked to warn him, but did not know how to do it. 'The spectacle of all that laborious little world is very pleasant to an old stick like myself. I do not know them,' he went on, raising his hand with an air of reserve – so as not to appear to be boasting of his own conquests, to testify to his own purity and not to allow any suspicion to rest upon that of the students – 'but they are most civil, they often go so far as to keep a place for me, since I am a very old gentleman. Yes indeed, my dear boy, do not protest, I am past forty,' said the Baron, who was past sixty. 'It is a trifle stuffy in the hall in which Brichot lectures, but it is always interesting.' Albeit the Baron preferred to mingle with the youth of the schools, in other words to be jostled by them, sometimes, to save him a long wait in the lecture-room, Brichot took him in by his own door. Brichot might well be at home in the Sorbonne, at the moment when the janitor, loaded with chains of office, stepped out before him, and the master admired by his young pupils followed, he could not repress a certain timidity, and much as he desired to profit by that moment in which he felt himself so important to show consideration for Charlus, he was nevertheless slightly embarrassed; so that the janitor should allow him to pass, he said to him, in an artificial tone and with a preoccupied air: 'Follow me, Baron, they'll find a place for you,' then, without paying any more attention to him, to make his own entry, he advanced by himself briskly along the corridor. On either side, a double hedge of young lecturers greeted him; Brichot, anxious not to appear to be posing in the eyes of these young men to whom he knew that he was a great pontiff, bestowed on them a thousand glances, a thousand little nods of connivance, to which his desire to remain martial, thoroughly French, gave the effect of a sort of cordial encouragement by an old soldier saying: 'Damn it all, we can face the foe.' Then the applause of his pupils broke out. Brichot sometimes extracted from this attendance by M. de Charlus at his lectures an opportunity for giving pleasure, almost for returning hospitality. He would say to some parent, or to one of his middle-class friends: 'If it would interest your wife or daughter, I may tell you that the Baron de Charlus, Prince de Carency, a scion of the House of Condé, attends my lectures. It is something to remember, having seen one of the last descendants of our aristocracy who preserves the type. If they care to come, they will know him because he will be sitting next to my chair. Besides he will be alone there, a stout man, with white hair and black moustaches, wearing the military medal.' 'Oh, thank you,' said the father. And, albeit his wife had other engagements, so as not to disoblige Brichot, he made her attend the lecture, while the daughter, troubled by the heat and the crowd, nevertheless devoured eagerly with her eyes the descendant of Condé, marvelling all the same that he was not crowned with strawberry-leaves and looked just like anybody else of the present day. He meanwhile had no eyes for her, but more than one student, who did not know who he was, was amazed at his friendly glances, became self-conscious and stiff, and the Baron left the room full of dreams and melancholy. 'Forgive me if I return to the subject,' I said quickly to M. de Charlus, for I could hear Brichot returning, 'but could you let me know by wire if you should hear that Mlle Vinteuil or her friend is expected in Paris, letting me know exactly how long they will be staying and without telling anybody that I asked you.' I had almost ceased to believe that she had been expected, but I wished to guard myself thus for the future. 'Yes, I will do that for you, first of all because I owe you a great debt of gratitude. By not accepting what, long ago, I had offered you, you rendered me, to your own loss, an immense service, you left me my liberty. It is true that I have abdicated it in another fashion,' he added in a melancholy tone beneath which was visible a desire to take me into his confidence; 'that is what I continue to regard as the important fact, a whole combination of circumstances which you failed to turn to your own account, possibly because fate warned you at that precise minute not to cross my Path. For always man proposes and God disposes. Who knows whether if, on the day when we came away together from Mme de Villeparisis', you had accepted, perhaps many things that have since happened would never have occurred?' In some embarrassment, I turned the conversation, seizing hold of the name of Mme de Villeparisis, and sought to find out from him, so admirably qualified in every respect, for what reasons Mme de Villeparisis seemed to be held aloof by the aristocratic world. Not only did he not give me the solution of this little social problem, he did not even appear to me to be aware of its existence. I then realised that the position of Mme de Villeparisis, if it was in later years to appear great to posterity, and even in the Marquise's lifetime to the ignorant rich, had appeared no less great at the opposite extremity of society, that which touched Mme de Villeparisis, that of the Guermantes. She was their aunt; they saw first and foremost birth, connections by marriage, the opportunity of impressing some sister-in-law with the importance of their own family. They regarded this less from the social than from the family point of view. Now this was more brilliant in the case of

Mme de Villeparisis than I had supposed. I had been impressed when I heard that the title Villeparisis was falsely assumed. But there are other examples of great ladies who have made degrading marriages and preserved a predominant position. M. de Charlus began by informing me that Mme de Villeparisis was a niece of the famous Duchesse de —, the most celebrated member of the great aristocracy during the July Monarchy, albeit she had refused to associate with the Citizen King and his family. I had so longed to hear stories about this Duchess! And Mme de Villeparisis, the kind Mme de Villeparisis, with those cheeks that to me had been the cheeks of an ordinary woman, Mme de Villeparisis who sent me so many presents and whom I could so easily have seen every day, Mme de Villeparisis was her niece brought up by her, in her home, at the Hôtel de —. 'She asked the Duc de Doudeauville,' M. de Charlus told me, 'speaking of the three sisters, "Which of the sisters do you prefer?" And when Doudeauville said: "Madame de Villeparisis", the Duchesse de — replied "Pig!" For the Duchess was extremely *witty*,' said M. de Charlus, giving the word the importance and the special pronunciation in use among the Guermantes. That he should have thought the expression so 'witty' did not, however, surprise me, for I had on many other occasions remarked the centrifugal, objective tendency which leads men to abdicate, when they are relishing the wit of others, the severity with which they would criticise their own, and to observe, to record faithfully, what they would have scorned to create. 'But what on earth is he doing, that is my greatcoat he is bringing,' he said, on seeing that Brichot had made so long a search to no better result. 'I would have done better to go for it myself. However, you can put it on now. Are you aware that it is highly compromising, my dear boy, it is like drinking out of the same glass, I shall be able to read your thoughts. No, not like that, come, let me do it,' and as he put me into his greatcoat, he pressed it down on my shoulders, fastened it round my throat, and brushed my chin with his hand, making the apology: 'At his age, he doesn't know how to put on a coat, one has to titivate him, I have missed my vocation, Brichot, I was born to be a nurserymaid.' I wanted to go home, but as M. de Charlus had expressed his intention of going in search of Morel, Brichot detained us both. Moreover, the certainty that when I went home I should find Albertine there, a certainty as absolute as that which I had felt in the afternoon that Albertine would return home from the Trocadéro, made me at this moment as little impatient to see her as I had been then when I was sitting at the piano, after Françoise had sent me her telephone message. And it was this calm that enabled me, whenever, in the course of this conversation, I attempted to rise, to obey Brichot's injunctions who was afraid that my departure might prevent Charlus from remaining with him until the moment when Mme Verdurin was to come and fetch us. 'Come,' he said to the Baron, 'stay a little here with us, you shall give him the accolade presently,' Brichot added, fastening upon myself his almost sightless eyes to which the many operations that he had undergone had restored some degree of life, but which had not all the same the mobility necessary to the sidelong expression of malice. 'The accolade, how absurd!' cried the Baron, in a shrill and rapturous tone. 'My boy, I tell you, he imagines he is at a prize-giving, he is dreaming of his young pupils. I ask myself whether he don't sleep with them.' 'You wish to meet Mlle Vinteuil,' said Brichot, who had overheard the last words of our conversation. 'I promise to let you know if she comes, I shall hear of it from Mme Verdurin,' for he doubtless foresaw that the Baron was in peril of an immediate exclusion from the little clan. 'I see, so you think that I have less claim than yourself upon Mme Verdurin,' said M. de Charlus, 'to be informed of the coming of these terribly disreputable persons. You know that they are quite notorious. Mme Verdurin is wrong to allow them to come here, they are all very well for the fast set. They are friends with a terrible band of women. They meet in the most appalling places.' At each of these words, my suffering was increased by the addition of a fresh suffering, changing in form. 'Certainly not, I don't suppose that I have any better claim than yourself upon Mme Verdurin,' Brichot protested, punctuating his words, for he was afraid that he might have aroused the Baron's suspicions. And as he saw that I was determined to go, seeking to detain me with the bait of the promised entertainment: 'There is one thing which the Baron seems to me not to have taken into account when he speaks of the reputation of these two ladies, namely that a person's reputation may be at the same time appalling and undeserved. Thus for instance, in the more notorious group which I shall call parallel, it is certain that the errors of justice are many and that history has registered convictions for sodomy against illustrious men who were wholly innocent of the charge. The recent discovery of Michelangelo's passionate love for a woman is a fresh fact which should entitle the friend of Leo X to the benefit of a posthumous retrial. The Michelangelo case seems to me clearly indicated to excite the snobs and mobilise the Villette, when another case in which anarchism reared its head and became the fashionable sin of our worthy dilettantes, but which must not even be mentioned now for fear of stirring up quarrels, shall have run its course.' From the moment when Brichot began to speak of masculine reputations, M. de Charlus betrayed on every one of his features that special sort of impatience which one sees on the face of a medical or military expert when society people who know

nothing about the subject begin to talk nonsense about points of therapeutics or strategy. 'You know absolutely nothing about the matter,' he
said at length to Brichot. 'Quote me a single reputation that is undeserved.
Mention names. Oh yes, I know the whole story,' was his brutal retort to a
timid interruption by Brichot, 'the people who tried it once long ago out of
curiosity, or out of affection for a dead friend, and the man who, afraid he
has gone too far, if you speak to him of the beauty of a man, replies that that
is Chinese to him, that he can no more distinguish between a beautiful man
and an ugly one than between the engines of two motorcars, mechanics not
being in his line. That's all stuff and nonsense. Mind you, I don't mean to
say that a bad (or what is conventionally so called) and yet undeserved
reputation is absolutely impossible. It is so exceptional, so rare, that for
practical purposes it does not exist. At the same time I, who have a certain
curiosity in ferreting things out, have known cases which were not mythical.
Yes, in the course of my life, I have established (scientifically speaking, of
course, you mustn't take me too literally) two unjustified reputations. They
generally arise from a similarity of names, or from certain outward signs, a
profusion of rings, for instance, which persons who are not qualified to
judge imagine to be characteristic of what you were mentioning, just as
they think that a peasant never utters a sentence without adding: 'Jarnignié',
or an Englishman: 'Goddam'. Dialogue for the boulevard theatres. What
will surprise you is that the unjustified are those most firmly established in
the eyes of the public. You yourself, Brichot, who would thrust your hand
in the flames to answer for the virtue of some man or other who comes to
this house and whom the enlightened know to be a wolf in sheep's clothing,
you feel obliged to believe like every Tom, Dick and Harry in what is
said about some man in the public eye who is the incarnation of those
propensities to the common herd, when as a matter of fact, he doesn't care
twopence for that sort of thing. I say twopence, because if we were to offer
five-and-twenty louis, we should see the number of plaster saints dwindle
down to nothing. As things are, the average rate of sanctity, if you see any
sanctity in that sort of thing, is somewhere between thirty and forty per
cent.' If Brichot had transferred to the male sex the question of evil
reputations, with me it was, inversely, to the female sex that, thinking of
Albertine, I applied the Baron's words. I was appalled at his statistics, even
when I bore in mind that he was probably enlarging his figures to reach the
total that he would like to believe true, and had based them moreover upon
the reports of persons who were scandalmongers and possibly liars, and had
in any case been led astray by their own desire, which, coming in addition
to that of M. de Charlus, doubtless falsified the Baron's calculations.

'Thirty per cent!' exclaimed Brichot. 'Why, even if the proportions were reversed I should still have to multiply the guilty a hundredfold. If it is as you say, Baron, and you are not mistaken, then we must confess that you are one of those rare visionaries who discern a truth which nobody round them has ever suspected. Just as Barrés made discoveries as to parliamentary corruption, the truth of which was afterwards established, like the existence of Leverrier's planet. Mme Verdurin would prefer to cite men whom I would rather not name who detected in the Intelligence Bureau, in the General Staff, activities inspired, I am sure, by patriotic zeal, which I had never imagined. Upon freemasonry, German espionage, morphinomania, Léon Daudet builds up, day by day, a fantastic fairytale which turns out to be the barest truth. Thirty per cent!' Brichot repeated in stupefaction. It is only fair to say that M. de Charlus taxed the great majority of his contemporaries with inversion, always excepting those men with whom he himself had had relations, their case, provided that they had introduced the least trace of romance into those relations, appearing to him more complex. So it is that we see men of the world, who refuse to believe in women's honour, allow some remnants of honour only to the woman who has been their mistress, as to whom they protest sincerely and with an air of mystery: 'No, you are mistaken, she is not that sort of girl.' This unlooked-for tribute is dictated partly by their own self-respect which is flattered by the supposition that such favours have been reserved for them alone, partly by their simplicity which has easily swallowed everything that their mistress has given them to believe, partly from that sense of the complexity of life which brings it about that, as soon as we approach other people, other lives, ready-made labels and classifications appear unduly crude. 'Thirty per cent! But have a care; less fortunate than the historians whose conclusions the future will justify, Baron, if you were to present to posterity the statistics that you offer us, it might find them erroneous. Posterity judges only from documentary evidence, and will insist on being assured of your facts. But as no document would be forthcoming to authenticate this sort of collective phenomena which the few persons who are enlightened are only too ready to leave in obscurity, the best minds would be moved to indignation, and you would be regarded as nothing more than a slanderer or a lunatic. After having, in the social examination, obtained top marks and the primacy upon this earth, you would taste the sorrows of a blackball beyond the grave. That is not worth powder and shot, to quote – may God forgive me – our friend Bossuet.' 'I am not interested in history,' replied M. de Charlus, 'this life is sufficient for me, it is quite interesting enough, as poor Swann used to say.' 'What, you knew Swann, Baron, I was not aware of that. Tell me, was he that way inclined?' Brichot enquired with an air of misgiving! 'What a mind the man has! So you suppose that I only know men like that. No, I don't think so,' said Charlus, looking to the ground and trying to weigh the pros and cons. And deciding that, since he was dealing with Swann whose hostility to that sort of thing had always been notorious, a half-admission could only be harmless to him who was its object and flattering to him who allowed it to escape in an insinuation: 'I don't deny that long ago in our schooldays, once by accident,' said the Baron, as though unwillingly and as though he were thinking aloud, then recovering himself: 'But that was centuries ago, how do you expect me to remember, you are making a fool of me,' he concluded with a laugh. 'In any case, he was never what you'd call a beauty!' said Brichot who, himself hideous, thought himself good-looking and was always ready to believe that other men were ugly. 'Hold your tongue,' said the Baron, 'you don't know what you're talking about, in those days he had a peach-like complexion, and,' he added, finding a fresh note for each syllable, 'he was as beautiful as Cupid himself. Besides he was always charming. The women were madly in love with him.' 'But did you ever know his wife?' 'Why, it was through me that he came to know her. I thought her charming in her disguise one evening when she played Miss Sacripant; I was with some fellows from the club, each of us took a woman home with him, and, although all that I wanted was to go to sleep, slanderous tongues alleged, for it is terrible how malicious people are, that I went to bed with Odette. Only she took advantage of the slanders to come and worry me, and I thought I might get rid of her by introducing her to Swann. From that moment she never let me go, she couldn't spell the simplest word, it was I who wrote all her letters for her. And it was I who, afterwards, had to take her out. That, my boy, is what comes of having a good reputation, you see. Though I only half deserved it. She forced me to help her to betray him, with five, with six other men.' And the lovers whom Odette had had in succession (she had been with this man, then with that, those men not one of whose names had ever been guessed by poor Swann, blinded in turn by jealousy and by love, reckoning the chances and believing in oaths more affirmative than a contradiction which escapes from the culprit, a contradiction far more unseizable, and at the same time far more significant, of which the jealous lover might take advantage more logically than of the information which he falsely pretends to have received, in the hope of confusing his mistress), these lovers M. de Charlus began to enumerate with as absolute a certainty as if he had been repeating the list of the Kings of France. And indeed the jealous lover is, like the contemporaries of an historical event, too close, he knows nothing, and it is in the eyes of strangers that the comic aspect of adultery assumes the precision of history, and prolongs itself in lists of names which are, for that matter, unimportant and become painful only to another jealous lover, such as myself, who cannot help comparing his own case with that which he hears mentioned and asks himself whether the woman of whom he is suspicious cannot boast an equally illustrious list. But he can never know anything more, it is a sort of universal conspiracy, a 'blind man's buff' in which everyone cruelly participates, and which consists, while his mistress flits from one to another, in holding over his eyes a bandage which he is perpetually attempting to tear off without success, for everyone keeps him blindfold, poor wretch, the kind out of kindness, the wicked out of malice, the coarse-minded out of their love of coarse jokes, the well-bred out of politeness and good-breeding, and all alike respecting one of those conventions which are called principles. 'But did Swann never know that you had enjoyed her favours?' 'What an idea! If you had suggested such a thing to Charles! It's enough to make one's hair stand up on end. Why, my dear fellow, he would have killed me on the spot, he was as jealous as a tiger. Any more than I ever confessed to Odette, not that she would have minded in the least, that . . . but you must not make my tongue run away with me. And the joke of it is that it was she who fired a revolver at him, and nearly hit me. Oh! I used to have a fine time with that couple; and naturally it was I who was obliged to act as his second against d'Osmond, who never forgave me. D'Osmond had carried off Odette and Swann, to console himself, had taken as his mistress, or make-believe mistress, Odette's sister. But really you must not begin to make me tell you Swann's story, we should be here for ten years, don't you know, nobody knows more about him than I do. It was I who used to take Odette out when she did not wish to see Charles. It was all the more awkward for me as I have a quite near relative who bears the name Crécy, without of course having any manner of right to it, but still he was none too well pleased. For she went by the name of Odette de Crécy, as she very well might, being merely separated from a Crécy whose wife she still was, and quite an authentic person, a highly respectable gentleman out of whom she had drained his last farthing. But why should I have to tell you about this Crécy, I have seen you with him on the crawler, you used to have him to dinner at Balbec. He must have needed those dinners, poor fellow, he lived upon a tiny allowance that Swann made him; I am greatly afraid that, since my friend's death, that income must have stopped altogether. What I do not understand,' M. de Charlus said to me, 'is that, since you used often to go to Charles's, you did not ask me this evening to present you to the Queen of Naples. In fact I can see that you are less interested in *people* than in curiosities, and that continues to surprise me in a person who knew Swann, in whom that sort of interest was so far developed that it is impossible to say whether it was I who initiated him in these matters or he myself. It surprises me as much as if I met a person who had known Whistler and remained ignorant of what is meant by taste. By Jove, it is Morel that ought really to have been presented to her, he was passionately keen on it too, for he is the most intelligent fellow you could imagine. It is a nuisance that she has left. However, I shall effect the conjunction one of these days. It is indispensable that he should know her. The only possible obstacle would be if she were to die in the night. Well, we may hope that it will not happen.' All of a sudden Brichot, who was still suffering from the shock of the proportion 'thirty per cent' which M. de Charlus had revealed to him, Brichot who had continued all this time in the pursuit of his idea, with an abruptness which suggested that of an examining magistrate seeking to make a prisoner confess, but which was in reality the result of the Professor's desire to appear perspicacious and of the misgivings that he felt about launching so grave an accusation, spoke. 'Isn't Ski like that?' he enquired of M. de Charlus with a sombre air. To make us admire his alleged power of intuition, he had chosen Ski, telling himself that since there were only three innocent men in every ten, he ran little risk of being mistaken if he named Ski who seemed to him a trifle odd, suffered from insomnia, scented himself, in short was not entirely normal. *'Nothing of the sort!'* exclaimed the Baron with a bitter, dogmatic, exasperated irony. 'What you say is utterly false, absurd, fantastic. Ski is like that precisely to the people who know nothing about it; if he was, he would not look so like it, be it said without any intention to criticise, for he has a certain charm, indeed I find something very attractive about him.' 'But give us a few names, then,' Brichot pursued with insistence. M. de Charlus drew himself up with a forbidding air. 'Ah! my dear Sir, I, as you know, live in a world of abstraction, all that sort of thing interests me only from a transcendental point of view,' he replied with the touchy susceptibility peculiar to men of his kind, and the affectation of grandiloquence that characterised his conversation. 'To me, you understand, it is only general principles that are of any interest, I speak to you of this as I might of the law of gravitation.' But these moments of irritable reaction in which the Baron sought to conceal his true life lasted but a short time compared with the hours of continual progression in which he allowed it to be guessed, displayed it with an irritating complacency, the need to confide being stronger in him than the fear of divulging his secret. 'What I was trying to say,' he went on, 'is that for one evil reputation that is unjustified there are hundreds of good ones which are no less so. Obviously, the number of those who do not merit their reputations varies according to whether you rely upon what is said by men of their sort or by the others. And it is true that if the malevolence of the latter is limited by the extreme difficulty which they would find in believing that a vice as horrible to them as robbery or murder is being practised by men whom they know to be sensitive and sincere, the malevolence of the former is stimulated to excess by the desire to regard as – what shall I say? – accessible, men who appeal to them, upon the strength of information given them by people who have been led astray by a similar desire, in fact by the very aloofness with which they are generally regarded. I have heard a man, viewed with considerable disfavour on account of these tastes, say that he supposed that a certain man in society shared them. And his sole reason for believing it was that this other man had been polite to him! So many reasons for *optimism*,' said the Baron artlessly, 'in the computation of the number. But the true reason of the enormous difference that exists between the number calculated by the profane, and that calculated by the initiated, arises from the mystery with which the latter surround their actions, in order to conceal them from the rest, who, lacking any source of information, would be literally stupefied if they were to learn merely a quarter of the truth.' 'Then in our days, things are as they were among the Greeks,' said Brichot. 'What do you mean, among the Greeks? Do you suppose that it has not been going on ever since? Take the reign of Louis XIV, you have young Vermandois, Molière, Prince Louis of Baden, Brunswick, Charolais, Boufflers, the Great Condé, the Duc de Brissac.' 'Stop a moment, I knew about Monsieur, I knew about Brissac from Saint-Simon, Vendôme of course, and many, others as well. But that old pest Saint-Simon often refers to the Great Condé and Prince Louis of Baden and never mentions it.' 'It seems a pity, I must say, that it should fall to me to teach a Professor of the Sorbonne his history. But, my dear Master, you are as ignorant as a carp.' 'You are harsh, Baron, but just. And, wait a moment, now this will please you, I remember now a song of the period composed in macaronic verse about a certain storm which surprised the Great Condé as he was going down the Rhône in the company of his friend, the Marquis de La Moussaye. Condé says:

> Carus Amicus Mussaeus,
> Ah! Quod tempus, bonus Deus,
> > Landerirette
> Imbre sumus perituri.

And La Moussaye reassures him with:

> Securae sunt nostrae vitae
> Sumus enim Sodomitae
> Igne tantum perituri
>   Landeriri.'

'I take back what I said,' said Charlus in a shrill and mannered tone, 'you are a well of learning, you will write it down for me, won't you, I must preserve it in my family archives, since my great-great-great-grandmother was a sister of M. le Prince.' 'Yes, but, Baron, with regard to Prince Louis of Baden I can think of nothing. However, at that period, I suppose that generally speaking the art of war . . . ' 'What nonsense, Vendôme, Villars, Prince Eugène, the Prince de Conti, and if I were to tell you of all the heroes of Tonkin, Morocco, and I am thinking of men who are truly sublime, and pious, and "new generation", I should astonish you greatly. Ah! I should have something to teach the people who are making enquiries about the new generation which has rejected the futile complications of its elders, M. Bourget tells us! I have a young friend out there, who is highly spoken of, who has done great things, however, I am not going to tell tales out of school, let us return to the seventeenth century, you know that Saint-Simon says of the Maréchal d'Huxelles – one among many: "Voluptuous in Grecian debaucheries which he made no attempt to conceal, he used to get hold of young officers whom he trained to his purpose, not to mention stalwart young valets, and this openly, in the army and at Strasbourg." You have probably read Madame's *Letters*, all his men called him "Putain". She is quite outspoken about it.' 'And she was in a good position to know, with her husband.' 'Such an interesting character, Madame,' said M. de Charlus. 'One might base upon her the lyrical synthesis of "Wives of Aunties". First of all, the masculine type; generally the wife of an Auntie is a man, that is what makes it so easy for her to bear him children. Then Madame does not mention Monsieur's vices, but she does mention incessantly the same vice in other men, writing as a well-informed woman, from that tendency which makes us enjoy finding in other people's families the same defects as afflict us in our own, in order to prove to ourselves that there is nothing exceptional or degrading in them. I was saying that things have been much the same in every age. Nevertheless, our own is quite remarkable in that respect. And notwithstanding the instances that I have borrowed from the seventeenth century, if my great ancestor François C. de La Rochefoucauld were alive in these days, he might say of them with even more justification than of his own – come, Brichot, help me out: "Vices are common to every age; but if certain persons whom everyone knows had appeared in the first centuries of our era, would anyone speak today of the prostitutions of Heliogabalus?" "*Whom everyone knows*" appeals to me immensely. I see that my sagacious kinsman understood the tricks of his most illustrious contemporaries as I understand those of my own. But men of that sort are not only far more frequent today. They have also special characteristics.' I could see that M. de Charlus was about to tell us in what fashion these habits had evolved. The insistence with which M. de Charlus kept on reverting to this topic – into which, moreover, his intellect, constantly trained in the same direction, had acquired a certain penetration – was, in a complicated way, distinctly trying. He was as boring as a specialist who can see nothing outside his own subject, as irritating as a well-informed man whose vanity is flattered by the secrets which he possesses and is burning to divulge, as repellent as those people who, whenever their own defects are mentioned, spread themselves without noticing that they are giving offence, as obsessed as a maniac and as uncontrollably imprudent as a criminal. These characteristics which, at certain moments, became as obvious as those that stamp a madman or a criminal, brought me, as it happened, a certain consolation. For, making them undergo the necessary transposition in order to be able to draw from them deductions with regard to Albertine, and remembering her attitude towards Saint-Loup, and towards myself, I said to myself, painful as one of these memories and melancholy as the other was to me, I said to myself that they seemed to exclude the kind of deformity so plainly denounced, the kind of specialisation inevitably exclusive, it appeared, which was so vehemently apparent in the conversation as in the person of M. de Charlus. But he, as ill luck would have it, made haste to destroy these grounds for hope in the same way as he had furnished me with them, that is to say unconsciously. 'Yes,' he said, 'I am no longer in my teens, and I have already seen many things change round about me, I no longer recognise either society, in which the barriers are broken down, in which a mob, devoid of elegance and decency, dance the tango even in my own family, or fashions, or politics, or the arts, or religion, or anything. But I must admit that the thing which has changed most of all is what the Germans call homosexuality. Good God, in my day, apart from the men who loathed women, and those who, caring only for women, did the other thing merely with an eye to profit, the homosexuals were sound family men and never kept mistresses except to screen themselves. If I had had a daughter to give away, it is among them that I should have looked for my son-in-law if I had wished to be certain that she would not be unhappy. Alas! Things have changed entirely. Nowadays they are recruited also from the men who are the most insatiable with women. I thought I possessed a certain instinct, and that when I said to myself: 'Certainly not', I could not have been mistaken. Well, I give it up. One of my friends, who is well-known for that sort of thing, had a coachman whom my sister-in-law Oriane found for him, a lad from Combray who was something of a jack of all trades, but particularly in trading with women, and who, I would have sworn, was as hostile as possible to anything of that sort. He broke his mistress's heart by betraying her with two women whom he adored, not to mention the others, an actress and a girl from a bar. My cousin the Prince de Guermantes, who has that irritating intelligence of people who are too ready to believe anything, said to me one day: 'But why in the world does not X— have his coachman? It might be a pleasure to Théodore' (which is the coachman's name) 'and he may be annoyed at finding that his master does not make advances to him.' I could not help telling Gilbert to hold his tongue; I was overwrought both by that boasted perspicacity which, when it is exercised indiscriminately, is a want of perspicacity, and also by the silver-lined malice of my cousin who would have liked X— to risk taking the first steps so that, if the going was good, he might follow.' 'Then the Prince de Guermantes is like that, too?' asked Brichot with a blend of astonishment and dismay. 'Good God,' replied M. de Charlus, highly delighted, 'it is so notorious that I don't think I am guilty of an indiscretion if I tell you that he is. Very well, the year after this, I went to Balbec, where I heard from a sailor who used to take me out fishing occasionally, that my Théodore, whose sister, I may mention, is the maid of a friend of Mme Verdurin, Baroness Putbus, used to come down to the harbour to pick up now one sailor, now another, with the most infernal cheek, to go for a trip on the sea "with extras".' It was now my turn to enquire whether his employer, whom I had identified as the gentleman who at Balbec used to play cards all day long with his mistress, and who was the leader of the little group of four boon companions, was like the Prince of Guermantes. 'Why, of course, everyone knows about him, he makes no attempt to conceal it.' 'But he had his mistress there with him.' 'Well, and what difference does that make? How innocent these children are,' he said to me in a fatherly tone, little suspecting the grief that I extracted from his words when I thought of Albertine. 'She is charming, his mistress.' 'But then his three friends are like himself.' 'Not at all,' he cried, stopping his ears as though, in playing some instrument, I had struck a wrong note. 'Now he has gone to the other extreme. So a man has no longer the right to have friends? Ah! Youth, youth; it gets everything wrong. We shall have to begin your education over again, my boy. Well,' he went on, 'I admit that this case, and I know of many others, however open a mind I may try to keep for every form of audacity, does embarrass me. I may be very old-fashioned, but I fail to understand,' he said in the tone of an old Gallican speaking of some development of Ultramontanism, of a Liberal Royalist speaking of the *Action Française* or of a disciple of Claude Monet speaking of the Cubists. 'I do not reproach these innovators, I envy them if anything, I try to understand them, but I do not succeed. If they are so passionately fond of woman, why, and especially in this workaday world where that sort of thing is so frowned upon, where they conceal themselves from a sense of shame, have they any need of what they call "a bit of brown"? It is because it represents to them something else. What?' 'What else can a woman represent to Albertine,' I thought, and there indeed lay the cause of my anguish. 'Decidedly, Baron,' said Brichot, 'should the Board of Studies ever think of founding a Chair of Homosexuality, I shall see that your name is the first to be submitted. Or rather, no; an Institute of Psycho-physiology would suit you better. And I can see you, best of all, provided with a Chair in the Collège de France, which would enable you to devote yourself to personal researches the results of which you would deliver, like the Professor of Tamil or Sanskrit, to the handful of people who are interested in them. You would have an audience of two, with your assistant, not that I mean to cast the slightest suspicion upon our corps of janitors, whom I believe to be above suspicion.' 'You know nothing about them,' the Baron retorted in a harsh and cutting tone. 'Besides you are wrong in thinking that so few people are interested in the subject. It is just the opposite.' And without stopping to consider the incompatibility between the invariable trend of his own conversation and the reproach which he was about to heap upon other people: 'It is, on the contrary, most alarming,' said the Baron, with a scandalised and contrite air, 'people are talking about nothing else. It is a scandal, but I am not exaggerating, my dear fellow! It appears that, the day before yesterday, at the Duchesse d'Agen's, they talked about nothing else for two hours on end; you can imagine, if women have taken to discussing that sort of thing, it is a positive scandal! What is vilest of all is that they get their information,' he went on with an extraordinary fire and emphasis, 'from pests, regular harlots like young Châtellerault, who has the worst reputation in the world, who tell them stories about other men. I have been told that he said more than enough to hang me, but I don't care, I am convinced that the mud and filth flung by an individual who barely escaped being turned out of the Jockey for cheating at cards can only fall back upon himself. I am sure that if I were Jane d'Agen, I should have sufficient respect for my drawing-room not to allow such subjects to be discussed in it, nor to allow my own flesh and blood to be dragged through the mire in my house.

But there is no longer any society, any rules, any conventions, in conversation any more than in dress. Ah, my dear fellow, it is the end of the
world. Everyone has become so malicious. The prize goes to the man who
can speak most evil of his fellows. It is appalling.'

As cowardly still as I had been long ago in my boyhood at Combray when
I used to run away in order not to see my grandfather tempted with brandy
and the vain efforts of my grandmother imploring him not to drink it, I had
but one thought in my mind, which was to leave the Verdurins' house
before the execution of M. de Charlus occurred. 'I simply must go,' I said to
Brichot. 'I am coming with you,' he replied, 'but we cannot slip away,
English fashion. Come and say goodbye to Mme Verdurin,' the Professor
concluded, as he made his way to the drawing-room with the air of a man
who, in a guessing game, goes to find out whether he may 'come back'.

While we conversed, M. Verdurin, at a signal from his wife, had taken
Morel aside. Indeed, had Mme Verdurin decided, after considering the
matter in all its aspects, that it was wiser to postpone Morel's enlightenment,
she was powerless now to prevent it. There are certain desires, some of
them confined to the mouth, which, as soon as we have allowed them to
grow, insist upon being gratified, whatever the consequences may be; we are
unable to resist the temptation to kiss a bare shoulder at which we have been
gazing for too long and at which our lips strike like a serpent at a bird, to
bury our sweet tooth in a cake that has fascinated and famished it, nor can
we forego the delight of the amazement, anxiety, grief or mirth to which we
can move another person by some unexpected communication. So, in a
frenzy of melodrama, Mme Verdurin had ordered her husband to take
Morel out of the room and, at all costs, to explain matters to him. The
violinist had begun by deploring the departure of the Queen of Naples
before he had had a chance of being presented to her. M. de Charlus had
told him so often that she was the sister of the Empress Elisabeth and of
the Duchesse d'Alençon that Her Majesty had assumed an extraordinary
importance in his eyes. But the Master explained to him that it was not to
talk about the Queen of Naples that they had withdrawn from the rest, and
then went straight to the root of the matter. 'Listen,' he had concluded after
a long explanation; 'listen; if you like, we can go and ask my wife what she
thinks. I give you my word of honour, I've said nothing to her about it. We
shall see how she looks at it. My advice is perhaps not the best, but you know
how sound her judgment is; besides, she is extremely attached to yourself,
let us go and submit the case to her.' And while Mme Verdurin, awaiting
with impatience the emotions that she would presently be relishing as she
talked to the musician, and again, after he had gone, when she made her

husband give her a full report of their conversation, continued to repeat: 'But what in the world can they be doing? I do hope that my husband, in keeping him all this time, has managed to give him his cue,' M. Verdurin reappeared with Morel who seemed greatly moved. 'He would like to ask your advice,' M. Verdurin said to his wife, in the tone of a man who does not know whether his prayer will be heard. Instead of replying to M. Verdurin, it was to Morel that, in the heat of her passion, Mme Verdurin addressed herself. 'I agree entirely with my husband, I consider that you cannot tolerate this sort of thing for another instant,' she exclaimed with violence, discarding as a useless fiction her agreement with her husband that she was supposed to know nothing of what he had been saying to the violinist. 'How do you mean? Tolerate what?' stammered M. Verdurin, endeavouring to feign astonishment and seeking, with an awkwardness that was explained by his dismay, to defend his falsehood. 'I guessed what you were saying to him,' replied Mme Verdurin, undisturbed by the improbability of this explanation, and caring little what, when he recalled this scene, the violinist might think of the Mistress's veracity. 'No,' Mme Verdurin continued, 'I feel that you ought not to endure any longer this degrading promiscuity with a tainted person whom nobody will have in her house,' she went on, regardless of the fact that this was untrue and forgetting that she herself entertained him almost daily. 'You are the talk of the Conservatoire,' she added, feeling that this was the argument that carried most weight; 'another month of this life and your artistic future is shattered, whereas, without Charlus, you ought to be making at least a hundred thousand francs a year.' 'But I have never heard anyone utter a word, I am astounded, I am very grateful to you,' Morel murmured, the tears starting to his eyes. But, being obliged at once to feign astonishment and to conceal his shame, he had turned redder and was perspiring more abundantly than if he had played all Beethoven's sonatas in succession, and tears welled from his eyes which the Bonn Master would certainly not have drawn from him. 'If you have never heard anything, you are unique in that respect. He is a gentleman with a vile reputation and the most shocking stories are told about him. I know that the police are watching him and that is perhaps the best thing for him if he is not to end like all those men, murdered by hooligans,' she went on, for as she thought of Charlus the memory of Mme de Duras recurred to her, and in her frenzy of rage she sought to aggravate still further the wounds that she was inflicting on the unfortunate Charlie, and to avenge herself for those that she had received in the course of the evening. 'Anyhow, even financially, he can be of no use to you, he is completely ruined since he has become the prey of people who are blackmailing him, and who can't even make him fork out the price of the tune they call, still less can he pay you for your playing, for it is all heavily mortgaged, town house, country house, everything.' Morel was all the more ready to believe this lie since M. de Charlus liked to confide in him his relations with hooligans, a race for which the son of a valet, however debauched he may be, professes a feeling of horror as strong as his attachment to Bonapartist principles.

Already, in the cunning mind of Morel, a plan was beginning to take shape similar to what was called in the eighteenth century the reversal of alliances. Determined never to speak to M. de Charlus again, he would return on the following evening to Jupien's niece, and see that everything was made straight with her. Unfortunately for him this plan was doomed to failure, M. de Charlus having made an appointment for that very evening with Jupien, which the ex-tailor dared not fail to keep, in spite of recent events. Other events, as we shall see, having followed upon Morel's action, when Jupien in tears told his tale of woe to the Baron, the latter, no less wretched, assured him that he would adopt the forsaken girl, that she should assume one of the titles that were at his disposal, probably that of Mlle d'Oloron, that he would see that she received a thorough education, and furnish her with a rich husband. Promises which filled Jupien with joy and left his niece unmoved, for she was still in love with Morel, who, from stupidity or cynicism, used to come into the shop and tease her in Jupien's absence. 'What is the matter with you,' he would say with a laugh, 'with those black marks under your eyes? A broken heart? Gad, the years pass and people change. After all, a man is free to try on a shoe, all the more a woman, and if she doesn't fit him . . . ' He lost his temper once only, because she cried, which he considered cowardly, unworthy of her. People are not always very tolerant of the tears which they themselves have provoked.

But we have looked too far ahead, for all this did not happen until after the Verdurins' party which we have interrupted, and we must go back to the point at which we left off. 'I should never have suspected it,' Morel groaned, in answer to Mme Verdurin. 'Naturally people do not say it to your face, that does not prevent your being the talk of the Conservatoire,' Mme Verdurin went on wickedly, seeking to make it plain to Morel that it was not only M. de Charlus that was being criticised, but himself also. 'I can well believe that you know nothing about it; all the same, people are quite outspoken. Ask Ski what they were saying the other day at Chevillard's within a foot of us when you came into my box. I mean to say, people point you out. As far as I'm concerned, I don't pay the slightest attention, but what I do feel is that it makes a man supremely ridiculous and that he becomes a public laughing-stock for the rest of his life.' 'I don't know how to thank you,' said Charlie in the tone we use to a dentist who has just caused us terrible pain while we tried not to let him see it, or to a too bloodthirsty second who has forced us into a duel on account of some casual remark of which he has said: 'You can't swallow that.' 'I believe that you have plenty of character, that you are a man,' replied Mme Verdurin, 'and that you will be capable of speaking out boldly, although he tells everybody that you would never dare, that he holds you fast.' Charlie, seeking a borrowed dignity in which to cloak the tatters of his own, found in his memory something that he had read or, more probably, heard quoted, and at once proclaimed: 'I was not brought up to eat that sort of bread. This very evening I will break with M. de Charlus. The Queen of Naples has gone, hasn't she? Otherwise, before breaking with him, I should like to ask him . . . ' 'It is not necessary to break with him altogether,' said Mme Verdurin, anxious to avoid a disruption of the little nucleus. 'There is no harm in your seeing him here, among our little group, where you are appreciated, where no one speaks any evil of you. But insist upon your freedom, and do not let him drag you about among all those sheep who are friendly to your face; I wish you could have heard what they were saying behind your back. Anyhow, you need feel no regret, not only are you wiping off a stain which would have marked you for the rest of your life, from the artistic point of view, even if there had not been this scandalous presentation by Charlus, I don't mind telling you that wasting yourself like this in this sham society will make people suppose that you aren't serious, give you an amateur reputation, as a little drawing-room performer, which is a terrible thing at your age. I can understand that to all those fine ladies it is highly convenient to be able to return their friends' hospitality by making you come and play for nothing, but it is your future as an artist that would foot the bill. I don't say that you shouldn't go to one or two of them. You were speaking of the Queen of Naples – who has left, for she had to go on to another party – now she is a splendid woman, and I don't mind saying that I think she has a poor opinion of Charlus and came here chiefly to please me. Yes, yes, I know she was longing to meet us, M. Verdurin and myself. That is a house in which you might play. And then I may tell you that if I take you – because the artists all know me, you understand, they have always been most obliging to me, and regard me almost as one of themselves, as their Mistress – that is a very different matter. But whatever you do, you must never go near Mme de Duras! Don't go and make a stupid blunder like that! I know several artists who have come here and told me all about her. They know they can trust me,' she said, in the sweet and simple tone which she knew how to adopt in an instant, imparting an appropriate air of modesty to her features, an appropriate charm to her eyes, 'they come here, just like that, to tell me all their little troubles; the ones who are said to be most silent, go on chatting to me sometimes for hours on end and I can't tell you how interesting they are. Poor Chabrier used always to say: "There's nobody like Mme Verdurin for getting them to talk." Very well, don't you know, all of them, without one exception, I have seen them in tears because they had gone to play for Mme de Duras. It is not only the way she enjoys making her servants humiliate them, they could never get an engagement anywhere else again. The agents would say: "Oh yes, the fellow who plays at Mme de Duras's." That settled it. There is nothing like that for ruining a man's future. You know what society people are like, it's not taken seriously, you may have all the talent in the world, it's a dreadful thing to have to say, but one Mme de Duras is enough to give you the reputation of an amateur. And among artists, don't you know, well, you can ask yourself whether I know them, when I have been moving among them for forty years, launching them, taking an interest in them; very well, when they say that somebody is an amateur, that finishes it. And people were beginning to say it of you. Indeed, at times I have been obliged to take up the cudgels, to assure them that you would not play in some absurd drawing-room! Do you know what the answer was: "But he will be forced to go, Charlus won't even consult him, he never asks him for his opinion." Somebody thought he would pay him a compliment and said: "We greatly admire your friend Morel." Can you guess what answer he made, with that insolent air which you know? "But what do you mean by calling him my friend, we are not of the same class, say rather that he is my creature, my protégé." ' At this moment there stirred beneath the convex brows of the musical deity the one thing that certain people cannot keep to themselves, a saying which it is not merely abject but imprudent to repeat. But the need to repeat it is stronger than honour, than prudence. It was to this need that, after a few convulsive movements of her spherical and sorrowful brows, the Mistress succumbed: 'Someone actually told my husband that he had said "my servant", but for that I cannot vouch,' she added. It was a similar need that had compelled M. de Charlus, shortly after he had sworn to Morel that nobody should ever know the story of his birth, to say to Mme Verdurin: 'His father was a flunkey.' A similar need again, now that the story had been started, would make it circulate from one person to another, each of whom would confide it under the seal of a secrecy which would be promised and not kept by the hearer, as by the informant himself. These stories would end, as in the game called hunt-the-thimble, by being traced back to Mme Verdurin, bringing down upon her the wrath of the person concerned, who would at last have learned the truth. She knew this, but could not repress the words that were burning her tongue. Anyhow, the word 'servant' was bound to annoy Morel. She said 'servant' nevertheless, and if she added that she could not vouch for the word, this was so as at once to appear certain of the rest, thanks to this hint of uncertainty, and to show her impartiality. This impartiality that she showed, she herself found so touching that she began to speak affectionately to Charlie: 'For, don't you see,' she went on, 'I am not blaming him, he is dragging you down into his abyss, it is true, but it is not his fault, since he wallows in it himself, since he wallows in it,' she repeated in a louder tone, having been struck by the aptness of the image which had taken shape so quickly that her attention only now overtook it and was trying to give it prominence. 'No, the fault that I do find with him,' she said in a melting tone – like a woman drunken with her own success – 'is a want of delicacy towards yourself. There are certain things which one does not say in public. Well, this evening, he was betting that he would make you blush with joy, by telling you (stuff and nonsense, of course, for his recommendation would be enough to prevent your getting it) that you were to have the Cross of the Legion of Honour. Even that I could overlook, although I have never quite liked,' she went on with a delicate, dignified air, 'hearing a person make a fool of his friends, but, don't you know, there are certain little things that one does resent. Such as when he told us, with screams of laughter, that if you want the Cross it's to please your uncle and that your uncle was a footman.' 'He told you that!' cried Charlie, believing, on the strength of this adroitly interpolated quotation, in the truth of everything that Mme Verdurin had said! Mme Verdurin was overwhelmed with the joy of an old mistress who, just as her young lover was on the point of deserting her, has succeeded in breaking off his marriage, and it is possible that she had not calculated her lie, that she was not even consciously lying. A sort of sentimental logic, something perhaps more elementary still, a sort of nervous reflex urging her, in order to brighten her life and preserve her happiness, to stir up trouble in the little clan, may have brought impulsively to her lips, without giving her time to check their veracity, these assertions diabolically effective if not rigorously exact. 'If he had only repeated it to us, it wouldn't matter,' the Mistress went on, 'we know better than to listen to what he says, besides, what does a man's origin matter, you have your own value, you are what you make yourself, but that he should use it to make Mme de Portefin laugh' (Mme Verdurin named this lady on purpose because she knew that Charlie admired her) 'that is what vexes us: my husband said to me when he heard him: "I would sooner he had struck me in the face." For he is as fond of you as I am, don't you know, is Gustave' (from this we learn that M. Verdurin's name was

Gustave). 'He is really very sensitive.' 'But I never told you I was fond of him,' muttered M. Verdurin, acting the kind-hearted curmudgeon. 'It is Charlus that is fond of him.' 'Oh, no! Now I realise the difference, I was betrayed by a scoundrel and you, you are good,' Charlie exclaimed in all sincerity. 'No, no,' murmured Mme Verdurin, seeking to retain her victory, for she felt that her Wednesdays were safe, but not to abuse it: 'scoundrel is too strong; he does harm, a great deal of harm, unconsciously; you know that tale about the Legion of Honour was the affair of a moment. And it would be painful to me to repeat all that he said about your family,' said Mme Verdurin, who would have been greatly embarrassed had she been asked to do so. 'Oh, even if it only took a moment, it proves that he is a traitor,' cried Morel. It was at this moment that we returned to the drawing-room. 'Ah!' exclaimed M. de Charlus when he saw that Morel was in the room, advancing upon him with the alacrity of the man who has skilfully organised a whole evening's entertainment with a view to an assignation with a woman, and in his excitement never imagines that he has with his own hands set the snare in which he will presently be caught and publicly thrashed by bravoes stationed in readiness by her husband. 'Well, after all it is none too soon; are you satisfied, young glory, and presently young knight of the Legion of Honour? For very soon you will be able to sport your Cross,' M. de Charlus said to Morel with a tender and triumphant air, but by the very mention of the decoration endorsed Mme Verdurin's lies, which appeared to Morel to be indisputable truth. 'Leave me alone, I forbid you to come near me,' Morel shouted at the Baron. 'You know what I mean, all right, I'm not the first young man you've tried to corrupt!' My sole consolation lay in the thought that I was about to see Morel and the Verdurins pulverised by M. de Charlus. For a thousand times less an offence I had been visited with his furious rage, no one was safe from it, a king would not have intimidated him. Instead of which, an extraordinary thing happened. One saw M. de Charlus dumb, stupefied, measuring the depths of his misery without understanding its cause, finding not a word to utter, raising his eyes to stare at each of the company in turn, with a questioning, outraged, suppliant air, which seemed to be asking them not so much what had happened as what answer he ought to make. And yet M. de Charlus possessed all the resources, not merely of eloquence but of audacity, when, seized by a rage which had long been simmering against someone, he reduced him to desperation, with the most outrageous speeches, in front of a scandalised society which had never imagined that anyone could go so far. M. de Charlus, on these occasions, burned, convulsed with a sort of epilepsy, which left everyone trembling. But in these instances he had the initiative, he launched the attack, he said whatever came into his mind (just as Bloch was able to make fun of Jews and blushed if the word Jew was uttered in his hearing). Perhaps what struck him speechless was – when he saw that M. and Mme Verdurin turned their eyes from him and that no one was coming to his rescue – his anguish at the moment and, still more, his dread of greater anguish to come; or else that, not having lost his temper in advance, in imagination, and forged his thunderbolt, not having his rage ready as a weapon in his hand, he had been seized and dealt a mortal blow at the moment when he was unarmed (for, sensitive, neurotic, hysterical, his impulses were genuine, but his courage was a sham; indeed, as I had always thought, and this was what made me like him, his malice was a sham also: the people whom he hated, he hated because he thought that they looked down upon him; had they been civil to him, instead of flying into a furious rage with them, he would have taken them to his bosom, and he did not show the normal reactions of a man of honour who has been insulted); or else that, in a sphere which was not his own, he felt himself less at his ease and less courageous than he would have been in the Faubourg. The fact remains that, in this drawing-room which he despised, this great nobleman (in whom his sense of superiority to the middle classes was no less essentially inherent than it had been in any of his ancestors who had stood in the dock before the Revolutionary Tribunal) could do nothing, in a paralysis of all his members, including his tongue, but cast in every direction glances of terror, outraged by the violence that had been done to him, no less suppliant than questioning. In a situation so cruelly unforeseen, this great talker could do no more than stammer: 'What does it all mean, what has happened?' His question was not even heard. And the eternal pantomime of panic terror has so little altered, that this elderly gentleman, to whom a disagreeable incident had just occurred in a Parisian drawing-room, unconsciously repeated the various formal attitudes in which the Greek sculptors of the earliest times symbolised the terror of nymphs pursued by the Great Pan.

The ambassador who has been recalled, the under-secretary placed suddenly on the retired list, the man about town whom people began to cut, the lover who has been shown the door examine sometimes for months on end the event that has shattered their hopes; they turn it over and over like a projectile fired at them they know not whence or by whom, almost as though it were a meteorite. They would fain know the elements that compose this strange engine which has burst upon them, learn what hostilities may be detected in them. Chemists have at least the power of analysis; sick men suffering from a malady the origin of which they do not know can send for the doctor; criminal mysteries are more or less solved by the examining magistrate. But when it comes to the disconcerting actions of our fellow-men, we rarely discover their motives. Thus M. de Charlus, to anticipate the days that followed this party to which we shall presently return, could see in Charlie's attitude one thing alone that was self-evident. Charlie, who had often threatened the Baron that he would tell people of the passion that he inspired in him, must have seized the opportunity to do so when he considered that he had now sufficiently 'arrived' to be able to fly unaided. And he must, out of sheer ingratitude, have told Mme Verdurin everything. But how had she allowed herself to be taken in (for the Baron, having made up his mind to deny the story, had already persuaded himself that the sentiments for which he was blamed were imaginary)? Some friends of Mme Verdurin, who themselves perhaps felt a passion for Charlie, must have prepared the ground. Accordingly, M. de Charlus during the next few days wrote terrible letters to a number of the faithful, who were entirely innocent and concluded that he must be mad; then he went to Mme Verdurin with a long and moving tale, which had not at all the effect that he desired. For in the first place Mme Verdurin repeated to the Baron: 'All you need do is not to bother about him, treat him with scorn, he is a mere boy.' Now the Baron longed only for a reconciliation. In the second place, to bring this about, by depriving Charlie of everything of which he had felt himself assured, he asked Mme Verdurin not to invite him again; a request which she met with a refusal that brought upon her angry and sarcastic letters from M. de Charlus. Flitting from one supposition to another, the Baron never arrived at the truth, which was that the blow had not come from Morel. It is true that he might have learned this by asking him for a few minutes' conversation. But he felt that this would injure his dignity and would be against the interests of his love. He had been insulted, he awaited an explanation. There is, for that matter, almost invariably, attached to the idea of a conversation which might clear up a misunderstanding, another idea which, whatever the reason, prevents us from agreeing to that conversation. The man who is abased and has shown his weakness on a score of occasions, will furnish proofs of pride on the twenty-first, the only occasion on which it would serve him not to adopt a headstrong and arrogant attitude but to dispel an error which will take root in his adversary failing a contradiction. As for the social side of the incident, the rumour spread abroad that M. de Charlus had been turned out of the Verdurins' house at the moment when he was attempting to rape a young musician. The effect of this rumour was that nobody was surprised when M. de Charlus did not appear again at the Verdurins', and whenever he happened by chance to meet, anywhere else, one of the faithful whom he had suspected and insulted, as this person had a grudge against the Baron who himself abstained from greeting him, people were not surprised, realising that no member of the little clan would ever wish to speak to the Baron again.

While M. de Charlus, rendered speechless by Morel's words and by the attitude of the Mistress, stood there in the pose of the nymph a prey to Panic terror, M. and Mme Verdurin had retired to the outer drawing-room, as a sign of diplomatic rupture, leaving M. de Charlus by himself, while on the platform Morel was putting his violin in its case. 'Now you must tell us exactly what happened,' Mme Verdurin appealed avidly to her husband. 'I don't know what you can have said to him, he looked quite upset,' said Ski, 'there are tears in his eyes.' Pretending not to have understood: 'I'm sure, nothing that I said could make any difference to him,' said Mme Verdurin, employing one of those stratagems which do not deceive everybody, so as to force the sculptor to repeat that Charlie was in tears, tears which filled the Mistress with too much pride for her to be willing to run the risk that one or other of the faithful, who might not have heard what was said, remained in ignorance of them. 'No, it has made a difference, for I saw big tears glistening in his eyes,' said the sculptor in a low tone with a smile of malicious connivance, and a sidelong glance to make sure that Morel was still on the platform and could not overhear the conversation. But there was somebody who did overhear, and whose presence, as soon as it was observed, was to restore to Morel one of the hopes that he had forfeited. This was the Queen of Naples, who, having left her fan behind, had thought it more polite, on coming away from another party to which she had gone on, to call for it in person. She had entered the room quite quietly, as though she were ashamed of herself, prepared to make apologies for her presence, and to pay a little call upon her hostess now that all the other guests had gone. But no one had heard her come in, in the heat of the incident the meaning of which she had at once gathered, and which set her ablaze with indignation. 'Ski says that he had tears in his eyes, did you notice that? I did not see any tears. Ah, yes, I remember now,' she corrected herself, in the fear that her denial might not be believed. 'As for Charlus, he's not far off them, he ought to take a chair, he's tottering on his feet, he'll be on the floor in another minute,' she said with a pitiless laugh. At that moment Morel hastened towards her: 'Isn't that lady the Queen of Naples?' he asked (albeit he knew quite well that she was), pointing to Her Majesty who was making her way towards Charlus. 'After what has just happened, I can no longer, I'm afraid, ask the Baron to present me.' 'Wait, I shall take you to her myself,' said Mme Verdurin, and, followed by a few of the faithful, but not by myself and Brichot who made haste to go and call for our hats and coats, she advanced

upon the Queen who was talking to M. de Charlus. He had imagined that
the realisation of his great desire that Morel should be presented to the
Queen of Naples could be prevented only by the improbable demise of that
lady. But we picture the future as a reflection of the present projected into
empty space, whereas it is the result, often almost immediate, of causes
which for the most part escape our notice. Not an hour had passed, and now
M. de Charlus would have given everything he possessed in order that
Morel should not be presented to the Queen. Mme Verdurin made the
Queen a curtsey. Seeing that the other appeared not to recognise her: 'I am
Mme Verdurin. Your Majesty does not remember me.' 'Quite well,' said
the Queen as she continued so naturally to converse with M. de Charlus and
with an air of such complete indifference that Mme Verdurin doubted
whether it was to herself that this 'Quite well' had been addressed, uttered
with a marvellously detached intonation, which wrung from M. de Charlus,
despite his broken heart, a smile of expert and delighted appreciation of
the art of impertinence. Morel, who had watched from the distance the
preparations for his presentation, now approached. The Queen offered her
arm to M. de Charlus. With him, too, she was vexed, but only because he
did not make a more energetic stand against vile detractors. She was
crimson with shame for him whom the Verdurins dared to treat in this
fashion. The entirely simple civility which she had shown them a few hours
earlier, and the arrogant pride with which she now stood up to face them,
had their source in the same region of her heart. The Queen, as a woman
full of good nature, regarded good nature first and foremost in the form of
an unshakable attachment to the people whom she liked, to her own family,
to all the Princes of her race, among whom was M. de Charlus, and, after
them, to all the people of the middle classes or of the humblest populace
who knew how to respect those whom she liked and felt well-disposed
towards them. It was as to a woman endowed with these sound instincts that
she had shown kindness to Mme Verdurin. And, no doubt, this is a narrow
conception, somewhat Tory, and increasingly obsolete, of good nature. But
this does not mean that her good nature was any less genuine or ardent. The
ancients were no less strongly attached to the group of humanity to which
they devoted themselves because it did not exceed the limits of their city,
nor are the men of today to their country than will be those who in the
future love the United States of the World. In my own immediate
surroundings, I have had an example of this in my mother whom Mme de
Cambremer and Mme de Guermantes could never persuade to take part in
any philanthropic undertaking, to join any patriotic workroom, to sell or to
be a patroness at any bazaar. I do not go so far as to say that she was right in

doing good only when her heart had first spoken, and in reserving for her own family, for her servants, for the unfortunate whom chance brought in her way, her treasures of love and generosity, but I do know that these, like those of my grandmother, were unbounded and exceeded by far anything that Mme de Guermantes or Mme de Cambremer ever could have done or did. The case of the Queen of Naples was altogether different, but even here it must be admitted that her conception of deserving people was not at all that set forth in those novels of Dostoevsky which Albertine had taken from my shelves and devoured, that is to say in the guise of wheedling parasites, thieves, drunkards, at one moment stupid, at another insolent, debauchees, at a pinch murderers. Extremes, however, meet, since the nobleman, the brother, the outraged kinsman whom the Queen sought to defend, was M. de Charlus, that is to say, notwithstanding his birth and all the family ties that bound him to the Queen, a man whose virtue was hedged round by many vices. 'You do not look at all well, my dear cousin,' she said to M. de Charlus. 'Lean upon my arm. Be sure that it will still support you. It is firm enough for that.' Then, raising her eyes proudly to face her adversaries (at that moment, Ski told me, there were in front of her Mme Verdurin and Morel), 'You know that, in the past, at Gaeta, it held the mob in defiance. It will be able to serve you as a rampart.' And it was thus, taking the Baron on her arm and without having allowed Morel to be presented to her, that the splendid sister of the Empress Elisabeth left the house. It might be supposed, in view of M. de Charlus's terrible nature, the persecutions with which he terrorised even his own family, that he would, after the events of this evening, let loose his fury and practise reprisals upon the Verdurins. We have seen why nothing of this sort occurred at first. Then the Baron, having caught cold shortly afterwards, and contracted the septic pneumonia which was very rife that winter, was for long regarded by his doctors, and regarded himself, as being at the point of death, and lay for many months suspended between it and life. Was there simply a physical change, and the substitution of a different malady for the neurosis that had previously made him lose all control of himself in his outbursts of rage? For it is too obvious to suppose that, having never taken the Verdurins seriously, from the social point of view, but having come at last to understand the part that they had played, he was unable to feel the resentment that he would have felt for any of his equals; too obvious also to remember that neurotics, irritated on the slightest provocation by imaginary and inoffensive enemies, become on the contrary inoffensive as soon as anyone takes the offensive against them, and that we can calm them more easily by flinging cold water in their faces than by attempting to prove to them the inanity of their grievances. It is probably not in a physical change that we ought to seek the explanation of this absence of rancour, but far more in the malady itself. It exhausted the Baron so completely that he had little leisure left in which to think about the Verdurins. He was almost dead. We mentioned offensives; even those which have only a posthumous effect require, if we are to 'stage' them properly, the sacrifice of a part of our strength. M. de Charlus had too little strength left for the activity of a preparation. We hear often of mortal enemies who open their eyes to gaze upon one another in the hour of death and close them again, made happy. This must be a rare occurrence, except when death surprises us in the midst of life. It is, on the contrary, at the moment when we have nothing left to lose, that we are not bothered by the risks which, when full of life, we would lightly have undertaken. The spirit of vengeance forms part of life, it abandons us as a rule – notwithstanding certain exceptions which, occurring in the heart of the same person, are, as we shall see, human contradictions – on the threshold of death. After having thought for a moment about the Verdurins, M. de Charlus felt that he was too weak, turned his face to the wall, and ceased to think about anything. If he often lay silent like this, it was not that he had lost his eloquence. It still flowed from its source, but it had changed. Detached from the violence which it had so often adorned, it was no more now than an almost mystic eloquence decorated with words of meekness, words from the Gospel, an apparent resignation to death. He talked especially on the days when he thought that he would live. A relapse made him silent. This Christian meekness into which his splendid violence was transposed (as is in *Esther* the so different genius of *Andromaque*) provoked the admiration of those who came to his bedside. It would have provoked that of the Verdurins themselves, who could not have helped adoring a man whom his weakness had made them hate. It is true that thoughts which were Christian only in appearance rose to the surface. He implored the Archangel Gabriel to appear and announce to him, as to the Prophet, at what time the Messiah would come to him. And, breaking off with a sweet and sorrowful smile, he would add: 'But the Archangel must not ask me, as he asked Daniel, to have patience for "seven weeks, and threescore and two weeks", for I should be dead before then.' The person whom he awaited thus was Morel. And so he asked the Archangel Raphael to bring him to him, as he had brought the young Tobias. And, introducing more human methods (like sick Popes who, while ordering masses to be said, do not neglect to send for their doctors), he insinuated to his visitors that if Brichot were to bring him without delay his young Tobias, perhaps the Archangel Raphael would consent to restore Brichot's sight, as he had done to the father of Tobias, or as had happened in the sheep-pool of Bethesda. But, notwithstanding these human lapses, the moral purity of M. de Charlus's conversation had none the less become alarming. Vanity, slander, the insanity of malice and pride, had alike disappeared. Morally M. de Charlus had been raised far above the level at which he had lived in the past. But this moral perfection, as to the reality of which his oratorical art was for that matter capable of deceiving more than one of his compassionate audience, this perfection vanished with the malady which had laboured on its behalf. M. de Charlus returned along the downward slope with a rapidity which, as we shall see, continued steadily to increase. But the Verdurins' attitude towards him was by that time no more than a somewhat distant memory which more immediate outbursts prevented from reviving.

To turn back to the Verdurins' party, when the host and hostess were by themselves, M. Verdurin said to his wife: 'You know where Cottard has gone? He is with Saniette: he has been speculating to put himself straight and has gone smash. When he got home just now after leaving us, and learned that he hadn't a penny in the world and nearly a million francs of debts, Saniette had a stroke.' 'But then, why did he gamble, it's idiotic, he was the last person in the world to succeed at that game. Cleverer men than he get plucked at it, and he was born to let himself be swindled by every Tom, Dick and Harry.' 'Why, of course, we have always known that he was an idiot,' said M. Verdurin. 'Anyhow, this is the result. Here you have a man who will be turned out of house and home tomorrow by his landlord, who is going to find himself utterly penniless; his family don't like him, Forcheville is the last man in the world to do anything for him. And so it occurred to me, I don't wish to do anything that doesn't meet with your approval, but we might perhaps be able to scrape up a small income for him so that he shan't be too conscious of his ruin, so that he can keep a roof over his head.' 'I entirely agree with you, it is very good of you to have thought of it. But you say 'a roof'; the imbecile has kept on an apartment beyond his means, he can't remain in it, we shall have to find him a couple of rooms somewhere. I understand that at the present moment he is still paying six or seven thousand francs for his apartment.' 'Six thousand, five hundred. But he is greatly attached to his home. In short, he has had his first stroke, he can scarcely live more than two or three years. Suppose we were to allow him ten thousand francs for three years. It seems to me that we should be able to afford that. We might for instance this year, instead of taking la Raspelière again, get hold of something on a simpler scale. With our income, it seems to me that to sacrifice ten thousand francs a year for three years is not out of the question.' 'Very well, there's only the nuisance that people will get to know about it, we shall be expected to do it again for others.' 'Believe me, I have thought about that. I shall do it only upon the express condition that nobody knows anything about it. Thank you, I have no desire that we should become the benefactors of the human race. No philanthropy! What we might do is to tell him that the money has been left to him by Princess Sherbatov.' 'But will he believe it? She consulted Cottard about her will.' 'If the worse comes to the worst, we might take Cottard into our confidence, he is used to professional secrecy, he makes an enormous amount of money, he won't be like one of those busybodies one is obliged to hush up. He may even be willing to say, perhaps, that it was himself that the Princess appointed as her agent. In that way we shouldn't even appear. That would avoid all the nuisance of scenes, and gratitude, and speeches.' M. Verdurin added an expression which made quite plain the kind of touching scenes and speeches which they were anxious to avoid. But it cannot have been reported to me correctly, for it was not a French expression, but one of those terms that are to be found in certain families to denote certain things, annoying things especially, probably because people wish to indicate them in the hearing of the persons concerned without being understood! An expression of this sort is generally a survival from an earlier condition of the family. In a Jewish family, for instance, it will be a ritual term diverted from its true meaning, and perhaps the only Hebrew word with which the family, now thoroughly French, is still acquainted. In a family that is strongly provincial, it will be a term in the local dialect, albeit the family no longer speaks or even understands that dialect. In a family that has come from South America and no longer speaks anything but French, it will be a Spanish word. And, in the next generation, the word will no longer exist save as a childish memory. They may remember quite well that their parents at table used to allude to the servants who were waiting, without being understood by them, by employing some such word, but the children cannot tell exactly what the word meant, whether it was Spanish, Hebrew, German, dialect, if indeed it ever belonged to any language and was not a proper name or a word entirely forged. The uncertainty can be cleared up only if they have a great-uncle, a cousin still surviving who must have used the same expression. As I never knew any relative of the Verdurins, I have never been able to reconstruct the word. All I know is that it certainly drew a smile from Mme Verdurin, for the use of this language less general, more personal, more secret, than their everyday speech inspires in those who use it among themselves a sense of self-importance which is always accompanied by a certain satisfaction. After this moment of mirth: 'But if Cottard talks,' Mme Verdurin objected. 'He will not talk.' He did mention it, to myself at least, for it was from him that

I learned of this incident a few years later, actually at the funeral of Saniette. I was sorry that I had not known of it earlier. For one thing the knowledge would have brought me more rapidly to the idea that we ought never to feel resentment towards other people, ought never to judge them by some memory of an unkind action, for we do not know all the good that, at other moments, their hearts may have sincerely desired and realised; no doubt the evil form which we have established once and for all will recur, but the heart is far more rich than that, has many other forms that will recur, also, to these people, whose kindness we refuse to admit because of the occasion on which they behaved badly. Furthermore, this revelation by Cottard must inevitably have had an effect upon me, because by altering my opinion of the Verdurins, this revelation, had it been made to me earlier, would have dispelled the suspicions that I had formed as to the part that the Verdurins might be playing between Albertine and myself, would have dispelled them, wrongly perhaps as it happened, for if M. Verdurin – whom I supposed, with increasing certainty, to be the most malicious man alive – had certain virtues, he was nevertheless tormenting to the point of the most savage persecution, and so jealous of his domination over the little clan as not to shrink from the basest falsehoods, from the fomentation of the most unjustified hatreds, in order to sever any ties between the faithful which had not as their sole object the strengthening of the little group. He was a man capable of disinterested action, of unostentatious generosity, that does not necessarily mean a man of feeling, nor a pleasant man, nor a scrupulous, nor a truthful, nor always a good man. A partial goodness, in which there persisted, perhaps, a trace of the family whom my great-aunt had known, existed probably in him in view of this action before I discovered it, as America or the North Pole existed before Columbus or Peary. Nevertheless, at the moment of my discovery, M. Verdurin's nature offered me a new and unimagined aspect; and so I am brought up against the difficulty of presenting a permanent image as well of a character as of societies and passions. For it changes no less than they, and if we seek to portray what is relatively unchanging in it, we see it present in succession different aspects (implying that it cannot remain still but keeps moving) to the disconcerted artist.

CHAPTER THREE

Flight of Albertine

Seeing how late it was, and fearing that Albertine might be growing impatient, I asked Brichot, as we left the Verdurins' party, to be so kind as to drop me at my door. My carriage would then take him home. He congratulated me upon going straight home like this (unaware that a girl was waiting for me in the house), and upon ending so early, and so wisely, an evening of which, on the contrary, all that I had done was to postpone the actual beginning. Then he spoke to me about M. de Charlus. The latter would doubtless have been stupefied had he heard the Professor, who was so kind to him, the Professor who always assured him: 'I never repeat anything', speaking of him and of his life without the slightest reserve. And Brichot's indignant amazement would perhaps have been no less sincere if M. de Charlus had said to him: 'I am told that you have been speaking evil of me.' Brichot did indeed feel an affection for M. de Charlus and, if he had had to call to mind some conversation that had turned upon him, would have been far more likely to remember the friendly feeling that he had shown for the Baron, while he said the same things about him that everyone was saying, than to remember the things that he had said. He would not have thought that he was lying if he had said: 'I who speak of you in so friendly a spirit', since he did feel a friendly spirit while he was speaking of M. de Charlus. The Baron had above all for Brichot the charm which the Professor demanded before everything else in his social existence, and which was that of furnishing real examples of what he had long supposed to be an invention of the poets. Brichot, who had often expounded the second Eclogue of Virgil without really knowing whether its fiction had any basis in reality, found later on in conversing with Charlus some of the pleasure which he knew that his masters, M. Mérimée and M. Renan, his colleague M. Maspéro had felt, when travelling in Spain, Palestine, and Egypt, upon recognising in the scenery and the contemporary peoples of Spain, Palestine and Egypt, the setting and the invariable actors of the ancient scenes which they themselves had expounded in their books. 'Be it said without offence to that knight of noble lineage,' Brichot declared to me in the carriage that was taking us home, 'he is simply prodigious when he illustrates his satanic catechism with a distinctly Bedlamite vigour and the persistence, I was going to say the candour, of Spanish whitewash and of a returned émigré. I can assure you, if I dare express myself like Mgr d'Hulst, I am by no means bored upon the days when I receive a visit from that feudal lord who, seeking to defend Adonis against our age of miscreants, has followed the instincts of his race, and, in all sodomist innocence, has gone crusading.' I listened to Brichot, and I was not alone with him. As, for that matter, I had never ceased to feel since I left home that evening, I felt myself, in however obscure a fashion, tied fast to the girl who was at that moment in her room. Even when I was talking to someone or other at the Verdurins', I had felt, confusedly, that she was by my side, I had that vague impression of her that we have of our own limbs, and if I happened to think of her it was as we think, with disgust at being bound to it in complete subjection, of our own body. 'And what a fund of scandal,' Brichot went on, 'sufficient to supply all the appendices of the *Causeries du Lundi*, is the conversation of that apostle. Imagine that I have learned from him that the ethical treatise which I had always admired as the most splendid moral composition of our age was inspired in our venerable colleague X by a young telegraph messenger. Let us not hesitate to admit that my eminent friend omitted to give us the name of this ephebe in the course of his demonstrations. He has shown in so doing more human respect, or, if you prefer, less gratitude than Phidias who inscribed the name of the athlete whom he loved upon the ring of his Olympian Zeus. The Baron had not heard that story. Needless to say, it appealed to his orthodox mind. You can readily imagine that whenever I have to discuss with my colleague a candidate's thesis, I shall find in his dialectic, which for that matter is extremely subtle, the additional savour which spicy revelations added, for Sainte-Beuve, to the insufficiently confidential writings of Chateaubriand. From our colleague, who is a goldmine of wisdom but whose gold is not legal tender, the telegraph-boy passed into the hands of the Baron, "all perfectly proper, of course", (you ought to hear his voice when he says it). And as this Satan is the most obliging of men, he has found his protégé a post in the Colonies, from which the young man, who has a sense of gratitude, sends him from time to time the most excellent fruit. The Baron offers these to his distinguished friends; some of the young man's pineapples appeared quite recently on the table at Quai Conti, drawing from Mme Verdurin, who at that moment put no malice into her words: "You must have an uncle or a nephew in America, M. de Charlus, to get pineapples like these!" I admit that if I had known the truth then I should have eaten them with a certain gaiety, repeating to myself *in petto* the opening lines of an Ode of Horace which Diderot loved to recall. In fact, like my colleague Boissier, strolling from the Palatine to Tibur, I derive from the Baron's conversation a singularly more vivid and more savoury idea of the writers of the Augustan age. Let us not even speak of those of the Decadence, nor let us hark back to the Greeks, although I have said to that excellent Baron that in his company I felt like Plato in the house of Aspasia. To tell the truth, I had considerably enlarged the scale of the two characters and, as La Fontaine says, my example was taken "from lesser animals". However it be, you do not, I imagine, suppose that the Baron took offence. Never have I seen him so ingenuously delighted. A childish excitement made him depart from his aristocratic phlegm. "What flatterers all these Sorbonnards are!" he exclaimed with rapture. "To think that I should have had to wait until my age before being compared to Aspasia! An old image like me! Oh, my youth!" I should like you to have seen him as he said that, outrageously powdered as he always is, and, at his age, scented like a young coxcomb. All the same, beneath his genealogical obsessions, the best fellow in the world. For all these reasons, I should be distressed were this evening's rupture to prove final. What did surprise me was the way in which the young man turned upon him. His manner towards the Baron has been, for some time past, that of a violent partisan, of a feudal vassal, which scarcely betokened such an insurrection. I hope that, in any event, even if (*Di omen avertant*) the Baron were never to return to Quai Conti, this schism is not going to involve myself. Each of us derives too much advantage from the exchange that we make of my feeble stock of learning with his experience.' (We shall see that if M. de Charlus, after having hoped in vain that Brichot would bring Morel back to him, showed no violent rancour against him, at any rate his affection for the Professor vanished so completely as to allow him to judge him without any indulgence.) 'And I swear to you that the exchange is so much in my favour that when the Baron yields up to me what his life has taught him, I am unable to endorse the opinion of Sylvestre Bonnard that a library is still the best place in which to ponder the dream of life.'

We had now reached my door. I got out of the carriage to give the driver Brichot's address. From the pavement, I could see the window of Albertine's room, that window, formerly quite black, at night, when she was not staying in the house, which the electric light inside, dissected by the slats of the shutters, striped from top to bottom with parallel bars of gold. This magic scroll, clear as it was to myself, tracing before my tranquil mind precise images, near at hand, of which I should presently be taking possession, was completely invisible to Brichot who had remained in the carriage, almost blind, and would moreover have been completely incomprehensible to him could he have seen it, since, like the friends who called upon me before dinner, when Albertine had returned from her drive, the Professor was unaware that a girl who was all my own was waiting for me in a bedroom adjoining mine. The carriage drove on. I remained for a moment alone upon the pavement. To be sure, these luminous rays which I could see from below and which to anyone else would have seemed merely superficial, I endowed with the utmost consistency, plenitude, solidity, in view of all the significance that I placed behind them, in a treasure unsuspected by the rest of the world which I had concealed there and from which those horizontal rays emanated, a treasure if you like, but a treasure in exchange for which I had forfeited my freedom, my solitude, my thought. If Albertine had not been there, and indeed if I had merely been in search of pleasure, I would have gone to demand it of unknown women, into whose life I should have attempted to penetrate, at Venice perhaps, or at least in some corner of nocturnal Paris. But now all that I had to do when the time came for me to receive caresses, was not to set forth upon a journey, was not even to leave my own house, but to return there. And to return there not to find myself alone, and, after taking leave of the friends who furnished me from outside with food for thought, to find myself at any rate compelled to seek it in myself, but to be on the contrary less alone than when I was at the Verdurins', welcomed as I should be by the person to whom I abdicated, to whom I handed over most completely my own person, without having for an instant the leisure to think of myself nor even requiring the effort, since she would be by my side, to think of her. So that as I raised my eyes to look for the last time from outside at the window of the room in which I should presently find myself, I seemed to behold the luminous gates which were about to close behind me and of which I myself had forged, for an eternal slavery, the unyielding bars of gold.

Our engagement had assumed the form of a criminal trial and gave Albertine the timidity of a guilty party. Now she changed the conversation whenever it turned upon people, men or women, who were not of mature years. It was when she had not yet suspected that I was jealous of her that I could have asked her to tell me what I wanted to know. We ought always to take advantage of that period. It is then that our mistress tells us of her pleasures and even of the means by which she conceals them from other people. She would no longer have admitted to me now as she had admitted at Balbec (partly because it was true, partly in order to excuse herself for not making her affection for myself more evident, for I had already begun to weary her even then, and she had gathered from my kindness to her that she need not show it to me as much as to other men in order to obtain more from me than from them), she would no longer have admitted to me now as she had admitted then: 'I think it stupid to let people see that one is in love; I'm just the opposite, as soon as a person appeals to me, I pretend not to take any notice of him. In that way, nobody knows anything about it.'

What, it was the same Albertine of today, with her pretensions to frankness and indifference to all the world who had told me this! She would never have informed me of such a rule of conduct now! She contented herself when she was talking to me with applying it, by saying of somebody or other who might cause me anxiety: 'Oh, I don't know, I never noticed them, they don't count.' And from time to time, to anticipate discoveries which I might make, she would proffer those confessions which their accent, before one knows the reality which they are intended to alter, to render innocent, denounces already as being falsehoods.

Albertine had never told me that she suspected me of being jealous of her, preoccupied with everything that she did. The only words – and that, I must add, was long ago – which we had exchanged with regard to jealousy seemed to prove the opposite. I remembered that, on a fine moonlight evening, towards the beginning of our intimacy, on one of the first occasions when I had accompanied her home, and when I would have been just as glad not to do so and to leave her in order to run after other girls, I had said to her: 'You know, if I am offering to take you home, it is not from jealousy; if you have anything else to do, I shall slip discreetly away.' And she had replied: 'Oh, I know quite well that you aren't jealous and that it's all the same to you, but I've nothing else to do except to stay with you.' Another occasion was at la Raspelière, when M. de Charlus, not without casting a covert glance at Morel, had made a display of friendly gallantry toward Albertine; I had said to her: 'Well, he gave you a good hug, I hope.' And as I had added half ironically: 'I suffered all the torments of jealousy', Albertine, employing the language proper either to the vulgar class from which she sprang or to that other, more vulgar still, which she frequented, replied: 'What a fusspot you are! I know quite well you're not jealous. For one thing, you told me so, and besides, it's perfectly obvious, get along with you!' She had never told me since then that she had changed her mind; but there must all the same have developed in her, upon that subject, a number of fresh ideas, which she concealed from me but which an accident might, in spite of her, betray, for this evening when, having gone indoors, after going to fetch her from her own room and taking her to mine, I had said to her (with a certain awkwardness which I did not myself understand, for I had indeed told Albertine that I was going to pay a call, and had said that I did not know

where, perhaps upon Mme de Villeparisis, perhaps upon Mme de Guermantes, perhaps upon Mme de Cambremer; it is true that I had not actually
mentioned the Verdurins): 'Guess where I have been, at the Verdurins',' I
had barely had time to utter the words before Albertine, a look of utter
consternation upon her face, had answered me in words which seemed to
explode of their own accord with a force which she was unable to contain: 'I
thought as much.' 'I didn't know that you would be annoyed by my going to
see the Verdurins.' It is true that she did not tell me that she was annoyed,
but that was obvious; it is true also that I had not said to myself that she
would be annoyed. And yet in the face of the explosion of her wrath, as in
the face of those events which a sort of retrospective second sight makes us
imagine that we have already known in the past, it seemed to me that I could
never have expected anything else. 'Annoyed? What do you suppose I care,
where you've been. It's all the same to me. Wasn't Mlle Vinteuil there?'
Losing all control of myself at these words: 'You never told me that you had
met her the other day,' I said to her, to show her that I was better informed
than she knew. Believing that the person whom I reproached her for having
met without telling me was Mme Verdurin, and not, as I meant to imply,
Mlle Vinteuil: 'Did I meet her?' she enquired with a pensive air, addressing
at once herself as though she were seeking to collect her fugitive memories
and myself as though it were I that ought to have told her of the meeting;
and no doubt in order that I might say what I knew, perhaps also in order to
gain time before making a difficult response. But I was preoccupied with the
thought of Mlle Vinteuil, and still more with a dread which had already
entered my mind but which now gripped me in a violent clutch, the dread
that Albertine might be longing for freedom. When I came home I had
supposed that Mme Verdurin had purely and simply invented, to enhance
her own renown, the story of her having expected Mlle Vinteuil and her
friend, so that I was quite calm. Albertine, merely by saying: 'Wasn't Mlle
Vinteuil there?' had shown me that I had not been mistaken in my original
suspicion; but anyhow my mind was set at rest in that quarter for the future,
since by giving up her plan of visiting the Verdurins' and going instead to
the Trocadéro, Albertine had sacrificed Mlle Vinteuil. But, at the Trocadéro,
from which, for that matter, she had come away in order to go for a drive
with myself, there had been as a reason to make her leave it the presence of
Léa. As I thought of this I mentioned Léa by name, and Albertine, distrustful,
supposing that I had perhaps heard something more, took the initiative and
exclaimed volubly, not without partly concealing her face: 'I know her quite
well; we went last year, some of my friends and I, to see her act: after the
performance we went behind to her dressing-room, she changed in front of

us. It was most interesting.' Then my mind was compelled to relinquish Mlle Vinteuil and, in a desperate effort, racing through the abysses of possible reconstructions, attached itself to the actress, to that evening when Albertine had gone behind to her dressing-room. On the other hand, after all the oaths that she had sworn to me, and in so truthful a tone, after the so complete sacrifice of her freedom, how was I to suppose that there was any evil in all this affair? And yet, were not my suspicions feelers pointing in the direction of the truth, since if she had made me a sacrifice of the Verdurins in order to go to the Trocadéro, nevertheless at the Verdurins' Mlle Vinteuil was expected, and, at the Trocadéro, there had been Léa, who seemed to me to be disturbing me without cause and whom all the same, in that speech which I had not demanded of her, she admitted that she had known upon a larger scale than that of my fears, in circumstances that were indeed shady? For what could have induced her to go behind like that to that dressing-room? If I ceased to suffer because of Mlle Vinteuil when I suffered because of Léa, those two tormentors of my day, it was either on account of the inability of my mind to picture too many scenes at one time, or on account of the interference of my nervous emotions of which my jealousy was but the echo. I could induce from them only that she had belonged no more to Léa than to Mlle Vinteuil and that I was thinking of Léa only because the thought of her still caused me pain. But the fact that my twin jealousies were dying down – to revive now and then, alternately – does not, in any way, mean that they did not on the contrary correspond each to some truth of which I had had a foreboding, that of these women I must not say to myself none, but all. I say a foreboding, for I could not project myself to all the points of time and space which I should have had to visit, and besides, what instinct would have given me the coordinate of one with another necessary to enable me to surprise Albertine, here, at one moment, with Léa, or with the Balbec girls, or with that friend of Mme Bontemps whom she had jostled, or with the girl on the tennis-court who had nudged her with her elbow, or with Mlle Vinteuil?

I must add that what had appeared to me most serious, and had struck me as most symptomatic, was that she had forestalled my accusation, that she had said to me: 'Wasn't Mlle Vinteuil there?' to which I had replied in the most brutal fashion imaginable: 'You never told me that you had met her.' Thus as soon as I found Albertine no longer obliging, instead of telling her that I was sorry, I became malicious. There was then a moment in which I felt a sort of hatred of her which only intensified my need to keep her in captivity.

'Besides,' I said to her angrily, 'there are plenty of other things which you hide from me, even the most trivial things, such as for instance when you went for three days to Balbec, I mention it in passing.' I had added the words 'I mention it in passing' as a complement to 'even the most trivial things' so that if Albertine said to me 'What was there wrong about my trip to Balbec?' I might be able to answer: 'Why, I've quite forgotten. I get so confused about the things people tell me, I attach so little importance to them.' And indeed if I referred to those three days which she had spent in an excursion with the chauffeur to Balbec, from where her postcards had reached me after so long an interval, I referred to them purely at random and regretted that I had chosen so bad an example, for in fact, as they had barely had time to go there and return, it was certainly the one excursion in which there had not even been time for the interpolation of a meeting at all protracted with anybody. But Albertine supposed, from what I had just said, that I was fully aware of the real facts, and had merely concealed my knowledge from her; so she had been convinced, for some time past, that, in one way or another, I was having her followed, or in short was somehow or other, as she had said the week before to Andrée, better informed than herself about her own life. And so she interrupted me with a wholly futile admission, for certainly I suspected nothing of what she now told me, and I was on the other hand appalled, so vast can the disparity be between the truth which a liar has disguised and the idea which, from her lies, the man who is in love with the said liar has formed of the truth. Scarcely had I uttered the words: 'When you went for three days to Balbec, I mention it in passing,' before Albertine, cutting me short, declared as a thing that was perfectly natural: 'You mean to say that I never went to Balbec at all? Of course I didn't! And I have always wondered why you pretended to believe that I had. All the same, there was no harm in it. The driver had some business of his own for three days. He didn't like to mention it to you. And so, out of kindness to him (it was my doing! Besides it is always I that have to bear the brunt), I invented a trip to Balbec. He simply put me down at Auteuil, with my friend in the Rue de l'Assomption, where I spent the three days bored to tears. You see it is not a serious matter, there's nothing broken. I did indeed begin to suppose that you perhaps knew all about it, when I saw how you laughed when the postcards began to arrive, a week late. I quite see that it was absurd, and that it would have been better not to send any cards. But that wasn't my fault. I had bought the cards beforehand and given them to the driver before he dropped me at Auteuil, and then the fathead put them in his pocket and forgot about them instead of sending them on in an envelope to a friend of his near Balbec who was to forward them to you. I kept on supposing that they would turn up. He forgot all about them for five days, and instead of telling me the idiot sent them on at once to Balbec. When he did tell me, I fairly broke it over him, I can tell you! And you go and make a stupid fuss, when it's all the fault of that great fool, as a reward for my shutting myself up for three whole days, so that he might go and look after his family affairs. I didn't even venture to go out into Auteuil for fear of being seen. The only time that I did go out, I was dressed as a man, and that was a funny business. And it was just my luck, which follows me wherever I go, that the first person I came across was your Yid friend Bloch. But I don't believe it was from him that you learned that my trip to Balbec never existed except in my imagination, for he seemed not to recognise me.'

I did not know what to say, not wishing to appear astonished, while I was appalled by all these lies. With a sense of horror, which gave me no desire to turn Albertine out of the house, far from it, was combined a strong inclination to burst into tears. This last was caused not by the lie itself and by the annihilation of everything that I had so stoutly believed to be true that I felt as though I were in a town that had been razed to the ground, where not a house remained standing, where the bare soil was merely heaped with rubble – but by the melancholy thought that, during those three days when she had been bored to tears in her friend's house at Auteuil, Albertine had never once felt any desire, the idea had perhaps never occurred to her to come and pay me a visit one day on the quiet, or to send a message asking me to go and see her at Auteuil. But I had not time to give myself up to these reflections. Whatever happened, I did not wish to appear surprised. I smiled with the air of a man who knows far more than he is going to say: 'But that is only one thing out of a thousand. For instance, you knew that Mlle Vinteuil was expected at Mme Verdurin's, this afternoon when you went to the Trocadéro.' She blushed: 'Yes, I knew that.' 'Can you swear to me that it was not in order to renew your relations with her that you wanted to go to the Verdurins'.' 'Why, of course I can swear. Why do you say renew, I never had any relations with her, I swear it.' I was appalled to hear Albertine lie to me like this, deny the facts which her blush had made all too evident. Her mendacity appalled me. And yet, as it contained a protestation of innocence which, almost unconsciously, I was prepared to accept, it hurt me less than her sincerity when, after I had asked her: 'Can you at least swear to me that the pleasure of seeing Mlle Vinteuil again had nothing to do with your anxiety to go this afternoon to the Verdurins' party?' she replied: 'No, that I cannot swear. It would have been a great pleasure to see Mlle Vinteuil again.' A moment earlier, I had been angry with her because she concealed her relations with Mlle Vinteuil, and now her admission of the pleasure that she would have felt in seeing her again turned my bones to water. For that matter, the mystery in which she had cloaked her intention of going to see the Verdurins ought to have been a sufficient proof. But I had not given the matter enough thought. Although she was now telling me the truth, why did she admit only half, it was even more stupid than it was wicked and wretched. I was so crushed that I had not the courage to insist upon this question, as to which I was not in a strong position, having no damning evidence to produce, and to recover my ascendancy, I hurriedly turned to a subject which would enable me to put Albertine to rout: 'Listen, only this evening, at the Verdurins', I learned that what you had told me about Mlle Vinteuil . . .' Albertine gazed at me fixedly with a tormented air, seeking to read in my eyes how much I knew. Now, what I knew and what I was about to tell her as to Mlle Vinteuil's true nature, it was true that it was not at the Verdurins' that I had learned it, but at Montjouvain long ago. Only, as I had always refrained, deliberately, from mentioning it to Albertine, I could now appear to have learned it only this evening. And I could almost feel a joy – after having felt, on the little tram, so keen an anguish – at possessing this memory of Montjouvain, which I postdated, but which would nevertheless be the unanswerable proof, a crushing blow to Albertine. This time at least, I had no need to 'seem to know' and to 'make Albertine speak'; I did know, I had seen through the lighted window at Montjouvain. It had been all very well for Albertine to tell me that her relations with Mlle Vinteuil and her friend had been perfectly pure, how could she when I swore to her (and swore without lying) that I knew the habits of these two women, how could she maintain any longer that, having lived in a daily intimacy with them, calling them 'my big sisters,' she had not been approached by them with suggestions which would have made her break with them, if on the contrary she had not complied? But I had no time to tell her what I knew. Albertine, imagining, as in the case of the pretended excursion to Balbec, that I had learned the truth, either from Mlle Vinteuil, if she had been at the Verdurins', or simply from Mme Verdurin herself who might have mentioned her to Mlle Vinteuil, did not allow me to speak but made a confession, the exact opposite of what I had supposed, which nevertheless, by showing me that she had never ceased to lie to me, caused me perhaps just as much grief (especially since I was no longer, as I said a moment ago, jealous of Mlle Vinteuil); in short, taking the words out of my mouth, Albertine proceeded to say: 'You mean to tell me that you found out this evening that I lied to you when I pretended that I had been more or less brought up by Mlle Vinteuil's friend. It is true that I did lie to you a little. But I felt that you despised me so, I saw too that you were so keen upon that man Vinteuil's music that as one of my school friends – this is true, I swear to you – had been a friend of

Mlle Vinteuil's friend, I stupidly thought that I might make myself seem interesting to you by inventing the story that I had known the girls quite well. I felt that I was boring you, that you thought me a goose, I thought that if I told you that those people used to see a lot of me, that I could easily tell you all sorts of things about Vinteuil's work, I should acquire a little importance in your eyes, that it would draw us together. When I lie to you, it is always out of affection for you. And it needed this fatal Verdurin party to open your eyes to the truth, which has been a bit exaggerated besides. I bet, Mlle Vinteuil's friend told you that she did not know me. She met me at least twice at my friend's house. But of course, I am not smart enough for people like that who have become celebrities. They prefer to say that they have never met me.' Poor Albertine, when she imagined that to tell me that she had been so intimate with Mlle Vinteuil's friend would postpone her own dismissal, would draw her nearer to me, she had, as so often happens, attained the truth by a different road from that which she had intended to take. Her showing herself better informed about music than I had supposed would never have prevented me from breaking with her that evening, on the little tram; and yet it was indeed that speech, which she had made with that object, which had immediately brought about far more than the impossibility of a rupture. Only she made an error in her interpretation, not of the effect which that speech was to have, but of the cause by virtue of which it was to produce that effect, a cause which was my discovery not of her musical culture, but of her evil associations. What had abruptly drawn me to her, what was more, merged me in her was not the expectation of a pleasure – and pleasure is too strong a word, a slight interest – it was a wringing grief.

Once again I had to be careful not to keep too long a silence which might have led her to suppose that I was surprised. And so, touched by the discovery that she was so modest and had thought herself despised in the Verdurin circle, I said to her tenderly: 'But, my darling, I would gladly give you several hundred francs to let you go and play the fashionable lady wherever you please and invite M. and Mme Verdurin to a grand dinner.' Alas! Albertine was several persons in one. The most mysterious, most simple, most atrocious revealed herself in the answer which she made me with an air of disgust and the exact words to tell the truth I could not quite make out (even the opening words, for she did not finish her sentence). I succeeded in establishing them only a little later when I had guessed what was in her mind. We hear things retrospectively when we have understood them. 'Thank you for nothing! Fancy spending a cent upon those old frumps, I'd a great deal rather you left me alone for once in a way so that I can go and get someone decent to break my . . . ' As she uttered the words, her face flushed crimson, a look of terror came to her eyes, she put her hand over her mouth as though she could have thrust back the words which she had just uttered and which I had completely failed to understand. 'What did you say, Albertine?' 'No, nothing, I was half asleep and talking to myself.' 'Not a bit of it, you were wide awake.' 'I was thinking about asking the Verdurins to dinner, it is very good of you.' 'No, I mean what you said just now.' She gave me endless versions, none of which agreed in the least, I do not say with her words which, being interrupted, remained vague, but with the interruption itself and the sudden flush that had accompanied it. 'Come, my darling, that is not what you were going to say, otherwise why did you stop short.' 'Because I felt that my request was indiscreet.' 'What request?' 'To be allowed to give a dinner-party.' 'No, it is not that, there is no need of discretion between you and me.' 'Indeed there is, we ought never to take advantage of the people we love. In any case, I swear to you that that was all.' On the one hand it was still impossible for me to doubt her sworn word, on the other hand her explanations did not satisfy my critical spirit. I continued to press her. 'Anyhow, you might at least have the courage to finish what you were saying, you stopped short at *break*.' 'No, leave me alone!' 'But why?' 'Because it is dreadfully vulgar, I should be ashamed to say such a thing in front of you. I don't know what I was thinking of, the words – I don't even know what they mean, I heard them used in the street one day by some very low people – just came to my lips without rhyme or reason. It had nothing to do with me or anybody else, I was simply dreaming aloud.' I felt that I should extract nothing more from Albertine. She had lied to me when she had sworn, a moment ago, that what had cut her short had been a social fear of being indiscreet, since it had now become the shame of letting me hear her use a vulgar expression. Now this was certainly another lie. For when we were alone together there was no speech too perverse, no word too coarse for us to utter among our embraces. Anyhow, it was useless to insist at that moment. But my memory remained obsessed by the word 'break.' Albertine frequently spoke of 'breaking sticks' or 'breaking sugar' over someone, or would simply say: 'Ah! I fairly broke it over him!' meaning 'I fairly gave it to him!' But she would say this quite freely in my presence, and if it was this that she had meant to say, why had she suddenly stopped short, why had she blushed so deeply, placed her hands over her mouth, given a fresh turn to her speech, and, when she saw that I had heard the word 'break', offered a false explanation. But as soon as I had abandoned the pursuit of an interrogation from which I received no response, the only thing to do was to appear to have lost interest in the matter, and, retracing my thoughts to Albertine's reproaches of me for having gone to the

Mistress's, I said to her, very awkwardly, making indeed a sort of stupid excuse for my conduct: 'Why, I had been meaning to ask you to come to the Verdurins' party this evening', a speech that was doubly maladroit, for if I meant it, since I had been with her all the day, why should I not have made the suggestion? Furious at my lie and emboldened by my timidity: 'You might have gone on asking me for a thousand years,' she said, 'I would never have consented. They are people who have always been against me, they have done everything they could to upset me. There was nothing I didn't do for Mme Verdurin at Balbec, and I've been finely rewarded. If she summoned me to her deathbed, I wouldn't go. There are some things which it is impossible to forgive. As for you, it's the first time you've treated me badly. When Françoise told me that you had gone out (she enjoyed telling me that, I don't think), you might have knocked me down with a feather. I tried not to show any sign, but never in my life have I been so insulted.' While she was speaking, there continued in myself, in the thoroughly alive and creative sleep of the unconscious (a sleep in which the things that barely touch us succeed in carving an impression, in which our hands take hold of the key that turns the lock, the key for which we have sought in vain), the quest of what it was that she had meant by that interrupted speech the end of which I was so anxious to know. And all of a sudden an appalling word, of which I had never dreamed, burst upon me: 'pot'. I cannot say that it came to me in a single flash, as when, in a long passive submission to an incomplete memory, while we try gently, cautiously, to draw it out, we remain fastened, glued to it. No, in contrast to the ordinary process of my memory, there were, I think, two parallel quests; the first took into account not merely Albertine's words, but her look of extreme annoyance when I had offered her a sum of money with which to give a grand dinner, a look which seemed to say: 'Thank you, the idea of spending money upon things that bore me, when without money I could do things that I enjoy doing!' And it was perhaps the memory of this look that she had given me which made me alter my method in discovering the end of her unfinished sentence. Until then I had been hypnotised by her last word: 'break', she had meant to say break what? Break wood? No. Sugar? No. Break, break, break. And all at once the look that she had given me at the moment of my suggestion that she should give a dinner-party, turned me back to the words that had preceded. And immediately I saw that she had not said 'break' but 'get someone to break'. Horror! It was this that she would have preferred. Twofold horror! For even the vilest of prostitutes, who consents to that sort of thing, or desires it, does not employ to the man who yields to her desires that appalling expression. She would feel the degradation too great. To a woman alone, if she loves women, she says this, as an excuse for giving herself presently to a man. Albertine had not been lying when she told me that she was speaking in a dream. Distracted, impulsive, not realising that she was with me, she had, with a shrug of her shoulders, begun to speak as she would have spoken to one of those women, to one, perhaps, of my young budding girls. And abruptly recalled to reality, crimson with shame, thrusting back between her lips what she was going to say, plunged in despair, she had refused to utter another word. I had not a moment to lose if I was not to let her see how desperate I was. But already, after my sudden burst of rage, the tears came to my eyes. As at Balbec, on the night that followed her revelation of her friendship with the Vinteuil pair, I must immediately invent a plausible excuse for my grief, and one that was at the same time capable of creating so profound an effect upon Albertine as to give me a few days' respite before I came to a decision. And so, at the moment when she told me that she had never received such an insult as that which I had inflicted upon her by going out, that she would rather have died than hear Françoise tell her of my departure, when, as though irritated by her absurd susceptibility, I was on the point of telling her that what I had done was nothing, that there was nothing that could offend her in my going out – as, during these moments, moving on a parallel course, my unconscious quest for what she had meant to say after the word 'break' had proved successful, and the despair into which my discovery flung me could not be completely hidden, instead of defending, I accused myself. 'My little Albertine,' I said to her in a gentle voice which was drowned in my first tears, 'I might tell you that you are mistaken, that what I did this evening is nothing, but I should be lying; it is you that are right, you have realised the truth, my poor child, which is that six months ago, three months ago, when I was still so fond of you, never would I have done such a thing. It is a mere nothing, and it is enormous, because of the immense change in my heart of which it is the sign. And since you have detected this change which I hoped to conceal from you, that leads me on to tell you this: My little Albertine' (and here I addressed her with a profound gentleness and melancholy), 'don't you see, the life that you are leading here is boring to you, it is better that we should part, and as the best partings are those that are ended at once, I ask you, to cut short the great sorrow that I am bound to feel, to bid me goodbye tonight and to leave in the morning without my seeing you again, while I am asleep.' She appeared stupefied, still incredulous and already disconsolate: 'Tomorrow? You really mean it?' And notwithstanding the anguish that I felt in speaking of our parting as though it were already in the past – partly perhaps because of that very anguish – I began to give Albertine the most precise instructions as to certain things which she would have to do after she left the house. And passing from one request to another, I soon found myself entering into the minutest details. 'Be so kind,' I said, with infinite melancholy, 'as to send me back that book of Bergotte's which is at your aunt's. There is no hurry about it, in three days, in a week, whenever you like, but remember that I don't want to have to write and ask you for it, that would be too painful. We have been happy together, we feel now that we should be unhappy.' 'Don't say that we feel that we should be unhappy,' Albertine interrupted me, 'don't say "we", it is only you who feel that.' 'Yes, very well, you or I, as you like, for one reason or another. But it is absurdly late, you must go to bed – we have decided to part tonight.' 'Pardon me, you have decided, and I obey you because I do not wish to cause you any trouble.' 'Very well, it is I who have decided, but that makes it none the less painful for me. I do not say that it will be painful for long, you know that I have not the faculty of remembering things for long, but for the first few days I shall be so miserable without you. And so I feel that it will be useless to revive the memory with letters, we must end everything at once.' 'Yes, you are right,' she said to me with a crushed air, which was enhanced by the strain of fatigue upon her features due to the lateness of the hour; 'rather than have one finger chopped off, then another, I prefer to lay my head on the block at once.' 'Heavens, I am appalled when I think how late I am keeping you out of bed, it is madness. However, it's the last night! You will have plenty of time to sleep for the rest of your life.' And as I suggested to her thus that it was time to say good-night I sought to postpone the moment when she would have said it. 'Would you like me, as a distraction during the first few days, to tell Bloch to send his cousin Esther to the place where you will be staying, he will do that for me.' 'I don't know why you say that' (I had said it in an endeavour to wrest a confession from Albertine); 'there is only one person for whom I care, which is yourself,' Albertine said to me, and her words filled me with comfort. But, the next moment, what a blow she dealt me! 'I remember, of course, that I did give Esther my photograph because she kept on asking me for it and I saw that she would like to have it, but as for feeling any liking for her or wishing ever to see her again . . . ' And yet Albertine was of so frivolous a nature that she went on: 'If she wants to see me, it is all the same to me, she is very nice, but I don't care in the least either way.' And so when I had spoken to her of the photograph of Esther which Bloch had sent me (and which I had not even received when I mentioned it to Albertine) my mistress had gathered that Bloch had shown me a photograph of herself, given by her to Esther. In my worst suppositions, I had never imagined that any such intimacy could have existed between Albertine and Esther. Albertine had found no words in which to answer me when I spoke of the photograph. And now, supposing me, wrongly, to be in the know, she thought it better to confess. I was appalled. 'And, Albertine, let me ask you to do me one more favour, never attempt to see me again. If at any time, as may happen in a year, in two years, in three years, we should find ourselves in the same town, keep away from me.' Then, seeing that she did not reply in the affirmative to my prayer: 'My Albertine, never see me again in this world. It would hurt me too much. For I was really fond of you, you know. Of course, when I told you the other day that I wanted to see the friend again whom I mentioned to you at Balbec, you thought that it was all settled. Not at all, I assure you, it was quite immaterial to me. You were convinced that I had long made up my mind to leave you, that my affection was all make-believe.' 'No indeed, you are mad, I never thought so,' she said sadly. 'You are right, you must never think so, I did genuinely feel for you, not love perhaps, but a great, a very great affection, more than you can imagine.' 'I can, indeed. And do you suppose that I don't love you!' 'It hurts me terribly to have to give you up.' 'It hurts me a thousand times more,' replied Albertine. A moment earlier I had felt that I could no longer restrain the tears that came welling up in my eyes. And these tears did not spring from at all the same sort of misery which I had felt long ago when I said to Gilberte: 'It is better that we should not see one another again, life is dividing us.' No doubt when I wrote this to Gilberte, I said to myself that when I should be in love not with her but with another, the excess of my love would diminish that which I might perhaps have been able to inspire, as though two people must inevitably have only a certain quantity of love at their disposal; of which the surplus taken by one is subtracted from the other, and that from her too, as from Gilberte, I should be doomed to part. But the situation was entirely different for several reasons, the first of which (and it had, in its turn, given rise to the others) was that the lack of will-power which my grandmother and mother had observed in me with alarm, at Combray, and before which each of them, so great is the energy with which a sick man imposes his weakness upon others, had capitulated in turn, this lack of will-power had gone on increasing at an ever accelerated pace. When I felt that my company was boring Gilberte, I had still enough strength left to give her up; I had no longer the same strength when I had made a similar discovery with regard to Albertine, and could think only of keeping her at any cost to myself. With the result that, whereas I wrote to Gilberte that I would not see her again, meaning quite sincerely not to see her, I said this to Albertine as a pure falsehood, and in the hope of bringing about a reconciliation. Thus we presented each to the other an appearance which was widely different from the reality. And no doubt it is always so when two people stand face to face, since each of them is ignorant of a part of what exists in the other (even what he knows, he can understand only in part) and since both of them display what is the least personal thing about them, whether because they have not explored themselves and regard as negligible what is most important, or because insignificant advantages which have no place in themselves seem to them more important and more flattering. But in love this misunderstanding is carried to its supreme pitch because, except perhaps when we are children, we endeavour to make the appearance that we assume, rather than reflect exactly what is in our mind, be what our mind considers best adapted to enable us to obtain what we desire, which in my case, since my return to the house, was to be able to keep Albertine as docile as she had been in the past, was that she should not in her irritation ask me for a greater freedom, which I intended to give her one day, but which at this moment, when I was afraid of her cravings for independence, would have made me too jealous. After a certain age, from self-esteem and from sagacity, it is to the things which we most desire that we pretend to attach no importance. But in love, our mere sagacity – which for that matter is probably not the true wisdom – forces us speedily enough to this genius for duplicity. All that I had dreamed, as a boy, to be the sweetest thing in love, what had seemed to me to be the very essence of love, was to pour out freely, before the feet of her whom I loved, my affection, my gratitude for her kindness, my longing for a perpetual life together. But I had become only too well aware, from my own experience and from that of my friends, that the expression of such sentiments is far from being contagious. Once we have observed this, we no longer 'let ourself go'; I had taken good care in the afternoon not to tell Albertine how grateful I was to her that she had not remained at the Trocadéro. And tonight, having been afraid that she might leave me, I had feigned a desire to part from her, a feint which for that matter was not suggested to me merely by the enlightenment which I supposed myself to have received from my former loves and was seeking to bring to the service of this.

The fear that Albertine was perhaps going to say to me: 'I wish to be allowed to go out by myself at certain hours, I wish to be able to stay away for a night,' in fact any request of that sort, which I did not attempt to define, but which alarmed me, this fear had entered my mind for a moment before and during the Verdurins' party. But it had been dispelled, contra-dicted moreover by the memory of how Albertine assured me incessantly how happy she was with me. The intention to leave me, if it existed in

Albertine, was made manifest only in an obscure fashion, in certain sorrowful glances, certain gestures of impatience, speeches which meant nothing of the sort, but which, if one analysed them (and there was not even any need of analysis, for we can immediately detect the language of passion, the lower orders themselves understand these speeches which can be explained only by vanity, rancour, jealousy, unexpressed as it happens, but revealing itself at once to the listener by an intuitive faculty which, like the 'good sense' of which Descartes speaks, is the most widespread thing in the world), revealed the presence in her of a sentiment which she concealed and which might lead her to form plans for another life apart from myself. Just as this intention was not expressed in her speech in a logical fashion, so the presentiment of this intention, which I had felt tonight, remained just as vague in myself. I continued to live by the hypothesis which admitted as true everything that Albertine told me. But it may be that in myself, during this time, a wholly contrary hypothesis, of which I refused to think, never left me; this is all the more probable since, otherwise, I should have felt no hesitation in telling Albertine that I had been to the Verdurins', and, indeed, my want of astonishment at her anger would not have been comprehensible. So that what probably existed in me was the idea of an Albertine entirely opposite to that which my reason formed of her, to that also which her own speech portrayed, an Albertine that all the same was not wholly invented, since she was like a prophetic mirror of certain impulses that occurred in her, such as her ill humour at my having gone to the Verdurins'. Besides, for a long time past, my frequent anguish, my fear of telling Albertine that I loved her, all this corresponded to another hypothesis which explained many things besides, and had also this to be said for it, that, if one adopted the first hypothesis, the second became more probable, for by allowing myself to give way to effusive tenderness for Albertine, I obtained from her nothing but irritation (to which moreover she assigned a different cause).

If I analyse my feelings by this hypothesis, by the invariable system of retorts expressing the exact opposite of what I was feeling, I can be quite certain that if, tonight, I told her that I was going to send her away, it was – at first, quite unconsciously – because I was afraid that she might desire her freedom (I should have been put to it to say what this freedom was that made me tremble, but anyhow some state of freedom in which she would have been able to deceive me, or, at least, I should no longer have been able to be certain that she was not) and wished to show her, from pride, from cunning, that I was very far from fearing anything of the sort, as I had done already, at Balbec, when I was anxious that she should have a good opinion of me, and later on, when I was anxious that she should not have time to feel bored with me. In short, the objection that might be offered to this second hypothesis – which I did not formulate – that everything that Albertine said to me indicated on the contrary that the life which she preferred was the life in my house, resting, reading, solitude, a loathing of Sapphic loves, and so forth, meed not be considered seriously. For if on her part Albertine had chosen to interpret my feelings from what I said to her, she would have learned the exact opposite of the truth, since I never expressed a desire to part from her except when I was unable to do without her, and at Balbec I had confessed to her that I was in love with another woman, first Andrée, then a mysterious stranger, on the two occasions on which jealousy had revived my love for Albertine. My words, therefore, did not in the least reflect my sentiments. If the reader has no more than a faint impression of these, that is because, as narrator, I reveal my sentiments to him at the same time as I repeat my words. But if I concealed the former and he were acquainted only with the latter, my actions, so little in keeping with my speech, would so often give him the impression of strange revulsions of feeling that he would think me almost mad. A procedure which would not, for that matter, be much more false than that which I have adopted, for the images which prompted me to action, so opposite to those which were portrayed in my speech, were at that moment extremely obscure; I was but imperfectly aware of the nature which guided my actions; at present, I have a clear conception of its subjective truth. As for its objective truth, that is to say whether the inclinations of that nature grasped more exactly than my reason Albertine's true intentions, whether I was right to trust to that nature or on the contrary it did not corrupt Albertine's intentions instead of making them plain, that I find difficult to say. That vague fear which I had felt at the Verdurins' that Albertine might leave me had been at once dispelled. When I returned home, it had been with the feeling that I myself was a captive, not with that of finding a captive in the house. But the dispelled fear had gripped me all the more violently when, at the moment of my informing Albertine that I had been to the Verdurins', I saw her face veiled with a look of enigmatic irritation which moreover was not making itself visible for the first time. I knew quite well that it was only the crystallisation in the flesh of reasoned complaints, of ideas clear to the person who forms and does not express them, a synthesis rendered visible but not therefore rational, which the man who gathers its precious residue from the face of his beloved, endeavours in his turn, so that he may understand what is occurring in her, to reduce by analysis to its intellectual elements. The approximate equation of that unknown quantity which Albertine's thoughts were to me, had given me, more or less: 'I knew his suspicions, I was sure that he would attempt to verify them, and so that I might not hinder him, he has worked out his little plan in secret.' But if this was the state of mind (and she had never expressed it to me) in which Albertine was living, must she not regard with horror, find the strength fail her to carry on, might she not at any moment decide to terminate an existence in which, if she was, in desire at any rate, guilty, she must feel herself exposed, tracked down, prevented from ever yielding to her instincts, without thereby disarming my jealousy, and if innocent in intention and fact, she had had every right, for some time past, to feel discouraged, seeing that never once, from Balbec, where she had shown so much perseverance in avoiding the risk of her ever being left alone with Andrée, until this very day when she had agreed not to go to the Verdurins' and not to stay at the Trocadéro, had she succeeded in regaining my confidence. All the more so as I could not say that her behaviour was not exemplary. If at Balbec, when anyone mentioned girls who had a bad style, she used often to copy their laughter, their wrigglings, their general manner, which was a torture to me because of what I supposed that it must mean to her girl friends, now that she knew my opinion on the subject, as soon as anyone made an allusion to things of that sort, she ceased to take part in the conversation, not only in speech but with the expression on her face. Whether it was in order not to contribute her share to the slanders that were being uttered about some woman or other, or for a quite different reason, the only thing that was noticeable then, upon those so mobile features, was that from the moment in which the topic was broached they had made their inattention evident, while preserving exactly the same expression that they had worn a moment earlier. And this immobility of even a light expression was as heavy as a silence; it would have been impossible to say that she blamed, that she approved, that she knew or did not know about these things. None of her features bore any relation to anything save another feature. Her nose, her mouth, her eyes formed a perfect harmony, isolated from everything else; she looked like a pastel, and seemed to have no more heard what had just been said than if it had been uttered in front of a portrait by Latour.

My serfdom, of which I had already been conscious when, as I gave the driver Brichot's address, I caught sight of the light in her window, had ceased to weigh upon me shortly afterwards, when I saw that Albertine appeared so cruelly conscious of her own. And in order that it might seem to her less burdensome, that she might not decide to break her bonds of her own accord, I had felt that the most effective plan was to give her the impression that it would not be permanent and that I myself was looking forward to its termination. Seeing that my feint had proved successful, I might well have thought myself fortunate, in the first place because what I had so greatly dreaded, Albertine's determination (as I supposed) to leave me, was shown to be non-existent, and secondly, because, quite apart from the object that I had had in mind, the very success of my feint, by proving that I was something more to Albertine than a scorned lover, whose jealousy is flouted, all of his ruses detected in advance, endowed our love afresh with a sort of virginity, revived for it the days in which she could still, at Balbec, so readily believe that I was in love with another woman. For she would probably not have believed that any longer, but she was taking seriously my feigned determination to part from her now and for ever. She appeared to suspect that the cause of our parting might be something that had happened at the Verdurins'. Feeling a need to soothe the anxiety into which I was worked by my pretence of a rupture, I said to her: 'Albertine, can you swear that you have never lied to me?' She gazed fixedly into the air before replying: 'Yes, that is to say no. I ought not to have told you that Andrée was greatly taken with Bloch, we never met him.' 'Then why did you say so?' 'Because I was afraid that you had believed other stories about her, that's all.' I told her that I had met a dramatist who was a great friend of Léa, and to whom Léa had told some strange things. I hoped by telling her this to make her suppose that I knew a great deal more than I cared to say about Bloch's cousin's friend. She stared once again into vacancy and then said: 'I ought not, when I spoke to you just now about Léa, to have kept from you a three weeks' trip that I took with her once. But I knew you so slightly in those days!' 'It was before Balbec?' 'Before the second time, yes.' And that very morning, she had told me that she did not know Léa, and, only a moment ago, that she had met her once only in her dressing-room! I watched a tongue of flame seize and devour in an instant a romance which I had spent millions of minutes in writing. To what end? To what end? Of course I understood that Albertine had revealed these facts to me because she thought that I had learned them indirectly from Léa; and that there was no reason why a hundred similar facts should not exist. I realised thus that Albertine's utterances, when one interrogated her, did not ever contain an atom of truth, that the truth she allowed to escape only in spite of herself, as though by a sudden combination in her mind of the facts which she had previously been determined to conceal with the belief that I had been informed of them. 'But two things are nothing,' I said to Albertine, 'let us have as many as four, so that you may leave me some memories of you. What other revelations have you got for me?' Once again she stared into vacancy. To what belief in a future life was she adapting her falsehood, with what Gods less unstable than she had supposed was she seeking to ally herself? This cannot have been an easy matter, for her silence and the fixity of her gaze continued for some time. 'No, nothing else,' she said at length. And, notwithstanding my persistence, she adhered, easily now, to 'nothing else.' And what a lie! For, from the moment when she had acquired those tastes until the day when she had been shut up in my house, how many times, in how many places, on how many excursions must she have gratified them! The daughters of Gomorrah are at once so rare and so frequent that, in any crowd of people, one does not pass unperceived by the other. From that moment a meeting becomes easy.

I remembered with horror an evening which at the time had struck me as merely absurd. One of my friends had invited me to dine at a restaurant with his mistress and another of his friends who had also brought his own. The two women were not long in coming to an understanding, but were so impatient to enjoy one another that, with the soup, their feet were searching for one another, often finding mine. Presently their legs were interlaced. My two friends noticed nothing; I was on tenterhooks. One of the women, who could contain herself no longer, stooped under the table, saying that she had dropped something. Then one of them complained of a headache and asked to go upstairs to the lavatory. The other discovered that it was time for her to go and meet a woman friend at the theatre. Finally I was left alone with my two friends who suspected nothing. The lady with the headache reappeared, but begged to be allowed to go home by herself to wait for her lover at his house, so that she might take a dose of antipyrin. They became great friends, used to go about together, one of them, dressed as a man, picking up little girls and taking them to the other, initiating them. One of them had a little boy who, she pretended, was troublesome, and handed him over for punishment to her friend, who set to work with a strong arm. One may say that there was no place, however public, in which they did not do what is most secret.

'But Léa behaved perfectly properly with me all the time,' Albertine told me. 'She was indeed a great deal more reserved than plenty of society women.' 'Are there any society women who have shown a want of reserve with you, Albertine?' 'Never.' 'Then what do you mean?' 'O, well, she was less free in her speech.' 'For instance?' 'She would never, like many of the women you meet, have used the expression "rotten", or say: "I don't care a damn for anybody." ' It seemed to me that a part of the romance which the flames had so far spared was crumbling at length in ashes.

My discouragement might have persisted. Albertine's words, when I thought of them, made it give place to a furious rage. This succumbed to a sort of tender emotion. I also, when I came home and declared that I wished to break with her, had been lying. And this desire for a parting, which I had feigned with perseverance, gradually affected me with some of the misery which I should have felt if I had really wished to part from Albertine.

Besides, even when I thought in fits and starts, in twinges, as we say of other bodily pains, of that orgiastic life which Albertine had led before she met me, I admired all the more the docility of my captive and ceased to feel any resentment.

No doubt, never, during our life together, had I failed to let Albertine know that such a life would in all probability be merely temporary, so that Albertine might continue to find some charm in it. But tonight I had gone further, having feared that vague threats of separation were no longer sufficient, contradicted as they would doubtless be, in Albertine's mind, by her idea of a strong and jealous love of her, which must have made me, she seemed to imply, go in quest of information to the Verdurins'.

Tonight I thought that, among the other reasons which might have made me decide of a sudden, without even realising except as I went on what I was doing, to enact this scene of rupture, there was above all the fact that, when, in one of those impulses to which my father was liable, I threatened another person in his security, as I had not, like him, the courage to carry a threat into practice, in order not to let it be supposed that it had been but empty words, I would go to a considerable length in pretending to carry out my threat and would recoil only when my adversary, having had a genuine illusion of my sincerity, had begun seriously to tremble. Besides, in these lies, we feel that there is indeed a grain of truth, that, if life does not bring any alteration of our loves, it is ourselves who will seek to bring or to feign one, so strongly do we feel that all love, and everything else evolves rapidly towards a farewell. We would like to shed the tears that it will bring long before it comes. No doubt there had been, on this occasion, in the scene that I had enacted, a practical value. I had suddenly determined to keep Albertine because I felt that she was distributed among other people whom I could not prevent her from joining. But had she renounced them all finally for myself, I should have been all the more firmly determined never to let her go, for a parting is, by jealousy, rendered cruel, but, by gratitude, impossible. I felt that in any case I was fighting the decisive battle in which I must conquer or fall. I would have offered Albertine in an hour all that I possessed, because I said to myself: 'Everything depends upon this battle, but such battles are less like those of old days which lasted for a few hours than a battle of today which does not end on the morrow, nor on the day after, nor in the following week. We give all our strength, because we steadfastly believe that we shall never need any strength again. And more than a year passes without bringing a 'decisive' victory. Perhaps an unconscious reminiscence of lying scenes enacted by M. de Charlus, in whose company I was when the fear of Albertine's leaving me had seized hold of me, was added to the rest. But, later on, I heard my mother say something of which I was then unaware and which leads me to believe that I found all the elements of this scene in myself, in those obscure reserves of heredity which certain emotions, acting in this respect as, upon the residue of our stored-up strength, drugs such as alcohol and coffee act, place at our disposal. When my aunt Léonie learned from Eulalie that Françoise, convinced that her mistress would never again leave the house, had secretly planned some outing of which my aunt was to know nothing, she, the day before, would pretend to have made up her mind that she would attempt an excursion on the morrow. The incredulous Françoise was ordered not only to prepare my aunt's clothes beforehand, to give an airing to those that had been put away for too long, but to order a carriage, to arrange, to within a quarter of an hour, all the details of the day. It was only when Françoise, convinced or at any rate shaken, had been forced to confess to my aunt the plan that she herself had formed, that my aunt would publicly abandon her own, so as not, she said, to interfere with Françoise's arrangements. Similarly, so that Albertine might not believe that I was exaggerating and to make her proceed as far as possible in the idea that we were to part, drawing myself the obvious deductions from the proposal that I had advanced, I had begun to anticipate the time which was to begin on the morrow and was to last for ever, the time in which we should be parted, addressing to Albertine the same requests as if we were not to be reconciled almost immediately. Like a general who considers that if a feint is to succeed in deceiving the enemy it must be pushed to extremes, I had employed in this feint almost as much of my store of sensibility as if it had been genuine. This fictitious parting scene ended by causing me almost as much grief as if it had been real, possibly because one of the actors, Albertine, by believing it to be real, had enhanced the other's illusion. While we were living, from day to day, in a day which, even if painful, was still endurable, held down to earth by the ballast of habit and by that certainty that the morrow, should it prove a day of torment, would contain the presence of the person who is all in all, here was I stupidly destroying all that oppressive life. I was destroying it, it is true, only in a fictitious fashion, but this was enough to make me wretched; perhaps because the sad words which we utter, even when we are lying, carry in themselves their sorrow and inject it deeply into us; perhaps because we do not realise that, by feigning farewells, we evoke by anticipation an hour which must inevitably come later on; then we cannot be certain that we have not released the mechanism which will make it strike. In every bluff there is an element, however small, of uncertainty as to what the person whom we are deceiving is going to do. If this make-believe of parting should lead to a parting! We cannot consider the possibility, however unlikely it may seem, without a clutching of the heart. We are doubly anxious, because the parting would then occur at the moment when it would be intolerable, when we had been made to suffer by the woman who would be leaving us before she had healed, or at least appeased us. In short, we have no longer the solid ground of habit upon which we rest, even in our sorrow. We have deliberately deprived ourselves of it, we have given the present day an exceptional importance, have detached it from the days before and after it; it floats without roots like a day of departure; our imagination ceasing to be paralysed by habit has awakened, we have suddenly added to our everyday love sentimental dreams which enormously enhance it, make indispensable to us a presence upon which, as a matter of fact, we are no longer certain that we can rely. No doubt it is precisely in order to assure ourselves of that presence for the future that we have indulged in the make-believe of being able to dispense with it. But this make-believe, we have ourselves been taken in by it, we have begun to suffer afresh because we have created something new, unfamiliar which thus resembles those cures that are destined in time to heal the malady from which we are suffering, but the first effects of which are to aggravate it.

I had tears in my eyes, like the people who, alone in their bedrooms, imagining, in the wayward course of their meditations, the death of someone whom they love, form so detailed a picture of the grief that they would feel that they end by feeling it. And so as I multiplied my advice to Albertine as to the way in which she would have to behave in relation to myself after we had parted, I seemed to be feeling almost as keen a distress as though we had not been on the verge of a reconciliation. Besides, was I so certain that I could bring about this reconciliation, bring Albertine back to the idea of a life shared with myself, and, if I succeeded for the time being, that in her, the state of mind which this scene had dispelled would not revive? I felt myself, but did not believe myself to be master of the future, because I realised that this sensation was due merely to the fact that the future did not yet exist, and that thus I was not crushed by its inevitability. In short, while I lied, I was perhaps putting into my words more truth than I supposed. I had just had an example of this, when I told Albertine that I should quickly forget her; this was what had indeed happened to me in the case of Gilberte, whom I now refrained from going to see in order to escape not a grief but an irksome duty. And certainly I had been grieved when I wrote to Gilberte that I would not come any more, and I had gone to see her only occasionally. Whereas the whole of Albertine's time belonged to me, and in love it is easier to relinquish a sentiment than to lose a habit. But all these painful words about our parting, if the strength to utter them had been given me because I knew them to be untrue, were on the other hand sincere upon Albertine's lips when I heard her exclaim: 'Ah! I promise, I will never see you again. Anything sooner than see you cry like that, my darling. I do not wish to cause you any grief. Since it must be, we will never meet again.' They were sincere, as they could not have been coming from me, because, for one thing, as Albertine felt nothing stronger for me than friendship, the renunciation that they promised cost her less; because, moreover, in a scene of parting, it is the person who is not genuinely in love that makes the tender speeches, since love does not express itself directly; because, lastly, my tears, which would have been so small a matter in a great love, seemed to her almost extraordinary and overwhelmed her, transposed into the region of that state of friendship in which she dwelt, a friendship greater than mine for her, to judge by what she had just said, which was perhaps not altogether inexact, for the thousand kindnesses of love may end by arousing, in the person who inspires without feeling it, an affection, a gratitude less selfish than the sentiment that provoked them, which, perhaps, after years of separation, when nothing of that sentiment remains in the former lover, will still persist in the beloved.

'My little Albertine,' I replied, 'it is very good of you to make me this promise. Anyhow, for the first few years at least, I shall avoid the places where I might meet you. You don't know whether you will be going to Balbec this year? Because in that case I should arrange not to go there myself.' But now, if I continued to progress thus, anticipating time to come in my lying inventions, it was with a view no less to inspiring fear in Albertine than to making myself wretched. As a man who at first had no serious reason for losing his temper, becomes completely intoxicated by the sound of his own voice, and lets himself be carried away by a fury engendered not by his grievance but by his anger which itself is steadily growing, so I was falling ever faster and faster down the slope of my wretchedness, towards an ever more profound despair, and with the inertia of a man who feels the cold grip him, makes no effort to resist it and even finds a sort of pleasure in shivering. And if I had now at length, as I fully supposed, the strength to control myself, to react and to reverse my engines, far more than from the grief which Albertine had caused me by so unfriendly a greeting on my return, it was from that which I had felt in imagining, so as to pretend to be outlining them, the formalities of an imaginary separation, in foreseeing its consequences, that Albertine's kiss, when the time came for her to bid me good-night, would have to console me now. In any case, it must not be she that said this good-night of her own accord, for that would have made more difficult the revulsion by which I would propose to her to abandon the idea of our parting. And so I continued to remind her that the time to say good-night had long since come and gone, a method which, by leaving the initiative to me, enabled me to put it off for a moment longer. And thus I scattered with allusions to the lateness of the hour, to our exhaustion, the questions with which I was plying Albertine. 'I don't know where I shall be going,' she replied to the last of these, in a worried tone. 'Perhaps I shall go to Touraine, to my aunt's.' And this first plan that she suggested froze me as though it were beginning to make definitely effective our final separation. She looked round the room, at the pianola, the blue satin armchairs. 'I still cannot make myself realise that I shall not see all this again, tomorrow, or the next day, or ever. Poor little room. It seems to me quite impossible; I cannot get it into my head.' 'It had to be; you were unhappy here.' 'No, indeed, I was not unhappy, it is now that I shall be unhappy.' 'No, I assure you, it is better for you.' 'For you, perhaps!' I began to stare fixedly into vacancy, as though, worried by an extreme hesitation, I was debating an idea which had occurred to my mind. Then, all of a sudden: 'Listen, Albertine, you say that you are happier here, that you are going to be unhappy.' 'Why, of course.' 'That appals me; would you like us to try to carry on for a few weeks? Who knows, week by week, we may perhaps go on for a long time; you know that there are temporary arrangements which end by becoming permanent.' 'Oh, how kind you are!' 'Only in that case it is ridiculous of us to have made ourselves wretched like this over nothing for hours on end, it is like making all the preparations for a long journey and then staying at home. I am shattered with grief.' I made her sit on my knee, I took Bergotte's manuscript which she so longed to have and wrote on the cover: 'To my little Albertine, in memory of a new lease of life.' 'Now,' I said to her, 'go and sleep until tomorrow, my darling, for you must be worn out.' 'I am very glad, all the same.' 'Do you love me a little bit?' 'A hundred times more than ever.'

I should have been wrong in being delighted with this little piece of play-acting, had it not been that I had carried it to the pitch of a real scene on the stage. Had we done no more than quite simply discuss a separation, even that would have been a serious matter. In conversations of this sort, we suppose that we are speaking not merely without sincerity, which is true, but freely. Whereas they are generally, though we know it not, murmured in spite of us; the first murmur of a storm which we do not suspect. In reality, what we express at such times is the opposite of our desire (which is to live for ever with her whom we love), but there is also that impossibility of living together which is the cause of our daily suffering, a suffering preferred by us to that of a parting, which will, however, end, in spite of ourselves, in parting us. Generally speaking, not, however, at once. As a rule, it happens – this was not, as we shall see, my case with Albertine – that, some time after the words in which we did not believe, we put into action a vague attempt at a deliberate separation, not painful, temporary. We ask the woman, so that afterwards she may be happier in our company, so that we on the other hand may momentarily escape from continual worries and fatigues, to go without us, or to let us go without her, for a few days elsewhere, the first days that we have – for a long time past – spent, as would have seemed to us impossible, away from her. Very soon she returns to take her place by our fireside. Only this separation, short, but made real, is not so arbitrarily decided upon, not so certainly the only one that we have in mind. The same sorrows begin afresh, the same difficulty in living together becomes accentuated, only a parting is no longer so difficult as before; we have begun mentioning it, and have then put it into practice in a friendly fashion. But these are only preliminary ventures whose nature we have not recognised. Presently, to the momentary and smiling separation will succeed the terrible and final separation for which we have, without knowing it, paved the way.

'Come to my room in five minutes and let me see something of you, my dearest boy. You are full of kindness. But afterwards I shall fall asleep at once, for I am almost dead.' It was indeed a dead woman that I beheld when, presently, I entered her room. She had gone to sleep immediately she lay down, the sheets wrapped like a shroud about her body had assumed, with their stately folds, a stony rigidity. One would have said that, as in certain Last Judgments of the Middle Ages, her head alone was emerging from the tomb, awaiting in its sleep the Archangel's trumpet. This head had been surprised by sleep almost flung back, its hair bristling. And as I saw the expressionless body extended there, I asked myself what logarithmic table it constituted so that all the actions in which it might have been involved, from the nudge of an elbow to the brushing of a skirt, were able to cause me, stretched out to the infinity of all the points that it had occupied in space and time, and from time to time sharply reawakened in my memory, so intense an anguish, albeit I knew those actions to have been determined in her by impulses, desires, which in another person, in herself five years earlier or five years later, would have left me quite indifferent. All this was a lie, but a lie for which I had not the courage to seek any solution other than my own death. And so I remained, in the fur coat which I had not taken off since my return from the Verdurins', before that bent body, that figure allegorical of what? Of my death? Of my love? Presently I began to hear her regular breathing. I went and sat down on the edge of her bed to take that soothing cure of fresh air and contemplation. Then I withdrew very gently so as not to awaken her.

It was so late that, in the morning, I warned Françoise to tread very softly when she had to pass by the door of Albertine's room. And so Françoise, convinced that we had spent the night in what she used to call orgies, ironically warned the other servants not to 'wake the Princess'. And this was one of the things that I dreaded, that Françoise might one day be unable to contain herself any longer, might treat Albertine with insolence, and that this might introduce complications into our life. Françoise was now no longer, as at the time when it distressed her to see Eulalie treated generously by my aunt, of an age to endure her jealousy with courage. It distorted, paralysed our old servant's face to such an extent that at times I asked myself whether she had not, after some outburst of rage, had a slight stroke. Having thus asked that Albertine's sleep should be respected, I was unable to sleep myself. I endeavoured to understand the true state of Albertine's mind. By that wretched farce which I had played, was it a real peril that I had averted, and, notwithstanding her assurance that she was so happy living with me, had she really felt at certain moments a longing for freedom, or on the contrary was I to believe what she said? Which of these two hypotheses was the truth? If it often befell me, if it was in a special case to befall me that I must extend an incident in my past life to the dimensions of history, when I made an attempt to understand some political event; inversely, this morning, I did not cease to identify, in spite of all the differences and in an attempt to understand its bearing, our scene overnight with a diplomatic incident that had just occurred. I had perhaps the right to reason thus. For it was highly probable that, without my knowledge, the example of M. de Charlus had guided me in that lying scene which I had so often seen him enact with such authority; on the other hand, was it in him anything else than an unconscious importation into the domain of his private life of the innate tendency of his Germanic stock, provocative from guile and, from pride, belligerent at need. Certain persons, among them the Prince of Monaco, having suggested the idea to the French Government that, if it did not dispense with M. Delcassé, a menacing Germany would indeed declare war, the Minister for Foreign Affairs had been asked to resign. So that the French Government had admitted the hypothesis of an intention to make war upon us if we did not yield. But others thought that it was all a mere 'bluff' and that if France had stood firm Germany would not have drawn the sword. No doubt the

scenario was not merely different but almost opposite, since the threat of a
rupture had not been put forward by Albertine; but a series of impressions
had led me to believe that she was thinking of it, as France had been led to
believe about Germany. On the other hand, if Germany desired peace, to
have provoked in the French Government the idea that she was anxious for
war was a disputable and dangerous trick. Certainly, my conduct had been
skilful enough, if it was the thought that I would never make up my mind to
break with her that provoked in Albertine sudden longings for independence.
And was it not difficult to believe that she did not feel them, to shut one's
eyes to a whole secret existence, directed towards the satisfaction of her vice,
simply on remarking the anger with which she had learned that I had gone to
see the Verdurins', when she exclaimed: 'I thought as much', and went on
to reveal everything by saying: 'Wasn't Mlle Vinteuil there?' All this was
corroborated by Albertine's meeting with Mme Verdurin of which Andrée
had informed me. But perhaps all the same these sudden longings for
independence (I told myself, when I tried to go against my own instinct)
were caused – supposing them to exist – or would eventually be caused by the
opposite theory, to wit that I had never had any intention of marrying her,
that it was when I made, as though involuntarily, an allusion to our
approaching separation that I was telling the truth, that I would whatever
happened part from her one day or another, a belief which the scene that I
had made overnight could then only have confirmed and which might end
by engendering in her the resolution: 'If this is bound to happen one day or
another, better to end everything at once.' The preparations for war which
the most misleading of proverbs lays down as the best way to secure the
triumph of peace, create first of all the belief in each of the adversaries that
the other desires a rupture, a belief which brings the rupture about, and,
when it has occurred, this further belief in each of them that it is the other
that has sought it. Even if the threat was not sincere, its success encourages a
repetition. But the exact point to which a bluff may succeed is difficult to
determine; if one party goes too far, the other which has previously yielded,
advances in its turn; the first party, no longer able to change its method,
accustomed to the idea that to seem not to fear a rupture is the best way of
avoiding one (which is what I had done overnight with Albertine), and
moreover driven to prefer, in its pride, to fall rather than yield, perseveres in
its threat until the moment when neither can draw back any longer. The
bluff may also be blended with sincerity, may alternate with it, and it is
possible that what was a game yesterday may become a reality tomorrow.
Finally it may also happen that one of the adversaries is really determined
upon war, it might be that Albertine, for instance, had the intention of,

sooner or later, not continuing this life any longer, or on the contrary that the idea had never even entered her mind and that my imagination had invented the whole thing from start to finish. Such were the different hypotheses which I considered while she lay asleep that morning. And yet as to the last I can say that I never, in the period that followed, threatened Albertine with a rupture unless in response to an idea of an evil freedom on her part, an idea which she did not express to me, but which seemed to me to be implied by certain mysterious dissatisfactions, certain words, certain gestures, of which that idea was the only possible explanation and of which she refused to give me any other. Even then, quite often, I remarked them without making any allusion to a possible separation, hoping that they were due to a fit of ill temper which would end that same day. But it continued at times without intermission for weeks on end, during which Albertine seemed anxious to provoke a conflict, as though there had been at the time, in some region more or less remote, pleasures of which she knew, of which her seclusion in my house was depriving her, and which would continue to influence her until they came to an end, like those atmospheric changes which, even by our own fireside, affect our nerves, even when they are occurring as far away as the Balearic islands.

This morning, while Albertine lay asleep and I was trying to guess what was concealed in her, I received a letter from my mother in which she expressed her anxiety at having heard nothing of what we had decided in this phrase of Mme de Sévigné: 'In my own mind I am convinced that he will not marry; but then, why trouble this girl whom he will never marry? Why risk making her refuse suitors at whom she will never look again save with scorn? Why disturb the mind of a person whom it would be so easy to avoid?' This letter from my mother brought me back to earth. 'What am I doing, seeking a mysterious soul, interpreting a face and feeling myself overawed by presentiments which I dare not explore?' I asked myself. 'I have been dreaming, the matter is quite simple. I am an undecided young man, and it is a question of one of those marriages as to which it takes time to find out whether they will happen or not. There is nothing in this peculiar to Albertine.' This thought gave me an immense but a short relief. Very soon I said to myself: 'One can after all reduce everything, if one regards it in its social aspect, to the most commonplace item of newspaper gossip. From outside, it is perhaps thus that I should look at it. But I know well that what is true, what at least is also true, is everything that I have thought, is what I have read in Albertine's eyes, is the fears that torment me, is the problem that I incessantly set myself with regard to Albertine. The story of the hesitating bridegroom and the broken engagement may correspond to this, as the report of a theatrical performance made by an intelligent reporter may give us the subject of one of Ibsen's plays. But there is something beyond those facts which are reported. It is true that this other thing exists perhaps, were we able to discern it, in all hesitating bridegrooms and in all the engagements that drag on, because there is perhaps an element of mystery in our everyday life.' It was possible for me to neglect it in the lives of other people, but Albertine's life and my own I was living from within.

Albertine no more said to me after this midnight scene than she had said before it: 'I know that you do not trust me, I am going to try to dispel your suspicions.' But this idea, which she never expressed in words, might have served as an explanation of even her most trivial actions. Not only did she take care never to be alone for a moment, so that I might not lack information as to what she had been doing, if I did not believe her own statements, but even when she had to telephone to Andrée, or to the garage, or to the livery stable or elsewhere, she pretended that it was such a bore to stand about by herself waiting to telephone, what with the time the girls took to give you your number, and took care that I should be with her at such times, or, failing myself, Françoise, as though she were afraid that I might imagine reprehensible conversations by telephone in which she would make mysterious assignations. Alas, all this did not set my mind at rest. I had a day of discouragement. Aimé had sent me back Esther's photograph, with a message that she was not the person. And so Albertine had other intimate friends as well as this girl to whom, through her misunderstanding of what I said, I had, when I meant to refer to something quite different, discovered that she had given her photograph. I sent this photograph back to Bloch. What I should have liked to see was the photograph that Albertine had given to Esther. How was she dressed in it? Perhaps with a bare bosom, for all I knew. But I dared not mention it to Albertine (for it would then have appeared that I had not seen the photograph), or to Bloch, since I did not wish him to think that I was interested in Albertine. And this life, which anyone who knew of my suspicions and her bondage would have seen to be agonising to myself and to Albertine, was regarded from without, by Françoise, as a life of unmerited pleasures of which full advantage was cunningly taken by that 'trickstress' and (as Françoise said, using the feminine form far more often than the masculine, for she was more envious of women) 'charlatante'. Indeed, as Françoise, by contact with myself, had enriched her vocabulary with fresh terms, but had adapted them to her own style, she said of Albertine that she had never known a person of such 'perfidity', who was so skilful at 'drawing my money' by play-acting (which Françoise, who was as prone to mistake the particular for the general as the general for the particular and who had but a very vague idea of the various kinds of dramatic art, called 'acting a pantomime'). Perhaps for this error as to the true nature of the life led by Albertine and myself, I was myself to some extent responsible owing to the vague confirmations of it which, when I was talking to Françoise, I skilfully let fall, from a desire either to tease her or to appear, if not loved, at any rate happy. And yet my jealousy, the watch that I kept over Albertine, which I would have given anything for Françoise not to suspect, she was not long in discovering, guided, like the thought-reader who, groping blindfold, finds the hidden object, by that intuition which she possessed for anything that might be painful to me, which would not allow itself to be turned aside by the lies that I might tell in the hope of distracting her, and also by that clairvoyant hatred which urged her – even more than it urged her to believe her enemies more prosperous, more skilful hypocrites than they really were – to discover the secret that might prove their undoing and to precipitate their downfall. Françoise certainly never made any scenes with Albertine. But I was acquainted with Françoise's art of insinuation, the advantage that she knew how to derive from a significant setting, and I cannot believe that she resisted the temptation to let Albertine know, day by day, what a degraded part she was playing in the household, to madden her by a description, cunningly exaggerated, of the confinement to which my mistress was subjected. On one occasion I found Françoise, armed with a huge pair of spectacles, rummaging through my papers and replacing among them a sheet on which I had jotted down a story about Swann and his utter inability to do without Odette. Had she maliciously left it lying in Albertine's room? Besides, above all Françoise's innuendoes which had merely been, in the bass, the muttering and perfidious orchestration, it is probable that there must have risen, higher, clearer, more pressing, the accusing and calumnious voice of the Verdurins, annoyed to see that Albertine was involuntarily keeping me and that I was voluntarily keeping her away from the little clan. As for the money that I was spending upon Albertine, it was almost impossible for me to conceal it from Françoise, since I was unable to conceal any of my expenditure from her. Françoise had few faults, but those faults had created in her, for their service, positive talents which she often lacked apart from the exercise of those faults. Her chief fault was her curiosity as to all money spent by us upon people other than herself. If I had a bill to pay, a gratuity to give, it was useless my going into a corner, she would find a plate to be put in the right place, a napkin to be picked up, which would give her an excuse for approaching. And however short a time I allowed her, before dismissing her with fury, this woman who had almost lost her sight, who could barely add up a column of figures, guided by the same expert sense which makes a tailor, on catching sight of you, instinctively calculate the price of the stuff of which your coat is made, while he cannot resist fingering it, or makes a painter responsive to a colour effect, Françoise saw by stealth, calculated instantaneously the amount that I was giving. And when, so that she might not tell Albertine that I was corrupting her chauffeur, I took the initiative and, apologising for the tip, said: 'I wanted to be generous to the chauffeur, I gave him ten francs'; Françoise, pitiless, to whom a glance, that of an old and almost blind eagle, had been sufficient, replied: 'No indeed, Monsieur gave him a tip of 43 francs. He told Monsieur that the charge was 45 francs, Monsieur gave him 100 francs, and he handed back only 12 francs.' She had had time to see and to reckon the amount of the gratuity which I myself did not know. I asked myself whether Albertine, feeling herself watched, would not herself put into effect that separation with which I had threatened her, for life in its changing course makes realities of our fables. Whenever I heard a door open, I felt myself shudder as my grandmother used to shudder in her last moments whenever I rang my bell. I did not believe that she would leave the house without telling me, but it was my unconscious self that thought so, as it was my grandmother's unconscious self that throbbed at the sound of the bell, when she was no longer conscious. One morning indeed, I felt a sudden misgiving that she not only had left the house but had gone for good: I had just heard the sound of a door which seemed to me to be that of her room. On tiptoe I crept towards the room, opened the door, stood upon the threshold. In the dim light the bedclothes bulged in a semicircle, that must be Albertine who, with her body bent, was sleeping with her feet and face to the wall. Only, overflowing the bed, the hair upon that head, abundant and dark, made me realise that it was she, that she had not opened her door, had not stirred, and I felt that this motionless and living semicircle, in which a whole human life was contained and which was the only thing to which I attached any value, I felt that it was there, in my despotic possession.

If Albertine's object was to restore my peace of mind, she was partly successful; my reason moreover asked nothing better than to prove to me that I had been mistaken as to her crafty plans, as I had perhaps been mistaken as to her vicious instincts. No doubt I added to the value of the arguments with which my reason furnished me my own desire to find them sound. But, if I was to be fair and to have a chance of perceiving the truth, unless we admit that it is never known save by presentiment, by a telepathic emanation, must I not say to myself that if my reason, in seeking to bring about my recovery, let itself be guided by my desire, on the other hand, so

far as concerned Mlle Vinteuil, Albertine's vices, her intention to lead a
different life, her plan of separation, which were the corollaries of her vices,
my instinct had been capable, in the attempt to make me ill, of being led
astray by my jealousy. Besides, her seclusion, which Albertine herself
contrived so ingeniously to render absolute, by removing my suffering,
removed by degrees my suspicion and I could begin again, when the night
brought back my uneasiness, to find in Albertine's presence the consolation
of earlier days. Seated beside my bed, she spoke to me of one of those
dresses or one of those presents which I never ceased to give her in the effort
to enhance the comfort of her life and the beauty of her prison. Albertine
had at first thought only of dresses and furniture. Now silver had begun to
interest her. And so I had questioned M. de Charlus about old French silver,
and had done so because, when we had been planning to have a yacht – a
plan which Albertine decided was impracticable, as I did also whenever I
had begun to believe in her virtue, with the result that my jealousy, as it
declined, no longer held in check other desires in which she had no place
and which also needed money for their satisfaction – we had, to be on the
safe side, not that she supposed that we should ever have a yacht, asked Elstir
for his advice. Now, just as in matters of women's dress, the painter was a
refined and sensitive critic of the furnishing of yachts. He would allow only
English furniture and old silver. This had led Albertine, since our return
from Balbec, to read books upon the silversmith's art, upon the handiwork
of the old chasers. But as our old silver was melted twice over, at the time of
the Treaty of Utrecht when the King himself, setting the example to his
great nobles, sacrificed his plate, and again in 1789, it is now extremely rare.
On the other hand, it is true that modern silversmiths have managed to copy
all this old plate from the drawings of Le Pont-aux-Choux; Elstir considered
this modern antique unworthy to enter the home of a woman of taste, even
a floating home. I knew that Albertine had read the description of the
marvels that Roelliers had made for Mme du Barry. If any of these pieces
remained, she was dying to see them, and I to give them to her. She had even
begun to form a neat collection which she installed with charming taste in a
glass case and at which I could not look without emotion and alarm, for the
art with which she arranged them was that born of patience, ingenuity,
homesickness, the need to forget, in which prisoners excel. In the matter of
dress, what appealed to her most at this time was everything that was made
by Fortuny. These Fortuny gowns, one of which I had seen Mme de
Guermantes wearing, were those of which Elstir, when he told us about the
magnificent garments of the women of Carpaccio's and Titian's day, had
prophesied the speedy return, rising from their ashes, sumptuous, for

everything must return in time, as it is written beneath the vaults of Saint Mark's, and proclaimed, where they drink from the urns of marble and jasper of the byzantine capitals, by the birds which symbolise at once death and resurrection. As soon as women had begun to wear them, Albertine had remembered Elstir's prophecy, she had desired to have one and we were to go and choose it. Now these gowns, even if they were not those genuine antiques in which women today seem a little too much 'in fancy dress' and which it is preferable to keep as pieces in a collection (I was in search of these also, as it happens, for Albertine), could not be said to have the chilling effect of the artificial, the sham antique. Like the theatrical designs of Sert, Bakst and Benoist who at that moment were recreating in the Russian ballet the most cherished periods of art – with the aid of works of art impregnated with their spirit and yet original – these Fortuny gowns, faithfully antique but markedly original, brought before the eye like a stage setting, with an even greater suggestiveness than a setting, since the setting was left to the imagination, that Venice loaded with the gorgeous East from which they had been taken, of which they were, even more than a relic in the shrine of Saint Mark suggesting the sun and a group of turbaned heads, the fragmentary, mysterious and complementary colour. Everything of those days had perished, but everything was born again, evoked to fill the space between them with the splendour of the scene and the hum of life, by the reappearance, detailed and surviving, of the fabrics worn by the Doges' ladies. I had tried once or twice to obtain advice upon this subject from Mme de Guermantes. But the Duchess cared little for garments which form a 'costume'. She herself, though she possessed several, never looked so well as in black velvet with diamonds. And with regard to gowns like Fortuny's, her advice was not of any great value. Besides, I felt a scruple, if I asked for it, lest she might think that I called upon her only when I happened to need her help, whereas for a long time past I had been declining several invitations from her weekly. It was not only from her, moreover, that I received them in such profusion. Certainly, she and many other women had always been extremely kind to me. But my seclusion had undoubtedly multiplied their hospitality tenfold. It seems that in our social life, a minor echo of what occurs in love, the best way for a man to make himself sought-after is to withhold himself. A man calculates everything that he can possibly cite to his credit, in order to find favour with a woman, changes his clothes all day long, pays attention to his appearance, she does not pay him a single one of the attentions which he receives from the other woman to whom, while he betrays her, and in spite of his appearing before her ill-dressed and without any artifice to attract, he has endeared himself for ever. Similarly, if a man were to regret that he was not sufficiently courted in society, I should not advise him to pay more calls, to keep an even finer carriage, I should tell him not to accept any invitation, to live shut up in his room, to admit nobody, and that then there would be a queue outside his door. Or rather I should not tell him so. For it is a certain road to success which succeeds only like the road to love, that is to say if one has not adopted it with that object in view, if, for instance, you confine yourself to your room because you are seriously ill, or are supposed to be, or are keeping a mistress shut up with you whom you prefer to society (or for all these reasons at once), this will justify another person, who is not aware of the woman's existence, and simply because you decline to see him, in preferring you to all the people who offer themselves, and attaching himself to you.

'We shall have to begin to think soon about your Fortuny gowns,' I said to Albertine one evening. Surely, to her who had long desired them, who chose them deliberately with me, who had a place reserved for them beforehand not only in her wardrobe but in her imagination, the possession of these gowns, every detail of which, before deciding among so many, she carefully examined, was something more than it would have been to an over-wealthy woman who has more dresses than she knows what to do with and never even looks at them. And yet, notwithstanding the smile with which Albertine thanked me, saying: 'You are too kind', I noticed how weary, and even wretched, she was looking.

While we waited for these gowns to be ready, I used to borrow others of the kind, sometimes indeed merely the stuffs, and would dress Albertine in them, drape them over her; she walked about my room with the majesty of a Doge's wife and the grace of a mannequin. Only my captivity in Paris was made more burdensome by the sight of these garments which suggested Venice. True, Albertine was far more of a prisoner than I. And it was curious to remark how, through the walls of her prison, destiny, which transforms people, had contrived to pass, to change her in her very essence, and turn the girl I had known at Balbec into a tedious and docile captive. Yes, the walls of her prison had not prevented that influence from reaching her; perhaps indeed it was they that had produced it. It was no longer the same Albertine, because she was not, as at Balbec, incessantly in flight upon her bicycle, never to be found owing to the number of little watering-places where she would go to spend the night with her girl friends and where moreover her untruths made it more difficult to lay hands upon her; because confined to my house, docile and alone, she was no longer even what at Balbec, when I had succeeded in finding her, she used to be upon the beach, that fugitive, cautious, cunning creature, whose presence was enlarged by the thought of all those assignations which she was skilled in concealing, which made one love her because they made one suffer, in whom, beneath her coldness to other people and her casual answers, one could feel yesterday's assignation and tomorrow's, and for myself a contemptuous, deceitful thought; because the sea breeze no longer buffeted her skirts, because, above all, I had clipped her wings, she had ceased to be a Victory, was a burdensome slave of whom I would fain have been rid.

Then, to change the course of my thoughts, rather than begin a game of cards or draughts with Albertine, I asked her to give me a little music. I remained in bed, and she went and sat down at the end of the room before the pianola, between the two bookcases. She chose pieces which were quite new or which she had played to me only once or twice, for, as she began to know me better, she had learned that I liked to fix my thoughts only upon what was still obscure to me, glad to be able, in the course of these successive renderings, to join together, thanks to the increasing but, alas, distorting and alien light of my intellect, the fragmentary and interrupted lines of the structure which at first had been almost hidden in the mist. She knew and, I think, understood the joy that my mind derived, at these first hearings, from this task of modelling a still shapeless nebula. She guessed that at the third or fourth repetition my intellect, having reached, having consequently placed at the same distance, all the parts, and having no longer any activity to spare for them, had reciprocally extended and arrested them upon a uniform plane. She did not, however, proceed at once to a fresh piece, for, without perhaps having any clear idea of the process that was going on in my mind, she knew that at the moment when the effort of my intellect had succeeded in dispelling the mystery of a work, it was very rarely that, in compensation, it did not, in the course of its task of destruction, pick up some profitable reflection. And when in time Albertine said: 'We might give this roll to Françoise and get her to change it for something else', often there was for me a piece of music less in the world, perhaps, but a truth the more. While she was playing, of all Albertine's multiple tresses I could see but a single loop of black hair in the shape of a heart trained at the side of her ear like the riband of a Velasquez Infanta. Just as the substance of that Angel musician was constituted by the multiple journeys between the different points in past time which the memory of her occupied in myself, and its different abodes, from my vision to the most inward sensations of my being, which helped me to descend into the intimacy of hers, so the music that she played had also a volume, produced by the inconstant visibility of the different phrases, accordingly as I had more or less succeeded in throwing a light upon them and in joining together the lines of a structure which at first had seemed to me to be almost completely hidden in the fog.

I was so far convinced that it was absurd to be jealous of Mlle Vinteuil and her friend, inasmuch as Albertine since her confession had made no attempt to see them and among all the plans for a holiday in the country which we had formed had herself rejected Combray, so near to Montjouvain, that, often, what I would ask Albertine to play to me, without its causing me any pain, would be some music by Vinteuil. Once only this music had been an indirect cause of my jealousy. This was when Albertine, who knew that I had heard it performed at Mme Verdurin's by Morel, spoke to me one evening about him, expressing a keen desire to go and hear him play and to make his acquaintance. This, as it happened, was shortly after I had learned of the letter, unintentionally intercepted by M. de Charlus, from Léa to Morel. I asked myself whether Léa might not have mentioned him to Albertine. The words: 'You bad woman, you naughty old girl' came to my horrified mind. But precisely because Vinteuil's music was in this way painfully associated with Léa – and no longer with Mlle Vinteuil and her friend – when the grief that Léa caused me was soothed, I could then listen to this music without pain; one malady had made me immune to any possibility of the others. In this music of Vinteuil, phrases that I had not noticed at Mme Verdurin's, obscure phantoms that were then indistinct, turned into dazzling architectural structures; and some of them became friends, whom I had barely made out at first, who at best had appeared to me to be ugly, so that I could never have supposed that they were like those people, unattractive at first sight, whom we discover to be what they really are only after we have come to know them well. From one state to the other was a positive transmutation. On the other hand, phrases that I had distinguished at once in the music that I had heard at Mme Verdurin's, but had not then recognised, I identified now with phrases from other works, such as that phrase from the Sacred Variation for the Organ which, at Mme Verdurin's, had passed unperceived by me in the septet, where nevertheless, a saint that had stepped down from the sanctuary, it found itself consorting with the composer's familiar fays. Finally, the phrase that had seemed to me too little melodious, too mechanical in its rhythm, of the swinging joy of bells at noon, had now become my favourite, whether because I had grown accustomed to its ugliness or because I had discovered its beauty. This reaction from the disappointment which great works of art cause at first may in fact be attributed to a weakening of the initial impression or to the effort necessary to lay bare the truth. Two hypotheses which suggest themselves in all important questions, questions of the truth of Art, of the truth of the Immortality of the Soul; we must choose between them; and, in the case of Vinteuil's music, this choice presented itself at every moment under a variety of forms. For instance, this music seemed to me to be something truer than all the books that I knew. Sometimes I thought that this was due to the fact that what we feel in life, not being felt in the form of ideas, its literary (that is to say an intellectual) translation in giving an account of it, explains it, analyses it, but does not recompose it as does music, in which the sounds seem to assume the inflection of the thing itself, to reproduce that interior and extreme point of our sensation which is the part that gives us that peculiar exhilaration which we recapture from time to time and which when we say: 'What a fine day! What glorious sunshine!' we do not in the least communicate to our neighbour, in whom the same sun and the same weather arouse wholly different vibrations. In Vinteuil's music, there were thus some of those visions which it is impossible to express and almost forbidden to record, since, when at the moment of falling asleep we receive the caress of their unreal enchantment, at that very moment in which reason has already deserted us, our eyes are already sealed, and before we have had time to know not merely the ineffable but the invisible, we are asleep. It seemed to me indeed when I abandoned myself to this hypothesis that art might be real, that it was something even more than the simply nervous joy of a fine day or an opiate night that music can give; a more real, more fruitful exhilaration, to judge at least by what I felt. It is not possible that a piece of sculpture, a piece of music which gives us an emotion which we feel to be more exalted, more pure, more true, does not correspond to some definite spiritual reality. It is surely symbolical of one, since it gives that impression of profundity and truth. Thus nothing resembled more closely than some such phrase of Vinteuil the peculiar pleasure which I had felt at certain moments in my life, when gazing, for instance, at the steeples of Martinville, or at certain trees along a road near Balbec, or, more simply, in the first part of this book, when I tasted a certain cup of tea.

Without pressing this comparison farther, I felt that the clear sounds, the blazing colours which Vinteuil sent to us from the world in which he composed, paraded before my imagination with insistence but too rapidly for me to be able to apprehend it, something which I might compare to the perfumed silkiness of a geranium. Only, whereas, in memory, this vagueness may be, if not explored, at any rate fixed precisely, thanks to a guiding line of circumstances which explain why a certain savour has been able to recall to us luminous sensations, the vague sensations given by Vinteuil coming not from a memory but from an impression (like that of the steeples of

Martinville), one would have had to find, for the geranium scent of his music, not a material explanation, but the profound equivalent, the unknown and highly coloured festival (of which his works seemed to be the scattered fragments, the scarlet-flashing rifts), the mode in which he 'heard' the universe and projected it far beyond himself. This unknown quality of a unique world which no other composer had ever made us see, perhaps it is in this, I said to Albertine, that the most authentic proof of genius consists, even more than in the content of the work itself. 'Even in literature?' Albertine enquired. 'Even in literature.' And thinking again of the monotony of Vinteuil's works, I explained to Albertine that the great men of letters have never created more than a single work, or rather have never done more than refract through various mediums an identical beauty which they bring into the world. 'If it were not so late, my child,' I said to her, 'I would show you this quality in all the writers whose works you read while I am asleep, I would show you the same identity as in Vinteuil. These typical phrases, which you are beginning to recognise as I do, my little Albertine, the same in the sonata, in the septet, in the other works, would be for instance, if you like, in Barbey d'Aurevilly, a hidden reality revealed by a material trace, the physiological blush of *l'Ensorcelée*, of *Aimée de Spens*, of *la Clotte*, the hand of the *Rideau Cramoisi*, the old manners and customs, the old words, the ancient and peculiar trades behind which there is the Past, the oral history compiled by the rustics of the manor, the noble Norman cities redolent of England and charming as a Scots village, the cause of curses against which one can do nothing, the Vellini, the Shepherd, a similar sensation of anxiety in a passage, whether it be the wife seeking her husband in *Une Vieille Maîtresse*, or the husband in *l'Ensorcelée* scouring the plain and the "Ensorcelée" herself coming out from Mass. There are other typical phrases in Vinteuil like that stonemason's geometry in the novels of Thomas Hardy.'

Vinteuil's phrases made me think of the 'little phrase' and I told Albertine that it had been so to speak the national anthem of the love of Swann and Odette, 'the parents of Gilberte whom you know. You told me that she was not a bad girl. But didn't she attempt to have relations with you? She has mentioned you to me.' 'Yes, you see, her parents used to send a carriage to fetch her from our lessons when the weather was bad, I believe she took me home once and kissed me,' she said, after a momentary pause, with a laugh, and as though it were an amusing confession. 'She asked me all of a sudden whether I was fond of women.' (But if she only believed that she remembered that Gilberte had taken her home, how could she say with such precision that Gilberte had asked her this odd question?) 'In fact, I don't know what absurd idea came into my head to make a fool of her, I told her that I was.'

(One would have said that Albertine was afraid that Gilberte had told me this and did not wish me to come to the conclusion that she was lying.) 'But we did nothing at all.' (It was strange, if they had exchanged confidences, that they should have done nothing, especially as, before this, they had kissed, according to Albertine.) 'She took me home like that four or five times, perhaps more, and that is all.' It cost me a great effort not to ply her with further questions, but, mastering myself so as to appear not to be attaching any importance to all this, I returned to Thomas Hardy. 'Do you remember the stonemasons in *Jude the Obscure*, in *The Well-Beloved*, the blocks of stone which the father hews out of the island coming in boats to be piled up in the son's studio where they are turned into statues; in *A Pair of Blue Eyes* the parallelism of the tombs, and also the parallel line of the vessel, and the railway coaches containing the lovers and the dead woman; the parallelism between *The Well-Beloved*, where the man is in love with three women, and *A Pair of Blue Eyes* where the woman is in love with three men, and in short all those novels which can be laid one upon another like the vertically piled houses upon the rocky soil of the island. I cannot summarise the greatest writers like this in a moment's talk, but you would see in Stendhal a certain sense of altitude combining with the life of the spirit: the lofty place in which Julien Sorel is imprisoned, the tower on the summit of which Fabrice is confined, the belfry in which the Abbé Blanès pores over his astrology and from which Fabrice has such a magnificent bird's-eye view. You told me that you had seen some of Vermeer's pictures, you must have realised that they are fragments of an identical world, that it is always, however great the genius with which they have been recreated, the same table, the same carpet, the same woman, the same novel and unique beauty, an enigma, at that epoch in which nothing resembles or explains it, if we seek to find similarities in subjects but to isolate the peculiar impression that is produced by the colour. Well, then, this novel beauty remains identical in all Dostoevsky's works, the Dostoevsky woman (as distinctive as a Rembrandt woman) with her mysterious face, whose engaging beauty changes abruptly, as though her apparent good nature had been but make-believe, to a terrible insolence (although at heart it seems that she is more good than bad), is she not always the same, whether it be Nastasia Philipovna writing love letters to Aglaé and telling her that she hates her, or in a visit which is wholly identical with this – as also with that in which Nastasia Philipovna insults Vania's family – Grouchenka, as charming in Katherina Ivanovna's house as the other had supposed her to be terrible, then suddenly revealing her malevolence by insulting Katherina Ivanovna (although Grouchenka is good at heart); Grouchenka, Nastasia, figures as original, as mysterious not merely as

Carpaccio's courtesans but as Rembrandt's Bathsheba. As, in Vermeer, there is the creation of a certain soul, of a certain colour of fabrics and places, so there is in Dostoevsky creation not only of people but of their homes, and the house of the Murder in *Crime and Punishment* with its *dvornik*, is it not almost as marvellous as the masterpiece of the House of Murder in Dostoevsky, that sombre house, so long, and so high, and so huge, of Rogojin in which he kills Nastasia Philipovna. That novel and terrible beauty of a house, that novel beauty blended with a woman's face, that is the unique thing which Dostoevsky has given to the world, and the comparisons that literary critics may make, between him and Gogol, or between him and Paul de Kock, are of no interest, being external to this secret beauty. Besides, if I have said to you that it is, from one novel to another, the same scene, it is in the compass of a single novel that the same scenes, the same characters reappear if the novel is at all long. I could illustrate this to you easily in *War and Peace*, and a certain scene in a carriage . . . ' 'I didn't want to interrupt you, but now that I see that you are leaving Dostoevsky, I am afraid of forgetting. My dear boy, what was it you meant the other day when you said: "It is, so to speak, the Dostoevsky side of Mme de Sévigné." I must confess that I did not understand. It seems to me so different.' 'Come, little girl, let me give you a kiss to thank you for remembering so well what I say, you shall go back to the pianola afterwards. And I must admit that what I said was rather stupid. But I said it for two reasons. The first is a special reason. What I meant was that Mme de Sévigné, like Elstir, like Dostoevsky, instead of presenting things in their logical sequence, that is to say beginning with the cause, shows us first of all the effect, the illusion that strikes us. That is how Dostoevsky presents his characters. Their actions seem to us as misleading as those effects in Elstir's pictures where the sea appears to be in the sky. We are quite surprised to find that some sullen person is really the best of men, or vice versa.' 'Yes, but give me an example in Mme de Sévigné.' 'I admit,' I answered her with a laugh, 'that I am splitting hairs very fine, but still I could find examples.' 'But did he ever murder anyone, Dostoevsky? The novels of his that I know might all be called *The Story of a Crime*. It is an obsession with him, it is not natural that he should always be talking about it.' 'I don't think so, dear Albertine, I know little about his life. It is certain that, like everyone else, he was acquainted with sin, in one form or another, and probably in a form which the laws condemn. In that sense he must have been more or less criminal, like his heroes (not that they are altogether heroes, for that matter), who are found guilty with attenuating circumstances. And it is not perhaps necessary that he himself should have been a criminal. I am not a novelist; it is possible that creative writers are tempted by certain forms of life of which they have no personal experience. If I come with you to Versailles as we arranged, I shall show you the portrait of the ultra-respectable man, the best of husbands, Choderlos de Laclos, who wrote the most appallingly corrupt book, and facing it that of Mme de Genlis who wrote moral tales and was not content with betraying the Duchesse d'Orléans but tormented her by turning her children against her. I admit all the same that in Dostoevsky this preoccupation with murder is something extraordinary which makes him very alien to me. I am stupefied enough when I hear Baudelaire say:

Si le viol, le poison, le poignard, l'incendie
N'ont pas encor brodé de leurs plaisants dessins
Le canevas banal de nos piteux destins,
C'est que notre âme, hélas! n'est pas assez hardie.

But I can at least assume that Baudelaire is not sincere. Whereas Dostoevsky . . . All that sort of thing seems to me as remote from myself as possible, unless there are parts of myself of which I know nothing, for we realise our own nature only in course of time. In Dostoevsky I find the deepest penetration but only into certain isolated regions of the human soul. But he is a great creator. For one thing, the world which he describes does really appear to have been created by him. All those buffoons who keep on reappearing, like Lebedev, Karamazov, Ivolghin, Segrev, that incredible procession, are a humanity more fantastic than that which peoples Rembrandt's *Night Watch*. And perhaps it is fantastic only in the same way, by the effect of lighting and costume, and is quite normal really. In any case it is at the same time full of profound and unique truths, which belong only to Dostoevsky. They almost suggest, those buffoons, some trade or calling that no longer exists, like certain characters in the old drama, and yet how they reveal true aspects of the human soul! What astonishes me is the solemn manner in which people talk and write about Dostoevsky. Have you ever noticed the part that self-respect and pride play in his characters? One would say that, to him, love and the most passionate hatred, goodness and treachery, timidity and insolence are merely two states of a single nature, their self-respect, their pride preventing Aglaé, Nastasia, the Captain whose beard Mitya pulls, Krassotkin, Alyosha's enemy-friend, from showing themselves in their true colours. But there are many other great passages as well. I know very few of his books. But is it not a sculpturesque and simple theme, worthy of the most classical art, a frieze interrupted and resumed on which the tale of vengeance and expiation is unfolded, the crime of old Karamazov getting the poor idiot with child, the mysterious, animal, unexplained impulse by which the mother, herself unconsciously the instrument of an avenging destiny, obeying also obscurely her maternal instinct, feeling perhaps a combination of physical resentment and gratitude towards her seducer, comes to bear her child on old Karamazov's ground. This is the first episode, mysterious, grand, august as a Creation of Woman among the sculptures at Orvieto. And as counterpart, the second episode more than twenty years later, the murder of old Karamazov, the disgrace brought upon the Karamazov family by this son of the idiot, Smerdyakov, followed shortly afterwards by another action, as mysteriously sculpturesque and unexplained, of a beauty as obscure and natural as that of the child-birth in old Karamazov's garden, Smerdyakov hanging himself, his crime accomplished. As for Dostoevsky, I was not straying so far from him as you thought when I mentioned Tolstoy who has imitated him closely. In Dostoevsky there is, concentrated and fretful, a great deal of what was to blossom later on in Tolstoy. There is, in Dostoevsky, that proleptic gloom of the primitives which their disciples will brighten and dispel.' 'My dear boy, what a terrible thing it is that you are so lazy. Just look at your view of literature, so far more interesting than the way we were made to study it; the essays that they used to make us write upon *Esther*: "Monsieur" – you remember,' she said with a laugh, less from a desire to make fun of her masters and herself than from the pleasure of finding in her memory, in our common memory, a relic that was already almost venerable. But while she was speaking, and I continued to think of Vinteuil, it was the other, the materialist hypothesis, that of there being nothing, that in turn presented itself to my mind. I began to doubt, I said to myself that after all it might be the case that, if Vinteuil's phrases seemed to be the expression of certain states of the soul analogous to that which I had experienced when I tasted the madeleine that had been dipped in a cup of tea, there was nothing to assure me that the vagueness of such states was a sign of their profundity rather than of our not having learned yet to analyse them, so that there need be nothing more real in them than in other states. And yet that happiness, that sense of certainty in happiness while I was drinking the cup of tea, or when I smelt in the Champs-Elysées a smell of mouldering wood, was not an illusion. In any case, whispered the spirit of doubt, even if these states are more profound than others that occur in life, and defy analysis for the very reason that they bring into play too many forces which we have not yet taken into consideration, the charm of certain phrases of Vinteuil's music makes us think of them because it too defies analysis, but this does not prove that it has the same depth; the beauty of a phrase of pure music can easily appear to be the image of or at least akin to an intellectual impression which we have received, but simply because it is unintellectual. And why then do we suppose to be specially profound those mysterious phrases which haunt certain works, including this septet by Vinteuil?

It was not, however, his music alone that Albertine played me; the pianola was to us at times like a scientific magic lantern (historical and geographical) and on the walls of this room in Paris, supplied with inventions more modern than that of Combray days, I would see, accordingly as Albertine played me Rameau or Borodin, extend before me now an eighteenth century tapestry sprinkled with cupids and roses, now the Eastern steppe in which sounds are muffled by boundless distances and the soft carpet of snow. And these fleeting decorations were as it happened the only ones in my room, for if, at the time of inheriting my aunt Léonie's fortune, I had vowed that I would become a collector like Swann, would buy pictures, statues, all my money went upon securing horses, a motorcar, dresses for Albertine. But did not my room contain a work of art more precious than all these – Albertine herself? I looked at her. It was strange to me to think that it was she, she whom I had for so long thought it impossible even to know, who now, a wild beast tamed, a rose bush to which I had acted as trainer, as the framework, the trellis of its life, was seated thus, day by day, at home, by my side, before the pianola, with her back to my bookcase. Her shoulders, which I had seen bowed and resentful when she was carrying her golf-clubs, were leaning against my books. Her shapely legs, which at first I had quite reasonably imagined as having trodden throughout her girlhood the pedals of a bicycle, now rose and fell alternately upon those of the pianola, upon which Albertine who had acquired a distinction which made me feel her more my own, because it was from myself that it came, pressed her shoes of cloth of gold. Her fingers, at one time trained to the handlebars, now rested upon the keys like those of a Saint Cecilia. Her throat the curve of which, seen from my bed, was strong and full, at that distance and in the lamplight appeared more rosy, less rosy, however, than her face presented in profile, to which my gaze, issuing from the innermost depths of myself, charged with memories and burning with desire, added such a brilliancy, such an intensity of life that its relief seemed to stand out and turn with almost the same magic power as on the day, in the hotel at Balbec, when my vision was clouded by my overpowering desire to kiss her; I prolonged each of its surfaces beyond what I was able to see and beneath what concealed it from me and made me feel all the more strongly – eyelids which half hid her eyes, hair that covered the upper part of her cheeks – the relief of those superimposed planes. Her eyes shone like, in a matrix in which the opal is still embedded, the two facets which alone have as yet been polished, which, become more brilliant than metal, reveal, in the midst of the blind matter that encumbers them, as it were the mauve, silken wings of a butterfly placed under glass. Her dark, curling hair, presenting a different appearance whenever she turned to ask me what she was to play next, now a splendid wing, sharp at the tip, broad at the base, feathered and triangular, now weaving the relief of its curls in a strong and varied chain, a mass of crests, of watersheds, of precipices, with its incisions so rich and so multiple, seemed to exceed the variety that nature normally realises and to correspond rather to the desire of a sculptor who accumulates difficulties in order to bring into greater prominence the suppleness, the fire, the moulding, the life of his execution, and brought out more strongly, by interrupting in order to resume them, the animated curve, and, as it were, the rotation of the smooth and rosy face, of the polished dullness of a piece of painted wood. And, in contrast with all this relief, by the harmony also which united them with her, which had adapted her attitude to their form and purpose, the pianola which half concealed her like the keyboard of an organ, the bookcase, the whole of that corner of the room seemed to be reduced to nothing more than the lighted sanctuary, the shrine of this angel musician, a work of art which, presently, by a charming magic, was to detach itself from its niche and offer to my kisses its precious, rosy substance. But no, Albertine was in no way to me a work of art. I knew what it meant to admire a woman in an artistic fashion, I had known Swann. For my own part, moreover, I was, no matter who the woman might be, incapable of doing so, having no sort of power of detached observation, never knowing what it was that I beheld, and I had been amazed when Swann added retrospectively for me an artistic dignity – by comparing her, as he liked to do with gallantry to her face, to some portrait by Luini, by finding in her attire the gown or the jewels of a picture by Giorgione – to a woman who had seemed to me to be devoid of interest. Nothing of that sort with me. The pleasure and the pain that I derived from Albertine never took, in order to reach me, the line of taste and intellect; indeed, to tell the truth, when I began to regard Albertine as an angel musician glazed with a marvellous patina whom I congratulated myself upon possessing, it was not long before I found her uninteresting; I soon became bored in her company, but these moments were of brief duration; we love only that in which we pursue something inaccessible, we love only what we do not possess, and very soon I returned to the conclusion that I did not possess Albertine. In her eyes I saw pass now the hope, now the memory, perhaps the regret of joys which I could not guess, which in that case she preferred to renounce rather than tell me of them, and which, gathering no more of them than certain flashes in her pupils, I no more perceived than does the spectator who has been refused admission to the theatre, and who, his face glued to the glass panes of the door, can take in nothing of what is happening upon the stage. I do not know whether this was the case with her, but it is a strange thing, and so to speak a testimony by the most incredulous to their belief in good, this perseverance in falsehood shown by all those who deceive us. It is no good our telling them that their lie hurts us more than a confession, it is no good their realising this for themselves, they will start lying again a moment later, to remain consistent with their original statement of how much we meant to them. Similarly an atheist who values his life will let himself be burned alive rather than allow any contradiction of the popular idea of his courage. During these hours, I used sometimes to see hover over her face, in her gaze, in her pout, in her smile, the reflection of those inward visions the contemplation of which made her on these evenings unlike her usual self, remote from me to whom they were denied. 'What are you thinking about, my darling?' 'Why, nothing.' Sometimes, in answer to this reproach that she told me nothing, she would at one moment tell me things which she was not unaware that I knew as well as anyone (like those statesmen who will never give you the least bit of news, but speak to you instead of what you could read for yourself in the papers the day before), at another would describe without the least precision, in a sort of false confidence, bicycle rides that she had taken at Balbec, the year before our first meeting. And as though I had guessed aright long ago, when I inferred from it that she must be a girl who was allowed a great deal of freedom, who went upon long jaunts, the mention of those rides insinuated between Albertine's lips the same mysterious smile that had captivated me in those first days on the front at Balbec. She spoke to me also of the excursions that she had made with some girlfriends through the Dutch countryside, of returning to Amsterdam in the evening, at a late hour, when a dense and happy crowd of people almost all of whom she knew, thronged the streets, the canal towpaths, of which I felt that I could see reflected in Albertine's brilliant eyes as in the glancing windows of a fast-moving carriage, the innumerable, flickering fires. Since what is called aesthetic curiosity would deserve rather the name of indifference in comparison with the painful, unwearying curiosity that I felt as to the places in which Albertine had stayed, as to what she might have been doing on a particular evening, her smiles, the expressions in her eyes, the words that she had uttered, the kisses that she had received. No, never would the jealousy that I had felt one day of Saint-Loup, if it had persisted, have caused me this immense uneasiness. This love of woman for woman was something too unfamiliar; nothing enabled me to form a certain, an accurate idea of its pleasures, its quality. How many people, how many places (even places which did not concern her directly, vague pleasure resorts where she might have enjoyed some pleasure), how many scenes (wherever there was a crowd, where people could brush against her) Albertine – like a person who, shepherding all her escort, a whole company, past the barrier in front of her, secures their admission to the theatre – from the threshold of my imagination or of my memory, where I paid no attention to them, had introduced into my heart! Now the knowledge that I had of them was internal, immediate, spasmodic, painful. Love, what is it but space and time rendered perceptible by the heart.

And yet perhaps, had I myself been entirely faithful, I should have suffered because of infidelities which I would have been incapable of conceiving, whereas what it tortured me to imagine in Albertine was my own perpetual desire to find favour with fresh ladies, to plan fresh romances, was to suppose her guilty of the glance which I had been unable to resist casting, the other day, even when I was by her side, at the young bicyclists seated at tables in the Bois de Boulogne. As we have no personal knowledge, one might almost say that we can feel no jealousy save of ourselves. Observation counts for little. It is only from the pleasure that we ourselves have felt that we can derive knowledge and grief.

At moments, in Albertine's eyes, in the sudden inflammation of her cheeks, I felt as it were a gust of warmth pass furtively into regions more inaccessible to me than the sky, in which Albertine's memories, unknown to me, lived and moved. Then this beauty which, when I thought of the various years in which I had known Albertine whether upon the beach at Balbec or in Paris, I found that I had but recently discovered in her, and which consisted in the fact that my mistress was developing upon so many planes and embodied so many past days, this beauty became almost heartrending. Then beneath that blushing face I felt that there yawned like a gulf the inexhaustible expanse of the evenings when I had not known Albertine. I might, if I chose, take Albertine upon my knee, take her head in my hands; I might caress her, pass my hands slowly over her, but, just as if I had been handling a stone which encloses the salt of immemorial oceans or the light of a star, I felt that I was touching no more than the sealed envelope of a person who inwardly reached to infinity. How I suffered from that position to which we are reduced by the carelessness of nature which, when instituting the division of bodies, never thought of making possible the interpenetration of souls (for if her body was in the power of mine, her mind escaped from the grasp of mine). And I became aware that Albertine was not even for me the marvellous captive with whom I had thought to enrich my home, while I concealed her presence there as completely, even from the friends who came to see me and never suspected that she was at the end of the corridor, in the room next to my own, as did that man of whom nobody knew that he kept sealed in a bottle the Princess of China; urging me with a cruel and fruitless pressure to the remembrance of the past, she resembled, if anything, a mighty goddess of Time. And if it was necessary that I should lose for her sake years, my fortune – and provided that I can say to myself, which is by no means certain, alas, that she herself lost nothing – I have nothing to regret. No doubt solitude would have been better, more fruitful, less painful. But if I had led the life of a collector which Swann counselled (the joys of which M. de Charlus reproached me with not knowing, when, with a blend of wit, insolence and good taste, he said to me: 'How ugly your rooms are!') what statues, what pictures long pursued, at length possessed, or even, to put it in the best light, contemplated with detachment, would, like the little wound which healed quickly enough, but which the unconscious clumsiness of Albertine, of people generally, or of my own thoughts was never long in reopening, have given me access beyond my own boundaries, upon that avenue which, private though it be, debouches upon the high road along which passes what we learn to know only from the day on which it has made us suffer, the life of other people?

Sometimes the moon was so bright that, an hour after Albertine had gone to bed, I would go to her bedside to tell her to look at it through the window. I am certain that it was for this reason that I went to her room and not to assure myself that she was really there. What likelihood was there of her being able, had she wished, to escape? That would have required an improbable collusion with Françoise. In the dim room, I could see nothing save on the whiteness of the pillow a slender diadem of dark hair. But I could hear Albertine's breath. Her slumber was so profound that I hesitated at first to go as far as the bed. Then I sat down on the edge of it. Her sleep continued to flow with the same murmur. What I find it impossible to express is how gay her awakenings were. I embraced her, shook her. At once she ceased to sleep, but, without even a moment's interval, broke out in a laugh, saying as she twined her arms about my neck: 'I was just beginning to wonder whether you were coming', and she laughed a tender, beautiful laugh. You would have said that her charming head, when she slept, was filled with nothing but gaiety, affection and laughter. And in waking her I had merely, as when we cut a fruit, released the gushing juice which quenches our thirst.

Meanwhile winter was at an end; the fine weather returned, and often when Albertine had just bidden me good-night, my room, my curtains, the wall above the curtains being still quite dark, in the nuns' garden next door I could hear, rich and precious in the silence like a harmonium in church, the modulation of an unknown bird which, in the Lydian mode, was already chanting matins, and into the midst of my darkness flung the rich dazzling note of the sun that it could see. Once indeed, we heard all of a sudden the regular cadence of a plaintive appeal. It was the pigeons beginning to coo. 'That proves that day has come already,' said Albertine; and, her brows almost knitted, as though she missed, by living with me, the joys of the fine weather, 'Spring has begun, if the pigeons have returned.' The resemblance between their cooing and the crow of the cock was as profound and as obscure as, in Vinteuil's septet, the resemblance between the theme of the *adagio* and that of the closing piece, which is based upon the same key-theme as the other but so transformed by differences of tonality, of measure, that the profane outsider if he opens a book upon Vinteuil is astonished to find that they are all three based upon the same four notes, four notes which for that matter he may pick out with one finger upon the piano without recapturing anything of the three fragments. So this melancholy fragment performed by the pigeons was a sort of cockcrow in the minor, which did not soar up into the sky, did not rise vertically, but, regular as the braying of a donkey, enveloped in sweetness, went from one pigeon to another along a single horizontal line, and never raised itself, never changed its lateral plaint into that joyous appeal which had been uttered so often in the *allegro* of the introduction and in the finale.

Presently the nights grew shorter still and before what had been the hour of daybreak, I could see already stealing above my window-curtains the daily increasing whiteness of the dawn. If I resigned myself to allowing Albertine to continue to lead this life, in which, notwithstanding her denials, I felt that she had the impression of being a prisoner, it was only because I was sure that on the morrow I should be able to set myself, at the same time to work and to leave my bed, to go out of doors, to prepare our departure for some property which we should buy and where Albertine would be able to lead more freely and without anxiety on my account, the life of country or seaside, of boating or hunting, which appealed to her. Only, on the morrow, that past which I loved and detested by turns in Albertine, it would so happen that (as, when it is the present, between himself and us, everyone, from calculation, or courtesy, or pity, sets to work to weave a curtain of falsehood which we mistake for the truth), retrospectively, one of the hours which composed it, and even those which I had supposed myself to know, offered me all of a sudden an aspect which someone no longer made any attempt to conceal from me and which was then quite different from that in which it had previously appeared to me. Behind some look in her eyes, in place of the honest thought which I had formerly supposed that I could read in it, was a desire, unsuspected hitherto, which revealed itself, alienating from me a fresh region of Albertine's heart which I had believed to be assimilated to my own. For instance, when Andrée left Balbec in the month of July, Albertine had never told me that she was to see her again shortly, and I supposed that she had seen her even sooner than she expected, since, in view of the great unhappiness that I had felt at Balbec, on that night of the fourteenth of September, she had made me the sacrifice of not remaining there and of returning at once to Paris. When she had arrived there on the fifteenth, I had asked her to go and see Andrée and had said to her: 'Was she pleased to see you again?' Now one day Mme Bontemps had called, bringing something for Albertine; I saw her for a moment and told her that Albertine had gone out with Andrée: 'They have gone for a drive in the country.' 'Yes,' replied Mme Bontemps, 'Albertine is always ready to go to the country. Three years ago, for instance, she simply had to go, every day, to the Buttes-Chaumont.' At the name Buttes-Chaumont, a place where Albertine had told me that she had never been, my breath stopped for a moment. The truth is the most cunning of enemies. It launches its attacks upon the points of our heart at which we were not expecting them, and have prepared no defence. Had Albertine been lying to her aunt, then, when she said that she went every day to the Buttes-Chaumont, or to myself, more recently, when she told me that she did not know the place? 'Fortunately,' Mme Bontemps went on, 'that poor Andrée will soon be leaving for a more bracing country, for the real country, she needs it badly, she is not looking at all well. It is true that she did not have an opportunity this summer of getting the fresh air she requires. Just think, she left Balbec at the end of July, expecting to go back there in September, and then her brother put his knee out, and she was unable to go back.' So Albertine was expecting her at Balbec and had concealed this from me. It is true that it was all the more kind of her to have offered to return to Paris with me. Unless . . . 'Yes, I remember Albertine's mentioning it to me' (this was untrue). 'When did the accident occur, again? I am not very clear about it.' 'Why, to my mind, it occurred in the very nick of time, for a day later the lease of the villa began, and Andrée's grandmother would have had to pay a month's rent for nothing. He hurt his leg on the fourteenth of September, she was in time to telegraph to Albertine on the morning of the fifteenth that she was not coming and Albertine was in time to warn the agent. A day later, the lease would have run on to the middle of October.' And so, no doubt, when

Albertine, changing her mind, had said to me: 'Let us go this evening', what she saw with her mind's eye was an apartment, that of Andrée's grandmother, where, as soon as we returned, she would be able to see the friend whom, without my suspecting it, she had supposed that she would be seeing in a few days at Balbec. Those kind words which she had used, in offering to return to Paris with me, in contrast to her headstrong refusal a little earlier, I had sought to attribute them to a reawakening of her good nature. They were simply and solely the effect of a change that had occurred in a situation which we do not know, and which is the whole secret of the variation of the conduct of the women who are not in love with us. They obstinately refuse to give us an assignation for the morrow, because they are tired, because their grandfather insists upon their dining with him: 'But come later,' we insist. 'He keeps me very late. He may want to see me home.' The whole truth is that they have made an appointment with some man whom they like. Suddenly it happens that he is no longer free. And they come to tell us how sorry they are to have disappointed us, that the grandfather can go and hang himself, that there is nothing in the world to keep them from remaining with us. I ought to have recognised these phrases in Albertine's language to me on the day of my departure from Balbec, but to interpret that language I should have needed to remember at the time two special features in Albertine's character which now recurred to my mind, one to console me, the other to make me wretched, for we find a little of everything in our memory; it is a sort of pharmacy, of chemical laboratory, in which our groping hand comes to rest now upon a sedative drug, now upon a dangerous poison. The first, the consoling feature was that habit of making a single action serve the pleasure of several persons, that multiple utilisation of whatever she did, which was typical of Albertine. It was quite in keeping with her character, when she returned to Paris (the fact that Andrée was not coming back might make it inconvenient for her to remain at Balbec, without any implication that she could not exist apart from Andrée), to derive from that single journey an opportunity of touching two people each of whom she genuinely loved, myself, by making me believe that she was coming in order not to let me be alone, so that I should not be unhappy, out of devotion to me, Andrée by persuading her that, as soon as there was no longer any question of her coming to Balbec, she herself did not wish to remain there a moment longer, that she had prolonged her stay there only in the hope of seeing Andrée and was now hurrying back to join her. Now, Albertine's departure with myself was such an immediate sequel, on the one hand to my grief, my desire to return to Paris, on the other hand to Andrée's telegram, that it was quite natural that Andrée and I, unaware, respectively, she of my grief, I of her telegram, should have supposed that Albertine's departure from Balbec was the effect of the one cause that each of us knew, which indeed it followed at so short an interval and so unexpectedly. And in this case, I might still believe that the thought of keeping me company had been Albertine's real object, while she had not chosen to overlook an opportunity of thereby establishing a claim to Andrée's gratitude. But unfortunately I remembered almost at once another of Albertine's characteristics, which was the vivacity with which she was gripped by the irresistible temptation of a pleasure. And so I recalled how, when she had decided to leave, she had been so impatient to get to the tram, how she had pushed past the Manager who, as he tried to detain us, might have made us miss the omnibus, the shrug of connivance that she had given me, by which I had been so touched, when, on the crawler, M. de Cambremer had asked us whether we could not 'postpone it by a week'. Yes, what she saw before her eyes at that moment, what made her so feverishly anxious to leave, what she was so impatient to see again was that emptied apartment which I had once visited, the home of Andrée's grandmother, left in charge of an old footman, a luxurious apartment, facing south, but so empty, so silent, that the sun appeared to have spread dustsheets over the sofa, the armchairs of the room in which Albertine and Andrée would ask the respectful caretaker, perhaps unsuspecting, perhaps an accomplice, to allow them to rest for a while. I could always see it now, empty, with a bed or a sofa, that room, to which, whenever Albertine seemed pressed for time and serious, she set off to meet her friend, who had doubtless arrived there before her since her time was more her own. I had never before given a thought to that apartment which now possessed for me a horrible beauty. The unknown element in the lives of other people is like that in nature, which each fresh scientific discovery merely reduces, but does not abolish. A jealous lover exasperates the woman with whom he is in love by depriving her of a thousand unimportant pleasures, but those pleasures which are the keystone of her life she conceals in a place where, in the moments in which he thinks that he is showing the most intelligent perspicacity and third parties are keeping him most closely informed, he never dreams of looking. Anyhow, Andrée was at least going to leave Paris. But I did not wish that Albertine should be in a position to despise me as having been the dupe of herself and Andrée. One of these days, I would tell her. And thus I should force her perhaps to speak to me more frankly, by showing her that I was informed, all the same, of the things that she concealed from me. But I did not wish to mention it to her for the moment, first of all because, so soon after her aunt's visit, she would guess from where my information came, would block that source and would not dread other, unknown sources. Also because I did not wish to risk, so long as I was not absolutely certain of keeping Albertine for as long as I chose, arousing in her too frequent irritations which might have the effect of making her decide to leave me. It is true that if I reasoned, sought the truth, prognosticated the future on the basis of her speech, which always approved of all my plans, assuring me how much she loved this life, of how little her seclusion deprived her, I had no doubt that she would remain with me always. I was indeed greatly annoyed by the thought, I felt that I was missing life, the universe, which I had never enjoyed, bartered for a woman in whom I could no longer find anything novel. I could not even go to Venice, where, while I lay in bed, I should be too keenly tormented by the fear of the advances that might be made to her by the gondolier, the people in the hotel, the Venetian women. But if I reasoned, on the other hand, upon the other hypothesis, that which rested not upon Albertine's speech, but upon silences, looks, blushes, sulks, and indeed bursts of anger, which I could quite easily have shown her to be unfounded and which I preferred to appear not to notice, then I said to myself that she was finding this life insupportable, that all the time she found herself deprived of what she loved, and that inevitably she must one day leave me. All that I wished, if she did so, was that I might choose the moment in which it would not be too painful to me, and also that it might be in a season when she could not go to any of the places in which I imagined her debaucheries, either at Amsterdam, or with Andrée whom she would see again, it was true, a few months later. But in the interval I should have grown calm and their meeting would leave me unmoved. In any case, I must wait before I could think of it until I was cured of the slight relapse that had been caused by my discovery of the reasons by which Albertine, at an interval of a few hours, had been determined not to leave, and then to leave Balbec immediately. I must allow time for the symptoms to disappear which could only go on diminishing if I learned nothing new, but which were still too acute not to render more painful, more difficult, an operation of rupture recognised now as inevitable, but in no sense urgent, and one that would be better performed 'in cold blood'. Of this choice of the right moment I was the master, for if she decided to leave me before I had made up my mind, at the moment when she informed me that she had had enough of this life, there would always be time for me to think of resisting her arguments, to offer her a larger freedom, to promise her some great pleasure in the near future which she herself would be anxious to await, at worst, if I could find no recourse save to her heart, to assure her of my grief. I was therefore quite at my ease from this point of view, without, however, being very logical with myself. For, in the hypotheses in which I left out of account the things which she said and announced, I supposed that, when it was a question of her leaving me, she would give me her reasons beforehand, would allow me to fight and to conquer them. I felt that my life with Albertine was, on the one hand, when I was not jealous, mere boredom, and on the other hand, when I was jealous, constant suffering. Supposing that there was any happiness in it, it could not last. I possessed the same spirit of wisdom which had inspired me at Balbec, when, on the evening when we had been happy together after Mme de Cambremer's call, I determined to give her up, because I knew that by prolonging our intimacy I should gain nothing. Only, even now, I imagined that the memory which I should preserve of her would be like a sort of vibration prolonged by a pedal from the last moment of our parting. And so I intended to choose a pleasant moment, so that it might be it which continued to vibrate in me. It must not be too difficult, I must not wait too long, I must be prudent. And yet, having waited so long, it would be madness not to wait a few days longer, until an acceptable moment should offer itself, rather than risk seeing her depart with that same sense of revolt which I had felt in the past when Mamma left my bedside without bidding me good-night, or when she said goodbye to me at the station. At all costs I multiplied the favours that I was able to bestow upon her. As for the Fortuny gowns, we had at length decided upon one in blue and gold lined with pink which was just ready. And I had ordered, at the same time, the other five which she had relenquished with regret, out of preference for this last. Yet with the coming of spring, two months after her aunt's conversation with me, I allowed myself to be carried away by anger one evening. It was the very evening on which Albertine had put on for the first time the indoor gown in gold and blue by Fortuny which, by reminding me of Venice, made me feel all the more strongly what I was sacrificing for her, who felt no corresponding gratitude towards me. If I had never seen Venice, I had dreamed of it incessantly since those Easter holidays which, when still a boy, I had been going to spend there, and earlier still, since the Titian prints and Giotto photographs which Swann had given me long ago at Combray. The Fortuny gown which Albertine was wearing that evening seemed to me the tempting phantom of that invisible Venice. It swarmed with Arabic ornaments, like the Venetian palaces hidden like sultanas behind a screen of pierced stone, like the bindings in the Ambrosian library, like the columns from which the Oriental birds that symbolised alternatively life and death were repeated in the mirror of the fabric, of an intense blue which, as my gaze extended over it, was changed into a malleable gold, by those same transmutations which, before the advancing gondolas, change into flaming metal the azure of the Grand Canal. And the sleeves were lined with a cherry pink which is so peculiarly Venetian that it is called Tiepolo pink.

In the course of the day, Françoise had let fall in my hearing that Albertine was satisfied with nothing, that when I sent word to her that I would be going out with her, or that I would not be going out, that the motorcar would come to fetch her, or would not come, she almost shrugged her shoulders and would barely give a polite answer. This evening, when I felt that she was in a bad temper, and when the first heat of summer had wrought upon my nerves, I could not restrain my anger and reproached her with her ingratitude. 'Yes, you can ask anybody,' I shouted at the top of my voice, quite beyond myself, 'you can ask Françoise, it is common knowledge.' But immediately I remembered how Albertine had once told me how terrifying she found me when I was angry, and had applied to myself the speech of Esther:

> Jugez combien ce front irrité contre moi
> Dans mon âme troublée a dû jeter d'émoi.
> Hélas sans frissonner quel coeur audacieux
> Soutiendrait les éclairs qui partent de ses yeux.

I felt ashamed of my violence. And, to make reparation for what I had done, without, however, acknowledging a defeat, so that my peace might be an armed and awe-inspiring peace, while at the same time I thought it as well to show her once again that I was not afraid of a rupture so that she might not feel any temptation to break with me: 'Forgive me, my little Albertine, I am ashamed of my violence, I don't know how to apologise. If we are not able to get on together, if we are to be obliged to part, it must not be in this fashion, it would not be worthy of us. We will part, if part we must, but first of all I wish to beg your pardon most humbly and from the bottom of my heart.' I decided that, to atone for my rudeness and also to make certain of her intention to remain with me for some time to come, at any rate until Andrée should have left Paris, which would be in three weeks, it would be as well, next day, to think of some pleasure greater than any that she had yet had and fairly slow in its fulfilment; also, since I was going to wipe out the offence that I had given her, perhaps I should do well to take advantage of this moment to show her that I knew more about her life than she supposed. The resentment that she would feel would be removed on the morrow by my kindness, but the warning would remain in her mind. 'Yes, my little Albertine, forgive me if I was violent. I am not quite as much to blame as you think. There are wicked people in the world who are trying to make us quarrel; I have always refrained from mentioning this, as I did not wish to torment you. But sometimes I am driven out of my mind by certain accusations. For instance,' I went on, 'they are tormenting me at present, they are persecuting me with reports of your relations, but with Andrée.' 'With Andrée?' she cried, her face ablaze with anger. And astonishment or the desire to appear astonished made her open her eyes wide. 'How charming! And may one know who has been telling you these pretty tales, may I be allowed to speak to these persons, to learn from them upon what they are basing their scandals?' 'My little Albertine, I do not know, the letters are anonymous, but from people whom you would perhaps have no difficulty in finding' (this to show her that I did not believe that she would try) 'for they must know you quite well. The last one, I must admit (and I mention it because it deals with a trifle, and there is nothing at all unpleasant in it), made me furious all the same. It informed me that if, on the day when we left Balbec, you first of all wished to remain there and then decided to go, that was because in the interval you had received a letter from Andrée telling you that she was not coming.' 'I know quite well that Andrée wrote to tell me that she wasn't coming, in fact she telegraphed; I can't show you the telegram because I didn't keep it, but it wasn't that day; what difference do you suppose it could make to me whether Andrée came or not?' The words 'what difference do you suppose it could make to me' were a proof of anger and that 'it did make' some difference, but were not necessarily a proof that Albertine had returned to Paris solely from a desire to see Andrée. Whenever Albertine saw one of the real or alleged motives of one of her actions discovered by a person to whom she had pleaded a different motive, she became angry, even if the person were he for whose sake she had really performed the action. That Albertine believed that this information as to what she had been doing was not furnished me in anonymous letters against my will but was eagerly demanded by myself, could never have been deduced from the words which she next uttered, in which she appeared to accept my story of the anonymous letters, but rather from her air of anger with myself, an anger which appeared to be merely the explosion of her previous ill humour, just as the espionage in which, by this hypothesis, she must suppose that I had been indulging would have been only the culmination of a supervision of all her actions as to which she had felt no doubt for a long time past. Her anger extended even to Andrée herself, and deciding no doubt that from now onwards I should never be calm again even when she went out with Andrée: 'Besides, Andrée makes me wild. She is a deadly bore. I never want to go anywhere with her again. You can tell that to the people who informed you that I came back to Paris for her sake.

Suppose I were to tell you that after all the years I've known Andrée, I couldn't even describe her face to you, I've hardly ever looked at it!' Now at Balbec, in that first year, she had said to me: 'Andrée is lovely.' It is true that this did not mean that she had had amorous relations with her, and indeed I had never heard her speak at that time save with indignation of any relations of that sort. But could she not have changed even without being aware that she had changed, never supposing that her amusements with a girl friend were the same thing as the immoral relations, not clearly defined in her own mind, which she condemned in other women? Was it not possible also that this same change, and this same unconsciousness of change, might have occurred in her relations with myself, whose kisses she had repulsed at Balbec with such indignation, kisses which afterwards she was to give me of her own accord every day, which (so, at least, I hoped) she would give me for a long time to come, and which she was going to give me in a moment? 'But, my darling, how do you expect me to tell them when I do not know who they are?' This answer was so forceful that it ought to have melted the objections and doubts which I saw crystallised in Albertine's pupils. But it left them intact. I was now silent, and yet she continued to gaze at me with that persistent attention which we give to someone who has not finished speaking. I begged her pardon once more. She replied that she had nothing to forgive me. She had grown very gentle again. But, beneath her sad and troubled features, it seemed to me that a secret had taken shape. I knew quite well that she could not leave me without warning me, besides she could not either wish to leave me (it was in a week's time that she was to try on the new Fortuny gowns), nor decently do so, as my mother was returning to Paris at the end of the week and her aunt also. Why, since it was impossible for her to depart, did I repeat to her several times that we should be going out together next day to look at some Venetian glass which I wished to give her, and why was I comforted when I heard her say that that was settled? When it was time for her to bid me good-night and I kissed her, she did not behave as usual, but turned aside – it was barely a minute or two since I had been thinking how pleasant it was that she now gave me every evening what she had refused me at Balbec – she did not return my kiss. One would have said that, having quarrelled with me, she was not prepared to give me a token of affection which might later on have appeared to me a treacherous denial of that quarrel. One would have said that she was attuning her actions to that quarrel, and yet with moderation, whether so as not to announce it, or because, while breaking off her carnal relations with me, she wished still to remain my friend. I embraced her then a second time, pressing to my heart the mirroring and gilded azure of the Grand Canal and the mating birds, symbols of death and resurrection. But for the second time she drew away and, instead of returning my kiss, withdrew with the sort of instinctive and fatal obstinacy of animals that feel the hand of death. This presentiment which she seemed to be expressing overpowered me also, and filled me with so anxious an alarm that when she had reached the door I had not the courage to let her go, and called her back, 'Albertine,' I said to her, 'I am not at all sleepy. If you don't want to go to sleep yourself, you might stay here a little longer, if you like, but I don't really mind, and I don't on any account want to tire you.' I felt that if I had been able to make her undress, and to have her there in her white nightgown, in which she seemed more rosy, warmer, in which she excited my senses more keenly, the reconciliation would have been more complete. But I hesitated for an instant, for the blue border of her gown added to her face a beauty, an illumination, a sky without which she would have seemed to me more harsh. She came back slowly and said to me very sweetly, and still with the same downcast, sorrowful expression: 'I can stay as long as you like, I am not sleepy.' Her reply calmed me, for, so long as she was in the room, I felt that I could take thought for the future and that moreover it implied friendship, obedience, but of a certain sort, which seemed to me to be bounded by that secret which I felt to exist behind her sorrowful gaze, her altered manner, partly in spite of herself, partly no doubt to attune them beforehand to something which I did not know. I felt that, all the same, I needed only to have her all in white, with her throat bare, in front of me, as I had seen her at Balbec in bed, to find the courage which would make her obliged to yield. 'Since you are so kind as to stay here a moment to console me, you ought to take off your gown, it is too hot, too stiff, I dare not approach you for fear of crumpling that fine stuff and we have those symbolic birds between us. Undress, my darling.' 'No, I couldn't possibly take off this dress here. I shall undress in my own room presently.' 'Then you won't even come and sit down on my bed?' 'Why, of course.' She remained, however, a little way from me, by my feet. We talked. I know that I then uttered the word death, as though Albertine were about to die. It seems that events are larger than the moment in which they occur and cannot confine themselves in it. Certainly they overflow into the future through the memory that we retain of them, but they demand a place also in the time that precedes them. One may say that we do not then see them as they are to be, but in memory are they not modified also?

When I saw that she deliberately refrained from kissing me, realising that I was merely wasting my time, that it was only after the kiss that the soothing, the genuine minutes would begin, I said to her: 'Good-night, it is too late', because that would make her kiss me and we could then continue.

But after saying: 'Good-night, see you sleep well', exactly as she had done twice already, she contented herself with letting me kiss her on the cheek. This time I dared not call her back, but my heart beat so violently that I could not lie down again. Like a bird that flies from one end of its cage to the other, without stopping I passed from the anxiety lest Albertine should leave the house to a state of comparative calm. This calm was produced by the argument which I kept on repeating several times every minute: 'She cannot go without warning me, she never said anything about going', and I was more or less calmed. But at once I reminded myself: 'And yet if tomorrow I find that she has gone. My very anxiety must be founded upon something; why did she not kiss me?' At this my heart ached horribly. Then it was slightly soothed by the argument which I advanced once more, but I ended with a headache, so incessant and monotonous was this movement of my thoughts. There are thus certain mental states, and especially anxiety, which, as they offer us only two alternatives, are in a way as atrociously circumscribed as a merely physical pain. I perpetually repeated the argument which justified my anxiety and that which proved it false and reassured me, within as narrow a space as the sick man who explores without ceasing, by an internal movement, the organ that is causing his suffering, and withdraws for an instant from the painful spot to return to it a moment later. Suddenly, in the silence of the night, I was startled by a sound apparently insignificant which, however, filled me with terror, the sound of Albertine's window being violently opened. When I heard no further sound, I asked myself why this had caused me such alarm. In itself there was nothing so extraordinary; but I probably gave it two interpretations which appalled me equally. In the first place it was one of the conventions of our life in common, since I was afraid of draughts, that nobody must ever open a window at night. This had been explained to Albertine when she came to stay in the house, and albeit she was convinced that this was a mania on my part and thoroughly unhealthy, she had promised me that she would never break the rule. And she was so timorous about everything that she knew to be my wish, even if she blamed me for it, that she would have gone to sleep with the stench of a chimney on fire rather than open her window, just as, however important the circumstances, she would not have had me called in the morning. It was only one of the minor conventions of our life, but from the moment when she violated it without having said anything to me, did not that mean that she no longer needed to take precautions, that she would violate them all just as easily? Besides, the sound had been violent, almost ill-bred, as though she had flung the window open crimson with rage, and saying: 'This life is stifling me, so that's that, I must have air!' I did not exactly say all this to myself, but I continued to think, as of a presage more mysterious and more funereal than the hoot of an owl, of that sound of the window which Albertine had opened. Filled with an agitation such as I had not felt perhaps since the evening at Combray when Swann had been dining downstairs, I paced the corridor for a long time, hoping, by the noise that I made, to attract Albertine's attention, hoping that she would take pity upon me and would call me to her, but I heard no sound come from her room. Gradually I began to feel that it was too late. She must long have been asleep. I went back to bed. In the morning, as soon as I awoke, since no one ever came to my room, whatever might have happened, without a summons, I rang for Françoise. And at the same time I thought: 'I must speak to Albertine about a yacht which I mean to have built for her.' As I took my letters I said to Françoise without looking at her: 'Presently I shall have something to say to Mlle Albertine; is she out of bed yet?' 'Yes, she got up early.' I felt arise in me, as in a sudden gust of wind, a thousand anxieties, which I was unable to keep in suspense in my bosom. The tumult there was so great that I was quite out of breath as though caught in a tempest. 'Ah! But where is she just now?' 'I expect she's in her room.' 'Ah! Good! Very well, I shall see her presently.' I breathed again, she was still in the house, my agitation subsided. Albertine was there, it was almost immaterial to me whether she was or not. Besides, had it not been absurd to suppose that she could possibly not be there? I fell asleep, but, in spite of my certainty that she would not leave me, into a light sleep and of a lightness relative to her alone. For by the sounds that could be connected only with work in the courtyard, while I heard them vaguely in my sleep, I remained unmoved, whereas the slightest rustle that came from her room, when she left it, or noiselessly returned, pressing the bell so gently, made me start, ran through my whole body, left me with a throbbing heart, albeit I had heard it in a profound slumber, just as my grandmother in the last days before her death, when she was plunged in an immobility which nothing could disturb and which the doctors called coma, would begin, I was told, to tremble for a moment like a leaf when she heard the three rings with which I was in the habit of summoning Françoise, and which, even when I made them softer, during that week, so as not to disturb the silence of the death-chamber, nobody, Françoise assured me, could mistake, because of a way that I had, and was quite unconscious of having, of pressing the bell, for the ring of anyone else. Had I then entered myself into my last agony, was this the approach of death?

That day and the next we went out together, since Albertine refused to go out again with Andrée. I never even mentioned the yacht to her. These excursions had completely restored my peace of mind. But she had continued at night to embrace me in the same novel fashion, which left me furious. I could interpret it now in no other way than as a method of showing me that she was cross with me, which seemed to me perfectly absurd after my incessant kindness to her. And so, no longer deriving from her even those carnal satisfactions on which I depended, finding her positively ugly in her ill humour, I felt all the more keenly my deprivation of all the women and of the travels for which these first warm days reawakened my desire. Thanks no doubt to the scattered memory of the forgotten assignations that I had had, while still a schoolboy, with women, beneath trees already in full leaf, this springtime region in which the endless round of our dwelling-place travelling through the seasons had halted for the last three days, beneath a clement sky, and from which all the roads pointed towards picnics in the country, boating parties, pleasure trips, seemed to me to be the land of women just as much as it was the land of trees, and the land in which a pleasure that was everywhere offered became permissible to my convalescent strength. Resigning myself to idleness, resigning myself to chastity, to tasting pleasure only with a woman whom I did not love, resigning myself to remaining shut up in my room, to not travelling, all this was possible in the Old World in which we had been only the day before, in the empty world of winter, but was no longer possible in this new universe bursting with green leaves, in which I had awaked like a young Adam faced for the first time with the problem of existence, of happiness, who is not bowed down beneath the weight of the accumulation of previous negative solutions. Albertine's presence weighed upon me, and so I regarded her sullenly, feeling that it was a pity that we had not had a rupture. I wanted to go to Venice, I wanted in the meantime to go to the Louvre to look at Venetian pictures and to the Luxembourg to see the two Elstirs which, as I had just heard, the Duchesse de Guermantes had recently sold to that gallery, those that I had so greatly admired, the *Pleasures of the Dance* and the *Portrait of the X Family*. But I was afraid that, in the former, certain lascivious poses might give Albertine a desire, a regretful longing for popular rejoicings, making her say to herself that perhaps a certain life which she had never led, a life of fireworks and country taverns, was not so bad. Already, in anticipation, I was afraid lest, on the Fourteenth of July, she would ask me to take her to a popular ball and I dreamed of some impossible event which would cancel the national holiday. And besides, there were also present, in Elstir's pictures, certain nude female figures in the leafy landscapes of the South which might make Albertine think of certain pleasures, albeit Elstir himself (but would she not lower the standard of his work?) had seen in them nothing more than plastic beauty, or rather the beauty of snowy monuments which is assumed by the bodies of women seated among verdure. And so I resigned myself to abandoning that pleasure and made up my mind to go to Versailles. Albertine had remained in her room, reading, in her Fortuny gown. I asked her if she would like to go with me to Versailles. She had the charming quality of being always ready for anything, perhaps because she had been accustomed in the past to spend half her time as the guest of other people, and, just as she had made up her mind to come to Paris, in two minutes, she said to me: 'I can come as I am, we shan't be getting out of the car.' She hesitated for a moment between two cloaks in which to conceal her indoor dress – as she might have hesitated between two friends in the choice of an escort – chose one of dark blue, an admirable choice, thrust a pin into a hat. In a minute, she was ready, before I had put on my greatcoat, and we went to Versailles. This very promptitude, this absolute docility left me more reassured, as though indeed, without having any special reason for uneasiness, I had been in need of reassurance. 'After all I have nothing to fear, she does everything that I ask, in spite of the noise she made with her window the other night. The moment I spoke of going out, she flung that blue cloak over her gown and out she came, that is not what a rebel would have done, a person who was no longer on friendly terms with me,' I said to myself as we went to Versailles. We stayed there a long time. The whole sky was formed of that radiant and almost pale blue which the wayfarer lying down in a field sees at times above his head, but so consistent, so intense, that he feels that the blue of which it is composed has been utilised without any alloy and with such an inexhaustible richness that one might delve more and more deeply into its substance without encountering an atom of anything but that same blue. I thought of my grandmother who – in human art as in nature – loved grandeur, and who used to enjoy watching the steeple of Saint-Hilaire soar into the same blue. Suddenly I felt once again a longing for my lost freedom as I heard a sound which I did not at first identify, a sound which my grandmother would have loved as well. It was like the buzz of a wasp. 'Why,' said Albertine, 'there is an aeroplane, it is high up in the sky, so high.' I looked in every direction but could see only, unmarred by any black spot, the unbroken pallor of the serene azure. I continued nevertheless to hear the humming of the wings which suddenly came into my field of vision. Up there a pair of tiny wings, dark and flashing, punctured the continuous blue of the unalterable sky. I had at length been able to attach the buzzing to its cause, to that little insect throbbing up there in the sky, probably quite five thousand feet above me; I could see it hum. Perhaps at a time when distances by land had not yet been habitually shortened by speed as they are today, the whistle of a passing train a mile off was endowed with that beauty which now and for some time to come will stir our emotions in the hum of an aeroplane five thousand feet up, with the thought that the distances traversed in this vertical journey are the same as those on the ground, and that in this other direction, where the measurements appeared to us different because it had seemed impossible to make the attempt, an aeroplane at five thousand feet is no farther away than a train a mile off, is indeed nearer, the identical trajectory occurring in a purer medium, with no separation of the traveller from his starting point, just as on the sea or across the plains, in calm weather, the wake of a ship that is already far away or the breath of a single zephyr will furrow the ocean of water or of grain.

'After all neither of us is really hungry, we might have looked in at the Verdurins',' Albertine said to me, 'this is their day and their hour.' 'But I thought you were angry with them?' 'Oh! There are all sorts of stories about them, but really they're not so bad as all that. Madame Verdurin has always been very nice to me. Besides, one can't keep on quarrelling all the time with everybody. They have their faults, but who hasn't?' 'You are not dressed, you would have to go home and dress, that would make us very late.' I added that I was hungry. 'Yes, you are right, let us eat by ourselves,' replied Albertine with that marvellous docility which continued to stupefy me. We stopped at a big pastrycook's, situated almost outside the town, which at that time enjoyed a certain reputation. A lady was leaving the place, and asked the girl in charge for her things. And after the lady had gone, Albertine cast repeated glances at the girl as though she wished to attract her attention while the other was putting away cups, plates, cakes, for it was getting late. She came near me only if I asked for something. And what happened then was that as the girl, who moreover was extremely tall, was standing up while she waited upon us and Albertine was seated beside me, each time, Albertine, in an attempt to attract her attention, raised vertically towards her a sunny gaze which compelled her to elevate her pupils to an even higher angle since, the girl being directly in front of us, Albertine had not the remedy of tempering the angle with the obliquity of her gaze. She was obliged, without raising her head unduly, to make her eyes ascend to that disproportionate height at which the girl's eyes were situated. Out of consideration for myself, Albertine lowered her own at once, and, as the girl had paid her no attention, began again. This led to a series of vain imploring elevations before an inaccessible deity. Then the girl had nothing left to do but to put straight a big table, next to ours. Now Albertine's gaze need only be natural. But never once did the girl's eyes rest upon my mistress. This did not surprise me, for I knew that the woman, with whom I was slightly acquainted, had lovers, although she was married, but managed to conceal her intrigues completely, which astonished me vastly in view of her prodigious stupidity. I studied the woman while we finished eating. Concentrated upon her task, she was almost impolite to Albertine, in the sense that she had not a glance to spare for her, not that Albertine's attitude was not perfectly correct. The other arranged things, went on arranging things, without letting anything distract her. The counting and putting away of the coffee-spoons, the fruit-knives, might have been entrusted not to this large and handsome woman, but, by a 'labour-saving' device, to a mere machine, and you would not have seen so complete an isolation from Albertine's attention, and yet she did not lower her eyes, did not let herself become absorbed, allowed her eyes, her charms to shine in an undivided attention to her work. It is true that if this woman had not been a particularly foolish person (not only was this her reputation, but I knew it by experience), this detachment might have been a supreme proof of her cunning. And I know very well that the stupidest person, if his desire or his pocket is involved, can, in that sole instance, emerging from the nullity of his stupid life, adapt himself immediately to the workings of the most complicated machinery; all the same, this would have been too subtle a supposition in the case of a woman as idiotic as this. Her idiocy even assumed the improbable form of impoliteness! Never once did she look at Albertine whom, after all, she could not help seeing. It was not very flattering for my mistress, but, when all was said, I was delighted that Albertine should receive this little lesson and should see that frequently women paid no attention to her. We left the pastrycook's, got into our carriage and were already on our way home when I was seized by a sudden regret that I had not taken the waitress aside and begged her on no account to tell the lady who had come out of the shop as we were going in my name and address, which she must know because of the orders I had constantly left with her. It was indeed undesirable that the lady should be enabled thus to learn, indirectly, Albertine's address. But I felt that it would be a waste of time to turn back for so small a matter, and that I should appear to be attaching too great an importance to it in the eyes of the idiotic and untruthful waitress. I decided, finally, that I should have to return there, in a week's time, to make this request, and that it was a great bore, since one always forgot half the things that one had to say, to have to do even the simplest things in instalments. In this connection, I cannot tell you how densely, now that I come to think of it, Albertine's life was covered in a network of alternate, fugitive, often contradictory desires. No doubt falsehood complicated this still further, for, as she retained no accurate memory of our conversations, when she had said to me: 'Ah! That's a pretty girl, if you like, and a good golfer,' and I had asked the girl's name, she had answered with that detached, universal, superior air of which no doubt there is always enough and to spare, for every liar of this category borrows it for a moment when he does not wish to answer a question, and it never fails him: 'Ah! That I don't know' (with regret at her inability to enlighten me). 'I never knew her name, I used to see her on the golf course, but I didn't know what she was called' – if, a month later, I said to her: 'Albertine, you remember that pretty girl you mentioned to me, who plays golf so well', 'Ah, yes,' she would answer without thinking: 'Emilie Daltier, I don't know what has become of her.' And the lie, like a line of earthworks, was carried back from the defence of the name, now captured, to the possibilities of meeting her again. 'Oh, I can't tell you, I never knew her address. I never see anybody who could tell you. Oh, no! Andrée never knew her. She wasn't one of our little band, now so scattered.' At other times the lie took the form of a base admission: 'Ah! If I had three hundred thousand francs a year . . . ' She bit her lip. 'Well? What would you do then?' 'I should ask you,' she said, kissing me as she spoke, 'to allow me to remain with you always. Where else could I be so happy?' But, even when one took her lies into account, it was incredible how spasmodic her life was, how fugitive her strongest desires. She would be mad about a person whom, three days later, she would refuse to see. She could not wait for an hour while I sent out for canvas and colours, for she wished to start painting again. For two whole days she was impatient, almost shed the tears, quickly dried, of an infant that has just been weaned from its nurse. And this instability of her feelings with regard to people, things, occupations, arts, places, was in fact so universal that, if she did love money, which I do not believe, she cannot have loved it for longer than anything else. When she said: 'Ah! If I had three hundred thousand francs a year!' or even if she expressed a bad but very transient thought, she could not have attached herself to it any longer than to the idea of going to Les Rochers, of which she had seen an engraving in my grandmother's edition of Mme de Sévigné, of meeting an old friend from the golf course, of going up in an aeroplane, of going to spend Christmas with her aunt, or of taking up painting again.

We returned home very late one evening while, here and there, by the roadside, a pair of red breeches pressed against a skirt revealed an amorous couple. Our carriage passed in through the Porte Maillot. For the monuments of Paris had been substituted, pure, linear, without depth, a drawing of the monuments of Paris, as though in an attempt to recall the appearance of a city that had been destroyed. But, round about this picture, there stood out so delicately the pale-blue mounting in which it was framed that one's greedy eyes sought everywhere for a further trace of that delicious shade which was too sparingly measured out to them: the moon was shining. Albertine admired the moonlight. I dared not tell her that I would have admired it more if I had been alone, or in quest of a strange woman. I repeated to her poetry or passages of prose about moonlight, pointing out to her how from 'silvery' which it had been at one time, it had turned 'blue' in Chateaubriand, in the Victor Hugo of *Eviradnus* and *La Fête chez Thérèse*, to become in turn yellow and metallic in Baudelaire and Leconte de Lisle. Then, reminding her of the image that is used for the crescent moon at the end of *Booz endormi*, I repeated the whole of that poem to her. And so we came to the house. The fine weather that night made a leap forwards as the mercury in the thermometer darts upward. In the early-rising mornings of spring that followed, I could hear the tramcars moving, through a cloud of perfumes, in an air with which the prevailing warmth became more and more blended until it reached the solidification and density of noon. When the unctuous air had succeeded in varnishing with it and isolating in it the scent of the washstand, the scent of the wardrobe, the scent of the sofa, simply by the sharpness with which, vertical and erect, they stood out in adjacent but distinct slices, in a pearly chiaroscuro which added a softer glaze to the shimmer of the curtains and the blue satin armchairs, I saw myself, not by a mere caprice of my imagination, but because it was physically possible, following in some new quarter of the suburbs, like that in which Bloch's house at Balbec was situated, the streets blinded by the sun, and finding in them not the dull butchers' shops and the white free-stone facings, but the country dining-room which I could reach in no time, and the scents that I would find there on my arrival, that of the bowl of cherries and apricots, the scent of cider, that of gruyère cheese, held in suspense in the luminous congelation of shadow which they delicately vein like the heart of an agate, while the knife-rests of prismatic glass scatter rainbows athwart the room or paint the wax cloth here and there with peacock-eyes. Like a wind that swells in a regular progression, I heard with joy a motorcar beneath the window. I smelt its odour of petrol. It may seem regrettable to the over-sensitive (who are always materialists) for whom it spoils the country, and to certain thinkers (materialists after their own fashion also) who, believing in the importance of facts, imagine that man would be happier, capable of higher flights of poetry, if his eyes were able to perceive more colours, his nostrils to distinguish more scents, a philosophical adaptation of the simple thought of those who believe that life was finer when men wore, instead of the black coats of today, sumptuous costumes. But to me (just as an aroma, unpleasant perhaps in itself, of naphthaline and flowering grasses would have thrilled me by giving me back the blue purity of the sea on the day of my arrival at Balbec), this smell of petrol which, with the smoke from the exhaust of the car, had so often melted into the pale azure, on those scorching days when I used to drive from Saint-Jean de la Haise to Gourville, as it had accompanied me on my excursions during those summer afternoons when I had left Albertine painting, called into blossom now on either side of me, for all that I was lying in my darkened bedroom, cornflowers, poppies and red clover, intoxicated me like a country scent, not circumscribed and fixed, like that which is spread before the hawthorns and, retained in its unctuous and dense elements, floats with a certain stability before the hedge, but like a scent before which the roads took flight, the sun's face changed, castles came hurrying to meet me, the sky turned pale, force was increased tenfold, a scent which was like a symbol of elastic motion and power, and which revived the desire that I had felt at Balbec, to enter the cage of steel and crystal, but this time not to go any longer on visits to familiar houses with a woman whom I knew too well, but to make love in new places with a woman unknown. A scent that was accompanied at every moment by the horns of passing motors, which I set to words like a military call: 'Parisian, get up, get up, come out and picnic in the country, and take a boat on the river, under the trees, with a pretty girl; get up, get up!' And all these musings were so agreeable that I congratulated myself upon the 'stern decree' which prescribed that until I should have rung my bell, no 'timid mortal', whether Françoise or Albertine, should dream of coming in to disturb me 'within this palace' where

> ' . . . a terrible
> Majesty makes me all invisible
> To my subjects.'

But all of a sudden the scene changed; it was the memory, no longer of old impressions, but of an old desire, quite recently reawakened by the Fortuny gown in blue and gold, that spread itself before me, another spring, a spring not leafy at all but suddenly stripped, on the contrary, of its trees and flowers by the name that I had just uttered to myself: 'Venice', a decanted spring, which is reduced to its essential qualities, and expresses the lengthening, the warming, the gradual maturing of its days by the progressive fermentation, not (this time) of an impure soil, but of a blue and virgin water, springlike without bud or blossom, which could answer the call of May only by gleaming facets, carved by that month, harmonising exactly with it in the radiant, unaltering nakedness of its dusky sapphire. And so, no more than the seasons to its unflowering inlets of the sea, do modern years bring any change to the Gothic city; I knew it, I could not imagine it, but this was what I longed to contemplate with the same desire which long ago, when I was a boy, in the very ardour of my departure had shattered the strength necessary for the journey; I wished to find myself face to face with my Venetian imaginings, to behold how that divided sea enclosed in its meanderings, like the streams of Ocean, an urbane and refined civilisation, but one that, isolated by their azure belt, had developed by itself, had had its own schools of painting and architecture, to admire that fabulous garden of fruits and birds in coloured stone, flowering in the midst of the sea which kept it refreshed, splashed with its tide against the base of the columns and, on the bold relief of the capitals, like a dark blue eye watching in the shadows, laid patches, which it kept perpetually moving, of light. Yes, I must go, the time had come. Now that Albertine no longer appeared to be cross with me, the possession of her no longer seemed to me a treasure in exchange for which we are prepared to sacrifice every other. For we should have done so only to rid ourselves of a grief, an anxiety which were now appeased. We have succeeded in jumping through the calico hoop through which we thought for a moment that we should never be able to pass. We have lightened the storm, brought back the serenity of the smile. The agonising mystery of a hatred without any known cause, and perhaps without end, is dispelled. Henceforward we find ourselves once more face to face with the problem, momentarily thrust aside, of a happiness which we know to be impossible. Now that life with Albertine had become possible once again, I felt that I could derive nothing from it but misery, since she did not love me; better to part from her in the pleasant moment of her consent which I should prolong in memory. Yes, this was the moment; I must make quite certain of the date on which Andrée was leaving Paris, use all my influence with Mme Bontemps to make sure that at that moment Albertine should not be able to go either to Holland or to Montjouvain. It would fall to our lot, were we better able to analyse our loves, to see that often women rise in our estimation only because of the dead weight of men with whom we have to compete for them, although we can hardly bear the thought of that competition; the counterpoise removed, the charm of the woman declines. We have a painful and salutary example of this in the predilection that men feel for the women who, before coming to know them, have gone astray, for those women whom they feel to be sinking in perilous quicksands and whom they must spend the whole period of their love in rescuing; a posthumous example, on the other hand, and one that is not at all dramatic, in the man who, conscious of a decline in his affection for the woman whom he loves, spontaneously applies the rules that he has deduced, and, to make sure of his not ceasing to love the woman, places her in a dangerous environment from which he is obliged to protect her daily. (The opposite of the men who insist upon a woman's retiring from the stage even when it was because of her being upon the stage that they fell in love with her.)

When in this way there could be no objection to Albertine's departure, I should have to choose a fine day like this – and there would be plenty of them before long – one on which she would have ceased to matter to me, on which I should be tempted by countless desires, I should have to let her leave the house without my seeing her, then, rising from my bed, making all my preparations in haste, leave a note for her, taking advantage of the fact that as she could not for the time being go to any place the thought of which would upset me, I might be spared, during my travels, from imagining the wicked things that she was perhaps doing – which for that matter seemed to me at the moment to be quite unimportant – and, without seeing her again, might leave for Venice.

I rang for Françoise to ask her to buy me a guidebook and a timetable, as I had done as a boy, when I wished to prepare in advance a journey to Venice, the realisation of a desire as violent as that which I felt at this moment; I forgot that, in the interval, there was a desire which I had attained, without any satisfaction, the desire for Balbec, and that Venice, being also a visible phenomenon, was probably no more able than Balbec to realise an ineffable dream, that of the Gothic age, made actual by a springtime sea, and coming at moments to stir my soul with an enchanted, caressing, unseizable, mysterious, confused image. Françoise having heard my ring came into the room, in considerable uneasiness as to how I would receive what she had to say and what she had done. 'It has been most awkward,' she said to me, 'that Monsieur is so late in ringing this morning. I didn't know what I ought to do. This morning at eight o'clock Mademoiselle Albertine asked me for her trunks, I dared not refuse her, I was afraid of Monsieur's scolding me if I came and waked him. It was no use my putting her through her catechism, telling her to wait an hour because I expected all the time that Monsieur would ring; she wouldn't have it, she left this letter with me for Monsieur, and at nine o'clock off she went.' Then – so ignorant may we be of what we have within us, since I was convinced of my own indifference to Albertine – my breath was cut short, I gripped my heart in my hands suddenly moistened by a perspiration which I had not known since the revelation that my mistress had made on the little tram with regard to Mlle Vinteuil's friend, without my being able to say anything else than: 'Ah! Very good, you did quite right not to wake me, leave me now for a little, I shall ring for you presently.'

The Sweet Cheat Gone

Translated by

C. K. SCOTT MONCRIEFF

ERNEST ROBERT CURTIUS

zugeeignet

Obwohl die arme Albertine verschwunden ist,
haben die Bruder Albrecht gut gewusst
wie uns zu trösten

C. K. S. M.

CHAPTER ONE

Grief and oblivion

'MADEMOISELLE ALBERTINE has gone!' How much farther farther does anguish penetrate in psychology than psychology itself! A moment ago, as I lay analysing my feelings, I had supposed that this separation without a final meeting was precisely what I wished, and, as I compared the mediocrity of the pleasures that Albertine afforded me with the richness of the desires which she prevented me from realising, had felt that I was being subtle, had concluded that I did not wish to see her again, that I no longer loved her. But now these words: 'Mademoiselle Albertine has gone!' had expressed themselves in my heart in the form of an anguish so keen that I would not be able to endure it for any length of time. And so what I had supposed to mean nothing to me was the only thing in my whole life. How ignorant we are of ourselves. The first thing to be done was to make my anguish cease at once. Tender towards myself as my mother had been towards my dying grandmother, I said to myself with that anxiety which we feel to prevent a person whom we love from suffering: 'Be patient for just a moment, we shall find something to take the pain away, don't fret, we are not going to allow you to suffer like this.' It was among ideas of this sort that my instinct of self-preservation sought for the first sedatives to lay upon my open wound: 'All this is not of the slightest importance, for I am going to make her return here at once. I must think first how I am to do it, but in any case she will be here this evening. Therefore, it is useless to worry myself.' 'All this is not of the slightest importance', I had not been content with giving myself this assurance, I had tried to convey the same impression to Françoise by not allowing her to see what I was suffering, because, even at the moment when I was feeling so keen an anguish, my love did not forget how important it was that it should appear a happy love, a mutual love, especially in the eyes of Françoise, who, as she disliked Albertine, had always doubted her sincerity. Yes, a moment ago, before Françoise came into the room, I had supposed that I was no longer in love with Albertine, I had supposed that I was leaving nothing out of account; a careful analyst, I had supposed that I knew the state of my own heart. But our intelligence, however great it may be, cannot perceive the elements that compose it and remain unsuspected so long as, from the volatile state in which they generally exist, a phenomenon capable of isolating them has not subjected them to the first stages of solidification. I had been mistaken in thinking that I could see clearly into my own heart. But this knowledge which had not been given me by the finest mental perceptions had now been brought to me, hard, glittering, strange, like a crystallised salt, by the abrupt reaction of grief. I was so much in the habit of seeing Albertine in the room, and I saw, all of a sudden, a fresh aspect of Habit. Hitherto I had regarded it chiefly as an annihilating force which suppresses the originality and even our consciousness of our perceptions; now I beheld it as a dread deity, so riveted to ourselves, its meaningless aspect so incrusted in our heart, that if it detaches itself, if it turns away from us, this deity which we can barely distinguish inflicts upon us sufferings more terrible than any other and is then as cruel as death itself.

The first thing to be done was to read Albertine's letter, since I was anxious to think of some way of making her return. I felt that this lay in my power, because, as the future is what exists only in our mind, it seems to us to be still alterable by the intervention, *in extremis*, of our will. But, at the same time, I remembered that I had seen act upon it forces other than my own, against which, however long an interval had been allowed me, I could never have prevailed. Of what use is it that the hour has not yet struck if we can do nothing to influence what is bound to happen. When Albertine was living in the house I had been quite determined to retain the initiative in our parting. And now she had gone. I opened her letter. It ran as follows:

MY DEAR FRIEND – Forgive me for not having dared to say to you in so many words what I am now writing, but I am such a coward, I have always been so afraid in your presence that I have never been able to force myself to speak. This is what I should have said to you. Our life together has become impossible; you must, for that matter, have seen, when you turned upon me the other evening, that there had been a change in our relations. What we were able to straighten out that night would become irreparable in a few days' time. It is better for us, therefore, since we have had the good fortune to be reconciled, to part as friends. That is why, my darling, I am sending you this line, and beg you to be so kind as to forgive me if I am causing you a little grief when you think of the immensity of mine. My dear old boy, I do not wish to become your enemy, it will be bad enough to become by degrees, and very soon, a stranger to you; and so, as

I have absolutely made up my mind, before sending you this letter by Françoise, I shall have asked her to let me have my boxes. Goodbye: I leave with you the best part of myself.

ALBERTINE

'All this means nothing,' I told myself, 'It is even better than I thought, for as she doesn't mean a word of what she says she has obviously written her letter only to give me a severe shock, so that I shall take fright, and not be horrid to her again. I must make some arrangement at once: Albertine must be brought back this evening. It is sad to think that the Bontemps are no better than blackmailers who make use of their niece to extort money from me. But what does that matter? Even if, to bring Albertine back here this evening, I have to give half my fortune to Mme Bontemps, we shall still have enough left, Albertine and I, to live in comfort.' And, at the same time, I calculated whether I had time to go out that morning and order the yacht and the Rolls-Royce which she coveted, quite forgetting, now that all my hesitation had vanished, that I had decided that it would be unwise to give her them. 'Even if Mme Bontemps' support is not sufficient, if Albertine refuses to obey her aunt and makes it a condition of her returning to me that she shall enjoy complete independence, well, however much it may distress me, I shall leave her to herself; she shall go out by herself, whenever she chooses. One must be prepared to make sacrifices, however painful they may be, for the thing to which one attaches most importance, which is, in spite of everything that I decided this morning, on the strength of my scrupulous and absurd arguments, that Albertine shall continue to live here.' Can I say for that matter that to leave her free to go where she chose would have been altogether painful to me? I should be lying. Often already I had felt that the anguish of leaving her free to behave improperly out of my sight was perhaps even less than that sort of misery which I used to feel when I guessed that she was bored in my company, under my roof. No doubt at the actual moment of her asking me to let her go somewhere, the act of allowing her to go, with the idea of an organised orgy, would have been an appalling torment. But to say to her: 'Take our yacht, or the train, go away for a month, to some place which I have never seen, where I shall know nothing of what you are doing' – this had often appealed to me, owing to the thought that, by force of contrast, when she was away from me, she would prefer my society, and would be glad to return. 'This return is certainly what she herself desires; she does not in the least insist upon that freedom upon which, moreover, by offering her every day some fresh pleasure, I should easily succeed in imposing, day by day, a further restriction. No, what Albertine has wanted is that I shall no longer make myself unpleasant to her, and most of all – like Odette with Swann – that I shall make up my mind to marry her. Once she is married, her independence will cease to matter; we shall stay here together, in perfect happiness.' No doubt this meant giving up any thought of Venice. But the places for which we have most longed, such as Venice (all the more so, the most agreeable hostesses, such as the Duchesse de Guermantes, amusements such as the theatre), how pale, insignificant, dead they become when we are tied to the heart of another person by a bond so painful that it prevents us from tearing ourselves away. 'Albertine is perfectly right, for that matter, about our marriage. Mamma herself was saying that all these postponements were ridiculous. Marrying her is what I ought to have done long ago, it is what I shall have to do, it is what has made her write her letter without meaning a word of it; it is only to bring about our marriage that she has postponed for a few hours what she must desire as keenly as I desire it: her return to this house. Yes, that is what she meant, that is the purpose of her action,' my compassionate judgment assured me; but I felt that, in telling me this, my judgment was still maintaining the same hypothesis which it had adopted from the start. Whereas I felt that it was the other hypothesis which had invariably proved correct. No doubt this second hypothesis would never have been so bold as to formulate in so many words that Albertine could have had intimate relations with Mlle Vinteuil and her friend. And yet, when I was overwhelmed by the invasion of those terrible tidings, as the train slowed down before stopping at Parville station, it was the second hypothesis that had already been proved correct. This hypothesis had never, in the interval, conceived the idea that Albertine might leave me of her own accord, in this fashion, and without warning me and giving me time to prevent her departure. But all the same if, after the immense leap forwards which life had just made me take, the reality that confronted me was as novel as that which is presented by the discovery of a scientist, the inquiries of an examining magistrate or the researches of a historian into the mystery of a crime or a revolution, this reality while exceeding the meagre previsions of my second hypothesis nevertheless fulfilled them. This second hypothesis was not an intellectual feat, and the panic fear that I had felt on the evening when Albertine had refused to kiss me, the night when I had heard the sound of her window being opened, that fear was not based upon reason. But – and the sequel will show this more clearly, as several episodes must have indicated it already – the fact that our intellect is not the most subtle, the most powerful, the most appropriate instrument for grasping the truth, is only a reason the more for beginning with the intellect, and not with a subconscious intuition, a ready-made faith in presentiments. It is life that, little by little, case by case, enables us to observe that what is most important to our heart, or to our mind, is learned not by reasoning but by other powers. And then it is the intellect itself which, taking note of their superiority, abdicates its sway to them upon reasoned grounds and consents to become their collaborator and their servant. It is faith confirmed by experiment. The unforeseen calamity with which I found myself engaged, it seemed to me that I had already known it also (as I had known of Albertine's friendship with a pair of Lesbians), from having read it in so many signs in which (notwithstanding the contrary affirmations of my reason, based upon Albertine's own statements) I had discerned the weariness, the horror that she felt at having to live in that state of slavery, signs traced as though in invisible ink behind her sad, submissive eyes, upon her cheeks suddenly inflamed with an unaccountable blush, in the sound of the window that had suddenly been flung open. No doubt I had not ventured to interpret them in their full significance or to form a definite idea of her immediate departure. I had thought, with a mind kept in equilibrium by Albertine's presence, only of a departure arranged by myself at an undetermined date, that is to say a date situated in a non-existent time; consequently I had had merely the illusion of thinking of a departure, just as people imagine that they are not afraid of death when they think of it while they are in good health and actually do no more than introduce a purely negative idea into a healthy state which the approach of death would automatically destroy. Besides, the idea of Albertine's departure on her own initiative might have occurred to my mind a thousand times over, in the clearest, the most sharply defined form, and I should no more have suspected what, in relation to myself, that is to say in reality, that departure would be, what an unprecedented, appalling, unknown thing, how entirely novel a calamity. Of her departure, had I foreseen it, I might have gone on thinking incessantly for years on end, and yet all my thoughts of it, placed end to end, would not have been comparable for an instant, not merely in intensity but in kind, with the unimaginable hell the curtain of which Françoise had raised for me when she said: 'Mademoiselle Albertine has gone.' In order to form an idea of an unknown situation our imagination borrows elements that are already familiar and for that reason does not form any idea of it. But our sensibility, even in its most physical form, receives, as it were the brand of the lightning, the original and for long indelible imprint of the novel event. And I scarcely ventured to say to myself that, if I had foreseen this departure, I would perhaps have been incapable of picturing it to myself in all its horror, or indeed, with Albertine informing me of it, and myself threatening, imploring her, of preventing it! How far was any longing for Venice removed from me now! As far as, in the old days at Combray, was the longing to know Mme de Guermantes when the time came at which I longed for one thing only, to have Mamma in my room. And it was indeed all these anxieties that I had felt ever since my childhood, which, at the bidding of this new anguish, had come hastening to reinforce it, to amalgamate themselves with it in a homogeneous mass that was stifling me. To be sure, the physical blow which such a parting strikes at the heart, and which, because of that terrible capacity for registering things with which the body is endowed, makes our suffering somehow contemporaneous with all the epochs in our life in which we have suffered; to be sure, this blow at the heart upon which the woman speculates a little perhaps – so little compunction do we show for the sufferings of other people – who is anxious to give the maximum intensity to regret, whether it be that, merely hinting at an imaginary departure, she is seeking only to demand better terms, or that, leaving us for ever – for ever! – she desires to wound us, or, in order to avenge herself, or to continue to be loved, or to enhance the memory that she will leave behind her, to rend asunder the net of weariness, of indifference which she has felt being woven about her – to be sure, this blow at our heart, we had vowed that we would avoid it, had assured ourselves that we would make a good finish. But it is rarely indeed that we do finish well, for, if all was well, we would never finish! And besides, the woman to whom we show the utmost indifference feels nevertheless in an obscure fashion that while we have been growing tired of her, by virtue of an identical force of habit, we have grown more and more attached to her, and she reflects that one of the essential elements in a good finish is to warn the other person before one goes. But she is afraid, if she warns us, of preventing her own departure. Every woman feels that, if her power over a man is great, the only way to leave him is sudden flight. A fugitive because a queen, precisely. To be sure, there is an unspeakable interval between the boredom which she inspired a moment ago and, because she has gone, this furious desire to have her back again. But for this, apart from those which have been furnished in the course of this work and others which will be furnished later on, there are reasons. For one thing, her departure occurs as often as not at the moment when our indifference – real or imagined – is greatest, at the extreme point of the oscillation of the pendulum. The woman says to herself: 'No, this sort of thing cannot go on any longer', simply because the man speaks of nothing but leaving her, or thinks of nothing else; and it is she who leaves him. Then, the pendulum swinging back to its other extreme, the interval is all the greater. In an instant it returns to this point; once more, apart from all the reasons that have been given, it is so natural. Our heart still beats; and besides, the woman who has gone is no longer the same as the woman who was with us. Her life under our roof, all too well known, is suddenly enlarged by the addition of the lives with which she is inevitably to be associated, and it is perhaps to associate herself with them that she has left us. So that this novel richness of the life of the woman who has gone reacts upon the woman who was with us and was perhaps planning her departure. To the series of psychological facts which we are able to deduce and which form part of her life with us, our too evident boredom in her company, our jealousy also (the effect of which is that the men who have been left by a number of women have been left almost always in the same manner because of their character and of certain always identical reactions which can be calculated: each man has his own way of being betrayed, as he has his own way of catching cold), to this series not too mysterious for us, there corresponds doubtless a series of facts of which we were unaware. She must for some time past have been keeping up relations, written, or verbal or through messengers, with some man, or some woman, have been awaiting some signal which we may perhaps have given her ourselves, unconsciously, when we said: 'X called yesterday to see me,' if she had arranged with X that on the eve of the day when she was to join him he was to call upon me. How many possible hypotheses! Possible only. I constructed the truth so well, but in the realm of possibility only, that, having one day opened, and then by mistake, a letter addressed to my mistress, from this letter which was written in a code, and said: 'Go on waiting for a signal to go to the Marquis de Saint-Loup; let me know tomorrow by telephone,' I reconstructed a sort of projected flight; the name of the Marquis de Saint-Loup was there only as a substitute for some other name, for my mistress did not know Saint-Loup well enough, but had heard me speak of him, and moreover the signature was some sort of nickname, without any intelligible form. As it happened, the letter was addressed not to my mistress but to another person in the building who bore a different name which had been misread. The letter was written not in code, but in bad French, because it was written by an American woman, who was indeed a friend of Saint-Loup as he himself told me. And the odd way in which this American woman wrote certain letters had given the appearance of a nickname to a name which was quite genuine, only foreign. And so I had on that occasion been entirely at fault in my suspicions. But the intellectual structure which had in my mind combined these facts, all of them false, was itself the so accurate, so inflexible form of the truth that when three months later my mistress, who had at that time been meaning to spend the rest of her life with me, left me, it was in a fashion absolutely identical with that which I had imagined on the former occasion. A letter arrived, containing the same peculiarities which I had wrongly attributed to the former letter, but this time it was indeed meant as a signal.

This calamity was the greatest that I had experienced in my life. And, when all was said, the suffering that it caused me was perhaps even exceeded by my curiosity to learn the causes of this calamity which Albertine had deliberately brought about. But the sources of great events are like those of rivers, in vain do we explore the earth's surface, we can never find them. So Albertine had for a long time past been planning her flight; I have said (and at the time it had seemed to me simply a sign of affectation and ill humour, what Françoise called 'lifting her head') that, from the day upon which she had ceased to kiss me, she had gone about as though tormented by a devil, stiffly erect, unbending, saying the simplest things in a sorrowful tone, slow in her movements, never once smiling. I cannot say that there was any concrete proof of conspiracy with the outer world. Françoise told me long afterwards that, having gone into Albertine's room two days before her departure, she had found it empty, the curtains drawn, but had detected from the atmosphere of the room and the sounds that came in that the window was open. And indeed she had found Albertine on the balcony. But it is hard to say with whom she could have been communicating from there, and moreover the drawn curtains screening the open window could doubtless be explained by her knowing that I was afraid of draughts, and by the fact that, even if the curtains afforded me little protection, they would prevent Françoise from seeing from the passage that the shutters had been opened so early. No, I can see nothing save one trifling incident which proves merely that on the day before her departure she knew that she was going. For during the day she took from my room without my noticing it a large quantity of wrapping paper and cloth which I kept there, and in which she spent the whole night packing her innumerable wrappers and dressing-gowns so that she might leave the house in the morning; this was the only incident, it was more than enough. I cannot attach any importance to her having almost forced upon me that evening a thousand francs which she owed me, there is nothing peculiar in that, for she was extremely scrupulous about money. Yes, she took the wrapping paper overnight, but it was not only then that she knew that she was going to leave me! For it was not resentment that made her leave me, but her determination, already formed, to leave me, to abandon the life of which she had dreamed, that gave her that air of resentment. A resentful air, almost solemnly cold toward myself, except on the last evening when, after staying in my room longer than she had intended, she said – a remark which surprised me, coming from her who had always sought to postpone the moment of parting – she said to me from the door: 'Goodbye, my dear; goodbye, my dear.' But I did not take any notice of this, at the moment. Françoise told me that next morning when Albertine informed her that she was going (but this, for that matter, may be explained also by exhaustion, for she had spent the whole night in packing all her clothes, except the things for which she had to ask Françoise as they were not in her bedroom or her dressing-room), she was still so sad, so much more erect, so much stiffer than during the previous days that Françoise, when Albertine said to her: 'Goodbye, Françoise', almost expected to see her fall to the ground. When we are told anything like this, we realise that the woman who appealed to us so much less than any of the women whom we meet so easily in the course of the briefest outing, the woman who makes us resent our having to sacrifice them to herself, is on the contrary she whom now we would a thousand times rather possess. For the choice lies no longer between a certain pleasure – which has become by force of habit, and perhaps by the insignificance of its object, almost nothing – and other pleasures, which tempt and thrill us, but between these latter pleasures and something that is far stronger than they, compassion for suffering.

When I vowed to myself that Albertine would be back in the house before night, I had proceeded in hot haste to cover with a fresh belief the open wound from which I had torn the belief that had been my mainstay until then. But however rapidly my instinct of self-preservation might have acted, I had, when Françoise spoke to me, been left for an instant without relief, and it was useless my knowing now that Albertine would return that same evening, the pain that I had felt in the instant in which I had not yet assured myself of her return (the instant that had followed the words: 'Mademoiselle Albertine has asked for her boxes, Mademoiselle Albertine has gone'), this revived in me of its own accord as keen as it had been before, that is to say as if I had still been unaware of Albertine's immediate return. However, it was essential that she should return, but of her own accord. Upon every hypothesis, to appear to be taking the first step, to be begging her to return would be to defeat my own object. To be sure, I had not the strength to give her up as I had given up Gilberte. Even more than to see Albertine again, what I wished was to put an end to the physical anguish which my heart, less stout than of old, could endure no longer. Then, by dint of accustoming myself to not wishing anything, whether it was a question of work or of anything else, I had become more cowardly. But above all, this anguish was incomparably keener for several reasons, the most important of which was perhaps not that I had never tasted any sensual pleasure with Mme de

Guermantes or with Gilberte, but that, not seeing them every day, and at every hour of the day, having no opportunity and consequently no need to see them, there had been less prominent, in my love for them, the immense force of Habit. Perhaps, now that my heart, incapable of wishing and of enduring of its own free will what I was suffering, found only one possible solution, that Albertine should return at all costs, perhaps the opposite solution (a deliberate renunciation, gradual resignation) would have seemed to me a novelist's solution, improbable in real life, had I not myself decided upon it in the past when Gilberte was concerned. I knew therefore that this other solution might be accepted also and by the same man, for I had remained more or less the same. Only time had played its part, time which had made me older, time which moreover had kept Albertine perpetually in my company while we were living together. But I must add that, without my giving up the idea of that life, there survived in me of all that I had felt about Gilberte the pride which made me refuse to be to Albertine a repellent plaything by insisting upon her return; I wished her to come back without my appearing to attach any importance to her return. I got out of bed, so as to lose no more time, but was arrested by my anguish; this was the first time that I had got out of bed since Albertine had left me. Yet I must dress myself at once in order to go and make enquiries of her porter.

Suffering, the prolongation of a spiritual shock that has come from without, keeps on endeavouring to change its form; we hope to be able to dispel it by making plans, by seeking information; we wish it to pass through its countless metamorphoses, this requires less courage than retaining our suffering intact; the bed appears so narrow, hard and cold on which we lie down with our grief. I put my feet to the ground; I stepped across the room with endless precautions, took up a position from which I could not see Albertine's chair, the pianola upon the pedals of which she used to press her golden slippers, nor a single one of the things which she had used and all of which, in the secret language that my memory had imparted to them, seemed to be seeking to give me a fresh translation, a different version, to announce to me for the second time the news of her departure. But even without looking at them I could see them, my strength left me, I sank down upon one of those blue satin armchairs, the glossy surface of which an hour earlier, in the dimness of my bedroom anaesthetised by a ray of morning light, had made me dream dreams which then I had passionately caressed, which were so far from me now. Alas, I had never sat down upon any of them until this minute save when Albertine was still with me. And so I could not remain sitting there, I rose; and thus, at every moment there was one more of those innumerable and humble 'selves' that compose our personality which was still unaware of Albertine's departure and must be informed of it; I was obliged – and this was more cruel than if they had been strangers and had not borrowed my sensibility to pain – to describe to all these 'selves' who did not yet know of it, the calamity that had just occurred, it was necessary that each of them in turn should hear for the first time the words: 'Albertine has asked for her boxes' – those coffin-shaped boxes which I had seen put on the train at Balbec with my mother's – 'Albertine has gone'. To each of them I had to relate my grief, the grief which is in no way a pessimistic conclusion freely drawn from a number of lamentable circumstances, but is the intermittent and involuntary revival of a specific impression, come to us from without and not chosen by us. There were some of these 'selves' which I had not encountered for a long time past. For instance (I had not remembered that it was the day on which the barber called) the 'self' that I was when I was having my hair cut. I had forgotten this 'self', the barber's arrival made me burst into tears, as, at a funeral, does the appearance of an old pensioned servant who has not forgotten the deceased. Then all of a sudden I recalled that, during the last week, I had from time to time been seized by panic fears which I had not confessed to myself. At such moments, however, I had debated the question, saying to myself: 'Useless, of course, to consider the hypothesis of her suddenly leaving me. It is absurd. If I were to confess it to a sober, intelligent man' (and I should have done so to secure peace of mind, had not jealousy prevented me from making confidences) 'he would be sure to say to me: 'Why, you are mad. It is impossible.' And, as a matter of fact, during these last days we have not quarrelled once. People separate for a reason. They tell you their reason. They give you a chance to reply. They do not run away like that. No, it is perfectly childish. It is the only hypothesis that is absurd.' And yet, every day, when I found that she was still there in the morning when I rang my bell, I had heaved a vast sigh of relief. And when Françoise handed me Albertine's letter, I had at once been certain that it referred to the one thing that could not happen, to this departure which I had in a sense perceived many days in advance, in spite of the logical reasons for my feeling reassured. I had said this to myself almost with satisfaction at my own perspicacity in my despair, like a murderer who knows that his guilt cannot be detected, but is nevertheless afraid and all of a sudden sees his victim's name written at the head of a document on the table of the police official who has sent for him. My only hope was that Albertine had gone to Touraine, to her aunt's house where, after all, she would be fairly well guarded and could not do anything very serious in the interval before I brought her back. My worst fear was that she might be remaining in Paris, or have gone to Amsterdam or to Montjouvain, in other words that she had escaped in order to involve herself in some intrigue the preliminaries of which I had failed to observe. But in reality when I said to myself Paris, Amsterdam, Montjouvain, that is to say various names of places, I was thinking of places which were merely potential. And so, when Albertine's hall porter informed me that she had gone to Touraine, this place of residence which I supposed myself to desire seemed to me the most terrible of them all, because it was real, and because, tormented for the first time by the certainty of the present and the uncertainty of the future, I pictured to myself Albertine starting upon a life which she had deliberately chosen to lead apart from myself, perhaps for a long time, perhaps for ever, and in which she would realise that unknown element which in the past had so often distressed me when, nevertheless, I had enjoyed the happiness of possessing, of caressing what was its outer shell, that charming face impenetrable and captive. It was this unknown element that formed the core of my love. Outside the door of Albertine's house I found a poor little girl who gazed at me open-eyed and looked so honest that I asked her whether she would care to come home with me, as I might have taken home a dog with faithful eyes. She seemed pleased by my suggestion. When I got home, I held her for some time on my knee, but very soon her presence, by making me feel too keenly Albertine's absence, became intolerable. And I asked her to go away, giving her first a five-hundred franc note. And yet, a moment later, the thought of having some other little girl in the house with me, of never being alone, without the comfort of an innocent presence, was the only thing that enabled me to endure the idea that Albertine might perhaps remain away for some time before returning. As for Albertine herself, she barely existed in me save under the form of her name, which, but for certain rare moments of respite when I awoke, came and engraved itself upon my brain and continued incessantly to do so. If I had thought aloud, I should have kept on repeating it, and my speech would have been as monotonous, as limited as if I had been transformed into a bird, a bird like that in the fable whose song repeated incessantly the name of her whom, when a man, it had loved. We say the name to ourselves, and as we remain silent it seems as though we inscribed it on ourselves, as though it left its trace on our brain which must end by being, like a wall upon which somebody has amused himself by scribbling, entirely covered with the name, written a thousand times over, of her whom we love. We repeat it all the time in our mind, even when we are happy, all the more when we are unhappy. And to repeat this name, which gives us nothing in addition to what we already know, we feel an incessantly renewed desire, but, in the course of time, it wearies us. To carnal pleasure I did not even give a thought at this moment; I did not even see, with my mind's eye, the image of that Albertine, albeit she had been the cause of such an upheaval of my existence, I did not perceive her body and if I had wished to isolate the idea that was bound up – for there is always some idea bound up – with my suffering, it would have been alternately, on the one hand my doubt as to the intention with which she had left me, with or without any thought of returning, and on the other hand the means of bringing her back. Perhaps there is something symbolical and true in the minute place occupied in our anxiety by the person who is its cause. The fact is that the person counts for little or nothing; what is almost everything is the series of emotions, of agonies which similar mishaps have made us feel in the past in connection with her and which habit has attached to her. What proves this clearly is, even more than the boredom which we feel in moments of happiness, that the fact of seeing or not seeing the person in question, of being or not being admired by her, of having or not having her at our disposal will seem to us utterly trivial when we shall no longer have to set ourselves the problem (so superfluous that we shall no longer take the trouble to consider it) save in relation to the person herself – the series of emotions and agonies being forgotten, at least in so far as she is concerned, for it may have developed afresh but in connection with another person. Before this, when it was still attached to her, we supposed that our happiness was dependent upon her presence; it depended merely upon the cessation of our anxiety. Our subconscious was therefore more clairvoyant than ourselves at that moment, when it made the form of the beloved woman so minute, a form which we had indeed perhaps forgotten, which we might have failed to remember clearly and thought unattractive, in the terrible drama in which finding her again in order to cease from expecting her becomes an absolutely vital matter. Minute proportions of the woman's form, a logical and necessary effect of the fashion in which love develops, a clear allegory of the subjective nature of that love.

The spirit in which Albertine had left me was similar no doubt to that of the nations who pave the way by a demonstration of their armed force for the exercise of their diplomacy. She could not have left me save in the hope of obtaining from me better terms, greater freedom, more comfort. In that case the one of us who would have conquered would have been myself, had I had the strength to await the moment when, seeing that she could gain nothing, she would return of her own accord. But if at cards, or in war, where victory alone matters, we can hold out against bluff, the conditions are not the same that are created by love and jealousy, not to mention suffering. If, in order to wait, to 'hold out', I allowed Albertine to remain away from me for several days, for several weeks perhaps, I was ruining what had been my sole purpose for more than a year, never to leave her by herself for a single hour. All my precautions were rendered fruitless, if I allowed her the time, the opportunity to betray me as often as she might choose, and if in the end she did return to me, I should never again be able to forget the time when she had been alone, and even if I won in the end, nevertheless in the past, that is to say irreparably, I should be the vanquished party.

As for the means of bringing Albertine back, they had all the more chance of success the more plausible the hypothesis appeared that she had left me only in the hope of being summoned back upon more favourable terms. And no doubt to the people who did not believe in Albertine's sincerity, certainly to Françoise for instance, this was the more plausible hypothesis. But my reason, to which the only explanation of certain bouts of ill humour, of certain attitudes had appeared, before I knew anything, to be that she had planned a final departure, found it difficult to believe that, now that her departure had occurred, it was a mere feint. I say my reason, not myself. The hypothesis of a feint became all the more necessary to me the more improbable it was, and gained in strength what it lost in probability. When we find ourselves on the brink of the abyss, and it seems as though God has forsaken us, we no longer hesitate to expect a miracle of Him.

I realise that in all this I was the most apathetic, albeit the most anxious of detectives. But Albertine's flight had not restored to myself the faculties of which the habit of having her watched by other people had deprived me. I could think of one thing only: how to employ someone else upon the search for her. This other person was Saint-Loup, who agreed. The transference of the anxiety of so many days to another person filled me with joy and I quivered with the certainty of success, my hands becoming suddenly dry again as in the past, and no longer moist with that sweat in which Françoise had bathed me when she said: 'Mademoiselle Albertine has gone.'

The reader may remember that when I decided to live with Albertine, and even to marry her, it was in order to guard her, to know what she was doing, to prevent her from returning to her old habits with Mlle Vinteuil. It had been in the appalling anguish caused by her revelation at Balbec when she had told me, as a thing that was quite natural, and I succeeded, albeit it was the greatest grief that I had ever yet felt in my life, in seeming to find quite natural the thing which in my worst suppositions I had never had the audacity to imagine. (It is astonishing what a want of imagination jealousy, which spends its time in weaving little suppositions of what is untrue, shows when it is a question of discovering the truth.) Now this love, born first and foremost of a need to prevent Albertine from doing wrong, this love had preserved in the sequel the marks of its origin. Being with her mattered little to me so long as I could prevent her from 'being on the run', from going to this place or to that. In order to prevent her, I had had recourse to the vigilance, to the company of the people who went about with her, and they had only to give me at the end of the day a report that was fairly reassuring for my anxieties to vanish in good humour.

Having given myself the assurance that, whatever steps I might have to take, Albertine would be back in the house that same evening, I had granted a respite to the grief which Françoise had caused me when she told me that Albertine had gone (because at that moment my mind taken by surprise had believed for an instant that her departure was final). But after an interruption, when with an impulse of its own independent life the initial suffering revived spontaneously in me, it was just as keen as before, because it was anterior to the consoling promise that I had given myself to bring Albertine back that evening. This utterance, which would have calmed it, my suffering had not heard. To set in motion the means of bringing about her return, once again, not that such an attitude on my part would ever have proved very successful, but because I had always adopted it since I had been in love with Albertine, I was condemned to behave as though I did not love her, was not pained by her departure, I was condemned to continue to lie to her. I might be all the more energetic in my efforts to bring her back in that personally I should appear to have given her up for good. I decided to write Albertine a farewell letter in which I would regard her departure as final, while I would send Saint-Loup down to put upon Mme Bontemps, as though without my knowledge, the most brutal pressure to make Albertine return as soon as possible. No doubt I had had experience with Gilberte of the danger of letters expressing an indifference which, feigned at first, ends by becoming genuine. And this experience ought to have restrained me from writing to Albertine letters of the same sort as those that I had written to Gilberte. But what we call experience is merely the revelation to our own eyes of a trait in our character which naturally reappears, and reappears all the more markedly because we have already brought it into prominence once of our own accord, so that the spontaneous impulse which guided us on the first occasion finds itself reinforced by all the suggestions of memory. The human plagiarism which it is most difficult to avoid, for individuals (and even for nations which persevere in their faults and continue to aggravate them) is the plagiarism of ourselves.

Knowing that Saint-Loup was in Paris I had sent for him immediately; he came in haste to my rescue, swift and efficient as he had been long ago at

Doncières, and agreed to set off at once for Touraine. I suggested to him the following arrangement. He was to take the train to Châtellerault, find out where Mme Bontemps lived, and wait until Albertine should have left the house, since there was a risk of her recognising him. 'But does the girl you are speaking of know me, then?' he asked. I told him that I did not think so. This plan of action filled me with indescribable joy. It was nevertheless diametrically opposed to my original intention: to arrange things so that I should not appear to be seeking Albertine's return; whereas by so acting I must inevitably appear to be seeking it, but this plan had the inestimable advantage over 'the proper thing to do' that it enabled me to say to myself that someone sent by me was going to see Albertine, and would doubtless bring her back with him. And if I had been able to read my own heart clearly at the start, I might have foreseen that it was this solution, hidden in the darkness, which I felt to be deplorable, that would ultimately prevail over the alternative course of patience which I had decided to choose, from want of will-power. As Saint-Loup already appeared slightly surprised to learn that a girl had been living with me through the whole winter without my having said a word to him about her, as moreover he had often spoken to me of the girl who had been at Balbec and I had never said in reply: 'But she is living here', he might be annoyed by my want of confidence. There was always the risk of Mme Bontemps's mentioning Balbec to him. But I was too impatient for his departure, for his arrival at the other end, to wish, to be able to think of the possible consequences of his journey. As for the risk of his recognising Albertine (at whom he had resolutely refrained from looking when he had met her at Doncières), she had, as everyone admitted, so altered and had grown so much stouter that it was hardly likely. He asked me whether I had not a picture of Albertine. I replied at first that I had not, so that he might not have a chance, from her photograph, taken about the time of our stay at Balbec, of recognising Albertine, though he had had no more than a glimpse of her in the railway carriage. But then I remembered that in the photograph she would be already as different from the Albertine of Balbec as the living Albertine now was, and that he would recognise her no better from her photograph than in the flesh. While I was looking for it, he laid his hand gently upon my brow, by way of consoling me. I was touched by the distress which the grief that he guessed me to be feeling was causing him. For one thing, however final his rupture with Rachel, what he had felt at that time was not yet so remote that he had not a special sympathy, a special pity for this sort of suffering, as we feel ourselves more closely akin to a person who is afflicted with the same malady as ourselves. Besides, he had so strong an affection for myself that the thought of my

suffering was intolerable to him. And so he conceived, towards her who was
the cause of my suffering, a rancour mingled with admiration. He regarded
me as so superior a being that he supposed that if I were to subject myself to
another person she must be indeed extraordinary. I quite expected that he
would think Albertine, in her photograph, pretty, but as at the same time I
did not imagine that it would produce upon him the impression that Helen
made upon the Trojan elders, as I continued to look for it, I said modestly:
'Oh! you know, you mustn't imagine things, for one thing it is a bad
photograph, and besides there's nothing startling about her, she is not a
beauty, she is merely very nice.' 'Oh, yes, she must be wonderful,' he said
with a simple, sincere enthusiasm as he sought to form a mental picture of
the person who was capable of plunging me in such despair and agitation. 'I
am angry with her because she has hurt you, but at the same time one can't
help seeing that a man who is an artist to his fingertips like you, that
you, who love beauty in everything and with so passionate a love, were
predestined to suffer more than the ordinary person when you found it in a
woman.' At last I managed to find her photograph. 'She is bound to be
wonderful,' still came from Robert, who had not seen that I was holding out
the photograph to him. All at once he caught sight of it, he held it for a
moment between his hands. His face expressed a stupefaction which
amounted to stupidity. 'Is this the girl you are in love with?' he said at length
in a tone from which astonishment was banished by his fear of making me
angry. He made no remark upon it, he had assumed the reasonable, prudent,
inevitably somewhat disdainful air which we assume before a sick person –
even if he has been in the past a man of outstanding gifts, and our friend –
who is now nothing of the sort, for, raving mad, he speaks to us of a celestial
being who has appeared to him, and continues to behold this being where
we, the sane man, can see nothing but a quilt on the bed. I at once
understood Robert's astonishment and that it was the same in which the
sight of his mistress had plunged me, with this difference only that I had
recognised in her a woman whom I already knew, whereas he supposed that
he had never seen Albertine. But no doubt the difference between our
respective impressions of the same person was equally great. The time was
past when I had timidly begun at Balbec by adding to my visual sensations
when I gazed at Albertine sensations of taste, of smell, of touch. Since then,
other more profound, more pleasant, more indefinable sensations had been
added to them, and afterwards painful sensations. In short, Albertine was
merely, like a stone round which snow has gathered, the generating centre
of an immense structure which rose above the plane of my heart. Robert, to
whom all this stratification of sensations was invisible, grasped only a

residue of it which it prevented me, on the contrary, from perceiving. What had disconcerted Robert when his eyes fell upon Albertine's photograph was not the consternation of the Trojan elders when they saw Helen go by and said: 'All our misfortunes are not worth a single glance from her eyes', but the exactly opposite impression which may be expressed by: 'What, it is for this that he has worked himself into such a state, has grieved himself so, has done so many idiotic things!' It must indeed be admitted that this sort of reaction at the sight of the person who has caused the suffering, upset the life, sometimes brought about the death of someone whom we love, is infinitely more frequent than that felt by the Trojan elders, and is in short habitual. This is not merely because love is individual, nor because, when we do not feel it, finding it avoidable and philosophising upon the folly of other people come naturally to us. No, it is because, when it has reached the stage at which it causes such misery, the structure composed of the sensations interposed between the face of the woman and the eyes of her lover – the huge egg of pain which encases it and conceals it as a mantle of snow conceals a fountain – is already raised so high that the point at which the lover's gaze comes to rest, the point at which he finds his pleasure and his sufferings, is as far from the point which other people see as is the real sun from the place in which its condensed light enables us to see it in the sky. And what is more, during this time, beneath the chrysalis of griefs and affections which render invisible to the lover the worst metamorphoses of the beloved object, her face has had time to grow old and to change. With the result that if the face which the lover saw on the first occasion is very far removed from that which he has seen since he has been in love and has been made to suffer, it is, in the opposite direction, equally far from the face which may now be seen by the indifferent onlooker. (What would have happened if, instead of the photograph of one who was still a girl, Robert had seen the photograph of an elderly mistress?) And indeed we have no need to see for the first time the woman who has caused such an upheaval, in order to feel this astonishment. Often we know her already, as my great-uncle knew Odette. Then the optical difference extends not merely to the bodily aspect, but to the character, to the individual importance. It is more likely than not that the woman who is causing the man who is in love with her to suffer has already behaved perfectly towards someone who was not interested in her, just as Odette who was so cruel to Swann had been the sedulous 'lady in pink' to my great-uncle, or indeed that the person whose every decision is calculated in advance with as much dread as that of a deity by the man who is in love with her, appears as a person of no importance, only too glad to do anything that he may require of her, in the eyes of the man who is not in love with her, as Saint-Loup's mistress appeared to me who saw in her nothing more than that 'Rachel, when from the Lord' who had so repeatedly been offered me. I recalled my own stupefaction, that first time that I met her with Saint-Loup, at the thought that anybody could be tormented by not knowing what such a woman had been doing, by the itch to know what she might have said in a whisper to some other man, why she had desired a rupture. And I felt that all this past existence – but, in this case, Albertine's – toward which every fibre of my heart, of my life was directed with a throbbing, clumsy pain, must appear just as insignificant to Saint-Loup as it would one day, perhaps, appear to myself. I felt that I would pass perhaps gradually, so far as the insignificance or gravity of Albertine's past was concerned, from the state of mind in which I was at the moment to that of Saint-Loup, for I was under no illusion as to what Saint-Loup might be thinking, as to what anyone else than the lover himself might think. And I was not unduly distressed. Let us leave pretty women to men devoid of imagination. I recalled that tragic explanation of so many of us which is furnished by an inspired but not lifelike portrait, such as Elstir's portrait of Odette, which is a portrait not so much of a mistress as of our degrading love for her. There was lacking only what we find in so many portraits – that the painter should have been at once a great artist and a lover (and even then it was said that Elstir had been in love with Odette). This disparity, the whole life of a lover – of a lover whose acts of folly nobody understands – the whole life of a Swann goes to prove. But let the lover be embodied in a painter like Elstir and then we have the clue to the enigma, we have at length before our eyes those lips which the common herd have never perceived, that nose which nobody has ever seen, that unsuspected carriage. The portrait says: 'What I have loved, what has made me suffer, what I have never ceased to behold is this.' By an inverse gymnastic, I who had made a mental effort to add to Rachel all that Saint-Loup had added to her of himself, I attempted to subtract the support of my heart and mind from the composition of Albertine and to picture her to myself as she must appear to Saint-Loup, as Rachel had appeared to me. Those differences, even though we were to observe them ourselves, what importance would we attach to them? When, in the summer at Balbec, Albertine used to wait for me beneath the arcades of Incarville and spring into my carriage, not only had she not yet put on weight, she had, as a result of too much exercise, begun to waste; thin, made plainer by an ugly hat which left visible only the tip of an ugly nose, and a side-view, pale cheeks like white slugs, I recognised very little of her, enough however to know, when she sprang into the carriage, that it was she, that she had been punctual in keeping our appointment and had not gone somewhere else; and this was enough; what we love is too much in the past, consists too much in the time that we have spent together for us to require the whole woman; we wish only to be sure that it is she, not to be mistaken as to her identity, a thing far more important than beauty to those who are in love; her cheeks may grow hollow, her body thin, even to those who were originally most proud, in the eyes of the world, of their domination over beauty, that little tip of a nose, that sign in which is summed up the permanent personality of a woman, that algebraical formula, that constant, is sufficient to prevent a man who is courted in the highest society and is in love with her from being free upon a single evening because he is spending his evenings in brushing and entangling, until it is time to go to bed, the hair of the woman whom he loves, or simply in staying by her side, so that he may be with her or she with him, or merely that she may not be with other people.

'You are sure,' Robert asked me, 'that I can begin straight away by offering this woman thirty thousand francs for her husband's constituency? She is as dishonest as all that? You're sure you aren't exaggerating and that three thousand francs wouldn't be enough?' 'No, I beg of you, don't try to be economical about a thing that matters so much to me. This is what you are to say to her (and it is to some extent true): "My friend borrowed these thirty thousand francs from a relative for the election expenses of the uncle of the girl he was engaged to marry. It was because of this engagement that the money was given him. And he asked me to bring it to you so that Albertine should know nothing about it. And now Albertine goes and leaves him. He doesn't know what to do. He is obliged to pay back the thirty thousand francs if he does not marry Albertine. And if he is going to marry her, then if only to keep up appearances she ought to return immediately, because it will look so bad if she stays away for long." You think I've made all this up?' 'Not at all,' Saint-Loup assured me out of consideration for myself, out of discretion, and also because he knew that truth is often stranger than fiction. After all, it was by no means impossible that in this tale of the thirty thousand francs there might be, as I had told him, a large element of truth. It was possible, but it was not true and this element of truth was in fact a lie. But we lied to each other, Robert and I, as in every conversation when one friend is genuinely anxious to help another who is desperately in love. The friend who is being counsellor, prop, comforter, may pity the other's distress but cannot share it, and the kinder he is to him the more he has to lie. And the other confesses to him as much as is necessary in order to secure his help, but, simply perhaps in order to secure that help, conceals many things from him. And the happy one of the two is, when all is said, he who takes trouble, goes on a journey, executes a mission, but feels no anguish in his heart. I was at this moment the person that Robert had been at Doncières when he thought that Rachel had abandoned him. 'Very well, just as you like; if I get my head bitten off, I accept the snub in advance for your sake. And even if it does seem a bit queer to make such an open bargain, I know that in our own set there are plenty of duchesses, even the most stuffy of them, who if you offered them thirty thousand francs would do things far more difficult than telling their nieces not to stay in Touraine. Anyhow I am doubly glad to be doing you a service, since that is the only reason that will make you consent to see me. If I marry,' he went on, 'don't you think we might see more of one another, won't you look upon my house as your own . . . ' He stopped short, the thought having suddenly occurred to him (as I supposed at the time) that, if I too were to marry, his wife would not be able to make an intimate friend of Albertine. And I remembered what the Cambremers had said to me as to the probability of his marrying a niece of the Prince de Guermantes. He consulted the timetable, and found that he could not leave Paris until the evening. Françoise enquired: 'Am I to take Mlle Albertine's bed out of the study?' 'Not at all,' I said, 'you must leave everything ready for her.' I hoped that she would return any day and did not wish Françoise to suppose that there could be any doubt of her return. Albertine's departure must appear to have been arranged between ourselves, and not in any way to imply that she loved me less than before. But Françoise looked at me with an air, if not of incredulity, at any rate of doubt. She too had her alternative hypotheses. Her nostrils expanded, she could scent the quarrel, she must have felt it in the air for a long time past. And if she was not absolutely sure of it, this was perhaps because, like myself, she would hesitate to believe unconditionally what would have given her too much pleasure. Now the burden of the affair rested no longer upon my overwrought mind, but upon Saint-Loup. I became quite light-hearted because I had made a decision, because I could say to myself: 'I haven't lost any time, I have acted.' Saint-Loup can barely have been in the train when in the hall I ran into Bloch, whose ring I had not heard, and so was obliged to let him stay with me for a minute. He had met me recently with Albertine (whom he had known at Balbec) on a day when she was in bad humour. 'I met M. Bontemps at dinner,' he told me, 'and as I have a certain influence over him, I told him that I was grieved that his niece was not nicer to you, that he must make entreaties to her in that connection.' I boiled with rage; these entreaties, this compassion destroyed the whole effect of Saint-Loup's intervention and brought me into direct contact with Albertine herself whom I now seemed to be imploring to return. To make matters worse, Françoise, who was lingering in the hall, could hear every word. I heaped every imaginable reproach upon Bloch, telling him that I had never authorised him to do anything of the sort and that, besides, the whole thing was nonsense. Bloch, from that moment, continued to smile, less, I imagine, from joy than from self-consciousness at having made me angry. He laughingly expressed his surprise at having provoked such anger. Perhaps he said this hoping to minimise in my mind the importance of his indiscreet intervention, perhaps it was because he was of a cowardly nature, and lived gaily and idly in an atmosphere of falsehood, as jellyfish float upon the surface of the sea, perhaps because, even if he had not been of a different race, as other people can never place themselves at our point of view, they do not realise the magnitude of the injury that words uttered at random can do us. I had barely shown him out, unable to think of any remedy for the mischief that he had done, when the bell rang again and Françoise brought me a summons from the head of the Sûreté. The parents of the little girl whom I had brought into the house for an hour had decided to lodge a complaint against me for corruption of a child under the age of consent. There are moments in life when a sort of beauty is created by the multiplicity of the troubles that assail us, intertwined like Wagnerian *leitmotiv*, from the idea also, which then emerges, that events are not situated in the content of the reflections portrayed in the wretched little mirror which the mind holds in front of it and which is called the future, that they are somewhere outside, and spring up as suddenly as a person who comes to accuse us of a crime. Even when left to itself, an event becomes modified, whether frustration amplifies it for us or satisfaction reduces it. But it is rarely unaccompanied. The feelings aroused by each event contradict one another, and there comes to a certain extent, as I felt when on my way to the head of the Sûreté, an at least momentary revulsion which is as provocative of sentimental misery as fear. I found at the Sûreté the girl's parents who insulted me by saying: 'We don't eat this sort of bread', and handed me back the five hundred francs which I declined to take, and the head of the Sûreté who, setting himself the inimitable example of the judicial facility in repartee, took hold of a word from each sentence that I uttered, a word which enabled him to make a witty and crushing retort. My innocence of the alleged crime was never taken into consideration, for that was the sole hypothesis which nobody was willing to accept for an instant. Nevertheless the difficulty of a conviction enabled me to escape with an extremely violent reprimand, while the parents were in the room. But as soon as they had gone, the head of the Sûreté, who had a weakness for little girls, changed his tone and admonished me as one man to another: 'Next time, you must be more careful. Gad, you can't pick them up as easily as that, or you'll get into trouble. Anyhow, you can find dozens of girls better than that one, and far cheaper. It was a perfectly ridiculous amount to pay.' I felt him to be so incapable of understanding me if I attempted to tell him the truth that without saying a word I took advantage of his permission to withdraw. Every passer-by, until I was safely at home, seemed to me an inspector appointed to spy upon my behaviour. But this *leitmotiv*, like that of my anger with Bloch, died away, leaving the field clear for that of Albertine's departure. And this took its place once more, but in an almost joyous tone now that Saint-Loup had started. Now that he had undertaken to go and see Mme Bontemps, my sufferings had been dispelled. I believed that this was because I had taken action, I believed it sincerely, for we never know what we conceal in our heart of hearts. What really made me happy was not, as I supposed, that I had transferred my load of indecisions to Saint-Loup. I was not, for that matter, entirely wrong; the specific remedy for an unfortunate event (and three events out of four are unfortunate) is a decision; for its effect is that, by a sudden reversal of our thoughts, it interrupts the flow of those that come from the past event and prolong its vibration, and breaks that flow with a contrary flow of contrary thoughts, come from without, from the future. But these new thoughts are most of all beneficial to us when (and this was the case with the thoughts that assailed me at this moment), from the heart of that future, it is a hope that they bring us. What really made me so happy was the secret certainty that Saint-Loup's mission could not fail, Albertine was bound to return. I realised this; for not having received, on the following day, any answer from Saint-Loup, I began to suffer afresh. My decision, my transference to him of full power of action, were not therefore the cause of my joy, which, in that case, would have persisted; but rather the 'Success is certain' which had been in my mind when I said: 'Come what may'. And the thought aroused by his delay, that, after all, his mission might not prove successful, was so hateful to me that I had lost my gaiety. It is in reality our anticipation, our hope of happy events that fills us with a joy which we ascribe to other causes and which ceases, letting us relapse into misery, if we are no longer so assured that what we desire will come to pass. It is always this invisible belief that sustains the edifice of our world of sensation, deprived of which it rocks from its foundations. We have seen that it creates for us the merit or unimportance of other people, our excitement or boredom at seeing them. It creates similarly the possibility of enduring a grief which seems to us trivial, simply because we are convinced that it will presently be brought to an end, or its sudden enlargement until the presence of a certain person matters as much as, possibly more than our life itself. One thing however succeeded in making my heartache as keen as it had been at the first moment and (I am bound to admit) no longer was. This was when I read over again a passage in Albertine's letter. It is all very well our loving people, the pain of losing them, when in our isolation we are confronted with it alone, to which our mind gives, to a certain extent, whatever form it chooses, this pain is endurable and different from that other pain less human, less our own, as unforeseen and unusual as an accident in the moral world and in the region of our heart, which is caused not so much by the people themselves as by the manner in which we have learned that we are not to see them again. Albertine, I might think of her with gentle tears, accepting the fact that I should not be able to see her again this evening as I had seen her last night, but when I read over again: 'my decision is irrevocable', that was another matter, it was like taking a dangerous drug which might give me a heart attack which I could not survive. There is in inanimate objects, in events, in farewell letters a special danger which amplifies and even alters the nature of the grief that people are capable of causing us. But this pain did not last long. I was, when all was said, so sure of Saint-Loup's skill, of his eventual success, Albertine's return seemed to me so certain that I asked myself whether I had had any reason to hope for it. Nevertheless, I rejoiced at the thought. Unfortunately for myself, who supposed the business with the Sûreté to be over and done with, Françoise came in to tell me that an inspector had called to enquire whether I was in the habit of having girls in the house, that the porter, supposing him to refer to Albertine, had replied in the affirmative, and that from that moment it had seemed that the house was being watched. In future it would be impossible for me ever to bring a little girl into the house to console me in my grief, without the risk of being put to shame in her eyes by the sudden intrusion of an inspector, and of her regarding me as a criminal. And at the same instant I realised how far more we live for certain ideas than we suppose, for this impossibility of my ever taking a little girl on my knee again seemed to me to destroy all the value of my life, but what was more I understood how comprehensible it is that people will readily refuse wealth and risk their lives, whereas we imagine that pecuniary interest and the fear of death rule the world. For if I had thought that even a little girl who was a complete stranger might by the arrival of a policeman, be given a bad impression of myself, how much more readily would I have committed suicide. And yet there was no possible comparison between the two degrees of suffering. Now in everyday life we never bear in mind that the people to whom we offer money, whom we threaten to kill, may have mistresses or merely friends, to whose esteem they attach importance, not to mention their own self-respect. But, all of a sudden, by a confusion of which I was not aware (I did not in fact remember that Albertine, being of full age, was free to live under my roof and even to be my mistress), it seemed to me that the charge of corrupting minors might include Albertine also. Thereupon my life appeared to me to be hedged in on every side. And when I thought that I had not lived chastely with her, I found in the punishment that had been inflicted upon me for having forced an unknown little girl to accept money, that relation which almost always exists in human sanctions, the effect of which is that there is hardly ever either a fair sentence or a judicial error, but a sort of compromise between the false idea that the judge forms of an innocent action and the culpable deeds of which he is unaware. But then when I thought that Albertine's return might involve me in the scandal of a sentence which would degrade me in her eyes and would perhaps do her, too, an injury which she would not forgive me, I ceased to look forward to her return, it terrified me. I would have liked to telegraph to her not to come back. And immediately, drowning everything else, the passionate desire for her return overwhelmed me. The fact was that having for an instant considered the possibility of telling her not to return and of living without her, all of a sudden, I felt myself on the contrary ready to abandon all travel, all pleasure, all work, if only Albertine might return! Ah, how my love for Albertine, the course of which I had supposed that I could foretell, on the analogy of my previous love for Gilberte, had developed in an entirely opposite direction! How impossible it was for me to live without seeing her! And with each of my actions, even the most trivial, since they had all been steeped before in the blissful atmosphere which was Albertine's presence, I was obliged in turn, with a fresh expenditure of energy, with the same grief, to begin again the apprenticeship of separation. Then the competition of other forms of life thrust this latest grief into the background, and, during those days which were the first days of spring, I even found, as I waited until Saint-Loup should have seen Mme Bontemps, in imagining Venice and beautiful, unknown women, a few moments of pleasing calm. As soon as I was conscious of this, I felt in myself a panic terror. This calm which I had just enjoyed was the first apparition of that great occasional force which was to wage war in me against grief, against love, and would in the end prove victorious. This state of which I had just had a foretaste and had received the warning, was, for a moment only, what would in time to come be my permanent state, a life in which I should no longer be able to suffer on account of Albertine, in which I should no longer be in love with her. And my love, which had just seen and recognised the one enemy by whom it could be conquered, forgetfulness, began to tremble, like a lion which in the cage in which it has been confined has suddenly caught sight of the python that is about to devour it.

I thought of Albertine all the time and never was Françoise, when she came into my room, quick enough in saying: 'There are no letters', to curtail my anguish. From time to time I succeeded, by letting some current or other of ideas flow through my grief, in refreshing, in aerating to some slight extent the vitiated atmosphere of my heart, but at night, if I succeeded in going to sleep, then it was as though the memory of Albertine had been the drug that had procured my sleep, whereas the cessation of its influence would awaken me. I thought all the time of Albertine while I was asleep. It was a special sleep of her own that she gave me, and one in which, moreover, I should no longer have been at liberty, as when awake, to think of other things. Sleep and the memory of her were the two substances which I must mix together and take at one draught in order to put myself to sleep. When I was awake, moreover, my suffering went on increasing day by day instead of diminishing, not that oblivion was not performing its task, but because by the very fact of its doing so it favoured the idealisation of the regretted image and thereby the assimilation of my initial suffering to other analogous sufferings which intensified it. Still this image was endurable. But if all of a sudden I thought of her room, of her room in which the bed stood empty, of her piano, her motor car, I lost all my strength, I shut my eyes, let my head droop upon my shoulder like a person who is about to faint. The sound of doors being opened hurt me almost as much because it was not she that was opening them.

When it was possible that a telegram might have come from Saint-Loup, I dared not ask: 'Is there a telegram?' At length one did come, but brought with it only a postponement of any result, with the message: 'The ladies have gone away for three days.' No doubt, if I had endured the four days that had already elapsed since her departure, it was because I said to myself: 'It is only a matter of time, by the end of the week she will be here.' But this argument did not alter the fact that for my heart, for my body, the action to be performed was the same: living without her, returning home and not finding her in the house, passing the door of her room – as for opening it, I had not yet the courage to do that – knowing that she was not inside, going to bed without having said good-night to her, such were the tasks that my heart had been obliged to accomplish in their terrible entirety, and for all the world as though I had not been going to see Albertine. But the fact that my heart had already performed this daily task four times proved that it was now capable of continuing to perform it. And soon, perhaps, the consideration which helped me to go on living in this fashion – the prospect of Albertine's return – I should cease to feel any need of it (I should be able to say to myself: 'She is never coming back', and remain alive all the same as

I had already been living for the last four days), like a cripple who has recovered the use of his feet and can dispense with his crutches. No doubt when I came home at night I still found, taking my breath away, stifling me in the vacuum of solitude, the memories placed end to end in an interminable series of all the evenings upon which Albertine had been waiting for me; but already I found in this series my memory of last night, of the night before and of the two previous evenings, that is to say the memory of the four nights that had passed since Albertine's departure, during which I had remained without her, alone, through which nevertheless I had lived, four nights already, forming a string of memories that was very slender compared with the other, but to which every new day would perhaps add substance. I shall say nothing of the letter conveying a declaration of affection which I received at this time from a niece of Mme de Guermantes, considered the prettiest girl in Paris, nor of the overtures made to me by the Duc de Guermantes on behalf of her parents, resigned, in their anxiety to secure their daughter's happiness, to the inequality of the match, to an apparent misalliance. Such incidents which might prove gratifying to our self-esteem are too painful when we are in love. We feel a desire, but shrink from the indelicacy of communicating them to her who has a less flattering opinion of us, nor would that opinion be altered by the knowledge that we are able to inspire one that is very different. What the Duke's niece wrote to me could only have made Albertine angry. From the moment of waking, when I picked my grief up again at the point which I had reached when I fell asleep, like a book which had been shut for a while but which I would keep before my eyes until night, it could be only with some thought relating to Albertine that all my sensation would be brought into harmony, whether it came to me from without or from within. The bell rang: it is a letter from her, it is she herself perhaps! If I felt myself in better health, not too miserable, I was no longer jealous, I no longer had any grievance against her, I would have liked to see her at once, to kiss her, to live happily with her ever after. The act of telegraphing to her: 'Come at once' seemed to me to have become a perfectly simple thing, as though my fresh mood had changed not merely my inclinations but things external to myself, had made them more easy. If I was in a sombre mood, all my anger with her revived, I no longer felt any desire to kiss her, I felt how impossible it was that she could ever make me happy, I sought only to do her harm and to prevent her from belonging to other people. But these two opposite moods had an identical result: it was essential that she should return as soon as possible. And yet, however keen my joy at the moment of her return, I felt that very soon the same difficulties would crop up again and that to seek happiness in the satisfaction of a moral desire was as fatuous as to attempt to reach the horizon by walking straight ahead. The farther the desire advances, the farther does true possession withdraw. So that if happiness or at least freedom from suffering can be found it is not the satisfaction, but the gradual reduction, the eventual extinction of our desire that we must seek. We attempt to see the person whom we love, we ought to attempt not to see her, oblivion alone brings about an ultimate extinction of desire. And I imagine that if an author were to publish truths of this sort he would dedicate the book that contained them to a woman to whom he would thus take pleasure in returning, saying to her: 'This book is yours'. And thus, while telling the truth in his book, he would be lying in his dedication, for he will attach to the book's being hers only the importance that he attaches to the stone that came to him from her which will remain precious to him only so long as he is in love with her. The bonds that unite another person to ourselves exist only in our mind. Memory as it grows fainter relaxes them, and notwithstanding the illusion by which we would fain be cheated and with which, out of love, friendship, politeness, deference, duty, we cheat other people, we exist alone. Man is the creature that cannot emerge from himself, that knows his fellows only in himself; when he asserts the contrary, he is lying. And I should have been in such terror (had there been anyone capable of taking it) of somebody's robbing me of this need of her, this love for her, that I convinced myself that it had a value in my life. To be able to hear uttered, without being either fascinated or pained by them, the names of the stations through which the train passed on its way to Touraine, would have seemed to me a diminution of myself (for no other reason really than that it would have proved that Albertine was ceasing to interest me); it was just as well, I told myself, that by incessantly asking myself what she could be doing, thinking, longing, at every moment, whether she intended, whether she was going to return, I should be keeping open that communicating door which love had installed in me, and feeling another person's mind flood through open sluices the reservoir which must not again become stagnant. Presently, as Saint-Loup remained silent, a subordinate anxiety – my expectation of a further telegram, of a telephone call from him – masked the other, my uncertainty as to the result, whether Albertine was going to return. Listening for every sound in expectation of the telegram became so intolerable that I felt that, whatever might be its contents, the arrival of the telegram, which was the only thing of which I could think at the moment, would put an end to my sufferings. But when at length I had received a telegram from Robert in which he informed me that he had seen Mme Bontemps, but that, notwith-standing all his precautions, Albertine had seen him, and that this had upset everything, I burst out in a torrent of fury and despair, for this was what I would have done anything in the world to prevent. Once it came to Albertine's knowledge, Saint-Loup's mission gave me an appearance of being dependent upon her which could only dissuade her from returning, my horror of which was, as it happened, all that I had retained of the pride that my love had boasted in Gilberte's day and had since lost. I cursed Robert. Then I told myself that, if this attempt had failed, I would try another. Since man is able to influence the outer world, how, if I brought into play cunning, intelligence, pecuniary advantage, affection, should I fail to succeed in destroying this appalling fact: Albertine's absence. We believe that according to our desire we are able to change the things around about us, we believe this because otherwise we can see no favourable solution. We forget the solution that generally comes to pass and is also favourable: we do not succeed in changing things according to our desire, but gradually our desire changes. The situation that we hoped to change because it was intolerable becomes unimportant. We have not managed to surmount the obstacle, as we were absolutely determined to do, but life has taken us round it, led us past it, and then if we turn round to gaze at the remote past, we can barely catch sight of it, so imperceptible has it become. In the flat above ours, one of the neighbours was strumming songs. I applied their words, which I knew, to Albertine and myself, and was stirred by so profound a sentiment that I began to cry. The words were:

'Hélas, l'oiseau qui fuit ce qu'il croit l'esclavage,
d'un vol désespéré revient battre au vitrage'

and the death of Manon:

'Manon, réponds-moi donc,
Seul amour de mon âme, je n'ai su qu'aujourd'hui
la bonté de ton coeur.'

Since Manon returned to Des Grieux, it seemed to me that I was to Albertine the one and only love of her life. Alas, it is probable that, if she had been listening at that moment to the same air, it would not have been myself that she would have cherished under the name of Des Grieux, and, even if the idea had occurred to her, the memory of myself would have checked her emotion on hearing this music, albeit it was, although better and more distinguished, just the sort of music that she admired. As for myself, I had not the courage to abandon myself to so pleasant a train of thought, to imagine Albertine calling me her 'heart's only love' and realising that she had been mistaken over what she 'had thought to be bondage'. I knew that we can never read a novel without giving its heroine the form and features of the woman with whom we are in love. But be the ending as happy as it may, our love has not advanced an inch and, when we have shut the book, she whom we love and who has come to us at last in its pages, loves us no better in real life. In a fit of fury, I telegraphed to Saint-Loup to return as quickly as possible to Paris, so as to avoid at least the appearance of an aggravating insistence upon a mission which I had been so anxious to keep secret. But even before he had returned in obedience to my instructions it was from Albertine herself that I received the following letter: 'My dear – you have sent your friend Saint-Loup to my aunt, which was foolish. My dear boy, if you needed me why did you not write to me myself, I should have been only too delighted to come back, do not let us have any more of these absurd complications.' 'I should have been only too delighted to come back!' If she said this, it must mean that she regretted her departure, and was only seeking an excuse to return. So that I had merely to do what she said, to write to her that I needed her, and she would return.

I was going, then, to see her again, her, the Albertine of Balbec (for since her departure this was what she had once more become to me; like a seashell to which we cease to pay any attention while we have it on the chest of drawers in our room, once we have parted with it, either by giving it away or by losing it, and begin to think about it, a thing which we had ceased to do, she recalled to me all the joyous beauty of the blue mountains of the sea). And it was not only she that had become a creature of the imagination, that is to say desirable, life with her had become an imaginary life, that is to say a life set free from all difficulties, so that I said to myself: 'How happy we are going to be!' But, now that I was assured of her return, I must not appear to be seeking to hasten it, but must on the contrary efface the bad impression left by Saint-Loup's intervention, which I could always disavow later on by saying that he had acted upon his own initiative, because he had always been in favour of our marriage. Meanwhile, I read her letter again, and was nevertheless disappointed when I saw how little there is of a person in a letter. Doubtless the characters traced on the paper express our thoughts, as do also our features: it is still a thought of some kind that we see before us. But all the same, in the person, the thought is not apparent to us until it has been diffused through the expanded water-lily of her face. This modifies it considerably. And it is perhaps one of the causes of our perpetual disappointments in love, this perpetual deviation which brings it about that, in response to our expectation of the ideal person with whom we are in love, each meeting provides us with a person in flesh and blood in whom there is already so little trace of our dream. And then when we demand something of this person, we receive from her a letter in which even of the person very little remains, as in the letters of an algebraical formula there no longer remains the precise value of the arithmetical ciphers, which themselves do not contain the qualities of the fruit or flowers that they enumerate. And yet love, the beloved object, her letters, are perhaps nevertheless translations (unsatisfying as it may be to pass from one to the other) of the same reality, since the letter seems to us inadequate only while we are reading it, but we have been sweating blood until its arrival, and it is sufficient to calm our anguish, if not to appease, with its tiny black symbols, our desire which knows that it contains after all only the equivalent of a word, a smile, a kiss, not the things themselves.

I wrote to Albertine:

MY DEAR – I was just about to write to you, and I thank you for telling me that if I had been in need of you you would have come at once; it is like you to have so exalted a sense of devotion to an old friend, which can only increase my regard for you. But no, I did not ask and I shall not ask you to return; our meeting – for a long time to come – might not be painful, perhaps, to you, a heartless girl. To me whom at times you have thought so cold, it would be most painful. Life has driven us apart. You have made a decision which I consider very wise, and which you have made at the right moment, with a marvellous presentiment, for you left me on the day on which I had just received my mother's consent to my asking you to marry me. I would have told you this when I awoke, when I received her letter (at the same moment as yours). Perhaps you would have been afraid of distressing me by leaving immediately after that. And we should perhaps have united our lives in what would have been for us (who knows?) misery. If this is what was in store for us, then I bless you for your wisdom. We should lose all the fruit of it were we to meet again. This is not to say that I should not find it a temptation. But I claim no great credit for resisting it. You know what an inconstant person I am and how quickly I forget. You have told me often, I am first and foremost a man of habit. The habits which I am beginning to form in your absence are not as yet very strong. Naturally, at this moment, the habits that I had when you were with me, habits which your departure has upset, are still the stronger. They will not remain so for very long. For that reason, indeed, I had thought of taking advantage of these last few days in which our meeting would not yet be for me what it will be in a fortnight's time, perhaps even sooner (forgive my frankness): a disturbance – I had thought of taking advantage of them, before the final oblivion, in order to settle certain little material questions with you, in which you might, as a good and charming friend, have rendered a service to him who for five minutes imagined himself your future husband. As I never expected that my mother would approve, as on the other hand I desired that we should each of us enjoy all that liberty of which you had too generously and abundantly made a sacrifice which might be admissible had we been living together for a few weeks, but would have become as hateful to you as to myself now that we were to spend the rest of our lives together (it almost hurts me to think as I write to you that this nearly happened, that the news came only a moment too late), I had thought of organising our existence in the most independent manner possible, and, to begin with, I wished you to have that yacht in which you could go cruising while I, not being well enough to accompany you, would wait for you at the port (I had written to Elstir to ask for his advice, since you admire his taste), and on land I wished you to have a motor car to yourself, for your very own, in which you could go out, could travel wherever you chose. The yacht was almost ready; it is named, after a wish that you expressed at Balbec, *le Cygne*. And remembering that your favourite make of car was the Rolls, I had ordered one. But now that we are never to meet again, as I have no hope of persuading you to accept either the vessel or the car (to me they would be quite useless), I had thought – as I had ordered them through an agent, but in your name – that you might perhaps by countermanding them, yourself, save me the expense of the yacht and the car which are no longer required. But this, and many other matters, would need to be discussed. Well, I find that so long as I am capable of falling in love with you again, which will not be for long, it would be madness, for the sake of a sailing-vessel and a Rolls-Royce, to meet again and to risk the happiness of your life since you have decided that it lies in your living apart from myself. No, I prefer to keep the Rolls and even the yacht. And as I shall make no use of them and they are likely to remain for ever, one in its dock, dismantled, the other in its garage, I shall have engraved upon the yacht (Heavens, I am afraid of misquoting the title and committing a heresy which would shock you) those lines of Mallarmé which you used to like:

> Un cygne d'autrefois se souvient que c'est lui
> Magnifique mais qui sans espoir se délivre
> Pour n'avoir pas chanté la région où vivre
> Quand du stérile hiver a resplendi l'ennui.

You remember – it is the poem that begins:

> Le vierge, le vivace et le bel aujourd'hui . . .

Alas, today is no longer either virginal or fair. But the men who know, as I know, that they will very soon make of it an endurable 'tomorrow' are seldom *endurable* themselves. As for the Rolls, it would deserve rather those other lines of the same poet which you said you could not understand:

> Dis si je ne suis pas joyeux
> Tonnerre et rubis aux moyeux
> De voir en l'air que ce feu troue
>
> Avec des royaumes épars
> Comme mourir pourpre la roue
> Du seul vespéral de mes chars.

'Farewell for ever, my little Albertine, and thanks once again for the charming drive which we took on the eve of our parting. I retain a very pleasant memory of it.

'P.S. I make no reference to what you tell me of the alleged suggestions which Saint-Loup (whom I do not for a moment believe to be in Touraine) may have made to your aunt. It is just like a Sherlock Holmes story. For what do you take me?

No doubt, just as I had said in the past to Albertine: 'I am not in love with you', in order that she might love me; 'I forget people when I do not see them', in order that she might come often to see me; 'I have decided to leave you', in order to forestall any idea of a parting, now it was because I was absolutely determined that she must return within a week that I said to her: 'Farewell for ever'; it was because I wished to see her again that I said to her: 'I think it would be dangerous to see you'; it was because living apart from her seemed to me worse than death that I wrote to her: 'You were right, we should be wretched together.' Alas, this false letter, when I wrote it in order to appear not to be dependent upon her and also to enjoy the pleasure of saying certain things which could arouse emotion only in myself and not in her, I ought to have foreseen from the start that it was possible that it would result in a negative response, that is to say one which confirmed what I had said; that this was indeed probable, for even had Albertine been less intelligent than she was, she would never have doubted for an instant that what I said to her was untrue. Indeed without pausing to consider the intentions that I expressed in this letter, the mere fact of my writing it, even if it had not been preceded by Saint-Loup's intervention, was enough to prove to her that I desired her return and to prompt her to let me become more and more inextricably ensnared. Then, having foreseen the possibility of a reply in the negative, I ought also to have foreseen that this reply would at once revive in its fullest intensity my love for Albertine. And I ought, still before posting my letter, to have asked myself whether, in the event of Albertine's replying in the same tone and refusing to return, I should have sufficient control over my grief to force myself to remain silent, not to telegraph to her: 'Come back', not to send her some other messenger, which, after I had written to her that we would not meet again, would make it perfectly obvious that I could not get on without her, and would lead to her refusing more emphatically than ever, whereupon I, unable to endure my anguish for another moment, would go down to visit her and might, for all I knew, be refused admission. And, no doubt, this would have been, after three enormous blunders, the worst of all, after which there would be nothing left but to take my life in front of her house. But the disastrous manner in which the psychopathic universe is constructed has decreed that the clumsy action, the action which we ought most carefully to have avoided, should be precisely the action that will calm us, the action that, opening before us, until we learn its result, fresh avenues of hope, relieves us for the moment of the intolerable pain which a refusal has aroused in us. With the result that, when the pain is too keen, we dash headlong into the blunder that consists in writing, sending somebody to intercede, going in person, proving that we cannot get on without the woman we love. But I foresaw nothing of all this. The probable result of my letter seemed to me on the contrary to be that of making Albertine return to me at once. And so, as I thought of this result, I greatly enjoyed writing the letter. But at the same time I had not ceased, while writing it, from shedding tears; partly, at first, in the same way as upon the day when I had acted a pretence of separation, because, as the words represented for me the idea which they expressed to me, albeit they were aimed in the opposite direction (uttered mendaciously because my pride forbade me to admit that I was in love), they carried their own load of sorrow. But also because I felt that the idea contained a grain of truth.

As this letter seemed to me to be certain of its effect, I began to regret that I had sent it. For as I pictured to myself the return (so natural, after all) of Albertine, immediately all the reasons which made our marriage a thing disastrous to myself returned in their fullest force. I hoped that she would refuse to come back. I was engaged in calculating that my liberty, my whole future depended upon her refusal, that I had been mad to write to her, that I ought to have retrieved my letter which, alas, had gone, when Françoise, with the newspaper which she had just brought upstairs, handed it back to me. She was not certain how many stamps it required. But immediately I changed my mind; I hoped that Albertine would not return, but I wished the decision to come from her, so as to put an end to my anxiety, and I handed the letter back to Françoise. I opened the newspaper; it announced a performance by Berma. Then I remembered the two different attitudes in which I had listened to Phèdre, and it was now in a third attitude that I thought of the declaration scene. It seemed to me that what I had so often repeated to myself, and had heard recited in the theatre, was the statement of the laws of which I must make experience in my life. There are in our soul things to which we do not realise how strongly we are attached. Or else, if we live without them, it is because we put off from day to day, from fear of failure, or of being made to suffer, entering into possession of them. This was what had happened to me in the case of Gilberte when I thought that I had given her up. If before the moment in which we are entirely detached from these things – a moment long subsequent to that in which we suppose ourselves to have been detached from them – the girl with whom we are in love becomes, for instance, engaged to someone else, we are mad, we can no longer endure the life which appeared to us to be so sorrowfully calm. Or else, if we are in control of the situation, we feel that she is a burden, we would gladly be rid of her. Which was what had happened to me in the case of Albertine. But let a sudden departure remove the unloved creature from us, we are unable to survive. But did not the plot of *Phèdre* combine these two cases? Hippolyte is about to leave. Phèdre, who until then has taken care to court his hostility, from a scruple of conscience, she says, or rather the poet makes her say, because she is unable to foresee the consequences and feels that she is not loved, Phèdre can endure the situation no longer. She comes to him to confess her love, and this was the scene which I had so often repeated to myself: 'On dit qu'un prompt départ vous éloigne de nous . . .' Doubtless this reason for the departure of Hippolyte is less decisive, we may suppose, than the death of Thésée. And similarly when, a few lines farther on, Phèdre pretends for a moment that she has been misunderstood: 'Aurais-je perdu tout le soin de ma gloire?' we may suppose that it is because Hippolyte has repulsed her declaration.

> Madame, oubliez-vous
> Que Thésée est mon père, et qu'il est votre époux?

But there would not have been this indignation unless, in the moment of a consummated bliss, Phèdre could have had the same feeling that it amounted to little or nothing. Whereas, as soon as she sees that it is not to be consummated, that Hippolyte thinks that he has misunderstood her and makes apologies, then, like myself when I decided to give my letter back to Françoise, she decides that the refusal must come from him, decides to stake everything upon his answer: 'Ah! cruel, tu m'as trop entendue.' And there is nothing, not even the harshness with which, as I had been told, Swann had treated Odette, or I myself had treated Albertine, a harshness which substituted for the original love a new love composed of pity, emotion, of the need of effusion, which is only a variant of the former love, that is not to be found also in this scene:

> Tu me haïssais plus, je ne t'aimais pas moins.
> Tes malheurs te prêtaient encor de nouveaux charmes.

What proves that it is not to the 'thought of her own fame' that Phèdre attaches most importance is that she would forgive Hippolyte and turn a deaf ear to the advice of Oenone had she not learned at the same instant that Hippolyte was in love with Aricie. So it is that jealousy, which in love is equivalent to the loss of all happiness, outweighs any loss of reputation. It is then that she allows Oenone (which is merely a name for the baser part of herself) to slander Hippolyte without taking upon herself the 'burden of his defence' and thus sends the man who will have none of her to a fate the calamities of which are no consolation, however, to herself, since her own suicide follows immediately upon the death of Hippolyte. Thus at least it was, with a diminution of the part played by all the 'Jansenist scruples', as Bergotte would have said, which Racine ascribed to Phèdre to make her less guilty, that this scene appeared to me, a sort of prophecy of the amorous episodes in my own life. These reflections had, however, altered nothing of my determination, and I handed my letter to Françoise so that she might post it after all, in order to carry into effect that appeal to Albertine which seemed to me to be indispensable, now that I had learned that my former attempt had failed. And no doubt we are wrong when we suppose that the accomplishment of our desire is a small matter, since as soon as we believe that it cannot be realised we become intent upon it once again, and decide that it was not worth our while to pursue it only when we are quite certain that our attempt will not fail. And yet we are right also. For if this accomplishment, if our happiness appear of small account only in the light of certainty, nevertheless they are an unstable element from which only trouble can arise. And our trouble will be all the greater the more completely our desire will have been accomplished, all the more impossible to endure when our happiness has been, in defiance of the law of nature, prolonged for a certain period, when it has received the consecration of habit. In another sense as well, these two tendencies, by which I mean that which made me anxious that my letter should be posted, and, when I thought that it had gone, my regret that I had written it, have each of them a certain element of truth. In the case of the first, it is easily comprehensible that we should go in pursuit of our happiness – or misery – and that at the same time we should hope to keep before us, by this latest action which is about to involve us in its consequences, a state of expectancy which does not leave us in absolute despair, in a word that we should seek to convert into other forms, which, we imagine, must be less painful to us, the malady from which we are suffering. But the other tendency is no less important, for, born of our belief in the success of our enterprise, it is simply an anticipation of the disappointment which we should very soon feel in the presence of a satisfied desire, our regret at having fixed for ourselves, at the expense of other forms which are necessarily excluded, this form of happiness. I had given my letter to Françoise and had asked her to go out at once and post it. As soon as the letter had gone, I began once more to think of Albertine's return as imminent. It did not fail to introduce into my mind certain pleasing images which neutralised somewhat by their attractions the dangers that I foresaw in her return. The pleasure, so long lost, of having her with me was intoxicating.

Time passes, and gradually everything that we have said in falsehood becomes true; I had learned this only too well with Gilberte; the indifference that I had feigned when I could never restrain my tears had ended by becoming real; gradually life, as I told Gilberte in a lying formula which retrospectively had become true, life had driven us apart. I recalled this, I said to myself: 'If Albertine allows an interval to elapse, my lies will become the truth. And now that the worst moments are over, ought I not to hope that she will allow this month to pass without returning? If she returns, I shall have to renounce the true life which certainly I am not in a fit state to enjoy as yet, but which as time goes on may begin to offer me attractions while my memory of Albertine grows fainter.'

I have said that oblivion was beginning to perform its task. But one of the effects of oblivion was precisely – since it meant that many of Albertine's less pleasing aspects, of the boring hours that I had spent with her, no longer figured in my memory, ceased therefore to be reasons for my desiring that she should not be with me as I used to wish when she was still in the house – that it gave me a curtailed impression of her, enhanced by all the love that I had ever felt for other women. In this novel aspect of her, oblivion which nevertheless was engaged upon making me accustomed to our separation, made me, by showing me a more attractive Albertine, long all the more for her return.

Since her departure, very often, when I was confident that I showed no trace of tears, I would ring for Françoise and say to her: 'We must make sure that Mademoiselle Albertine hasn't left anything behind her. Don't forget to do her room, it must be ready for her when she comes.' Or merely: 'Only the other day Mademoiselle Albertine said to me, let me think now, it was the day before she left . . . ' I was anxious to diminish Françoise's abominable pleasure at Albertine's departure by letting her see that it was not to be prolonged. I was anxious also to let Françoise see that I was not afraid to speak of this departure, to proclaim it – like certain generals who describe a forced retreat as a strategic withdrawal in conformity with a prearranged plan – as intended by myself, as constituting an episode the true meaning of which I concealed for the moment, but in no way implying the end of my friendship with Albertine. By repeating her name incessantly I sought in short to introduce, like a breath of air, something of herself into that room in which her departure had left a vacuum, in which I could no longer breathe. Then, moreover, we seek to reduce the dimensions of our grief by making it enter into our everyday speech between ordering a suit of clothes and ordering dinner.

While she was doing Albertine's room, Françoise, out of curiosity, opened the drawer of a little rosewood table in which my mistress used to put away the ornaments which she discarded when she went to bed. 'Oh! Monsieur, Mademoiselle Albertine has forgotten to take her rings, she has left them in the drawer.' My first impulse was to say: 'We must send them after her.' But this would make me appear uncertain of her return. 'Very well,' I replied after a moment of silence, 'it is hardly worth while sending them to her as she is coming back so soon. Give them to me, I shall think about it.' Françoise handed me the rings with a distinct misgiving. She loathed Albertine, but, regarding me in her own image, supposed that one could not hand me a letter in the handwriting of my mistress without the risk of my opening it. I took the rings. 'Monsieur must take care not to lose them,' said Françoise, 'such beauties as they are! I don't know who gave them to her, if it was Monsieur or someone else, but I can see that it was someone rich, who had good taste!' 'It was not I,' I assured her, 'besides, they don't both come from the same person, one was given her by her aunt and the other she bought for herself.' 'Not from the same person!' Françoise exclaimed, 'Monsieur must be joking, they are just alike, except that one of them has had a ruby added to it, there's the same eagle on both, the same initials inside . . . ' I do not know whether Françoise was conscious of the pain that she was causing me, but she began at this point to curve her lips in a smile which never left them. 'What, the same eagle? You are talking nonsense. It is true that the one without the ruby has an eagle upon it, but on the other it is a sort of man's head.' 'A man's head, where did Monsieur discover that? I had only to put on my spectacles to see at once that it was one of the eagle's wings; if Monsieur will take his magnifying glass, he will see the other wing on the other side, the head and the beak in the middle. You can count the feathers. Oh, it's a fine piece of work.' My intense anxiety to know whether Albertine had lied to me made me forget that I ought to maintain a certain dignity in Françoise's presence and deny her the wicked pleasure that she felt, if not in torturing me, at least in disparaging my mistress. I remained breathless while Françoise went to fetch my magnifying glass, I took it from her, asked her to show me the eagle upon the ring with the ruby, she had no difficulty in making me see the wings, conventionalised in the same way as upon the other ring, the feathers, cut separately in relief, the head. She pointed out to me also the similar inscriptions, to which, it is true, others were added upon the ring with the ruby. And on the inside of both was Albertine's monogram. 'But I'm surprised that it should need all this to make Monsieur see that the rings are the same,' said Françoise. 'Even without examining them, you can see that it is the same style, the same way of turning the gold, the same form. As soon as I looked at them I could have sworn that they came from the same place. You can tell it as you can tell the dishes of a good cook.' And indeed, to the curiosity of a servant, whetted by hatred and trained to observe details with a startling precision, there had been added, to assist her in this expert criticism, the taste that she had, that same taste in fact which she showed in her cookery and which was intensified perhaps, as I had noticed when we left Paris for Balbec, in her attire, by the coquetry of a woman who was once good-looking, who has studied the jewels and dresses of other women. I might have taken the wrong box of medicine and, instead of swallowing a few capsules of veronal on a day when I felt that I had drunk too many cups of tea, might have swallowed as many capsules of caffeine; my heart would not have throbbed more violently. I asked Françoise to leave the room. I would have liked to see Albertine immediately. To my horror at her falsehood, to my jealousy of the unknown donor, was added grief that she should have allowed herself to accept such presents. I made her even more presents, it is true, but a woman whom we are keeping does not seem to us to be a kept woman so long as we do not know that she is being kept by other men. And yet since I had continued to spend so much money upon her, I had taken her notwithstanding this moral baseness; this baseness I had maintained in her, I had perhaps increased, perhaps created it. Then, just as we have the faculty of inventing fairy tales to soothe our grief, just as we manage, when we are dying of hunger, to persuade ourselves that a stranger is going to leave us a fortune of a hundred millions, I imagined Albertine in my arms, explaining to me in a few words that it was because of the similarity of its workmanship that she had bought the second ring, that it was she who had had her initials engraved on it. But this explanation was still feeble, it had not yet had time to thrust into my mind its beneficent roots, and my grief could not be so quickly soothed. And I reflected that many men who tell their friends that their mistresses are very kind to them must suffer similar torments. Thus it is that they lie to others and to themselves. They do not altogether lie; they do spend in the woman's company hours that are really pleasant; but think of all that the kindness which their mistresses show them before their friends and which enables them to boast, and of all that the kindness which their mistresses show when they are alone with them, and which enables their lovers to bless them, conceal of unrecorded hours in which the lover has suffered, doubted, sought everywhere in vain to discover the truth! It is to such sufferings that we attach the pleasure of loving, of delighting in the most insignificant remarks of a woman, which we know to be insignificant, but which we perfume with her scent. At this moment I could no longer find any delight in inhaling, by an act of memory, the scent of Albertine. Thunderstruck, holding the two rings in my hand, I stared at that pitiless eagle whose beak was rending my heart, whose wings, chiselled in high relief, had borne away the confidence that I retained in my mistress, in whose claws my tortured mind was unable to escape for an instant from the incessantly recurring questions as to the stranger whose name the eagle doubtless symbolised, without however allowing me to decipher it, whom she had doubtless loved in the past, and whom she had doubtless seen again not so long ago, since it was upon that day so pleasant, so intimate, of our drive together through the Bois that I had seen, for the first time, the second ring, that upon which the eagle appeared to be dipping his beak in the bright blood of the ruby.

If, however, morning, noon and night, I never ceased to grieve over Albertine's departure, this did not mean that I was thinking only of her. For one thing, her charm having acquired a gradual ascendancy over things which, in course of time, were entirely detached from her, but were nevertheless electrified by the same emotion that she used to give me, if something made me think of Incarville or of the Verdurins, or of some new part that Léa was playing, a flood of suffering would overwhelm me. For another thing, what I myself called thinking of Albertine, was thinking of how I might bring her back, of how I might join her, might know what she was doing. With the result that if, during those hours of incessant martyrdom, there had been an illustrator present to represent the images which accompanied my sufferings, you would have seen pictures of the Gare d'Orsay, of the bank notes offered to Mme Bontemps, of Saint-Loup stooping over the sloping desk of a telegraph office at which he was writing out a telegram for myself, never the picture of Albertine. Just as, throughout the whole course of our life, our egoism sees before it all the time the objects that are of interest to ourselves, but never takes in that Ego itself which is incessantly observing them, so the desire which directs our actions descends towards them, but does not reascend to itself, whether because, being unduly utilitarian, it plunges into the action and disdains all knowledge of it, or because we have been looking to the future to compensate for the disappointments of the past, or because the inertia of our mind urges it down the easy slope of imagination, rather than make it reascend the steep slope of introspection. As a matter of fact, in those hours of crisis in which we would stake our whole life, in proportion as the person upon whom it depends reveals more clearly the immensity of the place that she occupies in our life, leaving nothing in the world which is not overthrown by her, so the image of that person diminishes until it is no longer perceptible. In everything we find the effect of her presence in the emotion that we feel; herself, the cause, we do not find anywhere. I was during these days so incapable of forming any picture of Albertine that I could almost have believed that I was not in love with her, just as my mother, in the moments of desperation in which she was incapable of ever forming any picture of my grandmother (save once in the chance encounter of a dream the importance of which she felt so intensely that she employed all the strength that remained to her in her sleep to make it last), might have accused and did in fact accuse herself of not regretting her mother, whose death had been a mortal blow to her but whose features escaped her memory.

Why should I have supposed that Albertine did not care for women? Because she had said, especially of late, that she did not care for them: but did not our life rest upon a perpetual lie? Never once had she said to me: 'Why is it that I cannot go out when and where I choose, why do you always ask other people what I have been doing?' And yet, after all, the conditions of her life were so unusual that she must have asked me this had she not herself guessed the reason. And to my silence as to the causes of her claustration, was it not comprehensible that she should correspond with a similar and constant silence as to her perpetual desires, her innumerable memories and hopes? Françoise looked as though she knew that I was lying when I made an allusion to the imminence of Albertine's return. And her belief seemed to be founded upon something more than that truth which generally guided our old housekeeper, that masters do not like to be humiliated in front of their servants, and allow them to know only so much of the truth as does not depart too far from a flattering fiction, calculated to maintain respect for themselves. This time, Françoise's belief seemed to be founded upon something else, as though she had herself aroused, kept alive the distrust in Albertine's mind, stimulated her anger, driven her in short to the point at which she could predict her departure as inevitable. If this was true, my version of a temporary absence, of which I had known and approved, could be received with nothing but incredulity by Françoise. But the idea that she had formed of Albertine's venal nature, the exasperation with which, in her hatred, she multiplied the 'profit' that Albertine was supposed to be making out of myself, might to some extent give a check to that certainty. And so when in her hearing I made an allusion, as if to something that was altogether natural, to Albertine's immediate return, Françoise would look me in the face, to see whether I was not inventing, in the same way in which, when the butler, to make her angry, read out to her, changing the words, some political news which she hesitated to believe, as for instance the report of the closing of the churches and expulsion of the clergy, even from the other end of the kitchen, and without being able to read it, she would fix her gaze instinctively and greedily upon the paper, as though she had been able to see whether the report was really there.

When Françoise saw that after writing a long letter I put on the envelope the address of Mme Bontemps, this alarm, hitherto quite vague, that Albertine might return, increased in her. It grew to a regular consternation when one morning she had to bring me with the rest of my mail a letter upon the envelope of which she had recognised Albertine's handwriting. She asked herself whether Albertine's departure had not been a mere make-believe, a supposition which distressed her twice over as making definitely certain for the future Albertine's presence in the house, and as bringing upon myself, and thereby, in so far as I was Françoise's master, upon herself, the humiliation of having been tricked by Albertine. However great my impatience to read her letter, I could not refrain from studying for a moment Françoise's eyes from which all hope had fled, inducing from this presage the imminence of Albertine's return, as a lover of winter sports concludes with joy that the cold weather is at hand when he sees the swallows fly south. At length Françoise left me, and when I had made sure that she had shut the door behind her, I opened, noiselessly so as not to appear anxious, the letter which ran as follows:

My dear, thank you for all the nice things that you say to me, I am at your orders to countermand the Rolls, if you think that I can help in any way, as I am sure I can. You have only to let me know the name of your agent. You would let yourself be taken in by these people whose only thought is of selling things, and what would you do with a motor car, you who never stir out of the house? I am deeply touched that you have kept a happy memory of our last drive together. You may be sure that for my part I shall never forget that drive in a twofold twilight (since night was falling and we were about to part) and that it will be effaced from my memory only when the darkness is complete.

I felt that this final phrase was merely a phrase and that Albertine could not possibly retain until her death any such pleasant memory of this drive from which she had certainly derived no pleasure since she had been impatient to leave me. But I was impressed also, when I thought of the bicyclist, the golfer of Balbec, who had read nothing but *Esther* before she made my acquaintance, to find how richly endowed she was and how right I had been in thinking that she had in my house enriched herself with fresh qualities which made her different and more complete. And thus, the words that I had said to her at Balbec: 'I feel that my friendship would be of value to you, that I am just the person who could give you what you lack' – I had written this upon a photograph which I gave her – 'with the certainty that I was being providential' – these words, which I uttered without believing them and simply that she might find some advantage in my society which would outweigh any possible boredom, these words turned out to have been true as well. Similarly, for that matter, when I said to her that I did not wish to see her for fear of falling in love with her, I had said this because on the contrary I knew that in frequent intercourse my love grew cold and that separation kindled it, but in reality our frequent intercourse had given rise to a need of her that was infinitely stronger than my love in the first weeks at Balbec.

Albertine's letter did not help matters in any way. She spoke to me only of writing to my agent. It was necessary to escape from this situation, to cut matters short, and I had the following idea. I sent a letter at once to Andrée in which I told her that Albertine was at her aunt's, that I felt very lonely, that she would be giving me an immense pleasure if she came and stayed with me for a few days and that, as I did not wish to make any mystery, I begged her to inform Albertine of this. And at the same time I wrote to Albertine as though I had not yet received her letter:

My dear, forgive me for doing something which you will understand so well, I have such a hatred of secrecy that I have chosen that you should be informed by her and by myself. I have acquired, from having you staying so charmingly in the house with me, the bad habit of not being able to live alone. Since we have decided that you are not to come back, it has occurred to me that the person who would best fill your place, because she would make least change in my life, would remind me most strongly of yourself, is Andrée, and I have invited her here. So that all this may not appear too sudden, I have spoken to her only of a short visit, but between ourselves I am pretty certain that this time it will be permanent. Don't you agree that I am right? You know that your little group of girls at Balbec has always been the social unit that has exerted the greatest influence upon me, in which I have been most happy to be eventually included. No doubt it is this influence which still makes itself felt. Since the fatal incompatibility of our natures and the mischances of life have decreed that my little Albertine can never be my wife, I believe that I shall nevertheless find a wife – less charming than herself, but one whom greater conformities of nature will enable perhaps to be happier with me – in Andrée.

But after I had sent this letter to the post, the suspicion occurred to me suddenly that, when Albertine wrote to me: 'I should have been only too delighted to come back if you had written to me myself', she had said this only because I had not written to her, and that, had I done so, it would not have made any difference; that she would be glad to know that Andrée was staying with me, to think of her as my wife, provided that she herself remained free, because she could now, as for a week past, stultifying the hourly precautions which I had adopted during more than six months in Paris, abandon herself to her vices and do what, minute by minute, I had prevented her from doing. I told myself that probably she was making an improper use, down there, of her freedom, and no doubt this idea which I formed seemed to me sad but remained general, showing me no special details, and, by the indefinite number of possible mistresses which it allowed me to imagine, prevented me from stopping to consider any one of them, drew my mind on in a sort of perpetual motion not free from pain but tinged with a pain which the absence of any concrete image rendered endurable. It ceased however to be endurable and became atrocious when Saint-Loup arrived. Before I explain why the information that he gave me made me so unhappy, I ought to relate an incident which I place immediately before his visit and the memory of which so distressed me afterwards that it weakened, if not the painful impression that was made on me by my conversation with

Saint-Loup, at any rate the practical effect of this conversation. This incident was as follows. Burning with impatience to see Saint-Loup, I was waiting for him upon the staircase (a thing which I could not have done had my mother been at home, for it was what she most abominated, next to 'talking from the window') when I heard the following speech: 'Do you mean to say you don't know how to get a fellow sacked whom you don't like? It's not difficult. You need only hide the things that he has to take in. Then, when they're in a hurry and ring for him, he can't find anything, he loses his head. My aunt will be furious with him, and will say to you: 'Why, what is the man doing?' When he does show his face, everybody will be raging, and he won't have what is wanted. After this has happened four or five times, you may be sure that they'll sack him, especially if you take care to dirty the things that he has to bring in clean, and all that sort of thing.' I remained speechless with astonishment, for these cruel, Machiavellian words were uttered by the voice of Saint-Loup. Now I had always regarded him as so good, so tender-hearted a person that this speech had the same effect upon me as if he had been acting the part of Satan in a play: it could not be in his own name that he was speaking. 'But after all a man has got to earn his living,' said the other person, of whom I then caught sight and who was one of the Duchesse de Guermantes's footmen. 'What the hell does that matter to you so long as you're all right?' Saint-Loup replied callously. 'It will be all the more fun for you, having a scapegoat. You can easily spill ink over his livery just when he has to go and wait at a big dinner-party, and never leave him in peace for a moment until he's only too glad to give notice. Anyhow, I can put a spoke in his wheel, I shall tell my aunt that I admire your patience in working with a great lout like that, and so dirty too.' I showed myself, Saint-Loup came to greet me, but my confidence in him was shaken since I had heard him speak in a manner so different from anything that I knew. And I asked myself whether a person who was capable of acting so cruelly towards a poor and defenceless man had not played the part of a traitor towards myself, on his mission to Mme Bontemps. This reflection was of most service in helping me not to regard his failure as a proof that I myself might not succeed, after he had left me. But so long as he was with me, it was nevertheless of the Saint-Loup of long ago and especially of the friend who had just come from Mme Bontemps that I thought. He began by saying: 'You feel that I ought to have telephoned to you more often, but I was always told that you were engaged.' But the point at which my pain became unendurable was when he said: 'To begin where my last telegram left you, after passing by a sort of shed, I entered the house and at the end of a long passage was shown into a drawing-room.' At these words, shed, passage, drawing-room, and before he had even finished uttering them, my heart was shattered more swiftly than by an electric current, for the force which girdles the earth many times in a second is not electricity, but pain. How I repeated them to myself, renewing the shock as I chose, these words, shed, passage, drawing-room, after Saint-Loup had left me! In a shed one girl can lie down with another. And in that drawing-room who could tell what Albertine used to do when her aunt was not there? What was this? Had I then imagined the house in which she was living as incapable of possessing either a shed or a drawing-room? No, I had not imagined it at all, except as a vague place. I had suffered originally at the geographical identification of the place in which Albertine was. When I had learned that, instead of being in two or three possible places, she was in Touraine, those words uttered by her porter had marked in my heart as upon a map the place in which I must at length suffer. But once I had grown accustomed to the idea that she was in a house in Touraine, I had not seen the house. Never had there occurred to my imagination this appalling idea of a drawing-room, a shed, a passage, which seemed to be facing me in the retina of Saint-Loup's eyes, who had seen them, these rooms in which Albertine came and went, was living her life, these rooms in particular and not an infinity of possible rooms which had cancelled one another. With the words shed, passage, drawing-room, I became aware of my folly in having left Albertine for a week in this cursed place, the existence (instead of the mere possibility) of which had just been revealed to me. Alas! when Saint-Loup told me also that in this drawing-room he had heard someone singing at the top of her voice in an adjoining room and that it was Albertine who was singing, I realised with despair that, rid of me at last, she was happy! She had regained her freedom. And I who had been thinking that she would come to take the place of Andrée! My grief turned to anger with Saint-Loup. 'That is the one thing in the world that I asked you to avoid, that she should know of your coming.' 'If you imagine it was easy! They had assured me that she was not in the house. Oh, I know very well that you aren't pleased with me, I could tell that from your telegrams. But you are not being fair to me, I did all that I could.' Set free once more, having left the cage from which, here at home, I used to remain for days on end without making her come to my room, Albertine had regained all her value in my eyes, she had become once more the person whom everyone pursued, the marvellous bird of the earliest days. 'However, let us get back to business. As for the question of the money, I don't know what to say to you, I found myself addressing a woman who seemed to me to be so scrupulous that I was afraid of shocking her. However, she didn't say no when I mentioned the money to her. In fact, a little later she told me that she was touched to find that we understood one another so well. And yet everything that she said after that was so delicate, so refined, that it seemed to me impossible that she could have been referring to my offer of money when she said: "We understand one another so well", for after all I was behaving like a cad.' 'But perhaps she did not realise what you meant, she cannot have heard you, you ought to have repeated the offer, for then you would certainly have won the battle.' 'But what do you mean by saying that she cannot have heard me, I spoke to her as I am speaking to you, she is neither deaf nor mad.' 'And she made no comment?' 'None.' 'You ought to have repeated the offer.' 'How do you mean, repeat it? As soon as we met I saw what sort of person she was, I said to myself that you had made a mistake, that you were letting me in for the most awful blunder, and that it would be terribly difficult to offer her the money like that. I did it, however, to oblige you, feeling certain that she would turn me out of the house.' 'But she did not. Therefore, either she had not heard you and you should have started afresh, or you could have developed the topic.' 'You say: "She had not heard", because you were here in Paris, but, I repeat, if you had been present at our conversation, there was not a sound to interrupt us, I said it quite bluntly, it is not possible that she failed to understand.' 'But anyhow is she quite convinced that I have always wished to marry her niece?' 'No, as to that, if you want my opinion, she did not believe that you had any intention of marrying the girl. She told me that you yourself had informed her niece that you wished to leave her. I don't really know whether now she is convinced that you wish to marry.' This reassured me slightly by showing me that I was less humiliated, and therefore more capable of being still loved, more free to take some decisive action. Nevertheless I was in torments. 'I am sorry, because I can see that you are not pleased.' 'Yes, I am touched by your kindness, I am grateful to you, but it seems to me that you might . . . ' 'I did my best. No one else could have done more or even as much. Try sending some one else.' 'No, as a matter of fact, if I had known, I should not have sent you, but the failure of your attempt prevents me from making another.' I heaped reproaches upon him: he had tried to do me a service and had not succeeded. Saint-Loup as he left the house had met some girls coming in. I had already and often supposed that Albertine knew other girls in the country; but this was the first time that I felt the torture of that supposition. We are really led to believe that nature has allowed our mind to secrete a natural antidote which destroys the suppositions that we form, at once without intermission and without danger. But there was nothing to render me immune from these girls whom Saint-Loup had met. All these details, were they not precisely what I had sought to learn from everyone with regard to Albertine, was it not I who, in order to learn them more fully, had begged Saint-Loup, summoned back to Paris by his colonel, to come and see me at all costs, was it not therefore I who had desired them, or rather my famished grief, longing to feed and to wax fat upon them? Finally Saint-Loup told me that he had had the pleasant surprise of meeting, quite near the house, the only familiar face that had reminded him of the past, a former friend of Rachel, a pretty actress who was taking a holiday in the neighbourhood. And the name of this actress was enough to make me say to myself: 'Perhaps it is with her'; was enough to make me behold, in the arms even of a woman whom I did not know, Albertine smiling and flushed with pleasure. And after all why should not this have been true? Had I found fault with myself for thinking of other women since I had known Albertine? On the evening of my first visit to the Princesse de Guermantes, when I returned home, had I not been thinking far less of her than of the girl of whom Saint-Loup had told me who frequented disorderly houses and of Mme Putbus's maid? Was it not in the hope of meeting the latter of these that I had returned to Balbec, and, more recently, had been planning to go to Venice? Why should not Albertine have been planning to go to Touraine? Only, when it came to the point, as I now realised, I would not have left her, I would not have gone to Venice. Even in my own heart of hearts, when I said to myself: 'I shall leave her presently', I knew that I would never leave her, just as I knew that I would never settle down again to work, or make myself live upon hygienic principles, or do any of the things which, day by day, I vowed that I would do upon the morrow. Only, whatever I might feel in my heart, I had thought it more adroit to let her live under the perpetual menace of a separation. And no doubt, thanks to my detestable adroitness, I had convinced her only too well. In any case, now, things could not go on like this. I could not leave her in Touraine with those girls, with that actress, I could not endure the thought of that life which was escaping my control. I would await her reply to my letter: if she was doing wrong, alas! a day more or less made no difference (and perhaps I said this to myself because, being no longer in the habit of taking note of every minute of her life, whereas a single minute in which she was unobserved would formerly have driven me out of my mind, my jealousy no longer observed the same division of time). But as soon as I should have received her answer, if she was not coming back, I would go to fetch her; willy-nilly, I would tear her away from her women friends. Besides, was it not better for me to go down in person, now that I had discovered the duplicity, hitherto unsuspected by me, of Saint-Loup; he might, for all I knew, have organised a plot to separate me from Albertine.

And at the same time, how I should have been lying now had I written to her, as I used to say to her in Paris, that I hoped that no accident might befall her. Ah! if some accident had occurred, my life, instead of being poisoned for ever by this incessant jealousy, would at once regain, if not happiness, at least a state of calm through the suppression of suffering.

The suppression of suffering? Can I really have believed it, have believed that death merely eliminates what exists, and leaves everything else in its place, that it removes the grief from the heart of him for whom the other person's existence has ceased to be anything but a source of grief, that it removes the grief and substitutes nothing in its place. The suppression of grief! As I glanced at the paragraphs in the newspapers, I regretted that I had not had the courage to form the same wish as Swann. If Albertine could have been the victim of an accident, were she alive I should have had a pretext for hastening to her bedside, were she dead I should have recovered, as Swann said, my freedom to live as I chose. Did I believe this? He had believed it, that subtlest of men who thought that he knew himself well. How little do we know what we have in our heart. How clearly, a little later, had he been still alive, I could have proved to him that his wish was not only criminal but absurd, that the death of her whom he loved would have set him free from nothing.

I forsook all pride with regard to Albertine, I sent her a despairing telegram begging her to return upon any conditions, telling her that she might do anything she liked, that I asked only to be allowed to take her in my arms for a minute three times a week, before she went to bed. And had she confined me to once a week, I would have accepted the restriction. She did not, ever, return. My telegram had just gone to her when I myself received one. It was from Mme Bontemps. The world is not created once and for all time for each of us individually. There are added to it in the course of our life things of which we have never had any suspicion. Alas! it was not a suppression of suffering that was wrought in me by the first two lines of the telegram: 'My poor friend, our little Albertine is no more; forgive me for breaking this terrible news to you who were so fond of her. She was thrown by her horse against a tree while she was out riding. All our efforts to restore her to life were unavailing. If only I were dead in her place!' No, not the suppression of suffering, but a suffering until then unimagined, that of learning that she would not come back. And yet, had I not told myself, many times, that, quite possibly, she would not come back? I had indeed told myself so, but now I saw that never for a moment had I believed it. As I needed her presence, her kisses, to enable me to endure the pain that my suspicions wrought in me, I had formed, since our Balbec days, the habit of being always with her. Even when she had gone out, when I was left alone, I was kissing her still. I had continued to do so since her departure for Touraine. I had less need of her fidelity than of her return. And if my reason might with impunity cast a doubt upon her now and again, my imagination never ceased for an instant to bring her before me. Instinctively I passed my hand over my throat, over my lips which felt themselves kissed by her lips still after she had gone away, and would never be kissed by them again; I passed my hands over them, as Mamma had caressed me at the time of grandmother's death, when she said: 'My poor boy, your grandmother, who was so fond of you, will never kiss you again.' All my life to come seemed to have been wrenched from my heart. My life to come? I had not then thought at times of living it without Albertine? Why, no! All this time had I, then, been vowing to her service every minute of my life until my death? Why, of course! This future indissolubly blended with hers I had never had the vision to perceive, but now that it had just been shattered, I could feel the place that it occupied in my gaping heart. Françoise, who still knew nothing, came into my room; in a sudden fury I shouted at her: 'What do you want?' Then (there are sometimes words which set a different reality in the same place as that which confronts us; they stun us as does a sudden fit of giddiness) she said to me: 'Monsieur has no need to look cross. I've got something here that will make him very happy. Here are two letters from Mademoiselle Albertine.' I felt, afterwards, that I must have stared at her with the eyes of a man whose mind has become unbalanced. I was not even glad, nor was I incredulous. I was like a person who sees the same place in his room occupied by a sofa and by a grotto: nothing seeming to him more real, he collapses on the floor. Albertine's two letters must have been written at an interval of a few hours, possibly at the same moment, and, anyhow, only a short while before the fatal ride. The first said: 'My dear, I must thank you for the proof of your confidence which you give me when you tell me of your plan to get Andrée to stay with you. I am sure that she will be delighted to accept, and I think that it will be a very good thing for her. With her talents, she will know how to make the most of the companionship of a man like yourself, and of the admirable influence which you manage to secure over other people. I feel that you have had an idea from which as much good may spring for her as for yourself. And so, if she should make the least shadow of difficulty (which I don't suppose), telegraph to me, I undertake to bring pressure to bear upon her.' The second was dated on the following day. (As a matter of fact, she must have written her two letters at an interval of a few minutes, possibly without any interval, and must have antedated the first. For, all the time, I had been forming an absurd idea of her intentions, which had been only this: to return to me, and which anyone with no direct interest in the matter, a man lacking in imagination, the plenipotentiary in a peace treaty, the merchant who has to examine a deal, would have judged more accurately than myself.) It contained only these words: 'Is it too late for me to return to you? If you have not yet written to Andrée, would you be prepared to take me back? I shall abide by your decision, but I beg you not to be long in letting me know it, you can imagine how impatiently I shall be waiting. If it is telling me to return, I shall take the train at once. With my whole heart, yours, Albertine.'

For the death of Albertine to be able to suppress my suffering, the shock of the fall would have had to kill her not only in Touraine but in myself. There, never had she been more alive. In order to enter into us, another person must first have assumed the form, have entered into the surroundings of the moment; appearing to us only in a succession of momentary flashes, he has never been able to furnish us with more than one aspect of himself at a time, to present us with more than a single photograph of himself. A great weakness, no doubt, for a person to consist merely in a collection of moments; a great strength also: it is dependent upon memory, and our memory of a moment is not informed of everything that has happened since; this moment which it has registered endures still, lives still, and with it the person whose form is outlined in it. And moreover, this disintegration does not only make the dead man live, it multiplies him. To find consolation, it was not one, it was innumerable Albertines that I must first forget. When I had reached the stage of enduring the grief of losing this Albertine, I must begin afresh with another, with a hundred others.

So, then, my life was entirely altered. What had made it – and not owing to Albertine, concurrently with her, when I was alone – attractive, was precisely the perpetual resurgence, at the bidding of identical moments, of moments from the past. From the sound of the rain I recaptured the scent of the lilacs at Combray, from the shifting of the sun's rays on the balcony the pigeons in the Champs-Elysées, from the muffling of all noise in the heat of the morning hours, the cool taste of cherries, the longing for Brittany or Venice from the sound of the wind and the return of Easter. Summer was at hand, the days were long, the weather warm. It was the season when, early in the morning, pupils and teachers resort to the public gardens to prepare for the final examinations under the trees, seeking to extract the sole drop of coolness that is let fall by a sky less ardent than in the midday heat but already as sterilely pure. From my darkened room, with a power of evocation equal to that of former days but capable now of evoking only pain, I felt that outside, in the heaviness of the atmosphere, the setting sun was plastering the vertical fronts of houses and churches with a tawny distemper. And if Françoise, when she came in, parted, by accident, the inner curtains, I stifled a cry of pain at the gash that was cut in my heart by that ray of long-ago sunlight which had made beautiful in my eyes the modern front of Marcouville l'Orgueilleuse, when Albertine said to me: 'It is restored.' Not knowing how to account to Françoise for my groan, I said to her: 'Oh, I am so thirsty.' She left the room, returned, but I turned sharply away, smarting under the painful discharge of one of the thousand invisible memories which at every moment burst into view in the surrounding darkness: I had noticed that she had brought in a jug of cider and a dish of cherries, things which a farm-lad had brought out to us in the carriage, at Balbec, 'kinds' in which I should have made the most perfect communion, in those days, with the prismatic gleam in shuttered dining-rooms on days of scorching heat. Then I thought for the first time of the farm called Les Ecorres, and said to myself that on certain days when Albertine had told me, at Balbec, that she would not be free, that she was obliged to go somewhere with her aunt, she had perhaps been with one or another of her girl friends at some farm to which she knew that I was not in the habit of going, and, while I waited desperately for her at Marie-Antoinette, where they told me: 'No, we have not seen her today,' had been using, to her friend, the same words that she used to say to myself when we went out together: 'He will never think of looking for us here, so that there's no fear of our being disturbed.' I told Françoise to draw the curtains together, so that I should not see that ray of sunlight. But it continued to filter through, just as corrosive, into my memory. 'It doesn't appeal to me, it has been restored, but we shall go tomorrow to Saint-Mars le Vêtu, and the day after to . . . ' Tomorrow, the day after, it was a prospect of life shared in common, perhaps for all time, that was opening; my heart leaped towards it, but it was no longer there, Albertine was dead.

I asked Françoise the time. Six o'clock. At last, thank God, that oppressive heat would be lifted of which in the past I used to complain to Albertine, and which we so enjoyed. The day was drawing to its close. But what did that profit me? The cool evening air came in; it was the sun setting in my memory, at the end of a road which we had taken, she and I, on our way home, that I saw now, more remote than the farthest village, like some distant town not to be reached that evening, which we would spend at Balbec, still together. Together then; now I must stop short on the brink of that same abyss; she was dead. It was not enough now to draw the curtains, I tried to stop the eyes and ears of my memory so as not to see that band of orange in the western sky, so as not to hear those invisible birds responding from one tree to the next on either side of me who was then so tenderly embraced by her that now was dead. I tried to avoid those sensations that are given us by the dampness of leaves in the evening air, the steep rise and fall of mule-tracks. But already those sensations had gripped me afresh, carried far enough back from the present moment so that it should have gathered all the recoil, all the resilience necessary to strike me afresh, this idea that Albertine was dead. Ah! never again would I enter a forest, I would stroll no more beneath the spreading trees. But would the broad plains be less cruel to me? How many times had I crossed, going in search of Albertine, how many times had I entered, on my return with her, the great plain of Cricqueville, now in foggy weather when the flooding mist gave us the illusion of being surrounded by a vast lake, now on limpid evenings when the moonlight, dematerialising the earth, making it appear, a yard away, celestial, as it is, in the daytime, on far horizons only, enshrined the fields, the woods, with the firmament to which it had assimilated them, in the moss-agate of a universal blue.

Françoise was bound to rejoice at Albertine's death, and it should, in justice to her, be said that by a sort of tactful convention she made no pretence of sorrow. But the unwritten laws of her immemorial code and the tradition of the mediaeval peasant woman who weeps as in the romances of chivalry were older than her hatred of Albertine and even of Eulalie. And so, on one of these late afternoons, as I was not quick enough in concealing my distress, she caught sight of my tears, served by the instinct of a little old peasant woman which at one time had led her to catch and torture animals, to feel only amusement in wringing the necks of chickens and in boiling lobsters alive, and, when I was ill, in observing, as it might be the wounds that she had inflicted upon an owl, my suffering expression which she afterwards proclaimed in a sepulchral tone and as a presage of coming disaster. But her Combray 'Customary' did not permit her to treat lightly tears, grief, things which in her judgment were as fatal as shedding one's flannels in spring or eating when one had no 'stomach'. 'Oh, no, Monsieur, it doesn't do to cry like that, it isn't good for you.' And in her attempt to stem my tears she showed as much uneasiness as though they had been torrents of blood. Unfortunately I adopted a chilly air that cut short the effusions in which she was hoping to indulge and which might quite well, for that matter, have been sincere. Her attitude towards Albertine had been, perhaps, akin to her attitude towards Eulalie, and, now that my mistress could no longer derive any profit from me, Françoise had ceased to hate her. She felt bound, however, to let me see that she was perfectly well aware that I was crying, and that, following the deplorable example set by my family, I did not wish to 'let it be seen'. 'You mustn't cry, Monsieur,' she adjured me, in a calmer tone, this time, and intending to prove her own perspicacity rather than to show me any compassion. And she went on: 'It was bound to happen; she was too happy, poor creature, she never knew how happy she was.'

How slow the day is in dying on these interminable summer evenings. A pallid ghost of the house opposite continued indefinitely to sketch upon the sky its persistent whiteness. At last it was dark indoors; I stumbled against the furniture in the hall, but in the door that opened upon the staircase, in the midst of the darkness which I had supposed to be complete, the glazed panel was translucent and blue, with the blue of a flower, the blue of an insect's wing, a blue that would have seemed to me beautiful if I had not felt it to be a last reflection, trenchant as a blade of steel, a supreme blow which in its indefatigable cruelty the day was still dealing me. In the end, however, the darkness became complete, but then a glimpse of a star behind one of the trees in the courtyard was enough to remind me of how we used to set out in a carriage, after dinner, for the woods of Chantepie, carpeted with moonlight. And even in the streets it would so happen that I could isolate upon the back of a seat, could gather there the natural purity of a moonbeam in the midst of the artificial lights of Paris, of that Paris over which it enthroned, by making the town return for a moment, in my imagination, to a state of nature, with the infinite silence of the suggested fields, the heart-rending memory of the walks that I had taken in them with Albertine. Ah! when would the night end? But at the first cool breath of dawn I shuddered, for it had revived in me the delight of that summer when, from Balbec to Incarville, from Incarville to Balbec, we had so many times escorted each other home until the break of day. I had now only one hope left for the future – a hope far more heartrending than any dread – which was that I might forget Albertine. I knew that I should one day forget her; I had quite forgotten Gilberte, Mme de Guermantes; I had quite forgotten my grand-mother. And it is our most fitting and most cruel punishment, for that so complete oblivion, as tranquil as the oblivion of the graveyard, by which we have detached ourself from those whom we no longer love, that we can see this same oblivion to be inevitable in the case of those whom we love still. To tell the truth, we know it to be a state not painful, a state of indifference. But not being able to think at the same time of what I was and of what I should one day be, I thought with despair of all that covering mantle of caresses, of kisses, of friendly slumber, of which I must presently let myself be divested for all time. The rush of these tender memories sweeping on to break against the knowledge that Albertine was dead oppressed me by the incessant conflict of their baffled waves so that I could not keep still; I rose, but all of a sudden I stopped in consternation; the same faint daybreak that I used to see at the moment when I had just left Albertine, still radiant and warm with her kisses, had come into the room and bared, above the curtains, its blade now a sinister portent, whose whiteness, cold, implacable and compact, entered the room like a dagger thrust into my heart.

Presently the sounds from the streets would begin, enabling me to tell from the qualitative scale of their resonance the degree of the steadily increasing heat in which they were sounding. But in this heat which, a few hours later, would have saturated itself in the fragrance of cherries, what I found (as in a medicine which the substitution of one ingredient for another is sufficient to transform from the stimulant and tonic that it was into a debilitating drug) was no longer the desire for women but the anguish of Albertine's departure. Besides, the memory of all my desires was as much impregnated with her, and with suffering, as the memory of my pleasures. That Venice where I had thought that her company would be a nuisance (doubtless because I had felt in a confused way that it would be necessary to me), now that Albertine was no more, I preferred not to go there. Albertine had seemed to me to be an obstacle interposed between me and everything else, because she was for me what contained everything, and it was from her as from an urn that I might receive things. Now that this urn was shattered, I no longer felt that I had the courage to grasp things; there was nothing now from which I did not turn away, spiritless, preferring not to taste it. So that my separation from her did not in the least throw open to me the field of possible pleasures which I had imagined to be closed to me by her presence. Besides, the obstacle which her presence had perhaps indeed been in the way of my travelling, of my enjoying life, had only (as always happens) been a mask for other obstacles which reappeared intact now that this first obstacle had been removed. It had been in the same way that, in the past, when some friend had called to see me and had prevented me from working, if on the following day I was left undisturbed, I did not work any better. Let an illness, a duel, a runaway horse make us see death face to face, how richly we should have enjoyed the life of pleasure, the travels in unknown lands which are about to be snatched from us. And no sooner is the danger past than what we find once again before us is the same dull life in which none of those delights had any existence for us.

No doubt these nights that are so short continue for but a brief season. Winter would at length return, when I should no longer have to dread the memory of drives with her, protracted until the too early dawn. But would not the first frosts bring back to me, preserved in their cold storage, the germ of my first desires, when at midnight I used to send for her, when the time seemed so long until I heard her ring the bell: a sound for which I might now wait everlastingly in vain? Would they not bring back to me the germ of my first uneasiness, when, upon two occasions, I thought that she was not coming? At that time I saw her but rarely, but even those intervals that there were between her visits which made her emerge, after many weeks, from the heart of an unknown life which I made no effort to possess, ensured my peace of mind by preventing the first inklings, constantly interrupted, of my jealousy from coagulating, from forming a solid mass in my heart. So far as they had contrived to be soothing, at that earlier time, so far, in retrospect, were they stamped with the mark of suffering, since all the unaccountable things that she might, while those intervals lasted, have been doing had ceased to be immaterial to me, and especially now that no visit from her would ever fall to my lot again; so that those January evenings on which she used to come, and which, for that reason, had been so dear to me, would blow into me now with their biting winds an uneasiness which then I did not know, and would bring back to me (but now grown pernicious) the first germ of my love. And when I considered that I would see again presently that cold season, which since the time of Gilberte and my play-hours in the Champs-Elysées, had always seemed to me so depressing; when I thought that there would be returning again evenings like that evening of snow when I had vainly, far into the night, waited for Albertine to come; then as a consumptive chooses the best place, from the physical point of view, for his lungs, but in my case making a moral choice, what at such moments I still dreaded most for my grief, for my heart, was the return of the intense cold, and I said to myself that what it would be hardest to live through was perhaps the winter. Bound up as it was with each of the seasons, in order for me to discard the memory of Albertine I should have had first to forget them all, prepared to begin again to learn to know them, as an old man after a stroke of paralysis learns again to read; I should have had first to forego the entire universe. Nothing, I told myself, but an actual extinction of myself would be capable (but that was impossible) of consoling me for hers. I did not realise that the death of oneself is neither impossible nor extraordinary; it is effected without our knowledge, it may be against our will, every day of our life, and I should have to suffer from the recurrence of all sorts of days which not only nature but adventitious circumstances, a purely conventional order introduce into a season. Presently would return the day on which I had gone to Balbec in that earlier summer when my love, which was not yet inseparable from jealousy and did not perplex itself with the problem of what Albertine would be doing all day, had still to pass through so many evolutions before becoming that so specialised love of the latest period, that this final year, in which Albertine's destiny had begun to change and had received its quietus, appeared to me full, multiform, vast, like a whole century. Then it would be the memory of days more slow in reviving but dating from still earlier years; on the rainy Sundays on which nevertheless everyone else had gone out, in the void of the afternoon, when the sound of wind and rain would in the past have bidden me stay at home, to 'philosophise in my garret', with what anxiety would I see the hour approach at which Albertine, so little expected, had come to visit me, had fondled me for the first time, breaking off because Françoise had brought in the lamp, in that time now doubly dead when it had been Albertine who was interested in me, when my affection for her might legitimately nourish so strong a hope. Even later in the season, those glorious evenings when the windows of kitchens, of girls' schools, standing open to the view like wayside shrines, allow the street to crown itself with a diadem of those demi-goddesses who, conversing, ever so close to us, with their peers, fill us with a feverish longing to penetrate into their mythological existence, recalled to me nothing now but the affection of Albertine whose company was an obstacle in the way of my approaching them.

Moreover, to the memory even of hours that were purely natural would inevitably be added the moral background that makes each of them a thing apart. When, later on, I should hear the goatherd's horn, on a first fine, almost Italian morning, the day that followed would blend successively with its sunshine the anxiety of knowing that Albertine was at the Trocadéro, possibly with Léa and the two girls, then her kindly, domestic gentleness, almost that of a wife who seemed to me then an embarrassment and whom Françoise was bringing home to me. That telephone message from Françoise which had conveyed to me the dutiful homage of an Albertine who was returning with her, I had thought at the time that it made me swell with pride. I was mistaken. If it had exhilarated me, that was because it had made me feel that she whom I loved was really mine, lived only for me, and even at a distance, without my needing to occupy my mind with her, regarded me as her lord and master, returning home upon a sign from myself. And so that telephone message had been a particle of sweetness, coming to me from afar, sent out from that region of the Trocadéro where there were proved to be for me sources of happiness directing towards me molecules of comfort, healing balms, restoring to me at length so precious a liberty of spirit that I need do no more, surrendering myself without the restriction of a single care to Wagner's music, than await the certain arrival of Albertine, without fever, with an entire absence of impatience in which I had not had the perspicacity to recognise true happiness. And this happiness that she should return, that she should obey me and be mine, the cause of it lay in love and not in pride. It would have been quite immaterial to me now to have at my behest fifty women returning, at a sign from myself, not from the Trocadéro but from the Indies. But that day, conscious of Albertine who, while I sat alone in my room playing music, was coming dutifully to join me, I had breathed in, where it lay scattered like motes in a sunbeam, one of those substances which, just as others are salutary to the body, do good to the soul. Then there had been, half an hour later, Albertine's return, then the drive with Albertine returned, a drive which I had thought tedious because it was accompanied for me by certainty, but which, on account of that very certainty, had, from the moment of Françoise's telephoning to me that she was bringing Albertine home, let flow a golden calm over the hours that followed, had made of them as it were a second day, wholly unlike the first, because it had a completely different moral basis, a moral basis which made it an original day, which came and added itself to the variety of the days that I had previously known, a day which I should never have been able to imagine – any more than we could imagine the delicious idleness of a day in summer if such days did not exist in the calendar of those through which we had lived – a day of which I could not say absolutely that I recalled it, for to this calm I added now an anguish which I had not felt at the time. But at a much later date, when I went over gradually, in a reversed order, the times through which I had passed before I was so much in love with Albertine, when my scarred heart could detach itself without suffering from Albertine dead, then I was able to recall at length without suffering that day on which Albertine had gone shopping with Françoise instead of remaining at the Trocadéro; I recalled it with pleasure, as belonging to a moral season which I had not known until then; I recalled it at length exactly, without adding to it now any suffering, rather, on the contrary, as we recall certain days in summer which we found too hot while they lasted, and from which only after they have passed do we extract their unalloyed standard of fine gold and imperishable azure.

With the result that these several years imposed upon my memory of Albertine, which made them so painful, the successive colouring, the different modulations not only of their seasons or of their hours, from late afternoons in June to winter evenings, from seas by moonlight to dawn that broke as I was on my way home, from snow in Paris to fallen leaves at Saint-Cloud, but also of each of the particular ideas of Albertine that I successively formed, of the physical aspect in which I pictured her at each of those moments, the degree of frequency with which I had seen her during that season, which itself appeared consequently more or less dispersed or compact, the anxieties which she might have caused me by keeping me waiting, the desire which I had felt at a given moment for her, the hopes formed and then blasted; all of these modified the character of my retrospective sorrow fully as much as the impressions of light or of scents which were associated with it, and completed each of the solar years through which I had lived – years which, simply with their springs, their trees, their breezes, were already so sad because of the indissociable memory of her – complementing each of them with a sort of sentimental year in which the hours were defined not by the sun's position, but by the strain of waiting for a tryst, in which the length of the days, in which the changes of temperature were determined not by the seasons but by the soaring flight of my hopes, the progress of our intimacy, the gradual transformation of her face, the expeditions on which she had gone, the frequency and style of the letters that she had written me during her absence, her more or less eager anxiety to see me on her return. And lastly if these changes of season, if these different days furnished me each with a fresh Albertine, it was not only by recalling to me similar moments. The reader will remember that always, even before I began to be in love, each day had made me a different person, swayed by other desires because he had other perceptions, a person who, whereas he had dreamed only of cliffs and tempests overnight, if the indiscreet spring dawn had distilled a scent of roses through the gaping portals of his house of sleep, would awake alert to set off for Italy. Even in my love, had not the changing state of my moral atmosphere, the varying pressure of my beliefs, had they not one day diminished the visibility of the love that I was feeling, had they not another day extended it beyond all bounds, one day softened it to a smile, another day condensed it to a storm? We exist only by virtue of what we possess, we possess only what is really present to us, and so many of our memories, our humours, our ideas set out to voyage far away from us, until they are lost to sight! Then we can no longer make them enter into our reckoning of the total which is our personality. But they know of secret paths by which to return to us. And on certain nights, having gone to sleep almost without regretting Albertine any more – we can regret only what we remember – on awakening I found a whole fleet of memories which had come to cruise upon the surface of my clearest consciousness, and seemed marvellously distinct. Then I wept over what I could see so plainly, what overnight had been to me non-existent. In an instant, Albertine's name, her death, had changed their meaning; her betrayals had suddenly resumed their old importance.

How could she have seemed dead to me when now, in order to think of her, I had at my disposal only those same images one or other of which I used to recall when she was alive, each one being associated with a particular moment? Rapid and bowed above the mystic wheel of her bicycle, tightly strapped upon rainy days in the amazonian corslet of her waterproof which made her breasts protrude, while serpents writhed in her turbaned hair, she scattered terror in the streets of Balbec; on the evenings on which we had taken champagne with us to the woods of Chantepie, her voice provoking, altered, she showed on her face that pallid warmth colouring only over her cheekbones so that, barely able to make her out in the darkness of the carriage, I drew her face into the moonlight in order to see her better, and which I tried now in vain to recapture, to see again in a darkness that would never end. A little statuette as we drove to the island, a large, calm, coarsely grained face above the pianola, she was thus by turns rain-soaked and swift, provoking and diaphanous, motionless and smiling, an angel of music. So that what would have to be obliterated in me was not one only, but countless Albertines. Each of these was thus attached to a moment, to the date of which I found myself carried back when I saw again that particular Albertine. And the moments of the past do not remain still; they retain in our memory the motion which drew them towards the future, towards a future which has itself become the past, and draw us on in their train. Never had I caressed the waterproofed Albertine of the rainy days, I wanted to ask her to divest herself of that armour, that would be to know with her the love of the tented field, the brotherhood of travel. But this was no longer possible, she was dead. Never either, for fear of corrupting her, had I shown any sign of comprehension on the evenings when she seemed to be offering me pleasures which, but for my self-restraint, she would not perhaps have sought from others, and which aroused in me now a frantic desire. I should not have found them the same in any other woman, but she who would fain have offered me them I might scour the whole world now without encountering, for Albertine was dead. It seemed that I had to choose between two sets of facts, to decide which was the truth, so far was the fact of Albertine's death – arising for me from a reality which I had not known, her life in Touraine – a contradiction of all my thoughts of her, my desires, my regrets, my tenderness, my rage, my jealousy. So great a wealth of memories, borrowed from the treasury of her life, such a profusion of sentiments evoking, implicating her life, seemed to make it incredible that Albertine should be dead. Such a profusion of sentiments, for my memory, while preserving my affection, left to it all its variety. It was not Albertine alone that was simply a series of moments, it was also myself. My love for her had not been simple: to a curious interest in the unknown had been added a sensual desire and to a sentiment of an almost conjugal mildness, at one moment indifference, at another a jealous fury. I was not one man only, but the steady advance hour after hour of an army in close formation, in which there appeared, according to the moment, impassioned men, indifferent men, jealous men – jealous men no two of whom were jealous of the same woman. And no doubt it would be from this that one day would come the healing which I should not expect. In a composite mass, these elements may, one by one, without our noticing it, be replaced by others, which others again eliminate or reinforce, until in the end a change has been brought about which it would be impossible to conceive if we were a single person. The complexity of my love, of my person, multiplied, diversified my sufferings. And yet they could always be ranged in the two categories, the option between which had made up the whole life of my love for Albertine, swayed alternately by trust and by a jealous suspicion.

If I had found it difficult to imagine that Albertine, so vitally alive in me (wearing as I did the double harness of the present and the past), was dead, perhaps it was equally paradoxical in me that Albertine, whom I knew to be dead, could still excite my jealousy, and that this suspicion of the misdeeds of which Albertine, stripped now of the flesh that had rejoiced in them, of the heart that had been able to desire them, was no longer capable, nor responsible for them, should excite in me so keen a suffering that I should only have blessed them could I have seen in those misdeeds the pledge of the moral reality of a person materially non-existent, in place of the reflection, destined itself too to fade, of impressions that she had made on me in the past. A woman who could no longer taste any pleasure with other people ought not any longer to have excited my jealousy, if only my affection had been able to come to the surface. But this was just what was impossible, since it could not find its object, Albertine, save among memories in which she was still alive. Since, merely by thinking of her, I brought her back to life, her infidelities could never be those of a dead woman; the moments at which she had been guilty of them became the present moment, not only for Albertine, but for that one of my various selves who was thinking of her. So that no anachronism could ever separate the indissoluble couple, in which, to each fresh culprit, was immediately mated a jealous lover, pitiable and always contemporaneous. I had, during the last months, kept her shut up in my own house. But in my imagination now, Albertine was free, she was abusing her freedom, was prostituting herself to this friend or to that. Formerly, I used constantly to dream of the uncertain future that was unfolding itself before us, I endeavoured to read its message. And now, what lay before me, like a counterpart of the future – as absorbing as the future because it was equally uncertain, as difficult to decipher, as mysterious, more cruel still because I had not, as with the future, the possibility or the illusion of influencing it, and also because it unrolled itself to the full extent of my own life without my companion's being present to soothe the anguish that it caused me – was no longer Albertine's Future, it was her Past. Her Past? That is the wrong word, since for jealousy there can be neither past nor future, and what it imagines is invariably the present.

Atmospheric changes, provoking other changes in the inner man, awaken forgotten variants of himself, upset the somnolent course of habit, restore their old force to certain memories, to certain sufferings. How much the more so with me if this change of weather recalled to me the weather in which Albertine, at Balbec, under the threat of rain, it might be, used to set out, heaven knows why, upon long rides, in the clinging mail-armour of her waterproof. If she had lived, no doubt today, in this so similar weather, she would be setting out, in Touraine, upon a corresponding expedition. Since she could do so no longer, I ought not to have been pained by the thought; but, as with amputated cripples, the slightest change in the weather revived my pains in the member that had ceased, now, to belong to me.

All of a sudden it was an impression which I had not felt for a long time – for it had remained dissolved in the fluid and invisible expanse of my memory – that became crystallised. Many years ago, when somebody mentioned her bath-wrap, Albertine had blushed. At that time I was not jealous of her. But since then I had intended to ask her if she could remember that conversation, and why she had blushed. This had worried me all the more because I had been told that the two girls, Léa's friends, frequented the bathing establishment of the hotel, and, it was said, not merely for the purpose of taking baths. But, for fear of annoying Albertine, or else deciding to await some more opportune moment, I had always refrained from mentioning it to her and in time had ceased to think about it. And all of a sudden, some time after Albertine's death, I recalled this memory, stamped with the mark, at once irritating and solemn, of riddles left for ever insoluble by the death of the one person who could have interpreted them. Might I not at least try to make certain that Albertine had never done anything wrong in that bathing establishment? By sending someone to Balbec I might perhaps succeed. While she was alive, I should doubtless have been unable to learn anything. But people's tongues become strangely loosened and they are ready to report a misdeed when they need no longer fear the culprit's resentment. As the constitution of our imagination, which has remained rudimentary, simplified (not having passed through the countless transformations which improve upon the primitive

models of human inventions, barely recognisable, whether it be the barometer, the balloon, the telephone, or anything else, in their ultimate
perfection), allows us to see only a very few things at one time, the memory
of the bathing establishment occupied the whole field of my inward vision.

Sometimes I came in collision in the dark lanes of sleep with one of those
bad dreams, which are not very serious for several reasons, one of these
being that the sadness which they engender lasts for barely an hour after we
awake, like the weakness that is caused by an artificial soporific. For another
reason also, namely that we encounter them but very rarely, no more than
once in two or three years. And moreover it remains uncertain whether we
have encountered them before, whether they have not rather that aspect of
not being seen for the first time which is projected over them by an illusion,
a subdivision (for duplication would not be a strong enough term).

Of course, since I entertained doubts as to the life, the death of Albertine,
I ought long since to have begun to make enquiries, but the same weariness,
the same cowardice which had made me give way to Albertine when she was
with me prevented me from undertaking anything since I had ceased to see
her. And yet from a weakness that had dragged on for years on end, a flash of
energy sometimes emerged. I decided to make this investigation which,
after all, was perfectly natural. One would have said that nothing else had
occurred in Albertine's whole life. I asked myself whom I could best send
down to make enquiries on the spot, at Balbec. Aimé seemed to me to be
a suitable person. Apart from his thorough knowledge of the place, he
belonged to that category of plebeian folk who have a keen eye to their own
advantage, are loyal to those whom they serve, indifferent to any thought of
morality, and of whom – because, if we pay them well, in their obedience to
our will, they suppress everything that might in one way or another go
against it, showing themselves as incapable of indiscretion, weakness or
dishonesty as they are devoid of scruples – we say: 'They are good fellows.'
In such we can repose an absolute confidence. When Aimé had gone, I
thought how much more to the point it would have been if, instead of
sending him down to try to discover something there, I had now been able
to question Albertine herself. And at once the thought of this question
which I would have liked, which it seemed to me that I was about to put to
her, having brought Albertine into my presence – not thanks to an effort of
resurrection but as though by one of those chance encounters which, as is
the case with photographs that are not posed, with snapshots, always make
the person appear more alive – at the same time in which I imagined our
conversation, I felt how impossible it was; I had just approached a fresh
aspect of the idea that Albertine was dead, Albertine who inspired in me that

affection which we have for the absent the sight of whom does not come to correct the embellished image, inspiring also sorrow that this absence must be eternal and that the poor child should be deprived for ever of the joys of life. And immediately, by an abrupt change of mood, from the torments of jealousy I passed to the despair of separation.

What filled my heart now was, in the place of odious suspicions, the affectionate memory of hours of confiding tenderness spent with the sister whom death had really made me lose, since my grief was related not to what Albertine had been to me, but to what my heart, anxious to participate in the most general emotions of love, had gradually persuaded me that she was; then I became aware that the life which had bored me so – so, at least, I thought – had been on the contrary delicious, to the briefest moments spent in talking to her of things that were quite insignificant, I felt now that there was added, amalgamated a pleasure which at the time had not – it is true – been perceived by me, but which was already responsible for making me turn so perseveringly to those moments to the exclusion of any others; the most trivial incidents which I recalled, a movement that she had made in the carriage by my side, or to sit down facing me in my room, dispersed through my spirit an eddy of sweetness and sorrow which little by little overwhelmed it altogether.

This room in which we used to dine had never seemed to me attractive, I had told Albertine that it was attractive merely in order that my mistress might be content to live in it. Now the curtains, the chairs, the books, had ceased to be unimportant. Art is not alone in imparting charm and mystery to the most insignificant things; the same power of bringing them into intimate relation with ourselves is committed also to grief. At the moment I had paid no attention to the dinner which we had eaten together after our return from the Bois, before I went to the Verdurins', and towards the beauty, the solemn sweetness of which I now turned, my eyes filled with tears. An impression of love is out of proportion to the other impressions of life, but it is not when it is lost in their midst that we can take account of it. It is not from its foot, in the tumult of the street and amid the thronging houses, it is when we are far away, that from the slope of a neighbouring hill, at a distance from which the whole town has disappeared, or appears only as a confused mass upon the ground, we can, in the calm detachment of solitude and dusk, appreciate, unique, persistent and pure, the height of a cathedral. I tried to embrace the image of Albertine through my tears as I thought of all the serious and sensible things that she had said that evening.

One morning I thought that I could see the oblong shape of a hill swathed in mist, that I could taste the warmth of a cup of chocolate, while my heart

was horribly wrung by the memory of that afternoon on which Albertine
had come to see me and I had kissed her for the first time: the fact was that
I had just heard the hiccough of the hot-water pipes, the furnace having just
been started. And I flung angrily away an invitation which Françoise brought
me from Mme Verdurin; how the impression that I had felt when I went to
dine for the first time at la Raspelière, that death does not strike us all at the
same age, overcame me with increased force now that Albertine was dead,
so young, while Brichot continued to dine with Mme Verdurin who was still
entertaining and would perhaps continue to entertain for many years to
come. At once the name of Brichot recalled to me the end of that evening
party when he had accompanied me home, when I had seen from the street
the light of Albertine's lamp. I had already thought of it upon many
occasions, but I had not approached this memory from the same angle.
Then when I thought of the void which I should now find upon returning
home, that I should never again see from the street Albertine's room, the
light in which was extinguished for ever, I realised how, that evening, in
parting from Brichot, I had thought that I was bored, that I regretted my
inability to stroll about the streets and make love elsewhere, I realised how
greatly I had been mistaken, that it was only because the treasure whose
reflections came down to me in the street had seemed to be entirely in my
possession that I had failed to calculate its value, which meant that it seemed
to me of necessity inferior to pleasures, however slight, of which however, in
seeking to imagine them, I enhanced the value. I realised how much that
light which had seemed to me to issue from a prison contained for me of
fullness, of life and sweetness, all of which was but the realisation of what
had for a moment intoxicated me and had then seemed for ever impossible:
I began to understand that this life which I had led in Paris in a home which
was also her home, was precisely the realisation of that profound peace of
which I had dreamed on the night when Albertine had slept under the same
roof as myself, at Balbec. The conversation which I had had with Albertine
after our return from the Bois before that party at the Verdurins', I should
not have been consoled had it never occurred, that conversation which had
to some extent introduced Albertine into my intellectual life and in certain
respects had made us one. For no doubt if I returned with melting affection
to her intelligence, to her kindness to myself, it was not because they were
any greater than those of other persons whom I had known. Had not Mme
de Cambremer said to me at Balbec: 'What! You might be spending your
days with Elstir, who is a genius, and you spend them with your cousin!'
Albertine's intelligence pleased me because, by association, it revived in me
what I called its sweetness as we call the sweetness of a fruit a certain

sensation which exists only in our palate. And in fact, when I thought of
Albertine's intelligence, my lips instinctively protruded and tasted a memory
of which I preferred that the reality should remain external to me and
should consist in the objective superiority of another person. There could be
no denying that I had known people whose intelligence was greater. But the
infinitude of love, or its egoism, has the result that the people whom we
love are those whose intellectual and moral physiognomy is least defined
objectively in our eyes, we alter them incessantly to suit our desires and fears,
we do not separate them from ourselves: they are only a vast and vague place
in which our affections take root. We have not of our own body, into which
flow perpetually so many discomforts and pleasures, as clear an outline as we
have of a tree or house, or of a passer-by. And where I had gone wrong was
perhaps in not making more effort to know Albertine in herself. Just as, from
the point of view of her charm, I had long considered only the different
positions that she occupied in my memory in the procession of years, and
had been surprised to see that she had been spontaneously enriched with
modifications which were due merely to the difference of perspective, so I
ought to have sought to understand her character as that of an ordinary
person, and thus perhaps, finding an explanation of her persistence in
keeping her secret from me, might have averted the continuance between us,
with that strange desperation, of the conflict which had led to the death of
Albertine. And I then felt, with an intense pity for her, shame at having
survived her. It seemed to me indeed, in the hours when I suffered least, that
I had derived a certain benefit from her death, for a woman is of greater
service to our life if she is in it, instead of being an element of happiness, an
instrument of sorrow, and there is not a woman in the world the possession
of whom is as precious as that of the truths which she reveals to us by causing
us to suffer. In these moments, thinking at once of my grandmother's death
and of Albertine's, it seemed to me that my life was stained with a double
murder from which only the cowardice of the world could absolve me. I had
dreamed of being understood by Albertine, of not being scorned by her,
thinking that it was for the great happiness of being understood, of not being
scorned, when so many other people might have served me better. We wish
to be understood, because we wish to be loved, and we wish to be loved
because we are in love. The understanding of other people is immaterial and
their love importunate. My joy at having possessed a little of Albertine's
intelligence and of her heart arose not from their intrinsic worth, but from
the fact that this possession was a stage farther towards the complete
possession of Albertine, a possession which had been my goal and my
chimera, since the day on which I first set eyes on her. When we speak of the

'kindness' of a woman, we do no more perhaps than project outside ourselves the pleasure that we feel in seeing her, like children when they say: 'My dear little bed, my dear little pillow, my dear little hawthorns'. Which explains incidentally why men never say of a woman who is not unfaithful to them: 'She is so kind', and say it so often of a woman by whom they are betrayed. Mme de Cambremer was right in thinking that Elstir's intellectual charm was greater. But we cannot judge in the same way the charm of a person who is, like everyone else, exterior to ourselves, painted upon the horizon of our mind, and that of a person who, in consequence of an error in localisation which has been due to certain accidents but is irreparable, has lodged herself in our own body so effectively that the act of asking ourselves in retrospect whether she did not look at a woman on a particular day in the corridor of a little seaside railway-tram makes us feel the same anguish as would a surgeon probing for a bullet in our heart. A simple crescent of bread, but one which we are eating, gives us more pleasure than all the ortolans, young rabbits and barbavelles that were set before Louis XV, and the blade of grass which, a few inches away, quivers before our eye, while we are lying upon the mountain-side, may conceal from us the sheer summit of another peak, if it is several miles away.

Furthermore, our mistake is our failure to value the intelligence, the kindness of a woman whom we love, however slight they may be. Our mistake is our remaining indifferent to the kindness, the intelligence of others. Falsehood begins to cause us the indignation, and kindness the gratitude which they ought always to arouse in us, only if they proceed from a woman with whom we are in love, and bodily desire has the marvellous faculty of restoring its value to intelligence and a solid base to the moral life. Never should I find again that divine thing, a person with whom I might talk freely of everything, in whom I might confide. Confide? But did not other people offer me greater confidence than Albertine? Had I not had with others more unrestricted conversations? The fact is that confidence, conversation, trivial things in themselves, what does it matter whether they are more or less imperfect, if only there enters into them love, which alone is divine. I could see Albertine now, seated at her pianola, rosy beneath her dark hair, I could feel, against my lips which she was trying to part, her tongue, her motherly, inedible, nourishing and holy tongue whose secret flame and dew meant that even when Albertine let it glide over the surface of my throat or stomach, those caresses, superficial but in a sense offered by her inmost flesh, turned outward like a cloth that is turned to show its lining, assumed even in the most external touches as it were the mysterious delight of a penetration.

All these so pleasant moments which nothing would ever restore to me again, I cannot indeed say that what made me feel the loss of them was despair. To feel despair, we must still be attached to that life which could end only in disaster. I had been in despair at Balbec when I saw the day break and realised that none of the days to come could ever be a happy day for me, I had remained fairly selfish since then, but the self to which I was now attached, the self which constituted those vital reserves that were set in action by the instinct of self-preservation, this self was no longer alive; when I thought of my strength, of my vital force, of the best elements in myself, I thought of a certain treasure which I had possessed (which I had been alone in possessing since other people could not know exactly the sentiment, concealed in myself, which it had inspired in me) and which no one could ever again take from me since I possessed it no longer.

And, to tell the truth, when I had ever possessed it, it had been only because I had liked to think of myself as possessing it. I had not merely committed the imprudence, when I cast my eyes upon Albertine and lodged her in my heart, of making her live within me, nor that other imprudence of combining a domestic affection with sensual pleasure. I had sought also to persuade myself that our relations were love, that we were mutually practising the relations that are called love, because she obediently returned the kisses that I gave her, and, having come in time to believe this, I had lost not merely a woman whom I loved but a woman who loved me, my sister, my child, my tender mistress. And in short, I had received a blessing and a curse which Swann had not known, for after all during the whole of the time in which he had been in love with Odette and had been so jealous of her, he had barely seen her, having found it so difficult, on certain days when she put him off at the last moment, to gain admission to her. But afterwards he had had her to himself, as his wife, and until the day of his death. I, on the contrary, while I was so jealous of Albertine, more fortunate than Swann, had had her with me in my own house. I had realised as a fact the state of which Swann had so often dreamed and which he did not realise materially until it had ceased to interest him. But after all I had not managed to keep Albertine as he had kept Odette. She had fled from me, she was dead. For nothing is ever repeated exactly, and the most analogous lives which, thanks to the kinship of the persons and the similarity of the circumstances, we may select in order to represent them as symmetrical, remain in many respects opposite.

By losing my life I should not have lost very much; I should have lost now only an empty form, the empty frame of a work of art. Indifferent as to what I might in the future put in it, but glad and proud to think of what it had contained, I dwelt upon the memory of those so pleasant hours, and this moral support gave me a feeling of comfort which the approach of death itself would not have disturbed.

How she used to hasten to see me at Balbec when I sent for her, lingering only to sprinkle scent on her hair to please me. These images of Balbec and Paris which I loved to see again were the pages still so recent, and so quickly turned, of her short life. All this which for me was only memory had been for her action, action as precipitate as that of a tragedy towards a sudden death. People develop in one way inside us, but in another way outside us (I had indeed felt this on those evenings when I remarked in Albertine an enrichment of qualities which was due not only to my memory), and these two ways do not fail to react upon each other. Albeit I had, in seeking to know Albertine, then to possess her altogether, obeyed merely the need to reduce by experiment to elements meanly similar to those of our own self the mystery of every other person, I had been unable to do so without exercising an influence in my turn over Albertine's life. Perhaps my wealth, the prospect of a brilliant marriage had attracted her, my jealousy had kept her, her goodness or her intelligence, or her sense of guilt, or her cunning had made her accept, and had led me on to make harsher and harsher a captivity in chains forged simply by the internal process of my mental toil, which had nevertheless had, upon Albertine's life, reactions, destined themselves to set, by the natural swing of the pendulum, fresh and ever more painful problems to my psychology, since from my prison she had escaped, to go and kill herself upon a horse which but for me she would not have owned, leaving me, even after she was dead, with suspicions the verification of which, if it was to come, would perhaps be more painful to me than the discovery at Balbec that Albertine had known Mlle Vinteuil, since Albertine would no longer be present to soothe me. So that the long plaint of the soul which thinks that it is living shut up within itself is a monologue in appearance only, since the echoes of reality alter its course and such a life is like an essay in subjective psychology spontaneously pursued, but furnishing from a distance its 'action' to the purely realistic novel of another reality, another existence, the vicissitudes of which come in their turn to inflect the curve and change the direction of the psychological essay. How highly geared had been the mechanism, how rapid had been the evolution of our love, and, notwithstanding the sundry delays, interruptions and hesitations of the start, as in certain of Balzac's tales or Schumann's ballads, how sudden the catastrophe! It was in the course of this last year, long as a century to me, so many times had Albertine changed her appearance in my mind between Balbec and her departure from Paris, and also, independently of me and often without my knowledge, changed in herself, that I must place the whole of that happy life of affection which had lasted so short a while, which yet appeared to me with an amplitude, almost an immensity, which now was for ever impossible and yet was indispensable to me. Indispensable without perhaps having been in itself and at the outset a thing that was necessary since I should not have known Albertine had I not read in an archaeological treatise a description of the church at Balbec, had not Swann, by telling me that this church was almost Persian, directed my taste to the Byzantine Norman, had not a financial syndicate, by erecting at Balbec a hygienic and comfortable hotel, made my parents decide to hear my supplication and send me to Balbec. To be sure, in that Balbec so long desired I had not found the Persian church of my dreams, nor the eternal mists. Even the famous train at one twenty-two had not corresponded to my mental picture of it. But in compensation for what our imagination leaves us wanting and we give ourselves so much unnecessary trouble in trying to find, life does give us something which we were very far from imagining. Who would have told me at Combray, when I lay waiting for my mother's good-night with so heavy a heart, that those anxieties would be healed, and would then break out again one day, not for my mother, but for a girl who would at first be no more, against the horizon of the sea, than a flower upon which my eyes would daily be invited to gaze, but a flower that could think, and in whose mind I should be so childishly anxious to occupy a prominent place, that I should be distressed by her not being aware that I knew Mme de Villeparisis? Yes, it was the good-night, the kiss of a stranger like this, that, in years to come, was to make me suffer as keenly as I had suffered as a child when my mother was not coming up to my room. Well, this Albertine so necessary, of love for whom my soul was now almost entirely composed, if Swann had not spoken to me of Balbec, I should never have known her. Her life would perhaps have been longer, mine would have been unprovided with what was now making it a martyrdom. And also it seemed to me that, by my entirely selfish affection, I had allowed Albertine to die just as I had murdered my grandmother. Even later on, even after I had already known her at Balbec, I should have been able not to love her as I was to love her in the sequel. When I gave up Gilberte and knew that I would be able one day to love another woman, I scarcely ventured to entertain a doubt whether, considering simply the past, Gilberte was the only woman whom I had been capable of loving. Well, in the case of Albertine I had no longer any doubt at all, I was sure that it need not have been herself that I loved, that it might have been someone else. To prove this, it would have been sufficient that Mlle de Stermaria, on the evening when I was going to take her to dine on the island in the Bois, should not have put me off. It was still not too late, and it would have been upon Mlle de Stermaria that I would have trained that activity of the imagination which makes us extract from a woman so special a notion of the individual that she appears to us unique in herself and predestined and necessary for us. At the most, adopting an almost physiological point of view, I could say that I might have been able to feel this same exclusive love for another woman but not for any other woman. For Albertine, plump and dark, did not resemble Gilberte, tall and ruddy, and yet they were fashioned of the same healthy stuff, and over the same sensual cheeks shone a look in the eyes of both which it was difficult to interpret. They were women of a sort that would never attract the attention of men who, for their part, would do the most extravagant things for other women who made no appeal to me. A man has almost always the same way of catching cold, and so forth; that is to say, he requires to bring about the event a certain combination of circumstances; it is natural that when he falls in love he should love a certain class of woman, a class which for that matter is very numerous. The two first glances from Albertine which had set me dreaming were not absolutely different from Gilberte's first glances. I could almost believe that the obscure personality, the sensuality, the forward, cunning nature of Gilberte had returned to tempt me, incarnate this time in Albertine's body, a body quite different and yet not without analogies. In Albertine's case, thanks to a wholly different life shared with me into which had been unable to penetrate – in a block of thoughts among which a painful preoccupation maintained a permanent cohesion – any fissure of distraction and oblivion, her living body had indeed not, like Gilberte's, ceased one day to be the body in which I found what I subsequently recognised as being to me (what they would not have been to other men) feminine charms. But she was dead. I should, in time, forget her. Who could tell whether then, the same qualities of rich blood, of uneasy brooding would return one day to spread havoc in my life, but incarnate this time in what feminine form I could not foresee. The example of Gilberte would as little have enabled me to form an idea of Albertine and guess that I should fall in love with her, as the memory of Vinteuil's sonata would have enabled me to imagine his septet. Indeed, what was more, on the first occasions of my meeting Albertine, I might have supposed that it was with other girls that I should fall in love. Besides, she might indeed quite well have appeared to me, had I met her a year earlier, as dull as a grey sky in which dawn has not yet broken. If I had changed in relation to her, she herself had changed also, and the girl who had come and sat upon my bed on the day of my letter to Mlle de Stermaria was no longer the same girl that I had known at Balbec, whether by a mere explosion of the woman which occurs at the age of puberty, or because of some incident which I have never been able to discover. In any case if she whom I was one day to love must to a certain extent resemble this other, that is to say if my choice of a woman was not entirely free, this meant nevertheless that, trained in a manner that was perhaps inevitable, it was trained upon something more considerable than a person, upon a type of womankind, and this removed all inevitability from my love for Albertine. The woman whose face we have before our eyes more constantly than light itself, since, even when our eyes are shut, we never cease for an instant to adore her beautiful eyes, her beautiful nose, to arrange opportunities of seeing them again, this unique woman – we know quite well that it would have been another woman that would now be unique to us if we had been in another town than that in which we made her acquaintance, if we had explored other quarters of the town, if we had frequented the house of a different hostess. Unique, we suppose; she is innumerable. And yet she is compact, indestructible in our loving eyes, irreplaceable for a long time to come by any other. The truth is that the woman has only raised to life by a sort of magic spell a thousand elements of affection existing in us already in a fragmentary state, which she has assembled, joined together, bridging every gap between them, it is ourselves who by giving her her features have supplied all the solid matter of the beloved object. Whence it comes about that even if we are only one man among a thousand to her and perhaps the last man of them all, to us she is the only woman, the woman towards whom our whole life tends. It was indeed true that I had been quite well aware that this love was not inevitable since it might have occurred with Mlle de Stermaria, but even without that from my knowledge of the love itself, when I found it to be too similar to what I had known with other women, and also when I felt it to be vaster than Albertine, enveloping her, unconscious of her, like a tide swirling round a tiny rock. But gradually, by dint of living with Albertine, the chains which I myself had forged I was unable to fling off, the habit of associating Albertine's person with the sentiment which she had not inspired made me nevertheless believe that it was peculiar to her, as habit gives to the mere association of ideas between two phenomena, according to a certain school of philosophy, an illusion of the force, the necessity of a law of causation. I had thought that my social relations, my wealth, would dispense me from suffering, and too effectively perhaps since this seemed to dispense me from feeling, loving, imagining; I envied a poor country girl whom her absence of social relations, even by telegraph, allows to ponder for months on end upon a grief which she cannot artificially put to sleep. And now I began to realise that if, in the case of Mme de Guermantes, endowed with everything that could make the gulf infinite between her and myself, I had seen that gulf suddenly bridged by the opinion that social advantages are nothing more than inert and transmutable matter, so, in a similar albeit converse fashion, my social relations, my wealth, all the material means by which not only my own position but the civilisation of my age enabled me to profit, had done no more than postpone the conclusion of my struggle against the contrary inflexible will of Albertine upon which no pressure had had any effect. True, I had been able to exchange telegrams, telephone messages with Saint-Loup, to remain in constant communication with the office at Tours, but had not the delay in waiting for them proved useless, the result nil? And country girls, without social advantages or relations, or human beings enjoying the perfections of civilisation, do they not suffer less, because all of us desire less, because we regret less what we have always known to be inaccessible, what for that reason has continued to seem unreal? We desire more keenly the person who is about to give herself to us; hope anticipates possession; but regret also is an amplifier of desire. Mme de Stermaria's refusal to come and dine with me on the island in the Bois was what had prevented her from becoming the object of my love. This might have sufficed also to make me fall in love with her if afterwards I had seen her again before it was too late. As soon as I had known that she was not coming, entertaining the improbable hypothesis – which had been proved correct – that perhaps she had a jealous lover who prevented her from seeing other men, that I should never see her again, I had suffered so intensely that I would have given anything in the world to see her, and it was one of the keenest anguishes that I had ever felt that Saint-Loup's arrival had soothed. After we have reached a certain age our loves, our mistresses, are begotten of our anguish; our past, and the physical lesions in which it is recorded, determine our future. In Albertine's case, the fact that it would not necessarily be she that I must love was, even without the example of those previous loves, inscribed in the history of my love for her, that is to say for herself and her friends. For it was not a single love like my love for Gilberte, but was created by division among a number of girls. That it was on her account and because they appeared to me more or less similar to her that I had amused myself with her friends was quite possible. The fact remains that for a long time hesitation among them all was possible, my choice strayed from one to another, and when I thought that I preferred one, it was enough that another should keep me waiting, should refuse to see me, to make me feel the first premonitions of love for her. Often at that time when Andrée was coming to see me at Balbec, if, shortly before Andrée was expected, Albertine failed to keep an appointment, my heart throbbed without ceasing, I felt that I would never see her again and that it was she whom I loved. And when Andrée came it was in all seriousness that I said to her (as I said it to her in Paris after I had learned that Albertine had known Mlle Vinteuil) what she supposed me to be saying with a purpose, without sincerity, what I would indeed have said and in the same words had I been enjoying myself the day before with Albertine: 'Alas! If you had only come sooner, now I am in love with some-one else.' Again, in this case of Andrée, replaced by Albertine after I learned that the latter had known Mlle Vinteuil, my love had alternated between them, so that after all there had been only one love at a time. But a case had occurred earlier in which I had more or less quarrelled with two of the girls. The one who took the first step towards a reconciliation would restore my peace of mind, it was the other that I would love, if she remained cross with me, which does not mean that it was not with the former that I would form a definite tie, for she would console me – albeit ineffectively – for the harshness of the other, whom I would end by forgetting if she did not return to me again. Now, it so happened that, while I was convinced that one or the other at least would come back to me, for some time neither of them did so. My anguish was therefore twofold, and twofold my love, while I reserved to myself the right to cease to love the one who came back, but until that happened continued to suffer on account of them both. It is the lot of a certain period in life which may come to us quite early that we are made less amorous by a person than by a desertion, in which we end by knowing one thing and one thing only about that person, her face having grown dim, her heart having ceased to exist, our preference of her being quite recent and inexplicable; namely that what we need to make our suffering cease is a message from her: 'May I come and see you?' My separation from Albertine on the day when Françoise informed me: 'Mademoiselle Albertine has gone' was like an allegory of countless other separations. For very often in order that we may discover that we are in love, perhaps indeed in order that we may fall in love, the day of separation must first have come. In the case when it is an unkept appointment, a written refusal that dictates our choice, our imagination lashed by suffering sets about its work so swiftly, fashions with so frenzied a rapidity a love that had scarcely begun, and had been quite featureless, destined, for months past, to remain a rough sketch, that now and again our intelligence which has not been able to keep pace with our heart, cries out in astonishment: 'But you must be mad, what are these strange thoughts that are making you so miserable? That is not real life.' And indeed at that moment, had we not been roused to action by the betrayer, a few healthy distractions that would calm our heart physically would be sufficient to bring our love to an end. In any case if this life with

Albertine was not in its essence necessary, it had become indispensable to me. I had trembled when I was in love with Mme de Guermantes because I used to say to myself that, with her too abundant means of attraction, not only beauty but position, wealth, she would be too much at liberty to give herself to all and sundry, that I should have too little hold over her. Albertine had been penniless, obscure, she must have been anxious to marry me. And yet I had not been able to possess her exclusively. Whatever be our social position, however wise our precautions, when the truth is confessed we have no hold over the life of another person. Why had she not said to me: 'I have those tastes'? I would have yielded, would have allowed her to gratify them. In a novel that I had been reading there was a woman whom no objurgation from the man who was in love with her could induce to speak. When I read the book, I had thought this situation absurd; had I been the hero, I assured myself, I would first of all have forced the woman to speak, then we could have come to an understanding; what was the good of all this unnecessary misery? But I saw now that we are not free to abstain from forging the chains of our own misery, and that however well we may know our own will, other people do not obey it.

And yet those painful, those ineluctable truths which dominated us and to which we were blind, the truth of our sentiments, the truth of our destiny, how often without knowing it, without meaning it, we have expressed them in words in which we ourselves doubtless thought that we were lying, but the prophetic value of which has been established by subsequent events. I could recall many words that each of us had uttered without knowing at the time the truth that they contained, which indeed we had said thinking that each was deceiving the other, words the falsehood of which was very slight, quite uninteresting, wholly confined within our pitiable insincerity, compared with what they contained that was unknown to us. Lies, mistakes, falling short of the reality which neither of us perceived, truth extending beyond it, the truth of our natures the essential laws of which escape us and require time before they reveal themselves, the truth of our destinies also. I had supposed that I was lying when I said to her at Balbec: 'The more I see you, the more I shall love you' (and yet it was that intimacy at every moment that had, through the channel of jealousy, attached me so strongly to her), 'I know that I could be of use to you intellectually'; and in Paris: 'Do be careful. Remember that if you met with an accident, it would break my heart.' And she: 'But I may meet with an accident'; and I in Paris on the evening when I pretended that I wished to part from her: 'Let me look at you once again since presently I shall not be seeing you again, and it will be for ever!' and when, that same evening, she looked round the room: 'To think that I shall never see this room again, those books, that pianola, the whole house, I cannot believe it and yet it is true.' In her last letters again, when she wrote – probably saying to herself: 'This is the stuff to tell him' – 'I leave with you the best part of myself' (and was it not now indeed to the fidelity, to the strength, which too was, alas, frail, of my memory that were entrusted her intelligence, her goodness, her beauty?) and 'that twofold twilight (since night was falling and we were about to part) will be effaced from my thoughts only when the darkness is complete', that phrase written on the eve of the day when her mind had indeed been plunged in complete darkness, and when, it may well have been, in the last glimmer, so brief but stretched out to infinity by the anxiety of the moment, she had indeed perhaps seen again our last drive together and in that instant when everything forsakes us and we create a faith for ourselves, as atheists turn Christian upon the battlefield, she had perhaps summoned to her aid the friend whom she had so often cursed but had so deeply respected, who himself – for all religions are alike – was so cruel as to hope that she had also had time to see herself as she was, to give her last thought to him, to confess her sins at length to him, to die in him. But to what purpose, since even if, at that moment, she had had time to see herself as she was, we had both of us understood where our happiness lay, what we ought to do, only because that happiness was no longer possible, and because we could no longer realise it. So long as things are possible we postpone them, and they cannot assume that force of attraction, that apparent ease of realisation save when, projected upon the ideal void of the imagination, they are removed from their burdensome, degrading submersion in the vital medium. The thought that we must die is more painful than the act of dying, but less painful than the thought that another person is dead, which, becoming once more a plane surface after having engulfed a person, extends without even an eddy at the point of disappearance, a reality from which that person is excluded, in which there exists no longer any will, any knowledge, and from which it is as difficult to reascend to the thought that the person has lived, as it is difficult, with the still recent memory of her life, to think that she is now comparable with the unsubstantial images, with the memories left us by the characters in a novel which we have been reading.

At any rate I was glad that, before she died, she had written me that letter, and above all had sent me that final message which proved to me that she would have returned had she lived. It seemed to me that it was not merely more soothing, but more beautiful also, that the event would have been incomplete without this note, would not have had so markedly the form of art and destiny. In reality it would have been just as markedly so had it been different; for every event is like a mould of a particular shape, and, whatever it be, it imposes, upon the series of incidents which it has interrupted and seems to have concluded, a pattern which we believe to be the only one possible, because we do not know the other which might have been substituted for it. I repeated to myself: 'Why had she not said to me: "I have those tastes", I would have yielded, would have allowed her to gratify them, at this moment I should be kissing her still.' What a sorrow to have to remind myself that she had lied to me thus when she swore to me, three days before she left me, that she had never had with Mlle Vinteuil's friend those relations which at the moment when Albertine swore it her blush had confessed. Poor child, she had at least had the honesty to refuse to swear that the pleasure of seeing Mlle Vinteuil again had no part in her desire to go that day to the Verdurins'. Why had she not made her admission complete, why had she then invented that inconceivable tale? Perhaps however it was partly my fault that she had never, despite all my entreaties which were powerless against her denial, been willing to say to me: 'I have those tastes.' It was perhaps partly my fault because at Balbec, on the day when, after Mme de Cambremer's call, I had had my first explanation with Albertine, and when I was so far from imagining that she could have had, in any case, anything more than an unduly passionate friendship with Andrée, I had expressed with undue violence my disgust at that kind of moral lapse, had condemned it in too categorical a fashion. I could not recall whether Albertine had blushed when I had innocently expressed my horror of that sort of thing, I could not recall it, for it is often only long afterwards that we would give anything to know what attitude a person adopted at a moment when we were paying no attention to it, an attitude which, later on, when we think again of our conversation, would elucidate a poignant difficulty. But in our memory there is a blank, there is no trace of it. And very often we have not paid sufficient attention, at the actual moment, to the things which might even then have seemed to us important, we have not properly heard a sentence, have not noticed a gesture, or else we have forgotten them. And when later on, eager to discover a truth, we reascend from deduction to deduction, turning over our memory like a sheaf of written evidence, when we arrive at that sentence, at that gesture, which it is impossible to recall, we begin again a score of times the same process, but in vain: the road goes no farther. Had she blushed? I did not know whether she had blushed, but she could not have failed to hear, and the memory of my speech had brought her to a halt later on when perhaps she had been on the point of making her confession to me. And now she no longer existed anywhere, I might scour the earth from pole to pole without finding Albertine. The reality which had closed over her was once more unbroken, had obliterated every trace of the creature who had sunk into its depths. She was no more now than a name, like that Mme de Charlus of whom the people who had known her said with indifference: 'She was charming.' But I was unable to conceive for more than an instant the existence of this reality of which Albertine had no knowledge, for in myself my mistress existed too vividly, in myself in whom every sentiment, every thought bore some reference to her life. Perhaps if she had known, she would have been touched to see that her lover had not forgotten her, now that her own life was finished, and would have been moved by things which in the past had left her indifferent. But as we would choose to refrain from infidelities, however secret they might be, so fearful are we that she whom we love is not refraining from them, I was alarmed by the thought that if the dead do exist anywhere, my grandmother was as well aware of my oblivion as Albertine of my remembrance. And when all is said, even in the case of a single dead person, can we be sure that the joy which we should feel in learning that she knows certain things would compensate for our alarm at the thought that she knows *all*; and, however agonising the sacrifice, would we not sometimes abstain from keeping after their death as friends those whom we have loved, from the fear of having them also as judges?

My jealous curiosity as to what Albertine might have done was unbounded. I suborned any number of women from whom I learned nothing. If this curiosity was so keen, it was because people do not die at once for us, they remain bathed in a sort of *aura* of life in which there is no true immortality but which means that they continue to occupy our thoughts in the same way as when they were alive. It is as though they were travelling abroad. This is a thoroughly pagan survival. Conversely, when we have ceased to love her, the curiosity which the person arouses dies before she herself is dead. Thus I would no longer have taken any step to find out with whom Gilberte had been strolling on a certain evening in the Champs-Elysées. Now I felt that these curiosities were absolutely alike, had no value in themselves, were incapable of lasting, but I continued to sacrifice everything to the cruel satisfaction of this transient curiosity, albeit I knew in advance that my enforced separation from Albertine, by the fact of her death, would lead me to the same indifference as had resulted from my deliberate separation from Gilberte.

If she could have known what was about to happen, she would have stayed with me. But this meant no more than that, once she saw herself dead, she would have preferred, in my company, to remain alive. Simply in view of the contradiction that it implied, such a supposition was absurd. But it was not innocuous, for in imagining how glad Albertine would be, if she could know, if she could retrospectively understand, to come back to me, I saw her before me, I wanted to kiss her; and alas, it was impossible, she would never come back, she was dead. My imagination sought for her in the sky, through the nights on which we had gazed at it when still together; beyond that moonlight which she loved, I tried to raise up to her my affection so that it might be a consolation to her for being no longer alive, and this love for a being so remote was like a religion, my thoughts rose towards her like prayers. Desire is very powerful, it engenders belief; I had believed that Albertine would not leave me because I desired that she might not. Because I desired it, I began to believe that she was not dead; I took to reading books upon table-turning, I began to believe in the possibility of the immortality of the soul. But that did not suffice me. I required that, after my own death, I should find her again in her body, as though eternity were like life. Life, did I say! I was more exacting still. I would have wished not to be deprived for ever by death of the pleasures of which however it is not alone in robbing us. For without her death they would eventually have grown faint, they had begun already to do so by the action of long-established habit, of fresh curiosities. Besides, had she been alive, Albertine, even physically, would gradually have changed, day by day I should have adapted myself to that change. But my memory, calling up only detached moments of her life, asked to see her again as she would already have ceased to be, had she lived; what it required was a miracle which would satisfy the natural and arbitrary limitations of memory which cannot emerge from the past. With the simplicity of the old theologians, I imagined her furnishing me not indeed with the explanations which she might possibly have given me but, by a final contradiction, with those that she had always refused me during her life. And thus, her death being a sort of dream, my love would seem to her an unlooked-for happiness; I saw in death only the convenience and optimism of a solution which simplifies, which arranges everything. Sometimes it was not so far off, it was not in another world that I imagined our reunion. Just as in the past, when I knew Gilberte only from playing with her in the Champs-Elysées, at home in the evening I used to imagine that I was going to receive a letter from her in which she would confess her love for me, that she was coming into the room, so a similar force of desire, no more embarrassed by the laws of nature which ran counter to it than on the former occasion in the case of Gilberte, when after all it had not been mistaken since it had had the last word, made me think now that I was going to receive a message from Albertine, informing me that she had indeed met with an accident while riding, but that for romantic reasons (and as, after all, has sometimes happened with people whom we have long believed to be dead) she had not wished me to hear of her recovery and now, repentant, asked to be allowed to come and live with me for ever. And, making quite clear to myself the nature of certain harmless manias in people who otherwise appear sane, I felt coexisting in myself the certainty that she was dead and the incessant hope that I might see her come into the room,

I had not yet received any news from Aimé, albeit he must by now have reached Balbec. No doubt my enquiry turned upon a secondary point, and one quite arbitrarily selected. If Albertine's life had been really culpable, it must have contained many other things of far greater importance, which chance had not allowed me to touch, as it had allowed me that conversation about the wrapper, thanks to Albertine's blushes. It was quite arbitrarily that I had been presented with that particular day, which many years later I was seeking to reconstruct. If Albertine had been a lover of women, there were thousands of other days in her life her employment of which I did not know and about which it might be as interesting for me to learn; I might have sent Aimé to many other places in Balbec, to many other towns than Balbec. But these other days, precisely because I did not know how she had spent them, did not represent themselves to my imagination. They had no existence. Things, people, did not begin to exist for me until they assumed in my imagination an individual existence. If there were thousands of others like them, they became for me representative of all the rest. If I had long felt a desire to know, in the matter of my suspicions with regard to Albertine, what exactly had happened in the baths, it was in the same manner in which, in the matter of my desires for women, and although I knew that there were any number of girls and lady's-maids who could satisfy them and whom chance might just as easily have led me to hear mentioned, I wished to know – since it was of them that Saint-Loup had spoken to me – the girl who frequented houses of ill fame and Mme Putbus's maid. The difficulties which my health, my indecision, my 'procrastination', as M. de Charlus called it, placed in the way of my carrying out any project, had made me put off from day to day, from month to month, from year to year, the elucidation of certain suspicions as also the accomplishment of certain desires. But I kept them in my memory promising myself that I would not forget to learn the truth of them, because they alone obsessed me (since the others had no form in my eyes, did not exist), and also because the very accident that had chosen them out of the surrounding reality gave me a guarantee that it was indeed in them that I should come in contact with a trace of reality, of the true and coveted life.

Besides, from a single fact, if it is certain, can we not, like a scientist making experiments, extract the truth as to all the orders of similar facts? Is not a single little fact, if it is well chosen, sufficient to enable the experimenter to deduce a general law which will make him know the truth as to thousands of analogous facts?

Albertine might indeed exist in my memory only in the state in which she had successively appeared to me in the course of her life, that is to say subdivided according to a series of fractions of time, my mind, reestablishing unity in her, made her a single person, and it was upon this person that I sought to bring a general judgment to bear, to know whether she had lied to me, whether she loved women, whether it was in order to be free to associate with them that she had left me. What the woman in the baths would have to say might perhaps put an end for ever to my doubts as to Albertine's morals.

My doubts! Alas, I had supposed that it would be immaterial to me, even pleasant, not to see Albertine again, until her departure revealed to me my error. Similarly her death had shown me how greatly I had been mistaken when I believed that I hoped at times for her death and supposed that it would be my deliverance. So it was that, when I received Aimé's letter, I realised that, if I had not until then suffered too painfully from my doubts as to Albertine's virtue, it was because in reality they were not doubts at all. My happiness, my life required that Albertine should be virtuous, they had laid it down once and for all time that she was. Furnished with this preservative belief, I could without danger allow my mind to play sadly with suppositions to which it gave a form but added no faith. I said to myself, 'She is perhaps a woman-lover', as we say, 'I may die tonight'; we say it, but we do not believe it, we make plans for the morrow. This explains why, believing mistakenly that I was uncertain whether Albertine did or did not love women, and believing in consequence that a proof of Albertine's guilt would not give me anything that I had not already taken into account, I was able to feel before the pictures, insignificant to anyone else, which Aimé's letter called up to me, an unexpected anguish, the most painful that I had ever yet felt, and one that formed with those pictures, with the picture, alas! of Albertine herself, a sort of precipitate, as chemists say, in which the whole was invisible and of which the text of Aimé's letter, which I isolate in a purely conventional fashion, can give no idea whatsoever, since each of the words that compose it was immediately transformed, coloured for ever by the suffering that it had aroused.

MONSIEUR – Monsieur will kindly forgive me for not having written sooner to Monsieur. The person whom Monsieur instructed me to see had gone away for a few days, and, anxious to justify the confidence which

Monsieur had placed in me, I did not wish to return empty-handed. I have just spoken to this person who remembers (Mlle A.) quite well.' Aimé who possessed certain rudiments of culture meant to italicise *Mlle A.* between inverted commas. But when he meant to write inverted commas, he wrote brackets, and when he meant to write something in brackets he put it between inverted commas. Thus it was that Françoise would say that someone *stayed* in my street meaning that he abode there, and that one could *abide* for a few minutes, meaning *stay*, the mistakes of popular speech consisting merely, as often as not, in interchanging – as for that matter the French language has done – terms which in the course of centuries have replaced one another. 'According to her the thing that Monsieur supposed is absolutely certain. For one thing, it was she who looked after (Mlle A.) whenever she came to the baths. (Mlle A.) came very often to take her bath with a tall woman older than herself, always dressed in grey, whom the bath-woman without knowing her name recognised from having often seen her going after girls. But she took no notice of any of them after she met (Mlle A.). She and (Mlle A.) always shut themselves up in the dressing-box, remained there a very long time, and the lady in grey used to give at least 10 francs as a tip to the person to whom I spoke. As this person said to me, you can imagine that if they were just stringing beads, they wouldn't have given a tip of ten francs. (Mlle A.) used to come also sometimes with a woman with a very dark skin and long-handled glasses. But (Mlle A.) came most often with girls younger than herself, especially one with a high complexion. Apart from the lady in grey, the people whom (Mlle A.) was in the habit of bringing were not from Balbec and must indeed often have come from quite a distance. They never came in together, but (Mlle A.) would come in, and ask for the door of her box to be left unlocked – as she was expecting a friend, and the person to whom I spoke knew what that meant. This person could not give me any other details, as she does not remember very well, which is easily understood after so long an interval.' Besides, this person did not try to find out, because she is very discreet and it was to her advantage, for (Mlle A.) brought her in a lot of money. She was quite sincerely touched to hear that she was dead. It is true that so young it is a great calamity for her and for her friends. I await Monsieur's orders to know whether I may leave Balbec where I do not think that I can learn anything more. I thank Monsieur again for the little holiday that he has procured me, and which has been very pleasant especially as the weather is as fine as could be. The season promises well for this year. We hope that Monsieur will come and put in a little appearance.

I can think of nothing else to say that will interest Monsieur.

To understand how deeply these words penetrated my being, the reader must bear in mind that the questions which I had been asking myself with regard to Albertine were not subordinate, immaterial questions, questions of detail, the only questions as a matter of fact which we ask ourselves about anyone who is not ourselves, whereby we are enabled to proceed, wrapped in an impenetrable thought, through the midst of suffering, falsehood, vice or death. No, in Albertine's case, they were essential questions: 'In her heart of hearts what was she? What were her thoughts? What were her loves? Did she lie to me? Had my life with her been as lamentable as Swann's life with Odette?' And so the point reached by Aimé's reply, even although it was not a general reply – and precisely for that reason – was indeed in Albertine, in myself, the uttermost depths.

At last I saw before my eyes, in that arrival of Albertine at the baths along the narrow lane with the lady in grey, a fragment of that past which seemed to me no less mysterious, no less alarming than I had feared when I imagined it as enclosed in the memory, in the facial expression of Albertine. No doubt anyone but myself might have dismissed as insignificant these details, upon which my inability, now that Albertine was dead, to secure a denial of them from herself, conferred the equivalent of a sort of likelihood. It is indeed probable that for Albertine, even if they had been true, her own misdeeds, if she had admitted them, whether her conscience thought them innocent or reprehensible, whether her sensuality had found them exquisite or distinctly dull, would not have been accompanied by that inexpressible sense of horror from which I was unable to detach them. I myself, with the help of my own love of women, albeit they could not have been the same thing to Albertine, could more or less imagine what she felt. And indeed it was already a first degree of anguish, merely to picture her to myself desiring as I had so often desired, lying to me as I had so often lied to her, preoccupied with one girl or another, putting herself out for her, as I had done for Mlle de Stermaria and ever so many others, not to mention the peasant girls whom I met on country roads. Yes, all my own desires helped me to understand, to a certain degree, what hers had been; it was by this time an intense anguish in which all my desires, the keener they had been, had changed into torments that were all the more cruel; as though in this algebra of sensibility they reappeared with the same coefficient but with a minus instead of a plus sign. To Albertine, so far as I was capable of judging her by my own standard, her misdeeds, however anxious she might have been to conceal them from me – which made me suppose that she was conscious of her guilt or was afraid of grieving me – her misdeeds because she had planned them to suit her own taste in the clear light of imagination in which desire plays, appeared to her nevertheless as things of the same nature as the rest of life, pleasures for herself which she had not had the courage to deny herself, griefs for me which she had sought to avoid causing me by concealing them, but pleasures and griefs which might be numbered among the other pleasures and griefs of life. But for me, it was from without, without my having been forewarned, without my having been able myself to elaborate them, it was from Aimé's letter that there had come to me the visions of Albertine arriving at the baths and preparing her gratuity.

No doubt it was because in that silent and deliberate arrival of Albertine with the woman in grey I read the assignation that they had made, that convention of going to make love in a dressing-box which implied an experience of corruption, the well-concealed organisation of a double life, it was because these images brought me the terrible tidings of Albertine's guilt that they had immediately caused me a physical grief from which they would never in time to come be detached. But at once my grief had reacted upon them: an objective fact, such as an image, differs according to the internal state in which we approach it. And grief is as potent in altering reality as is drunkenness. Combined with these images, suffering had at once made of them something absolutely different from what might be for anyone else a lady in grey, a gratuity, a bath, the street which had witnessed the deliberate arrival of Albertine with the lady in grey. All these images – escaping from a life of falsehood and misconduct such as I had never conceived – my suffering had immediately altered in their very substance, I did not behold them in the light that illuminates earthly spectacles, they were a fragment of another world, of an unknown and accursed planet, a glimpse of Hell. My Hell was all that Balbec, all those neighbouring villages from which, according to Aimé's letter, she frequently collected girls younger than herself whom she took to the baths. That mystery which I had long ago imagined in the country round Balbec and which had been dispelled after I had stayed there, which I had then hoped to grasp again when I knew Albertine because, when I saw her pass me on the beach, when I was mad enough to desire that she might not be virtuous, I thought that she must be its incarnation, how fearfully now everything that related to Balbec was impregnated with it. The names of those stations, Toutainville, Epreville, Parville, grown so familiar, so soothing, when I heard them shouted at night as I returned from the Verdurins', now that I thought how Albertine had been staying at the last, had gone from there to the second, must often have ridden on her bicycle to the first, they aroused in me an anxiety more cruel than on the first occasion, when I beheld the places with such misgivings, before arriving at a Balbec which I did not yet know. It is one of the faculties of jealousy to reveal to us the extent to which the reality of external facts and the sentiments of the heart are an unknown element which lends itself to endless suppositions. We suppose that we know exactly what things are and what people think, for the simple reason that we do not care about them. But as soon as we feel the desire to know, which the jealous man feels, then it becomes a dizzy kaleidoscope in which we can no longer make out anything. Had Albertine been unfaithful to me? With whom? In what house? Upon what day? The day on which she had said this or that to me? When I remembered that I had in the course of it said this or that? I could not tell. Nor did I know what were her sentiments towards myself, whether they were inspired by financial interest, by affection. And all of a sudden I remembered some trivial incident, for instance that Albertine had wished to go to Saint-Mars le Vêtu, saying that the name interested her, and perhaps simply because she had made the acquaintance of some peasant girl who lived there. But it was nothing that Aimé should have found out all this for me from the woman at the baths, since Albertine must remain eternally unaware that he had informed me, the need to know having always been exceeded, in my love for Albertine, by the need to show her that I knew; for this abolished between us the partition of different illusions, without having ever had the result of making her love me more, far from it. And now, after she was dead, the second of these needs had been amalgamated with the effect of the first: I tried to picture to myself the conversation in which I would have informed her of what I had learned, as vividly as the conversation in which I would have asked her to tell me what I did not know; that is to say, to see her by my side, to hear her answering me kindly, to see her cheeks become plump again, her eyes shed their malice and assume an air of melancholy; that is to say, to love her still and to forget the fury of my jealousy in the despair of my loneliness. The painful mystery of this impossibility of ever making her know what I had learned and of establishing our relations upon the truth of what I had only just discovered (and would not have been able, perhaps, to discover, but for the fact of her death) substituted its sadness for the more painful mystery of her conduct. What? To have so keenly desired that Albertine should know that I had heard the story of the baths, Albertine who no longer existed! This again was one of the consequences of our utter inability, when we have to consider the matter of death, to picture to ourselves anything but life. Albertine no longer existed. But to me she was the person who had concealed from me that she had assignations with women at Balbec, who imagined that she had succeeded in keeping me in ignorance of them. When we try to consider what happens to us after our own death, is it not still our living self which by mistake we project before us? And is it much more absurd, when all is said, to regret that a woman who no longer exists is unaware that we have learned what she was doing six years ago than to desire that of ourselves, who will be dead, the public shall still speak with approval a century hence? If there is more real foundation in the latter than in the former case, the regrets of my retrospective jealousy proceeded none the less from the same optical error as in other men the desire for posthumous fame. And yet this impression of all the solemn finality that there was in my separation from Albertine, if it had been substituted for a moment for my idea of her misdeeds, only aggravated them by bestowing upon them an irremediable character.

I saw myself astray in life as upon an endless beach where I was alone and, in whatever direction I might turn, would never meet her. Fortunately, I found most appropriately in my memory – as there are always all sorts of things, some noxious, others salutary in that heap from which individual impressions come to light only one by one – I discovered, as a craftsman discovers the material that can serve for what he wishes to make, a speech of my grandmother's. She had said to me, with reference to an improbable story which the bath-woman had told Mme de Villeparisis: 'She is a woman who must suffer from a disease of mendacity.' This memory was a great comfort to me. What importance could the story have that the woman had told Aimé? Especially as, after all, she had seen nothing. A girl can come and take baths with her friends without having any evil intention. Perhaps for her own glorification the woman had exaggerated the amount of the gratuity. I had indeed heard Françoise maintain once that my aunt Léonie had said in her hearing that she had 'a million a month to spend', which was utter nonsense; another time that she had seen my aunt Léonie give Eulalie four thousand-franc notes, whereas a fifty-franc note folded in four seemed to me scarcely probable. And so I sought – and, in course of time, managed – to rid myself of the painful certainty which I had taken such trouble to acquire, tossed to and fro as I still was between the desire to know and the fear of suffering. Then my affection might revive afresh, but, simultaneously with it, a sorrow at being parted from Albertine, during the course of which I was perhaps even more wretched than in the recent hours when it had been jealousy that tormented me. But my jealousy was suddenly revived, when I thought of Balbec, because of the vision which at once reappeared (and which until then had never made me suffer and indeed appeared one of the most innocuous in my memory) of the dining-room at Balbec in the evening, with, on the other side of the windows, all that populace crowded together in the dusk, as before the luminous glass of an aquarium, producing a contact (of which I had never thought) in their conglomeration, between the fishermen and girls of the lower orders and the young ladies jealous of that splendour new to Balbec, that splendour from which, if not their means, at any rate avarice and tradition debarred their parents, young ladies among whom there had certainly been almost every evening Albertine whom I did not then know and who doubtless used to accost some little girl whom she would meet a few minutes later in the dark, upon the sands, or else in a deserted bathing hut at the foot of the cliff. Then it was my sorrow that revived, I had just heard like a sentence of banishment the sound of the lift which, instead of stopping at my floor, went on higher. And yet the only person from whom I could have hoped for a visit would never come again, she was dead. And in spite of this, when the lift did stop at my floor, my heart throbbed, for an instant I said to myself: 'If, after all, it was only a dream! It is perhaps she, she is going to ring the bell, she has come back, Françoise will come in and say with more alarm than anger – for she is even more superstitious than vindictive, and would be less afraid of the living girl than of what she will perhaps take for a ghost – "Monsieur will never guess who is here." ' I tried not to think of anything, to take up a newspaper. But I found it impossible to read the articles written by men who felt no real grief. Of a trivial song, one of them said: 'It moves one to *tears*', whereas I myself would have listened to it with joy had Albertine been alive. Another, albeit a great writer, because he had been greeted with cheers when he alighted from a train, said that he had received 'an *unforgettable* welcome', whereas I, if it had been I who received that welcome, would not have given it even a moment's thought. And a third assured his readers that, but for its tiresome politics, life in Paris would be 'altogether delightful' whereas I knew well that even without politics that life could be nothing but atrocious to me, and would have seemed to me delightful, even with its politics, could I have found Albertine again. The sporting correspondent said (we were in the month of May): 'This season of the year is positively painful, let us say rather disastrous, to the true sportsman, for there is nothing, absolutely nothing in the way of game', and the art critic said of the Salon: 'In the face of this method of arranging an exhibition we are overwhelmed by an immense discouragement, by an infinite regret . . . ' If the force of the regret that I was feeling made me regard as untruthful and colourless the expressions of men who had no true happiness or sorrow in their lives, on the other hand the most insignificant lines which could, however remotely, attach themselves either to Normandy, or to Touraine, or to hydropathic establishments, or to Léa, or to the Princesse de Guermantes, or to love, or to absence, or to infidelity, at once set before my eyes, without my having the time to turn them away from it, the image of Albertine, and my tears started afresh.

Besides, in the ordinary course, I could never read these newspapers, for the mere act of opening one of them reminded me at once that I used to open them when Albertine was alive, and that she was alive no longer; I let them drop without having the strength to unfold their pages. Each impression called up an impression that was identical but marred, because there had been cut out of it Albertine's existence, so that I had never the courage to live to the end these mutilated minutes. Indeed, when, little by little, Albertine ceased to be present in my thoughts and all-powerful over my heart, I was stabbed at once if I had occasion, as in the time when she was there, to go into her room, to grope for the light, to sit down by the pianola. Divided among a number of little household gods, she dwelt for a long time in the flame of the candle, the doorbell, the back of a chair, and other domains more immaterial such as a night of insomnia or the emotion that was caused me by the first visit of a woman who had attracted me. In spite of this the few sentences which I read in the course of a day or which my mind recalled that I had read, often aroused in me a cruel jealousy. To do this, they required not so much to supply me with a valid argument in favour of the immorality of women as to revive an old impression connected with the life of Albertine. Transported then to a forgotten moment, the force of which my habit of thinking of it had not dulled, and in which Albertine was still alive, her misdeeds became more immediate, more painful, more agonising. Then I asked myself whether I could be certain that the bath-woman's revelations were false. A good way of finding out the truth would be to send Aimé to Touraine, to spend a few days in the neighbourhood of Mme Bontemps's villa. If Albertine enjoyed the pleasures which one woman takes with others, if it was in order not to be deprived of them any longer that she had left me, she must, as soon as she was free, have sought to indulge in them and have succeeded, in a district which she knew and to which she would not have chosen to retire had she not expected to find greater facilities there than in my house. No doubt there was nothing extraordinary in the fact that Albertine's death had so little altered my preoccupations. When our mistress is alive, a great part of the thoughts which form what we call our loves come to us during the hours when she is not by our side. Thus we acquire the habit of having as the object of our meditation an absent person, and one who, even if she remains absent for a few hours only, during those hours is no more than a memory. And so death does not make any great difference. When Aimé returned, I asked him to go down to Châtellerault, and thus not only by my thoughts, my sorrows, the emotion caused me by a name connected, however remotely, with a certain person, but even more by all my actions, by the enquiries that I undertook, by the use that I made of my money, all of which was devoted to the discovery of Albertine's actions, I may say that throughout this year my life remained filled with love, with a true bond of affection. And she who was its object was a corpse. We say at times that something may survive of a man after his death, if the man was an artist and took a certain amount of pains with his work. It is perhaps in the same way that a sort of cutting taken from one person and grafted on the heart of another continues to carry on its existence, even when the person from whom it had been detached has perished. Aimé established himself in quarters close to Mme Bontemps's villa; he made the acquaintance of a maidservant, of a job-master from whom Albertine had often hired a carriage by the day. These people had noticed nothing. In a second letter, Aimé informed me that he had learned from a young laundress in the town that Albertine had a peculiar way of gripping her arm when she brought back the clean linen. 'But,' she said, 'the young lady never did anything more.' I sent Aimé the money that paid for his journey, that paid for the harm which he had done me by his letter, and at the same time I was making an effort to discount it by telling myself that this was a familiarity which gave no proof of any vicious desire when I received a telegram from Aimé: 'Have learned most interesting things have abundant proofs letter follows.' On the following day came a letter the envelope of which was enough to make me tremble; I had guessed that it came from Aimé, for everyone, even the humblest of us, has under his control those little familiar spirits at once living and couched in a sort of trance upon the paper, the characters of his handwriting which he alone possesses. 'At first the young laundress refused to tell me anything, she assured me that Mlle Albertine had never done anything more than pinch her arm. But to get her to talk, I took her out to dinner, I made her drink. Then she told me that Mlle Albertine used often to meet her on the bank of the Loire, when she went to bathe, that Mlle Albertine who was in the habit of getting up very early to go and bathe was in the habit of meeting her by the water's edge, at a spot where the trees are so thick that nobody can see you, and besides there is nobody who can see you at that hour in the morning. Then the young laundress brought her friends and they bathed and afterwards, as it was already very hot down here and the sun scorched you even through the trees, they used to lie about on the grass getting dry and playing and caressing each other. The young laundress confessed to me that she loved to amuse herself with her young friends and that seeing Mlle Albertine was always wriggling against her in her wrapper she made her take it off and used to caress her with her tongue along the throat and arms, even on the soles of her feet which Mlle Albertine stretched out to her. The laundress undressed too, and they played at pushing each other into the water; after that she told me nothing more, but being entirely at your orders and ready to do anything in the world to please you, I took the young laundress to bed with me. She asked me if I would like her to do to me what she used to do to Mlle Albertine when she took off her bathing-dress. And she said to me: "If you could have seen how she used to quiver, that young lady, she said to me: (oh, it's just heavenly) and she got so excited that she could not keep from biting me." I could still see the marks on the girl's arms. And I can understand Mlle Albertine's pleasure, for the girl is really a very good performer.'

I had indeed suffered at Balbec when Albertine told me of her friendship with Mlle Vinteuil. But Albertine was there to comfort me. Afterwards when, by my excessive curiosity as to her actions, I had succeeded in making Albertine leave me, when Françoise informed me that she was no longer in the house and I found myself alone, I had suffered more keenly still. But at least the Albertine whom I had loved remained in my heart. Now, in her place – to punish me for having pushed farther a curiosity to which, contrary to what I had supposed, death had not put an end – what I found was a different girl, heaping up lies and deceits one upon another, in the place where the former had so sweetly reassured me by swearing that she had never tasted those pleasures which, in the intoxication of her recaptured liberty, she had gone down to enjoy to the point of swooning, of biting that young laundress whom she used to meet at sunrise on the bank of the Loire, and to whom she used to say: 'Oh, it's just heavenly.' A different Albertine, not only in the sense in which we understand the word different when it is used of other people. If people are different from what we have supposed, as this difference cannot affect us profoundly, as the pendulum of intuition cannot move outward with a greater oscillation than that of its inward movement, it is only in the superficial regions of the people themselves that we place these differences. Formerly, when I learned that a woman loved other women, she did not for that reason seem to me a different woman, of a peculiar essence. But when it is a question of a woman with whom we are in love, in order to rid ourselves of the grief that we feel at the thought that such a thing is possible, we seek to find out not only what she has done, but what she felt while she was doing it, what idea she had in her mind of the thing that she was doing; then descending and advancing farther and farther, by the profundity of our grief we attain to the mystery, to the essence. I was pained internally, in my body, in my heart – far more than I should have been pained by the fear of losing my life – by this curiosity with which all the force of my intellect and of my subconscious self collaborated;

and similarly it was into the core of Albertine's own being that I now projected everything that I learned about her. And the grief that had thus caused to penetrate to so great a depth in my own being the fact of Albertine's vice, was to render me later on a final service. Like the harm that I had done my grandmother, the harm that Albertine had done me was a last bond between her and myself which outlived memory even, for with the conservation of energy which belongs to everything that is physical, suffering has no need of the lessons of memory. Thus a man who has forgotten the charming night spent by moonlight in the woods, suffers still from the rheumatism which he then contracted. Those tastes which she had denied but which were hers, those tastes the discovery of which had come to me not by a cold process of reasoning but in the burning anguish that I had felt on reading the words: 'Oh, it's just heavenly', a suffering which gave them a special quality of their own, those tastes were not merely added to the image of Albertine as is added to the hermit-crab the new shell which it drags after it, but, rather, like a salt which comes in contact with another salt, alters its colour, and, what is more, its nature. When the young laundress must have said to her young friends: 'Just fancy, I would never have believed it, well, the young lady is one too!' to me it was not merely a vice hitherto unsuspected by them that they added to Albertine's person, but the discovery that she was another person, a person like themselves, speaking the same language, which, by making her the compatriot of other women, made her even more alien to myself, proved that what I had possessed of her, what I carried in my heart, was only quite a small part of her, and that the rest which was made so extensive by not being merely that thing so mysteriously important, an individual desire, but being shared with others, she had always concealed from me, she had kept me aloof from it, as a woman might have concealed from me that she was a native of an enemy country and a spy; and would indeed have been acting even more treacherously than a spy, for a spy deceives us only as to her nationality, whereas Albertine had deceived me as to her profoundest humanity, the fact that she did not belong to the ordinary human race, but to an alien race which moves among it, conceals itself among it and never blends with it. I had as it happened seen two paintings by Elstir showing against a leafy background nude women. In one of them, one of the girls is raising her foot as Albertine must have raised hers when she offered it to the laundress. With her other foot she is pushing into the water the other girl, who gaily resists, her hip bent, her foot barely submerged in the blue water. I remembered now that the raising of the thigh made the same swan's-neck curve with the angle of the knee that was made by the droop of Albertine's thigh when she was lying by my side on the bed, and I had often meant to tell her that she reminded me of those paintings. But I had refrained from doing so, in order not to awaken in her mind the image of nude female bodies. Now I saw her, side by side with the laundress and her friends, recomposing the group which I had so admired when I was seated among Albertine's friends at Balbec. And if I had been an enthusiast sensitive to absolute beauty, I should have recognised that Albertine re-composed it with a thousand times more beauty, now that its elements were the nude statues of goddesses like those which consummate sculptors scattered about the groves of Versailles or plunged in the fountains to be washed and polished by the caresses of their eddies. Now I saw her by the side of the laundress, girls by the water's edge, in their twofold nudity of marble maidens in the midst of a grove of vegetation and dipping into the water like bas reliefs of Naiads. Remembering how Albertine looked as she lay upon my bed, I thought I could see her bent hip, I saw it, it was a swan's neck, it was seeking the lips of the other girl. Then I beheld no longer a leg, but the bold neck of a swan, like that which in a frenzied sketch seeks the lips of a Leda whom we see in all the palpitation peculiar to feminine pleasure, because there is nothing else but a swan, and she seems more alone, just as we discover upon the telephone the inflections of a voice which we do not distinguish so long as it is not dissociated from a face in which we materialise its expression. In this sketch, the pleasure, instead of going to seek the face which inspires it and which is absent, replaced by a motionless swan, is concentrated in her who feels it. At certain moments the communication was cut between my heart and my memory. What Albertine had done with the laundress was indicated to me now only by almost algebraical abbreviations which no longer meant anything to me; but a hundred times in an hour the interrupted current was restored, and my heart was pitilessly scorched by a fire from hell, while I saw Albertine, raised to life by my jealousy, really alive, stiffen beneath the caresses of the young laundress, to whom she was saying: 'Oh, it's just heavenly.' As she was alive at the moment when she committed her misdeeds, that is to say at the moment at which I myself found myself placed, it was not sufficient to know of the misdeed, I wished her to know that I knew. And so, if at those moments I thought with regret that I should never see her again, this regret bore the stamp of my jealousy, and, very different from the lacerating regret of the moments in which I loved her, was only regret at not being able to say to her: 'You thought that I should never know what you did after you left me, well, I know everything, the laundress on the bank of the Loire, you said to her: "Oh, it's just heavenly", I have seen the bite.' No doubt I said to myself: 'Why torment myself? She who took her pleasure with the laundress no longer exists, and consequently was not a person whose actions retain any importance. She is not telling herself that I know. But no more is she telling herself that I do not know, since she tells herself nothing.' But this line of reasoning convinced me less than the visual image of her pleasure which brought me back to the moment in which she had tasted it. What we feel is the only thing that exists for us, and we project it into the past, into the future, without letting ourselves be stopped by the fictitious barriers of death. If my regret that she was dead was subjected at such moments to the influence of my jealousy and assumed this so peculiar form, that influence extended over my dreams of occultism, of immortality, which were no more than an effort to realise what I desired. And so at those moments if I could have succeeded in evoking her by turning a table as Bergotte had at one time thought possible, or in meeting her in the other life as the Abbé X thought, I would have wished to do so only in order to repeat to her: 'I know about the laundress. You said to her: "Oh, it's just heavenly", I have seen the bite.' What came to my rescue against this image of the laundress, was – certainly when it had endured for any while – the image itself, because we really know only what is novel, what suddenly introduces into our sensibility a change of tone which strikes us, the things for which habit has not yet substituted its colourless facsimiles. But it was, above all, this subdivision of Albertine in many fragments, in many Albertines, which was her sole mode of existence in me. Moments recurred in which she had merely been good, or intelligent, or serious, or even addicted to nothing but sport. And this subdivision, was it not after all proper that it should soothe me? For if it was not in itself anything real, if it depended upon the successive form of the hours in which it had appeared to me, a form which remained that of my memory as the curve of the projections of my magic lantern depended upon the curve of the coloured slides, did it not represent in its own manner a truth, a thoroughly objective truth too, to wit that each one of us is not a single person, but contains many persons who have not all the same moral value and that if a vicious Albertine had existed, it did not mean that there had not been others, she who enjoyed talking to me about Saint-Simon in her room, she who on the night when I had told her that we must part had said so sadly: 'That pianola, this room, to think that I shall never see any of these things again' and, when she saw the emotion which my lie had finally com-municated to myself, had exclaimed with a sincere pity: 'Oh, no, anything rather than make you unhappy, I promise that I will never try to see you again.' Then I was no longer alone. I felt the wall that separated us vanish. At the moment in which the good Albertine had returned, I had found again the one person from whom I could demand the antidote to the sufferings which Albertine was causing me. True, I still wanted to speak to her about the story of the laundress, but it was no longer by way of a cruel triumph, and to show her maliciously how much I knew. As I should have done had Albertine been alive, I asked her tenderly whether the tale about the laundress was true. She swore to me that it was not, that Aimé was not truthful and that, wishing to appear to have earned the money which I had given him, he had not liked to return with nothing to show, and had made the laundress tell him what he wished to hear. No doubt Albertine had been lying to me throughout. And yet in the flux and reflux of her contradictions, I felt that there had been a certain progression due to myself. That she had not indeed made me, at the outset, admissions (perhaps, it is true, involuntary in a phrase that escaped her lips) I would not have sworn. I no longer remembered. And besides she had such odd ways of naming certain things, that they might be interpreted in one sense or the other, but the feeling that she had had of my jealousy had led her afterwards to retract with horror what at first she had complacently admitted. Anyhow, Albertine had no need to tell me this. To be convinced of her innocence it was enough for me to embrace her, and I could do so now that the wall was down which parted us, like that impalpable and resisting wall which after a quarrel rises between two lovers and against which kisses would be shattered. No, she had no need to tell me anything. Whatever she might have done, whatever she might have wished to do, the poor child, there were sentiments in which, over the barrier that divided us, we could be united. If the story was true, and if Albertine had concealed her tastes from me, it was in order not to make me unhappy. I had the pleasure of hearing this Albertine say so. Besides, had I ever known any other? The two chief causes of error in our relations with another person are, having ourselves a good heart, or else being in love with the other person. We fall in love for a smile, a glance, a bare shoulder. That is enough; then, in the long hours of hope or sorrow, we fabricate a person, we compose a character. And when later on we see much of the beloved person, we can no longer, whatever the cruel reality that confronts us, strip off that good character, that nature of a woman who loves us, from the person who bestows that glance, bares that shoulder, than we can when she has grown old eliminate her youthful face from a person whom we have known since her girlhood. I called to mind the noble glance, kind and compassionate, of that Albertine, her plump cheeks, the coarse grain of her throat. It was the image of a dead woman, but, as this dead woman was alive, it was easy for me to do immediately what I should inevitably have done if she had been by my side in her living body (what I should do were I ever to meet her again in another life), I forgave her.

The moments which I had spent with this Albertine were so precious to me that I would not have let any of them escape me. Now, at times, as we recover the remnants of a squandered fortune, I recaptured some of these which I had thought to be lost; as I tied a scarf behind my neck instead of in front, I remembered a drive of which I had never thought again, before which, in order that the cold air might not reach my throat, Albertine had arranged my scarf for me in this way after first kissing me. This simple drive, restored to my memory by so humble a gesture, gave me the same pleasure as the intimate objects once the property of a dead woman who was dear to us which her old servant brings to us and which are so precious to us; my grief found itself enriched by it, all the more so as I had never given another thought to the scarf in question.

And now Albertine, liberated once more, had resumed her flight; men, women followed her. She was alive in me. I became aware that this prolonged adoration of Albertine was like the ghost of the sentiment that I had felt for her, reproduced its various elements and obeyed the same laws as the sentimental reality which it reflected on the farther side of death. For I felt quite sure that if I could place some interval between my thoughts of Albertine, or if, on the other hand, I had allowed too long an interval to elapse, I should cease to love her; a clean cut would have made me unconcerned about her, as I was now about my grandmother. A period of any length spent without thinking of her would have broken in my memory the continuity which is the very principle of life, which however may be resumed after a certain interval of time. Had not this been the case with my love for Albertine when she was alive, a love which had been able to revive after a quite long interval during which I had never given her a thought? Well, my memory must have been obedient to the same laws, have been unable to endure longer intervals, for all that it did was, like an aurora borealis, to reflect after Albertine's death the sentiment that I had felt for her, it was like the phantom of my love.

At other times my grief assumed so many forms that occasionally I no longer recognised it; I longed to be loved in earnest, decided to seek for a person who would live with me; this seemed to me to be the sign that I no longer loved Albertine, whereas it meant that I loved her still; for the need to be loved in earnest was, just as much as the desire to kiss Albertine's plump cheeks, merely a part of my regret. It was when I had forgotten her that I might feel it to be wiser, happier to live without love. And so my regret for Albertine, because it was it that aroused in me the need of a sister, made that need insatiable. And in proportion as my regret for Albertine grew fainter, the need of a sister, which was only an unconscious form of that regret, would become less imperious. And yet these two residues of my love did not proceed to shrink at an equal rate. There were hours in which I had made up my mind to marry, so completely had the former been eclipsed, the latter on the contrary retaining its full strength. And then, later on, my jealous memories having died away, suddenly at times a feeling welled up into my heart of affection for Albertine, and then, thinking of my own love affairs with other women, I told myself that she would have understood, would have shared them – and her vice became almost a reason for loving her. At times my jealousy revived in moments when I no longer remembered Albertine, albeit it was of her that I was jealous. I thought that I was jealous of Andrée, of one of whose recent adventures I had just been informed. But Andrée was to me merely a substitute, a bypath, a conduit which brought me indirectly to Albertine. So it is that in our dreams we give a different face, a different name to a person as to whose underlying identity we are not mistaken. When all was said, notwithstanding the flux and reflux which upset in these particular instances the general law, the sentiments that Albertine had left with me were more difficult to extinguish than the memory of their original cause. Not only the sentiments, but the sensations. Different in this respect from Swann who, when he had begun to cease to love Odette, had not even been able to recreate in himself the sensation of his love, I felt myself still reliving a past which was no longer anything more than the history of another person; my ego in a sense cloven in twain, while its upper extremity was already hard and frigid, burned still at its base whenever a spark made the old current pass through it, even after my mind had long ceased to conceive Albertine. And as no image of her accompanied the cruel palpitations, the tears that were brought to my eyes by a cold wind blowing as at Balbec upon the apple trees that were already pink with blossom, I was led to ask myself whether the renewal of my grief was not due to entirely pathological causes and whether what I took to be the revival of a memory and the final period of a state of love was not rather the first stage of heart disease.

There are in certain affections secondary accidents which the sufferer is too apt to confuse with the malady itself. When they cease, he is surprised to find himself nearer to recovery than he has supposed. Of this sort had been the suffering caused me – the complication brought about – by Aimé's letters with regard to the bathing establishment and the young laundress. But a healer of broken hearts, had such a person visited me, would have found that, in other respects, my grief itself was on the way to recovery. No doubt in myself, since I was a man, one of those amphibious creatures who are plunged simultaneously in the past and in the reality of the moment, there still existed a contradiction between the living memory of Albertine and my consciousness of her death. But this contradiction was so to speak the opposite of what it had been before. The idea that Albertine was dead, this idea which at first used to contest so furiously with the idea that she was alive that I was obliged to run away from it as children run away from a breaking wave, this idea of her death, by the very force of its incessant onslaught, had ended by capturing the place in my mind that, a short while ago, was still occupied by the idea of her life. Without my being precisely aware of it, it was now this idea of Albertine's death – no longer the present memory of her life – that formed the chief subject of my unconscious musings, with the result that if I interrupted them suddenly to reflect upon myself, what surprised me was not, as in earlier days, that Albertine so living in myself could be no longer existent upon the earth, could be dead, but that Albertine, who no longer existed upon the earth, who was dead, should have remained so living in myself. Built up by the contiguity of the memories that followed one another, the black tunnel, in which my thoughts had been straying so long that they had even ceased to be aware of it, was suddenly broken by an interval of sunlight, allowing me to see in the distance a blue and smiling universe in which Albertine was no more than a memory, unimportant and full of charm. Is it this, I asked myself, that is the true Albertine, or is it indeed the person who, in the darkness through which I have so long been rolling, seemed to me the sole reality? The person that I had been so short a time ago, who lived only in the perpetual expectation of the moment when Albertine would come in to bid him good-night and to kiss him, a sort of multiplication of myself made this person appear to me as no longer anything more than a feeble part, already half-detached from myself, and like a fading flower I felt the rejuvenating refreshment of an exfoliation. However, these brief illuminations succeeded perhaps only in making me more conscious of my love for Albertine, as happens with every idea that is too constant and has need of opposition to make it affirm itself. People who were alive during the war of 1870, for instance, say that the idea of war ended by seeming to them natural, not because they were not thinking sufficiently of the war, but because they could think of nothing else. And in order to understand how strange and important a fact war is, it was necessary that, some other thing tearing them from their permanent obsession, they should forget for a moment that war was being waged, should find themselves once again as they had been in a state of peace, until all of a sudden upon the momentary blank there stood out at length distinct the monstrous reality which they had long ceased to see, since there had been nothing else visible.

If, again, this withdrawal of my different impressions of Albertine had at least been carried out not in echelon but simultaneously, equally, by a general retirement, along the whole line of my memory, my impressions of her infidelities retiring at the same time as those of her kindness, oblivion would have brought me solace. It was not so. As upon a beach where the tide recedes unevenly, I would be assailed by the rush of one of my suspicions when the image of her tender presence had already withdrawn too far from me to be able to bring me its remedy. As for the infidelities, they had made me suffer, because, however remote the year in which they had occurred, to me they were not remote; but I suffered from them less when they became remote, that is to say when I pictured them to myself less vividly, for the remoteness of a thing is in proportion rather to the visual power of the memory that is looking at it than to the real interval of the intervening days, like the memory of last night's dream which may seem to us more distant in its vagueness and obliteration than an event which is many years old. But albeit the idea of Albertine's death made headway in me, the reflux of the sensation that she was alive, if it did not arrest that progress, obstructed it nevertheless and prevented its being regular. And I realise now that during this period (doubtless because of my having forgotten the hours in which she had been cloistered in my house, hours which, by dint of relieving me from any pain at misdeeds which seemed to me almost unimportant because I knew that she was not committing them, had become almost tantamount to so many proofs of her innocence), I underwent the martyrdom of living in the constant company of an idea quite as novel as the idea that Albertine was dead (previously I had always started from the idea that she was alive), with an idea which I should have supposed it to be equally impossible to endure and which, without my noticing it, was gradually forming the basis of my consciousness, was substituting itself for the idea that Albertine was innocent: the idea that she was guilty. When I believed that I was doubting her, I was on the contrary believing in her; similarly I took as the starting point of my other ideas the certainty – often proved false as the contrary idea had been – the certainty of her guilt, while I continued to imagine that I still felt doubts. I must have suffered intensely during this period, but I realise that it was inevitable. We are healed of a suffering only by experiencing it to the full. By protecting Albertine from any contact with the outer world, by forging the illusion that she was innocent, just as later on when I adopted as the basis of my reasoning the thought that she was alive, I was merely postponing the hour of my recovery, because I was postponing the long hours that must elapse as a preliminary to the end of the necessary sufferings. Now with regard to these ideas of Albertine's guilt, habit, were it to come into play, would do so according to the same laws that I had already experienced in the course of my life. Just as the name Guermantes had lost the significance and the charm of a road bordered with flowers in purple and ruddy clusters and of the window of Gilbert the Bad, Albertine's presence, that of the blue undulations of the sea, the names of Swann, of the lift-boy, of the Princesse de Guermantes and ever so many others had lost all that they had signified for me – that charm and that significance leaving in me a mere word which they considered important enough to live by itself, as a man who has come to set a subordinate to work gives him his instructions and after a few weeks withdraws – similarly the painful knowledge of Albertine's guilt would be expelled from me by habit. Moreover, between now and then, as in the course of an attack launched from both flanks at once, in this action by habit two allies would mutually lend a hand. It was because this idea of Albertine's guilt would become for me an idea more probable, more habitual, that it would become less painful. But on the other hand, because it would be less painful, the objections raised to my certainty of her guilt, which were inspired in my mind only by my desire not to suffer too acutely, would collapse one by one, and as each action precipitates the next, I should pass quickly enough from the certainty of Albertine's innocence to the certainty of her guilt. It was essential that I should live with the idea of Albertine's death, with the idea of her misdeeds, in order that these ideas might become habitual, that is to say that I might be able to forget these ideas and in the end to forget Albertine herself.

I had not yet reached this stage. At one time it was my memory made more clear by some intellectual excitement – such as reading a book – which revived my grief, at other times it was on the contrary my grief – when it was aroused, for instance, by the anguish of a spell of stormy weather – which raised higher, brought nearer to the light, some memory of our love.

Moreover these revivals of my love for Albertine might occur after an interval of indifference interspersed with other curiosities, as after the long interval that had dated from her refusal to let me kiss her at Balbec, during which I had thought far more about Mme de Guermantes, about Andrée, about Mme de Stermaria; it had revived when I had begun again to see her frequently. But even now various preoccupations were able to bring about a separation – from a dead woman, this time – in which she left me more indifferent. And even later on when I loved her less, this remained nevertheless for me one of those desires of which we soon grow tired, but which resume their hold when we have allowed them to lie quiet for some time. I pursued one living woman, then another, then I returned to my dead. Often it was in the most obscure recesses of myself, when I could no longer form any clear idea of Albertine, that a name came by chance to stimulate painful reactions, which I supposed to be no longer possible, like those dying people whose brain is no longer capable of thought and who are made to contract their muscles by the prick of a needle. And, during long periods, these stimulations occurred to me so rarely that I was driven to seek for myself the occasions of a grief, of a crisis of jealousy, in an attempt to re-attach myself to the past, to remember her better. Since regret for a woman is only a recrudescence of love and remains subject to the same laws, the keenness of my regret was enhanced by the same causes which in Albertine's lifetime had increased my love for her and in the front rank of which had always appeared jealousy and grief. But as a rule these occasions – for an illness, a war, can always last far longer than the most prophetic wisdom has calculated – took me unawares and caused me such violent shocks that I thought far more of protecting myself against suffering than of appealing to them for a memory.

Moreover a word did not even need to be connected, like 'Chaumont', with some suspicion (even a syllable common to different names was sufficient for my memory – as for an electrician who is prepared to use any substance that is a good conductor – to restore the contact between Albertine and my heart) in order to reawaken that suspicion, to be the password, the triumphant 'Open, Sesame' unlocking the door of a past which one had ceased to take into account, because, having seen more than enough of it, strictly speaking one no longer possessed it; one had been shorn of it, had supposed that by this subtraction one's own personality had changed its form, like a geometrical figure which by the removal of an angle would lose one of its sides; certain phrases for instance in which there occurred the name of a street, of a road, where Albertine might have been, were sufficient to incarnate a potential, non-existent jealousy, in the quest of a body, a dwelling, some material location, some particular realisation. Often it was simply during my sleep that these 'repetitions', these 'da capo' of our dreams which turn back in an instant many pages of our memory, many leaves of the calendar, brought me back, made me return to a painful but remote impression which had long since yielded its place to others but which now became present once more. As a rule, it was accompanied by a whole stage-setting, clumsy but appealing, which, giving me the illusion of reality, brought before my eyes, sounded in my ears what thenceforward dated from that night. Besides, in the history of a love-affair and of its struggles against oblivion, do not our dreams occupy an even larger place than our waking state, our dreams which take no account of the infinitesimal divisions of time, suppress transitions, oppose sharp contrasts, undo in an instant the web of consolation so slowly woven during the day, and contrive for us, by night, a meeting with her whom we would eventually have forgotten, provided always that we did not see her again. For whatever anyone may say, we can perfectly well have in a dream the impression that what is happening is real. This could be impossible only for reasons drawn from our experience which at that moment is hidden from us. With the result that this improbable life seems to us true. Sometimes, by a defect in the internal lighting which spoiled the success of the play, the appearance of my memories on the stage giving me the illusion of real life, I really believed that I had arranged to meet Albertine, that I was seeing her again, but then I found myself incapable of advancing to meet her, of uttering the words which I meant to say to her, to rekindle in order to see her the torch that had been quenched, impossibilities which were simply in my dream the immobility, the dumbness, the blindness of the sleeper – as suddenly one sees in the faulty projection of a magic lantern a huge shadow, which ought not to be visible, obliterate the figures on the slide, which is the shadow of the lantern itself, or that of the operator. At other times Albertine appeared in my dream, and proposed to leave me once again, without my being moved by her determination. This was because from my memory there had been able to filter into the darkness of my dream a warning ray of light which, lodged in Albertine, deprived her future actions, the departure of which she informed me, of any importance, this was the knowledge that she was dead. Often this memory that Albertine was dead was combined, without destroying it, with the sensation that she was alive. I conversed with her; while I was speaking, my grandmother came and went at the other end of the room. Part of her chin had crumbled away like a corroded marble, but I found nothing unusual in that. I told Albertine that I had various questions to ask her with regard to the bathing establishment at Balbec and to a certain laundress in Touraine, but I postponed them to another occasion since we had plenty of time and there was no longer any urgency. She assured me that she was not doing anything wrong and that she had merely, the day before, kissed Mlle Vinteuil on the lips. 'What? Is she here?' 'Yes, in fact it is time for me to leave you, for I have to go and see her presently.' And since, now that Albertine was dead, I no longer kept her a prisoner in my house as in the last months of her life, her visit to Mlle Vinteuil disturbed me. I sought to prevent Albertine from seeing her. Albertine told me that she had done no more than kiss her, but she was evidently beginning to lie again as in the days when she used to deny everything. Presently she would not be content, probably, with kissing Mlle Vinteuil. No doubt from a certain point of view I was wrong to let myself be disturbed like this, since, according to what we are told, the dead can feel, can do nothing. People say so, but this did not explain the fact that my grandmother, who was dead, had continued nevertheless to live for many years, and at that moment was passing to and fro in my room. And no doubt, once I was awake, this idea of a dead woman who continued to live ought to have become as impossible for me to understand as it is to explain. But I had already formed it so many times in the course of those transient periods of insanity which are our dreams, that I had become in time familiar with it; our memory of dreams may become lasting, if they repeat themselves sufficiently often. And long after my dream had ended, I remained tormented by that kiss which Albertine had told me that she had bestowed in words which I thought that I could still hear. And indeed, they must have passed very close to my ear since it was I myself that had uttered them.

All day long, I continued to converse with Albertine, I questioned her, I forgave her, I made up for my forgetfulness of the things which I had always meant to say to her during her life. And all of a sudden I was startled by the thought that to the creature invoked by memory to whom all these remarks were addressed, no reality any longer corresponded, that death had destroyed the various parts of the face to which the continual urge of the will to live, now abolished, had alone given the unity of a person. At other times, without my having dreamed, as soon as I awoke, I felt that the wind had changed in me; it was blowing coldly and steadily from another direction, issuing from the remotest past, bringing back to me the sound of a clock striking far-off hours, of the whistle of departing trains which I did not ordinarily hear. One day I tried to interest myself in a book, a novel by Bergotte, of which I had been especially fond. Its congenial characters appealed to me strongly, and very soon, reconquered by the charm of the book, I began to hope, as for a personal pleasure, that the wicked woman might be punished; my eyes grew moist when the happiness of the young lovers was assured. 'But then,' I exclaimed in despair, 'from my attaching so much importance to what Albertine may have done, I must conclude that her personality is something real which cannot be destroyed, that I shall find her one day in her own likeness in heaven, if I invoke with so many prayers, await with such impatience, learn with such floods of tears the success of a person who has never existed save in Bergotte's imagination, whom I have never seen, whose appearance I am at liberty to imagine as I please!' Besides, in this novel, there were seductive girls, amorous correspondences, deserted paths in which lovers meet, this reminded me that one may love clandestinely, it revived my jealousy, as though Albertine had still been able to stroll along deserted paths. And there was also the

incident of a man who meets after fifty years a woman whom he loved in her
youth, does not recognise her, is bored in her company. And this reminded
me that love does not last for ever and crushed me as though I were destined
to be parted from Albertine and to meet her again with indifference in my
old age. If I caught sight of a map of France, my timorous eyes took care not
to come upon Touraine so that I might not be jealous, nor, so that I might
not be miserable, upon Normandy where the map marked at least Balbec
and Doncières, between which I placed all those roads that we had traversed
so many times together. In the midst of other names of towns or villages of
France, names which were merely visible or audible, the name of Tours for
instance seemed to be differently composed, no longer of immaterial images,
but of venomous substances which acted in an immediate fashion upon my
heart whose beatings they quickened and made painful. And if this force
extended to certain names, which it had made so different from the rest,
how when I remained more shut up in myself, when I confined myself to
Albertine herself, could I be astonished that, emanating from a girl who was
probably just like any other girl, this force which I found irresistible, and to
produce which any other woman might have served, had been the result of
a confusion and of the bringing in contact of dreams, desires, habits,
affections, with the requisite interference of alternate pains and pleasures?
And this continued after her death, memory being sufficient to carry on the
real life, which is mental. I recalled Albertine alighting from a railway-
carriage and telling me that she wanted to go to Saint-Mars le Vêtu, and I
saw her again also with her 'polo' pulled down over her cheeks, I found once
more possibilities of pleasure, towards which I sprang saying to myself: 'We
might have gone on together to Incarville, to Doncières.' There was no
watering-place in the neighbourhood of Balbec in which I did not see her,
with the result that that country, like a mythological land which had been
preserved, restored to me, living and cruel, the most ancient, the most
charming legends, those that had been most obliterated by the sequel of my
love. Oh! what anguish were I ever to have to lie down again upon that bed
at Balbec around whose brass frame, as around an immovable pivot, a fixed
bar, my life had moved, had evolved, bringing successively into its compass
gay conversations with my grandmother, the nightmare of her death,
Albertine's soothing caresses, the discovery of her vice, and now a new life in
which, looking at the glazed bookcases upon which the sea was reflected, I
knew that Albertine would never come into the room again! Was it not, that
Balbec hotel, like the sole indoor set of a provincial theatre, in which for
years past the most diverse plays have been performed, which has served for
a comedy, for one tragedy, for a second, for a purely poetical drama, that

hotel which already receded quite far into my past? The fact that this part alone remained always the same, with its walls, its bookcases, its glass panes, through the course of fresh epochs in my life, made me more conscious that, in the total, it was the rest, it was myself that had changed, and gave me thus that impression that the mysteries of life, of love, of death, in which children imagine in their optimism that they have no share, are not set apart, but that we perceive with a dolorous pride that they have embodied themselves in the course of years in our own life.

I tried at times to take an interest in the newspapers. But I found the act of reading them repellent, and moreover it was not without danger to myself. The fact is that from each of our ideas, as from a clearing in a forest, so many roads branch in different directions that at the moment when I least expected it I found myself faced by a fresh memory. The title of Fauré's melody *le Secret* had led me to the Duc de Broglie's *Secret du Roi*, the name Broglie to that of Chaumont, or else the words 'Good Friday' had made me think of Golgotha, Golgotha of the etymology of the word which is, it seems, the equivalent of *Calvus Mons*, Chaumont. But, whatever the path by which I might have arrived at Chaumont, at that moment I received so violent a shock that I could think only of how to guard myself against pain. Some moments after the shock, my intelligence, which like the sound of thunder travels less rapidly, taught me the reason. Chaumont had made me think of the Buttes-Chaumont to which Mme Bontemps had told me that Andrée used often to go with Albertine, whereas Albertine had told me that she had never seen the Buttes-Chaumont. After a certain age our memories are so intertwined with one another that the thing of which we are thinking, the book that we are reading are of scarcely any importance. We have put something of ourself everywhere, everything is fertile, everything is dangerous, and we can make discoveries no less precious than in Pascal's *Pensées* in an advertisement of soap.

No doubt an incident such as this of the Buttes-Chaumont which at the time had appeared to me futile was in itself far less serious, far less decisive evidence against Albertine than the story of the bath-woman or the laundress. But, for one thing, a memory which comes to us by chance finds in us an intact capacity for imagining, that is to say in this case for suffering, which we have partly exhausted when it is on the contrary ourselves that deliberately applied our mind to recreating a memory. And to these latter memories (those that concerned the bath-woman and the laundress) ever present albeit obscured in my consciousness, like the furniture placed in the semi-darkness of a gallery which, without being able to see them, we avoid as we pass, I had grown accustomed. It was, on the contrary, a long time since I had given a

thought to the Buttes-Chaumont, or, to take another instance, to Albertine's
scrutiny of the mirror in the casino at Balbec, or to her unexplained delay on
the evening when I had waited so long for her after the Guermantes party, to
any of those parts of her life which remained outside my heart and which I
would have liked to know in order that they might become assimilated,
annexed to it, become joined with the more pleasant memories which
formed in it an Albertine internal and genuinely possessed. When I raised a
corner of the heavy curtain of habit (the stupefying habit which during the
whole course of our life conceals from us almost the whole universe, and in
the dead of night, without changing the label, substitutes for the most
dangerous or intoxicating poisons of life some kind of anodyne which does
not procure any delight), such a memory would come back to me as on the
day of the incident itself with that fresh and piercing novelty of a recurring
season, of a change in the routine of our hours, which, in the realm of
pleasures also, if we get into a carriage on the first fine day in spring, or leave
the house at sunrise, makes us observe our own insignificant actions with a
lucid exaltation which makes that intense minute worth more than the sum-
total of the preceding days. I found myself once more coming away from the
party at the Princesse de Guermantes's and awaiting the coming of Albertine.
Days in the past cover up little by little those that preceded them and are
themselves buried beneath those that follow them. But each past day has
remained deposited in us, as, in a vast library in which there are older books,
a volume which, doubtless, nobody will ever ask to see. And yet should this
day from the past, traversing the lucidity of the subsequent epochs, rise to
the surface and spread itself over us whom it entirely covers, then for a
moment the names resume their former meaning, people their former
aspect, we ourselves our state of mind at the time, and we feel, with a vague
suffering which however is endurable and will not last for long, the problems
which have long ago become insoluble and which caused us such anguish at
the time. Our ego is composed of the superimposition of our successive
states. But this superimposition is not unalterable like the stratification of a
mountain. Incessant upheavals raise to the surface ancient deposits. I found
myself as I had been after the party at the Princesse de Guermantes's,
awaiting the coming of Albertine. What had she been doing that evening?
Had she been unfaithful to me? With whom? Aimé's revelations, even if I
accepted them, in no way diminished for me the anxious, despairing interest
of this unexpected question, as though each different Albertine, each fresh
memory, set a special problem of jealousy, to which the solutions of the
other problems could not apply. But I would have liked to know not only
with what woman she had spent that evening, but what special pleasure the

action represented to her, what was occurring in that moment in herself. Sometimes, at Balbec, Françoise had gone to fetch her, had told me that she had found her leaning out of her window, with an uneasy, questing air, as though she were expecting somebody. Supposing that I learned that the girl whom she was awaiting was Andrée, what was the state of mind in which Albertine awaited her, that state of mind concealed behind the uneasy, questing gaze? That tendency, what importance did it have for Albertine? How large a place did it occupy in her thoughts? Alas, when I recalled my own agitation, whenever I had caught sight of a girl who attracted me, sometimes when I had merely heard her mentioned without having seen her, my anxiety to look my best, to enjoy every advantage, my cold sweats, I had only, in order to torture myself, to imagine the same voluptuous emotion in Albertine. And already it was sufficient to torture me, if I said to myself that, compared with this other thing, her serious conversations with me about Stendhal and Victor Hugo must have had very little weight with her, if I felt her heart attracted towards other people, detach itself from mine, incarnate itself elsewhere. But even the importance which this desire must have had for her and the reserve with which she surrounded it could not reveal to me what, qualitatively, it had been, still less how she qualified it when she spoke of it to herself. In bodily suffering, at least we do not have ourselves to choose our pain. The malady decides it and imposes it on us. But in jealousy we have to some extent to make trial of sufferings of every sort and degree, before we arrive at the one which seems appropriate. And what could be more difficult, when it is a question of a suffering such as that of feeling that she whom we loved is finding pleasure with persons different from ourselves who give her sensations which we are not capable of giving her, or who at least by their configuration, their aspect, their ways, represent to her anything but ourselves. Ah! if only Albertine had fallen in love with Saint-Loup! How much less, it seemed to me, I should have suffered! It is true that we are unaware of the peculiar sensibility of each of our fellow-creatures, but as a rule we do not even know that we are unaware of it, for this sensibility of other people leaves us cold. So far as Albertine was concerned, my misery or happiness would have depended upon the nature of this sensibility; I knew well enough that it was unknown to me, and the fact that it was unknown to me was already a grief – the unknown desires and pleasures that Albertine felt, once I was under the illusion that I beheld them, when, some time after Albertine's death, Andrée came to see me.

For the first time she seemed to me beautiful, I said to myself that her almost woolly hair, her dark, shadowed eyes, were doubtless what Albertine had so dearly loved, the materialisation before my eyes of what she used to take with her in her amorous dreams, of what she beheld with the prophetic eyes of desire on the day when she had so suddenly decided to leave Balbec.

Like a strange, dark flower that was brought to me from beyond the grave, from the innermost being of a person in whom I had been unable to discover it, I seemed to see before me, the unlooked-for exhumation of a priceless relic, the incarnate desire of Albertine which Andrée was to me, as Venus was the desire of Jove. Andrée regretted Albertine, but I felt at once that she did not miss her. Forcibly removed from her friend by death, she seemed to have easily taken her part in a final separation which I would not have dared to ask of her while Albertine was alive, so afraid would I have been of not succeeding in obtaining Andrée's consent. She seemed on the contrary to accept without difficulty this renunciation, but precisely at the moment when it could no longer be of any advantage to me. Andrée abandoned Albertine to me, but dead, and when she had lost for me not only her life but retrospectively a little of her reality, since I saw that she was not indispensable, unique to Andrée who had been able to replace her with other girls.

While Albertine was alive, I would not have dared to ask Andrée to take me into her confidence as to the nature of their friendship both mutually and with Mlle Vinteuil's friend, since I was never absolutely certain that Andrée did not repeat to Albertine everything that I said to her. But now such an enquiry, even if it must prove fruitless, would at least be unattended by danger. I spoke to Andrée not in a questioning tone but as though I had known all the time, perhaps from Albertine, of the fondness that Andrée herself had for women and of her own relations with Mlle Vinteuil's friend. She admitted everything without the slightest reluctance, smiling as she spoke. From this avowal, I might derive the most painful consequences; first of all because Andrée, so affectionate and coquettish with many of the young men at Balbec, would never have been suspected by anyone of practices which she made no attempt to deny, so that by analogy, when I discovered this novel Andrée, I might think that Albertine would have confessed them with the same ease to anyone other than myself whom she felt to be jealous. But on the other hand, Andrée having been Albertine's dearest friend, and the friend for whose sake she had probably returned in haste from Balbec, now that Andrée was proved to have these tastes, the conclusion that was forced upon my mind was that Albertine and Andrée had always indulged them together. Certainly, just as in a stranger's presence, we do not always dare to examine the gift that he has brought us, the wrapper of which we shall not unfasten until the donor has gone, so long as Andrée was with me I did not retire into myself to examine the grief that she had brought me, which, I could feel, was already causing my bodily servants, my nerves, my heart, a keen disturbance which, out of good breeding, I pretended not to notice, speaking on the contrary with the utmost affability to the girl who was my guest without diverting my gaze to these internal incidents. It was especially painful to me to hear Andrée say, speaking of Albertine: 'Oh yes, she always loved going to the Chevreuse valley.' To the vague and non-existent universe in which Albertine's excursions with Andrée occurred, it seemed to me that the latter had, by a posterior and diabolical creation, added an accursed valley. I felt that Andrée was going to tell me everything that she was in the habit of doing with Albertine, and, while I endeavoured from politeness, from force of habit, from self-esteem, perhaps from gratitude, to appear more and more affectionate, while the space that I had still been able to concede to Albertine's innocence became smaller and smaller, I seemed to perceive that, despite my efforts, I presented the paralysed aspect of an animal round which a steadily narrowing circle is slowly traced by the hypnotising bird of prey which makes no haste because it is sure of reaching when it chooses the victim that can no longer escape. I gazed at her nevertheless, and, with such liveliness, naturalness and assurance as a person can muster who is trying to make it appear that he is not afraid of being hypnotised by the other's stare, I said casually to Andrée: 'I have never mentioned the subject to you for fear of offending you, but now that we both find a pleasure in talking about her, I may as well tell you that I found out long ago all about the things of that sort that you used to do with Albertine. And I can tell you something that you will be glad to hear although you know it already: Albertine adored you.' I told Andrée that it would be of great interest to me if she would allow me to see her, even if she simply confined herself to caresses which would not embarrass her unduly in my presence, performing such actions with those of Albertine's friends who shared her tastes, and I mentioned Rose-monde, Berthe, each of Albertine's friends, in the hope of finding out something. 'Apart from the fact that not for anything in the world would I do the things you mention in your presence,' Andrée replied, 'I do not believe that any of the girls whom you have named have those tastes.' Drawing closer in spite of myself to the monster that was attracting me, I answered: 'What! You are not going to expect me to believe that, of all your band, Albertine was the only one with whom you did that sort of thing!' 'But I have never done anything of the sort with Albertine.' 'Come now, my dear Andrée, why deny things which I have known for at least three years, I see no harm in them, far from it. Talking of such things, that evening when she was so anxious to go with you the next day to Mme Verdurin's, you may remember perhaps . . . ' Before I had completed my sentence, I saw in Andrée's eyes, which it sharpened to a pinpoint like those stones which for that reason jewellers find it difficult to use, a fleeting, worried stare, like the heads of persons privileged to go behind the scenes who draw back the edge of the curtain before the play has begun and at once retire in order not to be seen. This uneasy stare vanished, everything had become quite normal, but I felt that anything which I might see hereafter would have been specially arranged for my benefit. At that moment I caught sight of myself in the mirror; I was struck by a certain resemblance between myself and Andrée. If I had not long since ceased to shave my upper lip and had had but the faintest shadow of a moustache, this resemblance would have been almost complete. It was perhaps when she saw, at Balbec, my moustache which had scarcely begun to grow, that Albertine had suddenly felt that impatient, furious desire to return to Paris. 'But I cannot, all the same, say things that are not true, for the simple reason that you see no harm in them. I swear to you that I never did anything with Albertine, and I am convinced that she detested that sort of thing. The people who told you were lying to you, probably with some ulterior motive,' she said with a questioning, defiant air. 'Oh, very well then, since you won't tell me,' I replied. I preferred to appear to be unwilling to furnish a proof which I did not possess. And yet I uttered vaguely and at random the name of the Buttes-Chaumont. 'I may have gone to the Buttes-Chaumont with Albertine, but is it a place that has a particularly evil reputation?' I asked her whether she could not mention the subject to Gisèle who had at one time been on intimate terms with Albertine. But Andrée assured me that after the outrageous way in which Gisèle had behaved to her recently, asking a favour of her was the one thing that she must absolutely decline to do for me. 'If you see her,' she went on, 'do not tell her what I have said to you about her, there is no use in making an enemy of her. She knows what I think of her, but I have always preferred to avoid having violent quarrels with her which only have to be patched up afterwards. And besides, she is a dangerous person. But you can understand that when one has read the letter which I had in my hands a week ago, and in which she lied with such absolute treachery, nothing, not even the noblest actions in the world, can wipe out the memory of such a thing.' In short, if, albeit Andrée had those tastes to such an extent that she made no pretence of concealing them, and Albertine had felt for her that strong affection which she had undoubtedly felt, notwithstanding this Andrée had never had any carnal relations with Albertine and had never been aware that Albertine had those tastes, this meant that Albertine did not have them, and had never enjoyed with anyone those relations which, rather than with anyone else, she would have enjoyed with Andrée. And so when Andrée had left me, I realised that so definite a statement had brought me peace of mind. But perhaps it had been dictated by a sense of the obligation, which Andrée felt that she owed to the dead girl whose memory still survived in her, not to let me believe what Albertine had doubtless, while she was alive, begged her to deny.

Novelists sometimes pretend in an introduction that while travelling in a foreign country they have met somebody who has told them the story of a person's life. They then withdraw in favour of this casual acquaintance, and the story that he tells them is nothing more or less than their novel. Thus the life of Fabrice del Dongo was related to Stendhal by a Canon of Padua. How gladly would we, when we are in love, that is to say when another person's existence seems to us mysterious, find some such well-informed narrator! And undoubtedly he exists. Do we not ourselves frequently relate, without any trace of passion, the story of some woman or other, to one of our friends, or to a stranger, who has known nothing of her love-affairs and listens to us with keen interest? The person that I was when I spoke to Bloch of the Duchesse de Guermantes, of Mme Swann, that person still existed, who could have spoken to me of Albertine, that person exists always . . . but we never come across him. It seemed to me that, if I had been able to find women who had known her, I should have learned everything of which I was unaware. And yet to strangers it must have seemed that nobody could have known so much of her life as myself. Did I even know her dearest friend, Andrée? Thus it is that we suppose that the friend of a Minister must know the truth about some political affair or cannot be implicated in a scandal. Having tried and failed, the friend has found that whenever he discussed politics with the Minister the latter confined himself to generalisations and told him nothing more than what had already appeared in the newspapers, or that if he was in any trouble, his repeated attempts to secure the Minister's help have ended invariably in an: 'It is not in my power' against which the friend is himself powerless. I said to myself: 'If I could have known such and such witnesses!' from whom, if I had known them, I should probably have been unable to extract anything more than from Andrée, herself the custodian of a secret which she refused to surrender. Differing in this respect also from Swann who, when he was no longer jealous, ceased to feel any curiosity as to what Odette might have done with Forcheville, even after my jealousy had subsided, the thought of making the acquaintance of Albertine's laundress, of the people in her neighbourhood, of reconstructing her life in it, her intrigues, this alone had any charm for me. And as desire always springs from a preliminary sense of

value, as had happened to me in the past with Gilberte, with the Duchesse
de Guermantes, it was, in the districts in which Albertine had lived in the
past, the women of her class that I sought to know, and whose presence
alone I could have desired. Even without my being able to learn anything
from them, they were the only women towards whom I felt myself attracted,
as being those whom Albertine had known or whom she might have known,
women of her class or of the classes with which she liked to associate, in a
word those women who had in my eyes the distinction of resembling her or
of being of the type that had appealed to her. As I recalled thus either
Albertine herself, or the type for which she had doubtless felt a preference,
these women aroused in me an agonising feeling of jealousy or regret, which
afterwards when my grief had been dulled changed into a curiosity not
devoid of charm. And among them especially the women of the working
class, on account of that life, so different from the life that I knew, which is
theirs. No doubt it is only in our mind that we possess things, and we do not
possess a picture because it hangs in our dining-room if we are incapable of
understanding it, or a landscape because we live in front of it without even
glancing at it. But still I had had in the past the illusion of recapturing
Balbec, when in Paris Albertine came to see me and I held her in my arms.
Similarly I obtained a contact, restricted and furtive as it might be, with
Albertine's life, the atmosphere of workrooms, a conversation across a
counter, the spirit of the slums, when I kissed a seamstress. Andrée, these
other women, all of them in relation to Albertine – as Albertine herself had
been in relation to Balbec – were to be numbered among those substitutes
for pleasures, replacing one another, in a gradual degradation, which enable
us to dispense with the pleasure to which we can no longer attain, a holiday
at Balbec, or the love of Albertine (as the act of going to the Louvre to look
at a Titian which was originally in Venice consoles us for not being able to
go there), for those pleasures which, separated one from another by
indistinguishable gradations, convert our life into a series of concentric,
contiguous, harmonic and graduated zones, encircling an initial desire
which has set the tone, eliminated everything that does not combine with it
and spread the dominant colour (as had, for instance, occurred to me also in
the cases of the Duchesse de Guermantes and of Gilberte). Andrée, these
women, were to the desire, for the gratification of which I knew that it was
hopeless, now, to pray, to have Albertine by my side, what one evening,
before I knew Albertine save by sight, had been the many-faceted and
refreshing lustre of a bunch of grapes.

   Associated now with the memory of my love, Albertine's physical and
social attributes, in spite of which I had loved her, attracted my desire on the

contrary towards what at one time it would least readily have chosen: dark girls of the lower middle class. Indeed what was beginning to a certain extent to revive in me was that immense desire which my love for Albertine had not been able to assuage, that immense desire to know life which I used to feel on the roads round Balbec, in the streets of Paris, that desire which had caused me so much suffering when, supposing it to exist in Albertine's heart also, I had sought to deprive her of the means of satisfying it with anyone but myself. Now that I was able to endure the thought of her desire, as that thought was at once aroused by my own desire, these two immense appetites coincided, I would have liked us to be able to indulge them together, I said to myself: 'That girl would have appealed to her', and led by this sudden digression to think of her and of her death, I felt too unhappy to be able to pursue my own desire any further. As, long ago, the Méséglise and Guermantes ways had established the conditions of my liking for the country and had prevented me from finding any real charm in a village where there was no old church, nor cornflowers, nor buttercups, so it was by attaching them in myself to a past full of charm that my love for Albertine made me seek out exclusively a certain type of woman; I began again, as before I was in love with her, to feel the need of things in harmony with her which would be interchangeable with a memory that had become gradually less exclusive. I could not have found any pleasure now in the company of a golden-haired and haughty duchess, because she would not have aroused in me any of the emotions that sprang from Albertine, from my desire for her, from the jealousy that I had felt of her love-affairs, from my sufferings, from her death. For our sensations, in order to be strong, need to release in us something different from themselves, a sentiment which will not find any satisfaction in pleasure, but which adds itself to desire, enlarges it, makes it cling desperately to pleasure. In proportion as the love that Albertine had felt for certain women ceased to cause me pain, it attached those women to my past, gave them something that was more real, as to buttercups, to hawthorn blossom the memory of Combray gave a greater reality than to unfamiliar flowers. Even of Andrée, I no longer said to myself with rage: 'Albertine loved her', but on the contrary, so as to explain my desire to myself, in a tone of affection: 'Albertine loved her dearly'. I could now understand the widowers whom we suppose to have found consolation and who prove on the contrary that they are inconsolable because they marry their deceased wife's sister. Thus the decline of my love seemed to make fresh loves possible for me, and Albertine like those women long loved for themselves who, later, feeling their lover's desire grow feeble, maintain their power by confining themselves to the office of panders, provided me, as the Pompadour provided Louis XV, with fresh damsels. Even in the past, my time had been divided into periods in which I desired this woman or that. When the violent pleasures afforded by one had grown dull, I longed for the other who would give me an almost pure affection until the need of more sophisticated caresses brought back my desire for the first. Now these alternations had come to an end, or at least one of the periods was being indefinitely prolonged. What I would have liked was that the newcomer should take up her abode in my house, and should give me at night, before leaving me, a friendly, sisterly kiss. In order that I might have believed – had I not had experience of the intolerable presence of another person – that I regretted a kiss more than a certain pair of lips, a pleasure more than a love, a habit more than a person, I would have liked also that the newcomers should be able to play Vinteuil's music to me like Albertine, to talk to me as she had talked about Elstir. All this was impossible. Their love would not be equivalent to hers, I thought, whether because a love to which were annexed all those episodes, visits to picture galleries, evenings spent at concerts, the whole of a complicated existence which allows correspondences, con-versations, a flirtation preliminary to the more intimate relations, a serious friendship afterwards, possesses more resources than love for a woman who can only offer herself, as an orchestra possesses more resources than a piano, or because, more profoundly, my need of the same sort of affection that Albertine used to give me, the affection of a girl of a certain culture who would at the same time be a sister to me, was – like my need of women of the same class as Albertine – merely a recrudescence of my memory of Albertine, of my memory of my love for her. And once again, I discovered, first of all that memory has no power of invention, that it is powerless to desire anything else, even anything better than what we have already possessed, secondly that it is spiritual in the sense that reality cannot furnish it with the state which it seeks, lastly that, when applied to a person who is dead, the resurrection that it incarnates is not so much that of the need to love in which it makes us believe as that of the need of the absent person. So that the resemblance to Albertine of the woman whom I had chosen, the resemblance of her affection even, if I succeeded in winning it, to Albertine's, made me all the more conscious of the absence of what I had been unconsciously seeking, of what was indispensable to the revival of my happiness, that is to say Albertine herself, the time during which we had lived together, the past in quest of which I had unconsciously gone. Certainly, upon fine days, Paris seemed to me innumerably aflower with all these girls, whom I did not desire, but who thrust down their roots into the obscurity of the desire and the mysterious nocturnal life of Albertine. They were like the girls of whom she had said to me at the outset, when she had not begun to distrust me: 'That girl is charming, what nice hair she has.' All the curiosity that I had felt about her life in the past when I knew her only by sight, and on the other hand all my desires in life were blended in this sole curiosity, to see Albertine in company with other women, perhaps because thus, when they had left her, I should have remained alone with her, the last and the master. And when I observed her hesitations, her uncertainty when she asked herself whether it would be worth her while to spend the evening with this or that girl, her satiety when the other had gone, perhaps her disappointment, I should have brought to the light of day, I should have restored to its true proportions the jealousy that Albertine inspired in me, because seeing her thus experience them I should have taken the measure and discovered the limit of her pleasures. Of how many pleasures, of what an easy life she has deprived us, I said to myself, by that stubborn obstinacy in denying her instincts! And as once again I sought to discover what could have been the reason for her obstinacy, all of a sudden the memory came to me of a remark that I had made to her at Balbec on the day when she gave me a pencil. As I rebuked her for not having allowed me to kiss her, I had told her that I thought a kiss just as natural as I thought it degrading that a woman should have relations with another woman. Alas, perhaps Albertine had never forgotten that imprudent speech.

I took home with me the girls who had appealed to me least, I stroked their virginal tresses, I admired a well-modelled little nose, a Spanish pallor. Certainly, in the past, even with a woman of whom I had merely caught sight on a road near Balbec, in a street in Paris, I had felt the individuality of my desire and that it would be adulterating it to seek to assuage it with another person. But life, by disclosing to me little by little the permanence of our needs, had taught me that, failing one person, we must content ourselves with another – and I felt that what I had demanded of Albertine another woman, Mme de Stermaria, could have given me. But it had been Albertine; and what with the satisfaction of my need of affection and the details of her body, an interwoven tangle of memories had become so inextricable that I could no longer detach from a desire for affection all that embroidery of my memories of Albertine's body. She alone could give me that happiness. The idea of her uniqueness was no longer a metaphysical *a priori* based upon what was individual in Albertine, as in the case of the women I passed in the street long ago, but an *a posteriori* created by the contingent and indissoluble overlapping of my memories. I could no longer desire any affection without feeling a need of her, without grief at her absence. Also the mere resemblance of the woman I had selected, of the affection that I asked of her to the happiness that I had known made me all the more conscious of all that was lacking before that happiness could revive. The same vacuum that I had found in my room after Albertine had left, and had supposed that I could fill by taking women in my arms, I found in them. They had never spoken to me, these women, of Vinteuil's music, of Saint-Simon's memoirs, they had not sprayed themselves with too strong a scent before coming to visit me, they had not played at interlacing their eyelashes with mine, all of which things were important because, apparently, they allow us to weave dreams round the sexual act itself and to give ourselves the illusion of love, but in reality because they formed part of my memory of Albertine and it was she whom I would fain have seen again. What these women had in common with Albertine made me feel all the more clearly what was lacking of her in them, which was everything, and would never be anything again since Albertine was dead. And so my love for Albertine which had drawn me towards these women made me indifferent to them, and perhaps my regret for Albertine and the persistence of my jealousy, which had already outlasted the period fixed for them in my most pessimistic calculations, would never have altered appreciably, had their existence, isolated from the rest of my life, been subjected merely to the play of my memories, to the actions and reactions of a psychology applicable to immobile states, and had it not been drawn into a vaster system in which souls move in time as bodies move in space. As there is a geometry in space, so there is a psychology in time, in which the calculations of a plane psychology would no longer be accurate because we should not be taking into account time and one of the forms that it assumes, oblivion; oblivion, the force of which I was beginning to feel and which is so powerful an instrument of adaptation to reality because it gradually destroys in us the surviving past which is a perpetual contradiction of it. And I ought really to have discovered sooner that one day I should no longer be in love with Albertine. When I had realised, from the difference that existed between what the importance of her person and of her actions was to me and what it was to other people, that my love was not so much a love for her as a love in myself, I might have deduced various consequences from this subjective nature of my love and that, being a mental state, it might easily long survive the person, but also that having no genuine connection with that person, it must, like every mental state, even the most permanent, find itself one day obsolete, be 'replaced', and that when that day came everything that seemed to attach me so pleasantly, indissolubly, to the memory of Albertine would no longer exist for me. It is the tragedy of other people that they are to us merely showcases for the very perishable collections of our own mind. For this very reason we base upon them projects which have all the ardour of our mind; but our mind grows tired, our memory crumbles, the day would arrive when I would readily admit the first comer to Albertine's room, as I had without the slightest regret given Albertine the agate marble or other gifts that I had received from Gilberte.

Translator's note:
In the French text of *Albertine Disparue*, Volume I ends with this chapter.

CHAPTER TWO

Mademoiselle de Forcheville

It was not that I was not still in love with Albertine, but no longer in the same fashion as in the final phase. No, it was in the fashion of the earliest times, when everything that had any connection with her, places or people, made me feel a curiosity in which there was more charm than suffering. And indeed I was quite well aware now that before I forgot her altogether, before I reached the initial stage of indifference, I should have, like a traveller who returns by the same route to his starting-point, to traverse in the return direction all the sentiments through which I had passed before arriving at my great love. But these fragments, these moments of the past are not immobile, they have retained the terrible force, the happy ignorance of the hope that was then yearning towards a time which has now become the past, but which a hallucination makes us for a moment mistake retrospectively for the future. I read a letter from Albertine, in which she had said that she was coming to see me that evening, and I felt for an instant the joy of expectation. In these return journeys along the same line from a place to which we shall never return, when we recall the names, the appearance of all the places which we have passed on the outward journey, it happens that, while our train is halting at one of the stations, we feel for an instant the illusion that we are setting off again, but in the direction of the place from which we have come, as on the former journey. Soon the illusion vanishes, but for an instant we felt ourselves carried away once again: such is the cruelty of memory.

At times the reading of a novel that was at all sad carried me sharply back, for certain novels are like great but temporary bereavements, they abolish our habits, bring us in contact once more with the reality of life, but for a few hours only, like a nightmare, since the force of habit, the oblivion that it creates, the gaiety that it restores to us because our brain is powerless to fight against it and to recreate the truth, prevails to an infinite extent over the almost hypnotic suggestion of a good book which, like all suggestions, has but a transient effect.

And yet, if we cannot, before returning to the state of indifference from which we started, dispense ourselves from covering in the reverse direction the distances which we had traversed in order to arrive at love, the trajectory, the line that we follow, are not of necessity the same. They have this in common, that they are not direct, because oblivion is no more capable than love of progressing along a straight line. But they do not of necessity take the same paths. And on the path which I was taking on my return journey, there were in the course of a confused passage three halting-points which I remember, because of the light that shone round about me, when I was already nearing my goal, stages which I recall especially, doubtless because I perceived in them things which had no place in my love for Albertine, or at most were attached to it only to the extent to which what existed already in our heart before a great passion associates itself with it, whether by feeding it, or by fighting it, or by offering to our analytical mind a contrast with it.

The first of these halting-points began with the coming of winter, on a fine Sunday, which was also All Saints' Day, when I had ventured out of doors. As I came towards the Bois, I recalled with sorrow how Albertine had come back to join me from the Trocadéro, for it was the same day, only without Albertine. With sorrow and yet not without pleasure all the same, for the repetition in a minor key, in a despairing tone, of the same motif that had filled my day in the past, the absence even of Françoise's telephone message, of that arrival of Albertine which was not something negative, but the suppression in reality of what I had recalled, of what had given the day a sorrowful aspect, made of it something more beautiful than a simple, unbroken day, because what was no longer there, what had been torn from it, remained stamped upon it as on a mould.

In the Bois, I hummed phrases from Vinteuil's sonata. I was no longer hurt by the thought that Albertine had fooled me, for almost all my memories of her had entered into that secondary chemical state in which they no longer cause any anxious oppression of the heart, but rather comfort. Now and then, at the passages which she used to play most often, when she was in the habit of uttering some reflection which I had thought charming at the time, of suggesting some reminiscence, I said to myself: 'Poor little girl', but without melancholy, merely adding to the musical phrase an additional value, a value that was so to speak historic and curious like that which the portrait of Charles I by Van Dyck, so beautiful already in itself, acquires from the fact that it found its way into the national collection because of Mme du Barry's desire to impress the King. When the little phrase, before disappearing altogether, dissolved into its various elements in which it floated still for a moment in scattered fragments, it was not for me as it had been for Swann a messenger from Albertine who was vanishing. It was not altogether the same association of ideas that the little phrase had aroused in me as in Swann. I had been impressed, most of all, by the elaboration, the attempts, the repetitions, the 'outcome' of a phrase which persisted throughout the sonata as that love had persisted throughout my life. And now, when I realised how, day by day, one element after another of my love departed, the jealous side of it, then some other, drifted gradually back in a vague remembrance to the feeble bait of the first outset, it was my love that I seemed, in the scattered notes of the little phrase, to see dissolving before my eyes.

As I followed the paths separated by undergrowth, carpeted with a grass that diminished daily, the memory of a drive during which Albertine had been by my side in the carriage, from which she had returned home with me, during which I felt that she was enveloping my life, floated now round about me, in the vague mist of the darkening branches in the midst of which the setting sun caused to gleam, as though suspended in the empty air, a horizontal web embroidered with golden leaves. Moreover my heart kept fluttering at every moment, as happens to anyone in whose eyes a rooted idea gives to every woman who has halted at the end of a path, the appearance, the possible identity of the woman of whom he is thinking. 'It is perhaps she!' We turn round, the carriage continues on its way and we do not return to the spot. These leaves, I did not merely behold them with the eyes of my memory, they interested me, touched me, like those purely descriptive pages into which an artist, to make them more complete, introduces a fiction, a whole romance; and this work of nature thus assumed the sole charm of melancholy which was capable of reaching my heart. The reason for this charm seemed to me to be that I was still as much in love with Albertine as ever, whereas the true reason was on the contrary that oblivion was continuing to make such headway in me that the memory of Albertine was no longer painful to me, that is to say, it had changed; but however clearly we may discern our impressions, as I then thought that I could discern the reason for my melancholy, we are unable to trace them back to their more remote meaning. Like those maladies the history of which the doctor hears his patient relate to him, by the help of which he works back to a more profound cause, of which the patient is unaware, similarly our impressions, our ideas, have only a symptomatic value. My jealousy being held aloof by the impression of charm and agreeable sadness which I was feeling, my senses reawakened. Once again, as when I had ceased to see Gilberte, the love of woman arose in me, rid of any exclusive association with any particular woman already loved, and floated like those spirits that have been liberated by previous destructions and stray suspended in the springtime air, asking only to be allowed to embody themselves in a new creature. Nowhere do there bud so many flowers, forget-me-not though they be styled, as in a cemetery. I looked at the girls with whom this fine day so countlessly blossomed, as I would have looked at them long ago from Mme de Villeparisis' carriage or from the carriage in which, upon a similar Sunday, I had come there with Albertine. At once, the glance which I had just cast at one or other of them was matched immediately by the curious, stealthy, enterprising glance, reflecting unimaginable thoughts, which Albertine had furtively cast at them and which, duplicating my own with a mysterious, swift, steel-blue wing, wafted along these paths which had hitherto been so natural the tremor of an unknown element with which my own desire would not have sufficed to animate them had it remained alone, for it, to me, contained nothing that was unknown.

Moreover at Balbec, when I had first longed to know Albertine, was it not because she had seemed to me typical of those girls the sight of whom had so often brought me to a standstill in the streets, upon country roads, and because she might furnish me with a specimen of their life? And was it not natural that now the cooling star of my love in which they were condensed should explode afresh in this scattered dust of nebulae? They all of them seemed to me Albertines – the image that I carried inside me making me find copies of her everywhere – and indeed, at the turning of an avenue, the girl who was getting into a motorcar recalled her so strongly, was so exactly of the same figure, that I asked myself for an instant whether it were not she that I had just seen, whether people had not been deceiving me when they sent me the report of her death. I saw her again thus at the corner of an avenue, as perhaps she had been at Balbec, getting into a car in the same way, when she was so full of confidence in life. And this other girl's action in climbing into the car, I did not merely record with my eyes, as one of those superficial forms which occur so often in the course of a walk: become a sort of permament action, it seemed to me to extend also into the past in the direction of the memory which had been superimposed upon it and which pressed so deliciously, so sadly against my heart. But by this time the girl had vanished.

A little farther on I saw a group of three girls slightly older, young women perhaps, whose fashionable, energetic style corresponded so closely with what had attracted me on the day when I first saw Albertine and her friends, that I hastened in pursuit of these three new girls and, when they stopped a carriage, looked frantically in every direction for another. I found one, but it was too late. I did not overtake them. A few days later, however, as I was coming home, I saw, emerging from the portico of our house, the three girls whom I had followed in the Bois. They were absolutely, the two dark ones especially, save that they were slightly older, the type of those young ladies who so often, seen from my window or encountered in the street, had made me form a thousand plans, fall in love with life, and whom I had never been able to know. The fair one had a rather more delicate, almost an invalid air, which appealed to me less. It was she nevertheless that was responsible for my not contenting myself with glancing at them for a moment, but, becoming rooted to the ground, staring at them with a scrutiny of the sort which, by their fixity which nothing can distract, their application as though to a problem, seem to be conscious that the true object is hidden far beyond what they behold. I should doubtless have allowed them to disappear as I had allowed so many others, had not (at the moment when they passed by me) the fair one – was it because I was scrutinising them so closely? – darted a stealthy glance at myself, then, having passed me and turning her head, a second glance which fired my blood. However, as she ceased to pay attention to myself and resumed her conversation with her friends, my ardour would doubtless have subsided, had it not been increased a hundredfold by the following incident. When I asked the porter who they were: 'They asked for Mme la Duchesse,' he informed me. 'I think that only one of them knows her and that the others were simply seeing her to the door. Here's the name, I don't know whether I've taken it down properly.' And I read: 'Mlle Déporcheville', which it was easy to correct to 'd'Éporcheville', that is to say the name, more or less, so far as I could remember, of the girl of excellent family, vaguely connected with the Guermantes, whom Robert had told me that he had met in a disorderly house, and with whom he had had relations. I now understood the meaning of her glance, why she had turned round, without letting her companions see. How often I had thought about her, imagining her in the light of the name that Robert had given me. And, lo and behold, I had seen her, in no way different from her friends, save for that concealed glance which established between me and herself a secret entry into the parts of her life which, evidently, were concealed from her friends, and which made her appear more accessible – almost half my own – more gentle than girls of noble birth generally are. In the mind of this girl, between me and herself, there was in advance the common ground of the hours that we might have spent together, had she been free to make an appointment with me. Was it not this that her glance had sought to express to me with an eloquence that was intelligible to myself alone? My heart throbbed until it almost burst, I could not have given an exact description of Mlle d'Éporcheville's appearance, I could picture vaguely a fair complexion viewed from the side, but I was madly in love with her. All of a sudden I became aware that I was reasoning as though, of the three girls, Mlle d'Éporcheville could be only the fair one who had turned round and had looked at me twice. But the porter had not told me this. I returned to his lodge, questioned him again, he told me that he could not enlighten me, but that he would ask his wife who had seen them once before. She was busy at the moment scrubbing the service stair. Which of us has not experienced in the course of his life these uncertainties more or less similar to mine, and all alike delicious? A charitable friend to whom we describe a girl that we have seen at a ball, concludes from our description that she must be one of his friends and invites us to meet her. But among so many girls, and with no guidance but a mere verbal portrait, may there not have been some mistake? The girl whom we are about to meet, will she not be a different girl from her whom we desire? Or on the contrary are we not going to see holding out her hand to us with a smile precisely the girl whom we hoped that she would be? This latter case which is frequent enough, without being justified always by arguments as conclusive as this with respect to Mlle d'Éporcheville, arises from a sort of intuition and also from that wind of fortune which favours us at times. Then, when we catch sight of her, we say to ourself: 'That is indeed the girl.' I recall that, among the little band of girls who used to parade along the beach, I had guessed correctly which was named Albertine Simonet. This memory caused me a keen but transient pang, and while the porter went in search of his wife, my chief anxiety – as I thought of Mlle d'Éporcheville and since in those minutes spent in waiting in which a name, a detail of information which we have, we know not why, fitted to a face, finds itself free for an instant, ready if it shall adhere to a new face to render, retrospectively, the original face as to which it had enlightened us strange, innocent, imperceptible – was that the porter's wife was perhaps going to inform me that Mlle d'Éporcheville was, on the contrary, one of the two dark girls. In that event, there would vanish the being in whose existence I believed, whom I already loved, whom I now thought only of possessing, that fair and sly Mlle d'Éporcheville whom the fatal answer must then separate into two distinct elements, which I had arbitrarily united after the fashion of a novelist who blends together diverse elements borrowed from reality in order to create an imaginary character, elements which, taken separately – the name failing to corroborate the supposed intention of the glance – lost all their meaning. In that case my arguments would be stultified, but how greatly they found themselves, on the contrary, strengthened when the porter returned to tell me that Mlle d'Éporcheville was indeed the fair girl.

From that moment I could no longer believe in a similarity of names. The coincidence was too remarkable that of these three girls one should be named Mlle d'Éporcheville, that she should be precisely (and this was the first convincing proof of my supposition) the one who had gazed at me in that way, almost smiling at me, and that it should not be she who frequented the disorderly houses.

Then began a day of wild excitement. Even before starting to buy all the bedizenments that I thought necessary in order to create a favourable impression when I went to call upon Mme de Guermantes two days later, when (the porter had informed me) the young lady would be coming again to see the Duchess, in whose house I should thus find a willing girl and make an appointment (or I should easily be able to take her into a corner for a moment), I began, so as to be on the safe side, by telegraphing to Robert to ask him for the girl's exact name and for a description of her, hoping to have his reply within forty-eight hours (I did not think for an instant of anything else, not even of Albertine), determined, whatever might happen to me in the interval, even if I had to be carried down in a chair were I too ill to walk, to pay a long call upon the Duchess. If I telegraphed to Saint-Loup it was not that I had any lingering doubt as to the identity of the person, or that the girl whom I had seen and the girl of whom he had spoken were still distinct personalities in my mind. I had no doubt whatever that they were the same person. But in my impatience at the enforced interval of forty-eight hours, it was a pleasure, it gave me already a sort of secret power over her to receive a telegram concerning her, filled with detailed information. At the telegraph office, as I drafted my message with the animation of a man who is fired by hope, I remarked how much less disconcerted I was now than in my boyhood and in facing Mlle d'Éporcheville than I had been in facing Gilberte. From the moment in which I had merely taken the trouble to write out my telegram, the clerk had only to take it from me, the swiftest channels of electric communication to transmit it across the extent of France and the Mediterranean, and all Robert's sensual past would be set to work to identify the person whom I had seen in the street, would be placed at the service of the romance which I had sketched in outline, and to which I need no longer give a thought, for his answer would undertake to bring about a happy ending before twenty-four hours had passed. Whereas in the old days, brought home by Françoise from the Champs-Elysées, brooding alone in the house over my impotent desires, unable to employ the practical devices of civilisation, I loved like a savage, or indeed, for I was not even free to move about, like à flower. From this moment I was in a continual fever; a request from my father that I would go away with him for a couple of days, which would have obliged me to forego my visit to the Duchess, filled me with such rage and desperation that my mother interposed and persuaded my father to allow me to remain in Paris. But for many hours my anger was unable to subside, while my desire for Mlle d'Éporcheville was increased a hundredfold by the obstacle that had been placed between us, by the fear which I had felt for a moment that those hours, at which I smiled in constant anticipation, of my call upon Mme de Guermantes, as at an assured blessing of which nothing could deprive me, might not occur. Certain philosophers assert that the outer world does not exist, and that it is in ourselves that we develop our life. However that may be, love, even in its humblest beginnings, is a striking example of how little reality means to us. Had I been obliged to draw from memory a portrait of Mlle d'Éporcheville, to furnish a description, an indication of her, or even to recognise her in the street, I should have found it impossible. I had seen her in profile, on the move, she had struck me as being simple, pretty, tall and fair, I could not have said anything more. But all the reactions of desire, of anxiety, of the mortal blow struck by the fear of not seeing her if my father took me away, all these things, associated with an image which, after all, I did not remember and as to which it was enough that I knew it to be pleasant, already constituted a state of love. Finally, on the following morning, after a night of happy sleeplessness I received Saint-Loup's telegram: 'de l'Orgeville, *de* preposition, *orge* the grain, barley, *ville* town, small, dark, plump, is at present in Switzerland.' It was not she!

A moment before Françoise brought me the telegram, my mother had come into my room with my letters, had laid them carelessly on my bed, as though she were thinking of something else. And withdrawing at once to leave me by myself, she had smiled as she left the room. And I, who was familiar with my dear mother's little subterfuges and knew that one could always read the truth in her face, without any fear of being mistaken, if one took as a key to the cipher her desire to give pleasure to other people, I smiled and thought: 'There must be something interesting for me in the post, and Mamma has assumed that indifferent air so that my surprise may be complete and so as not to be like the people who take away half your pleasure by telling you of it beforehand. And she has not stayed with me because she is afraid that in my pride I may conceal the pleasure that I shall feel and so feel it less keenly.' Meanwhile, as she reached the door she met Françoise who was coming into the room, the telegram in her hand. As soon as she had handed it to me, my mother had forced Françoise to turn back, and had taken her out of the room, startled, offended and surprised. For Françoise considered that her office conferred the privilege of entering my room at any hour of the day and of remaining there if she chose. But already, upon her features, astonishment and anger had vanished beneath the dark and sticky smile of a transcendent pity and a philosophical irony, a viscous liquid that was secreted, in order to heal her wound, by her outraged self-esteem. So that she might not feel herself despised, she despised us. Also she considered that we were masters, that is to say capricious creatures, who do not shine by their intelligence and take pleasure in imposing by fear upon clever people, upon servants, so as to show that they are the masters, absurd tasks such as that of boiling water when there is illness in the house, of mopping the floor of my room with a damp cloth, and of leaving it at the very moment when they intended to remain in it. Mamma had left the post by my side, so that I might not overlook it. But I could see that there was nothing but newspapers. No doubt there was some article by a writer whom I admired, which, as he wrote seldom, would be a surprise to me. I went to the window, and drew back the curtains. Above the pale and misty daylight, the sky was all red, as at the same hour are the newly lighted fires in kitchens, and the sight of it filled me with hope and with a longing to pass the night in a train and awake at the little country station where I had seen the milk-girl with the rosy cheeks.

Meanwhile I could hear Françoise who, indignant at having been banished from my room, into which she considered that she had the right of entry, was grumbling: 'If that isn't a tragedy, a boy one saw brought into the world. I didn't see him when his mother bore him, to be sure. But when I first knew him, to say the most, it wasn't five years since he was birthed!'

I opened the *Figaro*. What a bore! The very first article had the same title as the article which I had sent to the paper and which had not appeared, but not merely the same title . . . why, there were several words absolutely identical. This was really too bad. I must write and complain. But it was not merely a few words, there was the whole thing, there was my signature at the foot. It was my article that had appeared at last! But my brain which, even at this period, had begun to show signs of age and to be easily tired, continued for a moment longer to reason as though it had not understood that this was my article, just as we see an old man obliged to complete a movement that he has begun even if it is no longer necessary, even if an unforeseen obstacle, in the face of which he ought at once to draw back, makes it dangerous. Then I considered the spiritual bread of life that a newspaper is, still hot and damp from the press in the murky air of the morning in which it is distributed, at break of day, to the housemaids who bring it to their masters with their morning coffee, a miraculous, self-multiplying bread which is at the same time one and ten thousand, which remains the same for each person while penetrating innumerably into every house at once.

What I am holding in my hand is not a particular copy of the newspaper, it is any one out of the ten thousand, it is not merely what has been written for me, it is what has been written for me and for everyone. To appreciate exactly the phenomenon which is occurring at this moment in the other houses, it is essential that I read this article not as its author but as one of the ordinary readers of the paper. For what I held in my hand was not merely what I had written, it was the symbol of its incarnation in countless minds. And so, in order to read it, it was essential that I should cease for a moment to be its author, that I should be simply one of the readers of the *Figaro*. But then came an initial anxiety. Would the reader who had not been forewarned catch sight of this article? I open the paper carelessly as would this not forewarned reader, even assuming an air of not knowing what there is this morning in my paper, of being in a hurry to look at the social paragraphs and the political news. But my article is so long that my eye which avoids it (to remain within the bounds of truth and not to put chance on my side, as a person who is waiting counts very slowly on purpose) catches a fragment of it in its survey. But many of those readers who notice the first article and even read it do not notice the signature; I myself would be quite incapable of saying who had written the first article of the day before. And I now promise myself that I will always read them, including the author's name, but, like a jealous lover who refrains from betraying his mistress in order to believe in her fidelity, I reflect sadly that my own future attention will not compel the reciprocal attention of other people. And besides there are those who are going out shooting, those who have left the house in a hurry. And yet after all some of them will read it. I do as they do, I begin. I may know full well that many people who read this article will find it detestable, at the moment of reading it, the meaning that each word conveys to me seems to me to be printed on the paper, I cannot believe that each other reader as he opens his eyes will not see directly the images that I see, believing the author's idea to be directly perceived by the reader, whereas it is a different idea that takes shape in his mind, with the simplicity of people who believe that it is the actual word which they have uttered that proceeds along the wires of the telephone; at the very moment in which I mean to be a reader, my mind adjusts, as its author, the attitude of those who will read my article. If M. de Guermantes did not understand some sentences which would appeal to Bloch, he might, on the other hand, be amused by some reflection which Bloch would scorn. Thus for each part which the previous reader seemed to overlook, a fresh admirer presenting himself, the article as a whole was raised to the clouds by a swarm of readers and so prevailed over my own mistrust of myself which had no longer any need to analyse it. The truth of the matter is that the value of an article, however remarkable it may be, is like that of those passages in parliamentary reports in which the words: 'Wait and see!' uttered by the Minister, derive all their importance only from their appearing in the setting: The President of the Council, Minister of the Interior and of Religious Bodies: 'Wait and see!' (Outcry on the extreme Left. 'Hear, hear!' from the Left and Centre) – the main part of their beauty dwells in the minds of the readers. And it is the original sin of this style of literature, of which the famous Lundis are not guiltless, that their merit resides in the impression that they make on their readers. It is a synthetic Venus, of which we have but one truncated limb if we confine ourselves to the thought of the author, for it is realised in its completeness only in the minds of his readers. In them it finds its fulfilment. And as a crowd, even a select crowd, is not an artist, this final seal of approval which it sets upon the article must always retain a certain element of vulgarity. Thus Sainte-Beuve, on a Monday, could imagine Mme de Boigne in her bed with its eight columns reading his article in the *Constitutionnel*, appreciating some charming phrase in which he had long delighted and which might never, perhaps, have flowed from his pen had he not thought it expedient to load his article with it in order to give it a longer range. Doubtless the Chancellor, reading it for himself, would refer to it during the call which he would pay upon his old friend a little later. And as he took her out that evening in his carriage, the Duc de Noailles in his grey pantaloons would tell her what had been thought of it in society, unless a word let fall by Mme d'Herbouville had already informed her.

I saw thus at that same hour, for so many people, my idea or even failing my idea, for those who were incapable of understanding it, the repetition of my name and as it were a glorified suggestion of my personality, shine upon them, in a daybreak which filled me with more strength and triumphant joy than the innumerable daybreak which at that moment was blushing at every window.

I saw Bloch, M. de Guermantes, Legrandin, extracting each in turn from every sentence the images that it enclosed; at the very moment in which I endeavour to be an ordinary reader, I read as an author, but not as an author only. In order that the impossible creature that I am endeavouring to be may combine all the contrary elements which may be most favourable to me, if I read as an author, I judge myself as a reader, without any of the scruples that may be felt about a written text by him who confronts in it the ideal which he has sought to express in it. Those phrases in my article, when I wrote them, were so colourless in comparison with my thought, so complicated and opaque in comparison with my harmonious and transparent vision, so full of gaps which I had not managed to fill, that the reading of them was a torture to me, they had only accentuated in me the sense of my own impotence and of my incurable want of talent. But now, in forcing myself to be a reader, if I transferred to others the painful duty of criticising me, I succeeded at least in making a clean sweep of what I had attempted to do in first reading what I had written. I read the article forcing myself to imagine that it was written by someone else. Then all my images, all my reflections, all my epithets taken by themselves and without the memory of the check which they had given to my intentions, charmed me by their brilliance, their amplitude, their depth. And when I felt a weakness that was too marked taking refuge in the spirit of the ordinary and astonished reader, I said to myself: 'Bah! How can a reader notice that, there is something missing there, it is quite possible. But, be damned to them, if they are not satisfied! There are plenty of pretty passages, more than they are accustomed to find.' And resting upon this ten-thousandfold approval which supported me, I derived as much sense of my own strength and hope in my own talent from the article which I was reading at that moment as I had derived distrust when what I had written addressed itself only to myself.

No sooner had I finished this comforting perusal than I who had not had the courage to reread my manuscript, longed to begin reading it again immediately, for there is nothing like an old article by oneself of which one can say more aptly that 'when one has read it one can read it again'. I decided that I would send Françoise out to buy fresh copies, in order to give them to my friends, I should tell her, in reality so as to touch with my finger the miracle of the multiplication of my thought and to read, as though I were another person who had just opened the *Figaro*, in another copy the same sentences. It was, as it happened, ever so long since I had seen the Guer-mantes, I must pay them, next day, the call which I had planned with such agitation in the hope of meeting Mlle d'Éporcheville, when I telegraphed to Saint-Loup. I should find out from them what people thought of my article. I imagined some female reader into whose room I would have been so glad to penetrate and to whom the newspaper would convey if not my thought, which she would be incapable of understanding, at least my name, like a tribute to myself. But these tributes paid to one whom we do not love do not enchant our heart any more than the thoughts of a mind which we are unable to penetrate reach our mind. With regard to other friends, I told myself that if the state of my health continued to grow worse and if I could not see them again, it would be pleasant to continue to write to them so as still to have, in that way, access to them, to speak to them between the lines, to make them share my thoughts, to please them, to be received into their hearts. I told myself this because, social relations having previously had a place in my daily life, a future in which they would no longer figure alarmed me, and because this expedient which would enable me to keep the attention of my friends fixed upon myself, perhaps to arouse their admiration, until the day when I should be well enough to begin to see them again, consoled me. I told myself this, but I was well aware that it was not true, that if I chose to imagine their attention as the object of my pleasure, that pleasure was an internal, spiritual, ultimate pleasure which they themselves could not give me, and which I might find not in conversing with them, but in writing remote from them, and that if I began to write in the hope of seeing them indirectly, so that they might have a better idea of myself, so as to prepare for myself a better position in society, perhaps the act of writing would destroy in me any wish to see them, and that the position which literature would perhaps give me in society, I should no longer feel any wish to enjoy, for my pleasure would be no longer in society, but in literature.

After luncheon when I went down to Mme de Guermantes, it was less for the sake of Mlle d'Éporcheville who had been stripped, by Saint-Loup's telegram, of the better part of her personality, than in the hope of finding in the Duchess herself one of those readers of my article who would enable me to form an idea of the impression that it had made upon the public – subscribers and purchasers – of the *Figaro*. It was not however without pleasure that I went to see Mme de Guermantes. It was all very well my telling myself that what made her house different to me from all the rest was the fact that it had for so long haunted my imagination, by knowing the reason for this difference I did not abolish it. Moreover, the name Guermantes existed for me in many forms. If the form which my memory had merely noted, as in an address-book, was not accompanied by any poetry, older forms, those which dated from the time when I did not know Mme de Guermantes, were liable to renew themselves in me, especially when I had not seen her for some time and when the glaring light of the person with human features did not quench the mysterious radiance of the name. Then once again I began to think of the home of Mme de Guermantes as of something that was beyond the bounds of reality, in the same way as I began to think again of the misty Balbec of my early dreams, and as though I had not since then made that journey, of the one twenty-two train as though I had never taken it. I forgot for an instant my own knowledge that such things did not exist, as we think at times of a beloved friend forgetting for an instant that he is dead. Then the idea of reality returned as I set foot in the Duchess's hall. But I consoled myself with the reflection that in spite of everything it was for me the actual point of contact between reality and dreams.

When I entered the drawing-room, I saw the fair girl whom I had supposed for twenty-four hours to be the girl of whom Saint-Loup had spoken to me. It was she who asked the Duchess to 'reintroduce' me to her. And indeed, the moment I came into the room I had the impression that I knew her quite well, which the Duchess however dispelled by saying: 'Oh! You have met Mlle de Forcheville before.' I myself, on the contrary, was certain that I had never been introduced to any girl of that name, which would certainly have impressed me, so familiar was it in my memory ever since I had been given a retrospective account of Odette's love affairs and Swann's jealousy. In itself my twofold error as to the name, in having remembered 'de l'Orgeville' as 'd'Éporcheville' and in having reconstructed as 'd'Éporcheville' what was in reality 'Forcheville', was in no way extraordinary. Our mistake lies in our supposing that things present themselves ordinarily as they are in reality, names as they are written, people as photography and psychology give an unalterable idea of them. As a matter of fact this is not at all what we ordinarily perceive. We see, we hear, we conceive the world quite topsy-turvy. We repeat a name as we have heard it spoken until experience has corrected our mistake, which does not always happen. Everyone at Combray had spoken to Françoise for five-and-twenty years of Mme Sazerat and Françoise continued to say 'Mme Sazerin', not from that deliberate and proud perseverance in her mistakes which was habitual with her, was strengthened by our contradiction and was all that she had added of herself to the France of Saint-André-des-Champs (of the equalitarian principles of 1789 she claimed only one civic right, that of not pronouncing words as we did and of maintaining that 'hôtel', 'été' and 'air' were of the feminine gender), but because she really did continue to hear 'Sazerin'.*

This perpetual error which is precisely 'life', does not bestow its thousand forms merely upon the visible and the audible universe but upon the social universe, the sentimental universe, the historical universe, and so forth. The Princesse de Luxembourg is no better than a prostitute in the eyes of the Chief Magistrate's wife, which as it happens is of little importance; what is slightly more important, Odette is a difficult woman to Swann, whereupon he builds up a whole romance which becomes all the more painful when he discovers his error; what is more important still, the French are thinking only of revenge in the eyes of the Germans. We have of the universe only formless, fragmentary visions, which we complete by the association of arbitrary ideas, creative of dangerous suggestions. I should therefore have

* See Swann's Way, p. 84, where, however, this, error is attributed to Eulalie. C. K. S. M.

had no reason to be surprised when I heard the name Forcheville (and I was already asking myself whether she was related to the Forcheville of whom I had so often heard) had not the fair girl said to me at once, anxious no doubt to forestall tactfully questions which would have been unpleasant to her: 'You don't remember that you knew me quite well long ago . . . you used to come to our house . . . your friend Gilberte. I could see that you didn't recognise me. I recognised you immediately.' (She said this as if she had recognised me immediately in the drawing-room, but the truth is that she had recognised me in the street and had greeted me, and later Mme de Guermantes informed me that she had told her, as something very odd and extraordinary, that I had followed her and brushed against her, mistaking her for a prostitute.) I did not learn until she had left the room why she was called Mlle de Forcheville. After Swann's death, Odette, who astonished everyone by her profound, prolonged and sincere grief, found herself an extremely rich widow. Forcheville married her, after making a long tour of various country houses and ascertaining that his family would acknowledge his wife. (The family raised certain objections, but yielded to the material advantage of not having to provide for the expenses of a needy relative who was about to pass from comparative penury to opulence.) Shortly after this, one of Swann's uncles, upon whose head the successive demise of many relatives had accumulated an enormous fortune, died, leaving the whole of his fortune to Gilberte who thus became one of the wealthiest heiresses in France. But this was the moment when from the effects of the Dreyfus case there had arisen an anti-semitic movement parallel to a more abundant movement towards the penetration of society by Israelites. The politicians had not been wrong in thinking that the discovery of the judicial error would deal a fatal blow to anti-semitism. But provisionally at least a social anti-semitism was on the contrary enhanced and exacerbated by it. Forcheville who, like every petty nobleman, had derived from conversations in the family circle the certainty that his name was more ancient than that of La Rochefoucauld, considered that, in marrying the widow of a Jew, he had performed the same act of charity as a millionaire who picks up a prostitute in the street and rescues her from poverty and mire; he was prepared to extend his bounty to Gilberte, whose prospects of marriage were assisted by all her millions but were hindered by that absurd name 'Swann'. He declared that he would adopt her. We know that Mme de Guermantes, to the astonishment – which however she liked and was accustomed to provoke – of her friends, had, after Swann's marriage, refused to meet his daughter as well as his wife. This refusal had been apparently all the more cruel inasmuch as what had long made marriage with Odette seem possible to Swann was the prospect of introducing his daughter to Mme de Guermantes. And doubtless he ought to have known, he who had already had so long an experience of life, that these pictures which we form in our mind are never realised for a diversity of reasons. Among these there is one which meant that he seldom regretted his inability to effect that introduction. This reason is that, whatever the image may be, from the trout to be eaten at sunset which makes a sedentary man decide to take the train, to the desire to be able to astonish, one evening, the proud lady at a cash-desk by stopping outside her door in a magnificent carriage which makes an unscrupulous man decide to commit murder, or to long for the death of rich relatives, according to whether he is bold or lazy, whether he goes ahead in the sequence of his ideas or remains fondling the first link in the chain, the act which is destined to enable us to attain to the image, whether that act be travel, marriage, crime . . . that act modifies us so profoundly that we cease to attach any importance to the reason which made us perform it. It may even happen that there never once recurs to his mind the image which the man formed who was not then a traveller, or a husband, or a criminal, or a recluse (who has bound himself to work with the idea of fame and has at the same moment rid himself of all desire for fame). Besides even if we include an obstinate refusal to seem to have desired to act in vain, it is probable that the effect of the sunlight would not be repeated, that feeling cold at the moment we would long for a bowl of soup by the chimney-corner and not for a trout in the open air, that our carriage would leave the cashier unmoved who perhaps for wholly different reasons had a great regard for us and in whom this sudden opulence would arouse suspicion. In short we have seen Swann, when married, attach most importance to the relations of his wife and daughter with Mme Bontemps.

To all the reasons, derived from the Guermantes way of regarding social life, which had made the Duchess decide never to allow Mme and Mlle Swann to be introduced to her, we may add also that blissful assurance with which people who are not in love hold themselves aloof from what they condemn in lovers and what is explained by their love. 'Oh! I don't mix myself up in that, if it amuses poor Swann to do stupid things and ruin his life, it is his affair, but one never knows with that sort of thing, it may end in great trouble, I leave them to clear it up for themselves.' It is the *Suave mari magno* which Swann himself recommended to me with regard to the Verdurins, when he had long ceased to be in love with Odette and no longer formed part of the little clan. It is everything that makes so wise the judgments of third persons with regard to the passions which they do not feel and the complications of behaviour which those passions involve.

Mme de Guermantes had indeed applied to the ostracism of Mme and Mlle Swann a perseverance that caused general surprise. When Mme Molé, Mme de Marsantes had begun to make friends with Mme Swann and to bring a quantity of society ladies to see her, Mme de Guermantes had remained intractable but had made arrangements to blow up the bridges and to see that her cousin the Princesse de Guermantes followed her example. On one of the gravest days of the crisis when, during Rouvier's Ministry, it was thought that there was going to be war with Germany, upon going to dine with M. de Bréauté at Mme de Guermantes's, I found the Duchess looking worried. I supposed that, since she was always dabbling in politics, she intended to show that she was afraid of war, as one day when she had appeared at the dinner-table so pensive, barely replying in monosyllables, upon somebody's enquiring timidly what was the cause of her anxiety, she had answered with a grave air: 'I am anxious about China.' But a moment later Mme de Guermantes, herself volunteering an explanation of that anxious air which I had put down to fear of a declaration of war, said to M. de Bréauté: 'I am told that Marie-Aynard means to establish the Swanns. I simply must go and see Marie-Gilbert tomorrow and make her help me to prevent it. Otherwise, there will be no society left. The Dreyfus case is all very well. But then the grocer's wife round the corner has only to call herself a Nationalist and expect us to invite her to our houses in return.' And I felt at this speech, so frivolous in comparison with the speech that I expected to hear, the astonishment of the reader who, turning to the usual column of the *Figaro* for the latest news of the Russo-Japanese war, finds instead the list of people who have given wedding-presents to Mlle de Mortemart, the importance of an aristocratic marriage having displaced to the end of the paper battles upon land and sea. The Duchess had come in time moreover to derive from this perseverance, pursued beyond all normal limits, a satisfaction to her pride which she lost no opportunity of expressing. 'Babal,' she said, 'maintains that we are the two smartest people in Paris, because he and I are the only two people who do not allow Mme and Mlle Swann to bow to us. For he assures me that smartness consists in not knowing Mme Swann.' And the Duchess ended in a peal of laughter.

However, when Swann was dead, it came to pass that her determination not to know his daughter had ceased to furnish Mme de Guermantes with all the satisfaction of pride, independence, self-government, persecution which she was capable of deriving from it, which had come to an end with the passing of the man who had given her the exquisite sensation that she was resisting him, that he was unable to make her revoke her decrees.

Then the Duchess had proceeded to the promulgation of other decrees which, being applied to people who were still alive, could make her feel that she was free to act as she might choose. She did not speak to the Swann girl, but, when anyone mentioned the girl to her, the Duchess felt a curiosity, as about some place that she had never visited, which could no longer be suppressed by her desire to stand out against Swann's pretensions. Besides, so many different sentiments may contribute to the formation of a single sentiment that it would be impossible to say whether there was not a lingering trace of affection for Swann in this interest. No doubt – for in every grade of society a worldly and frivolous life paralyses our sensibility and robs us of the power to resuscitate the dead – the Duchess was one of those people who require a personal presence – that presence which, like a true Guermantes, she excelled in protracting – in order to love truly, but also, and this is less common, in order to hate a little. So that often her friendly feeling for people, suspended during their lifetime by the irritation that some action or other on their part caused her, revived after their death. She then felt almost a longing to make reparation, because she pictured them now – though very vaguely – with only their good qualities, and stripped of the petty satisfactions, of the petty pretensions which had irritated her in them when they were alive. This imparted at times, notwith-standing the frivolity of Mme de Guermantes, something that was distinctly noble – blended with much that was base – to her conduct. Whereas three-fourths of the human race flatter the living and pay no attention to the dead, she would often do, after their death, what the people would have longed for her to do whom she had maltreated while they were alive.

As for Gilberte, all the people who were fond of her and had a certain respect for her dignity, could not rejoice at the change in the Duchess's attitude towards her except by thinking that Gilberte, scornfully rejecting advances that came after twenty-five years of insults, would be avenging these at length. Unfortunately, moral reflexes are not always identical with what common sense imagines. A man who, by an untimely insult, thinks that he has forfeited for all time all hope of winning the friendship of a person to whom he is attached finds that on the contrary he has established his position. Gilberte, who remained quite indifferent to the people who were kind to her, never ceased to think with admiration of the insolent Mme de Guermantes, to ask herself the reasons for such insolence; once indeed (and this would have made all the people who showed some affection for her die with shame on her account) she had decided to write to the Duchess to ask her what she had against a girl who had never done her any injury. The Guermantes had assumed in her eyes proportions which their birth would have been powerless to give them. She placed them not only above all the nobility, but even above all the royal houses.

Certain women who were old friends of Swann took a great interest in Gilberte. When the aristocracy learned of her latest inheritance, they began to remark how well bred she was and what a charming wife she would make. People said that a cousin of Mme de Guermantes, the Princesse de Nièvre, was thinking of Gilberte for her son. Mme de Guermantes hated Mme de Nièvre. She announced that such a marriage would be a scandal. Mme de Nièvre took fright and swore that she had never thought of it. One day, after luncheon, as the sun was shining, and M. de Guermantes was going to take his wife out, Mme de Guermantes was arranging her hat in front of the mirror, her blue eyes gazing into their own reflection, and at her still golden hair, her maid holding in her hand various sunshades among which her mistress might choose. The sun came flooding in through the window and they had decided to take advantage of the fine weather to pay a call at Saint-Cloud, and M. de Guermantes, ready to set off, wearing pearl-grey gloves and a tall hat on his head said to himself: 'Oriane is really astounding still. I find her delicious', and went on, aloud, seeing that his wife seemed to be in a good humour: 'By the way, I have a message for you from Mme de Virelef. She wanted to ask you to come on Monday to the Opéra, but as she's having the Swann girl, she did not dare and asked me to explore the ground. I don't express any opinion, I simply convey the message. But really, it seems to me that we might . . . ' he added evasively, for their attitude towards anyone else being a collective attitude and taking an identical form in each of them, he knew from his own feelings that his wife's hostility to Mlle Swann had subsided and that she was anxious to meet her. Mme de Guermantes settled her veil to her liking and chose a sunshade. 'But just as you like, what difference do you suppose it can make to me, I see no reason against our meeting the girl. I simply did not wish that we should appear to be countenancing the dubious establishments of our friends. That is all.' 'And you were perfectly right,' replied the Duke. 'You are wisdom incarnate, Madame, and you are more ravishing than ever in that hat.' 'You are very kind,' said Mme de Guermantes with a smile at her husband as she made her way to the door. But, before entering the carriage, she felt it her duty to give him a further explanation: 'There are plenty of people now who call upon the mother, besides she has the sense to be ill for nine months of the year . . . It seems that the child is quite charming. Everybody knows that we were greatly attached to Swann. People will think it quite natural', and they set off together for Saint-Cloud.

A month later, the Swann girl, who had not yet taken the name of

Forcheville, came to luncheon with the Guermantes. Every conceivable subject was discussed; at the end of the meal, Gilberte said timidly: 'I believe you knew my father quite well.' 'Why of course we did,' said Mme de Guermantes in a melancholy tone which proved that she understood the daughter's grief and with a deliberate excess of intensity which gave her the air of concealing the fact that she was not sure whether she did remember the father. 'We knew him quite well, I remember him *quite well*.' (As indeed she might, seeing that he had come to see her almost every day for twenty-five years.) 'I know quite well who he was, let me tell you,' she went on, as though she were seeking to explain to the daughter whom she had had for a father and to give the girl information about him, 'he was a great friend of my mother-in-law and besides he was very intimate with my brother-in-law Palamède.' 'He used to come here too, indeed he used to come to luncheon here,' added M. de Guermantes with an ostentatious modesty and a scrupulous exactitude. 'You remember, Oriane. What a fine man your father was. One felt that he must come of a respectable family; for that matter I saw once, long ago, his own father and mother. They and he, what worthy people!'

One felt that if they had, parents and son, been still alive, the Duc de Guermantes would not have had a moment's hesitation in recommending them for a post as gardeners! And this is how the Faubourg Saint-Germain speaks to any bourgeois of the other bourgeois, whether in order to flatter him with the exception made – during the course of the conversation – in favour of the listener, or rather and at the same time in order to humiliate him. Thus it is that an anti-Semite in addressing a Jew, at the very moment when he is smothering him in affability, speaks evil of Jews, in a general fashion which enables him to be wounding without being rude.

But while she could shower compliments upon a person, when she met him, and could then never bring herself to let him take his leave, Mme de Guermantes was also a slave to this need of personal contact. Swann might have managed, now and then, in the excitement of conversation, to give the Duchess the illusion that she regarded him with a friendly feeling, he could do so no longer. 'He was charming,' said the Duchess with a wistful smile and fastening upon Gilberte a kindly gaze which would at least, supposing the girl to have delicate feelings, show her that she was understood, and that Mme de Guermantes, had the two been alone together and had circumstances allowed it, would have loved to reveal to her all the depth of her own feelings. But M. de Guermantes, whether because he was indeed of the opinion that the circumstances forbade such effusions, or because he considered that any exaggeration of sentiment was a matter for women and that men had no more part in it than in the other feminine departments, save the kitchen and the wine-cellar which he had reserved to himself, knowing more about them than the Duchess, felt it incumbent upon him not to encourage, by taking part in it, this conversation to which he listened with a visible impatience.

Moreover Mme de Guermantes, when this outburst of sentiment had subsided, added with a worldly frivolity, addressing Gilberte: 'Why, he was not only a great friend of my brother-in-law Charlus, he was also a great favourite at Voisenon' (the country house of the Prince de Guermantes), as though Swann's acquaintance with M. de Charlus and the Prince had been a mere accident, as though the Duchess's brother-in-law and cousin were two men with whom Swann had happened to be intimate for some special reason, whereas Swann had been intimate with all the people in that set, and as though Mme de Guermantes were seeking to make Gilberte understand who, more or less, her father had been, to 'place' him by one of those character sketches by which, when we seek to explain how it is that we happen to know somebody whom we would not naturally know, or to give an additional point to our story, we name the sponsors by whom a certain person was introduced.

As for Gilberte, she was all the more glad to find that the subject was dropped, in that she herself was anxious only to change it, having inherited from Swann his exquisite tact combined with an intellectual charm that was appreciated by the Duke and Duchess who begged her to come again soon. Moreover, with the minute observation of people whose lives have no purpose, they would discern, one after another, in the people with whom they associated, the most obvious merits, exclaiming their wonder at them with the artless astonishment of a townsman who on going into the country discovers a blade of grass, or on the contrary magnifying them as with a microscope, making endless comments, taking offence at the slightest faults, and often applying both processes alternately to the same person. In Gilberte's case it was first of all upon these minor attractions that the idle perspicacity of M. and Mme de Guermantes was brought to bear: 'Did you notice the way in which she pronounced some of her words?' the Duchess said to her husband after the girl had left them; 'it was just like Swann, I seemed to hear him speaking.' 'I was just about to say the very same, Oriane.' 'She is witty, she is just like her father.' 'I consider that she is even far superior to him. Think how well she told that story about the sea-bathing, she has a vivacity that Swann never had.' 'Oh! but he was, after all, quite witty.' 'I am not saying that he was not witty, I say that he lacked vivacity,' said M. de Guermantes in a complaining tone, for his gout made him irritable, and when he had no one else upon whom to vent his irritation, it was to the Duchess that he displayed it. But being incapable of any clear understanding of its causes, he preferred to adopt an air of being misunderstood.

This friendly attitude on the part of the Duke and Duchess meant that, for the future, they might at the most let fall an occasional 'your poor father' to Gilberte, which, for that matter, was quite unnecessary, since it was just about this time that Forcheville adopted the girl. She addressed him as 'Father', charmed all the dowagers by her politeness and air of breeding, and it was admitted that, if Forcheville had behaved with the utmost generosity towards her, the girl had a good heart and knew how to reward him for his pains. Doubtless because she was able, now and then, and desired to show herself quite at her ease, she had reintroduced herself to me and in conversation with me had spoken of her true father. But this was an exception and no one now dared utter the name Swann in her presence.

I had just caught sight, in the drawing-room, of two sketches by Elstir which formerly had been banished to a little room upstairs in which it was only by chance that I had seen them. Elstir was now in fashion, Mme de Guermantes could not forgive herself for having given so many of his pictures to her cousin, not because they were in fashion, but because she now appreciated them. Fashion is, indeed, composed of the appreciations of a number of people of whom the Guermantes are typical. But she could not dream of buying others of his pictures, for they had long ago begun to fetch absurdly high prices. She was determined to have something, at least, by Elstir in her drawing-room and had brought down these two drawings which, she declared, she 'preferred to his paintings'.

Gilberte recognised the drawings. 'One would say Elstir,' she suggested. 'Why, yes,' replied the Duchess without thinking, 'it was, as a matter of fact, your fa . . . some friends of ours who made us buy them. They are admirable. To my mind, they are superior to his paintings.' I who had not heard this conversation went closer to the drawings to examine them. 'Why, this is the Elstir that . . . ' I saw Mme de Guermantes's signals of despair. 'Ah, yes! The Elstir that I admired upstairs. It shows far better here than in that passage. Talking of Elstir, I mentioned him yesterday in an article in the *Figaro*. Did you happen to read it?' 'You have written an article in the *Figaro*?' exclaimed M. de Guermantes with the same violence as if he had exclaimed: 'Why, she is my cousin.' 'Yes, yesterday.' 'In the *Figaro*, you are certain? That is a great surprise. For we each of us get our *Figaro*, and if one of us had missed it, the other would certainly have noticed it. That is so, ain't it, Oriane, there was nothing in the paper.' The Duke sent for the *Figaro* and accepted the facts, as though, previously, the probability had been that I had made a mistake as to the newspaper for which I had written. 'What's that, I don't understand, do you mean to say, you have written an article in the *Figaro*,' said the Duchess, making an effort in order to speak of a matter which did not interest her. 'Come, Basin, you can read it afterwards.' 'No, the Duke looks so nice like that with his big beard sweeping over the paper,' said Gilberte. 'I shall read it as soon as I am at home.' 'Yes, he wears a beard now that everybody is clean-shaven,' said the Duchess, 'he never does anything like other people. When we were first married, he shaved not only his beard but his moustaches as well. The peasants who didn't know him by sight thought that he couldn't be French. He was called at that time the Prince des Laumes.' 'Is there still a Prince des Laumes?' asked Gilberte, who was interested in everything that concerned the people who had refused to bow to her during all those years. 'Why, no!' the Duchess replied with a melancholy, caressing gaze. 'Such a charming title! One of the finest titles in France!' said Gilberte, a certain sort of banality emerging inevitably, as a clock strikes the hour, from the lips of certain quite intelligent persons. 'Yes, indeed, I regret it too. Basin would have liked his sister's son to take it, but it is not the same thing; after all it is possible, since it is not necessarily the eldest son, the title may pass to a younger brother. I was telling you that in those days Basin was clean-shaven; one day, at a pilgrimage – you remember, my dear,' she turned to her husband, 'that pilgrimage at Paray-le-Monial – my brother-in-law Charlus who always enjoys talking to peasants, was saying to one after another: 'Where do you come from?' and as he is extremely generous, he would give them something, take them off to have a drink. For nobody was ever at the same time simpler and more haughty than Même. You'll see him refuse to bow to a Duchess whom he doesn't think duchessy enough, and shower compliments upon a kennelman. And so, I said to Basin: "Come, Basin, say something to them too." My husband, who is not always very inventive – ' 'Thank you, Oriane,' said the Duke, without interrupting his reading of my article in which he was immersed – 'approached one of the peasants and repeated his brother's question in so many words: "Where do you come from?" "I am from Les Laumes." "You are from Les Laumes. Why, I am your Prince." Then the peasant looked at Basin's smooth face and replied: " 's not true. You're an English." ' * One saw thus in these anecdotes told by the Duchess those great and eminent titles, such as that of the Prince des Laumes, rise to their true position, in their original state and their local

---

* Translator's footnote: Mme de Guermantes forgets that she has already told this story at the expense of the Prince de Léon. See *The Captive*, pp. 473–4.

colour, as in certain Books of Hours one sees, amid the mob of the period, the soaring steeple of Bourges.

Some cards were brought to her which a footman had just left at the door. 'I can't think what has come over her, I don't know her. It is to you that I am indebted for this, Basin. Not that they have done you any good, all these people, my poor dear', and, turning to Gilberte: 'I really don't know how to explain to you who she is, you certainly have never heard of her, she calls herself Lady Rufus Israel.'

Gilberte flushed crimson: 'I do not know her,' she said (which was all the more untrue in that Lady Israel and Swann had been reconciled two years before the latter's death and she addressed Gilberte by her Christian name), 'but I know quite well, from hearing about her, who it is that you mean.' The truth is that Gilberte had become a great snob. For instance, another girl having one day, whether in malice or from a natural want of tact, asked her what was the name of her real – not her adoptive – father, in her confusion, and as though to mitigate the crudity of what she had to say, instead of pronouncing the name as 'Souann' she said 'Svann', a change, as she soon realised, for the worse, since it made this name of English origin a German patronymic. And she had even gone on to say, abasing herself so as to rise higher: 'All sorts of stories have been told about my birth, but of course I know nothing about that.'

Ashamed as Gilberte must have felt at certain moments when she thought of her parents (for even Mme Swann represented to her and was a good mother) of such an attitude towards life, we must, alas, bear in mind that its elements were borrowed doubtless from her parents, for we do not create the whole of our own personality. But with a certain quantity of egoism which exists in the mother, a different egoism, inherent in the father's family, is combined, which does not invariably mean that it is added, nor even precisely that it serves as a multiple, but rather that it creates a fresh egoism infinitely stronger and more redoubtable. And, in the period that has elapsed since the world began, during which families in which some defect exists in one form have been intermarrying with families in which the same defect exists in another, thereby creating a peculiarly complex and detestable variety of that defect in the offspring, the accumulated egoisms (to confine ourselves, for the moment, to this defect) would have acquired such force that the whole human race would have been destroyed, did not the malady itself bring forth, with the power to reduce it to its true dimensions, natural restrictions analogous to those which prevent the infinite proliferation of the infusoria from destroying our planet, the unisexual fertilisation of plants from bringing about the extinction of the vegetable kingdom, and so forth. From time to time a virtue combines with this egoism to produce a new and disinterested force.

The combinations by which, in the course of generations, moral chemistry thus stabilises and renders inoffensive the elements that were becoming too formidable, are infinite and would give an exciting variety to family history. Moreover with these accumulated egoisms such as must have been embodied in Gilberte there coexists some charming virtue of the parents; it appears for a moment to perform an interlude by itself, to play its touching part with an entire sincerity.

No doubt Gilberte did not always go so far as when she insinuated that she was perhaps the natural daughter of some great personage, but as a rule she concealed her origin. Perhaps it was simply too painful for her to confess it and she preferred that people should learn of it from others. Perhaps she really believed that she was hiding it, with that uncertain belief which at the same time is not doubt, which reserves a possibility for what we would like to think true, of which Musset furnishes an example when he speaks of Hope in God. 'I do not know her personally,' Gilberte went on. Had she after all, when she called herself Mlle de Forcheville, a hope that people would not know that she was Swann's daughter? Some people, perhaps, who, she hoped, would in time become everybody. She could not be under any illusion as to their number at the moment, and knew doubtless that many people must be murmuring: 'Isn't that Swann's daughter?' But she knew it only with that information which tells us of people taking their lives in desperation while we are going to a ball, that is to say a remote and vague information for which we are at no pains to substitute a more precise knowledge, founded upon a direct impression. Gilberte belonged, during these years at least, to the most widespread variety of the human ostrich, the kind which buries its head in the hope not of not being seen, which it considers hardly probable, but of not seeing that other people see it, which seems to it something to the good and enables it to leave the rest to chance. As distance makes things smaller, more uncertain, less dangerous, Gilberte preferred not to be near other people at the moment when they made the discovery that she was by birth a Swann.

And as we are near the people whom we picture to ourselves, as we can picture people reading their newspaper, Gilberte preferred the papers to style her Mlle de Forcheville. It is true that with the writings for which she herself was responsible, her letters, she prolonged the transition for some time by signing herself 'G. S. Forcheville'. The real hypocrisy in this signature was made manifest by the suppression not so much of the other letters of the word 'Swann' as of those of the word 'Gilberte'. In fact, by reducing the innocent Christian name to a simple G, Mlle de Forcheville seemed to insinuate to her friends that the similar amputation applied to the name 'Swann' was due merely to the necessity of abbreviation. Indeed she gave a special importance to the S, and gave it a sort of long tail which ran across the 'G', but which one felt to be transitory and destined to disappear like the tail which, still long in the monkey, has ceased to exist in man.

Notwithstanding this, in her snobbishness, there remained the intelligent curiosity of Swann. I remember that, during this same afternoon, she asked Mme de Guermantes whether she could meet M. du Lau, and that when the Duchess replied that he was an invalid and never went out, Gilberte asked what sort of man he was, for, she added with a faint blush, she had heard a great deal about him. (The Marquis du Lau had indeed been one of Swann's most intimate friends before the latter's marriage, and Gilberte may perhaps herself have seen him, but at a time when she was not interested in such people.) 'Would M. de Bréauté or the Prince d'Agrigente be at all like him?' she asked. 'Oh! not in the least,' exclaimed Mme de Guermantes, who had a keen sense of these provincial differences and drew portraits that were sober, but coloured by her harsh, golden voice, beneath the gentle blossoming of her violet eyes. 'No, not in the least. Du Lau was the gentleman from the Périgord, charming, with all the good manners and the absence of ceremony of his province. At Guermantes, when we had the King of England, with whom du Lau was on the friendliest terms, we used to have a little meal after the men came in from shooting . . . It was the hour when du Lau was in the habit of going to his room to take off his boots and put on big woollen slippers. Very well, the presence of King Edward and all the Grand Dukes did not disturb him in the least, he came down to the great hall at Guermantes in his woollen slippers, he felt that he was the Marquis du Lau d'Ollemans who had no reason to put himself out for the King of England. He and that charming Quasimodo de Breteuil, they were the two that I liked best. They were, for that matter, great friends of . . . ' (she was about to say 'your father' and stopped short). 'No, there is no resemblance at all, either to Gri-gri, or to Bréauté. He was the genuine nobleman from the Périgord. For that matter, Même quotes a page from Saint-Simon about a Marquis d'Ollemans, it is just like him.' I repeated the opening words of the portrait: 'M. d'Ollemans who was a man of great distinction among the nobility of the Périgord, from his own birth and from his merit, and was regarded by every soul alive there as a general arbiter to whom each had recourse because of his probity, his capacity and the suavity of his manners, as it were the cock of his province.' 'Yes, he's like that,' said Mme de Guermantes, 'all the more so as du Lau was always as

red as a cock.' 'Yes, I remember hearing that description quoted,' said
Gilberte, without adding that it had been quoted by her father, who was, as
we know, a great admirer of Saint-Simon.

She liked also to speak of the Prince d'Agrigente and of M. de Bréauté, for
another reason. The Prince d'Agrigente was prince by inheritance from the
House of Aragon, but his Lordship was Poitevin. As for his country house,
the house that is to say in which he lived, it was not the property of his own
family, but had come to him from his mother's former husband, and was
situated almost halfway between Martinville and Guermantes. And so
Gilberte spoke of him and of M. de Bréauté as of neighbours in the country
who reminded her of her old home. Strictly speaking there was an element
of falsehood in this attitude, since it was only in Paris, through the Comtesse
Molé, that she had come to know M. de Bréauté, albeit he had been an old
friend of her father. As for her pleasure in speaking of the country round
Tansonville, it may have been sincere. Snobbishness is, with certain people,
analogous to those pleasant beverages with which they mix nutritious
substances. Gilberte took an interest in some lady of fashion because she
possessed priceless books and portraits by Nattier which my former friend
would probably not have taken the trouble to inspect in the National
Library or at the Louvre, and I imagine that notwithstanding the even
greater proximity, the magnetic influence of Tansonville would have had
less effect in drawing Gilberte towards Mme Sazerat or Mme Goupil than
towards M. d'Agrigente.

'Oh! poor Babal and poor Gri-gri,' said Mme de Guermantes, 'they are in
a far worse state than du Lau, I'm afraid they haven't long to live, either of
them.'

When M. de Guermantes had finished reading my article, he paid me
compliments which however he took care to qualify. He regretted the
slightly hackneyed form of a style in which there were 'emphasis, metaphors
as in the antiquated prose of Chateaubriand'; on the other hand he
congratulated me without reserve upon my 'occupying myself': 'I like a man
to do something with his ten fingers. I do not like the useless creatures who
are always self-important or agitators. A fatuous breed!'

Gilberte, who was acquiring with extreme rapidity the ways of the world
of fashion, announced how proud she would be to say that she was the friend
of an author. 'You can imagine that I shall tell people that I have the
pleasure, the honour of your acquaintance.'

'You wouldn't care to come with us, tomorrow, to the Opéra-Comique?'
the Duchess asked me; and I thought that it would be doubtless in that same
box in which I had first beheld her, and which had seemed to me then as

inaccessible as the submarine realm of the Nereids. But I replied in a melancholy tone: 'No, I am not going to the theatre just now; I have lost a friend to whom I was greatly attached.' The tears almost came to my eyes as I said this, and yet, for the first time, I felt a sort of pleasure in speaking of my bereavement. It was from this moment that I began to write to all my friends that I had just experienced great sorrow, and to cease to feel it.

When Gilberte had gone, Mme de Guermantes said to me: 'You did not understand my signals, I was trying to hint to you not to mention Swann.' And, as I apologised: 'But I quite understand. I was on the point of mentioning him myself, I stopped short just in time, it was terrible, fortunately I bridled my tongue. You know, it is a great bore,' she said to her husband, seeking to mitigate my own error by appearing to believe that I had yielded to a propensity common to everyone, and difficult to resist. 'What do you expect me to do,' replied the Duke. 'You have only to tell them to take those drawings upstairs again, since they make you think about Swann. If you don't think about Swann, you won't speak about him.'

On the following day I received two congratulatory letters which surprised me greatly, one from Mme Goupil whom I had not seen for many years and to whom, even at Combray, I had not spoken more than twice. A public library had given her the chance of seeing the *Figaro*. Thus, when anything occurs in our life which makes some stir, messages come to us from people situated so far outside the zone of our acquaintance, our memory of whom is already so remote that these people seem to be placed at a great distance, especially in the dimension of depth. A forgotten friendship of our school days, which has had a score of opportunities of recalling itself to our mind, gives us a sign of life, not that there are not negative results also. For example, Bloch, from whom I would have been so glad to learn what he thought of my article, did not write to me. It is true that he had read the article and was to admit it later, but by a counter-stroke. In fact, he himself contributed, some years later, an article to the Figaro and was anxious to inform me immediately of the event. As he ceased to be jealous of what he regarded as a privilege, as soon as it had fallen to him as well, the envy that had made him pretend to ignore my article ceased, as though by the raising of a lever; he mentioned it to me but not at all in the way in which he hoped to hear me mention his article: 'I know that you too,' he told me, 'have written an article. But I did not think that I ought to mention it to you, for fear of hurting your feelings, for we ought not to speak to our friends of the humiliations that occur to them. And it is obviously a humiliation to supply the organ of sabres and aspergills with "five-o'clocks", not forgetting the holy-water-stoup.' His character remained unaltered, but his style had become less precious, as happens to certain people who shed their mannerisms, when, ceasing to compose symbolist poetry, they take to writing newspaper serials.

To console myself for his silence, I read Mme Goupil's letter again; but it was lacking in warmth, for if the aristocracy employ certain formulas which slip into watertight compartments, between the initial *'Monsieur'* and the *'sentiments distingués'* of the close, cries of joy, of admiration may spring up like flowers, and their clusters waft over the barriers their entrancing fragrance. But middle-class conventionality enwraps even the content of letters in a net of 'your well-deserved success', at best 'your great success'. Sisters-in-law, faithful to their upbringing and tight-laced in their respectable stays, think that they have overflowed into the most distressing enthusiasm if they have written: 'my kindest regards'. 'Mother joins me' is a superlative of which they are seldom wearied.

I received another letter as well as Mme Goupil's, but the name of the writer was unknown to me. It was an illiterate hand, a charming style. I was desolate at my inability to discover who had written to me.

While I was asking myself whether Bergotte would have liked this article, Mme de Forcheville had replied that he would have admired it enormously and could not have read it without envy. But she had told me this while I slept: it was a dream.

Almost all our dreams respond thus to the questions which we put to ourselves with complicated statements, presentations of several characters on the stage, which however lead to nothing.

As for Mlle de Forcheville, I could not help feeling appalled when I thought of her. What? The daughter of Swann who would so have loved to see her at the Guermantes', for whom they had refused their great friend the favour of an invitation, they had now sought out of their own accord, time having elapsed which refashions everything for us, instils a fresh personality, based upon what we have been told about them, into people whom we have not seen during a long interval, in which we ourselves have grown a new skin and acquired fresh tastes. I recalled how, to this girl, Swann used to say at times as he hugged her and kissed her: 'It is a comfort, my darling, to have a child like you; one day when I am no longer here, if people still mention your poor papa, it will be only to you and because of you.' Swann in anticipating thus after his own death a timorous and anxious hope of his survival in his daughter was as greatly mistaken as the old banker who having made a will in favour of a little dancer whom he is keeping and who behaves admirably, tells himself that he is nothing more to her than a great friend, but that she will remain faithful to his memory. She did behave admirably, while her feet under the table sought the feet of those of the old banker's friends who appealed to her, but all this was concealed, beneath an excellent exterior. She will wear mourning for the worthy man, will feel that she is well rid of him, will enjoy not only the ready money, but the real estate, the motor cars that he has bequeathed to her, taking care to remove the monogram of the former owner, which makes her feel slightly ashamed, and with her enjoyment of the gift will never associate any regret for the giver. The illusions of paternal affection are perhaps no less deceiving than those of the other kind; many girls regard their fathers only as the old men who are going to leave them a fortune. Gilberte's presence in a drawing-room, instead of being an opportunity for speaking occasionally still of her father, was an obstacle in the way of people's seizing those opportunities, increasingly more rare, that they might still have had of referring to him. Even in connection with the things that he had said, the presents that he had made, people acquired the habit of not mentioning him, and she who ought to have refreshed, not to say perpetuated his memory, found herself hastening and completing the process of death and oblivion.

And it was not merely with regard to Swann that Gilberte was gradually completing the process of oblivion, she had accelerated in me that process of oblivion with regard to Albertine.

Under the action of desire, and consequently of the desire for happiness which Gilberte had aroused in me during those hours in which I had supposed her to be someone else, a certain number of miseries, of painful preoccupations, which only a little while earlier had obsessed my mind, had been released, carrying with them a whole block of memories, probably long since crumbled and become precarious, with regard to Albertine. For if many memories, which were connected with her, had at the outset helped to keep alive in me my regret for her death, in return that regret had itself fixed those memories. So that the modification of my sentimental state, prepared no doubt obscurely day by day by the constant disintegration of oblivion, but realised abruptly as a whole, gave me the impression which I remember that I felt that day for the first time, of a void, of the suppression in myself of a whole portion of my association of ideas, which a man feels in whose brain an artery, long exhausted, has burst, so that a whole section of his memory is abolished or paralysed.

The vanishing of my suffering and of all that it carried away with it, left me diminished as does often the healing of a malady which occupied a large place in our life. No doubt it is because memories are not always genuine that love is not eternal, and because life is made up of a perpetual renewal of our cells. But this renewal, in the case of memories, is nevertheless retarded by the attention which arrests, and fixes a moment that is bound to change. And since it is the case with grief as with the desire for women that we increase it by thinking about it, the fact of having plenty of other things to do should, like chastity, make oblivion easy.

By another reaction (albeit it was the distraction – the desire for Mlle d'Éporcheville – that had made my oblivion suddenly apparent and perceptible), if the fact remains that it is time that gradually brings oblivion, oblivion does not fail to alter profoundly our notion of time. There are optical errors in time as there are in space. The persistence in myself of an old tendency to work, to make up for lost time, to change my way of life, or rather to begin to live gave me the illusion that I was still as young as in the past; and yet the memory of all the events that had followed one another in my life (and also of those that had followed one another in my heart, for when we have greatly changed, we are led to suppose that our life has been longer) in the course of those last months of Albertine's existence, had made them seem to me much longer than a year, and now this oblivion of so many things, separating me by gulfs of empty space from quite recent events which they made me think remote, because I had had what is called 'the time' to forget them, by its fragmentary, irregular interpolation in my memory – like a thick fog at sea which obliterates all the landmarks – confused, destroyed my sense of distances in time, contracted in one place, extended in another, and made me suppose myself now farther away from things, now far closer to them than I really was. And as in the fresh spaces, as yet unexplored, which extended before me, there would be no more trace of my love for Albertine than there had been, in the time past which I had just traversed, of my love for my grandmother, my life appeared to me – offering a succession of periods in which, after a certain interval, nothing of what had sustained the previous period survived in that which followed – as something so devoid of the support of an individual, identical and permanent self, something so useless in the future and so protracted in the past, that death might just as well put an end to its course here or there, without in the least concluding it, as with those courses of French history which, in the Rhetoric class, stop short indifferently, according to the whim of the curriculum or the professor, at the Revolution of 1830, or at that of 1848, or at the end of the Second Empire.

Perhaps then the fatigue and distress which I was feeling were due not so much to my having loved in vain what I was already beginning to forget, as to my coming to take pleasure in the company of fresh living people, purely social figures, mere friends of the Guermantes, offering no interest in themselves. It was easier perhaps to reconcile myself to the discovery that she whom I had loved was nothing more, after a certain interval of time, than a pale memory, than to the rediscovery in myself of that futile activity which makes us waste time in decorating our life with a human vegetation that is alive but is parasitic, which likewise will become nothing when it is dead, which already is alien to all that we have ever known, which, nevertheless, our garrulous, melancholy, conceited senility seeks to attract. The newcomer who would find it easy to endure the prospect of life without Albertine had made his appearance in me, since I had been able to speak of her at Mme de Guermantes's in the language of grief without any real suffering. These strange selves which were to bear each a different name, the possibility of their coming had, by reason of their indifference to the object of my love, always alarmed me, long ago in connection with Gilberte when her father told me that if I went to live in Oceania I would never wish to return, quite recently when I had read with such a pang in my heart the passage in Bergotte's novel where he treats of the character who, separated by the events of life from a woman whom he had adored when he was young, as an old man meets her without pleasure, without any desire to see her again. Now, on the contrary, he was bringing me with oblivion an almost complete elimination of suffering, a possibility of comfort, this person so dreaded, so beneficent who was none other than one of those spare selves whom destiny holds in reserve for us, and, without paying any more heed to our entreaties than a clear-sighted and so all the more authoritative physician, substitutes without our aid, by an opportune intervention, for the self that has been too seriously injured. This renewal, as it happens, nature performs from time to time, as by the decay and refashioning of our tissues, but we notice this only if the former self contained a great grief, a painful foreign body, which we are surprised to find no longer there, in our amazement at having become another self to whom the sufferings of his precursor are nothing more than the sufferings of a stranger, of which we can speak with compassion because we do not feel them. Indeed we are unaffected by our having undergone all those sufferings, since we have only a vague remembrance of having suffered them. It is possible that similarly our dreams, during the night, may be terrible. But when we awake we are another person to whom it is of no importance that the person whose place he takes has had to fly during our sleep from a band of cutthroats.

No doubt this self had maintained some contact with the old self, as a friend, unconcerned by a bereavement, speaks of it nevertheless, to those who come to the house, in a suitable tone of sorrow, and returns from time to time to the room in which the widower who has asked him to receive the company for him may still be heard weeping. I made this contact even closer when I became once again for a moment the former friend of Albertine. But it was into a new personality that I was tending to pass altogether. It is not because other people are dead that our affection for them grows faint, it is because we ourselves are dying. Albertine had no cause to rebuke her friend. The man who was usurping his name had merely inherited it. We may be faithful to what we remember, we remember only what we have known. My new self, while it grew up in the shadow of the old, had often heard the other speak of Albertine; through that other self, through the information that it gathered from it, it thought that it knew her, it found her attractive, it was in love with her, but this was merely an affection at second hand.

Another person in whom the process of oblivion, so far as concerned Albertine, was probably more rapid at this time, and enabled me in return to realise a little later a fresh advance which that process had made in myself (and this is my memory of a second stage before the final oblivion), was Andrée. I can scarcely, indeed, refrain from citing this oblivion of Albertine as, if not the sole cause, if not even the principal cause, at any rate a conditioning and necessary cause of a conversation between Andrée and myself about six months after the conversation which I have already reported, when her words were so different from those that she had used on the former occasion. I remember that it was in my room because at that moment I found a pleasure in having semi-carnal relations with her, because of the collective form originally assumed and now being resumed by my love for the girls of the little band, a love that had long been undivided among them, and for a while associated exclusively with Albertine's person during the months that had preceded and followed her death.

We were in my room for another reason as well which enables me to date this conversation quite accurately. This was that I had been banished from the rest of the apartment because it was Mamma's day. Notwithstanding its being her day, and after some hesitation, Mamma had gone to luncheon with Mme Sazerat thinking that as Mme Sazerat always contrived to invite one to meet boring people, she would be able without sacrificing any pleasure to return home in good time. And she had indeed returned in time and without regret, Mme Sazerat having had nobody but the most deadly people who were frozen from the start by the special voice that she adopted when she had company, what Mamma called her Wednesday voice. My mother was, nevertheless, extremely fond of her, was sorry for her poverty – the result of the extravagance of her father who had been ruined by the Duchesse de X – a poverty which compelled her to live all the year round at Combray, with a few weeks at her cousin's house in Paris and a great 'pleasure-trip' every ten years.

I remember that the day before this, at my request repeated for months past, and because the Princess was always begging her to come, Mamma had gone to call upon the Princesse de Parme who, herself, paid no calls, and at whose house people as a rule contented themselves with writing their names, but who had insisted upon my mother's coming to see her, since the rules and regulations prevented her from coming to us. My mother had come home thoroughly cross: 'You have sent me on a fool's errand,' she told me, 'the Princesse de Parme barely greeted me, she turned back to the ladies to whom she was talking without paying me any attention, and after ten minutes, as she hadn't uttered a word to me, I came away without her even offering me her hand. I was extremely annoyed; however, on the doorstep, as I was leaving, I met the Duchesse de Guermantes who was very kind and spoke to me a great deal about you. What a strange idea that was to tell her about Albertine. She told me that you had said to her that her death had been such a grief to you. I shall never go near the Princesse de Parme again. You have made me make a fool of myself.'

Well, the next day, which was my mother's at-home day, as I have said, Andrée came to see me. She had not much time, for she had to go and call for Gisèle with whom she was very anxious to dine. 'I know her faults, but she is after all my best friend and the person for whom I feel most affection,' she told me. And she even appeared to feel some alarm at the thought that I might ask her to let me dine with them. She was hungry for people, and a third person who knew her too well, such as myself, would, by preventing her from letting herself go, at once prevent her from enjoying complete satisfaction in their company.

The memory of Albertine had become so fragmentary in me that it no longer caused me any sorrow and was no more now than a transition to fresh desires, like a chord which announces a change of key. And indeed the idea of a momentary sensual caprice being ruled out, in so far as I was still faithful to Albertine's memory, I was happier at having Andrée in my company than I would have been at having an Albertine miraculously restored to life. For Andrée could tell me more things about Albertine than Albertine herself had ever told me. Now the problems concerning Albertine still remained in my mind when my affection for her, both physical and moral, had already vanished. And my desire to know about her life, because it had diminished less, was now relatively greater than my need of her presence. On the other hand, the thought that a woman had perhaps had relations with Albertine no longer provoked in me anything save the desire to have relations myself also with that woman. I told Andrée this, caressing her as I spoke. Then, without making the slightest effort to harmonise her speech with what she had said a few months earlier, Andrée said to me with a lurking smile: 'Ah! yes, but you are a man. And so we can't do quite the same things as I used to do with Albertine.' And whether it was that she considered that this increased my desire (in the hope of extracting confidences, I had told her that I would like to have relations with a woman who had had them with Albertine) or my grief, or perhaps destroyed a sense of superiority to herself which she might suppose me to feel at being the only person who had had relations with Albertine: 'Ah! we spent many happy hours together, she was so caressing, so passionate. Besides, it was not only with me that she liked to enjoy herself. She had met a nice boy at Mme Verdurin's, Morel. They understood each other at once. He undertook (with her permission to enjoy himself with them too, for he liked virgins) to procure little girls for her. As soon as he had set their feet on the path, he left them. And so he made himself responsible for attracting young fisher-girls in some quiet watering-place, young laundresses, who would fall in love with a boy, but would not have listened to a girl's advances. As soon as the girl was well under his control, he would bring her to a safe place, where he handed her over to Albertine. For fear of losing Morel, who took part in it all too, the girl always obeyed, and yet she lost him all the same, for, as he was afraid of what might happen and also as once or twice was enough for him, he would slip away leaving a false address. Once he had the nerve to bring one of these girls, with Albertine, to a brothel at Corliville, where four or five of the women had her at once, or in turn. That was his passion, and Albertine's also. But Albertine suffered terrible remorse afterwards. I believe that when she was with you she had conquered her passion and put off indulging it from day to day. Then her affection for yourself was so strong that she felt scruples. But it was quite certain that, if she ever left you, she would begin again. She hoped that you would rescue her, that you would marry her. She felt in her heart that it was a sort of criminal lunacy, and I have often asked myself whether it was not after an incident of that sort, which had led to a suicide in a family, that she killed herself on purpose. I must confess that in the early days of her life with you she had not entirely given up her games with me. There were days when she seemed to need it, so much so that once, when it would have been so easy elsewhere, she could not say goodbye without taking me to bed with her, in your house. We had no luck, we were very nearly caught. She had taken her opportunity when Françoise had gone out on some errand, and you had not come home. Then she had turned out all the lights so that when you let yourself in with your key it would take you some time to find the switch, and she had not shut the door of her room. We heard you come upstairs, I had just time to make myself tidy and begin to come down. Which was quite unnecessary, for by an incredible accident you had left your key at home and had to ring the bell. But we lost our heads all the same, so that to conceal our awkwardness we both of us, without any opportunity of discussing it, had the same idea: to pretend to be afraid of the scent of syringa which as a matter of fact we adored. You were bringing a long branch of it home with you, which enabled me to turn my head away and hide my confusion. This did not prevent me from telling you in the most idiotic way that perhaps Françoise had come back and would let you in, when a moment earlier I had told you the lie that we had only just come in from our drive and that when we arrived Françoise had not left the house and was just going on an errand. But our mistake was – supposing you to have your key – turning out the light, for we were afraid that as you came upstairs you would see it turned on again, or at least we hesitated too long. And for three nights on end Albertine could not close an eye, for she was always afraid that you might be suspicious and ask Françoise why she had not turned on the light before leaving the house. For Albertine was terribly afraid of you, and at times she would assure me that you were wicked, mean, that you hated her really. After three days she gathered from your calm that you had said nothing to Françoise, and she was able to sleep again. But she never did anything with me after that, perhaps from fear, perhaps from remorse, for she made out that she did really love you, or perhaps she was in love with some other man. In any case, nobody could ever mention syringa again in her hearing without her turning crimson and putting her hand over her face in the hope of hiding her blushes.'

As there are strokes of good fortune, so there are misfortunes that come too late, they do not assume all the importance that they would have had in our eyes a little earlier. Among these was the calamity that Andrée's terrible revelation was to me. No doubt, even when bad tidings ought to make us unhappy, it so happens that in the diversion, the balanced give and take of conversation, they pass by us without stopping, and that we ourselves, preoccupied with a thousand things which we have to say in response, transformed by the desire to please our present company into someone else protected for a few moments in this new environment against the affections, the sufferings that he has discarded upon entering it and will find again when the brief spell is broken, have not the time to take them in. And yet if those affections, those sufferings are too predominant, we enter only distractedly into the zone of a new and momentary world, in which, too faithful to our sufferings, we are incapable of becoming another person, and then the words that we hear said enter at once into relation with our heart, which has not remained out of action. But for some time past words that concerned Albertine, had, like a poison that has evaporated, lost their toxic power. She was already too remote from me.

As a wayfarer seeing in the afternoon a misty crescent in the sky, says to himself: 'That is it, the vast moon,' so I said to myself: 'What, so that truth which I have sought so earnestly, which I have so dreaded, is nothing more than these few words uttered in the course of conversation, words to which we cannot even give our whole attention since we are not alone!' Besides, it took me at a serious disadvantage, I had exhausted myself with Andrée. With a truth of such magnitude, I would have liked to have more strength to devote to it; it remained outside me, but this was because I had not yet found a place for it in my heart. We would like the truth to be revealed to us by novel signs, not by a phrase similar to those which we have constantly repeated to ourselves. The habit of thinking prevents us at times from feeling reality, makes us immune to it, makes it seem no more than another thought.

There is no idea that does not carry in itself a possible refutation, no word that does not imply its opposite. In any case, if all this was true, how futile a verification of the life of a mistress who exists no longer, rising up from the depths and coming to the surface just when we are no longer able to make any use of it. Then, thinking doubtless of some other woman whom we now love and with regard to whom the same change may occur (for to her whom we have forgotten we no longer give a thought), we lose heart. We say to ourselves: 'If she were alive!' We say to ourselves: 'If she who is alive could understand all this and that when she is dead I shall know everything that she is hiding from me.' But this is a vicious circle. If I could have brought Albertine back to life, the immediate consequence would have been that Andrée would have revealed nothing. It is the same thing as the everlasting: 'You'll see what it's like when I no longer love you' which is so true and so absurd, since as a matter of fact we should elicit much if we were no longer in love, but when we should no longer think of enquiring. It is precisely the same. For the woman whom we see again when we are no longer in love with her, if she tells us everything, the fact is that she is no longer herself, or that we are no longer ourselves: the person who was in love has ceased to exist. There also death has passed by, and has made everything easy and unnecessary. I pursued these reflections, adopting the hypothesis that Andrée had been telling the truth – which was possible – and had been prompted to sincerity with me, precisely because she now had relations with me, by that Saint-André-des-Champs side of her nature which Albertine, too, had shown me at the start. She was encouraged in this case by the fact that she was no longer afraid of Albertine, for other people's reality survives their death for only a short time in our mind, and after a few years they are like those gods of obsolete religions whom we insult without fear, because people have ceased to believe in their existence. But the fact that Andrée no longer believed in the reality of Albertine might mean that she no longer feared (any more than to betray a secret which she had promised not to reveal) to invent a falsehood which slandered retrospectively her alleged accomplice. Had this absence of fear permitted her to reveal at length, in speaking as she did, the truth, or rather to invent a falsehood, if, for some reason, she supposed me to be full of happiness and pride, and wished to pain me? Perhaps the sight of me caused her a certain irritation (held in suspense so long as she saw that I was miserable, unconsoled) because I had had relations with Albertine and she envied me, perhaps – supposing that I considered myself on that account more highly favoured than her – an advantage which she herself had never, perhaps, obtained, nor even sought. Thus it was that I had often heard her say how ill they were looking to people whose air of radiant health, and what was more their consciousness of their own air of radiant health, exasperated her, and say in the hope of annoying them that she herself was very well, a fact that she did not cease to proclaim when she was seriously ill until the day when, in the detachment of death, it no longer mattered to her that other fortunate people should be well and should know that she was dying. But this day was still remote. Perhaps she had turned against me, for what reason I knew not, in one of those rages in which she used, long ago, to turn against the young man so learned in sporting matters, so ignorant of everything else, whom we had met at Balbec, who since then had been living with Rachel, and at the mention of whom Andrée overflowed in defamatory speeches, hoping to be sued for libel in order to be able to launch against his father disgraceful accusations the falsehood of which he would not be able to prove. Quite possibly this rage against myself had simply revived, having doubtless ceased when she saw how miserable I was. Indeed, the very same people whom she, her eyes flashing with rage, had longed to disgrace, to kill, to send to prison, by false testimony if need be, she had only to know that they were unhappy, crushed, to cease to wish them any harm, and to be ready to overwhelm them with kindnesses. For she was not fundamentally wicked, and if her non-apparent, somewhat buried nature was not the kindness which one divined at first from her delicate attentions, but rather envy and pride, her third nature, buried more deeply still, the true but not entirely realised nature, tended towards goodness and the love of her neighbour. Only, like all those people who, being in a certain state of life, desire a better state, but knowing it only by desire, do not realise that the first condition is to break away from the former state – like the neurasthenics or morphinomaniacs who are anxious to be cured, but at the same time do not wish to be deprived of their manias or their morphine, like the religious hearts or artistic spirits attached to the world who long for solitude but seek nevertheless to imagine it as not implying an absolute renunciation of their former existence – Andrée was prepared to love all her fellow-creatures, but on the condition that she should first of all have succeeded in not imagining them as triumphant, and to that end should have humiliated them in advance. She did not understand that we ought to love even the proud, and to conquer their pride by love and not by a more overweening pride. But the fact is that she was like those invalids who wish to be cured by the very means that prolong their malady, which they like and would cease at once to like if they renounced them. But people wish to learn to swim and at the same time to keep one foot on the ground. As for the young sportsman, the Verdurins' nephew, whom I had met during my two visits to Balbec, I am bound to add, as an accessory statement and in anticipation, that some time after Andrée's visit, a visit my account of which will be resumed in a moment, certain events occurred which caused a great sensation. First of all, this young man (perhaps remembering Albertine with whom I did not then know that he had been in love) became engaged to Andrée and married her, notwithstanding the despair of Rachel to which he paid not the slightest attention. Andrée no longer said then (that is to say some months after the visit of which I have been speaking) that he was a wretch, and I realised later on that she had said so only because she was madly in love with him and thought that he did not want to have anything to do with her. But another fact impressed me even more. This young man produced certain sketches for the theatre, with settings and costumes designed by himself, which have effected in the art of today a revolution at least equal to that brought about by the Russian ballet. In fact, the best qualified critics regarded his work as something of capital importance, almost as works of genius and for that matter I agree with them, confirming thus, to my own astonishment, the opinion long held by Rachel. The people who had known him at Balbec, anxious only to be certain whether the cut of the clothes of the men with whom he associated was or was not smart, who had seen him spend all his time at baccarat, at the races, on the golf course or on the polo ground, who knew that at school he had always been a dunce, and had even been expelled from the lycée (to annoy his parents, he had spent two months in the smart brothel in which M. de Charlus had hoped to surprise Morel), thought that perhaps his work was done by Andrée who, in her love for him, chose to leave him the renown, or that more probably he was paying, out of his huge private fortune at which his excesses had barely nibbled, some inspired but needy professional to create it. People in this kind of wealthy society, not purified by mingling with the aristocracy, and having no idea of what constitutes an artist – a word which to them is represented only by an actor whom they engage to recite monologues at the party given for their daughter's betrothal, at once handing him his fee discreetly in another room, or by a painter to whom they make her sit after she is married, before the children come and when she is still at her best – are apt to believe that all the people in society who write, compose or paint, have their work done for them and pay to obtain a reputation as an author as other men pay to make sure of a seat in Parliament. But all this was false, and the young man was indeed the author of those admirable works. When I learned this, I was obliged to hesitate between contrary suppositions. Either he had indeed been for years on end the 'coarse brute' that he appeared to be, and some physiological cataclysm had awakened in him the dormant genius, like a Sleeping Beauty, or else at the period of his tempestuous schooldays, of his failures to matriculate in the final examination, of his heavy gambling losses at Balbec, of his reluctance to show himself in the tram with his aunt Verdurin's faithful, because of their unconventional attire, he was already a man of genius, distracted perhaps from his genius, having left its key beneath the doormat in the effervescence of juvenile passions; or again, already a conscious man of genius, and at the bottom of his classes, because, while the master was uttering platitudes about Cicero, he himself was reading Rimbaud or Goethe. Certainly, there was no ground for any such hypothesis when I met him at Balbec, where his interests seemed to me to be centred solely in turning out a smart carriage and pair and in mixing cocktails. But even this is not an insuperable objection. He might be extremely vain, and this may be allied to genius, and might seek to shine in the manner which he knew to be dazzling in the world in which he lived, which did not mean furnishing a profound knowledge of elective affinities, but far rather a knowledge of how to drive four-in-hand. Moreover, I am not at all sure that later on, when he had become the author of those fine and so original works, he would have cared greatly, outside the theatres in which he was known, to greet anyone who was not in evening dress, like the 'faithful' in their earlier manner, which would be a proof in him not of stupidity, but of vanity, and indeed of a certain practical sense, a certain clairvoyance in adapting his vanity to the mentality of the imbeciles upon whose esteem he depended and in whose eyes a dinner-jacket might perhaps shine with a more brilliant radiance than the eyes of a thinker. Who can say whether, seen from without, some man of talent, or even a man devoid of talent, but a lover of the things of the mind, myself for instance, would not have appeared, to anyone who met him at Rivebelle, at the hotel at Balbec, or on the beach there, the most perfect and pretentious imbecile. Not to mention that for Octave matters of art must have been a thing so intimate, a thing that lived so in the most secret places of his heart that doubtless it would never have occurred to him to speak of them, as Saint-Loup, for instance, would have spoken, for whom the fine arts had the importance that horses and carriages had for Octave. Besides, he may have had a passion for gambling, and it is said that he has retained it. All the same, even if the piety which brought to light the unknown work of Vinteuil arose from amid the troubled life of Montjouvain, I was no less impressed by the thought that the masterpieces which are perhaps the most extraordinary of our day have emerged not from the university certificate, from a model, academic education, upon Broglie lines, but from the frequentation of 'paddocks' and fashionable bars. In any case, in those days at Balbec, the reasons which made me anxious to know him, which made Albertine and her friends anxious that I should not know him, were equally detached from his merit, and could only have brought into prominence the eternal misunderstanding between an 'intellectual' (represented in this instance by myself) and people in society (represented by the little band) with regard to a person in society (the young golfer). I had no inkling of his talent, and his prestige in my eyes, like that, in the past, of Mme Blatin, had been that of his being – whatever they might say – the friend of my girl friends, and more one of their band than myself. On the other hand, Albertine and Andrée, symbolising in this respect the incapacity of people in society to bring a sound judgment to bear upon the things of the mind and their propensity to attach themselves in that connection to false appearances, not only thought me almost idiotic because I took an interest in such an imbecile, but were astonished beyond measure that, taking one golfer with another, my choice should have fallen upon the poorest player of them all. If, for instance, I had chosen to associate with young Gilbert de Belloeuvre; apart from golf, he was a boy who had the gift of conversation, who had secured a *proxime* in the examinations and wrote quite good poetry (as a matter of fact he was the stupidest of them all). Or again if my object had been to 'make a study for a book', Guy Saumoy who was completely insane, who had abducted two girls, was at least a singular type who might 'interest' me. These two might have been allowed me, but the other, what attraction could I find in him, he was the type of the 'great brute', of the 'coarse brute'. To return to Andrée's visit, after the disclosure that she had just made to me of her relations with Albertine, she added that the chief reason for which Albertine had left me was the thought of what her friends of the little band might think, and other people as well, when they saw her living like that with a young man to whom she was not married. 'Of course I know, it was in your mother's house. But that makes no difference. You can't imagine what all those girls are like, what they conceal from one another, how they dread one another's opinion. I have seen them being terribly severe with young men simply because the men knew their friends and they were afraid that certain things might be repeated, and those very girls, I have happened to see them in a totally different light, much to their disgust.' A few months earlier, this knowledge which Andrée appeared to possess of the motives that swayed the girls of the little band would have seemed to me the most priceless thing in the world. What she said was perhaps sufficient to explain why Albertine, who had given herself to me afterwards in Paris, had refused to yield to me at Balbec where I was constantly meeting her friends, which I had absurdly supposed to be so great an advantage in winning her affection. Perhaps indeed it was because she had seen me display some sign of intimacy with Andrée or because I had rashly told the latter that Albertine was coming to spend the night at the Grand Hotel, that Albertine who perhaps, an hour earlier, was ready to let me take certain favours, as though that were the simplest thing in the world, had abruptly changed her mind and threatened to ring the bell. But then, she must have been accommodating to lots of others. This thought rekindled my jealousy and I told Andrée that there was something that I wished to ask her. 'You did those things in your grandmother's empty apartment?' 'Oh, no, never, we should have been disturbed.' 'Why, I thought . . . it seemed to me . . . ' 'Besides, Albertine loved doing it in the country.' 'And where, pray?' 'Originally, when she hadn't time to go very far, we used to go to the Buttes-Chaumont. She knew a house there. Or else we would lie under the trees, there is never anyone about; in the grotto of the Petit Trianon, too.' 'There, you see; how am I to believe you? You swore to me, not a year ago, that you had never done anything at the Buttes-Chaumont.' 'I was afraid of distressing you.' As I have said, I thought (although not until much later) that on the contrary it was on this second occasion, the day of her confessions, that Andrée had sought to distress me. And this thought would have occurred to me at once, because I should have felt the need of it, if I had still been as much in love with Albertine. But Andrée's words did not hurt me sufficiently to make it indispensable to me to dismiss them immediately as untrue. In short if what Andrée said was true, and I did not doubt it at the time, the real Albertine whom I discovered, after having known so many diverse forms of Albertine, differed very little from the young Bacchanal

who had risen up and whom I had detected, on the first day, on the front at
Balbec, and who had offered me so many different aspects in succession, as
a town gradually alters the position of its buildings so as to overtop, to
obliterate the principal monument which alone we beheld from a distance,
as we approach it, whereas when we know it well and can judge it exactly, its
true proportions prove to be those which the perspective of the first glance
had indicated, the rest, through which we passed, being no more than that
continuous series of lines of defence which everything in creation raises
against our vision, and which we must cross one after another, at the cost of
how much suffering, before we arrive at the heart. If, however, I had no
need to believe absolutely in Albertine's innocence because my suffering
had diminished, I can say that reciprocally if I did not suffer unduly at this
revelation, it was because, some time since, for the belief that I feigned in
Albertine's innocence, there had been substituted gradually and without my
taking it into account the belief, ever present in my mind, in her guilt. Now
if I no longer believed in Albertine's innocence, it was because I had already
ceased to feel the need, the passionate desire to believe in it. It is desire that
engenders belief and if we fail as a rule to take this into account, it is because
most of the desires that create beliefs end – unlike the desire which had
persuaded me that Albertine was innocent – only with our own life. To all
the evidence that corroborated my original version I had stupidly preferred
simple statements by Albertine. Why had I believed them? Falsehood is
essential to humanity. It plays as large a part perhaps as the quest of pleasure
and is moreover commanded by that quest. We lie in order to protect our
pleasure or our honour if the disclosure of our pleasure runs counter to our
honour. We lie all our life long, especially indeed, perhaps only, to those
people who love us. Such people in fact alone make us fear for our pleasure
and desire their esteem. I had at first thought Albertine guilty, and it was
only my desire devoting to a process of doubt the strength of my intelligence
that had set me upon the wrong track. Perhaps we live surrounded by
electric, seismic signs, which we must interpret in good faith in order to
know the truth about the characters of other people. If the truth must be
told, saddened as I was in spite of everything by Andrée's words, I felt it to
be better that the truth should at last agree with what my instinct had
originally foreboded, rather than with the miserable optimism to which I
had since made a cowardly surrender. I would have preferred that life
should remain at the high level of my intuitions. Those moreover which I
had felt, that first day upon the beach, when I had supposed that those girls
embodied the frenzy of pleasure, were vice incarnate, and again on the
evening when I had seen Albertine's governess leading that passionate girl

home to the little villa, as one thrust into its cage a wild animal which nothing in the future, despite appearances, will ever succeed in taming, did they not agree with what Bloch had told me when he had made the world seem so fair to me by showing me, making me palpitate on all my walks, at every encounter, the universality of desire. Perhaps, when all was said, it was better that I should not have found those first intuitions verified afresh until now. While the whole of my love for Albertine endured, they would have made me suffer too keenly and it was better that there should have subsisted of them only a trace, my perpetual suspicion of things which I did not see and which nevertheless happened continually so close to me, and perhaps another trace as well, earlier, more vast, which was *my love itself*. Was it not indeed, despite all the denials of my reason, tantamount to knowing Albertine in all her hideousness, merely to choose her, to love her; and even in the moments when suspicion is lulled, is not love the persistence and a transformation of that suspicion, is it not a proof of clairvoyance (a proof unintelligible to the lover himself), since desire going always in the direction of what is most opposite to ourselves forces us to love what will make us suffer? Certainly there enter into a person's charm, into the attraction of her eyes, her lips, her figure, the elements unknown to us which are capable of making us suffer most intensely, so much so that to feel ourselves attracted by the person, to begin to love her, is, however innocent we may pretend it to be, to read already, in a different version, all her betrayals and her faults. And those charms which, to attract me, materialised thus the noxious, dangerous, fatal parts of a person, did they perhaps stand in a more direct relation of cause to effect to those secret poisons than do the seductive luxuriance and the toxic juice of certain venomous flowers? It was perhaps, I told myself, Albertine's vice itself, the cause of my future sufferings, that had produced in her that honest, frank manner, creating the illusion that one could enjoy with her the same loyal and unrestricted comradeship as with a man, just as a parallel vice had produced in M. de Charlus a feminine refinement of sensibility and mind. Through a period of the most utter blindness, perspicacity persists beneath the very form of predilection and affection. Which means that we are wrong in speaking of a bad choice in love, since whenever there is a choice it can only be bad. 'Did those excursions to the Buttes-Chaumont take place when you used to call for her here?' I asked Andrée. 'Oh! no, from the day when Albertine came back from Balbec with you, except the time I told you about, she never did anything again with me. She would not even allow me to mention such things to her.' 'But, my dear Andrée, why go on lying to me? By the merest chance, for I never try to find out anything, I have learned in the minutest details things of that sort which Albertine did, I can tell you exactly, on the bank of the river with a laundress, only a few days before her death.' 'Ah! perhaps after she had left you, that I can't say. She felt that she had failed, that she would never again be able to regain your confidence.' These last words appalled me. Then I thought again of the evening of the branch of syringa, I remembered that about a fortnight later, as my jealousy kept seeking a fresh object, I had asked Albertine whether she had ever had relations with Andrée, and she had replied: 'Oh! never! Of course, I adore Andrée; I have a profound affection for her, but as though we were sisters, and even if I had the tastes which you seem to suppose, she is the last person that would have entered my head. I can swear to you by anything you like, by my aunt, by my poor mother's grave.' I had believed her. And yet even if I had not been made suspicious by the contradiction between her former partial admissions with regard to certain matters and the firmness with which she had afterwards denied them as soon as she saw that I was not unaffected, I ought to have remembered Swann, convinced of the platonic nature of M. de Charlus's friendships and assuring me of it on the evening of the very day on which I had seen the tailor and the Baron in the courtyard. I ought to have reflected that if there are, one covering the other, two worlds, one consisting of the things that the best, the sincerest people say, and behind it the world composed of those same people's successive actions, so that when a married woman says to you of a young man: 'Oh! It is perfectly true that I have an immense affection for him, but it is something quite innocent, quite pure, I could swear it upon the memory of my parents', we ought ourselves, instead of feeling any hesitation, to swear that she has probably just come from her bathroom to which, after every assignation that she has with the young man in question, she dashes, to prevent any risk of his giving her a child. The spray of syringa made me profoundly sad, as did also the discovery that Albertine could have thought or called me cruel and hostile; most of all perhaps, certain lies so unexpected that I had difficulty in grasping them. One day Albertine had told me that she had been to an aerodrome, that the airman was in love with her (this doubtless in order to divert my suspicion from women, thinking that I was less jealous of other men), that it had been amusing to watch Andrée's raptures at the said airman, at all the compliments that he paid Albertine, until finally Andrée had longed to go in the air with him. Now this was an entire fabrication; Andrée had never visited the aerodrome in question.

When Andrée left me, it was dinner-time. 'You will never guess who has been to see me and stayed at least three hours,' said my mother. 'I call it three hours, it was perhaps longer, she arrived almost on the heels of my first visitor, who was Mme Cottard, sat still and watched everybody come and go – and I had more than thirty callers – and left me only a quarter of an hour ago. If you hadn't had your friend Andrée with you, I should have sent for you.' 'Why, who was it?' 'A person who never pays calls.' 'The Princesse de Parme?' 'Why, I have a cleverer son than I thought I had. There is no fun in making you guess a name, for you hit on it at once.' 'Did she come to apologise for her rudeness yesterday?' 'No, that would have been stupid, the fact of her calling was an apology. Your poor grandmother would have thought it admirable. It seems that about two o'clock she had sent a footman to ask whether I had an at-home day. She was told that this was the day and so up she came.' My first thought, which I did not dare mention to Mamma, was that the Princesse de Parme, surrounded, the day before, by people of rank and fashion with whom she was on intimate terms and enjoyed conversing, had when she saw my mother come into the room felt an annoyance which she had made no attempt to conceal. And it was quite in the style of the great ladies of Germany, which for that matter the Guermantes had largely adopted, this stiffness, for which they thought to atone by a scrupulous affability. But my mother believed, and I came in time to share her opinion, that all that had happened was that the Princesse de Parme, having failed to recognise her, had not felt herself bound to pay her any attention, that she had learned after my mother's departure who she was, either from the Duchesse de Guermantes whom my mother had met as she was leaving the house, or from the list of her visitors, whose names, before they entered her presence, the servants recorded in a book. She had thought it impolite to send word or to say to my mother: 'I did not recognise you', but – and this was no less in harmony with the good manners of the German courts and with the Guermantes code of behaviour than my original theory – had thought that a call, an exceptional action on the part of a royal personage, and what was more a call of several hours' duration, would convey the explanation to my mother in an indirect but no less convincing form, which is just what did happen. But I did not waste any time in asking my mother to tell me about the Princess's call, for I had just recalled a number of incidents with regard to Albertine as to which I had meant but had forgotten to question Andrée. How little, for that matter, did I know, should I ever know, of this story of Albertine, the only story that could be of particular interest to me, or did at least begin to interest me afresh at certain moments. For man is that creature without any fixed age, who has the faculty of becoming, in a few seconds, many years younger, and who, surrounded by the walls of the time through which he has lived, floats within them but as though in a basin the surface-level of which is constantly changing, so as to bring him into the range now of one epoch now of another. I wrote to Andrée asking her to come again. She was unable to do so until a week had passed. Almost as soon as she entered the room, I said to her: 'Very well, then, since you maintain that Albertine never did that sort of thing while she was staying here, according to you, it was to be able to do it more freely that she left me, but for which of her friends?' 'Certainly not, it was not that at all.' 'Then because I was too unkind to her?' 'No, I don't think so. I believe that she was forced to leave you by her aunt who had designs for her future upon that guttersnipe, you know, the young man whom you used to call "I am in the soup", the young man who was in love with Albertine and had proposed for her. Seeing that you did not marry her, they were afraid that the shocking length of her stay in your house might prevent the young man from proposing. Mme Bontemps, after the young man had brought continual pressure to bear upon her, summoned Albertine home. Albertine after all needed her uncle and aunt, and when she found that they expected her to make up her mind she left you.' I had never in my jealousy thought of this explanation, but only of Albertine's desire for other women and of my own vigilance, I had forgotten that there was also Mme Bontemps who might presently regard as strange what had shocked my mother from the first. At least Mme Bontemps was afraid that it might shock this possible husband whom she was keeping in reserve for Albertine, in case I failed to marry her. Was this marriage really the cause of Albertine's departure, and out of self-respect, so as not to appear to be dependent on her aunt, or to force me to marry her, had she preferred not to mention it? I was beginning to realise that the system of multiple causes for a single action, of which Albertine showed her mastery in her relations with her girl friends when she allowed each of them to suppose that it was for her sake that she had come, was only a sort of artificial, deliberate symbol of the different aspects that an action assumes according to the point of view that we adopt. The astonishment, I might almost say the shame that I felt at never having even once told myself that Albertine, in my house, was in a false position, which might give offence to her aunt, it was not the first, nor was it the last time that I felt it. How often has it been my lot, after I have sought to understand the relations between two people and the crises that they bring about, to hear, all of a sudden, a third person speak to me of them from his own point of view, for he has even closer relations with one of the two, a point of view which has perhaps been the cause of the crisis. And if people's actions remain so indefinite, how should not the people themselves be equally indefinite? If I listened to the people who maintained that Albertine was a schemer who had tried to get one man after another to marry her, it was not difficult to imagine how they would have defined her life with me. And yet to my mind she had been a victim, a victim who perhaps was not altogether pure, but in that case guilty for other reasons, on account of vices to which people did not refer. But we must above all say to ourselves this: on the one hand, lying is often a trait of character; on the other hand, in women who would not otherwise be liars, it is a natural defence, improvised at first, then more and more organised, against that sudden danger which would be capable of destroying all life: love. On the other hand again, it is not the effect of chance if men who are intelligent and sensitive invariably give themselves to insensitive and inferior women, and are at the same time so attached to them that the proof that they are not loved does not in the least cure them of the instinct to sacrifice everything else in the attempt to keep such a woman with them. If I say that such men need to suffer, I am saying something that is accurate while suppressing the preliminary truths which make that need – involuntary in a sense – to suffer a perfectly comprehensible consequence of those truths. Without taking into account that, complete natures being rare, a man who is highly sensitive and highly intelligent will generally have little will-power, will be the plaything of habit and of that fear of suffering in the immediate present which condemns us to perpetual suffering – and that in those conditions he will never be prepared to repudiate the woman who does not love him. We may be surprised that he should be content with so little love, but we ought rather to picture to ourselves the grief that may be caused him by the love which he himself feels. A grief which we ought not to pity unduly, for those terrible commotions which are caused by an unrequited love, by the departure, the death of a mistress, are like those attacks of paralysis which at first leave us helpless, but after which our muscles begin by degrees to recover their vital elasticity and energy. What is more, this grief does not lack compensation. These sensitive and intelligent men are as a rule little inclined to falsehood. This takes them all the more by surprise inasmuch as, intelligent as they may be, they live in the world of possibilities, react little, live in the grief which a woman has just inflicted on them, rather than in the clear perception of what she had in mind, what she was doing, of the man with whom she was in love, a perception granted chiefly to deliberate natures which require it in order to prepare against the future instead of lamenting the past. And so these men feel that they are betrayed without quite knowing how. Wherefore the mediocre woman with whom we were surprised to see them fall in love enriches the universe for them far more than an intelligent woman would have done. Behind each of her words, they feel that a lie is lurking, behind each house to which she says that she has gone, another house, behind each action, each person, another action, another person. Doubtless they do not know what or whom, have not the energy, would not perhaps find it possible to discover. A lying woman, by an extremely simple trick, can beguile, without taking the trouble to change her method, any number of people, and, what is more, the very person who ought to have discovered the trick. All this creates, in front of the sensitive and intelligent man, a universe all depth which his jealousy would fain plumb and which is not without interest to his intelligence.

Albeit I was not exactly a man of that category, I was going perhaps, now that Albertine was dead, to learn the secret of her life. Here again, do not these indiscretions which occur only after a person's life on earth is ended, prove that nobody believes, really, in a future state? If these indiscretions are true, we ought to fear the resentment of her whose actions we are revealing fully as much on the day when we shall meet her in heaven, as we feared it so long as she was alive, when we felt ourselves bound to keep her secret. And if these indiscretions are false, invented because she is no longer present to contradict them, we ought to be even more afraid of the dead woman's wrath if we believed in heaven. But no one does believe in it. So that it was possible that a long debate had gone on in Albertine's heart between staying with me and leaving me, but that her decision to leave me had been made on account of her aunt, or of that young man, and not on account of women to whom perhaps she had never given a thought. The most serious thing to my mind was that Andrée, albeit she had nothing now to conceal from me as to Albertine's morals, swore to me that nothing of the sort had ever occurred between Albertine on the one hand and Mlle Vinteuil or her friend on the other. (Albertine herself was unconscious of her own instincts when she first met the girls, and they, from that fear of making a mistake in the object of our desire, which breeds as many errors as desire itself, regarded her as extremely hostile to that sort of thing. Perhaps later on they had learned that her tastes were similar to their own, but by that time they knew Albertine too well and Albertine knew them too well for there to be any thought of their doing things together.) In short I did not understand any better than before why Albertine had left me. If the face of a woman is perceived with difficulty by our eyes which cannot take in the whole of its moving surface, by our lips, still more by our memory, if it is shrouded in obscurity according to her social position, according to the level at which we are situated, how much thicker is the veil drawn between the actions of her whom we see and her motives. Her motives are situated in a more distant plane, which we do not perceive, and engender moreover actions other than those which we know and often in absolute contradiction to them. When has there not been some man in public life, regarded as a saint by his friends, who is discovered to have forged documents, robbed the State, betrayed his country? How often is a great nobleman robbed by a steward, whom he has brought up from childhood, ready to swear that he was an honest man, as possibly he was? Now this curtain that screens another person's motives, how much more impenetrable does it become if we are in love with that person, for it clouds our judgment and also obscures the actions of her who, feeling that she is loved, ceases at once to attach any value to what otherwise would doubtless have seemed to her important, such as wealth for example. Perhaps moreover she is impelled to pretend, to a certain extent, this scorn of wealth in the hope of obtaining more money by making us suffer. The bargaining instinct also may be involved. And so with the actual incidents in her life, an intrigue which she has confided to no one for fear of its being revealed to us, which many people might, for all that, have discovered, had they felt the same passionate desire to know it as ourselves, while preserving freer minds, arousing fewer suspicions in the guilty party, an intrigue of which certain people have not been unaware – but people whom we do not know and should not know how to find. And among all these reasons for her adopting an inexplicable attitude towards us, we must include those idiosyncrasies of character which impel a person, whether from indifference to his own interests, or from hatred, or from love of freedom, or from sudden bursts of anger, or from fear of what certain people will think, to do the opposite of what we expected. And then there are the differences of environment, of upbringing, in which we refuse to believe because, when we are talking together, they are effaced by our speech, but which return, when we are apart, to direct the actions of each of us from so opposite a point of view that there is no possibility of their meeting. 'But, my dear Andrée, you are lying again. Remember – you admitted it to me yourself – I telephoned to you the evening before; you remember Albertine had been so anxious, and kept it from me as though it had been something that I must not know about, to go to the afternoon party at the Verdurins' at which Mlle Vinteuil was expected.' 'Yes, but Albertine had not the slightest idea that Mlle Vinteuil was to be there.' 'What? You yourself told me that she had met Mme Verdurin a few days earlier. Besides, Andrée, there is no point in our trying to deceive one another. I found a letter one morning in Albertine's room, a note from Mme Verdurin begging her to come that afternoon.' And I showed her the note which, as a matter of fact, Françoise had taken care to bring to my notice by placing it on the surface of Albertine's possessions a few days before her departure, and, I am afraid, leaving it there to make Albertine suppose that I had been rummaging among her things, to

let her know in any case that I had seen it. And I had often asked myself
whether Françoise's ruse had not been largely responsible for the departure
of Albertine, who saw that she could no longer conceal anything from me,
and felt disheartened, vanquished. I showed Andrée the letter: 'I feel no
compunction, everything is excused by this strong family feeling . . . ' 'You
know very well, Andrée, that Albertine used always to say that Mlle Vinteuil's
friend was indeed a mother, an elder sister to her.' 'But you have misinterpreted this note. The person that Mme Verdurin wished Albertine to
meet that afternoon was not at all Mlle Vinteuil's friend, it was the young
man you call 'I am in the soup', and the strong family feeling is what Mme
Verdurin felt for the brute who is after all her nephew. At the same time I
think that Albertine did hear afterwards that Mlle Vinteuil was to be there,
Mme Verdurin may have let her know separately. Of course the thought of
seeing her friend again gave her pleasure, reminded her of happy times in
the past, but just as you would be glad, if you were going to some place, to
know that Elstir would be there, but no more than that, not even as much.
No, if Albertine was unwilling to say why she wanted to go to Mme
Verdurin's, it is because it was a rehearsal to which Mme Verdurin had
invited a very small party, including that nephew of hers whom you had met
at Balbec, to whom Mme Bontemps was hoping to marry Albertine and to
whom Albertine wanted to talk. A fine lot of people!' And so Albertine, in
spite of what Andrée's mother used to think, had had after all the prospect of
a wealthy marriage. And when she had wanted to visit Mme Verdurin, when
she spoke to her in secret, when she had been so annoyed that I should have
gone there that evening without warning her, the plot that had been woven
by her and Mme Verdurin had had as its object her meeting not Mlle
Vinteuil but the nephew with whom Albertine was in love and for whom
Mme Verdurin was acting as go-between, with the satisfaction in working
for the achievement of one of those marriages which surprise us in certain
families into whose state of mind we do not enter completely, supposing
them to be intent upon a rich bride. Now I had never given another thought
to this nephew who had perhaps been the initiator thanks to whom I had
received her first kiss. And for the whole plane of Albertine's motives which
I had constructed, I must now substitute another, or rather superimpose it,
for perhaps it did not exclude the other, a preference for women did not
prevent her from marrying. 'And anyhow there is no need to seek out all
these explanations,' Andrée went on. 'Heaven only knows how I loved
Albertine and what a good creature she was, but really, after she had typhoid
(a year before you first met us all) she was an absolute madcap. All of a
sudden she would be disgusted with what she was doing, all her plans would

have to be changed at once, and she herself probably could not tell you why. You remember the year when you first came to Balbec, the year when you met us all? One fine day she made someone send her a telegram calling her back to Paris, she had barely time to pack her trunks. But there was absolutely no reason for her to go. All the excuses that she made were false. Paris was impossible for her at the moment. We were all of us still at Balbec. The golf club wasn't closed, indeed the heats for the cup which she was so keen on winning weren't finished. She was certain to win it. It only meant staying on for another week. Well, off she went. I have often spoken to her about it since. She said herself that she didn't know why she had left, that she felt home-sick (the home being Paris, you can imagine how likely that was), that she didn't feel happy at Balbec, that she thought that there were people there who were laughing at her.' And I told myself that there was this amount of truth in what Andrée said that, if differences between minds account for the different impressions produced upon one person and another by the same work, for differences of feeling, for the impossibility of captivating a person to whom we do not appeal, there are also the differences between characters, the peculiarities of a single character, which are also motives for action. Then I ceased to think about this explanation and said to myself how difficult it is to know the truth in this world. I had indeed observed Albertine's anxiety to go to Mme Verdurin's and her concealment of it and I had not been mistaken. But then even if we do manage to grasp one fact like this, there are others which we perceive only in their outward appearance, for the reverse of the tapestry, the real side of the action, of the intrigue – as well as that of the intellect, of the heart – is hidden from us and we see pass before us only flat silhouettes of which we say to ourselves: it is this, it is that; it is on her account, or on someone's else. The revelation of the fact that Mlle Vinteuil was expected had seemed to me an explanation all the more logical seeing that Albertine had anticipated it by mentioning her to me. And subsequently had she not refused to swear to me that Mlle Vinteuil's presence gave her no pleasure? And here, with regard to this young man, I remembered a point which I had forgotten; a little time earlier, while Albertine was staying with me, I had met him, and he had been – in contradiction of his attitude at Balbec – extremely friendly, even affectionate with me, had begged me to allow him to call upon me, which I had declined to do for a number of reasons. And now I realised that it was simply because, knowing that Albertine was staying in the house, he had wished to be on good terms with me so as to have every facility for seeing her and for carrying her off from me, and I concluded that he was a scoundrel. Some time later, when I attended the first performances of this young man's works, no doubt I continued to think that if he had been so anxious to call upon me, it was for Albertine's sake, but, while I felt this to be reprehensible, I remembered that in the past if I had gone down to Doncieres, to see Saint-Loup, it was really because I was in love with Mme de Guermantes. It is true that the situation was not identical, since Saint-Loup had not been in love with Mme de Guermantes, with the result that there was in my affection for him a trace of duplicity perhaps, but no treason. But I reflected afterwards that this affection which we feel for the person who controls the object of our desire, we feel equally if the person controls that object while loving it himself. No doubt, we have then to struggle against a friendship which will lead us straight to treason. And I think that this is what I have always done. But in the case of those who have not the strength to struggle, we cannot say that in them the friendship that they affect for the controller is a mere ruse; they feel it sincerely and for that reason display it with an ardour which, once the betrayal is complete, means that the betrayed husband or lover is able to say with a stupefied indignation: 'If you had heard the protestations of affection that the wretch showered on me! That a person should come to rob a man of his treasure, that I can understand. But that he should feel the diabolical need to assure him first of all of his friendship, is a degree of ignominy and perversity which it is impossible to imagine.' Now, there is no such perversity in the action, nor even an absolutely clear falsehood. The affection of this sort which Albertine's pseudo-fiancé had manifested for me that day had yet another excuse, being more complex than a simple consequence of his love for Albertine. It had been for a short time only that he had known himself, confessed himself, been anxious to be proclaimed an intellectual. For the first time values other than sporting or amatory existed for him. The fact that I had been regarded with esteem by Elstir, by Bergotte, that Albertine had perhaps told him of the way in which I criticised writers which led her to imagine that I might myself be able to write, had the result that all of a sudden I had become to him (to the new man who he at last realised himself to be) an interesting person with whom he would like to be associated, to whom he would like to confide his plans, whom he would ask perhaps for an introduction to Elstir. With the result that he was sincere when he asked if he might call upon me, expressing a regard for me to which intellectual reasons as well as the thought of Albertine imparted sincerity. No doubt it was not *for that* that he was so anxious to come and see me and would have sacrificed everything else with that object. But of this last reason which did little more than raise to a sort of impassioned paroxysm the two other reasons, he was perhaps unaware himself, and the other two existed really, as might have existed really in Albertine when she had been anxious to go, on the afternoon of the rehearsal, to Mme Verdurin's, the perfectly respectable pleasure that she would feel in meeting again friends of her childhood, who in her eyes were no more vicious than she was in theirs, in talking to them, in showing them, by the mere fact of her presence at the Verdurins', that the poor little girl whom they had known was now invited to a distinguished house, the pleasure also that she might perhaps have felt in listening to Vinteuil's music. If all this was true, the blush that had risen to Albertine's cheeks when I mentioned Mlle Vinteuil was due to what I had done with regard to that afternoon party which she had tried to keep secret from me, because of that proposal of marriage of which I was not to know. Albertine's refusal to swear to me that she would not have felt any pleasure in meeting Mlle Vinteuil again at that party had at the moment intensified my torment, strengthened my suspicions, but proved to me in retrospect that she had been determined to be sincere, and even over an innocent matter, perhaps simply because it was an innocent matter. There remained what Andrée had told me about her relations with Albertine. Perhaps, however, even without going so far as to believe that Andrée had invented the story solely in order that I might not feel happy and might not feel myself superior to her, I might still suppose that she had slightly exaggerated her account of what she used to do with Albertine, and that Albertine, by a mental restriction, diminished slightly also what she had done with Andrée, making use systematically of certain definitions which I had stupidly formulated upon the subject, finding that her relations with Andrée did not enter into the field of what she was obliged to confess to me and that she could deny them without lying. But why should I believe that it was she rather than Andrée who was lying? Truth and life are very arduous, and there remained to me from them, without my really knowing them, an impression in which sorrow was perhaps actually dominated by exhaustion.

As for the third occasion on which I remember that I was conscious of approaching an absolute indifference with regard to Albertine (and on this third occasion I felt that I had entirely arrived at it), it was one day, at Venice, a long time after Andrée's last visit.

CHAPTER THREE

Venice

My mother had brought me for a few weeks to Venice and – as there may be beauty in the most precious as well as in the humblest things – I was receiving there impressions analogous to those which I had felt so often in the past at Combray, but transposed into a wholly different and far richer key. When at ten o'clock in the morning my shutters were thrown open, I saw ablaze in the sunlight, instead of the black marble into which the slates of Saint-Hilaire used to turn, the Golden Angel on the Campanile of San Marco. In its dazzling glitter, which made it almost impossible to fix it in space, it promised me with its outstretched arms, for the moment, half an hour later, when I was to appear on the Piazzetta, a joy more certain than any that it could ever in the past have been bidden to announce to men of good will. I could see nothing but itself, so long as I remained in bed, but as the whole world is merely a vast sundial, a single lighted segment of which enables us to tell what o'clock it is, on the very first morning I was reminded of the shops in the Place de l'Eglise at Combray, which, on Sunday mornings, were always on the point of shutting when I arrived for mass, while the straw in the market place smelt strongly in the already hot sunlight. But on the second morning, what I saw, when I awoke, what made me get out of bed (because they had taken the place in my consciousness and in my desire of my memories of Combray), were the impressions of my first morning stroll in Venice, Venice whose daily life was no less real than that of Combray, where as at Combray on Sunday mornings one had the delight of emerging upon a festive street, but where that street was paved with water of a sapphire blue, refreshed by little ripples of cooler air, and of so solid a colour that my tired eyes might, in quest of relaxation and without fear of its giving way, rest their gaze upon it. Like, at Combray, the worthy folk of the Rue de l'Oiseau, so in this strange town also, the inhabitants did indeed emerge from houses drawn up in line, side by side, along the principal street, but the part played there by houses that cast a patch of shade before them was in Venice entrusted to palaces of porphyry and jasper, over the arched door of which the head of a bearded god (projecting from its

alignment, like the knocker on a door at Combray) had the effect of
darkening with its shadow, not the brownness of the soil but the splendid
blue of the water. On the *piazza*, the shadow that would have been cast at
Combray by the linen-draper's awning and the barber's pole, turned into
the tiny blue flowers scattered at its feet upon the desert of sun-scorched
tiles by the silhouette of a Renaissance façade, which is not to say that, when
the sun was hot, we were not obliged, in Venice as at Combray, to pull down
the blinds between ourselves and the Canal, but they hung behind the
quatrefoils and foliage of Gothic windows. Of this sort was the window in
our hotel behind the pillars of which my mother sat waiting for me, gazing
at the Canal with a patience which she would not have displayed in the old
days at Combray, at that time when, reposing in myself hopes which had
never been realised, she was unwilling to let me see how much she loved me.
Nowadays she was well aware that an apparent coldness on her part would
alter nothing, and the affection that she lavished upon me was like those
forbidden foods which are no longer withheld from invalids, when it is
certain that they are past recovery. To be sure, the humble details which
gave an individuality to the window of my aunt Léonie's bedroom, seen
from the Rue de l'Oiseau, the asymmetry of its position not midway
between the windows on either side of it, the exceptional height of its
wooden ledge, the slanting bar which kept the shutters closed, the two
curtains of glossy blue satin, divided and kept apart by their rod, the
equivalent of all these things existed in this hotel in Venice where I could
hear also those words, so distinctive, so eloquent, which enable us to
recognise at a distance the house to which we are going home to luncheon,
and afterwards remain in our memory as testimony that, during a certain
period of time, that house was ours; but the task of uttering them had, in
Venice, devolved not, as at Combray, and indeed, to a certain extent,
everywhere, upon the simplest, that is to say the least beautiful things, but
upon the almost oriental arch of a façade which is reproduced among the
casts in every museum as one of the supreme achievements of the domestic
architecture of the middle ages; from a long way away and when I had barely
passed San Giorgio Maggiore, I caught sight of this arched window which
had already seen me, and the spring of its broken curves added to its smile of
welcome the distinction of a loftier, scarcely comprehensible gaze. And
since, behind those pillars of differently coloured marble, Mamma was
sitting reading while she waited for me to return, her face shrouded in a tulle
veil as agonising in its whiteness as her hair to myself who felt that my
mother, wiping away her tears, had pinned it to her straw hat, partly with
the idea of appearing 'dressed' in the eyes of the hotel staff, but principally

so as to appear to me less 'in mourning', less sad, almost consoled for the death of my grandmother; since, not having recognised me at first, as soon as I called to her from the gondola, she sent out to me, from the bottom of her heart, a love which stopped only where there was no longer any material substance to support it on the surface of her impassioned gaze which she brought as close to me as possible, which she tried to thrust forward to the advanced post of her lips, in a smile which seemed to be kissing me, in the framework and beneath the canopy of the more discreet smile of the arched window illuminated by the midday sun; for these reasons, that window has assumed in my memory the precious quality of things that have had, simultaneously, side by side with ourselves, their part in a certain hour that struck, the same for us and for them; and however full of admirable tracery its mullions may be, that illustrious window retains in my sight the intimate aspect of a man of genius with whom we have spent a month in some holiday resort, where he has acquired a friendly regard for us; and if, ever since then, whenever I see a cast of that window in a museum, I feel the tears starting to my eyes, it is simply because the window says to me the thing that touches me more than anything else in the world: 'I remember your mother so well.'

And as I went indoors to join my mother who had left the window, I did indeed recapture, coming from the warm air outside, that feeling of coolness that I had known long ago at Combray when I went upstairs to my room, but at Venice it was a breeze from the sea that kept the air cool, and no longer upon a little wooden staircase with narrow steps, but upon the noble surfaces of blocks of marble, splashed at every moment by a shaft of greenish sunlight, which to the valuable instruction in the art of Chardin, acquired long ago, added a lesson in that of Veronese. And since at Venice it is to works of art, to things of priceless beauty, that the task is entrusted of giving us our impressions of everyday life, we may sketch the character of this city, using the pretext that the Venice of certain painters is coldly aesthetic in its most celebrated parts, by representing only (let us make an exception of the superb studies of Maxime Dethomas) its poverty-stricken aspects, in the quarters where everything that creates its splendour is concealed, and to make Venice more intimate and more genuine give it a resemblance to Aubervilliers. It has been the mistake of some very great artists, that, by a quite natural reaction from the artificial Venice of bad painters, they have attached themselves exclusively to the Venice which they have found more realistic, to some humble *campo*, some tiny deserted *rio*. It was this Venice that I used often to explore in the afternoon, when I did not go out with my mother. The fact was that it was easier to find there women of the industrial class, matchmakers, pearl-stringers, workers in glass or lace, working women

in black shawls with long fringes. My gondola followed the course of the
small canals; like the mysterious hand of a Genie leading me through the
maze of this oriental city, they seemed, as I advanced, to be carving a road
for me through the heart of a crowded quarter which they clove asunder,
barely dividing with a slender fissure, arbitrarily carved, the tall houses with
their tiny Moorish windows; and, as though the magic guide had been
holding a candle in his hand and were lighting the way for me, they kept
casting ahead of them a ray of sunlight for which they cleared a path.

One felt that between the mean dwellings which the canal had just parted
and which otherwise would have formed a compact whole, no open space
had been reserved. With the result that the belfry of the church, or the
garden-trellis rose sheer above the *rio* as in a flooded city. But with churches
as with gardens, thanks to the same transposition as in the Grand Canal, the
sea formed so effective a way of communication, a substitute for street or
alley, that on either side of the *canaletto* the churches rose from the water in
this ancient, plebeian quarter, degraded into humble, much frequented
mission chapels, bearing upon their surface the stamp of their necessity, of
their use by crowds of simple folk, that the gardens crossed by the line of the
canal allowed their astonished leaves or fruit to trail in the water and that on
the doorstep of the house whose roughly hewn stone was still wrinkled as
though it had only just been sawn, little boys surprised by the gondola and
keeping their balance allowed their legs to dangle vertically, like sailors
seated upon a swing-bridge the two halves of which have been swung apart,
allowing the sea to pass between them.

Now and again there appeared a handsomer building that happened to be
there, like a surprise in a box which we have just opened, a little ivory temple
with its Corinthian columns and its allegorical statue on the pediment,
somewhat out of place among the ordinary buildings in the midst of which
it had survived, and the peristyle with which the canal provided it resembled
a landing-stage for market gardeners.

The sun had barely begun to set when I went to fetch my mother from the
Piazzetta. We returned up the Grand Canal in our gondola, we watched the
double line of palaces between which we passed reflect the light and angle of
the sun upon their rosy surfaces, and alter with them, seeming not so much
private habitations and historic buildings as a chain of marble cliffs at the
foot of which people go out in the evening in a boat to watch the sunset. In
this way, the mansions arranged along either bank of the canal made one
think of objects of nature, but of a nature which seemed to have created its
works with a human imagination. But at the same time (because of the
character of the impressions, always urban, which Venice gives us almost in

the open sea, upon those waves whose flow and ebb make themselves felt twice daily, and which alternately cover at high tide and uncover at low tide the splendid outside stairs of the palaces), as we should have done in Paris upon the boulevards, in the Champs-Elysées, in the Bois, in any wide thoroughfare that was a fashionable resort, in the powdery evening light, we passed the most beautifully dressed women, almost all foreigners, who, propped luxuriously upon the cushions of their floating vehicle, took their place in the procession, stopped before a palace in which there was a friend whom they wished to see, sent to enquire whether she was at home; and while, as they waited for the answer, they prepared to leave a card, as they would have done at the door of the Hôtel de Guermantes, they turned to their guidebook to find out the period, the style of the palace, not without being shaken, as though upon the crest of a blue wave, by the thrust of the flashing, prancing water, which took alarm on finding itself pent between the dancing gondola and the slapping marble. And thus any excursion, even when it was only to pay calls or to go shopping, was threefold and unique in this Venice where the simplest social coming and going assumed at the same time the form and the charm of a visit to a museum and a trip on the sea.

Several of the palaces on the Grand Canal had been converted into hotels, and, feeling the need of a change, or wishing to be hospitable to Mme Sazerat whom we had encountered – the unexpected and inopportune acquaintance whom we invariably meet when we travel abroad – and whom Mamma had invited to dine with us, we decided one evening to try an hotel which was not our own, and in which we had been told that the food was better. While my mother was paying the gondolier and taking Mme Sazerat to the room which she had engaged, I slipped away to inspect the great hall of the restaurant with its fine marble pillars and walls and ceiling that were once entirely covered with frescoes, recently and badly restored. Two waiters were conversing in an Italian which I translate: 'Are the old people going to dine in their room? They never let us know. It's the devil, I never know whether I am to reserve their table (*non so se bisogna conservargli la loro tavola*). And then, suppose they come down and find their table taken! I don't understand how they can take in *forestieri* like that in such a smart hotel. They're not our style.'

Notwithstanding his contempt, the waiter was anxious to know what action he was to take with regard to the table, and was going to get the lift-boy sent upstairs to enquire, when, before he had had time to do so, he received his answer: he had just caught sight of the old lady who was entering the room. I had no difficulty, despite the air of melancholy and weariness that comes with the burden of years, and despite a sort of eczema, a red leprosy that covered her face, in recognising beneath her bonnet, in her black jacket, made by W—, but to the untutored eye exactly like that of an old charwoman, the Marquise de Villeparisis. As luck would have it, the spot upon which I was standing, engaged in studying the remains of a fresco, between two of the beautiful marble panels, was directly behind the table at which Mme de Villeparisis had just sat down.

'Then M. de Villeparisis won't be long. They've been here a month now, and it's only once that they didn't have a meal together,' said the waiter.

I was asking myself who the relative could be with whom she was travelling, and who was named M. de Villeparisis, when I saw, a few moments later, advance towards the table and sit down by her side, her old lover, M. de Norpois.

His great age had weakened the resonance of his voice, but had in compensation given to his language, formerly so reserved, a positive intemperance. The cause of this was to be sought, perhaps, in certain ambitions for the realisation of which little time, he felt, remained to him, and which filled him all the more with vehemence and ardour; perhaps in the fact that, having been discarded from a world of politics to which he longed to return, he imagined, in the simplicity of his desire, that he could turn out of office, by the pungent criticisms which he launched at them, the men whose places he was anxious to fill. Thus we see politicians convinced that the Cabinet of which they are not members cannot hold out for three days. It would, however, be an exaggeration to suppose that M. de Norpois had entirely lost the traditions of diplomatic speech. Whenever 'important matters' were involved, he at once became, as we shall see, the man whom we remember in the past, but at all other times he would inveigh against this man and that with the senile violence of certain octogenarians which hurls them into the arms of women to whom they are no longer capable of doing any serious damage.

Mme de Villeparisis preserved, for some minutes, the silence of an old woman who in the exhaustion of age finds it difficult to rise from memories of the past to consideration of the present. Then, turning to one of those eminently practical questions that indicate the survival of a mutual affection: 'Did you call at Salviati's?'

'Yes.'

'Will they send it tomorrow?'

'I brought the bowl back myself. You shall see it after dinner. Let us see what there is to eat.'

'Did you send instructions about my Suez shares?'

'No; at the present moment the market is entirely taken up with oil shares.

But there is no hurry, they are still fetching an excellent price. Here is the bill of fare. First of all, there are red mullets. Shall we try them?'

'For me, yes, but you are not allowed them. Ask for a risotto instead. But they don't know how to cook it.'

'That doesn't matter. Waiter, some mullets for Madame and a risotto for me.'

A fresh and prolonged silence.

'Why, I brought you the papers, the *Corrière della Sera*, the *Gazzetta del Popolo*, and all the rest of them. Do you know, there is a great deal of talk about a diplomatic change, the first scapegoat in which is to be Paléologue, who is notoriously inadequate in Serbia. He will perhaps be succeeded by Lozé, and there will be a vacancy at Constantinople. But,' M. de Norpois hastened to add in a bitter tone, 'for an Embassy of such scope, in a capital where it is obvious that Great Britain must always, whatever may happen, occupy the chief place at the council-table, it would be prudent to turn to men of experience better armed to resist the ambushes of the enemies of our British ally than are diplomats of the modern school who would walk blindfold into the trap.' The angry volubility with which M. de Norpois uttered the last words was due principally to the fact that the newspapers, instead of suggesting his name, as he had requested them to do, named as a 'hot favourite' a young official of the Foreign Ministry. 'Heaven knows that the men of years and experience may well hesitate, as a result of all manner of tortuous manoeuvres, to put themselves forward in the place of more or less incapable recruits. I have known many of these self-styled diplomats of the empirical method who centred all their hopes in a soap bubble which it did not take me long to burst. There can be no question about it, if the Government is so lacking in wisdom as to entrust the reins of state to turbulent hands, at the call of duty an old conscript will always answer "Present!" But who knows' (and here M. de Norpois appeared to know perfectly well to whom he was referring) 'whether it would not be the same on the day when they came in search of some veteran full of wisdom and skill. To my mind, for everyone has a right to his own opinion, the post at Constantinople should not be accepted until we have settled our existing difficulties with Germany. We owe no man anything, and it is intolerable that every six months they should come and demand from us, by fraudulent machinations, and extort by force and fear, the payment of some debt or other, always hastily offered by a venal press. This must cease, and naturally a man of high distinction who has proved his merit, a man who would have, if I may say so, the Emperor's ear, would wield greater authority than any ordinary person in bringing the conflict to an end.'

A gentleman who was finishing his dinner bowed to M. de Norpois.

'Why, there is Prince Foggi,' said the Marquis.

'Ah, I'm not sure that I know whom you mean,' muttered Mme de Villeparisis.

'Why, of course you do. It is Prince Odone. The brother-in-law of your cousin Doudeauville. You cannot have forgotten that I went shooting with him at Bonnétable?'

'Ah! Odone, that is the one who went in for painting?'

'Not at all, he's the one who married the Grand Duke N—'s sister.'

M. de Norpois uttered these remarks in the cross tone of a schoolmaster who is dissatisfied with his pupil, and stared fixedly at Mme de Villeparisis out of his blue eyes.

When the Prince had drunk his coffee and was leaving his table, M. de Norpois rose, hastened towards him and with a majestic wave of his arm, himself retiring into the background, presented him to Mme de Villeparisis. And during the next few minutes while the Prince was standing beside their table, M. de Norpois never ceased for an instant to keep his azure pupils trained on Mme de Villeparisis, from the weakness or severity of an old lover, principally from fear of her making one of those mistakes in Italian which he had relished but which he dreaded. Whenever she said anything to the Prince that was not quite accurate he corrected her mistake and stared into the eyes of the abashed and docile Marquise with the steady intensity of a hypnotist.

A waiter came to tell me that my mother was waiting for me, I went to her and made my apologies to Mme Sazerat, saying that I had been interested to see Mme de Villeparisis. At the sound of this name, Mme Sazerat turned pale and seemed about to faint. Controlling herself with an effort: 'Mme de Villeparisis, who was Mlle de Bouillon?' she enquired.

'Yes.'

'Couldn't I just get a glimpse of her for a moment? It has been the desire of my life.'

'Then there is no time to lose, Madame, for she will soon have finished her dinner. But how do you come to take such an interest in her?'

'Because Mme de Villeparisis was, before her second marriage, the Duchesse d'Havre, beautiful as an angel, wicked as a demon, who drove my father out of his senses, ruined him and then forsook him immediately. Well, she may have behaved to him like any girl out of the gutter, she may have been the cause of our having to live, my family and myself, in a humble position at Combray; now that my father is dead, my consolation is to think that he was in love with the most beautiful woman of his generation, and as I have never set eyes on her, it will, after all, be a pleasure . . .'

I escorted Mme Sazerat, trembling with emotion, to the restaurant and pointed out Mme de Villeparisis.

But, like a blind person who turns his face in the wrong direction, so Mme Sazerat did not bring her gaze to rest upon the table at which Mme de Villeparisis was dining, but, looking towards another part of the room, said: 'But she must have gone, I don't see her in the place you're pointing to.'

And she continued to gaze round the room, in quest of the loathed, adored vision that had haunted her imagination for so long.

'Yes, there she is, at the second table.'

'Then we can't be counting from the same point. At what I call the second table there are only two people, an old gentleman and a little hunchbacked, red-faced woman, quite hideous.'

'That is she!'

In the meantime, Mme de Villeparisis having asked M. de Norpois to make Prince Foggi sit down, a friendly conversation followed among the three of them; they discussed politics, the Prince declared that he was not interested in the fate of the Cabinet and would spend another week at least at Venice. He hoped that in the interval all risk of a ministerial crisis would have been obviated. Prince Foggi supposed for a moment that these political topics did not interest M. de Norpois, for the latter who until then had been expressing himself with such vehemence had become suddenly absorbed in an almost angelic silence which he seemed capable of breaking, should his voice return, only by singing some innocent melody by Mendelssohn or César Franck. The Prince supposed also that this silence was due to the reserve of a Frenchman who naturally would not wish to discuss Italian affairs in the presence of an Italian. Now in this, the Prince was completely mistaken. Silence, an air of indifference were, in M. de Norpois, not a sign of reserve but the regular prelude to an intervention in important affairs. The Marquis had his eye upon nothing less (as we have seen) than Constantinople, with a preliminary settlement of the German question, with a view to which he hoped to force the hand of the Rome Cabinet. He considered, in fact, that an action on his part of international range might be the worthy crown of his career, perhaps even an avenue to fresh honours, to difficult tasks to which he had not relinquished his pretensions. For old age makes us incapable of performing our duties but not, at first, of desiring them. It is only in a third period that those who live to a very great age have relinquished desire, as they have had already to forego action. They no longer present themselves as candidates at futile elections which they tried so often to win, the Presidential election, for instance. They content themselves with taking the air, eating, reading the newspapers, they have outlived themselves.

The Prince, to put the Marquis at his ease and to show him that he regarded him as a compatriot, began to speak of the possible successors to the Prime Minister then in office. A successor who would have a difficult task before him. When Prince Foggi had mentioned more than twenty names of politicians who seemed to him suitable for office, names to which the ex-ambassador listened with his eyelids drooping over his blue eyes and without moving a muscle, M. de Norpois broke his silence at length to utter those words which were for a score of years to supply the Chanceries with food for conversation, and afterwards, when they had been forgotten, would be exhumed by some personage signing himself 'One Who Knows' or 'Testis' or 'Machiavelli' in a newspaper in which the very oblivion into which they had fallen entitled them to create a fresh sensation. As I say, Prince Foggi had mentioned more than twenty names to the diplomat who remained as motionless and mute as though he were stone deaf when M. de Norpois raised his head slightly, and, in the form that had been assumed by those of his diplomatic interventions which had had the most far-reaching consequences, albeit this time with greater audacity and less brevity, asked shrewdly: 'And has no one mentioned the name of Signor Giolitti?' At these words the scales fell from Prince Foggi's eyes; he could hear a celestial murmur. Then at once M. de Norpois began to speak about one thing and another, no longer afraid to make a sound, as, when the last note of a sublime aria by Bach has been played, the audience are no longer afraid to talk aloud, to call for their hats and coats in the cloakroom. He made the difference even more marked by begging the Prince to pay his most humble respects to Their Majesties the King and Queen when next he should see them, a phrase of dismissal which corresponds to the shout for a coachman at the end of a concert: 'Auguste, from the Rue de Belloy.' We cannot say what exactly were Prince Foggi's impressions. He must certainly have been delighted to have heard the gem: 'And Signor Giolitti, has no one mentioned his name?' For M. de Norpois, in whom age had destroyed or deranged his most outstanding qualities, had on the other hand, as he grew older, perfected his bravura, as certain aged musicians, who in all other respects have declined, acquire and retain until the end, in the matter of chamber-music, a perfect virtuosity which they did not formerly possess.

However that may be, Prince Foggi, who had intended to spend a fortnight in Venice returned to Rome that very night and was received a few days later in audience by the King in connection with the property which, as we may perhaps have mentioned already, the Prince owned in Sicily. The Cabinet hung on for longer than could have been expected. When it fell, the King consulted various statesmen as to the most suitable head of the new Cabinet. Then he sent for Signor Giolitti who accepted. Three months later a newspaper reported Prince Foggi's meeting with M. de Norpois. The conversation was reported as we have given it here, with the difference that, instead of: 'M. de Norpois asked shrewdly', one read: 'M. de Norpois said with that shrewd and charming smile which is so characteristic of him.' M. de Norpois considered that 'shrewdly' had in itself sufficient explosive force for a diplomat and that this addition was, to say the least, untimely. He had even asked the Quai d'Orsay to issue an official contradiction, but the Quai d'Orsay did not know which way to turn. As a matter of fact, ever since the conversation had been made public, M. Barrère had been telegraphing several times hourly to Paris, pointing out that there was already an accredited Ambassador at the Quirinal and describing the indignation with which the incident had been received throughout the whole of Europe. This indignation was nonexistent, but the other Ambassadors were too polite to contradict M. Barrère when he assured them that there could be no question about everybody's being furious. M. Barrère, listening only to his own thoughts, mistook this courteous silence for assent. Immediately he telegraphed to Paris: 'I have just had an hour's conversation with the Marchese Visconti-Venosta', and so forth. His secretaries were worn to skin and bone. M. de Norpois, however, could count upon the devotion of a French newspaper of very long standing, which indeed in 1870, when he was French Minister in a German capital, had rendered him an important service. This paper (especially its leading article, which was unsigned) was admirably written. But the paper became a thousand times more interesting when this leading article (styled 'premier-Paris' in those far off days and now, no one knows why, 'editorial') was on the contrary badly expressed, with endless repetitions of words. Everyone felt then, with emotion, that the article had been 'inspired'. Perhaps by M. de Norpois, perhaps by some other leading man of the hour. To give an anticipatory idea of the Italian incident, let us show how M. de Norpois made use of this paper in 1870, to no purpose, it may be thought, since war broke out nevertheless – most efficaciously, according to M. de Norpois, whose axiom was that we ought first and foremost to prepare public opinion. His articles, every word in which was weighed, resembled those optimistic bulletins which are at once followed by the death of the patient. For instance, on the eve of the declaration of war, in 1870, when mobilisation was almost complete, M. de Norpois (remaining, of course, in the background) had felt it to be his duty to send to this famous newspaper the following 'editorial':

The opinion seems to prevail in authoritative circles, that since the afternoon hours of yesterday, the situation, without of course being of an alarming nature, might well be envisaged as serious and even, from certain angles, as susceptible of being regarded as critical. M. le Marquis de Norpois would appear to have held several conversations with the Prussian Minister, in order to examine in a firm and conciliatory spirit, and in a wholly concrete fashion, the different causes of friction that, if we may say so, exist. Unfortunately, we have not yet heard, at the hour of going to press, that Their Excellencies have been able to agree upon a formula that may serve as base for a diplomatic instrument.

Latest intelligence: 'We have learned with satisfaction in well-informed circles that a slight slackening of tension appears to have occurred in Franco-Prussian relations. We may attach a specially distinct importance to the fact that M. de Norpois is reported to have met the British Minister "unter den Linden" and to have conversed with him for fully twenty minutes. This report is regarded as highly satisfactory.' (There was added, in brackets, after the word 'satisfactory' its German equivalent '*befriedigend*'.) And on the following day one read in the editorial: 'It would appear that, notwithstanding all the dexterity of M. de Norpois, to whom everyone must hasten to render homage for the skill and energy with which he has managed to defend the inalienable rights of France, a rupture is now, so to speak, virtually inevitable.'

The newspaper could not refrain from following an editorial couched in this vein with a selection of comments, furnished of course by M. de Norpois. The reader may perhaps have observed in these last pages that the 'conditional mood' was one of the Ambassador's favourite grammatical forms, in the literature of diplomacy. ('One would attach a special import-ance' for 'it appears that people attach a special importance.') But the 'present indicative' employed not in its regular sense but in that of the old 'optative' was no less dear to M. de Norpois. The comments that followed the editorial were as follows:

'Never have the public shown themselves so admirably calm' (M. de Norpois would have liked to believe that this was true but feared that it was precisely the opposite of the truth). 'They are weary of fruitless agitation and have learned with satisfaction that His Majesty's Government would assume their responsibilities according to the eventualities that might occur. The public ask' (optative) 'nothing more. To their splendid coolness, which is in itself a token of victory, we shall add a piece of intelligence amply qualified to reassure public opinion, were there any need of that. We are, indeed, assured that M. de Norpois who, for reasons of health, was ordered long ago to return to Paris for medical treatment, would appear to have left Berlin where he considered that his presence no longer served any purpose.

Latest intelligence: 'His Majesty the Emperor left Compiègne this morning for Paris in order to confer with the Marquis de Norpois, the Minister for War and Marshal Bazaine upon whom public opinion relies with absolute confidence. H. M. the Emperor has cancelled the banquet which he was about to give for his sister-in-law the Duchess of Alba. This action created everywhere, as soon as it became known, a particularly favourable impression. The Emperor has held a review of his troops whose enthusiasm is indescribable. Several Corps, by virtue of a mobilisation order issued immediately upon the Sovereign's arrival in Paris, are, in any contingency, ready to move in the direction of the Rhine.

*   *   *

Sometimes at dusk as I returned to the hotel I felt that the Albertine of long ago invisible to my eyes was nevertheless enclosed within me as in the dungeons of an internal Venice, the solid walls of which some incident occasionally slid apart so as to give me a glimpse of that past.

Thus for instance one evening a letter from my stockbroker reopened for me for an instant the gates of the prison in which Albertine abode within me alive, but so remote, so profoundly buried that she remained inaccessible to me. Since her death I had ceased to take any interest in the speculations that I had made in order to have more money for her. But time had passed; the wisest judgments of the previous generation had been proved unwise by this generation, as had occurred in the past to M. Thiers who had said that railways could never prove successful. The stocks of which M. de Norpois had said to us: 'even if your income from them is nothing very great, you may be certain of never losing any of your capital', were, more often than not, those which had declined most in value. Calls had been made upon me for considerable sums and in a rash moment I decided to sell out everything and found that I now possessed barely a fifth of the fortune that I had had when Albertine was alive. This became known at Combray among the survivors of our family circle and their friends, and, as they knew that I went about with the Marquis de Saint-Loup and the Guermantes family, they said to themselves: 'Pride goes before a fall!' They would have been greatly astonished to learn that it was for a girl of Albertine's humble position that I had made these speculations. Besides, in that Combray world in which everyone is classified for ever according to the income that he is known to enjoy, as in an Indian caste, it would have been impossible for anyone to form any idea of the great freedom that prevailed in the world of the Guermantes where people attached no importance to wealth, and where poverty was regarded as being as disagreeable, but no more degrading, as having no more effect on a person's social position than would a stomach-ache. Doubtless they imagined, on the contrary, at Combray that Saint-Loup and M. de Guermantes must be ruined aristocrats, whose estates were mortgaged, to whom I had been lending money, whereas if I had been ruined they would have been the first to offer in all sincerity to come to my assistance. As for my comparative penury, it was all the more awkward at the moment inasmuch as my Venetian interests had been concentrated for some little time past on a rosy-cheeked young glass-vendor who offered to the delighted eye a whole range of orange tones and filled me with such a longing to see her again daily that, feeling that my mother and I would soon be leaving Venice, I had made up my mind that I would try to create some sort of position for her in Paris which would save me the distress of parting from her. The beauty of her seventeen summers was so noble, so radiant, that it was like acquiring a genuine Titian before leaving the place. And would the scant remains of my fortune be sufficient temptation to her to make her leave her native land and come to live in Paris for my sole convenience? But as I came to the end of the stockbroker's letter, a passage in which he said: 'I shall look after your credits' reminded me of a scarcely less hypocritically professional expression which the bath-attendant at Balbec had used in speaking to Aimé of Albertine. 'It was I that looked after her,' she had said, and these words which had never again entered my mind acted like an 'Open, sesame!' upon the hinges of the prison door. But a moment later the door closed once more upon the immured victim – whom I was not to blame for not wishing to join, since I was no longer able to see her to call her to mind, and since other people exist for us only to the extent of the idea that we retain of them – who had for an instant seemed to me so touching because of my desertion of her, albeit she was unaware of it, that I had for the duration of a lightning-flash thought with longing of the time, already remote, when I used to suffer night and day from the companionship of her memory. Another time at San Giorgio degli Schiavoni, an eagle accompanying one of the Apostles and conventionalised in the same manner revived the memory and almost the suffering caused by the two rings the similarity of which Françoise had revealed to me, and as to which I had never learned who had given them to Albertine. Finally, one evening, an incident occurred of such a nature that it seemed as though my love must revive. No sooner had our gondola stopped at the hotel steps than the porter handed me a telegram which the messenger had already brought three times to the hotel, for owing to the inaccurate rendering of the recipient's name (which I recognised nevertheless, through the corruptions introduced by Italian clerks, as my own) the post-office required a signed receipt certifying that the telegram was addressed to myself. I opened it as soon as I was in my own room, and, as I cast my eye over the sheet covered with inaccurately transmitted words, managed nevertheless to make out: 'My dear, you think me dead, forgive me, I am quite alive, should like to see you, talk about marriage, when do you return? Love. Albertine.' Then there occurred in me in inverse order a process parallel to that which had occurred in the case of my grandmother: when I had learned the fact of my grandmother's death, I had not at first felt any grief. And I had been really grieved by her death only when spontaneous memories had made her seem to me to be once again alive. Now that Albertine was no longer alive for me in my mind, the news that she was alive did not cause me the joy that I might have expected. Albertine had been nothing more to me than a bundle of thoughts, she had survived her bodily death so long as those thoughts were alive in me; on the other hand, now that those thoughts were dead, Albertine did not in any way revive for me, in her bodily form. And when I realised that I felt no joy at the thought of her being alive, that I no longer loved her, I ought to have been more astounded than a person who, looking at his reflection in the glass, after months of travel, or of sickness, discovers that he has white hair and a different face, that of a middle-aged or an old man. This appals us because its message is: 'the man that I was, the fair young man no longer exists, I am another person.' And yet, was not the impression that I now felt the proof of as profound a change, as total a death of my former self and of the no less complete substitution of a new self for that former self, as is proved by the sight of a wrinkled face capped with a snowy poll instead of the face of long ago? But we are no more disturbed by the fact of our having become another person, after a lapse of years and in the natural order of events, than we are disturbed at any given moment by the fact of our being, one after another, the incompatible persons, crafty, sensitive, refined, coarse, disinterested, ambitious, which we are, in turn, every day of our life. And the reason why this does not disturb us is the same, namely that the self which has been eclipsed – momentarily in this latter case and when it is a question of character, permanently in the former case and when it is a matter of passions – is not present to deplore the other, the other which is for the moment, or for all time, our whole self; the coarse self laughs at his own coarseness, for he is a coarse person, and the forgetful man does not worry about his loss of memory, simply because he has forgotten.

I should have been incapable of resuscitating Albertine because I was incapable of resuscitating myself, of resuscitating the self of those days. Life, according to its habit which is, by incessant, infinitesimal labours, to change the face of the world, had not said to me on the morrow of Albertine's death: 'Become another person', but, by changes too imperceptible for me to be conscious even that I was changing, had altered almost every element in me, with the result that my mind was already accustomed to its new master – my new self – when it became aware that it had changed; it was upon this new master that it depended. My affection for Albertine, my jealousy depended, as we have seen, upon the irradiation by the association of ideas of certain pleasant or painful impressions, upon the memory of Mlle Vinteuil at Montjouvain, upon the precious good-night kisses that Albertine used to bestow on my throat. But in proportion as these impressions had grown fainter, the vast field of impressions which they coloured with a hue that was agonising or soothing began to resume its neutral tint. As soon as oblivion had taken hold of certain dominant points of suffering and pleasure, the resistance offered by my love was overcome, I was no longer in love with Albertine. I tried to recall her image to my mind. I had been right in my presentiment when, a couple of days after Albertine's flight, I was appalled by the discovery that I had been able to live for forty-eight hours without her. It had been the same thing when I wrote to Gilberte long ago saying to myself: 'If this goes on – for a year or two, I shall no longer be in love with her.' And if, when Swann asked me to come and see Gilberte again, this had seemed to me as embarrassing as greeting a dead woman, in Albertine's case death – or what I had supposed to be death – had achieved the same result as a prolonged rupture in Gilberte's. Death acts only in the same way as absence. The monster at whose apparition my love had trembled, oblivion, had indeed, as I had feared, ended by devouring that love. Not only did the news that she was alive fail to revive my love, not only did it allow me to realise how far I had already proceeded on the way towards indifference, it at once and so abruptly accelerated that process that I asked myself whether in the past the converse report, that of Albertine's death, had not in like manner, by completing the effect of her departure, exalted my love and delayed its decline. And now that the knowledge that she was alive and the possibility of our reunion made her all of a sudden so worthless in my sight, I asked myself whether Françoise's insinuations, our rupture itself, and even her death (imaginary, but supposed to be true) had not prolonged my love, so true is it that the efforts of third persons and even those of fate, in separating us from a woman, succeed only in attaching us to her. Now it was the contrary process that had occurred. Anyhow, I tried to recall her image and perhaps because I had only to raise my finger to have her once more to myself, the memory that came to me was that of a very stout, masculine girl from whose colourless face protruded already, like a sprouting seed, the profile of Mme Bontemps. What she might or might not have done with Andrée or with other girls no longer interested me. I no longer suffered from the malady which I had so long thought to be incurable and really I might have foreseen this. Certainly, regret for a lost mistress, jealousy that survives her death are physical maladies fully as much as tuberculosis or leukaemia. And yet among physical maladies it is possible to distinguish those which are caused by a purely physical agency, and those which act upon the body only through the channel of the mind. If the part of the mind which serves as carrier is the memory – that is to say if the cause is obliterated or remote – however agonising the pain, however profound the disturbance to the organism may appear to be, it is very seldom (the mind having a capacity for renewal or rather an incapacity for conservation which the tissues lack) that the prognosis is not favourable. At the end of a given period after which a man who has been attacked by cancer will be dead, it is very seldom that the grief of an inconsolable widower or father is not healed. Mine was healed. Was it for this girl whom I saw in my mind's eye so fleshy and who had certainly grown older as the girls whom she had loved had grown older, was it for her that I must renounce the dazzling girl who was my memory of yesterday, my hope for tomorrow (to whom I could give nothing, any more than to any other, if I married Albertine), renounce that new Albertine not 'such as hell had beheld her' but faithful, and 'indeed a trifle shy'? It was she who was now what Albertine had been in the past: my love for Albertine had been but a transitory form of my devotion to girlhood. We think that we are in love with a girl, whereas we love in her, alas! only that dawn the glow of which is momentarily reflected on her face. The night passed. In the morning I gave the telegram back to the hotel porter explaining that it had been brought to me by mistake and that it was not addressed to me. He told me that now that it had been opened he might get into trouble, that it would be better if I kept it; I put it back in my pocket, but determined that I would act as though I had never received it. I had definitely ceased to love Albertine. So that this love after departing so widely from the course that I had anticipated, when I remembered my love for Gilberte, after obliging me to make so long and painful a detour, itself too ended, after furnishing an exception, by merging itself, just like my love for Gilberte, in the general rule of oblivion.

But then I reflected: I used to value Albertine more than myself; I no longer value her now because for a certain time past I have ceased to see her. But my desire not to be parted from myself by death, to rise again after my death, this desire was not like the desire never to be parted from Albertine, it still persisted. Was this due to the fact that I valued myself more highly than her, that when I was in love with her I loved myself even more? No, it was because, having ceased to see her, I had ceased to love her, whereas I had not ceased to love myself because my everyday attachments to myself had not been severed like my attachments to Albertine. But if the attachments to my body, to my self were severed also . . . ? Obviously, it would be the same. Our love of life is only an old connection of which we do not know how to rid ourself. Its strength lies in its permanence. But death which severs it will cure us of the desire for immortality.

After luncheon, when I was not going to roam about Venice by myself, I went up to my room to get ready to go out with my mother. In the abrupt angles of the walls I could read the restrictions imposed by the sea, the parsimony of the soil. And when I went downstairs to join Mamma who was waiting for me, at that hour when, at Combray, it was so pleasant to feel the sun quite close at hand, in the darkness guarded by closed shutters, here, from top to bottom of the marble staircase as to which one knew no better than in a Renaissance picture, whether it was built in a palace or upon a galley, the same coolness and the same feeling of the splendour of the scene outside were imparted, thanks to the awning which stirred outside the ever-open windows through which, upon an incessant stream of air, the cool shade and the greenish sunlight moved as though over a liquid surface and suggested the weltering proximity, the glitter, the mirroring instability of the sea.

After dinner, I went out by myself, into the heart of the enchanted city where I found myself wandering in strange regions like a character in the *Arabian Nights*. It was very seldom that I did not, in the course of my wanderings, hit upon some strange and spacious piazza of which no guidebook, no tourist had ever told me.

I had plunged into a network of little alleys, *calli* dissecting in all directions by their ramifications the quarter of Venice isolated between a canal and the lagoon, as if it had crystallised along these innumerable, slender, capillary lines. All of a sudden, at the end of one of these little streets, it seemed as though a bubble had occurred in the crystallised matter. A vast and splendid *campo* of which I could certainly never, in this network of little streets, have guessed the importance, or even found room for it, spread out before me flanked with charming palaces silvery in the moonlight. It was one of those architectural wholes towards which, in any other town, the streets converge, lead you and point the way. Here it seemed to be deliberately concealed in a labyrinth of alleys, like those palaces in oriental tales to which mysterious agents convey by night a person who, taken home again before daybreak, can never again find his way back to the magic dwelling which he ends by supposing that he visited only in a dream.

On the following day I set out in quest of my beautiful nocturnal *piazza*, I followed *calli* which were exactly alike one another and refused to give me any information, except such as would lead me farther astray. Sometimes a vague landmark which I seemed to recognise led me to suppose that I was about to see appear, in its seclusion, solitude and silence, the beautiful exiled *piazza*. At that moment, some evil genie which had assumed the form of a fresh *calle* made me turn unconsciously from my course, and I found myself suddenly brought back to the Grand Canal. And as there is no great difference between the memory of a dream and the memory of a reality, I ended by asking myself whether it was not during my sleep that there had occurred in a dark patch of Venetian crystallisation that strange interruption which offered a vast *piazza* flanked by romantic palaces, to the meditative eye of the moon.

On the day before our departure, we decided to go as far afield as Padua where were to be found those Vices and Virtues of which Swann had given me reproductions; after walking in the glare of the sun across the garden of the Arena, I entered the Giotto chapel the entire ceiling of which and the background of the frescoes are so blue that it seems as though the radiant day has crossed the threshold with the human visitor, and has come in for a moment to stow away in the shade and coolness its pure sky, of a slightly deeper blue now that it is rid of the sun's gilding, as in those brief spells of respite that interrupt the finest days, when, without our having noticed any cloud, the sun having turned his gaze elsewhere for a moment, the azure, more exquisite still, grows deeper. In this sky, upon the blue-washed stone, angels were flying with so intense a celestial, or at least an infantile ardour, that they seemed to be birds of a peculiar species that had really existed, that must have figured in the natural history of biblical and Apostolic times, birds that never fail to fly before the saints when they walk abroad; there are always some to be seen fluttering above them, and as they are real creatures with a genuine power of flight, we see them soar upwards, describe curves, 'loop the loop' without the slightest difficulty, plunge towards the earth head downwards with the aid of wings which enable them to support themselves in positions that defy the law of gravitation, and they remind us far more of a variety of bird or of young pupils of Garros practising the *vol-plané*, than of the angels of the art of the Renaissance and later periods whose wings have become nothing more than emblems and whose attitude is generally the same as that of heavenly beings who are not winged.

* * *

When I heard, on the very day upon which we were due to start for Paris, that Mme Putbus, and consequently her maid, had just arrived in Venice, I asked my mother to put off our departure for a few days; her air of not taking my request into consideration, of not even listening to it seriously, reawakened in my nerves, excited by the Venetian springtime, that old desire to rebel against an imaginary plot woven against me by my parents (who imagined that I would be forced to obey them), that fighting spirit, that desire which drove me in the past to enforce my wishes upon the people whom I loved best in the world, prepared to conform to their wishes after I had succeeded in making them yield. I told my mother that I would not leave Venice, but she, thinking it more to her purpose not to appear to believe that I was saying this seriously, did not even answer. I went on to say that she would soon see whether I was serious or not. And when the hour came at which, accompanied by all my luggage, she set off for the station, I ordered a cool drink to be brought out to me on the terrace overlooking the canal, and installed myself there, watching the sunset, while from a boat that had stopped in front of the hotel a musician sang 'sole mio'.

The sun continued to sink. My mother must be nearing the station. Presently, she would be gone, I should be left alone in Venice, alone with the misery of knowing that I had distressed her, and without her presence to comfort me. The hour of the train approached. My irrevocable solitude was so near at hand that it seemed to me to have begun already and to be complete. For I felt myself to be alone. Things had become alien to me. I was no longer calm enough to draw from my throbbing heart and introduce into them a measure of stability. The town that I saw before me had ceased to be Venice. Its personality, its name, seemed to me to be lying fictions which I no longer had the courage to impress upon its stones. I saw the palaces reduced to their constituent parts, lifeless heaps of marble with nothing to choose between them, and the water as a combination of hydrogen and oxygen, eternal, blind, anterior and exterior to Venice, unconscious of Doges or of Turner. And yet this unremarkable place was as strange as a place at which we have just arrived, which does not yet know us – as a place which we have left and which has forgotten us already. I could not tell it anything more about myself, I could leave nothing of myself imprinted upon it, it left me diminished, I was nothing more than a heart that throbbed, and an attention strained to follow the development of 'sole mio'. In vain might I fix my mind despairingly upon the beautiful and characteristic arch of the Rialto, it seemed to me, with the mediocrity of the obvious, a bridge not merely inferior to but as different from the idea that I possessed of it as an actor with regard to whom, notwithstanding his fair wig and black garments, we know quite well that in his essential quality he is not Hamlet. So the palaces, the canal, the Rialto became divested of the idea that created their individuality and disintegrated into their common material elements. But at the same time this mediocre place seemed to me remote. In the basin of the arsenal, because of an element which itself also was scientific, namely latitude, there was that singularity in things which, even when similar in appearance to those of our own land, reveal that they are aliens, in exile beneath a foreign sky; I felt that that horizon so close at hand, which I could have reached in an hour, was a curve of the earth quite different from those made by the seas of France, a remote curve which, by the accident of travel, happened to be moored close to where I was; so that this arsenal basin, at once insignificant and remote, filled me with that blend of disgust and alarm which I had felt as a child when I first accompanied my mother to the Deligny baths; indeed in that fantastic place consisting of a dark water reflecting neither sky nor sun, which nevertheless amid its fringe of cabins one felt to be in communication with invisible depths crowded with human bodies in bathing dresses, I had asked myself whether those depths, concealed from mortal eyes by a row of cabins which prevented anyone in the street from suspecting that they existed, were not the entry to arctic seas which began at that point, whether the Poles were not comprised in them and whether that narrow space was not indeed the open water that surrounds the Pole. This Venice without attraction for myself in which I was going to be left alone, seemed to me no less isolated, no less unreal, and it was my distress which the sound of 'sole mio', rising like a dirge for the Venice that I had known, seemed to be calling to witness. No doubt I ought to have ceased to listen to it if I wished to be able to overtake my mother and to join her on the train, I ought to have made up my mind without wasting another instant that I was going, but this is just what I was powerless to do; I remained motionless, incapable not merely of rising, but even of deciding that I would rise from my chair.

My mind, doubtless in order not to have to consider the question of making a resolution, was entirely occupied in following the course of the successive lines of 'sole mio', singing them mentally with the singer, in anticipating for each of them the burst of melody that would carry it aloft, in letting myself soar with it, and fall to earth again with it afterwards.

No doubt this trivial song which I had heard a hundred times did not interest me in the least degree. I could afford no pleasure to anyone else, or to myself, by listening to it religiously like this to the end. In fact, none of the elements, familiar beforehand, of this popular ditty was capable of furnishing me with the resolution of which I stood in need; what was more, each of these phrases when it came and passed in its turn, became an obstacle in the way of my making that resolution effective, or rather it forced me to adopt the contrary resolution not to leave Venice, for it made me too late for the train. Wherefore this occupation, devoid of any pleasure in itself, of listening to 'sole mio', was charged with a profound, almost despairing melancholy. I knew very well that in reality it was the resolution not to go that I had adopted by the mere act of remaining where I was; but to say to myself: 'I am not going', a speech which in that direct form was impossible, became possible in this indirect form: 'I am going to listen to one more line of "sole mio" '; but the practical significance of this figurative language did not escape me and, while I said to myself: 'After all, I am only listening to another line', I knew that the words meant: 'I shall remain by myself at Venice.' And it was perhaps this melancholy, like a sort of numbing cold, that constituted the desperate but fascinating charm of the song. Each note that the singer's voice uttered with a force and ostentation that were almost muscular came and pierced my heart; when he had uttered his last flourish and the song seemed to be at an end, the singer had not had enough and repeated it an octave higher as though he needed to proclaim once again my solitude and despair.

My mother must by now have reached the station. In a little while she would be gone. My heart was wrung by the anguish that was caused me by – with the view of the canal that had become quite tiny now that the soul of Venice had escaped from it, of that commonplace Rialto which was no longer the Rialto – the wail of despair that 'sole mio' had become, which, declaimed thus before the unsubstantial palaces, reduced them to dust and ashes and completed the ruin of Venice; I looked on at the slow realisation of my misery built up artistically, without haste, note by note, by the singer as he stood beneath the astonished gaze of the sun arrested in its course beyond San Giorgio Maggiore,* with the result that the fading light was to combine for ever in my memory with the throb of my emotion and the bronze voice of the singer in a dubious, unalterable and poignant alloy.

---

*   Translator's footnote: The geography of this chapter is confusing, but it is evident that Proust has transferred the name of San Giorgio Maggiore to one of the churches on the Grand Canal. Compare also page 958.

Thus I remained motionless with a disintegrated will power, with no apparent decision; doubtless at such moments our decision has already been made: our friends can often predict it themselves. But we, we are unable to do so, otherwise how much suffering would we be spared!

But at length, from caverns darker than that from which flashes the comet which we can predict – thanks to the unimaginable defensive force of inveterate habit, thanks to the hidden reserves which by a sudden impulse habit hurls at the last moment into the fray – my activity was roused at length; I set out in hot haste and arrived, when the carriage doors were already shut, but in time to find my mother flushed with emotion, overcome by the effort to restrain her tears, for she thought that I was not coming. Then the train started and we saw Padua and Verona come to meet us, to speed us on our way, almost on to the platforms of their stations, and, when we had drawn away from them, return – they who were not travelling and were about to resume their normal life – one to its plain, the other to its hill.

The hours went by. My mother was in no hurry to read two letters which she had in her hand and had merely opened, and tried to prevent me from pulling out my pocketbook at once so as to take from it the letter which the hotel porter had given me. My mother was always afraid of my finding journeys too long, too tiring, and put off as long as possible, so as to keep me occupied during the final hours, the moment at which she would seek fresh distractions for me, bring out the hard-boiled eggs, hand me newspapers, untie the parcel of books which she had bought without telling me. We had long passed Milan when she decided to read the first of her two letters. I began by watching my mother who sat reading it with an air of astonishment, then raised her head, and her eyes seemed to come to rest upon a succession of distinct, incompatible memories, which she could not succeed in bringing together. Meanwhile I had recognised Gilberte's hand on the envelope which I had just taken from my pocketbook. I opened it. Gilberte wrote to inform me that she was marrying Robert de Saint-Loup. She told me that she had sent me a telegram about it to Venice but had had no reply. I remembered that I had been told that the telegraphic service there was inefficient, I had never received her telegram. Perhaps, she would refuse to believe this. All of a sudden, I felt in my brain a fact which had installed itself there in the guise of a memory leave its place which it surrendered to another fact. The telegram that I had received a few days earlier, and had supposed to be from Albertine, was from Gilberte. As the somewhat laboured originality of Gilberte's handwriting consisted chiefly, when she wrote one line, in introducing into the line above the strokes of her t's which appeared to be underlining the words, or the dots over her i's which appeared to be punctuating the sentence above them, and on the other hand in interspersing the line below with the tails and flourishes of the words immediately above it, it was quite natural that the clerk who dispatched the telegram should have read the tail of an s or z in the line above as an '-ine' attached to the word 'Gilberte'. The dot over the i of Gilberte had risen above the word to mark the end of the message. As for her capital G, it resembled a Gothic A. Add that, apart from this, two or three words had been misread, dovetailed into one another (some of them as it happened had seemed to me incomprehensible), and this was quite enough to explain the details of my error and was not even necessary. How many letters are actually read into a word by a careless person who knows what to expect, who sets out with the idea that the message is from a certain person, how many words into the sentence? We guess as we read, we create; everything starts from an initial mistake; the mistakes that follow (and not only in the reading of letters and telegrams, not only in reading as a whole), extra-ordinary as they may appear to a person who has not begun at the same starting-point, are all quite natural. A large part of what we believe to be true (and this applies even to our final conclusions) with a persistence equalled only by our sincerity, springs from an original misconception of our premises.

CHAPTER FOUR

A fresh light upon Robert de Saint-Loup

'Oh, it is unheard-of,' said my mother. 'Listen, at my age, one has ceased to be astonished at anything, but I assure you that there could be nothing more unexpected than what I find in this letter.' 'Listen, first, to me,' I replied, 'I don't know what it is, but however astonishing it may be, it cannot be quite so astonishing as what I have found in my letter. It is a marriage. It is Robert de Saint-Loup who is marrying Gilberte Swann.' 'Ah!' said my mother, 'then that is no doubt what is in the other letter, which I have not yet opened, for I recognised your friend's hand.' And my mother smiled at me with that faint trace of emotion which, ever since she had lost her own mother, she felt at every event however insignificant, that concerned human creatures who were capable of grief, of memory, and who themselves also mourned their dead. And so my mother smiled at me and spoke to me in a gentle voice, as though she had been afraid, were she to treat this marriage lightly, of belittling the melancholy feelings that it might arouse in Swann's widow and daughter, in Robert's mother who had resigned herself to parting from her son, all of whom my mother, in her kindness of heart, in her gratitude for their kindness to me, endowed with her own faculty of filial, conjugal and maternal emotion. 'Was I right in telling you that you would find nothing more astonishing?' I asked her. 'On the contrary!' she replied in a gentle tone, 'it is I who can impart the most extraordinary news, I shall not say the greatest, the smallest, for that quotation from Sévigné which everyone makes who knows nothing else that she ever wrote used to distress your grandmother as much as "what a charming thing it is to smoke". We scorn to pick up such stereotyped Sévigné. This letter is to announce the marriage of the Cambremer boy.' 'Oh!' I remarked with indifference, 'to whom? But in any case the personality of the bridegroom robs this marriage of any sensational element.' 'Unless the bride's personality supplies it.' 'And who is the bride in question?' 'Ah, if I tell you straight away, that will spoil everything; see if you can guess,' said my mother who, seeing that we had not yet reached Turin, wished to keep something in reserve for me as meat and drink for the rest of the journey. 'But how do you expect me to know? Is it anyone brilliant? If Legrandin and his sister are satisfied, we may be sure that it is a brilliant marriage.' 'As for Legrandin, I cannot say, but the person who informs me of the marriage says that Mme de Cambremer is delighted. I don't know whether you will call it a brilliant marriage. To my mind, it suggests the days when kings used to marry shepherdesses, though in this case the shepherdess is even humbler than a shepherdess, charming as she is. It would have stupefied your grandmother, but would not have shocked her.' 'But who in the world is this bride?' 'It is Mlle d'Oloron.' 'That sounds to me tremendous and not in the least shepherdessy, but I don't quite gather who she can be. It is a title that used to be in the Guermantes family.' 'Precisely, and M. de Charlus conferred it, when he adopted her, upon Jupien's niece.' 'Jupien's niece! It isn't possible!' 'It is the reward of virtue. It is a marriage from the last chapter of one of Mme Sand's novels,' said my mother. 'It is the reward of vice, it is a marriage from the end of a Balzac novel,' thought I. 'After all,' I said to my mother, 'when you come to think of it, it is quite natural. Here are the Cambremers established in that Guermantes clan among which they never hoped to pitch their tent; what is more, the girl, adopted by M. de Charlus, will have plenty of money, which was indispensable now that the Cambremers have lost theirs; and after all she is the adopted daughter, and, in the Cambremers' eyes, probably the real daughter – the natural daughter – of a person whom they regard as a Prince of the Blood Royal. A bastard of a semi-royal house has always been regarded as a flattering alliance by the nobility of France and other countries. Indeed, without going so far back, only the other day, not more than six months ago, don't you remember, the marriage of Robert's friend and that girl, the only possible justification of which was that she was supposed, rightly or wrongly, to be the natural daughter of a sovereign prince.' My mother, without abandoning the caste system of Combray which meant that my grandmother would have been scandalised by such a marriage, being principally anxious to echo her mother's judgment, added: 'Anyhow, the girl is worth her weight in gold, and your dear grandmother would not have had to draw upon her immense goodness, her unbounded indulgence, to keep her from condemning young Cambremer's choice. Do you remember how distinguished she thought the girl, years ago, one day when she went into the shop to have a stitch put in her skirt? She was only a child then. And now, even if she has rather run to seed, and become an old maid, she is a different woman, a thousand times more perfect. But your grandmother saw all that at a glance. She found the little niece of a jobbing tailor more "noble" than the Duc de Guermantes.' But even more necessary than to extol my grandmother was it for my mother to decide that it was 'better' for her that she had not lived to see the day. This was the supreme triumph of her filial devotion, as though she were sparing my grandmother a final grief. 'And yet, can you imagine for a moment,' my mother said to me, 'what old father Swann – not that you ever knew him, of course – would have felt if he could have known that he would one day have a great-grandchild in whose veins the blood of mother Moser who used to say: "Ponchour Mezieurs" would mingle with the blood of the Duc de Guise!' 'But listen, Mamma, it is a great deal more surprising than that. For the Swanns were very respectable people, and, given the position that their son occupied, his daughter, if he himself had made a decent marriage, might have married very well indeed. But all her chances were ruined by his marrying a courtesan.' 'Oh, a courtesan, you know, people were perhaps rather hard on her, I never quite believed.' 'Yes, a courtesan, indeed I can let you have some startling revelations one of these days.' Lost in meditation, my mother said: 'The daughter of a woman to whom your father would never allow me to bow marrying the nephew of Mme de Villeparisis, upon whom your father wouldn't allow me to call at first because he thought her too grand for me!' Then: 'The son of Mme de Cambremer to whom Legrandin was so afraid of having to give us a letter of introduction because he didn't think us smart enough, marrying the niece of a man who would never dare to come to our flat except by the service stairs! . . . All the same your poor grandmother was right – you remember – when she said that the great nobility could do things that would shock the middle classes and that Queen Marie-Amélie was spoiled for her by the overtures that she made to the Prince de Condé's mistress to persuade him to leave his fortune to the Duc d'Aumale. You remember too, it shocked her that for centuries past daughters of the House of Gramont who have been perfect saints have borne the name Corisande in memory of Henri IV's connection with one of their ancestresses. These are things that may happen also, perhaps, among the middle classes, but we conceal them better. Can't you imagine how it would have amused her, your poor grandmother?' said Mamma sadly, for the joys of which it grieved us to think that my grandmother was deprived were the simplest joys of life, a tale, a play, something more trifling still, a piece of mimicry, which would have amused her, 'Can't you imagine her astonishment? I am sure, however, that your grandmother would have been shocked by these marriages, that they would have grieved her, I feel that it is better that she never knew about them,' my mother went on, for, when confronted with any event, she liked to think that my grandmother would have received a unique impression of it which would have been caused by the marvellous singularity of her nature and had an extraordinary importance. Did anything painful occur, which could not have been foreseen in the past, the disgrace or ruin of one of our old friends, some public calamity, an epidemic, a war, a revolution, my mother would say to herself that perhaps it was better that Grandmamma had known nothing about it, that it would have distressed her too keenly, that perhaps she would not have been able to endure it. And when it was a question of something startling like this, my mother, by an impulse directly opposite to that of the malicious people who like to imagine that others whom they do not like have suffered more than is generally supposed, would not, in her affection for my grandmother, allow that anything sad, or depressing, could ever have happened to her. She always imagined my grandmother as raised above the assaults even of any malady which ought not to have developed, and told herself that my grandmother's death had perhaps been a good thing on the whole, inasmuch as it had shut off the too ugly spectacle of the present day from that noble character which could never have become resigned to it. For optimism is the philosophy of the past. The events that have occurred being, among all those that were possible, the only ones which we have known, the harm that they have caused seems to us inevitable, and, for the slight amount of good that they could not help bringing with them, it is to them that we give the credit, imagining that without them it would not have occurred. But she sought at the same time to form a more accurate idea of what my grandmother would have felt when she learned these tidings, and to believe that it was impossible for our minds, less exalted than hers, to form any such idea. 'Can't you imagine,' my mother said to me first of all, 'how astonished your poor grandmother would have been!' And I felt that my mother was pained by her inability to tell her the news, regretted that my grandmother could not learn it, and felt it to be somehow unjust that the course of life should bring to light facts which my grandmother would never have believed, rendering thus retrospectively the knowledge which my grandmother had taken with her of people and society false, and incomplete, the marriage of the Jupien girl and Legrandin's nephew being calculated to modify my grandmother's general ideas of life, no less than the news – had my mother been able to convey it to her – that people had succeeded in solving the problems, which my grandmother had regarded as insoluble, of aerial navigation and wireless telegraphy.

The train reached Paris before my mother and I had finished discussing these two pieces of news which, so that the journey might not seem to me too long, she had deliberately reserved for the latter part of it, not mentioning them until we had passed Milan. And my mother continued the discussion after we had reached home: 'Just imagine, that poor Swann who was so anxious that his Gilberte should be received by the Guermantes, how happy he would be if he could see his daughter become a Guermantes!' 'Under another name, led to the altar as Mlle de Forcheville, do you think he would be so happy after all?' 'Ah, that is true. I had not thought of it. That is what makes it impossible for me to congratulate the little chit, the thought that she has had the heart to give up her father's name, when he was so good to her. – Yes, you are right, when all is said and done, it is perhaps just as well that he knows nothing about it.' With the dead as with the living, we cannot tell whether a thing would cause them joy or sorrow. 'It appears that the Saint-Loups are going to live at Tansonville. Old father Swann, who was so anxious to show your poor grandfather his pond, could he ever have dreamed that the Duc de Guermantes would see it constantly, especially if he had known of his son's marriage? And you yourself who have talked so often to Saint-Loup about the pink hawthorns and lilacs and irises at Tansonville, he will understand you better. They will be his property.' Thus there developed in our dining-room, in the lamplight that is so congenial to them, one of those talks in which the wisdom not of nations but of families, taking hold of some event, a death, a betrothal, an inheritance, a bankruptcy, and slipping it under the magnifying glass of memory, brings it into high relief, detaches, thrusts back one surface of it, and places in perspective at different points in space and time what, to those who have not lived through the period in question, seems to be amalgamated upon a single surface, the names of dead people, successive addresses, the origins and changes of fortunes, transmissions of property. Is not this wisdom inspired by the Muse whom it is best to ignore for as long as possible, if we wish to retain any freshness of impressions, any creative power, but whom even those people who have ignored her meet in the evening of their life in the nave of the old country church, at the hour when all of a sudden they feel that they are less moved by eternal beauty as expressed in the carvings of the altar than by the thought of the vicissitudes of fortune which those carvings have undergone, passing into a famous private collection, to a chapel, from there to a museum, then returning at length to the church, or by the feeling as they tread upon a marble slab that is almost endowed with thought, that it covers the last remains of Arnault or Pascal, or simply by deciphering (forming perhaps a mental picture of a fair young worshipper) on the brass plate of the wooden prayer-desk, the names of the daughters of country squire or leading citizen? The Muse who has gathered up everything that the more exalted Muses of philosophy and art have rejected, everything that is not founded upon truth, everything that is merely contingent, but that reveals other laws as well, is History.

What I was to learn later on – for I had been unable to keep in touch with all this affair from Venice – was that Mlle de Forcheville's hand had been sought first of all by the Prince de Silistrie, while Saint-Loup was seeking to marry Mlle d'Entragues, the Duc de Luxembourg's daughter. This is what had occurred. Mlle de Forcheville possessing a hundred million francs, Mme de Marsantes had decided that she would be an excellent match for her son. She made the mistake of saying that the girl was charming, that she herself had not the slightest idea whether she was rich or poor, that she did not wish to know, but that even without a penny it would be a piece of good luck for the most exacting of young men to find such a wife. This was going rather too far for a woman who was tempted only by the hundred millions, which blinded her eyes to everything else. At once it was understood that she was thinking of the girl for her own son. The Princesse de Silistrie went about uttering loud cries, expatiated upon the social importance of Saint-Loup, and proclaimed that if he should marry Odette's daughter by a Jew then there was no longer a Faubourg Saint-Germain. Mme de Marsantes, sure of herself as she was, dared not advance farther and retreated before the cries of the Princesse de Silistrie, who immediately made a proposal in the name of her own son. She had protested only in order to keep Gilberte for herself. Meanwhile Mme de Marsantes, refusing to own herself defeated, had turned at once to Mlle d'Entragues, the Duc de Luxembourg's daughter. Having no more than twenty millions, she suited her purpose less, but Mme de Marsantes told everyone that a Saint-Loup could not marry a Mlle Swann (there was no longer any mention of Forcheville). Some time later, somebody having carelessly observed that the Duc de Châtellerault was thinking of marrying Mlle d'Entragues, Mme de Marsantes who was the most captious woman in the world mounted her high horse, changed her tactics, returned to Gilberte, made a formal offer of marriage on Saint-Loup's behalf, and the engagement was immediately announced. This engagement provoked keen comment in the most different spheres. Some old friends of my mother, who belonged more or less to Combray, came to see her to discuss Gilberte's marriage, which did not dazzle them in the least. 'You know who Mlle de Forcheville is, she is simply Mlle Swann. And her witness at the marriage, the "Baron" de Charlus, as he calls himself, is the old man who used to keep her mother at one time, under Swann's very nose, and no doubt to his advantage.' 'But what do you mean?' my mother protested. 'In the first place, Swann was extremely rich.' 'We must assume that he was not as rich as all that if he needed other people's money. But what is there in the woman, that she keeps her old lovers like that? She has managed to persuade the third to marry her and she drags out the second when he has one foot in the grave to make him act at the marriage of the daughter she had by the first or by someone else, for how is one to tell who the father was? She can't be certain herself! I said the third, it is the three hundredth I should have said. But then, don't you know, if she's no more a Forcheville than you or I, that puts her on the same level as the bridegroom who of course isn't noble at all. Only an adventurer would marry a girl like that. It appears he's just a plain Monsieur Dupont or Durand or something. If it weren't that we have a Radical mayor now at Combray, who doesn't even lift his hat to the priest, I should know all about it. Because, you understand, when they published the banns, they were obliged to give the real name. It is all very nice for the newspapers or for the stationer who sends out the intimations, to describe yourself as the Marquis de Saint-Loup. That does no harm to anyone, and if it can give any pleasure to those worthy people, I should be the last person in the world to object! What harm can it do me? As I shall never dream of going to call upon the daughter of a woman who has let herself be talked about, she can have a string of titles as long as my arm before her servants. But in an official document it's not the same thing. Ah, if my cousin Sazerat were still deputy-mayor, I should have written to him, and he would certainly have let me know what name the man was registered under.'

Other friends of my mother who had met Saint-Loup in our house came to her 'day', and enquired whether the bridegroom was indeed the same person as my friend. Certain people went so far as to maintain, with regard to the other marriage, that it had nothing to do with the Legrandin Cambremers. They had this on good authority, for the Marquise, *née* Legrandin, had contradicted the rumour on the very eve of the day on which the engagement was announced. I, for my part, asked myself why M. de Charlus on the one hand, Saint-Loup on the other, each of whom had had occasion to write to me quite recently, had made various friendly plans and proposed expeditions, which must inevitably have clashed with the wedding ceremonies, and had said nothing whatever to me about these. I came to the conclusion, forgetting the secrecy which people always preserve until the last moment in affairs of this sort, that I was less their friend than I had supposed, a conclusion which, so far as Saint-Loup was concerned, distressed me. Though why, when I had already remarked that the affability, the 'one-man-to-another' attitude of the aristocracy was all a sham, should I be surprised to find myself its victim? In the establishment for women – where men were now to be procured in increasing numbers – in which M. de Charlus had surprised Morel, and in which the 'assistant matron', a great reader of the *Gaulois*, used to discuss the social gossip with her clients, this lady, while conversing with a stout gentleman who used to come to her incessantly to drink champagne with young men, because, being already very stout, he wished to become obese enough to be certain of not being 'called up', should there ever be a war, declared: 'It seems, young Saint-Loup is "one of those" and young Cambremer too. Poor wives! – In any case, if you know the bridegrooms, you must send them to us, they will find everything they want here, and there's plenty of money to be made out of them.' Whereupon the stout gentleman, albeit he was himself 'one of those', protested, replied, being something of a snob, that he often met Cambremer and Saint-Loup at his cousins the Ardouvillers, and that they were great womanisers, and quite the opposite of 'all that'. 'Ah!' the assistant matron concluded in a sceptical tone, but without any proof of the assertion, and convinced that in our generation the perversity of morals was rivalled only by the absurd exaggeration of slanderous rumours. Certain people whom I no longer saw wrote to me and asked me 'what I thought' of these two marriages, precisely as though they had been inviting a public discussion of the height of women's hats in the theatre or the psychological novel. I had not the heart to answer these letters. Of these two marriages, I thought nothing at all, but I did feel an immense melancholy, as when two parts of our past existence, which have been anchored near to us, and upon which we have perhaps been basing idly from day to day an unacknowledged hope, remove themselves finally, with a joyous crackling of flames, for unknown destinations, like two vessels on the high seas. As for the prospective bridegrooms themselves, they regarded their own marriages from a point of view that was quite natural, since it was a question not of other people but of themselves. They had never tired of mocking at such 'grand marriages' founded upon some secret shame. And indeed the Cambremer family, so ancient in its lineage and so modest in its pretensions, would have been the first to forget Jupien and to remember only the unimaginable grandeur of the House of Oloron, had not an exception occurred in the person who ought to have been most gratified by this marriage, the Marquise de Cambremer-Legrandin. For, being of a malicious nature, she reckoned the pleasure of humiliating her family above that of glorifying herself. And so, as she had no affection for her son, and was not long in taking a dislike to her daughter-in-law, she declared that it was calamity for a Cambremer to marry a person who had sprung from heaven knew where, and had such bad teeth. As for young Cambremer, who had already shown a certain tendency to frequent the society of literary people, we may well imagine that so brilliant an alliance had not the effect of making him more of a snob than before, but that feeling himself to have become the successor of the Ducs d'Oloron – 'sovereign princes' as the newspapers said – he was sufficiently persuaded of his own importance to be able to mix with the very humblest people. And he deserted the minor nobility for the intelligent bourgeoisie on the days when he did not confine himself to royalty. The notices in the papers, especially when they referred to Saint-Loup, invested my friend, whose royal ancestors were enumerated, in a fresh importance, which however could only depress me – as though he had become someone else, the descendant of Robert the Strong, rather than the friend who, only a little while since, had taken the back seat in the carriage in order that I might be more comfortable in the other; the fact that I had had no previous suspicion of his marriage with Gilberte, the prospect of which had been revealed to me suddenly in a letter, so different from anything that I could have expected of either him or her the day before, and the fact that he had not let me know pained me, whereas I ought to have reflected that he had had a great many other things to do, and that moreover in the fashionable world marriages are often arranged like this all of a sudden, generally as a substitute for a different combination which has come to grief – unexpectedly – like a chemical precipitation. And the feeling of sadness, as depressing as a household removal, as bitter as jealousy, that these marriages caused me by the accident of their sudden impact was so profound, that later on people used to remind me of it, paying absurd compliments to my perspicacity, as having been just the opposite of what it was at the time, a twofold, nay a threefold and fourfold presentiment.

The people in society who had taken no notice of Gilberte said to me with an air of serious interest: 'Ah! It is she who is marrying the Marquis de Saint-Loup' and studied her with the attentive gaze of people who not merely relish all the social gossip of Paris but are anxious to learn, and believe in the profundity of their own introspection. Those who on the other hand had known Gilberte alone gazed at Saint-Loup with the closest attention, asked me (these were often people who barely knew me) to introduce them and returned from their presentation to the bridegroom radiant with the bliss of fatuity, saying to me: 'He is very nice looking.' Gilberte was convinced that the name 'Marquis de Saint-Loup' was a thousand times more important than 'Duc d'Orléans'.

'It appears that it is the Princesse de Parme who arranged young Cambremer's marriage,' Mamma told me. And this was true. The Princess had known for a long time, on the one hand, by his works, Legrandin whom she regarded as a distinguished man, on the other hand Mme de Cambremer who changed the conversation whenever the Princess asked her whether she was not Legrandin's sister. The Princess knew how keenly Mme de

Cambremer felt her position on the doorstep of the great aristocratic world, in which she was invited nowhere. When the Princesse de Parme, who had undertaken to find a husband for Mlle d'Oloron, asked M. de Charlus whether he had ever heard of a pleasant, educated man who called himself Legrandin de Méséglise (thus it was that M. Legrandin now styled himself), the Baron first of all replied in the negative, then suddenly a memory occurred to him of a man whose acquaintance he had made in the train, one night, and who had given him his card. He smiled a vague smile. 'It is perhaps the same person,' he said to himself. When he discovered that the prospective bridegroom was the son of Legrandin's sister, he said: 'Why, that would be really extraordinary! If he takes after his uncle, after all, that would not alarm me, I have always said that they make the best husbands.' 'Who are they?' enquired the Princess. 'Oh, Ma'am, I could explain it all to you if we met more often. With you one can talk freely. Your Highness is so intelligent,' said Charlus, seized by a desire to confide in someone which, however, went no farther. The name Cambremer appealed to him, although he did not like the boy's parents, but he knew that it was one of the four Baronies of Brittany and the best that he could possibly hope for his adopted daughter; it was an old and respected name, with solid connections in its native province. A Prince would have been out of the question and, moreover, not altogether desirable. This was the very thing. The Princess then invited Legrandin to call. In appearance he had considerably altered, and, of late, distinctly to his advantage. Like those women who deliberately sacrifice their faces to the slimness of their figures and never stir from Marienbad, Legrandin had acquired the free and easy air of a cavalry officer. In proportion as M. de Charlus had grown coarse and slow, Legrandin had become slimmer and moved more rapidly, the contrary effect of an identical cause. This velocity of movement had its psychological reasons as well. He was in the habit of frequenting certain low haunts where he did not wish to be seen going in or coming out: he would hurl himself into them. Legrandin had taken up tennis at the age of fifty-five. When the Princesse de Parme spoke to him of the Guermantes, of Saint-Loup, he declared that he had known them all his life, making a sort of composition of the fact of his having always known by name the proprietors of Guermantes and that of his having met, at my aunt's house, Swann, the father of the future Mme de Saint-Loup, Swann upon whose wife and daughter Legrandin, at Combray, had always refused to call. 'Indeed, I travelled quite recently with the brother of the Duc de Guermantes, M. de Charlus. He began the con-versation spontaneously, which is always a good sign, for it proves that a man is neither a tongue-tied lout nor stuck-up. Oh, I know all the things that people say about him. But I never pay any attention to gossip of that sort. Besides, the private life of other people does not concern me. He gave me the impression of a sensitive nature, and a cultivated mind.' Then the Princesse de Parme spoke of Mlle d'Oloron. In the Guermantes circle people were moved by the nobility of heart of M. de Charlus who, generous as he had always been, was securing the future happiness of a penniless but charming girl. And the Duc de Guermantes, who suffered from his brother's reputation, let it be understood that, fine as this conduct was, it was wholly natural. 'I don't know if I make myself clear, everything in the affair is natural,' he said, speaking ineptly by force of habit. But his object was to indicate that the girl was a daughter of his brother whom the latter was acknowledging. This accounted at the same time for Jupien. The Princesse de Parme hinted at this version of the story to show Legrandin that after all young Cambremer would be marrying something in the nature of Mlle de Nantes, one of those bastards of Louis XIV who were not scorned either by the Duc d'Orléans or by the Prince de Conti. These two marriages which I had already begun to discuss with my mother in the train that brought us back to Paris had quite remarkable effects upon several of the characters who have figured in the course of this narrative. First of all upon Legrandin; needless to say that he swept like a hurricane into M. de Charlus's town house for all the world as though he were entering a house of ill-fame where he must on no account be seen, and also, at the same time, to display his activity and to conceal his age – for our habits accompany us even into places where they are no longer of any use to us – and scarcely anybody observed that when M. de Charlus greeted him he did so with a smile which it was hard to intercept, harder still to interpret; this smile was similar in appearance, and in its essentials was diametrically opposite to the smile which two men, who are in the habit of meeting in good society, exchange if they happen to meet in what they regard as disreputable surroundings (such as the Elysée where General de Froberville, whenever, in days past, he met Swann there, would assume, on catching sight of him, an expression of ironical and mysterious complicity appropriate between two frequenters of the drawing-room of the Princesse des Laumes who were compromising themselves by visiting M. Grevy). Legrandin had been cultivating obscurely for a long time past – ever since the days when I used to go as a child to spend my holidays at Combray – relations with the aristocracy, productive at the most of an isolated invitation to a sterile house party. All of a sudden, his nephew's marriage having intervened to join up these scattered fragments, Legrandin stepped into a social position which retroactively derived a sort of solidity from his former relations with

people who had known him only as a private person but had known him
well. Ladies to whom people offered to introduce him informed them that
for the last twenty years he had stayed with them in the country for a
fortnight annually, and that it was he who had given them the beautiful old
barometer in the small drawing-room. It so happened that he had been
photographed in 'groups' which included Dukes who were related to them.
But as soon as he had acquired this social position, he ceased to make any use
of it. This was not merely because, now that people knew him to be received
everywhere, he no longer derived any pleasure from being invited, it was
because, of the two vices that had long struggled for the mastery of him, the
less natural, snobbishness, yielded its place to another that was less artificial,
since it did at least show a sort of return, albeit circuitous, towards nature.
No doubt the two are not incompatible, and a nocturnal tour of exploration
of a slum may be made immediately upon leaving a Duchess's party. But the
chilling effect of age made Legrandin reluctant to accumulate such an
abundance of pleasures, to stir out of doors except with a definite purpose,
and had also the effect that the pleasures of nature became more or less
platonic, consisting chiefly in friendships, in conversations which took up
time, and made him spend almost all his own among the lower orders, so
that he had little left for a social existence. Mme de Cambremer herself
became almost indifferent to the friendly overtures of the Duchesse de
Guermantes. The latter, obliged to call upon the Marquise, had noticed, as
happens whenever we come to see more of our fellow-creatures (that is to
say combinations of good qualities which we end by discovering with
defects to which we end by growing accustomed) that Mme de Cambremer
was a woman endowed with an innate intelligence and an acquired culture
of which for my part I thought but little, but which appeared remarkable to
the Duchess. And so she often came, late in the afternoon, to see Mme de
Cambremer and paid her long visits. But the marvellous charm which her
hostess imagined as existing in the Duchesse de Guermantes vanished as
soon as she saw that the other sought her company, and she received her
rather out of politeness than for her own pleasure. A more striking change
was manifest in Gilberte, a change at once symmetrical with and different
from that which had occurred in Swann after his marriage. It is true that
during the first few months Gilberte had been glad to open her doors to the
most select company. It was doubtless only with a view to an eventual
inheritance that she invited the intimate friends to whom her mother was
attached, but on certain days only when there was no one but themselves,
secluded apart from the fashionable people, as though the contact of Mme
Bontemps or Mme Cottard with the Princesse de Guermantes or the

Princesse de Parme might, like that of two unstable powders, have produced irreparable catastrophes. Nevertheless the Bontemps, the Cottards and such, although disappointed by the smallness of the party, were proud of being able to say: 'We were dining with the Marquise de Saint-Loup', all the more so as she ventured at times so far as to invite, with them, Mme de Marsantes, who was emphatically the 'great lady' with a fan of tortoiseshell and ostrich feathers, this again being a piece of legacy-hunting. She only took care to pay from time to time a tribute to the discreet people whom one never sees except when they are invited, a warning with which she bestowed upon her audience of the Cottard-Bontemps class her most gracious and distant greeting. Perhaps I should have preferred to be included in these parties. But Gilberte, in whose eyes I was now principally a friend of her husband and of the Guermantes (and who – perhaps even in the Combray days, when my parents did not call upon her mother – had, at the age when we do not merely add this or that to the value of things but classify them according to their species, endowed me with that prestige which we never afterwards lose), regarded these evenings as unworthy of me, and when I took my leave of her would say: 'It has been delightful to see you, but come again the day after tomorrow, you will find my aunt Guermantes, and Mme de Poix; today I just had a few of Mamma's friends, to please Mamma.' But this state of things lasted for a few months only, and very soon everything was altered. Was this because Gilberte's social life was fated to exhibit the same contrasts as Swann's? However that may be, Gilberte had been only for a short time Marquise de Saint-Loup (in the process of becoming, as we shall see, Duchesse de Guermantes)* when, having attained to the most brilliant and most difficult position, she decided that the name Saint-Loup was now embodied in herself like a glowing enamel and that, whoever her associates might be, from now onwards she would remain for all the world Marquise de Saint-Loup, wherein she was mistaken, for the value of a title of nobility, like that of shares in a company, rises with the demand and falls when it is offered in the market.

Everything that seems to us imperishable tends to destruction; a position in society, like anything else, is not created once and for all time, but, just as much as the power of an Empire, reconstructs itself at every moment by a sort of perpetual process of creation, which explains the apparent anomalies in social or political history in the course of half a century. The creation of the world did not occur at the beginning of time, it occurs every day. The

---

* Translator's footnote: This is quite inexplicable. Gilberte reappears as Saint-Loup's widow while the Duc de Guermantes and his wife are still alive.

Marquise de Saint-Loup said to herself, 'I am the Marquise de Saint-Loup', she knew that, the day before, she had refused three invitations to dine with Duchesses. But if, to a certain extent, her name exalted the class of people, as little aristocratic as possible, whom she entertained, by an inverse process, the class of people whom the Marquise entertained depreciated the name that she bore. Nothing can hold out against such processes, the greatest names succumb to them in the end. Had not Swann known a Duchess of the House of France whose drawing-room, because any Tom, Dick or Harry was welcomed there, had fallen to the lowest rank? One day when the Princesse des Laumes had gone from a sense of duty to call for a moment upon this Highness, in whose drawing-room she had found only the most ordinary people, arriving immediately afterwards at Mme Leroi's, she had said to Swann and the Marquis de Modène: 'At last I find myself upon friendly soil. I have just come from Mme la Duchesse de X—, there weren't three faces I knew in the room.' Sharing, in short, the opinion of the character in the operetta who declares: 'My name, I think, dispenses me from saying more', Gilberte set to work to flaunt her contempt for what she had so ardently desired, to proclaim that all the people in the Faubourg Saint-Germain were idiots, people to whose houses one could not go, and, suiting the action to the word, ceased to go to them. People who did not make her acquaintance until after this epoch, and who, in the first stages of that acquaintance, heard her, by that time Duchesse de Guermantes, make the most absurd fun of the world in which she could so easily have moved, seeing that she never invited a single person out of that world, and that if any of them, even the most brilliant, ventured into her drawing-room, she would yawn openly in their faces, blush now in retrospect at the thought that they themselves could ever have seen any claim to distinction in the fashionable world, and would never dare to confess this humiliating secret of their past weaknesses to a woman whom they suppose to have been, owing to an essential loftiness of her nature, incapable from her earliest moments of understanding such things. They hear her poke such delicious fun at Dukes, and see her (which is more significant) make her behaviour accord so entirely with her mockery! No doubt they do not think of enquiring into the causes of the accident which turned Mlle Swann into Mlle de Forcheville, Mlle de Forcheville into the Marquise de Saint-Loup, and finally into the Duchesse de Guermantes. Possibly it does not occur to them either that the effects of this accident would serve no less than its causes to explain Gilberte's subsequent attitude, the habit of mixing with upstarts not being regarded quite in the same light in which Mlle Swann would have regarded it by a lady whom everybody addresses as 'Madame la

Duchesse' and the other Duchesses who bore her as 'cousin'. We are always ready to despise a goal which we have not succeeded in reaching, or have permanently reached. And this contempt seems to us to form part of the character of people whom we do not yet know. Perhaps if we were able to retrace the course of past years, we should find them devoured, more savagely than anyone, by those same weaknesses which they have succeeded so completely in concealing or conquering that we reckon them incapable not only of having ever been attacked by them themselves, but even of ever excusing them in other people, let alone being capable of imagining them. Anyhow, very soon the drawing-room of the new Marquise de Saint-Loup assumed its permanent aspect, from the social point of view at least, for we shall see what troubles were brewing in it in another connection; well, this aspect was surprising for the following reason: people still remembered that the most formal, the most exclusive parties in Paris, as brilliant as those given by the Duchesse de Guermantes, were those of Mme de Marsantes, Saint-Loup's mother. On the other hand, in recent years, Odette's drawing-room, infinitely lower in the social scale, had been no less dazzling in its elegance and splendour. Saint-Loup, however, delighted to have, thanks to his wife's vast fortune, everything that he could desire in the way of comfort, wished only to rest quietly in his armchair after a good dinner with a musical entertainment by good performers. And this young man who had seemed at one time so proud, so ambitious, invited to share his luxury old friends whom his mother would not have admitted to her house. Gilberte, on her side, put into effect Swann's saying: 'Quality doesn't matter, what I dread is quantity.' And Saint-Loup, always on his knees before his wife, and because he loved her, and because it was to her that he owed these extremes of comfort, took care not to interfere with tastes that were so similar to his own. With the result that the great receptions given by Mme de Marsantes and Mme de Forcheville, given year after year with an eye chiefly to the establishment, upon a brilliant footing, of their children, gave rise to no reception by M. and Mme de Saint-Loup. They had the best of saddle-horses on which to go out riding together, the finest of yachts in which to cruise – but they never took more than a couple of guests with them. In Paris, every evening, they would invite three or four friends to dine, never more; with the result that, by an unforeseen but at the same time quite natural retrogression, the two vast maternal aviaries had been replaced by a silent nest.

The person who profited least by these two marriages was the young Mademoiselle d'Oloron who, already suffering from typhoid fever on the day of the religious ceremony, was barely able to crawl to the church and died a few weeks later. The letter of intimation that was sent out some time after her death blended with names such as Jupien's those of almost all the greatest families in Europe, such as the Vicomte and Vicomtesse de Montmorency, H. R. H. the Comtesse de Bourbon-Soissons, the Prince of Modena-Este, the Vicomtesse d'Edumea, Lady Essex, and so forth. No doubt even to a person who knew that the deceased was Jupien's niece, this plethora of grand connections would not cause any surprise. The great thing, after all, is to have grand connections. Then, the *casus foederis* coming into play, the death of a simple little shop-girl plunges all the princely families of Europe in mourning. But many young men of a later generation, who were not familiar with the facts, might, apart from the possibility of their mistaking Marie-Antoinette d'Oloron, Marquise de Cambremer, for a lady of the noblest birth, have been guilty of many other errors when they read this communication. Thus, supposing their excursions through France to have given them some slight familiarity with the country round Combray, when they saw that the Comte de Méséglise figured among the first of the signatories, close to the Duc de Guermantes, they might not have felt any surprise. 'The Méséglise way', they might have said, 'converges with the Guermantes way, old and noble families of the same region may have been allied for generations. Who knows? It is perhaps a branch of the Guermantes family which bears the title of Comte de Méséglise.' As it happened, the Comte de Méséglise had no connection with the Guermantes and was not even enrolled on the Guermantes side, but on the Cambremer side, since the Comte de Méséglise, who by a rapid advancement had been for two years only Legrandin de Méséglise, was our old friend Legrandin. No doubt, taking one false title with another, there were few that could have been so disagreeable to the Guermantes as this. They had been connected in the past with the authentic Comtes de Méséglise, of whom there survived only one female descendant, the daughter of obscure and unassuming parents, married herself to one of my aunt's tenant fanners named Ménager, who had become rich and bought Mirougrain from her and now styled himself 'Ménager de Mirougrain', with the result that when you said that his wife was born 'de Méséglise' people thought that she must simply have been born at Méséglise and that she was 'of Méséglise' as her husband was 'of Mirougrain'.

Any other sham title would have caused less annoyance to the Guermantes family. But the aristocracy knows how to tolerate these irritations and many others as well, the moment that a marriage which is deemed advantageous, from whatever point of view, is in question. Shielded by the Duc de Guermantes, Legrandin was, to part of that generation, and will be to the whole of the generation that follows it, the true Comte de Méséglise.

Yet another mistake which any young reader not acquainted with the facts might have been led to make was that of supposing that the Baron and Baronne de Forcheville figured on the list in their capacity as parents-in-law of the Marquis de Saint-Loup, that is to say on the Guermantes side. But on this side, they had no right to appear since it was Robert who was related to the Guermantes and not Gilberte. No, the Baron and Baronne de Forcheville, despite this misleading suggestion, did figure on the wife's side, it is true, and not on the Cambremer side, because not of the Guermantes, but of Jupien, who, the reader must now be told, was a cousin of Odette.

All M. de Charlus's favour had been lavished since the marriage of his adopted niece upon the young Marquis de Cambremer; the young man's tastes which were similar to those of the Baron, since they had not prevented the Baron from selecting him as a husband for Mlle d'Oloron, made him, as was only natural, appreciate him all the more when he was left a widower. This is not to say that the Marquis had not other qualities which made him a charming companion for M. de Charlus. But even in the case of a man of real merit, it is an advantage that is not disdained by the person who admits him into his private life and one that makes him particularly useful that he can also play whist. The intelligence of the young Marquis was remarkable and as they had already begun to say at Féterne when he was barely out of his cradle, he 'took' entirely after his grandmother, had the same enthusiasms, the same love of music. He reproduced also some of her peculiarities, but these more by imitation, like all the rest of the family, than from atavism. Thus it was that, some time after the death of his wife, having received a letter signed 'Léonor', a name which I did not remember as being his, I realised who it was that had written to me only when I had read the closing formula: '*Croyez à ma sympathie vraie*', the word '*vraie*', coming in that order, added to the Christian name Léonor the surname Cambremer.

About this time I used to see a good deal of Gilberte with whom I had renewed my old intimacy: for our life, in the long run, is not calculated according to the duration of our friendships. Let a certain period of time elapse and you will see reappear (just as former Ministers reappear in politics, as old plays are revived on the stage) friendly relations that have been revived between the same persons as before, after long years of interruption, and revived with pleasure. After ten years, the reasons which made one party love too passionately, the other unable to endure a too exacting despotism, no longer exist. Convention alone survives, and everything that Gilberte would have refused me in the past, that had seemed to her intolerable, impossible, she granted me quite readily – doubtless because

I no longer desired it. Although neither of us avowed to himself the reason for this change, if she was always ready to come to me, never in a hurry to leave me, it was because the obstacle had vanished: my love.

I went, moreover, a little later to spend a few days at Tansonville. The move I found rather a nuisance, for I was keeping a girl in Paris who slept in the bachelor flat which I had rented. As other people need the aroma of forests or the ripple of a lake, so I needed her to sleep near at hand during the night and by day to have her always by my side in the carriage. For even if one love passes into oblivion, it may determine the form of the love that is to follow it. Already, in the heart even of the previous love, daily habits existed, the origin of which we did not ourselves recall. It was an anguish of a former day that had made us think with longing, then adopt in a permanent fashion, like customs the meaning of which has been forgotten, those homeward drives to the beloved's door, or her residence in our home, our presence or the presence of someone in whom we have confidence upon all her outings, all these habits, like great uniform highroads along which our love passes daily and which were forged long ago in the volcanic fire of an ardent emotion. But these habits survive the woman, survive even the memory of the woman. They become the pattern, if not of all our loves, at least of certain of our loves which alternate with the others. And thus my home had demanded, in memory of a forgotten Albertine, the presence of my mistress of the moment whom I concealed from visitors and who filled my life as Albertine had filled it in the past. And before I could go to Tansonville I had to make her promise that she would place herself in the hands of one of my friends who did not care for women, for a few days.

I had heard that Gilberte was unhappy, betrayed by Robert, but not in the fashion which everyone supposed, which perhaps she herself still supposed, which in any case she alleged. An opinion that was justified by self-esteem, the desire to hoodwink other people, to hoodwink herself, not to mention the imperfect knowledge of his infidelities which is all that betrayed spouses ever acquire, all the more so as Robert, a true nephew of M. de Charlus, went about openly with women whom he compromised, whom the world believed and whom Gilberte supposed more or less to be his mistresses. It was even thought in society that he was too barefaced, never stirring, at a party, from the side of some woman whom he afterwards accompanied home, leaving Mme de Saint-Loup to return as best she might. Anyone who had said that the other woman whom he compromised thus was not really his mistress would have been regarded as a fool, incapable of seeing what was staring him in the face, but I had been pointed, alas, in the direction of the truth, a truth which caused me infinite distress, by a few words let fall by

Jupien. What had been my amazement when, having gone, a few months before my visit to Tansonville, to enquire for M. de Charlus, in whom certain cardiac symptoms had been causing his friends great anxiety, and having mentioned to Jupien, whom I found by himself, some love-letters addressed to Robert and signed Bobette which Mme de Saint-Loup had discovered, I learned from the Baron's former factotum that the person who used the signature Bobette was none other than the violinist who had played so important a part in the life of M. de Charlus. Jupien could not speak of him without indignation: 'The boy was free to do what he chose. But if there was one direction in which he ought never to have looked, that was the Baron's nephew. All the more so as the Baron loved his nephew like his own son. He has tried to separate the young couple, it is scandalous. And he must have gone about it with the most devilish cunning, for no one was ever more opposed to that sort of thing than the Marquis de Saint-Loup. To think of all the mad things he has done for his mistresses! No, that wretched musician may have deserted the Baron as he did, by a mean trick, I don't mind saying; still, that was his business. But to take up with the nephew, there are certain things that are not done.' Jupien was sincere in his indignation; among people who are styled immoral, moral indignation is quite as violent as among other people, only its object is slightly different. What is more, people whose own hearts are not directly engaged, always regard unfortunate entanglements, disastrous marriages as though we were free to choose the inspiration of our love, and do not take into account the exquisite mirage which love projects and which envelops so entirely and so uniquely the person with whom we are in love that the 'folly' with which a man is charged who marries his cook or the mistress of his best friend is as a rule the only poetical action that he performs in the course of his existence.

I gathered that Robert and his wife had been on the brink of a separation (albeit Gilberte had not yet discovered the precise nature of the trouble) and that it was Mme de Marsantes, a loving, ambitious and philosophical mother, who had arranged and enforced their reconciliation. She moved in those circles in which the inbreeding of incessantly crossed strains and a gradual impoverishment bring to the surface at every moment in the realm of the passions, as in that of pecuniary interest, inherited vices and compromises. With the same energy with which she had in the past protected Mme Swann, she had assisted the marriage of Jupien's niece and brought about that of her own son to Gilberte, employing thus on her own account, with a pained resignation, the same primeval wisdom which she dispensed throughout the Faubourg. And perhaps what had made her at a certain moment expedite Robert's marriage to Gilberte – which had certainly caused her less trouble and cost fewer tears than making him break with Rachel – had been the fear of his forming with another courtesan – or perhaps with the same one, for Robert took a long time to forget Rachel – a fresh attachment which might have been his salvation. Now I understood what Robert had meant when he said to me at the Princesse de Guermantes's: 'It is a pity that your young friend at Balbec has not the fortune that my mother insists upon. I believe she and I would have got on very well together.' He had meant that she belonged to Gomorrah as he belonged to Sodom, or perhaps, if he was not yet enrolled there, that he had ceased to enjoy women whom he could not love in a certain fashion and in the company of other women. Gilberte, too, might be able to enlighten me as to Albertine. If then, apart from rare moments of retrospect, I had not lost all my curiosity as to the life of my dead mistress, I should have been able to question not merely Gilberte but her husband. And it was, after all, the same thing that had made both Robert and myself anxious to marry Albertine (to wit, the knowledge that she was a lover of women). But the causes of our desire, like its objects for that matter, were opposite. In my case, it was the desperation in which I had been plunged by the discovery, in Robert's the satisfaction; in my case to prevent her, by perpetual vigilance, from indulging her predilection; in Robert's to cultivate it, and by granting her her freedom to make her bring her girl friends to him. If Jupien traced back to a quite recent origin the fresh orientation, so divergent from their original course, that Robert's carnal desires had assumed, a conversation which I had with Aimé and which made me very miserable showed me that the head waiter at Balbec traced this divergence, this inversion to a far earlier date. The occasion of this conversation had been my going for a few days to Balbec, where Saint-Loup himself had also come with his wife, whom during this first phase he never allowed out of his sight. I had marvelled to see how Rachel's influence over Robert still made itself felt. Only a young husband who has long been keeping a mistress knows how to take off his wife's cloak as they enter a restaurant, how to treat her with befitting courtesy. He has, during his illicit relations, learned all that a good husband should know. Not far from him at a table adjoining my own, Bloch among a party of pretentious young university men, was assuming a false air of being at his ease and shouted at the top of his voice to one of his friends, as he ostentatiously passed him the bill of fare with a gesture which upset two water-bottles: 'No, no, my dear man, order! Never in my life have I been able to make head or tail of these documents. I have never known how to order dinner!' he repeated with a pride that was hardly sincere and, blending literature with gluttony, decided at once upon a bottle of champagne which he liked to see 'in a purely symbolic fashion' adorning a conversation. Saint-Loup, on the other hand, did know how to order dinner. He was seated by the side of Gilberte – already pregnant (he was, in the years that followed, to keep her continually supplied with offspring)* – as he would presently lie down by her side in their double bed in the hotel. He spoke to no one but his wife, the rest of the hotel appeared not to exist for him, but at the moment when a waiter came to take his order, and stood close beside him, he swiftly raised his blue eyes and darted a glance at him which did not last for more than two seconds, but in its limpid penetration seemed to indicate a kind of curiosity and investigation entirely different from that which might have animated any ordinary diner studying, even at greater length, a page or messenger, with a view to making humorous or other observations which he would communicate to his friends. This little quick glance, apparently quite disinterested, revealed to those who had intercepted it that this excellent husband, this once so passionate lover of Rachel, possessed another plane in his life, and one that seemed to him infinitely more interesting than that upon which he moved from a sense of duty. But it was to be discerned only in that glance. Already his eyes had returned to Gilberte who had seen nothing, he introduced a passing friend and left the room to stroll with her outside. Now, Aimé was speaking to me at that moment of a far earlier time, the time when I had made Saint-Loup's acquaintance, through Mme de Villeparisis, at this same Balbec. 'Why, surely, Sir,' he said to me, 'it is common knowledge, I have known it for ever so long. The year when Monsieur first came to Balbec, M. le Marquis shut himself up with my lift-boy, on the excuse of developing some photographs of Monsieur's grand-mother. The boy made a complaint, we had the greatest difficulty in hushing the matter up. And besides, Monsieur, Monsieur remembers the day, no doubt, when he came to luncheon at the restaurant with M. le Marquis de Saint-Loup and his mistress, whom M. le Marquis was using as a screen. Monsieur doubtless remembers that M. le Marquis left the room, pretending that he had lost his temper. Of course I don't suggest for a moment that Madame was in the right. She was leading him a regular dance. But as to that day, no one will ever make me believe that M. le Marquis's anger wasn't put on, and that he hadn't a good reason to get away from Monsieur and Madame.' So far as this day was concerned, I am convinced that, if Aimé was not lying consciously, he was entirely mistaken. I remembered quite well the state Robert was in, the blow he struck the

---

* *Dis aliter visum.* We shall see, in the sequel, that the widowed Gilberte appears to be the mother of an only daughter. C. K. S. M.

journalist. And, for that matter, it was the same with the Balbec incident; either the lift-boy had lied, or it was Aimé who was lying. At least, I supposed so; certainty I could not feel, for we never see more than one aspect of things. Had it not been that the thought distressed me, I should have found a refreshing irony in the fact that, whereas to me sending the lift-boy to Saint-Loup had been the most convenient way of conveying a letter to him and receiving his answer, to him it had meant making the acquaintance of a person who had taken his fancy. Everything, indeed, is at least twofold. Upon the most insignificant action that we perform, another man will graft a series of entirely different actions; it is certain that Saint-Loup's adventure with the lift-boy, if it occurred, no more seemed to me to be involved in the commonplace dispatch of my letter than a man who knew nothing of Wagner save the duet in *Lohengrin* would be able to foresee the prelude to *Tristan*. Certainly to men, things offer only a limited number of their innumerable attributes, because of the paucity of our senses. They are coloured because we have eyes, how many other epithets would they not merit if we had hundreds of senses? But this different aspect which they might present is made more comprehensible to us by the occurrence in life of even the most trivial event of which we know a part which we suppose to be the whole, and at which another person looks as though through a window opening upon another side of the house and offering a different view. Supposing that Aimé had not been mistaken, Saint-Loup's blush when Bloch spoke to him of the lift-boy had not, perhaps, been due after all to my friend's pronouncing the word as 'lighft'. But I was convinced that Saint-Loup's physiological evolution had not begun at that period and that he then had been still exclusively a lover of women. More than by any other sign, I could tell this retrospectively by the friendship that Saint-Loup had shown for myself at Balbec. It was only while he was in love with women that he was really capable of friendship. Afterwards, for some time at least, to the men who did not attract him physically he displayed an indifference which was to some extent, I believe, sincere – for he had become very curt – and which he exaggerated as well in order to make people think that he was interested only in women. But I remember all the same that one day at Doncières, as I was on my way to dine with the Verdurins, and after he had been gazing rather markedly at Morel, he had said to me: 'Curious, that fellow, he reminds me in some ways of Rachel. Don't you notice the likeness? To my mind, they are identical in certain respects. Not that it can make any difference to me.' And nevertheless his eyes remained for a long time gazing abstractedly at the horizon, as when we think, before returning to the card-table or going

out to dinner, of one of those long voyages which we shall never make, but
for which we feel a momentary longing. But if Robert found certain traces
of Rachel in Charlie, Gilberte, for her part, sought to present some
similarity to Rachel, so as to attract her husband, wore like her bows of
scarlet or pink or yellow ribbon in her hair, which she dressed in a similar
style, for she believed that her husband was still in love with Rachel, and so
was jealous of her. That Robert's love may have hovered at times over the
boundary which divides the love of a man for a woman from the love of a
man for a man was quite possible. In any case, the part played by his
memory of Rachel was now purely aesthetic. It is indeed improbable that it
could have played any other part. One day Robert had gone to her to ask
her to dress up as a man, to leave a long tress of hair hanging down, and
nevertheless had contented himself with gazing at her without satisfying
his desire. He remained no less attached to her than before and paid her
scrupulously but without any pleasure the enormous allowance that he had
promised her, not that this prevented her from treating him in the most
abominable fashion later on. This generosity towards Rachel would not
have distressed Gilberte if she had known that it was merely the resigned
fulfilment of a promise which no longer bore any trace of love. But love
was, on the contrary, precisely what he pretended to feel for Rachel.
Homosexuals would be the best husbands in the world if they did not make
a show of being in love with other women. Not that Gilberte made any
complaint. It was the thought that Robert had been loved, for years on end,
by Rachel that had made her desire him, had made her refuse more eligible
suitors; it seemed that he was making a sort of concession to her when he
married her. And indeed, at first, any comparison between the two women
(incomparable as they were nevertheless in charm and beauty) did not
favour the delicious Gilberte. But the latter became enhanced later on in
her husband's esteem whereas Rachel grew visibly less important. There
was another person who contradicted herself: namely, Mme Swann. If, in
Gilberte's eyes, Robert before their marriage was already crowned with the
twofold halo which was created for him on the one hand by his life with
Rachel, perpetually proclaimed in Mme de Marsantes's lamentations, on
the other hand by the prestige which the Guermantes family had always
had in her father's eyes and which she had inherited from him, Mme de
Forcheville would have preferred a more brilliant, perhaps a princely
marriage (there were royal families that were impoverished and would have
accepted the dowry – which, for that matter, proved to be considerably less
than the promised millions – purged as it was by the name Forcheville) and
a son-in-law less depreciated in social value by a life spent in comparative

seclusion. She had not been able to prevail over Gilberte's determination, had complained bitterly to all and sundry, denouncing her son-in-law. One fine day she had changed her tune, the son-in-law had become an angel, nothing was ever said against him except in private. The fact was that age had left unimpaired in Mme Swann (become Mme de Forcheville) the need that she had always felt of financial support, but, by the desertion of her admirers, had deprived her of the means. She longed every day for another necklace, a new dress studded with brilliants, a more sumptuous motor car, but she had only a small income, Forcheville having made away with most of it, and – what Israelite strain controlled Gilberte in this? – she had an adorable, but a fearfully avaricious daughter, who counted every penny that she gave her husband, not to mention her mother. Well, all of a sudden she had discerned, and then found her natural protector in Robert. That she was no longer in her first youth mattered little to a son-in-law who was not a lover of women. All that he asked of his mother-in-law was to smoothe down some little difficulty that had arisen between Gilberte and himself, to obtain his wife's consent to his going for a holiday with Morel. Odette had lent her services, and was at once rewarded with a magnificent ruby. To pay for this, it was necessary that Gilberte should treat her husband more generously. Odette preached this doctrine to her with all the more fervour in that it was she herself who would benefit by her daughter's generosity. Thus, thanks to Robert, she was enabled, on the threshold of her fifties (some people said, of her sixties) to dazzle every table at which she dined, every party at which she appeared, with an unparalleled splendour without needing to have, as in the past, a 'friend' who now would no longer have stood for it, in other words have paid the piper. And so she had entered finally, it appeared, into the period of ultimate chastity, and yet she had never been so smart.

It was not merely the malice, the rancour of the once poor boy against the master who has enriched him and has moreover (this was in keeping with the character and still more with the vocabulary of M. de Charlus) made him feel the difference of their positions, that had made Charlie turn to Saint-Loup in order to add to the Baron's sorrows. He may also have had an eye to his own profit. I formed the impression that Robert must be giving him a great deal of money. After an evening party at which I had met Robert before I went down to Combray, and where the manner in which he displayed himself by the side of a lady of fashion who was reputed to be his mistress, in which he attached himself to her, never leaving her for a moment, enveloped publicly in the folds of her skirt, made me think, but with an additional nervous trepidation, of a sort of involuntary rehearsal of an ancestral gesture which I had had an opportunity of observing in M. de Charlus, when he appeared to be robed in the finery of Mme Molé or some other woman, the banner of a gynaecophil cause which was not his own but which he loved, albeit without having the right to flaunt it thus, whether because he found it useful as a protection or aesthetically charming, I had been struck, as we came away, by the discovery that this young man, so generous when he was far less rich, had become so stingy. That a man clings only to what he possesses, and that he who used to scatter money when he so rarely had any now hoards that with which he is amply supplied, is no doubt a common enough phenomenon, and yet in this instance it seemed to me to have assumed a more individual form. Saint-Loup refused to take a cab, and I saw that he had kept a tramway transfer-ticket. No doubt in so doing Saint-Loup was exercising, with a different object, talents which he had acquired in the course of his intimacy with Rachel. A young man who has lived for years with a woman is not as inexperienced as the novice for whom the girl that he marries is the first. Similarly, having had to enter into the minutest details of Rachel's domestic economy, partly because she herself was useless as a housekeeper, and afterwards because his jealousy made him determined to keep a firm control over her private life, he was able, in the administration of his wife's property and the management of their house-hold, to continue playing the part with a skill and experience which Gilberte would perhaps have lacked, who gladly relinquished the duties to him. But no doubt he was doing this principally in order to be able to support Charlie with every penny saved by his cheeseparing, maintaining him in affluence without Gilberte's either noticing or suffering by his peculations. Tears came to my eyes when I reflected that I had felt in the past for a different Saint-Loup an affection which had been so great and which I could see quite well, from the cold and evasive manner which he now adopted, that he no longer felt for me, since men, now that they were capable of arousing his desires, could no longer inspire his friendship. How could these tastes have come to birth in a young man who had been so passionate a lover of women that I had seen him brought to a state of almost suicidal frenzy because 'Rachel, when from the Lord' had threatened to leave him? Had the resemblance between Charlie and Rachel – invisible to me – been the plank which had enabled Robert to pass from his father's tastes to those of his uncle, in order to complete the physiological evolution which even in that uncle had occurred quite late in life? At times however Aimé's words came back to my mind to make me uneasy; I remembered Robert that year at Balbec; he had had a trick, when he spoke to the lift-boy, of not paying any attention to him which strongly resembled M. de Charlus's manner when

he addressed certain men. But Robert might easily have derived this from
M. de Charlus, from a certain stiffness and a certain bodily attitude proper
to the Guermantes family, without for a moment sharing the peculiar tastes
of the Baron. For instance, the Duc de Guermantes, who was free from any
taint of the sort, had the same nervous trick as M. de Charlus of turning his
wrist, as though he were straightening a lace cuff round it, and also in his
voice certain shrill and affected intonations, mannerisms to all of which, in
M. de Charlus, one might have been tempted to ascribe another meaning,
to which he would have given another meaning himself, the individual
expressing his peculiarities by means of impersonal and atavistic traits which
are perhaps nothing more than ingrained peculiarities fixed in his gestures
and voice. By this latter hypothesis, which borders upon natural history, it
would not be M. de Charlus that we ought to style a Guermantes marked
with a blemish and expressing it to a certain extent by means of traits
peculiar to the Guermantes race, but the Duc de Guermantes who would be
in a perverted family the exceptional example, whom the hereditary malady
has so effectively spared that the outward signs which it has left upon him
lose all their meaning. I remembered that on the day when I had seen Saint-
Loup for the first time at Balbec, so fair complexioned, fashioned of so rare
and precious a substance, gliding between the tables, his monocle fluttering
in front of him, I had found in him an effeminate air which was certainly not
suggested by what I was now learning about him, but sprang rather from the
grace peculiar to the Guermantes, from the fineness of that Dresden china
in which the Duchess too was moulded. I recalled his affections for myself,
his tender, sentimental way of expressing it, and told myself that this also,
which might have deceived anyone else, meant at the time something quite
different, indeed the direct opposite of what I had just learned about him.
But from when did the change date? If it had occurred before my return to
Balbec, how was it that he had never once come to see the lift-boy, had
never once mentioned him to me? And as for the first year, how could he
have paid any attention to the boy, passionately enamoured as he then was
of Rachel? That first year, I had found Saint-Loup peculiar, as was every
true Guermantes. Now he was even more individual than I had supposed.
But things of which we have not had a direct intuition, which we have
learned only through other people, we have no longer any opportunity, the
time has passed in which we could inform our heart of them; its communications with reality are suspended; and so we cannot profit by the
discovery, it is too late. Besides, upon any consideration, this discovery
pained me too intensely for me to be able to derive spiritual advantage from
it. No doubt, after what M. de Charlus had told me in Mme Verdurin's

house – in Paris, I no longer doubted that Robert's case was that of any number of respectable people, to be found even among the best and most intelligent of men. To learn this of anyone else would not have affected me, of anyone in the world save Robert. The doubt that Aimé's words had left in my mind tarnished all our friendship at Balbec and Doncières, and albeit I did not believe in friendship, nor did I believe that I had ever felt any real friendship for Robert, when I thought about those stories of the lift-boy and of the restaurant in which I had had luncheon with Saint-Loup and Rachel, I was obliged to make an effort to restrain my tears.

I should, as it happens, have no need to pause to consider this visit which I paid to the Combray district, which was perhaps the time in my life when I gave least thought to Combray, had it not furnished what was at least a provisional verification of certain ideas which I had formed long ago of the 'Guermantes way', and also a verification of certain other ideas which I had formed of the 'Méséglise way'. I repeated every evening, in the opposite direction, the walks which we used to take at Combray, in the afternoon, when we went the 'Méséglise way'. We dined now at Tansonville at an hour at which in the past I had long been asleep at Combray. And this on account of the heat of the sun. And also because, as Gilberte spent the afternoon painting in the chapel attached to the house, we did not take our walks until about two hours before dinner. For the pleasure of those earlier walks which was that of seeing as we returned home the purple sky frame the Calvary or mirror itself in the Vivonne, there was substituted the pleasure of setting forth when dusk had already gathered, when we encountered nothing in the village save the blue-grey, irregular and shifting triangle of a flock of sheep being driven home. Over half the fields night had already fallen; above the evening star the moon had already lighted her lamp which presently would bathe their whole extent. It would happen that Gilberte let me go without her, and I would move forward, trailing my shadow behind me, like a boat that glides across enchanted waters. But as a rule Gilberte came with me. The walks that we took thus together were very often those that I used to take as a child: how, then, could I help feeling far more keenly now than in the past on the 'Guermantes way' the conviction that I would never be able to write anything, combined with the conviction that my imagination and my sensibility had grown more feeble, when I found how little interest I took in Combray? And it distressed me to find how little I relived my early years. I found the Vivonne a meagre, ugly rivulet beneath its towpath. Not that I noticed any material discrepancies of any magnitude from what I remembered. But, separated from the places which I happened to be revisiting by the whole expanse of a different life, there was not, between them and myself, that contiguity from which is born, before even we can perceive it, the immediate, delicious and total deflagration of memory. Having no very clear conception, probably, of its nature, I was saddened by the thought that my faculty of feeling and imagining things must have diminished since I no longer took any pleasure in these walks. Gilberte herself, who understood me even less than I understood myself, increased my melancholy by sharing my astonishment. 'What,' she would say, 'you feel no excitement when you turn into this little footpath which you used to climb?' And she herself had so entirely altered that I no longer thought her beautiful, which indeed she had ceased to be. As we walked, I saw the landscape change, we had to climb hillocks, then came to a downward slope. We conversed, very pleasantly for me – not without difficulty however. In so many people there are different strata which are not alike (there were in her her father's character, and her mother's); we traverse first one, then the other. But, next day, their order is reversed. And finally we do not know who is going to allot the parts, to whom we are to appeal for a hearing. Gilberte was like one of those countries with which we dare not form an alliance because of their too frequent changes of government. But in reality this is a mistake. The memory of the most constant personality establishes a sort of identity in the person, with the result that he would not fail to abide by promises which he remembers even if he has not endorsed them. As for intelligence, it was in Gilberte, with certain absurdities that she had inherited from her mother, very keen. I remember that, in the course of our conversations while we took these walks, she said things which often surprised me greatly. The first was: 'If you were not too hungry and if it was not so late, by taking this road to the left and then turning to the right, in less than a quarter of an hour we should be at Guermantes.' It was as though she had said: 'Turn to the left, then the first turning on the right and you will touch the intangible, you will reach the inaccessibly remote tracts of which we never upon earth know anything but the direction, but' (what I thought long ago to be all that I could ever know of Guermantes, and perhaps in a sense I had not been mistaken) 'the "way".' One of my other surprises was that of seeing the 'source of the Vivonne' which I imagined as something as extraterrestrial as the Gates of Hell, and which was merely a sort of rectangular basin in which bubbles rose to the surface. And the third occasion was when Gilberte said to me: 'If you like, we might go out one afternoon, and then we can go to Guermantes, taking the road by Méséglise, it is the nicest walk,' a sentence which upset all my childish ideas by informing me that the two 'ways' were not as irreconcilable as I had supposed. But what struck me most forcibly was how little, during this visit,

I lived over again my childish years, how little I desired to see Combray, how meagre and ugly I thought the Vivonne. But where Gilberte made some of the things come true that I had imagined about the Méséglise way was during one of those walks which after all were nocturnal even if we took them before dinner – for she dined so late. Before descending into the mystery of a perfect and profound valley carpeted with moonlight, we stopped for a moment, like two insects about to plunge into the blue calyx of a flower. Gilberte then uttered, perhaps simply out of the politeness of a hostess who is sorry that you are going away so soon and would have liked to show you more of a country which you seem to appreciate, a speech of the sort in which her practice as a woman of the world skilled in putting to the best advantage silence, simplicity, sobriety in the expression of her feelings, makes you believe that you occupy a place in her life which no one else could fill. Showering abruptly over her the sentiment with which I was filled by the delicious air, the breeze that was wafted to my nostrils, I said to her: 'You were speaking the other day of the little footpath, how I loved you then!' She replied: 'Why didn't you tell me? I had no idea of it. I was in love with you. Indeed, I flung myself twice at your head.' 'When?' 'The first time at Tansonville, you were taking a walk with your family, I was on my way home, I had never seen such a dear little boy. I was in the habit,' she went on with a vague air of modesty, 'of going out to play with little boys I knew in the ruins of the keep of Roussainville. And you will tell me that I was a very naughty girl, for there were girls and boys there of all sorts who took advantage of the darkness. The altar-boy from Combray church, Théodore, who, I am bound to confess, was very nice indeed (Heavens, how charming he was!) and who has become quite ugly (he is the chemist now at Méséglise), used to amuse himself with all the peasant girls of the district. As they let me go out by myself, whenever I was able to get away, I used to fly there. I can't tell you how I longed for you to come there too; I remember quite well that, as I had only a moment in which to make you understand what I wanted, at the risk of being seen by your people and mine, I signalled to you so vulgarly that I am ashamed of it to this day. But you stared at me so crossly that I saw that you didn't want it.' And, all of a sudden, I said to myself that the true Gilberte – the true Albertine – were perhaps those who had at the first moment yielded themselves in their facial expression, one behind the hedge of pink hawthorn, the other upon the beach. And it was I who, having been incapable of understanding this, having failed to recapture the impression until much later in my memory after an interval in which, as a result of our conversations, a dividing hedge of sentiment had made them afraid to be as frank as in the first moments – had ruined everything by my clumsiness. I had lost them more completely – albeit, to tell the truth, the comparative failure with them was less absurd – for the same reasons that had made Saint-Loup lose Rachel.

'And the second time,' Gilberte went on, 'was years later when I passed you in the doorway of your house, a couple of days before I met you again at my aunt Oriane's, I didn't recognise you at first, or rather I did unconsciously recognise you because I felt the same longing that I had felt at Tansonville.' 'But between these two occasions there were, after all, the Champs-Elysées.' 'Yes, but there you were too fond of me, I felt that you were spying upon me all the time.' I did not ask her at the moment who the young man was with whom she had been walking along the Avenue des Champs-Elysées, on the day on which I had started out to call upon her, on which I would have been reconciled with her while there was still time, that day which would perhaps have changed the whole course of my life, if I had not caught sight of those two shadowy forms advancing towards me side by side in the dusk. If I had asked her, I told myself, she would perhaps have confessed the truth, as would Albertine had she been restored to life. And indeed when we are no longer in love with women whom we meet after many years, is there not the abyss of death between them and ourselves, just as much as if they were no longer of this world, since the fact that we are no longer in love makes the people that they were or the person that we were then as good as dead? It occurred to me that perhaps she might not have remembered, or that she might have lied to me. In any case, it no longer interested me in the least to know, since my heart had changed even more than Gilberte's face. This last gave me scarcely any pleasure, but what was most striking was that I was no longer wretched, I should have been incapable of conceiving, had I thought about it again, that I could have been made so wretched by the sight of Gilberte tripping along by the side of a young man, and thereupon saying to myself: 'It is all over, I shall never attempt to see her again.' Of the state of mind which, in that far off year, had been simply an unending torture to me, nothing survived. For there is in this world in which everything wears out, everything perishes, one thing that crumbles into dust, that destroys itself still more completely, leaving behind still fewer traces of itself than Beauty: namely Grief.

And so I am not surprised that I did not ask her then with whom she had been walking in the Champs-Elysées, for I have already seen too many examples of this incuriosity that is brought about by time, but I am a little surprised that I did not tell Gilberte that, before I saw her that evening, I had sold a bowl of old Chinese porcelain in order to buy her flowers. It had indeed been, during the dreary time that followed, my sole consolation to think that one day I should be able without danger to tell her of so delicate an intention. More than a year later, if I saw another carriage bearing down upon mine, my sole reason for wishing not to die was that I might be able to tell this to Gilberte. I consoled myself with the thought: 'There is no hurry, I have a whole lifetime in which to tell her.' And for this reason I was anxious not to lose my life. Now it would have seemed to me a difficult thing to express in words, almost ridiculous, and a thing that would 'involve consequences'. 'However,' Gilberte went on, 'even on the day when I passed you in the doorway, you were still just the same as at Combray; if you only knew how little you have altered!' I pictured Gilberte again in my memory. I could have drawn the rectangle of light which the sun cast beneath the hawthorns, the trowel which the little girl was holding in her hand, the slow gaze that she fastened on myself. Only I had supposed, because of the coarse gesture that accompanied it, that it was a contemptuous gaze because what I longed for it to mean seemed to me to be a thing that little girls did not know about and did only in my imagination, during my hours of solitary desire. Still less could I have supposed that so easily, so rapidly, almost under the eyes of my grandfather, one of them would have had the audacity to suggest it.

Long after the time of this conversation, I asked Gilberte with whom she had been walking along the Avenue des Champs-Elysées on the evening on which I had sold the bowl: it was Léa in male attire. Gilberte knew that she was acquainted with Albertine, but could not tell me any more. Thus it is that certain persons always reappear in our life to herald our pleasures or our griefs.

What reality there had been beneath the appearance on that occasion had become quite immaterial to me. And yet for how many days and nights had I not tormented myself with wondering who the man was, had I not been obliged, when I thought of him, to control the beating of my heart even more perhaps than in the effort not to go downstairs to bid Mamma goodnight in that same Combray. It is said, and this is what accounts for the gradual disappearance of certain nervous affections, that our nervous system grows old. This is true not merely of our permanent self which continues throughout the whole duration of our life, but of all our successive selves which after all to a certain extent compose the permanent self.

And so I was obliged, after an interval of so many years, to add fresh touches to an image which I recalled so well, an operation which made me quite happy by showing me that the impassable gulf which I had then supposed to exist between myself and a certain type of little girl with golden hair was as imaginary as Pascal's gulf, and which I felt to be poetic because of the long series of years at the end of which I was called upon to perform it. I felt a stab of desire and regret when I thought of the dungeons of Roussainville. And yet I was glad to be able to say to myself that the pleasure towards which I used to strain every nerve in those days, and which nothing could restore to me now, had indeed existed elsewhere than in my mind, in reality, and so close at hand, in that Roussainville of which I spoke so often, which I could see from the window of the orris-scented closet. And I had known nothing! In short Gilberte embodied everything that I had desired upon my walks, even my inability to make up my mind to return home, when I thought I could see the tree-trunks part asunder, take human form. The things for which at that time I so feverishly longed, she had been ready, if only I had had the sense to understand and to meet her again, to let me taste in my boyhood. More completely even than I had supposed, Gilberte had been in those days truly part of the 'Méséglise way'.

And indeed on the day when I had passed her in a doorway, albeit she was not Mlle de l'Orgeville, the girl whom Robert had met in houses of assignation (and what an absurd coincidence that it should have been to her future husband that I had applied for information about her), I had not been altogether mistaken as to the meaning of her glance, nor as to the sort of woman that she was and confessed to me now that she had been. 'All that is a long time ago,' she said to me, 'I have never given a thought to anyone but Robert since the day of our engagement. And, let me tell you, that childish caprice is not the thing for which I blame myself most.'

Time Regained

Translated by
STEPHEN HUDSON

We are grateful to
Dr S. Beddington-Behrens
for permission to use Stephen Hudson's
translation of *Time Regained*

CHAPTER ONE

Tansonville

TANSONVILLE seemed little more than a place to rest in between two walks or a refuge during a shower. Rather too countrified, it was one of those rural dwellings where every sitting-room is a cabinet of greenery, and where the roses and the birds out in the garden keep you company in the curtains; for they were old and each rose stood out so clearly that it might have been picked like a real one and each bird put in a cage, unlike those pretentious modern decorations in which, against a silver background, all the apple trees in Normandy are outlined in the Japanese manner, to trick the hours you lie in bed. I spent the whole day in my room, the windows of which opened upon the beautiful verdure of the park, upon the lilacs of the entrance, upon the green leaves of the great trees beside the water and in the forest of Méséglise. It was a pleasure to contemplate all this, I was saying to myself: 'How charming to have all this greenery in my window' until suddenly in the midst of the great green picture I recognised the clock tower of the Church of Combray toned in contrast to a sombre blue as though it were far distant, not a reproduction of the clock tower but its very self which, defying time and space, thrust itself into the midst of the luminous greenery as if it were engraved upon my window-pane. And if I left my room, at the end of the passage, set towards me like a band of scarlet, I perceived the hangings of a little sitting-room which though only made of muslin, were of a scarlet so vivid that they would catch fire if a single sun-ray touched them.

During our walks Gilberte alluded to Robert as though he were turning away from her but to other women. It was true that his life was encumbered with women as masculine attachments encumber that of women-loving men, both having that character of forbidden fruit, of a place vainly usurped, which unwanted objects have in most houses.

Once I left Gilberte early and in the middle of the night, while still half-asleep, I called Albertine. I had not been thinking or dreaming of her, nor had I mistaken her for Gilberte. My memory had lost its love for Albertine but it seems there must be an involuntary memory of the limbs, pale and sterile imitation of the other, which lives longer as certain mindless animals or plants live longer than man. The legs, the arms are full of blunted memories; a reminiscence germinating in my arm had made me seek the bell behind my back, as I used to in my room in Paris and I had called Albertine, imagining my dead friend lying beside me as she so often did at evening when we fell asleep together, counting the time it would take Françoise to reach us, so that Albertine might without imprudence pull the bell I could not find.

Robert came to Tansonville several times while I was there. He was very different from the man I had known before. His life had not coarsened him as it had M. de Charlus, but, on the contrary, had given him more than ever the easy carriage of a cavalry officer although at his marriage he had resigned his commission. As gradually M. de Charlus had got heavier, Robert (of course he was much younger, yet one felt he was bound to approximate to that type with age like certain women who resolutely sacrifice their faces to their figures and never abandon Marienbad, believing, as they cannot hope to keep all their youthful charms, that of the outline to represent best the others) had become slimmer, swifter, the contrary effect of the same vice. This velocity had other psychological causes: the fear of being seen, the desire not to seem to have that fear, the feverishness born of dissatisfaction with oneself and of boredom. He had the habit of going into certain haunts of ill-fame, where as he did not wish to be seen entering or coming out, he effaced himself so as to expose the least possible surface to the malevolent gaze of hypothetical passers-by, and that gust-like motion had remained and perhaps signified the apparent intrepidity of one who wants to show he is unafraid and does not take time to think.

To complete the picture one must reckon with the desire, the older he got, to appear young, and also the impatience of those who are always bored and *blasé*, yet being too intelligent for a relatively idle life, do not sufficiently use their faculties. Doubtless the very idleness of such people may display itself by indifference but especially since idleness, owing to the favour now accorded to physical exercise, has taken the form of sport, even when the latter cannot be practised, feverish activity leaves boredom neither time nor space to develop in.

He had become dried up and gave friends like myself no evidence of sensibility. On the other hand, he affected with Gilberte an unpleasant sensitiveness which he pushed to the point of comedy. It was not that Robert was indifferent to Gilberte; no, he loved her. But he always lied to her and this spirit of duplicity, if it was not the actual source of his lies, was constantly emerging. At such times he believed he could only extricate himself by exaggerating to a ridiculous degree the real pain he felt in giving pain to her. When he arrived at Tansonville he was obliged, he said, to leave the next morning on business with a certain gentleman of those parts, who was expecting him in Paris and who, encountered that very evening near Combray, unhappily revealed the lie, Robert having failed to warn him, by the statement that he was back for a month's holiday and would not be in Paris before. Robert blushed, saw Gilberte's faint melancholy smile, and after revenging himself on the unfortunate culprit by an insult, returned earlier than his wife and sent her a desperate note telling her he had lied in order not to pain her, for fear that when he left for a reason he could not tell her, she should think that he had ceased to love her; and all this, written as though it were a lie, was actually true. Then he sent to ask if he could come to her room, and there, partly in real sorrow, partly in disgust with the life he was living, partly through the increasing audacity of his successive pretences, he sobbed and talked of his approaching death, sometimes throwing himself on the floor as though he were ill. Gilberte, not knowing to what extent to believe him, thought him a liar on each occasion, but, disquieted by the presentiment of his approaching death and believing in a general way that he loved her, that perhaps he had some illness she knew nothing about, did not dare to oppose him or ask him to relinquish his journeys. I was unable to understand how he came to have Morel received as though he were a son of the house wherever the Saint-Loups were, whether in Paris or at Tansonville.

Françoise, knowing all that M. de Charlus had done for Jupien and Robert Saint-Loup for Morel, did not conclude that this was a trait which reappeared in certain generations of the Guermantes, but rather – seeing that Legrandin much loved Théodore – came to believe, prudish and narrow-minded as she was, that it was a custom which universality made respectable. She would say of a young man, were it Morel or Théodore: 'He is fond of the gentleman who is interested in him and who has so much helped him.' And as in such cases it is the protectors who love, who suffer, who forgive, Françoise did not hesitate between them and the youths they debauched, to give the former the *beau role*, to discover they had a 'great deal of heart'. She did not hesitate to blame Théodore who had played a great many tricks on Legrandin, yet seemed to have scarcely a doubt as to the nature of their relationship, for she added, 'The young man understands he's got to do his share as he says: "take me away with you, I will be fond of you and pet you", and, *ma foi*, the gentleman has so much heart that Théodore is sure to find him kinder than he deserves, for he's a hothead while the gentleman is so good that I often say to Jeannette (Theodore's fiancée), "My dear, if ever you're in trouble go and see that gentleman, he would lie on the ground to give you his bed, he is too fond of Théodore to throw him out and he will never abandon him".' It was in the course of one of these colloquies that, having enquired the name of the family with whom Théodore was living in the south, I suddenly grasped that he was the person unknown to me who had asked me to send him my article in the *Figaro* in a letter the calligraphy of which was of the people but charmingly expressed.

In the same fashion Françoise esteemed Saint-Loup more than Morel and expressed the opinion, in spite of the ignoble behaviour of the latter, that the marquis had too good a heart ever to desert him unless great reverses happened to himself.

Saint-Loup insisted I should remain at Tansonville and once let fall, although plainly he was not seeking to please me, that my visit was so great a happiness for his wife that she had assured him, though she had been wretched the whole day, that she was transported with joy the evening I unexpectedly arrived, that, in fact, I had miraculously saved her from despair, 'perhaps from something worse'. He begged me to try and persuade her that he loved her, assuring me that the other woman he loved was less to him than Gilberte and that he intended to break with her very soon. 'And yet,' he added, in such a feline way and with so great a longing to confide that I expected the name of Charlie to pop out at any moment, in spite of himself, like a lottery number, 'I had something to be proud of. This woman, who has proved her devotion to me and whom I must sacrifice for Gilberte's sake, never accepted attention from a man, she believed herself incapable of love; I am the first. I knew she had refused herself to everyone, so much so that when I received an adorable letter from her, telling me there could be no happiness for her without me, I could not resist it. Wouldn't it be natural for me to be infatuated with her, were it not intolerable for me to see poor little Gilberte in tears? Don't you think there is something of Rachel in her?' As a matter of fact, it had struck me that there was a vague resemblance between them. This may have been due to a certain similarity of feature, owing to their common Jewish origin, which was little marked in Gilberte, and yet when his family wanted him to marry, drew Robert towards her. The likeness was perhaps due also to Gilberte coming across photographs of Rachel and wanting to please Robert by imitating certain of the actress's habits, such as always wearing red bows in her hair, a black ribbon on her arm and dyeing her hair to appear dark. Then, fearing her sorrows affected her appearance, she tried to remedy it by occasionally exaggerating the artifice. One day, when Robert was to come to Tansonville for twenty-four hours, I was amazed to see her come to table looking so strangely different from her present as well as from her former self, that I was as bewildered as if I were facing an actress, a sort of Theodora. I felt that in my curiosity to know what it was that was changed about her, I was looking at her too fixedly. My curiosity was soon satisfied when she blew her nose, for in spite of all her precautions, the assortment of colours upon the handkerchief would have constituted a varied palette and I saw that she was completely painted. To this was due the bleeding appearance of her mouth which she forced into a smile, thinking it suited her, while the knowledge that the hour was approaching when her husband ought to arrive without knowing whether or not he would send one of those telegrams of which the model had been wittily invented by M. de Guermantes: 'Impossible to come, lie follows,' paled her cheeks and ringed her eyes.

'Ah, you see,' Robert said to me with a deliberately tender accent which contrasted with his former spontaneous affection, with an alcoholic voice and the inflection of an actor. 'To make Gilberte happy! What wouldn't I do to secure that? You can never know how much she has done for me.' The most unpleasant of all was his vanity, for Saint-Loup, flattered that Gilberte loved him, without daring to say that he loved Morel, gave her details about the devotion the violinist pretended to have for him, which he well knew were exaggerated if not altogether invented seeing that Morel demanded more money of him every day. Then confiding Gilberte to my care, he left again for Paris.

To anticipate somewhat (for I am still at Tansonville), I had the opportunity of seeing him once again in society, though at a distance, when his words, in spite of all this, were so lively and charming that they enabled me to recapture the past. I was struck to see how much he was changing. He resembled his mother more and more, but the proud and well-bred manner he inherited from her and which she possessed to perfection, had become, owing to his highly accomplished education, exaggerated and stilted; the penetrating look common to the Guermantes, gave him, from a peculiar animal-like habit, a half-unconscious air of inspecting every place he passed through. Even when motionless, that colouring which was his even more than it was the other Guermantes', a colouring which seemed to have a whole golden day's sunshine in it, gave him so strange a plumage, made of him so rare a creature, so unique, that one wanted to own him for an ornithological collection; but when, besides, this bird of golden sunlight put itself in motion, when, for instance, I saw Robert de Saint-Loup at a party, he had a way of throwing back his head so joyously and so proudly, under the golden plumage of his slightly ruffled hair, the movement of his neck was so much more supple, proud and charming than that of other men, that, between the curiosity and the half-social, half-zoological admiration he inspired, one asked oneself whether one had found him in the Faubourg Saint-Germain or in the Jardin des Plantes and whether one was looking at a *grand seigneur* crossing a drawing-room or a marvellous bird walking about in its cage. With a little imagination the warbling no less than the plumage lent itself to that interpretation. He spoke in what he believed the *grand-siècle* style and thus imitated the manners of the Guermantes, but an indefinable trifle caused them to become those of M. de Charlus. 'I must leave you an instant,' he said during that party, when M. de Marsantes was some distance away, 'to pay court to my niece a moment.'

As to that love of which he never ceased telling me, there were others besides Charlie, although he was the only one that mattered to him. Whatever kind of love a man may have, one is always wrong about the number of his *liaisons*, because one interprets friendships as *liaisons*, which is an error of addition, and also because it is believed that one proved *liaison* excludes another, which is a different sort of mistake. Two people may say, 'I know X's mistress,' and each be pronouncing a different name, yet neither be wrong. A woman one loves rarely suffices for all our needs, so we deceive her with another whom we do not love. As to the kind of love which Saint-Loup had inherited from M. de Charlus, the husband who is inclined that way generally makes his wife happy. This is a general law, to which the Guermantes were exceptions, because those of them who had that taste wanted people to believe they were women-lovers and, advertising themselves with one or another, caused the despair of their wives. The Courvoisiers acted more sensibly. The young Vicomte de Courvoisier believed himself the only person on earth and since the beginning of the world to be tempted by one of his own sex. Imagining that the preference came to him from the devil, he fought against it and married a charming woman by whom he had several children. Then one of his cousins taught him that the practice was fairly common, even went to the length of taking him to places where he could satisfy it. M. de Courvoisier only loved his wife the more for this and redoubled his uxorious zeal so that the couple were cited as the best *ménage* in Paris. As much could not be said for Saint-Loup, because Robert, not content with inversion, caused his wife endless jealousy by running after mistresses without getting any pleasure from them.

It is possible that Morel, being exceedingly dark, was necessary to Saint-Loup, as shadow is to sunlight. In this ancient family, one could well imagine a *grand seigneur*, blonde, golden, intelligent, dowered with every prestige, acquiring and retaining in the depths of his being, a secret taste, unknown to everyone, for negroes.

Robert, moreover, never allowed conversation to touch his peculiar kind of love affair. If I said a word he would answer, with a detachment that caused his eye-glass to fall, 'Oh! I don't know, I haven't an idea about such things. If you want information about them, my dear fellow, I advise you to go to someone else. I am a soldier, nothing more. I'm as indifferent to matters of that kind as I am passionately interested in the Balkan Wars. Formerly the history of battles interested you. In those days I told you we should again witness typical battles, even though the conditions were completely different, such, for instance, as the great attempt of envelopment by the wing in the Battle of Ulm. Well, special as those Balkan Wars may be, Lullé Burgas is again Ulm, envelopment by the wing. Those are matters you can talk to me about. But I know no more about the sort of thing you are alluding to than I do about Sanscrit.'

On the other hand, when he had gone, Gilberte referred voluntarily to the subjects Robert thus disdained when we talked together. Certainly not in connection with her husband, for she was unaware, or pretended to be unaware, of everything. But she enlarged willingly upon them when they concerned other people, whether because she saw in their case a sort of indirect excuse for Robert or whether, divided like his uncle between a severe silence on these subjects and an urge to pour himself out and to slander, he had been able to instruct her very thoroughly about them. Amongst those alluded to, no one was less spared than M. de Charlus; doubtless this was because Robert, without talking to Gilberte about Morel, could not help repeating to her in one form or another what had been told him by the violinist who pursued his former benefactor with his hatred. These conversations which Gilberte affected, permitted me to ask her if in similar fashion Albertine, whose name I had for the first time heard on her lips when the two were school friends, had the same tastes. Gilberte refused to give me this information. For that matter, it had for a long time ceased to afford me the slightest interest. Yet I continued to concern myself mechanically about it, just like an old man who has lost his memory now and then wants news of his dead son.

Another day I returned to the charge and asked Gilberte again if Albertine loved women. 'Oh, not at all,' she answered. 'But you formerly said that she was very bad form.' 'I said that? You must be mistaken. In any case, if I did say it – but you are mistaken – I was on the contrary speaking of little love affairs with boys and, at that age, those don't go very far.' Did Gilberte say this to hide that she herself, according to Albertine, loved women and had made proposals to her, or (for others are often better informed about our life than we think) did Gilberte know that I had loved and been jealous of

Albertine and (others being apt to know more of the truth than we believe, exaggerating it and so erring by excessive suppositions, while we were hoping they were mistaken through lack of any supposition at all) did she imagine that I was so still, and was she, out of kindness, blindfolding me which one is always ready to do to jealous people? In any case, Gilberte's words, since the 'bad form' of former days leading to the certificate of moral life and habits of today, followed an inverse course to the affirmations of Albertine, who had almost come to avowing half-relationship with Gilberte herself. Albertine had astonished me in this, as had also what Andrée told me, for, respecting the whole of that little band, I had at first, before knowing its perversity, convinced myself that my suspicions were unjustified, as happens so often when one discovers an innocent girl, almost ignorant of the realities of life, in a milieu which one had wrongly supposed the most depraved. Afterwards I retraced my steps in the contrary sense, accepting my original suspicions as true. And perhaps Albertine told me all this so as to appear more experienced than she was and to astonish me with the prestige of her perversity in Paris, as at first by the prestige of her virtue at Balbec. So, quite simply, when I spoke to her about women who loved women, she answered as she did, in order not to seem to be unaware of what I meant, as in a conversation one assumes an understanding air when somebody talks of Fourier or of Tobolsk without even knowing what these names mean. She had perhaps associated with the friend of Mlle Vinteuil and with Andrée, isolated from them by an airtight partition and, while they believed she was not one of them, she only informed herself afterwards (as a woman who marries a man of letters seeks to cultivate herself) in order to please me, by enabling herself to answer my questions, until she realised that the questions were inspired by jealousy when, unless Gilberte was lying to me, she reversed the engine. The idea came to me, that it was because Robert had learnt from her in the course of a flirtation of the kind that interested him, that she, Gilberte, did not dislike women, that he married her, hoping for pleasures which he ought not to have looked for at home since he obtained them elsewhere. None of these hypotheses were absurd, for in the case of women such as Odette's daughter or of the girls of the little band there is such a diversity, such an accumulation of alternating tastes, that if they are not simultaneous, they pass easily from a *liaison* with a woman to a passion for a man, so much so that it becomes difficult to define their real and dominant taste. Thus Albertine had sought to please me in order to make me marry her but she had abandoned the project herself because of my undecided and worrying disposition. It was in this too simple form that I judged my affair with Albertine at a time when I only saw it from the outside.

What is curious and what I am unable wholly to grasp, is that about that period all those who had loved Albertine, all those who would have been able to make her do what they wanted, asked, entreated, I would even say, implored me, failing my friendship, at least, to have some sort of relations with them. It would have been no longer necessary to offer money to Mme Bontemps to send me Albertine. This return of life, coming when it was no longer any use, profoundly saddened me, not on account of Albertine whom I would have received without pleasure if she had been brought to me, not only from Touraine but from the other world, but because of a young woman whom I loved and whom I could not manage to see. I said to myself that if she died or if I did not love her any more, all those who would have been able to bring her to me would have fallen at my feet. Meanwhile, I attempted in vain to work upon them, not being cured by experience which ought to have taught me, if it ever taught anyone anything, that to love is a bad fate like that in fairy stories, against which nothing avails until the enchantment has ceased.

'I've just reached a point,' Gilberte continued, 'in the book which I have here where it speaks of these things. It's an old Balzac I'm raking over to be on equal terms with my uncles, *La Fille aux Yeux d'Or*, but it's incredible, a beautiful nightmare. Maybe a woman can be controlled in that way by another woman, but never by a man.' 'You are mistaken, I knew a woman who was loved by a man who veritably succeeded in isolating her; she could never see anyone and only went out with trusted servants.' 'Indeed! How that must have horrified you who are so kind. Just recently Robert and I were saying you ought to get married, your wife would cure you and make you happy.' 'No, I've got too bad a disposition.' 'What nonsense.' 'I assure you I have. For that matter I have been engaged, but I could not marry.'

I did not want to borrow *La Fille aux Yeux d'Or* from Gilberte because she was reading it, but on the last evening that I stayed with her, she lent me a book which produced a lively and mingled impression upon me. It was a volume of the unpublished diary of the Goncourts. I was sad that last evening, in going up to my room, to think that I had never gone back one single time to see the Church of Combray which seemed to be awaiting me in the midst of greenery framed in the violet-hued window. I said to myself, 'Well, it must be another year, if I do not die between this and then', seeing no other obstacle but my death and not imagining that of the church, which, it seemed to me, must last long after my death as it had lasted long before my birth.

When, before blowing out my candle, I read the passage which I transcribe further on, my lack of aptitude for writing – presaged formerly during my walks on the Guermantes side, confirmed during the visit of which this was the last evening, those eves of departure, when the routine of habits which are about to end is ceasing and one begins to judge oneself – seemed to me less regrettable; it was as though literature revealed no profound truth while at the same time it seemed sad that it was not what I believed it. The infirm state which was to confine me in a sanatorium seemed less regrettable to me if the beautiful things of which books speak were no more beautiful than those I had seen. But, by a strange contradiction, now that this book spoke of them, I longed to see them. Here are the pages which I read until fatigue closed my eyes.

The day before yesterday, who should drop in here, to take me to dinner with him but Verdurin, the former critic of the *Revue*, author of that book on Whistler in which truly the doings, the artistic atmosphere of that highly original American are often rendered with great delicacy by that lover of all the refinements, of all the prettinesses of the thing painted which Verdurin is. And while I dress myself to follow him, every now and then, he gives vent to a regular recitation, like the frightened spelling out of a confession by Fromentin on his renunciation of writing immediately after his marriage with 'Madeleine', a renunciation which was said to be due to his habit of taking morphine, the result of which, according to Verdurin, was that the majority of the habitués of his wife's salon, not even knowing that her husband had ever written, spoke to him of Charles Blanc, St Victor, St Beuve, and Burty, to whom they believed him completely inferior. 'You Goncourt, you well know, and Gautier knew also that my *Salons* was a very different thing from those pitiable *Maîtres d'autrefois* believed to be masterpieces in my wife's family.' Then, by twilight, while the towers of the Trocadéro were lit up with the last gleams of the setting sun which made them look just like those covered with currant jelly of the old-style confectioners, the conversation continues in the carriage on our way to the Quai Conti where their mansion is, which its owner claims to be the ancient palace of the Ambassadors of Venice and where there is said to be a smoking-room of which Verdurin talks as though it were the drawing-room, transported just as it was in the fashion of the *Thousand and One Nights*, of a celebrated Palazzo, of which I forget the name, a Palazzo with a well-head representing the crowning of the Virgin which Verdurin asserts to be absolutely the finest of Sansovinos and which is used by their guests to throw their cigar ashes into. And, *ma foi*, when we arrive, the dull green diffusion of moonlight, verily like that under which classical painting shelters Venice and under which the silhouetted cupola of the Institute makes one think of the Salute in the pictures of Guardi, I have somewhat the illusion of being beside the Grand Canal, the illusion reinforced by the construction of the mansion, where from the first floor, one does not see the quay, and by the effective remark of the master of the house, who affirms that the name of the rue du Bac – I am hanged if I had ever thought of it – came from the ferry upon which the religious of former days, the Miramiones, went to mass at Notre Dame. I took to reloving the whole quarter where I wandered in my youth when my Aunt de Courmont lived there on finding almost contiguous to the mansion of Verdurin, the sign of 'Petit Dunkerque', one of those rare shops surviving otherwise than vignetted in the chalks and rubbings of Gabriel de St Aubin in which that curious eighteenth century individual came in and seated himself during his moments of idleness to bargain about pretty little French and foreign 'trifles' and the newest of everything produced by Art, as a bill-head of the 'Petit Dunkerque' has it, a bill-head of which I believe we alone, Verdurin and I, possess an example and which is one of those shuttlecock masterpieces of ornamented paper upon which, in the reign of Louis XV accounts were delivered, with its title-head representing a raging sea swarming with ships, a sea with waves which had the appearance of an illustration in the *Edition des Fermiers Généraux de l'Huître et des Plaideurs*. The mistress of the house, who places me beside her, says amiably that she has decorated her table with nothing but Japanese chrysanthemums, but these chrysanthemums are disposed in vases which are the rarest works of art, one of them of bronze upon which petals of red copper seemed to be the living efflorescence of the flower. There is Cottard the doctor, and his wife, the Polish sculptor Viradobetski, Swann the collector, a Russian *grande dame*, a Princess with a golden name which escapes me, and Cottard whispers in my ear that it is she who had shot point blank at the Archduke Rudolf. According to her I have an absolutely exceptional literary position in Galicia and in the whole north of Poland, a girl in those parts never consenting to promise her hand without knowing if her betrothed is an admirer of La Faustin.

'You cannot understand, you western people,' exclaims by way of conclusion the princess who gives me the impression, *ma foi*, of an altogether superior intelligence, 'that penetration by a writer into the intimate life of a woman.' A man with shaven chin and lips, with whiskers like a butler, beginning with that tone of condescension of a secondary professor preparing first form boys for the Saint-Charlemagne, that is Brichot, the university don. When my name was mentioned by Verdurin he did not say a word to show that he knew our books, which means for me anger, discouragement aroused by this conspiracy the Sorbonne organises against us, bringing contradiction and hostile silence even into the charming house where I am being entertained. We proceed to table and there is then an extraordinary procession of plates which are simply masterpieces of the art of the porcelain-maker. The connoisseur, whose attention is delicately tickled during the dainty repast, listens all the more complacently to the artistic chatter – while before him pass plates of Yung Tsching with their nasturtium rims yielding to the bluish centre with its rich flowering of the water-iris, a really decorative passage with its dawn-flight of kingfishers and cranes, a dawn with just that matutinal tone which I gaze at lazily when I awake daily at the Boulevard Montmorency – Dresden plates more finical in the grace of their fashioning, whether in the sleepy anaemia of their roses turning to violet in the crushed wine-lees of a tulip or with their rococo design of carnation and myosotis. Plates of Sèvres trellissed by the delicate vermiculation of their white fluting, verticillated in gold or bound upon the creamy plane of their *pâte tendre* by the gay relief of a golden ribbon, finally a whole service of silver on which are displayed those Lucinian myrtles which Dubarry would recognise. And what is perhaps equally rare is the really altogether remarkable quality of the things which are served in it, food delicately manipulated, a stew such as the Parisians, one can shout that aloud, never have at their grandest dinners and which reminds me of certain *cordons bleus* of Jean d'Heurs. Even the *foie gras* has no relation to the tasteless froth which is generally served under that name, and I do not know many places where a simple potato salad is thus made with potatoes having the firmness of a Japanese ivory button and the patina of those little ivory spoons with which the Chinese pour water on the fish that they have just caught. A rich red bejewelling is given to the Venetian goblet which stands before me by an amazing Léoville bought at the sale of M. Montalivet and it is a delight for the imagination and for the eye, I do not fear to say it, for the imagination of what one formerly called the jaw, to have served to one a brill which has nothing in common with that kind of stale brill served on the most luxurious tables which has received on its back the imprint of its bones during the delay of the journey, a brill not accompanied by that sticky glue generally called *sauce blanche* by so many of the chefs in great houses, but by a veritable *sauce blanche* made out of butter at five francs the pound; to see this brill in a wonderful Tching Hon dish graced by the purple rays of a setting sun on a sea which an amusing band of lobsters is navigating, their rough tentacles so realistically pictured that they seem to have been modelled upon the living carapace, a dish of which the handle is a little Chinaman catching with his line a fish which makes the silvery azure of his stomach an enchantment of mother of pearl. As I speak to Verdurin of the delicate satisfaction it must be for him to have this refined repast amidst a collection which no prince possesses at the present time, the mistress of the house throws me the melancholy remark: 'One sees how little you know him', and she speaks of her husband as a whimsical oddity, indifferent to all these beauties, 'an oddity' she repeats, 'that's the word, who has more gusto for a bottle of cider drunk in the rough coolness of a Norman farm'. And the charming woman, in a tone which is really in love with the colours of the country, speaks to us with overflowing enthusiasm of that Normandy where they have lived, a Normandy which must be like an enormous English park, with the fragrance of its high woodlands à la Lawrence, with its velvet cryptomeria in their enamelled borders of pink hortensia, with its natural lawns diversified by sulphur-coloured roses falling over a rustic gateway flanked by two intertwined pear trees resembling with its free-falling and flowering branches the highly ornamental insignia of a bronze appliqué by Gauthier, a Normandy which must be absolutely unsuspected by Parisians on holiday, protected as it is by the barrier of each of its enclosures, barriers which the Verdurins confess to me they did not commit the crime of removing. At the close of day, as the riot of colour was sleepily extinguished and light only came from the sea curdled almost to a skim-milk blue. 'Ah! Not the sea you know – ' protests my hostess energetically in answer to my remark that Flaubert had taken my brother and me to Trouville, 'That is nothing, absolutely nothing. You must come with me, without that you will never know' – they would go back through real forests of pink-tulle flowers of the rhododendrons, intoxicated with the scent of the gardens, which gave her husband abominable attacks of asthma. 'Yes,' she insisted, 'it is true, real crises of asthma.' Afterwards, the following summer, they returned, housing a whole colony of artists in an admirable dwelling of the Middle Ages, an ancient cloister leased by them for nothing, and *ma foi*, listening to this woman who after moving in so many distinguished circles, had yet kept some of that freedom of speech of a woman of the people, a speech which shows you things with the colour imagination gives to them, my mouth watered at the thought of the life which she confessed to living down there, each one working in his cell or in the salon which was so large that it had two fireplaces. Everyone came in before luncheon for altogether superior conversation interspersed with parlour games, reminding me of those evoked by that masterpiece of Diderot, his *Letters to Mlle Volland*. Then after luncheon everyone went out, even on days of sunny showers, when the sparkling of the raindrops luminously filtering through the knots of a magnificent avenue of centenarian beech trees which offered in front of the gates the vista of growth dear to the eighteenth century, and shrubs bearing drops of rain on their flowering buds suspended on their boughs, lingering to watch the delicate dabbling of a bullfinch enamoured of coolness, bathing itself in the tiny Nymphenbourg basin shaped like the corolla of a white rose. And as I talk to Mme Verdurin of the landscapes and of the flowers down there, so delicately pastelled by Elstir: 'But it is I who made all that known to him,' she exclaims with an indignant lifting of the head, 'everything, you understand; wonder-provoking nooks, all his themes; I threw them in his face when he left us, didn't I, Auguste? All those themes he has painted. Objects he always knew, to be fair, one must admit that. But flowers he had never seen; no, he did not know the difference between a marshmallow and a hollyhock. It was I who taught him, you will hardly believe me, to recognise the jasmine.' And it is, one must admit, a strange reflection that the painter of flowers, whom the connoisseurs of today cite to us as the greatest, superior even to Fantin-Latour, would perhaps never have known how to paint jasmine without the woman who was beside me. 'Yes, upon my word, the jasmine; all the roses he produced were painted while he was staying with me, if I did not bring them to him myself. At our house we just called him "M. Tiche". Ask Cottard or Brichot or any of them if he was ever treated here as a great man. He would have laughed at it himself. I taught him how to arrange his flowers; at the beginning he had no idea of it. He never knew how to make a bouquet. He had no natural taste for selection. I had to say to him, "No, do not paint that; it is not worth while, paint this." Oh! If he had listened to us for the arrangement of his life as he did for the arrangement of his flowers, and if he had not made that horrible marriage!' And abruptly, with eyes fevered by their absorption in a reverie of the past, with a nerve-racked gesture, she stretched forth her arms with a frenzied cracking of the joints from the silk sleeves of her bodice, and twisted her body into a suffering pose like some admirable picture which I believe has never been painted, wherein all the pent-up revolt, all the enraged susceptibilities of a friend outraged in her delicacy and in her womanly modesty can be read. Upon that she talks to us about the admirable portrait which Elstir made for her, a portrait of the Cottard family, a portrait given by her to the Luxembourg when she quarrelled with the painter, confessing that it was she who had given him the idea of painting the man in evening dress in order to obtain that beautiful expanse of linen, and she who chose the velvet dress of the woman, a dress offering support in the midst of all the fluttering of the light shades of the curtains, of the flowers, of the fruit, of the gauze dresses of the little girls like ballet-dancers' skirts. It was she, too, who gave him the idea of painting her in the act of arranging her hair, an idea for which the artist was afterwards honoured, which consisted, in short, in painting the woman, not as though on show, but surprised in the intimacy of her everyday life. 'I said to him, "When a woman is doing her hair or wiping her face, or warming her feet, she knows she is not being seen, she executes a number of interesting movements, movements of an altogether Leonardo-like grace." '

But upon a sign from Verdurin, indicating that the arousing of this state of indignation was unhealthy for that highly-strung creature which his wife was, Swann drew my admiring attention to the necklace of black pearls worn by the mistress of the house and bought by her quite white at the sale of a descendant of Mme de La Fayette to whom they had been given by Henrietta of England, pearls which had become black as the result of a fire which destroyed part of the house in which the Verdurins were living in a street the name of which I can no longer remember, a fire after which the casket containing the pearls was found but they had become entirely black. 'And I know the portrait of those pearls on the very shoulders of Mme de La Fayette, yes, exactly so, their portrait,' insisted Swann in the face of the somewhat wonderstruck exclamations of the guests. 'Their authentic portrait, in the collection of the Duc de Guermantes. A collection which has not its equal in the world,' he asserts and that I ought to go and see it, a collection inherited by the celebrated Duc who was the favourite nephew of Mme de Beausergent his aunt, of that Mme de Beausergent who afterwards became Mme d'Hayfeld, sister of the Marquise de Villeparisis and of the Princess of Hanover. My brother and I used to be so fond of him in the old days when he was a charming boy called Basin, which as a matter of fact, is the first name of the Duc. Upon that, Doctor Cottard, with that delicacy which reveals the man of distinction, returns to the history of the pearls and informs us that catastrophes of that kind produce in the mind of people distortions similar to those one remarks in organic matter and relates in really more philosophical terms than most physicians can command, how the footman of Mme Verdurin herself, through the horror of this fire where he nearly perished, had become a different man, his handwriting having so changed that on seeing the first letter which his masters, then in Normandy, received from him, announcing the event, they believed it was the invention of a practical joker. And not only was his handwriting different, Cottard asserts that from having been a completely sober man he had become an abominable drunkard whom Mme Verdurin had been obliged to discharge. This suggestive dissertation continued, on a gracious sign from the mistress of the house, from the dining-room into the Venetian smoking-room where Cottard told me he had witnessed actual duplications of personality, giving as example the case of one of his patients whom he amiably offers to bring to see me, in whose case Cottard has merely to touch his temples to usher him into a second life, a life in which he remembers nothing of the other, so much so that, a very honest man in this one, he had actually been arrested several times for thefts committed in the other during which he had been nothing less than a disgraceful scamp. Upon which Mme Verdurin acutely remarks that medicine could furnish subjects truer than a theatre where the humour of an imbroglio is founded upon pathological mistakes, which from thread to needle brought Mme Cottard to relate that a similar notion had been made use of by an amateur who is the prime favourite at her children's evening parties, the Scotchman Stevenson, a name which forced from Swann the peremptory affirmation: 'But Stevenson is a great writer, I can assure you, M. de Goncourt, a very great one, equal to the greatest.' And upon my marvelling at the escutcheoned panels of the ceiling in the room where we are smoking, panels which came from the ancient Palazzo Barberini, I express my regret at the progressive darkening of a certain vase through the ashes of our *londrès*, Swann having recounted that similar stains on the leaves of certain books attest their having belonged to Napoleon I, books owned, despite his anti-Bonapartist opinions by the Duc de Guermantes, owing to the fact that the Emperor chewed tobacco, Cottard, who reveals himself as a man of penetrating curiosity in all matters, declares that these stains do not come at all from that: 'Believe me, not at all,' he insists with authority, 'but from his habit of having always near at hand, even on the field of battle, some pastilles of Spanish liquorice to calm his liver pains. For he had a disease of the liver and it is of that he died,' concluded the doctor.

I stopped my reading there for I was leaving the following day, moreover, it was an hour when the other master claimed me, he under whose orders we are for half our time. We accomplish the task to which he obliges us with our eyes closed. Every morning he surrenders us to our other master knowing that otherwise we should be unable to yield ourselves to his service. It would be curious, when our spirit has reopened its eyes, to know what we could have been doing under that master who clouds the minds of his slaves before putting them to his immediate business. The most cunning, before their task is finished, try to peep out surreptitiously. But slumber speedily struggles to efface the traces of what they long to see. And, after all these centuries we know little about it. So I closed the Goncourt journal. Glamour of literature! I wanted to see the Cottards again, to ask them so many details about Elstir, I wanted to go and see if the 'Petit Dunkerque' shop still existed, to ask permission to visit that mansion of the Verdurins where I had dined. But I experienced a vague apprehension. Certainly I did not disguise from myself that I had never known how to listen nor, when I was with others, to observe; to my eyes no old woman exhibited a pearl necklace and my ears heard nothing that was said about it. Nevertheless, I had known these people in my ordinary life, I had often dined with them; whether it was the Verdurins, or the Guermantes, or the Cottards, each had seemed to me as commonplace as did that Basin to my grandmother who little supposed he was the beloved nephew, the charming young hero, of Mme de Beausergent. All had seemed to me insipid; I remembered the numberless vulgarities of which each one was composed . . . 'Et que tout cela fasse un astre dans la nuit!'

I resolved to put aside provisionally the objections against literature which these pages of Goncourt had aroused in me. Apart from the peculiarly striking naiveté of the memoir-writer, I was able to reassure myself from different points of view. To begin with, in regard to myself, the inability to observe and to listen of which the journal I have quoted had so painfully reminded me was not complete. There was in me a personage who more or less knew how to observe, but he was an intermittent personage who only came to life when some general essence common to many things which are its nourishment and its delight, manifested itself. Then the personage remarked and listened, but only at a certain depth and in such a manner that observation did not profit. Like a geometrician who in divesting things of their material qualities, only sees their linear substratum, what people said escaped me, for that which interested me was not what they wanted to say but the manner in which they said it in so far as it revealed their characters or their absurdities. Or rather that was an object which had always been my particular aim because I derived specific pleasure from identifying the denominator common to one person and another. It was only when I perceived it that my mind – until then dozing even behind the apparent activity of my conversation the animation of which masked to the outside world a complete mental torpor – started all at once joyously in chase, but that which it then pursued – for example the identity of the Verdurin's salon at diverse places and periods – was situated at half-depth, beyond actual appearance, in a zone somewhat withdrawn. Also the obvious transferable charm of people escaped me because I no longer retained the faculty of confining myself to it, like the surgeon who, beneath the lustre of a female abdomen, sees the internal disease which is consuming it. It was all very well for me to go out to dinner. I did not see the guests because when I thought I was observing them I was radiographing them.

From that it resulted that in collating all the observations I had been able to make about the guests in the course of a dinner, the design of the lines traced by me would form a unity of psychological laws in which the interest pertaining to the discourse of a particular guest occupied no place whatever. But were my portraits denuded of all merit because I did not compose them merely as portraits? If in the domain of painting one portrait represents truths relative to volume, to light, to movement, does that necessarily make it inferior to another quite dissimilar portrait of the same person in which a thousand details omitted in the first will be minutely related to each other, a second portrait from which it would be concluded that the model was beautiful while that of the first would be considered ugly, which might have a documentary and even historical importance but might not necessarily be an artistic truth.

Again my frivolity, the moment when I was with others, made me anxious to please and I desired more to amuse people with my chatter than to learn from listening unless I went out to interrogate someone upon a point of art or unless some jealous suspicion preoccupied me. But I was incapable of seeing a thing unless a desire to do so had been aroused in me by reading; unless it was a thing of which I wanted a previous sketch to confront later with reality. Even had that page of the Goncourts not enlightened me, I knew how often I had been unable to give my attention to things or to people, whom afterwards, once their image had been presented to me in solitude by an artist, I would have gone leagues and risked death to rediscover. Then my imagination started to work, had begun to paint. And the very thing I had yawned at the year before I desired when I again contemplated it and with anguish said to myself, 'Can I never see it again? What would I not give for it?'

When one reads articles about people, even about mere society people, qualifying them as 'the last representatives of a society of which there is no other living witness', doubtless some may exclaim, 'to think that he says so much about so insignificant a person and praises him as he does', but it is precisely such a man I should have deplored not having known if I had only read papers and reviews and if I had never seen the man himself, and I was more inclined, in reading such passages in the papers, to think, 'What a pity! And all I cared about then was getting hold of Gilberte and Albertine and I paid no attention to that gentleman whom I simply took for a society bore, for a pure façade, a marionnette.'

The pages of the Goncourt Journal that I had read made me regret that attitude. For perhaps I might have concluded from them that life teaches one to minimise the value of reading and shows us that what the writer exalts for us is not worth much; but I could equally well conclude the contrary, that reading enhances the value of life, a value we have not realised until books make us aware of how great that value is. Strictly, we can console ourselves for not having much enjoyed the society of a Vinteuil or of a Bergotte, because the awkward middle-classness of the one, the unbearable defects of the other prove nothing against them, since their genius is manifested by their works; and the same applies to the pretentious vulgarity of an Elstir in early days. Thus the journal of the Goncourts made me discover that Elstir was none other than the 'M. Tiche' who had once inflicted upon Swann such exasperating lectures at the Verdurins. But what man of genius has not adopted the irritating conversational manner of artists of his own circle before acquiring (as Elstir did, though it happens rarely) superior taste. Are not the letters of Balzac, for instance, smeared with vulgar terms which Swann would rather have died than use? And yet, it is probable that Swann, so sensitive, so completely exempt from every dislikeable idiosyncrasy, would have been incapable of writing *Cousine Bette* and *Le Curé de Tours*. Therefore, whether or no memoirs are wrong to endow with charm a society which has displeased us, is a problem of small importance, since, even if the writer of these memoirs is mistaken, that proves nothing against the value of a society which produces such genius and which existed no less in the works of Vinteuil, of Elstir and of Bergotte.

Quite at the other extremity of experience, when I remarked that the very curious anecdotes which are the inexhaustible material of the journal of the Goncourts and a diversion for solitary evenings, had been related to him by those guests whom in reading his pages we should have envied him knowing, it was not so very difficult to explain why they had left no trace of interesting memory in my mind. In spite of the ingenuousness of Goncourt, who supposed that the interest of these anecdotes lay in the distinction of the man who told them, it can very well be that mediocre people might have experienced during their lives or heard tell of curious things which they related in their turn. Goncourt knew how to listen as he knew how to observe, and I do not.

Moreover, it was necessary to judge all these happenings one by one. M. de Guermantes certainly had not given me the impression of that adorable model of juvenile grace whom my grandmother so much wanted to know and set before my eyes as inimitable according to the *Mémoires of Mme de Beausergent*. One must remember that Basin was at that time seven years old, that the writer was his aunt and that even husbands who are going to divorce their wives a few months later are loud in praise of them. One of the most charming poems of Sainte-Beuve is consecrated to the apparition beside a fountain of a young child crowned with gifts and graces, the youthful Mlle de Champlâtreux who was not more than ten years old. In spite of all the tender veneration felt by that poet of genius, the Comtesse de Noailles, for her mother-in-law the Duchesse de Noailles, born Champlâtreux, it is possible, if she were to paint her portrait, that it would contrast rather piquantly with the one Sainte-Beuve drew fifty years earlier.

What may perhaps be regarded as more disturbing, is something in between, personages in whose case what is said implies more than a memory which is able to retain a curious anecdote yet without one's having, as in the case of the Vinteuils, the Bergottes, the resource of judging them by their work; they have not created, they have only – to our great astonishment, for we found them so mediocre – inspired. Again it happens that the salon which, in public galleries, gives the greatest impression of elegance in great paintings of the Renaissance and onwards, is that of a little ridiculous bourgeoise whom after seeing the picture, I might, if I had not known her, have yearned to approach in the flesh, hoping to learn from her precious secrets that the painter's art did not reveal to me in his canvas, though her majestic velvet train and laces formed a passage of painting comparable to the most splendid of Titians. If only in bygone days I had understood that it is not the wittiest man, the best educated, the man with the best social relationships who becomes a Bergotte but he who knows how to become a mirror and is thereby enabled to reflect his own life, however commonplace, (though his contemporaries might consider him less gifted than Swann and less erudite than Bréauté) and one can say the same, with still more reason, of an artist's models. The awakening of love of beauty in the artist who can paint everything may be stimulated, the elegance in which he could find such beautiful motifs may be supplied, by people rather richer than himself – at whose houses he would find what he was not accustomed to in his studio of an unknown genius selling his canvases for fifty francs; for instance, a drawing-room upholstered in old silk, many lamps, beautiful flowers and fruit, handsome dresses – relatively modest folk (or who would appear that to people of fashion who are not even aware of the others' existence) who for that very reason are more in a position to make the acquaintance of an obscure artist, to appreciate him, to invite him and buy his pictures, than aristocrats who get themselves painted like a Pope or a Prime Minister by academic painters. Would not the poetry of an elegant interior and of the beautiful dresses of our period be discovered by posterity in the drawing-room of the publisher Charpentier by Renoir rather than in the portrait of the Princesse de Sagan or of the Comtesse de La Rochefoucauld by Cot or Chaplin? The artists who have given us the most resplendent visions of elegance have collected the elements at the homes of people who were rarely the leaders of fashion of their period; for the latter are seldom painted by the unknown depositary of a beauty they are unable to distinguish on his canvases, disguised as it is by the interposition of a vulgar burlesque of superannuated grace which floats before the public eye in the same way as the subjective visions which an invalid believes are actually before him. But that these mediocre models whom I had known could have inspired, advised certain arrangements which had enchanted me, that the presence of such an one of them in the picture was less that of a model, than of a friend whom a painter wishes to figure in his canvas, was like asking oneself whether we regret not having known all these personages because Balzac painted them in his books or dedicated his books to them as the homage of his admiration, to whom Sainte-Beuve or Baudelaire wrote their loveliest verses, still more if all the Récamiers, all the Pompadours would not have seemed to me insignificant people, whether owing to a temperamental defect which made me resent being ill and unable to return and see the people I had misjudged, or because they might only owe their prestige to the illusory magic of literature which forced me to change my standard of values and consoled me for being obliged from one day to the other, on account of the progress which my illness was making, to break with society, renounce travel and going to galleries and museums in order that I could be nursed in a sanatorium. Perhaps, however, this deceptive side, this artificial illumination, only exists in memoirs when they are too recent, too close to reputations, whether intellectual or fashionable, which will quickly vanish, (and if erudition then tries to react against this burial, will it succeed in dispelling one out of a thousand of these oblivions which keep on accumulating?)

These ideas tending some to diminish, others to increase my regret that I had no gift for literature, no longer occupied my mind during the long years I spent as an invalid in a sanatorium far from Paris, and I had altogether renounced the project of writing until the sanatorium was unable to find medical staff at the beginning of 1916.

I then returned, as will be seen, to a very different Paris from the Paris where I returned in August, 1914, when I underwent medical examination, after which I went back to the sanatorium.

CHAPTER TWO

M. de Charlus during the war, his opinions, his pleasure

On one of the first evenings after my return to Paris in 1916, wanting to hear about the only thing that interested me, the war, I went out after dinner to see Mme Verdurin, for she was, together with Mme Bontemps, one of the queens of that Paris of the war which reminded one of the Directory. As the leavening by a small quantity of yeast appears to be a spontaneous germination, young women were running about all day wearing cylindrical turbans on their heads as though they were contemporaries of Mme Tallien. As a proof of public spirit they wore straight Egyptian tunics, dark and very 'warlike' above their short skirts, they were shod in sandals, recalling Talma's buskin or high leggings like those of our beloved combatants. It was, they said, because they did not forget it was their duty to rejoice the eyes of those combatants that they still adorned themselves not only with *flou* dresses but also with jewels evoking the armies by their decorative theme, if indeed their material did not come from the armies and had not been worked by them. Instead of Egyptian ornaments recalling the campaign of Egypt, they wore rings or bracelets made out of fragments of shell or beltings of the 'seventy-fives', cigarette-lighters consisting of two English halfpennies to which a soldier in his dug-out had succeeded in giving a patina so beautiful that the profile of Queen Victoria might have been traced on it by Pisanello. It was again, they said, because they never ceased thinking of their own people, that they hardly wore mourning when one of them fell, the pretext being that he was proud to die, which enabled them to wear a close bonnet of white English crêpe (graceful of effect and encouraging to aspirants) while the invincible certainty of final triumph enabled them to replace the earlier cashmere by satins and silk muslins and even to wear their pearls 'while observing that tact and discretion of which it is unnecessary to remind French women'.

The Louvre and all the museums were closed and when one read at the head of an article 'Sensational Exhibition' one might be certain it was not an exhibition of pictures but of dresses destined to quicken 'those delicate artistic delights of which Parisian women have been too long deprived'. It was thus that elegance and pleasure had regained their hold; fashion, in default of art, sought to excuse itself, just as artists exhibiting at the revolutionary salon in 1793 proclaimed that it would be a mistake if it were regarded as 'inappropriate by austere Republicans that we should be engaged in art when coalesced Europe is besieging the territory of liberty'. The dressmakers acted in the same spirit in 1916 and asserted with the self-conscious conceit of the artist, that 'to seek what was new, to avoid banality, to prepare for victory, by disengaging a new formula of beauty for the generations after the war, was their absorbing ambition, the chimera they were pursuing as would be discovered by those who came to visit their salons delightfully situated in such and such a street, where the exclusion of the mournful preoccupations of the moment with the restraint imposed by circumstances and the substitution of cheerfulness and brightness was the order of the day.

The sorrows of the hour might, it is true, have got the better of feminine energy if we had not such lofty examples of courage and endurance to meditate. So, thinking of our combatants in the trenches who dream of more comfort and coquetry for the dear one at home, let us unceasingly labour to introduce into the creation of dresses that novelty which responds to the needs of the moment. Fashion, it must be conceded, is especially associated with the English, consequently with allied firms and this year the really smart thing is the *robe-tonneau* the charming freedom of which gives to all our young women an amusing and distinguished *cachet*. "It will indeed be one of the happiest consequences of this sad war" the delightful chronicler added (while awaiting the recapture of the lost provinces and the rekindling of national sentiment) "to have secured such charming results in the way of dress with so little material and to have created coquetry out of nothing without ill-timed luxury and bad style. At the present time dresses made at home are preferred to those made in several series by great dressmakers, because each one is evidence of the intelligence, taste and individuality of the maker." '

As to charity, when we remember all the unhappiness born of the invasion, of the many wounded and mutilated, obviously it should become 'ever more ingenious' and compel the ladies in the high turbans to spend the afternoon taking tea at the bridge-table commenting on the news from the front while their automobiles await them at the door with a handsome soldier on the seat conversing with the *chasseur*. For that matter it was not only the high cylindrical hats which were new but also the faces they surmounted. The ladies in the new hats were young women come one hardly knew whence, who had become the flower of fashion, some during the last six months, others during the last two years, others again during the last four. These differences were as important for them as, when I made my first appearance in society, were those between two families like the Guermantes and the Rochefoucaulds with three or four centuries of ancient lineage. The lady who had known the Guermantes since 1914 considered another who had been introduced to them in 1916 a parvenue, gave her the nod of a dowager duchess while inspecting her through her *lorgnon*, and avowed with a significant gesture that no one in society knew whether the lady was even married. 'All this is rather sickening,' concluded the lady of 1914, who would have liked the cycle of the newly-admitted to end with herself. These newcomers whom young men considered decidedly elderly and whom certain old men who had not been exclusively in the best society, seemed to recognise as not being so new as all that, did something more than offer society the diversions of political conversation and music in suitable intimacy; it had to be they who supplied such diversions for, so that things should seem new, whether they are so or not, in art or in medicine as in society, new names are necessary (in certain respects they were very new indeed). Thus Mme Verdurin went to Venice during the war and like those who want at any cost to avoid sorrow and sentiment, when she said it was 'épatant', what she admired was not Venice nor St Mark's nor the palaces, all that had given me delight and which she cheapened, but the effect of the searchlights in the sky, searchlights about which she gave information supported by figures. (Thus from age to age a sort of realism is reborn out of reaction against the art which has been admired till then.)

The Sainte-Euverte salon was a back number and the presence there of the greatest artists or the most influential ministers attracted no one. On the other hand, people rushed to hear a word uttered by the Secretary of one Government, by the Under-Secretary of another, at the houses of the new ladies in turbans whose winged and chattering invasions filled Paris. The ladies of the first Directory had a queen who was young and beautiful called Mme Tallien; those of the second had two who were old and ugly and who were called Mme Verdurin and Mme Bontemps. Who reproached Mme Bontemps because her husband had been bitterly criticised by the *Echo de Paris* for the part he played in the Dreyfus affair? As the whole Chamber had at an earlier period become revisionist, it was necessarily among the old revisionists and the former socialists that the party of social order, of religious toleration and of military efficiency had to be recruited. M. Bontemps would have been detested in former days because the anti-patriots were then given the name of Dreyfusards, but that name had soon been forgotten and had been replaced by that of the adversary of the three-year law. M. Bontemps on the other hand, was one of the authors of that law, therefore he was a patriot.

In society (and this social phenomenon is only the application of a much more general psychological law) whether novelties are reprehensible or not, they only excite consternation until they have been assimilated and defended by reassuring elements. As it had been with Dreyfusism, so it was with the marriage of Saint-Loup and Odette's daughter, a marriage people protested against at first. Now that people met everyone they knew at the Saint-Loups', Gilberte might have had the morals of Odette herself, people would have gone there just the same and would have agreed with Gilberte in condemning undigested moral novelties like a dowager-duchess. Dreyfusism was now integrated in a series of highly respectable and customary things. As to asking what it amounted to in itself, people now thought as little about accepting as formerly about condemning it. It no longer shocked anyone and that was all about it. People remembered it as little as they do whether the father of a young girl they know was once a thief or not. At most they might say: 'The man you're talking about is the brother-in-law or somebody of the same name, there was never anything against this one.' In the same way there had been different kinds of Dreyfusism and the man who went to the Duchesse de Montmorency's and got the Three-Year Law passed could not be a bad sort of man. In any case, let us be merciful to sinners. The oblivion allotted to Dreyfus was *a fortiori* extended to Dreyfusards. Besides, there was no one else in politics, since everyone had to be Dreyfusards at one time or another if they wanted to be in the Government, even those who represented the contrary of what Dreyfusism had incarnated when it was new and dreadful (at the time that Saint-Loup was considered to be going wrong) namely, anti-patriotism, irreligion, anarchy, etc. Thus M. Bontemps' Dreyfusism, invisible and contemplative like that of all politicians, was as little observable as the bones under his skin. No one remembered he had been Dreyfusard, for people of fashion are absent-minded and forgetful and also because time had passed which they affected to believe longer than it was and it had become fashionable to say that the pre-war period was separated from the war period by a gulf as deep, implying as much duration, as a geological period; and even Brichot the nationalist in alluding to the Dreyfus affair spoke of 'those prehistoric days'.

The truth is that the great change brought about by the war was in inverse ratio to the value of the minds it touched, at all events up to a certain point; for, quite at the bottom, the utter fools, the voluptuaries, did not bother about whether there was a war or not; while quite at the top, those who create their own world, their own interior life, are little concerned with the importance of events. What profoundly modifies the course of their thought is rather something of no apparent importance which overthrows the order of time and makes them live in another period of their lives. The song of a bird in the Park of Montboissier, or a breeze laden with the scent of mignonette, are obviously matters of less importance than the great events of the Revolution and of the Empire; nevertheless they inspired in Chateaubriand's *Mémoires d'Outre-Tombe* pages of infinitely greater value.

M. Bontemps did not want to hear peace spoken of until Germany had been divided up as it was during the Middle Ages, the doom of the house of Hohenzollern pronounced, and William II sentenced to be shot. In a word, he was what Brichot called a Diehard; this was the finest brevet of citizenship one could give him. Doubtless, for the three first days Mme Bontemps had been somewhat bewildered to find herself among people who asked Mme Verdurin to present her to them, and it was in a slightly acid tone that Mme Verdurin replied: 'the Comte, my dear', when Mme Bontemps said to her, 'Was that not the Duc d'Haussonville you just introduced to me?' whether through entire ignorance and failure to associate the name of Haussonville with any sort of title, or whether, on the contrary, by excess of knowledge and the association of her ideas with the *Parti des Ducs* of which she had been told M. d'Haussonville was one of the Academic members.

After the fourth day she began to be firmly established in the Faubourg Saint-Germain. Sometimes she could be observed among the fragments of an obscure society which as little surprised those who knew the egg from which Mme Bontemps had been hatched as the debris of a shell around a chick. But after a fortnight, she shook them off and by the end of the first month, when she said, 'I am going to the Lévi's', everyone knew, without her being more precise, that she was referring to the Lévis-Mirepoix, and not a single duchess who was there would have gone to bed without having first asked her or Mme Verdurin, at least by telephone, what was in the evening's communiqué, how things were going with Greece, what offensive was being prepared, in a word, all that the public would only know the following day or later and of which, in this way, they had a sort of dress rehearsal. Mme Verdurin, in conversation, when she communicated news, used 'we' in speaking of France: 'Now, you see, we exact of the King of Greece that he should retire from the Peloponnesse, etc. We shall send him etc.' And in all her discourses G. H. Q. occurred constantly ('I have telephoned to G. H. Q., etc.') an abbreviation in which she took as much pleasure as women did formerly who, not knowing the Prince of Agrigente, asked if it was 'Grigri' people were speaking of, to show they were *au courant*, a pleasure known only to society in less troubled times but equally enjoyed by the masses at times of great crisis. Our butler, for instance, when the King of Greece was discussed, was able, thanks to the papers, to allude to him like William II, as 'Tino', while until now his familiarity with kings had been more ordinary and invented by himself when he called the King of Spain 'Fonfonse'. One may further observe that the number of people Mme Verdurin named 'bores' diminished in direct ratio with the social importance of those who made advances to her. By a sort of magical transformation, every bore who came to pay her a visit and solicited an invitation, suddenly became agreeable and intelligent. In brief, at the end of a year the number of 'bores' was reduced to such proportions that 'the dread and unendurableness of being bored' which occurred so often in Mme Verdurin's conversation and had played such an important part in her life, almost entirely disappeared. Of late, one would have said that this unendurableness of boredom (which she had formerly assured me she never felt in her first youth) caused her less pain, like headaches and nervous asthmas, which lose their strength as one grows older; and the fear of being bored would doubtless have entirely abandoned Mme Verdurin owing to lack of bores, if she had not in some measure replaced them by other recruits amongst the old 'faithfuls'.

Finally, to have done with the duchesses who now frequented Mme Verdurin, they came there, though they were unaware of it, in search of exactly the same thing as during the Dreyfus period, a fashionable amusement so constituted that its enjoyment satisfied political curiosity and the need of commenting privately upon the incidents read in the newspapers. Mme Verdurin would say, 'Come in at five o'clock to talk about the war', as she would have formerly said 'to talk about *l'affaire* and in the interval you shall hear Morel'.

Now Morel had no business to be there for he had not been in any way exempted. He had simply not joined up and was a deserter, but nobody knew it. Another star of the Salon, 'Dans-les-choux', had, in spite of his sporting tastes, got himself exempted. He had become for me so exclusively the author of an admirable work about which I was constantly thinking, that it was only when, by chance, I established a transversal current between two series of souvenirs, that I realised it was he who had brought about Albertine's departure from my house. And again this transversal current ended, so far as those reminiscent relics of Albertine were concerned, in a channel which was dammed in full flow several years back. For I never thought any more about her. It was a channel unfrequented by memories, a line I no longer needed to follow. On the other hand the works of 'Dans-les-choux' were recent and that line of souvenirs was constantly frequented and utilised by my mind.

I must add that acquaintance with the husband of Andrée was neither very easy nor very agreeable and that the friendship one offered him was doomed to many disappointments. Indeed he was even then very ill and spared himself fatigues other than those which seemed likely to give him pleasure. He only thus classified meeting people as yet unknown to him whom his vivid imagination represented as being potentially different from the rest. He knew his old friends too well, was aware of what could be expected of them and to him they were no longer worth a dangerous and perhaps fatal fatigue. He was in short a very bad friend. Perhaps, in his taste for new acquaintances, he regained some of the mad daring which he used to display in sport, gambling and the excesses of the table in the old days at Balbec. Each time I saw Mme Verdurin, she wanted to introduce me to Andrée, apparently unable to admit that I had known her long before. As it happened, Andrée rarely came with her husband but she remained my excellent and sincere friend. Faithful to the aesthetic of her husband, who reacted against Russian ballets, she remarked of the Marquis de Polignac, 'He has had his house decorated by Bakst. How can one sleep in it? I should prefer Dubufe.'

Moreover the Verdurins, through that inevitable progress of aestheticism which ends in biting one's own tail, declared that they could not stand the modern style (besides, it came from Munich) nor white walls and they only liked old French furniture in a sombre setting.

It was very surprising at this period when Mme Verdurin could have whom she pleased at her house, to see her making indirect advances to a person she had completely lost sight of, Odette. One thought the latter could add nothing to the brilliant circle which the little group had become. But a prolonged separation, in soothing rancour, sometimes revives friendship. And the phenomenon which makes the dying utter only names formerly familiar to them and causes old people's complaisance with childish memories, has its social equivalent. To succeed in the enterprise of bringing Odette back to her, it must be understood that Mme Verdurin did not employ the 'ultras' but the less faithful *habitués* who had kept a foot in each salon. To them she said, 'I don't know why she doesn't come here any more. Perhaps she has quarrelled with me, I haven't quarrelled with her. What have I ever done to her? It was at my house she met both her husbands. If she wants to come back, let her know that my doors are open to her.' These words, which might have cost the pride of '*the patronne*' a good deal if they had not been dictated by her imagination, were passed on but without success. Mme Verdurin awaited Odette but the latter did not come until certain events which will be seen later brought her there for quite other reasons than those which could have been put forward by the embassy of the faithless, zealous as it was; few successes are easy, many checks are decisive.

Things were so much the same, although apparently different, that one came across the former expressions 'right-thinking' and 'ill-thinking' quite naturally. And just as the former communards had been anti-revisionist, so the strongest Dreyfusards wanted everybody to be shot with the full support of the generals just as at the time of the Affaire they had been against Galliffet. Mme Verdurin invited to such parties some rather recent ladies, known for their charitable works, who at first came strikingly dressed, with great pearl necklaces. Odette possessed one as fine as any and formerly had rather overdone exhibiting it but now she was in war dress, and imitating the ladies of the Faubourg, she eyed them severely. But women know how to adapt themselves. After wearing them three or four times, these ladies observed that the dresses they considered *chic* were for that very reason proscribed by the people who were *chic* and they laid aside their golden gowns and resigned themselves to simplicity.

Mme Verdurin said, 'It is deplorable, I shall telephone to Bontemps to do what is necessary tomorrow. They have again "censored" the whole end of Norpois' article simply because he let it be understood that they had "*limogé*" Percin.' For all these women got glory out of using the shibboleth current at the moment and believed they were in the fashion, just as a middle-class woman, when M. de Bréauté or M. de Charlus was mentioned, exclaimed: 'Who's that you're talking about? Babel de Bréauté, Même de Charlus?' For that matter, duchesses got the same pleasure out of saying '*limogé*', for like *roturiers un peu poètes* in that respect, it is the name that matters but they express themselves in accordance with their mental category in which there is a great deal that is middle-class. Those who have minds have no regard for birth.

All those telephonings of Mme Verdurin were not without ill-effects. We had forgotten to say that the Verdurin salon though continuing in spirit, had been provisionally transferred to one of the largest hotels in Paris, the lack of coal and light having rendered the Verdurin receptions somewhat difficult in the former very damp abode of the Venetian ambassadors. Nevertheless, the new salon was by no means unpleasant. As in Venice the site selected for its water supply dictates the form the palace shall take, as a bit of garden in Paris delights one more than a park in the country, the narrow dining-room which Mme Verdurin had at the hotel was a sort of lozenge with the radiant white of its screen-like walls against which every Wednesday, and indeed every day, the most various and interesting people and the smartest women in Paris stood out, happy to avail themselves of the luxury of the Verdurins, thanks to their fortune increasing at a time when the richest were restricting their expenditure owing to difficulty in getting their incomes. This somewhat modified style of reception enchanted Brichot who, as the social relations of the Verdurins developed, obtained additional satisfaction from their concentration in a small area, like surprises in a Christmas stocking. On certain days guests were so numerous that the dining-room of the private apartment was too small and dinner had to be served in the enormous dining-room of the hotel below where the 'faithful', while hypocritically pretending to miss the intimacy of the upper floor, were in reality delighted (constituting a select group as formerly in the little railway) to be a spectacular object of envy to neighbouring tables. In peacetime a society paragraph, surreptitiously sent to the *Figaro* or the *Gaulois*, would doubtless have announced to a larger audience than the dining-room of the Majestic could hold that Brichot had dined with the Duchesse de Duras, but since the war, society reporters having discontinued that sort of news (they got home on funerals, investitures and Franco-American banquets), the only publicity attainable was that primitive and restricted one, worthy of the dark ages prior to the discovery of Gutenberg, of being seen at the table of Mme Verdurin. After dinner, people went up to the Patronne's suite and the telephoning began again. Many of the large hotels were at that time full of spies, who daily took note of the news telephoned by M. Bontemps with an indiscretion fortunately counter-balanced by the complete inaccuracy of his information which was always contradicted by the event.

Before the hour when afternoon teas had finished, at the decline of day, one could see from afar in the still, clear sky, little brown spots which, in the twilight, one might have taken for gnats or birds. Just as, when we see a mountain far away which we might take for a cloud, we are impressed because we know it really to be solid, immense and resistant, so I was moved because the brown spots in the sky were neither gnats nor birds but aeroplanes piloted by men who were keeping watch over Paris. It was not the recollection of the aeroplanes I had seen with Albertine in our last walk near Versailles that affected me for the memory of that walk had become indifferent to me.

At dinner-time the restaurants were full and if, passing in the street, I saw a poor fellow home on leave, freed for six days from the constant risk of death, fix his eyes an instant upon the brilliantly illuminated windows, I suffered as at the hotel at Balbec when the fishermen looked at us while we dined. But I suffered more because I knew that the misery of a soldier is greater than that of the poor for it unites all the miseries and is still more moving because it is more resigned, more noble, and it was with a philosophical nod of his head, without resentment, that he who was ready to return to the trenches, observing the *embusqués* elbowing each other to reserve their tables, remarked: 'One would not say there was a war going on here.' At half-past nine, before people had time to finish their dinner, the lights were suddenly put out on account of police regulations, and at nine-thirty-five there was a renewed hustling of *embusqués* seizing their overcoats from the hands of the *chasseurs* of the restaurant where I had dined with Saint-Loup one evening of his leave, in a mysterious interior twilight like that in which magic lantern slides are shown or films at one of those cinemas towards which men and women diners were now hurrying. But after that hour, for those who, like myself, on the evening of which I am speaking, had remained at home for dinner and went out later to see friends, certain quarters of Paris were darker than the Combray of my youth; visits were like those one made to neighbours in the country.

Ah! if Albertine had lived, how sweet it would have been, on the evenings when I dined out, to make an appointment with her under the arcades. At first I should have seen nobody, I should have had the emotion of believing she would not come, when all at once I should have seen one of her dear grey dresses in relief against the black wall, her smiling eyes would have perceived me and we should have been able to walk arm-in-arm without anyone recognising or interfering with us and to have gone home together. Alas, I was alone and it was as though I were making a visit to a neighbour in the country, one of those calls such as Swann used to pay us after dinner, without meeting more passers-by in the obscurity of Tansonville as he walked down that little twisting path to the street of St Esprit, than I encountered this evening in the alley between the rue Clothilde and the rue Bonaparte, now a sinuous, rustic path. And as sections of countryside played upon by rough weather are unspoiled by a change in their setting, on evenings swept by icy winds, I felt myself more vividly on the shore of an angry sea than when I was at that Balbec of which I so often dreamed. And there were other elements which had not before existed in Paris and made one feel as though one had arrived from the train for a holiday in the open country, such as the contrast of light and shade at one's feet on moonlit evenings. Moonlight produces effects unknown to towns even in full winter; its rays played on the snow of the Boulevard Haussman unswept by workmen as on an Alpine glacier. The outlines of the trees were sharply reflected against the golden-blue snow as delicately as in certain Japanese pictures or in some backgrounds by Raphael. They lengthened on the ground at the foot of the trees as in nature when the setting sun reflects the trees which rise at regular intervals in the fields. But by a refinement of exquisite delicacy, the meadow upon which these shadows of ethereal trees were cast, was a field of Paradise, not green but of a white so brilliant on account of the moon shedding its rays on the jade-coloured snow, that one would have said it was woven of petals from the blossoms of pear trees. And in the squares the divinities of the public fountains holding a jet of ice in their hands seemed made of a twofold substance and, as though the artist had married bronze to crystal to produce it. On such rare days all the houses were black; but in spring, braving the police regulation once in a while, a particular house, perhaps only one floor of a particular house, or even only one room on that floor, did not close its shutters and seemed suspended by itself on impalpable shadows like a luminous projection, like an apparition without consistency. And the woman one's raised eyes perceived, isolated in the golden penumbra of the night in which oneself seemed lost, in which she too seemed abandoned, was endowed with the veiled, mysterious charm of an Eastern vision. At length one passed on and no living thing interrupted the rhythm of monotonous and hygienic tramping in the darkness.

*   *   *

I was reflecting that it was a long time since I had seen any of the personages with whom this work has been concerned. In 1914, during the two months I passed in Paris, I had once perceived M. de Charlus and had met Bloch and Saint-Loup, the latter only twice. It was certainly on the second occasion that he seemed to be most himself, and to have overcome that unpleasant lack of sincerity I had noticed at Tansonville to which I referred earlier. On this occasion, I recognised all his lovable qualities of former days. The first time I had seen him was at the beginning of the week that followed the declaration of war and while Bloch displayed extremely chauvinistic sentiments, Saint-Loup alluded to his own failure to join up with an irony that rather shocked me. Saint-Loup was just back from Balbec. 'All who don't go and fight,' he exclaimed with forced gaiety, 'whatever reason they give, simply don't want to be killed, it's nothing but funk.' And with a more emphatic gesture than when he alluded to others, 'And if I don't rejoin my regiment, it's for the same reason.' Before that, I had noticed in different people that the affectation of laudable sentiments is not the only disguise of unworthy ones, that a more original way is to exhibit the latter so that, at least, one does not seem to be disguising them. In Saint-Loup this tendency was strengthened by his habit, when he had done something for which he might have been censured, of proclaiming it as though it had been done on purpose, a habit he must have acquired from some professor at the War School with whom he had lived on terms of intimacy and for whom he professed great admiration. So I interpreted this outbreak as the affirmation of sentiments he wanted to exhibit as having inspired his evasion of military service in the war now beginning. 'Have you heard,' he asked as he left me, 'that my Aunt Oriane is about to sue for divorce? I know nothing about it myself. People have often said it before and I've heard it announced so often that I shall wait until the divorce is granted before I believe it. I may add that it isn't surprising; my uncle is a charming man socially and to his friends and relations and in one way he has more heart than my aunt. She's a saint, but she takes good care to make him feel it. But he's an awful husband; he has never ceased being unfaithful to his wife, insulting her, ill-treating her and depriving her of money into the bargain. It would be so natural if she left him that it's a reason for its being true and also for its not being true just because people keep on saying so. And after all, she has stood it for so long ... Of course, I know there are ever so many false reports which are denied and afterwards turn out to be true.' That made me ask him whether, before he married Gilberte, there had ever been any question of his marrying Mlle de Guermantes. He started at this and assured me it was not so, that it was only one of those society rumours born, no one knows how, which disappear as they come, the falsity of which does not make those who believe them more cautious, for no sooner does another rumour of an engagement, of a divorce or of a political nature arise than they give it immediate credence and pass it on. Forty-eight hours had not passed before certain facts proved that my interpretation of Robert's words was completely wrong when he said, 'All those who are not at the front are in a funk.' Saint-Loup had only said this to show off and appear psychologically original while he was uncertain whether his services would be accepted. But at that very moment he was moving heaven and earth to be accepted, showing less originality in the sense he had given to that word, but that he was more profoundly French, more in conformity with all that was best in the French of St André-des-Champs, gentlemen, bourgeois, respectable servants of gentlemen, or those in revolt against gentlemen, two equally French divisions of the same family, a Françoise offshoot and a Sauton offshoot, from which two arrows flew once more to the same target which was the frontier. Bloch was delighted to hear this avowal of cowardice by a Nationalist (who, in truth, was not much of a Nationalist) and when Saint-Loup asked him if he was going to join up, he made a grimace like a high-priest and replied 'shortsighted'.

But Bloch had completely changed his opinion about the war when he came to see me in despair some days later for, although he was shortsighted, he had been passed for service. I was taking him back to his house when we met Saint-Loup. The latter had an appointment with a former officer, M. de Cambremer, who was to present him to a colonel at the Ministry of War, he told me. 'Cambremer is an old acquaintance of yours, you know Cancan as well as I do.' I replied that, as a fact, I did know him and his wife too, but that I did not greatly appreciate them. Yet I was so accustomed, ever since I first made their acquaintance, to consider his wife an unusual person with a thorough knowledge of Schopenhauer who had access to an intellectual *milieu* closed to her vulgar husband, that I was at first surprised when Saint-Loup remarked: 'His wife is an idiot, you can have her; but he's an excellent fellow, gifted and extremely agreeable.' By the idiocy of the wife, no doubt Saint-Loup meant her mad longing to get into the best society, which that society severely condemned and, by the qualities of the husband, those his niece implied when she called him the best of the family. Anyhow, he did not bother himself about duchesses but that sort of intelligence is as far removed from the kind that characterises thinkers as is the intelligence the public respects because it has enabled a rich man 'to make his pile'. But the words of Saint-Loup did not displease me since they recalled that pretentiousness is closely allied to stupidity and that simplicity has a subtle but agreeable flavour. It is true I had no occasion to savour that of M. de Cambremer. But that is exactly why one being is so many different beings apart from differences of opinion. I had only known the shell of M. de Cambremer and his charm, attested by others, was unknown to me.

Bloch left us in front of his door, overflowing with bitterness against Saint-Loup, telling him that those 'beautiful red tabs' parading about at Staff Headquarters run no risk and that he, an ordinary second class private had no wish to 'get a bullet through his skin for the sake of William'. 'It seems that the Emperor William is seriously ill,' Saint-Loup answered. Bloch, who like all those people who have something to do with the Stock Exchange, received any sensational news with peculiar credulity, added, 'it is said even that he is dead.' On the Stock Exchange every sovereign who is ill, whether Edward VII or William II, is dead; every city on the point of being besieged, is taken. 'It is only kept secret,' Bloch went on, 'so that German public opinion should not be depressed. But he died last night. My father has it from "the best sources".' 'The best sources' were the only ones of which M. Bloch senior took notice, when, through the luck of possessing certain 'influential connections' he received the as yet secret news that the Exterior Debt was going to rise or de Beers fall. Moreover, if at that very moment there was a rise in de Beers or there were offers of Exterior Debt, if the market of the first was 'firm and active' and that of the second 'hesitating and weak', 'the best sources' remained nevertheless 'the best sources.' Bloch too announced the death of the Kaiser with a mysteriously important air, but also with rage. He was particularly exasperated to hear Robert say the 'Emperor William'. I believe under the knife of the guillotine Saint-Loup and M. de Guermantes would not have spoken of him otherwise. Two men in society who were the only living souls on a desert island where they would not have to give proof of good breeding to anyone, would recognise each other by those marks of breeding just as two Latinists would recognise each other's qualifications through correct quotations from Virgil. Saint-Loup would never, even under torture, have said other than 'Emperor William'; yet the *savoir vivre* is all the same a bondage for the mind. He who cannot reject it remains a mere man of society. Yet elegant mediocrity is charming – especially for the generosity and unexpressed heroism that go with it – in comparison with the vulgarity of Bloch, at once braggart and mountebank, who shouted at Saint-Loup: 'Can't you say simply "William"? That's it, you're in a funk, even here you're ready to crawl on your stomach to him. Pshaw! they'll make nice soldiers at the front, they'll lick the boots of the Boches. You red-tabs are fit to parade in a circus, that's all.'

'That poor Bloch will have it that I can do nothing but parade,' Saint-Loup remarked with a smile when we left our friend. And I felt that parading was not at all what Robert was after, though I did not then realise his intention as I did later when the cavalry being out of action, he applied to serve as an infantry officer, then as a *chasseur á pied* and finally when the sequel came which will be read later. But Bloch had no idea of Robert's patriotism simply because the latter did not express it. Though Bloch made professions of nefarious anti-militarism once he had been passed for service, he had declared the most chauvinistic opinions when he believed he would be exempted for shortsightedness. Saint-Loup would have been incapable of making such declarations, because of a certain moral delicacy which prevents one from expressing the depth of sentiments which are natural to us. My mother would not have hesitated a second to sacrifice her life for my grandmother's and would have suffered intensely from being unable to do so. Nevertheless I cannot imagine retrospectively a phrase on her lips such as 'I would give my life for my mother'. Robert was equally silent about his love for France and in that he seemed to me much more Saint-Loup (as I imagined his father to have been) than Guermantes. He would also have been incapable of such expressions owing to his mind having a certain moral bias. Men who do their work intelligently and earnestly have an aversion to those who want to make literature out of what they do, to make it important. Saint-Loup and I had not been either at the Lycée or at the

Sorbonne together, but each of us had separately attended certain lectures by the same masters and I remember his smile when he alluded to those who, because, undeniably, their lectures were exceptional tried to make themselves out men of genius by giving ambitious names to their theories. Little as we spoke of it, Robert laughed heartily. Our natural predilection was not for the Cottards or Brichots, though we had a certain respect for those who had a thorough knowledge of Greek or medicine and did not for that reason consider they need play the charlatan. Just as all my mother's actions were based upon the feeling that she would have given her life for her mother, as she had never formulated this sentiment which in any case she would have considered not only useless and ridiculous but indecent and shameful to express to others, so it was impossible to imagine Saint-Loup (speaking to me of his equipment, of the different things he had to attend to, of our chances of victory, of the little value of the Russian army, of what England would do) enunciating one of those eloquent periods to which even the most sympathetic minister is inclined to give vent when he addresses deputies and enthusiasts. I cannot, however, deny, on this negative side which prevented his expressing the beautiful sentiments he felt that there was a certain effect of the 'Guermantes spirit' of which so many examples were afforded by Swann. For if I found him a Saint-Loup more than anything else, he remained a Guermantes as well and owing to that, among the many motives which excited his courage there were some dissimilar to those of his Doncières friends, those young men with a passion for their profession with whom I had dined every evening and of whom so many were killed leading their men at the Battle of the Marne or elsewhere.

Such young socialists as might have been at Doncières when I was there, whom I did not know because they were not in Saint-Loup's set, were able to satisfy themselves that the officers in that set were in no way 'aristos' in the arrogantly proud and basely pleasure-loving sense which the 'populo' officers from the ranks, and the Freemasons, gave to the word. And equally, the aristocratic officer discovered the same patriotism amongst those Socialists whom when I was at Doncières in the midst of the Affair Dreyfus, I heard them accuse of being anti-patriotic. The deep and sincere patriotism of soldiers had taken a definite form which they believed intangible and which it enraged them to see aspersed, whereas the Radical-Socialists who were, in a sense, unconscious patriots, independents, without a defined religion of patriotism, did not realise what a profound reality underlay what they believed to be vain and hateful formulas.

Without doubt, Saint-Loup, like them, had grown accustomed to developing as the truest part of himself, the exploration and the conception of better schemes in view of greater strategic and tactical success, so that for him as for them the life of the body was of relatively small importance and could be lightly sacrificed to that inner life, the vital kernel around which personal existence had only the value of a protective epidermis. I told Saint-Loup about his friend, the director of the Balbec Grand Hotel, who, it appeared had, at the outbreak of war, alleged that there had been disaffection in certain French regiments which he called 'defectuosity' and had accused what he termed 'Prussian militarists' of provoking it, remarking with a laugh, 'My brother's in the trenches. They're only thirty metres from the Boches' until it was discovered that he was a Boche himself and they put him in a concentration camp.

'Apropos of Balbec, do you remember the former lift-boy of the hotel?' Saint-Loup asked me in the tone of one who seems not to know much about the person concerned and was counting upon me for enlightenment. 'He's joining up and wrote me to get him entered in the aviation corps.' Doubtless the lift-boy was tired of going up and down in the closed cage of the lift and the heights of the staircase of the Grand Hotel no longer sufficed for him. He was going to 'get his stripes' otherwise than as a concierge, for our destiny is not always what we had believed. 'I shall certainly support his application,' Saint-Loup said, 'I told Gilberte again this morning, we shall never have enough aeroplanes. It is through them we shall observe what the enemy is up to; they will deprive him of the chief advantage m an attack, surprise; the best army will perhaps be the one that has the best eyes. Has poor Françoise succeeded in getting her nephew exempted?'

Françoise who had for a long while done everything in her power to get her nephew exempted, on a recommendation through the Guermantes to General de St Joseph being proposed to her, had replied despairingly: 'Oh! That would be no use; there's nothing to be done with that old fellow, he's the worst sort of all, he's patriotic!' From the beginning of the war, Françoise whatever sorrow it had brought her, was of opinion that the 'poor Russians' must not be abandoned since we were 'allianced'. The butler, persuaded that the war would not last more than ten days and would end by the signal victory of France, would not have dared, for fear of being contradicted by event to predict a long and indecisive one, nor would he have had enough imagination. But, out of this complete and immediate victory he tried to extract beforehand whatever might cause anxiety to Françoise. 'It may turn out pretty rotten; it appears there are many who don't want to go to the front, boys of sixteen are crying about it.' He also tried to provoke her by saying all sorts of disagreeable things, what he called 'pulling her leg' by 'pitching an apostrophe at her' or 'flinging her a pun'. 'Sixteen years old! Sainted Mary!' exclaimed Françoise, and then, with momentary suspicion, 'But they said they only took them after they were twenty, they're only children at sixteen.' 'Naturally, the papers are ordered to say that. For that matter, the whole youth of the country will be at the front and not many will come back. In one way that will be a good thing, a good bleeding is useful from time to time, it makes business better. Yes, indeed, if some of these boys are a bit soft and chicken-hearted and hesitate, they shoot them immediately, a dozen bullets through the skin and that's that. In a way it's got to be done and what does it matter to the officers? They get their *pesetas* all the same and that's all they care about.' Françoise got so pale during these conversations that one might well fear the butler would cause her death from heart disease.

But she did not on that account lose her defects. When a girl came to see me, however much the old servant's legs hurt her, if ever I went out of my room for a moment I saw her on the top of the steps, in the hanging cupboard, in the act, she pretended, of looking for one of my coats to see if the moths had got into it, in reality to spy upon us. In spite of all my remonstrances, she kept up her insidious manner of asking indirect questions and for some time had been making use of the phrase 'because doubtless'. Not daring to ask me, 'Has that lady a house of her own?' she would say with her eyes lifted timidly like those of a gentle dog, 'Because doubtless that lady has a house of her own', avoiding the flagrant interrogation in order to be polite and not to seem inquisitive.

And further, since those servants we most care for – especially if they can no longer render us much service or even do their work – remain, alas, servants and mark more clearly the limits (which we should like to efface) of their caste in proportion to the extent to which they believe they are penetrating ours, Françoise often gave vent to strange comments about my person (in order to tease me, the butler would have said) which people in our own world would not make. For instance, with a delight as dissimulated but also as deep as if it had been a case of serious illness, if I happened to be hot and the perspiration (to which I paid no attention) was trickling down my forehead, she would say, 'My word! You're drenched' as though she were astonished by a strange phenomenon, smiling with that contempt for something indecorous with which she might have remarked, 'Why, you're going out without your collar!' while adopting a concerned tone intended to cause one discomfort. One would have thought I was the only person in the universe who had ever been 'drenched'. For, in her humility, in her tender admiration for beings infinitely inferior to her, she adopted their ugly forms of expression. Her daughter complained of her to me, 'She's always got something to say, that I don't close the doors properly and *patatipatali et patatapatala*.' Françoise doubtless thought it was only her insufficient education that had deprived her until now of this beautiful expression. And on her lips, on which formerly flowered the purest French, I heard several times a day, '*Et patati patall patata patala*'. As to that it is curious how little variation there is not only in the expressions but in the thoughts of the same individual. The butler, being accustomed to declare that M. Poincaré had evil motives, not of a venal kind but because he had absolutely willed the war, repeated this seven or eight times a day before the same ever-interested audience, without modifying a single word or gesture or intonation. Although it only lasted about two minutes, it was invariable like a performance. His mistakes in French corrupted the language of Françoise quite as much as the mistakes of her daughter.

She hardly slept, she hardly ate, she had the communiqués read to her, though she did not understand them, by the butler who understood them little better and in whom the desire to torment Françoise was often dominated by a superficial sort of patriotism; he remarked with a sympathetic chuckle when speaking of the Germans, 'That will stir them up a bit, our old Joffre is planning a comet to fall on them.' Françoise did not understand what comet he was talking about but felt none the less that this phrase was one of those charming and original extravagances to which a well-bred person must reply, so with good humour and urbanity, shrugging her shoulders with the air of saying 'He's always the same', she tempered her tears with a smile. At all events she was happy that her new butcher boy who in spite of his calling was somewhat timorous (although he had begun in the slaughterhouse), was too young to join up; otherwise, she would have been capable of going to the Minister of War about him.

The butler could not believe the communiqués were other than excellent and that the troops were not approaching Berlin, as he had read, 'We have repulsed the enemy with heavy losses on their side', actions that he celebrated as though they were new victories. For my part, I was horrified by the rapidity with which the theatre of these victories approached Paris and I was astonished that even the butler, who had seen in a communiqué that an action had taken place close to Lens, had not been alarmed by reading in the next day's paper that the result of this action had turned to our advantage at Jouy-le-Vicomte to which we firmly held the approaches. The butler very well knew the name of Jouy-le-Vicomte which was not far from Combray. But one reads the papers as one wants to with a bandage over one's eyes without trying to understand the facts, listening to the soothing words of the editor as to the words of one's mistress. We are beaten and happy because we believe ourselves unbeaten and victorious.

I did not stay long in Paris and returned fairly soon to my sanatorium. Though in principle the doctor treated his patients by isolation, I had received on two different occasions letters from Gilberte and from Robert. Gilberte wrote me (about September, 1914) that much as she would have liked to remain in Paris in order to get news from Robert more easily, the perpetual *taube* raids over Paris had given her such a fright, especially on her little girl's account, that she had fled from Paris by the last train which left for Combray, that the train did not even reach Combray and it was only thanks to a peasant's cart upon which she had made a ten hours journey in atrocious discomfort that she had at last been able to get to Tansonville. 'And what do you think awaited your old friend there?' Gilberte closed her letter by saying. 'I had left Paris to get away from the German aeroplanes, imagining that at Tansonville I should be sheltered from everything. I had not been there two days when what do you think happened! The Germans were invading the region after beating our troops near La Fère and a German staff, followed by a regiment, presented themselves at the gate of Tansonville and I was obliged to take them in without a chance of escaping, not a train, nothing.' Had the German staff behaved well or was one supposed to read into the letter of Gilberte the contagious effect of the spirit of the Guermantes who were of Bavarian stock and related to the highest aristocracy in Germany, for Gilberte was inexhaustible about the perfect behaviour of the staff and of the soldiers who had only asked 'permission to pick one of the forget-me-nots which grew at the side of the lake', good behaviour she contrasted with the unbridled violence of the French fugitives who had traversed the estate and sacked everything before the arrival of the German generals. Anyhow, if Gilberte's letter was, in certain respects, impregnated with the 'Guermantes spirit' – others would say it was her Jewish internationalism, which would probably not be true, as we shall see – the letter I received some months later from Robert was much more Saint-Loup than Guermantes for it reflected all the liberal culture he had acquired and was altogether sympathetic. Unhappily he told me nothing about the strategy as he used to in our conversations at Doncières and did not mention to what extent he considered the war had confirmed or disproved the principles which he then expounded to me.

The most he told me was that since 1914, several wars had succeeded each other, the lessons of each influencing the conduct of the following one. For instance, the theory of the 'breakthrough' had been completed by the thesis that before the 'breakthrough' it was necessary to overwhelm the ground occupied by the enemy with artillery. Later it was discovered, on the contrary, that this destruction made the advance of infantry and artillery impossible over ground so pitted with thousands of shell-holes that they became so many obstacles. 'War,' he said, 'does not escape the laws of our old Hegel. It is a state of perpetual becoming.'

This was little enough of all I wanted to know. But what disappointed me more was that he had no right to give me the names of the generals. And indeed, from what little I could glean from the papers, it was not those of whom I was so much concerned to know the value in war, who were conducting this one. Geslin de Bourgogne, Galliffet, Négrier were dead, Pau had retired from active service almost at the beginning of the war. We had never talked about Joffre or Foch or Castlenau or Pétain. 'My dear boy,' Robert wrote, 'if you saw what these soldiers are like, especially those of the people, the working class, small shopkeepers who little knew the heroism of which they were capable and would have died in their beds without ever being suspected of it, facing the bullets to succour a comrade, to carry off a wounded officer and, themselves struck, smile at the moment they are going to die because the staff surgeon tells them that the trench had been recaptured from the Germans; I can assure you, my dear boy, that it gives one a wonderful idea of what a Frenchman is and makes us understand the historic epochs which seemed rather extraordinary to us when we were at school.

'The epic is so splendid that, like myself, you would find words useless to describe it. In contact with such grandeur the word "*poilu*" has become for me something which I can no more regard as implying an allusion or a joke than when we read the word "*chouans*". I feel that the word "*poilu*" is awaiting great poets like such words as "Deluge" or "Christ" or "Barbarians" which were saturated with grandeur before Hugo, Vigny and the rest used them.

'To my mind, the sons of the people are the best of all but everyone is fine. Poor Vaugoubert, the son of the Ambassador, was wounded seven times before being killed and each time he came back from an expedition without being "scooped", he seemed to be excusing himself and saying that it was not his fault. He was a charming creature. We had seen a great deal of each other and his poor parents obtained permission to come to his funeral on condition that they didn't wear mourning nor stop more than five minutes on account of the bombardment. The mother, a great horse of a woman, whom you perhaps know, may have been very unhappy but one would not have thought so. But the father was in such a state, I assure you, that I, who have become almost insensible through getting accustomed to seeing the head of a comrade I was talking to shattered by a bomb or severed from his trunk, could hardly bear it when I saw the collapse of poor Vaugoubert who was reduced to a rag. It was all very well for the general to tell him it was for France that his son died a hero's death, that only redoubled the sobs of the poor man who could not tear himself away from his son's body. Well, that is why we can say, "they will not get through". Such men as these, my poor valet or Vaugoubert, have prevented the Germans from getting through. Perhaps you have thought we do not advance much, but that is not the way to reason; an army feels itself victorious by intuition as a dying man knows he is done for. And we know that we are going to be the victors and we will it so that we may dictate a just peace, not only for ourselves, but a really just peace, just for the French and just for the Germans.' As heroes of mediocre and banal mind, writing poems during their convalescence, placed themselves, in order to describe the war, not on the level of the events which in themselves are nothing, but on the level of the banal aesthetic of which they had until then followed the rules, speaking as they might have done ten years earlier of the 'bloody dawn', of the 'shuddering flight of victory', Saint-Loup, himself much more intelligent and artistic, remained intelligent and artistic and for my benefit noted with taste the landscapes while he was immobilised at the edge of a swampy forest, just as though he had been shooting duck. To make me grasp contrasts of shade and light which had been 'the enchantment of the morning', he referred to certain pictures we both of us loved and alluded to a page of Romain Rolland or of Nietzsche with the independence of those at the front who unlike those at the rear, were not afraid to utter a German name, and with much the same coquetry that caused Colonel du Paty de Clam to declaim in the witnesses' room during the Zola affair as he passed by Pierre Quillard, a Dreyfusard poet of the extremest violence whom he did not know, verses from the latter's symbolic drama *La Fille aux Mains coupées*, Saint-Loup, when he spoke to me of a melody of Schumann gave it its German title and made no circumlocution to tell me, when he had heard the first warble at the edge of a forest, that he had been intoxicated as though the bird of that 'sublime Siegfried' which he hoped to hear again after the war, had sung to him.

And now on my second return to Paris I had received on the day following my arrival another letter from Gilberte who without doubt had forgotten the one she had previously written me, to which I have alluded above, for her departure from Paris at the end of 1914 was represented retrospectively in quite different fashion. 'Perhaps you do not realise, my dear friend,' she wrote me, 'that I have now been at Tansonville two years. I arrived there at the same time as the Germans. Everybody wanted to prevent me going, I was treated as though I were mad. "What," they said to me, "you are safe in

Paris and you want to leave for those invaded regions just as everybody else is trying to get away from them?" I recognised the justice of this reasoning but what was to be done? I have only one quality, I am not a coward or, if you prefer, I am faithful, and when I knew that my dear Tansonville was menaced I did not want to leave our old steward there to defend it alone; it seemed to me that my place was by his side. And it is, in fact, thanks to that resolution that I was able to save the Château almost completely – when all the others in the neighbourhood, abandoned by their terrified proprietors, were destroyed from roof to cellar – and not only was I able to save the Château but also the precious collections which my dear father so much loved.' In a word, Gilberte was now persuaded that she had not gone to Tansonville, as she wrote me in 1914, to fly from the Germans and to be in safety, but, on the contrary, in order to meet them and to defend her Château from them. As a matter of fact, they (the Germans) had not remained at Tansonville, but she did not cease to have at her house a constant coming and going of officers which much exceeded that which reduced Françoise to tears in the streets of Combray and to live, as she said this time with complete truth, the life of the front. Also she was referred to eulogistically in the papers because of her admirable conduct and there was a proposal to give her a decoration. The end of her letter was perfectly accurate: 'You have no idea of what this war is, my dear friend, the importance of a road, a bridge or a height. How many times, during these days in this ravaged countryside, have I thought of you, of our walks you made so delightful, while tremendous fights were going on for the capture of a hillock you loved and where so often we had been together. Probably you, like myself, are unable to imagine that obscure Roussainville and tiresome Méséglise, whence our letters were brought and where one went to fetch the doctor when you were ill, are now celebrated places. Well, my dear friend, they have for ever entered into glory in the same way as Austerlitz or Valmy. The Battle of Méséglise lasted more than eight months, the Germans lost more than one hundred thousand men there, they destroyed Méséglise but they have not taken it. The little road you so loved, the one we called the stiff hawthorn climb, where you professed to be in love with me when you were a child, when all the time I was in love with you, I cannot tell you how important that position is. The great wheatfield in which it ended is the famous "slope 307" the name you have so often seen recorded in the communiqués. The French blew up the little bridge over the Vivonne which, you remember, did not bring back your childhood to you as much as you would have liked. The Germans threw others across; during a year and a half, they held one half of Combray and the French the other.'

The day following that on which I received this letter, that is to say the evening before the one when, walking in the darkness, I heard the sound of my footsteps while reflecting on all these memories, Saint-Loup, back from the front and on the point of returning there, had paid me a visit of a few minutes only, the mere announcement of which had greatly stirred me. Françoise at first was going to throw herself upon him, hoping she would be able to get the butcher boy exempted; his class was going to the front in a year's time. But she restrained herself, realising the uselessness of the effort, since, for some time the timid animal-killer had changed his butcher-shop and, whether the owner of ours feared she would lose our custom, or whether it was simply in good faith, she declared to Françoise that she did not know where this boy 'who for that matter would never make a good butcher' was employed. Françoise had looked everywhere for him, but Paris is big, there are a large number of butchers' shops and however many she went into she never was able to find the timid and blood-stained young man.

When Saint-Loup entered my room I had approached him with that diffidence, with that sense of the supernatural one felt about those on leave as we feel in approaching a person attacked by a mortal disease, who nevertheless gets up, dresses himself and walks about. It seemed that there was something almost cruel in these leaves granted to combatants, at the beginning especially, for those who had not like myself lived far from Paris, had acquired the habit which removes from things frequently experienced the root-deep impression which gives them their real significance. The first time one said to oneself, 'They will never go back, they will desert' – and indeed they did not come from places which seemed to us unreal merely because it was only through the papers we had heard of them and where we could not realise they had been taking part in Titanic combats and had come back with only a bruise on the shoulder – they came back to us for a moment from the shores of death itself and would return there, incomprehensible to us, filling us with tenderness, horror and a sentiment of mystery like the dead who appear to us for a second and whom, if we dare to question them, at most reply, 'You cannot imagine.' For it is extraordinary, in those who have been resurrected from the front, for among the living that is what men on leave are, or in the case of the dead whom a hypnotised medium evokes, that the only effect of this contact with the mystery is to increase, were that possible, the insignificance of our intercourse with them. Thus, approaching Robert who had a scar on his forehead more august and mysterious to me than a footprint left upon the earth by a giant, I did not dare ask him a question and he only said a few simple words. And those words were little different from what they would have been before the war, as though people, in spite of the war, continued to be what they were; the tone of intercourse remains the same, the matter differs and even then I gathered that Robert had found resources at the front which had made him little by little forget that Morel had behaved as badly to him as to his uncle. Nevertheless he had preserved a great friendship for him and now and then had a sudden longing to see him again which he kept on postponing. I thought it more considerate towards Gilberte not to inform Robert, if he wanted to find Morel, he had only to go to Mme Verdurin's.

On my remarking to Robert with a sense of humility how little one felt the war in Paris, he said that even there it was sometimes 'rather extraordinary'. He was alluding to a raid of zeppelins there had been the evening before and asked me if I had had a good view of it in the same way as he would formerly have referred to a piece of great aesthetic beauty at the theatre. One can imagine that at the front there is a sort of coquetry in saying, 'It's marvellous! What a pink – and that pale green!' when at that instant one can be killed, but it was not that which moved Saint-Loup about an insignificant raid on Paris. When I spoke to him about the beauty of the aeroplanes rising in the night, he replied, 'And perhaps the descending ones are still more beautiful. Of course they are marvellous when they soar upwards, when they're about to form *constellation* thus obeying laws as precise as those which govern astral constellations, for what is a spectacle to you is the assemblage of squadrons, orders being given to them, their despatch on scout duty, etc. But don't you prefer the moment when, mingling with the stars, they detach themselves from them to start on a chase or to return after the maroon sounds? When they "loop the loop", even the stars seem to change their position. And aren't the sirens rather Wagnerian, as they should be, to salute the arrival of the Germans, very like the national hymn, very "Wacht am Rhein" with the Crown Prince and the Princesses in the Imperial box; one wonders whether aviators or Walkyries are up there.' He seemed to get pleasure out of comparing aviators with Walkyries, and explained them on entirely musical principles. 'Dammit! the music of sirens is like the prancing of horses; we shall have to await the arrival of the Germans to hear Wagner in Paris.'

From certain points of view the comparison was not false. The city seemed a formless and black mass which all of a sudden passed from the depth of night into a blaze of light, and in the sky, where one after another, the aviators rose amidst the shrieking wail of the sirens while, with a slower movement, more insidious and therefore more alarming, for it made one think they were seeking an object still invisible but perhaps close to us, the searchlights swept unceasingly, scenting the enemy, encircling him with their beams until the instant when the pointed planes flashed like arrows in his wake. And in squadron after squadron the aviators darted from the city into the sky like Walkyries. Yet close to the ground, at the base of the houses, some spots were in highlight and I told Saint-Loup, if he had been at home the evening before, he would have been able, while he contemplated the apocalypse in the sky, to see on the earth, as in the burial of the Comte d'Orgaz by Greco, where those contrasting planes are parallel, a regular vaudeville played by personages in nightgowns, whose well-known names ought to have been sent to some successor of that Ferrari whose fashionable notes it had so often amused him and myself to parody. And we should have done so again that day as though there had been no war, although about a very 'war-subject', the dread of zeppelins realised, the Duchesse de Guermantes superb in her night-dress, the Duc de Guermantes indescribable in his pink pyjamas and bath-gown, etc., etc. 'I am sure,' he said, 'that in all the large hotels one might have seen American Jewesses in their chemises hugging to their bursting breasts pearl necklaces which would buy them a "busted" duke. On such nights, the Hotel Ritz must resemble an exchange and mart emporium.'

I asked Saint-Loup if this war had confirmed our conclusions at Doncières about war in the past. I reminded him of the proposition which he had forgotten, for instance about the parodies of former battles by generals of the future. 'The feint,' I said to him, 'is no longer possible in these operations where the advance is prepared with such accumulation of artillery and what you have since told me about reconnaissance by aeroplane which obviously you could not have foreseen, prevents the employment of Napoleonic ruses.' 'How mistaken you are,' he answered, 'obviously this war is new in relation to former wars for it is itself composed of successive wars of which the last is an innovation on the preceding one. It is necessary to adapt oneself to the enemy's latest formula so as to defend oneself against him; then he starts a fresh innovation and yet, as in other human things, the old tricks always come off. No later than yesterday evening the most intelligent of our military critics wrote: "When the Germans wanted to deliver East Prussia they began the operation by a powerful demonstration in the south against Warsaw, sacrificing ten thousand men to deceive the enemy. When at the beginning of 1915 they created the mass manoeuvre of the Arch-Duke Eugène in order to disengage threatened Hungary, they spread the report that this mass was destined for an operation against Serbia. Thus, in 1800 the army which was about to operate against Italy was definitely indicated as a reserve army which was not to cross the Alps but to support the armies engaged in the northern theatres of war. The ruse of Hindenburg attacking Warsaw to mask the real attack on the Mazurian Lakes, imitates the strategy of Napoleon in 1812." You see that M. Bidou repeats almost the exact words of which you remind me and which I had forgotten. And as the war is not yet finished, these ruses will be repeated again and again and will succeed because they are never completely exposed and what has done the trick once will do it again because it was a good trick.'

And in fact, for a long time after that conversation with Saint-Loup, while the eyes of the Allies were fixed upon Petrograd against which capital it was believed the Germans were marching, they were preparing a most powerful offensive against Italy. Saint-Loup gave me many other examples of military parodies or, if one believes that there is not a military art but a military science, of the application of permanent laws. 'I will not say, there would be contradiction in the words,' added Saint-Loup, 'that the art of war is a science. And if there is a science of war there is diversity, dispute and contradiction between its professors, diversity partly projected into the category of Time. That is rather reassuring, for, as far as it goes, it indicates that truth rather than error is evolving.' Later he said to me, 'See in this war the ideas on the possibility of the breakthrough, for instance. First it is believed in, then we come back to the doctrine of invulnerability of the fronts, then again to the possible but risky breakthrough, to the necessity of not making a step forward until the objective has been first destroyed (the dogmatic journalist will write that to assert the contrary is the greatest foolishness), then, on the contrary, to that of advancing with a very light preparation by artillery, then to the invulnerability of the fronts as a principle in force since the war of 1870, from that the assertion that it is a false principle for this war and therefore only a relative truth. False in this war because of the accumulation of masses and of the perfecting of engines (see Bidou of the 2nd July, 1918), an accumulation which at first made one believe that the next war would be very short, then very long, and finally made one again believe in the possibility of decisive victories. Bidou cites the Allies on the Somme, the Germans marching on Paris in 1918. In the same way, at each victory of the Germans, it is said: "the ground gained is nothing, the towns are nothing, what is necessary is to destroy the military force of the adversary." Then the Germans in their turn adopt this theory in 1918 and Bidou curiously explains (and July, 1918) that the capture of certain vital points, certain essential areas, decides the victory. It is moreover a particular turn of his mind. He has shown how, if Russia were blockaded at sea, she would be defeated and that an army enclosed in a sort of vast prison camp is doomed to perish.'

Nevertheless, if the war did not modify the character of Saint-Loup, his intelligence, developed through an evolution in which heredity played a great part, had reached a degree of brilliancy which I had never seen in him

before. How far away was the young golden-haired man formerly courted
or who aspired to be, by fashionable ladies and the dialectician, the
doctrinaire who was always playing with words. To another generation of
another branch of his family, much as an actor taking a part formerly played
by Bressant or Delaunay, he, blonde, pink and golden was like a successor to
M. de Charlus, once dark, now completely white. However much he failed
to agree with his uncle about the war, identified as he was with that part of
the aristocracy which was for France first and foremost whereas M. de
Charlus was fundamentally a defeatist, to those who had not seen the
original 'creator of the part' he displayed his powers as a controversialist. 'It
seems that Hindenburg is a revelation,' I said to him. 'An old revelation of
tit-for-tat or a future one. They ought, instead of playing with the enemy, to
let Mangin have his way, beat Austria and Germany to their knees and
Europeanise Turkey instead of Montenegrinising France.' 'But we shall
have the help of the United States,' I suggested. 'At present all I see is the
spectacle of Divided States. Why not make greater concessions to Italy and
frighten them with dechristianising France?' 'If your Uncle Charlus could
hear you!' I said. 'Really you would not be sorry to offend the Pope a bit
more and he must be in despair about what may happen to the throne of
Francis Joseph. For that matter he's in the tradition of Talleyrand and the
Congress of Vienna.' 'The era of the Congress of Vienna has gone full
circle,' he answered; 'one must substitute concrete for secret diplomacy. My
uncle is at bottom an impenitent monarchist who would swallow carps like
Mme Molé or scarps like Arthur Meyer as long as his carps and scarps were
cooked *à la Chambord*. Through hatred of the tricolour flag I believe he
would rather range himself under the red rag, which he would accept in
good faith instead of the white standard.'

Of course, these were only words and Saint-Loup was far from having the
occasionally basic originality of his uncle. But his disposition was as affable
and delightful as the other's was suspicious and jealous and he remained, as
at Balbec, charming and pink under his thick golden hair. The only thing in
which his uncle would not have surpassed him was in that mental attitude of
the Faubourg Saint-Germain with which those who believe themselves the
most detached from it are saturated and which simultaneously gives them
respect for men of intelligence who are not of noble birth (which only
flourishes in the nobility and makes revolution so unjust) and silly self-
complacency. It was through this mixture of humility and pride, of acquired
curiosity of mind and inborn sense of authority, that M. de Charlus and
Saint-Loup by different roads and holding contrary opinions had become to
a generation of transition, intellectuals interested in every new idea and

talkers whom no interrupter could silence. Thus a rather commonplace individual would, according to his disposition, consider both of them either dazzling or bores.

While recalling Saint-Loup's visit I had made a long detour on my way to Mme Verdurin's and I had nearly reached the Bridge of the Invalides. The lamps (few and far between, on account of Gothas) were lighted a little too early, for the change of hours had been prematurely determined for the summer season (like the furnaces which are lighted and extinguished at fixed dates) while night still came quickly and above the partly-illumined city, in one whole part of the sky – a sky which ignored summer and winter and did not deign to observe that half-past eight had become half-past nine – it still continued to be daylight. In all that part of the city, dominated by the towers of the Trocadéro, the sky had the appearance of an immense turquoise-tinted sea, which, at low tide, revealed a thin line of black rocks or perhaps only fishermen's nets aligned next each other and which were tiny clouds. A sea, now the colour of turquoise which was bearing unknowing man with it in the immense revolution of an earth upon which they are mad enough to continue their own revolutions, their vain wars such as this one now drenching France in blood. In fact one became giddy looking at the lazy, beautiful sky which deigned not to change its timetable and prolonged in its blue tones the lengthened day above the lighted city; it was no longer a spreading sea, but a vertical gradation of blue glaciers. And the towers of the Trocadéro seeming so close to those turquoise heights were in reality as far away from them as those twin towers in a town of Switzerland which, from far away, seem to neighbour the mountain slopes. I retraced my steps but as I left the Bridge of the Invalides behind me there was no more day in the sky, nor scarcely a light in all the city, and stumbling here and there against the dustbins, mistaking my road, I found myself, unexpectedly and after following a labyrinth of obscure streets, upon the Boulevards. There the impression of the East renewed itself and to the evocation of the Paris of the Directoire succeeded that of the Paris of 1815. As then, the disparate procession of uniforms of Allied troops, Africans in baggy red trousers, white-turbaned Hindus, created for me, out of that Paris where I was walking, an exotic imaginary city in an East minutely exact in costume and colour of the skins but arbitrarily chimerical in scenery, just as Carpaccio made of his own city a Jerusalem or a Constantinople by assembling therein a crowd whose marvellous medley of colour was not more varied than this. Walking behind two Zouaves who did not seem to notice him, I perceived a great stout man in a soft, felt hat and a long cloak, to whose mauve-coloured face I hesitated to put the name of an actor or of a painter equally well-known for innumerable sodomite scandals.

In any case feeling certain I did not know the promenader, I was greatly
surprised, when his glance met mine, to notice that he was embarrassed and
made as though to stop and speak to me, like one who wants to show you that
you are not surprising him in an occupation he would rather have kept secret.
For a second I asked myself who was saying good evening to me. It was M. de
Charlus. One could say of him that the evolution of his disease or the
revolution of his vice had reached that extreme point where the small
primitive personality of the individual, his ancestral qualities, were entirely
obscured by the interposition of the defect or generic evil which accompanied
them. M. de Charlus had gone as far as it was possible for him to go, or rather,
he was so completely marked by what he had become, by habits that were not
his alone but also those of many other inverts, that, at first, I had taken him
for one of these following the Zouaves on the open boulevard; in fact, for
another of their kind who was not M. de Charlus, not a *grand seigneur*, not a
man of mind and imagination and who only resembled the baron through
that appearance common to them all and to him as well which, until one
looked closer, had covered everything.

It was thus that, having wanted to go to Mme Verdurin's, I met M. de
Charlus. And certainly I should not have found him as I used to at her house;
their quarrel had only become accentuated and Mme Verdurin often made
use of present conditions to discredit him further. Having said for a long
time that he was used up, finished, more old-fashioned in his pretended
audacities than the most pompous nonentities, she now comprised that
condemnation in a general indictment by saying that he was 'pre-war'.
According to the little clan, the war had placed between him and the
present, a gulf which relegated him to a past that was completely dead.

Moreover – and that concerned rather the political world which was less
well-informed – Mme Verdurin represented him as done for, as complete a
social as an intellectual outsider. 'He sees no one, no one receives him,' she
told M. Bontemps, whom she easily convinced. Moreover there was some
truth in what she said. The situation of M. de Charlus had changed. Caring
less and less about society, having quarrelled with everybody owing to his
petulant disposition and, having through conviction of his own social
importance, disdained to reconcile himself with most of those who
constituted the flower of society, he lived in a relative isolation which, unlike
that in which Mme de Villeparisis died, was not caused by the ostracism of
the aristocracy but by something which appeared to the eyes of the public
worse, for two reasons. M. de Charlus's bad reputation, now well-known,
caused the ill-informed to believe that that accounted for people not
frequenting his society, while actually it was he who, of his own accord,

refused to frequent them, so that the effect of his own atrabilious humour appeared to be that of the hostility of those upon whom he exercised it. Besides that, Mme de Villeparisis had a great rampart: her family. But M. de Charlus had multiplied the quarrels between himself and his family, which moreover appeared to him uninteresting, especially the old Faubourg side, the Courvoisier set. He who had made so many bold sallies in the field of art, unlike the Courvoisiers, had no notion that what would have most interested a Bergotte was his relationship with that old Faubourg, his having the means of describing the almost provincial life lived by his cousins in the rue de la Chaise or in the Place du Palais Bourbon and the rue Garancière.

A point of view less transcendent and more practical was represented by Mme Verdurin who affected to believe that he was not French. 'What is his exact nationality? Is he not an Austrian?' M. Verdurin innocently enquired. 'Oh, no, not at all,' answered the Comtesse Molé, whose first gesture rather obeyed her good sense than her rancour. 'Nothing of the sort, he's a Prussian,' pronounced *la Patronne*: 'I know, I tell you. He told us often enough he was a hereditary peer of Prussia and a "Serene Highness".' 'All the same, the Queen of Naples told me – ' 'As to her, you know she's an awful spy,' exclaimed Mme Verdurin who had not forgotten the attitude which the fallen sovereign had displayed at her house one evening. 'I know it most positively. She only lives by spying. If we had a more energetic Government, all those people would be in a concentration camp. And in any case you would do well not to receive that charming kind of society, for I happen to know that the Minister of the Interior has got his eye on them and your house will be watched. Nothing will convince me that during two years Charlus was not continually spying at my house.' And thinking probably, that there might be some doubt as to the interest the German Government might take, even in the most circumstantial reports on the organisation of the 'little clan', Mme Verdurin, with the soft, confidential manner of a person who knows the value of what she is imparting and that it seems more significant if she does not raise her voice, 'I tell you, from the first day I said to my husband, "the way in which this man has inveigled himself into our house is not to my liking. There's something suspicious about it." Our estate was on a very high point at the back of a bay. I am certain he was entrusted by the Germans to prepare a base there for their submarines. Certain things surprised me and now I understand them. For instance, at first he would not come by train with the other guests. I had offered in the nicest way to give him a room in the château. Well, not a bit of it, he preferred living at Doncières where there were an enormous number of troops. All that stank in one's nostrils of espionage.'

As to the first of these accusations directed against the Baron de Charlus, that of being out of fashion, society people were quite ready to accept Mme Verdurin's point of view. This was ungrateful of them, for M. de Charlus who had been, up to a point their poet, had the art of extracting from social surroundings a sort of poetry into which he wove history, beauty, the picturesque, comedy and frivolous elegance. But fashionable people, incapable of understanding poetry, of which they saw none in their own lives, sought it elsewhere and placed a thousand feet above M. de Charlus men infinitely inferior to him, who affected to despise society and, on the other hand, professed social and political-economic theories. M. de Charlus delighted in an unprofessedly lyrical form of wit with which he described the knowing grace of the Duchesse of X's dresses and alluded to her as a sublime creature. This caused him to be looked upon as an idiot by those women in society who thought that the Duchesse of X was an uninteresting fool, that dresses are made to be worn without drawing attention to them and who, thinking themselves more intelligent, rushed to the Sorbonne or to the Chamber if Deschanel was going to speak.

In short, people in society were disillusioned with M. de Charlus, not because they had got through him but because they had never grasped his rare intellectual value. He was considered pre-war, old-fashioned, just because those least capable of judging merit, most readily accept the edicts of passing fashion; so far from exhausting, they have hardly even skimmed the surface of men of quality in the preceding generation whom they now condemn en bloc because they are offered the label of a new generation they will understand just as little.

As to the second accusation against M. de Charlus, that of Germanism, the happy-medium mentality of people in society made them reject it, but they encountered an indefatigable and particularly cruel interpreter in Morel, who, having managed to retain in the press and even in society the position which M. de Charlus had succeeded in getting him by expending twice as much trouble as he would have taken in depriving him of it, pursued the Baron with implacable hatred; this was not only cruel on the part of Morel, but doubly wrong, for whatever his relations with the Baron might have been, Morel had experienced the rare kindness his patron hid from so many people. M. de Charlus had treated the violinist with such generosity, with such delicacy, had shown such scruple about not breaking his word, that the idea of him which Charlie had retained was not at all that of a vicious man (at most he considered the Baron's vice a disease) but of one with the noblest ideas and the most exquisite sensibility he had ever known, a sort of saint. He denied it so little that though he had quarrelled with him he said sincerely enough to his relations, 'You can confide your son to him, he would only have the best influence upon him.' Indeed when he tried to injure him by his articles, in his mind he jeered, not at his vices but at his virtues.

Before the war, certain little broadsheets, transparent to what are called the 'initiates', had begun to do the greatest harm to M. de Charlus. Of one of these entitled *The Misadventure of a pedantic Duchess, the Old Age of the Baroness* Mme Verdurin had bought fifty copies, in order to lend them to her acquaintances, and M. Verdurin, declaring that Voltaire himself never wrote anything better, read them aloud to his friends. Since the war it was not the inversion of the Baron alone that was denounced, but also his alleged Germanic nationality. 'Frau Bosch', 'Frau von der Bosch' were the customary surnames of M. de Charlus. One effusion of poetic character had borrowed from certain dance melodies in Beethoven, the title 'Une Allemande'. Finally, two little novels, *Oncle d'Amérique et Tante de Francfort*, and *Gaillard d'arrière*, read in proof by the little clan, had given delight to Brichot himself who remarked, 'Take care the most noble and puissant Anastasia doesn't do us in.'

The articles themselves were better done than their ridiculous titles would have led one to suppose. Their style derived from Bergotte but in a way which perhaps only I could recognise, for this reason. The writings of Bergotte had had no influence upon Morel. Fecundation had occurred in so peculiar and exceptional a fashion that I must register it here. I have indicated in its place the special way Bergotte had of selecting his words and pronouncing them when he talked. Morel, who had met him in early days, gave imitations of him at the time in which he mimicked his speech perfectly, using the same words as Bergotte would have used. So now Morel transcribed conversations *à la Bergotte* but without transmuting them into what would have represented Bergotte's style of writing. As few people had talked with Bergotte, they did not recognise the tonality which was quite different from his style. That oral fertilisation is so rare that I wanted to mention it here; for that matter, it produces only sterile flowers.

Morel, who was at the Press Bureau and whose irregular situation was unknown, made the pretence, with his French blood boiling in his veins like the juice of the grapes of Combray, that to work in an office during the war was not good enough and that he wanted to join up (which he could have done at any moment he pleased) while Mme Verdurin did everything in her power to persuade him to remain in Paris. Certainly she was indignant that M. de Cambremer, in spite of his age, had a staff job, and she remarked about every man who did not come to her house, 'Where has he found means of hiding?' And if anyone affirmed that so and so had been in the front line from the first day she answered, lying unscrupulously or from the mere habit of falsehood, 'Not a bit of it, he has never stirred from Paris, he is doing something about as dangerous as promenading around the Ministries. I tell you I know what I am talking about because I have got it from someone who has seen him.' But in the case of 'the faithful' it was different. She did not want them to go and alluded to the war as a 'boring business' that took them away from her; and she took all possible steps to prevent them going which gave her the double pleasure of having them at dinner and, when they did not come or had gone, of abusing them behind their backs for their pusillanimity. The 'faithful' had to lend themselves to this *embusquage* and she was distressed when Morel pretended to be recalcitrant and told him, 'By serving in the Press Bureau you are doing your bit, and more so than if you were at the front. What is required is to be useful, really to take part in the war, to be of it. There are those who are of it and *embusqués*; you are of it and don't you bother, everyone knows you are and no one can have a word to say against you.' Under different circumstances, when men were not so few and when she was not obliged as now to have chiefly women, if one of them lost his mother she did not hesitate to persuade him that he could un-hesitatingly continue to go to her receptions. 'Sorrow is felt in the heart. If you were to go to a ball (she never gave any) I should be the first to advise you not to, but here at my little Wednesdays or in a box at the theatre, no one can be shocked. Everybody knows how grieved you are.' Now, however, men were fewer, mourning more frequent, she did not have to prevent them from going into society, the war saw to that. But she wanted to persuade them that they were more useful to France by stopping in Paris, in the same way as she would formerly have persuaded them that the defunct would have been more happy to see them enjoying themselves. All the same she got very few men, and sometimes, perhaps, she regretted having brought about the rupture with M. de Charlus, which could never be repaired.

But if M. de Charlus and Mme Verdurin no longer saw each other, each of them – with certain minor differences – continued as though nothing had changed, Mme Verdurin to receive and M. de Charlus to go about his own pleasures. For example, at Mme Verdurin's house, Cottard was present at the receptions in the uniform of a Colonel of *l'Ile du Rêve* rather similar to that of a Haitian Admiral, and upon the lapel of which a broad sky-blue ribbon recalled that of the *Enfants de Marie*; as to M. de Charlus, finding himself in a city where mature men who had up to then been his taste had disappeared, he had, like certain Frenchmen who run after women when they are in France but who live in the Colonies, at first from necessity, then from habit, acquired a taste for little boys.

Furthermore, one of the characteristic features of the Salon Verdurin disappeared soon after, for Cottard died 'with his face to the enemy' the papers said, though he had never left Paris; the fact was he had been overworked for his time of life and he was followed shortly afterwards by M. Verdurin, whose death caused sorrow to one person only – would one believe it? – Elstir. I had been able to study his work from a point of view which was in a measure final. But, as he grew older, he associated it superstitiously with the society which had supplied his models and, after the alchemy of his intuitions had transmuted them into works of art, gave him his public. More and more inclined to the belief that a large part of beauty resides in objects as, at first, he had adored in Mme Elstir that rather heavy type of beauty he had studied in tapestries and handled in his pictures, M. Verdurin's death signified to him the disappearance of one of the last traces of the perishable social framework, falling into limbo as swiftly as the fashions in dress which form part of it – that framework which supports an art and certifies its authenticity like the revolution which, in destroying the elegancies of the eighteenth century, would have distressed a painter of *fêtes galantes* or afflicted Renoir when Montmartre and the Moulin de la Galette disappeared. But, above all, with M. Verdurin disappeared the eyes, the brain, which had had the most authentic vision of his painting, wherein that painting lived, as it were, in the form of a cherished memory. Without doubt young men had emerged who also loved painting, but another kind of painting, and they had not, like Swann, like M. Verdurin, received lessons in taste from Whistler, lessons in truth from Monet, which enabled them to judge Elstir with justice! Also he felt himself more solitary when M. Verdurin, with whom he had, nevertheless, quarrelled years ago, died and it was as though part of the beauty of his work had disappeared with some of that consciousness of beauty which had until then, existed in the world.

The change which had been effected in M. de Charlus's pleasures remained intermittent. Keeping up a large correspondence with the front, he did not lack mature men home on leave.

Therefore, in a general way, Mme Verdurin continued to receive and M. de Charlus to go about his pleasures as if nothing had happened. And still for two years the immense human entity called France, of which even from a purely material point of view one can only feel the tremendous beauty if one perceives the cohesion of millions of individuals who, like cellules of various forms fill it like so many little interior polygons up to the extreme limit of its perimeter, and if one saw it on the same scale as infusoria or cellules see a human body, that is to say, as big as Mont Blanc, was facing a tremendous collective battle with that other immense conglomerate of individuals which is Germany.

At a time when I believed what people told me, I should have been tempted to believe Germany, then Bulgaria, then Greece when they proclaimed their pacific intentions. But since my life with Albertine and with Françoise had accustomed me to suspect those motives they did not express, I did not allow any word, however right in appearance of William II, Ferdinand of Bulgaria or Constantine of Greece to deceive my instinct which divined what each one of them was plotting. Doubtless my quarrels with Françoise and with Albertine had only been little personal quarrels, mattering only to the life of that little spiritual cellule which a human being is. But in the same way as there are bodies of animals, human bodies, that is to say, assemblages of cellules, which, in relation to one of them alone, are as great as a mountain, so there exist enormous organised groupings of individuals which we call nations; their life only repeats and amplifies the life of the composing cellules and he who is not capable of understanding the mystery, the reactions and the laws of those cellules, will only utter empty words when he talks about struggles between nations. But if he is master of the psychology of individuals, then these colossal masses of conglomerate individuals facing one another will assume in his eyes a more formidable beauty than a fight born only of a conflict between two characters, and he will see them on the scale on which the body of a tall man would be seen by infusoria of which it would require more than ten thousand to fill one cubic millimetre. Thus for some time past the great figure of France, filled to its perimeter with millions of little polygons of various shapes and the other figure of Germany filled with even more polygons were having one of those quarrels which, in a smaller measure, individuals have.

But the blows that they were exchanging were regulated by those number-less boxing-matches of which Saint-Loup had explained the principles to me. And because, even in considering them from the point of view of individuals they were gigantic assemblages, the quarrel assumed enormous and magnificent forms like the uprising of an ocean which with its millions of waves seeks to demolish a secular line of cliffs or like giant glaciers which, with their slow and destructive oscillation, attempt to disrupt the frame of the mountain by which they are circumscribed.

In spite of this, life continued almost the same for many people who have figured in this narrative, notably for M. de Charlus and for the Verdurins, as though the Germans had not been so near to them; a permanent menace in spite of its being concentrated in one immediate peril leaving us entirely unmoved if we do not realise it. People pursue their pleasures from habit without ever thinking, were etiolating and moderating influences to cease, that the proliferation of the infusoria would attain its maximum, that is to say, making a leap of many millions of leagues in a few days and passing from a cubic millimetre to a mass a million times larger than the sun, at the same time destroying all the oxygen of the substances upon which we live, that there would no longer be any humanity or animals or earth, and, without any notion that an irremediable and quite possible catastrophe might be determined in the ether by the incessant and frantic energy hidden behind the apparent immutability of the sun, they go on with their business, without thinking of these two worlds, one too small, the other too large for them to perceive the cosmic menace which hovers around us.

Thus the Verdurins gave their dinners (soon, after the death of M. Verdurin, Mme Verdurin alone) and M. de Charlus went about his pleasures, without realising that the Germans – immobilised, it is true, by a bleeding barrier which was always being renewed – were at an hour's automobile drive from Paris. One might say the Verdurins did, nevertheless, think about it, since they had a political salon where the situation of the armies and of the fleets was discussed every day. As a matter of fact, they thought about those hecatombs of annihilated regiments, of engulfed seafarers, but an inverse operation multiplies to such a degree what concerns our welfare and divides by such a formidable figure what does not concern it, that the death of millions of unknown people hardly affects us more unpleasantly than a draught. Mme Verdurin, who suffered from headaches on account of being unable to get *croissants* to dip into her coffee, had obtained an order from Cottard which enabled her to have them made in the restaurant mentioned earlier. It had been almost as difficult to procure this order from the authorities as the nomination of a general. She started her first *croissant* again on the morning the papers an-announced the wreck of the *Lusitania*. Dipping it into her coffee, she arranged her newspaper so that it would stay open without her having to deprive her other hand of its function of dipping, and exclaimed with horror, 'How awful! It's more frightful than the most terrible tragedies.' But those drowning people must have seemed to her reduced a thousandfold, for, while she indulged in these saddening reflections, she was filling her mouth and the expression on her face, induced, one supposes, by the savour of the *croissant*, precious remedy for her headache, was rather that of placid satisfaction.

M. de Charlus went beyond not passionately desiring the victory of France; without avowing it, he wanted, if not the triumph of Germany, at least that she should not, as everybody desired, be destroyed. The reason of this was that in quarrels the great assemblages of individuals called nations behave, in a certain measure, like individuals. The logic which governs them is within them and is perpetually remoulded by passion like that of people engaged in a love-quarrel or in some domestic dispute, such as that of a son with his father, of a cook with her mistress, of a woman with her husband. He who is in the wrong believes himself in the right, as was the case with Germany, and he who is in the right supports it with arguments which only appear irrefutable to him because they respond to his anger. In these quarrels between individuals, in order to be convinced that one of the parties is in the right – the surest plan is to be that party; no onlooker will ever be so completely convinced of it. And an individual, if he be an integral part of a nation, is himself merely a cellule of an individual which is the nation. Stuffing people's heads full of words means nothing. If, at a critical period in the war, a Frenchman had been told that his country was going to be beaten, he would have been desperate as though he were himself about to be killed by the 'Berthas'. Really, one fills one's own head with hope which is a sort of instinct of self-preservation in a nation if one is really an integral member of it. To remain blind to what is false in the claims of the individual called Germany, to see justice in every claim of the individual called France, the surest way was not for a German to lack judgment and for a Frenchman to possess it but for both to be patriotic. M. de Charlus, who had rare moral qualities, who was accessible to pity, generous, capable of affection and of devotion, was in contrast, for various reasons, amongst them that a Bavarian duchess had been his mother, without patriotism. In consequence he belonged as much to the body of Germany as to the body of France. If I had been devoid of patriotism myself, instead of feeling myself one of the cellules in the body of France, I think my way of judging the quarrel would not have been the same as formerly. In my adolescence, when I believed exactly what I was told, doubtless, on hearing the German Government protest its good faith, I should have been inclined to believe it, but now for a long time I had realised that our thoughts do not always correspond with our words.

But actually I can only imagine what I should have done if I had not been a member of the agent, France, as in my quarrels with Albertine, when my sad appearance and my choking throat were, as parts of my being, too passionately interested on my own behalf for me to reach any sort of detachment. That of M. de Charlus was complete. Since he was only a spectator, everything had the inevitable effect of making him Germanophile because, though not really French, he lived in France. He was very keen-witted and in all countries fools outnumber the rest; no doubt, if he had lived in Germany the German fools defending an unjust cause with passionate folly would have equally irritated him; but living in France, the French fools, defending a just cause with passionate folly, irritated him no less. The logic of passion, even in the service of justice, is never irrefutable by one who remains dispassionate. M. de Charlus acutely noted each false argument of the patriots. The satisfaction a brainless fool gets out of being in the right and out of the certainty of success, is particularly irritating. M. de Charlus was maddened by the triumphant optimism of people who did not know Germany and its power as he did, who every month were confident that she would be crushed the following month, and when a year had passed were just as ready to believe in a new prognostic as if they had not with equal confidence credited the false one they had forgotten, or if they were reminded of it, replied that, 'it was not the same thing'. M. de Charlus, whose mind contained some depth, might perhaps not have understood in Art that the 'it isn't the same thing' offered as an argument by the detractors of Monet in opposition to those who contended that 'they said the same thing about Delacroix', corresponded to the same mentality.

And then M. de Charlus was merciful, the idea of a vanquished man pained him, he was always for the weak, and could not read the accounts of trials in the papers without feeling in his own flesh the anguish of the prisoner and a longing to assassinate the judge, the executioner and the mob who delighted in 'seeing justice done'. In any case, it was now certain that France could not be beaten and he knew that the Germans were famine-stricken and would be obliged sooner or later to surrender at discretion. This idea was also more unpleasant to him owing to his living in France. His memories of Germany were, after all, dimmed by time, whereas the French who unpleasantly gloated in the prospect of crushing Germany, were people whose defects and antipathetic countenances were familiar to him. In such a case we feel more compassionate towards those unknown to us, whom we can only imagine, than towards those whose vulgar daily life is lived close to us, unless we feel completely one of them, one flesh with them; patriotism works this miracle, we stand by our country as we do by ourselves in a love quarrel.

The war, too, acted on M. de Charlus as an extraordinarily fruitful culture of those hatreds of his which were born from one instant to another, lasted a very short time, but during it were exceedingly violent. Reading the papers, the triumphant tone of the articles daily representing Germany laid low, 'the beast at bay, reduced to impotence', at a time when the contrary was only too true, drove him mad with rage by their irresponsible and ferocious stupidity. The papers were in part edited at that time by well-known people who thus found a way of 'doing their bit'; by the Brichots, the Norpois, by the Legrandins. M. de Charlus longed to meet and pulverise them with his bitterest irony. Always particularly well informed about sexual taints, he recognised them in others who, imagining themselves unsuspected, delighted in denouncing the sovereigns of the 'Empires of prey', Wagner et cetera as culprits in this respect. He yearned to encounter them face to face so that he could rub their noses in their own vices before the world and leave these insulters of a fallen foe demolished and dishonoured.

Finally M. de Charlus had a still further reason for being the Germanophile he was. One was that as a man of the world he had lived much amongst people in society, amongst men of honour who will not shake hands with a scamp; he knew their niceties and also their hardness, he knew they were insensible to the tears of a man they expel from a club, with whom they refuse to fight a duel, even if their act of 'moral purity' caused the death of the black sheep's mother. Great as his admiration had been for England, that impeccable England incapable of lies preventing corn and milk from entering Germany was in a way a nation of chartered gentlemen, of licensed witnesses and arbiters of honour, whilst to his mind some of Dostoevsky's disreputable rascals were better. But I never could understand why he identified such characters with the Germans since the latter do not appear to us to have displayed the goodness of heart which, in the case of the former, lying and deceit failed to prejudice.

Finally, a last trait will complete the Germanophilism of M. de Charlus, which he owed through a peculiar reaction to his 'Charlisme'. He considered Germans very ugly, perhaps because they were a little too close to his own blood, he was mad about Moroccans but above all about Anglo-Saxons whom he saw as living statues of Phidias. In him sexual gratification was inseparable from the idea of cruelty and (how strong this was I did not then realise) the man who attracted him seemed like a kind of delightful executioner. He would have thought, if he had sided against the Germans, that he was acting as he only did in his hours of self-indulgence, that is, in a sense contrary to his naturally merciful nature, in other words, impassioned; by seductive evil and desiring to crush virtuous ugliness. He was like that at the time of the murder of Rasputin at a supper party *à la* Dostoevsky, which impressed people by its strong Russian flavour (an impression which would have been much stronger if the public had been aware of all that M. de Charlus knew), because life deceives us so much that we come to believing that literature has no relation with it and we are astonished to observe that the wonderful ideas books have presented to us are gratuitously exhibited in everyday life, without risk of being spoilt by the writer, that for instance, a murder at a supper-party, a Russian incident, should have something Russian about it.

The war continued indefinitely and those who had announced years ago from a reliable source that negotiations for peace had begun, specifying even the clauses of the armistice, did not take the trouble, when they talked with you, to excuse themselves for their false information. They had forgotten it and were ready sincerely to circulate other information which they would forget equally quickly. It was the period when there were continuous raids of Gothas. The air perpetually quivered with the vigilant and sonorous vibration of the French aeroplanes. But sometimes the siren rang forth like a harrowing appeal of the Walkyries, the only German music one had heard since the war – until the hour when the firemen announced that the alarm was finished, while the maroon, like an invisible newsboy, communicated the good news at regular intervals and cast its joyous clamour into the air.

M. de Charlus was astonished to discover that even men like Brichot who, before the war, had been militarist and reproached France for not being sufficiently so, were not satisfied with blaming Germany for the excesses of her militarism, but even condemned her for admiring her army. Doubtless, they changed their view when there was a question of slowing down the war against Germany and rightly denounced the pacifists. Yet Brichot, as an example of inconsistency, having agreed in spite of his failing sight, to give lectures on certain books which had appeared in neutral countries, exalted the novel of a Swiss in which two children, who fell on their knees in admiration of the symbolic vision of a dragoon, are denounced as the seed of militarism. There were other reasons why this denunciation should displease M. de Charlus, who considered that a dragoon can be exceedingly beautiful. But still more he could not understand the admiration of Brichot, if not for the book which the baron had not read, at all events for its spirit which was so different from that which distinguished Brichot before the war. Then everything that was soldierlike was good, whether it was the irregularities of a General de Boisdeffre, the travesties and machinations of a Colonel du Paty de Clam or the falsifications of Colonel Henry. But by that extra-ordinary *volte-face* (which was in reality only another face of that most noble passion, patriotism, necessarily militarised when it was fighting against Dreyfusism which then had an anti-militarist tendency and now was almost anti-militarist since it was fighting against Germany, the super-militarist country), Brichot now cried: 'Oh! What an admirable exhibition, how seemly, to appeal to youth to continue brutality for a century, to recognise no other culture than that of violence: a dragoon! One can imagine the sort of vile soldiery we can expect of a generation brought up to worship these manifestations of brute force.'

'Now, look here,' M. de Charlus said to me, 'you know Brichot and Cambremer. Every time I see them, they talk to me about the extraordinary lack of psychology in Germany. Between ourselves, do you believe that until now they have cared much about psychology or that even now they are capable of proving they possess any? But, believe me, I am not exaggerating. Even when the greatest Germans are in question, Nietzsche or Goethe, you will hear Brichot say "with that habitual lack of psychology which characterises the Teutonic race". Obviously there are worse things than that to bear but you must admit that it gets on one's nerves. Norpois is more intelligent, I admit, though he has never been other than wrong from the beginning. But what is one to say about those articles which excite universal enthusiasm? My dear Sir, you know as well as I do what Brichot's value is, and I have a liking for him even since the feud which has separated me from his little tabernacle, on account of which I see him much less. Still, I have a certain respect for this college dean, a fine speaker and an erudite, and I avow that it is extremely touching, at his age and in bad health as he is, for he has become sensibly so in these last years, that he should have given himself up to what he calls service. But whatever one may say, good intention is one thing, talent another and Brichot never had talent. I admit that I share his admiration for certain grandeurs of the war. At most, however, it is extraordinary that a blind partisan of antiquity like Brichot, who never could be ironical enough about Zola seeing more beauty in a workman's home, in a mine than in historic palaces or about Goncourt putting Diderot above Homer and Watteau above Raphael, should repeat incessantly that Thermopylae or Austerlitz were nothing in comparison with Vauquois. This time the public, which resisted the modernists of Art and Literature, follows those of the war, because it's the fashion to think like that and small minds are not overwhelmed by the beauty but by the enormous scale of the war. They never write Kolossal without a K but at bottom what they bow down to is indeed colossal.'

'It is a curious thing,' added M. de Charlus, with that little high voice he adopted at times, 'I hear people who look quite happy all day long and drink plenty of excellent cocktails, say they will never be able to see the war through, that their hearts aren't strong enough, that they cannot think of anything else and that they will die suddenly, and the extraordinary thing is that it actually happens; how curious! Is it a matter of nourishment, because they only eat things which are badly cooked or because, to prove their zeal, they harness themselves to some futile task which interferes with the diet that preserved them? Anyhow, I have registered a surprising number of these strange premature deaths, premature at all events, so far as the desire of the dead person was concerned. I do not remember exactly what I was saying to you about Brichot and Norpois admiring this war but what a singular way to talk about it. To begin with, have you remarked that pullulation of new idioms used by Norpois which, exhausted by daily use – for really he is indefatigable and I believe the death of my Aunt Villeparisis gave him a second youth – are immediately replaced by others that are in general use. Formerly, I remember you used to be amused by noting these modes of language which appear, are kept going for a time, and then disappear: "He who sows the wind shall reap the whirlwind", "The dog barks, the caravan passes", "Find me a good politic and I shall produce good finance for you, said Baron Louis". These are symptoms which it would be exaggerated to take too tragically but which must be taken seriously, "To work for the King of Prussia" (for that matter this last has been revived as was inevitable). Well, since, alas, I have seen so many of them die we have had the "Scrap of paper", "the Robber Empires", "the famous Kultur which consists in assassinating defenceless women and children", "Victory, as the Japanese say, will be to him who can endure a quarter of an hour longer than the other", "The Germano-Turanians", "Scientific barbarity", "if we want to win the war in accordance with the strong expression of Mr Lloyd George", in fact, there are no end of them; the *mordant* of the troops, and the *cran* of the troops. Even the sentiments of the excellent Norpois undergo, owing to the war, as complete a modification as the composition of bread or the rapidity of transport. Have you observed that the excellent man, anxious to proclaim his desires as though they were a truth on the point of being realised, does not, all the same, dare to use the future tense which might be contradicted by events, but has adopted instead the verb "know".' I told M. de Charlus that I did not understand what he meant.

I must observe here that the Duc de Guermantes did not in the least share the pessimism of his brother. He was, moreover, as Anglophile as M. de Charlus was Anglophobe. For instance, he considered M. Caillaux a traitor who deserved to be shot a thousand times over. When his brother asked him for proofs of this treason, M. de Guermantes answered that if one only condemned people who signed a paper on which they declared 'I have betrayed', one would never punish the crime of treason. But in case I should not have occasion to return to it, I will also remark that two years later the Duc de Guermantes, animated by pure anti-Caillauxism, made the acquaintance of an English military attaché and his wife, a remarkably well-read couple, with whom he made friends as he did with the three charming ladies at the time of the Dreyfus Affair and that from the first day he was astounded, in talking of Caillaux, whose conviction he held to be certain and his crime patent, to hear one of the charming and well-read couple remark, 'He will probably be acquitted, there is absolutely nothing against him.' M. de Guermantes tried to allege that M. de Norpois, in his evidence had exclaimed, looking the fallen Caillaux in the face, 'You are the Giolitti of France, yes, M. Caillaux, you are the Giolitti of France.' But the charming couple smiled and ridiculed M. de Norpois, giving examples of his senility and concluded that he had thus addressed a M. Caillaux overthrown according to the *Figaro*, but probably in reality a very sly M. Caillaux. The opinions of the Duc de Guermantes soon changed. To attribute this change to the influence of an Englishwoman is not as extreme as it might have seemed if one had prophesied even in 1919, when the English called the Germans Huns and demanded a ferocious sentence on the guilty, that their opinion was to change and that every decision which could sadden France and help Germany would be supported by them.

To return to M. de Charlus. 'Yes,' he said, in reply to my not understanding him, ' "to know" in the articles of Norpois takes the place of the future tense, that is, expresses the wishes of Norpois, all our wishes, for that matter,' he added, perhaps not with complete sincerity. 'You understand that if "know" had not replaced the simple future tense one might, if pressed, admit that the subject of this verb could be a country. For instance, every time Brichot said "America 'would not know' how to remain indifferent to these repeated violations of right", "the two-headed Monarchy 'would not know' how to fail to mend its ways", it is clear that such phrases express the wishes of Norpois (his and ours) but, anyhow, the word can still keep its original sense in spite of its absurdity, because a country can "know", America can "know", even the two-headed Monarchy itself can "know" (in spite of its eternal lack of psychology) but that sense can no longer be admitted when Brichot writes "the systematic devastations 'would not know' how to persuade the neutrals", or "the region of the Lakes 'would not know' how to avoid shortly falling into the hands of the Allies", or "the results of the elections in the neutral countries 'would not know' how to reflect the opinion of the great majority in those countries". Now it is clear that these devastations, these Lakes and these results of elections are inanimate things which cannot "know". By that formula Norpois is simply addressing his injunctions to the neutrals (who, I regret to observe, do not seem to obey him) to emerge from their neutrality or exhorts the Lakes no longer to belong to the "Boches".' (M. de Charlus put the same sort of arrogance into his tone in pronouncing the word *boches* as he did formerly in the train to Balbec when he alluded to men whose taste is not for women.)

'Moreover, did you observe the tricks Norpois made use of in opening his articles on neutrals ever since 1914? He begins by declaring emphatically that France has no right to mix herself up in the politics of Italy, Roumania, Bulgaria, et cetera. It is "for those powers alone to decide with complete independence, consulting only their national interests, whether or not they are to abandon their neutrality." But if the preliminary declarations of the article (which would formerly have been called the exordium) are so markedly disinterested, what follows is generally much less so. Anyhow, as he goes on M. de Norpois says substantially, "it follows that those powers only who have allied themselves with the side of Right and Justice will secure material advantages from the conflict. It cannot be expected that the Allies will compensate those nations which, following the line of least resistance, have not placed their sword at the service of the Allies, by granting them territories from which, for centuries, the cry of their oppressed brethren has been raised in supplication". Norpois, having taken this first step towards advising intervention, nothing stops him and he now offers advice more and more thinly disguised, not only as to the principle but also as to the appropriate moment for intervention. "Naturally," he says, playing as he would himself call it, the good apostle, "it is for Italy, for Roumania alone to decide the proper hour and the form under which it will suit them to intervene. They cannot, however, be unaware that if they delay too long, they run the risk of missing the crucial moment. Even now Germany trembles at the thud of the Russian cavalry. It is obvious that the nations which have only flown to help in the hour of victory of which the resplendent dawn is already visible, can in no wise have a claim to the rewards they can still secure by hastening, et cetera, et cetera". It is like at the theatre when they say, "the last remaining seats will very soon be gone. This is a warning to the dilatory", an argument which is the more stupid that Norpois serves it up every six months and periodically admonishes Roumania: "The hour has come for Roumania to make up her mind whether she desires or not to realise her national aspirations. If she waits much longer, she will risk being too late". And though he has repeated the admonition for two years, the "too late" has not yet come to pass and they keep on increasing their offers to Roumania. In the same way he invites France et cetera to intervene in Greece as a protective power because the treaty which bound Greece to Serbia has not been maintained. And, really and truly, if France were not at war and did not desire the assistance of the benevolent neutrality of Greece, would she think of intervening as a protective power and would not the moral sentiment which inspires her reprobation of Greece for not keeping her engagements with Serbia, be silenced the moment the question arose of an equally flagrant violation in the case of Roumania and Italy who, like Greece, I believe with good reason, have not fulfilled their obligations, which were less imperative and extensive than is supposed, as allies of Germany. The truth is that people see everything through their newspaper and how can they do otherwise, seeing that they themselves know nothing about the peoples or the events in question. At the time of the "Affaire" which stirred all passions during that period from which it is now the right thing to say we are separated by centuries, for the war-philosophers have agreed that all links with the past are broken, I was shocked at seeing members of my own family give their esteem to anti-clericals and former Communists whom their paper represented as anti-Dreyfusards and insult a general of high birth and a Catholic who was a revisionist. I am no less shocked to see the whole French people execrate the Emperor Francis Joseph, whom they used rightly to venerate; I am able to assure you of this, for I used to know him well and he honoured me by treating me as his cousin. Ah! I have not written to him since the war,' he added as though avowing a fault for which he knew he could not be blamed. 'Yes, let me see, I did write once, only the first year. But it doesn't matter. It doesn't in the least change my respect for him, but I have many young relatives fighting in our lines and they would, I know, consider that I was acting very badly if I kept up a correspondence with the head of a nation at war with us. Let him who wishes criticise me,' he added, as if he were boldly exposing himself to my reproof; 'I did not want a letter signed Charlus to arrive at Vienna in such times as these. The chief criticism that I should direct against the old sovereign is that a *Seigneur* of his rank, head of one of the most ancient and illustrious houses in Europe, should have allowed himself to be led by the nose by that little upstart of a country squire, very intelligent for that matter but a pure *parvenu*, like William of Hohenzollern. That is not the least shocking of the anomalies of this war.' And as, once he adopted the nobiliary point of view which for him overshadowed everything else, M. de Charlus was capable of the most childish extravagances, he told me, in the same serious tone as if he were speaking of the Marne or of Verdun, that there were most interesting and curious things which should not be excluded by any historian of this war. 'For instance,' he said, 'people are so ignorant that no one has observed this remarkable point: the Grand-Master of the Order of Malta, who is a pure-bred Boche, does not on that account cease living at Rome where, as Grand-Master of our Order he enjoys exterritorial privileges. Isn't that interesting?' he added with the air of saying, 'You see you have not wasted your evening by meeting me.' I thanked him and he assumed the modest air of one who is not asking for payment. 'Ah! What was I telling you? Oh, yes, that people now hated Francis Joseph according to their paper. In the cases of the King Constantine of Greece and the Czar of Bulgaria the public has wavered between aversion and sympathy according to reports that they were going to join the Entente or what Norpois calls "the Central Empires". It is like when he keeps on telling us every moment that the hour of Venizelos is going to strike. I do not doubt that Venizelos is a man of much capacity but how do we know that his country wants him so much? He desired, we are informed, that Greece should keep her engagements with Serbia. So we ought to know what those engagements were and if they were more binding than those which Italy and Roumania thought themselves justified in violating. We display an anxiety about the way in which Greece executes her treaties and respects her constitution that we certainly should not have were it not to our interest. If there had been no war, do you believe that the guaranteeing powers would even have paid the slightest attention to the dissolution of the Chamber? I observe that one by one they are withholding their support from the King of Greece so as to be able to throw him out or imprison him the day that he has no army to defend him. I was telling you that the public only judges the King of Greece and the Czar of Bulgaria by the papers, and how could they do otherwise since they do not know them? I used to see a great deal of them and knew them well. When Constantine of Greece was Crown Prince he was a marvel of beauty. I have always believed that the Emperor Nicholas had a great deal of sentiment for him. *Honi soit qui mal y pense*, of course. Princess Christian spoke of it openly, but she's a fiend. As to the Czar of the Bulgarians, he's a sly hussy, a regular show-figure, but very intelligent, a remarkable man. He's very fond of me.'

M. de Charlus, who could be so pleasant, became odious when he touched on these subjects. His self-complacency irritated one like an invalid who keeps on assuring you how well he is. I have often thought that the 'faithful' who so much wanted the avowals withheld by the tortuous personage of Balbec, could not have put up with his ostentatious but uneasy display of his mania and would have felt as uncomfortable as if a morphino-maniac took out his syringe in front of them; probably they would soon have had enough of the confidences they thought they would relish. Besides, one got sick of hearing everybody relegated without proof to a category to which he belonged himself though he denied it. In spite of his intelligence, he had constructed for himself in that connection a narrow little philosophy (at the base of which there was perhaps a touch of that peculiar way of looking at life which characterised Swann) which attributed everything to special causes and, as always happens when a man is conscious of bordering on his own particular defect, he was unworthy of himself and yet unusually self-satisfied. So it came about that so earnest, so noble-minded a man could wear that idiotic smile when he enunciated: 'as there are strong presumptions of the same character in regard to Ferdinand of Coburg's relations with the Emperor William, that might be the reason why Czar Ferdinand placed himself by the side of the Robber-Empires. Dammit, after all, that is quite comprehensible. One is generous to one's sister, one doesn't refuse her anything. To my mind it would be a very charming explanation of the alliance of Germany and Bulgaria.' And M. de Charlus laughed as long over this stupid explanation as though it had been an ingenious one which, even if there had been any justification for it, was as puerile as the observations he made about the war when he judged it from the feudal point of view or from that of a Knight of the Order of Jerusalem. He finished with a sensible observation: 'It is astonishing that the public, though it only judges men and things in the war by the papers, is convinced that it is exercising its own initiative.'

M. de Charlus was right about that. I was told that Mme de Forcheville's silences and hesitations were worth witnessing for the sake of her facial expression when she announced with deep personal conviction: 'No, I do not believe that they will take Warsaw', 'I am under the impression that it will not last a second winter.' 'What I do not want is a lame peace.' 'What alarms me, if you care for my opinion, is the Chamber.' 'Yes, I believe, all the same, they can break through.' In enunciating these phrases, Odette's features assumed a knowing look which was emphasised when she remarked: 'I don't say that the German armies don't fight well, but they lack that *cran* as we call it.' In using that expression (or the word *mordant* in connection with the troops) she made a gesture of kneading with her hand, putting her head on one side and half-closing her eyes like an art-student. Her language bore more traces than ever of her admiration for the English whom she was no longer content to call as she used to 'our neighbours across the Channel', or 'our friends the English', but nothing less than 'our loyal allies'. Unnecessary to say that she never neglected to use in all contexts the expression 'fair play' in order to show that the English considered the Germans unfair players. 'Fair play is what is needed to win the war, as our brave allies say.' And she rather awkwardly associated the name of her son-in-law with everything that concerned the English soldiers and alluded to the pleasure he found in living on intimate terms with the Australians, as also with the Scottish, the New Zealanders and the Canadians. 'My son-in-law, Saint-Loup, knows the slang of all those brave "tommies". He knows how to make himself understood by those who came from the far "Dominions" and he would just as soon fraternise with the most humble private as with the general commanding the base.'

Let this digression about Mme de Forcheville, while I am walking along the boulevard side by side with M. de Charlus, justify a longer one, to elucidate the relations of Mme Verdurin with Brichot at this period. If poor Brichot, like Norpois, was judged with little indulgence by M. de Charlus (because the latter was at once extremely acute and, unconsciously, more or less Germanophile) he was actually treated much worse by the Verdurins. The latter were, of course, chauvinist, and they ought to have liked Brichot's articles which, for that matter, were not inferior to many publications considered delectable by Mme Verdurin. The reader will, perhaps, recall that, even in the days of La Raspelière, Brichot had become, instead of the great man they used to think him, if not a Turk's head like Saniette, at all events the object of their thinly disguised raillery. Nevertheless, he was still one of the 'faithful' which assured him some of the advantages tacitly allotted by the statutes to all the foundation and associated members of the little group. But as, gradually, perhaps owing to the war or through the rapid crystallisation of the long-delayed fashionableness with which all the necessary but till then invisible elements had long since saturated the Verdurin Salon, that salon had been opened to a new society and as the 'faithful', at first the bait for this new society, had ended by being less and less frequently invited, so a parallel phenomenon was taking place in Brichot's case. In spite of the Sorbonne, in spite of the Institute, his fame had, until the war, not outgrown the limits of the Verdurin salon. But when almost daily he began writing articles embellished with that false brilliance we have so often seen him lavishly dispensing for the benefit of the 'faithful' and as he possessed a real erudition which, as a true Sorbonian, he did not seek to hide under some of the graces he gave to it, society was literally dazzled. For once, moreover, it accorded its favour to a man who was far from being a nonentity and who could claim attention owing to the fertility of his intelligence and the resources of his memory. And while three duchesses went to spend the evening at Mme Verdurin's, three others contested the honour of having the great man at their table; and when the invitation of one of them was accepted, she felt herself the freer because Mme Verdurin, exasperated by the success of his articles in the Faubourg Saint-Germain, had taken care not to have him at her house when there was any likelihood of his encountering there some brilliant personage whom he did not yet know and who would hasten to capture him. Brichot in his old age was satisfied to bestow on journalism in exchange for liberal emoluments, all the distinction he had wasted gratis and unrecognised in the Verdurins' salon (for his articles gave him no more trouble than his conversation, so good a talker and so learned was he) and this might have brought him unrivalled fame and at one moment seemed on the eve of doing so, had it not been for Mme Verdurin. Certainly Brichot's articles were far from being as remarkable as society people believed them to be. The vulgarity of the man was manifest at every instant under the pedantry of the scholar. And over and above imagery which meant nothing at all ('the

Germans can no longer look the statue of Beethoven in the face', 'Schiller must have turned in his grave', 'the ink which initialled the neutrality of Belgium was hardly dry', 'Lenin's words mean no more than the wind over the steppes') there were trivialities such as 'Twenty thousand prisoners, that's something like a figure'. 'Our Command will know how to keep its eyes open once for all'. 'We mean to win; one point, that's all'. But mixed up with that nonsense, there were so much knowledge, intelligence and good reasoning. Now Mme Verdurin never began one of Brichot's articles without the anticipatory satisfaction of expecting to find absurdities in it and read it with concentrated attention so as to be certain not to let any of them escape her. Unfortunately there always were some, one hardly had to wait. The most felicitous quotation from an almost unknown author, unknown at all events, by the writer of the work Brichot referred to, was made use of to prove his unjustifiable pedantry and Mme Verdurin awaited the dinner-hour with impatience so that she could let loose her guests' shrieks of laughter, 'Well! What about our Brichot this evening? I thought of you when I was reading the quotation from Cuvier. Upon my word, I believe he's going crazy.' 'I haven't read it yet,' said a 'faithful'. 'What, you haven't read it yet? You don't know the delights in store for you. It's so perfectly idiotic that I nearly died of laughing.' And delighted that someone or other had not yet read the particular article so that she could expose Brichot's absurdities herself, Mme Verdurin told the butler to bring the *Temps* and began to read it aloud, emphasising the most simple phrases. After dinner, throughout the evening, the anti-Brichot campaign continued, but with a pretence of reserve. 'I'm not reading this too loud because I'm afraid that down there,' she pointed at the Comtesse Molé, 'there's a lingering admiration for this rubbish. Society people are simpler than one would think.' While they wanted Mme Molé to hear what they were saying about her, they pretended the contrary by lowering their voices, and she, in cowardly fashion, disowned Brichot whom in reality she considered the equal of Michelet. She agreed with Mme Verdurin and yet, so as to end on a note which seemed to her incontrovertible, added, 'One cannot deny that it is well written.' 'You call that well written,' rejoined Mme Verdurin, 'I consider that it's written like a pig,' a sally which raised a society laugh, chiefly because Mme Verdurin, rather abashed by the word 'pig', had uttered it in a whisper, with her hand over her lips. Her vindictiveness towards Brichot increased the more because he naively displayed satisfaction at his success in spite of ill-humour provoked by the censorship each time, as he said, with his habitual use of slang to show he was not too don-like, it had *caviardé* a part of his article. To his face Mme Verdurin did not let him perceive how poor an opinion she had of his articles except by a sullen demeanour which would have enlightened a more perceptive man. Once only she reproached him with using 'I' so often. As a matter of fact he did so partly from professional habit; expressions like: 'I admit that', 'I am aware that the enormous development of the fronts necessitates', et cetera, et cetera imposed themselves on him, but still more because as a former militant anti-Dreyfusard who had surmised the German preparations long before the war, he had grown accustomed to continually writing: 'I have denounced them since 1897', 'I pointed it out in 1901', 'I warned them in my little brochure, very scarce today "*habent sua fata libelli*" ' and thus the habit had taken root. He blushed deeply at Mme Verdurin's bitter observation. 'You are right, madame. One who loved the Jesuits as little as M. Combes, before he had been privileged with a preface by our charming master in delightful scepticism, Anatole France, who, unless I err, was my adversary – before the deluge, said that the "I" was always detestable.' From that moment Brichot replaced 'I' by 'we', but 'we' did not prevent the reader from seeing that the writer was speaking about himself, on the contrary it enabled him never to cease talking about himself, making a running commentary out of his least significant sentences and composing an article simply on a negation, invariably protected by 'we'. For instance, Brichot had stated, maybe, in another article that the German armies had lost some of their value, he would then begin as follows: ' "We" are not going to disguise the truth. "We" have said that these German armies had lost some of their value. "We" have not said that they were not still of great value. Still less shall "we" say that they have no value at all, any more than "we" should say that ground is gained which is not gained, et cetera, et cetera.' In short, Brichot would have been able, merely by enunciating everything he would not say and by recalling everything that he had been saying for years and what Clausewitz, Ovid, Apollonius of Tyana had said so and so many centuries ago, easily to constitute the material of a large volume. It is a pity he did not publish it because those articles crammed with erudition are now difficult to obtain. The Faubourg Saint-Germain, instructed by Mme Verdurin, began laughing at Brichot at her house, but, once they got away from the little clan, they continued to admire him. Then laughing at him became the fashion as it had been the fashion to admire him, and even those ladies who continued to be secretly interested in him, had no sooner read one of his articles, than they stopped and laughed at them in company, so as not to appear less intelligent than others. Brichot had never been so much talked about in the little clan as at this period, but with derision. The criterion of the intelligence of every newcomer was his opinion of Brichot's articles; if he responded unsatisfactorily the first time, they soon taught him how to judge people's intelligence.

'Well, my dear friend,' continued M. de Charlus, 'all this is appalling and there's a good deal more to deplore than tiresome articles. They talk about vandalism, about the destruction of statues, but is not the destruction of so many wonderful young men who were polychrome statues of incomparable beauty also vandalism? Is not a city in which there are no more beautiful men like a city in which all the statuary has been destroyed? What pleasure can I have in going to dinner at a restaurant where I am served by old moss-grown pot-bellies who look like Père Didon, if not by women in mob caps who make me think I am at a Bouillon Duval. Exactly, my dear fellow, and I think I have the right to say so, for the Beautiful is as much the Beautiful in living matter. A fine pleasure to be served by rickety creatures with spectacles the reason of whose exemption can be read in their faces. Nowadays, if one wants to gratify one's eyes with the sight of a good-looking person in a restaurant, one must no longer seek him among the waiters but among the customers. And one may see a servant again, often as they are changed, but what about that English lieutenant who has been to the restaurant for the first time and will perhaps be killed tomorrow? When Augustus of Poland, as Morand, the delightful author of *Clarisse* narrates, exchanged one of his regiments against a collection of Chinese pots, in my opinion he did a bad business. To think that all those splendid footmen six feet high, who adorned the monumental staircases of our beautiful lady friends, have all been killed, most of them having joined up because people kept on telling them that the war would only last two months. Ah! little did they know, as I did, the power of Germany, the valour of the Prussian race,' he added, forgetting himself.

And then, noticing that he had allowed his point of view to be too clearly seen, he continued: 'It is not so much Germany as the war itself that I fear for France. People imagine that the war is only a gigantic boxing-match at which they are gazing from afar, thanks to the papers. But that is completely untrue. It is a disease which, when it seems cured at one spot crops up in another. Today, Noyon will be relieved, tomorrow we shall have neither bread nor chocolate, the day after, he who believed himself safe and would, if needs must, be ready to die an unimagined death, will be horrified to read in the papers that his class has been called up. As to monuments, the destruction of a unique masterpiece like Rheims is not so terrible to me as to witness the destruction of such numbers of *ensembles* which made the smallest village of France instructive and charming.'

Immediately I began thinking of Combray and how in former days I had thought myself diminished in the eyes of Mme de Guermantes by avowing the modest situation which my family occupied there. I wondered if it had not been revealed to the Guermantes and to M. de Charlus whether by Legrandin or Swann or Saint-Loup or Morel. But that this might have been divulged was less painful to me than retrospective explanations. I only hoped that M. de Charlus would not allude to Combray.

'I do not want to speak ill of the Americans, monsieur,' he continued, 'it seems they are inexhaustibly generous and, since there has been no orchestral conductor in this war and each entered the dance considerably after the other and the Americans began when we were almost finished, they may have an ardour which four years of war has quenched among us. Even before the war they loved our country and our art and paid high prices for our masterpieces of which they have many now. But it is precisely this deracinated art, as M. Barrès would say, which is the reverse of everything which made the supreme charm of France. The Chateau explained the church which in its turn, because it had been a place of pilgrimage, explained the *chanson de geste*. As an illustration, I need not elaborate my own origin and my alliances; for that matter we are not concerned with that, but recently I had to settle some family interests and in spite of a certain coolness which exists between myself and the Saint-Loup family, I had to pay a visit to my niece who lives at Combray. Combray was only a little town like so many others, but our ancestors were represented as patrons in many of the painted windows of the church, in others our arms were inscribed. We had our chapel there and our tombs. This church was destroyed by the French and by the English because it served as an observation post for the Germans. All that medley of surviving history and of art which was France is being destroyed and it is not over yet. Of course I am not so ridiculous as to compare for family reasons the destruction of the Church of Combray with that of the Cathedral of Rheims which was a miracle of a Gothic cathedral in its spontaneous purity of unique statuary, or that of Amiens. I do not know if the raised arm of St Firmin is smashed to atoms today. If it is, the most noble affirmation of faith and of energy has disappeared from this world.' 'The symbol of it, monsieur,' I answered, 'I love symbols as you do, but it would be absurd to sacrifice to the symbol the reality which it symbolises. The cathedrals must be adored until the day when in order to preserve them, it would be necessary to deny the truths which they teach. The raised arm of St Firmin, with an almost military gesture, said: "Let us be broken if honour demands it. Do not sacrifice men to stones whose beauty arises from having for a moment established human verities." ' 'I understand what you mean,' answered M. de Charlus, 'and M. Barrès who alas! has been the cause of our making too many pilgrimages to the statue of Strasbourg and to the tomb of M. Deroulède, was moving and graceful when he wrote that the Cathedral of Rheims itself was less dear to us than the life of one of our infantrymen. This assertion makes the rage of our newspapers against the German general who said that the Cathedral of Rheims was less precious to him than the life of a German soldier, rather ridiculous. And what is so exasperating and harrowing is that every country says the same thing. The reasons given by the industrialist associations of Germany for retaining possession of Belfort as indispensable for the preservation of their country against our ideas of revenge are the same as those of Barrès exacting Mayence to protect us against the velleities of invasion by the Boches. How is it that the restitution of Alsace-Lorraine appeared to France an insufficient motive for a war and yet a sufficient motive for continuing it and for declaring it anew each year? You seem to believe the victory of France certain; I hope so with all my heart, you don't doubt that, but ever since, rightly or wrongly, the Allies believe that their own victory is assured (for my own part, of course, I should be delighted with such a solution, but I observe a great many paper victories, pyrrhic victories at a cost not revealed to us) and that the Boches are no longer confident of victory, we see Germany seeking peace and France wanting to prolong the war; that just France rightly desiring to make the voice of justice heard should be also France the compassionate, and make words of pity heard, were it only for the sake of her children, so that when spring-days come round and flowers bloom again, they will brighten other things than tombs. Be frank, my dear friend, you yourself expounded the theory to me that things only exist thanks to a perpetually renewed creation. You used to say that the creation of the world did not take place once and for all, but necessarily continues day by day. Well, if you said that in good faith you cannot except the war from that theory. It is all very well for our excellent Norpois to write (trotting out one of those rhetorical accessories he loves, like "the dawn of victory" and "General Winter") "now that Germany has wanted war, the die is cast" the truth is that every day war is declared anew. Therefore he who wants to continue it is as culpable as he who began it, perhaps more, for the latter could not perhaps foresee all its horrors.

And there is nothing to show that so prolonged a war, even if it has a victorious issue, will not have perils. It is difficult to talk about things which have no precedent and of repercussions on the organism of an operation which is attempted for the first time. Generally, it is true, we get over these novelties we're alarmed about quite well. The shrewdest Republican thought it mad to bring about the Disestablishment of the Church and it passed like a letter through the post. Dreyfus was rehabilitated, Picquart was made Minister of War without anybody saying a word. Nevertheless, what may not happen after such an exhaustion as that induced by an uninterrupted war lasting for several years? What will the men do when they come back? Will they be tired out? Will fatigue have broken them or driven them mad? All this may turn out badly, if not for France, at least for the Government and perhaps for the form of Government. Formerly you made me read the admirable *Aimée de Coigny* by Maurras. I should be much surprised if some Aimée de Coigny did not anticipate from the war which our Republic is making, developments expected by Aimée de Coigny in 1812 from the war the Empire was then making. If that Aimée de Coigny actually does exist, will her hopes be realised? I hope not.

To return to the war itself: did the Emperor William begin it? I strongly doubt it and if so, what act has he committed that Napoleon, for instance, did not commit? Acts I, personally, consider abominable but I am astonished they should inspire so much horror in the Napoleonic incense-burners, in those who, on the day of the declaration of war, shrieked like General X: "I have been awaiting this day for forty years. It is the greatest day of my life." Heaven knows if anyone protested more loudly than I when society gave a disproportionate position to the Nationalists, to soldiers, when every friend of the Arts was accused of doing things which were injurious to the Fatherland, when every unwarlike civilisation was considered deleterious. Hardly an authentic social figure counted in comparison with a general. Some crazy woman or other nearly introduced me to M. Syveton! You will tell me that all I was concerned to uphold were laws of society; but, in spite of their apparent frivolity, they might perhaps have prevented many excesses. I have always honoured those who defend grammar and logic and it is only realised fifty years later that they have averted great dangers. And our Nationalists are the most Germanophobe, the most Diehard of men, but during the last fifteen years their philosophy has entirely changed. As a fact, they are now urging the continuation of the war, but it is only to exterminate a belligerent race and from love of peace. For the warlike civilisation they thought so beautiful fifteen years ago now horrifies them; not only do they reproach Prussia with having allowed the military element in her country to predominate, but they consider that at all periods military civilisations were destructive of everything they have now discovered to be precious, including in the Arts that of gallantry. It suffices for one of their critics to be converted to nationalism for him to become at once a friend of peace; he is persuaded that in all warlike civilisations women play a humiliating and lowly part. One does not venture to reply that the ladies of the Knights in the Middle Ages and Dante's Beatrice were perhaps placed on a throne as elevated as M. Becque's heroines. I am expecting one of these days to find myself placed at table below a Russian revolutionary or perhaps only below one of our generals who make war because of their horror of war and in order to punish a people for cultivating an ideal which they themselves considered the only invigorating one fifteen years ago. The unhappy Czar was still honoured some months ago because he called the Conference of the Hague, but now that we are saluting free Russia we forget her only title to glory; thus the wheel of the world turns.

'And yet Germany uses so many of the same expressions as France that one might think that she's copying her. She never stops saying that she is fighting for her existence. When I read: "We are fighting against an implacable and cruel enemy until we have obtained a peace which will guarantee our future against all aggression and in order that the blood of our brave soldiers should not have been shed in vain", or "who is not with us is against us", I do not know if this phrase is Emperor William's or M. Poincaré's, for each one has used the same words with variations twenty times, though to tell you the truth I must confess that the Emperor in this case was the imitator of the President of the Republic. France would not perhaps have held to prolonging the war if she had remained weak, but neither would Germany perhaps have been in such a hurry to finish it if she had not ceased to be strong, I mean, to be as strong as she was, for you will see she is still strong enough.'

He had got into the habit of talking very loud from nervousness, from seeking relief from impressions which, having never cultivated any art, he felt impelled to cast forth, as an aviator his bombs, into an open field where his words struck no one, and especially in society where they fell haphazard and where he was listened to with attention owing to snobbishness and where he so tyrannised his audience that one could say it was intimidated. On the boulevards this harangue was, moreover, a mark of his scorn for passers-by on whose account he no more lowered his voice than he would have moved aside for them. But there his voice exploded and astounded, and, especially when his remarks were sufficiently intelligible for passers-by to turn round, the latter might have had us arrested as defeatists. I drew M. de Charlus' attention to this but succeeded only in exciting his hilarity: 'Admit that it really would be funny,' he said. 'After all, one never knows, any one of us risks every evening being in the news column the following day; and, if it comes to that, why shouldn't I be shot in the ditch of Vincennes? The same thing happened to my great-uncle the Duc d'Enghien. Thirst for noble blood delights the populace which in this respect displays more refinement than lions. As to those animals, you know, if Mme Verdurin only had a scratch on her nose, she'd say they had sprung upon, what in my youth one would have called her *pif*.' And he began to laugh with his mouth wide open as though he had been alone in a room.

At moments, seeing certain rather suspicious individuals emerging from a gloomy passage near where M. de Charlus was passing and congregating at some distance from him, I wondered whether he would prefer me to leave him alone or stay with him. Thus, one who met an old man subject to epileptic fits whose incoherent behaviour foreshadowed the probable imminence of an attack, would ask himself whether his company is desired as a support or feared as that of a witness from whom he might wish to hide the attack and whose mere presence perhaps might induce it whereas complete quiet might prevent it, while the possible event from which he cannot decide whether to fly or not, is revealed by the zigzag walk of the patient, similar to that of a drunken man. In the present case of M. de Charlus, the various divergent positions, signs of a possible incident of which I was not sure whether he wished it to happen or feared that my presence would prevent it, were, by an ingenious setting, not assumed by the baron himself who was walking straight on, but by a whole company of actors. All the same I think he preferred avoiding the encounter for he drew me into a side street more obscure than the boulevard and where there was a constant stream of soldiers of every army and of every nation, a juvenile influx compensating and consoling M. de Charlus for the reflux of all those men to the frontier which had caused that frightful void in Paris in the first days of the mobilisation. M. de Charlus unceasingly admired the brilliant uniforms passing before us which made Paris as cosmopolitan as a port, as unreal as a painted scene composed of architectural forms making a background for the most varied and seductive costumes.

He retained all his respect and affection for certain *grandes dames* who were accused of defeatism, just as he did for those who had formerly been accused of Dreyfusism. He only regretted that in condescending to be political, they should have given a hold to 'the polemics of journalists'. His view was unchanged so far as they were concerned. For his frivolity was so systematic that birth combined with beauty and other glamours was the lasting thing, and the war, like the Dreyfus Affair, a vulgar and fugitive fashion. Had the Duchesse de Guermantes been shot as an overture to a separate peace with Austria, he would have considered it heroic and no more degrading than it seems today that Marie Antoinette was sentenced to decapitation. At that moment, M. de Charlus, looking as noble as a St Vallier or a St Mégrin, was erect, rigid, solemn, spoke gravely, making none of those gestures and movements which reveal those of his kind. Yet why is it there are none whose voice is just right? At the very moment when he was talking of the most serious things, there was still that false note which needed tuning.

And M. de Charlus literally did not know which way to look next, raising his head as though he felt the need of an opera-glass, which, however, would not have been much use to him, for, on account of the zeppelin raid of the previous day having aroused the vigilance of the public authorities, there were soldiers right up to the sky. The aeroplanes I had seen some hours earlier, like insects or brown spots upon the evening blue, continued to pass into the night deepened still more by the partial extinction of the street lamps like luminous faggots. The greatest impression of beauty given us by these flying human stars was perhaps that of making us look at the sky whither one rarely turned one's eyes in that Paris of which in 1914 I had seen the almost defenceless beauty awaiting the menace of the approaching enemy. Certainly there was now, as then, the ancient unchanged splendour of a moon cruelly, mysteriously serene, which poured upon the still intact monuments the useless loveliness of her light, but, as in 1914, and more than in 1914, there was something else, other lights and intermittent beams which, one realised, whether they came from aeroplanes or from the searchlights of the Eiffel Tower, were directed by an intelligent will, by a protective vigilance which caused that same emotion, inspired that same gratitude and calm I had experienced in Saint-Loup's room, in the cell of that military cloister where so many fervent and disciplined hearts were being prepared for the day when without a single hesitation they were to consummate their sacrifice in the fullness of youth.

During the raid of the evening before the sky was more agitated than the earth; when it was over, the sky became comparatively calm but, like the sea after a tempest, not completely so. Aeroplanes rose like rockets into the sky to rejoin the stars, and searchlights moved slowly across the sky divided into sections by their pale star dust like wandering Milky Ways. The aeroplanes so mingled with the stars that one could almost imagine oneself in another hemisphere looking at new constellations.

M. de Charlus expressed his admiration for these aviators and, as he could no more help giving free play to his Germanophilism than to his other inclinations, although he denied both, said to me: 'Moreover, I must add that I admire the Germans in their Gothas just as much. And think of the courage that is needed to go in those zeppelins. They are simply heroes. And if they do throw their bombs upon civilians, don't our batteries fire upon theirs? Are you afraid of Gothas and cannon?' I avowed that I was not, but perhaps I was wrong. Having got into the habit, through idleness, of postponing my work from day to day, I doubtless supposed death might deal in the same way with me. How could one be afraid of a shell which you are convinced will not strike you that day? Moreover, these isolated ideas of bombs thrown, of possible death, added nothing tragic to the image I had formed of the passing German airships, until, one evening, I might see a bomb thrown towards us from one of them as it was tossed and segmented in the storm-clouds or from an aeroplane which, though I knew its murderous errand, I had till then regarded as celestial. For the ultimate reality of danger is only perceived through something new and irreducible to what one has previously known which we call an impression and which is often, as was the case now, summed up in a line, a line which would disclose a purpose, a line in which there was a latent power of action which modified it; thus upon the Pont de la Concorde around the menacing and pursued aeroplane, as though the fountains of the Champs Elysées, of the Place de la Concorde, of the Tuileries, were reflected in the clouds, searchlights like jets of luminous water pierced the sky like arrows, lines full of purpose, the foreseeing and protective purpose of powerful and wise men towards whom I felt that same gratitude as on the night in quarters at Doncières when their power deigned to watch over us with such splendid precision.

The night was as beautiful as in 1914 when Paris was equally menaced. The moonbeams seemed like soft, continuous magnesium light offering for the last time nocturnal visions of beautiful sites such as the Place Vendôme and the Place de la Concorde, to which my fear of shells which might destroy them lent a contrasting richness of as yet untouched beauty as though they were offering up their defenceless architecture to the coming blows. 'You are not afraid?' repeated M. de Charlus. 'Parisians do not seem to realise their danger. I am told that Mme Verdurin gives parties every day. I only know it by hearsay for I know absolutely nothing about them; I have entirely broken with them,' he added, lowering not only his eyes as if a telegraph boy had passed by, but also his head and his shoulders and lifting his arms with a gesture that signified: 'I wash my hands of them!' 'At least I can tell you nothing about them' (although I had not asked him). 'I know that Morel goes there a great deal' (it was the first time he had spoken to me about him). 'It is suggested that he much regrets the past, that he wants to make it up with me again,' he continued, showing simultaneously the credulity of a suburban who remarks: 'It is commonly said that France is negotiating more than ever with Germany, even that *pourparlers* are taking place' and of the lover whom the worst rebuffs cannot discourage. 'In any case, if he wants to, he has only to say so. I am older than he is and it is not for me to take the first step.' And indeed the uselessness of his saying so was abundantly evident. But, besides, he was not even sincere and for that reason one was embarrassed about M. de Charlus because, when he said it was not for him to take the first step, he was, on the contrary, making one and was hoping that I should offer to bring about a reconciliation. Certainly I knew the naive or assumed credulity of those who care for someone or even who are simply not invited by him, and impute to that person a wish he has never expressed in spite of fulsome importunities.

It must here be noted, that, unhappily, the very next day, M. de Charlus suddenly found himself face to face with Morel in the street. The latter in order to excite his jealousy took him by the arm and told him some tales that were more or less true and when M. de Charlus, bewildered and urgently wanting Morel to stay with him that evening, entreated him not to go away, the other, catching sight of a friend, said goodbye. M. de Charlus, in a fury, hoping that the threat which, as may be imagined, he was never likely to execute, would make Morel remain with him, said to him: 'Take care, I shall be revenged', and Morel turned away with a laugh, smacking his astonished friend on the back and putting his arm round him. From the sudden tremulous intonation with which M. de Charlus, in talking of Morel, had emphasised his words, from the pained expression in the depth of his eyes, I had the impression that there was something more behind his words than ordinary insistence. I was not mistaken and I will relate at once the two incidents which later proved it. (I am anticipating by many years in regard to the second of these incidents, which was after the death of M. de Charlus and that only occurred at a much later period. We shall have occasion to see him again several times, very different from the man we have hitherto known and in particular, when we see him the last time, it will be at a period when he had completely forgotten Morel.)

The first of these events happened only two years after the evening when I was walking down the boulevards, as I say, with M. de Charlus. I met Morel. Immediately I thought of M. de Charlus, of the pleasure it would give him to see the violinist, and I begged the latter to go and see him, were it only once. 'He has been good to you,' I told Morel. 'He is now old, he might die, one must liquidate old quarrels and efface their memory.' Morel appeared entirely to share my view as to the desirability of a reconciliation. Nevertheless, he refused categorically to pay a single visit to M. de Charlus. 'You are wrong,' I said to him. 'Is it obstinacy or indolence or perversity or ill-placed pride or virtue (be sure that won't be attacked), or is it coquetry?' Then the violinist, distorting his face into an avowal which no doubt cost him dear, answered with a shiver: 'No, it is none of those reasons. As to virtue, I don't care a damn, as to perversity, on the contrary, I'm beginning to pity him, nor is it from coquetry, that would be futile. It is not from idleness, there are days together when I do nothing but twiddle my thumbs. No, it has nothing to do with all that, it is – I beg you tell no one, and it is folly for me to tell you – it's – it's because I'm afraid.' He began trembling in all his limbs. I told him I did not understand what he meant. 'Don't ask me; don't let us say any more about it. You don't know him as I do. I could tell you things you've no idea of.' 'But what harm could he do you? Less still if there were no resentment between you. And, besides, you know at bottom he is very kind.' 'Yes, indeed, I know it. I know that he is kind and full of delicacy and right feeling. But leave me alone, don't talk about it, I beg you, I'm ashamed that I'm afraid of him.'

The second incident dates from after the death of M. de Charlus. There were brought to me several *souvenirs* which he had left me and a letter enclosed in three envelopes written at least ten years before his death. But he had at that time been so seriously ill that he had made his will, then he had partially recovered before falling into the condition in which we shall see him later on the day of an afternoon party at the Princesse de Guermantes'. The letter had remained in a casket with objects he had left to certain friends, for seven years; seven years during which he had completely forgotten Morel.

The letter written in a very fine yet firm hand was as follows: 'My dear friend, the ways of Providence are sometimes inscrutable. It makes use of the sin of an inferior individual to prevent a just man's fall from virtue. You know Morel, you know where he came from, from what fate I wanted to raise him, so to speak, to my own level. You know that he preferred to return, not merely to the dust and ashes from which every man, for man is veritably a phoenix, can be reborn, but into the slime and mud where the viper has its being. He let himself sink and thus preserved me from falling into the pit. You know that my arms contain the device of Our Lord Himself: "*Inculcabis super leonem et aspidem*", with a man represented with a lion and a serpent at his feet as a heraldic support. Now if the lion in me has permitted itself to be trampled on, it is because of the serpent and its prudence which is sometimes too lightly called a defect, because the profound wisdom of the Gospel has made of it a virtue, at least a virtue for others. Our serpent whose hisses were formerly harmoniously modulated when he had a charmer – himself greatly charmed for that matter – was not only a musical reptile but possessed to the point of cowardice that virtue which I now hold for divine, prudence. It was this divine prudence which made him resist the appeals which I sent him to come and see me. And I shall have neither peace in this world nor hope of forgiveness in the next if I do not make this avowal to you. It is he who in this matter was the instrument of divine wisdom, for I had resolved that he should not leave me alive. It was necessary that one or the other of us should disappear. I had decided to kill him. God himself inspired his prudence to preserve me from a crime. I do not doubt but that the intercession of the Archangel Michael, my patron saint, played a great part in this matter, and I implore him to forgive me for having so much neglected him during many years and for having requited him so ill for the innumerable bounties he has shown me, especially in my fight against evil. I owe to his service, I say it from the fullness of my faith and my intelligence, that the Celestial Father inspired Morel not to come and see me. And now it is I who am dying. Your faithful and devoted *Semper idem*, P. G. Charlus.'

Then I understood Morel's fear. Certainly there were both pride and literature in that letter, but the avowal was true. And Morel knew better than I did that 'almost mad side' which Mme de Guermantes recognised in her brother-in-law and which was not limited, as I had supposed until then, to momentary outbursts of superficial and futile passion.

But we must retrace our steps. I am still walking down the boulevards beside M. de Charlus, who is using me as a vague intermediary for overtures of peace between him and Morel. Observing that I did not reply, he thus continued: 'As to that, I do not know why he doesn't play any more. Apparently there is no more music, under the pretext of the war, but they dance and dine out. These fêtes represent what will be perhaps, if the Germans advance further, the last days of our Pompeii. It only needs the lava of some German Vesuvius (their naval guns are not less terrible than a volcano) to surprise them at their toilet and eternalise their gesture by interrupting it; children will later on be educated by illustrations of Mme Molé about to put the last layer of paint on her face before going to dine with her sister-in-law, or Sosthène de Guermantes finishing painting her false eyebrows. It will be lecturing material for the Brichots of the future; the frivolity of a period after ten centuries is worthy of the most serious erudition, especially if it has been preserved intact by a volcanic irruption in which matter akin to lava was thrown by bombardment. What documents for future history! When asphyxiating gases analogous to those emitted by Vesuvius and earthquakes like those which buried Pompeii will preserve intact all the remaining imprudent women who have not fled to Bayonne with their pictures and their statues. Moreover, has it not been Pompeii, a bit at a time every evening, for more than a year? These people flying to their cellars, not to bring out an old bottle of Mouton-Rothschild or of St Emilion, but to hide themselves and their most precious possessions like the priests of Herculaneum surprised by death at the moment when they were carrying off the sacred vessels. Attachment to an object always brings death to the possessor. Paris was not, like Herculaneum, founded by Hercules. But what similarities force themselves upon one and that lucidity which has come to us is not only of our period, every period possessed it. If we think that tomorrow we may share the fate of the cities of Vesuvius, the women of those days believed they were menaced with the fate of the Cities of the Plain. They have discovered on the walls of one of the houses of Pompeii the inscription: "Sodom and Gomorra".' I do not know if it was this name of Sodom and the ideas which it aroused in him, or whether it was that of the bombardment which made M. de Charlus lift for an instant his eyes to Heaven, but he soon brought them down to earth again. 'I admire all the heroes of this war,' he said. 'My dear fellow, take all those English soldiers whom I thought of somewhat lightly at the beginning of the war as mere football-players presumptuous enough to measure themselves against professionals – and what professionals! Well, merely aesthetically they are athletes of Greece, yes, of Greece, my dear fellow, these are the youths of Plato or rather of the Spartans. A friend of mine went to their camp at Rouen and saw marvels of which one has no idea. It is no longer Rouen, it is another town. Of course there is still the old Rouen with the emaciated saints of the Cathedral. That is beautiful also, but it is another thing. And our *poilus*! I cannot tell you what a savour I find in our *poilus*, in our little "*parigots*". There, like that one who is passing so free and easy in that droll, wide-awake manner. I often stop and have a word with them. What quick intelligence, what good sense! And the boys from the Provinces, how nice they are with their rolling r's and their country jargon. I have always lived a great deal in the country, I have slept in the farms, I know how to talk to these people. But our admiration for the French must not allow us to underestimate our enemies, that diminishes ourselves. And you don't know what a German soldier is, you've never seen them as I have, on parade doing the goose-step in "Unter den Linden".' In returning to the ideal of virility he had touched on at Balbec which in the course of time had taken a philosophic form, he made use of absurd arguments and at moments, even when he showed superiority, these forced one to perceive the limitations of a mere man of fashion, even though he was an intelligent man of fashion; 'You see,' he said, 'that superb fellow, the German soldier, is a strong, healthy being, who only thinks of the greatness of his country, "Deutschland über Alles" which isn't as stupid as it sounds, and while they prepare themselves in virile fashion we are steeped in dilettantism.' That word probably signified to M. de Charlus something analogous to literature, for immediately, recalling without doubt that I loved literature and, for a time, had the intention of devoting myself to it, he tapped me on the shoulder (taking the opportunity of leaning on it until I felt as bad as I used to during my military service from the recoil of a '76') and remarked, as though to soften the reproach: 'Yes, we have ruined ourselves by dilettantism, all of us, you too, remember, you can repeat your *mea culpa* like me. We have all been too dilettante.' Through surprise at the reproach, lack of the spirit of repartee, deference towards my interlocutor and touched by his friendly kindness, I replied, as though, at his invitation, I ought also to strike my breast. And this was perfectly senseless, for I had not a shadow of dilettantism to reproach myself with. 'Well,' he said, 'I'll leave you', the knot of men which had escorted us some distance having at last disappeared, 'I'm going home to bed like an old gentleman, the war seems to have changed all our habits – one of Norpois' aphorisms.' As to that, I knew that M. de Charlus would not be less surrounded by soldiers because he was at home for he had transformed his mansion into a military hospital, yielding in that less to his obsession than to his good heart.

It was a clear, still night and, in my imagination, the Seine, flowing between its circular bridges, circular through a combination of structure and reflection, resembled the Bosphorus, the moon symbolising, maybe, that invasion which the defeatism of M. de Charlus predicted or the cooperation of our Mussulman brothers with the armies of France, thin and curved like a sequin, seemed to be placing the Parisian sky under the oriental sign of the crescent.

For an instant longer M. de Charlus stopped, facing a Senegalese and, in farewell took my hand and crushed it, a German habit, peculiar to people of the baron's sort, continuing for some minutes to knead it, as Cottard would have said, as though the baron wanted to impart to my joints a suppleness they had not lost. In the case of blind people touch supplements the vision to a certain extent; I hardly know which sense this kneading took the place of. Perhaps he believed he was only pressing my hand, as, no doubt, he also believed he was only glancing at the Senegalese who passed into the shadows and did not deign to notice he was being admired. But in both cases M. de Charlus made a mistake; there was an excess of contact and of staring. 'Is not the whole Orient of Decamps, of Fromentin, of Ingres, of Delacroix in all this?' he remarked, still immobilised by the departure of the Senegalese. 'You know that I am never interested in things and people except as a painter or as a philosopher. Besides, I'm too old. But what a pity, to complete the picture, that one of us two is not an odalisque.'

It was not the Orient of Decamps or even of Delacroix which began haunting my imagination when the baron left me, but the old Orient of the *Thousand and One Nights* which I had so much loved. Losing myself more and more in the network of black streets, I was thinking of the Caliph

Haroun Al Raschid in quest of adventures in the lost quarters of Bagdad. Moreover, heat, due to the weather and to my walking, had made me thirsty, but all the bars had been closed long since and on account of the shortage of petrol the few taxis I met, driven by Levantines or negroes, did not even trouble to respond to my signs. The only place where I could have obtained something to drink and have regained the strength to return home, would have been a hotel. But in the street, rather far from the centre, I had now reached, all the hotels had been closed since the Gothas began hurling their bombs on Paris. The same applied to nearly all the shops whose proprietors, owing to the dearth of employees or because they themselves had taken fright and had fled to the country, had left upon their doors the usual notice, written by hand, announcing their reopening at a distant and problematical date. Those establishments which survived, announced in the same fashion they they would only open twice a week, and one felt that misery, desolation and fear inhabited the whole quarter. I was the more surprised to observe, amongst these abandoned houses, one where, in contrast, life seemed to have conquered fear and failure and which seemed to be full of activity and opulence. Behind the closed shutters of every window, lights, shaded to conform to police regulations, revealed complete indifference to economy and every few moments the door opened to admit some new visitor. This hotel must have excited the jealousy of the neighbouring shopkeepers (on account of the money which its owners must be making) and my curiosity was aroused on noticing an officer emerge from it at a distance of some fifteen paces which was too far for me to be able to recognise him in the darkness.

Yet something about him struck me. It was not his face for I could not see it nor was it his uniform which was disguised in an ample cloak, it was the extraordinary disproportion between the number of different points past which his body flitted and the minute number of seconds employed in an exit, which resembled an attempted sortie by someone besieged. This made me believe, though I could not formally recognise him – whether by his outline, his slimness or his gait, or – even by his velocity but by a sort of ubiquity peculiar to him – that it was Saint-Loup. Whoever he was, the officer with this gift of occupying so many different points in space in so short a time, had disappeared, without noticing me, in a cross street, and I stood asking myself whether or not I should enter this hotel the modest appearance of which made me doubt if it was really Saint-Loup who had emerged from it.

I now remembered that Saint-Loup had got himself unhappily mixed up in an espionage affair owing to the appearance of his name in some letters seized upon a German officer. Full justice had been rendered him by the military authority but in spite of myself I related that fact to what I now saw. Was that hotel used as a meeting-place by spies? The officer had been gone some moments when I saw several privates of various arms enter and this added to my suspicions; and I was extremely thirsty. 'It is probable I can get something to drink here,' I said to myself and I took advantage of that to try and satisfy my curiosity in spite of my apprehensions.

I do not think, however, that it was curiosity which decided me to climb up the several steps of the little staircase at the end of which the door of a sort of vestibule was open, no doubt on account of the heat. I believed at first that I should not be able to satisfy it for I saw several people come and ask for rooms, to whom the reply was given that there was not a single one vacant. Soon I grasped that all the people of the place had against them was that they did not belong to that nest of spies, for an ordinary sailor presented himself and they immediately gave him No. 28. I was able, thanks to the darkness, without being seen myself, to observe several soldiers and two men of the working class who were talking quietly in a small, stuffy room showily decorated with coloured portraits of women out of magazines and illustrated reviews. The men were expressing patriotic opinions: 'There's no help for it, one must do like the rest,' said one. 'Certainly, I don't think I'm going to be killed,' another said in answer to a wish I had not heard, and who, I gathered, was leaving the following day for a dangerous post. 'Just think of it, at twenty-two! It would be pretty stiff after only doing six months!' he cried in a tone revealing, more even than a desire to live, the justice of his reasoning as though being only twenty-two ought to give him a better chance of not being killed, in fact, that it was impossible he should be. 'In Paris it's wonderful,' said another, 'one wouldn't think there was a war on. Are you joining up, Julot?' 'Of course I'm joining up. I want to go and have a smack at those dirty Boches.' 'That Joffre! He's a chap who slept with Minister's wives, he's not done anything.' 'It's rotten to hear that sort of stuff,' interrupted an aviator who was somewhat older, turning towards the last speaker, a workman. 'I advise you not to talk like that when you get to the front or the *poilus* will very soon have you out of it.' The banality of this conversation gave me no great desire to hear more and I was about to go up or down when my attention was roused by hearing the following words which made me tremble. 'It is extraordinary that the *patron* has not come back yet, at this time of night. I don't know where he'll find those chains.' 'But the other is already chained up.' 'Yes, of course he's chained – in a way. If I were chained like that I'd pretty soon free myself.' 'But the padlock is locked.' 'Oh! It's locked all right but if one tried, one could force it open. The trouble is the chains aren't long enough. You aren't going to explain that sort of thing to me, considering I was beating him the whole night till my hands bled.' 'Well, you'll have to take a turn at it tonight.' 'No, it's not my turn, it's Maurice's. It will be my turn on Sunday. The patron promised me.' Now I knew why the sailor's strong arms were needed. If peaceful citizens had been refused admittance, it was not because the hotel was a nest of spies. An atrocious crime was going to be consummated if someone did not arrive in time to discover it and have the guilty arrested. On this threatened yet peaceful night all this seemed like a dream story and I deliberately entered the hotel with the determination of one who wants to see justice done with the enthusiasm of a poet.

I lightly touched my hat and those present, without disturbing themselves, answered my salute more or less politely. 'Will you please tell me whom I can ask for a room and for something to drink?' 'Wait a minute, the *patron* has gone out.' 'But the chief is upstairs,' suggested one of them. 'You know perfectly well you can't disturb him.' 'Do you think they'll give me a room?' 'Yes, I believe so, 43 must be free,' said the young man who was sure of not being killed because he was only twenty-two, making room for me on the sofa beside him. 'It would be a good thing to open the window, there's an awful lot of smoke here,' said the aviator, and indeed each of them had a pipe or a cigarette. 'Yes, that's all right, but shut the shutters first; you know lights are forbidden on account of zeppelins.' 'There won't be any more zeppelins, the papers said that they'd all been shot down.' 'They won't come! They won't come! What do you know about it? When you've been fifteen months at the front as I have, when you've shot down your five German aeroplanes, then you'll be able to talk. It's absurd to believe the papers. They were over Compiègne yesterday and killed a mother with her two children.' The young man who hoped not to be killed and who had an energetic, open and sympathetic face spoke with ardent eyes and with profound pity. 'There's no news of big Julot. His godmother hasn't had a letter from him for eight days and it's the first time he has been so long without giving her any news.' 'Who's his godmother?' 'The lady who keeps the place of convenience below Olympia.' 'Do they sleep together?' 'What are you talking about, she's a perfectly respectable married woman. She sends him money every week because she's got a good heart. She's a jolly good sort.' 'So you know big Julot?' 'Do I know him?' The young man of twenty-two answered hotly. 'He's one of my most intimate friends. There aren't many I think as much of as I do of him, he's a good pal, always ready to do one a turn. It would be a bad look out if anything happened to him.' Someone proposed a game of dice and from the fevered fashion in which the young man cast them and called out the results with his eyes starting out of his head, it was easy to see that he had the temperament of a gambler. I could not quite grasp what someone else said to him just then but he suddenly cried in a tone of deep resentment. 'Julot a pimp! He may say he is but he bloody well isn't. I've seen him pay his women. Yes I have. I don't say that Algerian Jeanne hasn't ever given him a bit. But never more than five francs, a woman in a house, earning more than fifty francs a day. To think of a man letting a woman give him only five francs. And now she's at the front, she's having a pretty hard life, I admit, but she earns what she likes and she never sends him anything. Julot a pimp, indeed there'd be plenty of pimps at that rate. Not only he isn't a pimp, but I think he's a fool into the bargain.' The oldest of the party, whom no doubt the *patron* had entrusted with keeping a certain amount of order, having gone out for a moment, only heard the end of the conversation but he stared at me and seemed visibly annoyed at the effect which it might have produced upon me. Without specially addressing the young man of twenty-two who had been exposing and developing his theory of venal love, he remarked in a general way: 'You're talking too much and too loud. The window is open. People are asleep at this hour. You know, if the *patron* heard you, there would be trouble.'

Just at that moment there was a sound of a door opening, and everybody kept quiet, thinking it was the *patron*. But it was only a foreign chauffeur, whom everybody welcomed. When the young man of twenty-two, seeing the superb watch-chain extending across the newcomer's waistcoat, bestowed on him a questioning and laughing glance followed by a frown of his eyebrows at the same time giving me a severe wink, I understood that the first glance meant 'Hullo! Where did you steal that? All my congratulations!' and the second 'Don't say anything. We don't know this chap, so look out.' Suddenly the *patron* came in sweating, carrying several yards of heavy chains, strong enough to chain up several prisoners and said: 'I've got a nice load here. If all of you were not so lazy, I shouldn't be obliged to go myself.' I told him I wanted a room for some hours only, 'I could not find a carriage and I am not very well, but I should like to have something taken up to my room to drink.' 'Pierrot, go to the cellar and fetch some cassis and tell them to prepare No. 43. There's No. 7 ringing. They say they're ill! Nice sort of illness! They're after cocaine, they look half-doped. They ought to be chucked out. Have a pair of sheets been put in No. 22? There you are, there's No. 7 ringing again. Run and see. What are you doing there, Maurice? You know very well you're expected, go up to 14 bis, and look sharp!' Maurice went out rapidly, following the *patron* who was evidently annoyed that I had seen his chains. 'How is it you're so late?' enquired the young man of twenty-two of the chauffeur. 'What do you mean, so late, I'm an hour too early. But it's too hot to walk about, my appointment's only at midnight.' 'But who are you here for?' 'For Pamela la Charmeuse,' answered the oriental chauffeur, whose laugh disclosed beautiful white teeth. 'Ah!' exclaimed the young man of twenty-two.

Soon I was shown up to No. 43 but the atmosphere was so unpleasant and my curiosity so great that, having drunk my cassis, I descended the stairs, then, seized with another idea, I went up again and, without stopping at the floor where my room was, I went right up to the top. All of a sudden, from a room which was isolated at the end of the corridor, I seemed to hear stifled groans. I went rapidly towards them and applied my ear to the door. 'I implore you, pity, pity, unloose me, unchain me, do not strike me so hard,' said a voice. 'I kiss your feet, I humiliate myself, I won't do it again, have pity.' 'I won't, you blackguard,' replied another voice, 'and as you're screaming and dragging yourself about on your knees like that, I'll tie you to the bed. No mercy!' And I heard the crack of a cat-o'nine-tails, probably loaded with nails for it was followed by cries of pain. Then I perceived that there was a lateral peep-hole in the room, the curtain of which they had forgotten to draw. Creeping softly in that direction, I glided up to the peep-hole and there on the bed, like Prometheus bound to his rock, squirming under the strokes of a cat-o-nine-tails, which was, as a fact, loaded with nails, wielded by Maurice, already bleeding and covered with bruises which proved he was not submitting to the torture for the first time, I saw before me M. de Charlus. All of a sudden the door opened and someone entered who, happily, did not see me. It was Jupien. He approached the Baron with an air of respect and an intelligent smile. 'Well! Do you need me?' The Baron requested Jupien to send Maurice out for a moment. Jupien put him out with the greatest heartiness. 'We can't be heard, I suppose?' asked the Baron. Jupien assured him that they could not. The Baron knew that Jupien, though he was as intelligent as a man of letters, had no sort of practical sense, and talked in front of designing people with hidden meanings that deceived no one, mentioning surnames everyone knew.

'One second,' interrupted Jupien who had heard a bell ring in room No. 3. It was a Liberal Deputy who was going away. Jupien did not need to look at the number of the bell, he knew the sound of it, as the deputy came after luncheon every day. That particular day he had been obliged to change his hour because he had to attend his daughter's marriage at midday at St Pierre de Chaillot So he had come in the evening, but wanted to get away in good time because of his wife who got anxious if he came home late, especially in these times of bombardment. Jupien made a point of accompanying him to the door so as to show deference towards the honourable gentleman without any eye to his own advantage. For while the deputy repudiating the exaggerations of the Action Française (he would for that matter have been incapable of understanding a line of Charles Maurras or of Léon Daudet), was on good terms with Ministers who were flattered at being invited to his shooting parties, Jupien would never have dared to solicit the slightest help from him in his occasional difficulties with the police. He fully understood, if he had risked talking about such matters to the wealthy and timid legislator, he would not have been spared the most harmless raid but would instantly have lost the most generous of his customers. Having accompanied the deputy to the door, the latter pulled his hat over his eyes, raised his collar and gliding rapidly away as he did in his electoral campaigns, believed he was hiding his face. Jupien – going up again to M. de Charlus, said: 'It was M. Eugène.' At Jupien's, as in lunatic asylums, people were only called by their first names, but, to satisfy the curiosity of the habitués and increase the prestige of his house, he took care to add the surnames in a whisper. Sometimes, however, Jupien did not know the identity of his clients, so he invented them and said that this one was a stockbroker, another a man of title or an artist; trifling and amusing mistakes so far as those whom he wrongly named were concerned. He finally quite resigned himself to ignorance as to the identity of M. Victor. Jupien further had the habit of pleasing the Baron by doing the contrary of what is considered the right thing at certain parties: 'I am going to introduce M. Lebrun to you' (in his ear: 'he calls himself M. Lebrun but in reality he's a Russian Grand-Duke.') In another sense, Jupien did not think it interesting enough to introduce a milkman to M. de Charlus, but, with a wink: 'He's a sort of milkman, but over and above that he's one of the most dangerous *apaches* in Belleville.' (The rollicking way in which Jupien said '*apache*' was worth seeing). And as though this observation were not enough, he added others such as: 'He has been sentenced several times for stealing and burgling houses. He was sent to Fresnes for fighting (the same jolly air) with people in the street whom he half crippled and he has been in an African battalion where he killed his sergeant.'

The Baron was slightly annoyed with Jupien because he knew that everybody more or less in that house he had charged his factotum to buy and have run by an underling, owing to the indiscretions of the uncle of Mlle d'Oloran late Mme de Cambremer, was aware of his personality and his name (fortunately many believed it was a pseudonym and so deformed it that the Baron was protected by their stupidity, not by Jupien's discretion). Eased by the knowledge that they could not be overheard, the Baron said to him: 'I did not want to speak before that little fellow. He's very nice and does his best but he's not brutal enough. His face pleases me but he calls me a low debauchee as though he had learnt it by heart.' 'Oh dear no! No one has said a word to him,' Jupien answered without realising the unlikelihood of the assertion. 'As a matter of fact he was mixed up in the murder of a concierge in La Villette.' 'Indeed? That is rather interesting,' said the Baron with a smile. 'But I've just secured a butcher, a slaughterer, who looks rather like him; by a bit of luck he happened to look in. Would you like to try him?' 'Yes, with pleasure.' I watched the man of the slaughterhouse enter. He did look a little like 'Maurice' but, what was more curious, both of them were of a type that I had never been able to define but which I then realised was also exemplified in Morel; if not in his face as I knew it, at least in a cast of features that the eyes of love, seeing Morel differently from me, might have fitted into his countenance. From the moment that I had made within myself a model with features borrowed from my recollections of what Morel might represent to someone else, I realised that those two young men, of whom one was a jeweller's boy and the other a hotel employee, were vaguely his successors. Must one conclude that M. de Charlus, at all events on one side of his love-affairs, was always faithful to the same type and that the lust which caused him to select these two young men was the same which had caused him to stop Morel on the platform of the station of Doncières, that all three resembled a little that youth whose form, engraved in the sapphire eyes of M. de Charlus, gave to his gaze the peculiar something which had frightened me on that first day at Balbec? Or, was it that his love for Morel had modified the type he favoured and he was now seeking men who resembled Morel to console himself for the latter's desertion? Another supposition was that perhaps in spite of appearances there had never been between Morel and himself any relations but those of friendship and that M. de Charlus had made Jupien procure these young men because they sufficiently resembled Morel for him to have the illusion that Morel was taking pleasure with him. It is true, bearing in mind all that M. de Charlus had done for Morel, that this supposition seems improbable, if one did not know that love forces great sacrifices from us for the being we love and sometimes the sacrifice of our very desire which, moreover, is the less easily exorcised because the being we love feels that we love him the more.

What takes away the likelihood of such a supposition was the highly strung and profoundly passionate temperament of M. de Charlus, similar in that respect to Saint-Loup, which might at first have played the same part in his relations with Morel, though a more decent and negative part, as his nephew's early relations with Rachel. The relations one has with a woman one loves (and that can apply also to love for a youth) can remain platonic for other reasons than the chastity of the woman or the unsensual nature of the love she inspires. The reason may be that the lover is too impatient and by the very excess of his love is unable to await the moment when he will obtain his desires by sufficient pretence of indifference. Continually, he returns to the charge, he never ceases writing to her whom he loves, he is always trying to see her, she refuses herself, he becomes desperate. From that time she knows, if she grants him her company, her friendship, that these benefits will seem so considerable to one who believed he was going to be deprived of them, that she need grant nothing more and that she can take advantage of the moment when he can no longer bear being unable to see her and when, at all costs, he must put an end to the struggle by accepting a truce which will impose upon him a platonic relationship as its preliminary condition. Moreover, during all the time that preceded this truce, the lover, in a constant state of anxiety, ceaselessly hoping for a letter, a glance, has long ceased thinking of the physical desire which at first tormented him but which has been exhausted by waiting and has been replaced by another order of longings more painful still if left unsatisfied. The pleasure formerly anticipated from caresses will later be accorded but transmuted into friendly words and promises of intercourse which brings delicious moments after the strain of uncertainty or after a look impregnated with such coldness that it seemed to remove the loved one beyond hope of his ever seeing her again. Women divine all this and know they can afford the luxury of never yielding to those who, from the first, have betrayed their inextinguishable desire. A woman is enchanted if, without giving anything, she can receive more than she generally gets when she does give herself. On that account highly-strung men believe in the chastity of their idol. And the halo with which they surround her is also a product, but, as we see, an indirect one, of their excessive love. There is in woman something of the unconscious function of drugs which are cunning without knowing it, like morphine. They are not indispensable in the case of those to whom they give the blessings of sleep and real wellbeing. By such they will not be bought at their weight in gold, taken in exchange for everything the sick man possesses, it is by those other unfortunates (they may, indeed, be the same but altered in the course of years) to whom the drug brings no sleep, gives them no pleasure but who, without it, are a prey to an agitation to which they must at all costs put an end, even though to do so means death.

And M. de Charlus, whose case, with the slight difference due to the similarity of sex, can be included in the general laws of love, though he belonged to a family more ancient than the Capets themselves, rich and sought after by the most exclusive society, while Morel was nobody, might say to him as he had said to me: 'I am a prince and I desire your welfare', nevertheless Morel was his master if he did not yield to him. And perhaps, to know he was loved was sufficient to make him determine not to. The disgust of distinguished people for snobs who want to force themselves upon them, the virile man has for the invert, the woman for every man who is too much in love with her. M. de Charlus not only had every advantage, he might perhaps have offered immense bribes to Morel, yet it is likely that they would have been unavailing in opposition to the latter's will. M. de Charlus had something in common with the Germans to whom he belonged by his origin and who, in the war now proceeding, were, as the Baron too often repeated, conquerors on every front. But what use were their victories since each one left the Allies more resolved than ever to refuse them the peace and reconciliation they wanted? Thus Napoleon invaded Russia and magnanimously invited the authorities to present themselves to him. But no one came.

I went downstairs and entered the little ante-room where Maurice, uncertain whether they would call him back or not and whom Jupien had told to wait, was about to join in a game of cards with one of his friends. They were much excited about a croix-de-guerre which had been found on the floor and did not know who had lost it or to whom to send it back so that the rightful owner should not be worried about it. They then started talking about the bravery of an officer who had been killed trying to save his orderly. 'All the same there are good people amongst the rich. I would have got killed with pleasure for such a man as that!' exclaimed Maurice who evidently only managed to inflict his ghastly flagellations on the Baron from mechanical habit, ignorance, need of money and preference for making it without working although, perhaps, it gave him more trouble. And as M. de Charlus had feared, he was possibly a good-hearted fellow, and certainly he seemed plucky. Tears almost came into his eyes when he spoke of the death of the officer and the young man of twenty-two was equally moved. 'Ah! They're fine fellows! Poor devils like us have nothing to lose. But a gentleman who's got lots of stuff, who can go and take his *aperitif* every day at six o'clock, it's really a bit thick. One can jaw as much as one likes, but when one sees chaps like that die, really it's pretty stiff. God oughtn't to let rich people like that die, besides, they're useful to working people. The damned Boches ought to be killed to the last man of them for doing in a man like that. And look what they've done at Louvain, cutting off the heads of little children! I don't know, I am not any better than anyone else but I'd rather have my throat cut than obey savages like that; they aren't men, they are out and out savages, you can't deny it.' In fact all these boys were patriots. One, only slightly wounded in the arm, was not on such a high level as the others as he said, having shortly to return to the front: 'Damn it, I wish it had been a proper wound' (one which procures exemption) just as Mme Swann formerly used to say, 'I've succeeded in catching a tiresome influenza.'

The door opened again for the chauffeur who had gone to take the air for a moment. 'Hullo!' he said, 'is it over already? It wasn't long!' noticing Maurice who, he supposed, was engaged in whipping the man they nicknamed after a newspaper of that period, 'The man in chains'. 'It may not seem long to you who've been out for a walk,' answered Maurice, annoyed for it to be known that he had not pleased the customer upstairs, 'but if you'd been obliged to keep on whipping like me in this heat! If it weren't for the fifty francs he gives – !' 'Besides, he's a man who talks well, one feels he's had an education. Did he say it would soon be over?' 'He said we shan't get them, that it will end without either side winning.' '*Bon sang de bon sang*! He must be a Boche.' 'I told you you were talking too loud,' said a man older than the others, noticing me. 'Have you done with your room?' 'Shut up, you're not master here.' 'Yes, I've finished and I've come to pay.' 'You'd better pay the *patron*. Maurice, go and fetch him.' 'I don't want to disturb you.' 'It doesn't disturb me.' Maurice went upstairs and came back. 'The *patron* is coming down,' he said. I gave him two francs for his trouble. He blushed with pleasure: 'Thank you very much. I shall send them to my brother who's a prisoner. No, he's all right, it depends on the camp.'

Meanwhile, two extremely elegant customers in dress coats and white ties under their overcoats, they seemed Russians from their slight accent, were standing in the doorway deliberating if they should enter. It was visibly the first time they had come there. They must have been told where the place was and seemed divided between desire, temptation and extreme fright. One of the two, a handsome young man, kept repeating every minute to the other, with a half-questioning, half-persuasive smile, 'After all, we don't care a damn.' He might say he did not mind the consequences, but he was not so indifferent as his words suggested for his remark did not result in his entering but on the contrary, in another glance at his friend, followed by the same smile and the same, 'After all we don't care a damn.' It was this 'we don't care a damn', an example among thousands of that expressive language so different from what we generally speak, in which emotion makes us vary what we meant to say and in its place make use of phrases emerging from an unknown lake where live expressions without relation to one's thought and for that very reason reveal it. I remember that Albertine once, when Françoise noiselessly entered the room just at the moment when my friend was lying beside me naked, exclaimed in spite of herself, to warn me: 'Ah! here's that beauty Françoise.' Françoise, whose sight was not good, and who was crossing the room some distance from us, apparently saw nothing. But the abnormal words 'that beauty Françoise' which Albertine had never used in her life, spontaneously revealed their origin; Françoise knew they had escaped Albertine through emotion and understanding without seeing, went off muttering in her patois, the word '*poutana*'. Much later on, when Bloch having become the father of a family, married one of his daughters to a Catholic, an ill-bred person informed her that he had heard she was the daughter of a Jew and asked her what her name had been. The young woman who had been Miss Bloch since her birth, answered, pronouncing Bloch in the German fashion as the Duc de Guermantes might have done, that is, pronouncing the Ch not like 'K' but with the Germanic 'ch'.

To go back to the scene of the hotel (into which the two Russians had finally decided to penetrate – 'after all we don't care a damn') the *patron* had not yet come back when Jupien entered and rated them for talking too loud, saying that the neighbours would complain. But he stood dumbfounded on seeing me. 'Get out all of you this instant!' he cried. Immediately all of them jumped up, whereupon I said: 'It would be better if these young men stayed here and I went outside with you a moment.' He followed me, much troubled, and I explained to him why I had come. One could hear customers asking the *patron* if he could not introduce them to a footman, a choir boy, a negro chauffeur. All professions interested these old madmen; soldiers of all arms and the allies of all nations. Some especially favoured Canadians, feeling the charm of their accent which was so slight that they did not know whether it was of old France or of England. On account of their kilts and because of the lacustrine dreams associated with such lusts, Scotchmen were at a premium, and as every mania owes its peculiar character, if not its aggravation, to circumstances, an old man, whose prurient cravings had all been sated, demanded with insistence to be made acquainted with a mutilated soldier. Steps were heard on the stairs. With the indiscretion which was natural to him, Jupien could not resist telling me it was the Baron who was coming down, that he must not on any account see me but if I would enter the little room contiguous to the passage where the young men were, he would open the shutter, a trick he had invented for the Baron to see and hear without being seen and which would now operate in my favour against him. 'Only don't make a noise,' he said. And half pushing me into the darkness, he left me. Moreover, he had no other room to offer me, his hotel, in spite of the war, being full. The room I had just left had been taken by the Vicomte de Courvoisier who, having been able to leave the Red Cross at X— for two days, had come to amuse himself for an hour in Paris before returning to the Chateau de Courvoisier where he would tell the Vicomtesse he had been unable to catch the last train. He had no notion that M. de Charlus was only a few yards away from him and the former had as little, never having encountered his cousin at Jupien's house, the latter being ignorant of the carefully disguised identity of the Vicomte.

The Baron soon came in, walking with some difficulty on account of his bruises which he must, nevertheless, have got used to. Although his debauch was finished and he was only going in to give Maurice the money he owed him, he directed a circular glance upon the young men gathered there which was at once tender and inquisitive and evidently expected to have the pleasure of a quite platonic but amorously prolonged chat with each of them. I noticed in all the lively frivolity he displayed towards the harem by which he seemed almost intimidated, those twistings of the body and tossings of the head, those sensitive glances I had noticed on the evening of his first arrival at La Raspelière, graces inherited from one of his grandmothers whom I had not known and which, masked in ordinary life by more virile expressions, were coquettishly displayed when he wanted to please an inferior audience by appearing a *grande dame*.

Jupien had recommended them to the goodwill of the Baron by telling him they were hooligans of Belleville and that they would go to bed with their own sisters for a louis. In actual fact, Jupien was both lying and telling the truth. Better and more sensitive than he told the Baron they were, they did not belong to a class of miscreants. But those who believed them so talked to them with entire good faith as if these terrible fellows were doing the same. However much a sadist may believe he is with an assassin, his own pure sadist soul is not on that account changed and he is hypnotised by the lies of these fellows who aren't in the least assassins but who, wanting to turn an easy penny, wordily bring their father, their mother or their sister to life and kill them again, turn and turn about, because they get interrupted in their conversation with the customer they are trying to please. The customer is bewildered in his simplicity and, in his absurd conception of the guilty gigolo revelling in mass-murders, is astounded at the culprit's lies and contradictions.

All of them seemed to know M. de Charlus who stayed some time talking to each of them in what he thought was his vernacular, from pretentious affectation of local colour and also from the sadistic pleasure of mixing himself up in a crapulous life. 'It's disgusting,' he said, 'I saw you in front of Olympia with two street-women, just to get some coppers out of them. That's a nice way of deceiving me.' Happily for the young man who was thus addressed, he had no time to declare that he had never accepted coppers from a woman, which would have diminished the excitement of M. de Charlus, and he reserved his protest for the end of the latter's sentence, replying, 'Oh, no! I do not deceive you.' These words caused M. de Charlus a lively pleasure and as, in his own despite, his natural intelligence prevailed over his affectation, he turned to Jupien: 'It's nice of him to say that and he says it so charmingly, one would think it was true. And, after all, what does it matter whether it's true or not if he makes one believe it. What sweet little eyes he's got. Come here, boy, I'm going to give you two big kisses for your trouble. You'll think of me in the trenches, won't you? Is it very hard?' 'Oh, my God. There are days when a shell passes close to you!' and the young man began imitating the noise of a shell, of aeroplanes and so on. 'But one must do like the rest and you can be sure we shall go on to the end.' 'Till the end,' replied the pessimistic Baron in a melancholy tone. 'Haven't you read in the papers that Sarah Bernhardt said France would go on till the end? The French will let themselves be killed to the last man.' 'I don't doubt for a single instant that the French will bravely be killed to the last man,' M. de Charlus answered as though it were the most natural thing in the world, in spite of his having no intention of doing anything whatever, but with the intention of correcting any impression of pacifism he might give in moments of forgetfulness. 'I don't doubt it, but I am asking myself to what extent Mme Sarah Bernhardt is qualified to speak in the name of France – Ah, I seem to know this charming young man', pointing at another whom he had probably never seen. He saluted him as he would have saluted a prince at Versailles and, so as to profit by the opportunity and have a supplementary pleasure gratis, like when I was small and went with my mother to give an order to Boissier or Gouache and one of the ladies offered me a bonbon from one of the glass vases in the midst of which she presided, he took the hand of the charming young man and pressed it for a long time in his Prussian fashion, fixing his eyes upon him and smiling for the interminable time photographers used to take in posing us when the light was bad. 'Monsieur, I am charmed, I am enchanted to make your acquaintance. He has such lovely hair,' he said, turning to Jupien. Then he moved over to Maurice to give him his fifty francs and put his arm round his waist. 'You never told me you had lined an old Belleville bitch,' M. de Charlus guffawed with ecstasy, sticking his face close to that of Maurice. 'Oh, monsieur le Baron,' protested the gigolo whom they had forgotten to warn, 'how can you believe such a thing?' Whether it was false or whether the alleged culprit really thought it was an abominable thing he had to deny, the boy went on: 'To touch my own kind, even a German as it is war is one thing, but a woman and an old woman at that!' This declaration of virtuous principles had the effect of a cold water douche upon the Baron, who moved coldly away from Maurice, none the less giving him his money, but with the air of one who is 'put off', someone who has been 'done' but who doesn't want to make a fuss, one who pays but is dissatisfied.

The bad impression produced upon the Baron was, moreover, increased by the way in which the beneficiary thanked him: 'I am going to send this to my old people and I shall keep a little for my pal at the front.' These

touching sentiments disappointed M. de Charlus almost as much as did his
rather conventional peasant-like expression. Jupien sometimes warned them
that they had to be 'more vicious'. Then one of them with the air of
confessing something satanic would adventure: 'I'll tell you something,
Baron, but you won't believe me. When I was a boy I looked through the
keyhole and saw my parents embracing each other. Isn't that vicious? You
seem to believe that I'm drawing the long bow but I swear I'm not. It's the
exact truth.' This fictitious attempt at perversity which only revealed
stupidity and innocence, exasperated M. de Charlus. The most determined
burglar, robber or assassin would not have satisfied him for they do not talk
about their crimes, and, moreover, there is in the sadist – good as he may be,
indeed the better he is – a thirst for evil that malefactors cannot satisfy. The
handsome young man, realising his mistake, might say, 'he'd let him have it
hot and heavy', and push audacity to the point of telling the Baron to
'bloody well make a date' with him, the charm was dissipated. The humbug
was as transparent as in books whose authors insist on writing slang. In vain
the young man gave him details of all his obscenities with his women, M. de
Charlus was only struck by how little they amounted to. For that matter that
was not only the result of insincerity, for nothing is more limited than vice.
In that sense one can really use a common expression and say that one is
always turning in the same vicious circle.

'How simple he is, one would never say he was a Prince,' the habitués
commented when M. de Charlus had gone escorted downstairs by Jupien to
whom the Baron did not cease complaining about the decency of the young
man. From the dissatisfied manner of Jupien, he had been trying to train the
young man in advance and one felt that the false assassin would presently
get a good dressing down. 'He's quite contrary to what you told me,' added
the Baron so that Jupien should profit by the lesson for another time. 'He
seems to have a nice nature, he expresses sentiments of respect for his
family.' 'All the same, he doesn't get on with his father at all,' objected
Jupien, 'they live together but each goes to a different bar.' Obviously that
was rather a feeble crime in comparison with assassination but Jupien found
himself taken aback. The Baron said nothing more because, though he
wanted his pleasures prepared for him, he also needed the illusion that they
were not prepared. 'He's an out-and-out ruffian, he told you all that to take
you in, you're too simple,' Jupien added, to exculpate himself but in so doing
only wounded the pride of M. de Charlus the more. While talking of M. de
Charlus being a prince the young men in the establishment were deploring
the death of someone about whom the gigolos said, 'I don't know his name
but it appears he is a baron,' and who was no other than the Prince de Foux

(the father of Saint-Loup's friend). While the Prince's wife believed he was spending most of his time at the Club, in reality he was spending hours with Jupien chattering and telling stories about society in the presence of blackguards. He was a fine, handsome man like his son. It is extraordinary that M. de Charlus did not know that he shared his tastes; doubtless this was because the Baron had only seen him in society. People went so far as to say that he had actually gone to the length of practising these tastes upon his son when he was still at College, which was probably false. On the other hand, very well informed about habits many are ignorant of, he kept a careful watch upon the people his son frequented. One day a man of low extraction followed the young Prince de Foux as far as his father's mansion and threw a missive through a window which the father had picked up. But though this follower was not, aristocratically speaking, of the same society as M. de Foux, he was from another point of view, and he had no difficulty in finding among their common associates an intermediary who made M. de Foux hold his tongue by proving that it was the young man who had provoked the advance from a man much older than himself. And that was quite credible, the Prince de Foux having succeeded in protecting his son from bad company outside, but not from his heredity. It may be added that young Prince de Foux, like his father, unsuspected in this respect by people in society, went to extreme lengths with another class.

'He's said to have a million a year to spend,' said the young man of twenty-two to whom this statement did not seem incredible. Soon the sound of M. de Charlus's carriage was heard. At that moment I perceived someone accompanied by a soldier leaving a neighbouring room with a slow step, a person who looked to me like an old lady in a black dress. I soon saw my mistake, it was a priest; that rare and in France extremely exceptional thing, a bad priest. Apparently the soldier was chaffing his companion about the incompatability of his conduct with his cloth for the priest, holding his finger in front of his hideous face with the grave gesture of a doctor of theology, answered sententiously: 'Well, what do you expect of me, I am not' (I was expecting him to say a saint) 'an angel.' There was nothing for him to do but go and he took leave of Jupien, who, having returned from escorting the Baron, was going upstairs, but, owing to his bewilderment, the bad priest had forgotten to pay for his room. Jupien, whose presence of mind never abandoned him, rattling the box in which the customers' contributions were put remarked: 'For the expenses of the service, Monsieur l'Abbé'. The repulsive personage apologised, handed over his money and departed.

Jupien came and fetched me from the obscure cavern whence I had not dared move. 'Go into the vestibule for a moment where the young men are sitting – it's quite all right as you're a lodger – while I go and shut up your room.' The *patron* was there and I paid him. At that moment, a young man in a dinner-jacket entered and with an air of authority demanded of the *patron*: 'Can I have Léon tomorrow morning at a quarter to eleven instead of eleven because I'm lunching out?' 'That depends on how long the Abbé keeps him,' the *patron* answered. This appeared to dissatisfy the young man in the dinner-jacket who seemed about to curse the Abbé but his anger took another form when he perceived me. Going straight up to the *patron*, he asked in an angry voice: 'Who's that? What does this mean?' The *patron*, much embarrassed, explained that my presence was of no importance, I was merely a lodger. The young man in the dinner-jacket was by no means appeased by this explanation and kept on repeating: 'This is extremely unpleasant; it's the sort of thing that ought not to happen. You know I hate it and I shan't put my foot inside this place again.' The execution of the threat did not seem, however, to be imminent for though he went away in a rage, he again expressed the wish that Léon should be free at a quarter to eleven if not at half-past ten. Jupien returned and took me downstairs. 'I don't want you to have a bad opinion of me,' he said, 'this house doesn't bring in as much money as you might think. I'm obliged to have respectable lodgers, though, if I depended only on them, I should lose money. Here to the contrary of the Mount Carmels, it is thanks to vice that virtue can exist. If I've taken this house, or rather, if I have had it taken by the *patron* whom you've seen, it's only to render service to the Baron and to distract his old age.' Jupien did not want to talk only about sadistic performances like those I had seen or about the Baron's vices. The latter even for conversation, for company or to play cards with, now only liked common people who exploited him. Doubtless, snobbishness about low company is just as comprehensible as the opposite. In the case of M. de Charlus, the two kinds had long been interchangeable; no one in society was smart enough to associate with and in the underworld, no one was base enough. 'I hate anything middling,' he said, 'the bourgeois comedy is irksome. Give me either princesses of classical tragedy or broad farce, no half-and-half, *Phèdre* or *Les Saltimbanques*. But, talk as he might, the equilibrium between these two forms of snobbery had been upset. Whether owing to an old man's fatigue or the extension of sensuality to the most banal intercourse, the Baron only lived now with inferiors. Thus unconsciously he was accepting succession from such of his great ancestors as the Duc de La Rochefoucauld, the Prince d'Harcourt, the Duc de Berry whom Saint-Simon exhibits as spending their lives with their lackeys who got enormous sums out of them, to such a point that when people went to see these great gentlemen they were shocked to find them familiarly playing cards and drinking with their servants. 'It's chiefly,' added Jupien, 'to save him being bored, because, you see, the Baron is a great baby. Even now, when he has got everything here he wants, he must run after adventures and play the villain. And, generous though he is, some time or other this behaviour may lead to trouble. Only the other day the *chasseur* of a hotel nearly died of fright because of the money the Baron offered him. Fancy! To come to his house, what imprudence! This lad, who only liked women, was very relieved when he understood what the Baron wanted. The Baron's promises of money made the lad believe he was a spy and he was consoled when he knew that he was not being asked to betray his country but only to surrender his body which is perhaps not any more moral but less dangerous and certainly easier.' Listening to Jupien I said to myself: 'What a pity M. de Charlus is not a novelist or a poet, not in order to describe what he sees, but the stage reached by M. de Charlus in relation to desire causes scandals to arise round him, forces him to take life seriously, to emotionalise pleasure, prevents him from becoming static through taking a purely ironical and exterior view of things, reopens in him a constant source of pain. Almost every time he makes overtures, he risks outrage if not prison. Not the education of children but that of poets is accomplished by blows. Had M. de Charlus been a novelist, the protection the house controlled by Jupien afforded him (though a police raid was always on the cards) by reducing the risks he ran from casual street encounters, would have been a misfortune for him. But M. de Charlus was only a dilettante in Art who did not dream of writing and had no gift for it.

'Moreover, I'll admit to you,' continued Jupien, 'that I haven't much scruple about making money out of this sort of job. I can't disguise from you that I like it, that it's to my taste. And is it a crime to get a salary for things one doesn't consider wrong? You are better educated than I am and doubtless you will tell me that Socrates did not consider he was justified in receiving money for his lessons. But in our day professors of philosophy are not like that, nor are doctors nor painters nor playwrights nor theatrical managers. Don't imagine that this business forces one to associate only with low people. It is true that the manager of an establishment of this kind, like a great courtesan, only receives men but he receives men who are important in all sorts of ways and who are generally on equal terms with the most refined, the most sensitive and the most amiable of their kind. This house might easily be transformed, I assure you, into an intellectual bureau and a news agency.' But I was still occupied with thinking of the blows I had seen M. de Charlus receive.

And, to tell the truth when one knew M. de Charlus, his pride, his satiation with social amusements, his caprices which changed so readily into passion for men of the worst class and of the lowest kind, one could easily understand that he was glad to possess the large fortune which, when enjoyed by a parvenu, enables him to marry his daughter to a duke and to invite Highnesses to his shooting parties, and permitted him to exercise authority in one, perhaps in several, establishments where there were permanently young men with whom he took his pleasure. Perhaps, indeed, he did not need to be vicious for that. He was the successor of so many great gentlemen and princes of the blood or dukes who, Saint-Simon tells us, never associated with anyone fit to speak to.

'Meanwhile,' I said to Jupien: 'this house is something very different, it is rather a pandemonium than a madhouse, since the madness of the lunatics who are there is placed upon the stage and visually reconstituted. I believed, like the Caliph in the *Thousand and One Nights*, that I had, at the critical moment, come to the rescue of a man who was being ill-treated and another story of the *Thousand and One Nights* was realised before my eyes, in which a woman is changed into a dog and allows herself to be beaten in order to regain her former shape.' Jupien, realising that I had seen the Baron being whipped, was much concerned. He remained silent a moment, then, suddenly, with that pretty wit of his own that had so often struck me when he greeted Françoise or myself in the courtyard of our house with such graceful phrases: 'You talk of stories in the *Thousand and One Nights*' he said. 'I know one which is not without relevance to the title of a book which I caught sight of at the Baron's house' (he was alluding to a translation of Ruskin's *Sesame and Lilies* which I had sent to M. de Charlus). 'If you ever wanted one evening to see, I won't say forty but ten thieves, you have only to come here; to be sure I'm there, you have only to look up and if my little window is left open and the light is on, it will mean that I am there and that you can come in; that is my Sesame. I only refer to Sesame; as to the Lilies, if you're seeking for them I advise you to look elsewhere', and saluting me somewhat cavalierly, for an aristocratic connection and a band of young men whom he controlled like a pirate-chief had given him a certain familiarity, he took leave of me. He had hardly left me when blasts of a siren were immediately followed by violent barrage firing. It was evident that a German aviator was hovering close over our heads and suddenly a violent explosion proved that he had hurled one of his bombs.

Many who had not wanted to run away had collected in the same room at Jupien's. Though they did not know each other they belonged more or less to the same wealthy and aristocratic society. The aspect of each inspired a repugnance due, doubtless, to their indulging in degrading vices. The face of one of them, an enormous fellow, was covered with red blotches like a drunkard's. I afterward learnt that, at first, he was not one but enjoyed making youths drink and that, later on, in fear of being mobilised, (though he seemed to be over fifty) as he was very fat, he started to drink without stopping until he exceeded the weight of a hundred kilos, beyond which men were exempted. And now the trick had turned into a passion, and however much people tried to prevent him, he always went back to the liquor-merchant. But the moment he spoke one could see, in spite of his mediocre intelligence, that he was a man of considerable education and culture. Another young society man of remarkably distinguished appearance, came in. In his case, there were as yet no exterior stigmata of vice but, what was worse, there were internal ones. Tall, with an attractive face, his manner of speech indicated a different order of intelligence to that of his alcoholic neighbour, indeed, without exaggeration, a very remarkable one. But whatever he said was accompanied by a facial expression suited to a different remark. Though he owned a complete storehouse of human expressions, he might have lived in another world, for he used them in the wrong order and seemed to scatter smiles and glances haphazard without relation to the remarks he was making or hearing. I hope for his sake if, as seems likely, he is still alive, that he was not the victim of an organic disease but of a passing disorder. Probably, if those men had been ordered to produce their visiting cards one would have been surprised to observe that they all belonged to the upper class of society. But every sort of vice and the greatest vice of all, lack of will which prevents a man from resisting it, brought them together there, in separate rooms, it is true, but every evening, I was told, so that if ladies in society still knew their names, they were gradually forgetting their faces. They still received invitations but habit always brought them back to that composite resort of evil repute. They concealed it but little from themselves, being in this respect different from the little chasseurs, workmen, etcetera, who ministered to their pleasure. And besides many obvious reasons this can be explained by the following one. For a commercial employee or a servant to go there was like a respectable woman going to a place of assignation. Some of them who had been there refused ever again to do so and Jupien himself telling lies to save their reputation or to prevent competition, declared: 'Oh, no, he doesn't come to my place and he wouldn't want to.' For men in society it is of less importance, in that other people in society do not go to such places and neither know anything about them nor concern themselves with other people's business.

At the beginning of the alarm I had left Jupien's house. The streets had become entirely dark. Only now and then an enemy aeroplane which was flying low enough cast a light on the spot where he was going to throw a bomb. I could no longer find my way and thought of that day when going to La Raspelière I had met an aviator like a god reining back his horse. I was thinking that this time the encounter would have a different end, that the God of Evil would kill me. I hurried my steps to escape like a traveller pursued by a waterspout, yet I turned in a circle round dark places from which I could not escape. At last the flames of a fire lighted me and I was able to rediscover my road whilst the cannon boomed unceasingly. But my thought turned elsewhere. I thought of Jupien's house now reduced perhaps to cinders for a bomb had fallen quite close to me just as I was coming out of that house upon which M. de Charlus might prophetically have written 'Sodom' as an unknown inhabitant of Pompeii had done with no less prescience when, possibly, as a prelude to the catastrophe, the volcanic eruption began. But what did sirens or Gothas matter to those who had come there bent on gratifying their lusts? We never think of the framework of nature which surrounds our passion. The tempest rages on the sea, the ship heaves and pitches on every side, avalanches fall from the windswept sky and, at most, we allow ourselves to pause a moment, to ward off an inconvenience caused us by that immense scene, in which both we and the human body we desire, are the tiniest atoms. The premonitory siren of the bombs troubled the inhabitants of Jupien's house as little as would an iceberg. More than that, the menace of a physical danger freed them from the fear by which they had been so long unhealthily obsessed. It is false to believe that the scale of fears corresponds to that of the dangers which inspire them. One might be frightened of sleeplessness and yet not of a duel, of a rat and not of a lion. For some hours the police would be concerned only for the lives of the population, a matter of small consequence, for it did not threaten to dishonour them.

Some of the habitués, recovering their moral liberty were the more tempted by the sudden darkness in the streets. Some of these Pompeians upon whom the fire of Heaven was already pouring, descended into the Métro passages which were as dark as catacombs. They knew, of course, that they would not be alone there. And the darkness which bathes everything as in a new element had the effect, an irresistibly tempting one for certain people, of eliminating the first phase of lust and enabling them to enter, without further ado the domain of caresses which as a rule demands preliminaries. Whether the libidinous aim is directed towards a woman or a man, assuming that approach is easy and that the sentimentalities that go on eternally in a drawing-room in the daytime can be dispensed with, even in the evening, however ill-lit the street, there must, at least, be a preamble when only the eyes can devour the corn within the ear, when the fear of passers-by or even of the one pursued prevents the follower getting further than vision and speech. But in darkness the whole bag of tricks goes by the board, hands, lips, bodies, come into immediate play. Then there is the excuse of the darkness itself and of the mistakes it engenders if a bad reception is met with, but if on the contrary, there is the immediate response of a body which, instead of withdrawing, comes closer, the inference that the woman or the man approached is equally licentious and vicious, adds the additional thrill of being able to bite into the fruit without lusting after it with the eyes and without asking permission. And still the darkness continued. Plunged in this new element Jupien's habitués imagined themselves travellers witnessing a phenomenon of nature such as a tidal wave or an eclipse, and instead of indulgence in a prearranged debauch, were seeking fortuitous adventures in the unknown, and celebrating, to the accompaniment of the volcanic thunder of bombs – as though in a Pompeian brothel – secret rites in the tenebrous shadows of the catacombs.

To such events the Pompeian paintings at Jupien's were appropriate for they recalled the end of the French Revolution at the somewhat similar period of the Directoire which was now beginning. Already in the anticipation of peace, new dances organised in darkness so as not too openly to infringe police regulations, were rioting in the night. And as an accompaniment certain artistic opinions, less anti-German than during the first years of the war, enabled stifled minds to expand though a brevet of civic virtue was needed by him who ventured to express them. A professor wrote a remarkable book on Schiller of which the papers took notice. But before mentioning the author, the publishers inscribed the volume with a statement like a printing licence, to the effect that he had been at the Marne and at Verdun, that he had had five mentions, and two sons killed. Upon that, there was loud praise of the lucidity and depth of the author's work upon Schiller, who could be qualified as great as long as he was alluded to as a great Boche and not as a great German, and thus the articles were passed by the Censor.

As I approached my home I was meditating on how quickly the consciousness ceases to collaborate with our habits, leaving them to develop on their own account without further concerning itself with them and how astonished we are, when we base our judgment of an individual merely on externals as though they comprehended the whole of him, at the actions of a man whose moral or intellectual value may develop independently in a completely different direction. Obviously it was a fault of upbringing or the entire lack of upbringing combined with a preference for earning money in the easiest way (many different kinds of work might be easier as it happens, but does not a sick man fabricate a far more painful existence out of manifold privations and remedies than the often comparatively mild illness against which he thinks he is thus defending himself?) or at all events, in the least laborious way, which had caused these youths, so to speak, in complete innocence and for small pay to do things which gave them no pleasure and must at first have inspired them with the strongest repugnance. Accordingly one might consider them fundamentally rotten, but they were not only wonderful soldiers in the war, brave to a degree, but often good-hearted fellows if not decent people in civil life. They no longer realised what was moral or immoral in the life they led because it was that of their surroundings.

Thus, in studying certain periods of ancient history we are sometimes amazed to observe that people who were individually good, participated without scruple in mass assassinations and human sacrifices, which probably seemed to them perfectly natural things. For him who reads the history of our period two thousand years hence, it will in the same way seem to have allowed gentle and pure consciences to be plunged in a vital environment to which they adapted themselves, though it will then appear just as monstrously pernicious. And what is more, I knew no man more gifted with intelligence and sensibility than Jupien, for those charming acquisitions which constituted the intellectual fabric of his discourse, did not come to him from school instruction or from university culture which might have made him remarkable, while so many young men in society got no profit from them whatever. It was his spontaneous, innate sense, his natural taste which enabled him from occasional haphazard and unguided readings in his spare moments to compose his way of speaking so rightly that all the symmetries of language were set off and showed their beauty in it. Yet the business in which he was engaged could with good reason be considered, if one of the most lucrative, one of the lowest imaginable. As to M. de Charlus, disdain as he might 'what people say', how was it that a feeling of personal dignity and self-respect had not forced him to resist sensual indulgences for which the only excuse was complete insanity? It could only be that in his case, as in that of Jupien, the habit of isolating morality from a whole order of actions (which, for that matter, must occur in a function such as that of a judge, sometimes in that of a statesman and others) had been acquired so long ago that, no longer demanding his judgment or moral sentiment, it had become aggravated from day to day until it had reached a point where this consenting Prometheus had allowed himself to be nailed by force to the rock of pure matter.

Certainly I realised that therein a new phase declared itself in the disease of M. de Charlus which, ever since I first perceived and judged it as stage by stage it revealed itself to my eyes, had continued to evolve with ever-increasing speed. The poor Baron could not now be far distant from the final term, from death, if indeed that was not preceded, according to the predictions and hopes of Mme Verdurin, by a poisoning which at his age could only hasten his death. Nevertheless, perhaps I used an inaccurate expression in saying rock of pure matter. It is possible that a little mind still survived in that pure matter. This madman knew, in spite of everything, that he was mad, that he was the prey at such moments of insanity, since he knew perfectly well that the man who was beating him was no wickeder than the little boys in battle-games who draw lots to decide which of them is to play the Prussian and upon whom all the others fall in true patriotic ardour and pretended hatred. A prey to insanity into which, nevertheless, some of M. de Charlus' personality entered; for even in its aberrations, human nature (as in our loves and in our journeys) still betrays the need of faith through the exactions of truth. When I told Françoise about a church in Milan – a city she would probably never see – or about the Cathedral of Rheims – even about that of Arras! – which she would never be able to see since they had been more or less destroyed, she envied the rich people who were able to afford the sight of such treasures and cried with nostalgic regret: 'Ah, how wonderful it must be!' Yet she, who had lived in Paris so many years, had never had the curiosity to go and see Notre Dame! It was just because Notre Dame belonged to Paris, to the city where her daily life was spent and where in consequence it was difficult for our old servant (as it would have been for me if the study of architecture had not modified in certain respects Combray instincts) to situate the objects of her dreams. There is immanent in those we love a certain dream which we cannot always discern but which we pursue. It was my belief in Bergotte and in Swann which made me love Gilberte, my belief in Gilbert the Bad which had made me fall in love with Mme de Guermantes. And what a great sweep of ocean had been included in my love, the saddest, the most jealous, the most personal ever, for Albertine. In that love of one creature towards whom one's whole being is urged, there is already something of aberration. And are not the very diseases of the body, at least those closely associated with the nervous system, in some measure peculiar tastes or peculiar fears contracted by our organs, by our articulation, which thus discover for themselves a horror of certain climates as inexplicable and as obstinate as the fancy certain men display for a woman who wears an eyeglass, or for circus-riders? Who shall ever say with what lasting and curious dream that desire aroused time after time at the sight of a circus rider, is associated; as unconscious and as mysterious as is, for example, the influence of a certain town, in appearance similar to others but in which a lifelong sufferer from asthma is able, for the first time, to breathe freely.

Aberrations are like passions which a morbid strain has overlaid, yet, in the craziest of them love can still be recognised. M. de Charlus' insistence that the chains which bound his feet and hands should be of attested strength, his demand to be tried at the bar of justice and, from what Jupien told me, for ferocious accessories there was great difficulty in obtaining even from sailors (the punishment they used to inflict having been abolished even where the discipline is strictest, on shipboard), at the base of all this there was M. de Charlus' constant dream of virility proved, if need be, by brutal acts and all the illumination the reflections of which within himself though to us invisible, he projected on judicial and feudal tortures which embellished an imagination coloured by the Middle Ages. This sentiment was in his mind each time he said to Jupien: 'There won't be any alarm this evening anyhow, for I can already see myself reduced to ashes by the fire of Heaven like an inhabitant of Sodom', and he affected to be frightened of the Gothas not because he really had the smallest fear of them but to have a pretext the moment the sirens sounded of dashing into the shelter of the Métropolitain, where he hoped to get a thrill from midnight frictions associated in his mind with vague dreams of prostrations and subterranean dungeons in the Middle Ages. Finally his desire to be chained and beaten revealed, with all its ugliness, a dream as poetic as the desire of others to go to Venice or to keep dancing girls. And M. de Charlus held so much to the illusion of reality which this dream gave him that Jupien was compelled to sell the wooden bed which was in room No. 43, and replace it by one of iron which went better with the chains.

At last the maroon sounded as I arrived home. The noise of approaching firemen was announced by a small boy and I met Françoise coming up from the cellar with the butler. She had thought me dead. She told me that Saint-Loup had excused himself for coming in to see if he had not let his *croix de guerre* fall when calling that morning. He had only just noticed he had lost it and having to rejoin his regiment the next day had wanted at all costs to see if it was not at my house. He and Françoise had searched everywhere without success. Françoise believed he must have lost it before coming to see me, for, she said, she could almost have sworn he did not have it on when she saw him; in this she was mistaken, which shows the value of witnesses and of recollections.

I felt immediately by the unenthusiastic way they spoke of him that Saint-Loup had not produced a good impression on Françoise and the butler. Saint-Loup's efforts to court danger were the exact opposite of those made by the butler's son and Françoise's nephew to get themselves exempted, but judging from their own standpoint, Françoise and the butler could not believe that. They were convinced that rich people are always protected. For that matter had they even known the truth about Robert's heroic bravery, they would not have been moved by it. He never talked of 'Boches', he praised the bravery of the Germans, he had not attributed our failure to secure victory from the first day, to treason. That was what they wanted to hear and that was what they would have considered a mark of courage. So, while they continued searching for the *croix de guerre*, I, who had not much doubt as to where that cross had been lost, found them cold on the subject of Robert. Though Saint-Loup had been amusing himself in equivocal fashion that evening, it was only while awaiting news of Morel; he had been seized with longing to see him again, and had made use of all his connections to discover the corps Morel was in, supposing him to have joined up, but, so far, he had received only contradictory answers. I advised Françoise and the butler to go to bed but the latter was never in any hurry to leave Françoise since, thanks to the war, he had found a still more efficacious way of tormenting her than telling her about the expulsion of the nuns and the Dreyfus affair. That evening and whenever I was near them during the time I spent in Paris, I heard the butler say to poor, frightened Françoise: 'They're not in a hurry, of course; they're waiting for the ripe pear, the day that they take Paris they'll have no mercy.' 'My God! Blessed Virgin Mary!' cried Françoise, 'isn't it enough for them to have conquered poor Belgium. She suffered enough at the time of her "invahition".' 'Belgium, Françoise. Why! What they did to Belgium is nothing to what they'll do here.' The war having thrown upon the people's conversation-market a number of new expressions which they only knew visually through reading the papers without being able to pronounce them, the butler added, 'You'll see, Françoise they are preparing a new attack of a greater *enverjure* than ever before.' In protest, if not out of pity for Françoise or from strategic common-sense, at least for grammar's sake, I told them that the right way to pronounce the word was *envergure*, but I only succeeded in making Françoise repeat the terrible word every time I entered the kitchen. The butler, much as he enjoyed frightening his fellow-servant, was equally pleased to show his master, though he was only a former gardener of Combray and now a butler, that he was a good Frenchman of the order of St-André-des-Champs and possessed the privilege, since the declaration of the rights of man, to pronounce *enverjure*, with complete independence and not to accept orders on a matter which had nothing to do with his service and, in regard to which, in consequence of the Revolution, no one had any right to correct him, since he was my equal.

I had, therefore, the irritation of hearing Françoise talk about an operation of great *enverjure* with an insistence which was intended to prove to me that

that pronunciation was, in fact, not that of ignorance but of maturely-considered determination. The butler indiscriminately applied a suspicious 'they' to the Government and the papers: 'They talk of the losses of the Boches, they don't talk of ours which, it appears, are ten times greater. They tell us that they're at the last gasp, that they've got nothing to eat. I believe they've got a hundred times more to eat than we have. It's all very well but they've no right to humbug us like that. If they had nothing to eat they wouldn't be able to fight like the other day when they killed a hundred thousand youngsters less than twenty years old.' He thus continually exaggerated the triumphs of the Germans as he did formerly those of the Radicals, and told tales of their atrocities so as to make the victories of the enemy still more painful to Françoise who kept on exclaiming: 'Sainted Mother of Angels! Sainted Mother of God!' Sometimes he tried being unpleasant to her in another way by saying: 'For that matter, we're no better than they are. What we're doing in Greece is no nicer than what they did in Belgium. You'll see, we shall have the whole world against us and we shall have to fight the lot', while, actually, the exact contrary was the truth. On days when news was good he revenged himself on Françoise by assuring her the war would last thirty-five years and that if, by chance, a possible peace came, it would not last more than a few months and would be succeeded by battles in comparison with which those of today were child's play and that after them nothing would be left of France.

The victory of the Allies if not close at hand, seemed at any rate assured, and unfortunately it must be admitted that this displeased the butler. For, having identified the world war and the rest of it with his campaign against Françoise (whom he liked, all the same, just as one likes a person whom one daily enrages by defeating him at dominoes) victory was represented to him in terms of the first conversation he would have with her thereafter when he would be irritated by hearing her say: 'Well, it's finished at last, and they'll have to give us a great deal more than we gave them in '71.' Really, he always believed this must happen in the end, for an unconscious patriotism made him think, like all Frenchmen, who were victims of an illusion similar to my own ever since I had been ill, that victory like my recovery was coming tomorrow. He took the upper hand of Françoise by announcing that though victory might come about, her heart would bleed from it, because a revolution would swiftly follow and then invasion. 'Ah! That bloody old war, the Boches will be the ones to recover quick from it! Why, Françoise! They've already made hundreds of millions out of it. But don't you imagine they're going to give us a penny of it. They may put that in the papers,' he added for prudence sake and to be on the safe side, 'to keep people quiet just as they've been saying for three years that the war would be finished the next day. I can't understand how people can be such fools as to believe it.' Françoise was the more worried by his comments because, as a matter of fact, she had believed the optimists in preference to the butler and had seen that the war, which was to end in a fortnight in spite of the 'invahition of poor Belgium', lasted for ever, that there was no advance, a phenomenon of fixation of the fronts the sense of which she could not understand, and that one of her innumerable godsons to whom she gave everything she received from us, had told her that this, that and the other things were concealed from the public. 'All that will fall upon the working-class,' the butler remarked in conclusion, 'and they'll take your field from you, Françoise.' 'Oh, my God!' But he preferred miseries that were close at hand and devoured the papers, hoping to announce a defeat to Françoise, and awaited news like Easter eggs, which should be bad enough to terrify Françoise without his suffering material disadvantages therefrom. Thus a Zeppelin raid enchanted him because he could watch Françoise hiding in the cellar while he felt convinced that in so large a city as Paris, bombs would not just fall upon our house.

Then Françoise began to get back her Combray pacifism. She even began doubting the 'German atrocities'. 'At the beginning of the war they told us the Germans were assassins, brigands, regular bandits – *bbboches*.' (If she put several b's to Boches it was because it seemed plausible enough to accuse the Germans of being assassins but to call them Boches seemed almost impossible in its enormity). Still, it was rather difficult to grasp what mysteriously horrible sense Françoise gave to the word Boche since she was talking about the beginning of the war and uttered the word so doubtfully. For the doubt that the Germans were criminals might be ill-founded in fact but did not in itself contain a contradiction from a logical point of view but how could anyone doubt that they were Boches since that word in the popular tongue means German and nothing else. Perhaps she was merely repeating violent comments she had heard at the time when a particular emphasis was given to the word Boche. 'I used to believe all that,' she said, 'but I'm now wondering if we aren't really just as big rogues as they are.' This blasphemous thought had been cunningly fostered in Françoise by the butler who, observing that his fellow-servant had a certain weakness for King Constantine of Greece, continually represented that we did not allow him to have any food until he surrendered. The abdication of the sovereign had further moved Françoise to declare: 'We're no better than they are. If we were in Germany we should do the same.'

I did not see much of her at that time as she often went to stay with cousins of hers about whom my mother one day said to me: 'You know, they're richer than you are.' In that connection a very beautiful thing happened, frequent enough at that period throughout the country, which, had there been historians to perpetuate its memory, would have borne witness to the grandeur of France, to the grandeur of her soul, that grandeur of St-André-des-Champs which was displayed no less by civilians at the rear than by the soldiers who fell at the Marne. A nephew of Françoise had been killed at Berry-au-Bac who was also a nephew of those millionaire cousins of Françoise, former café proprietors long since retired with a fortune. This young man of twenty-five, himself the proprietor of a little café, without other means, was called up and left his young wife to keep the little bar alone, hoping to return in a few months. He was killed and the following happened. These millionaire cousins of Françoise upon whom this young woman, widow of their nephew, had no claim whatever, left their home in the country to which they had retired ten years previously and again took over the café but without taking a penny. Every morning at six o'clock the millionaire wife, a true gentlewoman, dressed herself as did her young lady daughter to assist their niece and cousin by marriage, and for three years they washed glasses and served meals from early morning till half-past-nine at night without a day of rest. In this book in which there is not a single event which is not fictitious, in which there is not a single personage *à clef*, where I have invented every-thing to suit the requirements of my presentation, I must, in homage to my country, mention as personages who did exist in real life, these millionaire relations of Françoise who left their retirement to help their bereaved niece. And, persuaded that their modesty will not be offended for the excellent reason that they will never read this book, it is with childlike pleasure and deeply moved, that, unable to give the names of so many others who acted similarly and, thanks to whom France has survived, I here transcribe their name, a very French one, Larivière. If there were certain contemptible *embusqués* like the imperious young man in the dinner-jacket whom I saw at Jupien's and whose sole preoccupation was to know whether he could have Léon at half-past-ten because he was lunching out, they are more than made up for by the innumerable mass of Frenchmen of St-André-des-Champs, by all those superb soldiers beside whom I place the Larivières.

The butler, to quicken the anxieties of Françoise showed her some old *Readings for All* he had discovered somewhere, on the cover of which (the copies dated from before the war) figured 'The Imperial Family of Germany'. 'Here is our master of tomorrow,' said the butler to Françoise, showing her 'Guillaume'. She opened her eyes wide, then pointing at the feminine personage beside him in the picture, she added, 'And there is the Guillaumesse.'

My departure from Paris was retarded by news which, owing to the pain it caused me, rendered me incapable of moving for some time. I had learnt, in fact, of the death of Robert Saint-Loup, killed, protecting the retreat of his men, on the day following his return to the front. No man less than he, felt hatred towards a people (and as to the Emperor, for special reasons which may have been mistaken, he believed that William II had rather sought to prevent war than to unleash it). Nor did he hate Germanism; the last words I heard him utter six days before were those at the beginning of a Schumann song which he hummed to me in German on my staircase; indeed on account of neighbours I had to ask him to keep quiet. Accustomed by supreme good breeding to refrain from apologies, invective and phrase, in the face of the enemy he had avoided, as he did at the moment of mobilisation, whatever might have preserved his life by a self-effacement in action which his manners symbolised, even to his way of closing my cab door when he saw me out, standing bareheaded every time I left his house. For several days I remained shut up in my room thinking about him. I recalled his arrival at Balbec that first time when in his white flannels and his greenish eyes moving like water he strolled through the hall adjoining the large dining-room with its windows open to the sea. I recalled the uniqueness of a being whose friendship I had then so greatly desired. That desire had been realised beyond my expectation, yet it had given me hardly a moment's pleasure, and afterwards I had realised all the qualities as well as other things which were hidden under that elegant appearance. He had bestowed all, good and bad, without stint, day by day, and on the last he stormed a trench with utter generosity, putting all he possessed at the service of others, just as one evening he had run along the sofas of the restaurant so as not to inconvenience me. That I had, after all, seen him so little in so many different places, under so many different circumstances separated by such long intervals, in the hall of Balbec, at the café of Rivebelle, in the Doncières Cavalry barracks and military dinners, at the theatre where he had boxed a journalist's ears, at the Princesse de Guermantes', resulted in my retaining more striking and sharper pictures of his life, feeling a keener sorrow at his death than one often does in the case of those one has loved more but of whom one has seen so much that the image we retain of them is but a sort of vague average of an infinite number of pictures hardly different from each other and also that our sated affection has not preserved, as in the case of those we have seen for limited moments in the course of meetings unfulfilled in spite of them and of ourselves, the illusion of greater potential affection of which circumstances alone had deprived us. A few days after the one on which I had seen Saint-Loup tripping along behind his eye-glass and had

imagined him so haughty in the hall of Balbec there was another figure I had
seen for the first time upon the Balbec beach and who now also existed only
as a memory – Albertine – walking along the sand that first evening
indifferent to everybody and as akin to the sea as a seagull. I had so soon
fallen in love with her that, not to miss being with her every day I never left
Balbec to go and see Saint-Loup. And yet the history of my friendship with
him bore witness also to my having ceased at one time to love Albertine,
since, if I had gone away to stay with Robert at Doncières, it was out of grief
that Mme de Guermantes did not return the sentiment I felt for her. His life
and that of Albertine so late known to me, both at Balbec and both so soon
ended, had hardly crossed each other; it was he, I repeated to myself,
visualising that the flying shuttle of the years weaves threads between
memories which seemed at first to be completely independent of each
other, it was he whom I sent to Mme Bontemps when Albertine left me.
And then it happened that each of their two lives contained a parallel secret
I had not suspected. Saint-Loup's now caused me more sadness than
Albertine's for her life had become to me that of a stranger. But I could not
console myself that hers like that of Saint-Loup had been so short. She and
he both often said when they were seeing to my comfort: 'You are so ill', and
yet it was they who were dead, they whose last presentment I can visualise,
the one facing the trench, the other after her accident, separated by so short
an interval from the first, that even Albertine's was worth no more to me
than its association with a sunset on the sea.

Françoise received the news of Saint-Loup's death with more pity than
Albertine's. She immediately adopted her rôle of mourner and bewailed the
memory of the dead with lamentations and despairing comments. She
manifested her sorrow and turned her face away to dry her eyes only when I
let her see my own tears which she pretended not to notice. Like many
highly-strung people the agitation of others horrified her, doubtless because
it was too like her own. She wanted to draw attention to the slightest stiff
neck or giddiness she had managed to get afflicted with. But if I spoke of one
of my own pains she became stoical and grave and made a pretence of not
hearing me. 'Poor marquis!' she would say, although she could not help
thinking he had done everything in his power not to go to the front and,
once there, to escape danger.

'Poor lady!' she would say, alluding to Mme de Marsantes, 'how she must
have wept when she heard of the death of her son! If only she had been able
to see him again! But perhaps it was better she was not able to because his
nose was cut in two. He was completely disfigured.' And the eyes of
Françoise filled with tears through which nevertheless the cruel curiosity of

the peasant peered. Without doubt Françoise condoled with Mme de Marsantes with all her heart but she was sorry not to witness the form her grief had taken and that she could not luxuriate in the spectacle of her affliction. And as she liked crying and liked me to see her cry, she worked herself up by saying: 'I feel it dreadfully.' And she observed the traces of sorrow in my face with an eagerness which made me pretend to a kind of hardness when I spoke of Robert. In a spirit of imitation and because she had heard others say so, for there are *clichés* in the servants' quarters just as in coteries, she repeated, not without the complaisance of the poor: 'All his wealth did not prevent his dying like anyone else and it's no good to him now.' The butler profited by the opportunity to remark to Françoise that it was certainly sad but that it scarcely counted compared with the millions of men who fell every day in spite of all the efforts of the Government to hide it. But this time the butler did not succeed in causing Françoise more pain as he had hoped, for she answered: 'It's true they died for France too, but all of them are unknown and it's always more interesting when one has known people.' And Françoise who revelled in her tears, added: 'Be sure and let me know if the death of the marquis is mentioned in the paper.'

Robert had often said to me with sadness long before the war: 'Oh, don't let us talk about my life, I am doomed in advance.' Was he then alluding to the vice which he had until then succeeded in hiding from the world, the gravity of which he perhaps exaggerated as young people do who make love for the first time or who even earlier seek solitary gratification and imagine themselves like plants which cannot disseminate their pollen without dying? Perhaps in Saint-Loup's case this exaggeration arose as in that of children from the idea of an unfamiliar sin, a new sensation possessing an almost terrifying power which later on is attenuated. Or had he, owing to his father's early death, the presentiment of his premature end. Such a presentiment seems irrational and yet death seems subject to certain laws. One would think, for instance, that people born of parents who died very old or very young are almost forced to die at the same age, the former sustaining sorrows and incurable diseases till they are a hundred, the latter carried off, in spite of a happy, healthy existence at the inevitable and premature date by a disease so timely and accidental (however deep its roots in the organism) that it seems to be a formality necessary to the actuality of death. And is it not possible that accidental death itself – like that of Saint-Loup, linked as it was with his character in more ways than I have been able to say – is also determined beforehand, known only to gods invisible to man, but revealed by a special and semi-conscious sadness (and even expressed to others as sincerely as we announce misfortunes which, in our inmost hearts, we believe we shall escape and which nevertheless happen) in him who bears the fatal date and perceives it continuously within himself, like a device.

He must have been very beautiful in those last hours, he who in this life had seemed always, even when he sat or walked about in a drawing-room, to contain within himself the dash of a charge and to disguise smilingly the indomitable will-power centred in his triangle-shaped head when he charged for the last time. Disencumbered of its books, the feudal turret had become warlike again and that Guermantes was more himself in death – he was more of his breed, a Guermantes and nothing more and this was symbolised at his funeral in the church of Saint-Hilaire-de-Combray hung with black draperies where the 'G' under the closed coronet divested of initials and titles betokened the race of Guermantes which he personified in death.

Before going to the funeral, which did not take place at once, I wrote to Gilberte. Perhaps I ought to have written to the Duchesse de Guermantes but I imagined that she would have accepted the death of Robert with the indifference I had seen her display about so many others who had seemed so closely associated with her life, and perhaps even that, with her Guermantes spirit, she would want to show that superstition about blood ties meant nothing to her. I was too ill to write to everybody. I had formerly believed that she and Robert liked each other in the society sense, which is the same as saying that they exchanged affectionate expressions when they felt so disposed. But when he was away from her, he did not hesitate to say that she was a fool and if she sometimes found a selfish pleasure in his society, I had noticed that she was incapable of giving herself the smallest trouble, of using her power in the slightest degree to render him a service or even to prevent some misfortune happening to him. The spitefulness she had shown in refusing to recommend him to General Saint-Joseph when Robert was going back to Morocco proved that her goodwill towards him when he married was only a sort of compromise that cost her nothing. So that I was much surprised when I heard that, owing to her being ill when Robert was killed, her people considered it necessary to hide the papers from her for several days (under fallacious pretexts) for fear of the shock that would have been caused her by their announcement of his death. But my surprise was greater when I learnt that after she had been told the truth, the Duchesse de Guermantes wept the whole day, fell ill and took a long time – more than a week, which was long for her – to console herself. When I heard about her grief, I was touched and it enabled everyone to say, as I do, that there was a great friendship between them. But when I remember how many petty slanders, how much ill-will entered into that friendship, I realise how small a value society attaches to it.

Moreover somewhat later, under circumstances which were historically more important though they touched my heart less, Mme de Guermantes appeared, in my opinion, in a still more favourable light. It will be remembered that as a girl she had displayed audacious impertinence towards the Imperial family of Russia and after her marriage, spoke about them with a freedom amounting to social tactlessness, yet she was perhaps the only person, after the Russian Revolution, who gave proof of extreme devotion to the Grand-Dukes and Duchesses. The very year which preceded the war she had annoyed the Grande-Duchesse Vladimir by calling the Comtesse of Hohenfelsen, the morganatic wife of the Grand-Duc Paul, the 'Grande-Duchesse Paul'. But, no sooner had the Russian Revolution broken out, than our Ambassador at St Petersburg, M. Paléologue ('Paléo' for diplomatic society which, like the other, has its pseudo-witty abbreviations), was harassed by telegrams from the Duchesse de Guermantes who wanted news of the Grande-Duchesse Maria Pavlovna and for a long time the only marks of sympathy and respect which that Princess received came to her exclusively from Mme de Guermantes.

Saint-Loup caused, if not by his death, at least by what he had done in the weeks that preceded it, troubles greater than those of the Duchesse. What happened was that the day following the evening when I had seen M. de Charlus, the day on which he had said to Morel: 'I shall be revenged', Saint-Loup's hunt for Morel had ended by the general, under whose orders Morel ought to have been, discovering that he was a deserter and having him sought out and arrested. To excuse himself to Saint-Loup for the punishment which was going to be inflicted on a person he had been interested in, the general had written to inform Saint-Loup of it. Morel was convinced that his arrest was due to the rancour of M. de Charlus. He remembered the words 'I shall be revenged' and, thinking this was the revenge, he demanded to be heard. 'It is true,' he declared, 'that I deserted but, if I have been influenced to evil courses, is it altogether my fault?' Without compromising himself, he gave accounts of M. de Charlus and of M. d'Argencourt with whom he had also quarrelled, concerning matters which these two, with the twofold exuberance of lovers and of inverts, had told him, which caused the simultaneous arrest of M. de Charlus and M. d'Argencourt. This arrest caused, perhaps, less distress to these two than the knowledge that each had been the unwilling rival of the other, and the proceedings disclosed an enormous number of other and more obscure rivals picked up daily in the street. They were, moreover, quickly released as was Morel because the letter written to Saint-Loup by the general was returned to him with the mention: 'Dead on the field of honour'. The general, in honour of the dead, decided that Morel should simply be sent to the front; he there behaved bravely, escaped all dangers and, when the war was over, returned with the cross which, earlier, M. de Charlus had vainly solicited for him and which he thus got indirectly through the death of Saint-Loup.

I have since often thought, when recalling the croix-de-guerre lost at Jupien's, that if Saint-Loup had survived he would have been easily able to get elected deputy in the election which followed the war, thanks to the frothy idiocy and to the halo of glory which it left behind it, thanks also to centuries of prejudice being, on that account, abolished; and if the loss of a finger procured a brilliant marriage and entrance into an aristocratic family, the croix-de-guerre, though it were won in an office, took the place of a profession of faith and ensured a triumphant election to the Chamber of Deputies, almost to the French Academy. The election of Saint-Loup would, on account of his 'sainted' family, have made M. Arthur Meyer pour out floods of tears and ink. But perhaps Saint-Loup loved the people too sincerely to gain their suffrages although they would, doubtless, have forgiven him his democratic ideas for the sake of his noble birth. Saint-Loup would perhaps have exposed the former with success before a chamber composed of aviators, and those heroes would have understood him as would have done a few other elevated minds. But owing to the pacifying effect of the *Bloc National*, a lot of old political rascals had been fished up and were always elected. Those who were unable to enter a Chamber of aviators went about soliciting the votes of Marshals, of a President of the Republic, of a President of the Chamber, etc. in the hope of at least becoming members of the French Academy. They would not have favoured Saint-Loup but they did another of Jupien's customers, that deputy of Liberal Action, and he was re-elected unopposed. He did not stop wearing his territorial officer's uniform although the war had been over a long time. His election was joyfully welcomed by all the newspapers who had formed the Coalition on the strength of his name, with the help of rich and noble ladies who wore rags out of conventional sentimentality and fear of taxes, while men on the Stock Exchange ceaselessly bought diamonds, not for their wives but because, having no confidence in the credit of any country, they sought safety in tangible wealth, and incidentally made de Beers go up a thousand francs. Such imbecility was somewhat irritating but one was less indignant with the *Bloc National* when, suddenly, the victims of Bolshevism appeared on the scene; Grand-Duchesses in tatters whose husbands and sons had been in turn assassinated. Husbands in wheelbarrows, sons stoned and deprived of food, forced to labour amidst jeers and finally thrown into pits and buried alive because they were said to be sickening of the plague and might infect the community. The few who succeeded in escaping suddenly reappeared and added new and terrifying details to this picture of horror.

CHAPTER THREE

An afternoon party at the house of the Princesse de Guermantes

The new sanatorium to which I then retired did not cure me any more than the first one and a long time passed before I left it. During my railway-journey back to Paris the conviction of my lack of literary gifts again assailed me. This conviction which I believed I had discovered formerly on the Guermantes side, that I had recognised still more sorrowfully in my daily walks at Tansonville with Gilberte before going back to dinner or far into the night, and which on the eve of departure I had almost identified, after reading some pages of the memoirs of the Goncourts, as being synonymous with the vanity and lie of literature, a thought less sad perhaps but still more dismal if its reason was not my personal incompetence but the non-existence of an ideal in which I had believed, that conviction which had not for long re-entered my mind, struck me anew and with more lamentable force than ever. It was, I remember, when the train stopped in open country and the sun lit halfway down their stems the line of trees which ran alongside the railway. 'Trees,' I thought, 'you have nothing more to tell me, my cold heart hears you no more. I am in the midst of Nature, yet it is with boredom that my eyes observe the line which separates your luminous countenance from your shaded trunks. If ever I believed myself a poet I now know that I am not one. Perhaps in this new and barren stage of my life, men may inspire me as Nature no longer can and the years when I might perhaps have been able to sing her beauty will never return.' But in offering myself the consolation that possible observation of humanity might take the place of impossible inspiration, I was conscious that I was but seeking a consolation which I knew was valueless. If really I had the soul of an artist, what pleasure should I not be now experiencing at the sight of that curtain of trees lighted by the setting sun, of those little field-flowers lifting themselves almost to the footboard of the railway carriage, whose petals I could count and whose colours I should not dare describe as do so many excellent writers, for can one hope to communicate to the reader a pleasure one has not felt?

A little later I had observed with the same indifference, the lenses of gold and of orange into which the setting sun had transformed the windows of a house; and then, as the hour advanced, I had seen another house which seemed made of a strange pink substance. But I had made these various observations with the indifference I might have felt if, when walking in a garden with a lady, I had remarked a leaf of glass and further on an object like alabaster the unusual colour of which would not have distracted me from agonising boredom but which I had pointed at out of politeness to the lady and to show her that I had noticed them though they were coloured glass and stucco. In the same way as a matter of conscience I registered within myself as though to a person who was accompanying me and who would have been capable of getting more pleasure than I from them, the fiery reflections in the window-panes and the pink transparence of the house. But that companion whose notice I had drawn to these curious effects was doubtless of a less enthusiastic nature than many well-disposed people whom such a sight would have delighted, for he had observed the colours without any sort of joy.

Since my name was on their visiting-lists, my long absence from Paris had not prevented old friends from sending me invitations and when, on getting home, I found together with an invitation for the following day to a supper given by La Berma in honour of her daughter and her son-in-law, another for an afternoon reception at the Prince de Guermantes', my sad reflections in the train were not the least of the motives which counselled me to go there. I told myself it really was not worth while to deprive myself of society since I was either not equipped for or not up to the precious 'work' to which I had for so long been hoping to devote myself 'tomorrow' and which, maybe, corresponded to no reality. In truth, this reasoning was negative and merely eliminated the value of those which might have kept me away from this society function. But what made me go was that name of Guermantes which had so far gone out of my head that, when I saw it on the invitation card, it awakened a beam of attention and laid hold of a fraction of the past buried in the depths of my memory, a past associated with visions of the forest domain, its rich luxuriance once again assuming the charm and significance of the old Combray days when, before going home, I passed into the Rue de l'Oiseau and saw from outside, like dark lacquer, the painted window of Gilbert le Mauvais, Sire of Guermantes. For a moment the Guermantes seemed once more utterly different from society people, incomparable with them or with any living beings, even with a king, beings issuing from gestation in the austere and virtuous atmosphere of that sombre town of Combray where my childhood was spent, and from the whole past represented by the little street whence I gazed up at the painted window. I longed to go to the Guermantes' as though it would bring me back my childhood from the deeps of memory where I glimpsed it. And I continued to reread the invitation until the letters which composed the name, familiar and mysterious as that of Combray itself, rebelliously recaptured their independence and spelled to my tired eyes a name I did not know.

My mother was going to a small tea-party with Mme Sazerat so I had no scruple about attending the Princesse de Guermantes' reception. I ordered a carriage to take me there for the Prince de Guermantes no longer lived in his former mansion but in a magnificent new one which he had had built in the Avenue du Bois. One of the mistakes of people in society is that they do not realise, if they want us to believe in them, that they must first believe in themselves or at least that they must have some respect for the elements essential to our belief. At a time when I made myself believe even though I knew the contrary, that the Guermantes lived in their palace by virtue of hereditary privilege, to penetrate into the palace of a magician or a fairy, to have those doors open before me which are closed until the magical formula has been uttered seemed to me as difficult as to obtain an interview with the sorcerer and the fairy themselves. Nothing was easier than to convince myself that the old servant engaged the previous day at Potel and Chabot's was the son or grandson or descendant of those who served the family long before the revolution, and I had infinite good will in calling the picture which had been bought the preceding month at Bernheim junior's the portrait of an ancestor. But the charm must not be decanted, memories cannot be isolated and now that the prince de Guermantes had himself destroyed my illusion by going to live in the Avenue du Bois, there was little of it left. Those ceilings which I had feared would fall at the sound of my name and under which so much of my former awe and fantasy might still have lingered, now sheltered the evening parties of an American woman of no interest to me. Of course things have no power in themselves and since it is we who impart it to them, some middle-class schoolboy might at this moment be standing in front of the mansion in the Avenue du Bois and feeling as I did formerly about the earlier one. And this because he would still be at the age of faith which I had left far behind; I had lost that privilege as one loses the child's power to digest milk, which we can only consume in small quantities whilst babies can suck it down indefinitely without taking breath.

At least the Guermantes' change of domicile had the advantage for me that the carriage which had come to take me there and in which I was making these reflections had to pass through the streets which go towards the Champs Elysées. Those streets were at the time very badly paved, yet the moment the carriage entered them I was detached from my thoughts by a sensation of extreme sweetness; it was as though, all at once, the carriage was rolling along easily and noiselessly, like, when the gates of a park are opened, one seems to glide along a drive covered with fine gravel or dead leaves. There was nothing material about it but suddenly I felt emancipated from exterior obstacles as though I need no longer make an effort to adapt my attention as we do almost unconsciously when faced with something new; the streets through which I was then passing were those long forgotten ones which Françoise and I used to take when we were going to the Champs Elysées. The road itself knew where it was going, its resistance was overcome. And like an aviator who rolls painfully along the ground until, abruptly, he breaks away from it, I felt myself being slowly lifted towards the silent peaks of memory. Those particular streets of Paris will, for me, always be composed of a different substance from others.

When I reached the corner of the rue Royale where formerly an open-air streetseller used to display the photographs beloved of Françoise, it seemed to me that the carriage accustomed in the course of years to turning there hundreds of times was compelled to turn of itself. I was not traversing the same streets as those who were passing by, I was gliding through a sweet and melancholy past composed of so many different pasts that it was difficult for me to identify the cause of my melancholy. Was it due to those pacings to and fro awaiting Gilberte and fearing she would not come? Was it that I was close to a house where I had been told that Albertine had gone with Andrée or was it the philosophic significance a street seems to assume when one has used it a thousand times while one was obsessed with a passion which has come to an end and borne no fruit, like when after luncheon I made fevered expeditions to gaze at the playbills of *Phèdre* and of the *Black Domino* while they were still moist with the bill-sticker's paste?

Reaching the Champs Elysées and not much wanting to hear the whole of the concert at the Guermantes', I stopped the carriage and was able to get out of it to walk a few steps, when I noticed a carriage likewise about to stop. A man with glazed eyes and bent body was deposited rather than sitting in the back of it, and was making efforts to hold himself straight such as a child makes when told to behave nicely. An untouched forest of snow-white hair escaped from under his straw hat while a white beard like those snow attaches to statues in public gardens depended from his chin. It was M. de Charlus sitting beside Jupien (prodigal of attentions), convalescing from an attack of apoplexy (of which I was ignorant; all I had heard being that he had lost his eyesight, a passing matter, for he now saw clearly). He seemed, unless until then he had been in the habit of dyeing his hair and that he had been forbidden to do so because of the fatigue it involved, to have been subjected to some sort of chemical precipitation which had the effect of making his hair shine with such a brilliant and metallic lustre that the locks of his hair and beard spouted like so many geysers of pure silver and clad the aged and fallen prince with the Shakespearean majesty of a King Lear. The eyes had not remained unaffected by this total convulsion, this metallurgical alteration of the head; but by an inverse phenomenon they had lost all their lustre. What was most moving was the feeling that the lustre had been lent to them by moral pride and that owing to this having been lost, the physical and even the intellectual life of M. de Charlus survived his aristocratic hauteur which one had supposed to be embodied in it.

At that very moment there passed in a victoria, doubtless also going to the Prince de Guermantes', Mme de Sainte-Euverte whom formerly the Baron did not consider smart enough to be worth knowing. Jupien, who was taking care of him like a child, whispered in his ear that it was a personage he knew, Mme de Sainte-Euverte. Immediately, with infinite trouble and with the concentration of an invalid who wants to appear capable of movements still painful to him, M. de Charlus uncovered, bowed and wished Mme de Sainte-Euverte good-day with the respect he might have shown if she had been the Queen of France. The very difficulty of thus saluting her may have been the reason of it, through realising the poignancy of doing something painful and therefore doubly meritorious on the part of an invalid and doubly flattering to the lady to whom it was addressed. Like kings, invalids exaggerate politeness. Perhaps also there was a lack of co-ordination in the Baron's movements caused by disease of the marrow and brain and his gestures exceeded his intention. For myself I rather perceived therein a sort of quasi-physical gentleness, a detachment from the realities of life which strikes one in those about to enter the shadows of death. The profuse exposure of his silver-flaked head revealed a change less profound than this unconscious worldly humility which, reversing all social relationships, brought low in the presence of Mme de Sainte-Euverte, would have brought low – showing thereby its debility – in the presence of the least important American woman (who might at last have secured from the Baron a consideration until then withheld) a snobbishness which had seemed the most arrogant. For the Baron still lived, could still think; his intelligence survived. And, more than a chorus of Sophocles on the humbled pride of Oedipus, more even than death itself or any funeral speech, the Baron's humble and obsequious greeting of Mme de Sainte-Euverte proclaimed the perishable nature of earthly grandeurs and of all human pride. M. de

Charlus who, till then, would not have consented to dine with Mme de Sainte-Euverte, now bowed down to the ground before her. It may, of course, be that he thus bowed to her through ignorance of her rank (for the rules of the social code can be obliterated by a stroke like any other part of the memory), perhaps by an incoordination which transposed to the plane of apparent humility his uncertainty – which might otherwise have been haughty – regarding the identity of the passing lady. He saluted her, in fact, with the timid politeness of a child told by its mother to say good-morning to grown-up people. And a child he had become, without a child's pride.

For Mme de Sainte-Euverte to receive the homage of M. de Charlus was a world of gratified snobbery as, formerly, it was a world of snobbery for the Baron to refuse it her. And M. de Charlus had, at one blow, destroyed that precious and inaccessible character which he had succeeded in making Mme de Sainte-Euverte believe was an essential part of himself by the concentrated timidity, the frightened eagerness with which he raised his hat and let loose the foaming torrents of his silver hair as he stood uncovered before her with the eloquent deference of a Bossuet. After Jupien had assisted the Baron to descend, I saluted him and he began speaking to me very fast and so indistinctly that I could not understand him and when, for the third time, I asked him to repeat what he said, it provoked a gesture of impatience which surprised me because of the previous impassiveness of his face which was doubtless due to the effects of paralysis. But when I succeeded in grasping his whispered words I realised that the invalid's intelligence was completely intact.

There were moreover two M. de Charluses without counting others. Of the two the intellectual one spent the whole time complaining that he was approaching amnesia, that he was constantly pronouncing one word or one letter instead of another. But coincidentally, the other M. de Charlus, the subconscious one which wanted to be envied as much as the other to be pitied, stopped, like the leader of an orchestra at the beginning of a passage in which his musicians are floundering, and with infinite ingeniousness attached what followed to the word he had wrongly used but which he wanted one to believe he had deliberately chosen. Even his memory was uninjured; indeed he indulged in the exceedingly fatiguing coquetry of resuscitating some ancient and insignificant recollection in connection with myself to prove to me that he had preserved or recovered all his mental acuteness. For instance, without moving his head or his eyes and without varying his inflection, he said to me: 'Look! There's a post on which there's a notice exactly like the one where I was standing the first time I saw you at Avranches – no at Balbec, I mean.' And it was actually an advertisement of the same product.

At first I had difficulty in understanding what he said, as at first, one is unable to see in a darkened room, but like eyes which become accustomed to the dusk, my ears soon became accustomed to his pianissimo. I believe too that it got stronger as he went on speaking, whether because the weakness came partly from nervous apprehension which diminished while he was being distracted by someone or whether, on the contrary, the weakness was real and the strength of his voice was temporarily stimulated by excitement which was injurious to him and made strangers say: 'He's getting better, he mustn't think about his illness', whereas, on the contrary, it made him worse. Be this as it may, the Baron, at this particular moment, cast up his words with greater vigour like the tide does its waves in bad weather. An effect of his recent stroke was to make his voice sound like stones rolling under his words. And as he went on talking to me of the past, no doubt to show he had not lost his memory, he evoked it funereally, yet without sadness. He kept on enumerating the various members of his family or of his set who were dead, apparently less because he was sorry they had departed than because of his satisfaction at having survived them; in reminding himself of their death, he seemed to become more conscious of his own recovery. He enumerated almost triumphantly but in a monotonous tone accompanied by a slight stammer and with a sort of sepulchral resonance: 'Hannibal de Bréauté, dead! Antoine de Mouchy, dead! Charles Swann, dead! Adalbert de Montmorency, dead! Baron de Talleyrand, dead! Sosthène de Doudeauville, dead!' And each time the word 'dead' seemed to fall upon the defunct like a shovelful of earth, the heavier for the grave-digger wanting to press them ever deeper into the tomb.

The Duchesse de Létourville, who was not going to the reception of the Princesse de Guermantes because she had been ill for a long time, at that moment passed by us on foot and noticing the Baron whose attack she had not heard about, stopped to say good-day to him. But the illness from which she had been suffering did not make her better understand the illness of others, which she bore with an impatience and nervous irritation in which there was perhaps a good deal of pity. Hearing the Baron's defective pronunciation and the mistakes in some of his words and observing the difficulty with which he moved his arm, she glanced in turn at Jupien and at me as though she were asking the explanation of such a shocking phenomenon. As we did not answer she directed a long, sad, reproachful stare at M. de Charlus himself, apparently vexed at his being seen out with her in a condition as unusual as if he were wearing neither tie nor shoes. When the Baron made another mistake in his pronunciation, the distress and indignation of the Duchesse increased, and she cried at the Baron:

'Palamède?' in the interrogatory and exasperated tone of neurasthenic people who cannot bear waiting a moment and who, if one asks them in immediately and apologises for not being completely dressed, remark bitterly, not to excuse themselves but to accuse you: 'Oh, I see I'm disturbing you!' as though the person they are disturbing had done something wrong. Finally, she left us with a still more concerned air, saying to the Baron: 'You'd better go home.'

M. de Charlus wanted to sit down and rest in a chair while Jupien and I took a few steps together, and painfully extracted a book from his pocket which seemed to me to be a prayer-book. I was not sorry to learn some details about the Baron's health from Jupien. 'I am glad to talk to you, monsieur,' said Jupien, 'but we won't go further than the Rond-Point. Thank God, the Baron is better now, but I don't dare leave him long alone. He's always the same, he's too good-hearted, he'd give everything he has to others and that isn't all, he remains as much of a *coureur* as if he were a young man and I'm obliged to keep my eye on him.' 'The more so,' I replied, 'as he has recovered his own. I was greatly distressed when I was told that he had lost his eyesight.' 'His paralysis did, indeed, have that effect, at first he couldn't see at all. Just think that during the cure which, as a matter of fact, did him a lot of good, for several months he couldn't see any more than if he'd been blind from birth.' 'At least, that must have made part of your supervision unnecessary.' 'Not the least in the world! We had hardly arrived at a hotel than he asked me what such and such a person on the staff was like. I assured him they were all awful, but he knew it couldn't be as universal as I said and that I must be lying about some of them. There's that *petit polisson* again! And then he got a sort of intuition, perhaps from a voice, I don't know, and managed to send me away on some urgent commission. One day – excuse me for telling you all this, but as you once by chance entered the temple of impurity, I have nothing to hide from you;' (for that matter he always got a rather unpleasant satisfaction out of revealing secrets) 'I came back from one of those pretended urgent commissions quickly because I thought it had been arranged on purpose, when just as I approached the Baron's room I heard a voice ask: "What?" and the Baron's answer: "Do you mean to say it's the first time?" I entered without knocking and what was my horror! The Baron, misled by the voice which was indeed more mature than is habitual at that age (and at that time he was completely blind) – he, who formerly only liked grown men, was with a child not ten years old.'

I was told that at that period he was nearly every day a prey to attacks of mental depression characterised not exactly by divagation but by confessing at the top of his voice – in front of third parties whose presence and censoriousness he had forgotten – opinions he usually hid, such as his Germanophilism. So, long after the end of the war he was bewailing the defeat of the Germans, amongst whom he included himself and said bitterly: 'We shall have to be revenged. We have proved the power of our resistance and we were the best organised', or else his confidences took another form and he exclaimed in a rage: 'Don't let Lord X— or the Prince of *** come and tell me again what they said the other day for it was all I could do to prevent myself replying, "You know, because you're one of them, at least as much as I am." ' Needless to add that when M. de Charlus thus gave vent at times when he was, as they say, not all there, to these Germanophile and other avowals, people in his company such as Jupien or the Duchesse de Guermantes were in the habit of interrupting his imprudent words and giving to the third party who was less intimate and more indiscreet a forced but honourable interpretation of his words.

'Oh, my God,' called Jupien, 'I had good reason not to want to go far away. There he is starting a conversation with a gardener boy. Good-day, sir, it's better I should go, I can't leave my invalid alone a moment; he's nothing but a great baby.'

I got out of the carriage again a little before reaching the Princesse de Guermantes' and began thinking again of that lassitude, that weariness with which I had tried the evening before to note the railway line which separated the shadow from the light upon the trees in one of the most beautiful countrysides in France. Certainly such intellectual conclusions as I had drawn from these thoughts did not affect my sensibility so cruelly today, but they remained the same, for, as always happened when I succeeded in breaking away from my habits, going out at an unaccustomed hour to some new place, I derived a lively pleasure from it. Today, the pleasure of going to a reception at Mme de Guermantes' seemed to me purely frivolous, but since I now knew that I could expect to have no other than frivolous pleasures, what was the use of my not accepting them? I repeated to myself that in attempting this description I had experienced none of that enthusiasm which is not the only but the first criterion of talent. I began now to draw on my memory for 'snapshots', notably snapshots it had taken at Venice, but the mere mention of the word made Venice as boring to me as a photographic exhibition and I was conscious of no more taste or talent in visualising what I had formerly seen than yesterday in describing what I had observed with a meticulous and mournful eye. In a few minutes so many charming friends I had not seen for so long would doubtless be asking me not to cut myself off and to spend some time with them. I had no reason to refuse them since I now had the proof that I was good for nothing, that literature could no longer give me any joy whether because of my lack of talent or because it was a less real thing than I had believed.

When I remembered what Bergotte had said to me: 'You are ill but one cannot be sorry for you because you possess the delights of the mind', I saw how much he had been mistaken. How little delight I got out of this sterile lucidity. I might have added that if sometimes I had tasted pleasures – not those of the mind – I had always exhausted them with a different woman so that even if destiny were to grant me a hundred years of healthy life it would only be adding successive lengths to an existence already in a straight line which there was no object in lengthening further. As to the 'delights of the mind', could I thus name those cold and sterile reflections which my clear-sighted eye or my logical reasoning joylessly summarised?

But sometimes illumination comes to our rescue at the very moment when all seems lost; we have knocked at every door and they open on nothing until, at last, we stumble unconsciously against the only one through which we can enter the kingdom we have sought in vain a hundred years – and it opens.

Reviewing the painful reflections of which I have just been speaking, I had entered the courtyard of the Guermantes' mansion and in my distraction I had not noticed an approaching carriage; at the call of the linkman I had barely time to draw quickly to one side, and in stepping backwards I stumbled against some unevenly placed paving stones behind which there was a coach-house. As I recovered myself, one of my feet stepped on a flagstone lower than the one next it. In that instant all my discouragement disappeared and I was possessed by the same felicity which at different moments of my life had given me the view of trees which seemed familiar to me during the drive round Balbec, the view of the belfries of Martinville, the savour of the madeleine dipped in my tea and so many other sensations of which I have spoken and which Vinteuil's last works had seemed to synthesise. As at the moment when I tasted the madeleine, all my apprehensions about the future, all my intellectual doubts, were dissipated. Those doubts which had assailed me just before, regarding the reality of my literary gifts and even regarding the reality of literature itself were dispersed as though by magic.

This time I vowed that I should not resign myself to ignoring why, without any fresh reasoning, without any definite hypothesis, the insoluble difficulties of the previous instant had lost all importance as was the case when I tasted the madeleine. The felicity which I now experienced was undoubtedly the same as that I felt when I ate the madeleine, the cause of which I had then postponed seeking. There was a purely material difference in the images evoked. A deep azure intoxicated my eyes, a feeling of freshness, of dazzling light enveloped me and in my desire to capture the sensation, just as I had not dared to move when I tasted the madeleine because of trying to conjure back that of which it reminded me, I stood, doubtless an object of ridicule to the linkmen, repeating the movement of a moment since, one foot upon the higher flagstone, the other on the lower one. Merely repeating the movement was useless; but if, oblivious of the Guermantes' reception, I succeeded in recapturing the sensation which accompanied the movement, again the intoxicating and elusive vision softly pervaded me as though it said 'Grasp me as I float by you, if you can, and try to solve the enigma of happiness I offer you.' And then, all at once, I recognised that Venice which my descriptive efforts and pretended snapshots of memory had failed to recall; the sensation I had once felt on two uneven slabs in the Baptistry of St Mark had been given back to me and was linked with all the other sensations of that and other days which had lingered expectant in their place among the series of forgotten years from which a sudden chance had imperiously called them forth. So too the taste of the little madeleine had recalled Combray. But how was it that these visions of Combray and of Venice at one and at another moment had caused me a joyous certainty sufficient without other proofs to make death indifferent to me?

Asking myself this and resolved to find the answer this very day, I entered the Guermantes' mansion, because we always allow our inner needs to give way to the part we are apparently called upon to play and that day mine was to be a guest. On reaching the first floor a footman requested me to enter a small boudoir-library adjoining a buffet until the piece then being played had come to an end, the Princesse having given orders that the doors should not be opened during the performance. At that very instant a second premonition occurred to reinforce the one which the uneven paving-stones had given me and to exhort me to persevere in my task. The servant in his ineffectual efforts not to make a noise had knocked a spoon against a plate. The same sort of felicity which the uneven paving-stones had given me invaded my being; this time my sensation was quite different, being that of great heat accompanied by the smell of smoke tempered by the fresh air of a surrounding forest and I realised that what appeared so pleasant was the identical group of trees I had found so tiresome to observe and describe when I was uncorking a bottle of beer in the railway carriage and, in a sort of bewilderment, I believed for the moment, until I had collected myself, so

similar was the sound of the spoon against the plate to that of the hammer of
a railway employee who was doing something to the wheel of the carriage
while the train was at a standstill facing the group of trees, that I was now
actually there. One might have said that the portents which that day were to
rescue me from my discouragement and give me back faith in literature,
were determined to multiply themselves, for a servant, a long time in the
service of the Prince de Guermantes, recognised me and, to save me going
to the buffet, brought me some cakes and a glass of orangeade into the
library. I wiped my mouth with the napkin he had given me and immediately,
like the personage in the *Thousand and One Nights* who unknowingly
accomplished the rite which caused the appearance before him of a docile
genius, invisible to others, ready to transport him far away, a new azure
vision passed before my eyes; but this time it was pure and saline and swelled
into shapes like bluish udders. The impression was so strong that the
moment I was living seemed to be one with the past and (more bewildered
still than I was on the day when I wondered whether I was going to be
welcomed by the Princesse de Guermantes or whether everything was
going to melt away), I believed that the servant had just opened the window
upon the shore and that everything invited me to go downstairs and walk
along the sea-wall at high tide; the napkin upon which I was wiping my
mouth had exactly the same kind of starchiness as that with which I had
attempted with so much difficulty to dry myself before the window the first
day of my arrival at Balbec and within the folds of which, now, in that library
of the Guermantes mansion, a green-blue ocean spread its plumage like the
tail of a peacock. And I did not merely rejoice in those colours, but in that
whole instant which produced them, an instant towards which my whole life
had doubtless aspired, which a feeling of fatigue or sadness had prevented
my ever experiencing at Balbec but which now, pure, disincarnated and
freed from the imperfections of exterior perceptions, filled me with joy.

The piece they were playing might finish at any moment, and I should be
obliged to enter the drawing room. So I forced myself to try to penetrate as
quickly as possible into the nature of those identical sensations I had felt
three times within a few minutes so as to extract the lesson I might learn
from them. I did not stop to consider the extreme difference which there is
between the true impression which we have had of a thing and the artificial
meaning we give to it when we employ our will to represent it to ourselves,
for I remembered with what relative indifference Swann had been able to
speak formerly of the days when he was loved, because beneath the words,
he felt something else than them, and the immediate pain Vinteuil's little
phrase had caused him by giving him back those very days themselves as he

had formerly felt them, and I understood but too well that the sensation the uneven paving-stones, the taste of the madeleine, had aroused in me, bore no relation to that which I had so often attempted to reconstruct of Venice, of Balbec and of Combray with the aid of a uniform memory. Moreover, I realised that life can be considered commonplace in spite of its appearing so beautiful at particular moments because in the former case one judges and underrates it on quite other grounds than itself, upon images which have no life in them. At most I noted additionally that the difference there is between each real impression – differences which explain why a uniform pattern of life cannot resemble it – can probably be ascribed to this: that the slightest word we have spoken at a particular period of our life, the most insignificant gesture to which we have given vent, were surrounded, bore upon them the reflection of things which logically were unconnected with them, were indeed isolated from them by the intelligence which did not need them for reasoning purposes but in the midst of which – here, the pink evening-glow upon the floral wall-decoration of a rustic restaurant, a feeling of hunger, sexual desire, enjoyment of luxury – there, curling waves beneath the blue of a morning sky enveloping musical phrases which partly emerge like mermaids' shoulders – the most simple act or gesture remains enclosed as though in a thousand jars of which each would be filled with things of different colours, odours and temperature; not to mention that those vases placed at intervals during the growing years throughout which we ceaselessly change, if only in dream or in thought, are situated at completely different levels and produce the impression of strangely varying climates. It is true that these changes have occurred to us without our being aware of them; but the distance between the memory which suddenly returns and our present personality, as similarly between two memories of different years and places, is so great that it would suffice, apart from their specific uniqueness, to make comparison between them impossible. Yes, if a memory, thanks to forgetfulness, has been unable to contract any tie, to forge any link between itself and the present, if it has remained in its own place, of its own date, if it has kept its distance, its isolation in the hollow of a valley or on the peak of a mountain, it makes us suddenly breathe an air new to us just because it is an air we have formerly breathed, an air purer than that the poets have vainly called paradisiacal, which offers that deep sense of renewal only because it has been breathed before, inasmuch as the true paradises are paradises we have lost.

And on the way to it, I noted that there would be great difficulties in creating the work of art I now felt ready to undertake without its being consciously in my mind, for I should have to construct each of its successive parts out of a different sort of material. The material which would be suitable for memories at the side of the sea would be quite different from those of afternoons at Venice which would demand a material of its own, a new one, of a special transparency and sonority, compact, fresh and pink, different again if I wanted to describe evenings at Rivebelle where, in the dining-room open upon the garden, the heat was beginning to disintegrate, to descend and come to rest on the earth, while the rose-covered walls of the restaurant were lighted up by the last ray of the setting sun and the last watercolours of daylight lingered in the sky.

I passed rapidly over all these things, being summoned more urgently to seek the cause of that happiness with its peculiar character of insistent certainty, the search for which I had formerly adjourned. And I began to discover the cause by comparing those varying happy impressions which had the common quality of being felt simultaneously at the actual moment and at a distance in time, because of which common quality the noise of the spoon upon the plate, the unevenness of the paving-stones, the taste of the madeleine, imposed the past upon the present and made me hesitate as to which time I was existing in. Of a truth, the being within me which sensed this impression, sensed what it had in common in former days and now, sensed its extra-temporal character, a being which only appeared when through the medium of the identity of present and past, it found itself in the only setting in which it could exist and enjoy the essence of things, that is, outside time. That explained why my apprehensions on the subject of my death had ceased from the moment when I had unconsciously recognised the taste of the little madeleine, because at that moment the being that I then had been was an extra-temporal being and in consequence indifferent to the vicissitudes of the future. That being had never come to me, had never manifested itself except when I was inactive and in a sphere beyond the enjoyment of the moment, that was my prevailing condition every time that analogical miracle had enabled me to escape from the present. Only that being had the power of enabling me to recapture former days, time lost, in the face of which all the efforts of my memory and of my intelligence came to nought.

And perhaps, if just now I thought that Bergotte had spoken falsely when he referred to the joys of spiritual life it was because I then gave the name of spiritual life to logical reasonings which had no relation with it, which had no relation with what now existed in me – just as I found society and life wearisome because I was judging them from memories without truth while now that a veritable moment of the past had been born again in me three separate times, I had such a desire to live.

Nothing but a moment of the past? Much more perhaps; something which being common to the past and the present, is more essential than both. How many times in the course of my life reality had disappointed me because at the moment when I perceived it, my imagination, which was my only means of enjoying beauty, could not be applied to it by virtue of the inevitable law which only allows us to imagine that which is absent. And now suddenly the effect of this hard law had become neutralised, held in suspense by a marvellous expedient of nature which had caused a sensation to flash to me – sound of a spoon and of a hammer, uneven paving-stones – simultaneously in the past which permitted my imagination to grasp it and in the present in which the shock to my senses caused by the noise had effected a contact between the dreams of the imagination and that of which they are habitually deprived, namely, the idea of existence – and thanks to that stratagem had permitted that being within me to secure, to isolate and to render static for the duration of a lightning flash that which it can never wholly grasp, a fraction of time in its pure essence. When, with such a shudder of happiness, I heard the sound common, at once, to the spoon touching the plate, to the hammer striking the wheel, to the unevenness of the paving-stones in the courtyard of the Guermantes' mansion and the Baptistry of St Mark's, it was because that being within me can only be nourished on the essence of things and finds in them alone its subsistence and its delight. It languishes in the observation by the senses of the present sterilised by the intelligence awaiting a future constructed by the will out of fragments of the past and the present from which it removes still more reality, keeping that only which serves the narrow human aim of utilitarian purposes. But let a sound, a scent already heard and breathed in the past be heard and breathed anew, simultaneously in the present and in the past, real without being actual, ideal without being abstract, then instantly the permanent and characteristic essence hidden in things is freed and our true being which has for long seemed dead but was not so in other ways awakes and revives, thanks to this celestial nourishment. An instant liberated from the order of time has recreated in us man liberated from the same order, so that he should be conscious of it. And indeed we understand his faith in his happiness even if the mere taste of a madeleine does not logically seem to justify it; we understand that the name of death is meaningless to him for, placed beyond time, how can he fear the future?

But that illusion which brought near me a moment of the past incongruous to the present, would not last. Certainly we can prolong the visions of memory by willing it, which is no more than turning over an illustrated book. Thus formerly, when I was going for the first time to the Princesse de Guermantes' from the sunlit court of our house in Paris, I had lazily focused my mind at one moment on the square where the church of Combray stood, at another on the sea shore of Balbec, as I might have amused myself by turning over a folio of watercolours of different places I had visited and cataloguing these mnemonic illustrations with the egotistical pleasure of a collector, I might have said: 'After all, I have seen some beautiful things in my life.' Doubtless, in that event, my memory would have been asserting different sensations but it would only have been combining their homogeneous elements. That was a different thing from the three memories I had just experienced which, so far from giving me a more flattering notion of my personality, had, on the contrary, almost made me doubt its very existence. Thus, on the day when I dipped the madeleine in the hot infusion, in the heart of that place where I happened to be (whether that place was, as then, my room in Paris or, as today, the Prince de Guermantes' library) there had been the irradiation of a small zone within and around myself, a sensation (taste of the dipped madeleine, metallic sound, feeling of the uneven steps) common to the place where I then was and also to the other place (my Aunt Léonie's room, the railway carriage, the Baptistry of St Mark's). And, at the very moment when I was thus reasoning, the strident sound of a water-pipe, exactly like those long screeches which one heard on board excursion steamers at Balbec, made me experience (as had happened to me once in a large restaurant in Paris at the sight of a luxurious dining-room half empty, summerlike and hot) something more than a mere sensation like one I had, one late afternoon at Balbec, when, all the tables symmetrically laid with linen and silver, the large bow-windows wide open to the sun slowly setting on the sea with its wandering ships, I had only to step across the window-frame hardly higher than my ankle, to be with Albertine and her friends who were walking on the sea-wall. It was not only the echo, the duplication of a past sensation that the water-conduit had caused me to experience, it was the sensation itself. In that case as in all the preceding ones, the common sensation had sought to recreate the former place around itself whilst the material place in which the sensation occurred, opposed all the resistance of its mass to this immigration into a Paris mansion of a Norman seashore and a railway-embankment. The marine dining-room of Balbec with its damask linen prepared like altar cloths to receive the setting sun had sought to disturb the solidity of the Guermantes' mansion, to force its doors, and had made the sofas round me quiver an instant as on another occasion the tables of the restaurant in Paris had done. In all those resurrections, the distant place engendered by the sensation common to them all, came to grips for a second with the material place, like a wrestler. The material place was always the conqueror, and always the conquered seemed to me the more beautiful, so much so that I remained in a state of ecstasy upon the uneven pavement as I did with my cup of tea, trying to retain with the moment of their appearance, to make reappear as they escaped, that Combray, that Venice, that Balbec, invading, yet repelled, which came before my eyes only immediately to abandon me in the midst of a newer scene which yet was penetrable by the past. And if the material place had not been at once the conqueror I think I should have lost consciousness; for these resurrections of the past, for the second that they last, are so complete that they not only force our eyes to cease seeing the room which is before them in order to see the railway bordered by trees or the rising tide, they force our nostrils to breathe the air of those places which are, nevertheless, so far away, our will to choose between the diverse alternatives it offers us, our whole personality to believe itself surrounded by them, or at least to stumble between them and the material world, in the bewildering uncertainty we experience from an ineffable vision on the threshold of sleep.

So, that which the being within me, three or four times resurrected, had experienced, were perhaps fragments of lives snatched from time which, though viewed from eternity, were fugitive. And yet I felt that the happiness given me at those rare intervals in my life was the only fruitful and authentic one. Does not the sign of unreality in others consist in their inability to satisfy us, as, for instance, in the case of social pleasures which, at best, cause that discomfort which is provoked by unwholesome food, when friendship is almost a pretence, since, for whatever moral reasons he may seek it, the artist who gives up an hour of work to converse for that time with a friend knows that he is sacrificing a reality to an illusion (friends being friends only in the sense of a sweet madness which overcomes us in life and to which we yield, though at the back of our minds we know it to be the error of a lunatic who imagines the furniture to be alive and talks to it) owing to the sadness which follows its satisfaction – like that I felt the day I was first introduced to Albertine when I gave myself the trouble, after all not great, to obtain something – to make the acquaintance of the girl – which only seemed to me unimportant because I had obtained it. Even a deeper pleasure such as that which I might have felt when I loved Albertine was in reality only perceived by contrast with my anguish when she was no longer there, for when I was sure she would return as on the day when she came back from the Trocadéro, I only experienced a vague boredom, whereas the deeper I penetrated into the sound of the spoon on the plate or the taste of tea, the more exalted became my delight that my Aunt Léonie's chamber and later the whole of Combray and both its sides had entered my room. And now I was determined to concentrate my mind on that contemplation of the essence of things, to define it to myself, but how and by what means? Doubtless at the moment when the stiffness of the table-napkin had brought back Balbec to me and, for an instant, caressed my imagination not only with a view of the sea as it was that morning but with the scent of the room, with the swiftness of the wind, with an appetite for breakfast, with wavering between various walks, all those things attached to a sensation of space like winged wheels in their delirious race, doubtless at the moment when the unevenness of the two pavements had prolonged in all directions and dimensions my arid and crude visions of Venice and St Mark's, and all the emotions I had then experienced, relating the square to the church, the landing-stage to the square, the canal to the landing-stage, to everything the eye saw, to that whole world of longings which is in reality only perceived by the spirit, I had been tempted to set forth, if not to Venice because of the inclement season, at least to Balbec. But I did not stop an instant at that thought; not only did I realise that countries were not that which their name pictured to me and my imagination represented them but that it was only in my dreams, and hardly then, that a place consisting of pure matter was spread out before me clear and distinct from those common things one can see and touch. But even in regard to those images of another kind, of the memory, I knew that I had not found any beauty in Balbec when I went there and that the beauty memory had left in me was no longer the same at my second visit. I had too clearly proved the impossibility of expecting from reality that which was within myself. It was not in the Square of St Mark any more than during my second visit to Balbec or on my return to Tansonville to see Gilberte that I should find lost time and the journey which once more tempted me with the illusion that these old impressions existed outside myself and were situated in a certain spot could not be the means I was seeking. I would not allow myself to be lured again; it was necessary for me to know at last, if indeed it were possible to attain that which, disappointed as I had always been by places and people, I had (in spite of a concert-piece by Vinteuil which had seemed to say the contrary) believed unrealisable. I was not, therefore, going to attempt another experience on the road which I had long known to lead nowhere. Impressions such as those which I was attempting to render permanent could only vanish at the contact of a direct enjoyment which was powerless to give birth to them. The only way was to attempt to know them more completely where they existed, that is, within myself and by so doing to illuminate them in their depths. I had never known any pleasure at Balbec, any more than I had in living with Albertine, except what was perceptible afterwards. And if in recapitulating the disappointments of my life as I had so far lived it, they led me to believe that its reality must reside elsewhere than in action, and if, in following the vicissitudes of my life, I did not summarise them as a matter of pure hazard, I well knew that the disappointment of a journey and the disappointment of love were not different disappointments but varying aspects which, according to the conditions to which they apply, are inflicted upon us by the impotence, difficult for us to realise, of material pleasure and effective action. Again reflecting on that extra-temporal delight caused whether by the sound of the spoon or by the taste of the madeleine, I said to myself: 'Was this the happiness suggested by the little phrase of the Sonata, which Swann was deceived into identifying with the pleasure of love and was not endowed to find in artistic creation; that happiness which had made me respond as to a presentiment of something more supra-terrestrial still than the little phrase of the Sonata, to the red and mysterious appeal of that septet which Swann did not know, having died like so many others, before the truth, meant for them, had been revealed?' Moreover, it would have done him no good, for that phrase might symbolise an appeal but it could not create the force which would have made of Swann the writer he was not.

And yet I reminded myself after a moment and after having thought over those resurrections of memory, that in another way, obscure impressions had sometimes, as far back as Combray and on the Guermantes' side, demanded my thought in the same way as those mnemonic resurrections, yet they did not contain an earlier experience but a new truth, a precious image which I was trying to discover by efforts of the kind one makes to remember something, as though our loveliest ideas were like musical airs which might come to us without our having ever heard them and which we force ourselves to listen to and write down. I reminded myself with satisfaction (because it proved that I was the same then and that it represented a fundamental quality of my nature) and also with sadness in the thought that since then I had made no progress, that, as far back as at Combray, I was attempting to concentrate my mind on a compelling image, a cloud, a triangle, a belfry, a flower, a pebble, believing that there was perhaps something else under those symbols I ought to try to discover, a thought which these objects were expressing in the manner of hieroglyphic characters which one might imagine only represented material objects. Doubtless such deciphering was difficult, but it alone could yield some part of the truth. For the truths which the intelligence apprehends through direct and clear vision in the daylight world are less profound and less necessary than those which life has communicated to us unconsciously through an intuition which is material only in so far as it reaches us through our senses and the spirit of which we can elicit. In fact, in this case as in the other, whether it was a question of impressions given me by a view of the Martinville belfry or memories like those of the two uneven paving-stones or the taste of the madeleine, it was necessary to attempt to interpret them as symbols of so many laws and ideas, by trying to think, that is, by trying to educe my sensation from its obscurity and convert it into an intellectual equivalent. And what other means were open to me than the creation of a work of art? Already the consequences pressed upon my spirit; for whether it was a question of memories like the sound of the spoon and the taste of the madeleine or of those verities expressed in forms the meaning of which I sought in my brain, where, belfries, wild herbs, what not, they composed a complex illuminated scroll, their first characteristic was that I was not free to choose them, that they had been given to me as they were. And I felt that that must be the seal of their authenticity. I had not gone to seek the two paving-stones in the courtyard against which I had struck. But it was precisely the fortuitousness, the inevitablity of the sensation which safeguarded the truth of the past it revived, of the images it set free, since we feel its effort to rise upwards to the light and the joy of the real recaptured. That fortuitousness is the guardian of the truth of the whole series of contemporary impressions which it brings in its train, with that infallible proportion of light and shade, of emphasis and omission, of memory and forgetfulness, of which the conscious memory or observation are ignorant.

That book of unknown signs within me (signs in relief it seemed, for my concentrated attention, as it explored my unconscious in its search, struck against them, circled round them like a diver sounding) no one could help me read by any rule, for its reading consists in an act of creation in which no one can take our place and in which no one can collaborate. And how many turn away from writing it, how many tasks will one not assume to avoid that one! Every event, whether it was the Dreyfus affair or the war, furnished excuses to writers for not deciphering that book; they wanted to assert the triumph of Justice, to recreate the moral unity of the nation and they had no time to think of literature. But those were only excuses because either they did not possess or had ceased to possess genius, that is, instinct. For it is instinct which dictates duty and intelligence which offers pretexts for avoiding it. But excuses do not exist in art, intentions do not count there, the artist must at all times follow his instinct, which makes art the most real thing, the most austere school in life and the true last judgment. That book which is the most arduous of all to decipher is the only one which reality has dictated, the only one printed within us by reality itself. Whatever idea life has left in us, its material shape, mark of the impression it has made on us, is still the necessary pledge of its truth. The ideas formulated by the intellect have only a logical truth, a possible truth, their selection is arbitrary. Our only book is that one not made by ourselves whose characters are already imaged. It is not that the ideas we formulate may not be logically right but that we do not know if they are true. Intuition alone, however tenuous its consistency, however improbable its shape, is a criterion of truth and, for that reason, deserves to be accepted by the mind because it alone is capable, if the mind can extract that truth, of bringing it to greater perfection and of giving it pleasure without alloy. Intuition for the writer is what experiment is for the learned, with the difference that in the case of the learned the work of the intelligence precedes and in the case of the writer it follows. That which we have not been forced to decipher, to clarify by our own personal effort, that which was made clear before, is not ours. Only that issues from ourselves which we ourselves extract from the darkness within ourselves and which is unknown to others. And as art exactly recomposes life, an atmosphere of poetry surrounds those truths within ourselves to which we attain, the sweetness of a mystery which is but the twilight through which we have passed.

An oblique ray from the setting sun brings instantly back to me a time of which I had never thought again, when, in my childhood, my Aunt Léonie had a fever which Dr Percepied had feared was typhoid and they had made me stop for a week in the little room Eulalie had in the church square, where there was only a matting on the floor and a dimity curtain at the window humming in the sunlight to which I was unaccustomed. And when I think how the memory of that little room of an old servant suddenly added to my past life an extension so different from its other side and so delightful, I remember, as a contrast, the nullity of impressions left on my mind by the most sumptuous parties in the most princely mansions. The only thing that was distressing in Eulalie's room was that owing to the proximity of the viaduct, one heard the noise of passing trains at night. But as I knew that this roaring proceeded from regulated machines, it did not terrify me as much as the roars of a mammoth, prowling nearby in savage freedom, would have done in prehistoric days.

Thus I had already reached the conclusion that we are in no wise free in the presence of a work of art, that we do not create it as we please but that it pre-exists in us and we are compelled as though it were a law of nature to discover it because it is at once hidden from us and necessary. But is not that discovery, which art may enable us to make, most precious to us, a discovery of that which for most of us remains for ever unknown, our true life, reality as we have ourselves felt it and which differs so much from that which we had believed that we are filled with delight when chance brings us an authentic revelation of it? I was sure of this from the very falsity of so-called realistic art which would not be so deceptive if we had not in the course of life contracted the habit of giving what we feel an expression so different that, after a time, we believe it to be reality itself. I felt that it was not necessary for me to incommode myself with the diverse literary theories which had for a time troubled me – notably those that criticism had developed at the time of the Dreyfus affair and which had again resumed their sway during the war, which tended to 'make the artist come out of his ivory tower' and, instead of using frivolous or sentimental subjects as his material, to picture great working-class movements or if not the crowd, at all events rather than insignificant idlers ('I avow,' said Bloch, 'that the portraits of these futile people are indifferent to me') noble intellectuals or heroes.

Before even considering their logical content, these theories seemed to me to denote amongst those who entertained them, a proof of inferiority like a well-brought-up child, who, being sent out to lunch at a friend's house, hearing someone say: 'We speak out, we are frank', realises that the words signify a moral quality inferior to a pure and simple good act about which nothing is said. Authentic art does not proclaim itself for it is achieved in silence. Moreover, those who thus theorise, use ready-made expressions which singularly resemble those of the imbeciles they castigate. And perhaps it is rather by the quality of the language than by the particular aesthetic that we can judge the level which intellectual and moral work has reached. But inversely this quality of language (and we can study the laws of character equally well in a serious as in a frivolous subject, as an anatomist can study the laws of anatomy on the body of an imbecile just as well as on that of a man of talent; the great moral laws as well as those which govern the circulation of the blood or renal elimination making small difference between the intellectual value of individuals) with which theorists think they can dispense, those who admire theorists believe to be of no great intellectual value and in order to discern it, require it to be expressed in direct terms because they are unable to infer it from the beauty of imagery. Hence that vulgar temptation of an author to write intellectual works. A great indelicacy. A work in which there are theories is like an object upon which the price is marked. Further, this last only expresses a value which, in literature, is diminished by logical reasoning. We reason, that is, our mind wanders, each time our courage fails to force us to pursue an intuition through all the successive stages which end in its fixation, in the expression of its own reality.

The reality that must be expressed resides, I now realised, not in the appearance of the subject but in the degree of penetration of that intuition to a depth where that appearance matters little, as symbolised by the sound of the spoon upon the plate, the stiffness of the table-napkin, which were more precious for my spiritual renewal than many humanitarian, patriotic, international conversations. More style, I had heard said in those days, more literature of life. One can imagine how many of M. de Norpois' simple theories 'against flute-players' had flowered again since the war. For all those who, lacking artistic sensibility, that is, submission to the reality within, may be equipped with the faculty of reasoning for ever about art, and even were they diplomatists or financiers associated with the 'realities' of the present into the bargain, they will readily believe that literature is a sort of intellectual game which is destined to be eliminated more and more in the future. Some of them wanted the novel to be a sort of cinematographic procession. This conception was absurd. Nothing removes us further from the reality we perceive within ourselves than such a cinematographic vision.

Just now as I entered this library, I remembered what the Goncourts say about the beautiful original editions it contains and I promised myself to have a look at them whilst I was shut in here. And still following my argument, I took up one after another of the precious volumes without paying much attention to them when, inattentively opening one of them, *François le Champi*, by George Sand, I felt myself disagreeably affected as by some impression out of harmony with my thoughts, until I suddenly realised with an emotion which nearly brought tears to my eyes how much that impression was in harmony with them. It was as at the moment when in the mortuary vault the undertakers' men are lowering the coffin of a man who has rendered services to his country, and his son pressing the hands of the last friends who file past the tomb, suddenly hearing a flourish of trumpets under the windows, would be horrified by what he supposed a mockery designed to insult his sorrow, while another who had controlled himself until then, would be unable to restrain his tears because he realised that what he heard was the music of a regiment which was sharing his mourning and wanting to render homage to the remains of his father. Such was the painful impression I had experienced in reading the title of a book in the Prince de Guermantes' library, a title which communicated the idea to me that literature really does offer us that world of mystery I had no longer found in it. And yet, *François le Champi* was not a very remarkable book, but the name, like the name of Guermantes, was unlike those I had known later. The memory of what had seemed incomprehensible when my mother read it to me, was aroused by its title and in the same way that the name of

Guermantes (when I had not seen the Guermantes' for a long time) contained for me the whole of feudalism – so *François le Champi* contained the whole essence of the novel – dispossessing for an instant the commonplace ideas of which the stuffy novels of George Sand are composed. At a dinner party where thought is always superficial I might no doubt have spoken of *François le Champi* and the Guermantes' as though neither were associated with Combray. But when, as at this moment, I was alone, I plunged to a greater depth. At that time the idea that a particular individual whose acquaintance I had made in society was the cousin of Mme de Guermantes, that is to say, the cousin of a personage on a magic lantern slide, seemed to me incomprehensible, and just as much, that the finest books I had read should be, I do not even say superior which they nevertheless were, but equal to this extraordinary *François le Champi*. This was an old childish impression with which my memories of childhood and of my family were tenderly associated and which at first I had not recognised. At the first instant I had angrily asked myself who this stranger was who had done me a violence and the stranger was myself, the child I once was whom the book had revived in me, for recognising only the child in me, the book had at once summoned him, wanting only to be seen with his eyes, only to be loved with his heart and only to talk to him. And that book my mother had read aloud to me almost until morning at Combray, retained for me all the charm of that night. Certainly 'the pen' of George Sand, to use one of Brichot's expressions (he loved to say that a book was written by 'a lively pen'), did not appear to me a magical pen as it so long did to my mother before she modelled her literary tastes on mine. But it was a pen I had unconsciously electrified, as schoolboys sometimes amuse themselves by doing, and now a thousand trifles of Combray which I had not for so long seen, leaped lightly and spontaneously forth and came and hung on head over heels to the magnet in an endless chain vibrating with memories.

Certain minds which love mystery like to believe that objects preserve something of the eyes which have looked at them, that monuments and pictures are seen by us under an impalpable veil which the contemplative love of so many worshippers has woven about them through the centuries. That chimera would become true if they transposed it into the domain of the only reality there is for us all, into the domain of their own sensibility. Yes, in that sense and only in that sense, but much more so, for if we see again a thing which we looked at formerly it brings back to us, together with our past vision, all the imagery with which it was instinct. This is because objects – a book bound like others in its red cover – as soon as they have been perceived by us become something immaterial within us, partake of the same nature as our preoccupations or our feelings at that time and combine indissolubly with them. A name read in a book of former days contains within its syllables the swift wind and the brilliant sun of the moment when we read it. In the slightest sensation conveyed by the humblest aliment, the smell of coffee and milk, we recover that vague hope of fine weather which enticed us when the day was dawning and the morning sky uncertain; a sunray is a vase filled with perfumes, with sounds, with moments, with various humours, with climates. It is that essence which art worthy of the name must express and if it fails, one can yet derive a lesson from its failure (while one can never derive anything from the successes of realism) namely that that essence is in a measure subjective and incommunicable.

More than this, a thing we saw at a certain period, a book we read, does not remain for ever united only with what was then around us; it remains just as faithfully one with us as we then were and can only be recovered by the sensibility restoring the individual as he then was. If ever in thought I take up *François le Champi* in the library, immediately a child rises within me and replaces me, who alone has the right to read that title *François le Champi* and who reads it as he read it then with the same impression of the weather out in the garden, with the same old dreams about countries and life, the same anguish of the morrow. If I see a thing of another period, another young man will emerge. And my personality of today is only an abandoned quarry which believes that all it contains is uniform and monotonous, but from which memory, like a sculptor of ancient Greece, produces innumerable statues. I say, everything we see again, for books, behaving in that respect like things, through the way their cover opens, through the quality of the paper, can preserve within themselves as vivid a memory of how I then imagined Venice or of the wish I had to go there, as the sentences themselves. More vivid even, for the latter are sometimes an impediment like the photograph of a friend whom one recalls less after looking at it than when one contents oneself with thinking of him. Certainly in the case of many books of my youth, even, alas, those by Bergotte himself, when I happened to take them up on an evening I was tired, it was as though I had taken a train in the hope of obtaining repose by seeing different scenes and by breathing the atmosphere of former days. It often happens that the desired evocation is hindered by prolonged reading. There is one of Bergotte's books (the copy in this library contained a toadying and most platitudinous dedication to the Prince) which I read through one winter day some time ago when I could not see Gilberte, and I failed to discover those pages I formerly so much loved. Certain words made me think they were those pages but they were not. Where was the beauty I then found in them? Yet the snow which covered the Champs Elysées on the day I read it still covers the volume. I see it still.

And for that reason, had I been tempted to become a bibliophile like the Prince de Guermantes, I should only have been one in a way of my own, one who seeks a beauty independent of the value proper to the book and which consists for collectors in knowing the libraries through which it has passed, that it was given when such and such an event occurred to such and such a sovereign, to such and such a celebrity, in following its life from sale to sale; that beauty of a book which is in a sense historical, would not have been lost upon me. But I should extract that beauty with better will from the history of my own life, that is to say, not as a book-fancier; and it would often happen that I attached that beauty, not to the material volume itself but to a work such as this *François le Champi* contemplated for the first time in my little room at Combray during that night, perhaps the sweetest and the saddest of my life, when, alas, (at a time when the mysterious Guermantes seemed very inaccessible to me) I had wrung from my parents that first abdication from which I was able to date the decline of my health and of my will, my renunciation of a difficult task which every ensuing day made more painful – a task reassumed today in the library of those very Guermantes, on the most wonderful day when not only the former gropings of my thought but even the aim of my life and perhaps that of art were illuminated. Moreover, I should have been capable of interesting myself in the copies of books themselves in a living sense. The first edition of a work would have been more precious to me than the others but I should have understood by the first edition the one I read for the first time. I should seek original editions but by that I should mean books from which I got an original impression. For the impressions that follow are no longer original. I should collect the bindings of novels of former days, but they would be the days when I read my first novels, the days when my father repeated so often 'Sit up straight'. Like the dress in which we have seen a woman for the first time, they could help me to recover my love of then, the beauty which I had supplanted by so many images, ever less loved; in order to find it again, I who am no longer the self who felt it, must give place to the self I then was in order that he shall recall what he alone knew, what the self of today does not know.

The library which I should thus collect would have a greater value still, for the books I read formerly at Combray, at Venice, enriched now by memory with spacious illuminations representing the church of Saint-Hilaire, the gondola moored at the foot of San Giorgio Maggiore on the Grand Canal incrusted with flashing sapphires, would have become worthy of those medallioned scrolls and historic bibles which the collector never opens in order to read the text but only to be again enchanted by the colours with which some competitor of Fouquet has embellished them and which constitute all the value of the work. And yet to open those books read formerly only to look at the images which did not then adorn them would seem to me so dangerous that even in that sense, the only one I understand, I should not be tempted to become a bibliophile. I know too well how easily the images left by the mind are effaced by the mind. It replaces the old ones by new which have not the same power of resurrection. And if I still had the *François le Champi* which my mother selected one day from the parcel of books my grandmother was to give me for my birthday, I would never look at it; I should be too much afraid that, little by little, my impressions of today would insert themselves in it and blot out the earlier ones, I should be too fearful of its becoming so much a thing of the present that when I asked it to evoke again the child who spelt out its title in the little room at Combray, that child, unable to recognise its speech, would no longer respond to my appeal and would be for ever buried in oblivion.

The idea of a popular art like that of a patriotic art, even if it were not dangerous, seems to me absurd. If it were a matter of making it accessible to the masses one would have to sacrifice the delicacies of form 'suitable for idle people'; and I had frequented people in society enough to know that it is they who are the veritable unlettered, not the working electricians. In that respect a popular art-form should rather be intended for members of the Jockey Club than for those of the General Confederation of Labour; as to subjects, popular novels intoxicate the people like books written for children. They seek distraction through reading, and workmen are as inquisitive about princes as princes are about workmen. From the beginning of the war M. Barrés said that the artist (such as Titian) must above all work for the glory of his country. But he could only serve it as an artist, that is to say, on the condition, when he studies the laws of art, serves his apprenticeship and makes discoveries as intricate as those of science, that he must think of nothing – were it even his fatherland – except the truth he has to face. Do not let us imitate the revolutionaries who on account of their civic spirit despised when they did not destroy the works of Watteau and La Tour, painters who did more for the honour of France than all who took part in the Revolution. A soft-hearted person would not, perhaps, of his own accord choose anatomy as a subject of study. It was not the goodness of his virtuous heart, great though that was, which made Choderlos de Laclos write *Liaisons dangereuses* nor was it Flaubert's preference for the small or great *bourgeoisie* which made him select *Madame Bovary* and *L'Education sentimentale* as subjects. Some people say that the art of a period of speed must be brief, like those who said the war would be short, before it had taken place. By the same reasoning, the railway should have killed contemplation. Yet it was vain to regret the period of stagecoaches, for the automobile, in taking their place, still stops for tourists in front of abandoned churches.

A picture of life brings with it multiple and varied sensations. The sight, for instance, of the cover of a book which has been read spins from the character of its title the moonbeams of a distant summer-night. The taste of our morning coffee brings us that vague hope of a fine day which formerly so often smiled at us in the unsettled dawn from a fluted bowl of porcelain which seemed like hardened milk. An hour is not merely an hour, it is a vase filled with perfumes, with sounds, with projects, with climates. What we call reality is a relation between those sensations and those memories which simultaneously encircle us – a relation which a cinematographic vision destroys because its form separates it from the truth to which it pretends to limit itself – that unique relation which the writer must discover in order that he may link two different states of being together for ever in a phrase. In describing objects one can make those which figure in a particular place succeed each other indefinitely; the truth will only begin to emerge from the moment that the writer takes two different objects, posits their relationship, the analogue in the world of art to the only relationship of causal law in the world of science, and encloses it within the circle of fine style. In this, as in life, he fuses a quality common to two sensations, extracts their essence and in order to withdraw them from the contingencies of time, unites them in a metaphor, thus chaining them together with the indefinable bond of a verbal alliance. Was not nature herself from this point of view, on the track of art, was she not the beginning of art, she who often only permitted me to realise the beauty of one object long afterwards in another, midday at Combray only through the sound of its bells, mornings at Doncières only through the groans of our heating apparatus. The relationship may be of little interest, the objects commonplace, the style bad, but unless there is that relationship, there is nothing. A literature which is content with 'describing things', with offering a wretched summary of their lines and surfaces, is, in spite of its pretension to realism, the furthest from reality, the one which impoverishes us and saddens us the most, however much it may talk of glory and grandeur, for it abruptly severs communication between our present self, the past of which objects retain the essence and the future in which they encourage us to search for it again. But there is more. If reality were that sort of waste experience approximately identical in everyone because when we say: 'bad weather', 'war', 'cab-stand', 'lighted restaurant', 'flower garden', everybody knows what we mean – if reality were that, no doubt a sort of cinematographic film of these things would suffice and 'style', 'literature' isolating itself from that simple datum would be an artificial hors d'oeuvre. But is it so in reality? If I tried to render conscious to myself what takes place in us at the moment a circumstance or an event makes a certain impression, if, on the day I crossed the Vivonne bridge, the shadow of a cloud on the water made me jump for joy and ejaculate 'hullo!' if, listening to a phrase of Bergotte, all I could make of my impression were an expression such as 'Admirable!' which did not specially apply to it, if, annoyed by somebody's bad behaviour, Bloch uttered words with no particular relevance to so sordid an adventure: such as 'I consider it fantastic for a man to behave like that', or if flattered at being well received by the Guermantes and perhaps a little drunk on their wine, I could not help saying to myself in an undertone as I left them: 'After all, they're charming people whom it would be delightful to spend one's life with', I perceived that to express those impressions, to write that essential book, which is the only true one, a great writer does not, in the current meaning of the word, invent it, but, since it exists already in each one of us, interprets it. The duty and the task of a writer are those of an interpreter.

And if, where an inaccurate mode of expression inspired by the writer's self-esteem is concerned, the straightening-out of the oblique inner utterance (which diverges more and more from the original mental impression) until it makes one with the straight line which should have issued from that impression, if that straightening-out is an uneasy process against which our idleness rebels, there are other cases, of love, for instance, where that same straightening-out becomes painful. All our feigned indifferences, all our natural indignation at its inevitable lies, so like our own, in a word, all that we constantly said when we were unhappy or deceived, not only to the being we loved but even to ourselves while awaiting her, sometimes aloud in the silence of our chamber, marked by: 'No, really such behaviour is unbearable', and 'I've decided to see you for the last time. I can't deny the pain it causes,' to bring back what was really and truly felt from where it had strayed, is to abolish everything we most clung to, the matter of our passionate self-communion during fevered moments when, face to face with ourselves, we asked what letter we could write, what should be our next step.

Even when we seek artistic delights for the sake of the impression they make on us, we manage quickly to dispense with the impression itself and to fix our attention on that element in it which enables us to experience pleasure without penetrating to its depth, and thinking we can communicate it to others in conversation because we shall be talking to them about something common to them and to us, the personal root impression is eliminated. In the very moments when we are the most disinterested spectators of nature, of society, of love, of art itself – as all impression is twofold, half-sheathed in the object, prolonged in ourselves by another half which we alone can know – we hasten to neglect the latter, that is to say, the only one on which we should concentrate, and fasten merely on the other half which, being unfathomable because it is exterior to ourselves, causes us no fatigue; we consider the effort to perceive the little groove which a musical phrase or the view of a church has hollowed in ourselves too arduous. But we play the symphony over and over again, we go back to look at the church until – in that flight far away from our own life which we have not the courage to face called erudition – we get to know them as well, and in the same way as the most accomplished musical or archaeological amateur. And how many stop at that point, get nothing from their impression, and ageing useless and unsatisfied, remain sterile celibates of art! To them come the same discontents as to virgins and idlers whom the fecundity of labour would cure. They are more exalted when they talk about works of art than real artists, for their enthusiasm, not being an incentive to the hard task of penetrating to the depths, expands outwards, heats their conversation and empurples their faces; they think they are doing something by shrieking at the tops of their voices: 'Bravo! Bravo!' after the performance of a composition they like. But these manifestations do not force them to clarify the character of their admiration, so they learn nothing. Nevertheless, this futile admiration overflows in their most ordinary conversation and causes them to make gestures, grimaces and movements of the head when they talk of art: 'I was at a concert where they were playing music which I can assure you did not thrill me. Then they began the quartet. Ah! My word! That changed it! (The face of the amateur at that moment expresses anxious apprehension as if he were thinking: "I see sparks flying, there's a smell of burning, there's a fire!") Bless my soul! This is maddening! It's badly composed but it's flabbergasting! This is no ordinary work.'

But laughable as those amateurs may be, they are not altogether to be despised. They are the first attempts of nature to create an artist, as formless and unviable as the antediluvian animals which preceded those of today and which were not created to endure. These whimsical and sterile amateurs affect us much as did those first mechanical contrivances which could not leave the earth, in which, though the secret means remained to be discovered, was contained the aspiration of flight. 'And, old fellow,' adds the amateur, taking you by the arm, 'it's the eighth time I've heard it and I swear to you it won't be the last.' And in truth since they do not assimilate from art what is really nourishing, they perpetually need artistic stimulus, because they are a prey to a craving which can never be assuaged. So they will go on applauding the same work for a long time to come, believing that their presence is a duty, such as others fulfil at a board-meeting or a funeral. Then come other works whether of literature, of painting or of music which create opposition. For the faculty of starting ideas or systems and above all of assimilating them has always been much more frequent even amongst those who create, than real taste, but has been extended since the reviews, the literary papers, have multiplied (and with them the artificial profession of writers and artists). Thus the best of the young, the most intelligent, the most intense, preferred works of an elevated moral, sociological or religious tendency. They imagined that such considerations constitute the value of a work, thus renewing the error of the Davids, the Chenavards, the Brunetières; they prefer to Bergotte whose lightest phrases really exacted a much deeper return to oneself, writers who seemed more profound only because they wrote less well. The complexity of Bergotte's writing was only meant for society people, was the comment of these democrats, who thus did society people an honour they did not deserve. But from the moment that works of art are judged by reasoning, nothing is stable or certain, one can prove anything one likes. Whereas the reality of genius is a benefaction, an acquisition for the world at large, the presence of which must first be identified beneath the more obvious modes of thought and style; criticism stops at this point and assesses writers by the form instead of the matter. It consecrates as a prophet a writer who, while expressing in arrogant terms his contempt for the school which preceded him, brings no new message. This constant aberration of criticism has reached a point where a writer would almost prefer to be judged by the general public (were it not that it is incapable of understanding the researches an artist has been attempting in a sphere unknown to it). For there is more analogy between the instinctive life of the public and the genius of a great writer which is itself but instinct, realised and perfected, to be listened to in a religious silence imposed upon all others, than there is in the superficial verbiage and changing criteria of self-constituted judges. Their wrangling renews itself every ten years, for the kaleidoscope is not composed only of groups in society but of social, political and religious ideas which obtain a momentary expansion, thanks to their refraction in the masses, but survive only so long as their novelty influences minds which exact little in the way of proof. Again, parties and schools succeed each other, always catering to the same mentalities, men of relative intelligence prone to extravagances from which minds more scrupulous and more difficult to convince, abstain. Unhappily, just because the former are only half-minds they require action to complete themselves and as through this they exercise more influence than superior minds, they impose themselves on the mass and create a constituency not merely of unmerited reputations and unjustifiable rancours but also of civil and exterior warfare from which a little self-criticism might have saved them.

Now the enjoyment a well-balanced mind, a heart which is really alive, gets from the beautiful thought of a master, is undoubtedly wholesome, but valuable as are those who properly appreciate that thought (how many are there in twenty years?) they are reduced by their very enjoyment to being no more than the enlarged consciousness of another. A man may have done everything in his power to be loved by a woman who would only make him unhappy but has not succeeded, in spite of all his attempts during years, in obtaining an assignation with her. Instead of seeking to express his sufferings and the danger from which he has escaped, he ceaselessly rereads this thought of La Bruyère making it represent a thousand implications and the most moving memories of his own life: 'Men often want to love and do not know how to, they seek defeat without being able to encounter it and, if I may say so, are forced to remain free.' Whether this thought had this meaning or not for him who wrote it (for it to have that meaning he ought to have said 'to be loved' instead of 'to love' and it would have been more beautiful), it is certain that this sensitive man of letters endows the thought with life, swells it with significance until it bursts within him and he cannot repeat it without a feeling of immense satisfaction, so completely true and beautiful does it seem to him, although, after all, he has added nothing to it and it remains simply a thought of La Bruyère.

How can a literature of notations have any value since it is beneath the little things it notes that the reality exists (the grandeur in the distant sound of an aeroplane, in the outline of the belfry of Saint-Hilaire, the past in the savour of a madeleine) these being without significance in themselves if one does not disengage it from them?

Accumulated little by little in the memory, the chain of all the obscure impressions where nothing of what we actually experienced remains, constitutes our thought, our life, reality and it is that lie which a so-called 'lived art' would only reproduce, an art as crude as life, without beauty, a reproduction so wearisome and futile of what our eyes have seen and our intelligence has observed, that one asks oneself how he who makes that his aim can find in it the exultant stimulus which gives zest to work. The grandeur of veritable art, to the contrary of what M. de Norpois called 'a dilettante's amusement', is to recapture, to lay hold of, to make one with ourselves that reality far removed from the one we live in, from which we separate ourselves more and more as the knowledge which we substitute for it acquires a greater solidity and impermeability, a reality we run the risk of never knowing before we die but which is our real, our true life at last revealed and illumined, the only life which is really lived and which in one sense lives at every moment in all men as well as in the artist. But they do not see it because they do not seek to illuminate it. And thus their past is encumbered with innumerable 'negatives' which remain useless because the intelligence has not 'developed' them. To lay hold of our life; and also the life of others; for a writer's style and also a painter's are matters not of technique but of vision. It is the revelation, impossible by direct and conscious means, of the qualitative difference there is in the way in which we look at the world, a difference which, without art, would remain for ever each man's personal secret. By art alone we are able to get outside ourselves, to know what another sees of this universe which for him is not ours, the landscapes of which would remain as unknown to us as those of the moon. Thanks to art, instead of seeing one world, our own, we see it multiplied and as many original artists as there are, so many worlds are at our disposal, differing more widely from each other than those which roll round the infinite and which, whether their name be Rembrandt or Vermeer, send us their unique rays many centuries after the hearth from which they emanate is extinguished.

This labour of the artist to discover a means of apprehending beneath matter and experience, beneath words, something different from their appearance, is of an exactly contrary nature to the operation in which pride, passion, intelligence and habit are constantly engaged within us when we spend our lives without self-communion, accumulating as though to hide our true impressions, the terminology for practical ends which we falsely call life. In short, this complex art is precisely the only living art. It alone expresses for others, and makes us see, our own life, that life which cannot observe itself, the outer forms of which, when observed, need to be interpreted and often read upside down, in order to be laboriously deciphered. The work of our pride, our passion, our spirit of imitation, our abstract intelligence, our habits must be undone by art which takes the opposite course and returning to the depths where the real has its unknown being, makes us pursue it.

It is, of course, a great temptation to recreate true life, to renew impressions. But courage of all kinds is required, even emotional courage. For it means above all, abrogating our most cherished illusions, ceasing to believe in the objectivity of our own elaborations and, instead of soothing ourselves for the hundredth time with the words 'she was very sweet', reading into them

'I liked kissing her'. Of course what I had experienced in hours of love every other man experiences. But what one has experienced is like certain negatives which show black until they are placed under a lamp, and they too must be looked at from the back; we do not know what a thing is until we have approached it with our intelligence. Only when the intelligence illuminates it, when it has intellectualised it, we distinguish, and with how much difficulty, the shape of that which we have felt, and I realised also that the suffering I had formerly experienced with Gilberte in realising that our love has nothing to do with the being who inspires it, is salutary as a supplementary aid to knowledge. (For, however short a time our life may last it is only while we are suffering that our thoughts, in a constant state of agitation and change, cause the depths within us to surge as in a tempest to a height where we see that they are subject to laws which, until then, we could not observe, because the calm of happiness left those depths undisturbed. Perhaps only in the case of a few great geniuses is it possible for this movement to be constantly felt without their suffering turmoil and sadness; but again it is not certain, when we contemplate the spacious and uniform development of their serene achievements, that we are not too much taking for granted that the buoyancy of the work implies that of its creator, who perhaps, on the contrary, was continuously unhappy.) But principally because if our love is not only for a Gilberte, what gives us so much pain is not that it is also the love of an Albertine but because it is a more durable part of our soul than the various selves which successively die in us, each of which would selfishly retain it, a part of our soul which must, whatever the pain, detach itself from those beings so that we should understand and constitute their generality and impart the meaning of that love to all men, to the universal consciousness and not to one woman, then to another with which first one, then another of our successive selves has desired to unite.

It was, therefore, necessary for me to discover the meaning of the slightest signs that surrounded me (Guermantes, Albertine, Gilberte, Saint-Loup, Balbec, et cetera) which I had lost sight of owing to habit. We have to learn that to preserve and express reality when we have attained it, we must isolate it from everything that our habit of haste accumulates in opposition to it. Above all, I had, therefore to exclude words spoken by the lips but not by the mind; those humorous colloquialisms which after much social intercourse, we get accustomed to using artificially, which fill the mind with lies, those purely physical words uttered with a knowing smile by the writer who lowers himself by transcribing them, that little grimace which, for instance, constantly deforms the spoken phrase of a Sainte-Beuve, whereas real books must be children not of broad daylight and small-talk but of darkness and silence. And since art minutely reconstructs life round the verities one has apprehended in oneself, an atmosphere of poetry will always float round them, the sweetness of a mystery which is only the remains of twilight through which we have had to pass, the indication, like that of a measuring rod, of the depth of a work. (For that depth is not inherent in certain subjects as is believed by materialist-spiritual novelists, since they cannot penetrate beneath the world of appearances and their lofty intentions, like those virtuous tirades habitual to people who are incapable of the smallest kindly effort, must not prevent our observing that they have not even the mental power to throw off the ordinary banalities acquired by imitation.)

As to the verities which the intellect – even of highly endowed minds – gathers in the open road, in full daylight their value can be very great; but those verities have rigid outlines and are flat, they have no depth because no depths have been sounded to reach them – they have not been recreated. It often happens that writers who no longer exhibit these verities, as they grow old, only use their intelligence which has acquired more and more power; and though for this reason their mature works are more able, they have not the velvety quality of their youthful ones.

Nevertheless, I felt that the truths the intellect extracts from immediate reality are not to be despised for they might enshrine, with matter less pure but, nevertheless, vitalised by the mind, intuitions the essence of which, being common to past and present, carries us beyond time, but which are too rare and precious to be the only elements in a work of art. I felt a mass of truths pressing on my notice, relative to passions, characters and habits which could be thus used.

We can, perhaps, attach every creature who has caused us unhappiness to a divinity of which she is only the most fragmentary reflection, a divinity the contemplation of whom in the realm of idea will give us immediate happiness instead of our former pain. The whole art of living is to regard people who cause us suffering as, in a degree, enabling us to accept its divine form and thus to populate our daily life with divinities. The perception of these truths gave me joy albeit it reminded me that if I had discovered more than one of them through suffering, I had discovered as many in the course of the most commonplace indulgences.

Then a new light arose in me, less brilliant indeed than the one that had made me perceive that a work of art is the only means of regaining lost Time. And I understood that all the material of a literary work was in my past life, I understood that I had acquired it in the midst of frivolous amusements, in idleness, in tenderness and in pain, stored up by me without my divining its destination or even its survival, as the seed has in reserve all the ingredients which will nourish the plant. Like the seed I might die when the plant had developed and I might find I had lived for it without knowing it, without my life having ever seemed to require contact with the books I wanted to write and for which when I formerly sat down at my table, I could find no subject. Thus all my life up to that day might have been or might not have been summed up under the title: 'A vocation?' In one sense, literature had played no active part in my life. But, in another, my life, the memories of its sorrows, of its joys, had been forming a reserve like albumen in the ovule of a plant. It is from this that the plant draws its nourishment in order to transform itself into seed at a time when one does not yet know that the embryo of the plant is developing though chemical phenomena and secret but very active respirations are taking place in it. Thus my life had been lived in constant contact with the elements which would bring about its ripening. And those who would later derive nourishment from it would be as ignorant of the process that supplied it as those who eat the products of grain are unaware of the rich aliments it contains though they have manured the soil in which it was grown and have enabled it to reach maturity.

In this connection the comparisons which are false if one starts from them may be true if one ends by them. The writer envies the painter, he would like to make sketches and notes and, if he does so, he is lost. Yet, in writing, there is not a gesture of his characters, a mannerism, an accent, which has not impregnated his memory; there is not a single invented character to whom he could not give sixty names of people he has observed, of whom one poses for a grimace, another for an eyeglass, another for his temper, another for a particular movement of the arms. And the writer discovers that if his aspiration to be a painter could not be consciously realised, he has nevertheless filled his notebook with sketches without being aware of it.

For, owing to his instinct, the writer long before he knew he was going to be one, habitually avoided looking at all sorts of things other people noticed, and was, in consequence, accused by others of absentmindedness and by himself of being incapable of attention and observation, while all the time he was ordering his eyes and his ears to retain for ever what to others seemed puerile, the tone in which a phrase had been uttered, the facial expression and movement of the shoulders of a particular person at a particular moment perhaps years ago, who was otherwise unknown to him, and this because he had heard that tone before or felt he might hear it again, that it was a recurrent and permanent characteristic. It is the feeling for the general in the potential writer, which selects material suitable to a work of art because of its generality. He only pays attention to others, however dull and tiresome, because in repeating what their kind say like parrots, they are for that very reason prophetic birds, spokesmen of a psychological law. He recalls only what is general. Through certain ways of speaking, through a certain play of features and through certain movements of the shoulders even though they had been seen when he was a child, the life of others remains within himself and when later on he begins writing, that life will help to recreate reality, possibly by the use of that movement of the shoulders common to many people. This movement is as true to life as though it had been noted by an anatomist, but the writer expresses thereby a psychological verity by grafting on to the shoulders of one individual the neck of another, both of whom had only posed to him for a moment.

It is uncertain whether in the creation of a literary work the imagination and the sensibility are not interchangeable and whether the second, without disadvantage, cannot be substituted for the first just as people whose stomach is incapable of digesting entrust this function to their intestines. An innately sensitive man who has no imagination could, nevertheless write admirable novels. The suffering caused him by others and the conflict provoked by his efforts to protect himself against them, such experiences interpreted by the intelligence might provide material for a book as beautiful as if it were imagined and invented and as objective, as startling and unexpected as the author's imaginative fancy would have been, had he been happy and free from persecution.

The stupidest people unconsciously express their feelings by their gestures and their remarks and thus demonstrate laws they are unaware of which the artist brings to light. On account of this, the vulgar wrongly believe the writer to be mischievous for the artist sees an engaging generality in an absurd individual and no more imputes blame to him than a surgeon despises his patient for being affected with a chronic ailment of the circulation. Moreover, no one is less inclined to scoff at absurd people than the artist. Unfortunately he is more unhappy than mischievous where his own passions are concerned; though he recognises their generality just as much in his own case, he escapes personal suffering less easily. Obviously, we prefer to be praised rather than insulted and still more when a woman we love deceives us, what would we not give that it should be otherwise. But the resentment of the affront, the pain of the abandonment would in that event have been worlds we should never have known, the discovery of which, painful as it may be for the man, is precious for the artist. In spite of himself and of themselves, the mischievous and the ungrateful must figure in his work. The publicist involuntarily associates the rascals he has castigated with his own celebrity. In every work of art we can recognise the man the artist has most hated, and alas, even the women he has most loved. They were posing for the writer at the very moment when, against his will, they were making him suffer the most. When I was in love with Albertine I fully realised she did not love me and I had to resign myself to her only teaching me the pain of love even at its dawn.

And when we try to extract generality from our sorrow so as to write about it we are a little consoled, perhaps for another reason than those I have hitherto given, which is, that thinking in a general way, writing is a sanitary and indispensable function for the writer and gives him satisfaction in the same way that exercise, sweating and baths do a physical man. To tell the truth I revolted somewhat against this. However much I might believe that the supreme truth of life is in art, however little I was capable of the effort of memory needed to feel love for Albertine again as to mourn my grandmother anew, I asked myself whether, nevertheless, a work of art of which neither of them was conscious could be for those poor dead the fulfilment of their destiny. My grandmother whom I had watched with so much indifference while she lay near me in her last agony. Ah! could I, when my work is done, wounded beyond remedy, suffer, in expiation, long hours of abandonment by all as I lie dying! Moreover, I had an infinite pity for beings less dear, even indifferent to me, and of how many destinies had my thought used the sufferings, even only the absurdities in my attempts to understand them. All those beings who revealed truths to me and who were no longer there, seemed to me to have lived a life from which I alone profited and as though they had died for me.

It was sad for me to think that in my book, my love which was once everything to me, would be so detached from a being that various readers would apply it textually to the love they experienced for other women. But why should I be horrified by this posthumous infidelity, that this man or that should offer unknown women as the object of my sentiment, when that infidelity, that division of love between several beings began with my life and long before I began writing? I had indeed suffered successively through Gilberte, through Mme de Guermantes, through Albertine. Successively also I had forgotten them and only my love, dedicated at different times to different beings, had lasted. I had anticipated the profanation of my memories by unknown readers. I was not far from being horrified with myself as, perhaps, some nationalist party might be in whose name hostilities had been provoked and who alone had benefited from a war in which many noble victims had suffered and died without even knowing the issue of the struggle which, for my grandmother, would have been such a complete reward. And the single consolation she never knew, that at last I had set to work, was, such being the fate of the dead, that though she could not rejoice in my progress she had at least been spared consciousness of my long inactivity, of the frustrated life which had been such a pain to her. And certainly there were many others besides my grandmother and Albertine from whom I had assimilated a word, a glance, but of whom as individual beings I remembered nothing; a book is a great cemetery in which, for the most part, the names upon the tombs are effaced. Sometimes, on the other hand, one writes a well remembered name without knowing whether anything else survives of the being who bore it. That young girl with the deep sunken eyes, with the haunting voice, is she there? And if she is, in which part, where are we to look for her under the flowers?

But since we live remote from individual lives, since we no longer retain our deepest feelings such as my love for my grandmother and for Albertine, since they are now no more than meaningless words, since we can talk about these dead with people in society to whose houses it still gives us pleasure to go after the death of all we loved, if there is yet a means of learning to understand those forgotten words, should we not use it even though we had first to find a universal language in which to express them so that, thus rendered permanent, they would form the ultimate essence of those who are gone and remain an acquisition in perpetuity of every soul? Indeed, if we could explain that law of change which has made those words of the dead unintelligible to us, might not our inferiority become a new force? Furthermore the work in which our sorrows have collaborated, may perhaps be interpreted as an indication both of atrocious suffering and of happy consolation in the future. Indeed, if we say that the loves, the sorrows of the poet have served him, that they have aided him to construct his work, that the unknown women who least suspected, one with her mischief-making, the other with her raillery, that they were each contributing their stone towards the building of the monument they would never see, one does not sufficiently reflect that the life of the writer is not finished with that work, that the same nature which caused him the sorrow that coloured his work, will remain his after the work is finished, will cause him to love other women in circumstances which would be similar if they were not slightly changed by time which modifies conditions in the subject himself, in his appetite for love and in his resistance to suffering. From this first point of view his work must be considered only as an unhappy love which inevitably presages others and which causes his life to resemble it, so that the poet hardly needs to continue writing, so completely will he discover the semblance of what will happen anticipated in what he has written. Thus my love for Albertine and the degree in which it differed was already engrossed in my love for Gilberte in the midst of those joyous days when for the first time I heard Albertine's name mentioned by her aunt, without suspecting that that insignificant germ would one day develop and spread over my whole life.

But from another point of view, the work is an emblem of happiness because it teaches us that in all love the general has its being close beside the particular and passes from the second to the first by a gymnastic which strengthens the writer against sorrow through making him pass over its cause in order to probe to its essence. In fact, as I was to experience thereafter, when I had realised my vocation, even at a time of anguish caused by love, the object of one's passion becomes so completely merged in the universal during one's working hours, that for the time being, one forgets her existence and only feels one's heartache as a physical pain. It is true that it is a question of moments and that the effect seems to be the contrary if work comes afterwards. For when beings, who by their badness, their insignificance, succeed, in spite of ourselves, in destroying our illusions, are themselves reduced to impotence by being separated from the amorous chimera we had forged for ourselves, if we then put ourselves to work, our spirit raises them anew, identifies them, for the needs of self-analysis, with beings we once loved and in this case, literature doing over again the work undone by disillusion, bestows a sort of survival on sentiments which have ceased to exist.

Certainly we are obliged to relive our particular suffering with the courage of a physician who tries over again upon himself an experiment with a dangerous serum. But we ought to think of it under a general form which enables us to some extent to escape from its control by making all men co-partners in our sorrow, and this is not devoid of a certain gratification. Where life closes round us, intelligence pierces an egress, for if there is no remedy for unrequited love, one emerges from the verification of suffering if only by drawing its relevant conclusions. The intellect does not recognise situations in life which have no issue.

And I had to resign myself, since nothing can last except by becoming general (unless the mind lies to itself) by accepting the idea that even those beings who were dearest to the writer have ultimately only posed to him as to painters.

Sometimes when a painful section has remained at the stage of a sketch, a new tenderness, a new suffering comes which enables us to finish it and fill it out. One has no need to complain of the lack of new and helpful sorrows for plenty are forthcoming and one will not have to wait long for them. All the same, it is necessary to hasten to profit by them for they do not last very long; either we console ourselves or if they are too strong and the heart is not too sound, one dies. In love our successful rival, as well call him our enemy, is our benefactor. He immediately adds to a being who only excited in us an insignificant physical desire, an enormously enhanced value which we confuse with it. If we had no rivals, physical gratification would not be transformed into love, that is to say, if we had no rivals or believed we had none, for they need not actually exist. That illusory life which our suspicion and jealousy give to rivals who have no existence, is sufficient for our good. Happiness is salutary for the body but sorrow develops the powers of the spirit. Moreover, does it not on each occasion reveal to us a law which is no less indispensable for the purpose of bringing us back to truth, of forcing us to take things seriously by pulling up the weeds of habit, scepticism, frivolity and indifference? It is true that that truth which is incompatible with happiness, with health, is not always compatible with life itself. Sorrow ends by killing. At each fresh overmastering sorrow one more vein projects and develops its mortal sinuousness across our brows and under our eyes. Thus, little by little, those terribly ravaged faces of Rembrandt, of Beethoven, are made, at which people once mocked. And those pockets under the eyes and wrinkles in the forehead would not be there if there had not been such suffering in the heart. But since forces can change into other forces, since heat which has duration becomes light and the electricity in a lightning-flash can photograph, since our heavy heartache can with each recurrent sorrow raise above itself like a flag, a visible and permanent symbol, let us accept the physical hurt for the sake of the spiritual knowledge and let our bodies disintegrate, since each fresh fragment which detaches itself now becomes more luminously revealing so that we may complete our task at the cost of suffering not needed by others more gifted, building it up and adding to it in proportion to the emotions that destroy our life. Ideas are substitutes for sorrows; when the latter change into ideas they lose part of their noxious action on our hearts and even at the first instant their very transformation disengages a feeling of joy. Substitutes only in the order of time, however, for it would seem that the first element is idea and that sorrow is only the mode in which certain ideas first enter us. But there are many families in the group of ideas, some are immediately joys.

These reflections made me discover a stronger and more accurate sense of the truth of which I had often had a presentiment, notably when Mme de Cambremer was surprised that I could abandon a remarkable man like Elstir for the sake of Albertine. Even from the intellectual point of view I felt she was wrong but I did not know that what she was misunderstanding were the lessons through which one makes one's apprenticeship as a man of letters. The objective value of the arts has little say in the matter; what it is necessary to extract and bring to light are our sentiments, our passions, which are the sentiments and passions of all men. A woman we need makes us suffer, forces from us a series of sentiments, deeper and more vital than a superior type of man who interests us. It remains to be seen, according to the plane on which we live, whether we shall discover that the pain the infidelity of a woman has caused us is a trifle when compared with the truths thereby revealed to us, truths that the woman delighted at having made us suffer would hardly have grasped. In any case, such infidelities are not rare. A writer need have no fear of undertaking a long labour. Let the intellect get to work; in the course of it there will be more than enough sorrows to enable him to finish it. Happiness serves hardly any other purpose than to make unhappiness possible. When we are happy, we have to form very tender and strong links of confidence and attachment for their rupture to cause us the precious shattering called misery. Without happiness, if only that of hoping, there would be no cruelty and, therefore, no fruit of misfortune.

And more than a painter who needs to see many churches in order to paint one church, a writer, to obtain volume, consistency, generality and literary reality, needs many beings in order to express one feeling, for if art is long and life is short one can say on the other hand, that if inspiration is short, the sentiments it has to express are not much longer. Our passions shape our books, repose writes them in the intervals. When inspiration is reborn, when we are able to take up our work again, the woman who posed to us for our emotional reaction can no longer make us feel it. We must continue to paint her from another model and if that is a treachery to the first, in a literary sense, thanks to the similarity of our sentiments which make a work at one and the same time a memory of our past loves and the starting point of new ones, there is no great disadvantage in the exchange. That is one of the reasons why studies in which an attempt is made to guess whom an author has been writing about, are fatuous. For even a direct confession is at the very least intercalated between different episodes in the life of the author, the early ones which inspired it, the later ones which no less inspired the successive loves whose peculiarities were a tracing of the preceding ones. For we are not as faithful to the being we have most loved as we are to ourselves and sooner or later we forget her – since that is one of our characteristics – so as to start loving another. At the very most, she whom we have so much loved has given a particular form to that love which will make us faithful to her even in our infidelity. We should feel a need to take the same morning walks with her successor and to bring her home in the same fashion in the evening and we should give her also much too much money. (That circulation of money we give to women is curious; because of it, they make us miserable and so help us to write books – one might almost say that works of literature arlike artesian wells, the deeper the suffering, the higher they rise.) These substitutions add something disinterested and more general to work, and are also a lesson in austerity; we ought not to attach ourselves to beings, it is not beings who exist in reality and are amenable to description, but ideas. And we must not lose time while we can still dispose of these models. For those who pose for happiness are not, as a rule, able to spare us many sittings. But those who pose to us for sorrow give us plenty of sittings in the studio we only use at those periods. That studio is within ourselves. Those periods are a picture of our life with its divers sufferings. For they contain others and just when we think we are calm, a new one is born, new in all senses of the word; perhaps because unforeseen situations force us to enter into deeper contact with ourselves, the painful dilemmas in which love places us at every instant, instruct us, disclose to us successively the matter of which we are made.

Moreover, even when suffering does not supply by its revelation the raw material of our work, it helps us by stimulating us to it. Imagination, thought, may be admirable mechanisms but they can also be inert. Suffering alone sets them going. Thus when Françoise, noticing that Albertine came in by any door of the house that happened to be open as a dog would, spreading disorder wherever she went, ruining me, causing me infinite unhappiness, she said (for at that time I had already done some articles and translations), 'Ah, if only monsieur had engaged a well-educated little secretary who would have put all monsieur's rolls of paper in order instead of that girl who only wastes his time', perhaps I was wrong in thinking she was talking good sense. Perhaps Albertine had been more useful to me, even from the literary point of view, in making me lose my time and in causing me sorrow than a secretary who would have arranged my papers. But all the same, when a creature is so badly constituted (perhaps in nature that being is man) that he cannot love unless he suffers and that he must suffer to learn truth, the life of such a being becomes in the end very exhausting. The happy years are those that are wasted; we must wait for suffering to drive us to work. The idea of preliminary suffering is associated with that of work, we dread every fresh undertaking because we are thereby reminded of the pain in store for us before we can conceive it. And, realising that suffering is the best thing life has to offer, we think of death without horror and almost as a deliverance.

And yet, if that thought was somewhat repellent to me, we have to be sure we have not played with life and profited by other people's lives to write books but the exact opposite. The case of the noble Werther was, alas, not mine. Without believing an instant in Albertine's love, twenty times I wanted to kill myself for her; I had ruined myself and destroyed my health for her. When it is a question of writing, we have to be scrupulous, look close and cast out what is not true. But when it is only a question of our own lives, we ruin ourselves, make ourselves ill, kill ourselves for the sake of lies. Of a truth, it is only out of the matrix of those lies (if one is too old to be a poet) that we can extract a little truth. Sorrows are obscure and hated servitors against whom we contend, under whose sway we fall more and more, sinister servitors whom we cannot replace but who by strange and devious ways lead us to truth and to death. Happy those who have encountered the former before the latter and for whom, closely as one may follow the other, the hour of truth sounds before the hour of death.

Furthermore, I realised that the most trivial episodes of my past life had combined to give me the lesson of idealism from which I was now going to profit. Had not my meetings with M. de Charlus, for instance, even before his Germanophilism had given me the same lesson, and better than my love for Mme de Guermantes or for Albertine, better than the love of Saint-Loup for Rachel, proved to me how little material matters, that everything can be made of it by thought, a verity that the phenomenon of sexual inversion, so little understood, so idly condemned, enhances even more than that of love of women, instructive as that is; the latter shows us beauty flying from the woman we no longer love and residing in a face which others consider extremely ugly, which indeed might have displeased us and probably will later on; but it is still more remarkable to observe such a face under the cap of an omnibus conductor, receiving all the homage of a *grand seigneur*, who has for that abandoned a beautiful princesse. Did not my astonishment each time that I again saw the face of Gilberte, of Mme de Guermantes, of Albertine in the Champs Elysées, in the street, on the shore, prove that a memory can only be prolonged in a direction which diverges from the impression with which it formerly coincided and from which it separates itself more and more.

The writer must not mind if the invert gives his heroines a masculine visage. This peculiar aberration is the only means open to the invert of applying generality to what he reads. If M. de Charlus had not given Morel's face to the unfaithful one over whom Musset sheds tears in the *Nuit d'Octobre* or in the *Souvenir*, he would neither have wept nor understood since it was by that road alone, narrow and tortuous though it might be, that he had access to the verities of love. It is only through a custom which owes its origin to the insincere language of prefaces and dedications that a writer says 'my reader'. In reality, every reader, as he reads, is the reader of himself. The work of the writer is only a sort of optic instrument which he offers to the reader so that he may discern in the book what he would probably not have seen in himself. The recognition of himself in the book by the reader is the proof of its truth and *vice versa*, at least in a certain measure, the difference between the two texts being often less attributable to the author than to the reader. Further, a book may be too learned, too obscure for the simple reader, and thus be only offering him a blurred glass with which he cannot read. But other peculiarities (like inversion) might make it necessary for the reader to read in a certain way in order to read well; the author must not take offence at that but must, on the contrary, leave the reader the greatest liberty and say to him: 'Try whether you see better with this, with that, or with another glass.'

If I have always been so much interested in dreams, is it not because, compensating duration with intensity they help us to understand better what is subjective in love? And this by the simple fact that they render real with prodigious speed what is vulgarly called *nous mettre une femme dans la peau* to the point of falling passionately in love for a few minutes with an ugly one, which in real life would require years of habit, of union and – as though they had been invented by some miraculous doctor – intravenous injections of love as they can also be of suffering; with equal speed the amorous suggestion is dissipated and sometimes not only the nocturnal beloved has ceased to be such and has again become the familiar ugly one but something more precious is also dissipated, a whole picture of ravishing sentiments, of tenderness, of delight, of regrets, vaguely communicated to the mind, a whole shipload of passion for Cythera of which we should take note against the moment of waking up, shades of a beautiful truth which are effaced like a painting too dim to restore. Well, perhaps it was also because of the extraordinary tricks dreams play with time that they fascinated me so much. Had I not in a single night, in one minute of a night, seen days of long ago which had been relegated to those great distances where we can distinguish hardly any of the sentiments we then felt, melt suddenly upon me, blinding me with their brightness as though they were giant aeroplanes instead of the pale stars we believed, making me see again all they had once held for me, giving me back the emotion, the shock, the vividness of their immediate nearness, then recede, when I woke, to the distance they had miraculously traversed, so that one believes, mistakenly however, that they are one of the means of recovering lost Time.

I had realised that only grossly erroneous observation places everything in the object while everything is in the mind; I had lost my grandmother in reality many months after I had lost her in fact, I had seen the aspect of people vary according to the idea that I or others formed of them, a single person become many according to the number of people who saw him (the various Swanns at the beginning of this work according to who met him; the

Princesse de Luxembourg according to whether she was seen by the first President or by me) even according to a single person over many years (the variations of Guermantes and Swann in my own experience). I had seen love endow another with that which is only in the one who loves. And I had realised all this the more because I had stretched to its extreme limits the distance between objective reality and love (Rachel from Saint-Loup's point of view and from mine, Albertine from mine and from Saint-Loup's, Morel or the omnibus conductor or other people from M. de Charlus' point of view). Finally, in a certain measure the Germanophilism of M. de Charlus, like the gaze of Saint-Loup at the photograph of Albertine, had helped me for a moment to detach myself, if not from my Germanophobia at least from my belief in its pure objectivity and to make me think that perhaps it was with hate as with love and that in the terrible sentence which France is now pronouncing on Germany, whom she regards as outside the pale of humanity, there is an objectivity of feeling like that which made Rachel and Albertine seem so precious, the one to Saint-Loup, the other to me. What made it seem possible, in fact, that this wickedness was not entirely intrinsic to Germany was that I myself had experienced successive loves at the end of which the object of each one appeared to have no value and I had also seen my country experience successive hates which had caused to appear as traitors – a thousand times worse than the Germans to whom these traitors were supposed to be betraying France – Dreyfusards like Reinach with whom patriots were now collaborating against a country every member of which was necessarily a liar, a ferocious beast and an imbecile except, of course, those Germans who had espoused the French cause such as the King of Roumania and the Empress of Russia. It is true that the anti-Dreyfusard would have replied: 'It is not the same thing.' But, as a matter of fact, it never is the same thing, any more than it is the same person; were that not so, in the presence of an identical phenomenon he who is its dupe could not believe that qualities or defects are inherent in it and would only blame his own subjective condition.

The intellect has no difficulty, then, in basing a theory upon this difference (the teaching of the congregations according to Radicals, is against nature, it is impossible for the Jewish race to assimilate nationalism, the secular hatred of the Germans for the Latin race, the yellow races being momentarily rehabilitated). That subjective influence was equally marked among neutral Germanophiles who had lost the faculty of understanding or even of listening, the instant the German atrocities in Belgium were spoken of. (And, after all, there were real ones.) I remarked that the subjective nature of hatred as in vision itself, did not prevent the object possessing real qualities or defects and in no way caused reality to disappear in a pure 'relativeness'.

And if, after so many years and so much lost time, I felt the stirring of this vital pool within humanity even in international relationships, had I not apprehended it at the very beginning of my life when I read one of Bergotte's novels in the Combray garden and even if today I turn those forgotten pages, and see the schemes of a wicked character, I cannot lay down the book until I assure myself, by skipping a hundred pages, that towards the end the villain is duly humiliated and lives long enough to know that his sinister purposes have been foiled. For I could no longer recall what happened to the characters, in that respect not unlike those who will be seen this afternoon at Mme de Guermantes', the past life of whom, at all events of many of them, is as shadowy as though I had read of them in a half-forgotten novel.

Did the Prince of Agrigente end by marrying Mlle X? Or was it not the brother of Mlle X who was to marry the sister of the Prince of Agrigente, or was I confusing them with something I had once read or dreamed? The dream remained one of the facts of my life which had most impressed me, which had most served to convince me of the purely mental character of reality, a help I should not despise in the composition of my work. When I lived for love in a somewhat more disinterested fashion, a dream would bring my grandmother singularly close to me, making her cover great spaces of lost time, and so with Albertine whom I began to love again because, in my sleep, she had supplied me with an attenuated version of the story of the laundress. I believed that dreams might sometimes in this way be the carriers of truths and impressions that my unaided effort or encounters in the outside world could not bring me, that they would arouse in me that desire or yearning for certain non-existent things which is the condition for work, for abstraction from habit and for detaching oneself from the concrete. I should not disdain this second, this nocturnal muse, who might sometimes replace the other.

I had seen aristocrats become vulgar when their minds (like that of the Duc de Guermantes for instance) were vulgar. 'You aren't shy?' he asked, as Cottard might have done. In medicine, in the Dreyfus affair, during the war, I had seen people believe that truth is a thing owned and possessed by ministers and doctors, a yea or a nay which has no need of interpretation, which enables a radiographic plate to indicate, without interpretation, what is the matter with an invalid, which enables those in power to know that Dreyfus was guilty, to know (without despatching Roques to investigate on the spot) whether Sarrail had the necessary resources to advance at the same time as the Russians. There had not been an hour of my life which might not have thus served to teach me, as I have said, that only crudely erroneous perception places everything in the object; while, to the contrary, everything is in the mind.

In short, if I reflected, the matter of my experience came to me from Swann, not simply through what concerned himself and Gilberte. It was he who, ever since the Combray days, had given me the desire to go to Balbec, where, but for him, my parents would never have had the notion of sending me and but for which I should never have known Albertine. True, I associated certain things with her face as I saw her first, gazing towards the sea. In one sense I was right in associating them with her for if I had not walked by the sea that day, if I had not known her, all those ideas would not have developed (unless, at least, they had been developed by another). I was wrong again because that inspiring pleasure we like to identify retro-spectively with the beautiful countenance of a woman, comes from our senses and, in any case, it was quite certain that Albertine, the then Albertine, would not have understood the pages I should write. But it was just on that account (and that is a warning not to live in too intellectual an atmosphere), because she was so different from me that she had made me productive through suffering, and, at first, even through the simple effort required to imagine that which differs from oneself. Had she been able to understand these pages, she would have been unable to inspire them. But without Swann I should not even have known the Guermantes, since my grand-mother would not have rediscovered Mme de Villeparisis, I should not have made the acquaintance of Saint-Loup and of M. de Charlus which in turn caused me to know the Duchesse de Guermantes and, through her, her cousin, so that my very presence at this moment at the Prince de Guer-mantes' from which suddenly sprang the idea of my work (thus making me owe Swann not only the matter but the decision) also came to me from Swann, a rather flimsy pedestal to support the whole extension of my life. (In that sense, this Guermantes side derived from Swann's side.) But very often the author of a determining course in our lives is a person much inferior to Swann, in fact, a completely indifferent individual. It would have sufficed for some schoolfellow or other to tell me about a girl it would be nice for me to meet at Balbec (where in all probability I should not have met her) to make me go there. So it often happens that later on one runs across a schoolfellow one does not like and shakes hands with him without realising that the whole subsequent course of one's life and work has sprung from his chance remark: 'You ought to come to Balbec.' We feel no gratitude toward him nor does that prove us ungrateful. For in uttering those words he in no wise foresaw the tremendous consequences they might entail for us. The first impulse having been given, one's sensibility and intelligence exploited the circumstances which engendered each other without his any more foreseeing my union with Albertine than the masked ball at the Guermantes'. Doubtless, his agency was necessary and, through it, the exterior form of our life, even the raw material of our work sprang from him. Had it not been for Swann, my parents would never have had the idea of sending me to Balbec but that did not make him responsible for the sufferings which he indirectly caused me; these were due to my own weakness as his had been responsible for the pain Odette caused him. But in thus determining the life I was to lead, he had thereby excluded all the lives I might otherwise have lived. If Swann had not told me about Balbec I should never have known Albertine, the hotel dining-room, the Guermantes. I should have gone elsewhere; I should have known other people, my memory like my books would have been filled with quite different pictures, which I cannot even imagine but whose unknowable novelty allures me and makes me sorry I was not drawn that way and that Albertine, the Balbec shore, Rivebelle and the Guermantes did not remain unknown to me for ever.

Jealousy is a good recruiting sergeant who, when there is an empty space in our picture, goes and finds the girl we want in the street. She may not be pretty at first, but she soon fills the blank and becomes so when we get jealous of her.

Once we are dead we shall get no pleasure from our picture being so complete. But this thought is in no way discouraging for we feel that life is rather more complex than is generally supposed, likewise circumstances and there is a pressing need of proving this complexity. Jealousy is not necessarily born from a look, from something we hear or as the result of reflection; we can find it ready for us between the leaves of a directory – what in Paris is called *Tout-Paris* and in the country the *Annuaire des Châteaux*. Absent-mindedly, we had heard that a certain pretty girl we no longer thought about, had gone to pay a visit of some days to her sister in the Pas-de-Calais. With equal indifference it had occurred to us previously that, possibly, this pretty girl had been made love to by M. E. whom she never saw now because she no longer frequented the bar where she used to meet him. Who and what might her sister be, a maid perhaps? From discretion, we had never asked her. And now, lo and behold! Opening by chance the *Annuaire des Châteaux* we discover that M. E. owns a country house in the Pas-de-Calais near Dunkerque. There is no further room for doubt; to please the pretty girl, he has taken her sister as a maid, and if the pretty girl does not see him any more in the bar it is because he has her come to his house and, though he lives in Paris nearly the whole year round, he cannot dispense

with her even while he is in the Pas-de-Calais. The paintbrushes, drunk
with rage and love, paint and paint. But supposing, after all, it is not that,
supposing that really M. E. did not any longer see the pretty girl and had
only recommended her sister to his brother who lives the whole year round
in the Pas-de-Calais, so that, by chance, she has gone to see her sister at a
time when M. E. is not there, seeing that they had ceased to care for each
other. Unless indeed the sister is not a maid in the Château or anywhere else
but that her family happens to live in the Pas-de-Calais. Our original
distress surrenders to the latest supposition which soothes our jealousy. But
what does that matter? Jealousy buried within the pages of the *Annuaire des
Châteaux* has come just at the right moment, for now the empty space in the
canvas has been filled and the whole picture has been capitally composed,
thanks to jealousy having evoked the apparition of the pretty girl whom we
neither care for nor are jealous of.

At that moment the butler came to tell me that the first piece was over and
that I could leave the library and enter the drawing-rooms. That reminded
me of where I was. But I was in no wise disturbed in my argument by the fact
that a fashionable entertainment, a return into society, provided the point of
departure towards a new life I had been unable to find the way to in solitude.
There was nothing extraordinary about this, an influence which had roused
the eternal man in me being no more necessarily linked to solitude than to
society (as I had once believed, as perhaps was the case formerly, as perhaps
it might still have been, if I had developed harmoniously instead of having
suffered that long break which only now seemed to be reaching its end).
For, as I only felt that impression of beauty when there was imposed
upon the actual sensation however insignificant, another akin to it which,
spontaneously reborn in me, expanded the first one simultaneously over
several periods and filled my soul, in which my ordinary single sensations left
a void, with a generalising essence, there was no reason why I should not just
as well receive such sensations from society as from nature, since they occur
haphazard, provoked doubtless by a peculiar excitement owing to which, on
days when one happens to be outside the normal course of one's life, even
the most simple things begin to cause reactions which habit spares our
nervous system. My purpose was to discover the objective reason of its being
exactly and only that class of sensations which must lead to a work of art, by
pursuing the reflections I had been bent on linking together in the library,
for I felt that the emancipation of my spiritual life was now complete enough
for me to be able to sustain my thought in the midst of guests in the drawing-

room just as well as alone in the library; I should know how to preserve my solitude from that point of view even in the midst of that numerous company. Indeed, for the same reason that great events in the outer world have no influence upon our mental powers and that a mediocre writer living in an epic period will, nevertheless, remain a mediocre writer, what was dangerous in society was the worldly disposition one brought to it. But, of itself, it will no more make us mediocre than a war of heroes can make a bad poet sublime.

In any case, whether it was theoretically advantageous or not that a work of art should be thus constituted, and awaiting the further examination of that question, it was undeniable so far as I was concerned, that when any really aesthetic intuitions came to me it had always been as a result of sensations of that nature. True, they had been rare enough in my life but they dominated it, and I could recover from the past some of those heights I had mistakenly allowed myself to lose sight of (and I did not mean to do so again). This much I could now say, that if in my case this was an idiosyncrasy due to the exclusive significance it had for me, I was reassured by discovering that it was related to characteristics less marked yet discernible and fundamentally analogous in the case of certain writers. Is not the most beautiful part of the *Mémoires d'Outre-Tombe* assimilable with my sensations relative to the madeleine: 'Yesterday evening I was walking alone . . . I was drawn from my reflections by the warbling of a thrush perched upon the highest branch of a birch tree. At that instant the magical sound brought my paternal home before my eyes; I forgot the catastrophes of which I had been a witness and, transported suddenly into the past, I saw again that country where I had so often heard the thrush sing.' And is not this one of the two or three most beautiful passages in the *Mémoires*: 'A delicate and subtle odour of heliotrope was exhaled by a cluster of scarlet runners in flower; that odour was not brought us by a breeze from the homeland but by a wild Newfoundland wind, without relation to the exiled plant, without sympathy with memory and joy. In that perfume which beauty had not breathed nor purified in its breast nor spread abroad upon its path, in that perfume permeated by the light of dawn, of culture and of life, there was all the melancholy of regret, of exile and of youth.' One of the masterpieces of French literature, *Sylvie* by Gérard de Nerval, contains, in regard to Combourg, just like the *Mémoires d'Outre-Tombe*, a sensation of the same order as the taste of the madeleine and the warbling of the thrush. Finally, in the case of Baudelaire, such reminiscences are still more numerous, evidently less fortuitous and consequently, in my opinion, decisive. It is the poet himself who with greater variety and leisure seeks consciously in the odour of a woman, of her hair and of her breast, those inspiring analogies which evoke for him '*l'azur du ciel immense et rond*' and '*un port rempli de flammes et de mâts*'. I was seeking to recall those of Baudelaire's verses which are based upon the transposition of such sensations, so that I might place myself in so noble a company and thus obtain confirmation that the work I no longer had any hesitation in undertaking, merited the effort I intended to consecrate to it, when, reaching the foot of the staircase leading from the library, I found myself all of a sudden in the great salon and in the midst of a fête which seemed to me entirely different from those I had formerly attended and which began to disclose a peculiar aspect and to assume a new significance. From the instant I entered the great salon, in spite of my firmly retaining within myself the point I had reached in the project I had been forming, a startlingly theatrical sensation burst upon my senses which was to raise the gravest obstacles to my enterprise. Obstacles I should, doubtless, surmount but which, while I continued to muse upon the conditions of a work of art, were about to interrupt my reasoning by the repetition a hundred times over of the consideration most calculated to make me hesitate.

At the first moment I did not understand why I failed to recognise the master of the house and his guests, why they all appeared to have 'made a head', generally powdered, which completely changed them. The Prince, receiving his guests, still preserved that air of a jolly king of the fairies he suggested to my mind the first time I saw him, but now, having apparently submitted to the disguise he had imposed upon his guests, he had tricked himself out in a white beard and dragged his feet heavily along as though they were soled with lead. He seemed to be representing one of the ages of man. His moustache was whitened as though the hoarfrost in Tom Thumb's forest clung to it. It seemed to inconvenience his stiffened mouth and once he had produced his effect, he ought to have taken it off. To tell the truth, I only recognised him by reasoning out his identity with himself from certain familiar features. I could not imagine what that little Lezensac had put on his face, but while others had grown white, some as to half of their beard, some only as to their moustaches, he had found means, without the help of dyes, to cover his face with wrinkles and his eyebrows with bristling hairs; moreover, all this suited him ill, his countenance seemed to have hardened and bronzed and he wore an appearance of solemnity that aged him so much that he could no longer be taken for a young man. At the same moment I was astonished to hear addressed as Duc de Châtellerault a little old man with the silver moustache of an ambassador of whom only the slightest likeness reminded me of the young man whom I had once met calling on Mme de Villeparisis. In the case of the first person whom I succeeded in identifying by abstracting his natural features from his travesty by an effort of memory, my first thought ought to have been and perhaps was, for an instant, to congratulate him on being so marvellously made up that, at first, one had the same sort of hesitation in recognising him as is felt by an audience which, though informed by the programme, remains for a moment dumbfounded and then bursts into applause when some great actor, taking a part in which he looks completely different from himself, walks on to the stage.

From that point of view the most extraordinary of all was my personal enemy M. d'Argencourt; he was, verily, the *clou* of the party. Not only had he replaced a barely silvered beard by one of incredible whiteness, he had so tricked himself out by those little material changes which reconstitute and exaggerate personality and, more than that, apparently modify character, that this man, whose pompous and starchy stiffness still lingered in my memory, had changed into an old beggar who inspired no respect, an aged valetudinarian so authentic that his limbs trembled and the swollen features, once so arrogant, kept on smiling with silly beatitude. Pushed to this degree, the art of disguise becomes something more, it becomes a transformation. Indeed, some trifles might certify that it was actually M. d'Argencourt who offered this indescribable and picturesque spectacle, but how many successive facial states should I not have had to trace if I wanted to reconstruct the physiognomy of M. d'Argencourt whom I had formerly known and who had now succeeded, although he only had the use of his own body, in producing something so entirely different. It was obviously the extreme limit that haughtiest of faces could reach without disintegration, while that stiffest of figures was no more than a boiled rag shaking about from one spot to another. It was only by the most fleeting memory of a particular smile which formerly sometimes tempered for an instant M. d'Argencourt's arrogant demeanour, that one realised the possibility that this smile of an old, broken-down, second-hand clothes-dealer might represent the punctilious gentleman of former days. But even admitting it was M. d'Argencourt's intention to use the old meaning smile, the prodigious transformation of his face, the very matter of the eye with which he expressed it had become so different that the expression was that of another. I almost burst into laughter as I looked at this egregious old guy, as emolliated in his comical caricature of himself as M. de Charlus, paralysed and polite, was tragical. M d'Argencourt, in his incarnation of a moribund buffoon by Regnard, exaggerated by Labiche, was as easy of access, as urbane as was the King Lear of M. de Charlus who uncovered himself with deference before the most commonplace acquaintance who saluted him. All the same, I refrained from expressing my admiration for the remarkable performance. It was less my former antipathy which prevented me than his having reached a condition so different from himself that I had the illusion of standing before another as amiable, disarming and inoffensive as the Argencourt of former days was supercilious, hostile and nefarious. So entirely a different personage that, watching this snowman imitating General Dourakine falling into second childhood, grinning so ineffably comic and white, it seemed to me that a human being could undergo metamorphoses as complete as those of certain insects. I had the impression of observing through the glass of a showcase in a natural history museum what the sharpest and most stable features of an insect had turned into and I could no longer feel the sentiments which M. d'Argencourt had always inspired in me when I stood looking at this soft chrysalis which rather vibrated than moved. So I kept my silence, I did not congratulate M. d'Argencourt on offering a spectacle which seemed to assign the limits within which the transformation of the human body can operate.

Certainly, in the wings of a theatre or during a costume ball, politeness inclines one to exaggerate the difficulty, even to go so far as to affirm the impossibility of recognising the person in travesty. Here, on the contrary an instinct warned me that dissimulation was demanded, that these compliments would have been the reverse of flattering because such a transformation was not intended and I realised what I had not dreamed of when I entered this drawing-room, that every entertainment, however simple, when it takes place long after one has ceased to go into society and however few of those one has formerly known it brings together, gives the effect of a costume ball and the most successful one of all, at which one is truly puzzled by others, for the heads have been in the making for a long time without their wishing it and cannot be got rid of by toilet operations when the party is over. Puzzled by others! Alas! We ourselves puzzle them. The difficulty I experienced in putting the required name to the faces around me seemed to be shared by all those who perceived mine, for they paid no more attention to me than if they had never seen me before or were trying to disentangle from my appearance the memory of someone else.

M. d'Argencourt's success with this astonishing 'turn', certainly the most striking picture in his burlesque I could possibly have of him, was like an actor who makes a last appearance on the stage before the curtain falls amidst roars of laughter. If I no longer felt any antagonism to him, it was because he had returned to the innocence of babyhood and had no recollection of his contemptuous opinion of me, no recollection of having seen M. de Charlus suddenly leave go of my arm, whether because none of those sentiments survived in him or because in order to reach me they would have been so deformed by physical refractions that their meaning would have completely changed on the way, so that M. d'Argencourt appeared to have become amiable because he no longer had the power to express his malevolence and to curb his chronic and irritating hilarity. To compare him with an actor is an overstatement for, having no conscious mind at all, he was like a shaky doll with a woollen beard stuck on his face pottering about the room, like a scientific or philosophical marionette mimicking a part in a funeral ceremony or a lecture at the Sorbonne, simultaneously illustrating the vanity of all things and representing a natural history specimen. A Punch and Judy show of puppets, of which one could only identify those one had known by viewing them simultaneously at several levels graded in the background, which gave them depth and forced one to the mental effort of combining eye and memory as one gazed at these old phantoms.

A Punch and Judy show of puppets bathed in the immaterial colours of years, of puppets which exteriorised Time, Time usually invisible, which to attain visibility seeks and fastens on bodies to exhibit wherever it can, with its magic lantern. Immaterial like Golo on the door-handle of my room at Combray, the new and unrecognisable M. d'Argencourt was a revelation of Time by rendering it partially visible. In the new elements composing M. d'Argencourt's face and personality one could read a sum of years, one could recognise the symbolical figure of life, not permanent as it appears to us, but as it is, a constantly changing atmosphere in which the haughty nobleman caricatures himself in the evening as an old clothes-dealer.

In the case of others these changes, these positive transformations seemed to proceed from the sphere of natural history and it was surprising to hear a name applied to a person, not, as in the case of M. d'Argencourt, with the characteristics of a new and different species but with the exterior features of another person altogether. As in the case of M. d'Argencourt there were unsuspected potentialities which time had elicited from such and such a young girl, and though these potentialities were purely physiognomical or corporeal, they seemed to have moral implications. If the features of a face change, if they unite differently, if they contract slowly but continuously, they assume, with that changed aspect, another significance. Thus, a particular woman who had formerly given one an impression of aridity and shallowness and who had now acquired an enlargement of the cheeks and an unforeseeable bridge on her nose occasioned the same surprise, often an agreeable one, as a sensitive and thoughtful remark, a fine and high-minded act which one would never have expected of her. Unhoped-for horizons opened around that new nose. Kindness and tenderness, formerly undreamed of, became possible with those cheeks. From that chin one might hope for things unimaginable from the preceding one. These new facial features implied altered traits of character; the hard, scraggy girl had become a buxom, generous dowager. It was not in the zoological sense like M. d'Argencourt, but in the social and moral sense that one could say she had become a different person.

In all these ways an afternoon party such as this was something much more valuable than a vision of the past for it offered me something better than the successive pictures I had missed of the past separating itself from the present, namely, the relationship between the present and the past; it was like what used to be called a panopticon but a panopticon of years, a view not of a moment but of a person situated in the modifying perspective of Time.

The woman whose lover M. d'Argencourt had been, was not much changed, if one reckoned the time that had passed, that is, her face was not so completely demolished into that of a creature which has continuously disintegrated throughout his journey into the abyss, the direction of which we can only express by equally vain comparisons since we can only borrow them from the world of space and which, whether we estimate them in terms of height or length or depth have only the merit of conveying to us that this inconceivable yet perceptible dimension exists. The need, so as to give a name to a face, of what amounted to climbing up the years, compelled me later to reconstruct retrospectively the years about which I had never thought, so as to give them their proper order. From this point of view and so as not to allow myself to be deceived by the apparent identity of space, the perfectly new aspect of a being like M. d'Argencourt was a striking revelation of the reality of the era which generally seems an abstraction, in the same way as dwarf trees or giant baobabs illustrate a change of latitude.

Then life appears to us like a fairyland where one can watch the baby becoming adolescent, man becoming mature and inclining to the grave. And, since it is through perpetual change that one grasps that these beings, observed at considerable intervals, are so different, one realises that one has been obeying the same law as these creatures which are so transformed that they no longer resemble, though they have never ceased to be – just because they have never ceased to be – what we thought them before.

A young woman I had formerly known, now snow-white and reduced to a little malevolent old woman, seemed to prove that, in the final act, it was necessary that characters should be made up to be unrecognisable. But her brother had remained so erect, so exactly as he was, that the whitening of his upturned moustache seemed surprising on so young a face. The snowy whiteness of beards which had been completely black made the human landscape of that afternoon party melancholy as do the first brown leaves of a summer one has hardly begun enjoying when autumn comes. Thus I who from infancy, had lived from day to day, with a sort of fixed idea of myself derived from others as well as myself, perceived for the first time, after witnessing the metamorphosis of all these people, that the time which had gone by for them, had gone by for me also and this revelation threw me into consternation. Indifferent as their ageing was to me, now that theirs heralded the approach of my own, I was disconsolate. This approach was indeed announced by one verbal blow after another at intervals, which sounded to my ears like blasts from the trumpets of Judgment Day. The first was uttered by the Duchesse de Guermantes; I had just seen her pass between a double row of gaping people who, without realising how the marvellous artifice of her dress and aesthetic worked on them, moved by the sight of her scarlet head, her salmon-like flesh strangled with jewels just emerging from its black lace fins, gazed at the hereditary sinuosity of her figure as they might have done at some ancient jewel-bedecked fish in which the protective genius of the Guermantes' family was incarnated. 'Ah!' she exclaimed on seeing me, 'what a joy to see you, you my oldest friend!' In my youthful vanity of Combray days which never permitted me to count myself among her friends who actually shared that mysterious Guermantes' life, one of her accredited friends like M. de Bréauté or M. de Forestille or Swann, like so many who were dead, I might have been flattered but, instead, I was extremely miserable. 'Her oldest friend!' I thought, 'She's exaggerating, perhaps one of the oldest but am I really – ' At that moment one of the Prince's nephews came up to me and remarked: 'You who are an old Parisian'. An instant later a note was brought me. I had, on my arrival, seen one of the young Létourvilles whose relationship to the Duchesse I could not remember but who knew me a little. He had just left Saint-Cyr and thinking to myself he would be a charming acquaintance like Saint-Loup, who could initiate me into military affairs and their incidental changes, I had told him I would find him later so that we could arrange to dine together, for which he thanked me effusively. But I had remained dreaming in the library too long and the note he had left was to tell me that he was not able to wait and gave me his address. This coveted comrade ended his letter thus: 'With respectful regard, your young friend, Létourville'. 'Young friend!' Thus I used formerly to address people thirty years older than myself, Legrandin, for instance. That sub-lieutenant whom I was regarding as a comrade called himself my young friend. So it was not only military methods which had changed since then and from M. de Létourville's standpoint I was not a comrade but an old gentleman and I was separated from M. de Létourville to whom I imagined that I appeared as I did to myself as though by the opening arms of an invisible compass which placed me at such a distance from that young sub-lieutenant that to him who called himself my young friend I was an elderly gentleman.

Almost immediately afterwards someone spoke of Bloch and I asked if they were talking of young Bloch or his father (of whose death during the war I was unaware). It was said he died of emotion when France was invaded. 'I did not know that he had any children, not even that he was married,' said the Duchesse, 'but evidently it is the father we're talking about for there's nothing young about him.' She added, laughing, 'He might have grown-up sons.' Then I realised she was talking about my old friend. As it happened, he came in a few minutes later and I had difficulty in recognising him. He had now adopted the name of Jacques du Rozier, under which it would have needed the nose of my grandfather to scent the sweet valley of Hebron and the bond of Israel which my friend seemed to have finally broken. A modish Englishness had completely changed his appearance and everything that could be effaced was moulded into the semblance of a plaster cast. His former curly hair was now smoothed out flat, was parted in the middle and shone with cosmetics. His nose was still red and prominent and appeared to be swollen by a sort of permanent catarrh which perhaps explained the nasal accent with which he lazily drawled his phrases, for, he had discovered, in addition to a way of doing his hair to suit his complexion, a voice to the former nasal tone of which he had added an air of peculiar disdain to suit the inflamed contours of his nose. And thanks to hairdressing, to the elimination of his moustache, to his smartness of style and to his will, that Jewish nose had disappeared as a hump can almost be made to look like a straight back by being carefully disguised. But the significance of Bloch's physiognomy was changed above all by a redoubtable eyeglass. The mechanical effect produced in Bloch's face by this monocle enabled him to dispense with all those difficult duties to which the human countenance must submit, that of looking amiable, of expressing humour, good nature and effort. Its mere presence in Bloch's face made it unnecessary to consider whether it was good-looking or not, like when a shop-assistant shows you an English object and says it is 'le grand chic', and you don't dare consider whether you like it or not. And then he installed himself behind his glass in a haughty, distant and comfortable attitude as though it were an eightfold mirror, and by making his face suit his flat hair and his eyeglass his features no longer expressed anything whatever. On that face of Bloch's were superimposed that vapid and self-opinionated expression, those feeble movements of the head which soon find their point of stasis, and with which I should have identified the outworn learning of a complacent old gentleman if I had not at last recognised that the man facing me was an old friend, whom my memories had endowed with the continuous vigour of youth which he seemed now completely to lack. I had known him on the threshold of life, he had been my schoolfellow and unconsciously, I was regarding him, like myself, as though we were both living in the period of our youth. I heard it said that he looked quite his age and I was surprised to notice some familiar signs of it in his face. Then I realised that, in fact, he was old and that life makes its old men out of adolescents who last many years.

Someone hearing I was not well asked if I was not afraid to catch the 'grippe' which was raging at that time while another benevolent individual reassured me by remarking: 'Don't be afraid, it only attacks the young, people of your age don't run much risk of it.' I noticed that the servants had recognised me and whispered my name, and a lady said she had heard them remark in their vernacular: 'There goes old – ' (This was followed by my name.)

On hearing the Duchesse de Guermantes say, 'Of course I knew the Marshal! But I knew others who were much more representative, the Duchesse de Galliera, Pauline de Périgord, Mgr. Dupanloup,' I naively regretted not having known those she called relics of the *ancien régime*. I ought to have remembered that we call *ancien regime* what we have only known the end of; what is perceived thus on the horizon assumes a mysterious grandeur and seems the last chapter of a world we shall never see again; but as we go on it is soon we ourselves who are on the horizon for the generations behind us, the horizon continues to recede and the world which seemed finished begins again. 'When I was a young girl,' added Mme de Guermantes, 'I even saw the Duchesse de Dino. I'm no longer twenty-five, you know.' Her last words displeased me; she need not have said that, it would have been all right for an old woman. 'As to yourself,' she continued, 'you're always the same, you haven't, so to speak, changed at all', and that gave me almost more pain than if she had said the contrary for it proved, by the mere fact of being remarkable, how much time had passed. 'You're astonishing, my dear friend. You're always young', a melancholy remark since there is only sense in it when we have, in fact, if not in appearance, become old. And she gave me a final blow by adding: 'I've always regretted you did not get married. But, who knows! After all, perhaps you're happier as it is. You would have been old enough to have sons in the war and if they had been killed like poor Robert Saint-Loup (I often think of him) with your sensitiveness, you would not have survived them.' And I could see myself as in the first truth-telling mirror I might encounter in the eyes of old men who had in their own opinion remained young as I believed I had, and who when I offered myself as an example of old age, in order that they should deny it, would by the look they gave me, show not the slightest pretence that they saw me otherwise than they saw themselves. For we do not see ourselves as we are, our age as it is, but each of us sees it in the other as though in a mirror. And, no doubt, many would have been less unhappy than I to realise they were old. At first, some face age as they do death, with indifference, not because they have more courage than others but because they have less imagination. But a man who since boyhood has had one single idea in his mind, whose idleness and delicate health, just because they cause the postponement of its realisation, annul each wasted day because the disease which hastens the ageing of his body retards that of his spirit, such a man is more overwhelmed when he realises that he has never ceased living in Time than another who, having no inner life, regulates himself by the calendar and does not suddenly discover the aggregate of years he has been daily though unconsciously adding up. But there was a graver reason for my pain; I discovered that destructive action of Time at the very moment when I wanted to elucidate, to intellectualise extra-temporal realities in a work of art.

In the case of certain people present at this party, the successive sub-stitution of cellules had brought about so complete a change during my absence from society, such an entire metamorphosis, that I could have dined opposite them in a restaurant a hundred times without any more imagining I had formerly known them than I could have guessed the royalty of an incognito sovereign or the vice of a stranger. The comparison is inadequate in the matter of names, for one can imagine an unknown seated in front of you being a criminal or a king whilst those I had known, or rather, the people I had known who bore their name, were so different that I could not believe them the same. Nevertheless, as I would have done in taking the idea of sovereignty or of vice as a starting-point which soon makes us discern in the stranger (whom one might so readily have treated with amiability or the reverse while one was blindfolded) a distinguished or suspicious appearance, I applied myself to introducing into the face of a woman entirely unknown to me the idea that she was Mme Sazerat. And I ended by establishing my former notion of this face which would have remained utterly unknown to me, entirely that of another woman, as it had lost as fully the human attributes I had known as though it were that of a man changed into a monkey, were it not that the name and the statement of her identity put me in the way of solving the problem in spite of its difficulty. Sometimes, however, the old picture came to life with sufficient precision for me to confront the two and like a witness in the presence of an accused person, I had to say: 'No, I do not recognise her.'

A young woman asked me: 'Shall we go and dine together at a restaurant?' and when I replied: 'With pleasure, if you don't mind dining alone with a young man,' I heard the people round me giggle and I added hastily, 'or rather with an old one.' I realised that the words which caused the laughter were of the kind my mother might have used in speaking of me; for my mother I always remained a child and I perceived that I was looking at myself from her point of view. Had I registered, as she did, changes since my childhood, they would have been very old ones for I had stopped at the point where people once used to say, almost before it was true, 'Now he really is almost a young man.' That was what I was now thinking but tremendously late. I had not perceived how much I had changed, but how did the people who laughed at me know? I had not a grey hair, my moustache was black. I should have liked to ask them how this awful fact revealed itself. And now I understood what old age was – old age, which, of all realities, is perhaps the one of which we retain a purely abstract notion for the longest time, looking at calendars, dating our letters, seeing our friends get married, the children of our friends, without realising its significance, whether through dread or through idleness, until the day when an unknown effigy like M. d'Argencourt teaches us that we are living in a new world; until the day when we, who seem to him like his grandfather, treat the grandson of one of our women friends as a comrade and he laughs as though at a joke. And then I understood what is meant by death, love, joys of the mind, usefulness of sorrow and vocation. For if names had lost their meaning for me, words had unfolded it. The beauty of images is lodged at the back of things, that of ideas in front, so that the first no longer cause us wonder when we reach them and we only understand the second when we have passed beyond them.

The cruel discovery I had now made regarding the lapse of Time could only enrich my ideas and add to the material of my book. Since I had decided that it could not consist only of pure intuitions, namely those beyond Time, amongst the verities with which I intended to frame them, those which are concerned with Time, Time, in which men, societies and nations bathe and change, would have an important place. I should not be mindful only of those alterations to which the aspect of human beings must submit, of which new examples presented themselves at every moment, for still considering my work now begun with decision strong enough to resist temporary distraction, I continued to say, 'How do you do?' and talk to people I knew. Age, moreover, had not marked all of them in similar fashion. Someone asked my name and I was told it was M. de Cambremer. To show he had recognised me he enquired: 'Do you still suffer from those feelings of suffocation?' On my replying in the affirmative, he went on: 'You see that that does not prevent longevity', as though I were a centenarian. I was speaking to him with my eyes fixed upon two or three features which my thought was reducing to a synthesis of my memories of his personality quite different from what he now represented. He half turned his head for a moment and I then perceived that he had become unrecognisable owing to the adjunction to his cheeks of enormous red pockets which prevented him from opening his mouth and his eyes properly, so much so that I stood stupefied not wanting to show that I noticed this sort of anthrax to which it was more becoming that he should allude first. But since, like a courageous invalid, he made no allusion to it and laughed, I feared to seem lacking in feeling if I did not enquire and in tact if I did. 'But don't they come more rarely as one grows old?' he asked, referring to the suffocated feeling. I told him not. 'Well, my sister has them much less now than formerly,' he remarked with an air of contradiction, as though it must be the same in my case, as though age were a remedy which had been good for Mme de Gaucourt and therefore salutary for me. Mme de Cambremer-Legrandin now approached and I felt more and more afraid of seeming insensitive in not deploring what I remarked on her husband's face and yet I did not dare speak first. 'You must be pleased to see him again,' she said. 'Is he well?' I answered hesitatingly. 'As you see,' she replied. She had never even noticed the growth which offended my vision and which was only another of the masks which Time had attached to the Marquis's face, but so gradually and progressively that the Marquise had noticed nothing. When M. de Cambremer had finished questioning me about my attacks of suffocation it was my turn to ask someone, in a whisper, if the Marquis's mother was still alive. She was. In appreciating the passage of time, it is only the first step that counts. At first it is painful to realise that so much time has passed, afterwards one is surprised it is not more. One begins by being unable to realise that the thirteenth century is so far away and afterwards finds difficulty in believing that any churches of that period survive though they are innumerable in France. In a few instants that slower process had taken place in me which happens to those who can scarcely believe a person they know is sixty and fifteen years later are equally incredulous when they hear he is still alive and no more than seventy-five. I asked M. de Cambremer how his mother was. 'Splendid as ever,' he answered, using an adjective which to the contrary of those tribes which treat aged parents without pity applies in certain families to old people whose use of the physical faculties, such as hearing, walking to church and bearing bereavement without feeling depressed, endows them with extreme moral beauty in the eyes of their children.

If certain women proclaimed their age by make-up, certain men on whose faces I had never noticed cosmetics accentuated their age by ceasing to use them, now that they were no longer concerned to charm. Amongst these was Legrandin. The disappearance of the pink in his lips and cheeks which I had never suspected of being an artifice, gave his skin a grey hue and his long-drawn and mournful features the sculptured and lapidary precision of an Egyptian god. A god! More like one who had come back from the dead. He had not only lost the courage to paint himself but to smile, to put life into his manner and to talk with animation. It was astonishing to see him so pale, so beaten, only emitting a word now and then which had the insignificance of those uttered by the dead when they are evoked. One wondered what prevented him from being lively, talkative and entertaining, as at a séance, one is struck by the insignificant replies of the spirit of a man who was brilliant when he was alive, to questions susceptible of interesting developments. And one realised that old age had substituted a pale and tenuous phantom for the highly-coloured and alert Legrandin. Certain people's hair had not gone white. I noticed this when the Prince de Guermantes' old footman went to speak to his master. The ample whiskers which stood out from his cheeks had like his neck retained that red-pink which he could not be suspected of obtaining by dye like the Duchesse de Guermantes. But he did not seem less old on that account. One only felt that there are species of man like mosses and lichens in the vegetable kingdom which do not change at the approach of winter.

In the case of guests whose faces had remained intact, age showed itself in other ways; they only seemed to be inconvenienced when they had to walk; at first, something seemed wrong with their legs, later only, one grasped that age had attached soles of lead to their feet. Some, like the Prince of Agrigente, had been embellished by age. This tall, thin, dispirited-looking man with hair which seemed to remain eternally red, had, by means of a metamorphosis analogous to that of insects, been succeeded by an old man whose red hair, like a worn-out tablecloth, had been replaced by white. His chest had assumed an unheard-of and almost warriorlike protuberance which must have necessitated a regular bursting of the frail chrysalis I had known; a self-conscious gravity tinged his eyes which beamed with a newly acquired benevolence towards all and sundry. And as, in spite of the change in him, there was still a certain resemblance between the vigorous prince of now and the portrait my memory preserved, I was filled with admiration of the recreative power of Time which, while respecting the unity of the being and the laws of life, finds means of thus altering appearance and of introducing bold contrasts in two successive aspects of the same individual. Many people could be immediately identified but like rather bad portraits of themselves in which an unconscientious and malevolent artist had hardened the features of one, taken away the freshness of complexion or slightness of figure of another and darkened the look of a third. Comparing these images with those retained by my memory, I liked less those displayed to me now, in the same way as we dislike and refuse the photograph of a friend because we don't consider it a pleasant likeness. I should have liked to say to each one of them who showed me his portrait: 'No, not that one, it doesn't do you justice, it isn't you.' I should not have ventured to add: 'Instead of your beautiful straight nose you have now got the hooked nose of your father'; it was, in fact, a new familial nose. In short, the artist Time had produced all these models in such a way as to be recognisable without being likenesses, not because he had flattered but because he had aged them. That particular artist works very slowly. Thus the replica of the face of Odette, a barely outlined sketch of which I perceived in that of Gilberte on the day I first saw Bergotte, had been worked by time into the most perfect resemblance (as will be seen shortly) like painters who keep a work a long time and add to it year by year.

In several cases I recognised not only the people themselves but themselves as they used to be, like Ski, for instance, who was no more changed than a dried flower or fruit, a type of those amateur 'celibates of art' who remain ineffectual and unfulfilled in their old age. Ski had, in thus remaining an incomplete experiment, confirmed my theories about art. Others similarly affected were in no sense amateurs; they were society people interested in nothing, whom age had not ripened and if it had drawn a curve of wrinkles round their faces and given them an arch of white hair, they yet remained chubby and retained the sprightliness of eighteen. They were not old men but extremely faded young men of eighteen. Little would have been needed to efface the withering effects of years, and death would have had no more trouble in giving youth back to their faces than is needed to restore a slightly soiled portrait to its original brightness. I reflected also on the illusion which dupes us into crediting an aged celebrity with virtue, justice and loveliness of soul, my feeling being that such famous people, forty years earlier, had been terrible young men and that there was no reason to suppose that they were not just as vain, cunning, self-sufficient and tricky now.

Yet in complete contrast with these last I was surprised when I conversed with men and women who were formerly unbearable, to discover that they had almost entirely lost their defects, whether because life had disappointed or satisfied their ambitions and thus freed them from presumption or from bitterness. A rich marriage which makes both effort and ostentation unnecessary, perhaps too the influence of a wife, a slowly-acquired sense of values other than those in which light-headed youth exclusively believes had enlarged their characters and brought out their qualities. With age such individuals seemed to have acquired a different personality like trees which seem to assume a new character with their autumnal tints. In their case age manifested itself as a form of morality they used not to possess, in the case of others it was physical in character and so new to me that a particular person such as Mme de Souvré, for instance, seemed simultaneously familiar and a stranger. A stranger for I could not believe it was she and, in responding to her bow, I could not help letting her notice my mental effort to establish which of three or four people (of whom Mme de Souvré was not one) I was bowing to with a warmth which must have astonished her for, in fear of being too distant if she were an intimate friend, I had made up for the uncertainty of my recognition by the warmth of my smiling handshake. On the other hand, her new aspect was familiar to me. It was one I had, in the course of my life, often observed in stout, elderly women without then suspecting that, many years before, they might have resembled Mme de Souvré. So different was this aspect from the one I had known in the past that I might have thought her a character in a fairy story which first appears as a young girl, then as a stout matron and finally, no doubt, turns into a tottering, bow-backed old woman. She looked like an exhausted swimmer far from shore who painfully manages to keep her head above the waves of time which were submerging her. After looking long at her irresolute face, wavering like a treacherous memory which cannot retain former appearances, I succeeded somehow in recovering something by indulging in a little game of eliminating the squares and hexagons which age had affixed to those cheeks. But it was by no means always geometrical figures that it affixed to the faces of the women. In the Duchesse de Guermantes' cheeks which had remained remarkably unchanged though they now seemed compounded of nougat, I distinguished a trace of verdigris, a tiny bit of crushed shell and a fleshiness difficult to define because it was slighter than a mistletoe-berry and less transparent than a glass bead.

Some men walked lame and one knew it was not on account of a carriage accident but of a stroke and that they had, as people say, one foot in the grave. This was gaping for half-paralysed women like Mme de Franquetot who seemed to be unable to pull away their raiment caught in the stones of the vault, as though they could not recover their footing; with their heads held low, their bodies bent into a curve like the one between life and death they were now descending to their final extinction. Nothing could resist the movement of the parabola which was carrying them off; trying tremblingly to rise, their quivering fingers failed them. Certain faces under the hood of their white hair wore the rigidity, the sealed eyelids of those about to die, their constantly moving lips seemed to be mumbling the prayer of the dying.

If a face retained its linear form, white hair replacing blond or black sufficed to make it look like that of another. Theatrical costumiers know that a powdered wig so disguises a person as to make him unrecognisable. The young Marquis de Beausergent whom I had met in Mme de Cambremer's box when he was a sub-lieutenant on the day when Mme de Guermantes was in her sister's box, still had perfectly regular features, even more so, because the physiological rigidity of arteriosclerosis exaggerated the impassive physiognomy of the dandy and gave his features the intense and almost grimacing immobility of a study by Mantegna or Michelangelo. His formerly brick-red skin had become gravely pale; silver hair, slight stoutness, Doge-like dignity and a chronic fatigue which gave him a constant longing for sleep, combined to produce a new and impressive majesty. A rectangle of white beard had replaced a similar rectangle of blond so perfectly that, noticing that my former sub-lieutenant now had five stripes, my first thought was to congratulate him not on having been promoted colonel but on being one so completely that he seemed to have borrowed not only the uniform but also the solemn and serious appearance of his father the colonel. In the case of another man, a white beard had succeeded a blond one but as his face had remained gay, smiling and youthful, it made him appear redder and more active and by increasing the brightness of his eyes, gave this worldling who had remained young the inspired appearance of a prophet.

The transformation which white hair and other elements had effected, particularly in women, would have claimed my attention less if it had involved a change of colour only, for that may charm the eyes whereas a change of personality troubles the mind. Actually to recognise someone, more still, to identify him you have been unable to recognise, is to think two contradictory things under a single denomination, it is the same as saying that he who was here, the being we recall, is here no longer and that he who is here is one we never knew, that means piercing a mystery almost as troubling as that of death of which it is indeed the preface and the herald. For I knew what these changes meant and what they preluded and so that whitening of the women's hair in addition to so many other changes deeply moved me. Somebody mentioned a name and I was stupefied to know it applied at one and the same time to my former blonde dance-partner and to the stout elderly lady who moved ponderously past me. Except for a certain pinkness of complexion their name was perhaps the only thing in common between these two women who differed so much – the one in my memory and this one at the Guermantes' reception – the young *ingénue* and the theatrical dowager. That my dancer had managed to annex that huge carcass, that she had succeeded in slowing down her cumbersome movements like a metronome, that all she should have preserved of her youth were her cheeks, fuller certainly but freckled as ever, that for the erstwhile dainty blonde there should have been substituted this old pot-bellied Marshal, life must have achieved more destruction and reconstruction than is needed to replace a spire by a dome, and when one remembered that the operation had been carried out not upon inert matter but upon flesh which only changes insensibly, the overwhelming contrast between this apparition and the being I remembered removed her into a past which, rather than remote, was almost incredible. It was difficult to reunite the two aspects, to think of the two creatures under the same denomination; for in the same way that one has difficulty in realising that a dead body was alive or that he who was alive is dead today, it is almost as difficult, and the difficulty is the same (for the annihilation of youth, the destruction of a personality full of strength and vitality is the beginning of a void), to conceive that she who was young is old, when the aspect of this old woman juxtaposed on that of the young one seems so completely to exclude it that in turn it is the old woman, then the young one, then again the old one which appear to you as in a dream and one cannot believe that this was ever that, that the matter of that one is herself which had not escaped elsewhere, but thanks to the adroit manipulations of time, had become this one, that the same matter has never left the same body – if one did not have the name as an indication as well as the affirmative testimony of friends to which the copperas, erstwhile exiguous between the gold of the wheat ears today buried beneath the snow, alone gives an appearance of credibility.

One was terrified on considering the periods which must have passed since such a revolution had been accomplished in the geology of the human countenance, to observe the erosions that had taken place beside the nose, the immense deposits on the cheeks which enveloped the face with their opaque and refractory mass. I had always thought of our own individuality at a given moment in time as a polypus whose eye, an independent organism, although associated with it, winks at a scatter of dust without orders from the mind, still more, whose intestines are infected by an obscure parasite without the intelligence being aware of it, and similarly of the soul as a series of selves juxtaposed in the course of life but distinct from each other which would die in turn or take turn about like those different selves which alternately took possession of me at Combray when evening came. But I had also observed that these moral cellules which constitute a being are more durable than itself. I had seen the vices and the bravery of the Guermantes return in Saint-Loup, as I had seen the strange and swift defects and then the loyal semitism of Swann. I could see it again in Bloch. After he had lost his father the idea, besides the strong familial sentiment which often exists in Jewish families, that his father was superior to everyone, had given the form of a cult to his love for him. He could not bear losing him and had shut himself up for nearly a year in a sanatorium. He had replied to my condolences in a deeply felt but almost haughty tone, so enviable did he consider me for having been acquainted with that distinguished man whose carriage and pair he would have gladly given to a historical museum. And at his family table (for contrary to what the Duchesse de Guermantes believed, he was married) the same anger which animated M. Bloch senior against M. Nissim Bernard animated Bloch against his father-in-law. He made the same attacks on him. In the same way when I listened to the talk of Cottard, Brichot and so many others I had felt that by culture and fashion a single undulation propagates identical modes of speech and thought in the whole expanse of space, and in the same way, throughout the duration of time, great fundamental currents raise from the depths of the ages the same angers, the same sorrows, the same boasts, the same manias, throughout superimposed generations, each section accepting the criteria of various levels of the same series and reproducing, like shadows upon successive screens, pictures similar to though often less insignificant than that which brought Bloch and his father-in-law, M. Bloch senior and M. Nissim Bernard and others I never knew, to blows.

There were men I knew there with whose relations I was also acquainted without ever realising that they had a feature in common; in admiring the white-haired old hermit into whom Legrandin had changed, I suddenly observed, I could say discovered with a zoologist's satisfaction, in his ironed-out cheeks, the same construction as in those of his young nephew, Léonor de Cambremer, who however, did not seem to bear any resemblance to him; to this preliminary common feature I added another I had not until now remarked, then others, none of which composed the synthesis his youthfulness ordinarily offered me, so that soon I had a sort of caricature of him, deeper and more lifelike than a literal resemblance would have been; his uncle now seemed to me young Cambremer who, for fun, had assumed the appearance of the old man he would eventually be, so completely indeed that it was not only what youth of the past had become but what youth of today would change into that had given me such an intensified sense of Time.

Women tried to keep touch with the particular charm which had most distinguished them but the fresh matter that time had added to their faces would not permit of it. The features moulded by beauty having disappeared in most cases, they tried to construct another one with the relics. By displacing the centre of perspective if not of gravity in the face and recomposing its features to accord with the new character, they began building up a new sort of beauty at fifty as a man takes up a new profession late in life or as soil no longer good for the vine is used to produce beetroot. This caused a new youth to flower round the new features. But those who had been too beautiful or too ugly could not accommodate themselves to these transformations. The former modelled like marble on definitive lines which cannot be changed, crumbled away like a statue, the latter who had some facial defect had even an advantage over them. To start with it was only they whom one immediately recognised. One knew there were not two mouths in Paris like theirs which enabled me to distinguish them in the course of a party at which I had recognised nobody. And they did not even appear to have aged. Age is human and being monsters they had no more changed than whales. There were other men and women who did not seem to have aged; their outlines were as slim, their faces as young as ever. But if one approached them closely so as to talk to them, the face with its smooth skin and delicate contours appeared different, and as happens when one examines a vegetable body under a microscope, watery or ensanguined spots exuded. I observed sundry greasy marks on skin I had believed to be smooth which gave me a feeling of disgust. The outline did not resist this enlargement; at a close view that of the nose had been deflected and rounded, had been invaded by the same oily patches as the rest of the face and when it met the eyes, the latter disappeared into pockets which destroyed the resemblance with the former face one thought one had rediscovered. Thus those guests who had an appearance of youth at a distance, became old as one got near to them and could observe the enlargement and distribution of the facial planes. In fact their age seemed to depend upon the spectator so placing himself as to envisage them as young by observing them only at a distance which, deprived of the glass supplied to a long-sighted person by an optician, diminishes the object; their age, like the presence of infusoria in a glass of water, was brought about less by the progress of years than by the scale of enlargement in the observer's vision.

In general the amount of white hair was an index of depth in time, like mountain summits which appear to be on the same level as others until the brilliance of their snowy whiteness reveals their height above them. And even that could not always be said, especially about women. Thus the Princesse de Guermantes' locks, when they were grey, had the brilliance of silvery silk round her protuberant brow but now having determined to become white seemed to be made of wool and stuffing and resembled soiled snow. It also occurred that blonde dancing girls had not merely annexed, together with their white hair, the friendship of duchesses they had not previously known, but having formerly done nothing but dance, art had touched them with its grace. And, like those illustrious ladies in the eighteenth century who became religious, they lived in flats full of cubist paintings, with a cubist painter working only for them and they living only for him.

Old men whose features had changed attempted to fix on them permanently the fugitive expressions adopted for a pose, thinking they would secure a better appearance or palliate its defects; they seemed to have become unchangeable snapshots of themselves.

All these people had taken so much time to make up their disguises that, as a rule, they escaped the notice of those who lived with them, indeed often a reprieve was granted them and, during the interval, they had been able to remain themselves until quite late in life. But this deferred disguise was then accomplished more quickly and was, in any case, inevitable. Thus I had always known Mme X charming and erect and for long she remained so, too long indeed, for like a person who must not forget to put on her Turkish disguise before dark, she had waited till the last moment and precipitately transformed herself into the old Turkish lady her mother formerly resembled.

At the party I discovered one of my early friends whom I had formerly seen nearly every day during ten years. Someone reintroduced us to each other. As I went near to him, he said with a voice I well remembered: 'What a joy for me after so many years!' But what a surprise for me! His voice seemed to be proceeding from a perfected phonograph for though it was that of my friend, it issued from a great greyish man whom I did not know and the voice of my old comrade seemed to have been housed in this fat old fellow by means of a mechanical trick. Yet I knew that it was he, the person who introduced us after all that time not being the kind to play pranks. He declared that I had not changed, by which I grasped that he did not think he had. Then I looked at him again and except that he had got so fat, he had kept a good deal of his former personality. Nevertheless, I found it impossible to realise it and I tried to recall him. In his youth he had blue eyes that were always smiling and moving, apparently searching for something I was unaware of, which may have been disinterested truth, perhaps pursued in perpetual doubt with a boy's fugitive respect for family friends. Having become an influential politician, capable and despotic, those blue eyes which had never succeeded in finding what they were after had become immobilised and this gave them a sharp expression like a frowning eyebrow, while gaiety, unconsciousness and innocence had changed into design and disingenuousness. Emphatically he had changed into another person – then suddenly, in reply to a word of mine, he burst into laughter, the jolly familiar laugh of former days which suited the perpetual gay mobility of his glance. Musical fanatics hold that Z's music orchestrated by X becomes something absolutely different. These are shades which ordinary people cannot grasp, but the wild stifled laugh of a child beneath an eye pointed like a well-sharpened blue pencil, though a little on one side, is something more than a difference in orchestration. When his laughter ceased I would have liked to reconstruct my friend, but like Ulysses in the Odyssey, throwing himself upon the body of his dead mother, like a medium vainly trying to obtain from an apparition a reply which shall identify it, like a visitor to an electrical exhibition who cannot accept the voice from a phonograph as the spontaneous utterance of a human being, I ceased to recognise my friend.

It is necessary, however, to make this reserve that the beat of time itself can in certain cases be accelerated or slowed down. Four or five years before, I had by chance met in the street Vicomtesse de St Fiacre (daughter-in-law of the Guermantes' friend). Her sculptured features had seemed to assure her eternal youth and indeed she still was young. But now, in spite of her smiles and greetings, I failed to recognise her in a lady whose features had so gone to pieces that the outline of her face could not be restored. What had happened was that for three years she had been taking cocaine and other drugs. Her eyes deeply and darkly rimmed were haggard, her mouth had a strange twitch. She had, it seems, got up for this reception though she was in the habit of remaining in bed or on a sofa for months. Time has these express and special trains which bring about premature old age but on a parallel line return trains circulate which are almost as rapid. I took M. de Courgivaux for his son; he looked younger and though he must have been past fifty, appeared to be no more than thirty. He had found an intelligent doctor, had avoided alcohol and salt and so had become thirty again, hardly even that because he had had his hair cut that morning.

A curious thing is that the phenomenon of age seemed in its modalities to take note of certain social customs. Great gentlemen who had been in the habit of wearing the plainest alpaca and old straw hats which a bourgeois would not have put on his head, had aged in the same way as the gardeners and peasants in the midst of whom they had lived. Their cheeks were stained brown in patches and their faces had grown yellow and had sunk flat like a book. And I thought, too, of those who were not there because they could not be, of how their secretary, in an attempt to give them the illusion of survival, would excuse them by one of those telegrams the Princess received on occasion from such as had been ill or dying for years, who can rise no more nor even move and, surrounded by frivolous or assiduous visitors, the former attracted like inquisitive tourists, the latter by the faith of pilgrims, lie, with closed eyes clasping their breviary, their bedclothes partly thrown back like a mortuary shroud, chiselled into a skeleton beneath the pale, distended skin like marble on a tomb.

Certainly, some women were recognisable because their faces had remained almost the same and they wore their grey hair to harmonise with the season like autumn leaves. But in others and in some men their identity was so impossible to establish – for instance between the dark voluptuary one remembered and the old monk of now – that their transformation made one think, rather than of the actor's art, of that of the amazing mimic of whom Fregoli remains the prototype. That old woman yonder is about to weep because she knows that the indefinable and melancholy smile which was formerly her charm cannot even irradiate the surface of the mask old age has affixed to her. Now, discouraged from attempts to please she more adroitly resigns herself to using it as though it were a theatrical mask to make people laugh. But in the case of nearly all the women there was no limit to their efforts to fight against age; they held the mirror of their faces towards beauty, vanishing like a setting sun whose last rays they passionately long to retain. Some sought to smooth out, to extend the white surface, renouncing the piquancy of menaced dimples, quelling the resistance of a smile doomed and disarmed, while others, realising that their beauty had finally departed, took refuge in expression, as one compensates the loss of the voice by the art of diction, and hung on to a pout, to a smirk, to a pensive gaze, or to a smile to which muscular incoordination gave the appearance of weeping.

A stout lady bade me good-afternoon during the moment that these varied thoughts were pressing upon my mind. For an instant I hesitated to reply to her, fearing she might be taking me for someone else, then her confidence making me think the contrary and fearing she was someone with whom I might at one time have been intimate, I exaggerated the affability of my smile while my gaze still sought in her features the name I could not find. Thus an uncertain candidate for matriculation searches the face of the examiner for the answer he would be wiser to seek in his own memory. So I smiled and stared at the features of the stout lady. They appeared to be those of Mme de Forcheville and my smile became tinged with respect and my indecision began to cease when a second later, the stout lady said: 'You were taking me for mamma, I know I'm getting to look exactly like her', and I recognised Gilberte.

Moreover, even among men who had been subjected to only a slight change, whose moustaches only had become white, one felt that the change was not purely material. One saw them as through a coloured mist or glass which affected their facial aspect with a sort of fogginess and revealed what they allowed one to observe as if it were life-size though in reality it was far away, not in the sense of space, but, fundamentally, like being on another shore whence they had as much trouble in recognising us as we them. Perhaps Mme de Forcheville who looked to me as though she had been injected with paraffin which swells the skin and prevents it from sagging, was unique in presenting the appearance of a courtesan of an earlier period who had been embalmed for eternity. 'You took me for my mother', Gilberte had said and it was true. For that matter it was a compliment to the daughter. Moreover, it was not only in the last-named that familiar features had reappeared, as invisible till then in her face as the inturned parts of a seed-pod, the eventual opening out of which would never be suspected. Thus the enormous maternal bridge in one as in the other transformed towards the fifties a nose till then inflexibly straight. In the case of another daughter of a banker, her complexion of flower-like freshness had become copper-coloured through the reflection of the gold which the father had so freely manipulated. Some even ended by resembling the quarter where they lived, bearing upon their countenances a sort of reflection of the rue de l'Arcade or the Avenue du Bois or the rue de l'Elysée. But they reproduced more than anything else the features of their parents.

One starts with the idea that people have remained the same and one discovers that they have got old. But if one starts by thinking them old, one does not find them so bad. In Odette's case it was not merely that her appearance, when one knew her age and expected her to be an old woman seemed a more miraculous challenge to the laws of chronology than the conservation of radium to those of nature. If I had not recognised her at first, it was not because she had changed but because she had not. Having realised in the course of the last hour what additions time made to people and the subtraction that was needed to rediscover their personalities, I rapidly added to the old Odette the number of years which had passed over her with the result that I found someone before my eyes who could not possibly be her precisely because this someone was the Odette of former days.

Which was the effect of paint and which of dye? With her flat golden hair arranged at the back like the ruffled chignon of a doll surmounting a face with a doll-like expression of surprise and superimposed upon that an equally flat sailor hat of straw of the period of the 1878 Exhibition (in which she certainly had figured and if she had then been as old as now, she would have been one of its choicest features) she looked as though she were a young woman playing a part in a Christmas revue featuring the Exhibition of 1878.

Close to us, a minister of the pre-Boulangist period who had again become a minister, passed by, bowing right and left to ladies with a tremulous and distant smile, as though imprisoned in the past like a little phantom figure manipulated by an unseen hand which had reduced his size and changed his substance so that he looked like a pumice-stone reproduction of himself. This former Prime Minister, now cultivated by the Faubourg Saint-Germain, had once been the object of criminal proceedings and had been execrated by society and by the populace. But thanks to the renewal of the social elements in both groupings and the extinction of individual passions, memories disappear, no one remembered and he was honoured. There is no disgrace great enough to make a man lose heart if he bears in mind that at the end of a certain number of years our buried mistakes will be but invisible dust upon which nature's flowers will smile peacefully. The individual momentarily under a cloud, through the equilibrium brought about by time between the new and the old social strata, will easily assert his authority over them and be the object of their deference and admiration. Only, this is time's business; and at the moment of his troubles, he was inconsolable because the young milkmaid opposite had heard the crowd call him a swindler and shake their fists at him when he was in the soup. The young milkmaid does not see things on the plane of time and is unaware that men to whom the morning paper offers the incense of flattery were yesterday of bad repute and that the man who just now escaped prison, while perhaps, he was thinking of that young milkmaid, and who had not the humility to utter conciliatory words which might have secured him sympathy, will one day be glorified by the press and sought after by duchesses. Time also heals family quarrels. At the Princesse de Guermantes' there was a couple, each of whom had had an uncle; these two uncles were not content merely to fight a duel but each had sent the other his concierge or his butler as his representative for the occasion, so as to humiliate him by showing he was not fit to be treated as a gentleman. Such tales were asleep in the papers of thirty years ago and nobody knew anything about them. Thus the Princesse de Guermantes' salon, illuminated and forgetful, flowered like a peaceful cemetery. There time had not only disintegrated those of the past, it had made possible and created new associations.

To return to our politician. In spite of the change in his physical substance, a change as complete as the moral transformation he now roused in the public, in a word, in spite of the many years gone by since he was Prime Minister, he had become a Minister again. The present Prime Minister had given the one of forty years ago a post in the new Cabinet much as theatrical managers entrust a part to one of their earlier women associates who has been long in retirement but whom they consider more capable than younger ones of performing it with delicacy, of whose embarrassed situation they are, moreover, aware and who, at nearly eighty, still shows that age has scarcely impaired an artistic integrity which amazes the public within a few days of her death.

Mme de Forcheville presented an appearance so miraculous that one would have said not that she had grown young, but that, with all her carmine and rouge, she had reflowered. Even more than an incarnation of the Universal Exhibition of 1878, she could have been the chief attraction of a horticultural exhibition today. To me, at all events, she did not seem to be saying: 'I am the Exhibition of 1878' but 'I am the *Allée des Acacias* of 1892.' To me it was as though she were still part of it. And, because she had not changed, she seemed hardly to be living, she was like a sterilised rose. When I wished her good-afternoon, she tried for a moment vainly to put a name to my face. I gave it her and at once, thanks to its evocative magic, I ceased to wear the appearance of a strawberry tree or a kangaroo apparently bestowed on me by age, and she began talking to me with that peculiar voice, applauded in the smaller theatres, which enchanted people so much when they were invited to meet her at lunch and discovered that they could have as much as they liked of it with every word she uttered. That voice had retained the same futile cordiality, the same slight English accent. And yet, just as her eyes seemed to be looking at me from a distant shore, her voice was sad, almost appealing like that of the dead in the Odyssey. Odette ought to have gone on acting. I paid her a compliment on her youth. She answered: 'You are charming, my dear, thanks.' And as it was difficult for her to express any sentiment, however sincere, without revealing her anxiety to be fashionable, she repeated several times: 'Thanks so much, thanks so much.' And I, who had formerly made long journeys only to catch a glimpse of her in the Bois, who, when first I went to her house, had listened to the words that fell from her lips as though they were pearls, found the moments now spent with her interminable; I knew not what to say and I left her.

Alas, she was not always to remain thus. Less than three years afterwards, I was to see her at an evening party given by Gilberte, not fallen into second childhood but somewhat decayed, no longer able to hide under a mask-like face what she was thinking – thinking is saying too much – what she was feeling, moving her head about, pursing her lips, shaking her shoulders at everything she felt, like a drunken man or a child or like certain inspired poets who, unconscious of their surroundings, compose their poems when they are in company or at table, and, to the alarm of their astonished hostess, knit their brows and make grimaces. Mme de Forcheville's feelings – except the one that brought her to Gilberte's party, tenderness for her beloved child, her pride in so brilliant an entertainment, a pride which could not veil the mother's melancholy that she no longer counted – these feelings were never happy and were inspired by her perpetual self-defence against rudeness meted out to her, the timid defence of a child. One constantly heard people say: 'I don't know if Mme de Forcheville recognises me, perhaps I ought to be introduced over again.' 'You can dispense with that,' (someone replied at the top of his voice neither knowing nor caring that Gilberte's mother could hear every word) 'you won't get any fun out of it. Leave her alone. She's a bit daft.' Furtively, Mme de Forcheville cast a glance from her still beautiful eyes at the insulting speakers, then quickly looked away, for fear of seeming to have heard, while, bowing beneath the blow, she restrained her weak resentment with quivering head and heaving breast, and glanced towards another equally ruthless guest. Nor did she seem too greatly overwhelmed for she had been ailing several days and had hinted to her daughter to postpone the party, which the latter had refused. Mme de Forcheville did not love her the less; the presence of the Duchesses, the admiration the company manifested for the new mansion, flooded her heart with joy, and when the Marquise de Sebran was announced, this lady representing, with much effort, the highest peak of fashion, Mme de Forcheville felt she had been a good and far-seeing mother and that her maternal task had been accomplished. A fresh lot of contemptuous guests brought on another solitary colloquy, if a mute language only expressed by gesticulation can be called talking. Beautiful still, she had become as never previously, an object of infinite sympathy, for now the whole world betrayed her who had once betrayed Swann and the rest; now that the rôles were reversed, she had become too weak to defend herself against men. And soon she would be unable to defend herself against death. After that anticipation, let us go back three years, to the reception at the Prince de Guermantes'.

Bloch having asked me to introduce him to the master of the house, I did

not make a shadow of difficulty. The embarrassment I had felt the first time
at the Prince de Guermantes' evening party seemed natural enough then
but now it seemed as simple a matter to introduce one of his guests to him
as to bring someone to his house who had not been invited. Was this
because, since those far-distant days, I had become an intimate though a
long-forgotten intimate, of a society in which I was once a stranger, or was
it because, not being a true man of the world, what causes that type
embarrassment had no existence for me, now my shyness had passed? Or
again, was it because these people had little by little shed their first, their
second and their third fictitious aspects in my presence and that I sensed,
under the Prince's disdainful manner, a human longing to know people, to
make the acquaintance of those even whom he affected to despise? Finally,
was it because the Prince had changed like those others, arrogant in their
youth and in their maturity, whom old age had softened (the more so that
they had for long known by sight men against whose antecedents they had
reacted and whom they now knew to be on good terms with their own
acquaintances) especially if old age is assisted by virtues or vices which
broaden social relationships or by a social revolution which causes a
political conversion such as the Prince's to Dreyfusism?

Bloch interrogated me as I formerly did others when I first entered
society, and as I still did, about people I formerly knew socially and who
were now as far away, as isolated, as those Combray folk I had often wanted
to place. But Combray was so distinct from and impossible to reconcile with
the outer world that it was like a piece of a jigsaw puzzle that could not be
fitted into the map of France. 'Then I can't have any idea of what the Prince
de Guermantes used to be like from my knowledge of Swann or M. de
Charlus?' Bloch asked. For some time I used to borrow his way of putting
things and now he often imitated mine. 'Not the least.' 'But how did they
actually differ?' 'You would have had to hear them talk together to grasp it.
Now Swann is dead and M. de Charlus is not far from it. But the difference
was enormous.' And while Bloch's eye gleamed as he thought of what the
conversation of these marvellous people must have been, I was thinking that
I had exaggerated my pleasure in their society, having never got any until I
was alone and could differentiate them in my imagination. Did Bloch realise
this? 'Perhaps you've coloured it all a bit too much,' he remarked. 'Look at
our hostess, the Princesse de Guermantes, I know she's no longer young
but, after all, it isn't so very long ago that you spoke of her incomparable
charm and her marvellous beauty. Certainly I admit she has the grand
manner and she also has the extraordinary eyes you described to me, but I
don't see that she's so wonderful as all that. Obviously she's high-bred but

still . . . ' I had to explain to Bloch that we weren't alluding to the same person. The Princesse de Guermantes was dead and the Prince, ruined by the German defeat, had married ex-Mme Verdurin whom Bloch had not recognised. 'You're mistaken, I've looked up the Gotha of this year,' Bloch naively confessed, 'and I found that the Prince de Guermantes was living in this very mansion and had married someone of great importance. Wait a minute, now I've got it, Sidonie, Duchesse de Duras, *née* des Beaux.' This was a fact, for Mme Verdurin, shortly after her husband's death married the old ruined Duc de Duras, who thus made her the Prince de Guermantes' cousin and died after they had been married two years. He had supplied a very useful means of transition for Mme Verdurin who by a third marriage had become Princesse de Guermantes and now occupied a great position in the Faubourg Saint-Germain which would have much astonished Combray where the ladies of the rue de l'Oiseau, Mme Goupil's daughter and Mme Sazerat's daughter-in-law had said with a laugh, years before Mme Verdurin became Princesse de Guermantes: 'The Duchesse de Duras!' as though Mme Verdurin were playing a part at the theatre. The caste principle maintained that she should die Mme Verdurin and that the title which, in their eyes, could never confer any new social prestige, merely produced the bad effect of getting herself 'talked about'; that expression which in all social categories is applied to a woman who has a lover, was also applied in the Faubourg Saint-Germain to people who published books and in the Combray bourgeoisie to those who make marriages which for one reason or another are considered unsuitable. When Mme Verdurin married the Prince de Guermantes they must have said he was a sham Guermantes, a swindler. For myself, the realisation that a Princesse de Guermantes still existed, who had nothing to do with her who had so much charmed me and who was now no more, whom death had left defenceless, was intensely saddening as it was to witness the objects once owned by Princesse Hedwige such as her Château and everything else, pass to another. Succession to a name is sad like all successions and seems like an usurpation; and the uninterrupted stream of new Princesses de Guermantes would flow until the millennium, the name held from age to age by different women would always be that of one living Princesse de Guermantes, a name that ignored death, that was indifferent to change and heartaches and which would close over those who had worn it like the sea in its serene and immemorial placidity.

But, in contradiction to that permanence, the former *habitués* asserted that society had completely changed, that people were now received who in their day would never have been and that, as one says, was 'true and not true'. It was not true because they were not taking the curve of time into consideration, the result of which is that the present generation see the new people at their point of arrival whereas those of the past saw them at their point of departure. And when the latter entered society, there were new arrivals whose point of departure was remembered by others. One generation brings about a change, while it took the bourgeois name of a Colbert centuries to become noble. On the other hand, it was true, for if the social position of people changes, the most ineradicable ideas and customs (as also fortunes, marriages and national hatreds) change also, amongst them even that of only associating with fashionable people. Not only does snobbishness change its form but it might be forgotten like the war, and Radicals and Jews be admitted to the Jockey Club.

Certainly even the exterior change in faces I had known was only the symbol of an internal change effected day by day. Perhaps these people continued doing the same things every day but the idea they had about these things and about the people they associated with having a little life in it, resulted after some years, in those things and people being different under the same names and it would have been strange if the faces of the latter had not changed.

If in these periods of twenty years, the conglomerates of coteries had been demolished and reconstructed to suit new stars, themselves destined to disappear and to reappear, crystallisations and dispersals followed by new crystallisations had taken place in people's souls. If the Duchesse de Guermantes had been many people to me, such and such a person had been a favourite of Mme de Guermantes or of Mme Swann at a period preceding the Dreyfus Affair, and a fanatic or imbecile afterwards because the Dreyfus Affair had changed their social valuations and regrouped people round parties which had since been unmade and remade. Time serves us powerfully by adding its influence to purely intellectual affinities; it is the passage of time that causes us to forget our antipathies, our contempts, and the very causes which gave birth to them. If anyone had formerly analysed the modish elegance of young Mme Léonor de Cambremer, he would have discovered that she was the niece of the shopkeeper in our courtyard, to wit, Jupien, and that what had especially added to her prestige was that her father procured men for M. de Charlus. Yet, in combination, all this had produced an effect of brilliance, the now distant causes being unknown to most of the newcomers in society and forgotten by those who had been aware of them and valued today's effulgence more highly than yesterday's disgrace, for we always take a name at its present-day valuation. So the interest of these social transformations was that they, too, were an effect of lost time and a phenomenon of memory.

Amongst the present company, there was a man of considerable importance who in a recent notorious trial, had given evidence depending for its value on his high moral probity, in deference to which Judge and Counsel had unanimously bowed and the conviction of two people had been brought about. There was a general movement of interest and respect when he entered. It was Morel. I was perhaps the only one present who knew that he had first been kept by M. de Charlus, then by Saint-Loup and simultaneously by a friend of Saint-Loup. In spite of our common recollections, he wished me good day with cordiality though with a certain reserve. He recalled the time when we met at Balbec and those memories represented for him the beauty and melancholy of youth.

But there were people whom I failed to recognise because I had not known them, for time had exercised its chemistry on the composition of society as it had upon people themselves. The milieu, the specific nature of which was defined by affinities which attracted to it the great princely names of Europe and by the repulsion which separated from it any element which was not aristocratic, where I had found a material refuge for that name of Guermantes to which it lent its ultimate reality, had itself been subjected to a profound modification in the essential constitution which I had believed stable. The presence of people whom I had seen in quite other social groupings and who, it had seemed to me, could never penetrate into this one, astonished me less than the intimate familiarity with which they were received and called by their first names; a certain *ensemble* of aristocratic prejudices, of snobbery which until recently automatically protected the name of Guermantes from everything that did not harmonise with it, had ceased to function.

Certain foreigners of distinction, who, when I made my *début* in society, gave grand dinner-parties to which they only invited the Princesse de Guermantes, the Duchesse de Guermantes and the Princesse de Parme, and when they went to those ladies' houses were accorded the place of honour, passing for what was most illustrious in the society of the time, which perhaps they were, had disappeared without leaving a trace. Were they on a diplomatic mission or were they remaining at home? Perhaps a scandal, a suicide, a revolution had prevented their return to society, or were they perhaps German? Anyhow, their name only derived its lustre from their former position and was no longer borne by anyone: people did not even know to whom I was alluding and if I tried to spell out their names believed they were *rastaquouères*.

The best friends of those who, according to the old social code, ought not to have been there, were to my great astonishment, extremely well-born people who only bothered to come to the Princesse de Guermantes' for their new acquaintances' sake. What most characterised this new society was its prodigious aptitude for breaking up class distinctions.

The springs of a machine which had been strained were bent or broken and no longer worked, a thousand strange bodies penetrated it, deprived it of its homogeneity, its distinction, its colour. The Faubourg Saint-Germain, like a senile duchess, responded with timid smiles to the insolent servants who invaded its drawing-rooms, drank its orangeade and introduced their mistresses to it. Again I had that sense of time having drained away, of the annihilation of part of my vanished past presented to me less vitally by the destruction of this coherent unity (which the Guermantes' salon had been) of elements whose presence, recurrence and co-ordination were explained by a thousand shades of meaning, by a thousand reasons, than by the fact that the consciousness of those shades and meanings which caused one who was present to be there because he belonged there, because he was there by right while another who elbowed him was a suspicious newcomer, had been itself destroyed. That ignorance was not only social but political and of every kind. For the memory of individuals is not coincident with their lives, and the younger ones who had never experienced what their elders remembered, now being members of society, very legitimately in the nobiliary sense, the beginnings of certain people being unknown or forgotten, took them where they found them, at the point of their elevation or fall, believing it had always been so, that the Princesse de Guermantes and Bloch had always occupied the highest position and that Clemenceau and Viviani had always been Conservatives. And, as certain facts have greater historic duration than others, the execrated memory of the Dreyfus Affair lingered vaguely in their minds owing to what their fathers had told them, and if they were informed that Clemenceau had been a Dreyfusard they replied: 'It's not possible; you're making a mistake, he was on the other side.' Ministers with a shady past and former prostitutes were held to be paragons of virtue. Someone having asked a young man of good family if there had not been something equivocal in the past of Gilberte's mother, the young aristocrat answered that, as a matter of fact, she had, early in life, married an adventurer called Swann, but afterwards she had married one of the most prominent men in society, the Comte de Forcheville. Doubtless some people in that drawing-room, the Duchesse de Guermantes for instance, would have smiled at this statement (the denial of social qualifications to Swann seeming preposterous to me although formerly at Combray I had believed in common with my great-aunt, that Swann could not possibly know princesses) and so would other women who might have been there, but who now hardly ever went into society, the Duchesses de Montmorency, de Mouchy, de Sagan, who

had been Swann's intimate friends, though they had never caught sight of
Forcheville who was unknown in society when they frequented it. But
society as it was only existed like faces which have changed and blonde hair
now white, in the memory of people whose numbers diminished every day.

During the war Bloch gave up going about and frequenting his former
haunts where he cut a poor figure. On the other hand, he kept on publishing
works, the sophistry of which I made a point of repudiating, so as not to be
beguiled by it, but which, nevertheless, gave young men and ladies in society
the impression of uncommon intellectual depth, even of a sort of genius. It
was only after making a complete break between his earlier and his present
worldliness that he had entered on a new phase of his life and presented the
appearance of a famous and distinguished man in a reconstructed society.
Young men were, of course, unaware of his early beginnings in society and
the few names he recalled were those of former friends of Saint-Loup,
which gave a sort of retrospective and undefined elasticity to his present
prestige. In any case, he seemed to them one of those men of talent who at
all periods have flourished in good society, and no one thought he had ever
been otherwise.

After I had finished talking to the Prince de Guermantes, Bloch took
possession of me and introduced me to a young woman who had often heard
the Duchesse de Guermantes speak of me. If those of the new generation
considered the Duchesse de Guermantes nothing particular because she
knew actresses and others, the ladies of her family, now old, always regarded
her as exceptional, partly because they were familiar with her high birth and
heraldic distinction and her intimacies with what Mme de Forcheville would
have called in her pseudo-English, 'royalties', but also because she disdained
going to family parties, was terribly bored by them and they knew they could
never count on her. Her theatrical and political associations, which were
completely misunderstood, only increased her preciousness in their eyes
and, therefore, her prestige. So that whereas in the political and artistic
spheres she was a somewhat indefinable being, a sort of *défroquée* of the
Faubourg Saint-Germain who goes about with under-secretaries of State
and theatrical stars, if anyone in the Faubourg Saint-Germain gave a grand
party, they said: 'Is it any use inviting Marie Sosthènes? She won't come.
Still, for the sake of appearances – but she won't turn up.' And if, late in the
evening, Marie Sosthènes appeared in a brilliant dress and stood in the
doorway with a look of hard contempt for all her relations, if, maybe, she
remained an hour, it was a most important party for the dowager who was
giving it, in the same way as in early days, when Sarah Bernhardt promised a
theatrical manager her assistance upon which he did not count, and not only

came but with infinite compliance and simplicity recited twenty pieces instead of one. The presence of Marie Sosthènes, to whom Ministers spoke condescendingly though she, nevertheless, continued to cultivate more and more of them (that being the way of the world) classified the dowager duchess's evening party attended by only the most exclusive ladies above all the other parties given by all the other dowager duchesses that 'season' (as again Mme de Forcheville would have said) at which Marie Sosthènes, one of the most fashionable women of the day, had not taken the trouble to put in an appearance. The name of the young woman to whom Bloch had introduced me was entirely unknown to me and those of the different Guermantes could not be very familiar to her, for she asked an American woman how Mme de Saint-Loup came to be so intimate with the most distinguished people at the reception. This American was married to the Comte de Furcy, an obscure relative of the Forchevilles who to her represented everything that was most brilliant in society. So she answered in a matter-of-course way: 'It's only because she was born a Forcheville, nothing is better than that.' Although Mme de Furcy naively believed the name of Forcheville to be superior to that of Saint-Loup, at least she knew who the latter was. But of this, the charming friend of Bloch and of the Duchesse de Guermantes was absolutely ignorant and being somewhat bewildered, when a young girl presently asked her how Mme de Saint-Loup was related to their host, the Prince de Guermantes, she replied in good faith: 'Through the Forchevilles', a piece of information which that young woman passed on, as though she knew all about it, to one of her friends who, having a bad temper and an excitable disposition, got as red as a turkey-cock when a gentleman told her it was not through the Forchevilles that Gilberte belonged to the Guermantes, while he, thinking he had made a mistake, adopted her version and did not hesitate to propagate it. For this American woman, dinner-parties and social functions were a sort of Berlitz school. She repeated names she heard without any knowledge of their significance. Someone was explaining to someone else that Gilberte had not inherited Tansonville from her father, M. de Forcheville, that it was a family property of her husband's, being close to the Guermantes' estate and originally in the possession of Mme de Marsantes, but owing to its being heavily mortgaged, had been bought back by Gilberte as a marriage dowry. Finally, a gentleman of the old school reminiscing about Swann being a friend of the Sagans and the Mouchys and Bloch's American friend asking him how I came to know Swann, Bloch informed her that I had met him at Mme de Guermantes', not being aware that I had known him through his being our neighbour in the country and through his being known to my grandfather as a boy. Such mistakes, which are considered serious in all conservative societies, have been made by the most famous men. St-Simon, to prove that Louis XIV's ignorance was so great that 'it caused him sometimes to commit himself in public to the grossest absurdities' only gives two examples of it; the first was that the King being unaware that Rénel belonged to the family of Clermont-Gallerande and that St-Hérem belonged to that of Montmorin, treated them as men of no standing. So far as St-Hérem was concerned we are consoled by knowing that the King did not die in error, for he was put right 'very late' by M. de la Rochefoucauld. 'Moreover,' adds St-Simon with some pity, 'he had to explain (to the King) what these families were whose name conveyed nothing to him.'

This oblivion which so quickly buries the recent past combined with general ignorance, result reactively in erudition being attributed to some little knowledge, the more precious for its rarity, concerning people's genealogies, their real social position, whether such and such a marriage was for love, for money or otherwise; this knowledge is much esteemed in societies where a conservative spirit prevails and my grandfather possessed it to a high degree regarding the bourgeoisdom of Combray and of Paris. St-Simon esteemed this knowledge so much that, in holding up the Prince de Conti's remarkable intelligence to admiration, before even mentioning the sciences, or rather as though it were the most important one, he eulogised him for possessing 'a very beautiful mind, luminous, just, exact, comprehensive, infinitely well-stored, which forgot nothing, which was acquainted with genealogy, its chimeras and realities of distinguished politeness respecting rank and merit, showing in every way what princes of the blood ought to be and what they no longer are. He even went into details regarding their usurpations and through historical literature and conversations, derived the means of judging what was commendable in their birth and occupation.' In less brilliant fashion but with equal accuracy, my grandfather was familiar with everything concerning the *bourgeoisie* of Combray and of Paris and savoured it with no less appreciation. Epicures of that kind who knew that Gilberte was not Forcheville nor Mme de Cambremer Méséglise nor the youngest Valintonais were few in number. Few, and perhaps not even recruited from the highest aristocracy (it is not necessarily the devout or even Catholics who are most learned in the Golden Legend or the stained windows of the thirteenth century) but often forming a secondary aristocracy, keener about that with which it hardly has any contact and which on that account it has the more leisure for studying, its members meeting and making each other's acquaintance with satis-faction, enjoying succulent repasts at which genealogies are discussed like the Society of Bibliophiles or the Friends of Rheims. Ladies are not asked to such gatherings, but when the husbands go home, they say to their wives: 'I have been to a most interesting dinner; M. de la Raspelière was there and charmed us by explaining that that Mme de Saint-Loup with the pretty daughter was not born Forcheville at all. It's a regular romance.'

The young woman who was a friend of Bloch and of the Duchesse de Guermantes was not only elegant and charming, she was also intelligent and conversation with her was agreeable but was a matter of difficulty to me because not only was the name of my questioner new to me but also those of many to whom she referred and who now apparently formed the basis of society. On the other hand, it was a fact that, in compliance with her wish that I should tell her things, I referred to many who meant nothing to her; they had fallen into oblivion, at all events, those who had shone only with the lustre of their personality and had not the generic permanence of some celebrated aristocratic family the exact title of which the young woman rarely knew, making inaccurate assumptions as to the birth of those whose names she had heard the previous evening at a dinner-party and which, in most cases, she had never heard before, as she only began to go into society some years after I had left it (partly because she was still young, but also because she had only been living in France a short time and had not got to know people immediately). So, if we had a vocabulary of names in common, the individuals we fitted to them were different. I do not know how the name of Mme Leroi fell from my lips, but by chance, my questioner had heard it mentioned by some old friend of Mme de Guermantes who was making up to her. Not as it should have been, however, as was clear from the disdainful answer of the snobbish young woman: 'Oh! I know who Mme Leroi is! She was an old friend of Bergotte's', in a tone which implied 'a person I should not want at my house.' I knew that Mme de Guermantes' old friend, as a thorough society man imbued with the Guermantes' spirit, of which one characteristic was not to seem to attach importance to aristocratic intercourse, had not been so ill-bred and anti-Guermantes as to say: 'Mme Leroi who knew all the Highnesses and Duchesses' but had referred to her as 'rather an amusing woman. One day she said so and so to Bergotte.' But for people who know nothing about these matters, such conversational information is equivalent to what the press gives to the public which believes, according to its paper, alternatively that M. Loubet or M. Reinach are robbers or honourable citizens. In the eyes of my young questioner Mme Leroi had been a sort of Mme Verdurin during her first period but with less prestige and the little *clan* limited to Bergotte. By pure chance, this young woman happened to be amongst the last who were likely to hear the name of Mme Leroi. Today nobody knows anything about her which actually is quite as it should be. Her name does not even figure in the index of Mme de Villeparisis' posthumous memoirs although Mme Leroi had been much in her mind. The Marquise did not omit mentioning Mme Leroi because the latter had not been particularly amiable to her during her lifetime but because neither Mme Leroi's life nor her death were of interest so that the Marquise's silence was dictated less by social umbrage than by literary tact. My conversation with Bloch's smart young friend was agreeable but the difference between our two vocabularies made her uneasy, though it was instructive to me. In spite of our knowing that the years go by, that old age gives place to youth, that the most solid fortunes and thrones vanish, that celebrity is a passing thing, our way of rendering this knowledge conscious to ourselves and, so to speak, of accepting the impress of this universe whirled along by time upon our mental retina, is static. So that we always see as young those we knew young and those whom we knew as old people we embellish retrospectively with the virtues of old age, so that we unreservedly pin our faith to the credit of a millionaire and to the protection of a king though our reason tells us that both may be powerless fugitives tomorrow. In the more restricted field of society as in a simple problem which leads up to a more complex one of the same order, the unintelligibleness resulting from my conversation with this young woman owing to our having lived in a particular society at an interval of twenty-five years, impressed me with the importance of history and may have strengthened my own sense of it.

The truth is that this ignorance of the real situation which every ten years causes the newly-elected to rise and seem as though the past had never existed, which prevents an American who has just landed knowing that M. de Charlus occupied the highest social position in Paris at a period when Bloch had none whatever, and that Swann who put himself about for M. Bontemps had been the Prince of Wales's familiar friend, that ignorance exists not only among newcomers but also amongst contiguous societies, and, in the case of the last named as in the case of the others is also an effect (now exercised upon the individual instead of on the social curve) of Time. Doubtless we may change our milieu and our manner of life, but our memory retaining the thread of our identical personality attaches to itself, at successive periods, the memory of societies in which we lived, were it forty years earlier. Bloch at the Prince de Guermantes' perfectly remembered the humble Jewish environment in which he had lived when he was eighteen, and Swann, when he no longer loved Mme Swann but a woman who served tea at Colombin's, which for a time Mme Swann considered fashionable as she had the Thé de la Rue Royale, perfectly well knew his own social value for he remembered Twickenham and knew why he preferred going to Colombin's rather than to the Duchesse de Broglie's and knew equally well, had he been a thousand times less '*chic*', that would not have prevented him going to Colombin's or to the Hotel Ritz since anyone can go there who pays. Doubtless too Bloch's or Swann's friends remembered the obscure Jewish society and the invitations to Twickenham and thus friends, like more shadowy selves, of Swann and Bloch did not in their memory separate the elegant Bloch of today from the sordid Bloch of formerly or the Swann who went to Colombin's in his old age from the Swann of Buckingham Palace. But, in life, those friends were, in some measure, Swann's neighbours, their lives had developed sufficiently near his for their memory to contain him; whereas in the case of others further away from Swann, not exactly socially but in intimacy, who had known him more vaguely and whose meetings with him had been rarer, memories as numerous had given rise to more superficial views of his personality. And such strangers, after thirty years, remember nothing accurately enough about a particular individual's past to modify what he represents to their view in the present. I had heard people in society say of Swann in his last years, as though it were his title to celebrity: 'Are you talking about the Swann who goes to Colombin's?' Now, I heard people who ought to have known better, remark in alluding to Bloch, 'Do you mean the Guermantes Bloch, the intimate friend of the Guermantes?' These mistakes, which cut a life in two and, isolating him in the present, construct another man, a creation of yesterday, a man who is the mere compendium of his present-day habits (whereas he bears within himself the continuity which links him to his past) these mistakes are also the effect of Time, but they are not a social phenomenon, they are a phenomenon of memory. At that instant an example presented itself of a quite different kind, it is true, but on that account the more striking, of those oblivions which modify our conception of people. Mme de Guermantes' young nephew, the Marquis de Villemandois, had formerly displayed a persistent insolence towards me which had induced me, in a spirit of reprisal, to adopt so offensive an attitude towards him that we had tacitly become enemies. Whilst I was reflecting about Time at this afternoon party at the Princesse de Guermantes' he asked to be introduced to me and then told me he was under the impression that I had been acquainted with his parents, that he had read some of my articles and wanted to make or remake my acquaintance. It is true that with increasing age he, like many overbearing people of a weightier sort, had become less supercilious and, moreover, I was being talked about in his set because of articles (of small importance for that matter) I had been writing. But these grounds for his cordiality and advances were only accessory. The chief one, or at least the one which brought others into play, was that, either because he had a worse memory than I or attached less significance to my reprisals than I to his attacks, owing to my being less important in his eyes than he in mine, he had entirely forgotten our hostility. At most, my name recalled to his mind that he had seen me or somebody belonging to me at one of his aunt's houses and not being quite certain whether he had met me before or not, he at once started talking about his aunt at whose house he thought he might have met me, remembering he had often heard me spoken of there but not remembering our quarrel. Often a name is all that remains to us of a being, not only when he is dead but even while he is alive. And our memories about him are so vague and peculiar, correspond so little to the reality of the past that though we entirely forget that we nearly fought a duel with him, we remember that, when he was a child, he wore odd-looking yellow gaiters in the Champs Elysées, of which, although we remind him of them, he has no recollection.

Bloch had come in, leaping like a hyena. I thought, 'He's coming into a drawing-room which he could never have penetrated twenty years ago.' But he was also twenty years older and he was nearer death, what good would it do him? Looking at him closely, I perceived in the face upon which the light now played, which from further away and when less illumined seemed to reflect youthful gaiety whether because it actually survived there or I evoked it, the almost alarming visage of an old Shylock anxiously awaiting in the wings the moment to appear upon the stage, reciting his first lines under his breath. In ten years he would limp into these drawing-rooms dragging his feet over their heavy piled carpets, a master at last, and would be bored to death by having to go to the La Trémouïlles. How would that profit him?

I could the better elicit from these social changes truths sufficiently important to serve as a unifying factor in a portion of my work that they were not, as I might at first have been tempted to believe, peculiar to our period. At the time when I had hardly reached the point of entering the Guermantes' circle, I was more of a newcomer than Bloch himself today and I must then have observed human elements which, though integrated in it, were entirely foreign to it, recently assembled elements which must have seemed strangely new to the older set from whom I did not differentiate them and who, believed by the dukes to have always been members of the Faubourg, had either themselves been *parvenus* or if not they, their fathers or grandfathers. So it was not the quality of its members which made that society brilliant but its power to assimilate more or less completely people who fifty years later would appear just as good as those who now belonged to it. Even in the past with which I associated the name of Guermantes in order to do it honour in the fullest measure, with reason moreover, for under Louis XIV the semi-royal Guermantes were more supreme than today, the phenomenon I had studied was equally apparent. For instance, had they not then allied themselves by marriage with the Colbert family, today considered of high degree, since a Rochefoucauld considers a Colbert a good match. But it was not because the Colberts, then plain bourgeois, were noble that the Guermantes formed alliances with them, it was they who became noble by marrying into the Guermantes family. If the name of Haussonville is extinguished with the death of the present representative of that family, he will perhaps derive his distinction from being descended from Mme de Staël, while, before the Revolution, M. d'Haussonville, one of the first gentlemen in the kingdom, gratified his vanity as towards M. de Broglie by not deigning to know M. de Staël's father and by no more condescending to introduce him to M. de Broglie than the latter would have done to M. d'Haussonville, never imagining that his own son would marry the daughter, his friend's son the granddaughter of the authoress of *Corinne*. I realised from the way that the Duchesse de Guermantes talked to me that I might have cut a figure in society as an untitled man of fashion who is accepted as having always belonged to the aristocracy, like Swann in former days and after him M. Lebrun and M. Ampère, all of them friends of the Duchesse de Broglie who herself at the beginning was, so to speak, hardly in the best society. The first times I had dined at Mme de Guermantes', how often I must have shocked men like M. de Beaucerfeuil, less by my presence than by remarks showing that I was entirely ignorant of the associations which constituted his past and gave form to his social experience. Bloch would, when very old, preserve memories of the Guermantes' salon as it appeared to him now, ancient enough for him to feel the same surprise and resentment as M. de Beaucerfeuil at certain intrusions and ignorances. And besides, he would have acquired and dispensed amongst those about him qualities of tact and discretion which I had believed to be the particular gift of men like M. de Norpois and which are incarnated in those who seem to us most likely to be deficient in them.

Moreover, I had supposed myself exceptional in being admitted into the Guermantes set. But when I got away from myself and my immediate ambience, I observed that this social phenomenon was not as isolated as it first seemed and that from the Combray basin where I was born many jets of water had risen, like myself, above the liquid pool which was their source. Of course, circumstances and individual character have always a share in the matter and it was in quite different ways that Legrandin (by the curious marriage of his nephew) had in his turn penetrated this *milieu*, that Odette's daughter had become related to it, that Swann and finally I myself, had entered it. To myself who had been enclosed within my life, seeing it from within, Legrandin's way appeared to have no relevance to mine and to have gone in another direction, in the same way as one who follows the course of a river through a deep valley does not see that, in spite of its windings, it is the same stream. But, from the bird's eye view of a statistician who ignores reasons of sentiment and the imprudences which lead to the death of an individual and only counts the number of people who die in a year, one could observe that many people starting from the same environment as that with which the beginning of this narrative has been concerned reach another quite different and it is likely that, just as in every year there are an average number of marriages, any other well-to-do and refined bourgeois *milieu* would have furnished about the same proportion of people like Swann, like Legrandin, like myself and like Bloch, who would be re-discovered in the ocean of 'Society'. Moreover they are recognisable, for if young Comte de Cambremer impressed society with his grace, distinction and modishness, I recognised in those qualities as in his good looks and ardent ambition, the characteristics of his uncle Legrandin, that is to say, an old and very bourgeois friend of my parents, though one who had an aristocratic bearing.

Kindness, which is simply maturity, ends in sweetening natures originally more acid than Bloch's, and is as prevalent as that sense of justice which, if we are in the right, should make us fear a prejudiced judge as little as one who is our friend. And Bloch's grandchildren would be well-mannered and discreet from birth. Bloch had perhaps not reached that point yet. But I remarked that he who formerly affected to be compelled to take a two hours' railway-journey to see someone who hardly wanted to see him, now that he received many invitations not only to luncheon and to dinner but to come and spend a fortnight here and there, refused many of them without talking about it or boasting he had received them. Discretion in action and in words had come to him with age and social position, a sort of social old age, one might say. Undoubtedly Bloch was formerly as indiscreet as he was incapable of kindness and friendly service. But certain defects and certain qualities belong less to one or another individual from the social point of view than to one or another period of his life. They are almost exterior to individuals, who pass through the projection of their light as at varying solstices which are pre-existent, universal and inevitable. Doctors who want to find out whether a particular medicine has diminished or increased the acidity of the stomach, whether it quickens or lessens its secretions, obtain results which differ, not according to the stomach from the secretions of which they have extracted a little gastric juice, but according to the effects disclosed at an early or late stage through the action of the medicine upon it.

* * *

Thus at each of the moments of its duration the name of Guermantes, considered as a unity of all the names admitted within and about itself, suffered some dispersals, recruited new elements like gardens where flowers only just in bud yet about to replace others already faded, are indistinguishable from the mass which seems the same, save to those who have not observed the newcomers and keep in their mind's eye the exact picture of those that have disappeared.

More than one of the persons whom this afternoon party had collected or whose memory it evoked, provided me with the successive appearances he had presented under widely dissimilar circumstances. The individual rose before me again as he had been and, in doing so, called forth the various aspects of my own life, like different perspectives in a countryside where a hill or a castle seems at one moment to be to the right, at another to the left, to dominate a forest or emerge from a valley, thus reminding the traveller of changes of direction and altitude in the road he has been following. As I went further and further back I finally discovered pictures of the same individual, separated by such long intervals, represented by such distinct personalities, with such different meanings that, as a rule, I eliminated them from my field of recollection when I believed I had made contact with them, and often ceased believing they were the same people I had formerly known. Chance illumination was required for me to be able to attach them, like in an etymology, to the original significance they had for me. Mlle Swann throwing some thorny roses to me from the other side of the hedge, with a look I had retrospectively attributed to desire; the lover, according to Combray gossip, of Mme Swann, staring at me from behind that same hedge with a hard look which also did not warrant the interpretation I gave to it then and who had changed so completely since I failed to recognise him at Balbec as the gentleman looking at a notice near the casino, and whom I happened to think of once every ten years, saying to myself: 'That was M. de Charlus, how curious!' Mme de Guermantes at Dr. Percepied's wedding, Mme Swann in pink at my great-uncle's, Mme de Cambremer, Legrandin's sister, who was so smart that he was afraid we should want him to introduce us to her, and so many more pictures of Swann, Saint-Loup, etc. which, when I recalled them, I liked now and then to use as a frontispiece on the threshold of my relations with these different people but which actually

seemed to me mere fancies rather than impressions left upon my mind by
the individual with whom there was no longer any link. It is not only that
certain people have the power of remembering and others not (without
living in a state of permanent oblivion like Turkish ambassadors) which
always enables the latter to find room – the new precedent having vanished
in a week or the following one having exorcised it – for a fresh item of news
contradicting the last. Even if memories are equal, two persons do not
remember the same things. One would hardly notice an act which another
would feel intense remorse about while he will grasp at a word almost
unconsciously let fall by the other as though it were a characteristic sign of
goodwill. Self-interest implicit in not being wrong in our prejudgment
limits the time we shall remember it and encourages us to believe we never
indulged in it. Finally, a deeper and more unselfish interest diversifies
memories so thoroughly that a poet who has forgotten nearly all the facts of
which one reminds him retains a fugitive impression of them. As a result
of all this, after twenty years' absence one discovers involuntary and
unconscious forgiveness instead of anticipated resentments and on the
other hand, hatreds the cause of which one cannot explain (because one has
forgotten the bad impression one had made). One forgets dates as one does
the history of people one has known best. And because twenty years had
passed since Mme de Guermantes had first seen Bloch, she would have
sworn that he was born in her set and had been nursed by the Duchesse de
Chartres when he was two years old.

How many times these people had returned to my vision in the course of
their lives, the differing circumstances of which seemed to offer identical
characteristics under diverse forms and for various ends; and the diversity of
my own life at its turning-points through which the thread of each of these
lives had passed was compounded of lives seemingly the most distant from
my own as if life itself only disposed of a limited number of threads for the
execution of the most varied designs. What, for instance, were more separate
in my various pasts than my visits to my Uncle Adolphe, than the nephew of
Mme de Villeparisis, herself cousin of the Marshal, than Legrandin and his
sister, than the former waistcoat maker, Françoise's friend in the courtyard
of our home. And now all these different threads had been united to
produce, here the woof of the Saint-Loup *ménage*, there, that of the young
Cambremers, not to mention Morel and so many others the conjunction of
which had combined to form circumstances so compact that they seemed to
make a unity of which the personages were mere elements. And my life was
already long enough for me to have found in more than one case a being to
complete another in the conflicting spheres of my memory. To an Elstir

whose fame was now assured I could add my earliest memories of the Verdurins, of the Cottards, of conversations in Rivebelle restaurant on the morning when I first met Albertine and many others. In the same way, a collector who is shown the wing of an altar screen, remembers the church or museum or private collection in which the others are dispersed (as also, by following sale-catalogues or searching among dealers in antiques, he finally discovers the twin object to the one he possesses which makes them a pair and thus can mentally reconstitute the predella and the entire altarpiece). As a bucket let down or hauled up a well by a windlass touches the rope or the sides every now and then, there was not a personage, hardly even an event in my life, which had not at one time or another played different parts. If, after years I rediscovered the simplest social relationship or even a material object in my memory, I perceived that life had been ceaselessly weaving threads about it which in the end became a beautiful velvet covering like the emerald sheath of a water-conduit in an ancient park.

It was not only in appearance that these people were like dream-figures, their youth and love had become to themselves a dream. They had forgotten their very resentments and hatreds and, to be sure that this individual was the one they had not spoken to for ten years, they would have needed a register which even then would have had the vagueness of a dream in which an insult has been offered them by one unknown. Such dreams account for those contrasts in political life where people who once accused each other of murder and treason are members of the same Government. And dreams become as opaque as death in the case of old men on days following those of lovemaking. On such days no one was allowed to ask the President of the Republic any questions; he had forgotten everything. After he had been allowed to rest for some days, the recollection of public affairs returned to him fortuitously as in a dream.

Sometimes it was not a single image only that presented itself to my mind of one whom I had since known to be so different. It was during the same years that Bergotte had seemed a sweet, divine old man to me that I had been paralysed at the sight of Swann's grey hat and his wife's violet cloak, by the glamour of race which surrounded the Duchesse de Guermantes even in a drawing-room as though I stood gazing at ghosts; almost fabulous origins of relationships subsequently so banal which these charming myths lengthened into the past with the brilliance projected into the heavens by the sparkling tail of a comet. And even relations such as mine with Mme de Souvré, which had not begun in mystery, which were today so hard and worldly, revealed themselves at their beginnings in a smile, calm, soft and flatteringly expressed in the fullness of an afternoon by the sea, on a spring evening in Paris in the midst of smart equipages, of clouds of dust, of sunshine moving like water. And perhaps Mme de Souvré would not have been worthwhile if she had been detached from her frame like those monuments – the Salute for instance – which, without any great beauty of their own are so perfectly adapted to their site, and she had her place in a collection of memories which I estimated at a certain price, taking one with another, without going too closely into the particular value of Mme de Souvré's personality.

A thing by which I was more impressed, in the case of people who had undergone physical and social change was the different notion they had of each other. In old days Legrandin despised Bloch and never spoke to him; now he was most amiable to him. It was not in the least owing to Bloch's more prominent position which in this case was negligible, for social changes inevitably bring about respective changes in position amongst those who have been subjected to them. No. It was that people, that is, people as we see them, do not retain the uniformity of a picture when we look back on them. They evolve in relation to our forgetfulness. Sometimes we even go so far as to confuse them with others. 'Bloch, that's the man who came from Combray', and when he said Bloch, the person meant me. Inversely Mme Sazerat was convinced that a historical thesis on Philippe II was by me whereas it was by Bloch. Apart from these substitutions one forgets the bad turns people have done us, their unpleasantness, one forgets that last time we parted without shaking hands and, in contrast, we remember an earlier period when we were on good terms. Legrandin's affability with Bloch was referable to that earlier period, whether because he had forgotten a phase of his past or that he judged it better to ignore it, a mixture, in fact, of forgiveness, forgetfulness and indifference which is also an effect of Time. Moreover, even in love, the memories we have of each other are not the same. I had known Albertine to remind me in the most remarkable way of something I had said to her during the early days of our acquaintance which I had completely forgotten while she had no recollection whatever of another fact implanted in my head like a stone for ever. Our parallel lives resemble paths bordered at intervals by flower-vases placed symmetrically but not facing each other. It is still more comprehensible that one hardly remembers who the people were one knew slightly or one remembers something else about them further back, something suggested by those amongst whom one meets them again who have only just made their acquaintance and endow them with qualities and a position they never had but which the forgetful person wholly accepts.

Doubtless life, in casting these people upon my path on different occasions, had presented them in surrounding circumstances which had shrunk my view of them and prevented my knowing their essential characters. Of those Guermantes even who had been the subject of such wonderful dreams, at my first approach to them, one had appeared in the guise of an old friend of my grandmother's, another in that of a gentleman who had stared at me so unpleasantly in the grounds of the casino (for, between us and other beings there is a borderland of contingencies, as, from my readings at Combray, I knew there was one of perceptions which prevent reality and mind being placed in absolute contact). So that it was only after the event, by relating them to a name, that my acquaintance with them had become to me acquaintance with the Guermantes. But perhaps it was that very thing which made life seem more poetic to me when I thought about that mysterious race with the piercing eyes and beaks of birds, that pink, golden, unapproachable race which the force of blind and differing circumstances had presented so naturally to my observation, to my intercourse, even to my intimacy, that when I wanted to know Mlle de Stermaria or to have dresses made for Albertine, I applied to the Guermantes, as to my most helpful friends. Certainly it bored me at times to go and see them as to go and see others I knew in society. The charm of the Duchesse de Guermantes, even, like that of certain of Bergotte's pages, was only discernible to me at a distance and disappeared when I was near her, for it lay in my memory and in my imagination, and yet the Guermantes, like Gilberte, were different from other people in society in that their roots were plunged more deeply in my past when I dreamed more and believed more in individuals. That past filled me with weariness while talking to one or the other of them, for it was associated with those imaginings of my childhood which had once seemed the most beautiful and inaccessible and I had to console myself by confusing the value of their possession with the price at which my desire had appraised them, like a merchant whose books are in disorder.

But my past relations with other beings were magnified by dreams more ardent and hopeless with which my life opened so richly, so entirely dedicated to them that I could hardly understand how it was that what they yielded was this exiguous, narrow, mournful ribbon of a despised and unloved intimacy in which I could discover no trace of what had once been their mystery, their fever and their loveliness.

* * *

'What has become of the Marquise d'Arpajon?' asked Mme de Cambremer. 'She's dead,' answered Bloch. 'You're confusing her with the Comtesse d'Arpajon who died last year,' the Princesse de Malte joined the discussion.

The young widow of a very wealthy old husband, the bearer of a great name, she had been much sought in marriage and from that had derived a great deal of self-assurance. 'The Marquise d'Arpajon died too about a year ago.' 'I can assure you it isn't a year,' answered Mme de Cambremer. 'I was at a musical party at her house less than a year ago.' Bloch could no more take part in the discussion than a society gigolo, for all these deaths of aged people were too far away from him, whether owing to the great difference in age or to his recent entry into a different society which he approached, as it were, from the side, at a period of its decline into a twilight in which the memory of an unfamiliar past could not illuminate it. And for those of the same age and of the same society death had lost its strange significance. Moreover every day people were at the point of death of whom some recovered while others succumbed, so that one was not certain whether a particular individual one rarely saw had recovered from his cold on the chest or whether he had passed away. Deaths multiplied and lives became increasingly uncertain in those aged regions. At these crossroads of two generations and two societies which for different reasons were ill-placed for identifying death, it became confused with life, the former had been socialised and become an incident, which qualified a person more or less without the tone in which it was mentioned signifying that this incident ended everything so far as that person was concerned. So people said: 'You've forgotten. So and so is dead,' as they might have said: 'He's decorated, he's a member of the Academy,' or – which came to the same thing as it prevented his coming to parties – 'he has gone to spend the winter in the south', or 'he's been ordered to the mountains'. In the case of well-known men, what they left helped people to remember they were dead. But in the case of ordinary members of society, people got muddled about whether they were dead or not, partly because they did not know them well and had forgotten their past but more because they bothered little about the future one way or the other. And the difficulty people had in sorting out marriages, absences, retirements to the country and deaths of old people in society equally illustrated the insignificance of the dead and the indifference of the living.

'But if she's not dead how is it one doesn't see her any more nor her husband either?' asked an old maid who liked to be thought witty. 'I tell you,' answered her mother who, though fifty years old, never missed a party, 'it's because they're old and at that age people don't go out.' It was as though there lay in front of the cemetery a closed city of the aged with lamps always alight in the fog. Mme de Sainte-Euverte closed the debate by saying that the Comtesse d'Arpajon had died the year before after a long illness, but the Marquise d'Arpajon had also died suddenly 'from some quite trifling cause', a death which thus resembled the lives of them all and, in the same fashion, explained that she had passed away without anyone being aware of it and excused those who had made a mistake. Hearing that Mme d'Arpajon was really dead, the old maid cast an alarmed glance at her mother fearing that the news of the death of one of her contemporaries might be a shock to her; she imagined in anticipation people alluding to her own mother's death by explaining that 'she died as the result of a shock through the death of Mme d'Arpajon'. But on the contrary, her mother's expression was that of having won a competition against formidable rivals whenever anyone of her own age passed away. Their death was her only means of being agreeably conscious of her own existence. The old maid, aware that her mother had not seemed sorry to say that Mme d'Arpajon was a recluse in those dwellings from which the aged and tired seldom emerge, noticed that she was still less upset to hear that the Marquise had entered that ultimate abode from which no one returns. This affirmation of her mother's indifference aroused the caustic wit of the old maid. And, later on, to amuse her friends, she gave a humorous imitation of the lively fashion with which her mother rubbed her hands as she said: 'Goodness me, so that poor Mme d'Arpajon is dead.' She thus pleased even those who did not need death to make them glad they were alive. For every death is a simplification of life for the survivors; it relieves them of being grateful and of being obliged to make visits. Nevertheless, as I have said, M. Verdurin's death was not thus welcomed by Elstir.

*   *   *

A lady went out for she had other afternoon receptions to go to and she was to take tea with two queens. She was the society courtesan I formerly knew, the Princesse de Nissau. Apart from her figure having shrunk – which gave her head the appearance of being lower than it was formerly, of having what is called 'one foot in the grave' – one would have said that she had hardly aged. She remained, with her Austrian nose and delightful mien, a Marie-Antoinette preserved, embalmed, thanks to a thousand cunningly combined cosmetics which gave her face the hue of lilac. Her face wore that regretful soft expression of being compelled to go with a sweet half-promise to return, of inconspicuous withdrawal because of numerous exclusive invitations. Born almost on the steps of a throne, married three times, protected long and luxuriously by great bankers, the confused memories of her innumerable pasts, not to speak of the caprices she had indulged, weighed on her as lightly as her beautiful round eyes, her painted face and her mauve dress. As, taking French leave, she passed me, I bowed and she, taking my hand, fixed her round violet orbs upon me as if to say:

'How long since we met, do let us talk of it next time.' She pressed my hand, not quite sure whether there had or had not been a passage between us that evening she drove me from the Duchesse de Guermantes'. She merely took a chance by seeming to suggest something that had never been, which was not difficult for she looked tender over a strawberry-tart and assumed, about her compulsion to leave before the music was over, an attitude of despairing yet reassuring abandonment. Moreover, in her uncertainty about the incident with me, her furtive pressure did not detain her long and she did not say a word. She only looked at me in a way that said: 'How long! How long!' as there passed across her vision her husbands, the different men who had kept her, two wars – and her star-like eyes, like astronomic dials carved in opal, registered in quick succession all those solemn hours of a far-away past she conjured back each time she uttered a greeting which was always an excuse. She left me and floated to the door so as not to disturb me, to show me that if she did not stop and talk to me it was because she had to make up the time she had lost pressing my hand so as not to keep the Queen of Spain waiting. She seemed to go through the door at racing-pace. And she was, as a fact, racing to her grave.

Meanwhile, the Princesse de Guermantes kept repeating in an excited way in the metallic voice caused by her false teeth: 'That's it, we'll form a group. I love the intelligence of youth, it so co-operates! Ah, what a "mugician" you are.' She was talking with her large eyeglass in a round eye which was partly amused and partly excusing itself for not being able to keep it up but till the end she decided to 'co-operate' and 'form a group'.

*   *   *

I sat down by the side of Gilberte de Saint-Loup. We talked a great deal about Robert. Gilberte alluded to him deferentially as to a superior being whom she wanted me to know she admired and understood. We reminded each other that many of the ideas he had formerly expressed about the art of war (for he had often exposed the same theses at Tansonville as at Doncières and later) had been verified by the recent one. 'I can't tell you how much the slightest thing he told me at Doncierès strikes me now as it did during the war. The last words I heard him say when we parted never to meet again were that he was expecting of Hindenburg, a Napoleonic General, a type of Napoleonic battle the object of which is to separate two adversaries, perhaps, he said, the English and ourselves. Now scarcely a year after Robert's death a critic whom he much admired and who obviously exercised great influence on his military ideas, M. Henri Bidou, said that Hindenburg's offensive in March, 1918 was "a battle of separation by one adversary massed against two in line, a manoeuvre which the Emperor successfully executed in 1796 on the Apennines and failed with in 1815 in Belgium". Some time before that Robert was comparing battles with plays in which it is sometimes difficult to know what the author means because he has changed his plot in the course of the action. Now, as to this interpretation of the German offensive of 1918, Robert would certainly not be of M. Bidou's opinion. But other critics think that Hindenburg's success in the direction of Amiens, then his forced halt then his success in Flanders, then again the halt, accidentally made Amiens and afterwards Boulogne objectives he had not previously planned. And as everyone can reconstruct a play in his own way, there are those who see in this offensive the threat of a terrific march on Paris, others disordered hammer blows to annihilate the English army. And even if the General's orders are opposed to one or the other conception, critics will always be able to say, as Mounet-Sully did to Coquelin who affirmed that *The Misanthrope* was not the depressing drama he made it appear (for Molière's contemporaries testify that his interpretation was comic and made people laugh): "Well, then, Molière made a mistake".'

'And you remember,' Gilberte replied, 'what he said about aeroplanes (he expressed himself so charmingly), "every army must be an Argus with a hundred eyes." Alas, he did not live to see the verification of his predictions.' 'Oh, yes, he did,' I answered, 'he knew very well that, at the battle of the Somme, they were beginning to blind the enemy by piercing his eyes, destroying his aeroplanes and captive balloons.' 'Oh yes! So they did.' Since she had taken to living in her mind, she had become somewhat pedantic. 'And it was he who foretold a return to the old methods. Do you know that the Mesopotamian expeditions in this war' (she must have read this at the time in Brichot's articles) 'keep reminding one of the retreat of Xenophon; to get from the Tigris to the Euphrates the English Commander made use of canoes, long narrow boats, the gondolas of that country, which the ancient Chaldeans had made use of.' Her words gave me that feeling of stagnation in the past which is immobilised in certain places by a sort of specific gravity to such a degree that one finds it just as it was.

I avow that, thinking of my readings at Balbec, not far from Robert, I had been much impressed – as I was when I discovered Mme de Sévigné's intrenchment in the French countryside – to observe, in connection with the siege of Kut-el-Amara (Kut-the-Emir just as we say Vaux-le-Vicomte, Boilleau-l'Evêque, as the curé of Combray would have said if his thirst for etymology had extended to Oriental languages) the recurrence, near Bagdad, of that name Bassorah about which we hear so much in the *Thousand and One Nights*, whence, long before General Townsend, Sinbad the Sailor, in the times of the Caliphs, embarked or disembarked whenever he left or returned to Bagdad.

'There was a side of the war he was beginning to perceive,' I said, 'which is that it is human, that it is lived like a love or a hatred, can be recounted like a romance, and consequently if people keep on repeating that strategy is a science, it does not help them to understand it because it is not strategic. The enemy no more knows our plans than we know the motive of a woman we love, and perhaps we do not know ours either. In the offensive of March, 1918 was the object of the Germans to take Amiens? We know nothing about it. Perhaps they did not either and it was their advance westwards towards Amiens which determined their plan. Even admitting that war is scientific it is still necessary to paint it like Elstir painted the sea, by the use of another sense and using imagination and beliefs as a starting-point, to rectify them little by little as Dostoevsky narrated a life. Moreover, it is but too obvious that war is rather medical than strategic since it brings in its train unforeseen accidents the clinician hopes to avoid, such as the Russian Revolution.'

Throughout this conversation, Gilberte had spoken of Robert with a deference which seemed rather addressed to my former friend than to her dead husband. She seemed to be saying: 'I know how much you admired him, believe me, I knew and understood what a superior creature he was.' And yet the love she certainly no longer felt for his memory may perhaps have been the distant cause of the peculiarities in her present life. For Andrée was now Gilberte's inseparable friend. Although the former had for some time, chiefly because of her husband's talent, begun to enter, not, of course, the Guermantes set but an infinitely more fashionable society than that which she formerly frequented, people were astonished that the Marquise de Saint-Loup condescended to become her best friend. That fact seemed to be a sign of Gilberte's preference for what she believed to be an artistic life and for a positive social forfeiture. That may be the true explanation. Another, however, came to my mind, always convinced that images assembled somewhere are generally the reflection or in some fashion the effect of a former grouping different from though symmetrical with other images extremely distant from the second group. I thought that if Andrée, her husband and Gilberte were seen together every evening it was possibly because many years earlier Andrée's future husband had lived with Rachel and then left her for Andrée. It is probable that Gilberte lived in a society too far removed from and above theirs to know anything about it. But she must have learned of it later when Andrée went up and she came down enough for them to meet. Then the woman for whom a man had abandoned Rachel although she, Rachel, preferred him to Robert, must have been dowered with much prestige in the eyes of Gilberte.

In the same way, perhaps, the sight of Andrée recalled to Gilberte the youthful romance of her love for Robert and also inspired her respect for Andrée who was still loved by the man so adored by Rachel whom Gilberte knew Saint-Loup had preferred to herself. Perhaps, on the other hand, these memories played no part in Gilberte's predilection for this artistic couple and it was only the result, as in many other cases, of the development of tastes common amongst society women for acquiring new experience and simultaneously lowering themselves. Perhaps Gilberte had forgotten Robert as completely as I had Albertine and even if she knew it was Rachel whom the artist had left for Andrée she never thought about it because it never played any part in her liking for them. The only way of ascertaining whether my first explanation was either possible or true would have been through the evidence of the interested parties and then only if they proffered their confidence with clarity and sincerity. And the first is rarely met with, the second never.

'But how is it that you are here at this crowded reception?' asked Gilberte. 'It's not like you to come to a massacre like this. I might have expected to meet you anywhere rather than in one of these omnium-gatherums of my aunt; she is my aunt you know,' she added subtly; for having become Mme de Saint-Loup considerably before Mme Verdurin entered the family, she considered herself a Guermantes from the beginning of time and, in consequence, affected by the *mésalliance* of her uncle with Mme Verdurin whom, it is true, she had heard the family laugh at a thousand times whereas, of course, it was only when she was not there that they alluded to the *mesalliance* of Saint-Loup and herself. She affected, moreover, the greater disdain for this undistinguished aunt because the Princesse de Guermantes, owing to a sort of perversity which impels intelligent people to escape from the bondage of fashion, also owing to the need displayed by ageing people of memories that will form a background to their newly acquired position, would say about Gilberte: 'That's no new relationship for me, I knew the young woman's mother very well; why, she was my cousin Marsantes' great friend. It was at my house she met Gilberte's father. As to poor Saint-Loup, I used to know all his family, his uncle was once an intimate friend of mine at La Raspelière.' 'You see, the Verdurins were not Bohemians at all,' people said to me when they heard the Princesse de Guermantes talk in that way, 'they were old friends of Mme de Saint-Loup's family.' I was, perhaps, the only one who knew, through my grandfather, that indeed the Verdurins were not Bohemians, but it was not exactly because they had known Odette.

But it is as easy to give accounts of the past which nobody knows anything about as it is of travels in countries where no one has ever been. 'Well,' concluded Gilberte, 'as you do sometimes emerge from your ivory tower, would not a little intimate party at my house amuse you? I should invite sympathetic souls who would be more to your taste. A big affair like this is not for you. I saw you talking to my Aunt Oriane who may have the best qualities in the world but we shouldn't be libelling her, should we, if we said she doesn't belong to the élite of the mind?'

I could not impart to Gilberte the thoughts which had occupied me during the last hour but I thought she might provide me with distraction which, however, I should not get from talking literature with the Duchesse de Guermantes nor with her either. Certainly I intended to start afresh from the next day to live in solitude but, this time, with a real object. Even at my own house I should not let people come to see me during my working hours, for my duty to my work was more important than that of being polite or even kind. Doubtless, those who had not seen me for a long time would come, and believing me restored to health, would be insistent. When their day's work was finished or interrupted, they would insist on coming, having need of me as I once had of Saint-Loup, because, as had happened at Combray when my parents reproached me just when, unknown to them, I was forming the most praiseworthy resolution, the internal timepieces allotted to mankind are not all regulated to the same hour; one strikes the hour of rest when another strikes that of work, one that of a judge's sentence when the guilty has repented and that of his inner perfectioning has struck long before. But to those who came to see me or sent for me, I should have the courage to answer that I had an urgent appointment about essential matters it was necessary for me to regulate without further delay, an appointment of capital importance with myself. And yet, though indeed there be little relation between our real self and the other – because of their homonymy and their common body, the abnegation which makes us sacrifice easier duties, pleasures even, seems to others egoism.

Moreover, was it not to concern myself with them that I was going to live far apart from those who would complain that they never saw me, to concern myself with them more fundamentally than I could have done in their presence, so that I might reveal them to themselves, make them realise themselves. How would it have profited if, for years longer, I had wasted my nights by letting the words they had just uttered fade into an equally vain echo of my own, for the sake of the sterile pleasure of a social contact which excludes all penetrating thought? Would it not be better I should try to describe the curve, to elicit the law that governed their gestures, their words, their lives, their nature? Unhappily, I should be compelled to fight against that habit of putting myself in another's place which, though it may favour the conception of a work retards its execution. For, through an excess of politeness it makes us sacrifice to others not merely our pleasure but our duty even though putting oneself in the place of others, duty, whatever form it may take, even, were it helpful, that of remaining at the rear when one can render no service at the front, appears (contrary to the truth) to be our pleasure.

And far from believing myself unhappy because of a life without friends, without conversation, as some of the greatest have believed, I realised that the force and elation spent in friendship are a sort of false passport to an individual intimacy that leads nowhere and turns us back from a truth to which they might have conducted us. But anyhow, should intervals of repose and social intercourse be necessary to me, I felt that instead of the intellectual conversations which society people believe interesting to writers, light loves with young flowering girls would be the nourishment I might, at the most, allow my imagination, like the famous horse which was fed on nothing but roses. All of a sudden I longed again for what I had dreamed of at Balbec, when I saw Albertine and Andrée disporting themselves with their friends on the seashore before I knew them. But alas, those I now so much longed for, I could find no more. The years which had transformed all those I had seen today including Gilberte herself must, beyond question, have made of the other survivors as, had she not perished, of Albertine, women very different from the girls I remembered. I suffered at the thought of their attaint for time's changes do not modify the images in our memory. There is nothing more painful than the contrast between the alteration in beings and the fixity of memory, than the realisation that what our memory keeps green has decayed and that there can be no exterior approach to the beauty within us which causes so great a yearning to see it once more. The intense desire for those girls of long ago which my memory excited, could never be quenched unless I sought its satisfaction in another being as young. I had often suspected that what seems unique in a creature we desire does not belong to that individual. But the passage of time gave me completer proof, since after twenty years I now wanted, instead of the girls I had known, those possessing their youth. Moreover, it is not only the awakening of physical desire that corresponds to no reality because it ignores the passing of time. At times I prayed that, by a miracle, my grandmother and Albertine had, in spite of my reason, survived and would come to me. I believed I saw them, my heart leaped towards them. But I forgot that, if they had been alive, Albertine would almost have the appearance of Mme

Cottard at Balbec and that my grandmother at ninety-five would not exhibit the beautiful, calm, smiling face I still imagined hers as arbitrarily as we picture God the Father with a beard or as, in the seventeenth century, the heroes of Homer were represented in the company of noblemen with no regard to chronology.

I looked at Gilberte and I did not think, 'I should like to see you again.' But I told her it would certainly give me pleasure if she invited me to meet young girls, of whom I should ask no more than to evoke reveries and sorrows of former days, perhaps, on some unlikely day, to allow me the privilege of one chaste kiss.

As Elstir loved to see incarnated in his wife the Venetian beauty he so often painted in his works, I excused myself for being attracted through a certain aesthetic egoism towards beautiful women who might cause me suffering, and I cultivated a sort of idolatry for future Gilbertes, future Duchesses de Guermantes and Albertines who I thought might inspire me like a sculptor in the midst of magnificent antique marbles. I ought, nevertheless, to have remembered that each experience had been preceded by my sense of the mystery which pervaded them and that, instead of asking Gilberte to introduce me to young girls I should have done better to journey to those shores where nothing binds them to us, where an impassable gulf lies between them and us, where, though they are about to bathe two paces away on the beach, they are separated from us by the impossible. It was thus that my sentiment of mystery had enshrined first Gilberte, then the Duchesse de Guermantes, Albertine, so many others. True, the unknown and almost unknowable had become the common, the familiar, the indifferent or the painful, yet it retained something of its former charm.

And, to tell the truth (as in those calendars the postman brings us when he wants his Christmas box), there was not one year of my life that did not have the picture of a woman I then desired as its frontispiece or interleaved in its days; a picture sometimes the more arbitrary that I had not even seen her, as for instance, Mme Putbus' maid, Mlle d'Orgeville or some other girl whose name I had noticed in a society column amongst those of other charming dancers. I imagined her beautiful, I fell in love with her, I created an ideal being, queen of the provincial countryside where, I gleaned from the *Annuaire des Châteaux*, her family owned an estate. In the case of women I had known, that countryside was at least a double one. Each one of them emerged at a different point of my life, standing like protective local divinities first in the midst of the countryside of my dreams, a setting which patterned my life and to which my imagination clung; then perceived by the memory in the various places where I had known her, places she recalled because of her association with them; for though our life wanders, our memory is sedentary and, project ourselves as we may, our memories riveted to places from which we are detached, remain at home like temporary acquaintances made by a traveller in some city in which he leaves them to live their lives and finish their days as though he were still standing beside the church, in front of the door, beneath the trees in the avenue. Thus the shadow of Gilberte lengthened from the front of a church in l'Ile de France where I had imagined her to the drive of a park on the Méséglise side, that of Mme de Guermantes from the damp path over which red and violet grapes hung in clusters to the morning-gold of a Paris pavement. And this second personality, not born of desire but of memory, was not in either case the only one. I had known each in different circumstances and periods and in each she was another for me or I was another, bathed in dreams of another colour. And the law which had governed the dreams of each year now gathered round them the memories of the woman I had each time known, that which concerned the Duchesse de Guermantes of my childhood was concentrated by magnetic energy round Combray and that which concerned the Duchesse de Guermantes who invited me to luncheon about a sensitive being of a different kind; there were several Duchesses de Guermantes as there had been several Mme Swanns since the lady in pink, separated from each other by the colourless ether of years, and I could no more jump from one to the other than I could fly from here to another planet. Not only separated but different, decked out with dreams at different periods as with flora indiscoverable in another planet. So true was this that, having decided not to go to luncheon either with Mme de Forcheville or with Mme de Guermantes, so completely would that have transported me into another world, I could only tell myself that the one was the Duchesse de Guermantes, descendant of Geneviève de Brabant and the other was the lady in pink, because within me an educated man asserted the fact with the same authority as a scientist who stated that a nebulous Milky Way was composed of particles of a single star. In the same way Gilberte, whom I nevertheless asked absentmindedly to introduce me to girls like her former self, was now nothing more to me than Mme de Saint-Loup. As I looked at her, I did not start dreaming of the part my admiration of Bergotte, whom she had also forgotten, had formerly played in my love of her, for I now only thought of Bergotte as the author of his books, without remembering, except during rare and isolated flashes, my emotion when I was introduced to him, my disappointment, my astonishment at his conversation in the drawing-room with the white rugs, full of violets, where such a number of lamps were brought so early and placed upon so many different tables. All the memories which composed the original Mlle Swann were, in fact, foreshortened by the Gilberte of now, held back by the magnetic attraction of another universe, united to a sentence of Bergotte and bathed in the perfume of hawthorn.

The fragmentary Gilberte of today listened smilingly to my request and setting herself to think, she became serious and appeared to be searching for something in her head. Of this I was glad as it prevented her from noticing a group seated not far from us, the sight of which would not have been agreeable to her. The Duchesse de Guermantes was engaged in an animated conversation with a horrible old woman whom I stared at without having the slightest idea who she was. 'How extraordinary to see Rachel here,' Bloch passing at that moment, whispered in my ear. The magic name instantly broke the spell which had laid the disguise of this unknown and foul old woman upon Saint-Loup's mistress and I recognised her at once. In this case as in others, as soon as names were supplied to faces I could not recognise, the spell was broken and I knew them. All the same, there was a man there I could not recognise even when I was supplied with his name and I believed it must be a homonym for he bore no sort of likeness to the one I had formerly known and come across afterwards. It was the same man, after all, only greyer and fatter but he had removed his moustache and with it, his personality. It was indeed Rachel, now a celebrated actress, who was to recite verses of Musset and La Fontaine during the reception, with whom Gilberte's aunt, the Duchesse de Guermantes, was then talking. The sight of Rachel could in no case have been agreeable to Gilberte and I was annoyed to hear she was going to recite because it would demonstrate her intimacy with the Duchesse. The latter, too long conscious of being the leader of fashion (not realising that a situation of that kind only exists in the minds of those who believe in it and that many newcomers would not believe she had any position at all unless they saw her name in the fashion-columns and knew she went everywhere) nowadays only visited the Faubourg Saint-Germain at rare intervals, saying that it bored her to death and went to the other extreme by lunching with this or that actress whose company pleased her.

The Duchesse still hesitated to invite Balthy and Mistinguette, whom she thought adorable, for fear of a scene with M. de Guermantes, but in any case Rachel was her friend. From this the new generation concluded, notwith-standing her name, that the Duchesse de Guermantes must be a *demi-castor* who had never been the 'real thing'. It is true that Mme de Guermantes still took the trouble to ask certain sovereigns for whose friendship two other great ladies were her rivals, to luncheon. But they rarely came to Paris and knew people of no particular position, and as the Duchesse, owing to the Guermantes partiality for old forms (for though well-bred people bored her, she liked good manners) announced, 'Her Majesty has commanded the Duchesse de Guermantes, has deigned, et cetera,' the newcomers, ignorant of these formulas, assumed that the Duchesse's position had diminished. From Mme de Guermantes' standpoint, her intimacy with Rachel might indicate that we were mistaken in believing her condemnation of fashion to be a hypocritical pose at a time when her refusal to go to Mme de Sainte-Euverte's seemed to be due to snobbishness rather than to intelligence and her objection to the marquise on the ground of stupidity to be attributable to the latter's failure to attain her snobbish ambitions. But this intimacy with Rachel might equally signify that the Duchesse's intelligence was meagre, unsatisfied and desirous, very late, of expressing itself, combined with a total ignorance of intellectual realities and a fanciful spirit which makes ladies of position say 'What fun it will be' and finish their evenings in what actually is the most excruciating boredom, forcing themselves on someone to whom they have nothing to say so as to stand a moment by his bedside in an evening cloak, after which, observing that it is very late, they go off to bed.

It may be added that for some little time, the versatile Duchesse had felt a strong antipathy towards Gilberte which might make her take particular pleasure in receiving Rachel, which moreover enabled her to proclaim one of the Guermantes' maxims, namely, that they were too numerous to take up a quarrel or to go into mourning among themselves, a sort of 'it's not my business' independence which it had been expedient to adopt in regard to M. de Charlus who, had they espoused his cause, would have made them quarrel with everybody. As to Rachel, if she had actually taken a good deal of trouble to make friends with the Duchesse (trouble which the Duchesse had been unable to detect in the affected disdain and pretentious rudeness which made her believe the actress was not at all a snob) doubtless it came about from the fascination exercised upon society people by hardened Bohemians which is parallel to that which Bohemians feel about people in society, a double reaction which corresponds, in the political order, to the reciprocal curiosity and desire to be allies displayed by nations who have fought against each other. But Rachel's wish to be friends with the Duchesse might have a more peculiar reason. It was at the house of Mme de Guermantes and from Mme de Guermantes herself that she once suffered her greatest humiliation. Rachel had not forgotten though, little by little, she had pardoned it, but the singular prestige the Duchesse had derived from it in her eyes, would never be effaced. The colloquy from which I wanted to draw Gilberte's attention was fortunately interrupted, for the mistress of the house came to fetch

Rachel, the moment having come for her recitation, so she left the Duchesse and appeared upon the platform.

While these incidents were taking place a spectacle of a very different kind was to be seen at the other end of Paris. La Berma had asked some people to come to tea with her in honour of her daughter and her son-in-law but the guests were apparently in no hurry to arrive. Having learned that Rachel was to recite poems at the Princesse de Guermantes' (which greatly shocked la Berma, a great artist to whom Rachel was still a courtesan given minor parts, because Saint-Loup paid for her stage-wardrobe, in plays in which la Berma took the principal rôle, more shocked still by the report in town that though the invitations were sent in the name of the Princesse de Guermantes, it was Rachel who was receiving there) la Berma had written insistently to some of her faithful friends not to fail to come to her tea party, knowing they were also friends of the Princesse de Guermantes when she was Mme Verdurin. But the hours passed and no one arrived. When Bloch was asked to go he replied naively: 'No, I prefer going to the Princesse de Guermantes'.' And, alas, everyone else had made up his mind to do likewise. La Berma, attacked by a mortal disease which prevented her from going into society except on rare occasions, had become worse, since, in order to satisfy her daughter's demand for luxuries which her ailing and idle son-in-law could not provide, she had again gone on the stage. She knew she was shortening her life, but only cared to please her daughter to whom she brought the great prestige of her fame as to her son-in-law whom she detested but flattered because, as she knew her daughter adored him, she feared, if she did not conciliate him, he would, out of spite, keep them apart. La Berma's daughter, who was not entirely cruel and was secretly loved by the doctor who was attending her mother, allowed herself to be persuaded that these performances of *Phèdre* were not very dangerous to the invalid. In a measure she had forced the doctor to say so and had retained only that out of the many things he forbade and which she ignored; in reality the doctor had said that there was no harm in la Berma's performances, to please the young woman whom he loved, and perhaps through ignorance as well, knowing that the disease was incurable anyhow, on the principle that one readily accepts the shortening of the sufferings of invalids when in doing so one is the gainer, perhaps also through stupidly supposing it would please la Berma herself and must, therefore, do her good, a foolish notion in which he felt justified when, a box being sent him by la Berma's children for which he left all his patients in the lurch, he had found her as full of life on the stage as she had appeared moribund in her own house. And our habits do, indeed, in large measure, enable even our organs to accommodate themselves to an existence which at first seemed impossible. We have all seen an old circus performer with a weak heart accomplish acrobatic tricks which no one would believe his heart could stand. La Berma was in the same degree a stage veteran to whose exactions her organs so much adapted themselves that forfeiting prudence, she could, without the public discerning it, produce the illusion of health only affected by an imaginary nervous ailment. After the scene of Hippolyte's declaration, though la Berma well knew the terrible night to which she was returning, her admirers applauded her to the echo and declared her more beautiful than ever. She went back in a state of horrible suffering but happy to bring her daughter the banknotes which, with the playfulness of a former child of the streets, she was in the habit of tucking into her stocking whence she proudly extracted them, hoping for a smile or a kiss. Unhappily, these notes only enabled son-in-law and daughter to add new decorations to their house adjoining that of their mother, in consequence of which, incessant hammering interrupted the sleep which the great tragedian so much needed. To conform to changes of fashion and to the taste of Messrs de X or de Y, whom they hoped to entertain, they redecorated every room in the house. La Berma, realising that the sleep which alone could have calmed her suffering, had fled, resigned herself to not sleeping any more, not without a secret contempt for elegancies which were hastening her death and making her last days a torture. Doubtless she despised such decrees of fashion owing to a natural resentment of things that injure us which we are powerless to avoid. But it was also because, conscious of the genius within her, she had acquired in her early youth the realisation of their futility and had remained faithful to the tradition she had always reverenced and of which she was the incarnation, which made her judge things and people as she would have done thirty years earlier – Rachel, for instance, not as the fashionable actress she had become but as the little prostitute she had been. In truth, la Berma was no better than her daughter; it was from her heredity and from the contagion of example which admiration had rendered more effective, that her daughter had derived her egotism, her pitiless raillery, her unconscious cruelty. But, la Berma, in thus saturating her daughter with her own defects, had delivered herself. And even if la Berma's daughter had not had workmen in her house she would have exhausted her mother through the ruthless and irresponsible force of attraction of youth which infects old age with the madness of trying to assimilate it. Every day there was a luncheon party and they would have considered la Berma selfish to deny them that pleasure, or even not to be there as they counted on the magical presence of the illustrious mother to attract, not without difficulty, new social relationships which had to be hauled in by the ears. They 'promised' her to these new acquaintances for some party elsewhere so as to show them 'civility'. And the poor mother, engaged in a grave colloquy with death who had taken up his abode in her, had to get up and go out. The more so that, at this period, Réjane, in all the lustre of her talent, was giving performances abroad with enormous success and the son-in-law, anxious that la Berma should not be eclipsed, wanted as profuse an effulgence for the family and forced la Berma to make tours during which she had to have injections of morphia which might cause her death at any moment because of the state of her kidneys. The same magnet of fashion and social prestige had on the day of the Princesse de Guermantes' party, acted as an air-pump and had drawn la Berma's most faithful habitués there with the power of hydraulic suction, while at her own house there was absolute void and death. One young man had come, being uncertain whether the party at la Berma's would be equally brilliant or not. When she saw the time pass and realised that everyone had thrown her over, she had tea served and sat down to table as though to a funereal repast. There was nothing left in la Berma's face to recall her whose photograph had so deeply moved me one mid-Lenten evening long ago; death, as people say, was written in it. At this moment she verily resembled a marble of Erechtheum. Her hardened arteries were half petrified, long sculptural ribbons were traced upon her cheeks with a mineral rigidity. The dying eyes were relatively living in contrast with the terrible ossified mask and shone feebly like a serpent asleep in the midst of stones. Nevertheless, the young man who had sat down to the table out of politeness was continually looking at the time, attracted as he was to the brilliant party at the Guermantes'.

La Berma had no word of reproach for the friends who had abandoned her naively hoping she was unaware they had gone to the Guermantes'. She only murmured: 'Fancy a Rachel giving a party at the Princesse de Guermantes'; one has to come to Paris to see a thing like that!' and silently and with solemn slowness ate forbidden cakes as though she were observing some funeral rite. The tea-party was the more depressing that the son-in-law was furious that Rachel, whom he and his wife knew well, had not invited them. His despair was the greater that the young man who had been invited, told him he knew Rachel well enough, if he went to the Guermantes' at once, to ask her to invite the frivolous couple at the last moment. But la Berma's daughter knew the low level to which her mother relegated Rachel and that, to solicit an invitation from the former prostitute, would have been tantamount to killing her, and she told the young man and her husband that such a thing was out of the question. But she revenged herself during tea by adopting an air of being deprived of amusement and bored by that tiresome mother of hers. The latter pretended not to notice her daughter's sulkiness and every now and then addressed an amiable word to the young man, their only guest, in a dying voice. But soon the whirlwind which was blowing everybody to the Guermantes' and had blown me there prevailed; he got up and left, leaving Phèdre or death, one did not know which, to finish eating the funeral cakes with her daughter and her son-in-law.

The conversation Gilberte and I were having was interrupted by the voice of Rachel who had just stood up. Her performance was intelligent, for it assumed the unity of the poem as pre-existent apart from the recital and that we were only listening to a fragment of it, as though we were for a moment within earshot of an artist walking along a road. But the audience was bewildered at the sight of the woman bending her knees and throwing out her arms as though she were holding some invisible being in them, before she uttered a sound, and then becoming suddenly bandy-legged and starting to recite very familiar lines in a tone of supplication.

The announcement of a poem which nearly everybody knew had given satisfaction. But when they saw Rachel before beginning, peering about like one who is lost, lifting imploring hands and giving vent to sobs with every word, everyone felt embarrassed and shocked by the exaggeration. No one had ever supposed that reciting verses was this sort of thing. But, by degrees, one gets accustomed to it and one forgets the first feeling of discomfort; one begins analysing the performance and mentally comparing various forms of recitation so as to say to oneself that one thing or the other is better or worse. It is like when, on seeing a barrister the first time in an ordinary lawsuit stand forward, lift his arm from the folds of his gown and begin in a threatening tone, one does not dare look at one's neighbours. One feels it is ridiculous, but perhaps, after all, it is magnificent and one waits to see

Everybody looked at each other, not knowing what sort of face to put on; some of the younger ones whose manners were less restrained stifled bursts of laughter. Each person cast a stealthy look at the one next to him, that furtive look one bestows on a guest more knowing than oneself at a fashionable dinner when at the side of one's plate one observes a strange instrument, a lobster fork or a sugar-sifter one does not know how to wield, hoping to watch him using it so that one can copy him. One behaves similarly when someone quotes a verse one does not know but wants to appear to know and which, like giving way to someone else at a door, one leaves to a better-informed person the pleasure of identifying as though we were doing him a favour. Thus those who were listening waited with bent head and inquisitive eye for others to take the initiative in laughter, criticism, tears or applause.

Mme de Forcheville, come expressly from Guermantes whence the Duchesse, as we shall see later on, had been virtually expelled, adopted an attentive and strained appearance which was all but positively disagreeable, either to show she knew all about it and was not present as a mere society woman, or out of hostility to those less versed in literature who might talk to her about something else or because she was trying by complete concentration, to make up her mind whether she liked it or not because though, perhaps, she thought it 'interesting', she did not 'approve' the manner in which certain verses were delivered. This attitude might more properly have been adopted, one would have thought, by the Princesse de Guermantes. But as it was her own house and she had become as miserly as she was rich she made up her mind to give just five roses to Rachel and see to the *claque* for her. She excited enthusiasm and created general approval by her loud exclamations of delight. Only in that respect did she become a Verdurin again; she conveyed the impression of listening to the verses for her own pleasure, of really preferring them to be recited to her alone and of its being a matter of chance that five hundred people had come by her permission to share her pleasure in secrecy.

I noticed, however, without its affording my vanity any satisfaction since she had become old and ugly, that Rachel gave me a surreptitious wink. Throughout the recital she let me perceive by a subtly conveyed yet expressive smile that she was soliciting my acquiescence in her advances. But certain old ladies, unaccustomed to poetic recitations, remarked *sotto voce* to their neighbours: 'Did you see that?' alluding to the actress's tragi-comic miming which was too much for them. The Duchesse de Guermantes sensed the wavering of opinion and determining to assure the performer's triumph, exclaimed 'Marvellous!' in the very middle of a poem which she believed finished. Upon this several guests emphasised the exclamation with a gesture of appreciation, less with the object of displaying their approval of the recital than the terms they were on with the Duchesse. When the poem was finished, we were close to Rachel who thanked Mme de Guermantes and as I was with the latter, took advantage of the opportunity to address me graciously. I then realised that, unlike the impassioned gaze of M. de Vaugoubert's son which I had assumed to be a salutation intended for another, Rachel's significant smile, instead of being meant as an invitation was only intended to provoke my recognition and the bow I now made to her. 'I am sure he does not know me,' the actress remarked to the Duchesse in a mincing manner. 'On the contrary,' I asserted, 'I recognised you immediately.'

If, while that woman was reciting some of La Fontaine's most beautiful verses, she had only been thinking, whether out of goodwill, stupidity or embarrassment, of the awkwardness of approaching me, during the same time Bloch had only thought of how he could bound, like one who is escaping from a beleaguered city, if not over the bodies at all events on the feet of his neighbours, to congratulate the actress the moment the recital was over, whether from a mistaken sense of obligation or from a desire to show off. 'It was beautiful,' he said to her and, having thus relieved himself, he turned his back on her and made such a noise in resuming his seat that Rachel had to wait several minutes before she could begin her second poem. It was 'Les Deux Pigeons' and when it was over, Mme de Monrieuval went up to Mme de Saint-Loup who she knew was well-read, but did not remember that she had her father's subtle and sarcastic wit, and asked her: 'It's one of La Fontaine's fables, isn't it?' thinking so but not being sure, for she only knew the fables slightly and believed they were children's tales unsuitable for recitation in society. Doubtless the good woman supposed that, to have such a success, the artist must have parodied them. Gilbert, till then impassive, confirmed the notion, for as she disliked Rachel and wanted to convey that with such a diction nothing of the fables remained, her answer was given with that tinge of malice which left simple people uncertain what Swann really meant. Though she was Swann's daughter, she was more modern than he – like a duck hatched by a chicken – and being as a rule rather *lakist*, might have contented herself with saying: 'I thought it most moving, a charming sensibility', but Gilberte answered Mme de Monrieuval in Swann's fanciful fashion which people often made the mistake of taking literally: 'A quarter is the interpreter's invention, a quarter crazy, a quarter meaningless, the rest La Fontaine,' which enabled Mme de Monrieuval to assert that what people had been listening to was not 'Les Deux Pigeons' of La Fontaine, but a composition of which at the most a quarter was La Fontaine, at which nobody was surprised owing to their extraordinary ignorance.

But one of Bloch's friends having arrived late, the former painted a wonderful picture of Rachel's performance, getting a peculiar pleasure out of exaggerating its merits and holding forth to someone about modernist diction though it had not given him the slightest satisfaction. Then Bloch again congratulated Rachel with overdone emotion in a squeaky voice, told her she was a genius and introduced his friend who declared he had never admired anyone so much and Rachel, who now knew ladies in the best society and unconsciously copied them, answered: 'I am flattered, honoured, by your appreciation.' Bloch's friend asked Rachel what she thought of la Berma.

'Poor woman! It appears she's in a state of poverty. I will not say she had no talent, though it was not real talent for, at bottom, she only liked horrors, but certainly she was useful, she played in a lively fashion and she was a well-meaning, generous creature and has ruined herself for others. She has made nothing for a long time because the public no longer cares for the things she plays in. To tell the truth,' she added with a laugh, 'I must tell you that my age did not enable me to hear her till her last period when I was too young to form an opinion.' 'Didn't she recite poetry well?' Bloch's friend ventured the question to flatter her: 'As to that,' she replied, 'she never could recite a single line, it was prose, Chinese, Volapuk, anything you like except verse. Moreover, as I tell you, I hardly heard her and only quite at the last', to appear youthful, 'but I've been told she was no better formerly, rather the reverse.'

I realised that the passing of time does not necessarily bring about progress in the arts. And in the same way that a seventeenth century writer who was without knowledge of the French Revolution, scientific discoveries and the war, can be superior to another of this period and that Fagon was, perhaps, as great a physician as du Boulbon (the superiority of genius compensating in this case the inferiority of knowledge) so la Berma was a hundred times greater than Rachel, and time, by placing her at the top of the tree together with Elstir, had consecrated her genius.

One must not be surprised that Saint-Loup's former mistress sneered at la Berma, she would have done so when she was young, so how would she not do so now? Let a society woman of high intelligence and of amiable disposition become an actress, displaying great talent in her new profession and meeting with nothing but success, if one happened to be in her company some time later, one would be surprised at hearing her talk a language which was not hers but that of people of the theatre, assume their peculiar kind of coarse familiarity towards their colleagues and all the rest of the habits acquired by those who have been on the stage for thirty years. Rachel behaved similarly without having been in society.

Mme de Guermantes, in her decline, had felt new curiosities rising within her. Society had nothing more to give her. The fact that she occupied the highest position in it was, as we have seen, as plain to her as the height of the blue sky above the earth. She did not consider that she had to assert a position she regarded as unassailable. On the other hand, she wanted to extend her reading and attend more performances. As in former days, all the choicest and most exclusive spirits gathered familiarly in the little garden to drink orangeade amidst the perfumed breezes and clouds of pollen, to be entertained of an evening by her taste for and understanding of what was best in society, now another sort of appetite made her want to know the reasons of some literary controversy, to make the acquaintance of its protagonists and of actresses. Her tired mind demanded a new stimulant. To know such people, she now made advances to women with whom formerly she would not have exchanged cards, and who made much of their intimacy with the director of some review or other in the hope of getting hold of the Duchesse. The first actress she invited believed herself to be the only one admitted to a wonderful social milieu which seemed less wonderful to the second when the latter saw who had preceded her. The Duchesse believed her position to be unchanged because she received royalties at some of her evening parties. In reality she, the only representative of stainless blood, herself a born Guermantes, who could sign 'Guermantes' when she did not sign 'Duchesse de Guermantes', she who represented to her own sisters-in-law something infinitely precious, like a Moses saved from the waters, a Christ escaped into Egypt, a Louis XVII fled from the Temple, purest of pure breeds, now sacrificed it all, doubtless for the sake of that congenital need of mental nourishment which caused the social desuetude of Mme de Villeparisis, and had herself become a sort of Mme de Villeparisis at whose house snobbish women were afraid of meeting this person or that and whom young men, observing the accomplished fact without knowing what had preceded it, believed to be a Guermantes of inferior vintage, of a poor year, a *déclassée* Guermantes. In her new environment she remained what she had been more than she supposed and went on believing that being bored implied intellectual superiority and expressed this sentiment with a violence that made her voice sound harsh. When I talked about Brichot to her she said: 'He bored me enough for twenty years', and when Mme de Cambremer suggested her re-reading 'what Schopenhauer said about music', she commented on the remark with asperity: 'Re-read! That's a gem! Please not that.' Then old Albon smiled because he recognised one of the forms of the Guermantes' spirit.

'People can say what they like, it's admirable, there's the right note and character in it, it's an intelligent rendering, nobody ever recited verses like it,' the Duchesse said of Rachel, for fear Gilberte would sneer at her. The latter moved away to another group to avoid conflict with her aunt who, indeed, was extremely dull when she talked about Rachel. But considering the best writers cease to display any talent with increase of age or from excess of production, one can excuse society women for having less sense of humour as they get old. Swann missed the Princesse des Laumes' delicacy in the hard wit of the Duchesse de Guermantes. Late in life, tired by the slightest effort, Mme de Guermantes gave vent to an immense number of stupid observations. It is true that every now and then, even in the course of this very afternoon, she was again the woman I once knew and talked about society matters with her former verve. But in spite of the sparkling words and the accompanying charm which for so many years had held under their sway the most distinguished men in Paris, her wit scintillated, so to speak, in a vacuum. When she was about to say something funny, she paused the same number of seconds as she used to but when the jest came, there was no point in it. However, few enough people noticed it. The continuity of the proceeding made them think the spirit survived, like people who have a fancy for particular kinds of cakes and go to the same shop for them without noticing that they have deteriorated. Even during the war the Duchesse had shown signs of this decay. If anyone used the word culture, she stopped, smiled, her beautiful face lighted up and she ejaculated: 'la KKKKultur' and made her friends, who were fervents of the Guermantes' spirit, roar with laughter. It was, of course, the same mould, the same intonation, the same smile that had formerly delighted Bergotte, who, for that matter, had he lived, would have kept his pithy phrases, his interjections, his periods of suspense, his epithets, to express nothing. But newcomers were sometimes taken aback and if they happened to turn up on a day when she was neither bright nor in full possession of her faculties, they said, 'What a fool she is.'

Moreover, the Duchesse so timed her descent into a lower sphere as not to allow it to affect those of her family from whom she drew aristocratic prestige. If, to play her part as protectress of the arts, she invited a minister or a painter to the theatre and he asked her naively whether her sister-in-law or her husband were in the audience, the Duchesse intimidated him by a show of audacity and answered disdainfully: 'I don't know. When I go out I don't bother about my family. For politicians and artists I'm a widow.' In this way she prevented the too obtrusive parvenu from getting rebuffs – and herself reprimands – from M. de Marsantes and Basin.

I told Mme de Guermantes I had met M. de Charlus. She thought him more deteriorated than he was, it being the habit of people in society to see differences of intelligence in various people in their world amongst whom it is about uniform and also in the same person at different periods of his life. She added: 'He was always the very image of my mother-in-law and the likeness is more striking than ever.' There was nothing remarkable in that. We know, as a matter of fact, that certain women are reproduced in certain men with complete fidelity, the only mistake being the sex. We cannot qualify this as *felix culpa*, for sex reacts upon personality and feminism becomes effeminacy, reserve suceptibility and so on. This does not prevent a man's face, even though bearded, from being modelled on lines transferable to the portrait of his mother. There was nothing but a ruin of the old

M. de Charlus left but under all the layers of fat and rice powder one could recognise the remnants of a beautiful woman in her eternal youth.

'I can't tell you how much pleasure it gives me to see you,' the Duchesse continued. 'Goodness, when was it we last met?' 'Calling upon Mme d'Agrigente where I often used to see you.' 'Ah, of course, I often went there, my dear friend, as Basin was in love with her then. I could always be found with his particular friend of the moment because he used to say: "Mind you go and see her". I must confess that sort of "digestion-call" he made me pay when he had satisfied his appetite was rather troublesome. I got accustomed to that, but the tiresome part was being obliged to keep these relationships up after he had done with them. That always made me think of Victor Hugo's verse *"Emporte le bonheur et laisse-moi l'ennui"*. I accepted it smilingly like poetry but it wasn't fair. At least he might have let me be fickle about his mistresses; making up his accounts with the series he had enough of didn't leave me an afternoon to myself. Well, those days seem sweet compared to the present. I can consider it flattering that he has started being unfaithful to me again because it makes me feel young. But I prefer his earlier manner. I suppose it was so long since he had done that sort of thing that he didn't know how to set about it. But all the same, we get on quite well together. We talk together and rather like each other.' The Duchesse said this for fear I might think they had completely separated and, just as people say when someone is very ill: 'He still likes to talk, I was reading to him for an hour this morning,' she added: 'I'll tell him you're here, he'd like to see you', and went up to the Duc who was sitting on a sofa talking to a lady. But when he saw his wife approaching him, he looked so angry that she had no alternative but to retire. 'He's engaged; I don't know what he is up to, we shall see presently,' Mme de Guermantes said, leaving me to make what I liked of the situation.

Bloch approached us and asked us in the name of his American friend who the young Duchesse over there was. I told him she was the niece of M. de Bréauté, about whom Bloch, who had never heard his name, wanted particulars. 'Ah, Bréauté!' exclaimed Mme de Guermantes, addressing me, 'you remember! Goodness, how long ago it is!' Then turning to Bloch, 'He was a snob if you like; his people lived near my mother-in-law. That won't interest you, it's amusing for my old friend,' she indicated me, 'he used to know all about them in the old days as I did.' These words and many things in Mme de Guermantes' manner showed the time that had passed since then. Her friendships and opinions had so changed since the time she was referring to that she had come to thinking her charming Babel a snob. He, on the other hand, had not only receded in time, but, a thing I had not realised when I entered society and believed him one of those notabilities of Paris which would always be associated with his social history like with that of Colbert in the reign of Louis XIV, he also had a provincial label as a country neighbour of the old Duchesse and it was in that capacity that the Princesse des Laumes had been associated with him. Nevertheless, this Bréauté, barren of his one time wit, relegated to a past which dated him and proved he had since been completely forgotten by the Duchesse and her circle, formed a link between the Duchesse and myself which I could never have believed that first evening at the Opéra Comique when he had appeared to me like a nautical god in his marine cave, because she recalled that I had known him, consequently that I had been her friend, if not of the same social circle as herself, that I had frequented that circle for a far longer time than most of the people present; she recalled him and yet not clearly enough to remember certain details which were then my vital concern, that I was not invited to the Guermantes' place in the country and was only a small bourgeois of Combray when she came to Mlle Percepied's marriage mass, that, in spite of all Saint-Loup's requests, she did not invite me to her house during the year following Bréauté's appearance with her at the Opéra Comique. To me that was of capital importance for it was exactly then that the life of the Duchesse de Guermantes seemed to me like a paradise I could not enter, but for her it was the same indifferent existence she was accustomed to, and owing to my having often dined at her house later on, and to my having, even earlier, been her aunt's and her nephew's friend, she no longer remembered at what period our intimacy had begun nor realised the anachronism of making it start several years too early. For that made it seem as though I had known the Mme de Guermantes of that marvellous Guermantes name, that I had been received by the name of golden syllables in the Faubourg Saint-Germain when I had merely dined with a lady who was even then nothing more to me than a lady like any other and who had invited me not to descend into the submarine kingdom of the nereids but to spend the evening in her cousin's box. 'If you want to know all about Bréauté, who isn't worth it,' she added to Bloch, 'ask my friend who is worth a hundred of him. He has dined fifty times at my house with Bréauté. Wasn't it at my house that you met him? Anyhow, you met Swann there.' And I was as surprised that she imagined I might have met M. de Bréauté elsewhere than at her house and frequented that circle before I knew her as I was to observe that she imagined I had first known Swann at her house. Less untruthfully than Gilberte when she said that Bréauté was 'one of my old neighbours in the country; I like talking to him about Tansonville', whereas he did not in those days go to the Swann's at

Tansonville, I might have remarked: 'He was a country neighbour who often came to see us in the evening', in reference to Swann, who in truth, recalled something very different from the Guermantes.

'It's rather difficult to explain,' she continued. 'He was a man to whom Highnesses meant everything. He told a lot of rather funny stories about Guermantes people and my mother-in-law and Mme de Varambon before she was in attendance on the Princesse de Parme. But who cares about Mme de Varambon now? My friend here knew about all this, but it's done with now, they're people whose names are forgotten and, for that matter, they didn't deserve to survive.' And I realised, in spite of that unified thing society seems to be, where, in fact, social relationships reach their greatest concentration, where everything gets known about everybody, that areas of it remain in which time causes changes that cannot be grasped by those who only enter it when its configuration has changed. 'Mme de Varambon was an excellent creature who said unbelievably stupid things,' continued the Duchesse, insensitive to that poetry of the incomprehensible which is an effect of time, and concerned only with extracting human elements assimilable with literature of the Meilhac kind and with the Guermantes spirit, 'at one time she had a mania for constantly chewing cough drops called' – she laughed to herself as she recalled the name so familiar formerly, so unknown now to those she was addressing – 'Pastilles Géraudel. "Mme de Varambon," my mother-in-law said to her, ' "if you go on swallowing those Géraudel pastilles, you'll get a stomach-ache." "But, Mme la Duchesse," answered Mme de Varambon, "how can I hurt my stomach since they go into the bronchial tubes?" It was she who said, "The Duchesse has a cow so beautiful that it looks like a stallion." ' Mme de Guermantes would have gladly gone on telling stories about Mme de Varambon, of which we knew hundreds, but the name did not evoke in Bloch's memory any of those associations rekindled in us by the mention of Mme de Varambon, of M. de Bréauté, of the Prince d'Agrigente, who perhaps, on that account, exercised a glamour in his eyes I knew to be exaggerated but understood, though not because I had felt it, since our own weaknesses and absurdities seldom make us more indulgent to those of others even when we have thrust them into the light.

The past had been so transformed in the mind of the Duchesse or the demarcations which existed in my own had always been so absent from hers, that what had been an important event for me had passed unperceived by her and she endowed me with a social past which she made recede too far. For the Duchesse shared that notion of time past which I had just acquired, and contrary to my illusion which shortened it, she lengthened it, notably in not reckoning with that undefined line of demarcation between the period when she represented a name to me, then the object of my love – and the period during which she had become merely a woman in society like any other. Moreover, I only went to her house during that second period when she had become another to me. But these differences escaped her eyes and she would not have thought it more singular that I should have been at her house two years earlier because she did not know that she was then another person to me, her personality not appearing to her, as to me, discontinuous.

I told the Duchesse that Bloch believed it was the former Princesse de Guermantes who was receiving today. 'That reminds me of the first evening when I went to the Princesse de Guermantes' and believed I was not invited and that they were going to turn me out, when you wore a red dress and red shoes.' 'Gracious, how long ago that is!' she answered, thus emphasising the passage of time. She gazed sadly into the distance but particularly insisted on the red dress. I asked her to describe it to me, which she did with complaisance. 'Those dresses aren't worn nowadays. They were the fashion then. But it was pretty, wasn't it?' She was always afraid of saying anything that might not be to her advantage. 'Yes, I thought it very pretty. It isn't the fashion now but it will be again. All fashions come back, in dress, in music, in painting,' she added with emphasis, imagining something original in this philosophy. But the sadness of growing old gave her a lassitude belied by her smile. 'You're sure they were red shoes; I thought they were gold ones?' I assured her that my memory was exact on the point without detailing the circumstances which enabled me to be so certain. 'You're charming to remember,' she said tenderly, for women call those charming who remember their beauty, as artists do those who remember their works. Moreover, however distant the past, so determined a woman as the Duchesse is unlikely to forget it. 'Do you remember,' she said, as she thanked me for remembering her dress and her shoes, 'Basin and I brought you back that evening and there was a girl coming to see you after midnight. Basin laughed heartily about your having visitors at that time of night.' I did, indeed, remember that Albertine came to see me that night after the evening party at the Princesse de Guermantes'. I remembered it quite as well as the Duchesse, I to whom Albertine was now as indifferent as she would have been to Mme de Guermantes, had the latter known that the young girl on whose account I had not gone to their house, was Albertine. Long after our hearts have forsaken the poor dead, their indifferent dust remains, like an alloy, mingled with events of the past and, though we love them no more, when we evoke a room, a path, a road they lived in or traversed with us, we are compelled, so that the place they occupied may not remain untenanted, to think of them though we neither regret nor name nor identify them. (Mme de Guermantes did not identify the girl who was to come that evening, had never known her name and only referred to her because of the hour and the circumstances.) Those are the final and least enviable forms of survival.

If the opinions the Duchesse subsequently expressed regarding Rachel were indifferent in themselves, they interested me because they, too, marked a new hour on the dial. For the Duchesse had no more forgotten her evening party in which Rachel figured than had the latter and the memory had not undergone the slightest transformation. 'I must tell you,' she said, 'that I am the more interested to hear her recite and to witness her success that I discovered her, appreciated her, treasured her, imposed her, at a time when she was ignored and laughed at. You may be surprised, my dear friend, to know that the first time she was heard in public was at my house. Yes, while all the would-be advanced people like my new cousin' – she ironically indicated the Princesse de Guermantes who to her was still Mme Verdurin, 'would have let her starve without condescending to listen to her, I considered her interesting and gave her the prestige of performing at my house before the smartest audience we could get together. I can say, though it sounds stupid and pretentious, for fundamentally talent doesn't need protection, that I launched her. Of course she didn't need me.' I made a gesture of protest and observed that Mme de Guermantes was quite ready to welcome it. 'You evidently think talent has need of support? Perhaps, after all, you're right. You're repeating what Dumas formerly told me. In this case, I am extremely flattered if I do count for something, however little, not in the talent, of course, but in the reputation of an artist like her.' Mme de Guermantes preferred to abandon her idea that talent bursts like an abscess because it was more flattering for herself, but also because for some time now, she had been receiving new people and being rather worn out, she had practised humility by seeking information and asking others their opinion in order to form one. 'It isn't necessary for me to tell you,' she resumed, 'that this intelligent public which is called society saw nothing in it. They objected to her and scoffed at her. I might tell them it was original and curious, something different from what had been done before, no one believed me, as they never did believe me in anything. It was the same with the thing she recited, a piece by Maeterlinck. Now it's well known, but then everyone laughed at it though I considered it admirable. It surprises even myself considering I was only a peasant with the education of a country-girl, that I spontaneously admired things of that kind. I could not, of course, have explained why, but it gave me pleasure, it moved me. Why,

Basin, who is anything but sensitive, was struck by its effect on me. At that time, he said: "I don't want you to listen to these absurdities any more, they make you ill, and it was true. They take me for a hard woman and really I am a bundle of nerves.'

*   *   *

At this moment an unexpected incident occurred. A footman came to tell Rachel that la Berma's daughter and son-in-law wanted to speak to her. We have seen that the daughter had opposed her husband when he wanted to get an invitation from Rachel. But, after the departure of the young man, the boredom of the young couple left alone with their mother had grown, the thought that others were amusing themselves tormented them; in brief, availing themselves of la Berma's retirement to her bedroom to spit blood, they had quickly put on their smartest clothes, called a carriage and had arrived at the Princesse de Guermantes' without being invited. Rachel hardly grasped the situation, but secretly flattered, adopted an arrogant tone and told the footman she could not be disturbed, they must write and explain the object of their unusual proceeding. The footman came back with a card on which la Berma's daughter had scribbled that she and her husband could not resist the pleasure of hearing Rachel recite and asked her to let them come in. Rachel gloated over the pretext and her own triumph and replied that she was very sorry but that the recitation was over. In the anteroom, the footmen were winking at each other while the couple in vain awaited admission. The shame of their humiliation, the consciousness of the insignificance, the nullity of Rachel in her mother's eyes, pushed la Berma's daughter into pursuing to the end the step she had risked simply for amusement. She sent a message to Rachel that she would take it as a favour, even if she could not hear her recite, to be allowed to shake hands with her. Rachel at the moment, was talking to an Italian Prince who was said to be after her large fortune, the source of which her social relationships somewhat concealed. She took stock of the reversal of situations which now placed the children of the illustrious Berma at her feet. After informing everyone about the incident in the most charming fashion, she sent the young couple a message to come in, which they did without being asked twice, ruining la Berma's social prestige at one blow as they had previously destroyed her health. Rachel had realised that her condescension would result in her being considered kinder and the young couple baser than her refusal. So she received them with open arms and with the affectation of a patroness in the limelight who can put aside her magnificence, said: 'But of course, I'm delighted to see you, the Princesse will be charmed.' As she did not know that at the theatre she was supposed to have done the inviting, she may have feared, if she refused entry to la Berma's children, that they might have doubted not her goodwill for that would have been indifferent to her – but her influence. The Duchesse de Guermantes moved away instinctively, for in proportion to anyone's appearing to court society, he diminished in her esteem. At the moment she only felt for Rachel's kindness and would have turned her back on la Berma's children if they had been introduced to her. Meanwhile, Rachel was composing the gracious phrases with which she, the following day, would overwhelm la Berma in the wings: 'I was harrowed, distressed that your daughter should have been kept waiting in the anteroom. If I had only known! She sent me card after card.' She was enchanted to offer this insult to la Berma. Perhaps, had she known it would be a mortal blow, she might have hesitated. People like to persecute others but without exactly putting themselves in the wrong and without hounding them to death. Moreover, where was she wrong? She might say laughingly a few days later: 'That's pretty thick, I meant to be far nicer to her children than she ever was to me, and now they nearly accuse me of killing her. I take the Duchesse to witness.' It seems as though the children of great actors inherit all the evil and pretence of stage-life without accomplishing the determined work that springs from it as did this mother. Great actresses frequently die the victims of domestic plots which are woven round them, as happens so often at the close of dramas they play in.

Gilberte, as we have seen, wanted to avoid a conflict with her aunt on the subject of Rachel. She did well; it was not an easy matter to undertake the defence of Odette's daughter in opposition to Mme de Guermantes, so great was her animosity owing to what the Duchesse told me about the new form the Duc's infidelity had taken, which, extraordinary as it might appear to those who knew her age, was with Mme de Forcheville.

The life of the Duchesse was a very unhappy one, and for a reason which simultaneously brought about the lowering of M. de Guermantes' social standard. He, sobered by advancing age though still robust, had long ceased being unfaithful to Mme de Guermantes, but had suddenly become infatuated with Mme de Forcheville without knowing how he had got involved in the liaison. When one remembered Mme de Forcheville's present age, it did, indeed, seem extraordinary. But Odette had probably begun the life of a courtesan very young. And we encounter women who reincarnate themselves every ten years in new love affairs and sometimes drive some young wife to despair because of her husband's deserting her for them when one actually thought they were dead.

It had assumed such proportions that the old man, in this last love affair, imitating his own earlier amative proceedings, so secluded his mistress that, if my love for Albertine had been a multiple variation of Swann's for Odette, M. de Guermantes' recalled mine for Albertine. She had to take all her meals with him and he was always at her house. She boasted of this to friends who, but for her, would never have known the Duc and who came to her house to make his acquaintance, as people visit a courtesan to get to know the king who is her lover. It is true that Mme de Forcheville had been in society for a long time. But beginning over again, late in life, to be kept by such a haughty old man who played the most important part in her life, she lowered herself by ministering only to his pleasure, buying peignoirs and ordering food he liked, flattering her friends by telling them that she had spoken to him about them, as she told my great-uncle she had spoken about him to the Grand-Duke who then sent him cigarettes, in a word, she once more tended, in spite of the position she had secured in society, to become, owing to force of circumstances, what she had been to me when I was a child, the lady in pink. Of course, my Uncle Adolphe had been dead many years. But does the substitution of new people for old prevent us from beginning the same life over again? Doubtless she adapted herself to the new conditions out of cupidity, but also because, somewhat sought-after socially when she had a daughter to marry, she had been left in the background when Gilberte married Saint-Loup. She knew that the Duc would do what she liked, that he would bring her any number of duchesses who would not be reluctant to score off their friend Oriane and, perhaps, was stimulated into the bargain by the prospect of gratifying her feminine sentiment of rivalry at the expense of the outraged Duchesse. The Duc de Guermantes' exclusive Courvoisier nephews, Mme de Marsantes, the Princesse de Trania, went to Mme de Forcheville's in the expectation of legacies without troubling whether or no this caused pain to Mme de Guermantes, about whom Odette, stung by Mme de Guermantes' disdain, said the most evil things.

This liaison with Mme de Forcheville, which was only an imitation of his early ones, caused the Duc de Guermantes to miss for the second time being elected President of the Jockey Club and honorary member of the Académie des Beaux Arts just as M. de Charlus' public association with Jupien was the cause of his failure to be elected President of the Union Club and of the Society of Friends of Old Paris. Thus the two brothers, so different in their tastes, had fallen into disrepute on account of the same indolence and lack of will, more pleasantly observable in the case of their grandfather, a member of the French Academy, which led to the normal proclivities of one and the abnormal habits of the other degrading both.

The old Duc did not go out any more, he spent his days and evenings at Odette's. But today, as she herself had come to the Princesse de Guermantes' party, he had dropped in to see her for a moment, in spite of the annoyance of meeting his wife. I dare say I should not have recognised him if the Duchesse had not drawn my attention to him. He was now nothing but a ruin, but a splendid one; grander than a ruin, he had the romantic beauty of a rock beaten by a tempest. Scourged from every side by the waves of suffering, by rage at his suffering, his face, slowly crumbling like a block of granite almost submerged by the towering seas, retained the style, the suavity I had always admired. It was defaced like a beautiful antique head we are glad to possess as an ornament in a library. But it seemed to belong to an earlier period than it did, not only because its matter had acquired a rude brokenness in the place of its former grace but also because an involuntary expression caused by failing health, resisting and fighting death, by the arduousness of keeping alive, had replaced the old delicacy of mien and exuberance. The arteries had lost all their suppleness and had imprinted a sculptured hardness on the once expressive features. And, unconsciously, the Duc revealed by the contours of his neck, his cheeks, his brow, a being forced to hold on grimly to every moment and as though tossed by a tragic storm, his sparse white locks dashed their spray over the invaded promontory of his visage. And like the weird and spectral reflection an approaching storm sweeping everything before it, gives to rocks till then of another colour, I knew that the leaden grey of his hard, worn cheeks, the woolly whiteness of his unkempt hair, the wavering light which lingered in his almost unseeing eyes, were the but too real pigment borrowed from a fantastic palette with which was inimitably painted the prophetic shadows of age and the terrifying proximity of death.

The Duc only stayed a few moments, but long enough for me to see that Odette made fun of him to her younger aspirants. But it was strange that he who used to be almost ridiculous when he assumed the pose of a stage-king, was now endowed with a noble mien, resembling in that his brother whom also old age had relieved of accessories. And like his brother, once so arrogant, though in a different way, he seemed almost respectful. For he had not suffered the eclipse of M. de Charlus, reduced to bowing with a forgetful invalid's politeness to those he had formerly disdained, but he was very old and when he went through the door and wanted to go down the stairs to go away, old age, that most miserable condition which casts men from their high estate as it did the kings of Greek tragedy, old age gripped him, forced him to halt on that road of the cross which is the life of an impotent menaced by death, so that he might wipe his streaming brow and tap to find the step which escaped his foothold because he needed help to ensure it, help against his swimming eyes, help he was unknowingly imploring ever so gently and timidly from others. Old age had made him more than august, it had made him a suppliant.

Unable to do without Odette, always at her house and in the same armchair from which old age and gout made it difficult for him to rise, M. de Guermantes let her receive her friends who were only too pleased to be introduced to the Duc, to give him the lead in conversation, and listen to his talk of former society, of the Marquise de Villeparisis and of the Duc de Chartres.

Thus in the Faubourg Saint-Germain the apparently impregnable positions of the Duc and Duchesse de Guermantes and of the Baron de Charlus had lost their inviolability, as everything changes in this world, through the action of an interior principle which had never occurred to them; in the case of M. de Charlus it was the love of Charlie who had enslaved him to the Verdurins and then gradual decay, in the case of Mme de Guermantes a taste for novelty and for art, in the case of M. de Guermantes an exclusive love, as he had had so many in his life, rendered more tyrannical by the feebleness of old age to which the austerity of the Duchesse's salon where the Duc no longer put in an appearance and which, for that matter, had almost ceased functioning, offered no resistance by its power of rehabilitation. Thus the face of things in life changes, the centre of empires, the register of fortunes, the chart of positions, all that seemed final, are perpetually remoulded and during his lifetime a man can witness the completest changes just where those seemed to him least possible.

At moments, beneath the old pictures collected by Swann which, with this *Restauration* Duc and his beloved courtesan, completed the old-fashioned picture, the lady in pink interrupted him with her chatter and he stopped short, and stared at her with a ferocious glare. Possibly he had discovered that she, as well as the duchesse, occasionally made stupid remarks, perhaps an old man's fancy made him think that one of Mme de Guermantes' intemperate passages of humour had interrupted what he was saying and he thought himself back in the Guermantes' mansion, as caged beasts may imagine themselves free in African wilds. Raising his head sharply, he fixed his little yellow eyes, which once had the gleam of a wild animal's, on her in one of those sustained scowls which made me shiver when Mme de Guermantes told me about them. Thus the Duc glared at the audacious lady in pink, but she held her own, did not remove her eyes from him and at the end of a moment which seemed long to the spectators, the old wild beast, tamed, remembered he was no longer at large in the Sahara of his own home, but in his cage in the Jardin des Plantes at Mme de Forcheville's and he withdrew his head, from which still depended a thick fringe of blonde-white hair, into his shoulders and resumed his discourse. Apparently he had not understood what Mme de Forcheville said, which as a rule, meant little. He permitted her to ask her friends to dinner with him. A mania which was a relic of his former love affairs and did not surprise Odette, accustomed as she was to the same habit in Swann and which reminded me of my life with Albertine, was to insist on people going early so that he could say good-night to Odette last. It is unnecessary to add that the moment he had gone she invited other people. But the Duc had no suspicion of that, or preferred not to seem to suspect it; the vigilance of old men diminishes with their sight and hearing. After a certain age Jupiter inevitably changes into one of Molière's characters – into the absurd Géronte – not into the Olympian lover of Alcmene. And Odette deceived M. de Guermantes and took care of him with neither charm nor generosity of spirit. She was commonplace in that as in everything else. Life had given her good parts but she could not play them and, meanwhile, she was playing at being a recluse.

It was a fact that whenever I wanted to see her, I could not, because M. de Guermantes, desirous of reconciling the exactions of his hygiene with those of his jealousy, only allowed her to have parties in the daytime and on the further condition that there was no dancing. She frankly avowed the seclusion in which she lived and this for various reasons. The first was that she imagined, although I had only published a few articles and studies, that I was a well-known author which caused her to remark naively, returning to the past when I went to see her in the Avenue des Acacias and later at her house: 'Ah, if I could have then foreseen that that boy would one day be a great writer.' And having heard that writers are glad to be with women in order to document themselves and hear love stories, she readopted her rôle of courtesan to entertain me: 'Fancy, once there was a man who was crazy about me and I adored him. We were having a divine time together. He had to go to America and I was to go with him. On the eve of his departure I thought it would be more beautiful not to risk that such a wonderful love should come to an end. We spent our last evening together. He believed I should go with him. It was a delirious night of infinite voluptuousness and despair, for I knew I should never see him again. In the morning I gave my ticket to a traveller I did not know. He wanted to buy it but I answered: "No, you are rendering me such service in accepting it that I do not want the money." ' There was another story: 'One day I was in the Champs Elysées. M. de Bréauté, whom I had only seen once, looked at me so significantly that I stopped and asked him how he dared look at me like that. He

answered: "I'm looking at you because you've got an absurd hat on." It was
true. It was a little hat with pansies on it and the fashions of that period were
awful. But I was furious and I said to him: "I don't permit you to talk to me
like that." It began to rain and I said: "I might forgive you if you had a
carriage." "Oh, well, that's all right, I've got one and I'll accompany you
home." "No, I shall be glad to accept your carriage but not you." I got into
the carriage and he departed in the rain. But that evening he came to my
house. We had two years of wild love together. Come and have tea with
me,' she went on 'and I'll tell you how I made M. de Forcheville's
acquaintance. Really,' with a melancholy air, 'my life has been a cloistered
one, for I've only had great loves for men who were terribly jealous of me. I
don't speak of M. de Forcheville; he was quite indifferent and I only cared
for intelligent men, but, you see, M. Swann was as jealous as this poor Duc
for whose sake I sacrifice my life because he is unhappy at home. But it was
M. Swann I loved madly, and one can sacrifice dancing and society and
everything to please a man one loves or even to spare him anxiety. Poor
Charles, he was so intelligent, so seductive, exactly the kind of man I liked.'
Perhaps it was true. There was a time when Swann pleased her and it was
exactly when she was not 'his kind'. To tell the truth, she never had been 'his
kind', then or later. And yet he had loved her so long and so painfully. He
was surprised afterwards when he realised the contradiction of it. But there
would be none if we consider how great a proportion of suffering women
who aren't 'their kind' inflict on men. That is probably due to several causes;
first because they are not our kind, we let ourselves be loved without loving;
through that we adopt a habit we should not acquire with a woman who is
our kind. The latter, knowing she was desired, would resist and only accord
occasional meetings and thus would not gain such a foothold in our lives
that if, later on, we came to love her and then, owing to a quarrel or a
journey, we found ourselves alone and without news of her, she would
deprive us not of one bond but a thousand. Again this habit is sentimental
because there is no great physical desire at its base and if love is born, the
brain works better; romance takes the place of a physical urge. We do not
suspect women who are not our kind, we allow them to love us and if we
afterwards love them we love them a hundred times more than the others,
without getting from them the relief of satisfied desire. For these reasons
and many others, the fact that we experience our greatest sorrows with
women who are not our kind, is not only due to that derisive illusion which
permits the realisation of happiness only under the form that pleases us
least. A woman who is our kind is rarely dangerous, for she does not care
about us, satisfies us, soon abandons us and does not install herself in our

lives. What is dangerous and produces suffering in love is not the woman herself, it is her constant presence, the eagerness to know what she is doing every moment; it is not the woman, it is habit.

I was coward enough to say that what she told me about Swann was kind, not to say noble on her part, but I knew it was not true and that her frankness was mixed up with lies. I reflected with horror, as little by little she told me her adventures, on all that Swann had been ignorant of and of how much he would have suffered, for he had associated his sensibility with that creature and had guessed to the point of certainty, from nothing but her glance at an unknown man or woman, that they attracted her. Actually she told me all this only to supply what she believed was a subject for novels. She was wrong, not because she could not at any time have furnished my imagination with abundant material, but it would have had to be in less intentional fashion and by my agency disengaging, unknown to her, the laws that governed her life.

M. de Guermantes kept his thunders for the Duchesse to whose mixed gatherings Mme de Forcheville did not hesitate to draw the irritated attention of the Duc. Moreover, the Duchesse was very unhappy. It is true that M. de Charlus to whom I had once spoken about it, suggested that the first offence had not been on his brother's side, that the legend of the Duchesse's purity was in reality composed of an incalculable number of skilfully dissimulated adventures. I had never heard of them. To nearly everyone Mme de Guermantes was nothing of the sort and the belief that she had always been irreproachable was universal. I could not decide which of the two notions was true, for truth is nearly always unknown to three-quarters of the world. I recalled certain azure and fugitive glances of the Duchesse de Guermantes in the nave of the Combray church but, in truth, they refuted neither of these opinions, for each could give a different and equally acceptable meaning to them. In the madness of boyhood I had for a moment taken them as messages of love to myself. Later, I realised that they were but the benevolent glances which a suzeraine such as the one in the stained windows of the church bestowed on her vassals. Was I now to believe that my first idea was the right one, and that if the Duchesse never spoke to me of love, it was because she feared to compromise herself with a friend of her aunt and of her nephew rather than with an unknown boy she had met by chance in the church of St Hilaire de Combray?

The Duchesse might have been pleased for the moment that her past seemed more consistent for my having shared it, but she resumed her attitude of a society woman who despises society in replying to a question I asked her about the provincialism of M. de Bréauté, whom at the earlier period I had placed in the same category as M. de Sagan or M. de Guermantes. As she spoke, the Duchesse took me round the house. In the smaller rooms, the more intimate friends of the hosts were sitting apart to enjoy the music. In one of them, a little Empire salon where one or two frock-coated gentlemen sat upon a sofa listening, there was a couch curved like a cradle placed alongside the wall close to a Psyche leaning upon a Minerva, in the hollow of which a young woman lay extended. Her relaxed and languid attitude, which the entrance of the Duchesse in no way disturbed, contrasted with the brilliance of her Empire dress of a glittering silk beside which the most scarlet of fuchsias would have paled, encrusted with a pearl tissue in the folds of which the floral design appeared to be embedded. She slightly bent her beautiful brown head to salute the Duchesse. Although it was broad daylight, she had had the heavy curtains drawn to give herself up to the music, and the servants had lighted an urn on a tripod to prevent people stumbling. In answer to my question the Duchesse told me she was Mme de Sainte-Euverte and I wanted to know what relation she was of the Mme de Sainte-Euverte I had known. She was the wife of one of her great-nephews and Mme de Guermantes appeared to suggest that she was born a La Rochefoucauld but emphasised that she herself had never known the Sainte-Euvertes. I recalled to her mind the evening party, of which, it is true, I was only aware by hearsay, when, as Princesse des Laumes, she had renewed her acquaintance with Swann. Mme de Guermantes affirmed she had never been to that party but she had always been rather a liar and had become more so. Madame de Sainte-Euverte's salon – somewhat faded with time – was one she preferred ignoring and I did not insist. 'No,' she said, 'the person you may have met at my house because he was amusing, was the husband of the woman you refer to. I never had any social relations with her.' 'But she was a widow?' 'You thought so because they were separated; he was much nicer than she.' At last I realised that a huge, extremely tall and strong man with snow-white hair, whom I met everywhere but whose name I never knew, was the husband of Mme de Sainte-Euverte and had died the year before. As to the niece, I never discovered whether she lay extended on the sofa listening to the music without moving for anyone because of some stomach trouble or because of her nerves or phlebitis or a coming accouchement or a recent one which had gone wrong. The likely explanation was that she thought she might as well play the part of a Récamier figure on her couch in that shimmering red dress. She little knew that she had given birth to a new development of that name of Sainte-Euverte which, at so many intervals, marked the distance and continuity of Time. It was Time she was rocking in that cradle where the name of Sainte-Euverte flowered in a fuchsia-red silk in the Empire style. Mme de Guermantes declared that she had always detested Empire style; that meant, she detested it now, which was true, because she followed the fashions though not closely. Without complicating the matter by alluding to David of whose work she knew something, when she was a girl she considered Ingres the most boring of draughtsmen, then suddenly the most beguiling of new masters, so much so that she detested Delacroix. By what process she had returned to this creed of reprobation matters little, since such shades of taste are reflected by art-critics ten years before these superior women talk about them. After criticising the Empire style, she excused herself for talking about such insignificant people as the Sainte-Euvertes and of rubbish like Bréauté's provincialism, for she was as far from realising the interest they had for me as Mme de Sainte-Euverte de la Rochefoucauld looking after her stomach or her Ingres pose, was from suspecting that her name was my joy, her husband's name, not the far more famous one of her family, and that to me it represented the function of cradling time in that room full of temporal associations.

'How can all this nonsense interest you?' the Duchesse remarked. She uttered these words under her breath and nobody could have caught what she said. But a young man (who was to be of interest to me later because of a name much more familiar to me formerly than Sainte-Euverte) rose with an exaggerated air of being disturbed and went further away to listen in greater seclusion. They were playing the Kreutzer Sonata but he, having read the programme wrong, believed it was a piece by Ravel which he had been told was as beautiful as Palestrina but difficult to understand. In his abrupt change of place, he knocked, owing to the half darkness, against a tea-table which made a number of people turn their heads and thus afforded them an agreeable diversion from the suffering they were undergoing in listening religiously to the Kreutzer Sonata. And Mme de Guermantes and I who were the cause of this little scene, hastened into another room. 'Yes,' she continued, 'how can such nonsense interest a man with your talent? Like just now when I saw you talking to Gilberte de Saint-Loup, it isn't worthy of you. For me that woman is just nothing, she isn't even a woman; she's unimaginably pretentious and bourgeoise', for the Duchesse mixed up her aristocratic prejudices with her championship of truth. 'Indeed, ought you to come to places like this? Today, after all, it may be worth while because of Rachel's recitation. But, well as she did it, she doesn't extend herself before such an audience. You must come and lunch alone with her and then you'll see what a wonderful creature she is. She's a hundred times superior to everyone here. And after luncheon she shall recite Verlaine to you and you'll tell me what you think of it.'

She boasted to me specially about these luncheon parties to which X and Y always came. For she had acquired the characteristic that distinguishes the type of woman who has a 'Salon' whom she formerly despised (though she denied it today), the chief sign of whose superior eclecticism is to have 'all the men' at their houses. If I told her that a certain great lady who went in for a 'Salon' spoke ill of Mme Rowland, the Duchesse burst out laughing at my simplicity and said: 'Of course, she had "all the men" at her house and the other tried to take them away from her.' Mme de Guermantes continued: 'It passes my comprehension that you can come to this sort of thing – unless it's for studying character'; she added the last words doubtfully and suspiciously, afraid to go too far because she was not sure what that strange operation consisted of.

'Don't you think,' I asked her, 'it's painful for Mme de Saint-Loup to have to listen, as she did just now, to her husband's former mistress?' I observed that oblique expression coming over Mme de Guermantes' face which connects what someone has said with unpleasant factors. These may remain unspoken, but words with serious implications do not always receive verbal or written answers. Only fools solicit twice an answer to a foolish letter which was a *gaffe*; for such letters are only answered by acts and the correspondent whom the fool thinks careless, will call him Monsieur the next time he meets him instead of by his first name. My allusion to Saint-Loup's liaison with Rachel was not so serious and could not have displeased Mme de Guermantes more than a second by reminding her that I had been Robert's friend, perhaps his confidant about the mortification he had been caused when he obtained the Duchesse's permission to let Rachel appear at her evening party. Mme de Guermantes' face did not remain clouded and she answered my question about Mme Saint-Loup: 'I may tell you that I believe it to be a matter of indifference to her, for Gilberte never loved her husband. She is a horrible little creature. All she wanted was the position, the name, to be my niece, to get out of the slime to which her one idea now is to return. I can assure you all that pained me deeply for poor Robert's sake because though he may not have been an eagle, he saw it all and a good many things besides. Perhaps I ought not to say so because, after all, she's my niece and I've no proof that she was unfaithful to him, but there were all sorts of stories about her. But supposing I tell you that I know Robert wanted to fight a duel with an officer of Méséglise. And it was on account of all that that Robert joined up. The war was a deliverance from his family troubles and if you care for my opinion, he was not killed, he took care to get himself killed. She feels no sort of sorrow, she even astonishes me by the cynicism with which she displays her indifference, and that greatly pains me because I was very fond of Robert. It may perhaps surprise you because people don't know me, but I still think of him. I forget no one. He told me nothing but he knew I guessed it all. But, dear me, if she loved her husband ever so little, could she bear with such complete indifference being in the same drawing-room with a woman whose passionate lover he was for years, indeed one might say always, for I know for certain it went on even during the war. Why, she would spring at her throat,' the Duchesse cried, quite forgetting that she herself had acted cruelly by inviting Rachel and staging the scene she regarded as inevitable if Gilberte loved Robert. 'No!' she concluded, 'that woman is a pig.' Such an expression was possible in the mouth of Mme de Guermantes owing to her easy and gradual descent from the Guermantes environment to the society of actresses, and with this she affected an eighteenth century manner she considered refreshing on the part of one who could afford herself any liberty she chose. But the expression was also inspired by her hatred of Gilberte, by the need of striking her in effigy in default of physically. And she thought she was thereby equally justifying her action towards Gilberte or rather against her, in society, in the family, even in connection with her interest in Robert's inheritance.

But sometimes facts of which we are ignorant and which we could not imagine supply an apparent justification of our judgments. Gilberte, who doubtless inherited some of her mother's traits (and I dare say I had unconsciously surmised this when I asked her to introduce me to girls) after reflecting on my request and so that any profits that might accrue should not go out of the family, a conclusion the effrontery of which was greater than I could have imagined, came up to me presently and said: 'If you'll allow me, I'll fetch my young daughter, she's over there with young Mortemart and other youngsters of no importance. I'm sure she'll be a charming little friend for you.' I asked her if Robert had been pleased to have a daughter. 'Oh, he was very proud of her but, of course, it's my belief, seeing what his tastes were,' Gilberte naively added, 'he would have preferred a boy.' This girl, whose name and fortune doubtless led her mother to hope she would marry a prince of the blood and thus crown the whole edifice of Swann and of his wife, later on married an obscure man of letters, for she was quite unsnobbish, and caused the family to fall lower in the social scale than the level from which she originated. It was afterwards very difficult to convince the younger generation that the parents of this obscure household had occupied a great social position.

The surprise and pleasure caused me by Gilberte's words were quickly replaced while Mme de Saint-Loup disappeared into another room, by the idea of past Time which Mlle de Saint-Loup had brought back to me in her particular way without my even having seen her. In common with most human beings, was she not like the centre of crossroads in a forest, the point where roads converge from many directions? Those which ended in Mlle de Saint-Loup were many and branched out from every side of her. First of all, the two great sides where I had walked so often and dreamt so many dreams, came to an end in her – through her father, Robert de Saint-Loup, the Guermantes side and through Gilberte, her mother, the side of Méséglise which was Swann's side. One, through the mother of the young girl and the Champs Elysées, led me to Swann, to my evenings at Combray, to the side of Méséglise, the other, through her father, to my afternoons at Balbec where I saw him again near the glistening sea. Transversal roads already linked those two main roads together. For through the real Balbec where I had known Saint-Loup and wanted to go, chiefly because of what Swann had told me about its churches, especially about the Persian church and again through Robert de Saint-Loup, nephew of the Duchesse de Guermantes, I reunited Combray to the Guermantes' side. But Mlle de Saint-Loup led back to many other points of my life, to the lady in pink who was her grandmother and whom I had seen at my great-uncle's house. Here there was a new cross-road, for my great-uncle's footman who had announced me that day and who, by the gift of a photograph, had enabled me to identify the lady in pink, was the uncle of the young man whom not only M. de Charlus but also Mlle de Saint-Loup's father had loved and on whose account her mother had been made unhappy. And was it not the grandfather of Mlle de Saint-Loup, Swann, who first told me about Vinteuil's music as Gilberte had first told me about Albertine? And it was through speaking to Albertine about Vinteuil's music that I had discovered who her intimate girlfriend was and had started that life with her which had led to her death and to my bitter sorrows. And it was again Mlle de Saint-Loup's father who had tried to bring back Albertine to me. And I saw again all my life in society, whether at Paris in the drawing-rooms of the Swanns and the Guermantes', or in contrast, at the Verdurins' at Balbec, uniting the two Combray sides with the Champs Elysées and the beautiful terraces of La Raspelière. Moreover, whom of those we have known are we not compelled inevitably to associate with various parts of our lives if we relate our acquaintance with them? The life of Saint-Loup described by myself would be unfolded in every kind of scene and would affect the whole of mine, even those parts of it to which he was a stranger, such as my grandmother or Albertine. Moreover, contrast them as one might, the Verdurins were linked to Odette through her past, with Robert de Saint-Loup through Charlie; and how great a part had Vinteuil's music played in their home! Finally, Swann had loved the sister of Legrandin and the latter had known M. de Charlus whose ward young Cambremer had married. Certainly, if only our hearts were in question, the poet was right when he spoke of the mysterious threads which life breaks. But it is still truer that life is ceaselessly weaving them between beings, between events, that it crosses those threads, that it doubles them to thicken the woof with such industry that between the smallest point in our past and all the rest, the store of memories is so rich that only the choice of communications remains.

It is possible to say, if I tried to make conscious use of it and to recall it as it was, that there was not a single thing that served me now which had not been a living thing, living its own personal life in my service though transformed by that use into ordinary industrial matter. And my introduction to Mlle de Saint-Loup was going to take place at Mme Verdurin's who had become Princesse de Guermantes! How I thought back on the charm of those journeys with Albertine, whose successor I was going to ask Mlle de Saint-Loup to be – in the little tram going towards Doville to call on Mme Verdurin, that same Mme Verdurin who had cemented and broken the love of Mlle de Saint-Loup's grandfather and grandmother before I loved Albertine. And all round us were the pictures of Elstir who introduced me to Albertine and as though to melt all my pasts into one, Mme Verdurin, like Gilberte, had married a Guermantes.

We should not be able to tell the story of our relations with another, however little we knew him, without registering successive movements in our own life. Thus every individual – and I myself am one of those individuals – measured duration by the revolution he had accomplished not only round himself but round others and notably by the positions he had successively occupied with relation to myself. And, without question, all those different planes, upon which Time, since I had regained it at this reception, had exhibited my life, by reminding me that in a book which gave the history of one, it would be necessary to make use of a sort of spatial psychology as opposed to the usual flat psychology, added a new beauty to the resurrections my memory was operating during my solitary reflections in the library, since memory, by introducing the past into the present without modification, as though it were the present, eliminates precisely that great Time-dimension in accordance with which life is realised.

I saw Gilberte coming towards me. I, to whom Saint-Loup's marriage and all the concern it then gave me (as it still did) were of yesterday, was astonished to see beside her a young girl whose tall, slight figure marked the lapse of time to which I had, until now, been blind. Colourless, incomprehensible time materialised itself in her, as it were, so that I could see and touch it, had moulded her into a graven masterpiece while upon me alas, it had but been doing its work. However, Mlle de Saint-Loup stood before me. She had deep cleanly-shaped, prominent and penetrating eyes. I noticed that the line of her nose was on the same pattern as her mother's and grandmother's, the base being perfectly straight, and though adorable, was a trifle too long. That peculiar feature would have enabled one to recognise it amongst thousands and I admired Nature for having, like a powerful and original sculptor, effected that decisive stroke of the chisel at exactly the right point as it had in the mother and grandmother. That charming nose, protruding rather like a beak, had the Saint-Loup not the Swann curve. The soul of the Guermantes' had vanished but the charming head with the piercing eyes of a bird on the wing was poised upon her shoulders and threw me, who had known her father, into a dream. She was so beautiful, so promising. Gaily smiling, she was made out of all the years I had lost; she symbolised my youth.

Finally, this idea of Time had the ultimate value of the hand of a clock. It told me it was time to begin if I meant to attain that which I had felt in brief flashes on the Guermantes' side and during my drives with Mme de Villeparisis, that indefinable something which had made me think life worth living. How much more so now that it seemed possible to illuminate that life lived in darkness, at last to make manifest in a book the truth one ceaselessly falsifies. Happy the man who could write such a book. What labour awaited him. To convey its scope would necessitate comparison with the noblest and most various arts. For the writer, in creating each character, would have to present it from conflicting standpoints so that his book should have solidity, he would have to prepare it with meticulous care, perpetually regrouping his forces as for an offensive, to bear it as a load, to accept it as the object of his life, to build it like a church, to follow it like a régime, to overcome it like an obstacle, to win it like a friendship, to nourish it like a child, to create it like a world, mindful of those mysteries which probably only have their explanation in other worlds, the presentiment of which moves us most in life and in art. Parts of such great books can be no more than sketched, for time presses and perhaps they can never be finished because of the very magnitude of the architect's design. How many great cathedrals remain unfinished? Such a book takes long to germinate, its weaker parts must be strengthened, it has to be watched over, but afterwards it grows of itself, it designates our tomb, protects it from evil report and somewhat against oblivion. But to return to myself. I was thinking more modestly about my book and it would not even be true to say that I was thinking of those who would read it as my readers. For, as I have already shown, they would not be my readers, but the readers of themselves, my book being only a sort of magnifying-glass like those offered by the optician of Combray to a purchaser. So that I should ask neither their praise nor their blame but only that they should tell me if it was right or not, whether the words they were reading within themselves were those I wrote (possible divergencies in this respect might not always arise from my mistake but sometimes because the reader's eyes would not be those to whom my book was suitable). And, constantly changing as I expressed myself better and got on with the task I had undertaken, I thought of how I should devote myself to it at that plain white table, watched over by Françoise. As all those unpretentious creatures who live near us have a certain intuition of what we are trying to do and as I had so far forgotten Albertine that I forgave Françoise for her hostility to her, I should work near her and almost like her (at least as she used to formerly for now she was so old that she could hardly see), for it would be by pinning supplementary leaves here and there that I should build up my book, so to speak, like a dress rather than like a cathedral. When I could not find all the sheets I wanted, all my '*paperoles*' as Françoise called them, when just that one was missing that I needed, Françoise would understand my apprehension, for she always said she could not sew if she had not got the exact thread-number and sort of button she wanted and because, from living with me, she had acquired a sort of instinctive understanding of literary work, more right than that of many intelligent people and still more than that of stupid ones. Thus when I used to write my articles for the *Figaro*, while the old butler with that exaggerated compassion for the severity of toil which is unfamiliar, which cannot be observed, even for a habit he had not got himself like people who say to you, 'How it must tire you to yawn like that', honestly pitied writers and said: 'What a head-breaking business it must be', Françoise, to the contrary, divined my satisfaction and respected my work. Only she got angry when I told Bloch about my articles before they appeared, fearing he would forestall me and said: 'You aren't suspicious enough of all these people, they're copyists.' And Bloch, in fact, did offer a prospective alibi by remarking each time that I sketched something he liked: 'Fancy! that's curious, I've written something very much like that; I must read it to you.' (He could not then have read it to me because he was going to write it that evening.)

In consequence of sticking one sheet on another, what Françoise called my *paperoles* got torn here and there. In case of need she would be able to help me mend them in the same way as she patched worn parts of her dresses, or awaiting the glazier as I did the printer, when she stuck a bit of newspaper in a window instead of the glass pane. Holding up my copybooks devoured like worm-eaten wood, she said: 'It's all motheaten, look, what a pity, here's the bottom of a page which is nothing but a bit of lace,' and, examining it like a tailor: 'I don't think I can mend it, it's done for, what a shame; perhaps those were your most beautiful ideas. As they said at Combray, there are no furriers who know their job as well as moths, they always go for the best materials.'

Moreover, since individualities (human or otherwise) would in this book be constructed out of numerous impressions which, derived from many girls, many churches, many sonatas, would serve to make a single sonata, a single church and a single girl, should I not be making my book as Françoise made that *boeuf à la mode* so much savoured by M. de Norpois, of which the jelly was enriched by many additional carefully selected bits of meat? And at last I should achieve that for which I had so much longed and believed impossible during my walks on the Guermantes' side as I had believed it was impossible, when I came home, to go to bed without embracing my mother, or later, that Albertine loved women, an idea I finally accepted unconsciously, for our greatest fears like our greatest hopes are not beyond our capacity and it is possible to end by dominating the first and realising the second.

Yes, this newly-formed idea of Time warned me that the hour had come to set myself to work. It was high time. The anxiety which had taken possession of me when I entered the drawing-room and the made-up faces gave me the notion of lost time, was justified. Was there still time? The mind has landscapes at which it is only given us to gaze for a time. I had lived like a painter climbing a road which overlooks a lake hidden by a curtain of rocks and trees. Through a breach he perceives it, it lies before him, he seizes his brushes, but already darkness has come and he can paint no longer, night upon which day will never dawn again.

A condition of my work as I had conceived it just now in the library was that I must fathom to their depths impressions which had first to be recreated through memory. And my memory was impaired. Therefore as I had not yet begun, I had reason for apprehension, for even though I thought, in view of my age, that I had some years before me, my hour might strike at any moment. I had, in fact, to regard my body as the point of departure, which meant that I was constantly under the menace of a twofold danger, without and within. And even when I say this it is only for convenience of expression. For the internal danger as in that of cerebral haemorrhage is also external, being of the body. And the body is the great menace of the mind. We are less justified in saying that the thinking life of humanity is a miraculous perfectioning of animal and physical life than that it is an imperfection in the organisation of spiritual life as rudimentary as the communal existence of protozoa in colonies or the body of the whale etc., so imperfect, indeed, that the body imprisons the spirit in a fortress; soon the fortress is assailed at all points and in the end the spirit has to surrender.

But in order to satisfy myself by distinguishing the two sorts of danger which threatened my spirit and beginning by the external one, I remembered that it had often already happened in the course of my life, at moments of intellectual excitement when some circumstance had completely arrested my physical activity, for instance when I was leaving the restaurant of Rivebelle in a half-intoxicated condition in order to go to a neighbouring casino, that I felt the immediate object of my thought with extreme vividness and realised that it was a matter of chance not only that the object had not yet entered my mind but that its survival depended upon my physical existence. I cared little enough then. In my light-hearted gaiety I was neither prudent nor apprehensive. It mattered little to me that this happy thought flew away in a second and disappeared in the void. But now it was no longer so because the joy I experienced was not derived from a subjective nervous tension which isolates us from the past, but, on the contrary, from an extension of the consciousness in which the past, recreated and actualised, gave me, alas but for a moment, a sense of eternity. I wished that I could leave this behind me to enrich others with my treasure. My experience in the library which I wanted to preserve was that of pleasure but not an egoistical pleasure or at all events it was a form of egoism which is useful to others (for all the fruitful altruisms of Nature develop in an egoistical mode; human altruism which is not egoism, is sterile, it is that of a writer who interrupts his work to receive a friend who is unhappy, to accept some public function or to write propaganda articles).

I was no longer indifferent as when I returned from Rivebelle; I felt myself enlarged by this work I bore within me (like something precious and fragile, not belonging to me, which had been confided to my care and which I wanted to hand over intact to those for whom it was destined). And to think that when, presently, I returned home, an accident would suffice to destroy my body and that my lifeless mind would have for ever lost the ideas it now contained and anxiously preserved within its shaky frame before it had time to place them in safety within the covers of a book. Now, knowing myself the bearer of such a work, an accident which might cost my life was more to be dreaded, was indeed (by the measure in which this work seemed to me indispensable and permanent) absurd, when contrasted with my wish, with my vital urge, but not less probable on that account since accidents due to material causes can take place at the very moment when an opposing will, which they unknowingly annihilate, renders them monstrous, like the ordinary accident of knocking over a water-jug placed too near the edge of a table and thus disturbing a sleeping friend one acutely desires not to waken.

I knew very well that my brain was a rich mineral basin where there was an enormous and most varied area of precious deposits. But should I have the time to exploit them? I was the only person capable of doing so, for two reasons. With my death not only would the one miner capable of extracting the minerals disappear, but with him, the mineral itself. And the mere collision of my automobile with another on my way home would suffice to obliterate my body and my spirit would have to abandon my new ideas for ever. And by a strange coincidence, that reasoned fear of danger was born at the very moment when the idea of death had become indifferent to me. The fear of no longer existing had formerly horrified me at each new love I experienced – for Gilberte, for Albertine – because I could not bear the thought that one day the being who loved them might not be there; it was a sort of death. But the very recurrence of this fear led to its changing into calm confidence.

If the idea of death had cast a shadow over love, the memory of love had for long helped me not to fear death. I realised that death is nothing new, ever since my childhood I had been dead numbers of times. To take a recent period, had I not cared more for Albertine than for my life? Could I then have conceived my existence without my love for her? And yet I no longer loved her, I was no longer the being who loved her but a different one who did not love her, and I had ceased to love her when I became that other being. And I did not suffer because I had become that other, because I no longer loved Albertine; and certainly it did not seem to me a sadder thing that one day I should have no body than it had formerly seemed not to love Albertine. And yet how indifferent it all was to me now. These successive deaths, so feared by the self they were to destroy, so indifferent, so sweet were they, once they were accomplished, when he who feared them was no longer there to feel them, had made me realise how foolish it would be to fear death. And now that it had been for a while indifferent to me I began fearing it anew, in another form, it is true, not for myself but for my book for the achievement of which that life, menaced by so many dangers, was, at least, for a period, indispensable. Victor Hugo says: 'The grass must grow and children die.' I say that the cruel law of art is that beings die and that we ourselves must die after we have exhausted suffering so that the grass, not of oblivion but of eternal life, should grow, fertilised by works upon which generations to come will gaily picnic without care of those who sleep beneath it.

I have spoken of external dangers but there were internal ones also. If I were preserved from an accident without, who knows whether I might not be prevented from profiting from my immunity by an accident within, by some internal disaster, some cerebral catastrophe, before the months necessary for me to write that book, had passed. A cerebral accident was not even necessary. I had already experienced certain symptoms, a curious emptiness in the head and a forgetfulness of things I only found by luck as one does on going through one's things and finding something one had not been looking for; I was a treasurer from whose broken coffer his riches were slipping away.

When presently I went back home by the Champs Elysées who could say that I should not be struck down by the same evil as my grandmother when one day she came for a walk with me which was to be her last, without her ever dreaming of such a thing, in that ignorance which is our lot when the hand of the clock reaches the moment when the spring is released that strikes the hour. Perhaps the fear of having already almost traversed the minute that precedes the first stroke of the hour, when it is already preparing to strike, perhaps the fear of that blow which was about to crash through my brain was like an obscure foreknowledge of what was coming to pass, a reflection in the consciousness of a precarious state of the brain whose arteries are about to give way, which is no less possible than the sudden acceptance of death by the wounded who, if their lucidity remains and both doctor and will to live deceive them, yet see what is coming and say: 'I am going to die, I am ready', and write their last farewells to their wife.

That obscure premonition of what had to be came to me in a singular form before I began my book. One evening I was at a party and people said I was looking better than ever and were astonished that I showed so little signs of age. But that evening I came near falling three times going downstairs. I had only gone out for a couple of hours but when I got home, my memory and power of thought had gone and I had neither strength nor life in me. If they had come to proclaim me King or arrest me, I should have allowed them to do what they liked with me without saying a word, without even opening my eyes, like those who at the extreme point of seasickness, crossing the Caspian Sea, would offer no resistance if they were going to be thrown into the sea. Properly speaking I was not ill but I was as incapable of taking care of myself as old people active the evening before, who have fractured their thigh and enter a phase of existence which is only a preliminary, be it short or long, to inevitable death. One of my selves – the one that recently went to one of those barbaric feasts which are called dinners in society attended by white cravated men and plumed, half-naked women whose values are so topsy-turvy that a person who does not go to a dinner to which he has accepted an invitation or only puts in an appearance at the roast commits in their eyes a greater crime than the most immoral acts as lightly discussed in the course of it as illness and death which provide the only excuse for not being there, as long as the hostess has been informed in time to notify the fourteenth guest that someone has died – that self had kept its scruples and lost its memory. On the other hand, the other self, the one who conceived this work, remembered I had received an invitation from Mme Molé and had heard that Mme Sazerat's son was dead. I had made up my mind to use an hour of respite after which I should not be able to utter a word or swallow a drop of milk, tongue-tied like my grandmother during her death agony, for the purpose of excusing myself to Mme Molé and expressing my condolences to Mme Sazerat. But shortly afterwards, I forgot I had to do it. Happy oblivion! For the memory of my work was on guard and was going to use that hour of survival to lay my first foundations. Unhappily, taking up a copybook, Mme Molé's invitation card slipped out of it. Instantly, the forgetful self which dominates the other in the case of all those scrupulous savages who dine out, put away the copybook and began writing to Mme Molé (who would doubtless have thought more of me had she known that I had put my reply to her invitation before my architectural work). Suddenly, as I was answering, I remembered that Mme Sazerat had lost her son, so I wrote her too and having thus sacrificed the real duty to the fictitious obligation of proving my politeness and reasonableness, I fell lifeless, closed my eyes and for a whole week was only able to vegetate. Yet, if all my useless duties to which I was prepared to sacrifice the real one, went out of my head in a few minutes, the thought of my edifice never left me for an instant. I did not know whether it would be a church where the faithful would gradually learn truth and discover the harmony of a great unified plan or whether it would remain, like a Druid monument on the heights of a desert island, unknown for ever. But I had made up my mind to consecrate to it the power that was ebbing away, reluctantly almost, as though to leave me time to elaborate the structure before the entrance to the tomb was sealed. I was soon able to show an outline of my project. No one understood it. Even those who sympathised with my perception of the truth I meant later to engrave upon my temple, congratulated me on having discovered it with a microscope when, to the contrary, I had used a telescope to perceive things which were indeed very small because they were far away but every one of them a world. Where I sought universal laws I was accused of burrowing into the 'infinitely insignificant'. Moreover, what was the use of it all, I had a good deal of facility when I was young and Bergotte had highly praised my schoolboy efforts. But instead of working I had spent my time in idleness and dissipation, in being laid up and taken care of and in obsessions and I was starting my work on the eve of death without even knowing my craft. I had no longer the strength to face either my human obligations or my intellectual ones, still less both. As to the first, forgetfulness of the letters I had to write somewhat simplified my task. Loss of memory helped to delete social obligations which were replaced by my work. But, at the end of a month, association of ideas suddenly brought back remorseful memories and I was overwhelmed by my feeling of impotence. I was surprised at my own indifference to criticisms of my work but from the time when my legs had given way when I went downstairs I had become indifferent to everything; I only longed for rest until the end came. It was not because I counted on posthumous fame that I was indifferent to the judgments of the eminent today. Those who pronounced upon my work after my death could think what they pleased of it. I was no more concerned about the one than the other. Actually, if I thought about my work and not about the letters which I ought to have answered, it had ceased to be because I considered the former so much more important as I did at the time when I was idle and afterwards when I tried to work, up to the day when I had had to hold on to the banisters of the staircase. The organisation of my memory, of my preoccupations, was linked to my work perhaps because, while the letters I received were forgotten an instant later, the idea of my work was continuously in my mind, in a state of perpetual becoming. But it too had become importunate. My work was like a son whose dying mother must still unceasingly labour in the intervals of inoculations and cuppings. She may love him still but she only realises it through the excess of her care of him. And my powers as a writer were no longer equal to the egoistical exactions of the work. Since the day on the staircase, nothing in the world, no happiness, whether it came from friendships, from the progress of my work or from hope of fame, reached me except as pale sunlight that had lost its power to warm me, to give me life or any desire whatever and yet was too brilliant in its paleness for my weary eyes which closed as I turned towards the wall. As much as I could tell from the movement of my lips, I might have had a very slight smile in the corner of my mouth when a lady wrote me: 'I was surprised not to get an answer to my letter.' Nevertheless, that reminded me and I answered it. I wanted to try, so as not to be thought ungrateful, to be as considerate to others as they to me. And I was crushed by imposing these superhuman fatigues on my dying body.

This idea of death installed itself in me definitively as love does. Not that I loved death, I hated it. But I dare say I had thought of it from time to time as one does of a woman one does not yet love and now the thought of it adhered to the deepest layer of my brain so thoroughly that I could not think of anything without its first traversing the death zone, and even if I thought of nothing and remained quite still, the idea of death kept me company as incessantly as the idea of myself. I do not think that the day when I became moribund, it was the accompanying factors such as the impossibility of going downstairs, of remembering a name, of getting up, which had by unconscious reasoning given me the idea that I was already all but dead, but rather that it had all come together, that the great mirror of the spirit reflected a new reality. And yet I did not see how I could pass straight from my present ills to death without some warning. But then I thought of others and how people die every day without it seeming strange to us that there should be no hiatus between their illness and their death. I thought even that it was only because I saw them from the inside (far more than through deceitful hope) that certain ailments did not seem to me necessarily fatal, taken one at a time, although I thought I was going to die, just like those who, certain that their time has come, are nevertheless easily persuaded that their not being able to pronounce certain words has nothing to do with apoplexy or heart failure but is due to the tongue being tired, to a nerve condition akin to stammering, owing to the exhaustion consequent on indigestion.

In my case it was not the farewell of a dying man to his wife that I had to write, it was something longer and addressed to more than one person. Long to write! At best I might attempt to sleep during the daytime. If I worked it would only be at night but it would need many nights perhaps a hundred, perhaps a thousand. And I should be harassed by the anxiety of not knowing whether the Master of my destiny, less indulgent than the Sultan Sheriar, would, some morning when I stopped work, grant a reprieve until the next evening. Not that I had the ambition to reproduce in any fashion the *Thousand and One Nights*, any more than the *Mémoires* of Saint-Simon, they too written by night, nor any of the books I had so much loved and which, superstitiously attached to them in my childish simplicity as I was to my later loves, I could not, without horror, imagine different from what they were. As Elstir said of Chardin, one can only recreate what one loves by repudiating it. Doubtless my books, like my fleshly being, would, some day, die. But one must resign oneself to death. One accepts the thought that one will die in ten years and one's books in a hundred. Eternal duration is no more promised to works than to men.

It might perhaps be a book as long as the *Thousand and One Nights*, but very different. It is true that when one loves a work one would like to do something like it, but one must sacrifice one's temporal love and not think of one's taste but of a truth which does not ask what our preferences are and forbids us to think of them. And it is only by obeying truth that one may someday encounter what one has abandoned and having forgotten the *Arabian Nights* or the *Mémoires* of Saint-Simon have written their counterpart in another period. But had I still time? Was it not too late?

In any case, if I had still the strength to accomplish my work, the circumstances, which had today in the course of the Princesse de Guermantes' reception simultaneously given me the idea of it and the fear of not being able to carry it out, would specifically indicate its form of which I had a presentiment formerly in Combray church during a period which had so much influence upon me, a form which, normally, is invisible, the form of Time. I should endeavour to render that Time-dimension by transcribing life in a way very different from that conveyed by our lying senses. Certainly, our senses lead us into other errors, many episodes in this narrative had proved to me that they falsify the real aspect of life. But I might, if it were needful, to secure the more accurate interpretation I proposed, be able to leave the locality of sounds unchanged, to refrain from detaching them from the source the intelligence assigns to them, although making the rain patter in one's room or fall in torrents into the cup from which we are drinking is, in itself, no more disconcerting than when as they often have, artists paint a sail or a peak near to or far away from us, according as the laws of perspective, variation in colour and ocular illusion make them appear, while our reason tells us that these objects are situated at enormous distances from us.

I might, although the error would be more serious, continue the fashion of putting features into the face of a passing woman, when instead of nose and cheeks and chin there was nothing there but an empty space in which our desire was reflected. And, a far more important matter, if I had not the leisure to prepare the hundred masks suitable to a single face, were it only as the eyes see it and in the sense in which they read its features, according as those eyes hope or fear or, on the other hand, as love and habit which conceal changes of age for many years, see them, indeed, even if I did not undertake, in spite of my liaison with Albertine proving that without it everything is fictitious and false, to represent people not from outside but from within ourselves where their smallest acts may entail fatal consequences, and to vary the moral atmosphere according to the different impressions on our sensibility or according to our serene sureness that an object is insignificant whereas the mere shadow of danger multiplies its size in a moment, if I could not introduce these changes and many others (the need for which, if one means to portray the truth, has constantly been shown in the course of this narrative) into the transcription of a universe which had to be completely redesigned, at all events I should not fail to depict therein man, as having the extension, not of his body but of his years, as being forced to the cumulatively heavy task which finally crushes him, of dragging them with him wherever he goes.

Moreover, everybody feels that we are occupying an unceasingly increasing place in Time, and this universality could only rejoice me since it is the truth, a truth suspected by each one of us, which it was my business to try to elucidate. Not only does everyone feel that we occupy a place in Time but the most simple person measures that place approximately as he might measure the place we occupy in space. Doubtless we often make mistakes in this measurement, but that one should believe it possible to do it proves that one conceives of age as something measurable.

And often I asked myself not only whether there was still time but whether I was in a condition to accomplish my work. Illness which had rendered me a service by making me die to the world ('for if the grain does not die when it is sown, it remains barren, but if it dies it will bear much fruit') was now perhaps going to save me from idleness as idleness had preserved me from facility. Illness had undermined my strength and, as I had long noticed, had sapped the power of my memory when I ceased to love Albertine. And was not the recreation of the memory of impressions it was afterwards necessary to fathom, to illuminate, to transform into intellectual equivalents, one of the conditions, almost the essential condition, of a work of art such as I had conceived just now in the library? Ah, if I only still had the powers that were intact on the evening I had evoked when I happened to notice François le Champi. My grandmother's lingering death and the decline of my will and of my health dated from that evening of my mother's abdication. It was all settled at the moment when, unable to await the morning to press my lips upon my mother's face, I had taken my resolution, I had jumped out of bed and had stood in my nightshirt by the window through which the moonlight shone, until I heard M. Swann go away. My parents had accompanied him, I had heard the door open, the sound of bell and closing door.

At that very moment, in the Prince de Guermantes' mansion, I heard the sound of my parents' footsteps and the metallic, shrill, fresh echo of the little bell which announced M. Swann's departure and the coming of my mother up the stairs; I heard it now, its very self, though its peal rang out in the far distant past. Then thinking of all the events which intervened between the instant when I had heard it and the Guermantes' reception I was terrified to think that it was indeed that bell which rang within me still, without my being able to abate its shrill sound, since, no longer remembering how the clanging used to stop, in order to learn, I had to listen to it and I was compelled to close my ears to the conversations of the masks around me. To get to hear it close I had again to plunge into myself. So that ringing must always be there and with it, between it and the present, all that indefinable past unrolled itself which I did not know I had within me. When it rang I already existed and since, in order that I should hear it still, there could be no discontinuity, I could have had no instant of repose or of non-existence, of non-thinking, of non-consciousness, since that former instant clung to me, for I could recover it, return to it, merely by plunging more deeply into myself. It was that notion of the embodiment of Time, the inseparableness from us of the past that I now had the intention of bringing strongly into relief in my work. And it is because they thus contain the past that human bodies can so much hurt those who love them, because they contain so many memories, so many joys and desires effaced within them but so cruel for him who contemplates and prolongs in the order of time the beloved body of which he is jealous, jealous to the point of wishing its destruction. For after death Time leaves the body and memories – indifferent and pale – are obliterated in her who exists no longer and soon will be in him they still torture, memories which perish with the desire of the living body.

I had a feeling of intense fatigue when I realised that all this span of time had not only been lived, thought, secreted by me uninterruptedly, that it was my life, that it was myself, but more still because I had at every moment to keep it attached to myself, that it bore me up, that I was poised on its dizzy summit, that I could not move without taking it with me. The day on which I heard the distant, faraway sound of the bell in the Combray garden was a landmark in that enormous dimension which I did not know I possessed. I was giddy at seeing so many years below and in me as though I were leagues high.

I now understood why the Duc de Guermantes, whom I admired when he was seated because he had aged so little although he had so many more years under him than I, had tottered when he got up and wanted to stand erect – like those old Archbishops surrounded by acolytes, whose only solid part is their metal cross – and had moved, trembling like a leaf on the hardly approachable summit of his eighty-three years, as though men were perched upon living stilts which keep on growing, reaching the height of church-towers, until walking becomes difficult and dangerous and, at last, they fall. I was terrified that my own were already so high beneath me and I did not think I was strong enough to retain for long a past that went back so far and that I bore within me so painfully. If, at least, time enough were allotted to me to accomplish my work, I would not fail to mark it with the seal of Time, the idea of which imposed itself upon me with so much force today, and I would therein describe men, if need be, as monsters occupying a place in Time infinitely more important than the restricted one reserved for them in space, a place, on the contrary, prolonged immeasurably since, simultaneously touching widely separated years and the distant periods they have lived through – between which so many days have ranged themselves – they stand like giants immersed in Time.

Synopsis to Volume Two

CITIES OF THE PLAIN

Part I

The narrator watches for the Duc and Duchesse de Guermantes, wanting to ask them if his invitation to the Princesse is genuine; the flower and the bee; an encounter between M. de Charlus and Jupien reveals M. de Charlus's true sexuality; the narrator spies on them; his reflections on inverts, and their classification; the narrator fails to observe the fertilisation of the flower by the bee.

Part II

Chapter One

An evening at the Princesse de Guermantes: arrival; fear of not having been invited; the kindness of the Princesse; the Duc de Châtellerault; the narrator looking for an introduction to the Prince; M. de Charlus and the Duc de Sidonia; Professor E. M. de Vaugobert, and Mme de Vaugobert; Mme de Souvré; Mme d'Arpajon; still no introduction to the Prince; M. de Charlus refuses, finally M. de Bréauté performs the introduction.

The Prince and the Duc compared; the Prince and Swann; the fountain; arrival of the Duc and Duchesse; they laugh at the narrator's anxieties about his invitation; M. de Vaugobert and M. de Charlus; Mme d'Amoncourt.

The salons of the Duchesse, the Princesse and Mme de Saint-Euverte; Swann and the Prince de Guermantes; M. de Guermantes and Swann's Dreyfusism; Mme de Guermantes refuses to meet Mme Swann and Gilberte; likewise to attend Mme de Saint-Euverte's garden-party; Mme de Surgis, the Duc's new mistress, and M. de Charlus's interest in her good-looking sons.

Arrival of Saint-Loup; his blindness to his uncle's sexuality; his change of mind about Dreyfus; M. de Charlus's rudeness to Mme de Saint-Euverte; Swann reports his earlier conversation with the Prince de Guermantes; the Prince's belief in Dreyfus's innocence; Mme de Surgis's social position.

The narrator declines a supper invitation because he is meeting Albertine later, and returns home with the Duc and Duchesse; waiting for Albertine; Françoise's dislike of Albertine; Albertine's telephone call; the narrator forces her to visit him; his 'need' for her; her visit; the Duc de Guermantes converted to Dreyfusism; Odette's salon, based on anti-Dreyfusism.

Second visit to Balbec: the manager of the hotel; the narrator's memories of his grandmother, and his remorse over the photograph taken there by Saint-Loup; his lack of enthusiasm for Albertine; his reflections on his own unhappiness; his renewed desire to see Albertine.

Chapter Two

Further reflections on the narrator's unhappiness; he wants to see Albertine; he doesn't want to see her; he sends for her; his suspicions of Albertine and other girls.

The young and the old Mme de Cambremer; their disagreements over the arts; Poussin and Chopin; more attempts to manipulate Albertine's emotions; Albertine's generous response; then more jealousy, and more suspicions – Bloch's sister and her friend; invitation to the Verdurins' at La Raspelière; visit to Saint-Loup at Doncières; the narrator objects to Albertine's behaviour towards Saint-Loup.

M. de Charlus meets Morel for the first time; an evening at the Verdurins'; the 'little train' and its occupants; the Princesse Sherbatoff; arrival of Morel and M. de Charlus; the narrator agrees to say nothing about Morel's lowly origins; Morel's subsequent rudeness to him.

Arrival of the Cambremers: Mme de Cambremer's observations on many subjects, interspersed with Brichot's lectures on etymology; the Verdurin's ignorance of protocol, and M. de Charlus's insolent response; the Verdurins' cruelty to Brichot; first hostilities between M. de Charlus and Mme Verdurin; departure; the train home.

Chapter Three

Reflections on sleep, memory and awaking; M. de Charlus dines at the Grand Hotel with a footman; Aimé surprised to learn the Baron's identity; touring by car wth Albertine; another visit to the Verdurins; comparison between the motor car and the railway; M. de Charlus and Morel, and Morel's plans to seduce a young girl; Morel's ingratitude to M. De Charlus.

The narrator's continuing jealousy over Albertine; he resolves to leave her – until his mother advises him to do so; daily anxiety over how Albertine is spending her time; trips in the car end when the chauffeur leaves Balbec; the narrator sees an aeroplane for the first time.

M. de Charlus and the Verdurins; more evenings at La Raspelière; Morel persuades the Verdurins to replace their coachman with the chauffeur; M. de Charlus now becomes, for a short time, a member of the 'little clan'; his mistaken belief that his sexuality is a secret; Mme Verdurin's comments on M. de Charlus; his unawareness what the Verdurins really think of him; M. de Charlus on Albertine's clothes; M. de Charlus tries to persuade Morel to change his name; he invents a duel so that Morel will persuade him to give it up.

The train's stopping-places on the way to La Raspelière; the brothel at Maineville; Morel's assignation with the Prince de Guermantes; attempt of M. de Charlus and Jupien to disrupt it; Morel's flight from the brothel; the narrator and the Comte de Crécy; M. de Chevregny.

Mme Verdurin's grievances against the Cambremers, who have invited M. de Charlus and Morel to dinner; Morel's rudeness to the Cambremers.

The train journey again: the narrator's social success and pretensions make him once more want to break with Albertine; he still does not trust Albertine alone with Saint-Loup, and in consequence he offends Bloch by refusing to meet Bloch's father; he finds the place-names along the railway line have lost their magic.

Chapter Four

The narrator is still planning to break with Albertine, when she reveals her friendship with Mlle Vinteuil and her friend; the narrator panics; he must, immediately and at all costs, stop Albertine being with Mlle Vinteuil's friend; by various lies and stratagems he persuades her to come to Paris with him.

THE CAPTIVE

Chapter One: Life with Albertine

Waking to street noises; a letter from Mamma, who does not approve of the plan to marry Albertine; the narrator does not love Albertine, but this does not stop him feeling jealous on her account.

Visits to Mme de Guermantes; he consults her on dresses for Albertine; M. de Charlus and Morel visit Jupien; Jupien's niece; M. de Charlus's plans to help Morel and Jupien's niece.

The narrator persuades himself that he does love Albertine; she is careful to avoid doing things which will make him jealous; the narrator less attracted now to Andrée, but still he tries to question her about Albertine's behaviour; memories of the 'free spirit', the Albertine of Balbec; Albertine's kisses remind him of his mother's.

A new day: more reflections on jealousy; Albertine plans to visit the Verdurins; the narrator asks Andrée to stop her going; when he announces he will accompany her, Albertine decides to go shopping instead; a visit to an aerodrome; he recommends the Trocadéro for Albertine the next day; he is now treating Albertine as his parents used to treat him.

A spring morning in winter: Albertine *will* go to the Trocadéro; the girl from the dairy; the narrator reads in the *Figaro* that Mlle Léa will be appearing at the Trocadéro, so now he must make Albertine leave the Trocadéro; he sends Françoise with a message, and Albertine agrees to leave; the narrator plays the piano.

From the window he sees Morel picking a quarrel with Jupien's niece; Albertine returns; they go by car to the Bois; the narrator's regret for all the girls he sees who are now inaccessible to him; yet another plan to break with Albertine.

News of Bergotte's death prompts thoughts about doctors, art, the artist's possible immortality, and Albertine's untruthfulness; Albertine's skill in lying.

Chapter Two: the Verdurins quarrel with M. de Charlus
The narrator goes out in the evening – to the Verdurins', Albertine stays at home; (yet another) decision to break with Albertine; the narrator meets Brichot, who reminisces about Mme Verdurin's old salon; they meet M. de Charlus; the Baron's moral decline and his now overt homosexuality.

M. de Charlus the organiser of this evening at the Verdurins'; he has chosen the guests and decided the details of Morel's performance; Mme Verdurin's anger because her suggestions are ignored; she is snubbed by the Baron and his guests.

Morel plays a new piece by Vinteuil; thoughts on music and joy, art and perversion; it was Mlle Vinteuil's friend who transcribed Vinteuil's music after his death.

M. Verdurin's cruelty to Saniette; the guests leave, thanking the Baron but not thanking Mme Verdurin; her fury, and decision to make trouble between M. de Charlus and Morel; she gets Brichot to distract the Baron while she and M. de Verdurin talk to Morel; Brichot, the Baron and the narrator have a long discussion which finally comes round to the topic of homosexuality; meanwhile the narrator forms a new plan – he will *pretend* to break with Albertine.

When M. de Charlus returns to the drawing room, Morel cuts him and will have nothing to do with him; M. de Charlus is escorted away by the Queen of Naples; he falls ill; some reflections on the occasional kindness or good nature of the Verdurins.

The narrator returns home; Albertine's anger when she discovers he has been to the Verdurins'; revelation that she once went away for three weeks with Mlle Léa; the narrator pretends to want a separation; he asks Albertine never to see him again, but is appalled when she says she will go to her aunt in Touraine.

Chapter Three: Flight of Albertine
A letter from the narrator's mother, who is concerned about his intentions towards Albertine; the hostility of Françoise (and no doubt the Verdurins) to Albertine; more reflections on art lead to the conclusion that art is irrelevant to life, and that his interest in Albertine is the result of his obsession with her past life.

He finds out why Albertine so easily agreed to come to Paris with him; he knows she will leave him, but wants it to be at a time of his choosing; further recriminations as he cross-examines her again about past events; she refuses to kiss him good-night.

In the morning he thinks Albertine may have left; finding her still there, he takes her to Versailles; she then wants to go to the Verdurins, but he takes her home instead; he awakes the following day wanting to go to Venice without her, and is then told by Françoise that she has left.

THE SWEET CHEAT GONE

Chapter One: Grief and oblivion
The narrator tries to come to terms with Albertine's departure; he can do so only by telling himself she will return immediately; Albertine's farewell letter; he tries to console himself with a little girl he finds in the street. Saint-Loup agrees to help him, and leaves for Touraine; his surprise when he sees a photograph of Albertine.

Encounter with the police and the parents of the little girl; Françoise tells him the police are watching the house. Saint-Loup's first telegram – Albertine and her aunt are away; the narrator convinces himself (again) of his need for Albertine; Saint-Loup's second telegram – his mission not successful; a telegram from Albertine saying she would have come back if he had written to ask her to do so; this persuades him she *will* come back, so he writes to her praising her wisdom in leaving.

Newspaper announcement of a performance by Berma prompts reflections on *Phèdre*; Françoise finds two rings left by Albertine; the narrator tells Albertine he is thinking of marrying Andrée; Saint-Loup returns; the narrator's suspicions of Saint-Loup; the narrator imagines that Albertine's death will put an end to his suffering; he sends her a telegram.

A telegram from Mme Bontemps informs him that Albertine is dead; it is followed by two letters from Albertine written before she died – one approving the marriage with Andrée, the other asking to return.

He abandons his plans to visit Venice; he fears his future recollections of Albertine, prompted by varying climates and surroundings – and not of one Albertine, but of a whole host of Albertines; he sends Aimé to Balbec to try and find evidence of her misbehaviour there.

His memories finally prompt him to notice Albertine's intelligence and sweet nature; he feels guilty, he says, and claims to have known a happiness Swann never knew; Albertine compared with Gilberte.

Continuing obsession with Albertine's Lesbian experiences; a letter from Aimé gives details of her behaviour at the public baths in Balbec; the narrator wants Albertine to know that he knows about the baths; as his jealousy, his affection for Albertine and his pain increase, he decides to send Aimé to Touraine to do some more spying.

Aimé's letter from Châtellerault – the laundress has shown him what she used to do to Albertine, and described Albertine's response ('Oh, it's just heavenly'); the narrator's pain at this discovery; Albertine is the only person who could lessen this pain, and she is dead.

His feelings and memories keep Albertine alive – or keep different Albertines alive; remembering the kind Albertine, he forgives her, though still tortured by the idea of her guilt; he sees Andrée, who admits to Lesbian behaviour, but not with Albertine; he looks for girls like Albertine, or who might have attracted Albertine; finally he tells himself he will one day forget Albertine.

Chapter Two: Mademoiselle de Forcheville
The narrator still looking at girls; one, a blonde, gives him a look in return; he learns her name, Mlle d'Eporcheville; he believes this is the aristocrat who frequents brothels, but Saint-Loup tells him he is mistaken.

The narrator's article has appeared in the *Figaro*; he is delighted with it; wanting to know what others think of it, he visits Mme de Guermantes, where he meets the blonde girl again – Mlle de Forcheville (Gilberte

Swann, who has been adopted by Mme Swann's second husband), Mme de Guermantes has finally agreed to accept Gilberte, though she is still determined never to mention Swann's name; Gilberte's popularity with the Guermantes; the Duc's astonishment on hearing of the narrator's article; he praises it, without much enthusiasm.

A conversation with Andrée brings further revelations – Morel used to pick up young girls for Albertine; Albertine hoped the narrator would save her from her vice; is Andrée now telling the truth? Andrée's coming marriage to Octave, nephew of the Verdurins; she mentions Mme Bontemps's plan to marry Albertine to Octave; was that why Albertine had wanted to go to the Verdurins? The narrator finds sorrow giving way to exhaustion, as perhaps does the reader.

Chapter Three: Venice
The narrator in Venice with his mother; she no longer feels she has to conceal her love for him; they dine with Mme Sazerat at a hotel where Mme de Villeparisis and M. de Norpois are staying; Prince Foggi; Mme Sazerat's interest in 'the woman who drove my father out of his senses'; M. de Norpois's hopes of returning to a position in the diplomatic world.

The narrator's inheritance now greatly reduced; his hopes of taking a Venetian girl back to Paris with him; a telegram from Albertine saying she is alive and would like to talk about marriage; the narrator refuses to leave Venice with his mother because he has just heard that Mme Putbus and her maid have arrived there; at the very last minute he changes his mind, hurries to the station and does join his mother; reading a letter from Gilberte, he realises, from the way she signs her name, that the telegram must have been from her and not from Albrtine; Gilberte is to marry Saint-Loup.

Chapter Four: a fresh light upon Robert de Saint-Loup
The narrator tells his mother about Gilberte and Saint-Loup; in return she tells him that the young de Cambremer is to marry Mlle d'Oloron (Jupien's niece, who has been adopted by M. de Charlus); reflections on social position.

The narrator visits Gilberte, who is unhappy with Saint-Loup; Saint-Loup has taken Morel away from M. de Charlus, finding a similarity between him and Rachel; Gilberte's attempts to be like Rachel; she tells the narrator of her interest in him when she saw him in childhood; he concludes that the happiness of which he had dreamed had not been unattainable, after all.

TIME REGAINED

Chapter One: Tansonville

The narrator is staying with Gilberte, just before the beginning of the first world war; Saint-Loup's feelings for Gilberte, and for Morel; in appearance Saint-Loup is becoming more like the other Guermantes; the narrator regrets not visiting the church at Combray, and tells himself he will do it another year; he starts reading the journal of the Goncourts; its references to the Verdurin circle make him want to see those people again, but persuade him he lacks the writer's power of observation.

Chapter Two: M. de Charlus during the war

In 1916, after some years in a sanatorium, the narrator returns to Paris; Mme Verdurin and Mme Bontemps are now leading figures in society; the Verdurin salon – its old and new members; he recalls an earlier visit to Paris, in 1914; Saint-Loup's courage and patriotism; letters from Gilberte, saying that she is in Tansonville (now occupied by the Germans) and that there is fighting around Combray. Saint-Loup in Paris on leave – his thoughts on strategy.

A visit to the Verdurins: their hostility to M. de Charlus; decline in his social position; Morel's cruelty towards him; this cruelty eventually explained as the result of Morel's fear (a fear which the narrator discounts until it is confirmed, after M. de Charlus's death, by a letter written by him ten years earlier); M. de Charlus's pro-German sentiments; his belief that France will be defeated; his interest in the young men who are doing the fighting.

As he walks through Paris one evening, the narrator stops for a rest at a hotel; it turns out to be a male brothel owned by M. de Charlus and run by Jupien; the young men, who all look like Morel, are not brutal enough for M. de Charlus's tastes; a *croix de guerre* is found in the ante-room.

Arriving home, he finds that Saint-Loup has visited him, looking for his *croix de guerre*, which he has lost; the spirit of France epitomised by the behaviour of Françoise's millionaire cousins, the Larivières; these, Proust tells us, are the only non-fictional characters in the entire work.

Immediately on his return to the front, Saint-Loup is killed; the narrator reflects on their friendship; similarity between Saint-Loup's secret life and that of Albertine; the grief of the Duchesse de Guermantes; Morel is arrested as a deserter, and sent to the front, where he wins the *croix de guerre*.

Chapter Three: An afternoon party at the house of the Princesse de Guermantes
The war has ended; the narrator returns to Paris, and is invited to an
afternoon party by the Princesse de Guermantes (formerly Mme Verdurin);
on his way there he meets M. de Charlus with M. Jupien; the Baron greets
Mme de Saint-Euverte, a thing he would never have done in the past.

On arrival the narrator stumbles on the uneven paving-stones in the
courtyard, and this prompts a flash of recollection, as the madeleine had
done so many years before; inside the house, as he waits for a piece of music
to end, he encounters further memories; 'the only true paradises are
paradises we have lost', hence memory rather than travel is the key to
finding real happiness, and reality is the relation between sensations and
memories; he therefore has all the materials for a work of literature in the
experiences of his past life.

The music ends, and he joins the party; failing to recognise any of his
fellow-guests, he wonders if they are all in disguise; then he recognises M.
d'Argencourt, greatly aged; also the Duchesse de Guermantes, Bloch, Mme
Sazerat; he realises that time and old age will supply the materials for his
book.

M. de Cambremer, the Prince d'Agrigente (much improved by age),
Legrandin, young Cambremer; only Mme de Forcheville (Odette) is
unchanged, though within three years she will be senile, and avoided by her
daughter's guests; Bloch and the Prince de Guermantes; Bloch's unawareness
that the the Princesse is Mme Verdurin (who since the death of M. Verdurin
has also found time to be Duchesse de Duras); people's ignorance of names
and genealogy; hence the social position of a Bloch or a Swann not
understood.

As he meets old friends, the narrator reviews the influences on his life –
Gilberte Swann, M. de Charlus, the Duchesse de Guermantes, Albertine;
the importance of death to the old; death an event like becoming a member
of the Academy, or being away for the winter; the inability of old people to
remember who is alive and who is dead.

The narrator finds the Duchesse de Guermantes talking to 'a horrible old
woman'; this turns out to be Rachel, who is to recite some poems; absent-
mindedly, the narrator asks Gilberte to introduce him to young girls; on the
other side of Paris, la Berma has invited some people to tea, but her friends
go to the Princesse de Guermantes instead; an opportunity for Rachel to
patronise la Berma in her absence; even la Berma's daughter and son-in-law
abandon her.

The Duc de Guermantes' liaison with Mme de Forcheville (Odette); seeing
Odette reminds the narrator of Albertine; the Duchesse de Guermantes'

contemptuous remarks about Gilberte; Gilberte introduces the narrator to her daughter, it seems to him that time has materialised itself in this girl, and the idea of time convinces him that he must make a beginning if he is to accomplish the task he has set himself; the form of his work will be the form of Time, in which man has the extension, 'not of his body but of his years . . . dragging them with him wherever he goes'.